BY ALEKSANDR SOLZHENITSYN

August 1914 [The Red Wheel / Knot I]

November 1916 [The Red Wheel / Knot II]

Cancer Ward

A Candle in the Wind

Détente: Prospects for Democracy and Dictatorship

East and West

The First Circle

The Gulag Archipelago

Lenin in Zurich

Letter to the Soviet Leaders

The Mortal Danger

Nobel Lecture

The Oak and the Calf

One Day in the Life of Ivan Denisovich

Prussian Nights

Rebuilding Russia

Stories and Prose Poems

Victory Celebrations, Prisoners,
and *The Love-Girl and the Innocent*

Warning to the West

A World Split Apart

THE RED WHEEL

■

A Narrative
in Discrete Periods of Time

ALEKSANDR SOLZHENITSYN

AUGUST 1914

THE RED WHEEL · KNOT I

TRANSLATED FROM THE RUSSIAN BY H. T. WILLETTS

FARRAR, STRAUS AND GIROUX NEW YORK

Farrar, Straus and Giroux
18 West 18th Street, New York 10011

Printed in the United States of America
Originally published in Russian under the title Krasnoe koleso. Uzel I: Avgust chetyrnadtsatogo, *world copyright © 1971, 1983 by Aleksandr Solzhenitsyn*
English translation published in the United States in 1989 by Farrar, Straus and Giroux
This paperback edition, 2014

The Library of Congress has cataloged the hardcover edition as follows:
Solzhenitsyn, Aleksandr Isaevich 1918–2008.
[Avgust chetyrnadtsatogo. English]
August 1914 / Aleksandr Solzhenitsyn ; translated by H. T. Willetts. — 1st ed.
p. cm.
Translation of: Avgust chetyrnadtsatogo.
Includes index.
(The red wheel / Aleksandr Solzhenitsyn ; knot 1)
1. Tannenberg, Battle of, Stebark, Poland, 1914—Fiction. 2. War stories. 3. Historical fiction. I. Title. II. Series: Solzhenitsyn, Aleksandr Isaevich, 1918–2008. Krasnoe koleso. English ; knot 1.

PG3488.O4 A9413 1989
891.73'44

88030966

Paperback ISBN: 978-0-374-53469-1

www.fsgbooks.com
www.twitter.com/fsgbooks • www.facebook.com/fsgbooks

1 3 5 7 9 10 8 6 4 2

Publisher's Note

The author began thinking of writing *August 1914* in 1937—at that time not as the first "knot" of the present work but as the introduction to a large-scale novel on the Russian revolution. It was then that he gathered all the information—and there was quite a lot of it—on the Samsonov catastrophe available in the Soviet Union, and wrote the first chapters, describing the arrival of a colonel from the Supreme Commander's staff at Samsonov's headquarters, the transfer of his headquarters to Neidenburg, and the lunch party there. The structure of these chapters remains almost unaltered in the final version. At the first stage of the work many chapters were allotted to Sasha Lenartovich but these have been dropped over the years. There were also some chapters on the Shcherbak family estate (that of the author's maternal grandfather) in which Stolypin's career and the significance of his assassination were touched on.

Work on the novel was then interrupted until 1963, when the author again began actively collecting material. (The results of his preliminary labors had been preserved throughout the war years and his term of imprisonment.) He finally decided on the title *The Red Wheel* in 1965, and on the division into "knots" (concentrated and minutely detailed accounts of events within strictly limited periods of time, with complete breaks between them) in 1967.

Work on *The Red Wheel* went on uninterrupted from March 1969—first on the later knots (chapters relating to the years 1919–20, and especially those about Tambov and about Lenin). That spring, however, the author changed direction to work exclusively on *August 1914*, completing some eighteen months later, in October 1970, what in the Russian edition constitutes Volume I and part of Volume II.

In this form Knot I was published in Russian in Paris, in June 1971, by the YMCA Press. Two rival editions appeared in the same year in Germany, then one in Holland, followed in 1972 by others in France, Britain, the United States, Spain, Denmark, Norway, Sweden, Italy, and in subsequent years in other European, Asian, and American countries.

The publication of the book in the West without official permission provoked attacks on the author in the Communist press.

After the author's expulsion from the U.S.S.R. he expanded on the previously written Lenin chapters, among them what is now Chapter 22 of *August 1914*, which was deliberately omitted from the first edition. It was included in a bundle of chapters published in 1975 by the YMCA Press in Paris under the title *Lenin v Tsyurikhe* (*Lenin in Zurich*).

In the spring of 1976 the author worked at the Hoover Institution in California and assembled a great deal of information on the story of Stolypin's assassination.

The chapters belonging to the Stolypin cycle (the present Chapters 8 and 60–73) were all written in Vermont in the summer and autumn of 1976. "Study of a Monarch" (now Chapter 74, published separately in *Vestnik Russkogo Khristianskogo Dvizheniya* No. 124 for 1978) was written at the beginning of 1977.

PUBLISHER'S NOTE

Knot I acquired its final form in Vermont in 1981, while it was being set up for the press. The representation of notable historical personages, important army officers, and revolutionaries mentioned by name, the material in the survey chapters and those on the Tsar, the whole story of Stolypin's assassination by Bogrov and the detailed descriptions of military operations, down to the fate of individual regiments and battalions, faithfully reproduce the historical record.

The author's father is introduced almost under his own name, and his mother's family are shown true to life. The Kharitonov (actually Andreev) and Arkhangorodsky families and Varya are real people, and Obodovsky (Pyotr Akimovich Palchinsky) is a figure well known to history.

In the "screen" sequences in this book, the four different margins are used to represent four sets of technical instructions for the shooting of a film. These, from left to right on the page, are sound effects, camera direction, action, dialogue. The symbol = indicates "cut to."

Dates in the Russian original were given in the Old Style, according to the Julian calendar used in Russia until 1918 (and used even now by the Church). In this translation they have been changed, in accordance with the author's wishes, to the Gregorian (Western) calendar. The new dates are twelve or thirteen days ahead of the old.

Contents

CONTENTS

CONTENTS

CONTENTS

CONTENTS

CONTENTS

CONTENTS

CONTENTS

CONTENTS

CONTENTS

ACT ONE

REVOLUTION

Only the ax can deliver us, and nothing other than the ax . . . Russia summons us to the ax.

From a letter to Aleksandr Herzen's newspaper, The Bell, *1860*

KNOT I

AUGUST 1914

(23 August–3 September)

[1]

They left the village in the clear dawn light. As the sun rose the mountains were dazzling white with dark blue hollows, every indentation could be seen, and they looked so close that a stranger might have thought them a two hours' drive away.

The Caucasus loomed huge and elemental in a world of small man-made things. If all the people who had ever lived had opened their arms as wide as they could to carry all that they had ever made, or ever thought of making, and piled it up in swelling heaps, they could not have raised such an unbelievable mountain range.

The road from the village to the station kept the mountains continually before them as though those snowy expanses, those bare crags, those shadows hinting at invisible ravines were their destination. But from one half hour to the next, as the snow began to thaw on the lower slopes, the range seemed to part company with the earth, and its upper third hung suspended in the sky. It became shrouded in mist, so that there were no ribs or seams to show that these were mountains, and they saw instead what looked like a vast white cloud bank. This broke into fragments indistinguishable from real clouds. Then they too were washed away. The range disappeared as though it had been a celestial mirage, and wherever they looked they saw only grayish, heat-blanched sky. They drove on till noon and beyond, for more than fifty versts,* without changing direction, until the giant mountains retreated as rounded foot-hills closed in—the Camel, the Bull, the bald Snake, and the wooded Iron Hill.

They had set out when the road was not yet dusty and the steppe was cool and wet with dew. They traveled through the hours when the steppe took wing and rang with birdcalls, and the hours when there were only low whistles, chirrups, rustlings in the grass. Now they were driving into Mineralnye Vody, trailing a lazy dust cloud, at the deadest hour of the afternoon, when there was nothing to be heard but the steady wooden rattle of their cart—the noise of hooves was muffled by the dust. The subtle scents of plants had faded in those few hours, and now there was only the heavy smell of sun-scorched air laced with dust. The cart, the hay strewn on its floor, and they themselves smelled the same, but they had been steppe dwellers from earliest childhood, they liked the smell, and the heat could not worry them.

Their father had grudged them the use of his sprung carriage, and they

* Verst—an old Russian measure, roughly two-thirds of a mile. [*Trans.*]

were so badly shaken and jolted when the horses trotted that they had come most of the way at walking pace. They drove between wheat fields and grazing herds, past barren salt flats, across shallow gullies and streambeds, some dry, some with a little water. They saw no real rivers, and not a single large village. It was Sunday morning, and the road was deserted—they met no one and no one overtook them; yet Isaaki, who was always patient and today even quieter and more thoughtful than usual, did not find those eight hours tedious but could have gone on for twice as long, with the unnecessary reins slack in his hand, gazing over horse's ears from under his battered straw hat.

Yevstrat, his younger half brother, who would have to travel all the way back by the same road that night, slept at first on the hay behind Isaaki's back, then stirred, rose to his feet, looking around for something in the hay, jumped down, ran a little way from the cart, and caught up again. He couldn't keep still a moment, he chattered, he asked questions: "Why do you feel as if you're going backwards when you close your eyes?"

Yevstrat had now moved into the second class of the Pyatigorsk high school, although his father had at first wanted him, as he had Isaaki, to attend only the nearby middle school. His other brothers and sisters had seen nothing and knew nothing except the land, and cattle, and sheep, and they had done well enough, hadn't they? Isaaki had been sent to school a year later than he should have been, and his father had held on to him for a year after high school, refusing at first to be persuaded that something called a university should come next. But oxen will move a heavy load not by tugging but by steady pulling, and Isaaki could always get his way with his father by patient insistence.

Isaaki loved his native Sablinskaya, their farm ten versts from the village, and farm work, and during this summer vacation he had joined with a will in the mowing and threshing. In his plan for the future he combined his original way of life with what he had accumulated as a student. But from year to year this became more unrealistic: his education was slowly but inexorably separating him from his past, the people in his village, and his family.

He was one of only two students in the village. The villagers found their appearance and their conversation strange and ridiculous. As soon as they got home they hurriedly changed into their old clothes. Isaaki was, however, pleased about one thing: village gossip distinguished him from the other student, calling him (humorously) "the Narodnik." Whoever first thought of it, and however it caught on, everyone started using the nickname. There had been no Populists in Russia for a long time, but Isaaki, though he would never have dared call himself that out loud, thought of himself as a Narodnik for want of a better word to describe one who obtains an education for the sake of the people, and "goes to the people" with his book learning, his eloquence, and his love.

In fact, even returning to his family was almost impossible. Having given in to the incomprehensible university three years earlier, his father did not retract his decision, but he came to feel that he had made a mistake and lost his son. The only use he got from him was during the vacations, when he could put him to work on the farm; but in the long months of Sanya's absences his father could not see the sense of all that book learning.

He and his father would have remained close but for his stepmother, Marfa, a bold, domineering, greedy woman who kept the whole household on a short rein, making sure that no one stood in the way of her own children. Isaaki's older brothers and sisters had already moved out, and because of his stepmother his father and his own home were becoming strange to him. While he was still a boy Sanya had eyed them and wondered what powerful urge compelled a man widowed in his forties to take a second wife in her twenties, and one so sharp that when he was touching sixty he still could not rule his own household or indeed have much say in its affairs.

Newly acquired views also helped to make Isaaki feel a stranger. As a child he had been naïvely, uncomprehendingly aware of fasts and saints' days, he had gone barefoot to night services—but later on almost everyone he met had tried to talk him out of the religion of most Russians. Sablinskaya itself and their whole district were dotted with sectarian communities—Molokane, Dukhobors, Stundists, Jehovah's Witnesses. His stepmother came from one such group, and his father's allegiance to the Church became weaker. Arguments about different faiths were a favorite pastime in their locality. Sanya used to go along and listen until the views of Count Tolstoy made all these rival creeds equally foreign to him. There was intellectual confusion in the cities too; even the educated did not always understand each other, and Tolstoy's teaching settled all things so convincingly, demanding only truthfulness. Alas, within the family he could not practice it. Tolstoy's truth made it necessary for him to tell a lie: having become a vegetarian, he could not possibly explain that it was for reasons of conscience without incurring the disgust and derision of his family and all the village. Instead, he had to begin by telling a lie: some German medical man had discovered that abstaining from meat ensured long life. When he had tossed enough sheaves around, his body craved meat, and it was hard work deluding himself that potatoes and beans were all he needed.

His estrangement from his family had made the decision to leave home easier, but he could not be open about his intentions. He told a lie about having to return to the university early to do some practical work—and then had to invent the practical work and make it comprehensible to his unschooled father.

All that their village knew of the war in its first three weeks were the

Tsar's manifestos declaring war on Germany and Austria—which were read out in church and then posted in the square outside—the departure of two parties of reservists, and an additional roundup of horses for dispatch to the district capital, because the villagers of Sablinskaya now counted not as Terek Cossacks but as Russians. Apart from this there might have been no war. Newspapers never reached the village, and it was too early for letters from the army in the field. Indeed the very concept was a strange one. To "get a letter" in their village was pretentious, ostentatious, and Sanya discouraged letter writers. None of the Lazhenitsyn family was called up: the oldest brother was overage and his son was already in the army, the middle brother had some fingers missing, Isaaki was a student, and his stepmother's children were too young.

Nor did they see any sign of war on their half day's ride over the wide steppe.

They had crossed the bridge over the Kuma, rattled over the sun-baked railway track by the stony crossing, drove along the grassy street of Kumskaya, now called Mineralnye Vody, and still they noticed no signs of war. Life was so reluctant to be turned upside down! Wherever it could it went on in its old, quiet way.

They pulled up in the shade of a big elm by a well. Yevstrat was to wait there while the horses cooled down, water them, and then drive on to the station. Sanya washed, splashing himself down to the waist, using up two bucketfuls, got Yevstrat to pour icy water on his back from a dark tin mug, toweled himself dry, put on a clean white shirt and a belt, then left his things in the cart and went off empty-handed toward the station, avoiding the dust.

A little garden had been planted a short while ago to beautify the station approach, but hens had pecked its edges ragged and it was covered with a layer of dust from charabancs and carts driving up to the long station building. But a light awning on slender painted columns shading the Mineralnye Vody platform and the cooling breeze that blew along it spoke of the nearby watering places and their delights. Wild vines twined around the columns, and the whole place had the look of a cheerful summer resort. Here too there was nothing to indicate that anyone had ever heard of the war. Ladies in bright dresses and men in tussore followed porters to the departure platform for Kislovodsk. You could buy ice cream, mineral water, colored balloons.

And newspapers. Sanya bought one, and after a moment's thought another, and began opening them even before he sat down on a bench near the platform. Contrary to his usual methodical way, he skipped from column to column, leaving news items half read, and his face brightened as he went along. Good, good! Major Russian victory at Gumbinnen! The enemy will be compelled to evacuate all Prussia. . . . Things are also going well in Austria. . . . The Serbs too have won a victory! . . .

True to his farm boy's habit of wasting nothing, he folded the papers up, taking care not to crumple or tear them, as if he expected to need them forever, rose, and went to the ticket office to inquire about trains. He was making his way steadily through the press of bustling passengers, looking at no one, when suddenly a girl dashed out of the crowd. He assumed that she was rushing for a train, did not turn to look, and realized that she was coming toward him only when she threw her arms around his neck, hugged him and kissed him—then recoiled as though amazed by her own boldness, and stood there red in the face but happy.

"Sanya! Is it really you? *Wha-at* a coincidence! All the way from Petersburg I've been . . ."

Her arms had been around him for only half a second, but she had scattered his thoughts and he stood there confused by the elusive feelings that her sudden swoop had stirred in him, feelings that had to do not only with the touch of sun-warmed lips.

Varya, an old friend from the Pyatigorsk high school. They had not seen each other since. They had written occasional letters at first. In those days, she had had the straight-combed hair of a motherless girl, but now her hair was bobbed and fluffed out and she wore an excited, triumphant expression.

"For some reason I kept thinking, what if I suddenly run into you! I knew it couldn't happen, but all the same . . . I even thought of sending a telegram to the village, but I knew you wouldn't like it . . ."

Sanya stood and smiled. He was taken aback by the change in her since she had left school, by the unexpectedness of it, by the frightening thought of the telegram (it would have exploded like a bomb in the Lazhenitsyn household), and by the warmth of her presence.

"I've been traveling for more than three days," she said happily. "My guardian is dying, and I have to go and say goodbye to him. It isn't the most comfortable time to be traveling, the trains are packed. . . . What about you? Are you going somewhere? Or just meeting somebody?"

He was tempted to say, "Yes, you." Her sudden descent on him, her unconstrained manner tempted him to make a silly joke of it. "I'm here because I had a dream about you. Can it really be you?" She stood there, still out of breath, leaning toward him.

Varya had never been beautiful, and had not become more so since her school days; her chin was a little too stubborn and masculine, her nose a little too long, but her flushed pleasure in meeting him made her pretty.

"Do you remember? Do you . . . ? How we met on the boulevard once, unexpectedly? It must be fate! Listen, Sanya, where are you going now? I'm sure you can make time if you want to. Let's spend a little while together. Shall I stay in Mineralnye a bit? Or if you like we'll both go to Pyatigorsk. I leave it to you to decide."

She spoke in rapid, jerky sentences, with the same palpitating excitement that had swept her toward him. The pure and lofty feelings with which Sanya had left home that morning and gazed upon the snow and the deep blues of the rugged range as he traveled were disturbed, blurred, confused. The mood he had cherished evaporated as suddenly as the range had dissolved into cloud.

Life is an eternal struggle with temptation: eat no meat, but, oh, how I want some; do no evil, but doing good is so difficult. . . . If he went for a walk with her in Mineralnye Vody people from the village would see him and tell tales at home. But going to Pyatigorsk would be a nonsensical digression. Hotels and restaurants were out of the question. He had just enough for his ticket and not a kopeck more.

He thought wistfully of his special morning. But he was surprised to find that he would have been sorry not to have met Varya. He felt that he was perfectly capable of going with her.

Her sharp features lit up when she saw that he was willing to go, but she could not check herself and asked with shrill insistence, "Where *are* you going? And why?"

She herself had reminded him why he could not listen to her.

He smiled vaguely, and said to humor her, "I'm on my way to Moscow." He looked down and sideways, guiltily. "I'm stopping off at Rostov first. I've got a friend there, Konstantin. Maybe you know him?"

"But the term doesn't start for another three weeks!" Her arm, bare to the elbow, reached out and caught him firmly, peremptorily, by his elbow. "Do you think they may call you up?" she said anxiously, tightening her grip. "A fourth-year student? Never! What *are* you going for?"

He couldn't tell her just like that, in so many words, it would trivialize his intention. He gave an embarrassed smile.

"Well, you see . . . I get restless back home on the farm."

She started, tossed her head like a startled horse, then clutched both his hands.

"You don't mean you're volunteering?"

It was true, they had met once before by chance. Varya, a pupil at the city school, had ventured out one evening onto the main avenue of Pyatigorsk, with secret hopes, and had seen coming toward her a schoolboy of her acquaintance, three years older than herself.

Their meetings became occasions for serious intellectual discussions, which were very important to Varya: she had never had a close friend older than herself. Even when it got so dark that there was no danger of teachers seeing them, and Sanya could very well have held her arm, he did not do so. She greatly respected him for his seriousness (but would not have minded having to respect him less).

Later, when she went on to high school herself, she began meeting

Sanya at school dances and other gatherings. They found a good deal to talk about, but never danced. Sanya said that holding each other close in a waltz aroused desires before there had been time for any genuine feeling to develop and that Count Tolstoy thought this a bad thing. Varya let herself be persuaded by his gentle excuses that she did not really want to dance herself.

Later still they had kept up a correspondence for a while. He wrote very sober, earnest letters. Although Varya's horizon had widened in St. Petersburg, although she knew many clever people now, she often thought of Sanya.

Three weeks ago, near the house she lived in on Vasilievsky Island, she had read the Tsar's manifesto pasted on a pillar, then crossed the Neva by tram and seen the patriotic mob wrecking the German embassy in St. Isaac's Square, breaking windows and throwing furniture, marbles, and slashed pictures out into the street, toppling the enormous bronze horses and the bronze giants leading them from the roof to the pavement, while all the onlookers rejoiced as though what had come to them was not war but a long-awaited happiness—and at that troubled moment by the black and brown columns of St. Isaac's Cathedral, Varya had felt a pang of longing to see Sanya. She always did think of him when she rode past St. Isaac's. Isaaki did not like his Christian name and jokingly said that Peter the Great was really his namesake. Peter too had been born on St. Isaac's day, hence the name of the cathedral, but the Emperor had been given a more pleasant-sounding name and the lad from the steppe had not.

Varya had been summoned to Pyatigorsk unexpectedly. Her guardian, or rather the benefactor at whose expense she and many other orphans had been educated, was seriously ill, and it was thought right that she should visit him, although he did not remember all those who had received his charity, and the arrival of an unknown student with belated thanks for his generosity could not do much to cheer him. During those four weary days in the train traveling from one end of the Empire to the other, she had found herself repeating Sanya's name like an incantation: "Sanya, please be there! Be there, Sanya!" Just as she had in the old days, walking the length of the avenue in Pyatigorsk.

It wasn't just Sanya—that Tolstoy had corrupted so many manly characters! Varya had traveled from St. Isaac's through Moscow, through Kharkov, through Mineralnye Vody—all places associated with Sanya. When war broke out she had suddenly felt lonely and unwanted. Her own life had not been very full before, but she had felt the fullness of the life all around her. Now it was as though a great crack had opened in the bottom of a lake and the water was draining away, whirling and gurgling, and she must hurry, hurry before it dried up altogether.

She could not understand why the world was suddenly at so odd an angle. Only a month ago—no, only three weeks ago—no thinking Russian citizen seemed to doubt that the head of the Russian state was a contemptible person, unworthy even of serious mention, and that nothing he said could conceivably be repeated except in mockery. Then everything had changed from one day to the next. What looked like educated and intelligent people had assembled quite voluntarily around the advertising pillars, finding nothing funny in the monarch's lengthy title cylindrically unrolled, and had listened without compulsion while ringing voices read his proclamation:

"Russia, answering the challenge of her foes, rises up to do battle, rises up to perform her feats of arms with steel in her hand and the cross on her breast. . . . The Lord God sees that we have not taken up arms with any design of conquest, nor for the sake of empty worldly fame, but to defend the honor and security of our Empire, which God holds in His hand. The cause for which we fight is a just one. . . ."

All the way from St. Petersburg, Varya had seen troops entraining and their families seeing them off. These Russian farewells were particularly wild at country stops, where reservists danced to the balalaika on the unpaved road, raising the dust and emitting random cries, obviously drunk, while their families wept and made the sign of the cross over them. When one freight train carrying reservists passed another a cheer arose from both, and the fraternal hurrah, wild and desperate and senseless, echoed along the whole length of both trains.

No one, anywhere, demonstrated against the Tsar.

Sanya, in his clean white shirt, looked more than ever a child of the steppes with his deep tan and his slicked-down, corn-colored hair bleached from working in the fields. She had flung herself at him the moment she saw him, on impulse, but also hoping by this one movement to dispel the timidity which had clogged their earlier meetings. They would both, she felt sure, drop what they had been meaning to do and go somewhere, anywhere, together.

But Sanya was one of those simpletons who make everything complicated.

There was a gentle, thoughtful smile on the lips between the light brown mustache and the growth that was not yet a beard. And, as always, the ceaseless working of his mind showed in his eyes. She could see in him the heightened emotion that seemed to be devouring everyone. *Was* he going? Volunteering?

She gripped his shoulders. "Sanya! Don't go! Don't go away!"

He was being sucked by the eddying waters into the crack in the bottom of the lake with the rest of them. She longed to restore to him the lucidity and good sense which she had once acquired from him, to pluck him from the whirlpool while there was still time. She didn't stop to think—the words came to her unsought. All those decades of civic literature, the ideals of the intelligentsia, the student's love of the people—was he going to throw all that away in one moment? To forget Lavrov, Mikhailovsky. . . . A fine thing! Surrendering to vulgar patriotic feeling, betraying all his principles. He was not a revolutionary, of course, but he had always been a pacifist.

Anyone watching them would have thought that she was the warmonger and that he was gently deprecating her bellicosity. Varya grew heated and her smile hardened. She rose in exasperation and her hat slipped to one side—a cheap, modest hat chosen simply to keep the sun off her, not to make her more attractive.

Sanya simply nodded. He had no arguments to use against her and did not try to defend himself. Sadly he said, "I feel sorry for Russia."

The water was gurgling out of the lake.

"Sorry for what? Sorry for Russia?" Varya jumped as if she had been stung. "When you say Russia do you mean the idiot Emperor? The Black Hundred grocers?* The long-skirted priests?"

Sanya did not answer. He could think of nothing to say. He just listened. But he did not lose his temper under the lash of her reproaches. Any argument was a chance for him to test himself.

"Anyway, who says you have the strength of character to be a soldier?" Varya was seizing any weapon that came to hand.

For the first time she felt cleverer, more mature, more acute than he was—and shivered as though she had lost something precious.

"And what about Tolstoy?" She had found the final argument. "Have you asked yourself what Lev Tolstoy would say? Where are your principles? Where is your consistency?"

The light blue eyes under the corn-colored brows and above the corn-colored mustache were sad and unsure of themselves.

He raised his shoulders slightly and said barely audibly, "I feel sorry for Russia."

Document No. 1

5 August

AMBASSADOR PALÉOLOGUE TO EMPEROR NIKOLAI II:

. . . The French army will have to withstand the terrible assault of 25 German corps. I beg Your Majesty to order your troops to begin their offensive immediately. Otherwise the French army is in danger of being crushed.

* Members of mass organizations such as the Union of the Russian People and the Union of Michael the Archangel which sprang up in 1905 to defend the autocracy against liberals and revolutionaries. With the connivance and sometimes the assistance of the police they organized attacks on the headquarters and meeting places of "unpatriotic" political groups, pogroms against "non-Russian" groups, particularly the Jews, and demonstrations against the bureaucracy, represented as a barrier between the Tsar and his people. [*Trans.*]

Document No. 2

13 August

Note by Marshal Joffre:

. . . Anticipating all our wishes, Russia went into battle at the same time as ourselves. For this act of loyal cooperation, which is particularly praiseworthy inasmuch as the Russians were still a long way from completing the concentration of their forces, the Tsar's army and the Grand Duke Nikolai have earned the gratitude of France.

Document No. 3

14 August

NIKOLAI II TO FOREIGN MINISTER SAZONOV:

. . . I have ordered the Grand Duke Nikolai Nikolaevich to open up the way to Berlin at whatever cost and as quickly as possible. We must aim at the destruction of the German army.

[2]

It was no new thing for Sanya to find himself entangled in contradictions, and his ideas at odds with his feelings. But although he had found it possible to reinforce his resistance to meat or dancing by refraining on every occasion, month in and month out, no one had ever offered him war or recommended it or tried to tempt him with it. It had seemed completely out of the question in such a civilized and enlightened age, so that there had been no opportunity to prepare himself for it. He had an ingrained belief that war was a sin. That belief was easy enough to hold when it had never been put to the test. But the first war he had ever known broke out—and there in the untroubled calm of the rolling steppe under a cloudless sky he had suddenly begun to fret. Sanya felt helplessly that this was a war he could not reject, not just that he would be made to take part in it but that it would be base to stay out of it, and indeed that he must hurry to volunteer. No one in the village questioned the war or thought of it as an event people like themselves could accept or prevent as they chose. Everyone there accepted war and the recruiting officer's summons as acts of God, like a blizzard or a dust storm. But joining up voluntarily was something equally beyond their comprehension. Even on the long journey today, painfully shaken by the cart and scorched by the sun, Sanya had not reached a final decision. He still had to talk it over with his friend in Rostov, Kotya. That he would be betraying Tolstoy was clear enough. But as he had listened to Varya and bowed his head to the hail of democratic and revolutionary arguments, Sanya had found nothing in them to help him make up his mind. They could throw no bridge over the dark abyss yawning ahead of Russia.

He parted from Varya more determined to volunteer than he had been before he met her.

Varya herself was another matter. He had scarcely been able to restrain himself. She had begged him to go with her, and he had longed to do so. As the peasant saying goes: Break straw when it crackles and girls when they prattle. But men were already dying in battle. It would be dishonorable. If he had gone he might have weakened in his resolve and perhaps even returned to the village.

On the Baku mail train he spent half the night turning these things over in his mind, lying on an upper side berth in which there was barely room for his whole length. They had left Mineralnye in the evening. The train was crowded because of the war, and there were very few bunks vacant in third class.

No sooner had they parted than he yearned to be with her again. He shouldn't have left her. He was tempted to go back and follow her. Now, of all times, when he was going into the army, how could he have turned her down?

As it was, meeting her had only left him miserable—so miserable that he thought of going to Kharkov to see black-haired Lyonochka with her guitar and her love songs. If Kharkov, though, why not Pyatigorsk? No, if he had stayed with her he would have lost the determination and the impetus to go on with his plan.

Sanya longed for and dreamed of the day when he would really fall in love. Love someone with all his being, and for all his life.

But for the present the war was the only prospect unfolding before him.

It was stuffy in the carriage. Sanya's bunk was to the right of the aisle, and he was allowed to pull his window down and let in a cross draft. He lowered the folding lattice so that he would not fall out of the train. At the frequent stops passengers walked through the carriage brushing against Sanya's student jacket, and there were people talking on the platform outside his window. He woke from time to time to a feeling of disaster—that it was not his own made it no easier to bear. He glanced now and then at the tallow candle behind glass which lit four compartments, trying to judge from the drip how the time was elapsing. The flame guttered when the train was in motion, and heavy shadows chased one another over the ceiling.

At times he caught the name of a station, or peered through a crack to read it. He could recite their names, including whistle stops, by heart all the way from Prokhladnaya to Rostov, and in reverse order if asked.

He loved all these stations. The whole area was dear to him. One married sister lived in Nagutskaya, another in Kursavka. But his allegiance had been divided in recent years, since he had got to know the real Russia, the forest Russia that begins only at Voronezh.

The Lazhenitsyns came in fact from somewhere near Voronezh, and Sanya had persuaded his father to let him go to see the homeland of his ancestors during his year of idleness between school and university (intending also to look in on Lev Tolstoy).

His grandfather Yefim had told him that Tsar Peter had visited his wrath upon a remote ancestor, Filipp, who had had the temerity to change his abode without permission, evicting him and burning the village of Bobrovskaya in his great anger. Grandfather's father was one of several peasants banished from Voronezh province for rebellion: they were not, however, fettered, or sent to a remote garrison, or attached to a fortress, but let loose on the untamed steppe beyond the Kuma, on the old Cossack boundary line, where they had lived comfortably enough with no shortage of land, no need to divide the steppe up into strips, plowing and sowing, scouring it in carts to shear their sheep, with no one to hinder them. They had put down roots there.

Through the gaps in the lattice Sanya could see nothing but black night outside. But gradually the sky brightened until the candle flame looked dim and the conductor came to put it out. When the pale sky was touched with pink Sanya gave up any attempt to sleep, raised the window screen to the ceiling, wriggled into his jacket, and, with the cold breeze blowing in his face, waited for the sun to rise. The pink became a spreading canopy, spangled with little white clouds, and glowed fiercer at its source until finally a molten red sun spilled into the sky. It lavished its rich red light on the broad plains, grudging not even the remotest spot on the western horizon its share.

In that other Russia there were so many places of modest beauty hemmed in by forests and hills but never such sunrises, flooding the whole world with blazing light.

On just such a fine morning four years ago, before 6 a.m. when the sun had only just risen, Sanya had left Kozlova Zaseka station on his way to see Tolstoy. The air was fresher and milder than it ever is on a summer morning in the Kuban. After asking his way at the station Sanya went down into a dip, then crossed a hillside and entered woods such as he had never seen in pictures and, living in the south, could never have imagined—well-timbered, beautifully kept parkland, with mature, thick-trunked trees. The woods, drenched in milky, then iridescent dew, invited him not just to pass through but to wander, sit, lie down, stay, never to find his way out—and it seemed all the more special because the spirit of the prophet hovered there. Tolstoy must walk or ride that way to the station, he must have been there often, those woods were the beginning of his estate.

He was wrong. The woods took him uphill to the Orel highroad and abruptly ended there. He realized his mistake: he had to cross the main road and go downhill to the grounds of Yasnaya Polyana. The park was separated from the road by a ditch and dense shrubbery. Around the bend the white stone pillars of the gate came in sight.

Sanya was overcome by shyness. He couldn't make himself go through the main gates and along the drive, where he might have to answer questions. More likely than not he would not be let in to see the great man. He found it easier to jump over the ditch, force his way through the shrubbery, walk aimlessly about the grounds where this time he could be sure that Tolstoy took his walks, and sit for a while where Tolstoy must sit.

There were meandering paths, an ornamental pool, then another one, little bridges over standing water mantled with weeds, a summerhouse. He could not see the house or any of its inhabitants. He wandered round and round the sun-dappled paths, sat down from time to time, saw all there was to see, and began to feel that this was all he wanted. He was tempted to let this count as his visit to Tolstoy and set off back to the south.

But he went along another, birch-lined avenue—long, straight, and narrow like a corridor. The birches gave way to maples, then limes. He came to what was not altogether an open space but a less thickly wooded rectangular area bounded by limes, with paths running lengthwise, breadthwise, and diagonally. He caught a glimpse of someone walking quite briskly along these paths, hid behind the thick trunk of a lime tree, peered out, and saw . . . the Gray-headed One! The Gray-bearded One! . . . wearing a long shirt with a belt around it: shorter than he had expected, but so like his portraits that Sanya almost shook his head to make sure that it was not a mirage.

Tolstoy had a walking stick and kept his eyes on the ground. At one moment he stopped, leaned on his stick, and stared at the same spot for almost a minute, then moved on again. When the head in the canvas cap emerged from deep early-morning shade into sunlight, it was ringed with a bright halo. He walked around all four sides of the rectangle, then went around again, coming quite close to Sanya at one corner.

Sanya drank in the sight. He could have stood there for an hour, leaning his chest against the lime, embracing its rugged trunk with both hands, and peeping out from behind it. He certainly had no urge to disturb the Prophet's morning meditations, but he was afraid that Tolstoy might go back to the house instead of coming that way again, or that someone would turn up to talk to him.

His heart pounding, he stepped onto the path far enough away from Tolstoy not to frighten him, took off his school cap (he had worn it all that year, waiting for his father to let him go to the university), and stood there speechless.

Tolstoy glanced at his open-necked shirt and the cap in his hand. He halted. His face was careworn and preoccupied. But it was he who had to speak first to his tongue-tied worshipper.

"Good day, schoolboy."

As though it were he who had come to see Sanya!

If the Lord of Hosts had spoken Sanya's throat could not have been drier.

"Good day, Lev Nikolaevich," he said weakly.

He couldn't think of anything more to say. This was Tolstoy and he, Sanya, was distracting him, forcing him to concentrate on something unexpected. Tolstoy had, of course, seen more than his share of visitors, schoolboys included. He knew the sort of thing they were likely to ask and had his answers ready. They could read it all in his books if they cared to, but for some reason they insisted on hearing it from his own lips.

"Where are you from, boy?" the great man asked politely, making no attempt to move on.

"From the Aleksandrov district, in Stavropol province," Sanya answered in a hoarse but more audible voice. He pulled himself together, cleared his throat, and began speaking rapidly. "Lev Nikolaevich, I know I'm interrupting your walk and your thoughts. Please forgive me! I've come such a long way just to hear a few words from you. Have I understood correctly what you say about the purpose of man's life on earth?"

He did not, however, say what he thought Tolstoy meant, but waited. Tolstoy's lips, which were not entirely smothered by his beard, parted automatically to utter words he had said a thousand times: "To serve the good. And so create the Kingdom of God on earth."

"Yes, I know that!" Sanya said eagerly. "But tell me—how are we to serve it? By loving? Must it be by loving?"

"Of course. That is the only way."

"The only way?" That was what Sanya had come to hear. He felt more at ease and began speaking more smoothly, in something like his usual unflustered way. What he said was framed as a question, but one which partly answered itself, because like any adolescent he wanted to give even this great man the benefit of his by no means insignificant opinion. "But are you sure, Lev Nikolaevich, that you don't exaggerate the power of human love? Or at any rate of what is left of it in modern man? What if love is not so strong, not necessarily present in all men, what if love cannot prevail . . . wouldn't that mean that your teaching lacks . . ."—he couldn't finish the phrase—"is extremely premature? If so, ought we not to envisage some intermediate stage, ask less of people to start with and then try to awaken them to universal benevolence?"

When Tolstoy did not immediately answer he added quickly, "Because from my observation mutual goodwill is certainly not general in the south, where I come from, Lev Nikolaevich, it most certainly is not!"

The old man's brow was still furrowed with his own cares—and now this schoolboy was asking a question which made them no easier. He looked hard at Sanya from under the shaggy brows, and repeated the lesson his whole life had taught him: "Love is the only way! The only way. No one will ever find a better."

He seemed unwilling to say more, as if he were saddened or offended by the doubt cast on the truth he had discovered. He obviously wanted to resume his walk around the rectangle and think his own thoughts.

It grieved Sanya to think that he had upset one whom he worshipped, but he hastened to ask his favorite question, hoping to mollify the old man and wheedle another crumb of wisdom out of him at the same time.

"For my part, I want to do just that—to do good by loving. That is what I intend to do. I shall make that my object in life—to do good. But there's another thing, Lev Nikolaevich. How are we to know what good is? You write that the rational and the moral are always identical . . ."

The Prophet paused. Yes, he had said so. He bored a small hole in the hard ground with the metal tip of his stick.

"You say that the good and the reasonable are one and the same, or have the same origin. And that evil does not come from an evil nature, that people are evil not by nature but out of ignorance. Am I right? But"—Sanya's temerity took his breath away, yet he had after all seen certain things for himself—"it isn't at all like that, Lev Nikolaevich, it just isn't so! Evil refuses to know the truth. Rends it with its fangs! Evil people usually know better than anybody else just what they are doing. And go on doing it. What are we to do with them?"

He clapped his hand to his mouth so that he would say no more, so that he could not hear himself say more.

The old man sighed deeply. "That's because no one has been clever enough to explain to them in a way they can understand. We must explain things patiently. Then they will understand. All men are born with the ability to understand."

He strode off with his walking stick, obviously put out.

Sanya stood still, even when Tolstoy had left the path and disappeared behind the house. He remained there for some time.

He had hoped that after three minutes with the great man he would *know*, he would *understand*. He understood no more than before.

He had not been bold or quick enough to seek his idol's ruling on poetry. Was it or was it not permissible to write verse? Provided you did it privately, just for yourself? Whatever the answer, he had a secret urge to put rhyming lines together. He had sometimes written verses in a girl's album for fun.

Sanya had never felt very sure of himself, and every year that passed knocked some of the ground from under his feet. He had often despaired of bending his father's will, and felt fated to remain an unschooled savage from the steppes. After his journey to see Tolstoy he had spent the rest of the year working on the farm, reading only what little came to hand—Tolstoy as often as not. In the end he was allowed to go to Kharkov, but as soon as he began studying in the Faculty of History and Literature he felt like an ignoramus, a bumpkin from the back of beyond among town-bred fellow students. After his first year at Kharkov he had summoned up the courage to transfer to Moscow University (carrying Kotya off with him), but it was some time before he stopped feeling immature, uneducated, incapable of reaching the nub of a question. He was confused by the multiplicity of truths, and exhausted by the struggle to find one more convincing than another. He had considered himself a Tolstoyan since the seventh form at school, and until he began handling so many books he had felt secure and comfortable in his belief. But he was given Lavrov and Mikhailovsky to read and what they said all seemed so true and so right! He was given Plekhanov—and that too was true, so smoothly written, so cogent. Kropotkin's ideas he also found to his liking—and true! Then he opened *Vekhi* and realized with a shock that here was something completely contrary to what he had read before, yet true! The truth of it pierced him to the quick!

Books no longer inspired reverent joy but dread—dread that he would never be able to hold his own with an author, that every new book he read would seduce and enslave him. Just as he was becoming brave enough to disagree with a book now and then, the war had come along. Now he would never learn. Never catch up.

The train was nearing Armavir. Sanya jumped down from his bunk just in time to wash before the washroom was locked. There would be a wait of twenty minutes at Armavir while the locomotive was changed. The platform was clear and quiet at that hour in the morning. Here too there was nothing to show that the country was at war. Sanya bought hot, strong, sweet tea in the buffet but made do with the food he had brought from home in his bag.

When the train moved out he remained near the carriage door. Soot from the engine was blowing along the sunny side of the train, so Sanya opened the door on the other side and hung halfway out of the carriage. He could never tire of watching the huge, motley expanses of ripened crops wheeling away from him. From every carriage an elongated black shadow shuddered across the fields, dipping into gullies as it went, but otherwise the steppe was bathed in the soft light of dawn, still pink rather than yellow.

And although his body was filled with the joyous strength of youth and the promise of abundant life, he knew that he might never again see this steppe and the morning sun shining on the sea of corn.

The train went through Kubanskaya station. Even then Sanya did not go back into the carriage but stood where he was by the open door, with the wind of the train blowing about him, and drank in the view, wondering how he could bear to part with it.

He could trace the boundaries of a big estate, or "economy" as it was called in the northern Caucasus. Its regular fields, thickly clad with tall wheat, stood out in contrast with the steppe. Heavily loaded wagons moved about it. Oxen were pulling a traction engine and a thresher. Dwellings and farm buildings seen through a gap in a plantation of poplars wheeled away from him. The top story of a brick house seemed to travel along with the train. There were Venetian blinds at the windows, and on a carved balcony at the corner of the building he could clearly see a woman in a white frock.

He felt sure that she was young and attractive. Then she was hidden from sight by the poplars. He would never see her again.

[3]

The moment her sleep was broken, and before she could tell herself that she was young, that there was a beautiful summer day ahead, that life could be happy, the memory of the quarrel came back like a cold, dull ache. She and her husband had started quarreling again the day before.

She opened her eyes. He wasn't in the bedroom. She was alone.

She threw open the shutters and looked out on the grounds. A beautiful morning! And the air was cool in the shade of the silvery Himalayan firs which brushed the windowsills on the second story.

Was she happy? It was at her wish that this beautiful park had come into being in the middle of the bare steppe. She had only to ask and any object in the world, any gown from St. Petersburg or Paris, would be brought to the door.

Their last big quarrel had gone on for three days—three days of silence, of ignoring each other, shunning each other. The Feast of the Transfiguration came around, and Irina went to church at Armavir with her mother-in-law. The soaring voices of the choir, the priest's moving sermon, the joyful ceremony of blessing the colorful pyramids of apples and the little pails and jugs of mead in the churchyard, the vestments, banners, and burnished censers brilliantly lit by a blazing sun, the drifting smoke of incense—all these together turned her mind to higher things. Her grievances against her husband seemed so trivial and petty when she considered God's world and God's purpose in it—and now there was the war. Irina resolved not only to ask his forgiveness this time, although she was not in the least to blame, but never to quarrel again, and to apologize first whenever there was the slightest danger of a quarrel—because that was the only way for a Christian. When she got home after Mass on the Feast of the Transfiguration, Irina had begged her husband to forgive her. Romasha was very happy—that was all he had been waiting for—and he magnanimously asked his wife's forgiveness in return.

They had lived in harmony from Wednesday to Sunday. Then they had quarreled again, so bitterly that they could not possibly go on talking to each other.

In the corridor the maidservant asked Irina in a whisper whether she wanted anything. For the present, nothing at all. She went into the red-and-white-marble bathroom.

Afterwards she prayed before an icon of the Virgin. But her heart was no lighter for it.

Nor did she feel any relief as she carried out her toilet before the three-leaved mirror and contemplated her naturally pink skin, her shapely shoulders, and her waist-length hair, which took four buckets of rainwater to wash.

She went over to the covered balcony on the sunny side of the house and squinted at the train—probably the Baku mail train. The Tomchaks had a fascinating view of the trains four or five hundred yards from the house. Irina never tired of watching them approach and vanish from sight. She would promise herself good luck if she guessed correctly whether the number of carriages was odd or even.

Many of those traveling now would converge at a single destination—the war.

That was why the quarrel had flared up yesterday. Irina had said too emphatically that Russia was in great trouble and that her sons should rally to her. She hadn't been thinking of her husband, and hadn't realized how it might sound. She was talking in a general way about the Teutonic menace. But Romasha had thought that it was meant for him, had been deeply wounded, had called her a patriotic dimwit, a benighted monarchist, as bad as her ignorant, pigheaded father, incapable of appreciating how short their barbarian country was of bright and enterprising minds like that of her husband.

Their quarrels were always the same—almost like quarrels between two men: sometimes over the Tsar, whom Romasha always ridiculed; sometimes about religious belief, which he had lost completely, though he discreetly concealed the fact.

But it would not have been nearly so hurtful if Romasha hadn't brought Irina's late father into it. Ignorant? True, he had started as a farm laborer, and *his* father had been a ranker in the army. Pigheaded? Well, he was the one, and not his daughter, to whom Roman had paid court. The old man had singled out Roman from among all the suitors: "That lad won't let go of money without a struggle."

Her father had been childless for many years. He had been an old man already when he paid 40,000 to the Bishop of Stavropol for permission to remarry. "Orina," or "Orya" as he always called her, was the child of that late love. When she was seventeen he had felt death approaching and had been in a hurry to see her married as soon as she left school. She knew now that it had been too soon, and regretted that he had not given her time to grow up a little. And enjoy herself a little. He might even have let her choose for herself.

Still, what was done was done. And Irina did not even allow herself to think wistfully of the different life she might have led, let alone blame her late father. Only those without faith pine for what might have been. A believer makes himself at home with things as they are, and finds sustenance in them.

What was done was done, and Irina dutifully accepted the husband she had not chosen. She turned over to him all the capital she had inherited, unconditionally, keeping nothing for herself. The independence Romasha now enjoyed, his inexhaustible wealth, his leisured life, his freedom to visit the capitals and travel abroad whenever he pleased, he owed entirely to Irina's father, not to his own. He might at least refrain from insulting remarks about him.

It was time to go down to breakfast. On the wooden staircase at the back of the house an idyllic view of Tsarskoye Selo looked down on the top step, and Tolstoy, plowing, on the bottom one, both painted by an Italian artist brought in from Rostov.

The dining-room walls were painted to look as though they were paneled with walnut; there was a huge walnut sideboard and furniture upholstered in moss-green or frog-green leather. Lemon trees in tubs shut out the view of the park. The table in the middle of the room could be expanded to seat twenty-four, but had been folded to take twelve and was laid for two, at one corner. Ksenia, her sister-in-law, was still in bed, Roman was never expected at breakfast, and her father-in-law often rose very early and rushed off in his brake to survey his two thousand desyatins* of steppe. On this occasion he had been away for two days in Yekaterinodar, where Romasha's fate was being decided. The old man's expedition was on everyone's mind, though no one mentioned it.

Irina bent over and gave her mother-in-law a good-morning kiss on

* A desyatin equals 2.7 acres. [*Trans.*]

her broad, plump cheek. Excessively fat and immutably placid—there was nothing more to be said about Yevdokia Grigorievna's face in her fifties. She seemed unperturbed by present worries, and past griefs had left no mark on her. Yet there had been a week in her life when scarlet fever robbed her of six of her children at once—only Ksenia, the littlest, had been snatched from death as from a burning house. (Roman and the oldest sister were already grown up.) When Irina felt impatient with her mother-in-law she sometimes reminded herself of that week.

She crossed herself before an icon showing the Last Supper (and so judged suitable for the dining-room wall) and sat down. The Tomchaks were observing the Feast of the Assumption, and there was nothing meaty or milky on the table. The manservant did not appear at breakfast, and a parlormaid served them their creamless coffee.

Yevdokia Grigorievna, daughter of a simple village blacksmith (in coarser clothes she would still be the humble peasant she once was), was still not used after all these years to sitting at the table in a lace shawl like a lady and having everything she needed set before her. It gave her pleasure to notice that something was missing and to fetch it herself, and there were days when she banished the cooks from the kitchen and made a great caldron of Ukrainian borsch with her own hands. Embarrassed by what the servants might think, her children tried to restrain her, and when there were guests they made her put away her eternal knitting and the ball of wool that was always under their feet.

She was at pains to check the expenditure of soap and charcoal in the washhouse, and would not let the washerwomen launder her daughter-in-law's delicate underwear ("Why wear expensive things where nobody can see them?"). She made it a rule that she and her husband, and anyone else in the house who could be forced to, should wear coarse linen made by nuns who brought it to the door. After all, she and this same husband had once lived in an adobe hovel with a dozen sheep to their name, and in her old age Yevdokia Grigorievna was still unconvinced that her husband's wealth would last. She could not keep track of all the losses, because there were leaks everywhere, people begged, borrowed, or stole from their exorbitant wealth, they had ten house servants, ten outdoor servants, not counting Cossacks, and who could say how many clerks, stewards, horsebreakers, storemen, stable hands, ox drivers, mechanics, gardeners. You can't drink without spilling! Irina's father-in-law, Zakhar Fyodorovich, understood that very well. One of his sayings was "Live and let live. I've got big hands, and people can pick up something from me when they could never find anything for themselves." Yevdokia Grigorievna had to reconcile herself to the uncontrollable outflow from the estate's abundance, but she kept a close check on cloth lengths and thread when the seamstress came along once a year. Zakhar Fyodorovich thought nothing of giving an old suit to a tramp, but if Yevdokia Grigorievna found out she would send someone in pursuit to reclaim it. On the other hand, nothing was too good for the nuns, monks, and pilgrims who knew where to find her from her sister Arkhelaia, herself in a convent, and if the household itself was not fasting the servants were set to work cooking a meatless meal for the black horde as well as the lavish family dinner. At one time Zakhar Fyodorovich himself had sent oxcarts loaded with provisions to the convent in Teberda. But Irina had persuaded her father-in-law that the nuns were work-shy scroungers, that God would be better pleased if all this food went to the workers instead, and particularly if they were given meat three times a day in summer. He had taken her advice.

"You and Romasha slept in different rooms again?" her mother-in-law asked with her invariable bluntness.

Irina bowed her head and blushed, not at the old woman's rudeness but because after eight years she had lost all hope of having a child. It was a torment to her. Her mother-in-law's tactlessness was understandable, and her husband had every right to be impatient with her.

The plain features over the massive shoulders expressed as much surprise as the old woman's habitual complacency allowed.

"A wife sleeping by herself just because she takes it into her head to? I never heard of such a thing. If he'd turned you out I wouldn't say a word."

This wasn't just because it concerned her son. She always took the side of any man against any woman. "This way we shall never see the day . . ."

The enormous grandfather clock chimed the hour and played "How Glorious Is the Lord." (They had bought it at an auction—the Treasury had been selling the escheated goods of an extinct princely family.)

"You have to curb your pride, Irina."

Oh, how she had tried to! But what did her mother-in-law know about pride? If Zakhar Fyodorovich was angry with her he could abuse her at mealtimes to his heart's content and Yevdokia Grigorievna would humbly endure it all. It was Irina who had jumped up on one such occasion crying, "Romasha! Let's get out of here! We can't go on living in this house!" Her father-in-law had thrown his fork on the floor, risen, and left the room himself. Husbands, of course, cool down quickly when wives are submissive, and the quarrel is over almost as soon as it begins. Zakhar Fyodorovich was soon fussing over his wife and calling her "my old darling."

Irina herself prayed to be made gentle and meek, but when her mother-in-law preached meekness a dark wave of anger welled up in her.

"Why did you spoil him? Why did you pamper your son so much? I'm the one who has to live with him."

"What's wrong with him?"

The older woman was so naïvely surprised, and her big eyes so frank and innocent, that Irina had not the heart to remind her of scenes like that at the study door with all the servants listening. It had begun with an argument over what should be sown in some field or other. Zakhar Fyodorovich had seen red, stamped his foot, and yelled, "Son of a bitch!" and Roman Zakharovich had shouted back, "You're another!" Father had struck son a stunning blow with his walnut crook, and the son, in a fit of the same primitive rage, had drawn a revolver from his pocket. If Irina had not hung on to her husband, crying, "Mama! Lock the door quickly!" there would have been no way of separating them. Roman had left home in a huff and his parents, greatly alarmed, immediately began sending telegrams begging their dear little son to come back to them.

Father and son were quarreling again now. They were at odds more often than not.

Breakfast was over. Irina rose and left the room, a stately figure in muslin, with the ladylike walk she had perfected in finishing school. Over the gold-embroidered carpet, which had not been taken up for the summer, past the glass cabinet, to the staircase, down the last few steps to ground level, passing yet another Lev Tolstoy on the way, this time in the act of mowing, and out through the front door.

All these Tolstoys had been painted at Roman's insistence. He had explained to old Tomchak that this was something all educated people went in for, and that Tolstoy was one of Russia's great men, and a count into the bargain. His private reason for revering and promoting Tolstoy was the great man's rejection of confession and Holy Communion, both of which Roman detested.

The park, and the adjoining outbuildings and kitchen gardens, occupied fifty desyatins. There was always something interesting to do: you could go and look at the washerwomen, inspect the stores in the cellars with the housekeeper, call on the wives of the seasonal workers in their barracks, or, if you felt like it, visit the hothouses.

Wherever she went, she still had to decide: Should she make up with him? Should she humble herself?

Irina set out across the park, forcing herself not to turn around and look at the bedroom balcony, from which *he* was probably looking out for her. When he was sulking he was capable of lurking there for a day, or a day and a night, making a prisoner of himself, not even moving about the house.

She went on under the Himalayan firs. Getting them to take root had been hard work. They had been brought, already well grown, from the garden of a grand duke in the Crimea, in baskets, with lumps of soil clinging to their roots, and a mark on each showing which side should face east when it was planted.

Farther on there were winding avenues of lilac, chestnut, and walnut.

"You've got to have brains to make money," Zakhar Fyodorovich used to say. But you needed them just as much, and needed good taste too, to spend your money sensibly. The neighboring Mordorenko family had any amount of money—but what did they spend it on? They still lived like newly rich peasants; Yakov Fomich had improved his appearance with a mouthful of platinum teeth, and his hobbledehoy sons played heads-or-tails with gold coins instead of coppers. When Tomchak and Chepurnykh were in St. Petersburg buying six thousand desyatins of Kuban land from the two Grabbe brothers, Zakhar Tomchak had wanted to do things in a big way. "Let's entertain the two counts. Only we won't give them the miserable stuff they give their guests." But once in Palkin's restaurant, he couldn't think what to offer them, and simply ordered "the best you've got and plenty of it."

Zakhar Fyodorovich was learning how to live from his son and daughter-in-law. On the side of the house facing the railway line they had planted balsam or pyramid poplars in avenues wide enough for two troikas to pass. The trees gave out a sweet scent at the end of a sunny day, and the uncouth lord of the steppe conceded that "it's lovely, Irina my dear, really lovely." The front courtyard was lined with plane trees. It had been Irina's idea to have an artificial pool made. The basin was lined with cement; it could be drained and refilled with piped water. There was a place for bathing, and the earth scooped out to make the pool became a mound on which they erected a summerhouse. So there came into being a park of the sort you might expect to find on the estate of some old family, but not on an "economy" out in the steppe. It stood out in sharp contrast to the surrounding countryside. All around there was nothing but steppe, forest, or marsh, but here there was parkland, another country, with separate laws of its own. Beyond the park they had planted an orchard, bringing two hundred or more fruit trees from their old place, from the Karamyk, near Holy Cross, and the trees had flourished in their new home. Beyond the orchard was a vineyard. Irina had had Moorish grass planted around the summerhouse, and in the front courtyard there was a lawn of emerald-green English rye grass, kept short by lawn mowers.

But the two hothouses were Irina's special concern: the little one for spring flowers, to decorate the table at Easter, however early it came; and the tall one, where oleanders, palms, yuccas, and araucarias wintered, together with hundreds of pots of small flowers with names known only to Irina and the man in charge (not the head gardener). All these delicate hothouse dwellers had to be inspected daily, assisted as necessary, put out for an airing in summer, and in winter carried to the conservatory while they were in full bloom, then back to the hothouse as soon as they began to fade.

Enjoying the variety of scents and colors and shapes, the delicacy and vigor of these flowers, Irina felt more sure of herself, less vulnerable to her husband's insults.

She had the fantastic notion that Roman would, in spite of everything, come looking for her once he awoke. Normally there would have been no possibility of that, but now that war had broken out and they might be parted, perhaps he would feel differently. She wanted him to come to her, not to triumph over him, but for his own sake. It would show that he had a heart.

[4]

No, there's no place like home! In the most comfortable of beds, in the brightest of bright blue rooms (darkened at present, but the sun's rays were beginning to steal through the Venetian blinds). And if she liked she could spend a day, a week, or even a month in undisturbed idleness.

As she emerged from a long and pleasant sleep to the long and pleasant life before her, Ksenia yawned with exquisite enjoyment, wriggled, stretched, and bunched her fists over her head.

It was, of course, a reprehensible way of life. You would soon go to pieces living like that. You certainly wouldn't boast about the details to your friends. It was bad, it was uncivilized—but it was so enjoyable! There was something nice that you would find only here, that only you and your family knew about, and that your friends simply could not understand. Of course, there was nothing to compare with the delights of Moscow, dancing classes, theaters, debates, public lectures, and even your studies. There you lived in a whirl. But here when you woke up in the morning you could lie in bed as long as you liked. It was pleasant to be one of the idle rich for a while.

Someone coughed outside her door and knocked.

"You awake, Ksenia?"

"I haven't decided yet. Why?"

"I want to get at the safe for a minute. But I can come back later if you want to sleep some more."

Lingering in bed when you've just woken up is the best part of it. But knowing that someone is waiting for you to get up spoils everything.

"All right," Ksenia shouted. She swung her strong legs to the floor and stood up without using her hands. She ran barefoot to the door, tripping over her long nightgown, and undid the catch. "Wait a bit, don't come in yet!" She dived back into bed, straightened her hairnet, and pulled the coverlet up to her chin.

"You can come in now."

Her brother opened the door and came in.

"Good morning. Are you sure I didn't wake you up? I'm sorry, I really do need to go to the safe. I can't see anything in this light. May I open one shutter?"

He crossed the room carefully, but the perfume bottles on the dressing table tinkled as he bumped into it. As he opened the outer shutter, the joyous day burst into the room and Ksenia stopped regretting that her slumbers were over. She had slept enough! She rolled over onto her side, rested her cheek on one hand, and gazed at her brother.

Now that there was light Roman's sunken eyes glared aggressively as though he expected to find an enemy as well as his sister in the room. His mustache was two straight spikes—it had always refused to curl.

But the enemy was not present. Roman discovered the keys to the wall safe in his hand and went to open it.

"This won't take a minute. I can close the shutters again afterward."

When the house had been constructed some years earlier this room was to have been Roman's study, which was why a steel safe had been built into the wall. Then they had decided that Roman would share his father's study on the ground floor and that this would be Ksenia's room, but they had left the safe where it was so that Roman could keep his money and his papers separately. In any case, his sister was there only during vacations.

Roman looked trim, lean, and agile in his close-fitting English-style sports jacket and knee breeches, but he was rather short. He was wearing a light brown cap to match his suit and gaiters.

"Are you going out in the car? Are you taking Irina and me for a drive today? Shall we go to town, or to the river, past Shtengel's place?"

Ksenia snuggled her disgracefully healthy, indecently suntanned little face into the pillow as she weighed the pros and cons: what would she have to sacrifice or postpone till tomorrow if she went for a drive? A centuries-old oak grove, a miracle out there in the steppes, bordered the estate of Baron von Shtengel, the unrivaled rival of all the local farmers. Roman's was no ordinary car, but a white Rolls-Royce, one of only nine in Russia, so they said. Roman had been given lessons by an Englishman, he drove the car himself and could even repair it, but he didn't like getting dirty in the inspection pit, and kept a chauffeur.

On this occasion, however, he looked put out, fumbled with the broad peak of the brown cap, and said, "No, I was just going down to the garage. I will take you for a drive, but not today. When we know what's in store for me."

"Yes, of course! I'm sorry, Romasha, I really am."

She had slept so deeply that she had lost her memory. Forgotten everything in a single night! Forgotten even that somewhere in the world there was a war on! And entirely forgotten that their father had gone to town to plead Romasha's cause, that his fate was being decided right then. The fate of his car too! It was ridiculous: he might have to hand over his Rolls-Royce! She could easily believe that her brother was in no mood for outings. It might even bring bad luck. Although, if she was honest with herself, Ksenia couldn't help thinking that a man ought to be ashamed of evading military service. The only breadwinner in a family should be exempt, of course, but who could call Roman a breadwinner? He needn't necessarily go on the firing line, but common decency demanded that he should at least join the army.

Still, if he couldn't see this for himself Ksenia couldn't bring herself to tell him, although they had been at ease with each other ever since she had ceased being a child.

"Where's Irina?"

"I don't know."

By now Roman had unlocked the outer and inner doors of the safe, and his head and shoulders were bowed over it.

"Didn't you go down to breakfast? Have they called the fast off yet?"

Roman acknowledged her chuckle with a slight turn of the head to show her the tip of his mustache and a one-sided grin. His nose was like his father's, curved and fleshy.

There was no danger of disagreement about that! Observing fasts was just one of the Tomchak household's stupid habits. And there were so many fasts to be observed! Lent was just about understandable: a priest was brought in, and for a solid week the whole estate prayed and fasted and took Communion so that all the servants and employees could be cleansed of their sins before the spring sowing began. Ksenia was always away for Lent, and Romasha visited the capitals, returning only at Easter. But as soon as the Feast of the Trinity was past the utterly nonsensical St. Peter's fast was upon them. And no sooner was that over than the Assumption fast set in. And before you could enjoy the Christmas festivities you had to get through the Advent fast. On top of all this, every Wednesday and Friday were fast days! Fasting was no additional hardship to a poor man, but when you had as much money as the Tomchaks and could take your pick of the most delicious dishes in the world, why waste half your life fasting? It was barbarous.

Brother and sister were united by the fact that they were the only members of the family to hold progressive and critical views. The others were all primitives, barbarians.

Still lying on her side, with her legs drawn up and her fist under her cheek, Ksenia went on thinking aloud.

"I don't know . . . This is my last chance to give up my studies . . . right now, this August, while I've only wasted one year . . . and while the dancing school is still taking pupils."

A proprietorial feeling toward the safe and the need to concentrate made Roman want to be alone with it. He did not want his sister to see what was inside or what he was doing, although she wouldn't have understood anyway and didn't want to know. But Roman hunched his shoulders to hide his hands from his sister as he rustled his papers.

"If only you would support me," Ksenia said with a sigh, "I'd take the plunge."

Roman silently busied himself.

"It would take Papa three years to find out, I'm sure of that. I would still be going to Moscow for university courses, for all he knew. However angry he was afterward, however much he shouted, he'd have to forgive me in the end, wouldn't he?"

Roman went on with what he was doing, his head almost inside the safe.

"Even if he wouldn't forgive me I still don't know what I ought to do." Ksenia pursed and unpursed her lips, assessing the alternatives. "Surely it would be better than ruining my life? What do I want with agricultural science? It's a crime to suppress your inclinations!"

Roman interrupted what he was doing and straightened up. He turned his head, still taking care to hide the open safe with his torso.

"He would never forgive you. Anyway, you're talking nonsense. There's every reason for you to finish your agronomy course, it's the only sensible thing you can do. You'd be invaluable around here."

His sharp, shrewd eyes studied her from under thick black brows and the English cap. Ksenia tossed her head and pulled a face. Roman didn't seem to understand how she felt. Once he had reached a verdict he always delivered it with stern, unsmiling directness. Other men of affairs were rather afraid of him: what chance had she?

"You'll be a farmer in your own right. You're sure of inheriting a quarter of the estate, whatever happens. And if Father and I fall out completely it will be more. Do you want to give it all up just to dance barefoot on the stage? It makes no sense. It isn't as if you were a silly little girl and your family all beggars."

But he did think she was a silly little girl, a child in need of guidance. She was a full seventeen years younger than her brother; he talked to her as father to daughter, and Ksenia listened, although she was unconvinced.

He turned back to his safe. If he had been mercenary he would have encouraged his sister to go to ballet school—he would only have to sympathize with her determination and praise her dancing once or twice. If Ksenia were to get married and present her father with a grandson, the old man might make everything over to the child in a fit of rage against his son. From a practical point of view, it would be to Roman's advantage if his sister joined a ballet school and fell out with her father. But he would never stoop so low—it was incompatible with the lifestyle which he had adopted, that of an English gentleman. He must try to make her see reason.

Having taken what he needed and locked each of the steel doors with a full turn of its own key, Roman looked at his silent sister again, and said sternly, "And when you get married it will be to a steppe farmer."

Ksenia jumped as if she had been stung.

"Wha-at? Never in the world! You can all take a running jump!" She tore off the net around her hair. The whites of her merry eyes flashed like those of a little Negro girl. She burst out laughing and raised her arm toward the ceiling in a ballerina's gesture. The thought of it was so frightening that you could only laugh. A farmer's idea of a beautiful woman was one who needed two chairs to sit down. "Go away, I'm getting up now."

As soon as the door closed behind him she shot out of bed, flung open the shutter of the other window, let in the day. The sunshine! Life! She bounded down onto the floor, darted to the gray bentwood dressing table (part of a suite made for her when she left high school). But whichever way she turned the swiveling mirror she could not see herself full-length.

And only when you did that, only when you saw her legs (strong legs, but not at all fat, and so nimble, with such tiny little feet!), only then did you realize what a beauty Ksenia was.

A leap! A bound! Another leap!

Then to the mirror for another close look. A round, ruddy, rather ordinary face—the face of a Ukrainian peasant girl, a steppe dweller, a Pecheneg, Yarik Kharitonov's teasing nickname for her when they were at school together, and one that hurt her feelings. But her hair was less dark than her hazel eyes led you to expect, and that made her face "interesting." And anyway, as she grew older her expression had become more refined, *much* more refined, *and* more intellectual, *and* more thoughtful. An abnormally healthy look, though, not a hint of pallor (must work on being pale!). A round, naïve, rustic face, unmistakably a steppe dweller's face. And those extraordinarily even, extraordinarily strong teeth only made it more unmistakably just that. Could such a face possibly show how educated you were? What an amazingly acute sense of beauty she had acquired? Would anyone ever guess from looking at that face how often she had been to the theater? How many photographs she had hung on her wall, how many statuettes she had installed both at home and in her room in Moscow? There was Leonid Andreev! Several Geltzers! Several Isadoras! And Ksenia herself, sometimes in riding habit and boots with spurs, sometimes barefoot, in gauzy voile, with a locket.

Light as a bird, with her fingers holding her skirt, the best dancer in Kharitonova's school, perhaps in any of the Rostov schools. How could she get her way? What other way of life was there? What else was there in life?

Except dancing? Except dance! Those floating arms, not a bit too long; those shoulders, so beautifully molded! If only the neck would grow a little, become just a little longer and slenderer! The neck has an eloquence of its own in the dance, it is very important.

Never mind washing! Never mind eating! Never mind drinking! Just let me dance! Let me dance!

Through the door, onto the balcony, from the balcony into the big room with the stupid old plush furniture that the old people couldn't bring themselves to throw out. Now, that was a real mirror, one in which you could see all of yourself! Humming to herself. A leap! Another leap! How beautifully she did it! She was like a bird. She had a remarkably small foot—a man could have hidden it in his hand. And such elevation! It was a barefoot-dancing school: they used the whole foot, they didn't dance on point. Their aim was to resurrect ancient Greece! In fact it wasn't dancing at all, it was or-che-stic illustration. Wearing a Greek tunic and drooping in despair over a burial urn. Then there was a dance representing a prayer before a sacrificial altar. Why, she was almost as good as Isadora. She wouldn't be second-best. And she had everything before her!

But here came a maidservant with a vacuum cleaner. And another, bringing the young mistress a towel warmed in the sunshine—very pleasant to dry yourself with after your bath.

There was this to be done, and that, and then breakfast, and meanwhile the steppe was getting hot, so hot that the broadest of hat brims was no protection, and the best thing was to lie in a hammock out in the garden, all in white.

The sky was drained of color, as though faint from the heat, and even in dense shade it was oppressively hot. The heat muffled the spluttering of the traction engines in the threshing yard, the whine of machines from the work yard, and the mingled buzzing of insects. There was not even the slightest breeze.

Gravel crunched under someone's foot. Ksenia twisted around and saw Irina approaching, erect and demure as ever. Ksenia stretched out both arms as though to embrace her, since this was the first they had seen of each other that morning. As Irina bent over, Ksenia's book shut itself, slipped out of her hand, and lodged against the frame of the hammock—but not before Irina had noticed. She nodded at it reprovingly.

"More French reading matter?"

The book was in English, but that wasn't the point. Lying there with her head thrown back so that her loosely gathered hair brushed the taut netting of the hammock, she wrinkled her nose pleadingly. "Irinka," she pleaded, "surely you don't expect me to read the life of Serafim of Sarov all the time?"

Irina stood close to the trunk of a chestnut tree without touching it, without shifting her weight from either foot. She seemed to have no wish to relax, but her look was one of humorous benevolence.

"Of course not," she said, "but as far as I can see your reading doesn't include anything Russian."

"Such as?" For one moment there was in Ksenia's voice a hint of annoyance that her idle enjoyment had been disturbed. "I've read all of Turgenev and got sick of him a hundred times over. Dostoevsky gets on my nerves, gives me the jitters. Hamsun and Przybyszewski and Lagerlöf none of us read, you needn't worry about that."

Irina had arrived in the family when Ksenia was a bashful eleven-year-old, and had taken charge of her till she left for school in Rostov at the age of thirteen. *That* Ksenia had been brought up to walk with God, and knew no greater ecstasy than emulating her sister-in-law in fasting, praying, and devotion to Russian tradition.

Irina's face clouded over and she nodded her head ruefully, over and over again.

"You're running away . . ."

The quick hazel eyes flashed.

"From what? From all this Ukrainian boorishness? I truly wish I could get away from it—but how? These suitors from other 'economies' stink of tar, I could die laughing when I have to talk to them! Yevstignei Mordorenko!" She choked with laughter at the very thought of him. "Remember how he wept because they were sending him off to Paris?"

Irina joined in, in her own way. Though her features were austere and solemn, the button nose suggested that she had a sense of humor, and her lips were apt to tremble when she saw or heard something funny. A slight smile on Irina's face meant as much as a loud peal of laughter from Ksenia.

The blockhead of the Mordorenko family kept his own racehorses, and they were due to run in Moscow, but he had somehow incurred his father's displeasure and by way of punishment was packed off to Paris instead.

Whereupon Yevstignei, who was as big and strong as a horse himself and in his time had overlooked not one of the girls on the estate, not even the governess, sat down and blubbered for two days and nights, begging not to be exiled.

"Or just think how they toss women in the air at the balls around here!" Ksenia said, shaking with laughter.

The guest of honor at an anniversary celebration is sometimes tossed to the cheers of his friends. At their wild parties drunken steppe farmers would grab young women, including their own wives and daughters-in-law, and a dozen hands would throw them up in the air. The object of the game was to insert a hand under fluttering garments and clutch a bare thigh. (Roman, who behaved arrogantly with other farmers, gave great offense by taking Irina home in good time.)

"Well, I suppose that's my lot. Ksenia Zakharovna Tomchak! Can you imagine it on a visiting card? It reeks of peasant carts or undressed sheepskin or something. You wouldn't get past the door in any decent house."

"If it wasn't for those sheep, Ksenia my dear, you would never have seen high school or your university course."

"It might have been better if I hadn't. I should never have known what I'd missed. I should have married some Pecheneg barbarian with ten mills, and had my photograph taken standing behind my husband's chair like a stone image."

"All the same," Irina quietly insisted, "Russia's roots are here."

"Here? You mean Russia has Pecheneg roots?"

Irina frowned slightly, and the blue veins stood out on her long, graceful neck.

"Everything around us here," she said doggedly, "is much closer to the nation's roots than your enlightened Kharitonovs, who don't care about Russia at all."

Ksenia wriggled impatiently, braced herself against the taut ropes of the hammock, and said heatedly, "For heaven's sake! Where do you get these rigid, dogmatic judgments from? You've never set eyes on any of the Kharitonovs. Why can't you stand the very thought of them? They're all honest people, all hard workers—what has the Kharitonov family done to displease you?"

Ksenia's abrupt movements caused the book to slip through the mesh of the hammock.

Irina shook her head knowingly. "I've never seen them, but I know their kind. They all swear by the *people*, but the country itself . . ."

"Well, let's leave the Kharitonovs out of it," Ksenia said, now really annoyed.

Irina realized that she had got off on the wrong foot. She regretted criticizing the Kharitonovs directly instead of . . .

"It saddens me, Ksenia my dear, that everything here inspires either shame or ridicule in you. There is, of course, a lot that is shameful and ridiculous, but still this is where you see how real Russian people live, where you can feel the bedrock under the soil. The grain for our daily bread is grown here, not in Petersburg. You even find the church fast days superfluous. But fasting helps people to grow spiritually."

"Let's leave it at that then," Ksenia begged plaintively. She felt too lazy to argue, and anyway, there was something in what Irina said.

"What I meant," said Irina, as disarmingly as she could, "is that we are only too ready to find everything funny. If we see a comet with two tails—that's funny. There was an eclipse of the sun last Friday—and that was funny."

But Ksenia had lost all desire to argue. Her anger had ebbed as quickly as it had welled up. She gazed up at the canopy of sun-dappled leaves through half-closed eyes.

"Really now . . . There is such a thing as astronomy."

"Astronomers can say what they like," Irina calmly insisted. "But there was an eclipse of the sun when Prince Igor set out on his campaign. There was an eclipse during the Battle of Kulikovo. There was an eclipse at the crucial stage of the Northern War. Whenever Russia faces the ordeal of war there is an eclipse."

She loved mystery.

Ksenia leaned over to grab her book and almost fell out of the hammock herself. Her hair hung down in disorder, and an opened envelope fell out of the book.

"Oh yes, I forgot to tell you. I got a letter from Yarik Kharitonov. Just imagine, his classes ended early, the day after the war began, and he wrote this letter from the army in the field. By the time it got here he was already in action somewhere. And it's a happy letter—he's delighted to be there!"

They had been in the same year at school, done their homework together. He was like a favorite brother, and Ksenia thought of him with pride and affection.

"Where was it posted?"

"Ostrolenka. I must look for it on Romasha's map."

Irina's straight eyebrows came together in embarrassed approval.

"Imagine a family like that producing an officer and a patriot! I regard that as an omen."

But what of her husband? What was his future to be?

[5]

Zakhar Fyodorovich was used to doing business in the crazy city of Rostov—but not that sort of business. His usual reason for going there was machinery: all the latest machines turned up in Rostov. You could take a good look at them, run a hand over them, and someone would explain how they worked in a way you could understand. Before any of his neighbors or even Baron von Shtengel got around to it he had bought Siemens seed drills, potato cultivators, and those new plows that ran on belts between two traction engines. He sometimes negotiated big grain sales in Rostov (there were even French buyers among his customers). And of course he bought things for himself—fish in particular (there was nowhere like Rostov for fish!), other foodstuffs, household goods. He had gone in once to buy a pair of gloves—he had to have squirrel fur inside, soft leather outside, and there had never been any gloves like that in Armavir—and the crafty devils had talked him into buying a car while he was at it, a "Russo-Baltic Carriage," for 7,500 rubles. He had always carried on about his son's "Thomas"—he firmly believed that driving the beastly thing around the fields caused storms that beat down the crops. And there he was himself, looking for a chauffeur. His vineyard manager's young son was a good driver—he'd learned in the army—and took the job.

Zakhar Fyodorovich's buying and selling in Rostov always went smoothly, and he enjoyed seeing how briskly Rostov people went about their business. But he didn't even know where the high schools were—school signs were not the sort of thing he noticed. So when Roman and Ira induced him to send Ksenia on from the boarding school at Pyatigorsk to high school in Rostov he had taken her to town with some misgivings. High schools were a commodity he knew nothing about. Somebody was sure to palm off a dud on him.

As it happened, he also had business with Ilya Isakovich Arkhangorodsky, a very clever Jew and a respectable person. This Arkhangorodsky was the supreme expert on flour mills, including the most up-to-date types, those powered by electricity, for instance. His reputation was such that no one installed a mill anywhere between Tsaritsyn and Baku without calling in his firm, and when the tycoon Paramonov thought he would like a five-story mill in Rostov it was Arkhangorodsky who erected it for him. It had occurred to Tomchak that Arkhangorodsky would not mislead him if asked about a school for his daughter. Arkhangorodsky had turned up trumps: there was, of course, the public high school and a number of others, but his advice was to send her to Kharitonova's private school, where his own daughter was in the fourth form. They compared ages: both girls were thirteen—splendid, they could sit together. Zakhar Fyodorovich was pleased that Ksenia would have a friend from the start. He was particularly pleased that it was a private school, not a state school. No business goes well unless whoever runs it also owns it. You could expect nothing good from the state and its employees.

Zakhar Fyodorovich always wore a suit when he went to Rostov—worsted or tussore, according to the time of year. He also wore a felt hat, or even took an umbrella for swank (but soon forgot about it, and strode along waving his arms about as if he were back home on the steppe and had just jumped down from his droshky in his cape and his dubbined boots). There was one other thing—his daughter-in-law had, shortly before all this, given him the idea of ordering a hundred visiting cards, as though they were absolutely necessary. Money down the drain, of course. None of the businessmen and professional people whom Tomchak visited, nobody in the banks or on the exchange, handed ridiculous scraps of pasteboard around, and the whole packet stayed intact in his pocket like an unused pack of cards. He had never broken into it until he pulled up outside Kharitonova's school and gave his first card to the doorman to take upstairs.

Aglaida Fedoseevna Kharitonova turned out to be a woman of character, and a sensible one, except for the pince-nez which kept slipping off her nose—she would have done better to wear ordinary glasses. The sort of serious woman you could trust to look after your daughter in a distant town, and be sure that she wouldn't be up to any tricks if you didn't see her for half a year at a time.

That he himself might not appeal to the headmistress did not enter

Zakhar Fyodorovich's head. The salient characteristics of the male Tomchaks had always been their awkwardness, their sulks, their bad language in the family circle, and their cheerfulness and ready conversation whenever they had guests or went visiting. There was no company, and no woman, whom Zakhar Fyodorovich could not charm when he felt like it.

The picturesque Ukrainian's rugged features, his bushy brows, his big rambling nose, his town-going fancy dress complete with watch chain in the most conspicuous place, and even more his frankness, his sense of humor, his patriarchal dignity, and above all the breezy forcefulness that almost blew the papers from her desk and caused the calendar to change the date, bowled Aglaida Fedoseevna over and left her spellbound. She moved among clever and knowledgeable people, but none of them had that sort of energy, that passionate urge to be up and doing. Tomchak could not lower his voice to a normal conversational level even in the headmistress's study. He would not have shouted or laughed much louder if he had been walking beside creaking oxcarts with herds of sheep and cattle bleating and bellowing around him. Yet Aglaida Fedoseevna, exquisitely mannered guardian of hushed decorum, was not, as you would expect, appalled but thrilled by this gust of fresh air. Even the obvious fib he told—that he had visited four schools, none of them to his liking, but had taken to this one as soon as he set foot on the stairs, indeed at his first glimpse of the doorman—even this naïve artfulness she found endearing. So although every place in the fourth form was taken and she had not intended to admit anyone else, least of all a wild girl who would certainly have been badly taught hitherto, she agreed after ten minutes to take Ksenia; then instead of puckering her brow as a sign that she had other things to do, she succumbed to the cheerful Ukrainian's simple good nature, began asking him about himself, and rang for coffee.

Zakhar Tomchak told his story as though she was there only to hear it, with lavish detail and plenty of jokes. He told her that in his childhood he had been a simple shepherd in the Taurida, pasturing other people's sheep and calves. He and others from the area had come to the Caucasus looking for casual employment, and he had earned less than he would now pay the lowliest migrant laborer, let alone one of his regular skilled hands. After ten years his employer had given him ten sheep, a heifer, and some piglets of his own, and from that beginning he had amassed his present fortune, by sweating and slaving. The headmistress asked how much schooling he had had: a year and a half in a parish school had taught him enough for his purposes—to read the Bible and the *Lives of the Saints* in Russian or in Church Slavonic, and to write, not very well, it was true, but no one could ever cheat him over a purchase. She asked about his family, and he told her of the trials God had sent him: six of his children had died in a week, all but the two oldest and the youngest of his progeny. He had tears in his eyes, and dabbed at them with his handkerchief. Then he told her about the estate. They had baked flawless iron-hard bricks in kilns they had built themselves—a million of them, they could sell any that were left over. He himself had helped the architect design his new house, and seen to it that there was no window without Venetian blinds *and* shutters, so that they needn't worry how hot it was. They had laid four water mains, they had their own generator ready for use, they were now planting trees in the park and would put lamps in it . . . Anyway, he invited the headmistress there and then to bring her children for a holiday the next summer.

She repaid his confidence by telling him that she had recently lost her husband, an inspector of state schools, that she had three children—her daughter had just left school and was going to study in Moscow, and her older son, Yaroslav, who was thirteen, was getting out of hand, wanted to give up school and become an empty-headed army cadet.

She informed him that the school fees were two hundred rubles a year. Five times more than in the state schools, because . . .

Tomchak almost took offense. "I know what it costs, you don't have to tell me. You haven't any cattle, you don't make sunflower oil or grow beans, you have to have something to support your children on." When she asked where the little girl would live Tomchak became plaintive: "She has nowhere to lay her head, poor little lamb. How will she manage in this busy town with nobody to keep an eye on her? Maybe she could live with you." (He had been thinking of it from the first. That was why he had exerted his charm and drunk coffee and invited the headmistress to come and drink kumiss, when all the time other matters were clamoring for his attention.)

"What exactly have you in mind?" This was the last thing Kharitonova had expected.

"Well, you aren't hard up for rooms, are you? You say your oldest has left school and is going to Moscow, you could take mine in instead. You could give me all three of yours. I'd soon find room for them."

Ridiculous and impertinent as the suggestion was, Aglaida Fedoseevna, after their friendly conversation and the jokes they had shared, could not suddenly revert to her original glacial manner, with which she so successfully put people off. She tried to make this uncouth Ukrainian see that it was impossible, that it just wasn't done for a pupil to lodge with her headmistress, told him that her own daughter had been educated not at home but in a state high school so that there could be no suspicion of favoritism; but the uncouth Ukrainian was unimpressed and treated her to more of his homespun wisdom and pathos. "Where can I put her, then? I can't leave her with strangers. She'll have to come home and mind the sheep. Pity, she's a mighty clever girl."

"Don't you regard me as a stranger?"

"You? Of course not! You're one of my sort, I feel I really know you." He was so sure of it, and so happy about it, that the headmistress had no time to wonder how she and this wild man of the steppes had become so close.

Tomchak saw clearly that the headmistress had taken to him, and would like his daughter, but that he should not push too hard. He laughingly changed the subject, asking only whether she could give his little girl shelter for three days, because he had contracts to sign, would be going from office to office, had to make a trip to Mariupol, couldn't leave her in a hotel with no one to look after her but would find somewhere for her to live when he came back. The headmistress found that she had somehow let herself be persuaded. Tomchak even kissed her hand (it was not one of his skills, but he had seen others do it) and dashed off. He returned with a timid little girl in a plain checked frock with a sash, too overawed by the grand lady in pince-nez to sit down or look around—but not before a big porcelain jar of caviar, a square yard of cake from Filippov's, and various other packages had been delivered at the other entrance (the headmistress's quarters were in the school building). A few extras wouldn't come amiss even to this educated personage in nose-pinchers. Anyway, paying people in advance what your conscience told you to wasn't the same as giving a bribe, trying to buy someone. Tomchak couldn't have put it into words, but he felt in his heart that paying generously, for whatever it might be, created friendship and goodwill between people.

The three days of Tomchak's absence was time enough for the headmistress's experienced eye to see that Ksenia was neat and tidy, obedient, quick to learn. Her daughter's room was unused, so there would be no need to disturb the boys. Aglaida Fedoseevna even decided that a girl growing up in the same house would have a good influence on her sons. The only thing was that the child prayed much more than one would wish, spending a long time on her knees morning and evening. Still, this made it all the more tempting to remove her from her benighted family and propel her along the road of progress. The condition she made was that Ksenia would go home only for vacations, and that during the school year her father would not interfere. Zakhar Fyodorovich asked nothing better. The headmistress's rules were strict—what more could a young girl need?

It did not occur to Tomchak that he had subjected his daughter to an ordeal from the start: that, lodging with the headmistress, she might be looked upon by her classmates as a sneak and a tattletale. The headmistress herself preserved Ksenia from this danger: she attached great importance to the liberal spirit of her school, did not resort to secret interrogation or encourage tale-telling, and did not allow her teachers to do so. In their years together she had never asked Ksenia a single question of that kind. She and her late husband both thought that the main purpose of education was to produce citizens—which meant people hostile to authority.

Ksenia's ability and application surpassed Aglaida Fedoseevna's anticipations. Other girls spent an hour each day moving between home and school, but Ksenia needed only a minute, and devoted the hour she saved to study. She enjoyed the process of learning, and this, not school prizes, was her incentive. Her end-of-term mark was never lower than A-minus in any subject. She did particularly well in foreign languages, though she hadn't known a word of anything but Russian when she arrived. Two foreign languages were obligatory at the school, and Ksenia, when she left with her gold medal, could read three with ease. (She loved her school so much, was so anxious not to miss a day's study, and remained for years so unsure of herself that she had refused Irina's invitation to join her and Roman on their European grand tour.)

More languages meant more books. There were many bookcases in the Kharitonov apartment, stocked with children's books and books not for children, and there was little overlap with Ksenia's reading at home, except for Gogol and Dickens. If you found a volume as thick as a Bible, and of the same thin paper, it would be not the Bible but Shakespeare with frightening pictures.

With every term, every month Ksenia spent at school, she saw more and more clearly how barbarous and benighted the world of her childhood was. Her father's tactlessness in billeting his daughter with her headmistress was embarrassing enough in itself. When she went home for vacations Ksenia was horrified by the unrelieved uncouthness of her father's household. On one occasion she took Sonya Arkhangorodskaya home, and was consumed with shame when she saw still more painfully through her friend's eyes how primitive it all was. If the agricultural course had not come her way she would have gone off to study no matter what, just so long as she could associate with civilized people.

No longer did she kneel night and morning to pray devoutly: her prayers at home were perfunctory, and she went to church only when she could not avoid it, with the whole family, standing through the service with her mind elsewhere, crossing herself awkwardly.

Too late, it dawned on Tomchak that he had forgotten to ask the headmistress one little thing: whether or not she believed in God.

Document No. 4

24 August

FROM THE FRENCH MINISTRY OF FOREIGN AFFAIRS TO AMBASSADOR PALÉOLOGUE IN ST. PETERSBURG:

. . . insist that the Russian armies advance on Berlin as a matter of urgent necessity. Warn the Russian government without delay that . . .

[6]

Roman could spend a week in his own company without feeling bored just as long as his meals were served and his needs attended to on time: he knew no one more interesting and agreeable than himself.

He gave the elderly manservant detailed instructions about what to bring him for lunch, out there on the veranda, before the sun found it. He paid particular attention to the selection of cold fish to start the meal. (A Rostov fishmonger regularly put a barrel or a package for the Tomchaks on a passenger train, in the care of the conductor. A Cossack rode down to the station to collect it and pay the conductor for his trouble.) It seemed sensible to enjoy lunch out on the veranda, where he could be by himself with no one to nag him, before the old man returned. He would probably be back in the early evening, when there were two trains in quick succession. But they were quarreling, and Roman had no intention of trying to ingratiate himself by meeting his father at the station.

His worries were shared by the servant, whose brother, Roman's chauffeur, was liable to be called up but might be granted exemption together with other important workers if old Tomchak succeeded in his endeavors.

Roman was a "sole breadwinner" (the only son of the family), and thus exempt from conscription. But there were rumors that this privilege was to be withdrawn where the "breadwinner" did not actually support a family, and the manifesto on the militia three days back had referred vaguely to men missed by previous drafts. His father had hurried off to the recruiting office to close any possible loophole. On the glassed-in veranda outside his bedroom stood Roman's favorite couch, commandeered from his wife's suite. The smooth curve of the headrest enabled him to recline comfortably without lying down. He had no need to sit up or prop himself up with cushions if he wanted to smoke or read the papers or do what he was doing now—studying the war map hanging where he could see it on the wall.

He had telephoned a shop in Rostov and ordered a batch of flags of the warring nations, which he could pin to the map to show the positions of the armies in the field. He had started doing this before rumors that his exemption might be canceled reached him and blew the appeal of the map away like a puff of cannon smoke. Now his heart sank when he looked at the meandering frontiers, the little circles representing towns, the foreign names.

Roman lit a made-to-measure cigarette with his gold lighter. While they were abroad on their honeymoon Irina had given her husband a long, slim, gold cigarette case, too long for any Russian cigarette. Roman, being a gentleman, could not let this precious gift, the first of their marriage, go to waste. Renouncing shop-bought cigarettes, he had ordered wrappers of the appropriate size from the Asmolov factory in Rostov, twenty thousand at a time, and a young lady was called in from Armavir specially to fill them.

This was a day when not even smoking gave him any pleasure. He sat at a card table, spread out the papers he had taken from the safe, and busied himself with his accounts. Roman had only an elementary education. Thirty years ago, in Mokry Karamyk, the family was just getting on its feet, and it did not occur to them that their son ought to go to high school. Later on he had entered a commercial school but had not finished the course. He did, however, have a head for figures. He was also a very talented manager, but it was beneath his dignity to take orders from an overbearing father who could not stand contradiction and, with his extraordinary flair, did very well unaided. Roman was waiting for the day when he would be his own master. In the meantime, he had his capital and could afford to take no part in his father's business. Every year he spent two months in Moscow and St. Petersburg and two months abroad. In Moscow he drove trotting horses, beat foreign tourists to the last deluxe compartment in the Elite on the Petrovka, and went dinner-jacketed to the Bolshoi, strolling down the aisle to the front row of the orchestra stalls after everyone else was seated. Roman admired himself particularly on his travels. He enjoyed dressing in such a way that even new acquaintances at the Pump Room in Kislovodsk took him for an Englishman. He enjoyed astounding Europeans with Russian stamina and Russian oddity. Going to the Louvre, and in the purple room in which the Venus de Milo stood and no one was supposed to sit, holding out a ten-franc note to the attendant and calling, "*La chaise!*" then moving on to the next room and pointing: "Now put the chair there please, right there!" because his wife would be looking at bits of broken crockery for some time yet and he was ready for a smoke, or maybe even for lunch.

But Irina too was splendid when she put on her feathered hat and glided, erect as the statue of some goddess, with only her bird-of-paradise plumes nodding overhead. A man wouldn't be ashamed to show himself even at court with her. He wished, though, that he was an inch or two taller himself, and that his hair was not falling out so quickly. If that went on he would have to have it close-clipped.

It was no good, he couldn't get on with the accounts. He would be on tenterhooks until he knew what news his father was bringing. He paced the veranda, smoking and thinking.

Roman never felt fonder of himself than when he was deep in thought, exercising his talents to the full, including those gifts of statesmanship which as yet were hidden from the world at large. One way in which he was certainly superior to many members of the Duma was in his outspokenness. The wildest and most undisciplined farmers in the region treated Roman Zakharovich with respect. They might not like him very much, but they were a little afraid of him. Not only did he never flatter anybody, he never made the slightest concession for the sake of politeness, never bestowed a smile just to be hospitable, but always conversed with lofty seriousness, keeping his keen gaze on his companion's face. It was a rule of his not to waste a single minute talking to anyone of no interest and no use to him. Even if such a person was a guest in his house Roman Zakharovich would rise abruptly and go to his own room. Uncompromising people like himself were, he knew, just what the government of Russia presently lacked, especially at the very top.

Roman's pacing grew more and more emphatic and purposeful. At one end of his transit a photograph of Maxim Gorky hung from the frame of the veranda. Roman looked with approval at the challengingly cocked head and squashed nose of the famous writer. Roman was always loud in his praises of Gorky's books and plays. He found in them one of his own characteristics: refusal to truckle to well-wishers. Roman was enchanted by the daring with which Gorky poured out his bile on industrial and commercial tycoons who in return rapturously applauded his pungent, tingling originality.

Beyond the park lay two thousand desyatins of Kuban black earth—his, if he ever inherited them. To think that a mere slip of paper from the recruiting officer could wreck this rich and secure life, a life so full of promise, and consign this clever and enlightened head of his to a muddy trench—at the mercy of a sergeant major. The barbarity of it!

The Kuban had not, so far, given Russia a single public figure of real importance. The Kuban had no claim to fame. Roman pictured the various ways in which he might rise in the world, one more interesting than another. He would, in principle, be bolder than the Constitutional Democrats. What was there to the left of them? The socialists. Gorky was, of course, a socialist. He might, in fact, have considered becoming a socialist himself if their cause did not involve robbery and the confiscation of lawful property. Roman's one personal recollection of socialism—in 1906—stuck in his throat. Never in his life had he felt such resentment. It wasn't just the loss. He could have reconciled himself to that, as he would have done to losses caused by storm or drought or a fluctuation in prices. Everybody has losses! But having to hand over with good grace money earned by the sweat of your brow to insolent wretches, leering villains with neither the wit nor the application to earn a twentieth as much for themselves! The nearest they ever got to work was writing letters in a clerkly hand with bold flourishes and circulating them to all the steppe farmers: "Dear Zakhar Fyodorovich! Your contribution to revolutionary funds has been set at 40,000 rubles." (Some people were asked for 50,000.) "Otherwise your death will not be long delayed."

Signed: "The Anarcho-Communists." To reinforce the message, the first to refuse were indeed killed—a whole family of them.

What else could they do? They were in the middle of a revolution, everyone was frightened, the authorities were unsure of themselves. And then there was public opinion to consider. Give to the revolution? Of course you must. It's your sacred duty to the exploited people. That was the attitude of educated society. (If it had been for a legitimate revolution, to overthrow the hated Tsar, Roman would have spared no expense.) The farms were cut off from one another, defenseless out in the middle of the steppe. (After this experience the Tomchaks started keeping four hired Cossacks.) There was nothing for it—they made the journey in a cart, wearing workaday clothes, three of them: Roman, the bailiff, and a countinghouse clerk. Roman's father did not go. He could not have surrendered the money with his own hands. The first thousand would have broken his heart.

They drove to a distant spot behind an acacia plantation. It was autumn. He had a vivid memory of broad mauve pods crunching under their wheels. The others arrived—from Armavir?—in a phaeton, dressed not at all modestly, indeed quite expensively. One of them was even wearing a morning coat with satin lapels and a bow tie. They chatted politely and patiently counted the notes. It was three against three. Roman and his companions could have flung themselves on the others, beaten them up, shot them. They could have had people lying in ambush. Roman was in fact carrying a revolver in his back pocket. But he lacked the resolve. All Russia, for some reason, thought that these splendid, frightening fellows had right on their side. All the same, he could not bring himself to hand over the whole 40,000; he dug in his heels, haggled, and wheedled a discount of 2,500 out of them. They were greatly amused—"What skinflints you farmers are!" (His father warmly congratulated him on this coup.) They had made their farewells most politely and driven off. Nobody ever discovered what they had done with the money—built barricades? bought rifles? They could have been three con men who made a killing and went off to spend it on booze and prostitutes in Baku.

* * *

RICH MEN'S SONS ARE LIKE BLUE HORSES:
THEY RARELY WIN RACES

* * *

[7]

(A GLANCE AT THE NEWSPAPERS)

The man who does not know the magical effect of Lecital is a LIVING CORPSE . . . The stimulant to cure **NEURASTHENIA IN MEN** . . .

MOSCOW MUTUAL-AID FUND FOR BRIDES . . .

Ladies' coconut-fiber hammocks . . .

Click-Click, the London perfume with the exquisite bouquet . . .

LUCK PLUS CHANCE BRINGS WEALTH! **Buy a ticket in the lottery . . .**

. . . that ethical idealism in social matters in which the Slavic soul is so rich, and in which the enlightened West has become so poor . . .

To welcome the PRESIDENT OF THE FRENCH REPUBLIC a cruise on the large, first-class steamer *Rus* has been arranged for 20 July. Music on board. Intended for the fashionable public only.

. . . indifference of French democracy to the danger threatening the country from without . . . triumph of the anti-patriotic parties in the French parliament . . .

ATTEMPT ON THE LIFE OF GRIGORI RASPUTIN . . . Under interrogation she would only say, "He is the Antichrist" . . . She has been identified as Khionia Kuzminichna Guseva, a peasant from Simbirsk province . . . Rasputin's life is no longer in danger . . .

. . . the order prohibiting the renting of stands at the Nizhni Novgorod Fair to Jews has been rescinded . . .

WHY BE FAT ANY LONGER? ***An ideal anatomical girdle to correct obesity, indispensable to the elegant man.***

FRANCO-RUSSIAN ALLIANCE CELEBRATES ITS SILVER ANNIVERSARY . . . Visit of M. Poincaré . . . Official banquet . . . On Her Imperial Majesty's right . . . On the Emperor's left . . .

M. Poincaré receives a delegation of Russian peasants . . . The leader of the delegation greets the President and asks him to convey to the peasants of France . . .

BANQUET on board the battleship *France* . . . Resounding confirmation of unbreakable alliance . . . Peace the common ideal . . .

LAST HOURS of the French visit . . . Asked whether the alarm shown by European public opinion over events in the Balkans was justified . . . Viviani replied that it was "undoubtedly exaggerated."

. . . The *Times* notes that the superiority of the Russian army over the German is greater than . . .

UNCLE KOSTYA cigarettes—10 for 6 kopecks, the height of elegance and good taste!

SHUSTOV'S INCOMPARABLE ROWANBERRY LIQUEUR!

FOR LOVERS OF BEAUTY! ***Paris-type photographs. Latest original pictures. As* NATURE *intended! Sent in PLAIN SEALED envelope.***

. . . Russia's love of peace is well known . . . But Russia is conscious of her historic obligations and therefore . . .

. . . in view of the continuing strike, industrialists in the Vyborg district close factories and mills for two weeks . . .

. . . no newspapers have appeared in Moscow . . . one-day strike of compositors . . .

R A C I N G today

YAR RESTAURANT

PEACE OR WAR? This morning the talk everywhere was of "peace" . . . Unhappy Serbia . . . Peace-loving Russia . . . Austria has presented the most humiliating demands . . . Over little Serbia's head the sword is pointed at great Russia, defender of the inviolable right of millions to work and live . . .

. . . instead of crushing depression, a new access of courage and confidence in their own strength. This is a psychological characteristic of all healthy peoples.

. . . This giant among nations, which has never been broken by the heaviest trials, has no fear of a bloody contest from whichever quarter the threat comes.

MANY DISHEARTENED WOMEN have regained their *joie de vivre* with the aid of this cream . . .

His Majesty the Emperor has ordered the army and the fleet to be put on a war footing. Mobilization will begin on 31 July 1914.

Hark, Siars, the thunder's deafening rattle
From out that misty northern land:
'Tis he, he girds himself for battle,
Your elder brother, cross in hand.

THE GERMAN AMBASSADOR IN ST. PETERSBURG HAS DELIVERED A DECLARATION OF WAR

Confident mood in St. Petersburg and Moscow . . . Sale of alcoholic spirits prohibited in both capitals.

GOD WILL PUNISH THE AGGRESSOR!

. . . At the Winter Palace, a crowd of 100,000 kneels with lowered flags . . .

. . . Arise, great Russian people! . . . Heroism before which any that the world has ever seen pales . . . to ensure a bright future for all mankind . . . dreams of the brotherhood of peoples . . . Now or never, bring the world Light from the East . . .

FOOD PRICES UP. The price of meat in St. Petersburg has risen in the last few days . . . from 25 to 35 kopecks . . . In Kiev a crowd of poor people took the law into their own hands when traders arbitrarily raised prices . . .

The exchange of treasury notes for gold is suspended . . . Visiting banks in the capital today . . . pleased to discover that . . . Economically, Russia has less reason to fear the war than Germany . . . The strike movement has immediately come to an end . . .

GOD WILL PUNISH THE AGGRESSOR!

. . . We delivered Germany from national humiliation in 1812–13, and Austria in 1848 . . .

PORTRAITS OF OUR ENEMIES: His Apostolic Majesty, Franz Josef I, Emperor of Austria and King of Hungary . . .

TRIUMPHAL ONE-DAY SESSION OF THE STATE DUMA, 8 August . . . On this historic day representatives of all ethnic groups and all parties were moved by a single thought, a single sentiment trembled in all voices . . . Hands off Holy Russia! . . . We are ready for any sacrifice to preserve the honor and dignity of the indivisible Russian state . . . For the Lithuanian people this is a holy war . . . We Jews rally to the defense of our motherland . . . moved by our great devotion . . . We Germans settled in Russia have always regarded her as our motherland . . . and are ready to a man to lay down our lives . . . We Poles . . . Permit me to declare on behalf of the Tatar, Chuvash, and Cheremyss population . . . as one man . . . to struggle against the invader . . . to lay down our lives . . . The whole of the motherland has closed ranks around its Tsar, moved by love . . . In complete unity with our Autocratic Ruler . . . All our thoughts, emotions, noble impulses . . . "God, Tsar, and People!" . . . and victory is assured . . .

THE LAST WAR IN EUROPEAN HISTORY . . . A protracted war in Europe is impossible . . . Our experience of previous wars . . . the decisive events took place within two months of . . .

BULLETPROOF VESTS

ANY LADY *can have an* IDEAL BUST, *that glory of womanhood! Marbor pills! Strictly reliable! No one disappointed.*

Many vacancies as a result of mobilization . . .

ENGLISH CLOTH 40 percent cheaper . . .

GUITAR lessons by mail, free of charge. Write Afromeev, at Tyumen . . .

SECOND FATHERLAND WAR . . . Communiqué from General Staff . . . Russian units have penetrated into Prussia . . . Our dashing cavalry . . .

. . . constructive aims of the war . . .

Nizhni Novgorod Fair, 14 August . . . All shops selling beer and spirits have been shut for two weeks, and the fair has taken on an unusual appearance . . . There are no drunks to be seen in the streets, no well-wined merchants asking to be robbed . . . hardly anyone has had his pocket picked . . .

TO THOSE DEPARTING

Go, dear ones, go, shed never a tear,
Go, dear ones, go, and have no fear
For those you leave behind you.

Poles! The hour has struck when the cherished dream of your fathers and grandfathers . . . May the Polish people be reunited under the Russian scepter . . .

BULLETPROOF VESTS

WE MUST WIN!

. . . Never before have Russo-Polish relations attained such a degree of moral purity and clarity . . .

Czechs! The twelfth hour is upon you! . . . For three centuries you have dreamed of a free and independent Czech homeland—it is now or never!

JEWISH RIGHTS . . . Orders telegraphed to all provincial and city governors to put a stop to mass or selective eviction of Jews . . .

FALL OF GERMAN EMPIRE FORETOLD. As a student at Bonn University, Wilhelm II once asked a gypsy . . . She answered dispassionately that "a cruel whirlwind will come upon Germany and sweep away . . ."

ST. PETERSBURG SAFE. The idea of a German landing . . . can be completely discounted . . .

IN THE LAND OF SAVAGES . . . The land of Schiller and Goethe, Kant and Hegel . . . under the fist of the Iron Chancellor, to whom they have erected monuments everywhere . . . No one will shed tears over the ruins of this land of lies and violence . . .

MILITARY CENSORSHIP. Military censorship comes into force in St. Petersburg at 7 p.m. on 17 August next . . .

. . . the Chief Administration of the General Staff is required to keep the population informed as far as possible. The public must reconcile itself to the paucity of the information issued, and take comfort in the thought that this sacrifice is dictated by military necessity . . .

VISIT TO MOSCOW BY HIS IMPERIAL MAJESTY . . . The Emperor's speech in the Kremlin . . . Their Imperial Majesties leaving the chapel of Our Lady of Iversk . . . Tens of thousands of loyal subjects in a demonstration on Red Square . . .

The glittering court in haste assembled,
The Serbs, our brothers, first to appear,
Troops trampled by, the city trembled
As thousands raised a heartfelt cheer.
From out the shrine his people heard the song,
Where, as of old, before the battle's stress
The Tsar prayed earnestly and long,
Then came among them, hand upraised to bless.

WE MUST WIN!

HEROISM OF DON COSSACK KOZMA KRYUCHKOV . . . He caught sight of the 22 horsemen . . . Charged at them with a battle cry . . . fearlessly plunged into their midst . . . cut his way through, spinning like a top . . . His comrades galloped to his aid . . . first winner of the St. George's Cross in this war . . .

. . . due to the interruption of exports . . . unprecedented fall in prices of bread grains . . . Grain dealers are having an extremely difficult time . . .

CHALIAPIN REAPPEARS! He successfully evaded capture by the Germans and is now . . .

Letter from an ensign: "Nine Austrian spies were brought in today . . . From what they say the Austrian army is in poor shape . . ."

WAR DIARY. The most important news of the day is our advance on a broad front into East Prussia . . . There is thick forest everywhere, but broad paths run through it . . . it presents no obstacle to cavalry or infantry . . . On 20 August came the news that Gumbinnen had been taken . . . The whole of East Prussia is now under our control . . . The shattered German corps are no longer capable of . . .

GOOD NEWS. We are informed by the most authoritative source that not a single unit in the Russian army is now under the honorary command of a member of the German or the Austrian ruling house.

[8]

Elderly female hands steered her into his bedroom. Still dazzled by the glare of a southern noon, she thought at first that the shuttered room was pitch dark.

There was a smell of incense, dried herbs, and medicines.

Then she saw the shafts of light coming through cracks in the shutters and motes dancing in them. In the light diffused by these radiant particles she began to see other things, dimly at first, then more clearly.

He was lying in the space between two windows on a high bed, propped up on high pillows, covered, because the room was so stuffy, by a single sheet. Except that it was not drawn up over his face, it looked like a shroud.

Varya went toward the bed, but stopped short of it. All the way from St. Petersburg she had been wondering what she would say. She was afraid that whatever she said would sound artificial. The darkness was something of a help, making it easier to remain silent while she got used to her surroundings.

He could probably see her clearly, but he did not even move his head. After a few deep sighs he spoke in a voice little louder than a whisper: "Who's there?"

"Matveeva," she answered. "Varya."

"Mat-ve-eva?" The feeble voice somehow expressed both surprise and affection. "Matveeva?" There were long pauses between his words. "You're . . . supposed . . . to be . . . in Petersburg."

"I came back to see you. I was told . . . and here I am."

He hadn't been told, and couldn't be told, that war had broken out. It was almost true that she had come for his sake—bullied into it, of course, by various ladies. But she felt uncomfortable saying so. Was she there to show her benefactor that she was grateful? There was always something shaming about charity, and gratitude for it might ring false. Charity was a way of buying exemption from your social duty, some people said. All the same, Varya had to admit to those ladies, and to herself, that but for Ivan Sergeevich Saratovkin she would never have got to high school or gone on to attend university courses.

During those minutes of silence he had had thoughts of his own. He spoke in a louder voice, and with more obvious warmth: "Thank you, Varya my dear. I wasn't expecting you. I'm glad you came."

When she was a little girl he might, just once, have patted her on the head. She couldn't remember him speaking to her affectionately or paying any special attention to her. Indeed, they had very rarely met. In St. Petersburg she would have passed him by in the street without recognizing him.

But now his voice moved her. She began to think that there had been some point in coming so far. All the way there she had been sure that it was pointless, ridiculous, stupid.

She would have been ashamed to confess to her educated friends at the Institute that she had made such a journey to see a benefactor on his deathbed, the proprietor of a grocery store and delicatessen—merchant, shopkeeper, call him what you like, a Black Hundreder in any case. (Gotz's grandfather, of course, had been a tea merchant—but had contributed hundreds of thousands to the revolution!)

Saratovkin's shop was on Staropochtovaya, a quiet back street well away from the heavy traffic. It had no plate-glass windows, it was rather small and rather dark, but all Pyatigorsk, Yessentuki, and Zheleznovodsk knew it. The whole world's eatables and drinkables could be found at Saratovkin's—foreign wines of all vintages and every known brand of Swiss chocolate side by side with Vologda butter and Nezhin gherkins. Saratovkin's counter hands would have taken it as a personal disgrace if they had ever needed to say, "Sorry, we don't carry it." It was not obvious what Saratovkin hoped to gain by stocking items for which there was no lively day-to-day demand. It was probably just a matter of pride with him that even the most eccentric customer would never be told, "We have none."

Her coming, then, had not been pointless. But what more was there to say? She had been told that there was no hope for Ivan Sergeevich, and that if she did not hurry she would be too late. She could not express unrealistic hopes for his recovery without sounding insincere, nor could she behave as though she knew that he was dying. Small talk would be hopelessly false.

Varya didn't move a step nearer, but stood shifting her weight from foot to foot in her embarrassment, waiting for the moment when she could decently withdraw. She held her handbag before her, gripping it with both hands, to give them something to do.

By now the room seemed much lighter and she could see Ivan Sergeevich's round head on the pillow, his sparse hair, the moon face, the big mustaches wearily drooping like a pair of damp tassels.

All the rest of him was under the shroud.

That shroud, drawn up to his chin, and not her awareness that he was close to death, sent a chill down her spine.

But he lay there peacefully, apparently unaware that he had anything to fear.

"Varya my dear," he said in the same affectionate tone, as though she were not one of two dozen, dimly remembered, but his favorite daughter. "Varya, God grant . . . your schooling . . . will bring good . . . to you—and to other people. The light of . . . learning . . . is . . . two-edged . . . you know it is . . ."

She did not understand that strange word. Two-edged? She didn't even try to understand, all she wanted was to remain for ten minutes as decency demanded, and it was a relief that he was talking and she need not. But his tone softened her heart.

"And may He send you . . . a good husband. Perhaps . . . there is a young man already?"

"No-o-o-o," Varya sighed.

Suddenly she felt genuinely grateful to him: he had not forgotten the most important thing, he had touched the sorest spot so very gently.

Merchant or not, he was a good man. There had to be merchants anyway. There had to be someone who would try single-handed to make their town as good as the capital.

But—after he was gone?

"Everything will be all right," the old man said, to comfort her—or himself.

Then he was silent. Had he forgotten her?

Varya too was silent, shifting from foot to foot like a tongue-tied four-year-old, wishing she could think of something to say, still clutching her bag, and suddenly she thought, not just automatically but with genuine emotion, that someday she would be old herself and lie, prostrate and helpless, dying.

It was as though Ivan Sergeevich, from his deathbed, was helping her to bear that moment.

"Thank you," he said again. "Thank you for coming. God bless you."

What a good thing her visit had unexpectedly turned out to be—not, as she had imagined on the way there, excruciatingly painful and futile.

She left the darkened room deeply moved.

Outside, the baked air was trembling. The sprawl of Pyatigorsk opened up before her.

Saratovkin's three-story house stood at the junction of Lermontov and Dvoryanskaya streets. This was where the little open trams packed with holidaymakers in spite of the war turned on their way to the Gap. Up and up they crawled, on the lower slopes of Mashuk, past luxurious white villas and chalets all the way to the Aeolian Harp and Lermontov's Grotto. In the other direction, roofs plunged into green foliage as Lermontov Street descended precipitately toward the market. To the south, she could see, over the low-lying part of the city, the mountains, a remote, elusive blue smudge.

The broad panorama of her native place warmed her heart. Pyatigorsk! Why had she ever left it for cold, inhospitable Petersburg? At the time she had thought that she would find happiness there.

She was an orphan. But even an orphan is better off at home. And then . . . though he wasn't her father, hadn't he been as good as a father to her? He was not her father, but he had done so much for her.

How kindly he had spoken to her! How discerning he had been!

Now she had lost him too.

The delightful scene she had known since childhood, over which the spirit of Lermontov hovered unseen, was like a chalice brimming with heat and happiness. She ached with unbearable longing as she looked at it.

That was how she had felt when she met Sanya. Here, on her native soil, all things were possible!

Being with him, though, had only exasperated her beyond endurance.

Such an improbable encounter, in the midst of the general turmoil and commotion, could, you might think, have had tremendous results. It should have meant everything to him and to her, meant the whole world. It had meant nothing! The dark water was draining away, gurgling, and Varya had wanted to fling herself over the hole and block it with her body. But nothing had come of their meeting. They had merely dawdled around Mineralnye Vody station for a few hours, irritating each other and getting nowhere. Even as a schoolgirl she had found his exaggerated rectitude and his plodding methodical mind tiresome. Now, in the blinding July sunlight, it was only too clear that Sanya was bent on destroying himself, and that she could do nothing to prevent it. In her frustration she had spoken with a harshness which nothing in their conversation warranted and gone on her way to Pyatigorsk by the local train.

She had hurried home eagerly, forgetting that the war was her traveling companion all the way, that she was hurrying to her guardian's deathbed, tingling to the soles of her feet in anticipation of the happiness awaiting her there.

Like a woman terrorist carrying pyroxylin about her person, hidden under her bodice where the police could not look for it, Varya bore within her an explosive force too dangerous to carry for long.

She had been lost in St. Petersburg, an undereducated provincial, unnoticed and unneeded. But here in the warm bosom of her native place she would surely find friends and acquaintances. Someone would surely understand her—and help her understand her destiny.

How grateful she would be! How generously she would repay!

Her visit could not end just like that, with nothing to show for it.

A highlander walked by. Looking at his Circassian coat, the narrow crossbelt decorated with tarnished silver disks, and the dagger hanging from it, Varya thought: I'm home. This is my world! (Although there was not a single highlander among her acquaintances.)

She walked on in her cheap straw hat along a hot sidewalk with no walls to give shade and, suddenly, across the sidewalk before her feet there was a carpet. A luxurious Tekin carpet, dark red, with tongues of orange flame in it, spread out before her.

Varya started, like someone beginning to doze and suddenly realizing that he is dreaming. Was she seeing things? No, a soft carpet had been laid down from the door of a carpet store right across the sidewalk and other pedestrians were also hesitating to step on it. But there in the doorway stood the proprietor, a thickset elderly Turk in a red skullcap, smoking a long Turkish pipe and smilingly inviting the passersby to "walk on it, please walk on it, you'll find it's easy on the feet."

Some people ignored him and went around it, but others laughed and walked over it. Varya stepped on it, enjoying the luxurious feel of the thick pile underfoot. This curious happening must be a lucky omen.

Laughing, she tilted her head and gave the Turk a sideways look. His eyes were cunning and imperious.

She was sorry when the game ended and she stepped off the carpet. Its warm glow had kindled in her a feeling that life was rich and beautiful and that her happiness was assured.

A row of temporary shops and workshops had been erected on the open space between Lermontov Square and the square beyond it—ramshackle wooden sheds, and booths with shutters raised to shade their counters in daytime.

Varya walked past slowly, idly peeping into each of them. There was a vendor of Turkish delight and halvah. A haberdasher's stall. A cobbler. A whitesmith. A repairer of Primuses and oil stoves. In the next booth was a tinsmith: a big galvanized basin hung above his counter by way of a shop sign, and the harsh, angry noise of hammer on tin from inside the booth made you want to cover your ears.

Varya quickened her pace to escape from the din, but glanced sideways at the tinsmith as he paused and drew himself up to his full height: a young man, wearing in spite of the heat a thick shirt the color of tin and a black apron standing out stiffly from his body. He was black-haired and swarthy like many southerners, and his one unusual feature was a pair of ears remarkably small for a head so broad at brow and chin.

Varya slowed down as she caught sight of him. Did she know him? . . . One more step and she halted, sure that she did.

The young man turned one eye on her, hammer in hand, showing not the usual shopkeeper's or artisan's eagerness to oblige a possible customer but sullen hostility. He could, of course, see that she had nothing for him to repair.

Varya gave him her broadest summer smile. "Don't you know me?"

It had happened a long time ago. She had only just moved from the municipal school to a middle form in the high school, changing her own black apron (with shoulder straps) for a green smock. But the two older school friends from out of town with whom, as an orphan, she shared lodgings already had dealings with a certain Yemmanuil Yenchman (he was always introduced for some reason as Yemmanuil, not Emmanuel). They swore Varya to secrecy one day and revealed that he was a famous anarchist and they themselves sympathizers with his cause. The apartment was too small in any case for them to keep secrets from her, but she felt the holy awe of one initiated into a great mystery. The girls would hide odd boxes for him, or a book by Bakunin, or a copy of the newspaper *Black Flag*, and because this was all clandestine and forbidden literature they read every word while they had it in safekeeping, everything from the fundamental doctrine—that the whole present structure of life must be completely destroyed and that they must dedicate themselves to unsparing and unremitting destruction—to the instructions for making "macédoines" ("funnel potassium chlorate into a length of lead pipe and insert an ampoule of sulphuric acid").

On two or three occasions Yenchman arrived with Zhora—a silent, powerful youth, still immature, but a promising autodidact according to Yemmanuil, who took him along as his aide, deputy, and errand boy. Zhora was then fifteen years old.

How long had it been? Seven years? Varya had seen neither of them since, had forgotten all about them, and had certainly never thought that Zhora might still be in Pyatigorsk.

He scowled at her from his dim cave of a stall.

"Don't you recognize me, Zhora? I'm Varya . . . one of the three schoolgirls you used to know at Grafskaya Street . . . Remember? . . . you used to come there with Yemmanuil."

She called him by his pet name without thinking about it. She had been only a child herself, of course, only thirteen. But he was no longer a boy in his teens, he was a grown man, and a strong one with brawny shoulders.

He scowled at her from the half-darkness. He obviously didn't like it one bit. He grunted, muttered something inaudible, sat down on a low chair with his head turned away from her, and began hammering out a kink in the rim of a tub, resting it on an iron projection, pausing from time to time to turn it slightly, then resuming his hammering, each heavy blow followed by several lighter ones. He hammered savagely as though he were angry with the tin tub, and banged and tapped with his head tilted to one side, which made him look still more sullen. He did not even glance at Varya.

She, however, was fixed to that dirty, dark wooden counter littered with bits of tin, white or yellow side uppermost, and sprinkled with filings. She leaned both elbows on it, peering in at the broad-faced craftsman.

"I can't believe you don't remember me," she insisted. "There were two older girls and I'm Varya, the youngest. I remember you so well!"

Five minutes earlier she had had no memory of him at all, but all at once a forgotten shaft had opened and a strong, warm current of feeling welled up from the depths of memory. She could even recall the dark red checked shirt he had worn, which chair he had sat on, the movements of his hands. This feat of memory excited her to further effort and she dragged up from the depths forgotten phrases from anarchist programs: "Destruction and creation are incompatible . . . Effective destruction *is* freedom . . . Struggle with all acknowledged authority . . . Blow up monuments . . ."

He went on furiously hammering his tub, as though he were landing blow after blow on his worst enemy. His strong, fleshy lips were twisted in a grimace.

By now Varya could make out more of the dusky interior. She could see his smooth black cowlick, but his eyes eluded her. She could see the long, rigid (rubberized?) black apron.

In those days she herself had worn a short black apron, but one which she could smooth down so that it clung to her.

He must be made to remember! She would not go away until he did.

She stayed. Remembered phrases were borne up through the newly opened shaft, and she retrieved them, as astonished as though she were hearing them for the first time.

"Only by overcoming culture can we realize our anarchist ideals. Down with the tyranny of learning, down with the universities, those synagogues of scholarship! For the anarchist, learning is the second target of terror. Once we have buried religion we must bury learning, relegating it to the archives of human superstition . . ."

Strange words, extraordinary words! But perhaps there was a certain one-sided truth in them? Learning was cold and dry and forbidding. Especially for a young woman. And even more for a lonely young woman.

But why had all this remained in her memory? What force had brought it back to her now?

"The means of struggle may vary . . . poison, the dagger, the noose, the revolver, dynamite . . . dynamite, dynamite."

He was hammering away angrily. Did he really not recognize her? The jarring crash of metal on metal buffeted Varya's ears.

Suddenly she realized he could not admit that he recognized her. For conspiratorial reasons! He must still be a member of some fearsome black-flag society. Or even if he wasn't, he had a past to conceal and was afraid of being recognized!

As though she would ever give him away! She might even be of assistance to him in some clandestine activity. Or help him with his reading, his self-education—he must surely have difficulties there.

A force outside herself seemed to press her harder than ever against the counter. It was as though the whole row of shops were spinning like a carousel and she was pinned by centrifugal force to the booth in which there were just the two of them.

"Zhora, I'll never give you away!" she cried above the metallic din and the hiss of Primuses from the next stall, but not loud enough for the neighbors to hear. "You can trust me completely . . ."

With the banging and the noises next door, and her fear that she would not convince him, she was left breathless. But he had heard and understood. He stopped and turned to look at her. She saw now how grown-up and manly and strong he had become in the years since she had known him. There was something secret and mysterious about him too. Stiff black stubble covered his broad chin and his upper lip.

"You can . . . rely on me."

"What do you mean, rely on you? What business have we got

with each other? You're a lady. Why don't you go where you were going."

His rough voice made it an order.

"You can rely on me!" Varya said, still more earnestly and enthusiastically, still leaning heavily on the counter, noticing briefly and forgetting at once that her bare elbow had crushed a stray smut from the Primus mender's booth.

People walked by behind her. None of them was a would-be customer. She stood, elbows on the counter, head in hands, staring at the desperate anarchist. She remembered more.

"A revolutionary knows only the science of destruction . . . All tender feelings must be suppressed with cold passion . . . He is no revolutionary if he feels pity for anything in this world . . ."

Of course! It was so obvious! He had voluntarily renounced everything in this world. But surely a sympathetic friend would not be in his way? A disinterested helper? Varya, an orphan herself, understood only too well how lonely an orphan could be.

She looked closely at him. There was so much bitterness, so much pent-up suffering in his brooding, unshaven face and his dark stare.

"You must have had a hard time of it since then?" she said, as though hearing it might comfort him.

He suddenly opened up. "I did," he said. "There are lots of traitors. Not many people aren't. I got caught for one job. We polished a prison warden off. I got put in a penal battalion."

(She had guessed something of the sort.) "How long for?"

"Well, then there was the amnesty, and they changed it to banishment. And chucked me out to lead this dog's life. Wait till they get a taste of it themselves . . ."

He was evidently not married.

A vicious hammer blow saved him the trouble of speaking further.

"I had no idea you were in Pyatigorsk," Varya said.

He had given her a glimpse of a secret, underground, persecuted world. He had suddenly grown in stature and she could not go on addressing him familiarly. She had no real wish to enter that terrible world, but perhaps, if he commanded her to . . . To become one with the people, by whatever means, was that not everyone's dream?

"The South Russian Federation?" she whispered, suddenly remembering.

Even when he was not hammering, the concerted hissing of Primuses in the next booth made it difficult to hear.

But Zhora did hear, and shushed her as though he were shooing a cat. She froze. But he had decided to trust her further.

"The Federation was sold," she heard him say. "Somebody in Kiev. It was their own fault. They started getting all sorts of crazy ideas.

Wouldn't even let us share out what we got from the exes. So they came unstuck."

"What about Yenchman?" she asked, merely to remind him of their common past.

He waved his hand.

"Became a Pan-anarchist. I'm an Anarcho-Communist. Too educated the Pan-anarchists are. An Anarcho-Communist mustn't read anything, so that he can't come under anybody's influence. He has to work out all his views for himself, that's the only way you get freedom of the personality."

Having said his piece, he went to work again on his wretched tub.

There was movement above his apron, but below, it reared up as sheer and immobile as a mountainside.

What strength of character he had! What power there was in this underground smith!

But if he did not even need to read, what use could she be to him? Maybe she could act as a go-between, take messages to places where he couldn't show himself? If, of course, he would trust her . . .

She still had the feeling that it had been a happy omen when the carpet was rolled out before her.

He stopped banging, but waved his hammer with a savage glare in his eyes.

"We'll make them all crawl to us! On their knees! We'll empty their money bags for them!"

The light of invincible conviction shone in those eyes.

"We'll shoot the bastards one at a time," he said, looking at her as though she was one of them. "They've gorged themselves till their necks are too fat for their starched collars. Squash one of the dogs and he's just a lump of meat."

Varya didn't know how she could mollify him, how to meet him halfway.

"Then there's the long-haired priests. We'll give them a good combing and hang them by their manes."

"Wouldn't you be sorry for them?" she asked hesitantly.

"We won't be sorry for anybody!" He smacked his thick lips with frank enjoyment. "They've got to learn that they're up against real power, that they need to be afraid!"

His words frightened her. But life itself was cruel. It was all very well for the comfortable few at the top, all very well for people like her in Bestuzhev courses* to apply rigid moral rules to everything.

* Courses intended to provide women with the equivalent of a university education (though not a university degree) were first established in 1878 in St. Petersburg. They owe their name to the historian K. N. Bestuzhev-Ryumin, who was from 1878 until 1882 chairman of the Pedagogic Council, which administered them. [*Trans.*]

Varya slumped over the counter, careless of her dress. Memory supplied what had been the favorite subject of debate in those days: Did a revolutionary have a right to personal happiness? Or must he consistently subordinate his private life to his revolutionary ideals?

Feeling sorry for this young man whom life had cheated and passed by, this lonely, hunted, subterranean creature, she leaned halfway across the counter and wailed, "Zho-ora! You shouldn't deny yourself . . ."

Deny himself what?

He stopped hammering and looked at her. His face was still sullen and resentful.

She did not leave, did not step backward, did not even take her weight off the counter. She seemed ready to stay there till the shutters came down.

He was no longer hammering, but silently watching her, turning something over in his mind.

There was fire in his hard black eyes. From some underground smithy? From a hidden furnace?

Looking straight into her eyes, he thought a little longer, then said, "All right, come on in."

The Primuses were noisier than ever.

She pried herself away from the counter, without noticing the dirty mark on her elbow and perhaps others on her dress, raised the leaf, and pressed through the narrow gap.

She couldn't go much farther. The booth was two yards by two, and saucepans and pails hanging from the ceiling or standing around in piles left no room for anything else.

Why had he told her to come inside?

He rose awkwardly, as though one foot had gone to sleep. He was taller by a head. He took a step back, pushed against a little door, and nodded toward it. "In there."

Of course! There was a cupboard hidden away at the back of the booth, and this little door, so low that Varya ducked as she went through it, was the entrance.

He wanted to tell her a secret.

She felt no fear as she squeezed past the anarchist's rampant apron and hunched shoulders.

Going into the cupboard was like going underground.

Had he decided to trust her? At last she felt needed.

The cupboard was so poky that she could hardly turn around. A tin bathtub hanging somewhere behind her gave a warning rumble. Something knocked off her straw hat and it flew away from her.

The boards had been nailed close together, but there were cracks here and there and some light came through them.

Zhora bent low as he came in. There was another rumble, like muffled thunder, as he brushed against some metal receptacle.

It was so cramped, with all those utensils suspended or stacked around them, that there was only just room to stand face to face.

What next?

She could see him in the light from the cracks.

The Primuses were making a terrible din!

But when he peeled off his apron it hit the floor with a hard, sharp sound.

She was beginning to understand but trying hard not to.

He was frighteningly silent.

She was breathing heavily with terror and from the heat in this tight black trap, this dark well.

She felt the pitiless pressure of his hands on her shoulders.

Down, down, down.

[9]

Some years the Tomchaks paid the management of the Vladikavkaz Railway six hundred rubles for express trains to stop on demand at their station, Kubanskaya, which saved them the long haul to Armavir, twenty versts away.

That year they hadn't paid, but the expresses still stopped as usual. Zakhar Fyodorovich, returning from Yekaterinodar, got on the first express instead of waiting for the mail train, sent immediately for the senior conductor, had two red ten-ruble notes ready on the table (one was for the driver), and explained where he wanted to get off. The senior conductor, not in the least surprised that a busy man wished to save time, promised and kept his promise. It was almost evening, but still very hot, when the train stopped, and puzzled passengers stuck their heads out of windows to see a single passenger climb down onto the unshaded tracks. The gravel gave off a sickly smell of train grease in the shimmering heat.

A phaeton had been waiting in the shade all day. (Tomchak had long ago given up his "Russo-Baltic Carriage," which, whether you looked at springs, spokes, or axles, was so like an ordinary cart, for a Mercedes—but that was only for swank, when he went visiting; at other times he almost always preferred horse-drawn carriages, in which he felt less self-conscious. He went to church and to the station, where people would see him, in the phaeton.) The coachman jumped to it, rushed to take his master's little case, and tightened the harness. The horses, badly bitten by flies, were glad to be away. His son, though, hadn't come to meet him. No son of mine! The devil must be his dad!

The stationmaster had emerged to shake Tomchak's hand, but was too slow crossing the tracks: the phaeton was already rolling off. Tomchak was always in a hurry, and on this occasion more so than ever because he had wasted three days on the trip and was itching to get down to neglected work. He couldn't wait to see how things were going at this busiest of seasons. What was behind him was over and done with. Zakhar Fyodorovich's thoughts were of business ahead, things not yet done, things not yet checked, things perhaps overlooked in his absence. Besides, he was seething because his son had not met him.

Not far off to the left, less than a verst away, he saw the first of the threshing machines, in a cloud of blowing chaff. He would have driven over to look at it there and then, in the phaeton just as he was, but he didn't want to make people laugh—he must change his clothes first and transfer to the droshky.

He thought about the threshing. Thought that he must send carbolic acid to the Lukyanov homesteads—they would be shearing the merinos for the second time soon—thought that it might be time to cut the corncobs and store them in the new barn, which would hold a million puds* and had slatted sides for ventilation. The walls could be opened up for a cross draft or shut tight to keep out the rain: this method of storage, taken over from the German colonists, promised big profits if it was properly handled.

Tomchak had borrowed a lot of ideas from the colonists, and they had been rewarding. He had always respected the Germans, and regarded war against Germany as tomfoolery—like the time when he and Afanasi Karpenko had laid into each other with their walking sticks in a first-class carriage because Karpenko had called his daughter-in-law, Tomchak's older daughter, a fool of a girl. She was a fool, true enough—she had been pulled out of elementary school in a hurry to become a rich man's bride—but serious men should be ashamed to fight over such a thing. Instead of fighting Germany, all Russia should be learning from her how to work and prosper. Russia had begun to ripen in recent years. This was no time to be fighting. The three emperors should have held a requiem for that archduke and drunk vodka at his wake instead.

So he saw no sense at all in sending off to the war either his son or his skilled craftsmen or the hired Cossacks who had served him so loyally, guarding his estate and his treasure after that business with the bandits. He had got exemptions for all those he wanted and was returning with the news. If they had been at the station to meet him, with his son at their head showing proper respect for his father, they could all have rejoiced together.

Still, some of them were there waiting for their master, squatting on the ground by the white stone pillar at the bottom of the drive: two Cossacks, the diesel engineer, one gardener, and Roman's chauffeur, the footman's brother. Tomchak stopped the phaeton as they rose to gather

* A pud equals approximately 36 pounds or 16.38 kilograms. [*Trans.*]

around, and said warmly, as though he was in their debt, not they in his, "It'll be all right, boys. You can tell the others too. Carry on with what you were doing, and light a candle to the Good Lord."

And off he went, as they mumbled their thanks. The horses clip-clopped over the flagged driveway and across the front yard, but only his wife looked out from an upper window. *He* could not be bothered even to do that.

The coachman swung around the crescent to the porch. Tomchak alighted and hurried into the house. He no longer had any wish to meet his son.

Not a single board in the strong, young staircase creaked under him as he went upstairs like a youngster, not a man of fifty-six.

His rotund wife was waiting for him on the upper landing, her hands held out hopefully, feebly toward him.

"Well, Father?" She had barely voice enough to ask.

It went against the grain to answer. He felt his humiliation all the more deeply here in his own home. He merely touched his lips to his wife's forehead and went silently into the bedroom suite, with her following.

Since Yevdokia had given up farmwork, gout and a dozen other complaints had plagued her. The more ailments she contracted, the more doctoring she thought she needed. (Tomchak knew better! Never, never take any notice of doctors. He never let them get anywhere near him: he knew better than all the doctors in the world how to treat himself.) They had begun by buying barrels of mud and engaging a resident nurse to prepare baths for her mistress; then they had realized that what she needed was a trip to Yeisk, to Goryachevodsk, to Yessentuki—where nothing would do but lace frocks and carriages to ride in, so the ailments got worse and worse.

Now, however, Yevdokia moved nimbly enough into her bedroom and, while her husband paused to cross himself before the icons in the corner, went around him and barred his way. She held on to him, hardly daring to ask, looking into his face with its heavy mustache, large nose, and bushy brows, as though he were the prophet Elijah. Would he strike her, or wouldn't he?

Tomchak didn't want to talk. He'd gone to all that trouble, come home with the goods—and that one just lay on his couch, couldn't be bothered to get up. What he would really have liked was to ride out into the steppe without a word to anybody. But he saw how the old woman was suffering, had pity on her, and growled, "The recruiting officer swore that he'd get an exemption for the whole war."

Yevdokia relaxed, glowed, turned around, and crossed herself before the most important of the icons.

"Blessed be the Mother of God, who has heard my prayers."

"No, no." Zakhar frowned as he tossed his hat aside and pulled off his dustcoat. "The Mother of God doesn't come into it. I had to grease the works a bit so they wouldn't creak." With which he went toward his own room, but turned around sharply and caught her hanging back. Fire flashed from under the heavy brows. "Where d'you think you're going? You will not! Devil take him, let him ask for himself." His wind-chapped hand clenched into a fist, the swollen veins standing out in dark knots. He shook it. "If he wants to know he can just come and ask."

"I wasn't going to Roman," Yevdokia lied happily. "Can I get you anything?"

"No. I'll drink some balsam. I'm going to the fields in a bit."

He stripped off his three-piece suit and stood in his underwear.

The fiery, resinous Riga balsam had been his favorite drink since he had got to know it recently in Moscow. A glazed jug of the stuff stood in the dining room, another in the bedroom, and Zakhar Fyodorovich drank one little silver tot of it at a time.

"Maybe just a little Lenten borsch," his wife suggested, suffused with happiness. "Shall I warm some up?"

"Warm what? Beans and sunflower oil? Give it to me cold. And send one of the Cossacks over to Semyon. I want the droshky ready quick."

Zakhar's bedroom was beyond his wife's, and had no separate exit. "Ah, but that way no draft will ever blow on me," he often said. He would rush about the steppe in foul weather, in rain and cold, unconcernedly, but at home he was afraid of drafts and liked to be warm in bed. Looking incongruously rustic in Zakhar's present luxurious surroundings, a broad-tiled bench had been built onto the stove and he slept on it in winter. Here too, set in the wall, was his big safe; he tossed things into it, or took things out, almost without pausing: some of his ledgers were in it, but Tomchak never received his employees there. Nor did he himself take much pleasure in figures on paper—he was money's master, not its servant. He did not hold on to money, it all went into land, cattle, or buildings. Gold the Tomchaks shunned, as did all the workers—a small golden coin so easily fell out of a pocket; in the bank they had to pay the cashier a little extra to give them notes instead of burdening them with gold.

Zakhar Tomchak never sat brooding over figures or gloating over his money. He lingered in his office only as long as it took to reach a decision. Everything that mattered in his business was out in the fields, or where the machines were, or with his flocks, or in the work yard—that was where things must be watched and orders given. What determined the success of his business was the division of the rolling plains into rectangular fields sheltered from the winds by belts of trees; a seven-field crop rotation, with wheat, horsetooth maize, sunflower, clover, and sainfoin following each other and giving a bigger and better crop from year to year; replacing his dairy cows with a German breed that gave three pails; killing hogs forty at a time for the smoking shed (the German colonist he employed made hams and sausages as good as Eidenbach's in Rostov); and above all, shearing sheep by the thousand and baling mountains of wool.

Tomchak was always on the spot when big shipments of grain, wool, or meat from his estate were dispatched to the railhead or across country in heavy wagons. This for him was the greatest of holiday treats—running his eyes over the bulk and weight of all he was bestowing on people. He liked to boast of that occasionally—"I feed all Russia!"—and to be praised for it by others.

While his wife was fetching the soup, Zakhar Fyodorovich changed into a linen suit and put on boots with a double soft sole ("so the feet can sleep"). He would have liked to eat some pink fatback, or shepherd's gruel, hot, with mutton, but he had to get through the Feast of the Assumption. Instead, he folded his wheaten bread three times, slit it from end to end with a long kitchen knife, and lowered his mustache over the big bowl of cold, thick Lenten soup.

His wife stood before him, her hands folded on her big belly, and watched him eat.

He was in a hurry to finish and drive over the steppe in his droshky (he didn't like the single-axled boneshaker). But there was a knock and his daughter-in-law came in.

Zakhar Fyodorovich looked up sharply and snarled like a dog over his food. "Well? Told Roman already, have you?"

His wife, looking guilty, tried to appease him. "No, no. Only Ira. That's all right, isn't it?"

Irina came in looking not at all guilty, but as erect as ever, with her long neck held proudly and her luxuriant hair piled high. She had heard nothing of her husband all day except that, according to the footman, he was not lying dead in his bedroom: he had eaten lunch and received the latest newspapers. She watched her father-in-law dipping his mustache in the soup. She did not thank him, but looked at him with silent approval and goodwill.

Zakhar Fyodorovich might shout and hurl thunderbolts at everyone else in the house, but never at her; from the very first day she had felt safe, and her behavior had shown it. True, she never crossed him. She did not even wear expensive dresses and "baubles" (diamonds) at home, because he did not like it. She could strike the right note and persuade him, when no one else could, to make peace with his family or with other steppe farmers. "You're a child of God, Ira," her father-in-law would say with a sigh, and give way. On important political events he never listened to his son with those newspapers of his, but to his daughter-in-law's explanation drawn from *New Times*.

"Come over here, then," he said, pointing. He paused in the middle of eating his soup, wiped his mouth and his mustache with a big, thick napkin, and kissed her inclined forehead. He did not invite her to sit down or say another kind word, but, smacking his lips loudly, taking a bite of the thickly folded bread in his hand, and chewing, he said angrily, between swallows, "I'm sorry I went and got him off. He should have gone to the war—it would have done him good to get a good hiding . . . That devil's cub has had things too easy . . ."

He chomped away.

Irina took this to mean that getting exemption for his son had gone against the grain, and that the only consolation was that he had got it for his workers too.

She protested, but not very emphatically. "How can you talk like that, Papa?"

He hadn't finished eating, but he seemed to be swallowing more air than food as he got more furious.

"And you can tell him he'd better build his own business up—he needn't think he'll ever get his hands on mine! I'd sooner leave it all to my nephew. Or else," he began hesitantly—but his features hardened, and he issued his decision between two big gulps—"or else I'll take Ksenia out of school right now and marry her off!"

"Papa, Papa," Irina protested, her eyebrows arched. "You're saying that in the heat of the moment. What was the point of letting her go at all if you mean to take her out in the middle of her studies? Where's the sense in that?"

More than once, when he had heard about the miscalculations of other farmers, Zakhar Fyodorovich had said, "You know, I wouldn't have known any better. You've got to have your own agronomist. I wish I could find one who knows his job, likes hard work, is easy to get on with, and isn't a crook." It was on one such occasion that Irina and Roman had persuaded him to let Ksenia study agriculture: he would have an agronomist of his own—why look any further? But the keen plainsman's eye under those shaggy brows was fixed on something different now: "I'll tell you where the sense is. In a year's time I'd have a grandson, and in fifteen years an heir."

He finished eating and wiped his face. Its lower half was concealed by the napkin; the upper half expressed his pain.

Zakhar Fyodorovich could not have put into words, even for himself let alone for his womenfolk, the reason for his dismay and despondency. It wasn't that the estate or his money was in danger. Roman was no frivolous waster. But the soul of the business was threatened. If whoever inherited was to carry on his work loyally there must be spiritual continuity. Why should this dark alien creature find everything ready and in working order?

But Irina was producing one of her female arguments: "Anyway, how could you marry her off without asking her first? And to whom?"

Tomchak rose. His Cossack figure was big and clumsy beside Irina's elegant form.

"Well, if she stays there, who will she marry? A student? Who'll be sent to Siberia sooner or later? I was a fool sending her to school. She can rattle away in all sorts of heathen languages, but she's stopped believing in God. If I had a real son she could study till she was forty, till people stopped wondering at it. It's your fault, old woman," he groaned, taking the light walking stick with a curved handle polished from long use. "Why didn't you give me another son?"

"It was not God's will," sighed his wife, but her plump face was serene.

"I don't know what God's will may be. I do know what I want."

He strode from the room with a firm, heavy step, and they could hear him running down the stairs.

Ira had always admired her father-in-law. Like her deceased father, he was one of the nation's doers. Dozens of people depended on him for their work and their keep. He knew how great a service he was performing and he grudged his workers nothing. There was no cowardly clinging to his wealth. Nor did he really make much use of that wealth for himself. He was no doubt what any ordinary hero in the workaday world should be.

The imaginary heroes of her youth had been quite different. From the age of nine she had secretly hero-worshipped Natty Bumppo, or Hawkeye, Fenimore Cooper's noble and fearless warrior. Only such a hero would win Ira, but no one the least bit like him had ever come her way. She did, though, true to her secret destiny, become fond of shooting. She always kept a Browning in her handbag or her dressing-table drawer, and a lady's sporting gun of English make hung against a rug on the wall. It would take bird shot or small bullets that could pierce two-inch-thick planks. When officers from the local garrison came visiting, a sheet was stretched between two posts behind the cattle shed, and Ira joined them in target practice, scoring as many points as any of them. If her hero ever came along she would be worthy of him.

But what do we know of the hidden currents in anyone's life?

What Ira liked most was the mysterious. She enjoyed the thought that supernatural powers are secretly at work beside and around us. Enjoyed remembering, for instance, that Halley's comet was overhead in the year when this house was built and this park laid out.

All that here is hidden from us
In that other life made clear . . .

She loved walking under the stars and dreaming. Or, better still, when the setting sun flooded the westernmost avenue, on the edge of the vineyards, and the golden radiance irresistibly drew her away from that house, that park, that husband, this world, into the sun where none could trouble her.

There was such a sunset that day. And she longed to go out there, to roam like a free soul, released from the body and all its vexations.

But if she did not go and tell Roman immediately her mother-in-law would be there first. Besides, she would not be humbling herself if she hurried to him with such good news.

Irina did not shuffle or cough or knock to warn him of her arrival. She walked quietly and opened the door quietly. A mingled pink and yellow light poured around her as soon as she opened the door. On this side of the house the light of the setting sun was still filtering through the treetops in the park, across the veranda, through the glass wall between the veranda and the bedroom, where it was reinforced by the pale pink wallpaper, the reflected light from the gold and pink coverlets, and the gleaming brass knobs on the two maple-wood bedsteads.

It was still light enough to read. And *he* was sitting in a low, deep armchair with his back to her, holding an open newspaper in his hands. He must have heard the door open, must have recognized her footsteps. But he did not look around.

He had to go on to the end showing how ill used he felt by the whole household, and also how firm he was.

He was sitting so that Irina could see only the bald patch in his black hair above the back of the chair.

Seeing how rapidly his hair was thinning at thirty-six, looking at the defenseless crown she knew so well, Irina suddenly softened. The trammels that had held her back fell away.

With a lighter step she went toward him as he turned his head, went toward the mixture of resentment, uncertainty, and dawning hope on the dark face, averted from the light and still unshaven.

"Everything is all right, Roman dear," she told him in a level voice. "Papa has arranged it all. They say we can rely on it."

She had gone right up to his chair before he could even sit up straight, but he seized her hands, kissed them, and said something with a catch in his voice. Not about the quarrel, and whether it was her fault or his. The quarrel might never have happened.

And his father might not have existed. Roman did not mention him, did not ask about him, showed no inclination to go and thank him.

Irina thought it best not to pass on his father's angry words and threats.

Irina's arms were bare above her elbows, and Roman kissed the dimples and the soft pink skin of her upper arm, where there was not a single blemish, until the tight sleeves would not push up any farther. Then he turned her around, sat her on his knees, and pressed his head against her breast.

She found herself looking again at the bald patch amid his sparse, wiry hair. She kissed it gently.

He talked and talked, happily, animatedly. At first Irina couldn't make sense of it. He was promising her that after America, where he had long wanted to go, because it was the best, most efficient, most sensible country on earth, or even before going there, anyway once the war ended, they would take the journey she longed to make—she had confessed it long ago, he had rejected the idea, and she had kept it to herself since—to Palestine and on to India.

"How shall we do our sightseeing?" Irina asked. "Like we did in Paris?"

(There was a fast elevator to the top of the Eiffel Tower. "What is there to see up there?" Roman had asked. He was afraid of heights. "I'll go up by myself, then!" she said, and he reluctantly tagged along. Napoleon's tomb? "Who cares about Napoleon? We Russians settled his hash.")

"No, no, we'll look at everything properly," he promised, but he was already easing her off his lap and fingering one of his long cigarettes as he went out onto the veranda, picking up a crumpled *Stock Exchange Gazette* on the way. "Ira my love, tell them to bring us supper here, something light, chicken maybe. We'll stay in and go to bed early."

There was still enough light on the veranda, but it was getting darker every minute in the bedroom and all the colors were fading, turning ashen. But Irina did not switch the light on.

She went into the windowless depths of the bedroom. Reluctantly she turned to one of the beds and lifted the coverlet, colorless now in the evening gloom, by one corner as though it were made of sheet iron, and stood holding it, motionless, as though it were beyond her strength to raise it any farther . . .

Irina's compassion for her husband had left her as quickly as it had come. She thought wistfully of the night she had just spent apart from him, and even of the day behind her. Wearisome and lonely as it had been, she had been free. If she drew back the coverlet she would lay bare the mine shaft, the dried-up well at the bottom of which she would lie on her back, sleepless, exhausted, yet with no voice to cry out and no dangling rope to clutch at. And her hero would never come . . .

As for Roman, he had pored stupidly over his newspapers for hours, but only now did he begin to understand them and take a lively interest. The newspapers seemed to have changed—the letters glowed and throbbed. It was not yet dark on the veranda, and he went up to his map to look at the little flags and the line that marked the frontier.

Since the frontier had been ratified at the Congress of Vienna the Prussian stump thrust toward Russia as though for amputation had never been touched: Russia and Germany had never been at war in all that time. Indeed, for longer than that, for a hundred and fifty years, there had been no war between them; in fact Germany itself had not existed for most of that time. Now their frontiers and defenses were being tested for the first time.

There was an old saying from the days of Frederick the Great: Russians have always beaten Prussians! "We are advancing, our armies are on the offensive!" Communiqués from the headquarters of the Supreme Commander did not identify armies, corps, and divisions by number, and Roman could not be sure where, exactly, to pin his flags. Nor was it clear what the flags signified: they were a product of his imagination, and there were as many of them as he found convenient. He could please himself whether or not to annex an additional ten or twenty versts of Prussia.

Taking care not to tear the map, he pinned the flags farther forward by two days' march.

His armies were on the move!

[10]

Darkness had fallen and the electric lamps had been lit outside the two-story building occupied by HQ 2nd Army in Ostrolenka. Strapping sentries stood at the gate and the front door, and two soldiers patrolled the street outside, moving in and out of the shadows cast by the trees.

The army directed from this headquarters had been advancing against the enemy for a week, but there was no anxious to-ing and fro-ing, no galloping in and out of messengers, no rumbling of carriages, no yelling of orders, no alarms, no turning out of the guard. As evening closed in, Army Headquarters was as quiet and sleepy as the rest of Ostrolenka. Some windows were already lit up. No other lights would now go on to disturb the scene. Nor was there the usual tangle of field telephone cables around headquarters: a double line to the telegraph pole outside connected it with the town exchange.

The townspeople had not been forbidden to walk the streets around HQ, and young Poles, some in black and white, some in brighter colors, were strolling along the pavements. Polish boys had already been called up, and the girls walked with each other except for a few who were with Russian officers. After a hot day the evening was still close and airless. Many windows were open, and singing could be heard from a gramophone not very far off.

A car came swaying and rattling around the corner a block away, the bright beams of its headlights startling the sleepy street, thundered up to headquarters in a whirl of dust, and drove through the gate past the saluting sentry. It was an open car and its occupant was a small and gloomy major general.

After his arrival the street was silent again. A plump priest in a cassock sailed past. Male passersby greeted him with a respect never shown to priests in Russia, bowing from the waist, hat in hand, arm extended.

A hansom cab appeared, bringing two officers to HQ. They paid the fare, alighted, and went inside.

The senior of the two, a colonel, found the duty officer (not in the entrance hall) and presented him with a piece of paper. It was evidently important. Steadying his sword with one hand, the duty officer hurried upstairs to report to the Chief of Staff.

He, in his turn, was so startled and perturbed that he almost went down to receive the newcomer personally, but thought better of it, almost summoned him to his private office, but changed his mind again and trotted off with steps surprisingly small for a man so large to the room of the Army Commander, General Samsonov.

During his long and successful career as ataman of the Don Cossacks, then as governor-general of Turkestan and ataman of the Semirechye Cossacks, Cavalry General Samsonov had learned to carry out his duties in an unhurried and deliberate fashion, giving his subordinates to understand that each of us should follow the Creator's example, get through his work in six days, sleep quietly in his bed for six nights, and spend the seventh day in restful contemplation. A ditherer will never make up for lost time by working on the Sabbath. But now he was kept busy on weekdays and Sundays alike. Indeed, he had lost count of the days: the previous day had been almost over before he remembered that it was Sunday. Every night he was kept from his sleep awaiting instructions from Army Group HQ and issuing orders of his own at peculiar hours. Moreover, there was a continuous buzzing in his head which made it difficult for him to think.

It was only three weeks since Samsonov had been recalled by imperial command from his work of putting the far eastern frontier regions in order and transferred immediately to the front line of the war just beginning in Europe. He had been in these parts long ago, just after the war with Japan, as Chief of Staff in the Warsaw Military District. That he had held this post years ago was the reason for his present appointment. Samsonov felt honored by His Majesty's confidence, and it was his wish to carry out this assignment, like any other, as well as possible. But he had been out of touch for so long. For the past seven years he had held administrative, not operational posts. He had never commanded so much as a corps in action, and all at once he found himself entrusted with an army.

It was a long time since he had given any thought at all to the East Prussian theater. Plans for war in this area had been made and changed over the years, but no one had acquainted him with them. Now he had been summoned by telegram from the Crimea, where he had been taking a cure, and ordered to carry out in a hurry a plan which he had not drawn up, or even had time to think about, according to which two Russian armies would advance into East Prussia, one westward from the Niemen, the other northward from the Narew, with the object of encircling and immobilizing all enemy forces there.

The new commander needed time for unhurried consideration and adjustment. He needed above all to be left alone, to collect himself, evaluate the plan, pore over maps, but he was given no time for any of this. The new commander needed to get to know his staff, to discover what use any of them were as aides and advisers, but no allowance was made for that either. When he looked at the staff assigned to him he found that he had been unfairly treated. Oranovsky, formerly Chief of Staff of the Warsaw District, had moved over to the Northwestern Army Group, taking all the best staff officers with him. Rennenkampf, commander of the Vilna Military District, had also carried off staff officers whom he had known for many years when he took command of the 1st Army. HQ 2nd Army had been packed before Samsonov's arrival with a random collection of officers from here, there, and everywhere, people who had never belonged to the same team and did not even know each other. Samsonov would never have chosen for himself that bumbling Chief of Staff or that peevish Quartermaster General, but they had been there to meet him when he arrived. The new commander further needed to make the round of the regiments, get to know at least the senior officers, take a look at the soldiers and let them see him, make sure that everybody was ready, and only then begin moving into alien territory, still taking his time, conserving the strength of his troops for battle, converting reservists into soldiers as he went along. If the commander was not ready, how much less so were his corps. Only three of them belonged to the Warsaw District—the others had been brought in from distant places. The army was to have been allowed twenty-nine days from mobilization day to get ready, but instead was ordered to advance on the fifteenth day, before its lines of communication were in order. Those who made the decision were gripped by hysterical anxiety for the safety of Paris. Not a single corps was up to strength, the cavalry assigned to the various corps had not yet moved up, the infantry had detrained too early and at the wrong places (destinations were sometimes changed after detraining, so that some regiments were marched sixty versts or so alongside the railway line), and the whole army was dispersed over an area larger than Belgium. When Samsonov arrived supplies and equipment were only just being unloaded: supply depots did not have portable stores for seven days of operations as they were supposed to, and, worst of all, there was insufficient transport to serve the inner regions. Only the left flank could rely on rail transport. Other corps had to make do with wagons but these too were inadequate: one-horse instead of two-horse wagons; town horses, not used to working in sandy terrain; and by order of some unknown person in the Department of Military Communications, the 13th Corps' transports had been taken off the train before they reached Bialystok, needlessly covering the remaining one hundred and fifty versts of sandy road to the frontier on their own wheels.

He was allowed time for nothing, schedules were ruthlessly tight, nagging telegrams poured in. The whole world must see the awesome might of Russia on the march. On 15 August, march they did, and on 19 August, the Feast of the Transfiguration (a happy omen), they crossed the frontier. They did not, however, encounter the enemy, but marched on day after day deeper and deeper into the void, wastefully leaving fighting units behind at fords and bridges and in small towns, because the second-line divisions were not moving up in support.

It was in Samsonov's nature to advance boldly and resolutely, but not rashly. There had been no fighting, but the rear was so disorganized that the speed of movement was disastrous in itself. It was essential to pause at least for a day or two, to let supplies catch up, give the fighting units a rest and time to look around, time to make themselves at home. HQ 2nd Army reported daily to Army Group HQ: the army had been eight or nine days on the march, four or five of them through East Prussia, a wasteland from which all provisions had been removed and in which all haystacks had been burned. Bread and fodder had to be brought up over longer and longer distances, it was more difficult all the time, transport was lacking, the army had already eaten two-thirds of its hardtack, exhausted men were marching in baking heat along sandy roads into emptiness!

The Army Group Commander, Zhilinsky, reading all this a hundred versts to the rear of Ostrolenka, took none of it in, turned a deaf ear, and went on squawking his parrot cry: "Advance with all speed! Only the speed of our legs can bring us victory! The enemy is slipping away from you!"

There were limits which General Samsonov did not allow himself to overstep even in his thoughts. He would never venture to criticize the imperial family—including, of course, the Supreme Commander. Nor would he risk any independent opinion on the higher interests of Russia. A directive from the Supreme Commander had explained that since war had been declared on Russia originally, and since France had given her immediate support, Russia's obligations to her ally made it necessary to advance into East Prussia with all possible speed: General Samsonov did not presume to question this directive. It had spoken, however, of "a steady advance according to plan," and if something different was happening that could reasonably be attributed to Army Group HQ, especially if you knew the cold, arrogant, sour, sarcastic General Zhilinsky. Army Group HQ reacted to Samsonov's progress reports with incredulity and even derision. His complaints were put down to slackness. He was incensed by telegrams from Zhilinsky, day in and day out, rebuking him for his slowness and hurrying him up—and where Zhilinsky was concerned Samsonov did not meekly refrain from judgment. Why should a senior officer who obstinately refuses to recognize the real situation be commended for his "willpower"? Why should a subordinate's reports on the way things were actually going be seen as signs of weakness?

Army Group HQ had one task and one task only: to coordinate the 1st and 2nd armies. Such a big staff, with ludicrously little to do, inevitably began interfering with arrangements made by the army commanders. Its actual efforts at coordination were from the start so many wrenches in the works. Neither Army Group HQ nor cavalry reconnaissance gave the 2nd Army the feeling that it was in touch with its neighbors to the right. Even during the last three days, while orders of the day from Army Group HQ, together with the whole Russian press, were lauding the 1st Army's victory at Gumbinnen, Samsonov's corps, advancing from the south, had never felt that somewhere beyond the forests and the lakes they had the support of Rennenkampf's troops as they advanced from the east, or even of his numerous cavalry (five divisions), nor did they catch sight of any Germans fleeing from east to west. The whole of Russia was rejoicing in Rennenkampf's victory, and only his neighbor in East Prussia gained nothing from it.

It might have been otherwise if certain posts had been filled by different people. But Zhilinsky and Oranovsky were alien beings, incapable of listening and unwilling to compromise. Samsonov had never had close contact with Zhilinsky until he had presented himself at Bialystok. In the first few minutes of their conversation he had realized that there was no chance at all of understanding between this general and himself. Zhilinsky had not uttered a single ordinary friendly sentence, had not treated him as a brother-in-arms. He had talked like a persnickety martinet, not a fellow officer. He had made it clear that he always knew best and had no intention of consulting subordinates. In his quiet office he had spoken in an unnecessarily peremptory way, even interrupting what Samsonov was saying. He probably felt humiliated by his lowly position as a mere army group commander with only two armies under him.

Zhilinsky, in fact, had been removed from the post of Chief of the General Staff that spring and, since he had to be found a job somewhere, put in command of the Warsaw Military District. (They had thought of bringing Samsonov back instead, but passed him over because he did not have the requisite knowledge of French. This was most unfortunate. Had Samsonov returned to the Warsaw District in the spring he would have had time to master the situation, and would have known about the war plans in advance.)

Bad people always support each other—that is their great strength. Zhilinsky had Sukhomlinov behind him. He had patrons still higher up—friends at the court of the Dowager Empress Maria Fyodorovna—and this made him independent even of the Supreme Commander. But here Samsonov had reached his limits: it was not for him to judge members of the royal family.

He did not envy men like Zhilinsky their advancement, he sought no family ties with the royal household, but whenever he thought of it he was deeply troubled: there were difficult times ahead for Russia, and when they came all these glittering schemers would be gone with the wind, never to be heard of again.

Let them go up and up—as long as they didn't damage Russia's cause.

Samsonov had quite enough on his hands, taking over, training, and leading the 2nd Army. But they never stopped pestering him, they wrecked everything he did. He could not even keep the same corps in his army for two days running: the 1st Corps had been given to him, but not the right to move it; the Guards corps had been given to him, and taken away again three days afterward (with no warning from Zhilinsky, so that Samsonov went on thinking that the corps was advancing under his orders until, twenty-four hours late, its commander told him differently); no sooner had the 23rd Corps been allotted to him than one infantry division (under General Sirelius) was transferred to the Army Group reserve, and another (under General Mingin) posted to Novogeorgievsk, while the corps' artillery was sent to Grodno, and its cavalry to the southwestern front. When they came to their senses and returned Mingin's division to him it had to move at an even more exaggerated pace than the other corps to catch up with them. The 2nd Corps had also been formally under his command, but was tucked away among the lakes and immobilized—Samsonov could send instructions to it only via Army Group HQ. The previous day a telegram had arrived ordering him to hand over the 2nd Corps to Rennenkampf, who would now have seven altogether, while Samsonov was left with three and a half.

He would have borne even this calmly if there had been any rhyme or reason in it. But it made no sense at all. Although Samsonov had arrived here so late, although he had had so little time to think and to find out what others had been thinking about East Prussia over the years, he took one glance at what looked like the stump of an arm thrust into Russian territory and knew that it should be amputated at the shoulder, not gnawed at the elbow, which meant that his southern army, on the Narew, and not Rennenkampf's eastern army, should be the stronger.

But the dispute between him and Army Group HQ over the 2nd Army's objectives and its line of march dragged on and on. If they couldn't come to an understanding around a table, how could they possibly do so by telegraph? Catching the devil by the tail would be no harder than trying to grasp Zhilinsky's plan, which presupposed that the Germans would now press eastward to the Masurian Lakes to confront Rennenkampf and wait there for Samsonov to take them in the rear. On that assumption Samsonov would do best to proceed diagonally northeastward. Zhilinsky, therefore, had made the 2nd Army detrain and concentrate farther to the right than necessary. When he later allowed it to move a little to the left he succeeded only in spreading it too thin. A glance at the map was enough to tell anyone that the army should have deployed much farther to the left—along the Novogeorgievsk–Mlawa railway line, the only one in the whole frontage of the advance, whereas the Germans had a dozen lines within reach. How could anyone be so foolish as to stop short of the one and only accessible line and make the whole army tramp through trackless sand and bog?

Although it was rather late for him to put forward a plan of his own and suggest an alternative line of march, Samsonov wrote back agreeing to advance diagonally, but northwestward, not along the northeastern diagonal wrongly favored by Zhilinsky and Oranovsky. Instead of rushing into a sterile embrace with Rennenkampf he should move rapidly to trap the Germans before they could cross the Vistula.

On this he simply could not yield without admitting that he was a complete idiot and a puppet on a string. Zhilinsky's daily order was: "Diagonally right!" Samsonov's daily request was: "Diagonally left!" Without pulling in his right flank he began surreptitiously bending very slightly leftward, each order to corps and divisions assigning them positions two or three villages farther to the left. They had crossed the German frontier and gone on for three whole days without seeing a single German, or hearing or firing a single shot, yet Zhilinsky was still obsessed with his nonsensical vision of the Germans mesmerized by Rennenkampf and waiting to be hit in the back by Samsonov. The Germans fatally cornered among the Masurian Lakes, in the slanting gap between Rennenkampf and Samsonov, patiently waiting for the mouth of the sack to be sewn up! To Samsonov it was now clear beyond all possible doubt that Zhilinsky was driving him into a void, that the Germans were pouring westward, eluding the two Russian armies, and that the only hope was to widen the jaws of the pincers.

That was what he did, bending the left jaw as far to the left as he could. Zhilinsky would not give way and clung to the right jaw. All their martial ardor went into this dispute. Meanwhile the corps marched on and on, and the tug-of-war between the generals wasted their legs on erratic zigzag marches. Samsonov suffered from those unnecessary versts as though he were a footslogger himself; the soles of his boots burned and galled his feet, the uppers parted company with the welts—but all the same he felt bound to resist the crackbrained orders from Army Group HQ.

Another result of the dispute was that the army's frontage was fanning out: three and a half corps were spread thinly over seventy versts. Zhilinsky nagged and nagged about this overextension: that he was right for once made it all the more annoying.

Samsonov would have been happier if he could have carried out orders just as he received them. But what if the orders made no sense? What if they were obviously detrimental to the motherland?

He had not been given a general objective and told to use his own method of achieving it; the way had been prescribed down to the minutest detail, and the slightest deviation brought a sharp rebuke. The Army Commander was left no more freedom than a hobbled horse.

In a final desperate attempt to clear up the telegraphic misunderstandings, Samsonov sent Quartermaster General Filimonov to discuss matters with Zhilinsky directly and seek permission to advance, if not diagonally leftward, then due north toward the Baltic. He was also to seek full discretion in the use on their left flank of the 1st Corps, which belonged to the Supreme Commander's reserve and which Samsonov had no authority to move. (As things were now, Samsonov was always told too late what orders it had been given.)

But while the Quartermaster General was on his way the telegraph keys tapped on, and tapped out two further directives from Zhilinsky, one of which had arrived yesterday, the other today. The earlier of the two repeated the old story: not to touch the 1st Corps but to advance rapidly with the other three and a half, taking care not to expose their flanks (you should try it yourself, you son of a bitch!), so as to occupy not later than 25 August the following positions . . . In other words, he was being asked to collide with Rennenkampf in a shoulder charge (if Rennenkampf was indeed in pursuit of fleeing Germans!) and relieve him of the town he had taken. Of all the crazy notions! Army Group HQ was telling them to shove the Germans out instead of surrounding them. Zhilinsky went on to complain that Samsonov was moving too slowly, that his orders were not given quickly enough, that his actions were halfhearted, that there were only insignificant screening forces ahead of him, and that he would never be in time to intercept the enemy's main force as it retreated.

The one scrap of truth in all this was that there were no Germans ahead of Samsonov (at least there had been none yesterday). Where, then, were they? That was the big question. He had not been able to probe, to reconnoiter, he had no cavalry to send forward, he had not taken a single prisoner: how could he possibly guess where the Germans were? Army HQ at least reported honestly that it did not know, whereas Army Group HQ assured everyone that it did.

Filimonov's conference with Army Group HQ did nothing to clear up the disagreement. Orders for that day, 24 August, arrived just an hour before his return: "I have previously called your attention to this and must now express my extreme disapproval of the overextension of the front and dispersal of corps in disregard of previous orders."

These telegraphed orders were, of course, drafted by Oranovsky, a handsome fellow with big lustrous eyes and a wavy mustache, impeccably dressed and full of his own importance. He and the Army Group Commander worked together in perfect harmony. Oranovsky did the drafting, Zhilinsky the signing.

"Extreme disapproval!" Of Samsonov's efforts at least to hook his left wing around the Germans and delay their flight. They were insisting that he should let the Germans get away unscathed . . .

Filimonov had now returned in the commander's car, and with not a minute's delay, without pausing even to wash (though not without checking that there would be a meat pie for supper as ordered), he bypassed the Army Chief of Staff (whom he did not regard as a real soldier) and knocked at Samsonov's door. There was an immediate shout from inside and he went in to find the commander lying on a sofa with his boots off. Filimonov stood to attention and saluted, but casually—they saw too much of each other to stand on ceremony. Omitting the formalities, he said simply, "I'm back, Aleksandr Vasilievich."

He sounded tired and sullen. He stood waiting for a while, then sat down. Filimonov was painfully aware of his lack of inches, which had held him back in his career. Whenever he could, he would sit down and hold on to his aiguillette. He always did his best to look imposing, but his hair, as close-clipped as that of a ranker, detracted greatly from the effect.

The commander had lain down because he was exhausted, and because however long he stood and stamped around in his heavy boots he could not make things any easier for his troops or help them along more quickly. So there he was, lying on his back, without his tunic, hands behind his head, feet raised on a bolster. His big, broad-browed face, one-third hidden by a beard and a mustache still only flecked with gray, always expressed a dignified consciousness of his rank, and was never disfigured by irritation or displeasure. He turned his large, placid eyes upon the new arrival but did not rise. He gave no sign that he had been anxiously awaiting Filimonov's return.

He had, in fact, been desperately eager to hear the news. But, toneless as Filimonov's voice was, those few words—"I'm back, Aleksandr Vasilievich"—pronounced with a dying fall, had told him everything.

The commander went on staring at the high, molded ceiling and listening to a faint buzzing audible only to himself. His domed forehead remained as smooth and unfurrowed as before. There was no narrowing of the eyes, no hunted look, no twitching of facial nerves. His still, thick lips remained hidden among the unruffled growth. But inside there was a dizzy feeling that the ground was sliding from under him. The commander would never admit it to anyone, but he was terrified by it. He had had no time to think any of his thoughts through to a conclusion, to let them ripen slowly, as sound ideas must ripen in a healthy mind, no time to formulate carefully any of the decisions which had now dribbled away along the telegraph wires. For the first time in thirty-eight years of service, beginning with command of a half squadron of hussars in the war with Turkey, Samsonov felt that he was no longer a man of action but only the mouthpiece of events which took their course regardless of him.

Filimonov could see what was going on in Samsonov's mind. Now, if he had been in his position, he wouldn't have talked to Zhilinsky like that. Nor would he be so hard on his corps commanders. But he had not been given authority. Choked by his high stiff collar, he sat drumming with his fingers on his aiguillette, glancing from time to time at his supine commander.

Filimonov, however, did not know what had happened while he was away. At last they had overtaken, or at any rate come into contact with, the fleeing enemy. These encounters had taken place yesterday, the news had arrived today, and it was particularly gratifying to learn that it was the *left* flank of the farthest *left* of the central corps, the 15th, that had made contact and swung *left* to give battle. The action had been successful. They had forced the Germans back!

It was only a few hours ago that a young officer with a bandaged head had arrived by car bringing a dispatch from General Martos. This final confirmation of his victory also proved for the first time that even in the silence of the wilderness Samsonov had read the Germans correctly. An hour ago he had answered Zhilinsky's insulting directive with a report on Martos's victory which should make the man ashamed of himself. He had included word for word Martos's report of a glorious episode in the history of the Chernigov Regiment. Its commander, Colonel Alekseev, had led the color guard in a bayonet charge. He had been killed almost immediately. There had been hand-to-hand fighting around the colors, but no German hand had touched them. The standard-bearer had been wounded three times, and the colors had been taken over by a lieutenant who had also been killed. In the night the Chernigov Regiment had made its way to neutral ground, bringing out the flag, the St. George's Cross from the top of the flagpole, and the wounded standard-bearer. The flag was now nailed to a Cossack lance.

It was after sending this report that Samsonov had removed his boots and lain down on the couch. Nothing had really happened to make things easier, but at least the Germans had shown themselves—and on his left! Army Group HQ had been made to look foolish!

That was why Samsonov lay there with an untroubled brow and untroubled eyes fixed on the ceiling, showing no interest in the details of what had happened at Army Group HQ. Instead he told his own news in leisurely fashion. It was, however, his duty to hear the worst. Filimonov heaped coals of fire on Samsonov's head, sparing him none of Zhilinsky's harsh words. He had been ordered to repeat them exactly: "I forbid you to call a halt. As it is, your army is advancing more slowly than I expected and to see the enemy where there is none is just cowardice. I shall not permit General Samsonov to be a coward!"

From his mustache to his graying temples Samsonov's calm, big-browed face flushed crimson. He swung his feet to the floor and looked at the Quartermaster General like a wounded man. Filimonov swore, and reviled the "Living Corpse"—the officers' nickname for Zhilinsky—but Samsonov did not join in. He had no breath for it. His agitation had brought on an attack of asthma.

What hurt most was that in normal times he would have challenged a man to a duel for an insult like that, but as things were he could neither complain about his superior officer nor avenge himself. A cavalryman from his youth up, he who had faced Turkish sabers and Japanese bullets could answer the offending party only by redoubled bravery on the field of battle. It was shaming to have to bow to him—but bow he must. Wounded and crimson in the face, he sat breathing noisily, and could not find his slippers with his feet.

At that point Postovsky, his Chief of Staff, came in. A large man to look at (though not bigger than Samsonov), this colorless, indecisive, but painstaking major general had never been on active service. He had served for many years in one staff job after another, more often than not "on special duties," and had been a general for eight years. Postovsky valued above all else undeviating observance of regulations and punctuality in collecting and dispatching directives, instructions, and reports. He had suffered only two real disasters in his military career: failure on one occasion to produce a piece of paper when it was asked for and an unfortunate misunderstanding with an influential person.

With his shoulders deferentially hunched he approached the commander, looking not so much at his sweaty forehead as at his unshod feet, and announced respectfully, "Aleksandr Vasilievich! A colonel has arrived from Supreme Headquarters with a letter from the Grand Duke."

Samsonov came out of his daze. More trouble! What was it this time? Had somebody managed to whisper in the Grand Duke's ear already? So far it had only been Zhilinsky—was he now going to get it from the Grand Duke as well?

"What does the letter say?"

"He still has it; I haven't read it. I wasn't sure how to deal with him."

"You should have taken it and read it."

The commander glanced miserably at Filimonov.

Filimonov was no happier. He could see the meat pie retreating into the distant future. He should have made time for it before coming to see the commander.

Samsonov called for his boots and tunic.

[11]

The commander expected neither help nor sense from the colonel. Just another pipsqueak of a staff officer sent to point him in the right direction. He made up his mind in advance to dislike the man: a decent officer doesn't scurry around from one headquarters to another, he stays put in a fighting unit. But when they all moved to the commander's office the new arrival asked permission to enter, neither presumptuously nor obsequiously, took a few steps into the middle of the room, in the regulation fashion but without swagger—and Samsonov decided in spite of himself that this officer, who seemed to be about forty years old, was not at all disagreeable. He had seated himself majestically at his big desk, but rose slightly to acknowledge Vorotyntsev's show of respect.

"Colonel Vorotyntsev, General Staff. From Supreme Commander's headquarters. I have a letter for Your Excellency." He drew the paper from his map case without fuss or flourish and held it out for whoever wished to take it.

Postovsky warily accepted it.

"What's it about?" Samsonov asked.

Relaxing his stance and gazing frankly into the commander's eyes with eyes just as large and clear, Vorotyntsev said, "The Grand Duke is disturbed by the shortage of information about the movements of your army."

Had the Supreme Commander really sent an officer to HQ 2nd Army, bypassing Army Group HQ, just to tell him that? A tyro might have felt flattered, but Samsonov answered, tight-lipped, "I thought I was more deserving of the Grand Duke's confidence."

The colonel quickly reassured him. "The Grand Duke's confidence in you is unshaken. But Supreme HQ cannot afford to know so little, so very little, about the course of military operations. Colonel Kotsebue has been sent simultaneously to General Rennenkampf's HQ. The 1st Army did not even report the battle at Gumbinnen until the fighting was all over."

He was keeping something back. But his gaze was candid and unsuspicious, as though he expected to hear of nothing worse than another victory virtually assured though as yet unannounced.

Samsonov did have a victory to boast of, as it happened. But modesty forbade it—and anyway the Supreme Commander's emissary had not swooped on them looking for victories but to scold them, teach them their job, put their house in order. It was impossible to convey in fifteen minutes the complexity of the problems in which each corps, in which the whole army was entangled, let alone the confusion in the commander's own head. It was useless even to start talking about it. Better to go and dine, as Filimonov had suggested, grudgingly including the colonel in his invitation.

Nonetheless, the commander asked with wary politeness what, exactly, his visitor wanted to know.

Vorotyntsev's quick and practiced eye had already surveyed the room, noting that it was furnished and equipped as though Samsonov's staff expected to spend the rest of the war in the same building. He had sized up the two generals who were supposed to embody the collective intelligence of the 2nd Army—the Chief of Staff and the Quartermaster General (according to a musty but still hardy tradition what should have been the nerve center was known as the "Quartermaster's Department," which showed how little importance was attached to it). As politeness demanded, his gaze returned to Samsonov, who was talking to him—but was soon wandering longingly to the two-miles-to-the-inch local maps pasted over the whole wall to form a single large map of East Prussia. Vorotyntsev's eye traveled over it, not with the idle curiosity of an outsider, but with a grave concern to match Samsonov's own.

Samsonov, tormented by the nagging feeling that he had overlooked something supremely important, suddenly saw a ray of hope: God had sent him the man his staff lacked, a man he could talk to.

He took a step toward the map.

Vorotyntsev took two tentative steps. His chest was adorned with the ribbon of the St. George's Cross, officer class, and the badge of the General Staff. As befitted an officer at the front, he wore no other decorations.

Vorotyntsev, Vorotyntsev . . . ? Samsonov tried to remember the name. There weren't so very many General Staff officers in Russia, but he didn't know many of the recent graduates. A corpulent figure with a slight paunch, he went up close to the map. In the empty space between desk and wall you could see that even standing before a division he would be impressive. There was a calm, statuesque dignity about him. His voice, too, was strong and pleasant. Vorotyntsev, solidly built but trim and light on his feet, moved in the same direction.

They stood close to the map, some distance from Postovsky and Filimonov, and with their backs to them. At waist level a large, bright flag, unsoiled and unrumpled, had been stuck into Ostrolenka, to mark HQ 2nd Army. At eye level tricolor flags represented the five corps: four of them Samsonov's, one belonging to the Supreme Commander's reserve. Higher still—you would have to stretch to move the pins—a meandering red silk thread purported to show where the front line ran that day.

Above it there were no black flags to indicate German positions. Up there all was silence. Those blue patches amid the great green expanse of forest were lakes, many, many lakes. On a map of that scale you could sense the depth of them. Of the enemy there was no sign.

Samsonov planted his outstretched hand on the wall. He liked big maps. He often said that the more difficult it was to draw an arrow on a map, the less likely you were to forget how hard it was for the soldier to cover the ground.

He came quickly to the point, which was to find out whose side the newcomer was on in the dispute between Zhilinsky and himself. Only in the context of this all-absorbing quarrel could he decide whether he was talking to a friend, as the colonel's eyes seemed to promise. Eyeing Vorotyntsev to see what effect he was having, he began hopefully explaining why he ought to be advancing northwestward, whereas Zhilinsky kept forcing him northeastward, so that as a result the army was moving more or less due north and its front was fanning out. He expounded all this in detail, as he would have done to the Grand Duke in person—to whom, of course, Vorotyntsev would be reporting tomorrow or the day after.

Samsonov spoke slowly, developing each thought exhaustively before moving on to the next. Like all generals, he disliked being interrupted.

Vorotyntsev did not interrupt. Not the slightest shadow of disagreement passed over the long, clean-cut features rounded off by a neatly trimmed, dark brown beard. But the quick, clear eyes did not look at Samsonov quite often enough, and did not always obediently follow his finger on the map.

Postovsky approached and stood behind them, but did not intervene. Filimonov's chair creaked disapprovingly in the background.

Samsonov quoted the Northwestern Army Group's intelligence summary as saying that according to information from local inhabitants the enemy was in full flight from the 1st Army.

The colonel's head jerked slightly. A somewhat embarrassed and apologetic look appeared on his face. Avoiding Samsonov's eyes and frowning into the dumb expanse at the top of the map, he said in a voice hardly louder than a sigh, "We mustn't be too sure about that, Your Excellency. What does your own reconnaissance tell you?"

Samsonov felt as though he had been stabbed in the heart. He had been expecting something nasty, and this was it.

"Well, you see . . . it's like this," he answered reluctantly, almost plaintively, "the 13th Corps, Klyuev's, still doesn't have its Cossack regiment. The cavalry divisions all have assignments on the flanks. So there's nothing available for reconnaissance. To make certain of intercepting the enemy the 13th and 15th corps should advance no farther to the right than this line due north to Allenstein. And it isn't far from there to the Baltic, a shorter distance than we've covered already."

Just as quietly, as though he didn't want Postovsky to hear, Vorotyntsev asked, "How far have you marched since deployment?"

"Let's see . . . some of the troops have done one hundred and fifty versts, some one hundred and eighty."

"Not including . . . zigzags?"

"The zigzags were caused by Army Group HQ pulling me off course."

"Yes," said Vorotyntsev, running his fingers along the bottom of the map. "But down here . . . before you got to the German frontier. Did you come all that way on foot too?"

He shouldn't have presumed to interrogate a full general in this impertinent way . . . but Samsonov could see that there was no disrespect in the eyes resting on him, only a consciousness of shared guilt. Samsonov could only assent.

"Yes. On foot. There are no railways anyhow . . ."

"Ten days," Vorotyntsev calculated. "How many rest days?"

These simple questions were painfully to the point. But it was just as well that he understood the situation.

"None at all! Zhilinsky doesn't allow us any. I keep asking. I keep telling them it's most important. Pyotr Ivanovich, bring me our dispatches."

Postovsky inclined his head and minced out. Filimonov, as though struck by the thought that his colleague would never find the things without him, sprang to his feet and stumped out after him.

"What I need more than anything is to stop and take a breather," the commander said. (He was glad that someone from Supreme HQ seemed to understand, instead of trying to hurry him up as they usually did.) "On the other hand, we mustn't let the enemy give us the slip. Army Group HQ keeps at us to prevent the Germans' crossing the Vistula. If we stop now we may lose them. Our brave men . . ."

"Crossing the Vistula" brought no reaction at all from Vorotyntsev.

Was the colonel familiar with the plan of campaign?

He was, he was. (But he did not seem very enthusiastic about it.) The idea was to outflank the Germans on both sides and prevent them from withdrawing either toward the Vistula or in the direction of Königsberg. They both knew the plan, but the underlying assumptions obviously needed rethinking.

"I almost produced a plan of my own," Samsonov said with a grin, "only it was too late."

The colonel pricked up his ears. "Tell me about it."

The general was always willing to confide in people to whom he had taken a liking.

"All right, if you want me to." The map stopped short of Samsonov's starting point. He moved to the left of it, placed both his great paws on the lower part of the wall, and drew them upward over the painted surface.

"I'd launch our two armies, side by side, along both banks of the Vistula. We should be shoulder to shoulder. The Germans wouldn't have the advantage of the dense East Prussian road system. In fact, they'd have to clear out of Prussia pretty smartly."

"A bold plan, that! I like it!" the colonel said; then, more soberly, "They'd never agree to Vilna and Riga being left unprotected."

"I know they wouldn't," Samsonov said with a sigh.

"And anyway," the colonel could not help adding, "we would be sticking our heads right into the jaws of the Polish trap. What if the Germans sprang it? While our rear was exposed? We would have to act very decisively!"

"Well, I didn't even submit it," Samsonov said with a wave of his hand. "I only gave them my views on the line of march. In a message addressed to the Supreme Commander on 11 August. I got no reply. Maybe you could find out why?"

"I shall indeed. You can depend on it."

Talking to Vorotyntsev was easier all the time. Wait a minute! He hadn't heard the most important thing yet: that the enemy had finally been sighted! "Yesterday. And where do you think? To the left, of course! There, look—at Orlau! About two divisions. Our Martos" (here Samsonov, unnecessarily, stuck the 15th Corps' flag in still more securely), "our Martos kept his head, deployed from the line of march, and gave battle. The fighting was fierce—the Germans had previously fortified positions—the whole field was covered with the dead, twenty-five hundred of them ours. But we won! We captured the enemy's heavy cannon and howitzers. And the Germans pulled out this morning."

"Congratulations!" the colonel said, though he did not seem as pleased as he might have been. "That's just what we need! And we've located the enemy! Whose corps was it?"

"Scholtz's."

"Scholtz's?" Then he added without a pause: "Did they pursue him?"

"How could they?" Samsonov sighed. "They're on their last legs."

This seemed a good time to tell the story of the Chernigov Regiment's colors (decorated with the St. George's Cross for 1812 and for Sevastopol). The regimental commander, Alekseev, charging with colors flying . . . the desperate battle around the flagpole . . . men lying on the ground prizing off the Cross with a breechblock . . . the colors now nailed to a Cossack lance.

Samsonov could picture the scene vividly, and he grew excited as he described it. He relished the single-minded chivalry of his soldiers in this episode.

Vorotyntsev, showing no surprise, nodded repeatedly as though he had heard about it long ago but shared Samsonov's feelings.

"Right, then." He examined the map again. "Over here to the left, you say? You've located the enemy—surely he won't get away now?"

"I keep saying it!" Samsonov boomed. "If the enemy has been sighted on our left and is withdrawing farther left, as any child can see, why order Blagoveshchensky's corps to defend the territory to the right as far as the lakes and occupy Bischofsburg tomorrow? All the way over here! Just to put Zhilinsky's mind at rest, we've split the corps off from the main body and rushed it to the right, all by itself. Where does that get us? We send one unit after another to covering positions, here, there, and everywhere . . . What shall we have left to attack with?"

"You've sighted them to your left, so you must advance to the left," Vorotyntsev advised unhesitatingly. "But what if their two divisions are just a covering force? Shouldn't you feel them out first?"

"But what do we attack with? Two and a half corps?"

"Why the half?"

"Because I've only got Klyuev and Martos. The 23rd has been pulled apart. Then there's Kondratovich in the offing somewhere, still getting his units together."

Meanwhile Vorotyntsev had performed an effortless knee bend, opened two fingers in a wide V, adjusted them like the arms of a compass to the scale of the map, then risen and begun measuring off the distance from waist level to eye level (from Ostrolenka to the corps). He seemed to be doing it for his own enlightenment, not to illustrate an unspoken criticism. But Samsonov hesitated and fell silent, while his eyes counted the miles with the colonel.

He turned red.

From Ostrolenka to the 13th Corps was six times the distance between the colonel's fingers.

No, Vorotyntsev was not trying to teach Samsonov his business. The look he gave the commander was not triumphant, not patronizing, but one of anxious inquiry. He was not reproaching him, only trying to understand why he hadn't moved up behind his corps.

"Well, communications with Bialystok are good here," said Samsonov. "You see, we've got this argument going on all the time. We have to get it worked out. Besides," he said, "it's easier to keep the supply columns rolling from here . . ."

But his cheeks and forehead were suffused with an even deeper flush. Zhilinsky's taunt had been unjust, dastardly—but the colonel sent by the Supreme Commander now had every right to think him a coward.

How had it come about? The commander could not understand it. How could he have failed to make that simple calculation himself, to measure off those six days of marching, long before this? It was obvious as soon as you looked at it . . . He could swear by Almighty God that he was not guilty of cowardice! He had not shrunk from accompanying the corps; but he had been sidetracked, hemmed in. Events had crowded in on him more quickly than his seething mind could assimilate them. He was in the murderous grip of this nonsensical argument day and night.

And all that time the corps had been marching on and on into the distance.

Till they had marched out of reach.

Vorotyntsev did not acknowledge this unspoken answer. His eyes continued to burn into the commander's. The lower part of Samsonov's face, he now saw, resembled that of the Emperor—the same mustache and beard almost hiding the same apparently calm, but far from self-assured lips.

Higher up, Samsonov's features—nose, eyes, and especially the brow—were stronger. He was turning gray. His whole face seemed frozen in an expression of eternal calm. But uneasiness smoldered beneath the immobile surface.

The commander thought a bit, and burst out: "I'm slandering myself! I got orders from Army Group HQ not to move my own HQ more often than was strictly necessary, and never without permission. It's no good arguing with them."

"How do you maintain contact with the corps?"

The colonel tried to sound like an interested friend, not an inspector. But the question brought a frown to Samsonov's face.

"Not very well. We've got mounted couriers. At a steady trot they can just about do it in twenty-four hours. Cars would only get stuck in the sand."

This colonel obviously thought himself cleverer than anyone at 2nd Army HQ or at Supreme HQ. He was probably thinking that he would make a better army commander himself. He would never believe how dizzy they could make a man—so dizzy that he failed to notice a six days' march!

"What about aerial reconnaissance?"

"The planes are always grounded. Under repair. Or else there's no fuel. The Germans are in the air all the time."

"What about the telegraph?"

Samsonov tutted regretfully. "All right some of the time. Cable gets broken. Not enough of it anyway. To tell you the truth, Neidenburg was taken on the 22nd, and I only heard of it on the 23rd. The fighting at Orlau started yesterday, but I didn't know till today. You don't even know what your own side's doing, let alone the Germans."

Postovsky returned, without Filimonov, carrying reports in two files.

Every day brought yesterday's reports on what the corps had done, for the most part, the day before that. Every evening orders were issued for the following day, which the corps might possibly carry out the day after that.

"Here, look at this!" Samsonov had grabbed the reports and was thumbing through them himself. "You asked about rest days . . ."

Vorotyntsev wouldn't be diverted. "What about wireless telegraph?"

"We've got it going," Postovsky said complacently. "Only yesterday, it's true. But we are transmitting."

That was something.

Eager to please, Postovsky went on: "We got a wireless telegram from the 13th Corps, for instance. Their vanguard has advanced beyond Lake Omulew, and still hasn't seen the enemy."

The thread marking the front line on the map still ran south of Omulew. They had forgotten to move it.

"Here you are." Samsonov had found what he was looking for. "I wanted to halt all the corps the day before yesterday and give them a chance to pull themselves together. And you know what? I got a telegram from Zhilinsky: 'The Supreme Commander'—not Zhilinsky himself, mind you, but the Supreme Commander—'insists that your corps continue to advance rapidly and without interruption. Not only the position on the northwestern front but the *general situation* makes this essential.' "

Leaving his finger where it had stopped, he stared at Vorotyntsev.

Right, my boy! Still fancy being in command? Would you have done better in my place? Lost your tongue, eh?

Vorotyntsev was indeed lost for words. He lowered his gaze to his boots, then raised them again to the map. A phrase can be like a cloudburst: wherever it overtakes you, you can only patiently submit to it. "The general situation!" No one can argue with that—neither the Army Commander nor Zhilinsky nor even the Grand Duke. That is the Emperor's preserve. The Emperor says France must be saved. We can only do his bidding.

Samsonov resumed his reading. " 'I find your plan of action for 22 August extremely timid and demand . . .' "

Vorotyntsev tilted his head to look at the mute northern expanse of East Prussia (no small country!).

Samsonov surrendered the files and joined him. He didn't tire easily! Postovsky's legs, however, were not those of a campaigner. He retreated with the files and sat down out of the way.

They did not know yet that Vorotyntsev had stolen a march on them. Instead of cooling his heels in the entrance hall while he was waiting to be received he had immediately located the Operations Department, called outside a captain he knew, and held a ten-minute whispered conversation with him behind a pillar. Young graduates of the General Staff Academy in recent years all knew each other and formed a secret brotherhood. Nearly all that he had been told in the commander's office he had learned beforehand from the captain. The one thing he was pleased about—and it had endeared the man to him—was that Samsonov had not lied or tried to embellish the truth.

Thanks to the friendly captain and the commander's map, Vorotyntsev was as thoroughly familiar with the situation as though he had been hanging around 2nd Army HQ for the whole three weeks, indeed as though his whole military career, his whole life had been spent preparing for this one operation.

With his imaginary pencil Vorotyntsev had converted all that had been said in that hour into rectangles, triangles, arcs, and arrows on the almost empty map, and he could easily visualize the total picture. He no longer cared which of the generals deserved blame or commendation, and even such important considerations as the exhaustion of the troops, tormented by the heat, short of water and of rest, the lack of cavalry, the poor communications, and the remoteness of headquarters from the scene of action were overshadowed by the supremely important task of locating the invisible Germans, divining their plan, feeling the bayonet point before it pricked your ribs, hearing the first cannon shot before the shell whistled overhead. A beautiful woman can feel a man's eyes on her without turning around and Vorotyntsev's flesh felt the ravening enemy tide racing toward the 2nd Army from the silent area of the map. He had merged with Samsonov's army—flesh of its flesh, bone of its bone. The chair he had left behind at Supreme HQ meant nothing, the scrap of paper signed by the Grand Duke gave him no right to move a single soldier, but he trembled to solve the riddle. He knew that he had been chosen by fate to take the decision. Samsonov must be tactfully persuaded that it was his own.

He saw a clock suspended over the whole of East Prussia, its lethal ten-verst pendulum audibly swinging to the left, to the right, to the Russian side, to the German side, to the Russian side.

"Your Excellency! Do you think they might try something like this?"

It was not pure guesswork. He had seen intelligence reports at GHQ on last year's German war games. (Samsonov probably hadn't had time.) The Germans had decided that their best plan was to cut off the Russian army on the Narew from the west. They were unlikely to have changed their minds, and unclear though the present situation was, much of what was known pointed in that direction.

The massive head, the big brow hung close to the map as the general followed Vorotyntsev's sweeping gesture and the dagger thrust of his broad palm. He blinked. "If only I had my 1st Corps! I could send Artamonov's corps to Soldau—if it *was* mine, and not part of the Supreme Commander's reserve. They won't let me have it!"

"Who won't? It's yours now."

"Yes, but they won't let me use it. Every time I ask they say no. I'm not allowed to move it beyond Soldau."

"I assure you that you're wrong." Vorotyntsev's hand was now a dagger pointed at his own breast. "I was there when the Grand Duke signed the order authorizing you to 'enlist the services of the 1st Corps in operations on the 2nd Army's front.' "

"Enlist its services . . .?"

"In your operations . . ."

"Yes, but can I move it beyond Soldau?"

"If it says 'on the 2nd Army's front' you can even switch it to the right if you want to. That's the way I see it."

"And they won't take it from me? Like the others? Like the Guards corps? First they said I couldn't move it beyond Warsaw, then they took it away from me altogether."

"On the contrary. You're required to use it in operations."

Samsonov stretched, expanded, his shoulders seemed to grow broader, he rocked on his heels. "When was that order signed?"

"When? . . . Wait a minute. Not the day before yesterday—the day before that. The evening of the 21st."

"Three whole days ago!" Samsonov roared. "Pyotr Ivanovich!"

Postovsky stood up.

"Do you hear that? Did we receive any such order about the 1st Corps?"

"Certainly not, Aleksandr Vasilievich. We were refused permission to move it."

"So the Northwestern Army Group is keeping it from me!" Samsonov thundered. In his anger he went beyond his usual limit. "Damn and blast it all! Why, oh why, did they inflict that damned Northwestern HQ on us? Why on earth do two armies need an army group HQ?"

Vorotyntsev raised his eyebrows, but not in surprise.

"Well—do two divisions need a corps HQ? Do every two brigades need a division HQ? Do we really need so many generals to a division?"

It was true. The whole thing had got out of hand. Commanding officers and staff officers were far too thick on the ground.

(Yes, God himself has sent this colonel. He understands it all, he's well disposed, he's quick on the uptake—and now he's put his hand in his pocket and made me a present of a whole army corps!)

Samsonov strode over to him. "My dear fellow!" He put both bear paws on Vorotyntsev's shoulders. "Let me . . ."

A hairy kiss.

They stood there, Samsonov, the taller, still with his hands on Vorotyntsev's shoulders.

"Only I shall have to check . . ."

"Please do. Mention my name. And the order of 21 August." Vorotyntsev gently released himself from the bear paws and turned to the map again.

Postovsky was still doubtful. "We don't really know what they mean by 'enlisting the services' of the 1st Corps in our operations. We shall have to ask."

"You don't have to do anything of the sort! Interpret it to suit yourselves. Issue a direct order, that's all you have to do. You needn't say 'Proceed north of Soldau,' just 'Hold a position north of Soldau.' We can get around it like that."

"But why did that odious creature hang on to the order for three days?" the general asked angrily.

"Why? He wanted to add a paragraph or two of his own, of course, otherwise Army Group HQ might look less important." Vorotyntsev spoke absently—his mind had moved to something else. "I tell you what. Don't ask for clarification. Just draft an order to Artamonov and I'll take it myself."

He was full of surprises!

"How can you? Aren't you going back to GHQ?"

"I've got a lieutenant with me. I'll send him back with my report. And in the meantime . . . ."

Vorotyntsev had had this possibility in mind all along. No one, not even the Grand Duke, realized that the idea of sending colonels to the 1st and 2nd armies had originated with Vorotyntsev, and that he had put it into other heads. Because it was unbearably boring and frustrating being a superior pen pusher on the highest of staffs with nothing to do but rustle maps and shuffle reports, all forty-eight hours out of date, or look out of the window at Mengden, the Guards cavalry officer who was the most active of the Grand Duke's six playboy adjutants, vainly whistling his pigeons back to the coop which stood under the windows of the Grand Duke's train. (The other adjutants hadn't even the energy for that.) You could burst with frustration pushing a pen at GHQ when the most hazardous and exciting of maneuvers had already begun in East Prussia, and both flanks of both converging armies were exposed; when stupendous and probably irreparable mistakes had already been committed on Rennenkampf's northern flank, and it would have been better if that victorious battle at Gumbinnen had never been fought. (Vorotyntsev did not, however, dare give Samsonov any bad news about the 1st Army, for fear of discouraging him.) And anyway, he could not go back to the Supreme Commander with what little he had so far discovered at 2nd Army HQ. The extreme left was the source of his most acute anxiety. That was the place for him to be.

"Your Excellency! Please regard me as a spare staff officer, seconded to you for operational purposes."

Samsonov gazed at him with the warmest approval.

Vorotyntsev went on, trying not to sound disrespectful. "I have to go to the 1st Corps because that's where things may begin to get clearer."

"Quite right, my dear fellow! Do go, and help me to get my hands on the 1st Corps."

"Have you got a liaison officer with the 1st Corps?"

"Yes, Colonel Krymov, my general for special duties."

"Oh, Krymov's there, is he?" Vorotyntsev said unenthusiastically. "Wasn't he with you in Turkestan?"

"Only for six months. But I took a liking to him. He's a good adviser and a good soldier." (Krymov was the only member of his staff with whom he felt any affinity.)

"Right," Vorotyntsev said after some hesitation. "Draft an order to him. Though there isn't much point . . . unless you can find a plane."

Postovsky looked apologetic. "They're under repair."

"And Krymov, as it happens, has one of our two cars," said Samsonov with a helpless gesture.

"Let's see"—Vorotyntsev was measuring it on the map—"as the crow flies it's ninety versts. By road it's a hundred and twenty."

"And it's very rough country," Postovsky warned him happily. "It was deliberately left rough as a barrier against the Germans. Quicksand, marshy streams, rickety bridges, hardly any drinking water."

Rough country! But their corps had been made to march across it.

"You'd best go by train" was the Chief of Staff's eminently sensible advice. "Change at Warsaw for the single-track line to Mlawa. You'd still be there by Wednesday morning—and you'd get some rest on the way."

Vorotyntsev briefly considered it. "No. No, thanks. Give me a good horse—no, two horses and a soldier, and I'll ride there."

"What difference does it make?" Postovsky asked in surprise. "Except that you'll get no sleep."

Vorotyntsev shook his head decidedly. "No. If I go by train I shall be none the wiser when I get there. This way I can see it all for myself."

They started getting ready. Orders for Artamonov were drawn up. (Though they couldn't for the life of them think how to word them. How could Samsonov "enlist the services" of the 1st Corps without having full command over it?) Vorotyntsev wrote his own letter to GHQ and explained things to the lieutenant. Two additional sheets were pasted into Vorotyntsev's folding map. This was in the Operations Department and in Filimonov's presence. Vorotyntsev asked for the cipher used in wireless messages to the 1st Corps. Filimonov knitted his brow. "Cipher? We don't use ciphers here." Vorotyntsev went to see Postovsky. The Chief of Staff was beginning to get tired of him, and wondering whether he would ever be allowed to have his dinner. "No. We don't use ciphers. What does that matter? Those codes can be the very devil. Our wireless operators aren't all high school boys, you know. They aren't properly trained yet; they'd get mixed up, garble the message, cause more confusion than ever."

"I don't understand," said Vorotyntsev. "You send everything uncoded—including the location and objectives of adjacent corps?"

"Well, the Germans don't know exactly when we might transmit." Postovsky was angry. There was some staff business into which outsiders shouldn't poke their noses! "Do you think they're trying to pick us up all around the clock? For all we know they can't receive us anyhow. God helps the bold!"

He saw Vorotyntsev's look of incredulous disapproval.

"Anyway, we don't send many wireless messages. We mainly use the telegraph. But if we can't get through by telegraph, what are we supposed to do? Send no messages at all?"

They were ready to dine. Samsonov admitted with a sigh that they had slipped up. They should have worked out a code and introduced it. That was really the responsibility of the Chief Signals Officer. There just hadn't been time. Anyway, they hadn't started sending messages by wireless till yesterday, so nothing terrible had happened.

Vorotyntsev looked from time to time at the handsome, affable commander, at the demonstratively hostile Filimonov, at the subdued and expressionless Postovsky—all three of them for the moment united in a single-minded desire to eat. Did the commander realize how unfairly he had been treated? It is the duty of a real staff officer to explore the morass of conjecture and raise the causeway over which a decision can advance. He must send an officer to check any doubtful report on the spot. He must give prominence to important information and make sure that it is not swamped by insignificant detail. A good staff officer does not preempt the commander's decisions, but does help him to make up his mind. Samsonov's staff was merely a hindrance.

They invited Vorotyntsev to choose the best soldier he could find, but he only wanted someone to accompany him part of the way and return. (His unspoken thought was that a regiment in the field, not HQ, was the place to look for "the best soldier.") He had no wish to join them in their leisurely meal at the elegantly laid table. Instead he had a hasty snack, washed down only with strong tea. He sat with them for a while out of politeness, oblivious of the famous meat pie, his mind elsewhere.

Samsonov hospitably pressed him to stay. "Just till tomorrow morning, my dear fellow! You must have a rest before you go on. You've hardly even sat down. You'll never win the war that way. Stay with us a bit! We can sit and talk things over comfortably."

He would dearly have liked a little more of Vorotyntsev's company, and was almost offended by his eagerness to be gone. He rose to see the colonel off, promising to move his headquarters to Neidenburg before dinnertime the next day.

It was not altogether clear what they had agreed on and how they intended to keep in touch. There were contingencies and dangers which they had deliberately left undiscussed—which superstition forbade them to discuss. They would know what to do when the time came.

Back at the dinner table Postovsky and Filimonov joined in urging the commander not to think of transferring his HQ. It would mean jettisoning all the work they had done. They would be no help to the corps barehanded.

What they had to do, now that the high-handed one-man raiding party from GHQ had dashed in and dashed out again, was consult Army Group HQ in the normal way, ask them to clear up doubtful points, then relay the information to their corps.

At that point a new order from Zhilinsky trickled in: previous orders to the commander of the 2nd Army were canceled and he now had permission to move his corps in a generally northern direction, but must not expose his right flank by diverting the 6th Corps (General Blagoveshchensky) or endanger his left flank by moving the 1st Corps. (It was still unclear to whom the 1st Corps was supposed to belong, but there was here a vague indication that it did, after all, belong to Samsonov.)

Only that morning Zhilinsky had been forbidding any extension of the front. Now he was recommending it. Whatever happened he would be in the right . . .

Still, he had given way on the line of march. Thank God for that! Now they must hold him to it.

They were busy far into the night converting the orders into detailed instructions for each corps. Even where telephone or telegraph lines existed they could not always get through. So as not to hold the corps up the next morning, they sent orders to such headquarters by wireless. Uncoded.

The Germans were not supposed to intercept those messages. They obviously wouldn't be out of bed all night listening in!

[1 2]

They had given Vorotyntsev a good bay stallion and a sergeant on a mare as escort. On this occasion he did not need to inquire the best way out of town—the sergeant knew it. Feeling uncomfortable in the still, warm night with his greatcoat and knapsack, Vorotyntsev hitched them to his saddle and rode at his ease.

He had cherished for years the dream of strategic perfection (someone, if not he himself, might achieve something like it once in a hundred years). He approached every general, entered every headquarters trembling with anticipation. This is the one! This is it! And every time he was disappointed. Almost always he saw despairingly that there was no common mind, no single purpose to unite the straggling thousands and steer them to victory.

It was a lesson he had learned, and taken to heart, over and over again—yet Vorotyntsev was dismayed by it every time. The more important the command, the higher it was on the army ladder, the more remote from events its staff would be, and the more surely and painfully you could expect to meet the same self-infatuated, careerist routineers, enthusiasts for the quiet life, interested only in eating and drinking their fill and rising effortlessly to the top. Not just a few individuals but a whole crowd of them saw the army as a comfortable, highly polished, and luxuriously carpeted stairway on which awards, great or small, were distributed at every step.

That was how it was at GHQ. Reports from the 1st Army in the last few days showed that things were much the same there—and Vorotyntsev had decided not to upset Samsonov with them. Rennenkampf's army consisted of only three corps, but five and a half cavalry divisions, the whole of the Guards cavalry (in other words, the fine flower of the Petersburg aristocracy), had been attached to it. The commander of the Guards cavalry, the Khan of Nakhichevan, had been ordered to pass along the rear of the enemy, disrupt his communications, and so deny him freedom of movement in East Prussia. But as soon as he moved off on 19 August a German force had appeared on his flank—a mere five battalions, an insignificant Landwehr brigade. Instead of screening himself and hurrying well to the rear of the main German forces, the Khan let himself be drawn into a ridiculous battle at Kauschen, where he deployed four of his divisions over a six-verst front and, instead of outflanking the German brigade on horseback, dismounted his men and hurled them at the German cannon head-on. He suffered horrifying losses, including more than forty officers. He himself sat the battle out at his remote headquarters, and toward evening pulled all his cavalry back—so far back that he was in effect inviting the Germans to move against Rennenkampf's infantry. The result the next day, 20 August, was the battle at Gumbinnen. Due credit had to be given to Rennenkampf. He defeated eight German divisions with six of his own, though his victory was incomplete and awaited consummation on the following day. But even this victory had not saved the situation, because, according to the Russian strategic plan, Rennenkampf was not supposed to give battle at that early stage, but was to act as a magnet to the East Prussian army, which Samsonov would then take in the rear—only, the morning after Gumbinnen, the Germans had disappeared! They had buried themselves in the depths of Prussia. Rennenkampf did not give chase, partly because of heavy losses to his infantry (but think how much cavalry he had!), partly because he had no shells left and none were being brought up (the supply services were completely unprepared, because of our suicidal haste to sacrifice ourselves for France!), and partly because he chose not to give in to Zhilinsky's chivying and hurry unduly. He asserted by way of excuse that the Germans had not withdrawn very far, but were digging in close to his own position. For two whole days after Gumbinnen, Rennenkampf had made no move. Vorotyntsev had left GHQ too early that morning to hear whether he had advanced the night before, and if so, how far.

Other things had strained relations between GHQ and 1st Army HQ in the past few days. In his anger after the battle at Kauschen, Rennenkampf had relieved the Khan of Nakhichevan of his command. The Khan, however, was a favorite of the Grand Duke's and the darling of the whole Guards fraternity in St. Petersburg. Nikolai Nikolaevich had, of course, "requested" Rennenkampf to reinstate him. Meanwhile thunderous condemnations of those responsible for the tragic fate of so many Guards officers began to arrive from Petersburg, all aimed at Rennenkampf. Rennenkampf had aggravated his offense by relieving Oranovsky's younger brother of his brigade—and Oranovsky senior, at Northwestern Army Group HQ, was indignant.

The main problem—where were the Germans hiding in East Prussia?—was lost sight of amid all these alarms and excursions. Any Russian not racked beyond endurance by the riddle (where have they got to? what has become of them?) had no drop of Suvorov's blood in his veins.

It was because of all this that Vorotyntsev had contrived Kotsebue's dispatch to the 1st Army and his own to the 2nd. There was a good deal of uncertainty about the 1st Army's doings, but the main puzzle concerned the 2nd.

And what had he found at 2nd Army HQ? That no one there had any grasp of the need for instant action in modern warfare, the need for immediate and appropriate response. The 2nd Army was embarking on a maneuver which called for a Suvorov—a headlong march to cut off East Prussia and begin the war with a stunning blow to Germany—and relying from the start on muddling through. Where was their reconnaissance? They simply waited for intelligence summaries from Army Group HQ, which passed on hearsay from the local population. For that matter, Samsonov had never been much good at reconnaissance. His cavalry had once missed Japanese infantry only twenty versts away from him. The story had got into print in Germany and could be read in Russian translation in St. Petersburg. The Germans knew whom they were up against and did not expect him to put them under pressure. He belonged to the Kuropatkin school of saintly passivity. "Remember—you are Kutuzov's heirs!" Asses! Imagine having three cavalry divisions—and not one of them out in front looking for the vanished Germans! How could they possibly hope to encircle this most formidable of enemies? A bear might try to bend a longbow but it would fly back in his face—as their plan would rebound on them.

That victory of theirs at Orlau—what did it amount to? They had made contact with the enemy. Hurrah! They had left 2,500 dead in order to discover that the enemy was not where the 2nd Army was heading—then trudged on in the wrong direction as before!

All this was Zhilinsky's doing . . . But there was no point in blowing up completely. The report had gone to the Grand Duke (who had, however, apparently left for St. Petersburg in the meantime).

Traffic from Ostrolenka station to the Janow road had been diverted to the other side of the bridge, evidently so that the rumble of traffic would not disturb 2nd Army HQ. The leading wagons of a long train were pouring onto the bridge at that moment. They were all two-horse wagons with sacks piled high above their sides and covered with tarpaulins. The wagon train had evidently only just moved out, and the carters had not yet taken their seats but were walking alongside. (With Army HQ in town you might easily bump into one of the top brass, who would want to know why you were tiring the horses unnecessarily.) Some of them walked in pairs, smoking, exchanging good-humored ruderies. They all seemed to be in high spirits. In peacetime a man might have been reluctant to start a journey in the middle of this moonless but still night, but they were actually enjoying it. Their horses were well fed, though perhaps not yet used to this heavy work, they had eaten well themselves, they did not expect to be in any danger in the immediate future (they were still two full days from the frontier), and they were all sturdy fellows who would have made perfectly good infantrymen. They waved their arms about in exaggerated gestures, and one of them even executed a neat little dance on the cobblestones to make his fellows laugh.

"Didn't finish the dance with your little Polish missy, eh?"

"I'm as miserable as can be, brothers," the dancer said, without a trace of regret in his voice. "They dragged me away on the night of nights."

"I tell you what, Oniska," a third wagoner said in a deep voice. "Your gray mare can pull the cart without you, she'll just follow my pair, so unhitch the bay, get permission from the sergeant major, and nip back quick to finish the job . . . You can catch up with us in the morning . . . You'll have an extra breadwinner for your old age . . ."

They all guffawed. But when they saw the rider on the thoroughbred stallion trying to pass them on the bridge they fell silent immediately.

Nothing in the army—weapons, uniforms, regulations—changes more slowly than soldiers' jokes. Vorotyntsev had heard jokes like these during the war with Japan. They had no doubt been told in the Crimea, and for that matter among Pozharsky's militia.* What made them amusing was not their content but the reckless gaiety with which they were roared out.

The sight of these high-spirited carters, with their relaxed confidence,

* That is, in the early seventeenth century. [*Trans.*]

was just what the despondent Vorotyntsev needed. Once across the bridge he stopped and unnecessarily called out to the nimble sergeant major who was running toward him along the wagon train yelling abuse at the leading cart. The sergeant major looked up quickly without stopping and in the faint light from the stars and the ribbon of river saw that this was a staff officer. He swerved sharply, stamped his feet smartly on the cobbled road, and halted precisely at the regulation distance, as though he had marched the whole way for no other purpose.

"Whose wagon train is this?"

"The 13th Army Corps, Your Honor."

"How long have you been on the road since you detrained?"

"Five days, Your Honor!"

"What are you carrying?"

"Hardtack, buckwheat, and oil, Your Honor!"

"No bread?"

"None at all, Your Honor!"

All these clumsy "Your Honors" were a terrible waste of a soldier's time in a twentieth-century war! But that was not something Vorotyntsev could change. He urged his horse on, with the sergeant following him. The sergeant major turned about, still according to the drill book, and broke into a trot, bawling at the leading carter louder than ever.

Ostrolenka station was one verst away—and by road it had taken them five days to get this far! Five days' journey behind them—and another six ahead! They hadn't enough horses for a six-day journey. Corps transport couldn't be expected to do the round trip, and army transport was nonexistent. Draw all the arrows you liked on the maps at Army HQ—the outcome of the battle was being quietly decided by these cartwheels.

All the same, these rough and jolly soldiers who had been judged unfit to serve in the line, their jaunty sergeant major, their sturdy horses, the tarpaulin covers tucked in to keep the rain out, the well-shod stallion under him, baring its teeth whenever the sergeant's mare fell behind—all these things together made Vorotyntsev feel calmer and more cheerful than he had been since leaving HQ. Russia's strength was inexhaustible. Feeling her strength he became stronger himself.

This war had begun with an astonishing show of national unity. There had been nothing like it, not for a single day, during the war with Japan, nor indeed at any time in Vorotyntsev's memory. He had been told that on the first day of the war people in St. Petersburg—even students—had joined in a spontaneous demonstration, leaving their homes and converging on the Winter Palace in the hope of seeing their Tsar. During Vorotyntsev's brief stay in Moscow people had walked in procession daily to the governor's residence, and the crowd in the streets had shown a remarkable unity of sentiment. Mobilization had come like a bolt from the blue, when the harvest was in full swing, yet peasants had besieged recruiting officers because "their Tsar had called them." Could the country squander this reserve of spontaneous patriotism? It could. From the very first days of the war the generals had begun pouring it down the drain.

Those who obtained promotion too easily never seriously considered that the art of war changes every decade and that it was their duty to keep learning, adjust to new developments, keep abreast of the times. When the War Minister himself boasted that he had never read a book in the thirty-five years since he left the Military Academy, what could be expected of anyone else? Once a man had obtained general's epaulets what else was there for him to aspire to? The ladder was so designed that the docile, the efficient routineers, those who knew how to please their superiors, ascended more easily than the strong-minded, the clever, and the efficient. Provided he acted in accordance with regulations, directives, and instructions a man could suffer any setback or defeat, retreat, be smashed, flee in disorder—and no one would blame him for it. Nor need he rack his brains trying to find reasons for his defeat. But woe betide him if he departed from instructions, used his own head, took some bold initiative—he might not even be forgiven his victories, and should he suffer a defeat he would be chewed up and spat out.

Another thing that helped to ruin the Russian army was the seniority rule, the unchallengeable authority of the date on an officer's commission, which brought him automatic promotion as the anniversaries rolled by. As long as he avoided any particularly unsavory misdemeanor and took care not to annoy his superiors, the mere passage of time would bring the desired promotion and a posting appropriate to his new rank. Only exceptionally distinguished service (as in the case of General Lechitsky) or friends at court could help a man to bypass the seniority rule. Everybody had come to regard it as right and inevitable, like the movements of the heavenly bodies, so much so that the first thing one colonel wanted to know about another colonel, or one general about another general, was not what battles he had fought in but the year, the month, the very day on which he had received his commission, and how close he was to further promotion.

The paved road ended abruptly just over the bridge, but the going was good for hooves. The track was clearly distinguishable in the starlight. It rose slightly at first, then went downhill, winding through the peacefully sleeping countryside, in which the last glimmers of light were dying out and treetops were only dimly discernible on either side. There was no need to ask the way. The riders went on at a brisk pace, but not too quickly, so that the horses would not be too tired by morning.

This brisk motion through the warm, dark stillness awoke in Vorotyntsev that joyous carefree feeling familiar to all soldiers (or at any rate officers, who live only for war). The tenuous ties with your normal place are severed, your body is eager for battle, your hands are free, your weapons weigh pleasurably upon you, your thoughts are all on the task at hand. It was a state of mind Vorotyntsev knew and loved.

He had refused to take the Warsaw train because he needed to "feel" every bit of ground the corps had passed over if he was to understand anything at all. It is not enough to be brave, quick-witted, and decisive: a real officer must be constantly aware of the soldier's hardships and his needs; the same burden must chafe his own shoulders until the last ranker has slipped off his pack and settled down for the night; every sip or morsel must stick in his throat if a single company in his division has nothing to eat or drink.

Vorotyntsev needed to "feel" it for himself because the scalding pain of the war with Japan had not diminished in the ten years since. Russia's mindless "educated public" might rejoice in that defeat, as an unthinking child rejoices in the illness which is his excuse for not doing something or not eating something that day, without realizing that it threatens him with disablement for life. The educated public might rejoice and put all the blame on the Tsar and Tsarism, but patriots could only grieve. Two or three such defeats in succession and the spine would be crooked forever. A thousand-year-old nation would perish. There had been two such defeats—the Crimean War and the war with Japan—with the not very great or glorious Turkish campaign as a slightly brighter interlude between them. The war which had now come upon her might therefore prove to be the beginning of a great florescence, but it might just as easily be the end of Russia altogether. That was why any true soldier must smart under the mistakes made in the Japanese war, dread their repetition, and strive to prevent it.

It was after the Japanese war that a "military renaissance" had flared up in the army, which was inflamed with the shame of defeat. A small, tightly knit group had come together in the General Staff Academy, consisting of soldiers with a feel for twentieth-century warfare, soldiers who realized that Peter the Great's banners and Suvorov's fame would do nothing to strengthen or protect Russia, that the need was for modern technology, modern organization, and fast and furious thinking.

Only this narrow brotherhood of General Staff officers, and perhaps a handful of engineers, knew that the whole world and Russia with it had slid without noticing into a New Age, in which everything, even the atmosphere of the planet, its oxygen supply, the rate of combustion, the very clockwork, was new and strange. All Russia, from the imperial family to the revolutionaries, naïvely thought that it was still breathing the same air as before and living on the same earth—and only those few engineers and soldiers were aware of the changed zodiac.

Barricades were raised, Dumas were convened and dissolved, emergency laws were enacted, mystics sought escape routes to the beyond—

and meanwhile this little group of captains and colonels, nicknamed the "Young Turks," developed their ideas, read the works of German generals, and gathered strength. No one persecuted them, but no one seemed to have any use for them either. The close ties between them were soon loosened because they could not stay on in the Academy forever, and the staff which could have accommodated all of them had not been created.

They had to take posts in different garrisons, perhaps never to see each other again, although each of them, wherever he was, felt himself part of a whole, a cell in the Russian military brain. A Young Turk nucleus lingered on (Professor Golovin's group), but in the past year the insidious Yanushkevich had gained control of the Academy, and his intractable rivals had been smashed or scattered. Not one of them had been given a command of real importance, not even a division. (Golovin had been banished to command a regiment of dragoons.) There was, of course, a long queue of officers entitled to promotion by length of service, proven incompetence, and connections at court. But in their own and in each other's eyes the Young Turks now had to answer for the future of the Russian army. Scattered about the operations departments of various headquarters, they hoped to turn the whole army in the right direction by the cogency of their proposals and the precision of their research.

It was they, the ones without rights or positions, who had taken up the Emperor Wilhelm's gauntlet. They, not the Baltic barons, not the intimates of the imperial family, not the generals bedizened with medals from neck to navel, they alone knew today's enemy—and admired him greatly! They knew that the German army was the strongest in the world at that time, and that it was an army in which patriotic sentiment was universal, an army with a superb administrative apparatus, an army which combined two incompatibles—the unmurmuring discipline of the Prussian and the initiative of the nimble-minded European. Officers exactly resembling this handful from the General Staff Academy were to be found in Germany in large numbers, right up to the level of army commander. Nor did the Germans change their Chief of the General Staff frequently. In Russia six generals had taken a turn at the post in nine years, whereas in Germany there had been only four chiefs in half a century, each inheriting from his predecessor (Moltke the Younger from Moltke the Elder) rather than replacing him. Nor had they waited until two days before mobilization to promulgate their "Field Service Regulations" as the Russians had. Nor had they left the adoption of a seven-year rearmament program until three weeks before the outbreak of war.

It would of course have been much jollier to stand side by side with Germany in an eternal alliance, as Dostoevsky had so fervently wished and advised. (Vorotyntsev, too, would have preferred it.) It would have been much more enjoyable developing and strengthening Russia as the

Germans had developed their own country. But now that it had come to war, their pride demanded that the Young Turks give a good account of themselves.

That meant not merely understanding and carrying out as well as possible the short-term tasks of a single day or night, but going right back to fundamentals; asking themselves where and when they should be advancing, and indeed whether they should be taking the offensive at all.

The military doctrine of the German General Staff was: Advance at all costs! Germany had good grounds for adopting it. But—allez oop!—the French had taken it over. Onward, ever onward! How splendid it sounded! The birdbrained Sukhomlinov was just as keen on it. There is, however, in military science a principle even more important than that of continual advance: your objective must match your resources.

Under the terms of her treaty with France, Russia was at liberty to choose whether she would attack Germany or Austria. The pros and cons of the two strategies had been discussed for years. The Austrian frontier was easily crossed, whereas in East Prussia the lakes gave an advantage to the defender and made things awkward for the attacker. An offensive against Germany would require large forces and offered no certain prospect of success. An attack on Austria promised great victories, the destruction of the whole Austrian army and of the Austro-Hungarian state itself, the reordering of half of Europe—and meanwhile Russia would need only small forces to defend herself against the Germans, inflicting on them the disadvantages of poor roads and Russian broad-gauge lines. That was the choice they had originally made. That was the thought behind Palitsyn's chain of forts: Kovno–Grodno–Osowiec–Novogeorgievsk.

(Vorotyntsev's horse, sinking deeper into the soft sand, offered further confirmation: that was why not a single road had been built in the region.)

But Sukhomlinov had become Chief of the General Staff, and with the ignorant rashness that looked so much like decisiveness had "reconciled" the rival plans: Russia would attack on both fronts at once! He had made the worst possible choice. Zhilinsky, who had replaced him two years ago, had gone so far as to give the French a firm undertaking that Russia would move against Germany (either in East Prussia or in the direction of Berlin) as well as Austria. And of course Russia was bound by her ancient military prowess and her word of honor not to disappoint her allies. Having examined the roots of the problem, you must still acquit yourself like a soldier.

The Russian mind soon tires of "either-or." "Either East Prussia . . . or Berlin?" Why make difficulties—let's go for both at once! So that when the 1st and 2nd armies had barely set foot in East Prussia and all their fighting was ahead of them, the plan for a 9th Army to move on Berlin was being cobbled together on the desks of the General Staff.

The individual must not allow friendship to degenerate into self-abasement—he will never be thanked for it—and this is even more true of the state. How long would France remember Russia's sacrifice, her blood tribute? Knowing all this, you must still show yourself worthy of your calling.

A hundred and fifty versts ahead of him, beyond the darkness, beyond this terrain which he had never previously seen except on a map, beyond the tossing of his stallion's powerful head, beyond the curvature of the earth over one degree of latitude, Vorotyntsev supposed that there must be dozens of staff officers just like himself—he could picture them—except that they were Germans. Except that they rode through the night in swift cars on hard roads, kept in touch by means of their ubiquitous telegraph network, and obtained precise data from aerial reconnaissance so that they could pin in flags and draw arrows showing precisely where the Russians were coming from and where they were going. Except that they had responsive and intelligent generals capable of taking rational decisions in the space of five minutes—whereas behind him there was Zhilinsky with his chin raised conceitedly skyward, Postovsky with his neatly kept files of two-day-old reports, Filimonov with his absurd pretensions and his futile energy, exerted only in his own interest, Samsonov slow and overburdened; while ahead of him were the corps lost in the sands and among the lakes. And all that Vorotyntsev could do as the fearful collision approached was scan the map burned into his memory and spur on his horse—and that not too hard, for fear that its strength would give out.

Speed! Speed, of course, was what this operation demanded, not footslogging all the way from Bialystok. Speed—but not the comic haste of a clown shedding shoes and trousers as he tumbles into the ring. Fasten your belt and do up your laces first! Imagine beginning with the two armies out of phase—sending Rennenkampf into the field before Samsonov was ready. The whole purpose of the plan had vanished into thin air . . . There was no time for conversation with the sergeant. They passed through populated places. If there was no one to tell them where they were, Vorotyntsev shone his flashlight on the map and worked it out for himself. After two hours of concentrated thought his mind began to wander. Blagoveshchensky's corps had strayed so far right that it might have been on its way to join Rennenkampf. Worse still, the 2nd Corps had got bogged down near the blank, forsaken lakes, where it was of no help to either the 1st or the 2nd Army. If you went by the names of its generals (Torklus, Baron Vietinghof, Sheideman, Rikhter, Shtempel, Mingin, Sirelius, Ropp), you would never guess that the 2nd Army was Russian . . . and only last spring it had narrowly missed being put under the command of Rausch-von-Traubenberg. Think how that would have sounded! Russians were so used to this German predominance that they never stopped to wonder whether Russia had had an independent national existence in the last two centuries, or whether she had been governed by Germans since the days of Peter the Great.

He thought, too, of Artamonov, the Russian general to whom he was now making his way and on whom Russia's honor might depend tomorrow. Artamonov was among other things Samsonov's contemporary, and would therefore resent taking orders from him. He had served for years as a staff officer, attached to General A "for special duties," or "at the disposal" of General B, had then for some reason commanded the Kronstadt naval base, although he was a landlubber, had been in charge of fortifications—and after all that suddenly found himself in command of an army corps.

The Germans took careful note of all these things and enjoyed the joke. These Russians had a General Staff to which the very concept of military specialization was unknown: as far as they were concerned what was neither a horse nor a cannon must be an infantryman!

Vorotyntsev thought also of Colonel Krymov, the General Staff officer who had gone on to the 1st Corps before him, and would now be either mending the situation or misreading it and spoiling everything. They had never met, but before leaving GHQ Vorotyntsev had looked up the records of all the generals and colonels whom he was likely to run into. Krymov was five years his senior and had been a colonel five years longer. His career had been a somewhat uneven one. At the turn of the century he had been in a rut as a battery quartermaster for eighteen months and things had not improved much afterward. He had nonetheless worked his way into the Academy, and graduated before the war with Japan. He had evidently fought bravely, winning medals in battle after battle. Then he had dozed off for another five years as head of a section in the Mobilization Department of the General Staff. Certain writings of his—on the subject of reserve armies—were also mentioned. Krymov's varied activities were all essential to a great army, but Vorotyntsev wondered yet again how any one officer could be equally good at all of them.

The path unrolled endlessly before them, tree-lined at times, unsheltered at others, but always sandy. They saw the dark, blurred shapes of occasional farmhouses, roofed wells, tall roadside calvaries. Northern Poland's sleep was quiet and peaceful, untroubled by the war.

They were challenged by sentries in two villages where wagon trains had halted for the night. But no one came along the road toward them, and no one overtook them. The horses were getting tired, and the sergeant was sagging in his saddle. Vorotyntsev intended to call a halt before dawn, feed the horses, take a couple of hours' sleep, then send the sergeant back and go on alone.

Gradually his thoughts stopped jumping about and tumbling over each other. Steadier and cooler thoughts came to him, and it was pleasant to be able to think them through calmly in this long soothing progress through the darkness.

Vorotyntsev was not disheartened by his sleepless night and the prospect of the long day's ride ahead of him, followed perhaps by a week of sheer insanity (for that was what the East Prussian battle seemed likely to be), with death perhaps bringing up the rear. This was what he was born to do. These were the greatest days of his life—the days for which every regular officer lives. He did not feel downcast, he felt buoyant and light-hearted. He was beyond caring whether or not he ate or slept.

[13]

If the truth be told there was another reason for his lightheartedness. He felt so free and easy partly because he had got away from home. He was slow to acknowledge it—and shocked by it. He had never before felt joy or relief at parting. But three weeks ago, when Moscow District HQ received the general mobilization order, though his head and heart had been full of the common concern, he was aware of a fleeting thought like a rainbow-hued lizard darting among the war ruins: there would now be nothing unnatural in a long absence from his wife. He needed more freedom, needed a rest from her.

Strange! He had never expected to feel like that. He had married on impulse—and been lucky. Until recently his happy home life had helped and inspired him in all his plans and actions. Intent as he was on a single goal, a single great cause, he could so easily have been unlucky, like so many others. Instead he had been extremely fortunate. A happy marriage usually demands care and effort. For Vorotyntsev it had been easy. His marriage had been a great success from the start. She was an excellent wife.

Long ago, in the last year of Aleksandr III's reign, Vorotyntsev, then in his first year at cadet school, stayed out late dallying with a girl in Neopalimov Lane, had to climb the fence, and was caught. The commandant, General Levachev (God rest his soul!) sent for him the next morning. "Right, then, Vorotyntsev. Forty-eight hours in the guardhouse." "Yes, sir." The tall, well-made general stood chatting for a while, looking at the cadet with a mischievous twinkle, then suddenly became serious. "Those forty-eight hours mean no more to you than they do to me. But you are an outstandingly able cadet, Vorotyntsev, you have flair. I'm told that the others call you 'the Chief of the General Staff.' " (Vorotyntsev saw nothing ridiculous in this. By the time he was fifty it might very well cease to be just a nickname.) "So please accept a little friendly advice from someone who knows. Gambling and drinking have been the ruin of a great many excellent officers, but although it isn't always so obvious women have ruined still more. Believe me, all these casual affairs and the personal upsets they cause are mere foolishness. They just waste a young man's time and energy. Don't throw yourself away. There's no hurry. I know they say 'eat when you're hungry and love while you're young'—but not too young if you have talent, because you haven't the time for it. You'll acquire a wife and family in due course. But you have to be something of a monk if you want to get to the top in the army."

Vorotyntsev had taken General Levachev's warning to heart—so much so that he came to think of it as an insight of his own.

Still earlier, in childhood, he had of course heard about the age-old dilemma: Love or Duty. He had made up his mind unhesitatingly and irrevocably: Duty every time! After the Levachev incident he had resolutely refused to flirt, or even to think of what some called "the vortex of passion." Even in leisure moments he discouraged the amorous confidences of brother officers or casual acquaintances, turning the conversation to something less time-wasting.

If the general's advice became a firm principle for the young Vorotyntsev it was largely because he had never heard anything definite on the subject from his father.

His father, in fact, never tried to give him the benefit of his own experience. The only way in which he had tried to influence his son's future was by sending him to a "modern school" instead of the cadet school to which Georgi himself was eager to go. But seven years of "modern" schooling had not cooled his enthusiasm, and he had gone on to the Aleksandrov Military School after all. In his own mind he was atoning for his grandfather's and his father's disloyalty to family tradition. They had both turned their backs on the army, and that in itself was enough to make Vorotyntsev regard his father with less than complete respect. Vorotyntsev senior could in any case hardly advise his son on marriage when his own experience of it had been so unfortunate. Why his parents had been on bad terms in recent years, living together in the same house like strangers, the young Vorotyntsev could not guess: he knew only that the air about him was heavy with the tedium of a joyless marriage from which there was no escape. Perhaps marriage was always like that? Perhaps it could never end any other way?

In Georgi's youth their house in Moscow had echoed to the sound of his mother's piano playing, a poignant, elegiac accompaniment to the silent hostility between husband and wife. She played frequently, for her own pleasure. Georgi thrilled to those strains and came to love them. He was sorry for his mother, but could think of no way to comfort her. She did her best to cultivate in him a chivalrous, worshipful attitude toward women, to make him feel that women have no adequate defense against the rude shocks of ordinary life and that masculine hands, which have strength and to spare, must raise them to a place of safety from the world's cruelty. Georgi readily absorbed this thought, which agreed so well with his natural inclinations; he had, he knew, such an abundance of strength that it would not be demeaning to put himself at the service of a weaker being.

He first saw and heard Alina in the Tambov Gentry Assembly—also seated at the piano, giving a recital. She was of medium height, exquisitely made, vivacious, with hair neither dark nor blond, and a charming smile, and she was, as it happened, playing the Chopin mazurkas which his mother often used to play. All these impressions fused into a single ardent conviction: before they were introduced, before she had finished the last mazurka, he knew that he had found her, he would marry her! No need for a closer look, no need for comparisons, for circumspection: Here she is, the one woman on this earth created specially for me!

Besides, it was just after the war with Japan. He was ecstatically happy to have survived, sure that he would now have a long life, determined to be happy. And he had just passed his thirtieth birthday.

It was such a lucky coincidence. He had never been in Tambov before, was there only for three days on a not very important inspection, and might never go there again, while Alina too was from Borisoglebsk, visiting friends in Tambov with her mother. Miraculously they had met!

Georgi had made up his own mind in a moment—he always knew at once what he wanted and what was right—and impetuously proposed to her. Alina was too taken aback to answer immediately. He had mounted a tempestuous courtship. When shortly afterward he stood before the altar with this ethereal, this wonderful creature in white, he was still afraid that she would change her mind at the last moment.

But it had all gone splendidly. You may love like that once in a lifetime, and there is no greater happiness than to lavish your love where you are loved tenderly in return. The world is complete, perfect, designed to ease your progress—petty disagreements do not count. That chivalrous worship of woman, that endless delight in her inculcated in you long ago—you know now on whom to bestow it!

The first years of their marriage were also his most strenuous years at the Academy, when the unbelievably crowded annual syllabus left no time and no room in his mind for anything else: in addition to the usual military curriculum he had to study several branches of mathematics, two foreign languages, two branches of law, three historical subjects, even Slavonic philology, even geology—and on top of all this write three dissertations. Those were the Academy's best years, when they were clearing away the old rubbish (not all of it, though, and not for long) and replacing the legend of Russia's congenital invincibility with the doctrine of hard work. (Every day on your way to the Academy you walked along Suvorov Prospect past Suvorov's church, and his glorious name reverberated in your head. What Russian officer did not dream of a destiny like his?)

Though the Academy dominated his life, evenings alone with Alina in their small and inexpensive apartment on Kostroma Street were a time of quiet happiness (Kostroma! The very name meant home!), Georgi at his desk, Alina at the piano or on the couch in the next room. Peace and stability banished from a troubled world any troubles of the heart. On his stipend of eighty rubles from the Academy they could hardly ever afford to go to the theater or a concert even on the very rare occasions when they had time, so they stayed at home night after night and enjoyed it all the more. Alina never complained. Those were unbelievably happy years! The more troubled his life as a citizen and a soldier, the more he appreciated the even tenor of a traditional home life with no need ever to change his habits. A deep, steady, unruffled happiness, day in and day out, free from shocks and explosions. They were unlucky with one child, and no second child followed, but even that did not cloud his happiness: life for him was meant to be movement and battle. Alina did not grieve too much over her loss and there, too, Georgi was fortunate. They agreed that they could be happy without children—their love had been decreed by heaven and was eternal.

His three years of study were followed by three years of teaching at the Academy, which were still fuller and happier. Then the Golovin group was dispersed and Vorotyntsev found himself in a remote garrison beyond Vyatka. For him of course, it was almost home—almost Kostroma. Surprisingly, Alina took banishment from Petersburg well, did not slink away to her mother in Borisoglebsk to wait for better times, but went with him to live in harsh and primitive conditions at the back of beyond, endured eighteen months of it unflinchingly, and was not too proud to cook and do the housework. He, at least, always had Schlieffen to pore over from day to day—but what had she got? What could she hope for at this low point in their lives? He knew how great her love and her sacrifice were and tried to make this dark time easier for her by being twice as considerate, twice as appreciative, twice as affectionate. She had, it is true, begun to pine toward the end, but he had managed to resurface and obtain a transfer to Moscow Military District HQ.

That had been less than six months ago. And strangely, during those comfortable last six months in Moscow, while Alina, humming happily, was busy making a new "little nest," Georgi had gradually become aware that there was something missing in their lives, that they had let something slip away from them. They no longer both began saying the same thing at once, no longer completed each other's sentences. Alina would arrange herself on the couch so that he could sit by her and tell her about fellow officers, incidents at headquarters, or what he had been thinking. There were so many new names, new ideas, books newly read—they had grown into a huge ball spinning like the earth itself. Vorotyntsev's bursting head could hardly contain them, and Alina was forever forgetting names, boring him, wasting his time, slowing him down by asking him to repeat things in which he felt sure she was not really interested anyway. Better to put in an evening's work at the office. He began evading her questions. And she began sulking.

She had every right to reprove him for his coldness, his lack of consideration for others, his fits of gloom, his absorption in himself—she rebuked him regularly and he could not blame her. But every scolding left a bitter taste in his mouth.

The truth was that as soon as they moved to Moscow, Alina had changed, become more demanding. After the Vyatka backwoods, after so many years of patient self-sacrifice, she felt that she was entitled to a little more color in her life. How much longer would she have to wait? Georgi had no answer. He was not ready for a change. He had shed none of his burdens. He had more on his hands than ever. And his real work, his greatest efforts, were still ahead of him. The truthful answer was "forever." He dreaded even to think what that new life with Alina would be like.

But of course he had wronged her. Not only in that way . . . there was something else. Something had happened to Georgi himself. It was as though his skin had become coarse and insensitive, had ceased to feel every stray wisp of hair. He found himself becoming indifferent to her soft, flimsy, fragrant garments—they were just something lying around or hanging up. When he kissed her it no longer had to be on her soft lips—the cheek was more convenient. Love's rituals became flat and tiresome. Would he have to go on with them forever? Had he become an old man before he was forty?

Still, it was the same with all living things. The bark of a tree thickens and grows rough. Love inevitably coarsens. Every marriage grows stale: it obviously could not be otherwise. As the years went by the ardors and the ecstasies and the very need for love were bound to cool. There are plenty of other sensations to enjoy at forty. Appreciation of a dewy morning can be as keen as it was in youth. You can mount a horse as nimbly as you did when you were twenty. There is the excitement of making notes in Schlieffen's margins . . .

And now there was the war. He was glad that he had left her in Moscow, where she would have company and concerts. It made things so much easier that his conscience was clear and his mind free for the things that mattered most.

He must not let her feel forgotten, he must write often, as she had begged him to, even if it was only half a page. He had made time to post a few words from Ostrolenka: "I love you, I love you, my incomparable wife!" And it was the truth.

But he was free, and on horseback. And all at once life was so simple, and interesting, and happy-go-lucky. If only it remained so!

A woman will generally claim exorbitant rights over her man, and take every opportunity to extend them from day to day if she can get away with it. At one time he had enjoyed that, later it had not worried him much, but now it had become hard to bear.

All in all, General Levachev had been right: love's problems, its agitations and its peripeties, all the trivial personal dramas it creates, are given much too much importance by women and by poets. The only sentiment the masculine heart can fittingly cherish is love of country or of community or of mankind at large.

Perhaps he had simply become housebound. Home is no place for warriors. He needed a change of air.

He rode and rode through the night. With his horse's strong surefooted stride he measured and got the feel of the endless versts between 2nd Army HQ and the corps—that terrible six-day march.

What a way to fight! War *had* once been like this, but those days were gone forever.

The enemy was nowhere to be seen. He had vanished into thin air.

Vorotyntsev remembered with a pang those uncoded wireless messages. How could they have done such a thing? Better to be without wireless than to put it in inefficient Russian hands.

Those invisible messages had outstripped the horsemen with their measured pace, leaked unprotected into the impenetrable darkness, and delivered the Russian 2nd Army into the hands of the despoiler.

[1 4]

Yaroslav Kharitonov graduated from the Aleksandrov Military School that summer. The order of events was to have been summer camp, then the graduation ceremony, then a month's leave at home in Rostov before he joined his regiment. In Rostov many pleasures awaited him. Yurik jumping for joy, his mother fussing over him, his boyhood home . . . He would see his school friends and, most important of all, together with Yurik, who was twelve now, and a friend, he would sail a boat, fitted out in readiness, up the Don to see something of Cossack life. They had been meaning to do this for a long time. To have been born in the territory of the Don Army and to think of Cossacks—that strong, brave, active breed of the soundest Russian stock—only as horsemen who dispersed demonstrators with whips was something to be ashamed of.

But he had to begin his army service before the scheduled date. War, and that was the only reason for any army's existence, burst upon him like a whirlwind, at once frightening and exhilarating. His class put on the coveted epaulets with stars on 1 August, and were not given time even to wait for their first photograph in officer's uniform to be delivered, let alone to go home and say goodbye. They were told to report to their units immediately, Yaroslav to the Narva Regiment, 13th Corps. He caught up with his regiment at Smolensk. Part of it was being loaded onto trains, part had not yet been mustered. (In Smolensk officers were applauded in the streets, and there were shouts of "Victory!" It was like walking in a warm hurricane.)

Although the four regiments in their division had the first four numbers in the Russian army, they lacked permanent cadres. The lower ranks were only just being brought up to strength with three reservists to every regular. Yaroslav was there in time to receive the new arrivals, dressed in their gray-black peasant clothes and carrying the remains of food brought from home tied up in white bundles, as though they were taking their Easter cakes to be blessed by the priest. After he had marched them to the bathhouse they were dressed in gray-green tunics and breeches, issued with rifles and ammunition, and loaded into freight cars, some still wearing their peasant caps. There was for some reason a shortage not only of regular private soldiers but of officers and NCOs. Who would ever have thought that Russia, a country at war throughout her history, could be so ill prepared? There were only three or four officers to a company. Kharitonov, as a newly fledged officer, was given only a platoon, but more experienced officers were put in command of two platoons, with an ensign to look after one of them.

Yaroslav went about his duties with a straight back and a firm, springy step, enjoying it all: the hurly-burly in Smolensk, getting the rustics into uniform, and, better still, the train journey. The engine hooted and tugged at its thirty wagons, buffers clanked, couplings creaked and tautened, the train jerked forward—and Yaroslav was riding not in the officers' carriage, but with his own (his own!) men, the forty members of the common people committed to his care, in a freight car. He had heard so much talk about loving "the people"—the Kharitonov family never talked of anything else. What else was there to live for except "the people"? But he had never had any opportunity to see the people. You couldn't even go to the nearest peasant market without permission, and if you did you had to wash your hands and change your shirt when you got home. In any case, you had no idea how to get into conversation with the people, you would be shy and tongue-tied in their presence. Now, in the most natural way possible, Yaroslav found himself, at the age of nineteen, acting almost as a father to these bearded peasants, who sought him out with their questions, their requests and reports. Once he had attended conscientiously to his duties all he had to do was look and listen eagerly, remember each man's name, where he came from, what he was leaving behind. Vyushkov there was a good talker, you could listen to him forever; the train went through the country he knew—"There's the market town on that high hill . . . where you're looking now there's nothing but gullies . . . that wooded hill over there is called Sharp Peak . . . you'd never believe the nightingales . . . the marvelous pastures . . ." Yaroslav felt that he had never been anywhere, he wanted to see it all for himself. This was happiness, this was what he had always longed for—to be at one with men like these, to join them in shutting out the rest of the world, to listen to the tinkling of the balalaika (a marvelous instrument, wild and poetic), to stand with them in the daytime leaning on the bar across the door space (some of them sat on the floor with their legs dangling over the side), to lie awake at night listening to their singing, their gossip, and to watch the glow of their cigarettes. You could expect no joy of the war—but the journey was enjoyable enough. Not only for Yaroslav: the soldiers were obviously in good spirits, they joked all the time, did little dances, wrestled with one another. At junctions crowds turned out to greet them with bands, flags, speeches, and presents. In this cheerful mood Yaroslav wrote his first letters: to his mother, to Yurik, to Oksana the Pecheneg, his beloved sister—his real sister, because Zhenya, now that she was married and had a child, had turned into a junior (but more remote) version of his mother. He told them that he had found what he had aspired to all his life, that this was just what he had wanted—to be a man, and a free man, at one with the common people.

Cheerfulness became more difficult as they went on. There was too much muddle and confusion. They were suddenly ordered off the train although it was going farther, and some joker quick-marched them, almost alongside the railway track, as far as Ostrolenka. Several days of this were hard on reservists, who were unused to such exertions, had not had time to break boots in or get used to their uniforms, and were carrying all their ammunition. They could not begin to guess the reason for it, and there was no one to ask. No doubt the corps' unlucky number was to blame. A general drove past and called out to them, "Germans may need trains, but Russians will get there on foot! Right, brothers?" "Right!" they yelled, Yaroslav among them.

The second-in-command of the battalion, Staff Captain Grokholets, a small, precise man with an upward-curving mustache, every inch a soldier (Yaroslav tried to imitate him), doubled up with laughter as he yelled at the column, "Onward goes the pilgrim band! Next stop Jerusalem!" It took a soldier's eye, Yaroslav thought, laughing himself, to see how apt the description was. The reservists trailed their rifles like heavy staffs to which they were chained, and their stiff new boots were another encumbrance—when the officers weren't looking they removed them, tied them together with twine, slung them around their necks, and trudged on barefoot. The battalion was strung out over a verst and there was no knowing where the rest of the regiment had got to. Officers were losing soldiers whom they did not yet know by sight and collaring soldiers from other battalions. Wagon trains, and herds of cows being driven along to provide the division with fresh food, barged into the straggling columns.

On the third day (21 August) after they had crossed the German frontier, there was a total eclipse of the sun. Officers had been ordered in advance to explain to the men that this was in the normal course of things, nothing to worry about, and that all they need do was keep a tight hold on the horses. The simple peasants, however, did not believe them. When it started getting dark in the middle of a sultry day, and birds flew about with frantic cries, and horses reared and tried to bolt in the sinister reddish twilight, the soldiers crossed themselves to a man and muttered, "It's a bad omen! It bodes no good!"

If there had been time to train them, to refresh their memories, to give them some shooting practice, these reservists could still have been turned into excellent soldiers. Yaroslav could tell as much from his own men. Take Kramchatkin, for instance, Ivan Feofanovich. He hadn't set foot outside his village for fifteen years, he was gray-bearded and, as his comrades put it, "old-looking." But Yaroslav was amazed at how well he remembered his drill, as though he had spent his whole life marching up to officers, putting everything he had into his salute—"Private Kramchatkin reporting, Your Honor, as ordered," with eyes as big as saucers and his waxed mustache stabbing at the sky. Yet he could not shoot at all. (He tried to conceal it, and they only found out by chance.)

This great war, Second Lieutenant Kharitonov's first, was beginning with blunders at every turn, the sorts of blunders for which in cadet school you would spend an eternity in the guardhouse. Everything that was done made a mockery of the regulations. Cadet school, and the smart young squad to which he had belonged, the brisk, precise arms drill, the short, sharp verbal reports, the clipped commands and the spirited songs, might have existed solely to show them how things never were and never could be in the army. Nothing that the future officers had been taught meant anything here: there was no reconnaissance, nothing was known of neighboring units, orders were changed with bewildering frequency, whole brigades in column of march were halted by galloping dispatch riders and turned about.

They had gone without their regulation rest day for two weeks now. The battalions were up at first light and ready to move in reasonably good time, but they would still be waiting under the merciless heat of the midmorning sun for the day's marching orders to arrive from Division via Brigade. Sometimes the brass didn't get around to it before noon, when a dispatch rider arrived with orders to move off not later than 8 a.m., and they had to make up for lost time by driving the battalions on all day without a rest. Then they would suddenly call a halt because a wagon train was blocking the road, or have to hold back the field kitchens to let the lagging advance guard through. Then they were driven on again. They marched until sunset, until twilight, until the middle of the night. Night was the time to sort themselves out and get something to eat, but it was not always easy. Sometimes the billeting officers who had been sent on ahead could not be found in the dark, and the battalions did not know where to settle. Sometimes senior officers wrangled over the placement of the units for the night, while the men hung around helplessly, or lit fires of twigs to make tea, unconcerned that they were giving their position away to the enemy. Then the field kitchens got busy by the light of kerosene flares which showered sparks into the night. Sometimes, when the kitchens went astray, they would go to bed at midnight hungry (officers as well as men shivering on the cold ground with nothing but their greatcoats to cover them) and be awakened at dawn to eat last night's supper. The night was always too short, and they never had enough sleep.

The soldiers would ask, "When are we going to get fresh-baked bread, Your Honor? This is our second week on hardtack, it scratches your insides to bits"—and there was no sensible explanation for the fact that their battalion had been unable to get bread in Bialystok, where there was any amount of it, because the commissariat there was "the wrong one." So that at the very beginning of the war, even before they got to the German frontier, and before a single shell had fallen or the first bullet whistled overhead, they were issued for ten days on end with stale hardtack smelling of mice, superannuated rusks, and soup that was often unsalted, because the supply services had not delivered.

As far as Ostrolenka there was only one road, and there could be no doubt about the route. But after Ostrolenka, where they were not allowed even a single day's rest, divisions and, beyond the frontier, even individual brigades took separate routes, and the corps command was later than ever with its orders, or got into such a muddle that a regiment might be marched ten versts out of its way without its being noticed from above—except by the German airmen who had started flying over the Russian columns before they left Poland. (No Russian planes were in the air: they were supposedly being saved for "the critical moment.") Once over the German frontier some units found themselves marching on firm graveled roads, but even on these the thousands of boots and hooves raised thick dust clouds and the grit got between the men's teeth. Once the road ran out, or turned off in the wrong direction, or where there was no road at all, men trudged and dragged cannon through deep dust and clinging sand in great heat which never let up in the day and was only once interrupted by a shower in the night, over country in which wells were far between, so that they went for hours without water. At other times they were floundering in boggy ground between crazily meandering streams. It was as though someone had deliberately chosen the most impassable route.

Horses, soldiers, and officers had only one thought, one aching wish—to rest. Colors had long ago been furled and were dragged along like spare cart shafts, drums had been put away with the baggage, no one gave the order to sing, men dropped behind their companies and were lost, and the others were kept going only by the hope that perhaps tomorrow they would be told to rest.

But the plan of which they were a part was obviously so important that there could be no thought of rest. They were hurried and hustled along at the same impossible speed, through German territory now—with not one real live German to be seen.

Staff Captain Grokholets, a narrow-shouldered man with a boyish figure in spite of his baldness, shared a joke with the other officers when they halted for a smoke. "This isn't war—we're on maneuvers. A dispatch rider from Army HQ has been looking for us for four days to tell us to stop because we've strayed into foreign territory. They've already sent Vasily Fyodorovich a note of apology."

This contemptuous Russification of the Kaiser's name, now generally used, somehow made them feel better.

They had been ready for battle as soon as they crossed the frontier at Chorzele (or "Khorzheley," as everyone in the regiment called it), expecting to be met with cannon or at least rifle fire before they had gone more than a yard or two into enemy territory. But neither then nor on the two following days did they hear a single shot or see a single German, soldier or civilian, or so much as a barnyard fowl. Barbed-wire barricades had been erected in places but left unmanned. Where they found half-dug trenches on the outskirts of a village they filled them in so that machine guns mounted on two-wheelers and other horse-drawn vehicles could pass. In one deserted village the main street had been blocked with carts and furniture. (Second Lieutenant Kozeko, who had never stopped whining till then, brightened up a little: "The Germans must be in a bad way!") In the next village someone found a bicycle and wheeled it out and the whole company crowded around to look. Many of them were seeing this wonderful contraption for the first time. A sergeant showed them how to ride it, with the crowd cheering him on.

The strangest thing of all to minds stupefied by heat and lack of sleep was that they were in Germany—but Germany was apparently uninhabited.

Yaroslav could never have imagined from the pictures he had seen in books what an extraordinary country Germany was, and how unlike his own. Steep roofs half the height of the houses were enough to make the view a foreign one, but even stranger were the villages of two-story brick houses, the stone byres, the concrete wellheads, the electric lighting (even in Rostov only a few streets had it), the electrical installations on farms, the telephones in peasant houses, the cleanliness—no smell of dung, no flies in spite of the heat. Nothing left half done, nothing spilled, nothing out of place—and the peasants of Prussia certainly hadn't made everything so spick and span for the benefit of their Russian visitors! Beards wagged in Yaroslav's company—the soldiers couldn't make out how the Germans kept their farms so tidy, with nothing lying around to show that any work had been done. How could you get to work in a yard so clean that you wouldn't dare throw your coat down? And why, when Germany was so rich, did Wilhelm covet Russian lath and plaster? They had seen Poland, and that was the sort of slovenly, slapdash place they were used to, but once across the German frontier they found everything—crops, roads, buildings—uncannily different.

This un-Russian orderliness was awe-inspiring in itself. And the fact that East Prussia was abandoned, a helpless prey, lifeless yet strangely menacing, filled the Russian soldiers with dread: they felt like naughty boys who had broken into a strange house and heard in the listening silence a warning that they would have to pay for their intrusion.

Even where there was something they could have purloined in passing they had no time to rummage about the houses. Nor was there room for loot in their knapsacks. Nor, knowing that they might be marching to their deaths, would they have had the heart to carry it.

Not all of the local people had run away. The first they met were not Germans but German Poles, who managed to make themselves understood in broken Russian. But they were treated with suspicion, and Kozeko's platoon was ordered to make a careful search of the farm buildings. ("Somebody wants to get me killed," Kozeko remarked to Kharitonov as he went off to carry out this operation. "There could be a platoon of Prussians hiding in the cellar.") They searched the place thoroughly, meeting no resistance, and found a brass instrument resembling a French horn in the house, another bicycle in the hayloft, and two rounds of Prussian rifle ammunition and a pair of boots with spurs in the bathhouse. Things began to look black for the Poles, and the general feeling was that they should be shot. They were marched off—a man of fifty or so and two lads of sixteen or seventeen—to regimental headquarters. As they were led past the battalion they pleaded with every officer and NCO in sight: "Spare our lives!" But Kozeko's sergeant, who was in charge of them, called out cheerfully, "Keep going, boys! Moscow doesn't believe in those tears!"

Soldiers crowded around to watch them go. "Serves them right! They're just the sort to take potshots at us out of the bushes. And go riding around the forest paths on their bicycles telling the Germans where to find us."

All the same, when they saw their first dead Germans on the roadside the reservists doffed their caps and crossed themselves. "God rest their souls!"

The day was not to pass with no shot fired. A German plane flew over (they often made two flights a day), and all the companies blazed away at it, but missed completely. Yaroslav noticed that some of the reservists closed their eyes to shoot. Then they saw three people in civilian dress dash out of a farmhouse, making for the woods, and opened fire and winged one of them. Later a Cossack galloped up to say that he had been fired on from the forest by a mounted patrol four versts away and half a company was detailed immediately to comb the forest. The soldiers tramped about among the trees, cursing the Cossack and their luck, but found nobody.

Kozeko, however, approved of the search: "Our main danger now is a bullet from the side." The two second lieutenants could not avoid talking to each other. Their appointment to neighboring platoons in the same company had thrown them together all the way from Bialystok. Kozeko was taciturn with the other officers, he was afraid of the battalion commander, he disliked the company commander, and he tried to avoid Grokholets, who seized every chance to poke fun at him. His observant mind and his urge to express himself found an outlet in the diary which, for want of anything else to write on, he kept in his officer's field-message pad. He took advantage of every free minute to add a few lines, always noting the exact time of the entry. "It's a heroic effort!" Grokholets said with mock amazement. "Nobody else is writing our regimental history. As soon as the war ends we shall commandeer your diary and have it bound in gold."

"Nobody can touch it!" Kozeko said in alarm. "The contents are private. It's my private property."

"Sorry, Second Lieutenant, it's army property," Grokholets said, rolling his eyes. "Every page of an officer's field-message pad belongs to headquarters."

Kozeko was older than Yaroslav and had held commissioned rank for two years before the war, but Yaroslav refused to be influenced by him. "I couldn't stay in the army a single day if I felt like you about it. Instead of cursing the war we ought to be putting all our effort into winning it. Anyway, how can a great people avoid big wars?"

Kozeko groaned like a man with a toothache, and looked around to make sure that no one could hear. "Let me tell you, everybody dodges it as best he can. Take Miloshevich, he's wangled a posting away from the front, or Nikodimov, he's got himself a job buying cattle. Don't you worry, nobody with brains gets stuck in a battalion."

"What I don't understand," Yaroslav said heatedly, "is why, thinking as you do, you ever wanted to become a regular officer."

Frowning unhappily, Kozeko sighed over his diary. "That's my secret . . . But wait till you've got a woman you dote on and a little home you love . . . It may be unpatriotic, but I can't live without my wife. And so I want peace. I tell you, it's better to be a stable hand and keep clear of the war than an officer in the Russian army."

Kozeko made life more miserable for those around him: he had nowhere to wash, he couldn't eat with dirty hands, he hated not being able to take his clothes off at night. Even without him the battalion grew gloomier and more despondent as the advance continued unopposed. Yaroslav had always imagined that an advancing army would be cheerful: We're going forward, we're taking prisoners, we're occupying territory—so we must be stronger than they are!

Armies are created, and officers trained, to take the offensive. But there was something depressing about this two weeks' advance without a single skirmish, with not a single German in sight, not a man wounded, and with the dull red glow of unexplained fires to right and left for company by night. What had become of the lightheartedness, the happiness which not only he but, from his observation, all the soldiers had experienced on their journey to the front in jolting boxcars, with the summer breeze in their faces? Kramchatkin, at least, had kept his do-or-die look, his shoulders were unbowed, he still devoured his platoon commander with his eyes, but Vyushkov now looked the other way, and his ready flow of stories had dried up. Not only was there no more singing in the battalion, but the bearded rankers avoided shouting and confined their remarks to the unavoidable minimum as though idle talk might anger God even further.

Movement became more and more difficult as the forest closed in on them. At first they sent platoons or half-companies to search the fringes, but soon the whole regiment was drifting into the forest and was swallowed up by it. It was quite unlike Russian woodland: no dead standing trees, no windfallen trunks, no rotting wood. The forest floor looked almost as if it had been swept, the brushwood was neatly piled, the cuttings were smooth, straight corridors. The roads running through the forest in various directions had been kept in good repair, though now they were rutted in places.

Every officer was supposed to have a map of the locality in his pouch, but there was not a single one in Yaroslav's company. Indeed, Grokholets was the only officer in the battalion with one. This was copied from a German original but it was insufficiently detailed and the place names were not always legible. Yaroslav, more than any of the other platoon commanders, hung around Grokholets and seized every opportunity to take a look at his map. The Germans had burned all the signposts, and the names of villages became hopelessly garbled as they were passed from officer to officer. "That was Saddek we just passed through, this is Kaltenborn, we shall be in Omulefoffen tonight." This great expanse of woodland with its sixty-foot pines was the Grünfliess Forest.

From midday on 23 August the whole forest began to resound with the noise of artillery fire on their left, fifteen versts to the west. A real, sustained bombardment—their first whiff of battle! But the regiments of the 13th Corps ignored it and pressed on through the forest to the north, where it was quiet, meeting no one on the way. They did spend the night in Omulefoffen.

Next morning they rose before the mist had cleared, breakfasted without hardtack for the first time, then went through the tedious performance of lining up and dressing by regiments, and even by brigades, with the artillery and supply wagons in their proper places. They took up their positions to continue the march northward from Omulefoffen, which meant skirting the outflung arm of Lake Omulew.

By the time they had gone through the lengthy business of forming up, said the usual preliminary prayer, and were ready to move, the late-morning heat was already beginning to take its toll—but at that very moment a dispatch rider galloped up and handed an envelope to the brigade commander. He immediately summoned the regimental commanders and gave orders for the Narva and Koporye regiments to change places: not, however, by the quickest means of turning about, but keeping the line of march of a brigade column, only with the head of the column now pointing westward, along another street. The August sun was blazing down full strength, and their dawn breakfast, unreinforced by hardtack, was a distant memory when the regiments moved off in their new direction, and two versts farther on ran into the rear of the Sofia Regiment, which was marching in the same direction. Shortly afterward they saw the dashing figure of Colonel Pervushin, whom everyone knew to be commander of the Neva Regiment, riding toward them along a cutting. The division was now complete. They streamed down the main forest road between colonnades of tall mastlike pines, first to Kaltenborn, through which they had marched yesterday, and then westward, toward Grünfliess. Once more, guns rumbled somewhere ahead of them, but not so loudly as the day before, whether because the sound did not carry in the heat or because the firing was dying down. The thought that they were marching toward gunfire was bracing: better the honest fight ahead of them than this eerie emptiness. (Kozeko, however, prayed that it would be all over before they got there.)

They reached a crossroads in the forest, at which they had to turn in loose sand and struggle up a slope. The wheels of the gun carriages sank in the sand and the horses, as exhausted and undernourished as the men, could not budge them, nor did the exertions of the gun crews help. Yaroslav led his men to the aid of the cheerful, bullet-headed sergeant major, and they got two of the guns moving, but the sergeant major had to harness eight horses instead of six to each of the others, and the whole column was held up yet again.

On and on they marched, and the firing up ahead stopped. Kozeko's prayer had been answered. They had marched some fifteen versts since morning and the sun was already declining from the meridian when the whole column stopped on the road in the middle of the forest, and the men sprawled in the shade under the trees to take their ease.

Anxious-looking officers on horseback galloped back and forth for an hour. Neither the rankers nor even the junior officers were told what was going on. Then the regimental commander called the senior officers together, and the creaking, the straining, the confused activity, the whipping-up of horses began all over again. The whole divisional column was swinging around to go back the way it had come.

Bellies were aching with hunger, the soles of men's feet were burning, the sun had disappeared behind the treetops, and there could have been no better time to settle down for the night and cook some supper. Instead, the division painfully retraced its steps, over the same crossroads, along the same forest road, all fifteen versts of it.

The pilgrims in uniform looked black and began muttering that the Russian army was commanded by Germans who meant to destroy it by exhaustion and starvation before it ever saw action.

They did not stop in the yellow sunset, which promised yet another bright, hot, dusty day tomorrow. They did not stop in the twilight, but faithfully counted the yards all the way back to the village of Omulefoffen again, arriving in the starry darkness, lighting their field kitchens in the same places as before, cooking their porridge (there was nothing else) after midnight, and lying down to sleep shortly before cockcrow.

Their bodies felt as heavy as lead when they rose and forced down their breakfast, porridge again, knowing that there would be no more that day. At least they now had a two days' supply of hardtack. They got themselves ready, dressed into line, and prepared to take the northward road out of Omulefoffen, which was originally to have been their route yesterday. The soldiers grumblingly predicted that they would be turned back yet again. Yaroslav, short of sleep as he was, tried to cheer himself and the others. "Never! Today will be different!"

But it was as though the prophets had cast a spell on the column: it stood there neither sleeping nor resting nor moving out. Then, when they had waited until the heat of the sun became even more exhausting, the invisible Germans on the staff (even Yaroslav had begun to believe in them by now) gave orders for the whole column to turn about yet again and form up to proceed out of the village along a quite different road midway between the other two.

Once again it took them a whole hour to re-form the ranks.

They moved off. It was as hot as the day before. Feet and wheels sank into the clogging sand as they had yesterday. But the road was worse and through wilder country, the bridges along it had all been blown up, and the Russians squandered all their strength struggling around impassable places and heaving themselves out of sand holes, up the embankment, and onto the road again. There was one new problem: the Germans had filled wells close to the road with earth, rubbish, and timber, and there was nowhere to get water except the great lake, which was inaccessible because the intervening ground was marshy.

There was no firing to be heard from any direction today. There was not a German to be seen—soldier or civilian, old man or woman. The whole Russian army had also gone to ground somewhere. All that remained of it was their division, driven on and on along the forsaken road through the wilderness. They did not even have Cossack scouts to ride on and see what was ahead of them.

The humblest illiterate soldier knew that his commanders were out of their depth.

It was 25 August, their fourteenth day of uninterrupted marching.

*

* *

Day and night where'er you fare
Cross and amulet you wear,
A wound that rankles hid beneath—
The thought that still you'll meet your death.

[1 5]

This was Neidenburg, a town that had taken remarkably little space from the fields and turned an enormous amount of stone into buildings. And this was its one and only square, hardly big enough to deserve the name. Three streets led from it, and its sides were irregular. At one sharp bend there was a two-storied house with smashed shop windows down below and smashed Venetian windows on the second floor. Smoke was pouring from it, and even thicker smoke was rising from the yard.

A half-platoon of soldiers were trying to quell the smoke without straining themselves. Buckets of water were being carried around the corner and through the gates (from which could be heard ax blows and the groan of planks as they were prized loose), where they were passed from hand to hand along a plank resting on a first-floor window ledge. Working out in the sun, the men had removed their tunics and frequently took off their caps to mop their brows.

It was far too hot to hurry, and anyway nothing was actually burning, in spite of the billowing smoke. There were no cries of encouragement, no buzz of excitement; many of the men were casually chatting, telling each other stories, even cracking jokes as they went about their work.

A sergeant was supervising the soldiers, while an ensign with a university graduate's badge, whose alert look was in contrast with his languid movements, was left with nothing to do, and took little interest in the work. He watched for a while, pacing the small, slippery cobbles, then made for the deep shade of a stone porch on the other side of the square, where a sheet with a red cross on it had been draped around a pillar. A two-wheeled field dispensary with no driver stood outside the building. A horse between its shafts shuddered from time to time.

Just then a black-browed, black-mustached doctor came out onto the porch, looking dazed and rubbing his head. The first deep breath he took turned into a heavy yawn that rocked him backward and forward. Then, noticing a plank lying on the polished stone step, he sat on it, letting his legs dangle and leaning back on his arms so that he was almost lying down.

The guns had moved on and there was no firing to be heard today. The only noise was that made by the soldiers. The sheet with the red cross, the foreignness of the high-gabled German buildings and their emptiness were the only reminders of the war.

There was nowhere for the ensign to sit except on one of the lower steps. A set determination, unusual for one of his age, showed in his face, but his uniform hung on him like a sack, and he looked at his soldiers with a bored expression, as though what they were doing had nothing to do with him.

The heavy smoke rose straight into the air. There was no wind to blow it toward the hospital building.

The doctor took several deep breaths and stopped yawning. He glanced at the soldiers putting the fire out, then sideways at his neighbor. "Don't sit on the stone step, Ensign. There's a plank here."

"The step's quite warm."

"Oh no, it isn't. You'll catch a chill!"

"I'm more worried about catching a bullet in the head."

"You may or you may not. The chill's a certainty." The ensign rose halfheartedly and went to sit by the doctor, a smooth, dignified man with a bushy mustache, a fine line of black side-whiskers running like a dark shadow down to his jawbone, and a look of exhaustion.

"What's wrong with you?"

"Been operating. Yesterday all night, again this morning."

"Have there been so many wounded?"

"What do you think? Germans as well as ours. Every kind of wound . . . shrapnel wound in the belly with prolapsed stomach, intestines and caul hanging out, man's fully conscious, lives for several hours, keeps begging us to put some ointment on his belly, inside . . . Bullet right through the skull, part of the brain coming out . . . The fighting was pretty rough, to judge by the wounds."

"Can you really tell from the wounds what the fighting was like?"

"Of course you can. If the wounds are mainly abdominal you know the fighting was heavy."

"Have you done them all now?"

"Yes—but you wouldn't believe how many there were!"

"So go and get some sleep."

"I shall have to pull myself together first." The doctor yawned. "I'm too tense now. Got to relax a bit."

"Gets on your nerves, does it?"

"Not really, but I still need to wind down. You don't react to death or to wounds—if you did you couldn't do your work. Man lies there, eyes like saucers, keeps asking whether he's going to live, and you just coldly take his pulse and plan the surgery. We could save a few more of the internal cases if we could get them to base for an operation. But what transport have we got? Two sledges and one covered wagon. The Germans have moved all their horses and carts out of reach. Anyway, where could we take them? Over the Narew? That's a hundred versts—ten on the highroad and ninety along murderous Russian back roads. The Germans send their wounded back by motor ambulance and within the hour they're in the finest operating theater you could hope to see."

The ensign looked sternly at the doctor.

"And what if the situation changes right now?" the doctor went on angrily. "What if we have to withdraw? We have absolutely no vehicles for an evacuation. The hospital would fall into German hands. And if we advance we shall have to bury the dead as we go along. Lying out in the fields in this heat they decompose quickly."

"The worse, the better," the ensign said bleakly.

"What do you mean by that?"

The ensign's eyes, lazy and indifferent a moment ago, lit up. "Individual instances of so-called compassion only obscure the issue and postpone a general solution. The worse things are in this war, and the worse things are for Russia, the better!"

The doctor's eyebrows rose and stayed up. "What are you talking about? You mean it doesn't matter if wounded Russian soldiers are tormented by fever and delirium? If they get infected? Let them suffer, let them die, so much the better—is that what you're saying?"

The ensign's keen, clever face became sterner and more earnest as he went on: "You have to look at the whole picture and see things in perspective if you don't want to make a fool of yourself. There isn't and never was any shortage of suffering in Russia. Let the sufferings of the wounded be added to the sufferings of the workers and peasants. The scandalous lack of facilities for treating them is a good thing because it brings the end so much nearer. The worse, the better!"

Speaking with his head tilted backward, the ensign seemed to be addressing not a single companion but a large gathering and asking, "Any more questions?"

The doctor had forgotten all about sleep. He stared wide-eyed at the brash young officer.

"So, according to you we shouldn't even operate? Shouldn't even dress their wounds? The more of them who die, the nearer we are to liberation? We've just been dealing with the standard-bearer from your Chernigov Regiment. Major arterial damage . . . lying out in no-man's-land for twelve hours before they brought him in . . . thready pulse. If you had your way we wouldn't bother with him. Is that what you mean by seeing things in perspective?"

The ensign's brown eyes flashed. "Did they have to flock after our ignorant brute of a colonel like panicking sheep? The flag is unfurled, and immediately the whole regiment has a lump in its throat. Imagine fighting for a bit of rag! And when that's gone, for the stick it was tied to. They've left a stack of corpses behind and that's all there is to be said. We could be tin soldiers the way they play with us."

Puzzled, the doctor asked, "Excuse me, but you're not a regular officer, are you? What are you?"

The ensign shrugged. "What does it matter? I'm a citizen."

"Your profession, I mean."

"I'm a lawyer, if you must know."

"Ah, a law-yer!" The doctor nodded his head as though he should have guessed as much. "A law-yer."

"What's wrong with that?" the ensign asked defensively.

"I might have known. Lawyers in Russia seem to breed like flies, if you'll excuse the expression."

"There are still far too few for such a lawless country."

The doctor ignored that. "Lawyers in the courts, lawyers in the Duma, lawyers in the political parties, lawyers in the press, lawyers at public meetings, lawyers writing pamphlets." He spread out his big hands. "I ask you, what sort of education does a lawyer get anyway?"

"I got a university education. Petersburg University," the ensign informed him with icy politeness.

"In the Law Faculty? I'm damned if I call that a higher education. You just memorize a dozen textbooks and take an exam, and that's all there is to it. Some education! I've known a few law students in my time—they frittered away their four years writing pamphlets, holding conferences, rabble-rousing . . ."

The ensign rebuked him, his face darkening. "That's a despicable way for an intellectual to talk. Why play *their* game? People with any claim to decency can't help sympathizing with the left."

The doctor realized that he had overstepped the mark, but the ensign had tried his patience.

"What I mean," he said, correcting himself, "is that if you had studied in the Medical or the Engineering Faculty you would have known what hard work exams can be. And when a man acquires some practical knowledge he doesn't sit back and do nothing. He works. Russia needs workers, people who get things done."

"You should be ashamed of yourself." The ensign stared at him with the same look of searing reproach. "You want to reinforce the present foul setup! We must tear it down without compunction and let in the light."

The doctor hadn't realized that he was reinforcing anything. Healing people was his sole concern. But before he could say so the fiery-eyed ensign fired a question at him.

"You graduated from the Army Medical Academy, I suppose?"

"Yes."

"What year?"

"1909."

"So-o-o." The ensign made a rapid calculation, and the nostrils of his long, straight nose quivered. "You must have been expelled in the critical year, 1905. Later on you capitulated and took an oath of loyalty, so they readmitted you. Am I right?"

The doctor's brow clouded. He turned the ends of his mustache downward, but they sprang back again. "Oath of loyalty! Trust you to pounce on that! What else could I do? I wanted to be an army doctor, and there's only one Army Medical Academy in the country. Anyway, if we had the most democratic government there could possibly be, it would rightly expect students not to hold antiwar meetings in the Army Medical Academy. That seems fair enough to me."

"What about wearing uniforms? What about students having to salute, like rankers?"

"Well, it's a military academy! I don't see anything terrible in that."

The ensign made an exasperated gesture. "Playing soldiers! We give way all along the line—and afterward we're surprised when . . ."

"What *we* do afterward is heal wounded men." It was the doctor's turn to get angry. "Just let me get on with it! Playing soldiers indeed! Wait till you're brought in tomorrow—with a smashed shoulder perhaps."

The ensign grinned. There was no malice in him. He was young, sincere, and passionate in his convictions, as the best Russian students always were.

"Nobody's against humanitarianism. Heal as many as you like! Let's look upon it as a form of mutual aid. But we can do without theoretical justifications of this obscene war."

"I don't remember producing any . . ."

"War of Liberation they call it! Anything to make people think it's worthwhile. 'To save our Serbian brothers.' We're so sorry for the Serbs, but we oppress all the non-Russian peoples of the Empire, and we aren't a bit sorry for them."

"All the same, it was Germany that started it." The doctor was having difficulty, as people in Russia usually did, in holding his own against youthful certitude.

"If you ask me, it's a pity Napoleon didn't beat us in 1812. He wouldn't have lasted long, and then we'd have been free."

As the lawyer, unsuccessfully disguised in a detested uniform, reeled off his carefully prepared arguments, the doctor, who had no ready answer, became more and more conciliatory.

"How did you come to be called up? Couldn't you get exemption or deferment?" he asked sympathetically.

"I just got stuck. I was doing basic training. Right turn, as you were, left turn, as you were . . . about face . . . on the double! I took the exam for ensign's rank in the reserve and that was it!"

"Well, let's get acquainted." The doctor extended a large, soft, but powerful hand. "My name's Fedonin."

The young lawyer offered him his thin, bony fingers and said, "Mine's Lenartovich."

"Lenartovich? Lenartovich? . . . Wait a minute, I seem to have heard that name in Petersburg somewhere . . . Could I have?"

"Depends what your interests are," Lenartovich replied, noncommittally. "My uncle was well known in revolutionary circles. He was executed."

"Of course, of course!" The doctor spoke apologetically, all the more impressed because he only vaguely remembered the affair and couldn't be sure whether the older Lenartovich had succeeded in shooting somebody, failed to blow somebody up, or been involved in a naval mutiny. "Yes, of course . . . Your name is partly German, isn't it?"

"Yes, one of my ancestors, also, incidentally, an army doctor, came here under Peter the Great. His descendants became completely Russian."

"Have you any family in Petersburg?"

"My parents are dead. I've got a sister in a Bestuzhev course. I had a letter from her today, as it happens. Written on the fourth day of the war, 5 August. Today's . . . what? 25 August. Call that a postal service?

Must come by oxcart. Or else the censors can't bear to part with it. It's the same with newspapers." He was getting more and more heated. "I've just got mine for 14 August. What sort of postal service is that? You don't know what to think! What's going on in Russia or in Germany or in Western Europe? We haven't the faintest idea. All we know is that we've taken Neidenburg more or less without a fight, which didn't stop us from bombarding it and setting fire to the place, and now good old Ivan is carrying buckets of water to put it out."

"Hold on, the Germans started some of the fires . . ."

"The Germans fired the big shops but it was the Cossacks who set fire to the outskirts. Fine. Anyway, the army on the Austrian front doesn't know a thing about us, and we know nothing about them. That's no way to fight a war. Rumors, that's all we ever hear. A cavalry officer rides by, whispers in somebody's ear, and that's all the news we get. Who shows any respect for the army in the field? Nobody. Everybody despises us. You talk as though it's just Russia versus Germany. If our boys break down the door of an abandoned apartment and carry something off, they've brought shame on a Christian army, they're punished and put in the guardhouse. But when Lieutenant Colonel Adamantov collects all the silver cream jugs and ewers he can lay his hands on, that's all right, nobody worries. That's Russia for you!"

Well, if it hadn't been for the filthy war, girls would never have dressed themselves all in white, never have concealed their foreheads so that only their eyebrows were showing, never have stepped out onto that porch looking so pure, so severe, and so . . . so new. Anonymous and unidentifiable, education, social status, and hair color all unknown, a nurse had appeared in the doorway in her new uniform.

"What is it, Tanya?"

"The patient with the broken jaw is restless, Valeryan Akimich. Can you come and look at him?"

The argument on the steps was over. The doctor sighed and went away with the swan-white nurse in tow, as was his right.

Her sad, lusterless eyes passed briefly over Lenartovich as she went.

Those white headdresses and uniforms were, of course, also play clothes for the privileged, and opium for the common soldier.

A lieutenant colonel mounted on a restive horse suddenly rode onto the square, bellowing—as was *his* right: "Who's in charge here?"

The soldiers started passing the buckets faster, and Lenartovich hurried down the steps as quickly as his dignity allowed, crossed the square, stood more or less to attention, saluted, rather crookedly, and said, "Ensign Lenartovich, 29th Chernigov Regiment!"

"Have you been told to put these fires out?"

"Yes. I mean yes, sir."

"So what d'you think this is, Ensign, a Christmas bazaar? Army HQ is on its way, it's moving in two doors from here, and you've been fooling around with these fires for three days now. It's enough to make a cat laugh—carrying buckets of water all that way. Surely you can find a pump somewhere?"

"Where can we get one, sir? Our battalion hasn't . . ."

"So use your brains for once. You're not at the university now, you know. What do you mean by wearing your men out like this? Follow me, I'll show you where you can get a pump and a hose. You should have looked around some of the barns."

The lieutenant colonel moved off on his magnificent horse, heading a triumphal procession, with Lenartovich trailing behind like a prisoner.

[1 6]

It took Vorotyntsev a night, a day, and another night to reach Soldau. He could have been quicker. He had sent the sergeant back earlier on, and was traveling light, but did not want to overtire his stallion, not knowing how long he would be needing it. The horse had been fed and watered when he rode into Soldau in the early morning of the 26th, before it was hot.

Like all German towns, Soldau occupied no more cultivable land than was necessary, and had no scruffy fringe of rubbish dumps, wasteland, and scattered habitations around it. By whichever road you entered you were immediately shut in by brick and tile: some of the houses were three or four stories high, and the walls supported pent roofs as high as themselves. In such little towns the streets are as regular as corridors, paved throughout with smooth, even cobbles or flags, and every house has something different about it—a turret perhaps or an unusual window. In small towns like Soldau a small area accommodates the town hall, the church, several miniature squares, a monument to somebody or other, perhaps more than one, all sorts of shops, beerhouses, a post office, a bank, and there may be a bijou park behind wrought-iron railings, then the streets and the town end just as abruptly, and you have scarcely passed the last house when you find a highroad lined with trees stretching before you with a neat grid of precisely demarcated fields on either side.

Soldau's inhabitants had deserted it completely and it was not overfull of Russian troops. Sentries had been posted here and there outside shops and storehouses—a necessary precaution. Vorotyntsev passed two looted buildings as he looked around the town. Instead of asking passersby where HQ was he followed his nose—it wouldn't let him down, though he might ride a little farther than necessary. Near a small house which nonetheless had iron railings, a little garden, a fountain, and a porch with two pillars, he caught sight of a car—a "Russo-Baltic Carriage." It didn't look much like HQ—there was nobody around—but the car told Vorotyntsev that this was where he might find the man he needed to see before calling at HQ.

He dismounted—and felt in his back how very tired he was. He hitched the horse to a tree beside the car, leaving his greatcoat on the saddle. No one was paying any attention to him. He pushed at the wrought-iron gate and went in.

The basin of the fountain was still wet from water that had only recently drained away. Flowers standing in regular formation in the dry soil were undamaged. It was only when he rounded a bush by the fountain that Vorotyntsev noticed a stone bench with heraldic beasts for armrests to one side of the porch, and sitting on it an elderly officer, with a dark growth on his face and untidy hair, smoking a crooked cigarette of his own rolling and looking displeased with life. From the waist down he was wearing an officer's uniform—wide riding breeches with yellow Trans-Baikal stripes—but up above he wore only a plain undervest, so that it was impossible to tell what his rank was. There was certainly nothing of the staff officer about him. He hardly stirred as the colonel approached.

Vorotyntsev saluted him casually, putting two fingers somewhere in the vicinity of his cap. "Can you tell me whether this is where Colonel Krymov is staying?"

The unshaven officer looked more miserable than ever, grunted and nodded, but otherwise did not stir.

"Are you Colonel Krymov?"

"Yes."

Ignoring rank and protocol yet again—the somnolent Krymov made it difficult not to—the newcomer held out, almost threw out, his right hand, palm open. "Vorotyntsev. I should like a word with you."

Krymov raised himself very slightly—just enough to avoid discourtesy, or on account of his bulk perhaps slightly less—briefly surrendered his rough, round hand, withdrew it, and pointed to a place beside himself on the bench. After which he went on smoking, showing no eagerness to learn anything further, although colonels from the General Staff were rarely glimpsed in the streets of Soldau.

While Vorotyntsev was taking his seat and mopping his brow he had already realized that it would be best to use as few words and as little formality as possible with Krymov, and realized too that although Krymov had not yet decided to like him, they would hit it off.

"I've just come from Aleksandr Vasilievich. He's told me about you . . ."

"I knew you had."

Vorotyntsev couldn't help looking surprised. "How?"

Krymov gave the merest nod at something beyond the fountain. "I know that stallion. I rode him last week . . . How did you get him here?"

It was Vorotyntsev's turn to laugh. "I didn't! He got me here."

Krymov looked startled, and dubious. "All the way from Ostrolenka? In the saddle?"

Vorotyntsev grunted—nothing remarkable in that. (But his sacrum ached and his back was stiff.)

Krymov looked a little more friendly but his eyes were still narrow. "Not ba-a-ad. Why not by train?"

"What can you see of the war from a train?" Vorotyntsev cheerfully retorted, but he divined from a slight movement of the heavy head that the question referred to the horse rather than the rider. "No, he hasn't worn himself out. And I've fed him regularly."

Krymov's next nod was more emphatic. "Right enough. You don't see much of the war from the train. Comfortable, though." He took a lacquered cigarette case from his pocket. "It's Daurian, wholeleaf. Good tobacco."

"I've given it up."

Krymov frowned disapproval. "Shouldn't have. You can't get through a war without tobacco. Yesterday, was it?"

"No, three years ago."

"When you left Ostrolenka, I mean."

"Oh—two days ago, in the evening."

Krymov blinked acknowledgment.

"Tell me—is Aleksandr Vasilievich getting my reports?"

"He didn't say."

"I've sent three. I'm working on the fourth. What about you?"

"I . . . er . . ." No, Vorotyntsev still only half understood the clipped utterances of this uncouth fellow with the sleepy, dissipated look. "Oh, I see what you mean. I'm from GHQ."

The worst possible credentials: obviously there to stick his nose in, to check up, obviously an outsider. One of the golden boys. A coxcomb. Why didn't he stay where he was wanted?

Krymov was looking grim again. "All right, let's have a wash and some breakfast. I'm only just out of bed myself. Got back in the middle of the night. Woke up—started thinking . . ."

"Back from where?"

"Er . . . cavalry division . . . Shtempel's . . ."

Vorotyntsev rose to this eagerly. "Tell me, are there two cavalry divisions here or not? Are they any use? What are they doing?"

"What are they doing? Cropping the grass! Lyubomirov had a hot time of it yesterday. Tried to take a town. Couldn't."

Vorotyntsev wouldn't be put off like that.

"The 2nd Army has three cavalry divisions, and not one of them up front. We're advancing blindly, with no reconnaissance. Klyuev doesn't have so much as one regiment of horse. Martos's Cossacks are Warsaw street cops—what sort of scouts will they make? Why is all the cavalry on the flanks?"

Krymov was not to be put out either. "Why, why, why? It's just happened that way. They thought they'd use the left wing to encircle the enemy. What else could they use for the job?"

They went inside. Only in the better St. Petersburg houses would you find such discreetly gleaming furniture, such bronze and such marble as here in the humble town of Soldau. The house had been picked over but not gutted: lace, ribbons, coral brooches, and combs had been scattered about the floor and left to lie there.

Krymov had the house to himself, with a single Cossack, who popped out of the kitchen at his master's ringing call—"Yevstafi!"

They went straight into the kitchen. Yevstafi, who was tall, not young but very energetic, already had a proprietorial attitude toward the numerous porcelain, tin, and wooden containers, jars, casks, and boxes of provisions with incomprehensible inscriptions. He was busying himself with Krymov's breakfast while sniffing and sampling all the jars in turn, shaking his head in wonder.

Krymov ordered breakfast for two and showed Vorotyntsev a bathroom with marble fittings and a mirror. The water had not been cut off! Men's and women's garments were hanging there, souvenirs of peacetime left behind two days ago.

"Maybe I'll have a shave as well," Vorotyntsev decided.

He did not, as he would normally have done, close the bathroom door behind him but removed his gun belt, hurriedly shed his tunic, and stood there in his undervest, like his host.

Instead of leaving him to himself, Krymov came in and sat on the edge of the bath. He rolled another crooked cigarette with one swift movement, and started spewing tar again.

Yevstafi brought hot water and Vorotyntsev, wielding his safety razor, explained to Krymov (who hadn't asked a single question) what had made him ride over to the 1st Corps. He could see now, he said, that he might have come for nothing.

He was not quite sure that he meant this, but he was regretfully inclined to think so. The thought had occurred to him only now while he was shaving; outside, on the bench with the animals' heads, he had felt different. When he had been warned at Army HQ that Krymov was here on the left flank, he had hesitated briefly. He should have obeyed his instinct and gone to see Blagoveshchensky on the right flank. But there was that unfortunate streak in Vorotyntsev's character: he made up his mind on the spur of the moment and then was slow to change it. He had it in mind to visit the 1st Corps even before he got to Ostrolenka, seeing it as the key to the whole operation.

Now neither horse nor train was of any use. He would have needed wings at his back to reach Blagoveshchensky in an hour.

Everything about Krymov made a more and more favorable impression, even the fact that he was in no hurry to get dressed and hide behind his epaulets but went on sitting on the edge of the bath in his undervest, emitting puffs of smoke. Whatever could be done for the 1st Corps, this rough diamond could do without Vorotyntsev's help.

Krymov heard his guest out and thawed again.

"Of course you aren't needed," he said. "Nor am I. This plaster saint of ours takes no notice even of the Army Commander. He knows that the Supreme Commander has a soft spot for his corps. They've taken the Guards regiment from us and he hopes they'll pull him out next. He came here via Vilna, and told the people in the cathedral there was nothing to be afraid of, because he was on his way to fight for them. He'll stand there like a dummy in a shop window waiting till the war ends and the prizes are given out."

Krymov sank into himself so that his legs dangled and the bath behind him looked like a boat without oars or a pole.

But his uncouthness and his somber words reassured Vorotyntsev as nothing else could.

"Well, we're about to give Artamonov a bit of a scare. I've brought him written orders from Samsonov. If he jibs we'll get on the phone to GHQ. It'll be best if we don't go through the usual channels. There's a man at GHQ who knows what's what. He'll do what's needed. You have to bypass Yanushkevich and Danilov and catch the Grand Duke at an opportune moment . . . There's no unity and no clarity at GHQ either. They're supposed to have transferred the 1st Corps to Samsonov on the 21st—but where's the order? Somebody's fouling things up again. It's ridiculous! A corps in the tightest corner of the front line, and not subordinated to anybody. Still Artamonov seems to be doing something. He's taken Soldau and continued to advance."

"What d'you mean, continued to advance? Might as well have a shave myself. Advance? Damned liar!" Krymov, purple with anger, waddled over to the mirror and looked back at Vorotyntsev, who had seated himself on a lady's chair. "He reported to Army HQ that there was a German division stationed in Soldau. He hadn't carried out reconnaissance, hadn't asked, just said they'd intercepted some sort of telephone message." Krymov flourished his razor. "He made it all up so he wouldn't have to attack the town. As it turned out, there were only two Landwehr regiments in Soldau, and they left of their own accord. He had to take the place willy-nilly. So he told another whopper." Krymov, lavishly lathered, was fuming again. "Told HQ that the Germans abandoned Neidenburg because he had taken Soldau."

"What about Usdau, then?"

"He didn't take Usdau, the cavalry division did. And he, poor soul, had to move up again."

"So that's how it is. I've never seen Artamonov myself."

"Who has? Even Aleksandr Vasilievich hasn't seen him. He became a general and got his gold-hilted sword for fighting bare-assed Chinamen. Like Kondratovich."

"Did you meet Kondratovich just now?"

"How could I? He's in the rear, trying to get the corps together. And happy about it. He's a well-known coward."

"Whom have you seen these last few days?"

"Martos."

"Now there's an excellent general."

"What's excellent about him? He's a nitpicker and he's worn his staff officers to a frazzle."

"No, he's just unusually punctilious. What do you think of Blagoveshchensky?"

"A sack of shit. A leaky sack of wet shit. And Klyuev is a nincompoop."

"What's the Chief of Staff, 1st Corps, like?"

"A complete numskull, not worth talking to."

Vorotyntsev could hold back his laughter no longer.

They went in to breakfast. Yevstafi had put a decanter of vodka on the table, and Krymov filled both glasses without asking.

Vorotyntsev declined at the risk of ruining their frank conversation. He had one un-Russian characteristic—he would not drink before doing business, only when all was satisfactorily settled. And in any case not in the morning.

Krymov clutched his glass in his fist. "An officer must be brave. In the face of the enemy. In the face of his own superiors. And in the face of vodka. If he isn't he's no officer."

He drank alone, looking sulky. But he finished what he had been saying about Artamonov. Yes, the 1st Corps was indeed two infantry regiments short. Of course, everybody was short, every unit was below strength. But Artamonov had drawn the conclusion that he couldn't fight at all. He was a smooth talker—"I shall reply to an attack by attacking!"—and a liar, that was the main thing about him. What could you do with such a liar? Smash his face in? Challenge him to a duel? That was why Krymov had gone to see Martos and arranged to borrow a column and attack Soldau from the east. Martos had found one for him. But the Germans had abandoned Soldau without waiting.

Vorotyntsev got onto the cavalry again: it was being misused and reduced to the role of protecting the army's flanks. Of course, all the generals were cavalrymen—Zhilinsky, Oranovsky, Rennenkampf, Samsonov . . .

"Leave Samsonov out of it," Krymov ordered him, "and don't talk about the cavalry when you know nothing about it! They were ordered to cut the Germans off from the Vistula. Now of course there's no way of shifting them."

He drained his second glass at a draft, irately insisting that the cavalry was good, that it had fought seriously and had suffered great losses. Should cavalry be expected to charge stone buildings and armored cars? What good was cavalry when the left hand doesn't know what the right hand's doing? They kept changing assignments, routes, making it ford the same stream three times, giving it orders it couldn't make head or tail of, sending it to wreck railway junctions somewhere in the rear, then telling it not to . . .

Vorotyntsev stuck to his guns. "There you are, you see. We don't know how to use cavalry. How are things in Rennenkampf's sector? And what about the Khan of Nakhichevan? Do you know about him?"

Krymov pricked up his ears. "What has he done?"

It was the last piece of news he had carried away in his head from GHQ.

It would have been wrong to upset Samsonov with it, but now he told Krymov all about the Khan's disgrace at Kauschen. Krymov might as well know that the cavalry weren't all he claimed . . .

". . . With such heavy losses the cavalry should at least have taken the fords over the Inster. But at the end of the day the Khan withdrew his cavalry eastward for a quiet night's rest. And gave the fords up."

Krymov frowned as though he had been insulted.

But Vorotyntsev was not finished yet. "The Germans," he went on, "have only one division of horse . . ."

"Plus regiments of horse with each corps."

"That's a different matter. And even so, the Khan couldn't close the gap on his flank and hold that single division back. It was right up alongside him in the engagement at Stallupönen on 17 August, it came from behind the 20th Corps, harried an infantry division, and withdrew just as easily as it had come."

Krymov turned scarlet. "Snob of a guardsman. I could wring his neck!"

"What is cavalry for, if not for engagements of that sort? Rennenkampf has five cavalry units, Samsonov three—they could have made mincemeat of East Prussia! Instead, our cavalry clings to the infantry's skirts. Rennenkampf not only failed to pursue the enemy after Gumbinnen, he doesn't even know where the Germans have got to. He reports that François's corps is smashed, and Mackensen's in disorder. It doesn't ring true somehow."

"But he did beat them?"

"I'm not sure. When I left GHQ no one had any idea what had become of the two German corps."

No, there was no avoiding the Russian ritual—at the third glass he found himself joining in. What drew them to each other was the knowledge that neither of them expected to get anything for himself out of this campaign.

After the cavalry they could not ignore the artillery.

"We were the first to realize, during the Japanese affair, that the next war would be decided by firepower, that what it would take was heavy artillery, lots of howitzers. But it was the Germans who acted, not ourselves. We have a hundred and eight guns to a corps, they have a hundred and sixty—of the best. With us there's always 'an acute shortage of funds,' there's never any money for the army. We want victory and glory without going to any expense."

"Well, the Duma did make some sort of offer," Krymov put in, though it was hardly the sort of thing anyone would expect from him. "It accused the War Ministry of failing to ask for adequate funds."

There might have been something of the sort, you couldn't keep track of all the twaddle in the newspapers. But that spring Vorotyntsev had read something rather different: "The Duma voted against the military budget and against the big program. There's somebody there called Sh . . . Shingarev. He made a speech: 'Militarization of the budget? After the millions will it be billions?' He should try living on an officer's pay."

Krymov was not a fanatical reader anyway.

"It could be like that. The Duma doesn't know what day of the week it is."

"No, the Duma did approve the program, but against the Kadet vote. They imagine that morale decides everything—Suvorov thought so, so did Dragomirov . . . and Tolstoy. Why waste money on weapons? But what have we got in our fortresses? Guns not much better than 'unicorns'!* Some of them use black gunpowder!"

Preaching to Krymov like this would alter nothing, but there were subjects on which Vorotyntsev once started could not stop. If he had tried to, the vodka would have set him off again. Krymov poured the next one.

"Now they've squandered the fortresses," he said mournfully.

He had not been fired by Vorotyntsev's fervor, he knew it all inside out. He nodded acquiescence as though he were listening to a recital of the laws of nature.

They became more and more friendly. First it was "Aleksandr Mikhailovich" and "Georgi Mikhailovich," then they got around to first names. (Vorotyntsev wouldn't have been in such a hurry, but that too was an unavoidable part of the Russian ritual.) Instead of going to see Artamonov they sat on and on over their breakfast.

* An ancient Russian artillery piece of the howitzer type, so called from the representation of that fabulous beast molded on its barrel. [*Trans.*]

They got onto the subject of looting on German territory. Krymov brought down his gnarled fist between the plates: he was for field courts-martial and exemplary executions! He had already approached Samsonov on the subject.

So he was a true soldier and a consistent disciplinarian. Vorotyntsev, however, pressed both palms to the table, spreading his fingers as wide as he could. "No, whatever you say I can't bring myself to shoot a Russian soldier. For what? Because he is poor and we have brought him into a rich country? Because we have never shown him anything better? Because he is hungry, and we don't feed him for a week at a time?"

Krymov's fist did not relax. It tightened, and thumped the table. "But it brings disgrace on Russia! And it's a sure way of ruining the army. If we're going to let that happen we shouldn't have come here. Army HQ's orders were 'properly organized requisitioning.' A strong requisitioning force moves up alongside the regiments, takes over all the cattle and distributes them, takes over all the threshing machines and all the mills, threshes, grinds, bakes bread, and distributes it to regiments. We ourselves take nothing."

"That's just fantasy, Aleksandr Mikhailovich, my friend! It might work for the Germans, but not with us! We should have to be something other than Russians."

He said "something other than Russians" but he knew that some Russians had the necessary qualities. He was secretly proud of what he felt to be his own German efficiency, his own unwavering German obstinacy, which always gave him the advantage over easily aroused and easily appeased people like Krymov.

It was time they finished breakfast and their aimless conversation, and went to give Artamonov a push, make him knuckle under to the 2nd Army's commander. Vorotyntsev was trying to find some way of getting his friend Svechin to the phone at Supreme Headquarters. Krymov was in no hurry to rise: he seemed to feel that after this morning of conversation nothing much remained to be done, and he might as well take a nap. But he would of course go along, and if he flared up Artamonov might have a rough time of it.

"Maybe afterward you could go and see where Mingin's division is and whether it's linked up with Martos?" Vorotyntsev made it a question, not a directive.

Krymov mumbled what might have been a noncommittal "yes," as though he had got tired of riding around these last few days and would sooner stay where he was. They both simultaneously heard a sharp burst of gunfire.

"Hey!"

"Hey!"

They went outside.

The firing was to the north of them—fifteen versts away. The air, already hot, muffled the distant sound. But there was quite a lot of artillery.

Artamonov would not have taken the initiative for anything.

Could it be the Germans then?

They had shown themselves. They were moving in.

"If only we knew," Vorotyntsev reflected, "if only we could find out right now which German division is out there we would have the answer to a lot of questions."

[1 7]

Postovsky and Filimonov had insisted there could be no thought of moving 2nd Army HQ on 25 August. The whole day went into planning and preparations and, more important, arranging and trying out a new telegraph link with Army Group HQ: it would be routed from Bialystok through Warsaw to Mlawa and from there, using German telegraph lines, to Neidenburg. Until it was sure that 2nd Army HQ would be at the end of a reliable line, always within reach of directives and always ready to report, Northwest Army Group HQ could not let it get any farther forward. The move was therefore scheduled for the morning of 26 August.

The 25th was another day of tension for Samsonov. His army corps were setting out on their seventh successive day's march—Zhilinsky was given detailed and copious reasons for allowing the two central corps, under Martos and Klyuev, a day's rest, but once more the request was refused: the enemy would escape, slip away. Rennenkampf was pursuing him! They themselves knew nothing about Rennenkampf except what Zhilinsky told them—that he was in pursuit. Reports reached them from field intelligence with the cavalry divisions on the left flank that there was a *large* enemy concentration ahead of them. This was further confirmation of Samsonov's idea that the enemy was concentrating on the left, but instead of rejoicing in being proved right he was tormented by doubt as to what he should do next. Simple common sense suggested that he should swing all his units leftward, instead of hurrying them forward. But his cheek still burned where the word "coward" had been branded on it the day before, and he was worn out by his wrangles with Zhilinsky. The battle with those above him was more exhausting than that with the enemy ahead and he valued the compromise which seemed to have been reached last night. He was further softened by Zhilinsky's first telegram, congratulating him on the victory at Orlau. And anyway, Army Group HQ must know something to be so positive, and cavalry reconnaissance might easily exaggerate enemy numbers. One division of the 13th Corps had moved left the night before to help Martos, at his request. It should, perhaps, have stayed there, but it had already hurried back to its own corps and was now on its way north again. It was a psychological impossibility to throw it off balance by switching it left again. In any case, diverting corps in this way was a very complicated thing. It meant holding up the advance and perhaps moving supply troops across each other's lines.

Meanwhile, to Samsonov's annoyance, Colonel Knox had arrived in Ostrolenka. Why, nobody knew—probably just to convey the goodwill of the British, who would not themselves be landing on the Continent for another six months. Samsonov disliked those artificial, ex officio European smiles at the best of times, and this visitor would be a hindrance and a distraction just at present. Samsonov still needed time to make sense of what was happening and to order his own thoughts in a head buzzing with worries. Now he had to put himself out to hold a diplomatic reception.

He avoided meeting Knox on the evening of the 25th, pretending that it was too late, but was compelled to invite the man to breakfast on the 26th. He received beforehand a disturbing report from Artamonov that large forces were massing opposite him. Without breaking his fast, he immediately assembled several of his staff officers around a map, and very nearly decided to switch the central corps leftward. He was dissuaded by his staff, who reminded him that the units just unloaded were approaching Soldau from the railway to catch up with the 23rd Corps, so that the best solution was to put them all under Artamonov's command for the time being. Meanwhile the central corps would continue their advance.

It was a solution of sorts, and a fairly simple one. They went off to breakfast. Samsonov put on his gold-hilted sword. They should have been leaving in a hurry, but instead there was this ceremonial breakfast with wine, handshakes, an exchange of polite messages with pauses for translation from English to Russian and from Russian to English. On and on it dragged. Knox, a man of good family with ten generations of breeding behind him, was still not all that old, and younger than his years in behavior. He needed no persuasion to drink, and in general seemed very much at his ease. The British uniform encourages informality—the neck moves freely in its turndown collar, the shoulders are hardly aware of those diminutive epaulets. Knox indeed looked more informal than most Britons in uniform, with a high decoration loosely dangling and the breast pocket of his tunic stuffed with papers. He even occasionally tucked his hands into the lower pockets, showing that his ideas on military bearing were quite different from those of his hosts.

Samsonov hoped that the breakfast would rid him of his guest and that Knox would immediately return to Zhilinsky or to the Grand Duke or to St. Petersburg—as long as he took himself off it didn't matter where. But it was not to be. Knox seated himself in Samsonov's car, carrying a rolled-up raincoat, and the interpreter explained that the colonel's orderly would bring the rest of his luggage along with the HQ baggage train.

The Army Commander exchanged a glance with his officers and announced that the Briton and his interpreter would ride in his car instead of Filimonov; while Postovsky sent a telegram by a circular route right across the whole kingdom of Poland to Neidenburg, ordering Staff Captain Ducimetière to arrange a special lunch, with the very best table linen and cutlery.

Then they were off, leaving the rest of the HQ staff to try to keep up with them in vans or charabancs or on horseback. The commander's open yellow car with its elongated hood and its high steering wheel was escorted by eight Cossacks, not, it must be said, crack troops—a division could not be robbed of one of its best squadrons for this purpose. The driver drove at a moderate speed so that the eight Cossack lances could keep up at a trot.

If ever Samsonov needed to be silent it was now, to inspect in silence the versts his troops had traveled, which he himself had never seen before: the fifty versts or so to Chorzele, the fifteen to Janow, the other ten along the German frontier, then the crossing point and the next dozen versts into enemy territory, conquered by his forces without a drop of blood shed or a shot fired.

The day was going to be as hot and stuffy as those before it, but the air disturbed by their motion fanned their faces and made thinking easy. This was just the time, as they sped, almost flew forward, when the long-awaited clarity might have come into the commander's head. He did not know himself what exactly he was unclear about. His orders had been relayed and were being carried out. But vagueness there was, a patch of undispelled fog, as though he were suffering from double vision. Samsonov was continually aware of this and tormented by it.

The commander held firmly on his knees a twenty-eight-inch map board, with a ten-verst map of the whole theater of operations stretched tight but ruffled by the wind. He had intended to look by turns at the map and to either side of the car throughout the journey. But now he had in the back seat this inquisitive Briton who also wanted to know everything, kept peeping over his shoulder, and before long was poking his finger at the map asking for explanations of every little thing.

What with the rumble of the engine and this importunate buzzing from behind, Samsonov despaired of settling down, clearing his mind, and thinking his own thoughts on the journey.

Knox was particularly interested in the 6th Corps on the right flank, because it had penetrated more deeply into enemy territory than the other units and had traveled more than halfway to the Baltic.

Yes, the 6th Corps had been due to occupy Bischofsburg the day before, and by now must obviously be to the north of it.

That was what the map showed, and that was the assumption he had to share with the Briton, because it was impossible to confess to a Western ally that whatever marks we might make on the map we did not really know; that not every wireless message got through, and that there were no other means of communication except by dispatch riders traveling without escort through enemy country. Blagoveshchensky's corps had veered so far right that it was no longer flanking the main body, no longer giving any cover. It had become a separate, isolated corps, the victim of Samsonov's disagreement with Zhilinsky.

But luckily Army Group HQ had listened to their pleas and had given permission that very morning for the 6th Corps to be switched leftward, closer to the central forces. In fact it was already on the move, passing Lake Dadey—that one there—and going on toward Allenstein.

What then of Rennenkampf? Was he advancing? Yes, there were reports to that effect.

And this, presumably, was a cavalry division? Yes, to secure the right flank.

Tolpygo's cavalry division, which he badly needed close at hand, had also been taken from him to close the same gap. It too was lost to the Army Commander.

How far should he confide in this uninvited guest? Tell him that none of the units was up to strength, and that the 23rd Corps had not been mustered at all? That he, Samsonov, ostensibly in command of a whole army, effectively controlled only the two and a half corps in the center, where he was now going? And that he did not precisely know their whereabouts?

It was the central units that the meticulous Knox particularly wanted to know about. Where were they?

Samsonov's blunt finger moved over the map: "The 13th Corps, Klyuev's, is here, more or less . . . yes, his new position will be roughly there, between those two lakes . . ."

"Northward, you mean?"

"Yes, he'll be going north . . . to Allenstein. He should take it today." (He should have taken it yesterday, but he hadn't got there in time.)

"What about the 15th?"

"The 15th, Martos's, should be up alongside and also advancing northward. Martos should have taken Hohenstein yesterday." (Had he, though?) "And today he should move well ahead of Klyuev."

"And the 23rd?"

If only the commander himself knew for sure when Kondratovich would get the 23rd together and bring it into the front line . . . Mingin's division had been rushed off its feet to catch up with Martos, and then thrown straight into battle.

As for the 23rd, it couldn't be far away either . . . It would cut the main road from Hohenstein to the northwest today.

But what would he say if Knox asked about the Germans? Where were *their* corps? How many were they? Where were they going? An empty, uninhabited expanse of lakes and forests, little towns, highways and railways—that was all that could be seen or heard of the Germans. East Prussia was a tempting and defenseless prey.

"Look," Samsonov told him, "it's like this. I've issued precise daily orders to each corps—where to go, which towns to take, and all this had to be harmonized with the wishes of those above, but you might as well know that these orders have not been welded together into a single clear plan as to *what exactly we should be doing.* Penetrating more deeply . . . cutting the enemy's line of march . . . denying the enemy this and that position . . . yes. But where is the general plan of campaign? Given the present uncertain disposition of forces, our own and the enemy's, what have we to go on?"

No sooner had Samsonov got into his stride than Knox interrupted again. "What about the 1st Corps? And those two cavalry divisions?"

Blast you! "They're all . . . covering the operation from the left flank . . . all part of a solid echelon formation."

Samsonov removed the map board from his knees and stood it on the floor against the car door, to put an end to these exchanges above the din of the engine . . .

After the struggle to explain, and in the growing heat, he felt his strength ebbing. He no longer wanted to think things out, but just to doze in an easy chair.

They kept the speed of the car down to that of the Cossacks, who changed horses once on the way. Whenever they overtook service wagons—a field hospital, the harness makers—they stopped while the commander patiently listened to reports. At Chorzele and Janow they inspected the command posts and checked who had left detachments there and for what purpose. Once they left the car to sit in the shade by a stream. The sun was past the zenith when with their smart Cossack escort, solemnly and at the alert, they descended the Polish bank to an ancient wooden bridge, mounted the Prussian bank, and entered a new land.

Brick-built villages flashed by. Every house was a fortress and could have withstood a siege. Yet they had all been surrendered without a shot fired. Shortly afterward they turned onto the excellent highroad from Willenberg to Neidenburg, which was completely undamaged. The highway brushed the southern spurs of the extensive Grünfliess Forest, then took them through open country, over rolling hills which never looked very high but gave a broad view.

What made the journey and the day particularly enjoyable for Knox was that he was the first Englishman to set foot on enemy soil in this war. In the course of the journey he had already begun composing several letters to England, which he intended to write that evening, in a German town of course. For the time being he was absorbing as many impressions as possible, since a good stylist must avoid repetition from one letter to another.

They caught a heavy smell of burning as Neidenburg rose before them. They could see from a long way off a big white-faced clock with filigreed hands in a green steeple, then pink, gray, and dark blue houses moved to let them in, and inscriptions on stone met their gaze. Before it became a center of military operations this had been a very comfortable little town. Now, although they could see nothing actually burning, there were many traces of fire: scorched apertures gaped where there had been windows, roofs had collapsed in places, there were blackened walls, splinters of shattered windowpanes littered the pavements, evil-smelling gray smoke poured from unextinguished fires, and the heat from stones, tiles, and iron which had not had time to cool aggravated the heat of the sun.

As they entered the town the commander was met by one of the billeting officers, who had been sent ahead. He ran in front along the street to show them the way. Around a turn, on the Rathaus square, the house selected for them came into view. It had escaped the fire and was surrounded by other unscathed buildings. Two Russian grenades had landed on it but had done no damage. It was a hospitable-looking little hotel, three stories high, with what looked like two German helmets at the corners of the roof. A lieutenant colonel ran down the steep steps from the porch and, standing to attention by the car, loudly reported that the building was ready, as were the telegraph line, lunch, and a place to sleep, and also that the town had been burning since the day of its capture, but that the fires had been brought under control by the efforts of troops assigned to that task.

Next to report was the commandant, a colonel appointed by Martos three days earlier. The majestic burgomaster also put in an appearance. (Other inhabitants were somewhere around, but invisible.) As they entered the town they had not immediately noticed the dull pounding noise, muffled by the heat but still heavy, as though hundreds of enormous pestles were pounding away all at once. Postovsky pricked up his ears once or twice, and was the first to comment: "That's close." Too close to the location of Army HQ. The commandant assured them that it was some way off.

Once again—to their left. A serious engagement. Who could it be? While the Englishman was looking the other way Samsonov and Postovsky got their bearings and consulted the map. The firing appeared to be to the left of Martos. Most probably it was Mingin and the unlucky half of the incomplete corps. But he was supposed to be farther away.

They went up some steps into the cool building. From outside, its dimensions seemed modest, but on the second floor it contained a sort of hall with armorial bearings in plaster on the walls and with three half-oval windows, a hall so spacious that it was hard to believe the building could hold it. There the table was already laid with ancient silver dishes and glasses with gilded crests. All they had to do was cross themselves and sit down to dine. (The commander, at least, crossed himself, leaving the others to do as they pleased.) They were served by German waiters.

All the time they were dining they could see gray-blue smoke drifting about in the dip between the church and the town hall.

And the distant pestles kept up their muffled pounding.

The abundance of wine called for many toasts, and Knox, savoring them in advance, rose first. It had not escaped his notice that the commander had been preoccupied throughout those hours on the road, that there was a sort of resigned sadness in his wide eyes rather than the conqueror's reckless joy in battle. Russia's ally considered it his agreeable duty to encourage her generals by explaining the importance of their successes.

"These are glorious pages in the history of the Russian army," he said. "Your descendants will mention the name of Samsonov side by side with that of . . . er . . . Suvorov. Your armies are advancing splendidly, to the delighted admiration of all civilized Europe. You are performing a great service to the common cause of the Triple Entente. At the fateful moment when defenseless Belgium has been lacerated by the claws of the leopard . . . when—I am a soldier and I must be frank—when Paris itself is threatened, your valiant offensive will give the enemy pause!"

The situation in France was indeed alarming. The might of Germany was poised to strike at Paris.

After that the drink flowed freely and there was no dodging the toasts that fell like shells all around: To His Majesty the Emperor! To His Majesty the King of England! To the Triple Entente itself!

But for his guest from overseas Samsonov would not have sat the lunch out. He would have liked to walk about the little town on his own two legs and take a good look at it. He was glad to be in Germany at last, nearer to what his units were doing and nearer to actual danger. He needed to mark his new position on the map and review all his dispositions: to determine who was nearest to him, what roads lay between, with whom he was in telegraphic communication, and where the lines ran. He needed to make sense of this new and heavy engagement to the northwest, send someone over to find out. He was gnawed by anxiety to think things through and reach a decision. The situation demanded a clear head. It was hard work swallowing those wines. None of them had any taste.

But he had to perform the rites of hospitality, had to behave politely to his ally. And wine, even when you swallow it without tasting it, still has its warming, blurring, soothing effect.

And after all, why see only the bad side when this far from stupid Briton saw only the good?

The commander lifted his heavy frame and proposed a short toast: "To the Russian soldier! To the saintly Russian soldier, who is used to enduring hardship patiently. As the saying goes, it's no good killing a Russian soldier, you still have to knock him down!"

Postovsky had not neglected to inform Army Group HQ immediately of their arrival, and had then tried the food on the waiters in case it was poisoned. Having relieved his mind in this way, he would have entered gaily into the spirit of the banquet if that gunfire had not been a little too close. He examined each bottle suspiciously before pouring (they had house labels which Staff Captain Ducimetière translated) and, overcoming his usual bashful taciturnity, responded warmly to the visitor's eulogies. Yes indeed! The Germans were obviously on the run! Yes indeed! It was a clear victory. If only the 1st Army would move at the same speed as the 2nd . . .

Then they were all speaking at once, including Filimonov, who had just arrived. Without benefit of a map they suddenly realized that they were at cross-purposes. They were all agreed that the 2nd Army was to outflank the Germans and head them off, but those in charge of the operation had different ideas about it: was the 2nd Army to move forward with its left or its right wing? It was difficult to see how anyone could encircle East Prussia without moving the left wing first—but what were they to make of reports that the left wing was standing fast while the right wing made its move?

All the same, the Englishman, after receiving the gist of the news from Postovsky and digesting it, found the energy to rise (he was obviously a sportsman) and declare in the next toast that the destruction of her army in Prussia would be the end of Germany! Because all its main forces were in the west and pinned down there. In the east, Germany would be laid bare and the Russian army would go on from East Prussia to force the Vistula and open up a short, direct, and unobstructed route to Berlin!

Glasses had been raised to this but not emptied when the duty officer came in and waited for a convenient moment to report. Samsonov nodded his assent and put down his glass without taking a sip.

"Your Excellency! General Artamonov has asked me to call you to the Hughes instrument."

The commander pushed his chair back noisily and stamped out without excusing himself.

His prescient heart knew . . .

The Chief of Staff, looking suddenly grave, minced after him over the parquet floor.

There was silence in the signals room except for the monotonous chatter of teleprinters. Samsonov took the weightless ribbon in his big, soft, white hands.

"Infantry General Artamonov greets Cavalry General Samsonov."

Who returns the compliment.

"General Artamonov considers it his duty to bring it to General Samsonov's notice that, acting jointly with Colonel Vorotyntsev of the General Staff, he has entered into telegraphic discussions with GHQ concerning the extent to which the 1st Corps is subordinate to 2nd Army HQ. GHQ are looking into it. The Supreme Commander's decision is not yet known."

(Looking into it again! More to-ing and fro-ing!)

"General Samsonov nevertheless hopes that General Artamonov has carried out the request of 2nd Army HQ to *remain* with his corps north of Soldau and so make the situation quite secure."

Yes. General Artamonov had done that without waiting to be asked. Positions beyond Usdau had been taken and were being held . . .

Usdau . . . (Check with the map.)

"Has any enemy resistance been encountered?"

"No, not yesterday. However, the substantial enemy forces which were the subject of a report this morning . . ."

"You have been reinforced with additional units . . ."

"Yes, yes, they have arrived . . . Those substantial forces attacked the corps today, which is the reason why General Artamonov considered it necessary to trouble General Samsonov."

"How substantial exactly are these enemy forces and what was the outcome of the fighting?"

"All attacks have been beaten off, all units valiantly stood their ground. The enemy forces, as far as we can judge, are larger than an army corps—probably three divisions. This is confirmed by aerial reconnaissance."

A great deal of tape had run unbroken through the commander's fingers into Postovsky's hands, then via the officer of the operations section onto the floor in tangled coils.

Samsonov lowered his large head and stared at the floor.

From which corner of that great empty expanse of Prussia could such a large force have suddenly appeared there, on the left? Did it mean that the enemy had already slipped out of East Prussia altogether, escaped from the sack which was to have closed about him, but instead of crossing the Vistula, instead of running away, was beginning to put pressure on the Russian left?

Or were these fresh forces, newly arrived from Germany proper?

What then was he to do? Order all his units that very minute to turn leftward?

He must reach a decision.

That very minute.

Perhaps, though, Artamonov was exaggerating—he was apt to panic. Yes, in all probability he was exaggerating.

He ought to go over to the offensive, but he had not concerted his plan with GHQ.

He had to restrain himself. He now had only a corps and a half to call his own.

The instrument was idling. Postovsky and the captain supported the tape and straightened it so that it would not get in a tangle.

"At all events General Samsonov urgently requests the commander of the 1st Corps to keep a firm hold on his present positions and not to withdraw an inch, because to do so might wreck the 2nd Army's whole operation."

"General Artamonov assures the Army Commander that his corps will not flinch and will not retreat one single step."

[18]

At about four in the afternoon Major General Nechvolodov was bringing his detachment up from the south to Bischofsburg, along the cobbled highway. Nechvolodov himself was on horseback (with a few other mounted men around him), moving at a brisk walking pace some three hundred meters ahead of his troops.

What his detachment consisted of he would have been ashamed to say, even if he had been sure.

Nechvolodov had really been posted to the 6th Corps to take command of an infantry brigade. He had held such commands in various divisions for the past six years. It was a superfluous post—with only two regimental commanders below and the division commander immediately above—created, in Nechvolodov's view, simply to make major generals forget all they knew about line service, and he had acted accordingly. But the 6th Corps had given him a big surprise: in Bialystok, the day before the war began, he had been appointed "commander of the corps reserve," without being relieved of his brigade. He knew what "commander of the reserve" usually meant—a reserve force might be created in the field for a particular operation or to cover other units in an emergency—but Nechvolodov had never heard of a permanent reserve being formed on the day of general mobilization. Could it be that General Blagoveshchensky did not know what to do with all the generals in his corps? Or perhaps he was preparing for the worst even before the war began? (That was probably the explanation, since he had kept a good dragoon regiment just to protect Corps HQ.)

The composition of the reserve was also strange. Nechvolodov's two regiments (the Schlüsselburg and the Ladoga regiments) simply had attached to them a variety of special units (a mortar battery, a pontoon battalion, a company of sappers, a signals company, and seven squadrons of Don Cossacks, including the squadron guarding Corps HQ and forbidden to move a single step away from it)—and there was Nechvolodov's reserve. No doubt all these auxiliaries were not a help but a hindrance, complicating life for the simple infantryman Blagoveshchensky, according to whose classification there were four companies to a battalion, four battalions to a regiment, four regiments to a division, two divisions to a corps. Fortune also bestowed on the 6th Corps a blessing which comes the way of very few corps: a heavy artillery battery with guns of a caliber unfamiliar to the Russian army—six-inch howitzers. Blagoveshchensky, of course, had not the slightest idea where to station this outlandish present, and assigned it, too, to the "reserve." (He was an old campaigner, and knew what he was about: if you lost those rare weapons there would be a heavy reckoning. He wouldn't even move machine guns into the front line if he could help it—they were too precious for that, so he usually kept them back around HQ or the field hospital.)

Nechvolodov, however, was not given the chance to assemble his reserve in one place. (Not that there would have been any point in doing so, even if it had been possible.) His very own Schlüsselburg Regiment was taken from him and sent forward, so that his original brigade ceased to exist, while Nechvolodov was held back to reinforce the rear, and the detachment which with him as its figurehead was in pursuit of the main forces consisted now of his Ladoga Regiment (one battalion short), together with the sappers, bridge builders, and telegraphists, but without either cavalry or artillery.

However, according to Nechvolodov's estimate, the two divisions ahead of him were just as seriously depleted. Each of them had lost a quarter of its forces along the road. One of them was short a whole regiment, and a dozen companies had been whittled away from the other.

There was nothing of the grandiose commander about Nechvolodov—no swelling chest, no well-fed face, no self-importance: lean and long-legged (even on a big stallion his stirrups hung low), always taciturn and serious, and just now gloomy, he looked more like an unsuccessful officer who had spent far too long in junior positions.

He had been morose for days because he had been doing nothing but idiotic commandant's work in the rear, and because the Schlüsselburg Regiment had been taken away from him. Today he was sulkier still because even the prudent Corps HQ staff had rushed ahead of him on its way to Bischofsburg that morning. Shortly afterward the roar of many cannon announced a close engagement. He had grown gloomier still in the last two hours, as he began to come upon empty carts with terrified drivers, two-wheelers carrying the wounded, a little herd of horses with legs and hooves smashed by vehicles. Farther on they met more and more wounded, some of them on foot, from the Olonets and Belozersk regiments, and some of them from companies torn out of the Ladoga Regiment. Nechvolodov recognized an old acquaintance, an NCO who had served his time but volunteered to stay with the colors. Several officers were also carried past. Nechvolodov stopped some of those he met, briefly questioned them, and from their abrupt, excited replies tried to piece together a picture of the battle which had begun that morning and was still going on.

The story that emerged was full of contradictions, as always happens hot on the heels of events, before witnesses from different parts of the battlefield have had time to exchange stories. Some said that unknowingly they had camped for the night right next to the Germans, who had also not realized it, others that they had been on the move that morning, suspecting nothing, and had bumped into the enemy and come under withering fire: they were in marching order, quite unprepared, with no chance to dig themselves in (and anyway, the Germans had fired on them from the side, not from in front!). A third group claimed that they had been deployed in battle order beforehand, and had even dug waist-high trenches. Of the officers some thought that their forces had been moving northward and stumbled upon a column of the retreating Germans on the flank—they were much more frightened at first than the Russians, but were then able to deploy a great deal of artillery and begin a hot bombardment. "We had been expecting them from the east, and had been ordered to post our covering force on that side." Others corrected this account: the Olonets Regiment in fact had been deployed to the west. "But as soon as the Germans began firing from so many guns ('fifty,' 'no, a hundred!,' 'two hundred!') and using shrapnel at that, they tore holes in the densest part of the column, taking our men out by the dozen, so that we took flight and there was total confusion." Thousands had fallen, only a dozen to a battalion were left. No, they had stood fast, and "our company of the Belozersk Regiment went over to the attack itself." "Went over to the attack? How could it, when we were pinned down with the lake behind us? We threw down our weapons, rifles and all, and swam for it."

But there was enough agreement to leave no doubt that losses had been large, that several battalions had been smashed completely (and every battalion meant around a thousand men), to leave no doubt that after two weeks without meeting the enemy, without sight or sound of him, they had got too used to racing ahead over enemy territory in a carefree fashion without reconnaissance, without even outposts. Stepping out in this lighthearted way, they had put more than five versts between themselves and Bischofsburg yesterday, crossing a railway line of the greatest importance to the Germans, one which could be called the horizontal axis of East Prussia, and had marched on without casting a look around them, just as if they had been at home in Smolensk province, fighting units all mixed up with supply troops, and as if the very last thing they were expecting was to meet troops other than Russians here in German territory. So when the battle suddenly began they had no advance plan, no orders. The rank and file sensed it immediately, and immediately collapsed.

But Nechvolodov did not come across a single wounded Schlüsselburg and could not make out at all what had become of his regiment.

He was unhappily aware that behind him soldiers of his detachment were meeting the same wounded men and had time even on the move to learn more than enough.

Occasional rumbles could still be heard to the north.

With things as they were it was time for Nechvolodov to post guard patrols, even though he was moving in the rear of Corps HQ.

The temperature did not seem to have fallen, but the sun had moved around to look over his left shoulder and burn his left ear.

He was beginning to get a clear view of the town, with its gray and red steeples and towers. It was unscathed, and no fires were burning. Then suddenly he caught sight of a dust cloud over to his left, moving along a dirt road which would cross his path, and decided that it was made by a column bigger than an infantry battalion, together with a battery. It was crawling slowly along, again without precautions.

As far as he knew there were no enemy forces on his left—but then no one was supposed to be there at all. It was so easy to run into trouble. No need to marvel at other people's blunders!

Using his binoculars, however, Nechvolodov assured himself that these were Russian troops. At the head of this column, too, rode an officer. The horse was restive, dancing sideways, chafing at the bit, tossing its head, baring its teeth while the rider tried hard to bring it under control. Nechvolodov also saw a conspicuous black-and-tan dog, with big winglike ears, running along the verge. The dog was a company mascot, and many people realized that this was Rikhter's division.

The speed at which they were moving brought the two riders together at the crossroads. When he noticed the general and the column behind him, the other rider turned his horse around, reining it in sharply as it took a few paces too many, and called out to his men in a ringing voice: "Suzdal Regiment, halt! Fall out for a smoke—ten minutes."

He sounded cheerful and not at all tired, but his men were very weary: they staggered off the road, stood their rifles in pyramids, and without even shedding their greatcoat rolls dropped onto the nearest patch of dusty grass, although it was only a hundred paces to forest shade and clean grass.

The officer rode up on his restive bay, gave a jaunty salute, and reported: "Captain Raitsev-Yartsev, Your Excellency! Adjutant of the 62nd Suzdal Regiment!"

His bold grin revealed a single gold tooth in front. The horse squinted sideways and tossed its head.

Nechvolodov nodded at it. "Not your own?"

"Captured two hours ago, Your Excellency, and not used to it yet."

"You're a cavalryman, I see."

"Was, Your Excellency, but God unhorsed me for my sins."

Nechvolodov recognized the high spirits, the fire and dash, which are the mark of a true professional officer: We were born for war, we cannot live without it! That flame had once burned in him, but had dimmed with the years.

"Where did you capture it?"

"There's an abandoned manor house back there, with splendid stables. It's worth a look! Near the lake—what's it called . . ."

Nechvolodov's hand had already reached for the map case at his side and was opening it.

"Oh, what a beautiful map you have! Here you are: Dadey Pool"—he completed the obscene jingle in a whisper—"just the place to wash your tool."

Nechvolodov allowed himself a slight smile.

"But how did you come to be there? What were you looking for?"

"Our division thinks nothing of a seven-verst detour. We set off for a walk, changed our minds, and back we came again."

His gaiety was disarming. But with his horse dancing under him he could not look at the map with Nechvolodov. And the sun was baking.

"Let's go into the shade," Nechvolodov suggested.

The gold-toothed captain readily agreed.

They handed over their horses.

Nechvolodov called out to his adjutant, the chubby, rosy-cheeked Lieutenant Roshko (his southern blood glowed through his skin). "Misha," he ordered, "the column can march on. You ride ahead and see whether there is any road around Bischofsburg. If there isn't, choose streets which won't take us past Corps HQ."

Round-faced, quick-witted Roshko understood just what was wanted and his group galloped off.

Nechvolodov and Raitsev-Yartsev sat down cross-legged under the cool, lacy canopy of the forest and the general pulled out his map and unfolded it. Raitsev-Yartsev closed his fist (there was a gold ring on his middle finger) and used the long, tapering nail of his little finger to point out places on the map while he briefed the general.

Yesterday their division, consisting of three regiments (one had fallen behind) had been in occupation of a front facing east, and people were saying that the enemy was caught in a vise and would try to break through that way. However, they had not needed to fire a single shot. Next, they were ordered to converge on Bischofsburg. They had spent the morning marking time there. Just before noon the Corps Commander had ordered their division to march west, go around the southern end of Lake Dadey and forward to Allenstein, nearly forty versts away. So they had set off without any lunch, met no one, fired not a shot, suffered torments of thirst, and after ten versts, when they had already rounded the lake, an orderly from Corps HQ had dashed up with new orders from Blagoveshchensky: return at once to Bischofsburg and take up positions *to the east* of it. The Suzdal Regiment was the last in the column, so it had turned first and was now on its way back. But in the meantime an officer had galloped up with yet a third set of orders: only the Suzdal Regiment, with two batteries, was to go forward, take up positions outside Bischofsburg, and await the orders of the Corps Commander. The rest of the division was to turn north, along the other shore of Lake Dadey, and advance to join up with Komarov's division on the other side of the lake. It was just as well that the Suzdal Regiment had been in the rear. If the Uglich Regiment had received such an order it would have had to struggle down the column past two others while the Suzdal Regiment struggled past it in the opposite direction.

Raitsev-Yartsev had set out to tell his story merrily, as though all this muddle gave him pleasure, but faced with the deadly serious Nechvolodov he stopped flashing his gold tooth and merely tapped on the buckle of his belt with his long nail.

What a daredevil of a corps commander they had! Bolder than Napoleon. He was not built to sit around a table in some philanthropic committee in the rear; here he was, boldly strolling about a foreign land, crisscrossing it with the movements of his regiments. A quarter of his corps are smashed in a frontal attack, so he sends half the corps off to the left! He fears nothing, no, not he! Had he not formed his reserve before the war had even begun? Now it was up to Nechvolodov to save the day for him.

Nechvolodov's detachment was already marching past on its way to Bischofsburg. Raitsev-Yartsev's battalion lay on the grass, the cannon stood in the roadway. The rest of the Suzdal Regiment had not yet appeared.

It was time to hurry on, look for his Schlüsselburg Regiment, look for the Division Commander—but it is not so easy to fold up a map when you have just been shown something new on it: the lines you have studied dozens of times and know so well hold you spellbound with new revelations and new menaces.

They missed no opportunity to wrest troops from their own units, to subordinate units to new commanders, as they had subordinated the

Suzdal Regiment to the Corps Commander himself. The structure of command and the jurisdiction of commanders were hopelessly confused. Take Rikhter: even if he did force his way past Lake Dadey, with whom would he join up? The Russian forces there had been dispersed. Tolpygo's cavalry division was on the right wing, but where? Its Uhlan regiment had been torn away for use as corps cavalry. The division's line of march and objectives were changed again and again. Where were the Germans who were supposed to be on the right? Long gone, of course. And where, also on the right, was Rennenkampf? Why should he hurry? He was savoring his victory, and risks lay ahead. Empty country. Not a sound, not a shot. Where was the 13th Corps?

Silence. Empty air.

"Right. Thank you, Captain." Nechvolodov's hard hand clasped the captain's. He jumped into his saddle and, accompanied by an orderly, trotted past his troops in the direction of Bischofsburg.

The Germans had obviously made preparations to defend the place. For two hundred meters before the road entered the town the bushes on both sides had been cut down to give a clear view and deny the enemy cover, and a dozen loopholes had been knocked into the wall of the first building by the roadside, a big brick warehouse.

But none of it had been needed.

A long column of walking wounded came toward them from the town. Nechvolodov didn't stop to question them. He merely called out, "Hey, boys! Are the Schlüsselburgers here?"

Apparently not.

Round-faced Roshko, unperturbed, was waiting for him by the warehouse. He reported that there was no ring road but that he had found the right sort of streets and put out marker lights.

Nechvolodov rode off to look for Corps HQ, through the cool, narrow streets of tight-packed houses.

His first impression was that the town was peopled by Russian wounded—everywhere, out in the street and through windows, he saw the whiteness of bandages. But there were local residents around too. One unwarlike German was being taken somewhere under escort. Two others were in the same plight. On a street corner a number of German women had surrounded a Uhlan officer and were talking angrily all at once, one after another of them pointing first to his sword then to her own breast. Farther on, two German women carried out enamel pails and gave water to some soldiers, who joked with them.

Nechvolodov recognized HQ by Blagoveshchensky's dark blue car and the Cossacks of his escort squadron. Roshko and the others remained outside while he strode up the granite steps and through the vaulted vestibule to look for the commander's office.

Inside HQ everything was crated and on the move, either because they had just arrived or because they were leaving shortly. He did not get to Blagoveshchensky, or to his Chief of Staff, but he did meet Colonel Nippenström from the Quartermaster General's Department.

"What are you doing here?" Nippenström sounded frightened. "Haven't you caught up with Komarov yet? He's been waiting for you long enough!"

Nechvolodov's answer was even slower and colder than usual. "I couldn't go any faster. I wanted to ask the Corps Commander . . ."

Nippenström flapped his hands: "If the Corps Commander sees you here he'll tear your head off. Go away as fast as you can!"

"But go where? I don't know what my assignment is."

"What? You haven't heard? Your orders are to collect your reserves and cover the corps' withdrawal. You can get it all from Serbinovich . . ."

"But where *are* my reserves? Where's my artillery?"

"It's there, it's there. It's all in place. They're only waiting for you."

"All I have with me are sappers, bridge builders, and signalmen."

"All of those you can leave here."

"And where is my Schlüsselburg Regiment?"

"Serbinovich is bound to know. Go and see Serbinovich. We're on our way out too. We've jumped too far forward . . ."

"What German units are facing you?"

"We don't know ourselves!"

Nippenström was in a hurry: he had to repeat his wireless message telling the 13th Corps that the 6th Corps had been attacked by large enemy forces and could not come to their aid at Allenstein. He had sent the message once, and the 13th Corps had acknowledged receipt, but had not otherwise reacted.

General Blagoveshchensky had lacked the forces to carry out this move toward Allenstein, but to avoid unpleasantness, and knowing that his refusal would be countermanded, he had given orders that it should be reported for the time being only to his neighbor, not to Army HQ.

Nechvolodov, tall, gaunt, and motionless, stood in the space between two Gothic windows like the forgotten statue of some Teutonic Knight, watching staff officers pack and drag about a big box like a portable safe.

He did not ask to see anyone else. He left the building, lifted himself into his saddle, and rode off a little way, listening to Roshko's report that the detachment was already moving out northward, but that the Schlüsselburg Regiment was nowhere to be found.

At that point they heard a noise from the direction of Corps HQ. Nechvolodov looked back. The engine of a staff car was being cranked up. General Blagoveshchensky flitted obliquely down the steps with no eyes for Nechvolodov or anyone else on the square. The Chief of Staff and others with rolled maps hurried after him.

They took their seats and slammed the doors. The car began turning in the little square for its journey to the rear. Blagoveshchensky removed his cap and crossed himself with a sweeping gesture.

The shuddering of the car, or the light breeze, stirred his graying hair. He had the head of an old woman—except that it would never have mastered the maneuvering of pots on a stove.

Nechvolodov led his retinue out of the town at a trot.

[19]

"Your Honor! Hallo, Your Honor!" a cheerful voice shouted. Yaroslav, in the queue at the well, turned toward the road.

A half-battery (four cannon) was filing past, and the voice hailing Yaroslav was that of his chance acquaintance, the bullet-headed sergeant major: was it the day before yesterday, or a month ago, that incident along the road when Kharitonov's platoon had helped to drag those very same cannon out of the sand?

Yaroslav was delighted to see him. "O-ho," he called, throwing up both hands in a schoolboy's rather than an officer's greeting. "Want some water?"

"What sort of water? Distilled from corn mash?" The stocky, barrel-chested sergeant major was as merry as last time.

"Take a sip—it's delicious," an unknown infantryman called out. "Muck on top, sand down below."

The sun had sunk some way over Yaroslav's left shoulder but it was still hot.

"Would you believe it? Somebody had blocked the well with planks but we cleared it," he shouted. He was ashamed of his piping schoolboy voice, but however he tried could not make it sound rougher. "And the water's quite tolerable, everybody's getting as much as he can."

The sergeant major took his hat off and waved it to halt his men. His head was almost hairless, perfectly round and yellow all over, like a cheese, only bigger. Corn-colored mustaches, bushy but sharp-pointed, were fixed to the front of the cheese.

The well was on the edge of a sprawling farm, with several buildings scattered over a broad clearing. The cannon were pushed to one side. Drivers carried pails of water for the horses, and the gun crews hauled up a great screw-topped drum, probably German. The artillery excited envy because it had wheels and could carry the little extra that everybody needed. But there were other reasons for envy.

"Your soldiers *are* soldiers, I must say! Mine came straight from the plow all the way to Germany. What can I do with them?"

The sergeant major smiled complacently. "Our men have to have some schooling. Plowboys won't do."

The sergeant major was such a dignified figure, so solid, and so much his senior in years that the young lieutenant felt embarrassed by his pips, embarrassed to be superior in rank, and also, though much slimmer, in stature. Yaroslav tried to make up for all this embarrassment by unsoldierly politeness. "Tell me, what should I call you?"

"Sergeant Major, of course!" the other man said with a smile, wiping the sweat from his sunburned face.

"Come on! I mean your name and patronymic!"

The cheese twitched its mustache. "Names and patronymics aren't used in the army."

"In the world of human beings they are."

"In the world of human beings I was never called anything but Terenti in my life."

"What's your surname?"

"Chernega. And yours?" he asked, but without much interest—his eyes and his small ears were intent on the farm buildings, beyond Yaroslav and the well. Barely turning around to look for him, he gave an order to the bombardier.

"Kolomyka! Those are hens clucking over there! Pop over with two of the boys. Take a sack, and drive them into it with sticks."

Yaroslav was dismayed. These fine artillerymen, this splendid sergeant major—even they were at it. If they did it, who would resist temptation? He tried to prevent them.

"The farm's been cleaned out. There's nobody living there, and they've wrung the last cock's neck. There are some apples in the orchard, though."

Soldiers were sauntering about the orchard. He could see them from where he was. Others drifted over there, without asking permission and with no one to stop them. Still, they weren't from Kharitonov's platoon. His men had lost the use of their legs, and were glad just to sit till somebody moved them.

Chernega wasn't taken in. "No, they're there, just back of the plantation. I can hear them. Take another two buckets and look around the corn bins. If there's any oats left give us a shout and we'll come and bag them."

Chernega gave his orders confidently, without consulting his officers. But seeing the distress of the freckle-faced lieutenant who had been so obliging, he offered an explanation. "What is it artillery can't do without? Oats and meat. Without them the horses can't pull the guns, and the men can't lift the shells. If you've got a roast goose up your sleeve, well, that's what I call a war."

These last words he added in a singsong, and his face glistened as he pictured the roast goose. It was hard to see anything sinful in that expression and that wish. But on the other hand, if you thought about it . . . Yaroslav was troubled.

"A soldier is a good man," said Chernega, to reassure him further, "but his greatcoat has a great appetite. We're light artillery, but light is just a nickname. One of our guns, mounted, weighs a hundred and twenty-five puds. And a shell is just under half a pud. Work it out for yourself."

Kozeko was sitting on a big square beam with the inevitable field-message pad on his knees, making notes. He had eyes and ears for everything and he watched Chernega closely. And disapprovingly.

The company commander shouted from a distance, "Lieutenant Kharitonov! Take over—I'll be back soon," strode off with two soldiers past the farm buildings, and turned sharply beyond the plantation where Chernega had sent his troops.

Kozeko looked daggers and wrote down this fresh item for the record. He frowned over his notes, either because the apple he was munching was sour or because he found the whole situation so unpleasant.

The well was concrete and had a domed roof which cast a long shadow. The same chained bucket banged hollowly in the cylinder again and again as the strong hands of soldiers lowered and raised it, turning the handle quickly and pulling on the chain. Just as quickly they poured the water into pots and buckets of their own, cursing and abusing each other—"useless sod," "clumsy oaf"—jostling, splashing, muddying the ground, and the pots were no sooner emptied than they were thrust out again to catch the stream. The men bore off their brimming buckets at a run, but without spilling a drop, and held them to the soft unbitted lips of their horses. People yelled at the artillerymen: "It's no good trying to store it! Those great drums of yours would drain any well dry! Don't stock up! Drink now, as much as your belly will stand. And stop pouring it on your heads, you clowns! Get over there to the lake, and wade in up to your necks."

Amid their own hubbub, all that cursing and clanking, they seemed to have got used to the background noise to their left, and to have stopped hearing the rumble of battle. It was many lakes away, if not many versts. All that day there had been lakes to the left of them, lakes big and small, so it was not only the will of their commanders but the lakes that had deflected them northward, screening their route from the battle near at hand.

There were lakes to their right also. Just an hour ago they had struggled along a wooded isthmus, no more than three hundred meters wide, between two lakes, Plautziger and Lansker, each so big that the naked eye could only dimly see its far side. They had wedged themselves into the long, tree-clad and deserted corridor between these lakes and told themselves their division had no concern except with what was in that corridor—and that was nothing and no one.

Someone brought Terenti water. It was so cold that it made his throat ache, and it was muddy, but his insides demanded more and more. He sat down alongside Kozeko and invited Yaroslav to join him. He got out a pouch containing bundles of makhorka, and shook one loose.

"I can pack all my troubles into a pipe of tobacco. Do you smoke, sir?"

Someone had lovingly stitched an ornate monogram on the black silk of the pouch—"T.C.," with curlicues in crimson.

"I don't know," Chernega said, looking toward the sunlit side. "The ground is shaking under us and here we are, going along without even beating the woods, when they're sure to be sitting up in the pines with their binoculars watching us—and ringing up all the time. They're sitting there right now, ringing up to tell German HQ we're here drinking water." Terenti spoke with conviction, gazing at the encircling forest. But his behavior contradicted his anxious words: he showed no eagerness to dash into the woods, or indeed the slightest agitation. Either he was lazy or full of confidence in his own strength.

Second Lieutenant Kozeko, though, looked up in alarm and spoke out. "We ought to have outposts! We're moving so fast that our lookouts on the flanks are absolutely level with their companies. And the main column sometimes overtakes the lookouts up in front. It would be the easiest thing in the world to mow us down with a machine gun."

Kharitonov was just as worried. "The worst of it is that nobody knows what's going on. We've chalked up another fifteen versts today. And from what they say we still have ten to go by evening. The most up-to-date news we get comes from the regimental commander's orderly. This morning somebody started a rumor that a Japanese division was coming to our aid!"

Chernega nodded, puffing complacently. "I heard that tale as well." He radiated strength. Excessive strength, perhaps, for the work to be done.

"Poppycock! How could it be Japanese? Maybe one of ours from out that way."

"And then some say Wilhelm is commanding the armies in East Prussia himself," Chernega put in, but he was obviously as little concerned about Wilhelm as about all the rest.

Kharitonov felt respect for the older man's honesty and loyalty. An officer was not supposed to complain to a sergeant major about his superiors, but still . . .

"What about the day before yesterday? They had us rushing there and back again, thirty versts, without rhyme or reason! Well, all right, we went there to help, and then we weren't needed after all, but why didn't they have the sense to send us back slantwise? Why all the way back to Omulefoffen again? We could have done without Omulefoffen! And we could have had a day's rest, like that other division."

Chernega smoked on, looking knowing and placidly nodding. Yaroslav very much wished that he could borrow Chernega's ability to accept so placidly whatever came along.

Kozeko again: "Did you hear that rifle fire behind us an hour ago? Likely as not the Germans have breached our rear."

Chernega switched his pipe to the corner of his mouth. "What's he writing about there? Is he writing down what we say?"

Yaroslav laughed. "Are you a regular?"

"Not me—I'm not such a fool as that."

His forage cap sat jauntily on one side of his bullet head but did not fall off.

"Do you live in a town? Or in the country?"

"Well . . . country town, let's say." The question seemed to give him some difficulty.

"In what province?"

"Kursk, could be. Or Kharkov," he said reluctantly.

Yaroslav didn't want to let this rich specimen of a pocket-size hero go, but did not know how to keep him talking.

"Married? Any children?" he asked in a friendly way, making it sound as though he had already answered affirmatively on Chernega's behalf.

Chernega looked at the second lieutenant with little, round eyes like marbles. "Who needs a wife when there's one next door?"

At that point the bombardier rushed up and reported to the sergeant major in a low voice so that the others would not overhear. "Oats as well! And smoked hams! And beehives! The owner isn't there, they left this morning. There's only the watchman, a Pole, he says take what you want. I've posted sentries for the time being. Better be quick. The infantry are grabbing the horses and killing poultry already."

Chernega at once became brisk and businesslike, shot up on his short sturdy legs as though this were all he was waiting for, and yelled, "Right, boys! To horse, at the double! Forward!" Then to Kolomyka: "Lead the column while I report to the captain." The perspiring cheeselike head, still glistening with sweat, looked silky and assured under the tilted cap.

They all put their backs into it, lugged the guns to the turn by the plantation, and hitched on the ammunition limbers.

Two two-horse carriages and a sprung trap rolled out from behind the plantation to meet them.

The suspicious Kozeko, who never missed a thing, recognized them from far off and informed the others. "There you are—first the battalion commander tears by in a carriage, now here come company commanders in carriages, and the chaplain's got himself a trap. They've got so many soldiers driving them there'll be nobody left to fight soon!"

"All right, all right!" said Yaroslav angrily. "But what about you? Why did you pick those apples?"

"The devil tempted me." Kozeko threw the half-eaten apple away with no sign of regret. "Just to get home alive, that's all I ask of Germany . . ."

"You'll come out of it alive! You're sure to."

Kozeko looked up hopefully from his diary. "What makes you think so? Of course, a direct hit isn't very likely, but all that shrapnel . . ."

"God helps those who help themselves. You'll be sent to buy cattle. Put your diary away and line up your men!"

The sun was not very high now, and even if there was no fighting they would be struggling along till dark and after dark. Another battalion had pulled up at the well, and the leading companies of their own had already formed up and marched off. Yaroslav began rallying his platoon and drawing them up.

From behind, overtaking and pushing through the struggling and stumbling infantry, came several staff officers and senior officers on horseback, escorted by six mounted Cossacks and with them two riders wearing fresh bandages. The colonel in front, grim and unshaven, reined in his horse as Kharitonov, slim and eager, ran over, stood to attention, and reported.

At that moment the unmistakable squeal of a pig, clear enough to be heard even farther away, reached them from beyond the plantation.

"Are those your soldiers looting, Second Lieutenant?"

"Certainly not, Colonel! Mine are all here."

"Well, why aren't you marching? Where's your company commander?"

Kharitonov shook his head. The company commander's carriage had vanished.

"I'm standing in," he remembered.

"You'll be punished," the colonel said, but absently, with no real anger. "Don't you know your orders? You should be forcing the pace. You have to get to the railway line, and proceed along it five versts to the right before the day is out, and here you are fooling about around a well. Where's the battalion commander?"

"Up front."

Yaroslav understood less than ever: the Germans are on our left, and we are to turn right?

The horsemen rode on. Could even they make any sense of this wandering in the woods between the lakes?

They were officers on the staff of the 13th Corps. They had narrowly escaped death an hour before: their own infantry had taken them for Germans and opened fire furiously. They had anticipated something of the sort. A staff car had been badly damaged when their own side fired on it the day before—which was why they had taken an escort of six Cossacks who would be recognized by their lances, in spite of which their own infantry had taken them at a distance of two hundred meters for its first, long-awaited Germans and had fallen upon them.

They were carrying the latest orders from Army HQ: to speed up the corps' movement toward Allenstein! From the 6th Corps, which was lost far away to the right, came an unexpected wireless message—evidently an important one, because it was transmitted twice in quick succession. Unfortunately no one on the staff of the 13th Corps could decipher it: their key didn't seem to fit the code. Corps HQ did not know what to think.

The riders stayed for a while with the guns, caught up with one battalion commander in a carriage, then another—and the colonel threatened them all and urged on them the need to force the pace.

They went ahead of the regiment, and three versts farther on through the woods they came across two Germans laid out by the roadside, civilians pierced by lances and disfigured by blows.

"The work of your Cossacks, no doubt," the colonel said to the senior NCO, who had been wounded trying to stop the infantry firing on them.

The NCO shrugged, but did not answer. His jaw was bandaged.

Away from the road thick smoke, the harbinger of a fierce fire, was pouring from a lonely house.

[2 0]

Division Commander Komarov waited just long enough to order Nechvolodov to take up his positions and hold on to them pending further instructions in writing, and at 5 p.m. left with his own staff in the wake of Corps HQ. He had briefed Nechvolodov, not with the help of the map, but with circular movements of his hand in the air, telling him that the German advance from the north earlier in the day was "extremely unexpected," indeed that he was not sure that this really was their line of march, maybe they had overextended their flank, but in any case the Belozersk Regiment was holding the defensive line to the north, where it must be relieved. He begged Nechvolodov, while he was about it, not to open fire by mistake on that half-division of Rikhter's which was now on its way around Lake Dadey from the west and would arrive at any moment to help out. The division's Chief of Staff, Colonel Serbinovich, was unable to explain not only the disposition and strength of the enemy but even the location and condition of Russian units still in position. He promised Nechvolodov a heavy artillery battery and a mortar battery later on, somewhere up ahead, and for some purpose unknown took one battalion of the Ladoga Regiment away from him. Just at present he had no precise information on the Schlüsselburg Regiment, which had been moved sideways, eastward, the night before, and he could not say precisely where Division HQ would now be, but he promised to dispatch riders to report regularly.

Whereupon Division HQ removed itself so swiftly that Nechvolodov failed to notice its departure. He came across a second lieutenant in the Belozersk Regiment who reported that he had just seen for himself the commanding officer of his regiment get in Komarov's car and set off with him for Bischofsburg. So what about the regiment itself? The Belozersk had sustained great losses that morning, and had now been ordered to withdraw completely. But there were still two battalions in place up ahead.

So Nechvolodov, left with two battalions of the Ladoga Regiment, moved forward in quest of his artillery. He advanced cautiously, posting lookouts, along the more or less undamaged railway line toward Rothfliess station, from which the track described a smooth arc to join the main east-west line. And there, behind a copse, he did indeed see one battery of 4.2-inch mortars, and farther on one battery of heavy howitzers in firing positions, and knew that the others must be somewhere around.

The crushing load on the general's mind was lightened.

No sooner had Nechvolodov reached the stone shelter at Rothfliess station than the commander of the mortar battery, with his ropelike black mustache, and Colonel Smyslovsky, commanding the heavy battery, a short man with a shining bald head, a long, yellow magician's beard, and a confident air, came to see him.

He had met them both on two occasions in the last few weeks, but this time he noticed particularly the joyful gleam in the colonel's eyes, which seemed to say that he had been longing for a chance to practice his gunnery and was radiantly happy that he had finally got it. (It was, of course, happiness enough not having to abandon a well-equipped position.)

"Battery all here?" Nechvolodov asked, shaking his hand.

"All twelve guns!" Smyslovsky rapped out.

"How many rounds?"

"Sixty to a muzzle. We've got more in Bischofsburg, they can be brought up."

"Are they all in position?"

"Yes. And connected by telephone."

This was an innovation in the last few years: connecting observers with the hidden positions of the batteries by telephone lines. Not everybody was good at it yet.

"Did you have enough line?"

"I can even stretch it this far. The mortar battery here helped."

Nechvolodov asked no more. There wasn't time. For all he cared they could have stolen it (he saw the colonel of the mortar battery pass a complacent hand over his walrus mustache).

"How many have *you* got?"

"Seventy to a gun."

The rest was left unspoken. Commanders like these, with such guns, and telephone communications into the bargain, would use their firepower and would not retreat unless ordered to.

Now he was on the knife edge: he had two, three, perhaps five minutes in which to study the terrain, mark the enemy's positions and his own, choose his defensive lines, dispatch the Ladoga battalions to occupy them, get his own telephone line laid, find the enemy's range . . . And if in those three minutes all this surveying and selecting and dispatching and ordering was done wrongly or in the wrong order, then nothing would be done correctly in the following half hour. (And if the Germans come pouring in or open fire in that half hour, our shining eyes, our telephone wires, our sixty rounds to a muzzle won't help at all: we shall run for it.)

This was one of those critical moments in war when time is compressed to explosive density: there is only *now*, and afterward nothing!

"There's a water tower here," Smyslovsky announced. "We've found the range of our farthest targets, only *he's* moved forward."

Nechvolodov silently ducked his head under the low lintel and left the shelter.

The artillerymen followed.

They crossed the sun-baked railbed, with its smell of hot oil, at a run.

Nechvolodov beckoned to a battalion commander (he had no regimental commander left, and no use for one anyway) and ordered him to go and relieve the Belozersk battalion immediately, redraw the line if it had been badly chosen, and make his men dig themselves in as best they could if they valued their lives.

A muffled thump was heard beyond the distant woods, the noise swelled, and a yellow cloud of German shrapnel tore the air in front of them, to the left of the water tower and above.

"They threw some stuff this way earlier today," Smyslovsky said appreciatively, "but we kept quiet and they stopped."

They climbed the wooden ladder inside the water tower, Nechvolodov freeing his binoculars from their straps as he went. At the top of the stairs they found a platform with a broad view to the west and the north. Two telephonists with buzzer phones were sitting there already. The western window was glassed, and the blinding light of the sinking yellow sun made it impossible to look that way. But the northern window gave a good view. Glass and frame had been knocked out and the Germans would see no reflected light from the binoculars.

They spread the map out on a chest in the space between the windows, near the telephones.

All they knew of the situation was what they could see with their own eyes and what their common sense told them.

The Germans put up one high-explosive shell, then a second. They were probably range-finding too. There was a large concentration of troops and a great deal of movement in Gross-Bössau, beyond the main railway line, and also on the fringe of the forest. But no column, or so much as a single file, was advancing in their direction.

They might, however, begin moving at any minute.

"There are none of our troops left anywhere around Gross-Bössau, are there? We shan't be blasting away at our own side?"

"You can be sure of that. I've looked into it."

"We have left some there—far too many," said the serious mortar man with the big mustache.

There had, in fact, been no Russian dead to be seen as far as Rothfliess. The dead were all up front. But they were not altogether relevant to his question.

"The sun's on our left, just right for shooting north," Smyslovsky averred. "They've got a trig point over there—I should love to topple it!"

A German battery opened up from time to time on their left, from the lake. There must also be an infantry unit of some sort over there, so it was no good waiting for Rikhter either.

Nechvolodov gave orders for the other battalion of the Ladoga Regiment to be drawn up facing westward. He also divided the regiment's machine gunners between the two flanks.

After which he had no more men left. There was still an unguarded semicircle on the right, facing northeast and east, but he had no one to station there, and he himself had let the Ladoga battalion go without a word.

At one time, as a young man, he had argued heatedly about everything. But during his long years of service his face had set in a sour grimace, and he held his peace, both when biting his tongue could make no difference and when he should have broken his silence.

Of course, the lances of Rennenkampf's cavalry might appear on the right at any moment; though in this, as in the Japanese war, the cavalry was not generally used in battle: they took good care not to waste it on war. A commander could earn high praise by keeping his cavalry intact.

Rennenkampf was lying low, or was dead, or had been struck dumb.

Obviously Blagoveshchensky had done the right thing. If he had not withdrawn, would there have been anyone for him to link up with?

If the 2nd Army had entered Prussia like the head of a charging bull, those now at Rothfliess station were the tip of its right horn. The horn had penetrated the body of East Prussia to two-fifths of its depth. While they held Rothfliess station they were cutting the main line, the last line but one by which the Germans could switch their forces laterally across Prussia. Clearly, the Germans would want that station at any price. It would have been sensible to put the whole of the 6th Corps right there.

But fate had been kind in one way: they no longer had any brainless busybodies over them. That was the worst possible position to be in. Their fragile handful was the tip of the horn, but it was at least in their power not to do silly things.

The two battery commanders reached their posts and began to shout out orders.

They could hold out till it got dark—if only there was somebody to station on the right.

From above they could see the Belozersk Regiment pulling back—the infantry marching and two-wheelers rolling along close to the woods away from the station. The German bombardment was becoming more menacing, and the troops withdrawing were glad to get out of an impossible situation.

Nechvolodov descended from the water tower.

A tall officer with desperation written on his honest, beefy face loped up to him. His last bound brought him to a halt before the general, whom he saluted with a wild sweep of the arm ending almost behind his ear. He reported in a bass voice: "Your Excellency! Lieutenant Colonel Kosachevsky, battalion commander, Belozersk Regiment! We consider it dishonorable to leave you. Beg permission not to retreat."

He was so unsteady on his feet that he almost collapsed on the general. But reckless bravery shone in the bold eyes under the handsome eyebrows.

Nechvolodov looked at him uncomprehendingly. Then his lips twisted in a savage grimace, and he answered grudgingly, "Hm—well—" and embraced Kosachevsky with his long arms to prevent him from falling.

A little way off the long, straggling column continued its retreat. Two-wheelers rolled by, men limped or hobbled or walked past.

Could they really want to stay on? Perhaps only the officers did? Or maybe only Kosachevsky?

"How many of you are there?"

"We've had a hole knocked in us. We've got two and a half companies."

"Wheel them around. Take up position over there. I'll show you . . . on the right . . ."

By now Russian shells were whistling merrily overhead, winging, one after another, to find the enemy's range. And German high-explosive shells were flying in from various places, each crack of the steel whip raising a black fountain of earth.

Then came the first salvos.

Russian guns answered salvo with salvo. Four guns at once—that was Smyslovsky; and six guns—that was the mortar battery.

The bald and bearded man, hopping and skipping and rubbing his hands, found Nechvolodov up on the water tower. "We've knocked it out, Your Excellency. Their trig point—we've knocked it out!"

But before Nechvolodov could congratulate him there was a rustle like a gigantic tree falling, and a fierce whistle came toward them.

The water tower shuddered and was enveloped in a cloud of dust.

[2 1]

When the artillery blazes away you know without reconnoitering that the enemy is not on the run, that the enemy is strong. When the artillery blazes away, the imagined strength of the enemy grows in proportion to the din it makes. You see in your mind's eye, beyond the woods and lakes there, ground forces to match—a division or a corps.

They may not be there at all. There may be only two battalions, both under strength and one badly battered, and their trenching tools may be only just beginning to gouge out foxholes.

But this happens only if the artillery fires sensibly, not stupidly, and does not run out of shells. And only if it is well placed, so that it cannot be located by puffs of smoke or flashes, either in sunlight or after sundown.

This was how things were with Smyslovsky and the colonel in command of the mortars. Nechvolodov, who had seen at first glance that they were natural commanders, expected no less of them. If a man is a natural commander the outcome of a military engagement is more than half dependent on him; not just a brave commander, but one who is cool and self-possessed and does not waste his men. They have faith only in such a commander: when he orders them to attack, they know that this is the decisive moment, that there is no avoiding it. Nechvolodov felt himself to be a natural commander of this sort, perhaps a born commander. This had given him the strength to leave cadet school at seventeen and volunteer for active service, reach the rank of second lieutenant no later than his hothouse-bred contemporaries, begin his military studies in the General Staff Academy itself, and, still only twenty-five, graduate not only with top marks but with promotion out of turn for special excellence in military science.

How lucky that the three of them had come together that day. And God had brought them Kosachevsky. Their pathetic handful had performed the impossible: in that bottleneck at Rothfliess station, they had held up throughout the early evening what were obviously large and constantly growing enemy forces with powerful artillery.

To begin with there had been a short bombardment, and then a little after 6 p.m. the Germans had advanced from the north in open column, not in narrow file, so confident had their success earlier in the day made them.

But then the two Russian batteries had opened up with their twenty-four guns from five concealed firing positions and caught the advancing forces in a slashing rain of shrapnel, pounded them with high-explosive shells which raised black columns of earth, and driven them back where the topography and the forests made them invisible.

Meanwhile the Russian battalions hastily dug themselves in.

The Germans subsided and fell silent.

The sun was slowly sliding down.

The will to remain right there and not retreat, to fight as though this were the last, crucial battle of his life, the crowning achievement of his whole military career, is natural to any born commander.

It was in that spirit that they stood there now, forced to do so by the enemy, by the disposition of their forces, by the situation. Still, it would have been no bad thing to have some sort of orders telling them how long they were to be stationed in this place, whether they could expect reinforcements, and what they were supposed to do next.

But nothing came. The promised dispatch rider did not appear with instructions or explanations or merely to see whether they were still alive. Having beaten a hasty retreat, Corps HQ and Division HQ seemed to have forgotten about the reserve force they had left behind. Or perhaps they themselves had ceased to exist.

At 6:20 Nechvolodov sent a note to the Division Commander seeking further instructions. Where the messenger was to deliver this note, nobody knew.

The Germans spent some time observing and regrouping. They inflated and began sending up a captive balloon, from which they would probably have been able to locate all the Russian batteries, but something went wrong and it would not rise. Then they opened fire from three positions, demolished the water tower completely, reduced the whole station to ruins (the reserve HQ took refuge in a safe stone cellar), and finally began advancing, but in single file, cautiously. The Russian batteries, which had not been discovered and suppressed, came into their own, blazed away at the boundary lines, and caught the German concentrations behind their protective screens in heavy mortar fire.

The sun had sunk across the lake. Immediately after, a sharp eye could have seen the young moon following it. The Russians saw it over the left shoulder, the Germans over the right.

It was getting dark, and very much colder. A night of starlight lay ahead. The fumes of gunfire, the stench of destruction, rose and were quickly dispersed by the chilly air. Everybody put his greatcoat on.

Around 8 p.m. the Germans fell silent: perhaps because men generally tend to take the evening as the end of the day's efforts, and perhaps because they were not yet quite ready.

Nechvolodov ordered that the men should immediately be given the food already cooked—it would be lunch and supper in one—and that the battalions should put out sentries. He then climbed onto the wall of the shattered station, and spent the last gray minutes scanning the terrain. The dial of his pocket watch was visible for a while: he looked at it and was surprised—at eight, and again at eight-fifteen. Someone should have turned up from Division Headquarters in the last three hours.

Then, climbing cautiously down from the ruined wall and into the cellar, casting a long shadow right to the end of the vaulted descent, Nechvolodov made his way to a candle on the ground, squatted on his heels, and used his knees as a desk to write to the Division Commander:

"2020 hours. Rothfliess station. Fighting has died down. Tried in vain to obtain instructions from you." (He could not say to his superior "because you were on the run.") "I am holding my position at Rothfliess station with two battalions of the Ladoga Regiment." (He must not mention Kosachevsky's battalion: his failure to withdraw was a breach of discipline.) "I am trying to establish contact with the 13th, 14th, and 15th regiments." (In other words, with all the rest of his division: he could hardly make it plainer.) "I await your instructions."

He left the cellar and dispatched a messenger.

It was nearly dark, but he recognized the short, bearded Smyslovsky hurrying toward him.

They embraced. The other man's forage cap jabbed Nechvolodov's chin.

They patted each other on the back.

"We haven't got much to laugh about," Smyslovsky said in a happy voice. "We've got about twenty shells to a gun left, and the mortars about the same. I've sent for more, but I'm not sure they'll bring any. I wonder what's going on in Bischofsburg."

Maybe they should put the batteries in marching order? But that would mean that they had already decided to retreat.

In one way they had been lucky: there were only a handful of wounded in the two batteries, and these were light wounds. Reports had been collected from the battalions, and there too the number of casualties was small, incomparably smaller than earlier that day.

The man who digs his heels in does not fall over. The man who runs away does.

"I've picked up some splinters," Smyslovsky said cheerfully. "They were firing at us with twenty-one-centimeter mortars—apparently. Pretty good going. One direct hit would wreck this cellar."

The wounded were coming in from the battalions. The blacked-out dressing station sent them on to Bischofsburg.

The subdued rattle of vehicles gave away the position of the highroad.

At the station, staff officers and messengers kept coming and going, telephonists and medical orderlies all talked at once. Nechvolodov's troops had met so many wounded and terrified men on the long day's march that they themselves felt like victors.

The still, quiet air was getting chillier. There was not a sound from the Germans. The ruined buildings were invisible in the darkness. The evening sky was a peaceful starry dome overhead.

"It'll be four hours at nine o'clock," Nechvolodov said, sitting down on the sloping, rounded roof of the cellar. "Is it nearly nine now?"

Smyslovsky, who had perched beside him, threw back his head to look at the sky and drawled, "Just a few minutes to go."

"How can you tell?"

"By the stars."

"As precisely as that?"

"I'm used to it. I can always tell to within a quarter of an hour."

"Have you made a special study of astronomy?"

"A decent artilleryman has to."

Nechvolodov knew that there were five Smyslovsky brothers, all five artillery officers, all good at their job, with a scientific approach to it. Nechvolodov had met one of them before.

"What are your name and patronymic?"

"Aleksei Konstantinovich."

"And where are your brothers?"

"One of them is here, in the 1st Corps."

Nechvolodov had forgotten the flashlight in his pocket till his hand suddenly encountered it—a neat little German flashlight which one of his sergeants had found and presented to him earlier that day. He shone it on his watch.

It was three minutes to nine.

Without climbing down from the cellar roof he quietly gave orders for a dispatch rider to get ready, and, moving the little circle of light over a piece of paper held against his map case, wrote a note with a pencil:

"To General Blagoveshchensky. 2100 hours. Rothfliess station. My two battalions of the Ladoga Regiment, together with a mortar battery and a heavy artillery battery, constitute the general reserve of the corps. I have led the Ladoga battalions into battle. No instructions from Division Commander since 1700 hours. Nechvolodov."

To whom else should he write? And how could he convey in correct military language what he really wanted to say: You've been running for four hours now, you cowards! Let's hear from you! We can hold on here, but where, oh where, are you all?

He read it to Smyslovsky. Roshko took it to the messenger. The messenger galloped off. Then Nechvolodov gave orders for the battalions to strengthen their guard.

After that he sat on the sloping roof of the cellar, clasping his raised knees, and was silent.

It was not easy to draw him into conversation. Though, as Smyslovsky knew, this was not the most ordinary of generals—he wrote books in his spare time.

"Am I disturbing you? Shall I go away?"

"No, stay here," Nechvolodov said.

Why he did so was not at all clear. He hung his head and remained silent.

Time dragged by. Some unknown factor, something now stirring stealthily in the darkness, could suddenly change the situation.

Put bluntly, it was frightening: to lose your life, to die. But nobody yet seemed to find it frightening that two thousand men should be sitting abandoned and forgotten in the tranquil darkness full of lurking destruction.

How quiet it was! It was difficult to believe that it had been deafeningly noisy a little while ago. It was difficult to believe that there was a war at all. The armies were lying low, concealing their movements, suppressing every sound, and the people who would be there in peacetime had gone. There was no light anywhere—not a sign of life. The earth lay dead in thick, impenetrable blackness under a living, shifting sky, where everything was in place and all things kept within their limits and obeyed their law.

Smyslovsky lolled backward to make himself comfortable on the sloping cellar roof, stroking his long beard and looking up. From where he lay he had before him Andromeda's necklace strung out across the sky toward the five brilliant scattered stars of Pegasus.

And gradually their eternal radiant purity stilled the anxiety that had brought the colonel here in such haste to tell Nechvolodov that his splendid heavy batteries could not remain in their firing positions without shells and almost without cover. There were invisible laws too.

He lay there a while longer and said, "Just think. Here we are fighting for this blessed Rothfliess station, when this whole earth of ours—"

He had a lively, nimble, fertile mind, which could not go for a minute without absorbing something or expressing something.

"—is the prodigal son of the ruling luminary. It lives only by the light and warmth its father bestows on it. But that diminishes from year to year, and the atmosphere becomes poorer in oxygen. A time will come when our warm coverlet will be threadbare, and all life on earth will perish . . . If we all continually remembered this, what would East Prussia matter to us? Or Serbia?"

Nechvolodov said nothing.

"And inside? . . . The molten magma struggles to break out. The thickness of the earth's crust is only fifty versts or so, it is like the thin peel of a Messina orange, like the skin on boiling milk. And we have no home or happiness anywhere else."

Nechvolodov did not deny it.

"There has already been one occasion, ten thousand years ago, when almost all living things were buried. But that has taught us nothing."

Nechvolodov did not let it disturb him.

A long, conspiratorial silence set in. Smyslovsky could not be ignorant of Nechvolodov's *Tales of the Russian Land,* intended for a popular audience, and belonging as he did to the educated class, he obviously could not approve of them. But the whole war seemed trivial beneath the majesty of the sky, and the differences between the two men were muted that evening. Muted, but not altogether forgotten. Smyslovsky had mentioned Serbia. Serbia had been crushed by a brutal predator, and the need to defend her was not diminished by the beauty of the stars. Nechvolodov felt bound to demur.

"Surely the Emperor's love of peace must have some limit? Surely he could not let Serbia be humiliated in that way?"

There was so much Smyslovsky could have said in reply. He had heard too much wild mystical nonsense about the "Slav idea." Where had they got it from? Why had they forced it on people? Anyway, there was no following all those Balkan intrigues. But at present he hadn't the heart for petty argument.

"Then again—where did life on earth come from? When the earth was regarded as the center of the universe it was natural to believe also that all the germs of life were peculiar to our planet. But now that it is an insignificant minor planet? All the scientists have been defeated by the riddle. Life was brought to us by an unknown force, from no one knows where, and no one knows why . . ."

This was more in Nechvolodov's line. Army life, depending as it did on unambiguous orders, permitted no duality of interpretation. But in the meditations of his leisure hours he believed in a dual reality which accounted for the miracles of Russian history. Talking about it, however, was harder than writing about it. Talking about it was almost impossible.

"Well . . ." Nechvolodov replied. "You take the broad view of everything. I can't look beyond Russia."

That was just the trouble. And it was worse still that a good general should be a writer of bad books and see that as his vocation. In his version, Orthodoxy was always right as against Catholicism, the rulers of Moscow as against Novgorod. Russian ways were gentler and purer than those of the West. It was much safer to discuss cosmology with him.

But Nechvolodov had decided that it was his turn. "You know, a lot of us don't understand even Russia. Nineteen out of twenty don't understand what 'fatherland' means. Our soldiers fight only for their religion and the Tsar—that's what holds the army together."

But what could you expect of ordinary soldiers when even officers were forbidden to discuss political matters? This was an order which applied to the whole army and it was not for Nechvolodov to condemn it since it had been approved by the All-Highest. All the same, when he had taken command of the 16th (Ladoga) Infantry Regiment he could not forget for a minute that, together with the Semyonovsky Guards Regiment and the 1st Grenadier Brigade, it had been the sole prop of the throne in Moscow during the 1905 rising.

"It's all the more important that the idea of the fatherland should be cherished in every heart."

In spite of himself he was in danger of quoting from his own book, and it was not the time or place to talk about it seriously. Aleksei Smyslovsky himself had outgrown both the Tsar and religion, but the fatherland was something he understood very well.

Had their conversation meandered by soundless paths in that direction Smyslovsky would have had to confess that he greatly respected his late father-in-law, General Malakhov, who as governor-general of Moscow had suppressed the rising.

"Aleksandr Dmitrievich, is what I have heard true, that you put forward proposals for the reform of the officer corps before the present Emperor's accession—proposals affecting the Guards and the system of promotion?"

"I did," Nechvolodov said unenthusiastically.

"And what happened?"

In a half-audible whisper: "I ended up swimming with the current. Like all the rest . . ."

He shone the flashlight on his watch.

Had the Germans gone to bed? Or were they slowly infiltrating, unobserved by the lookouts? Or circling around, to cut the Russians off tomorrow?

Ought he to be taking decisions? Acting? Or just submissively waiting? What should he be doing?

Nechvolodov did not move.

Suddenly they heard a noise close at hand, voices arguing, angry abuse, and Roshko led a figure up to the cellar roof. "Your Excellency! This dolt has been looking for you for the last four hours. If he hasn't been dreaming and isn't lying he almost ended up with the Germans."

He handed over a packet.

They opened it, and the two of them read it together by the flashlight.

"To Major General Nechvolodov. 26 August, 1730 hours." They read that bit again. Nechvolodov even rubbed the figures—yes, that was what it said: 1730 hours!

"The Division Commander has ordered you with the general corps reserve entrusted to you to cover the withdrawal of units of the 4th Infantry Division, which is in action to the north of Gross-Bössau . . ."

"To the north of Gross-Bössau." Nechvolodov echoed Smyslovsky in a flat expressionless voice.

To the north of Gross-Bössau. In the rear not only of the German infantry but of the guns which had been bombarding them for the past few hours, to the rear of their captive balloon, where only Russian corpses had lain through the heat of the day after the commotion early in the morning. "To the north of Gross-Bössau"—what delirious shadows were flickering in the writer's head?

There was no need to read on. There was nothing more to read except:

"Captain Kuznetsov. For the Division Chief of Staff."

Not the Division Commander, not even the Chief of Staff—they had just shouted something as they jumped into their car or charabanc, or while they were already on the move, and Captain Kuznetsov too, deputizing for all of them, was in such a hurry to follow that he had entrusted the dispatch to this hopeless dunce.

Nechvolodov shone the light on his watch, and wrote the time of receipt on the dispatch: 26 August, 2155 hours.

His instructions had been four and a half hours on the way. But they need never have been written at all. Nechvolodov had heard almost the same with his own ears from Komarov at five o'clock that evening.

In five whole hours they had not found a minute to consider what was to become of the reserve.

Nechvolodov threw back his head, as though listening for something.

Nothing there. Silence.

"Aleksei Konstantinovich," he said quietly, "leave two howitzers in position and put the others in line of march, facing south. The mortar battery will do the same." In a louder voice: "Misha! Get over to Bischofsburg, at a gallop. Find out for yourself exactly what units are there and what their orders are. I want to know who's the senior officer, whether any ammunition is being brought up for our guns, and where the Schlüsselburg Regiment is. Get back as fast as you can."

Roshko repeated all the questions fully, precisely, omitting nothing, then dashed off, summoning a few men to accompany him. They came running, and the muffled thud of hoofbeats on the soft ground was followed by silence.

That was what Smyslovsky had come to tell him an hour and a half ago: that the guns were doomed if they were kept in firing position without ammunition. But now that he had permission to do so he was reluctant to pull out.

It should have been the other way around: this quiet night would have given the whole corps time enough to move in and take up positions beside them.

If they withdrew, all his firing had been useless, all his shells had flown on a fool's errand, and his men had been wounded for nothing.

The night seemed so quiet, so free from danger.

Half an hour or more later Smyslovsky returned to reserve HQ and found Nechvolodov still on the cellar roof. He leaned on the vaulted brickwork beside him. "Aleksandr Dmitrievich, what about the infantry battalions?"

"I don't know. I can't decide," Nechvolodov said with an effort.

These things are always so easy to decide after the event. Of course you should have withdrawn, as quickly as you could! Of course you should have stayed, and put up a stiffer resistance! Perhaps they were being cut off at that very minute. Perhaps at that very minute help was no more than one verst away. But right now, abandoned by all those above him, knowing nothing about the army, or the corps, or the neighbors, or the enemy, in the silence, in the darkness, in the depths of a strange land, he had to make a decision, and it had to be the only sound one.

Smyslovsky stood silent, buttressing the vaulted roof of the cellar, with his shoulder, smoothing his beard, not hindering, not daring to offer advice.

Suddenly everything changed. The unpeopled darkness came to life—without a sound, though: milky white, thick, and immensely long, the beam of a German searchlight shone out from some high point.

With its blunt, malevolent, deadly hand it began slowly feeling for Nechvolodov's reserve.

Instantly, the whole world was changed, as though the enemy had begun raining fire from a dozen big guns at once.

Nechvolodov sprang lightly to his feet and ran to the highest point of the cellar roof. Smyslovsky bounded up to join him.

The beam continued its search.

Slowly, very slowly it traveled, reluctant to abandon each strip torn from the darkness. It had begun over to the left, by the lake, and it still had quite a long way to go.

Nechvolodov called men over and shouted orders to be transmitted to the battalions: under no circumstances must anyone move while the beam was on him.

They ran to telephone.

Just that one beam had changed everything. Obviously only the darkness was holding the Germans back. At first light, or a little later in the morning, they would advance.

If he delayed until morning he would have to stay on all the next day. If he did not mean to wait he must withdraw at once.

Then a second beam shone out, at an angle to the first, but at such a distance from it that the two would approach each other without intersecting. The second beam passed over the Belozersk battalion on Nechvolodov's right flank.

How large a force must he allow for behind those noiseless, luminous cudgels?

Obviously the Germans thought that the Russians too were in considerable force.

Once again Nechvolodov summoned a signals officer and stretched out a long arm to hand him a message.

"To Lieutenant Colonel Kosachevsky. As soon as the beam goes past withdraw your battalion from its present position and bring it up here to the railway."

They must not be held back any longer whatever happened.

"Let's get up on the station!" Smyslovsky suggested.

It was a pity to let the opportunity slip without taking a look themselves. They hurried down from the cellar roof, over to the ruins of the station, and with the help of the flashlight climbed over a heap of bricks to the sloping girder by which they could clamber up onto the wall.

But the sound of hooves from behind made them hesitate. Nechvolodov recognized Roshko's voice.

They went back.

Roshko was out of breath, but he still delivered his report in the robust young voice which went with his strong frame and his rosy cheeks.

"There's not a single senior commander in Bischofsburg. I couldn't find the leading echelon of the artillery. All the units are mixed up, and the houses are full of wounded. Nobody knows where to go. Some have orders to withdraw, others do not. The Schlüsselburg Regiment has turned up! They have just arrived in Bischofsburg from the east. They have orders from Komarov to withdraw to a position farther off than we were this morning. Tolpygo's cavalry division is also pulling into Bischofsburg and his orders are to carry on westward. While Rikhter's division, wagon train and all, is withdrawing from the west. They've got into a tangle, and nobody can force a way through the streets. They won't get it sorted out by morning. That's all."

The searchlights slowly probed deeper, then shifted sideways.

The beams were getting closer together.

It was 11:15 p.m. Nechvolodov's reserve force had held up the enemy south of Gross-Bössau for the whole of 26 August. They had no orders for 27 August. Nechvolodov would have to make them up for himself.

Standing on the pile of broken bricks amid the ruins of the station, and with one eye on the searchlight beams, he delivered his decision quietly, almost indolently.

"We shall withdraw, Aleksei Konstantinovich. Pull out the remaining guns. Move both artillery batteries up to the northern outskirts of Bischofsburg. Look out for some good positions, just in case, and wait for me."

"Right," Smyslovsky replied. "*Feci quod potui, faciant meliora potentes.*"*

He went away.

"Roshko—tell the Ladoga battalions to leave their defensive positions without a sound, wind in their telephone lines, and get over here."

Life suddenly stopped at the station: the deathly light, the ghostly pale spot, had reached it. Men stood or sat still behind buildings and trees.

* I have done what I could—let whoever can do better.

Horses in their places of concealment were restive, neighed, and tugged at the reins. The men had orders to keep a tight hold on them.

They felt helpless and humiliated in their forced immobility under the lingering beam: if it did not move on they might have to stay like that all night.

But the thought that the searchlight might crawl to a new position was more menacing still.

The beam went away.

They bestirred themselves. Nechvolodov went down into the cellar and wrote out his final order. Before extinguishing the candle he looked at the map, and looked again.

The 6th Corps was rolling back as easily as a billiard ball—round, smooth, and carefree, with no one to hampen its progress.

And it was exposing Samsonov's army to an unobstructed blow from the right, a blow against which it had no defense.

* * *

THERE WAS A HORN,
BUT GOD KNOCKED IT OFF

* * *

[2 2]

Yes, yes, yes, yes! It's a vice, this habit of plunging recklessly, of rushing full steam ahead, intent only on your goal, blind and deaf to all around, so that you fail to see the childishly obvious danger beside you. Like when he and Yuly Martov, the moment their three years of Siberian tedium were over and they were on their way abroad at last, carrying a basket of subversive literature and a letter with the plan for *Iskra* in invisible ink, chose that of all times to be too clever, too conspiratorial. The rule is to change trains en route, but they had forgotten that the second train would pass through Tsarskoye Selo, and were detained by the gendarmes as suspicious persons. Luckily the police with their salutary Russian sluggishness gave them time to get rid of the basket, took the letter at its face value because they could not be bothered to hold it over a flame—and *Iskra* was saved!

Later, in that year of tense struggle between the "majority" of twenty-one and the "minority" of twenty-two, the whole Party had let the Japanese war slip by almost unnoticed.

This new war he had neither written nor thought about. He had not reacted to Jaurès's appeal. Why? Because the *reunion movement* had spread like a plague, until in the last few years it had infected the whole of Russian social democracy. Nothing could be more dangerous and damaging to the proletariat than this epidemic: "conciliation," "reunification"—cretinous nonsense, it could ruin the Party! The leaders of the ditherers' International had seized the initiative. Let *them* "make peace," let *them* unify the two factions. They had summoned "the majority" to their sordid little unification conference in Brussels. How to wangle out of it? How to dodge it? Engrossed in this problem he had scarcely heard the pistol shot at Sarajevo. The International was due to hold its Congress in Vienna that same August, and never before had he been so absorbed in the life-and-death struggle with the Mensheviks. Suddenly, it was super-super-super-urgent to drum up in the few weeks left a delegation from inside Russia that would look representative of a genuinely large and active Party—which really meant organizing such a Party on the spot in Poronin—so as to appear in full force at the Congress. While he was busy improvising and bringing in his delegates (openly, over the frontier), Austria had declared war on Serbia, and he had hardly noticed. Even Germany's declaration of war on Russia had meant nothing to him. When you are locked in combat it is difficult to pause. Reports were put about that the German Social Democrats had voted war credits. Was that then the end of them? Had the mainspring of the International snapped? No. Once wound up it went on automatically convening its Congress.

In *principle,* of course, he had known that an imperialist war must break out. It had been theoretically predicted, infallibly foreseen. But not at that precise moment, not in that particular year. He had failed to see it coming. And landed in a mess.

Yes, yes, yes—he had had ten days to think about his ambiguous situation right there on the Russian frontier, to turn the delegates back, to get out of Poronin as quickly as possible now that the damned place was no good to anybody, to escape from the Austro-Hungarian mousetrap altogether. What work could he do in a country at war? He should have made a dash for the blessed haven of Switzerland, a neutral country, a safe country, a country where there were no restrictions, where policemen were intelligent and laws were laws! But no—mesmerized by the coming Congress he hadn't stirred an inch. Then, suddenly, Russia was at war with Austria and those of the delegates who had arrived were interned. Some of the Russians were of call-up age, and their presence raised awkward questions.

What a miscalculation! What an anxious three weeks he had lived through since! Now it was all behind him. He was walking along the platform of Nowy Targ station. As far as the engine, and back again. With Hanecki.

Hanecki's pleasant, clean-shaven, rather delicate face was calm enough now, but how he had raged at those Nowy Targ bureaucrats! Hanecki had not let him down in his hour of need. (He was of course quite at home in Nowy Targ. His rich father was a local man.) Whereas Zinoviev had slunk away at the critical moment. Nowy Targ was not Poronin. Not nearly so dangerous. Still, some of the Poronin fanatics might turn up, and anything could happen. Although there at the station, with a gendarme reassuringly pacing the platform, nobody was likely to attack him.

Looked at dialectically, a gendarme is sometimes a bad thing and sometimes a good thing.

The engine had a big red wheel, almost the height of a man.

However wary you are, however circumspect, however suspicious, in seven long years the abominable tranquillity of an essentially petit-bourgeois existence will lull your vigilance. In the shadow of something big, you lean against a massive iron wall without looking at it carefully—and suddenly it moves, it turns out to be a big red engine wheel driven by a long, naked piston rod, your spine is twisted and you are down! With your head banging against the rails, you belatedly realize that yet again some stupid danger has taken you unawares.

Lenin was in no danger from the Austrian authorities. He had a valid passport and the legal status of a political émigré, an enemy of Tsarism. As far as the Austrian police were concerned he was immaculate. But how could he have bungled such a promising operation? Let his handful of Party workers be arrested? An endless chain of stupidities. A wall of stupidities. How could he have been guilty of such an elementary, such a stupid, such a blind miscalculation? It was Tsarskoye Selo all over again. (Or like 1895 when they had been about to publish a newspaper but had been rounded up before they got a single issue out.) Yes, yes, yes, yes! A revolutionary must always be ready to go to jail (though it's cleverer to stay out) but not for such a silly reason! Not in such a humiliating way! He shouldn't have let them tie his hands just at the wrong moment. He had just got together the beginnings of a Party—and had let its members be jailed! Worse still, when people saw that the delegates had been arrested yet the organizer remained free, what conclusion would they draw?

That very evening he and Hanecki had sent telegrams to the Political Department of the Cracow police and to socialist friends in Vienna. Telegrams were necessary because it was not a simple matter for him to get out of Poronin himself. From the day war broke out railway tickets could be obtained only with the village headman's permission. If he wouldn't give it even the friendly police sergeant would not easily change his mind. And if you managed to get as far as Nowy Targ, you had to get another permit, you needed a new recommendation, and that was slow in coming, so you spent eleven days pacing the flagged floor of a tiny room in the police station from wall to wall or tossing restlessly on the creaking wire bed (there was no hotel in Nowy Targ), irritated and goaded by the thought that none of it need ever have happened! That it was all your own doing! That you had dug your own grave!

No accidental setback, no defeat, no dirty, underhand trick on the part of your enemies is ever so galling as your own miscalculations, however slight. They nag at you day and night, especially in confinement. Because they are *your own* mistakes—you cannot be objective about them, cannot live them down or forget them, cannot get away from the thought that it need never have happened. It *need* never have happened! But it *has* happened because of your own bungling! The blunder is all *yours*!

Hanecki (Kuba to his Party comrades) had been magnificent. He had not gone soft, not backed away, he had behaved like a bulldog sinking its teeth in policemen's trousers. He had showered Lenin with names—Social Democrats, parliamentarians, and other public figures. Write to them at once! Tell them the facts! Pester them! Get them to intervene. Two dozen letters were dispatched in all directions. There was no evening train, so Hanecki dashed off to Nowy Targ in a peasant cart. Rushed to Cracow, saw various people there (he could make up a yarn to fool any bureaucrat at a moment's notice), and sent more telegrams to Vienna. Any Slav in his place would have wearied, relaxed his efforts, given up, but Hanecki's stamina was inexhaustible, and he kept going. By then Lenin had given him one further commission: to get permission for him to leave for Switzerland.

Spurred on by Hanecki's urgent telegrams, the Social Democratic deputies Viktor Adler and Diamand had appealed to the Chancellor and the Ministry of the Interior, giving written guarantees that the Russian Social Democrat Ulyanov was not only loyal to the Austro-Hungarian Empire but was a worse enemy of the Russian government than the Chancellor himself. The Cracow police received their instructions: "Ulyanov could be of great service to us in present circumstances." The way was then clear for further negotiations to free the interned comrades. But how would their release affect Lenin? Would they not want to know why he had not been jailed? Kuba had a marvelous idea: that little room in the police station had really been a cell. *Of course* Lenin had been imprisoned!

Meanwhile another blunder, another danger overlooked! Things you could put into the heads of the Austrian Chancellor and of imbecile Austrian bureaucrats were less readily understood by Galician peasants, who were as obtuse as peasants the world over—in Europe, in Asia, or in Alakayevka. You can live in a place without realizing how you look to those about you. In the eyes of the benighted inhabitants of Poronin these were strange people, unlike other summer residents, picking up letters and packets by the sackful from day to day, always writing, writing, writing, receiving substantial money orders from Russia, and visitors who crossed the frontier without passports. The war came along—and obviously they were spies. Weren't they always walking in the mountains? What were they doing there? Making maps? The government warned everybody: If you see anyone behaving suspiciously, detain him. He may be taking photographs of roads, or poisoning wells. Ulyanov then—perhaps he was a spy? It was staggering, beyond all understanding! Peasant women coming out of church, whether or not they had seen Nadya and were doing it for her benefit, had deafened the whole street with their din. If the authorities had let him go, *they* would poke his eyes out for him, cut out his tongue! Nadya had come home pale and trembling all over. Her fright was contagious. They might very well poke his eyes out, he wouldn't be a bit surprised. There was nothing to stop them from cutting his tongue out either. Nothing could be simpler: they would come along with their pitchforks and knives. Never in his life had Lenin been exposed to such enormous danger. Nobody had ever treated him like this . . . But then history records many such obscene outbursts of mob fury. There were no guarantees against it even in civilized countries. You were safer in jail than among an ignorant rabble.

To feel alarm in the face of threats means only that you are prepared for battle, not that you are panicky.

So his last days and hours in Poronin had been darkened and troubled, and Lenin had no intention of going back. For two years this safe, peaceful little town had been crouched to spring. They kept to the house, they were unable to eat or sleep, they started feverishly packing, and of course Nadya made all sorts of new mistakes. Forgot to pack things, threw away highly secret papers. She was too agitated to understand what she was reading. Besides, tons and tons of paper had accumulated in the two seasons they had spent at the villa.

How could he have been so slow, lingered so close to the Russian frontier? Cossack raiders could have carried him off in a flash.

Here on the platform by the neat green train, in the presence of the gendarme and the station personnel, there could be no mob violence, and at last he felt at ease. The first bell had rung. Still twenty-three minutes before the train left. Everybody was more cheerful on this cheerful, sunny, cloudless morning. No military freight was being loaded, no newly mobilized soldiers were on the move, the platform and the train looked just as they always did in the summer holiday season. But tickets were available only with police permission, and so the carriages were half empty.

Nadya and his mother-in-law had already taken their seats and were looking out of the window. Vladimir Ilyich had taken Kuba's arm and they were walking backward and forward along the platform, both of them short men, both of them broad, only Lenin was big-boned and Kuba merely fat.

In appearance and behavior Kuba was the perfect businessman. His immense self-assurance, his ingeniously twisted shoelace mustache, and the steady, earnest gaze of his slightly protruding eyes were irresistible.

When a man displays such remarkable abilities you must listen carefully to what he says, however visionary it may seem to be. He had known Kuba a long time, ever since the Second Congress, but solely in connection with Polish affairs. It was only that summer that he had shown a new side of himself and become indispensable. He was worth his weight in gold: extraordinarily efficient and tight-lipped in all serious matters—no outsider would ever get a word out of him. They had spent much of June and July walking about the plateau near Poronin and discussing Kuba's pyrotechnic schemes for making money. Possibly because of his bourgeois origins, Hanecki had a remarkable financial flair, an extraordinary grasp of money matters—a quality as valuable as it was rare in a revolutionary. He had argued, correctly, that money was the Party's arms and legs, that without money any party was helpless, just a lot of hot air. If even parliamentary parties needed a great deal of money—for their electoral campaigns—it was infinitely more important to an underground revolutionary Party, which had to organize hiding places, safe meeting places, transport, literature, and weapons, train its fighters, support its professionals, and when the time was right carry out a revolution.

He was preaching to the converted. These were things which all Bolsheviks had understood ever since the Second Congress and their first steps as an independent Party: without money you can't move an inch, money is all-important. They had started by squeezing donations out of wealthy Russian merchants, like Mamontov, or Konovalov ("Give them a bun"), and Savva Morozov had kicked in a thousand a month to pay the expenses of the Petersburg committee, but others had shelled out irregularly, in a fit of businessman's benevolence or "intellectual" sympathy. (Garin-Mikhailovsky had just once given ten thousand.) Then you had to start begging again. A surer way was to take it for yourself. Perhaps screw a legacy out of somebody, as they had from Shmidt, the factory owner, or marry off Party members to heiresses, or swindle the Lbov gang out in the Urals by taking their money and not delivering the promised weapons. Or you could be more systematic about it and use the methods of scientific warfare. They had planned to print counterfeit money in Finland, and Krasin had obtained the watermarked paper. Krasin again had made bombs for the expropriations. The "exes" (expropriations) had gone off extraordinarily well: then because of Plekhanov's and Martov's squeamishness the Fifth Congress had banned them, but it was impossible to call a halt, and Kamo and Koba had triumphantly grabbed another 340,000 from the Treasury in Tiflis. But success had gone to their heads, and comrades had started changing crisp Tsarist five-hundred-ruble notes in Berlin, in Paris, in Stockholm. They should have been content with less. The Tsarist ministry had circulated the serial numbers, and so Litvinov was caught. So was Sara Ravich, in Munich, and a note she was trying to smuggle out of prison was intercepted. After their homes had been searched, thirteen Geneva Bolsheviks had been picked up, and Karpinsky and Semashko would have been put away for a spell if the liberals in Parliament hadn't helped. But worst of all, obscenest of all, Kautsky, with his false, hypocritical, sneaking devotion to "principle," had started squawking like an old hen. What a vile trick, setting up a "socialist court" to try the Russian Bolsheviks, and ordering them like a half-wit to burn the all-powerful five-hundred-ruble notes! (Lenin had only to see a picture of that hoary-headed holy man in his goggling glasses, and he retched as though he found himself swallowing a frog.) It's all right for you, the German workers are well off, they pay large dues, your party is legal, but what about us? (Of course they hadn't been such fools as to burn all of it.) Then they did another stupid thing, and made the malicious old man financial arbitrator between Bolsheviks and Mensheviks. They had to make a tactical pretense of accepting reunion, which meant pooling their funds—and the Mensheviks hadn't a bean. Since it was impossible to conceal the whole Shmidt inheritance, they had given part of it to Kautsky as arbitrator, and later on, when the new split came, he would not hand it back to the Bolsheviks.

This last summer Hanecki had captured Lenin's imagination with his plans to found a trading company of his own in Europe, or take a partnership in some existing firm and make guaranteed monthly remittances to the Party out of his profits. This was not a Russian pipe dream: every move had been worked out with impressive precision. Kuba hadn't thought of it himself, it was the brainchild of the elephantine genius Parvus, who had been writing to him from Constantinople. Parvus, once as poor as any other Social Democrat, had gone to Turkey to organize strikes, and now wrote frankly that he had all the money he needed (if rumor was right, he was fabulously wealthy) and that the time had come for the Party too to get rich. He had put it neatly. Their best hope of overthrowing capitalism was to become capitalists themselves. Socialists must start by becoming capitalists! The Socialists had laughed at him. Rosa, Klara, and Liebknecht had let him know how they despised him. But perhaps they had been in too much of a hurry. Sarcasm wilted in the face of Parvus's solid financial power.

It was partly because of Hanecki's schemes that the war had caught them napping.

They discussed them further in these last few minutes, and made arrangements to keep in touch. They would in any case be seeing each other soon; Zinoviev would follow after Lenin, and then Hanecki, as soon as he obtained exemption from Austrian military service.

. . . There went the second bell. Lenin hopped nimbly onto the step. Hatless, almost completely bald, in his shabby suit, with his sharp features, his habit of looking uneasily over his shoulder, and his neglected beard, he really did look rather like a spy. Hanecki wanted to tease him about it, but he knew that Lenin couldn't take a joke and refrained.

But what did he look like himself if not a spy, with his sad, wary eyes, and the shiny suit which did not go with his businessman's face?

The stationmaster stood stern and stiff in his tall red-and-black cap. There were three rings on the bell. The guard sounded his horn and started running.

People waved goodbye, and they waved back through the open window.

All in all, life in Poronin hadn't been too bad. A quiet, steady life, not like the mad rush of Paris. For all his homeless wanderings about Europe, he had never become a European. He found it easier to act if his surroundings were simple and narrow. They had lived through so many anxious moments here, so many joys.

So many disillusionments.

Malinovsky.

The platform, the station, and those left behind were snatched from sight. Even Hanecki, admirable and reliable comrade though he was, would be missing from the next stage of his life. At some future point he might very well become again the most important and useful of men, and desperately urgent letters with double and triple underlining would be dashed off in the small hours, but for the time being he had done a splendid job and ceased to exist.

There was an infallible law of revolutionary struggle, or perhaps of human life in general, which no one had yet put into words but which Lenin had often noticed at work. At any given time one or two people emerged to take their place at his side, people who for the moment were intellectually closer to him, more interesting, important, and useful than anyone else, people who particularly stimulated him to confide in them, to discuss things with them, to act in concert with them. But hardly any of them retained this position for long, because situations change every day, and we must change dialectically with them, change instantly or, rather, anticipate change—that is the meaning of political genius. It was natural that one after another, encountering the whirlwind that was Lenin, should be drawn immediately into his activities, should carry out his instructions at the prescribed moment and with the prescribed speed, by whatever means and at whatever personal sacrifice. Natural, because all this was done not for Vladimir Ilyich but for the compelling power which manifested itself through him, and of which he was only the infallible interpreter, who always knew precisely what was right just for today, and indeed by the evening was not always quite what it had been in the morning. Once one of these transitional people grew obstinate, ceased to understand why his duties were necessary and urgent, began to mention his mixed feelings or his own unique destiny, then it was just as natural to remove him from the main road, dismiss him, forget him, abuse and anathematize him if necessary—but even when he dismissed or damned someone Lenin was acting in obedience to the power which drew him on. The exiles on the Yenisei had occupied this position of intellectual intimacy for a long, long time, but only because there was no one geographically nearer. From afar he had imagined that Plekhanov would take their place, but after a few short meetings a cold, cruel lesson had put an abrupt end to that. Martov had been close—indeed dangerously, undesirably close—for years on end, but he too had had to give way. (From his bitter experience with Martov he had learned once and for all that there can be no such relationship between human beings as simple friendship transcending political, class, and material ties.) Bogdanov had been a close friend while he was fund-raising for the Party, but when this abruptly ended he had misjudged the sharp slope before him, while aspiring to set the course, and come crashing down. Some relationships proved quite durable. That with Krasin, for instance—he was indispensable as a fund-raiser. Meanwhile, new loyal followers were sucked into the whirlwind—Kamenev, Zinoviev, Malinovsky . . .

Only those who saw the Party's needs in correct perspective could hold their places and march at his side. But when the urgent need of the moment changed, the perspective usually changed too, so that all those recent collaborators remained helplessly rooted in the dull, stationary earth, like so many signposts receding from view until they vanished and were forgotten, though sometimes they loomed sharply at a new turning in the road, this time as enemies. There had been fellow spirits who were close for a week, a day, an hour, for the space of a single conversation, a single report, a single errand—and Lenin openheartedly lavished all his fervor, left the impress of his own sense of urgency on them, so that each one felt himself to be the most important person in the world; then, an hour later, they were already receding, and he would soon have clean forgotten who they were and why he had needed them. Thus, Valentinov had seemed close when he first arrived from Russia, though he had aroused misgivings with his stupid remark that some bit of metalwork he had made meant more to him, when he was working in a factory, than the political struggle. He had soon shown his true nature: he had lacked the stamina to stand up to Martov and become no better than a Menshevik himself.

The train was rolling down the incline, struggling around the mountain bends. Paths and cart tracks ran down the slopes, and higher up, beyond farmhouses, ricks, and standing crops, the mountain road was still visible. You could run up it with your eyes. In all his walks around Poronin he had never been there.

He sat down at last. He should be thinking, or working, not sentimentalizing.

His womenfolk, reading his looks and his movements aright, did not pester him with trifles or fidget unnecessarily, but sat quietly in their seats.

All those exhausting years from 1908 on, after the defeat of the revolution, had been one long story of desertions and dismissals. One after another they had gone: the *Vperyod* group, the Recallists, the Ultimatists, the Machists, the God-Builders . . . Lunacharsky, Bazarov, Aleksinsky, Brilliant, Rozhkov, Lyadov, Lozovsky, Manuilsky, Gorky, the whole old guard, knocked together during the split with the Mensheviks. There were moments when it seemed that there would be no one left, that the whole Bolshevik Party would consist of himself, a couple of women, and a dozen third-raters and washouts who used to come to Bolshevik meetings back in the Paris days; that if he got up to speak at a general meeting he would have not a single friend there and would be shoved off the platform. Away they went, one after another—and what iron certainty was needed not to start doubting himself, not to waver, not to run after them and make up, but, with this clear prophetic insight, to stand firm and wait for them to return of their own accord, to come to their senses. And those who didn't could go to hell.

In 1906 and 1907 defeat was not yet total, society was still on the boil, spinning around the rim of the maelstrom. Lenin had sat in Kuokkala, waiting in vain for the second wave. But from 1908, when the reactionary rabble had tightened its grip on the whole of Russia, the underground had shriveled to nothing, the workers had swarmed like ants out of their holes and into legal bodies—trade unions and insurance associations—and the decline of the underground had sapped the vitality of the emigration too, reduced it to a hothouse existence. *Back there* was the Duma, a legal press—and every émigré was eager to publish *there*.

That was why the outbreak of war was such a marvelous thing. He was overjoyed by it! *Back there*, all those Liquidators would be suppressed immediately, the importance of legal activity would sink sharply, whereas the importance of the emigration and its strength would increase. The center of gravity of Russian political life was shifting back abroad!

Lenin had sized up the situation in those first days of confinement in Nowy Targ. He would not let a personal mishap overshadow the general good fortune; he had absorbed and begun processing the fact that all Europe was at war. The result of this process in Lenin's brain was always the birth of slogans ready for use: the creation of slogans for present needs was the ultimate purpose of all his thinking. That, and the translation of his arguments into the Marxist vernacular: his supporters and followers would not understand him in any other language.

What emerged he had revealed after his release to Hanecki before anyone else: the thing to realize was that now that the war had begun, they should not wish it away or try to stop it, but take advantage of it. They must rise above the sanctimonious notion, sometimes insinuated even into proletarian heads, that war was a disaster or a sin. The slogan "Peace at any price" was for psalm-singing hypocrites. What line should revolutionary democrats everywhere follow in the present situation? The first need was to refute the fairy tale that the Central Powers were to blame for starting the war. The Entente would take refuge in the story that they were "innocent victims of aggression." They would even pretend that the *rentiers'* republic must be defended in the interests of democracy. These excuses must be stamped on, trampled underfoot! What did it matter who had attacked first? The propaganda line must be that *all* governments were equally to blame (the Germans perhaps less than others). What mattered was not who was to blame, but how to turn the war to the best advantage. "They're all to blame"—only if that was accepted could they go on working to bring down the Tsar's government.

This was a lucky war. It would greatly benefit international socialism—with one sharp jolt it would cleanse the workers' movement of the accumulated filth of peacetime! Instead of the previous division of Socialists into opportunists and revolutionaries—an ambiguous distinction which leaves loopholes for enemies—it would make unmistakably clear the real line of cleavage in the international movement, that between patriots and anti-patriots. We are anti-patriots!

It meant the end of the International's shabby schemes for reuniting Bolsheviks and Mensheviks. There would be no Vienna Congress now. There wouldn't be another peep out of them. The rift now yawned so wide that there could be no thought of reconciliation. Yet earlier in July they had had him by the throat: "We see no differences sufficient to justify a split." "Send a delegation to talk peace." Talk peace with the Menshevik scum! Ah, but now, now that you've voted war credits, your International is dead. It will never get on its feet again, it's a corpse. You'll keep up your skeleton's dance for a long time yet, but we must declare for all to hear: You're dead. Inessa's trip to Brussels was our last meeting with you, we've had enough!

At this point, his mother-in-law suddenly realized that they had left a suitcase behind. They hastily checked and counted the baggage under the seats and on the overhead racks. It wasn't there. How disgraceful! They might have been escaping from a burning building! Vladimir Ilyich was upset. Without order in the family and the home, work was impossible. It might sound comic, but an orderly household was itself a contribution to the Party cause. He didn't dare tell the older woman off. She could give as good as she got, and anyway they respected each other—he even gave her little presents to keep on the right side of her. But he reprimanded Nadya. What could you expect from her, though, when she couldn't sew on a button or remove a stain properly? He could do better himself! She wouldn't even give him a clean handkerchief unless he asked.

He never forgave a mistake. No matter who made it, he would remember it as long as he lived.

He turned his head to the window.

The train was gradually winding its way down from the mountains. Engine smoke, sometimes gray, sometimes white, swept past the windows. He was sick of mountains too, after all these years of emigration.

With Nadya, it was like water off a duck's back. All right, we've forgotten a case. We can't go back for it, can we? We'll write from Cracow and they'll send it on.

Nadya had a firm rule, often applied in the past. If she took Volodya's share of the blame on herself, he would cool off and come around. What vexed him most was to be found equally at fault.

He looked his age as he sat there gloomily, with his untrimmed beard and mustache and his anxiously arched ginger eyebrows, staring absently, unseeingly through the window. Nadya knew his changes of expression so well. Just now, she must be careful not to cross him, not even to speak to him, or distract him by exchanging a word with her mother. She must just let him sit there, sink into himself, bathe his hurts in soothing silence, recover from the frantic days in Nowy Targ, the threats in Poronin, the lost case. At such times, whether he took a solitary walk or sat silently thinking, after half an hour or an hour of meditation his brow would clear and the angry little wrinkles would be smoothed from around his eyes, leaving long, deep creases.

A split in the international socialist movement was long overdue but only the war had brought it into the open and made it unavoidable. It was absolutely marvelous. It might seem that the proletarian front had been weakened by the mass betrayal of Socialists: not so—it was *good* that they had betrayed! It was now so much the easier to insist on his own distinct line.

Whereas a month ago he hadn't known what to say or how to wriggle out of it. An inspiration—instead of going to Brussels himself he would send Inessa, leading a delegation! Inessa with her excellent French, with her incomparable poise—cool, calm, slightly disdainful. (Frenchmen in the presidium will be at your feet immediately. And the Germans won't understand you too well—and that's just fine. Every time a German speaks, call for a translation!) What a clever move! They'll be at their wits' end, those ultra-Socialist donkeys. Get on with it at once! Write and ask her. Will she go? Can she go? A holiday with the children on the Adriatic? Rubbish, find somebody to look after the children, we'll pay the expenses out of Party funds. Writing an article on free love? Without being rude (a woman can never give one hundred percent of herself to the Party, she's always up to some nonsense), your manuscript can wait. I'm sure you're one of those who are at their best and bravest doing a responsible job single-handed. Rubbish, rubbish, I don't listen to pessimists. You'll cope magnificently. I'm sure you have nerve enough for it. They'll all be furious I'm not there (that makes me happy!) and they'll probably want to avenge themselves on you, but I'm sure you'll show your claws in no uncertain fashion. We'll call you . . . let's see . . . Petrov. Why reveal your real name to Liquidators? (I'm "Petrov" too—you should remember, if nobody else does. So through our pseudonyms we shall face the public united in one person—openly yet secretly. You will actually be me.) My dear friend, I do beg you to say yes. Will you go? Of course you will! Of course you will! Yes, indeed, we must rehearse thoroughly. And be mighty quick about it. You must simply lie to the Liquidators: promise them that *maybe*, later on, we'll accept a majority decision. (But *of course* we shall never really accept anything. *Not a single one* of their proposals!) Then tell some fib about the children being ill, and say that you can't stay on any longer. We must convince the European Socialists, petit-bourgeois scum that they are, that the Bolsheviks are the most serious of the Russian parties. Slip them the bit about trade unions and insurance associations—that has a tremendous effect on them. When they ask questions, cut them short, avoid answering, fight them off. Take the offensive at all times! Get Rosa talking, show them that she has no proper party behind her, that Hanecki's opposition is the real party. You've got it now! You'll go! Warmest best wishes. Very truly (this in English), your own . . .

Then Hanecki had spoiled things. He'd delivered an ultimatum—not altogether unreasonable: 250 crowns for the Brussels trip or he wouldn't go. But party funds must be used carefully. (And Hanecki isn't the only one. There are plenty of people we could make use of, but we mustn't throw our money around . . .) So in Hanecki's absence the lousy Polish opposition had betrayed and voted with Rosa and Plekhanov for the rotten, idiotic conciliation scheme.

. . . All the same, Inessa, you did better than I could have done. Apart from the fact that I don't know the language, I should certainly have blown up. I couldn't have stood that farce! I should have called them a lot of crooks. But you carried it off calmly, firmly, you foiled all their tricks. You have done the Party a great service. I'm sending you 150 francs. (Probably not enough? Let me know how much more you spent and I'll send it.) Write to me. Are you very tired? Are you very angry with me? Why is it "extremely unpleasant" for you to write about the conference? Maybe you are ill? What is wrong with you? Do reply, or I shall have no peace.

Inessa was the only human being whose moods he sensed and responded to even at a distance. Indeed, at a distance the pull was stronger.

One thing to remember: with wartime censorship he must adopt a less intimate tone. It might give an opening for blackmail. Socialists must be prudent.

Their correspondence had been interrupted by the war, and now her letters would go to Poronin. Still, there was every reason to believe that once she had sent her children off to Russia, Inessa would return to Switzerland. Perhaps she was there already.

The women were quietly discussing how they were going to manage in Cracow. Nadya suggested that her mother and Volodya should stay with the luggage while she called on Inessa's former landlady. It would save trouble if they could move in that very day.

As she said it, her gaze traveled to the window, brushing Volodya's cheek. He remained impassive, didn't turn his head, made no comment, but all the same the tightening of his temples and the lowering of his eyelids assured Nadya that he had heard and approved.

It was convenient and quick, it would save them having to look, true enough. But still, there was no particular need for them to stay in Inessa's room. It was just that Volodya disliked the unfamiliar, and anyway it was only for a short time. These were the best excuses she could offer her mother.

She had always felt humiliated in her mother's eyes. The feeling was less painful now than it had been, but it was still there.

However, Nadya had schooled herself to follow rigid rules. Volodya must not be deflected from his path by so much as a hairsbreadth. She must do everything to make his life easier, and never hamper him. She must always be there, but ready at any moment to efface herself when she was unwanted.

She had made her choice, and she must stick to it. She had shouldered the burden and must bear it. She must not permit herself a single hard word about her rival, although there was plenty she could say. She must always welcome her warmly, like a girlhood friend, so as not to spoil Volodya's good humor, or his standing with his comrades. She must join in their rambles and their reading sessions—*à trois*.

When it had all started—indeed, earlier, when Inessa, then a Sorbonne student with a red feather in her hat (no Russian woman revolutionary would have had the nerve to wear it), although she had two husbands and five children behind her, had first walked into their Paris apartment—before Volodya was half out of his chair, Nadya had seen vividly what was to come. Seen, too, her powerlessness to prevent it. And that it was her duty not to try.

Nadya had volunteered to remove herself. She would not be an obstacle in the life of such a man—there were obstacles enough already. More than once she had been on the verge of leaving him. But Volodya, after some thought, had told her to stay. He had made up his mind. Once and for all.

She was needed, then. Certainly, nobody else would get on so well with him. Resignation was made easier by the realization that no woman could claim such a man all to herself. It was enough of a vocation that she, among others, was useful to him. No less than the other one. Indeed, in many ways she was closer to him.

So she had stayed, determined never to stand in his way, never to show her hurt. Indeed, to train herself not to feel it, so that the hurt would burn itself out and die down. Instead of treating it gently she had prodded and inflamed the wound so as to cauterize it. So if there was some practical advantage in staying in what not so long ago had been Inessa's room, then that was where she would stay, without fretting about all the time Volodya had spent there in the past.

But with her mother there to see it . . .

It would soon be Cracow. Volodya was brightening up. Obviously, he had made some headway in his thinking.

No, the trip to Brussels went off splendidly, you mustn't regret it. My one regret is that you had no time to strike up a correspondence with Kautsky, as I told you to . . . (You would have written under your own name, but I would have discreetly drafted the letters for you.) What a low character he is! I hate and despise him more than anyone on earth. What filthy, rotten hypocrisy! It really is a pity we couldn't get that game going, we'd have had some sport with him!

Volodya had cheered up, and even whistled a little tune. Completely forgetting the lost case, he suggested eating, and took out the pocketknife which he always carried.

They spread out a napkin and produced a chicken, hard-boiled eggs, a bottle of milk, Galician bread, butter in oilpaper, salt in a little box.

Volodya even made a bit of a joke about his mother-in-law being a capitalist and a blot on his revolutionary biography.

Seriously, though, they must get their financial affairs settled, and swiftly. They had a lot of money in a Cracow bank—who could have expected war so soon?—a legacy from Nadya's aunt in Novocherkassk, her mother's sister, more than 4,000 rubles. And now it was bound to be confiscated as enemy alien property. What a blunder! At all costs he must find someone smart enough to squeeze the money out of them, then convert it into something safe—into gold, or maybe some of it into Swiss francs. And they must take it with them.

Then—to Vienna without delay. They must hurry up the visas and testimonials for Switzerland, and get there quickly. Austria-Hungary was a belligerent, anything might happen.

One thing to be said for the opportunists' International was that it never refused help to anyone in difficulties. And in every country it had what amounted to ministers of its own. On this occasion, Kuba had insisted that he should pay courtesy calls on Adler and Diamand, thank them all over again in person for obtaining his release (although he had already telegraphed his heartfelt gratitude), and, whatever happened, keep a civil tongue . . . Volodya smiled wryly, with specks of egg white and yolk around his mouth. It was certainly a tricky corner for him—having to go and make himself agreeable to moldy old revisionists, petit-bourgeois scum. After all, it was only fair: if loyalty to political principles was beyond them they could at least help him to live. That provided a concrete, practical platform for a temporary tactical understanding with them. Even in Switzerland he wouldn't be able to do without this bunch. He wouldn't be admitted without sponsors—and who else would sponsor him? (Robert Grimm is an overgrown schoolboy—I met him in Bern last year, when you, Inessa, were in the hospital.)

Ridicule left not a scratch on Lenin, no humiliation could get him down, he never felt ashamed—but all the same it was not easy for a man of forty-four to humble himself to younger men, to be so dependent on other people, to have no strength of his own.

If they hadn't left Geneva for Paris in 1908, they would not now have to fight their way into Switzerland, they would have been firmly and safely established there, with their own printing press, with connections, with all they needed. What had possessed them to move to Paris?

(If they hadn't gone to Paris, he would not have met Inessa.)

Last year, when you went to Kocher for treatment, Inessa, and we discovered what a good doctor is (Volodya had read the literature on goiter himself, and checked Kocher's methods), we should have had the sense to stay in Bern right then. Why not? If a revolutionary has to outlive Tsarism, and he is no longer twenty-five, his health counts as one of his weapons. It is also Party property. The Party's funds should be used ungrudgingly for its maintenance. He should live where there are excellent doctors, indeed as close as possible to the most eminent men in the profession—and that could only mean in Switzerland. You wouldn't go to Semashko for treatment—that would be too silly! As doctors our revolutionary comrades are a lot of donkeys. You wouldn't trust one of them to poke about inside you.

You're still far from well, Inessa. You ought to be closer to Kocher.

Yes, but, Volodya, the atmosphere in Switzerland is dreadfully petit bourgeois, remember how stuffy we always found it. Remember how they all shied away from us after the Tiflis "ex." In their country, you see, the law is sacrosanct, and they will not stand for crimes against property. And they call themselves Social Democrats!

All very true, but in Switzerland you'll never be in a fix like mine in Nowy Targ. Getting Semashko and Karpinsky out was child's play.

And what libraries they have! What a pleasure it always is to work there! And now, with a war on . . . ! No other place is so civilized and so comfortable.

A clean, well-scrubbed country, pleasant mountains, friendly guesthouses, limpid lakes with waterfowl on them.

The settling tank of the Russian revolution.

And because it was a neutral country the only place from which he could keep up his international contacts.

When he thought about it, when he reflected, what a joy it was—all Europe involved in a war such as it had never known before! The war which Marx and Engels had expected, but not lived to see. Such a war was the surest way to world revolution. The spark which they had fanned in vain in 1905 would burst unaided into a conflagration. There would never be a more propitious moment.

A presentiment quickened within him; this is it, the event you have lived to interpret and complete! Twenty-seven years of political self-education, books, pamphlets, party squabbles. An apathetic and ineffectual spectator during the first revolution. Regarded by everyone in the International as a disturber of the peace, an impertinent sectarian, leading a feeble, constantly dwindling little group calling itself a Party. All the time, without knowing it, you were waiting for this moment, and now the moment has come! The heavy wheel turns, gathering speed—like the red wheel of the engine—and you must keep up with its mighty rush. He who had never yet stood before the crowd, directing the movement of the masses, how was he to harness them to the wheel, to his own racing heart, check their impetus, and put them into reverse?

Cracow.

They put their coats on and collected their things.

Lenin got ready absentmindedly, only vaguely aware of their arrival and of what must be done.

They carried the baggage themselves, without a porter.

They were deafened by the noise: they had grown unused to crowds. And this was a different, wartime crowd. There were five times as many people on the platform as there would have been on a working day, and they were five times more worried and all in a hurry. Nuns, who shouldn't have been there at all, elbowed the travelers, thrusting holy pictures and prayer cards on them. Lenin hastily drew back his hand as though from something dirty. A freight car stood incongruously at a passenger platform, and people were carrying into it an endless succession of big boxes labeled "Flea Powder." Soldiers, civilians, railwaymen, and passengers jostled each other. Slowly and with difficulty they elbowed their way along the densely thronged platform. There was a big streamer on the station wall, with a slogan in red letters on yellow fabric: JEDEM RUSS—EIN SCHUSS!*

This had nothing at all to do with them, but he couldn't suppress a shudder.

* A bullet for every Russian!

The station hall was packed and stifling. They found a shady spot on a raised place against the side wall, at an angle to the square. The crowd there was denser than ever, and there were a lot of women. They settled Nadya's mother on a bench, with the luggage all around her, and Nadya went off to see Inessa's landlady. Vladimir Ilyich ran to buy newspapers and came back reading them as he walked, bumping into people, then perched himself on a hard suitcase, gripping the pile of papers between his elbows and his knees.

There was nothing particularly cheerful in the news. Reports on the battles in Galicia and in East Prussia were equally evasive, which meant that the Russians weren't doing too badly. But there were battles in France! War in Serbia! Who among the older generation of Socialists would ever have dreamed of such a thing?

The Socialists would be completely at a loss. They couldn't rise above their calls for peace. Those who weren't "defenders of the fatherland" were incapable of anything except yap and blather about "stopping the war."

As though anyone could. As though anyone had the strength to seize the racing engine wheel with his bare hands.

Piss-poor, slobbering pseudo-Socialists with the petit-bourgeois worm in them would try to capture the masses by jabbering away "for peace" and even "against annexations." And everybody would find it quite natural: against war means "for peace," doesn't it? They must be hit first and hit hard.

Which of them had the vision to see and the strength of mind to embrace the great decision ahead: not to try to stop the war, but to step it up. To transfer it—*to your own country*!

We won't say so openly, but we are *for* the war.

"Peace" is a slogan for fatheads and traitors. What is the point of a hollow peace that nobody needs, unless you can convert it immediately into *civil war with no quarter given*? Anyone who does *not* come out in favor of civil war must be branded as a traitor!

The main thing is a sober grasp of the balance of forces, a sober assessment of alliances. It is no good standing like silly priests between the embattled armies, arms raised, sleeves flapping. Germany must be seen from the start not as just another imperialist country, but as a mighty ally. To make a revolution we need weapons, troops, money, so we must look for someone with an interest in giving them to us. We must find channels for negotiation, covertly reassure ourselves that if difficulties arise in Russia and she starts suing for peace, Germany will not agree to peace talks, will not abandon the Russian revolutionaries to the whim of fate.

Germany! What power! What weapons! And what resolution she had shown in striking through Belgium! They knew that there would be howls of indignation, but didn't let it worry them. If fight they must, then fight they would. How resolute are the orders of their high command! Not a hint of Russian shilly-shallying there. (They had shown the same decisiveness in grabbing the Russian Social Democrats, and still more in releasing them.)

Germany will undoubtedly win this war. And so she is the best, the natural ally against the Tsar.

The carrion crow in the Russian coat of arms is trapped at last. You're caught by the foot, you'll never pull free! This war was of your own choosing! Now you'll be cut down to size, shorn of everything as far as Kiev, as far as Kharkov, as far as Riga! We'll thrash the imperial spirit out of you! Die, damn you, die! All you're good for is oppressing others. Russia will be completely dismembered. Poland and Finland must be detached. And the Baltic lands. And the Ukraine. And the Caucasus. Die, damn you!

There was a hubbub on the concourse and the crowd surged in their direction, as far as the platform barrier, where the police held them back. What was going on? A train had pulled in. A hospital train. Perhaps the first such train, after the first major battle. A path was cleared through the crowd to give the file of waiting ambulances room to turn around. Hefty, grim-looking orderlies quickly passed stretcher after stretcher from the train to the ambulances. Women pressed forward from every side, trying to struggle through the crowd, eagerly, fearfully craning to catch a glimpse of gray faces barely visible among bandages and sheets, dreading to discover their men. There were shrieks of recognition or disappointment, and the crowd closed in tighter and pulsed like a single being.

Though the raised place where the Ulyanovs were sitting was some distance away, they could see it all. But Lenin, to get a better view, rose and went nearer to the parapet.

There weren't enough ambulances and stretchers, and instead of waiting some of the wounded were leaving the platform on their own feet, supported by nurses—pale figures in gray hospital smocks or blue greatcoats, with thickly bandaged heads, necks, shoulders, arms, some walking gingerly, some firmer on their feet—and now the waiting crowd would not be held, but swarmed toward them, shrilly, joyfully, yelling, embracing and kissing dear ones and strangers alike, taking them over from the nurses, carrying their kit bags, while above them, over all those heads, borne aloft by male hands, mugs of frothy beer and white plates of roast meat floated out from the restaurant.

By the parapet, refreshed and excited, stood the man in the black bowler, with his untrimmed ginger beard, his brows knit in concentration, his eyes sharp and eager, and he too had one hand raised, with the fingers splayed as though holding a great beer mug, he too swallowed painfully as though he had been in the trenches and was parched for want of that drink. His probing gaze widened and contracted, widened and contracted as he seized on every detail in the scene which might be turned to use.

A joyful inspiration took shape in his dynamic mind, one of the most powerful, swiftest, and surest decisions of his life. The smell of printer's ink from the newspapers, the smell of blood and medicines from the station hall evaporated—and suddenly, like a soaring eagle following the movements of a little golden lizard, you have eyes only for the one truth that matters, your heart pounds, like an eagle you swoop down on it, seize it by its trembling tail as it is vanishing into a crevice in the rock, and you tug and tug and rise into the air unfurling it like a ribbon, like a streamer bearing the slogan: TRANSFORM THIS WAR INTO CIVIL WAR! And this war, this war will bring all the governments of Europe down in ruins!

He stood by the parapet, looking down on the square with his hands raised, as though he had taken his place for a speech but was not quite ready to begin.

Daily, hourly, wherever you may be, *protest* angrily and uncompromisingly against the war! But . . . (The dialectic essence of the situation.) But . . . *will* it to continue! See that it does not stop short! That it drags on and is *transformed*! A war like this one must not be fumbled, must not be wasted.

Such a war is a gift from history!

[2 3]

(REVIEW OF EVENTS TO 26 AUGUST)

General Zhilinsky's bold raven eye took in only the corner of East Prussia around the Masurian Lakes. Yet a German schoolboy could have looked at the map and told him that this was not enough: that the whole East Prussian stump, thrust out eastward and caught under the armpit by the kingdom of Poland, was vulnerable to a Russian attack. Russia's plan should have been self-evident: it should have amputated Prussia. From the Niemen in the east, where the German army would in any case not take the offensive and so extend its vulnerable arm, the Russians should have deployed a modest covering force merely to draw off German troops from elsewhere. The main Russian force should have advanced northward from the Narew to squeeze the Germans under its arm.

The Germans, in such an unfavorable position, might have temporarily abandoned East Prussia—except that, far though it was from Germany, this was their very own land. Here were the roots of the Teutonic Order, here was the cradle of Prussia's kings. This land must be held whatever the inconveniences.

During the annual maneuvers the German High Command had more than once tested the situation that might arise, and devised a forceful counterstroke: they would use the network of highroads and railway lines, further developed with this in mind, to slip out of the trap in the first two or three days of the war, then strike a heavy blow at the flank of the main enemy concentration, stunning it, crushing it, or in some versions surrounding it.

True, they were less apprehensive after the Russo-Japanese war, and standing instructions included the following:

"We need not expect the Russian High Command either to exploit favorable circumstances quickly or to maneuver with speed and precision. Russian troops move extremely slowly, and there are great holdups in issuing, transmitting, and carrying out orders. We can permit ourselves maneuvers on the Russian front which would be impossible with any other enemy."

Low as their estimate was of this future enemy, Russian behavior in August 1914 astounded the Germans. What advanced from the east was not a covering force to distract the Germans but five infantry and six cavalry divisions, including the Guards division, the elite of St. Petersburg, while to the south the Russians made no effort to cross the frontier at all.

Here was a riddle. Why were the Russian armies not synchronizing their movements? Why was the southern army not hastening to anticipate the eastern and complete the encirclement? Should this be interpreted as a strategic innovation on the part of the Russians? Were they ignoring the fashionable theories of encirclement, intending simply to shove the enemy out, to send him reeling backward, which would obviously be in keeping with the ingenuous Russian national character (*das russische Gemüt*)?

However that might be, all they could do for the time being was strike at Rennenkampf's army on the Niemen. The quicker, the better—a protracted operation might be disastrous. General von Prittwitz, commanding the army in Prussia, threw almost all his forces to its eastern extremity. Victory should have been assured: Rennenkampf with all his underemployed cavalry was so unaware of the enemy's approach that he had declared 20 August—the day on which battle was joined—a day of rest. As a result his cavalry did not fight at all and each of his infantry divisions fought its own battle. All the same, the Germans were punished that day for their disrespect for the enemy: the standing instruction listing the failings of the Russian High Command had neglected to mention the Russian infantry's powers of endurance and its excellent marksmanship—losing the war with Japan had taught the Russians something. Prittwitz's army at Gumbinnen, in spite of its two-to-one superiority in artillery, was cut about and lost the battle.

On the evening of this dreadful day Prittwitz received a report that German planes had also spotted large Russian forces in the south. Even if he had won at Gumbinnen he would have had to pull back rapidly and disengage from Rennenkampf. After losing the battle, Prittwitz was inclined to withdraw all the way beyond the Vistula and abandon East Prussia.

But the disengagement went very smoothly. The Germans maneuvered as though the eastern Russian army did not exist; that same evening they left the front line, put a day's march between themselves and the enemy overnight, and then, unobserved by Russian planes, sank into the landscape and withdrew to the far end of Prussia. They left behind only one cavalry division and some weak Landwehr infantry to keep an eye on

Rennenkampf's army. Throughout the day following the battle, 21 August, again on the 22nd, and even on the morning of the 23rd, Rennenkampf (here was a second startling Russian riddle!) did not race after the enemy to trample and destroy him, to seize space, roads, and cities, but instead stood still, allowed a gap of sixty kilometers to develop, and even then moved only with the greatest caution.

In one night and one day Prittwitz had successfully pulled his three corps out of Rennenkampf's reach, and decided not to withdraw across the Vistula after all but to regroup and strike at the left flank of Samsonov's army as it approached from the south. Because—and this was the third Russian riddle!—the Russian southern army, which was under close aerial observation from day to day, was making no attempt either to probe Scholtz's corps, which was screening Prussia as with an obliquely held shield, or to encircle it, or even to attack head-on, but was confidently advancing slantwise into empty space, exposing its flank to Scholtz as it passed him by.

However, the situation report sent to his superiors by Prittwitz himself, and the wave of alarm caused in Berlin by the refugees streaming out of Prussia, stirred things up. On 22 August the German General Staff decided to replace Prittwitz. The new Chief of Staff of the Prussian army was the forty-nine-year-old Ludendorff, fresh from his triumph in Belgium: "You may yet save the situation for us and prevent the worst from happening." He was received by Wilhelm on the evening of the 22nd, decorated for the taking of Liège, and in the course of the night got together on a special eastbound train from Koblenz with the new army commander, Hindenburg, the crusty sixty-seven-year-old general who had on occasion criticized the Kaiser's conduct of maneuvers but had now been recalled from retirement. From the train they ordered the German forces to regroup—exactly as Prittwitz had already regrouped them. (All senior German officers without exception had been brought up on the military doctrine of Moltke the Elder: it told them that commanders of genius are rare exceptions, and that the fate of the nation cannot depend on such happy chances, but that military science enables even men of average ability to implement a victorious strategy.)

The picture as the outside world saw it was one of German defeat in Prussia, but the French Ministry of Foreign Affairs, faced with the irresistible breakthrough of German might from the north, succumbed to its own panicky imaginings or else to deliberate misinformation from somewhere and on 24 August sent a hysterical telegram to its ambassador in St. Petersburg: "According to information from a most reliable source," the Germans had transferred two front-line corps from Prussia to France, in view of which the ambassador should once more insist on an immediate Russian offensive against Berlin. The German General Staff had indeed withdrawn two corps—the Guards reserve corps and the 11th Army Corps—but in the opposite direction, from the battle on the Marne and the right wing of the German forces advancing on Paris, to Prussia. Count von Moltke the Younger had taken this difficult decision on receiving the news of the German defeat the day before at Orlau. That was an intolerable postscript to the defeat at Gumbinnen. Germany could not give up Prussia even temporarily. At the same time, according to the great Schlieffen Plan the main thrust was to be on Germany's right wing, with the object of taking Paris and getting the French off their hands in the first forty days of war. (After the "miracle on the Marne" Moltke too was dismissed.) Thus the German seizure of Paris, and in consequence the whole German war effort, was thwarted by the unsung General Martos's corps in a battle which history has mislaid.

Meanwhile, the Russians had set the Germans a fourth riddle with their uncoded wireless messages! A car overtook Ludendorff en route to pass to him intercepted messages, and he received others after his arrival—radio messages between 2nd Army HQ and Corps HQ as well as something like a dozen messages from the 1st Army on 24 August, indicating the exact positions of various Russian army corps, their objectives and their movements, the extent of their ignorance (total) about the enemy, followed on the morning of the 25th by a full set of the 2nd Army's redeployment orders. It became quite clear that the 1st Army would do nothing to save the 2nd from defeat.

But perhaps all this openness was intended to mislead? No—the reports from reconnaissance aircraft, from scouts left behind, from voluntary defense organizations and telephone calls from local residents, all concurred. Had any army in military history ever had such a clear view of the enemy, such a complete map of his movements? What might have been a complicated campaign in a country dotted with lakes and barricaded with forests of twenty-meter pines had been made as simple for the Germans as a training exercise.

The four riddles had a single solution: the Russians were incapable of coordinating the movements of large bodies of men. That being so, the Germans could risk abandoning their flanking movement in favor of encirclement. The map begged them, the map implored them, the map itself showed them how to plot a twentieth-century Cannae.

It was tempting to try to surround the whole of Samsonov's army, but it had spread out in all directions and the German forces were too small for the purpose. They decided therefore to push the outlying corps back from Usdau and Bischofsburg and so open corridors for the insertion of pincers. For this purpose, the German units had spent more than four days redeploying. General von François's corps was transferred by rail diagonally right across Prussia. Mackensen's corps and Below's (according to Rennenkampf's report both of these had been smashed, and their remnants had taken refuge in Königsberg) had covered eighty kilometers at normal marching speed, enjoyed a peaceful day's rest to put themselves in order, and on the morning of 26 August delivered a stunning blow to Komarov's carelessly exposed division.

This, 26 August, was the day on which Samsonov at last moved his headquarters to Neidenburg, where toasts were drunk to the capture of Berlin under the very tip of the unsheathed and fast-extending claw, and to the rumble of German artillery close at hand using its seven-to-one superiority against Mingin's division at Mühlen. The day when Martos's corps, in its dash past Scholtz, tangled with him more and more frequently, rounded on him, and harried him with great courage and success. The same day on which Klyuev's corps, totally unaware that there were enemy forces anywhere around, raced over sandy terrain to what should have been the empty north—and into a trap, a wolf pit; raced on verst after unretraceable verst, for each of which it would pay in battalions. The same day—26 August—on which the Russian General Staff was already elaborating its plan to pull Rennenkampf out of "conquered" East Prussia, and on which Zhilinsky informed Rennenkampf by telegram that his main objective should be to lay siege to Königsberg fortress (where superannuated Landsturm troops had taken shelter) and to pin down the Germans (who were not there to be pinned) on the coast, so as to prevent them from reaching the Vistula (which was not what they were trying to do).

In spite of which the Prussian High Command did not consider 26 August a very good day. One disappointment was that they had not intercepted a single uncoded Russian wireless message in twenty-four hours, so that their view of the Russian positions, which only a little while ago had been so clear, was clouded and confused by many unknown movements.

Although they had smashed Komarov's division, Mackensen and Below advanced in the region of Lake Dadey with the caution learned at Gumbinnen and this caution proved wise: at Rothfliess station on the evening of the 26th the Russians put up a stout resistance, apparently with considerable forces. (They had to wait for the morning of the 27th before German fliers discovered Blagoveshchensky's corps falling back in much greater disorder than would have seemed possible the previous day.) The resistance to the death of two Russian regiments south of Mühlen blinded Hindenburg to the fact that in this sector the gap he needed already yawned: in his orders he wrote that the Russians had more than a corps there. Failing to see this ready-made gap, the Germans tried forcing a way through at Usdau.

The ends of the thick pincers seemed reluctant to close.

The shadow of Providence (*Vorsehung*) fell too on that fortified line at Mühlen, on those lakeside cliffs, on the five-hundred-year-old firs of the beloved ancestral land where the Russian 2nd Army was now so violently and so vulnerably advancing: to this place the united forces of Slavdom had come in 1410 and shattered the Teutonic Knights near the little village of Tannenberg, between Hohenstein and Usdau.

Half a millennium later fate had so arranged things that Germany could exact retribution (*das Strafgericht*).

[2 4]

No natural gift brings nothing but joy. There is always some grief to go with it. But no one suffers more for his talent than a gifted officer. The army serves a brilliant man enthusiastically—once he has grasped his field marshal's baton. Before that, while he is only reaching for the baton, the army raps his fingers repeatedly. Discipline, on which the army is founded, is always hostile to a man of talent, and all that is pulsating in him and straining to break through must be contained, forced to conform and to submit. All those who are for the time being his superiors find such a self-willed subordinate intolerable. As a result, he is promoted more slowly than the mediocrities.

General von François had arrived in East Prussia as Chief of Staff of an army corps in 1903. Ten years later, now nearly sixty, he had been posted there again to command a corps—the best, it is true, in the German army.

In 1903 Count von Schlieffen had supervised a staff exercise there, and François had been put in command of one of the "Russian" armies. It was on him that Schlieffen had demonstrated his pincer movement. In his summary he had written: "The Russian army laid down its arms under threat of encirclement from the flank and the rear." François had cheekily protested: "Excellency! As long as I command it the Russian army will never lay down its arms!" Schlieffen laughed and added these words: "Realizing the hopelessness of his army's situation its commander sought and found death in the front line."

In real warfare that is just the sort of thing that never happens. But it is what General Hermann von François would have been ready to do to avoid disgrace. His Huguenot family did not regard the country which had given them shelter simply as a temporary refuge. They had come to know and to serve Germany and only Germany as their native land. François's great-grandfather had earned ennoblement in Germany before the guillotine was introduced in France. His father, also a general, wounded by the French in 1870, cried, "I am glad to be dying at a moment when Germany appears to be winning!"

In 1913 François had taken over his command in East Prussia with instructions to carry out a "defensive withdrawal": faced with superior enemy forces he would retreat, hitting back as he went. But that was a misinterpretation of the late Schlieffen's plan! Defensive action on the eastern front as a whole until the German armies in the west could disengage did not at all mean that withdrawal was the correct tactic in every sector. François compared the German and the Russian characters and decided that speedy attack best suited the German soldier and his training, whereas the Russian character was distinguished by aversion to any sort of methodical work, absence of any sense of duty, fear of responsibility, and total inability to value time and use it to the full. Hence the sluggishness of Russian generals, their inclination to act mechanically, their hankering after peace and comfort. François's choice in East Prussia was, therefore, to carry out an offensive defense, to attack the Russians first, wherever they appeared.

When the Great War began (a great war for Germany, and a great and eagerly awaited war for François, who now had a unique opportunity to prove himself his country's and perhaps Europe's best commander in the field), his intention was to make the most of Germany's rapid mobilization, and as soon as his corps was on a war footing to cross the frontier and attack Rennenkampf's forces while they were assembling in their usual leisurely fashion. He soon found that not even the German army can recognize and accept an excessively dynamic talent. Prittwitz vetoed François's plan: "We must reconcile ourselves to sacrificing part of the province" (Prussia). François could not accept that. He defiantly attacked Stallupönen, but at the height of a battle which seemed to him to be going well a car drove up with orders from Prittwitz to terminate the action and withdraw in the direction of Gumbinnen. But if the army had plans of its own, so did the Corps Commander! François answered the courier loudly enough for his officers to hear: "Inform General von Prittwitz that General von François will terminate the action as soon as the Russians are routed!" Alas, they were not routed, and his own Chief of Staff denounced him to Army HQ. That evening François tried to explain himself, but Prittwitz reported his insubordination to the Emperor, while François himself informed the Emperor that he could not fight with his present Chief of Staff! He was taking a risk. The Emperor had received many complaints already, and regarded the general as "an excessively independent character." Here was an excuse to get angry and relieve him of his command. At the same time, to tolerate a hostile Chief of Staff would hardly be the mark of an outstanding commander!

However hard he tried to renounce or suppress his inheritance, at heart he was still an ungovernable Frenchman.

But, separated as he was from the High Command, he owed it to himself to ensure that the scales of justice were held even. It was essential to explain every step as he took it, for history and for posterity. No one would do it for you if you did not attend to it yourself. So all the time he was fighting with an energy and agility extraordinary in one of his age, with skill and with relish, climbing church towers to inspect the terrain, superintending the unloading of shells (which would no doubt have been unloaded without his help), rushing by cart to wherever there was fighting to make sure that the situation was as described in his orders, sometimes swallowing no more than a single cup of cocoa all day (that was for the benefit of his memoirs—there was in fact the occasional beefsteak), sleeping two or three hours a night, François still did not neglect to make sure that every decision he took was recorded and explained three times over: in orders to his subordinates, in reports to his superiors, and in a detailed account for the military archives (and, if he survived, his own book), an account not just of his actions, but of intentions on which he was not always authorized to act. Before the fighting began he wrote it all down himself, and afterward he invariably took a special aide-de-camp with him in one of his two cars—his own son, a lieutenant, whose job was to keep the general's diary and record his thoughts as they came to him.

The general felt compelled to put his whole line of conduct into his own words. Nobody would deal more stylishly with the crucial question: Should one simply obey orders, which is always the easiest thing to do, or should one acknowledge a greater responsibility, a higher duty than simple obedience? Should one suppress all fear of failure, ignore the warnings of timid souls, and trust the promptings of instinct?

He found himself at odds with Prittwitz again in the battle of Gumbinnen. In its early hours François had already decided that the battle was a great victory (as he reported to Prittwitz, and Prittwitz to the General Staff). He stepped up his attack, outflanking Rennenkampf (though his critics maintain that he attacked head-on because he had misjudged the distribution of the Russian forces), took many prisoners, gave orders that evening to renew the attack on the following day—and at that point received Prittwitz's order that all corps were to withdraw in the night without making a sound, and not stop that side of the Vistula.

This was intolerably bad luck: to lose all at once everything that your talent had so far accomplished, just because Mackensen, your neighbor, was fighting unsuccessfully; to abandon tomorrow's success with its scent already in your nostrils; to cancel your own correct order and submit to an incorrect one.

But that's the army for you. Fresh from the field of victory, his victory, with his whole being still throbbing to the music of battle, he began the long "castling" movement by train via Königsberg.

That's the army. But there was more to the German army than that. The following day the central telephone service was busy hunting down François, linking one line to another, until it finally connected his dot on the map with Koblenz, and His Majesty the Emperor begged to be informed how the general saw the situation, and whether in his view the decision to transfer his corps was the correct one.

That was a high honor for a corps commander (and a plain indication that the Army Commander was about to be dismissed). But François's nimble mind did not dwell on his injured dignity and the way in which his correct views had been ignored the day before: what was correct yesterday was no longer correct today. As Napoleon had said, a general who lets his imagination run away with him cannot be a great commander in the field. The withdrawal once begun must be carried through to the end. Having abandoned the field to the army on the Niemen, he must now demonstrate his exceptional ability against the army on the Narew.

At some point no longer traceable, between telephone calls, the journeys by special train, and his meeting with the new commanders at the new HQ (they were all old acquaintances: François had once been Chief of Staff in Hindenburg's corps, while Ludendorff, now so exalted, was nine years his junior and had once been his subordinate on the General Staff), a new idea ripened: that of encircling the army on the Narew by a double pincer movement. Each of the three felt that he was its author ("It will be for history to prove that I, and no one else, produced it and carried it out").

On the evening of 24 August (just as Vorotyntsev appeared at the sleepy headquarters in Ostrolenka) General von François was already sitting in the Kronprinz Hotel, not far from the spot at which the first trains were unloading forces to confront Samsonov's left flank, and writing his order of the day.

"The brilliant victories of the corps at Stallupönen and Gumbinnen have prompted the Supreme Command to transfer you, soldiers of the 1st Army Corps, here by rail, so that you may by your invincible bravery smite this new foe who has appeared from Russian Poland. When we destroy this enemy we shall return to our previous position and deal with the Russian hordes there who are burning down our native towns in defiance of international law . . ."

François, looking forward to his inexorable return, was writing in the lower western corner of East Prussia, while his troops were still entraining in the upper eastern corner near Königsberg, and train after train chugged from one end of Prussia to the other. The Germans had faltered for twelve hours, and then performed another of their miracles: troop trains left at half-hour intervals, day and night, and even the German railway regulations lost their binding force—trains ran almost buffer to buffer on open track between stations, they entered sectors regardless of red signals, they took twenty-five minutes instead of two hours to unload at special military platforms. At François's request the trains pulled up as close as possible to tomorrow's battlefield, leaving the battalions with a mere five kilometers to walk, just far enough to stretch their legs.

The heavy-jowled ones, Hindenburg and Ludendorff, were no more appreciative of this miracle than of the others. They arrived at François's command post while nearly all of his artillery was still on the way, and demanded that he begin the offensive which they avidly awaited.

François's eyes, though he was quite unaware of it, always had a sarcastic glint. "If those are my orders," he said, "I shall begin, but my men will have to fight—I hardly like to say it—with the bayonet."

It was all right for the Russians to insist that "the bullet's a blunderer, the bayonet's the boy" (shells were of course even sillier), but Schlieffen's pupils should have understood by now that the era of heavy armaments had arrived, and that victory would go to those who had superior firepower. It was all right to talk about invincible bravery in orders to your troops, but your job was to add up batteries and rounds of ammunition.

Why, oh why were the ablest always subordinate to those of lesser talent? François's heart sank as he was compelled to contemplate, a meter before him and so far above him, these two "strong-willed," beefy faces mounted with the aid of thick, rigid necks on solid trunks. (Ludendorff's jaw was not yet so grimly set, his gaze not yet so stony and expressionless, but it already strongly resembled that of his commanding officer. Hindenburg's face was almost rectangular, his features coarse and heavy, the bags under his eyes bulged, his nose had no bridge, his mustaches seemed to droop under their own weight, his ears had amalgamated with his cheeks. What could these two know about the promptings of intuition, and calculated risk?)

(François omitted to change places with them mentally and examine himself with their eyes: This little whippersnapper doesn't *look* like a general, his eye movements are far too quick for a man of his age; worst of all, he has that bad habit of interrupting, evading the issue, changing the subject abruptly.)

Right now, for instance, the question was where to attack. François wouldn't listen to the instructions they gave him—he had suggestions of his own, he wanted to catch the Russian 1st Corps and the whole of Samsonov's army in the same trap. And he *would* argue! They were at it for a whole hour. They vetoed it. They ordered him to drive off the 1st Corps and once it was out of the way encircle the nucleus of the army. As to when he should attack, François had to bargain hard for half a day's postponement—from dawn till midday on 26 August.

Because it was neither the place nor the time he would have chosen, he began the attack halfheartedly, and on the first day his operations were perfunctory. He put pressure on the enemy's forward cover, and the Russian regiments took their stand in clearly visible positions on high ground: the line ran from the hill with a windmill through Usdau and on along the railway embankment. It was through Usdau that he must open up the way to Neidenburg on 27 August.

The preliminary skirmishes petered out at sunset. The rest of the artillery was to move in and take up position during the night, with bigger guns, and a more rapid rate of fire than the Russians had ever before experienced. Tomorrow at 4 a.m. he, General von François, would begin the main battle.

"But what if the Russians start first, in the night, *mein General*?" asked his son, who was still writing by a dark lantern.

They were in a hayloft. The general was too squeamish to sleep in a house in which Russians had previously made themselves at home. He wound up his alarm clock and put it under his pillow, pulled off his boots and stretched out his short legs to their full extent, and eased his creaky joints before replying with a yawning smile: "Remember this, my boy: the Russians never move before lunch if they can help it."

* * *

Con moto

Leader: *Jerry must have eaten henbane,*
Jerry's fighting mad!

Chorus: *Ooh you! Oh you! Eh you! Ah you!*
Jerry's fighting mad!

Leader: *Jerry's army's marching at us,*
Vas Cat-whiskers struts ahead!

Chorus: *Ooh you! Oh you! Eh you! Ah you!*
Vas Cat-whiskers struts ahead!

("Russian soldiers' song, 1914." A picture postcard shows our heroes marching to the drum, with the cat poor Wilhelm [conventionally translated into Russian as Vasily], and supplies the tune to these words.)

[2 5]

How irksome and inopportune it had all been: the war itself, which was an interruption to General Artamonov's career; the deployment of his corps dangerously far to the left, closest to Germany; being made to move still farther forward from Soldau; those reports of the enemy's great strength; their first attack on the very day when this colonel, this spy from GHQ, arrived; those telegraphic exchanges intended to tighten the noose around the general's neck.

Till then Artamonov had advanced smoothly from peak to peak, effortlessly collecting promotions and decorations (first-class) along the way. True, he had not shirked, he had worked zealously for his advancement. Everybody went to cadet school—he had attended two; everybody went to a military academy—he had done time in two (and indeed been admitted to three—at one he had failed). It was harder for him to sit still than for other people because his strong legs demanded movement and his sinews ached when he was not running around. But he had been lucky enough to serve for ten years on "special assignments," or as senior adjutant on the staff of a military district, or "at the disposal of the General Staff," and he had rushed around the Amur basin, rushed off to the Boers, rushed off to Abyssinia, and even rushed around the Central Asian provinces of his own country on camelback. He was tireless. He served honorably, gave of his best. He was in his element when traveling—setting off, arriving, moving on were what he enjoyed, not fighting; war involved not only movement but possible damage to his advancement if things went wrong. The war against the Boxer rebels, however, had brought both enjoyment and rewards. In the war with Japan too he had successfully jumped out of the Mukden cul-de-sac, abandoned half a hundred mud-hut hamlets to the yellow-skinned ones without regret. But this war was off to a bad start. Aerial reconnaissance had reported that Artamonov was faced by two divisions—then, suddenly, it was two corps. The Germans had some terrible scheme up their sleeves. How could he penetrate the riddle? How protect himself? Artamonov had been wearing a military uniform all his life, but only now did he feel menaced by the mysteriousness of war. The impossibility of guessing what the enemy intended to do to him tomorrow and of thinking what to do in reply kept him rushing frantically not just from room to room in his headquarters but over the whole area occupied by the corps. Twice a day his automobile enveloped the whole locality in dust. Ostensibly he was inspecting and encouraging his troops, but in reality he was totally perplexed and demoralized. He knew that he must keep morale up, but beyond that had no idea what to do—he honestly hadn't. In the middle of the day the Germans began their offensive and Artamonov in desperation decided for himself to do what his staff had been unable to force him to do—make a little attack: two regiments on the left flank advanced five versts still farther west and took a big village. But was it a good thing? Was it the right thing? It was beneath a corps commander to ask anyone's advice, least of all that of a colonel sent to spy on him by GHQ. He did, however, need to do some hard thinking and try to find out how influential this colonel was, how deep in the confidence of the Supreme Commander he was, and what intrigue had brought him here. So Artamonov said nothing to Vorotyntsev about his fears and his preoccupations, but put a brave front on it and made small talk: "They say Germany's strength lies in order and system, but that is also her weakness. Once we start fighting unsystematically, in a disorderly fashion, you'll see, they'll be completely at a loss."

This colonel stuck like a burr. When, late in the evening after the fighting had died down, the Corps Commander decided to make the rounds of his positions and encourage his troops, the colonel volunteered yet again to go along with him, and would not be put off. A bad omen. And indeed every question he asked, everything he said along the way was a malicious attempt to catch the general out. Leaving Soldau, they flashed their headlights as they passed some troops and the colonel put on an act, remarking that he didn't seem to see any fortifications, didn't see the trenches which the corps must have dug around the town during its four days there—but perhaps he had just failed to notice them? They talked about that day's fighting, and he started shaking his head because a regiment had been moved from the right flank, leaving a gap there. Artamonov took him down a peg by telling him that Shtempel's cavalry brigade had moved in to fill it, but immediately after that they drove into a village and found that Shtempel's brigade was spending the night there and had no thought of moving out before morning. Artamonov gave Shtempel a dressing-down. But if you rode around prying into everything you could find fault with everybody. The colonel from GHQ ended by asking point-blank, and with unconcealed disrespect, what plan the Corps Commander had for the following day.

Plan? (Not a very Russian word somehow!) The only possible plan, but I'm not such a simpleton as to mention it out loud! The plan was to pull the whole corps out of this tight corner safely and in such a way that the commander would get a medal, not a black mark. But he could not put such a simple plan into words. The colonel must certainly have great connections or he would not so casually come out with what were practically orders—telling the general that since his command was twice as large as a corps, and since his left flank with its cavalry divisions could maneuver freely, he could lash out at the German flank tomorrow with this extended and mobile flank of his—there was still time to distribute orders and realign his units. All of which was supposed to be for Artamonov's own good.

Thank you, we know very well what's good for us! But he had indeed suffered a great misfortune—the number of troops under his command had doubled that day, and his headache was twice as bad as before. He had been rash enough to raise the alarm and complain to Army HQ that the enemy was concentrating in his sector and Samsonov had replied by putting at his disposition the two cavalry divisions and all the troops (the Warsaw Guards division and a separate rifle brigade) which had arrived too late to join the still incomplete 23rd Corps. The Army Commander now "felt assured that even superior enemy forces will not be able to break the stubborn resistance of the glorious troops of the 1st Corps." Artamonov telegraphed a reply in the same high style, thanking "his valiant commander for his confidence." That confidence froze Artamonov's blood: how was he to bear such a cross?

This cock crowing, these cuckoo calls, filled Vorotyntsev with blind hatred. That the clipped and sober language of soldiers was replaced by the fulsomeness of courtiers complimenting each other on their valor was a fatal mark of weakness, unimaginable in the German army. This great force had been assembled on the left flank of Samsonov's army, and action must be taken without so much as half an hour's delay, yet there they were tapping out compliments to each other. The Kexholm Life Guards Regiment had detrained earlier and marched to the right, to Neidenburg, to try to overtake its own corps, the 23rd. But today the Lithuanian Life Guards had detrained in Mlawa, and that regiment would now find itself under Artamonov's command. (While two other regiments of the Warsaw "yellow" Guards were not in Warsaw at all, and nobody knew where the Division Commander, General Sirelius, was skulking.) As for the 1st Rifle Brigade, it was one of the newest and most highly trained fighting units in the whole Russian army. The troops which their car was now overtaking were battalions of the 1st Brigade moving up to forward positions.

If the left flank of the 2nd Army had stood firm, jutting out like a horn from its lines, the partial withdrawal during the past day would have given no cause for alarm, and it would not have been too terrible if they had closed their ranks even further. But by now the left flank was not so much a horn as a crushed shoulder.

But whatever you said to Artamonov there was no meeting of minds, and no hope of a response. All Vorotyntsev's hints and suggestions and ideas bounced off that smoothly sculpted marble brow. It was no use even discussing with him what they had learned that evening, that the German troops confronting them were François's 1st Corps, which though "shattered" by Rennenkampf at Gumbinnen had precipitately resurfaced right here. There was some sort of plan behind that, and a menacing one.

Vorotyntsev had spent the whole day with the corps command and seen all he needed of its bustling, fusspot general. A touch of gray at the temples and in the walrus mustache, epaulets and aiguillettes lend dignity and nobility to any idiot and make it hard to see the man as he really is and always has been. But if you try hard enough you will see that you have before you, disguised as a general, somebody who would make an excellent private soldier provided he had a strict NCO over him: keen, quick on his feet, never still for a minute, eager to be in on everything, and probably unafraid of bullets. Alternatively he would make a pretty good deacon: tall, well built, with quite a good voice, assiduously censing every nook and cranny, endowed with a certain histrionic talent, and perhaps also a genuine devotion to the service of God.

But why should he be an infantry general? Why should sixty thousand Russian fighting men be in the power of someone so imprudent?

Now, for instance, he had dashed off to make the rounds of his units by night—and what had he left behind at headquarters? Who was carrying out reconnaissance? What sort of linkup was there between the infantry and the artillery? How many rounds per gun had been brought up, and would there be wheels and boxes enough to move them backward and forward with the movement of the battle? Artamonov did not really know and did not even know that he ought to know. Why, in the day just over, had his corps been rolled back in places by an attack in moderate strength? Artamonov showed no anxiety to discover the reasons, and would not have relished hearing them from Vorotyntsev. Riding like this by car over the battlefield might have been a good way for a clever general to survey his unraveling forces, to visit every sector while there was still time for him to put everything right in person. But add motorcar wheels to nimble and senselessly active legs and you have a disaster. Yet nobody would suspect Artamonov of indecision. He appeared undaunted by his responsibilities. He took advice from no one and you needed a good ear to detect the bewilderment in his voice.

They drove along the dark road, headlights blazing. The trunks of trees lining the road, bushes, houses, barns, road barriers, marching troops, carts looked lifeless and unfamiliar in the white glare. Those coming toward them were dazzled. Now and then soldiers turned to look at them from the depths of the darkness, and individuals in their path hobbled quickly to safety or whipped up their horses.

If Vorotyntsev's journey had ever had any sense it was now exhausted. He was authorized only to carry out "staff reconnaissance": to acquaint himself personally with the situation and correct intelligence reports previously received. He had done more than enough for this purpose. The danger now was that his findings would reach HQ too late, and his soldierly duty was to rush back to Army HQ and GHQ. He had no authority to hang around the necks of staff officers and line commanders. He might, of course, do a great deal to improve matters by attaching himself to Artamonov like a limpet, looking over his shoulder while he made his decisions, and warning him against mistakes. Artamonov, however, suspiciously rejected such tutelage, and Vorotyntsev for that matter was having great difficulty in forcing himself to stay with Artamonov any longer. All things come to him who waits. But patience was not one of Vorotyntsev's virtues. No, he could not bring himself to complete this nocturnal round of inspection with the general. They had started it at Usdau, which was twenty versts away from Army HQ by the highroad—and that was where he decided to break off.

The village of Usdau was situated on a broad elevation, as the movement of the car told them. Oil lamps had been lit in some houses, while others were in darkness, but you could tell from the number of horses and soldiers that every house, barn, and yard must be crammed full. Low fires were burning in several field kitchens, screened from the enemy by a high wall.

They pulled up behind a red-brick Gothic church and extinguished the headlights. They had sent word ahead and Major General Savitsky hurried out to report. To disguise the untidiness of the arrangements, he was called "sector commander," but, simply put, he commanded a brigade with only one regiment on the spot (the 85th, Vyborg Regiment) —and that had a regimental commander of its own. The brigade's other regiment had got stuck in Warsaw. (The slovenliness did not end there: the Vyborg Regiment's neighbor to the left was another division short a regiment, which was also in Warsaw, and farther left still were two regiments belonging to the same division as the Vyborg, which had taken the offensive that day. The Division Commander, General Dushkevich, was there with them. It would have been hard to create a more intricate muddle deliberately.)

Artamonov expressed a wish to see the brigade's positions. Savitsky took them around the houses, by the diffused light from windows. He was gray-headed but his bearing was that of a fit young man. In the starlit darkness his voice and his sensible way of explaining things confirmed this impression. The Vyborg Regiment had occupied this strong key position after being forced back the previous day. A hundred meters in front of the village, where the high ground began to slope down toward the enemy, a continuous line of trenches had been drawn and the soldiers were still digging themselves in deeper.

The regiment was fresh. It had been brought in by rail, had never missed a meal, had suffered very few losses in the fighting earlier on, and the men worked with a will. The visitors heard the clatter of picks and shovels, and men exchanging jokes.

Savitsky saw clearly all the weaknesses and dangers of his position: he knew that there was a gaping hole on the Russian right and no one to fill it, that not enough artillery had been assigned to this important wing, only one battalion of light field artillery and—just to tease—two medium howitzers. The other ten howitzers belonging to the corps, and the whole heavy artillery battalion, were on the left. But Artamonov was too impatient to turn his mind to this—if he did he would never finish his rounds before morning. He broke in on Savitsky and Vorotyntsev and gave orders for a platoon—"those men over there, just as they are in their working clothes"—to be lined up for inspection. (He would have them know that he had been in charge of defense works at Kronstadt itself!) The platoon dropped their tools, climbed out of the trench, and lined up without arms. Artamonov strode along the rank.

"What do you say, then, boys? Are we going to beat them?"

A ragged roar told him that we were.

"Everything is all right, then?"

Everything was all right, they said.

"Your regiment once took Berlin. That's what you got your silver bugles for! You there"—to a broad-shouldered private—"what's your name?"

"Agafon, Your Excellency," the man answered smartly.

"Which Agafon are you called after? When's your name day?"

"The threshing-time Agafon, Your Excellency," said the soldier unhesitatingly.

"Idiot! Threshing time! What do you mean, threshing time?"

"You know, autumn time, Your Excellency, when the sheaves are in from the fields and all the work's on the threshing floor."

"Fathead! You ought to know who your own saint is! And say a prayer to him before the battle. Have you read the *Lives of the Saints*?"

"Y-yes, Your Excellency."

"Your saint is like a guardian angel, to watch over you and defend you. And you don't know which one he is! When's the patron saint's day in your village? I don't suppose you know that either?"

"Of course I do, Your Excellency. It's about the same time, on the Little Immaculate."

"There you go again! What's this Little Immaculate?"

Agafon was stumped. But a literate voice in the rear rank called out, "The Nativity of the Blessed Virgin Mary, Your Excellency!"

"Right then, pray to the Mother of God while you can!" Artamonov said in conclusion, and moved on to the fourth man along the line.

As it turned out, Mefodi Perepelyatnik didn't know his saint's life either.

"Are you all wearing crosses?" the general asked testily.

"Of course! We all are!" A dozen rather indignant voices answered for Russia.

"So don't forget to say your prayers. The Germans will attack tomorrow, so just you say your prayers!"

Vorotyntsev might have thought that this was all put on for his benefit, but Artamonov was always the same. Did it come from something deeply rooted in the general's heart, or was it simply that he had served long enough in the Petersburg Military District to know how much the Grand Duke liked to see icon lamps in every soldier's tent? Artamonov's face gave nothing away, it was a blank wall, and his nose a fixed handle that opened no door. His eyes were just as expressionless.

Now he too crossed himself. The sweep of his arm was visible against the sky. Just as he had dashed wildly from flank to flank of his corps, so now he flung his arm in a swift, sweeping movement across his brow, across his chest, as though he were brushing off a gadfly while he still had a bit of shoulder left. He made the sign of the cross over Savitsky too, and embraced him: "May God preserve you! May God preserve your Vyborg Regiment!"

He would have given it its full name perhaps, had it not been a little awkward: the Regiment of His Imperial and Royal Majesty Wilhelm II, Emperor of Germany and King of Prussia. The name was no longer used, but a new one had yet to be invented. Vorotyntsev knew this regiment of old. It had been at Liaoyang, on the Sha Ho, and at Mukden, always somewhere in his vicinity. The rankers, no doubt, had all been replaced since those days, but the regiment, a living thing, had somehow remained the same. And there were probably some officers left from that time, if you looked for them.

The Corps Commander took his leave and Savitsky went off to the right to post half a company of machine gunners where the front came to an abrupt end. Vorotyntsev went with him. To live is to suffer anxiety. No sooner was he rid of one worry, that the army would be outflanked from the left, than another began nagging—that there was an empty space and a draft blowing to the right of the corps.

Savitsky spoke briefly and to the point. He understood the whole situation. Why, though, was understanding never found at the same level as authority?

They walked between the village and the main line of trenches and came out by a windmill. Its gigantic black bulk stood alone in a windy, exposed place even higher up than the village, and its motionless sails could be seen against the starry sky like arms crossed in entreaty—"Go no farther"—or defiance—"You shall not pass."

Was there a lookout on the mill? There had been, but he had been ordered down: he was too good a target and the enemy had been firing in that direction in the early evening.

Farther on, the highway and the railway line, as they left the village side by side, turned sharply to the north between embankments, cutting across the front, and Savitsky went across the tracks to post machine guns. He offered Vorotyntsev a bed in the house where he would be sleeping himself. It was time, though, to part company. Vorotyntsev walked along the dark, deserted tracks, and where the highroad to Neidenburg reappeared from under the railway line he sat down on the dry, sparse grass of the embankment.

In the whole dark expanse to the east, as far as he could see from the northern to the southern extreme, no light winked except where Andromeda and Pegasus sprawled across the sky, and brilliant Capella had crept out in pursuit of sinuous Perseus, and the Pleiades clustered in their milky haze. There was no noise of artillery or of rifle fire, of hooves or of wheels—the earth was as it had been created, except that there were no animals and no people. Nearby, the coming clash of corps with corps was ripening. The fate of armies, and perhaps of the whole campaign, hung on it. A stone's throw away, Shtempel's brigade would go into action at dawn. And the Germans—had they guessed, would they try to infiltrate or not?

The best thing Vorotyntsev could do was to run down from the embankment and keep running along the road all the way to Neidenburg, find the Army Commander, explain to him that there was a weak spot very close to HQ, that the body of the army was being torn in two, that HQ itself was defenseless, obtain orders for the left flank to take the offensive—and come right back with them!

But it couldn't be done by morning. Even if he found a two-wheeler and charged full tilt over the twenty versts there was no hope of achieving anything before dawn. A patrol somewhere might put a bullet in him. Getting the sluggish commander out of bed in the middle of the night, stirring him up, persuading him to take emergency measures—it was too much to hope for.

So he would stay where he was in Usdau. What happened here would be decisive. But a colonel from GHQ no longer had any business here. Every one of the tens of thousands of officers and men at his back knew his duties—he alone had no specific obligation, only some indefinable duty imposed by his own conscience. The moment he alighted from Artamonov's car the purpose of his visit to the 1st Corps had vanished. And no new purpose had replaced it. He was sending no reports and could not influence the course of events. It was beginning to look as though he could have achieved more without leaving GHQ.

He was always so eager to find the best use for his abilities, and he had found the worst.

From his youth on, Vorotyntsev had craved one thing above all else: to influence his country's history for the good, to drag or hustle uncouth Russia along the road to better things. But no individual was granted such power and influence unless he stood in the shadow of the throne. Whatever position he grasped at, however desperately he struggled, it was all in vain.

Waves of sleepiness swept over him. He woke with a start. He had spent the last two nights swaying in the saddle. How long was it since he had breakfasted with Krymov? Was it only a few hours ago? It felt like a week.

It would be so easy to lean back just a little further and take a doze on the embankment. But the ground had grown cold.

Vorotyntsev went down from the embankment and made his way back to the village. His thoughts were as unsteady as his legs. He was in no condition to act, to make decisions, to think at all. Despising himself for his failure and for his helplessness, he stumbled to the house where he had been told to spend the night.

It was a rustic house, but the bedroom had an alcove. There was a weightless eiderdown in a pink silk cover on the double bed. At the front in the Japanese war he had spent his nights in mud huts or dugouts or tents.

A bronze clock with a top like a spire ticked away on the marble mantel. Probably an eight-day clock, wound up by the householders before they left. It agreed exactly with Vorotyntsev's watch: in a quarter of an hour's time it would be midnight.

It was stuffy in the room, and the kerosene lamp made it more so, but the warmth was pleasant. With his last remaining strength Vorotyntsev took off his belt, tugged off his boots, tucked his revolver under the feather pillow, put matches handy, blew out the lamp, and finally sank into the luxurious softness, his sense of failure and of helplessness still painfully awake. But the bed received him as though it had been waiting for him. The edges of his anxieties and his perplexity softened, his heartbeat, which he could hear through the pillow, slowed down and soon he ceased to hear it.

A lot later, or only a little later, he found himself in a room—a different room, with unlit corners. The light was poor, and he did not know where it was coming from. It illuminated only the spot he was meant to see. It fell now on her face and her breast.

She? Yes, it was she! He recognized her at once, though he had never seen her in his life. He marveled that he had found her so easily. It had always seemed impossible. They had never seen each other, but now they recognized each other at once, ran to take each other by the elbows. There was some sort of light, but not enough to see her face and her expression clearly, yet he knew her at once and thrilled to the knowledge. It was she! It really was! The inexpressibly dear one, who was all women to him!

He felt a painful tenderness for her. And astonishment—that she existed, and that his heart was capable of such powerful, such overwhelming emotion.

They rushed into each other's arms and spoke without saying a single word out loud, but they understood each other perfectly and at once. They could see only very dimly, but his sense of touch was very much alive, his hands moved from her elbows to her narrow, concave back; he pressed her to him, and they were happy with a sense of belonging, of homecoming.

No duty summoned him elsewhere, no cares weighed on him, there was nothing except lightness and the happiness of embracing her. And then, strangely, it was as though they were not seeing each other for the first time, as though they had come a long way together and had a perfect understanding. There was a bed in the room; he led her unhesitatingly toward it, and the light moved with them.

Suddenly she held back, stood still. Not out of shyness—they made no disguise of their feelings—but he knew at once that she had stopped because she could not, for some reason, turn down the covers.

Puzzled, he hurriedly pulled back the coverlet and saw lying half hidden by the pillow Alina's neatly folded nightgown—pink with lace trimming. He could distinguish no other color in the room—the color of the dress she was wearing, of her eyes, of her lips—but the pink nightgown he recognized at once.

It jolted his memory. Alina! Yes, there was Alina—and that was a hindrance. The strength drained out of him. He knew then that his place was not with *her*, that he was about to lose her. For the last few moments he clasped her tighter, tighter, with all the strength he had in him, engulfed by love.

There was a bang and the tinkle of broken glass. Georgi woke up, but had no strength at first to shake off his sweet reverie. The windowpanes had not been broken, but the Germans were landing their first shells very near. The gray light of dawn was in the room. He closed his eyes again—he hadn't the strength to keep them open.

Contact with her had been too powerful a sensation for him to believe now that it was just a dream. He was still lying there, utterly powerless. He could not move a finger even if it meant that the grass would never grow again, that the world would come to an end if he did not do something about it. He was still on fire with her, and did not at first even ask himself who she was. Had he really been looking for her? As far as he could remember he had never thought of her. Such thoughts were strange to him.

What amazed him was not that he had conjured up a nonexistent woman in a dream—there was nothing extraordinary in that—but the intensity of his emotion. He had never experienced anything like it in his waking hours.

Sinful weakness of the flesh! If he died for it he must go on lying there. The will to rise was not yet in him.

He was still so vividly aware of her that he was reluctant to part his knees and lose her warmth. He lay there blissfully helpless, incapable of moving if a shell knocked the wall down.

What could it mean? That he was going to die?

It was all coming back to him, this wasted journey, the battle ahead, his uselessness in this place. He ought to be hurrying off somewhere—to Samsonov? or to Artamonov? The noise of shells had not yet fused into a single scream: he could tell the caliber of each as it whistled through the chill early-morning air, and could distinguish explosions outside the village from those inside. That was a three-inch shell. And that a six-incher. And the next one perhaps still bigger.

How were things in the trenches? How was Agafon of the threshing floor getting on?

By now he could make out the clock on the mantelpiece. It was seven minutes past four. There was a nearer explosion. Doors were banged in the house. Somebody thumped on his door, and a brisk, round-faced cook brought him a little pot of porridge, still hot, though the soldiers no doubt had been given theirs an hour back. Thank you, my nameless friend! I've seen thousands of faces like yours in Russia and forgotten them, but you, God grant, I shall remember forever.

Vorotyntsev jumped out of bed and immediately forgot his dream. He ate his porridge quickly, with a wooden spoon uncomfortably wide for his mouth, wound up his pocket watch, put on his belt, binoculars, and greatcoat, and wondered where to go next.

The windows rattled, the house shook, but from inside it was, as always, difficult to decide from which direction the shells and bullets were coming.

He cleaned out the mess tin, and found the porridge cook waiting in the corridor for it—it was probably his own tin—clapped him on the shoulder—"Thank you, my friend"—and darted out of the house toward the trenches, almost cheerful.

It was a chilly morning. Mist trailed in the broad rolling expanse of low-lying ground to the west. A shell exploded, raising a black shower of earth, and fragments whistled through the air. Vorotyntsev took shelter from them behind the brick wall of a barn, then ran with long strides to the nearest trench and, as it happened, to the same platoon which had acquitted itself so badly in the eyes of General Artamonov. He jumped down into the trench between two soldiers. They had made a good job of their digging. The trench was the height of a man, with niches, and the rogues had even lugged benches and chairs down there, although flying wood splinters might hurt someone.

Over to the left, in a little channel specially made for it in the soil banked up to form a rampart, a sleek, tawny toy lion the size of a cat stood facing the enemy with his tail toward his own soldiers.

"Your Ex'ency, what's that beast called?"

"You've been told often enough."

All the same they waited for confirmation.

"It's a lion. Where did you get it?"

"Going through the town."

"Is it made of rag or is it solid?"

"It's solid."

Shells whizzed by and, though the bombardment was as yet neither heavy nor accurate, they promised with malicious glee a hot day ahead. Alone in the trench anyone would have crouched down, hidden his head behind the wall of earth, and kept silent, but with others around him every man was recklessly brave. Then there was that lion. Vorotyntsev liked it. His earlier helplessness and irresolution fell away like dross and the day began to take cheerful shape.

From where he was he had a broad view, but half of the area was afloat in mist, and flashes from the German batteries on higher ground touched the crests of its waves with fire. Here was something he could be usefully doing. Use his map case as a desk, mark the points of the compass on a piece of paper, take his bearings from the windmill—luckily it was fully visible from this point in the long, curving trench—and note the positions of the batteries, judging the distances with his bare eye or else with the aid of the ranging graticules in his binoculars. Vorotyntsev enjoyed artillery work; he had of his own wish attended a course one summer at the Luga School for Artillery Officers and learned a lot from it.

"What d'you think, boys—why aren't our men answering back?" they asked their comrades, but glancing at Vorotyntsev.

"Don't want to give away their positions," Vorotyntsev's stalwart neighbor in the trench answered for him, pursing his lips in mock solemnity and like the others keeping half an eye on the colonel.

Although the main weight of German fire was apparently meant for regiments to their left, shells were beginning to fall thick and fast around them. The soldiers' faces were tense, the jokes dried up in their parched mouths. One of them held a prayer book and whispered a prayer. The scream of steel whips on the upstroke shattered the air into showers of whimpering fragments. The soldier on Vorotyntsev's right shrank from every whistling noise even when no explosion followed. But the large-nosed man to his left followed each stroke of the colonel's pencil openmouthed, his protruding lower lip showing his amusement. His expression was full of goodwill. He watched the paper on the map case with parted lips, but keen eyes. He asked no questions, but seemed to be taking it all in so that he could start doing the same thing himself at any moment.

"See what I mean?" Vorotyntsev asked, taking a look through his binoculars and making a mark on the paper. "Before they really put the squeeze on us—"

"We ought to drive a few wedges into them," the soldier said, nodding confidently. His face showed that he thought he could work out directions and distances just as well for himself.

"What's your name?"

"Arseni."

"Surname?"

"Blagodarev."

A handy name, easy to get hold of, and the ready way he gave it warmed the cockles of the heart. Blagodarev—"Thankful." So easily moved to gratitude that it was evidently on the tip of his tongue to thank Vorotyntsev for asking.

Dawn was brightening beyond the village behind them, but the mist was thickening on the lower ground. For the next hour the height on which they stood would be obscured, screened from the German batteries firing from the west. Those to the north, however, would be able to aim more accurately. Whoo-oosh—that was a near one! They were using mostly howitzers, and firing high-explosive shells rather than shrapnel—quite rightly.

The company commander squeezed past behind them. "Lion not wounded yet?" he asked. They laughed in reply.

Vorotyntsev asked him to pass the diagram to the gunners through the battalion commander.

So far only three men in the whole company had been wounded, none of them seriously. From what they heard, a direct hit on the 1st Battalion, down below the mill, had laid low a dozen. As the mist shrank the morning brightened, illuminating the little clouds of shrapnel, the fountains of earth raised by high-explosive shells, and ten versts of battlefield over to the left on which the two 1st Corps, the Russian and the German, confronted each other. So far the battle had a date—27 August 1914—but no name. Would it be the Battle of Usdau? Or of Soldau? It was equally uncertain whether its fame would live on through the ages (and which side would win the glory) or whether it would be forgotten tomorrow.

What with his short night, his rude awakening by gunfire, and his brisk activity in the chilly morning air, Vorotyntsev had still not got around to thinking seriously about where his duty now lay. There was certainly no point in staying where he was, in that trench. Still, he felt exhilarated, his futile flitting around was over, and he was doing something positive at last. He no longer regretted this excursion in the least. Still less did he regret leaving GHQ, where they would not be waking up till nine o'clock. That day, 27 August 1914, saw the beginning of the second war in Colonel Vorotyntsev's life—a war of unknown duration and of uncertain outcome for Russian arms and for himself. The purpose of his studies and his past service had been to ensure that he would not go through that war without making a contribution.

"They're letting up a bit!" Blagodarev was the first to say it. Above the din of shell bursts he could hear individual guns firing, and distinguish those trained on their position from others farther along the front. Like an experienced concertgoer he detected the dying fall seconds before anyone else. True enough, the explosions in the sector occupied by their regiment were now farther between.

"You have a good ear," said Vorotyntsev approvingly. "Pity you aren't in the artillery, you'd be able to locate your targets by ear."

Blagodarev grinned, but not too broadly—just enough to gratify the colonel without seeming unduly flattered.

They straightened their backs and breathed more freely. Some of them sat down on chairs and rolled cigarettes. They examined the lion. He was unhurt. Not a single hole in him! There were guffaws: We really made fools of ourselves, hiding like we did!

"When's dinnertime?" the soldier who had asked about the artillery wanted to know.

They pounced on him happily.

"Listen to him! Hungry already!"

"By the light of the moon—or maybe not so soon!"

"If you get one through your belly first, you'll have nowhere to shove your dinner!"

The bombardment had been lifted from their sector only, and switched to the neighboring regiments on their left. An effectively coordinated artillery operation was something Vorotyntsev appreciated. Russian commanders could never have made all their gunners change targets simultaneously like that: telephones, cable, and training were all lacking. But what did it mean? An infantry attack on Usdau? They were facing northwest, but Vorotyntsev's field glasses probed due north—the enemy might wheel to attack from that direction, that was what he feared most. A crimson sun had broken through behind them, shining over the houses, through the trees, and beginning to play on their little hill. It was getting warmer. The men removed their greatcoats and rolled them up. Wilhelm's monogram had been picked off their shoulder straps, leaving them looking the worse for wear.

The order to have rifles at the ready was passed along the line.

But there was no attack. In fact, the Germans did not show themselves at all. Again Blagodarev was the first to spot what was happening.

"Hey! Hey, you! Look at that!" he said, stretching his long arm out over the parapet, fascinated by what he saw. It was hardly the way to address the colonel, but perhaps it was not meant for him. "There's something coming! Something coming!" Through his field glasses Vorotyntsev saw every detail. Two cars with their tops up, each carrying four men, had emerged from a copse. They were less than three versts away, and Vorotyntsev could distinguish with his powerful lenses their faces and their badges of rank. In the first sat a fidgety little general. The lenses of his binoculars flashed from time to time—he could have seen very little with the sun in his eyes. The road they were following ran from left to right beyond the dip in the ground and was visible above the ebbing mist. With no one to warn them or hold them back they were approaching rapidly.

"It's a general! We have a general coming to see us!" Vorotyntsev, in his excitement, shared the news with Blagodarev—of course. "It would be nice to throw a scare into him! I should love a little chat with him!"

He was in the wrong place, in the trench there. If he had been with Savitsky he could have got them all to hold their fire. He wondered whether they had noticed. In any case, it was too late to get to a telephone.

"A general!" Blagodarev's chest heaved—the hunter thrilled at the sight of his prey. "Get him, somebody! Get him!"

The road was running downhill, it would plunge into the mist and rise again as it approached Usdau and their trenches. But those outposts down in the dip which had not been flattened couldn't resist the temptation, and several rifles began shooting at the cars when they were something like four hundred meters away.

The German infantry returned their fire.

Those in the cars took fright, stopped, tried to turn, and stalled.

Just the time for a dose of shrapnel! But the spotter would be mumbling over the phone to battalion HQ and by the time word reached the battery . . .

Through his field glasses Vorotyntsev saw the general jump athletically from his car. His aides hopped out simultaneously, some of them without opening their doors, and they all took to their heels, heads well down.

"If only we could wing just one of them!" Vorotyntsev could not contain his frustration. Since there was nothing he could do anyway, he put the glasses to Blagodarev's eyes. He expected Blagodarev to be startled, but he peered through them without hesitation, burst out laughing, slapped his sides, and shouted loud enough for the whole battalion to hear, "He's lost his way, the bandy-legged old billy goat! Stop him! Ho ho ho . . . !"

The cars straightened themselves out and went back to pick up their passengers. But they had already run into the bushes, or slid down into a ditch or gully, and the general waved the cars on without them.

Only then did the first Russian three-inch gun open up over the village, over the heads of those in the trenches, quite close to that particular spot. At least they had found the range.

Who was that general? And why didn't he know that the place was full of Russians?

The incident put the soldiers in a good humor and broke down the last barrier between them and Vorotyntsev. Blagodarev lost all constraint and told everybody within forty meters of him how he had been in the right place to see the general skipping like a goat, and a mighty frisky one at that. The soldiers were surprised to hear that there were such generals.

Blagodarev was obviously a great one for laughing—everything amused him—but probably a great one for work as well. There was a certain awkwardness in his movements, the awkwardness of one whose hands are numb, whose feet itch, if they have nothing to do. He had said that he was twenty-five, but he still had the fresh, chubby cheeks of an infant and the naïve trustfulness you find only in country people.

"Hold on now, boys! And take good care of the lion! Our friend there is going to make it hot for us," Vorotyntsev promised cheerfully. "That's why he came looking around."

There was nothing to be cheerful about. Many of them would shortly be dead or wounded. But, as always in male societies, anyone who felt an urge to run for it while he was in one piece carefully concealed it, everyone joined in the jokes and guffaws, trying to impress his fellows with his unconcern.

"Remember, boys, the brave man dies once, the coward every minute!"

Vorotyntsev saw that this company had already accepted him and taken a liking to him. He was filled with a pleasurable pride in being the right man in the right place. New strength coursed through his veins, the strength forgotten during his years in Petersburg and Moscow, the strength of that stouthearted and inexhaustible Russia under every Russian greatcoat which has no fear at all of Germans.

"Where's the Thresher then, pals? Let's have a look at him by daylight!"

"Thresher! Hey, Thresher! Right away, sir! He must have heard the call of nature! We'll have him here in a minute!"

"Let's have Perepelyatnik, then!"

The skinny but lively Mefodi Perepelyatnik was only a few men away from Blagodarev, and was already pushing his way through to the colonel, sniffing, but Vorotyntsev had no time to look him over. Apart from the booming to the left of them, the crack of a dozen great whips aimed directly at them shattered the air ahead.

"All right! Have you all remembered your saints' names? Pra-a-ay!" Vorotyntsev shouted while he could. They remembered the visiting general yesterday and voices to right and left answered with what might be their last laugh.

"Pray to God, but row for the shore!"

"St. Nicholas will shield us all!"

"Goodbye, world! Goodbye, village!" Arseni roared as he dived to the bottom of the trench and hid his head in his arms—but not before crossing himself.

The Vyborg Regiment's trenches felt the hammer blows of German shells all along the line. Once again the taut German command and its infallible signal system had turned on that one hill the fire of dozens of cannon and howitzers, light, heavy, and heavier still—yes, those deafening thuds, those tremendous explosions, were made by something bigger than six-inch shells.

Shells tore at the ground nearby. The body of the earth shuddered, shaken loose from its soul. Every shell seemed to be flying straight at them, at colonel and ranker alike, God help us! But not a single one landed on them. They were shaken, deafened, showered with earth sometimes mixed with splinters, and they caught that heavy stench of burning that even the raw recruit associates with death.

You could no longer distinguish one explosion from another. There was one continuous, mingled roar, one long, trembling torment in the shadow of death.

Vorotyntsev himself had never experienced anything like it in his life. There had never been such heavy bombardments in the war with Japan. It was as if your own body, not the ground near you, were being lacerated. It cost a mental effort to remind yourself that if you could still hear and think, it could not be your body but must still be the ground. He had been preoccupied with war and little else for all those years, but in real life he had become unused to it. He seemed to be experiencing it all for the first time. Though a graduate of the Academy, he still had to remind himself again and again that it was theoretically impossible even in an hour-long bombardment of this intensity to flush more than a quarter of the defenders from a deep trench, so that there was a seventy-five percent chance of staying alive.

But how many minutes could nerves and mind hold out if you could see nothing of the enemy, if you could not put up any sort of fight, but were merely a passive target? He should be taking a reading and looking at his watch, but his eyes had instinctively closed tight. He opened them as soon as he realized it and saw, a couple of meters away, Blagodarev's head, wearing a crumpled cap, pressed, like his own, against the front wall of the trench halfway up. Blagodarev too was slow to open his eyes.

There were just the two of them, isolated in the deafening din, the only human beings left alive on earth, turning on each other what might be their last gaze.

Vorotyntsev winked encouragingly. Blagodarev tried to go one better and twist his mouth into a silly grin. But he could not manage it. He did not know about the seventy-five percent! He had not been told in time.

Now each minute was counted as it crawled by. Vorotyntsev clutched his warm pocket watch in his hand, but to keep his eyes on it was more than he could do; the second hand crept forward too slowly, sucking in avalanches of metal, thousands of splinters, and big lumps of earth each time around.

There was no sun now, no morning, only smoky, evil-smelling night.

Thoughts crowded into those narrow intervals, as close-packed as the soldiers in the trench. How are we to fight if we cannot match their artillery? We can't hit anything more than seven versts away, and the Germans have a range of ten . . . in the Japanese war there was nothing like this . . . during the Japanese war I wasn't married . . . Alina would cry a bit and marry again—a pity I shall leave no children . . . perhaps a good thing . . . a pity I never met *her*, the woman I saw in my dream last night . . . if my life is over, what have I done with it? . . . 27 August 1914 . . . if war is your profession you can have no qualms about dying . . . but what about these peasants? . . . what reward can a common soldier look for? Just to stay alive. What keeps me going?

Blagodarev seemed as interested in the watch as he had been just now in the map case. He crawled forward. Crawled? Was he wounded? No, he wanted to shout in Vorotyntsev's ear.

Vorotyntsev did not understand. Did he want to hold the watch and admire it? Was he boasting that he too was good at timing things?

Blagodarev roared again, showing off his lung power.

Still Vorotyntsev did not understand. Then it came to him. "Like on a threshing floor!" The soldiers lying low on the bottom of the trench were like sheaves laid flat on a barn floor waiting, each one of them, for his one and only body to be threshed. The gigantic flails passed down their ranks and winnowed out souls like grain, for a cause of which they knew nothing. All the victims could do was wait their turn. The untouched and the wounded could only await their second turn.

However did they endure this threshing without howling or going mad? The minutes nonetheless went by.

Five minutes had passed, without a doubt. Ten.

A soldier with his face dripping blood held the rags of skin together with all his fingers as he pushed his way past their backs in a frenzy.

Nearby one man was bandaging another.

But they were still an unbroken link in the chain of trenches.

It was one way of living—life under the threshing flail. They had begun to get used to it.

Looking at him, Vorotyntsev decided that Blagodarev was not afraid. He did not want to die, of course, and he must know that he ought to be afraid, that in such a situation anyone ought to be afraid, but all the same there was no longer any fear in him: his expression was not one of profound shock, his eyes were not protruding, his mind was not clouded, his heart had not jumped out of his breast.

Perhaps he had foreseen his meeting with this soldier when he had refused to accept an escort to the rear. This was a man he would gladly keep by him until the fighting was all over.

Blagodarev sat in the trench like someone sheltering from a downpour under a leaky roof. He had sized up the situation and was making himself at home. Now he was hunting for shell splinters and gouging out those that had not penetrated too deeply into the trench wall. He picked up a hot one, burned himself, tossed it from hand to hand, and gave it to the colonel to look at—a warm, jagged splinter, as warm to the body as a cross worn around the neck.

There was a primitive simplicity and uncouth naturalness about his behavior that antedated armies, ranks, classes, governments.

Suddenly Blagodarev stared past Vorotyntsev and over his head with a look of amazement on his face as though he had arrived in bast shoes not in a barn but in a palace. Vorotyntsev turned his head to look.

SCREEN

The mill has caught fire!

It can be seen clearly over the rim of the trench—directly in their line of sight though the view is sometimes obscured by smoke from explosions, dust clouds, showers of loose earth.

That crash—like a blow on the head! The whole world is quaking, collapsing in ruins.

Then—

the mill again, burning soundlessly. The mill is in flames—it has not been destroyed by the shell, but is completely enveloped in fire:

Tongues of flame lick at the cladding of its pyramidal base.

They light up the empty hillside and turn it crimson.

The sail arms are motionless. The fire races over the lower blades

and from the hub runs both ways to the tips.
= The whole mill is ablaze! All of it!
This is the way the fire works: first it devours the deal cladding, while the skeleton remains intact,
then the skeleton glows brighter and brighter, more and more golden—but still it holds out! The tie beams are still in place!
The ribs are all on fire—both those of the base and those of the sails!
= For some reason, perhaps because of the currents of hot air, the sails before they collapse begin slowly,
slowly,
slowly to turn. Without a wind! What miracle is this?
The red-gold spokes, ribs without flesh now, revolve in this strange motion
like a Catherine wheel.
It is collapsing.
Falling to pieces.
Disintegrating in fiery fragments.

What no one should be expected to stand for more than three minutes the Vyborg Regiment had endured for over an hour. They had ranged some of the dead along the trench wall, but had fallen behind with the work. The wounded were tended where they sat—often by other wounded men. There was no hope of carrying them away: the trenches were deep, and each battalion had only two narrow corridors to the village. So bandaged men stayed where they were. There were ashen, bloodstained faces everywhere, and here and there unwounded men with trembling lips and hands. The men of the Vyborg Regiment had been pounded for over an hour, but they showed no urge to run, and it probably did not enter their heads that they could choose not to cower there under shellfire. No, just as stones carried along by the ice cap survive its melting, survive centuries and civilizations, survive storms and scorching heat, and still obstinately lie where they were deposited, so did these soldiers sit and refuse to be dislodged. They had inherited it from their forefathers, this age-old, unbreakable, inescapable habit; men must suffer patiently, there is no escape.

Vorotyntsev cowered down like the rest of them. In this pounding, which he could have avoided, in his friendship with this regiment, which he did not command, he seemed to have found his final home.

No one dared hope that it would ever end. But suddenly the bombardment became lighter; whether the guns had changed their target in concert or stopped firing altogether was not certain. The stinking darkness began to clear and they saw the glow of morning over the field. The sun had shifted high overhead and the trench gave no shelter from its burning rays.

They began straightening their backs, stretching their legs, peering out. Absurdly hoarse voices returning from the dead took on sonority: it had been so-o-o much tougher than yesterday and hey, look, all that smo-o-oke over yonder, a lot worse than we got!

That somebody else was having a still harder time of it was a consolation. The Germans were blazing away over to the left, at the railway track and the other village, and amid those incessant explosions, those fountains of smoke, those black upheavals, it was more terrible to imagine those others sitting it out and to wonder how they would survive than to remember that they had been through it themselves.

It was difficult, so difficult to stop being a stone and become a living thing again, but what they ought to be doing was not flexing their stiff limbs, not gawking, but looking to their rifles, making sure that they were propped up safely, that they were not choked with dirt, that cartridges were handy, that bayonets were fixed. The Germans had obviously not changed targets to be merciful, they were probably getting ready right then to attack.

They seemed, though, to have blundered. Something had gone wrong. They had ceased fire, but the infantry was not moving. They were wasting invaluable minutes, letting the Vyborg Regiment recover its strength and its lust for battle.

The sun had burned off the last of the mist in the dip before them, and they could see clearly that the Germans were not coming. Ah! No! There they were! Over to the right! Rifles released a hail of bullets, and machine guns began chattering.

Vorotyntsev, with no distinct idea in mind, as though his head were not his own, intoxicated by the heavy smoke, seized a spare rifle and a cartridge belt from a dead soldier and, holding his sword to one side, squeezed past the dead, the wounded, and the living, bumping against the sides of the trench in his unsteady progress toward the battalion on the right flank, whose trench curved around the burned-out windmill. His head seemed heavy, yet his thoughts moved too lightly perhaps, too impetuously. Once you had been *there* you somehow thought differently. No theory required a staff colonel to squeeze his way through to help the battalion on the right flank with his rifle. But he so much wanted to!

Yes, the one-horned helmets were advancing, but . . .

"Look at those yokels!" Vorotyntsev shouted, to encourage those near enough to hear, and found himself a perch at the elbow of the trench. "Bumpkins! Not Europeans! Who fights like that?"

The Germans had waited too long again. They had not crept up close, ready for the moment when the artillery finished its work so that they could charge in the brief interval while the Russians were still stunned. Worse still, they were not pressing forward in little groups, not spreading out and taking cover as they ran, but advancing in unbroken ranks, offering a beautiful target and halting to fire from the shoulder. That's no good! Either shoot or move—never both at once! For us it's shoot! Shoot, shoot! The Japanese taught us not to advance like that, and gave us plenty of shooting practice.

All the time they had been taking such a cruel drubbing they had seen nothing of the enemy, but suddenly there he was, the deadly enemy, the eternal enemy! It's for his sake we've suffered torment all our lives—wake up, shoulder! Let's settle our account with him! He made us grovel—now it's his turn to take it lying down! Every one we bowl over will make one less!

The battalion on the right squared up, as good as new, and blazed away, firing thick and fast and true, happily exacting payment for their long inactivity in the trench. Vorotyntsev stood in the front rank with them, firing away just as happily, fishing out cartridges, loading, taking aim, firing, shifting his target, and when it looked as though *his* bullet had brought a German down, crowing with delight.

The fearsome sharp-spiked helmets came on. The Germans shot standing or on one knee. (Who needs helmets? Forage caps are good enough for us! The odd Russian clutches his head and spins around, but Russian heads are generally bulletproof!) The Vyborg Regiment stood its ground and kept firing without a tremor, without the slightest inclination to retreat. They had no fear of the spiked helmets—fifty meters away now. No one gave orders, no one so much as raised a hand, but the Vyborg Regiment stood fast and fired with a will.

Germans fell down with cries of pain, or flopped out of harm's way, deliberately rolling down the slope. The rest turned and ran, upright, and the Russians let them have it in the back.

Some keen hunters hoisted themselves out of the trench to pursue with bayonets. But a lieutenant seized one of them and hauled him back. Others too were halted. Quite rightly.

Vorotyntsev had stopped firing. He was delighted at the way the Russians were holding their ground. They would stand fast, he felt sure, waiting for their former colonel-in-chief, Kaiser Wilhelm, to arrive in person. Vorotyntsev, exulting in the heady smoke clouds, loved the Vyborg Regiment, loved that day—27 August—and loved already the Battle of Usdau, loved Savitsky—Savitsky especially! He struggled along the trench, trying to get near him.

A company commander shouted in his ear and pointed: "Over there! There's an arch under the railway line, the general's either under the arch or on the other side."

That was the right place for him. The quieter it was, the better he could hear the machine guns and deploy such forces as he had himself effectively. There was no point in going to Savitsky, or in dashing off to Neidenburg just now. Shtempel's brigade was somewhere in the dim distance. There was nothing for him to the right either. And he could do nothing for the Vyborg Regiment. Why was he there at all?

Guns boomed, off to the left, and a yellow layer of shrapnel covered the black smoke of bursting high-explosive shells. Five regiments, one behind another, were still holding the line over there and the battle might tilt either way. That was the place for him! The endurance and stalwartness of the Vyborg Regiment must not go for nothing. Their effort should inspire the whole corps in these crucial hours.

It was difficult to move along the trench, stepping over bodies and bumping into wounded men. Some of the soldiers had clambered up on top where there was more room. Vorotyntsev, hanging on to his rifle by its strap, jumped out and walked along the rim of the trench. Things seemed to be whistling by quite near him, but the going was easy and unobstructed. Anyway, his ears were no longer very receptive, and much of what he saw he hardly saw at all. Blood-soaked bandages and tourniquets littered the ground. There was a thick sprinkling of shrapnel bullets. There was the breech end of a shattered rifle; cartridge cases shone in the sun. There were tin cans, an abandoned belt with a brass buckle, a man crawling, another man, with a bandage that left his crown exposed, holding his forehead. Another, sitting on the ground, pulled his boot off and poured blood from it as if it were a jug. One man stared out from the trench with lifeless eyes, while nearby other men were laughing. He was not consciously seeing any of it. His eyes, and his mind, were unreceptive. His movements were those of a drunken man—pleasurably reckless, exaggeratedly forceful, arms suddenly flung outward, an unnecessary stamp of the foot, a sudden lurch; he was in that state in which you can prick yourself or cut yourself without feeling it. Strangely, thoughts came quickly and easily to his fuddled mind.

When he had gone off to the battalion on the right he had entirely forgotten his trench companion Blagodarev. Remembering him now on the way back, Vorotyntsev felt that no one was more important, more necessary to him. Was he still alive? Surely he could not be dead?

The 2nd Battalion had defended itself as successfully as the 1st. They were carrying or leading the wounded away, by the communication trench and along the top. Down in the trench they were putting their house in order. One group was freeing a man who looked as though a dozen gravediggers had tried to bury him. Vorotyntsev recognized his old place—first he saw the yellow lion's tail sticking out from a heap of earth, then, to the right of it, there was Blagodarev's wonderfully sagacious ugly mug. He was tidying up with a frown on his face, throwing out the wreckage of a chair and empty zinc cartridge containers.

Vorotyntsev asked the captain to let him have one private soldier and gave Blagodarev a cheery nod.

"Blagodarev? Want to come with me?"

"Why not?" he answered, no more surprised than if they had arranged to go for a stroll together. He tucked his tongue into his distended cheek, cast a rapid glance over the half square meter of hole in which his life had nearly ended, slung his tightly rolled greatcoat over his head and onto his shoulders, swung himself up out of the trench with a powerful heave, and in the same movement stood upright. "Where to, though?" He behaved as though he had grown up on the battlefield, shoulder to shoulder with Vorotyntsev. "Give me your gun—and your greatcoat. It'll make things easier for you."

He settled the greatcoat on top of his own, slung both rifles over the same shoulder, and stuffed a mess tin into his belt without stopping. They were away.

It was seven-thirty. GHQ had not woken up yet, had yet to drink its morning tea, while here a thousand men had been pulverized since day broke, and a whole day of battle lay ahead.

By the look of it, another stagnant, suffocating, scorching summer's day.

They walked along behind their own lines, beyond the railway, where they could move more quickly and easily. Now they could see what they had been deaf to in the trenches. Russian guns too were flashing, the gunners stripped to their undershirts and sweating profusely, busily loading shells and firing, but they could not silence the German barrage. Even here they were not safe from flying German shrapnel; twice it came so close that Arseni and the colonel dropped to the ground face downward—though after the bombardment they had gone through, it was almost a joke to them.

The Germans were still concentrating their fire mainly on the frontline regiments, behind which the two men were now walking.

"The Yenisei Regiment is holding on," Vorotyntsev said, rubbing his hands. "Just another hour could change the whole situation."

Not long ago a photograph of this very same Yenisei Regiment had gone around Russia: they had marched past Poincaré at Peterhof, the Grand Duke Nikolai Nikolaevich stepping it out on the right flank with his perfect martial bearing and an air of desperate bravery about him, saluting and giving this honored guest eyes right. That had been less than a week ago—and now the same heroes were being reduced to pulp in this place.

"The Irkutsk Regiment is standing up to them as well," said the colonel joyfully. "We can win this battle today, Arseni, if we use our heads."

That would suit Arseni fine. He didn't care how soon the war was over.

"What should our side be doing, sir?"

"Moving over to the left as quickly as possible. If we simply stand our ground, we shan't win."

Arseni had a longer stride than any crane, but the colonel was a very good walker too. He had nothing to carry, of course. But he made up for it by darting left and right to find out the name of each unit, how many rounds it had, and what its orders were.

Back there, the Germans were off again pounding the Vyborg Regiment, and heavily. There were smoke and flames here and there, and shell after shell soared into the air. Arseni was glad that they had left in time. The trench was a communal grave. You climbed into it of your own accord and stood trembling like a ram waiting to be poleaxed. Whereas moving over open ground you had the use of your hands and feet and could die a freer man. You might even still get something out of life. Arseni had been very ready to follow this businesslike colonel. He would not have taken on an orderly's job, but it was fine being a partner in an expedition. The colonel was not content just to get through the day alive. He meant to achieve something.

Vorotyntsev was looking for the reserve units which should have moved in. But he found none in the first few versts, and the artillery was thin on the ground too. The only surprise was the Grand Duchess Viktoria Fyodorovna's motorized ambulance unit, probably the only one of its kind in the Russian army: they saw seriously wounded men brought in from the dressing stations, loaded into motor vehicles, and carried straight off to Soldau.

At another bend in the railway line, where it turned sharply toward the rear and Soldau, they discovered the corps mortar battalion, shorn of the two howitzers given to Savitsky. In their position on a reverse slope were stacks of mortar bombs and more were being brought up, but they were not firing much. Their battalion was directly subordinate to the commander of the corps artillery, Masalsky, who was nowhere to be seen, and it had no clear instructions as to whom it should support and how. Lieutenant Colonel Smyslovsky, commanding the battalion, had intended only to defend himself if things got bad. Vorotyntsev quickly reached an understanding with him. He would if necessary turn his guns forty-five degrees until they fired northwestward, and would set up lateral observation posts to the west. Things might start happening over there—and that way they would be ready. They agreed on means of communication. Vorotyntsev wanted to know where the rifle brigade was. Smyslovsky supposed that it might be moving forward beyond the railway line. In a wood farther back to the right the Lithuanian Guards Regiment was assembling—these were fresh troops with nothing to do for the moment—they were not taking up defensive positions or digging a second line of trenches.

Senka's colonel debated with himself. Should he go to the Lithuanians or not? The way lay across a harvested field dotted with patches of black ash; every single stock of rye had been burned, not one kopeck's worth had been spared. The colonel made up his mind: "You, Arseni, will stay here, I shall be back soon." Then he glanced at his watch—no, better get over to the left flank, where the riflemen are.

They slipped over the track quickly. The colonel looked around, pointed—"They went that way"—and quickened his pace.

"What are howitzers for, Your Honor?"

"Don't keep saying 'Your Honor,' it wastes time."

"What should I call you then?"

"Nothing. You've seen what they're like—short, broad barrels, forty-eight lines."

"What d'you mean, lines?"

The colonel sighed. "Well, anyway, they provide curtain fire. They're good for bombarding sheltered positions."

Senka sighed too. "I'm sorry I'm not in the artillery."

"Would you like to be? If we come out of this alive I'll get you in."

Senka nodded, but did not take it seriously, of course. A man must say something. If they'd met earlier on, when Senka was doing his conscript service . . . But with a war on, bah, he'll go his way and I mine. By the Feast of the Patronage we'll be strangers.

An enormous potato field lay before them. Such beautiful potatoes! The Germans didn't let even gullies go to waste. They grew something or other on the slopes and fenced them off from cattle. Beyond the field were two houses standing all by themselves. They strode toward them with the potato haulms whipping their boots. It must be nice to live like that, with your own bit of land around you.

The colonel kept up a breathless pace, and if Senka's legs had been shorter he would have been exhausted. The colonel rushed ahead and kept looking through those glasses of his. Just outside the village stood a tall brick barn, and the colonel could make out a number of infantrymen standing around it, obviously the rifle brigade.

"What kind of troops are they, Your Hon . . . ?" Senka asked as they hurried on.

"Infantry, but crack troops. More machine guns. Stiffer training. Tough boys, like you. That's why they have only two battalions to a regiment instead of four. They manage just as well."

Senka sighed regretfully. "Pity we can't go back and tell our men we've got all this muscle back here. They'd feel a lot easier!"

They followed the curve in the line of the front. Before them was the Ruttkowitz estate, beyond it a little wood, and beyond that again, so Vorotyntsev understood, the Petrov and Neuschlott regiments, which had moved up yesterday. The German bombardment was much lighter here.

Yes, he had been right. That was their plan—the Germans dared not try to outflank the Russians with cavalry around. They intended instead to force a way through Usdau. And this was where the whole situation could be transformed—and saved. Who, though, was to rally the forces? One and a half cavalry divisions were twiddling their thumbs, kicking their heels—who would lead them?

The farm building turned out to be a cattle shed. A splendid building like that for cattle! The riflemen were big and fit and fresh. They were sitting eating whatever rations they had left, with nothing to drink. Senka felt the pangs of hunger. He had two rusks in his sack—better eat them before he was killed or wounded. Why was there such a hollow feeling in his belly? He hadn't been plowing or mowing, but something was gnawing his insides.

The riflemen were arguing about the cross-shaped gaps left between bricks at frequent intervals in the walls. Was it easier to lay the bricks like that? Was it just ornament? Was it to protect the cattle against evil spirits? They spoke approvingly of the steep, sloping roofs, too—no need to shovel the snow from them, it would slide off by itself.

Vorotyntsev had missed the regimental commander—he had gone to seek instructions from anyone he could find, the Corps Commander if necessary. But both battalion commanders and the regimental adjutant were on hand. The four of them sat down together. The rifle brigade had arrived in Soldau with no commander, no staff, no artillery, just four separate regiments, each of them moving as it thought best and looking for something to do. Didn't they have an assignment? Their general assignment from Corps HQ was to keep moving northwest—nothing more precise than that; they had not been told what line to occupy, how much space to leave between units, who their neighbors were to right and left . . .

"Right, gentlemen!" Vorotyntsev eagerly interrupted. "Corps HQ is ten versts away, and as you see, they have sent nobody over. Army regulations allow a 'council of the senior officers present' to take command when necessary. Let's set up such a council, for your four regiments to begin with. I'll give you the precise situation in a moment. We'll make the Ruttkowitz estate our concentration area for the present. One regiment is there already, you say? Splendid. Your battalions can go over there and carry on into the forest. How are we to concentrate all four regiments? Let each of them send a senior officer to Ruttkowitz, to make arrangements for the regiments to move in. Now, junior officers: can you let me have two or three for liaison? I want one to take a note to the Lithuanian Regiment—perhaps we can persuade them to move over farther to the left. Another to look for Colonel Krymov, and ask him, if he can be found, to bring his cavalry divisions over at once. He may be on the way already. And another one . . . where is that heavy artillery battalion?"

The heavy artillery battalion was two versts to the rear. Because of some peculiarity of the command structure it would not take orders even from the Corps Artillery Commander but did just as it pleased.

"They won't be able to do anything at that distance. They must close up this way. I'll go to them myself . . . No, I'd better go to Ruttkowitz. Have they strung telephone wires out here yet? Has anybody noticed? Surely they must have an observation post at Ruttkowitz? I'll write them a note too . . ."

The bright flame of his assurance kindled an answering glow in the senior infantry officers. They were not stick-in-the-muds—while the battle was being decided in the thunder of guns all around them impotent inaction was a torment. Notes were written using the map case for a desk. The writing was a hasty scrawl, but the contents were concise and clear. The young liaison officers hurried off, steadying their useless swords as they ran. Both rifle battalions got themselves ready with much rattling of ammunition, formed up, and left for Ruttkowitz.

Senka and the colonel were the only two left in the barn: the colonel was sitting against a wall, still thinking or perhaps just waiting for something.

Senka meanwhile had dipped his mess tin into a pond on which ducks were bobbing oblivious of the war and brought water back. His belly was aching. The rusks must have been lying around for five years in the stores, and you couldn't get your teeth in them without water. Funny thing nobody had taken a shot at those ducks from the road. It would have been nice to take his boots off and soak his feet in the pond, but a glance at the colonel told him that it couldn't be done, there wasn't time.

"Would you like a rusk, Your Hon . . . ?"

Vorotyntsev started, took it with a hand that seemed to belong to somebody else, but saw the mess tin and dipped the crust in it all the same.

"It's only nine o'clock," he said. "You ought to have kept it for midday."

They nibbled.

The colonel glanced at the map, at the road, at the map, and at the road again, where ammunition carts and supply wagons were trundling by behind the line of trees. He went on nibbling.

"Are you married, Arseni?" His voice seemed to belong to somebody else. Was he asking a question or not?

"Hasn't been much of a marriage so far. Less than a year we've had together. Married last Shrovetide."

"A good wife, is she?"

"They're all good the first year," said Senka, with feigned indifference, chewing hard. He was too proud to show his real feelings.

"What's she called?"

Senka's chewing became slower. "Ye-ka-te-ri-na."

In fact, she wasn't usually even called Katya. Her street name was

"Mitten"—insultingly suggesting not just that she was small but that she didn't really exist unless she was picked up by someone, and could be dropped without a second thought. Senka's reply to this was the old saying: "Hand and glove show us how to love." When they began courting the girls and the boys had all laughed at him: Couldn't he find himself a big strong girl with some work in her? What good would that tiny creature be to him? And to tease her they said he would crush all her ribs. But in spite of all the jeers he trusted his instinct and clung to her, he couldn't help himself—and what a warm and happy wife his little Katya had proved to be! You wouldn't find another like her in the whole Tambov district, let alone in little Kamenka. You can become very fond of a horse because it needs neither whip nor reins, because you don't have to say a word, you just have to think it and the horse knows almost before you which way to turn and how to pull. A woman like that—what price would you put on her? You can never be really sure when she sleeps or whether she eats: by the time you wake up she has flitted off and is going about her business, which is to see that her Senka is well fed and prosperous and at ease.

But even that was not the best of it: it was very sweet being with her, like sucking the marrow from a bone. And the things she thought of! Lovingly he gave her a big belly and got endless enjoyment out of watching and feeling its swelling roundness.

They had not been left to enjoy their happiness for long. Arseni ran his hand over his face to drive away these untimely thoughts. Russian soldiers were tramping, hiding, crawling over the whole area and every one of them had left a Katya behind; this was no time for moping. There was no knowing whether he himself would be alive at the end of the day.

"Can you ride a horse?"

"Nothing to it. Where I come from they're all old hands. We've got so many stud farms and so many horses in our district . . ."

The colonel jumped up as if he'd been scalded—"Could be the riflemen!"—and dashed down the oblique path to the road. The ensign he had sent ran to meet him halfway: the heavy artillery battalion was moving up on its own initiative.

"Right, then, we're off!" the colonel said happily. They caught up with the riflemen and went with them along the road to the estate. The regimental commander bent down from his saddle for a conference with Senka's colonel. The riflemen were handpicked, still unruffled, marching in strict order.

"Have you brought us our orders?" they asked Senka. "Where are we going—do you know?"

"Where you'll get the stuffing knocked out of you." He told them a little about the hammering they'd taken earlier.

Before they reached the estate there was a strange rumbling somewhere—what it was Senka couldn't make out at first. They hastily unslung their rifles and blazed away at the sky. Senka fell flat on his back. There he goes like one of hell's angels, with black crosses on his wings! But he didn't take a shot at it, he couldn't get his hand to his gun. He merely wondered, how does he do it, the hellhound, flying like that, with nothing to keep him up there? And what would it be like for him if somebody winged him and he came tumbling down?

The plane flew on.

The estate was a big one. There was an orchard with several hundred trees but it had been ruthlessly plundered, stripped of its fruit, and many branches were broken. Near the orchard the estate had a little wood of its own—hundred-year-old limes and oaks, carefully tended, well groomed, with little paths—and cattle were wandering about in it, purebred cattle. The stable doors were wide open. You could see clean floors, water troughs, but not a single horse. A gang of soldiers had dragged sofas and red plush armchairs out of the house and were lounging in them, smoking. They jumped up when they saw the colonel and made themselves scarce. Senka tried a chair for the fun of it. The colonel and two lieutenants of the rifle brigade took it into their heads to go up to the roof and look around. Senka volunteered to open up the attic for them. The house was full of wonders. There was a mirror that covered a whole wall—it had been smashed by soldiers who wanted pieces of glass to admire themselves in. Furniture had been overturned and broken. The floor was covered with broken china, faceted and flower-patterned. That was a funny sort of billiard table, with no cloth or cushions, smooth and black. How could the balls stay on it? "You bumpkin!" One of the lieutenants playfully pulled Senka's cap over his eyes. "That's not a billiard table, it's a grand piano." "What's that cracked thing on the wall?" "That's marble, it's a family tree to tell you who you're descended from." The floor was just as much of a shambles. Lace curtains had been torn down from the windows, cupboards rifled, clothing, toys, photographs, books, and papers lay scattered about. The lieutenant picked something up. "Racing certificates. He bred some good horses!"

Senka opened all the doors to the attic, and the attic window. Senka's colonel put his head out and before he had even focused his field glasses said, "That company on the other side of the park—tell the officer I would like to see him." Senka bounded down the stairs, two or three at a time: all that stuff and no time to run your hands over it or even look!

Senka found a Cossack lieutenant—it was a squadron of the 6th Don Cossack Regiment sent to replace the divisional cavalry and diverted here when the bombardment was intensified. Senka had the presence of mind to ask them for a mare. He harnessed her to a two-wheeler, threw an armful of straw into it, and rode back, urging the horse on with the reins along a well-rolled sandy path, overhung by branches which no rain could beat through.

The colonel had a word with the Cossack lieutenant and gave him written orders. All this time the noise, whatever it was, was getting louder and there was a stir of excitement. A unit of light field artillery stood between the manor house and the woods nearby—and suddenly they became frantic. How they went at it! It was as though all the dogs of a village had suddenly begun raving at a single wayfarer, every one of them barking fit to burst. The battle had taken a new turn.

Around the house too everything started happening at breakneck speed. The lieutenants rushed off to their regiments, hands on sword hilts. The colonel jumped into the two-wheeler, as though he had ordered it himself.

"The Petrov and Neuschlott regiments are attacking by themselves," he shouted in Senka's ear. "On their own! Without waiting for the rest of the corps! That's the stuff! The rifles will back them up. And the howitzers will be here any minute now." He looked as though he might jump out of the cart and beat the mare to it.

The Don Cossack squadron overtook them, also galloping toward the woods.

This was jolly! Senka would have rushed to do battle with the Germans with a cart shaft if he could! Settle up with them quick—and go home. Better than fighting the next village, this was. It did his heart good to see the lads go at it. Good for them! Attacking on their own! Why stand around, waiting to be ground to bits? It was a fine, blazing day, the fields were wide and open and not their own—no need to worry about trampling them. If they'd been fighting like this back home in Kamenka there'd be no joy in it, of course. There had never, thank God, been a fight like this in Kamenka, in all its days.

The cannon stood right behind the estate. They blazed away, without spacing their shots, enjoying themselves, boisterously, playfully. War is fond of fun lovers. Even in the bright daylight you could see the barrels lick their lips with tongues of fire at every shot. One gunner shook his fist in the direction of the wood each time he fired—"Take that, and damn you!" A captain nearby shouted to the colonel, "We're raising our sights." "That means our troops are advancing," the colonel explained to Senka.

Pile into them! You know we can get the better of them!

But the Germans too were feeling for their target—not the manor house, but these batteries. There was a meadow in front of the house with a light breeze ruffling the grass, and when a shell crashed a black fountain of earth spurted higher than a tall tree, thicker than an oak bole, and the crater it left was not a sand hole but a neat black cavity.

They had pinpointed one of our batteries! Right between the guns. Flash, bang! Up went a box of shells! Flash, bang again! And again!

Horses bolted in all directions, men, those who still could, crawled dazed from the wreckage. Senka's mare shied across the roadway—Senka could hardly straighten her out—and was away into the wood.

Limbers sped past them, to be hitched on and moved closer to the target. "Can't they lob one in from here?" Arseni asked. "They're going to fire point-blank," said the colonel, waving him on. "Whip her up, Arseni, let's get there."

The wood was not very big. They galloped through it, overtaking one regiment of rifles. Two others had already taken up position. A broad field, the village taken yesterday, scattered farmhouses, then more woods, a wall of trees this time—and that, the colonel said, was where the Petrov Regiment should be. This side of the wood puffs of shrapnel filled the air. As soon as they dispersed, others took their place in a continuous barrage, lashing the air to prevent the Russian forces from pushing forward.

"Hear them? Over to the right there. Howitzers! They're moving them up in front of the Petrov Regiment."

"The ones that were over by the railway?"

"That's right."

"So we're nearly back where we started."

Whee-ee-ee! Flame leapt from the path ahead. A black column thick as an oak stood up before them. The crash hurt their ears. They sprang out and lay flat (holding on to the reins, though) while showers of splinters hissed and whistled past. They could hardly believe the mare was in one piece, they themselves unhurt. But the cart was riddled. Nothing for it, though. They turned off the road and jolted over the field in their unsprung cart at a gallop—bump, bump, bump.

"Your Hon . . . sir, are we going the right way? Looks as though the rifles have halted over to the left." "Yes, but we'll go right, get around that shrapnel barrage to the Petrov Regiment. Get on with it!"

The place was still warm from the Germans. They had been there earlier that morning; their dead and Russian dead were lying side by side, and there were wounded men, but there was no time to do anything for them. There had been a German battery on the spot too, and some of its charges had exploded. Two guns had been smashed and the horses killed in the traces. The rest had been hauled away.

The shrapnel still barred their way.

"Bear right a bit!"

Then two deafening shell bursts—not ahead, but behind them. They should have passed overhead. "Hey, that's our lot pitching them short, the devils!"

The going was rough but they charged on. The colonel felt his shoulder. "Ah, I've got a bit of a scratch, Arseni." He unbuttoned his tunic. "Caught me here, in the shoulder. Could have been one of ours. More likely that German high-explosive shell back down the road. It's only just started hurting." "Want it bandaged, Your Honor?" "No, drive on faster."

The Germans had been there only half an hour ago. Ammunition pouches, cartridge clips, knapsacks, and machine-gun belts were strewn around, a headless corpse lay in one place and a corpse complete with head in another (someone had gone through their pockets and left the linings turned out); there were guns, broken and unbroken, and in a colorful wrapping what might very well be something edible—but the work wouldn't wait while they stopped to pick it up. Now they had reached the woods again, and machine guns were chattering somewhere near. Ours? Theirs? They couldn't go any farther with the horse. "Tie her to a tree. We can walk."

Wounded men staggered past them as they went through the woods, with a weary way ahead of them. One was waving his arms and crowing, "We've downed so many, our side is steamrollering them!" Another, with his chest swathed in bandages and his greatcoat draped around his shoulders, croaked, "They're flattening us!" An ensign stumbled by, wounded in the neck and unable to turn his head. He wept when he saw the colonel, but not from the pain. "We've got nothing to shoot with, we're using up our last cartridges. Why don't they bring us some? Who's using his ass instead of his head again?" "How many did you throw away?" the colonel asked him. The ensign flapped his hand, and coughed up blood. "All right, I know, the men squander cartridges, they're not careful enough with them."

A wide clearing ran slantwise across the wood. At its edge there was a ditch full of water. The Petrov Regiment had gone to ground behind it, keeping their heads down and not firing. Through the clearing ran a road, and something weird and wonderful was moving along it, not more than two hundred meters away. It moved as though it was on wheels, but no wheels were visible. It was like a living creature, but had neither head nor tail. It had a movable top, and you could hear it spraying machine-gun bullets and see the puffs of smoke.

What could it be? There were murmurs of alarm. Nobody had ever seen anything like it. Could it get at them in the wood or only move on the road? "It's just a heavy vehicle," Senka's colonel shouted. "It won't come over the ditch, it'll get stuck." "What's it got on it, though?" "It's armor-plated, and that makes it too heavy to get at us here." "What's it firing with—is it a cannon?" "A small-caliber, quick-firing gun—it sounds frightening but doesn't do much damage." "Why don't we capture it, Your Honor? We could dig across the road on both sides of it, or knock it out." "What are you going to knock it out with, when the cartridges have run out?" "They say there are some on the way if we hold on."

But before that happened a sergeant ran up: the Neuschlott Regiment over to the right had passed the order on—everybody to withdraw! "Use that word again and I'll have your head," Senka's colonel told him. "I'll do for you myself!" "It's not my idea, Your Honor. I'll take you to the lieutenant colonel, he's by the farmhouse over there. They sent him a note, they got the message over the phone . . ." "Battalion commander, please stay where you are, don't listen to this rubbish! When they get here with the cartridges, advance as and when you can, d'you hear? Hear that? That's our heavy artillery battalion going forward, firing its placing shots; you'll get more support than you've ever dreamed of now. I'll go to the farm with this sergeant to check his story—and maybe shoot him! Say you didn't mean it, you son of a bitch, let them all hear you!" "You can shoot me if you like, Your Honor, but they telephoned and said . . ." "Blagodarev, bring the cart around the back way!"

Back there in Usdau the relentless flailing had fractured and scattered Vorotyntsev's thoughts and there was no collecting them in the hours that followed. Ever since that bombardment he had moved at a pace unthinkable at any other time. He seemed to be furiously thinking for three, and at the same time it was as though the smoke from the explosions and the fires they started were drifting through his head, so that whatever he saw happening, whether to himself or to others, he saw in that blue-gray haze.

He had the map clearly in mind and understood exactly how the battle was going. As the pressure of the enemy from the left had eased, the pent-up Russian forces, impatient of restraint, had surged forward spontaneously. The impulse had not originated at division level, but in the companies themselves. (There was unmeasured strength in the Russian people. They were used to victory!) With nobody egging them on, the Petrov and Neuschlott regiments had gone into action, supported—and here Vorotyntsev had played a certain part—by the three rifle regiments, who broadened the advance to the left, and by the two artillery battalions. (He felt particularly proud that he had guessed an hour before the attack where it might begin.) After their initial success, they had looked into each other's faces and lost all sense of danger, and pressed forward still more boldly and fearlessly.

"Brilliant job, men," the battalion commander shouted, "thank you!" and gunners, bombardiers, and sergeants all shouted "Hurrah!" and threw their caps in the air. This self-generating victorious attack had lasted only one hour, till ten-thirty, but in that endless sixty minutes Vorotyntsev had experienced ecstatic happiness, not so much because they had advanced two or three versts, not so much because the enemy was on the run, as because of that spontaneous ferment which surely was the mark of an army deserving of victory.

And to show himself no less worthy, Vorotyntsev had during that hour kept one thought sharply focused in his mind—how could he help the attack to develop? How could he swing it to the right, to lash the German flank? Where could he find General Dushkevich? Where could he bring up the Lithuanian Guards? All the rest, the trivial things, were wrapped in mist: why had they sat nibbling rusks by a duck pond? They had been on foot—where had the two-wheeled cart suddenly come from? When, exactly, had his shoulder been grazed? Through the haze of happiness, of battle, of bafflement, Blagodarev's face was constantly before him, the face of a man who would serve his superior officer and humor him when necessary without obsequiousness, a man who would never show disrespect though he had a lively mind and a will of his own. Vorotyntsev was not too absorbed to realize how lucky he had been to chance on such a soldier.

All this was abruptly ended by the sergeant bringing the order to retreat. It was as though the road he was treading had been swept away by a rockfall. Vorotyntsev had yelled at the sergeant and could almost have shot him on the spot, not because he thought the man a liar but in despair. He suddenly realized that he had been dreading something of the sort all morning. The moment he heard the rumor it pierced him to the core—it was so obviously true. This was just what *would* happen! Anything else you might doubt, but this was so typically Russian!

The Petrov Regiment had received no such order, but the enfeebling thought ran through it like an electric current and on to the rifle regiments. The Neuschlott Regiment had already begun to pull back; all Vorotyntsev's efforts to dissuade its officers went for nothing when the telephonist, a calm and literate Ukrainian sergeant, received a message which he wrote down and repeated word for word: "To Division Commander. The Corps Commander has ordered immediate withdrawal to Soldau." There could be no mistake. The sergeant had recognized the voice of his immediate superior, the division signals officer, Lieutenant Struzer.

On the high ground at the southern edge of the mature pine forest, where they were now reeling in useless telephone lines, an observation platform rigged up by the Germans, and taken from them an hour ago, swayed at the top of a tall tree. Vorotyntsev climbed up to it, almost slipping off the precarious, hastily improvised ladder. That was when the pain in his shoulder made itself felt. The whole world gave a lurch and he almost decided not to go on. He was not sure what he would be looking for, but he had to cast an eye around. The platform, some seventeen meters up, had no rail around it, and he had either to tie himself to a branch or to hang on with one hand. He held on with his good hand, grasping his field glasses and adjusting the screw with the other. He looked first to what was now the far left, at the familiar hill at Usdau, the stone base of the burned-out mill, the trenches they had taken shelter in that morning, and the ground around them pockmarked with black shell holes. He also saw, strung out over the whole area and advancing in open order, upright, unopposed by bullet or bayonet, German infantry.

That was it then. The battle was over. The day was lost.

The Vyborg Regiment, obviously, was no more. All those bodies, all those heads, had been threshed to no purpose.

Somebody down below shouted that General Dushkevich was there and wanted to know what he could see. What he saw was something he couldn't shout out for everybody to hear. He said that he would come down. But first he turned his field glasses to the right, and there he saw that the Germans had already crossed the railway line. One Russian battalion was still resisting, firing from the other side of the track at a big bend in the line. And Smyslovsky's ten howitzers were giving it support from their former position, farther back. Still farther to the right the heavy artillery battery, hidden by a fold in the ground, could be located by the sound of its guns, and especially by the loud, rapid fire of its cannon. Their shots were falling on the very place beyond the big forest which should have been and very nearly had been the objective of the Russian attack. But it was no good . . . He could see for several versts around, and over the whole field units and individuals were scurrying about, obviously with no single will to direct them.

The strap of his field glasses was catching on branches, his shoulder ached, his foot was slipping. The descent was difficult, and he very nearly fell.

Vorotyntsev seemed to have gone deaf. He could not hear his own voice as he reported what he had seen, and did not hear what pudgy, excitable Dushkevich said in return. He seemed to be hearing the general's words and seeing his face in a dream but he understood: the division had begun to retreat as a result of the telephone call from Soldau without the Division Commander knowing anything about it. He had troops up ahead in exposed positions, half encircled, and he was going to join them. The order from Corps did not say who was to cover the retreat. Were they supposed to rush back higgledy-piggledy, without any cover? Luckily, good communications had been established with the two artillery battalions. Without their covering fire Dushkevich's troops had no hope of extricating themselves. Wounded men had been left over the whole battlefield—what was to become of them now?

Dushkevich disappeared, but Blagodarev turned up with the cart and they rolled off, sometimes following the road, sometimes striking out across country. An eight-gun field battery was getting ready to move, and its commanding officer was sitting on a stone, looking like a man with a head wound, shuddering from time to time. Supply wagons charged along the highroad, drawn by lathered horses (when they are advancing they barely crawl along). Infantry, a medley of units, were walking along, shouting and swearing. You could smell the bitterness soldiers feel when the top brass (not they themselves) have ruined everything.

They passed close to the barn where they had made their arrangement with the riflemen—and that was where they met a battalion of the Lithuanian Regiment: without orders, simply at Colonel Krymov's request, its commanding officer was on his way to occupy an outlying position. The guardsmen moved gravely on as the retreating mob rolled toward them, looking neither left nor right, apparently quite indifferent, thinking their own thoughts, husbanding their minutes.

The Corps Commander, however, was nowhere to be seen. Not a glimpse was caught of his ubiquitous car. But he it was whom Vorotyntsev was eager to see, now that he had no hope of stemming the retreat and saving this battle. First, to smack his stupid arrogant face, spit on him, knock him flying! He longed to do it. But what can a subordinate do? What does his uniform permit? Nothing. Not even to tell him the home truths he had never heard, and never would hear. Besides, it was a long way to Soldau and the road was choked when they set out. As soon as it was a little clearer, Blagodarev whipped the mare to a gallop. Half seeing the rise and fall of her haunches, Vorotyntsev knew what he could tell the Corps Commander, but along the road he began to think better of it. No, he would simply let the blockhead explain in his own words why he had thwarted the offensive which had started spontaneously at company level, how he had managed to let slip this opportunity to round out the dented and sagging left flank. Not that any sensible answer was to be expected, but it would be interesting to hear what nonsense he would think up.

The Corps Commander's car was now dormant outside headquarters.

Vorotyntsev flung himself out of the two-wheeler, ran at, sprang at, burst in at the heavy door just as he emerged from the signals room with his drooping mustache, his beaky nose, his stupid, staring eyes, his battering ram of a brow, his parade-ground chest and squared shoulders, his ever-readiness to do and die for God and his Emperor. How good it would be to split that thick head with a sword! Vorotyntsev had ceased to notice differences of rank, had ceased hearing his own voice even, but he saluted mechanically and bawled at the Corps Commander: "Your Excellency! How could you give the order to retreat when we had already won? How could you squander regiments like those?"

A shadow flickered over the coward's face as he disowned his action. "I . . . I gave no such order."

Liar! Traitor! With his fishy whiskers! Might have known he would deny it! Whose idea was it then—Lieutenant Struzer's?

Such a battle! Such a battle it had been! And this sheep's head had thrown it away!

* * *

In the signals room Artamonov had just been reporting to Samsonov: "All attacks repelled. Standing firm as a rock. Shall carry out orders in full." What else could he say without bringing disgrace on his name? He had answered firmly, proudly, like a soldier. The loose ends would all be tied up sooner or later—Artamonov had got used to that in his army career. Sure enough, communication with Neidenburg was cut just at that moment. Excellent! He would be able to report later on that he had withdrawn under pressure from two enemy corps. Two and a half, rather. Three hundred guns. No, four hundred. Armored cars too. Armed with cannon. It would all come right somehow.

His patrons would come to his rescue.

Still, he was troubled. It was not his life that he valued. He valued his career, his name, not his life. He would gladly die now, an honorable death, a glorious death.

He jumped into his car and told the driver to take him—as fast as he could—to the front, no matter where, wherever Russian troops were still in the field. He felt short of air behind the windshield. He lifted himself up and rode standing, gulping the breeze that blew in his face. The skirts of his red-lined greatcoat turned out and flapped behind him like two red flags.

He was riding toward the retreating Russian forces, to shame them: You're running away—but your fearless general is advancing! He gave no instructions—let somebody else tell them where to stand and defend themselves, what positions the batteries should take up, and what their targets should be. Instead, he rode on to inspire his men with the mere sight of him, and greedily to swallow fresh air.

His red skirts flapped, but he stood firm as a rock.

[26]

The leading battalion of His Majesty the King of the Hellenes' Own 1st Neva Regiment was the first Russian unit to enter the town of Allenstein on the afternoon of 27 August, without a shot fired, and without readying its guns for battle.

So many improbabilities came together that the town trembled like a mirage before the eyes of the Neva Regiment: did it really exist, or not? Were they walking about it on their own feet, or in a dream? For so many days they had dragged themselves along, through the deserted land, seeing not a single one of its fleeing inhabitants, only ruined farmhouses and occasional villages amid the trees, keeping well clear of towns, choosing, deliberately it seemed, the wildest forest ways between the lakes—and after all this they found themselves, hungry, dusty, bedraggled, entering one of Prussia's finest towns, a sparkling clean town with a holiday air about it, full not only of its own citizens but of newcomers in the thousands. And all this just one step away from the forest wilderness. For two weeks they had trudged on and on without fighting, seeing no evidence that there was a war. As they entered this town they could see for themselves that there was no war.

The inhabitants were walking the pavements, going about their business, secure in their numbers and their defenselessness, going into open shops, carrying their purchases, pushing prams, some of them not so much as glancing at the troops as they marched in so that it might have been thought that the battalion was returning from maneuvers to its age-old home, where everybody had stopped noticing it, except that the buildings here were a great change from those of modest little Roslavl, and the townspeople wore strange clothes. The soldiers goggled at them and forgot to march in step or in line.

In the midst of all this baffling foreignness (perhaps if you tried to grasp it it would vanish like a mirage) there was one thing real—the sight of Colonel Pervushin, the regiment's favorite. He marched beside them with his light step, swinging his left arm, gazing around him, and the very look of this strong, daring, and determined man, with his jaunty, knowing half-smile, seemed to promise that he knew it all, would miss nothing, would do what was best for his men. He halted the battalion in a shady spot, ordered the posting of sentries, especially by the open wineshops, and said, "Gentlemen, if any officer wants a shave or a haircut, or wants to go to the pastry cook's, please take it in turns."

After two weeks of painful marching it might have sounded like a joke, what with that mocking stare and the untrimmed mustache concealing the movement of his lips, but the officers, one after another, asked permission, went off, and laid their coins with the two-headed eagle on the counter just as if they had been in Smolensk or Poland. Shopkeepers or their assistants served them politely, charging at the rate of fifty kopecks to the mark. Not so long ago these Russians had been hunting down civilian signalers and militarized cyclists, but now the German razor moved gently over the Russian officer's throat. They had stopped seeing double, it was as if a turn of the screw on their binoculars had brought things back to their true size and shape. People in uniform were at war—but war of all against all was beyond the limits of the humanly possible. Someone had hung a sheet on a large building with an inscription in Russian: LUNATIC ASYLUM. PLEASE DO NOT ENTER AND DO NOT DISTURB THE PATIENTS. No one entered, and no one disturbed them. A German medical orderly in uniform saluted Russian officers. Some women overheard a passing officer speaking German, stopped him, and began arguing with him: "What are you hoping to achieve? Do you really think you can conquer a civilized people?" Nonetheless, they invited him for coffee and sandwiches.

The overcrowding of this tight, narrow little town had another novel result: nothing could have been more difficult than "occupying" it in the full sense of the word—there was nowhere to billet a single regiment, let alone almost a whole corps. Pervushin set off to look for the Division Commander and the commanders of other regiments already in the streets or at the gates of Allenstein, to suggest that they should bivouac outside the town, near the lake, near the river, and on the outskirts of the forest from which they had come.

He met his taciturn friend Kabanov, commanding the Dorogobuzh Regiment, who immediately agreed. Then he recognized Kakhovskoy, commander of the Kashir Regiment, by the anxious tilt of his head. He agreed just as readily, and the three of them, feeling no need to consult higher authority, decided between them which sector each would occupy.

Under the former Corps Commander, General Alekseev, regimental commanders had been encouraged to show initiative and coordinate their actions without waiting for orders from above. Relations between most of them were friendly and businesslike, without the usual jealousy and dirty tricks.

That, however, was where Pervushin ran out of luck. He went past a little square where a dozen horsemen had halted, some of whom stood holding the horses, while others sat on a bench near the fountain. He could not possibly pretend that he had not noticed the Corps Commander.

Pervushin was not one of fortune's darlings. The son of an ensign, with no property at all, he had married a merchant's daughter. He had won the Order of St. Vladimir and the St. George's Cross after being wounded at Mukden, but although he was nearly as old as the Corps Commander and the Army Commander, he had been eight years a colonel. There was no knowing exactly why, since the matter was never spoken of except in secret correspondence, but it seemed that he had been rude to some important personage and that undisclosed instructions had blocked his advancement ever since. In spite of this, he never sulked in the presence of his superiors and had never mentioned his grievance, even in peacetime.

There was no avoiding the Corps Commander, and Colonel Pervushin, whose supple figure, swift salute, and bright voice were hardly those of a man of sixty, gave his exalted contemporary, General Klyuev, more information than he really needed on guards posted and other measures taken. Klyuev had the facial appurtenances of a military man, especially the mustache without which no officer looks decent, but viewed closely this was not a soldier's face, indeed it was not a face at all—it had no real character. Not everyone in the corps, perhaps, thought precisely that, but where Klyuev was now they had all been used to seeing General Alekseev and his honest, knitted brow. He had been promoted just as the war broke out, to a post at HQ Southwest Army Group, and no one who had known him could report to Klyuev without thinking: You can try as hard as you like, you'll never be an Alekseev. Klyuev couldn't help reading this in the faces of officers standing before him and disliking them for it. From the first he had taken a particular dislike to Pervushin and that exaggerated look of unflagging courage in his insolently goggling eyes. Klyuev's antipathy had been reinforced four days earlier: as the noise of the bombardment from the left was reaching its peak Colonel Pervushin had the impertinence to appear unsummoned in the Corps Commander's tent, bypassing his Brigade Commander, bypassing his Division Commander, and request permission "in the name of the officers in his regiment" to attack leftward and go to the aid of the 15th Corps. Klyuev would never have expected such signal indiscipline from one of his subordinates, or indeed imagined that it could occur in the army at all. Perhaps this was only an example of the way things were done under Alekseev, but Klyuev's indignation was directed against Pervushin personally.

He had refused him permission. (But had used the idea for his own benefit, reporting to his superiors that he was ready to lead this whole corps to his neighbor's assistance.) He listened to Pervushin with the same hostility now, waiting for a chance to make him smart. Yet again Pervushin proved unable to remove himself without gratuitous suggestions. With the need to station regiments outside the town in mind, he asked the Corps Commander, not for instructions on that point (it could be managed better without them), but whether for safety's sake he would authorize the destruction of the four railway lines. (Allenstein was the junction at which the main East Prussian lines intersected.)

Klyuev answered contemptuously that this was not a matter for a regimental commander, but that if he really wanted to know, Army Group HQ had given instructions that German railway lines were not on any account to be destroyed but must be kept intact for the Russian advance. "The best thing you can do, Colonel (hand me the map, will you), is move one of your battalions north of the town, into the 'town forest,' and deploy it in a wide arc to guard the approaches."

Pervushin should have known that meeting senior officers, even accidentally, and, worse still, trying to do their thinking for them could only bring disaster. There was nothing for it now but to tilt his bold, broad face backward and repeat his orders, retorting with his eyes only: You'll never be an Alekseev. Three precise steps backward—then stroll off to move the battalion farther into Germany than any other Russian force would go at any time during the war.

The staff officers sat on their bench in the shade trying to calculate without the aid of quartermasters or paymasters how much bread they should order the town to have ready by evening if the needs of all the regiments were to be fully satisfied, how much they should pay for it, and whether they would have money left to buy additional provisions.

Many units were now without hardtack and salt, while others had only enough for a single day. The horses were no longer being given oats.

There in the shade it was not hot, just pleasantly warm. The little fountain with mythological figures around it played peacefully. German women in summer frocks passed nearby, leading children by the hand or wheeling them in prams. A haberdasher's shop was open for business across the road, and a cab carried an elderly couple past. Apart from the peaceful, muffled murmuring of a small town without trams or cars, no noise reached them, not even the rumble of distant guns, which sounds like stage thunder.

The 13th Corps had reached this idyllic spot after two weeks of unreal war, of cross-country rambles with never a shot fired. If only the war could have ended there and then!

General Klyuev had been forty years in the army and never seen anything of war—neither as a cadet, nor as an ensign, nor as commander of the Volynian Life Guards, nor, obviously, as a member of His Imperial Majesty's entourage. He had been kept back for "special duties" during the war with Turkey, had been "a general for special duties" in the Japanese war. As the much decorated and commended Chief of Staff of a military district, he could reasonably have hoped that he would end his career without ever going to war, but war had suddenly sought him out and he had had to take Alekseev's place as commander of a corps.

General Klyuev had, it is true, sometimes taken part in maneuvers. And, happily, his corps' movements in the past two weeks had been quite like peacetime maneuvers, even though complicated by shortage of food for the troops, poor communications, and the heavy firing on his left (he had only that morning offered fate a bribe by sending Martos a brigade made up of the Narva and Koporye regiments, which had made a previous unsuccessful attempt to join him and returned), but he bore no responsibility for happenings outside his own sector, and inside it everything had so far gone tolerably well. He was only afraid that some mistake, some incautious decision of his, might ruin his fragile well-being, or that some unforeseeable but dreadful *it* would suddenly burst in on him.

Klyuev suffered torments. He had no confidence in his own strength, he was an alien being to everyone in the corps and did not feel that the officers were behind him. About the enemy he knew nothing at all. He had not ordered his staff to find a suitable building for headquarters, because he still did not quite believe that he had taken the town and could spend the night there.

All at once (could this be the *it* he had feared?) a two-wheeler rolled up and an airman jumped out and hurried over to report. (He was made to sit in the sand at Klyuev's feet so that the whole street would not hear.) He had just returned from a reconnaissance flight thirty versts to the east, almost as far as Lake Dadey, and had seen there two columns, each the length of a division, marching in Klyuev's direction. He had not gone low enough to distinguish clearly whether or not they were Russian troops . . . but . . . but the staff officers, busily buzzing over the maps on their knees, and showing them to Generals Klyuev and Pestich, decided that it could not be otherwise. Blagoveshchensky's corps had been ordered by Samsonov to come to his assistance! The time, the direction, and the numbers all supported this supposition. By tomorrow they would be packing a real punch—two corps! And if they joined up with Martos the punch would be so much the more powerful.

Pestich, the corps' Chief of Staff, did suggest sending an older and more experienced airman to check it out, but Klyuev turned this down and ordered a letter to be written in his name to Blagoveshchensky, saying that he had arrived in Allenstein with three-quarters of his corps, that he would spend the night there, that the enemy was nowhere to be seen, and that at dawn he would make way in Allenstein for Blagoveshchensky and set off himself to join up with Martos.

He then told his staff to find a suitable building for headquarters.

Suddenly (this was *it*! this was *it*!) a heavy burst of rifle fire was heard somewhere near the town, and some small cannon opened up.

Klyuev turned pale. His mouth was dry. How and from where could the Germans have crept up on him unobserved? Would they cut off his retreat?

A horseman galloped off to find out what was happening.

Concerted firing continued for several minutes. The Germans in the street did not conceal their excitement. But the firing was in only one place, and it was petering out.

It stopped altogether.

Klyuev signed the letter, sealed the envelope, and handed it to the airman: he would land near one of the columns and give it to the nearest general.

The young pilot, proud to have been given this assignment, leapt into the two-wheeler and dashed off to his plane.

The horseman returned. What had happened was that a German armored train had unexpectedly approached the outlying buildings of Allenstein and opened fire on the encampments of the Neva and Sofia regiments. The Russians had kept their heads and repulsed the train.

"We must destroy the lines," Pestich ordered.

The airman had not returned an hour later, or two hours later, or by nightfall.

But no one felt any anxiety on that account. Flying machines often broke down.

A reconnaissance party including officers was sent to meet the advancing columns. In the early evening an officer galloped in to report that one of these (supposedly Russian) columns had opened fire on them.

Again, no one was alarmed: Russian troops often opened fire on their own side.

[27]

Infantry general Nikolai Nikolaevich Martos was what is sometimes called a "don't spill a drop" person. He could not tolerate Russian sloppiness, the Russian inclination to "wait and see," to "sleep on it" and leave God to take the decisions. Every cause for anxiety, every unexplained blemish, prompted him to active investigation, firm decision, effective response. He had the qualities of a true leader of men. He would assess any situation, however confusing the facts, rapidly, soberly, and precisely. The worse the situation, the more acute his judgment was, and the more vigorous his action. He could not go to sleep while the least little thing remained unexplained. As a result he slept very little and spent most of his time smoking. If he got little sleep, so did his staff: he could never forget or forgive that one spilled drop, could not understand how anyone could spill it, demanded that it should be mopped up at once. Every order not carried out, every question unanswered or unsatisfactorily answered, gave him pain. He tirelessly badgered his subordinates, demanding that every tiny detail should be laid before him like a burnished silver coin. Russian officers were unused to such a regime, and cursed Martos. Krymov too had thought it unbearable, and roughly criticized Martos for "nagging his staff to death." In his book no general could be more vexatious than Martos.

He had been in the army all his life (he had fought in the Turkish war at the age of nineteen) but was less like the ordinary ponderous Russian general than a masquerading civilian: lean, quick, looking younger than his fifty-six years, sharp-tongued, striding around in an unbuttoned greatcoat—which ill suited his rank badges—with a pointer in his hand.

He had commanded the 15th Corps for four years and knew every man in it. The corps was proud of its commander, and had learned from many winter and summer exercises, maneuvers, and training camps that it was superior. It was, moreover, a local unit, belonging to the Warsaw Military District; Martos had prepared it to operate in this particular theater. It was only right that his corps should find itself in the hottest spot in Prussia, should be fighting on 23 August while other corps were forging ahead into empty territory, and should be the one to feel the enemy's presence on its flanks. It was only right, too, that Martos should be the general to size up the situation which no one at the top had yet understood, and choose the right direction in which to strike.

It was not right that he should have been deprived of the 6th and 15th cavalry divisions, in which he knew personally every squadron commander, on the first day of mobilization. He had not even been left with the regiment he particularly asked for, the Glukhovo Dragoons, but had been fobbed off with the Orenburg Cossack Regiment, which had previously fought only when policing the streets of Warsaw and had carefully avoided active service. Thus the only corps in Samsonov's army ready to bear the brunt of a major battle was deprived of cavalry support and rushed off into the unknown wilderness without even mounted scouts. Nor was it right for the High Command to squander the 15th Corps' strength on futile to-ing and fro-ing before the fighting began, making it march quite unnecessarily east for the general concentration, then march back again with a detour of several days. (This was Martos's third war, but he had never before seen such confusion and such erratic haste.) All six planes in the air squadron attached to the corps were of obsolete types, and but for the heroic eagerness of the pilots to fly, the corps would have been left without aerial reconnaissance.

The timid urban Cossacks made their contribution to reconnaissance by collecting rumors from local inhabitants. As a result, the corps expected to have to fight for Neidenburg. When this did not happen Martos made 23 August the corps' first rest day—but then they stumbled on the Germans near Orlau and unexpectedly found themselves giving battle in the middle of the day. The corps' artillery had rounds enough for every gun and performed admirably. First the Simbirsk, then the Poltava Regiment flung themselves into the attack without waiting for the order (not always a good thing—they had heavy losses). The battle cost the corps two brigade commanders, three regimental commanders, several battalion commanders, many junior officers, and more than three thousand other ranks. The enemy turned out to have at least six regiments of infantry in positions chosen in advance and strongly fortified, together with sixteen batteries. In the course of a battle which went on for two days, with a close night none the fresher for light rain between them, the Russians took Orlau and Frankenau, ceded them, then recovered them in an attack at dawn. The enemy withdrew, badly mauled, leaving behind equipment, wounded and dead men, including standing corpses caught in the dense plantations of sturdy young fir trees.

The German force proved to be Scholtz's corps, which had been billeted in this area in peacetime and trained to defend it. So much for Army Group HQ's assurances that the enemy was on the run from East Prussia. As Martos continued his advance and his left flank collided with the Germans from day to day, he was the first to see the significance of Scholtz's slantwise position, and to begin veering leftward without waiting for instructions. His pilots helped him to discover and assess the fortified German position to the west of Lake Mühlen.

All this had to be done with a corps which had gone without rest days for two weeks, was weak with hunger because supplies were not being brought up, and was not always allowed to sleep at night, because that was when units were turned and moved around. Martos needed help from his neighbors if he was to dislodge Scholtz but Klyuev was still wandering around somewhere in the distance. When the battle for Orlau was raging on the 23rd Martos had scribbled Klyuev a note (the quickest and easiest procedure between neighboring commanders) asking him to send two regiments to help out at Orlau. Klyuev received the note at once and could hear the bombardment, but sent help only on the following day, and only after Martos had won the battle without it. To Martos's left there was an even more worrying vacuum: Kondratovich's corps had not closed up. There was only Mingin's division, which made a sudden assault on Mühlen on 26 August, knowing nothing about the enemy, failed to take the fortified position by storm, and rolled back southward more quickly than it had come. Then Martos was ordered by Army HQ on the 26th not to take Mühlen and not to make a frontal attack on Scholtz, but to proceed farther into the empty north, take Hohenstein, and veer northeastward, toward Allenstein! With a storm raging in his heart, Martos sent two right-wing regiments to take Hohenstein and with the rest continued veering steadily northwestward against Scholtz, until on the night of the 26th–27th, by a bold "castling" move, he turned the front completely around to face westward and the Mühlen line. (The roads were blocked by tangled supply columns for some time afterward.)

Martos knew by now that his bedraggled divisions could not by themselves overcome the German defenses, and on the evening of the 26th he wrote yet another hasty note to Klyuev, who was proceeding northward without fighting, asking him to send his two nearest regiments if he could not spare a division. There was no assurance that Klyuev would do even this, and the only way to make victory certain would have been to throw in the whole of Klyuev's corps, under Martos's command. When Army HQ materialized in Neidenburg and Martos put his request to it that same night, this was the moment, and the only moment, when, if they acted without delay, on 27 August, they could smash the whole German center, after which no combination of moves could save the German army in Prussia. But to make this possible Klyuev's corps would have to begin moving over to Martos on the night of the 26th–27th! One division should reach him before midday, and the other in the afternoon. Army HQ, however, little knowing that it was able to hold on in Neidenburg only because Martos was attacking the Germans, turned down his request.

That was no great surprise to Martos, who had reported to Samsonov in a Warsaw hotel a little while before (and had known him as a young officer, a year younger than himself). He saw no signs of ready understanding, speed, decisiveness. As for the pappy Postovsky, he was a complete disaster, no worse appointment could have been made.

Martos was the first corps commander to spend his time not at his headquarters but at a command post from which he could see the enemy, with shells bursting around him. He attached great importance to this, and felt that every absence was valuable time lost, so on the morning of the 27th, when the guns on both sides were already banging away in his sector and he calculated that Army HQ might just be rubbing the sleep out of its eyes, Martos sent a colonel to telephone from the village urgently requesting yet again the immediate diversion of Klyuev's corps to the area.

The battle for Mühlen was a heavy one: six Russian against nine German regiments. The Russians broke into the village, took prisoners, and retreated. Several hundred shrapnel shells and high-explosive shells had been fired, scores of stretchers carried to the rear, battalions pulled out and replaced by reserves, firing positions changed, batteries knocked out and towed away, and a Russian plane almost brought down by concentrated friendly fire before the colonel got back from making his call. His conversation, alas, had been with Postovsky—he could not very well insist on speaking to the commander directly—who had rejected Martos's request on the grounds that "the Army Commander does not wish to cramp General Klyuev's initiative."

Nothing could have sent Martos into a wilder spin than this answer. He threw down his field glasses, ran down from the attic, and charged around among the pines on the hillside like a madman, raging and cursing to himself, using up the useless energy of his frustrated legs. He did not make the mistake of believing that his request had been reported to the commander, who had then turned it over in his enormous head, looking at it from all angles before deciding not to interfere with Klyuev's initiative. No, he recognized at once the work of Postovsky, that ball of ink-soaked blotting paper. He recognized his dread of departing from Army Group HQ's instructions of two days back. He could see the contemptible, self-important look on the man's face as he spoke in the commander's name without consulting him. There had never been any chance that he would formalize the subordination of Klyuev's corps to Martos. Martos was a corps commander pure and simple, whereas not so long ago good old Klyuev had been Chief of Staff in a military district, where Postovsky had served under him as Quartermaster General.

What was Martos to do? Leave the field of battle in the early morning, when his troops had already crossed a fortified river, when a German battalion was fleeing in panic, and gallop to the rear himself to ring HQ and demand to be told whether the commander was awake yet? There are maddening moments, unavoidable in the army, when the dunderheads placed over you act more foolishly and more damagingly all the time—you feel like disowning your uniform completely, stripping yourself of every stitch, and drowning yourself naked!

He was called back and told that Klyuev's reply had arrived: the Narva and Koporye regiments had been sent to Hohenstein. The indefatigable Martos regained his equilibrium and geared himself to the battle again.

There at his command and observation post, where he had good communications with his regiments and his artillery, consuming three dozen cigarettes and doing without dinner, Martos might have had a reasonably good day. There was a lull in the fighting as units closed up and changed position. The Germans were also receiving fresh reserves and extra guns. Martos was informed that the two regiments sent by Klyuev had reached Hohenstein, and ordered them to continue in the same direction without delay. At 4 p.m., without giving the Germans time to get their breath or allowing his own men a rest, he launched a fresh attack with all his regiments. They made good progress, surrounding Mühlen. But Martos was not to enjoy the moment he had prayed for. A messenger galloped over to tell him that Army HQ was on the phone wanting to speak to him urgently.

Never was Martos's presence at the command post more necessary than at that moment. It was almost too great an effort to tear himself away and ride over to talk to them, even to be told that he was getting Klyuev's corps. But an old soldier's sense of self-preservation made insubordination impossible. He rode off to the telephone, leaving everything to his Chief of Staff and promising to be back soon.

Through the big, heavy receiver connected to the German civil telephone network Martos heard Postovsky's affected croak clearly. But his mind was not on the man's manner, he could not believe the words he was hearing, he shifted from foot to foot as though the ground were burning beneath him. "General Martos, your orders are as follows," the tiresome voice droned. "Tomorrow morning you will proceed toward Allenstein to link up with the 13th and the 16th Corps. A big 'fist' of three corps is being formed."

Martos, taken completely by surprise, did not understand at first. Did it mean that he must go to Klyuev instead of Klyuev coming to him?

Yes, that was just what it did mean. It was as though a hole had been torn in Martos's narrow chest by a direct hit. He could not breathe, could not go on living! The human paperweight at the other end of the phone did not and could not understand. Did not understand that the 15th Corps alone was fighting and winning a hot engagement with the whole of the enemy's live, visible force in East Prussia, with every enemy soldier who had so far shown himself! Did not understand that every hour of this battle was a golden opportunity for the whole Russian army, and that troops should be brought into this place, not taken away from it! Did not understand that this day was the most glorious in Martos's military career, in his whole life! Did not, indeed, speak ordinary human language. Said, believe it or not, that the 15th Corps had *still not carried out its orders and gone forward farther to the north!*

"Give me the commander!" Martos cried in a thin, imperious voice. "Call him at once!"

Postovsky refused. They would have to go from one room to another, you see, and all the way downstairs. Why did he want the commander? The order was in his name.

"No-o-o!" Martos yelled, while he could, yelled as though his throat were about to be cut. "No, I shall listen to nobody except the commander! Let the commander tell me which general I should hand over my men to, and release me from my command! I won't serve any longer! I'm retiring!"

Postovsky did not shout back. (He didn't know how to.) He lowered his voice till it was almost inaudible. "All right, all right," he said helplessly, "I'll inform him. I'll telephone in an hour."

You won't get through to me an hour from now. In an hour the wolves can have you for all I care!

The boyish figure moved lightly, bounced like a ball into the saddle, and galloped to the command post so fast that his adjutant could hardly keep up.

After dark the message came that Klyuev's whole corps had been put under Martos's command. Martos rushed to telephone the commander of his right division: he was to send a message to Klyuev to come to General Martos's assistance as soon as possible.

So much for Russian communications. Solitary riders galloped over strange country, with enemy detachments perhaps all around. There were telephone lines everywhere, and no engineers to put them in working order.

[2 8]

Neidenburg brought Samsonov no peace of mind and no opportunity to play a direct part. He awoke under a strange ceiling and saw through the window the roofs and spires of an ancient town built by the Teutonic Knights. The roar of cannon was inexplicably near and smoke from unextinguished fires hung in the air. Two different ways of life—that of German civilians and that of Russian soldiers—mingled in the town. Each side followed its own laws, which had no meaning for the other, but they had to exist side by side in the same narrow stone cells, and first thing in the morning, before his staff officers appeared, the Russian town commandant and the German burgomaster arrived together to seek an interview with the Army Commander. Flour had to be taken from the town's stocks to bake bread for the troops—and this meant bargaining, protests, evasions. Would the police service set up by the commandant involve the citizens in any loss? The Russians had taken over a well-equipped German hospital, but there were German doctors and German wounded in it. Buildings and transport were being requisitioned for Russian hospitals—on what conditions, and on what authority?

Samsonov made an honest attempt to get to the bottom of these matters and settle disagreements—which in any case were amicable enough on both sides—fairly. But he could not concentrate. He was uneasily aware of things happening out of sight and out of reach in the sands and the forests, over a sprawling area of a hundred versts, and all the more uneasy because his staff officers showed no eagerness to burst in and report on these happenings.

Nominally, the commander stands higher than his staff officers in the army hierarchy, he has authority over them, not they over him, but in a slow-moving situation it is often the other way around: it depends on the staff officers what their commander learns and does not learn, what he is allowed to pronounce on and what not.

The previous day had culminated like all others in the dispatch of the most rational of all possible instructions to each of the corps telling it what to do on the morrow, and the army staff had gone to bed assured that all was as well as it possibly could be. By morning some members of the staff had thought up objections to what they themselves had insisted on yesterday, but you take your time reporting second thoughts to the commander. It rather looked as though some of yesterday's orders should in fact be changed, but it was too late for that since the morning's battles were already being fought in accordance with them. So the commander was left to spend a leisurely morning, trusting that with God's aid things were developing as he had wished and as he had ordered—that is to say, for the best.

But there was no concealing from him events in Mingin's division connected with the gunfire nearby. That division had for some reason not been transported by rail from Novogeorgievsk to Mlawa but had footslogged for a hundred versts alongside the track, and another fifty away from it, then quick-marched straight into the offensive the day before. The right-wing regiments had nonetheless almost taken Mühlen, and the Reval and Estland regiments, on the left, had also made good headway but had come under heavy fire and withdrawn. On learning this, Mingin had pulled the right wing back too, and broken away from Martos, perhaps exposing his flank. On all other matters—how big were the losses? What new positions had the retreating troops taken up?—

information was vague. So vague that for the time being a less alarming construction could be put upon it, especially as the firing had become more distant since morning and shifted to the right, in Martos's direction.

Samsonov scrutinized the map placed before him. He gave orders that Mingin should be told not to withdraw his regiments beyond a certain village ten versts from Neidenburg whatever happened. He cherished the hope that Sirelius's Guards division would be in Mingin's neighborhood very shortly. He had been eagerly expecting either Sirelius or Kondratovich, the Corps Commander, to visit him that morning, but they had not appeared.

Perhaps it would be better if the Army Commander himself went and took a look, rather than sending an officer to make inquiries? But if he went off to Mingin's division something important was bound to pop up on the opposite side.

So Samsonov passed the first half of the day in suspense, deprived of reliable information and with nothing obviously worth doing; he spent part of the time with Knox again (they rode to high ground and gazed into the distance), part of it with the quartermasters, the hospital commandant, then Postovsky, or poring over telegrams from HQ Northwestern Army Group. Dinnertime was approaching when a Cossack patrol brought in a report from Blagoveshchensky, signed out at 2 a.m.

The report was so strange that blink, frown, huff and puff as he would, Samsonov, even with the help of his staff officers, understood nothing. Blagoveshchensky was apparently unaware that he had been ordered to help Klyuev out: he made no reference to it, and gave no excuse for not doing what he had been told. He knew even less about the Germans—according to one peculiar sentence, "reconnaissance produced no information about the enemy." And immediately after that came the news that in the fighting that morning at Gross-Bössau (what fighting? when had he reported any fighting?) Komarov had lost more than four thousand men. Lost one-quarter of his division! And *still* "no information about the enemy"! After all that he indicated that the corps was withdrawing to a point twenty versts south of Gross-Bössau. He was obviously abandoning Bischofsburg, yet there was not a word about it. What sort of forces did the Germans have there? If their flank had merely brushed Blagoveshchensky as they ran by, how could they have inflicted losses of four thousand? They were not running, though—Rennenkampf was not getting any nearer, so obviously they were holding him. There ought not to be any considerable force facing Blagoveshchensky. Where could it have come from?

If the Germans had moved away from Rennenkampf, where had he got to? He knew where he was well off, that one.

Escaping somehow from Knox, Samsonov went along the dark corridor of the Landrat building carrying the evasive report—evasive? lying was the word—like a perturbed bear and sat at a dark oak desk with his head in his hands.

How dismally different war looked nowadays! The change had turned an army commander into a rag doll. If you have a general view of the battlefield you can gallop over to a fainthearted commander or send for him—but where *was* the battlefield? In the war with Japan it was sometimes remote and obscured. But where was it now? Cossacks had ridden twelve hours, covered seventy versts of enemy territory, risking death or captivity, to deliver this base, mendacious, traitorous letter! And there was no way of getting through to the coward, to find out what he was about, reprove him, put some heart into him, confirm his orders, no way at all until the Cossacks had fed their horses, rested them, and made the twelve-hour ride back. The wireless telegraph stations could not find each other, the flying machines either couldn't take off or did not return. He didn't much like the idea of sending his one and only car with his reply to Blagoveshchensky, and anyway it would need a mounted escort. Whether it was seventy versts now or five in Kutuzov's time, a horse's hooves were no different, his stride no longer. Not until this time tomorrow would he be able to find out whether the 6th Corps could straighten itself out and join up with the others, or whether it would split away completely, lose contact, so that Samsonov's army would find its right arm amputated.

With this sensation—that his right arm had been amputated, his right wing fractured—Samsonov sat down to dine. He could eat nothing. He made no efforts to disguise his gloom from Knox, and answered his questions without thinking.

But halfway through lunch cheering news reached them: communications with the 1st Corps, interrupted early that morning, had been reestablished, and he was given Artamonov's report: "Attacked by large enemy force at Usdau this morning. All attacks repelled. Standing firm as a rock. Shall carry out orders in full."

The commander's high, sloping brow cleared. He looked years younger. The mood around the table lightened. Knox, full of goodwill, eagerly plied him with questions.

His right arm hung paralyzed but new power was surging through the left—now the important one. How unjust he had been to Artamonov those past few days, writing him off as a careerist and a busy fool! Now he was the spearhead of the offensive of the whole army, and he could not possibly be suspected of exaggerating—such a strong and vivid expression as "firm as a rock" would never have occurred to him if it were not true.

The last minutes of the lunch were pleasant. Samsonov wanted further details from Krymov or Vorotyntsev, whichever of them could get to the phone more easily, but the line had been cut again.

All the more reason why he should turn his mind to the corps in the center. Although it was not yet 3 p.m. it was obviously time to start drafting tomorrow's order of the day for the whole army: better too early than too late. It would of course be more sensible to issue instructions hourly as the situation changed, rather than for twenty-four hours at a time, but once in twenty-four hours was the generally accepted practice—he was not responsible for it and couldn't change it.

A map was unfolded on the oval table, and Samsonov, Filimonov, and two colonels, holding one corner each, bent over it, tracing imaginary lines with their fingers while a colonel from Operations read out passages from previous instructions and reports for their guidance.

For Samsonov this sort of teamwork was always a solemn ritual. The fate of whole battalions, regiments even, might depend on accidental factors—poor lighting, the blink of an eyelid, whether you were seated or standing at the table, the thickness of a finger, a blunt pencil. Doing his best to reconcile the pattern of lines and arrows with his own calculations and instructions from above, Samsonov strove as conscientiously as he could to reach a rational conclusion. Drops of sweat fell on the map, and Samsonov mopped his brow, perhaps not only because the air in the Landrat building with its small and narrow windows was hot and heavy.

The order of the day began as always with a statement of what had been achieved. It was not at all bad—the 1st Corps had repulsed German attacks at Usdau, Mingin's division would hold the position assigned to it whatever the cost, the 15th Corps had taken Hohenstein and would take Mühlen at any moment, the 13th Corps was in Allenstein, the 6th Corps . . . well, the 6th Corps too might yet pull itself together.

Tomorrow, then? Obviously, the central corps would accelerate their swing to the left, with Artamonov's corps standing fast and serving as the axis on which the whole army would turn. Artamonov's orders would diplomatically avoid any mention of the possibility of retreat. And if he were told to stand his ground "*before* Soldau" the Supreme Commander's wishes must not be flouted. Klyuev would be ordered to proceed by forced marches and to join Martos. As for Martos, Filimonov insisted on an ingenious formulation: "Slip leftward along your own lines so as to shake off the enemy and leave him on your flank."

There was one thing which they could not tell the corps commanders: how strong the enemy was, his positions, how many corps he had.

And there, nearly ready, lay tomorrow's order of the day. It would be hard work, for someone, struggling through the underbrush in the half-darkness—but the order lay there on paper without a blot, in a fair, sloping hand.

But Samsonov was still not sure that everything had been done. Moreover, he felt unwell, there was no air to breathe.

"I think I'll take a walk and get some fresh air, gentlemen. We can sign it later—there's plenty of time."

Filimonov and Colonel Vyalov asked permission to go with him. The Chief of Intelligence, an officer with a bald head like a shiny pumpkin, took the draft order to Postovsky in another chamber. He noticed at once that it contradicted the latest orders from the Northwestern Army Group—that they should continue the offensive strictly northward.

"What are you thinking of?" he asked. "Martos should be closing up to Klyuev, not Klyuev to Martos. That's how we shall make the 'big fist.' "

By now it was after four, the heat was letting up, but the stone streets and buildings were oven-hot and the commander still could not get enough air. He took his cap off and wiped his brow again.

"Shall we walk on to the end of the town, gentlemen? There's a grove of some sort or a cemetery out there." Although he had already seen it the day before, and although he was now out in the glaring sunshine, the commander stopped in front of the Bismarck monument: there were flower beds around a massive rough-hewn yellow-brown rock with a jagged upper edge.

Bismarck—one third of his actual girth—stood out in sharp, angular relief—a dark Bismarck, as though he were shrouded in black thoughts.

The street they had taken led to the northwestern highways. That was the way to Mingin's division, and it was perhaps not accidental that the commander had felt drawn in that direction. He was walking along with his hands behind his back, as was his habit. From in front this made him look impressive, but from behind he looked like a manacled convict, and his bowed head heightened the resemblance. He did not try to make conversation, and the other officers kept their distance.

Samsonov had a feeling that he was doing the wrong thing, or, rather, that there was something he should be doing, something that eluded him, something hidden behind an impenetrable veil. He wanted to gallop off somewhere, anywhere, with saber drawn—but that would be senseless, and unbecoming to one in his position.

He was dissatisfied with himself. And Filimonov was permanently dissatisfied with him—that was obvious. No doubt the corps commanders were also dissatisfied. Army Group HQ had called him a coward. GHQ too must be thinking ill of him.

But what he should be doing no one could tell him.

The grove began just past the last house on the street. They were about to turn into it when a two-wheeler came rattling along at a brisk pace, followed by another, and then by a two-horse cart. The drivers plied their whips as though they were fleeing from hot pursuit, moving at a speed quite improper in the precincts of Army HQ. Samsonov's escort rushed to stop the vehicles and Filimonov, tugging at his aiguillette and looking angry, stepped into the middle of the road. Samsonov had so far ignored the whole thing. He went into the grove and sat on a bench.

The noise from the street, however, did not diminish. The wheels had stopped, but other vehicles drove up. There was a babble of voices, hushed as they came closer. Filimonov could be heard angrily interrogating the soldiers and forbidding them to go on. Samsonov asked Vyalov to go and find out what it was all about. The courteous Vyalov returned after some delay, at a loss as to how to tell Samsonov. Meanwhile Filimonov's voice was rising as he sharply reproved someone.

Vyalov explained that these were the disorganized remnants of the Estland Regiment, with a few men from the Reval Regiment (who had been supposed to stand their ground *whatever the cost* some ten versts away). They had broken ranks and run for it and kept going all the way to Neidenburg, unaware, of course, that Army HQ was now in that town. They were in a mood to roll back still farther.

Samsonov rose, disconcerted, breathing hard, and went out bareheaded into the fierce sunlight, his cap dangling forgotten in his hand.

The runaways formed up after a fashion—several vehicles, four officers in a group of their own, some hundred and fifty soldiers, with others straggling in to join them. They were ordered to sort themselves out into four ranks—and what ranks they were! Wavy lines of men with inflamed faces, many without caps, as though they were at prayer, not on parade, some without greatcoat rolls, others with their rolls at their feet, and some seeming no longer to have rifles. The bulge at the side of that dark-haired fellow acting as right marker was a mess tin, which he had hung on to although it had been holed by a splinter. There were a couple of dozen wounded, some with open wounds on which the blood had dried. They had halted, but seemed still to be in motion, swaying, poised to resume their retreat. There was a dazed look about them, and it was amazing that they somehow remained in line.

As the Army Commander approached, Filimonov bellowed, "Attention!" (Samsonov waved a deprecating hand) and began reporting at the top of his voice, or, rather, abusing this craven herd who had ceased to behave like human beings, let alone soldiers . . . Until then Samsonov had heard his Quartermaster General only indoors. He had not expected this raucous, rasping fury. Filimonov stood before the ranks yelling with the long-pent-up self-importance of a desk soldier and the martinet zeal of generals low in stature.

Listening to him shouting, accusing the whole Estland Regiment of treason, cowardice, desertion, Samsonov studied the soldiers' flushed and defiant faces. It was the reckless defiance of men who feel that the end is near, men whose ears are impervious to any amount of scolding from generals. It was a miracle that they had let themselves be halted. A stone wall couldn't have stopped them in their present mood.

All the same, Samsonov saw at once that their desperation was different from the mutinous defiance he had seen in turbulent soldiers' meetings along the Trans-Siberian Railway in 1905, when committees were supplanting officers to loud cries of "Down with . . . !" and "Let's all go home!" and station buildings and buffets were sacked and locomotives seized and their wagons detached. "We're first! We're going home! Down with the lot of them!" Officers counted for nothing at all. A hundred mutinous voices yelled, "Down with them!" (Yes, you too, who were always good to the men, we don't need your kindness, damn you, just give us our birthright!)

But here, on these contorted faces, the faces of men who had never expected to return from death to life, there was an agonized appeal to the officers: Take our birthright, damn you, you can have it—what will you give us in return?

Samsonov felt himself turning red—perhaps nobody would notice in the bright sunshine—as he put out a great paw to stop the Quartermaster General's hectoring, and began quietly questioning them, first the officers, the nearest to hand (there was only one company commander among them), then the rankers . . .

These were no practiced storytellers, the words tumbled out confusedly, and anyway what had they understood except that death was whistling all around them? They had been shelled by hundreds of guns, with not so much as a ditch to cower in, only the shallow furrows of a beet field. Russian artillery was missing, or else couldn't get the range to reply. The few cannon that did take the field were swept away immediately. Nonetheless, our side had answered the enemy's big guns with long-distance rifle and machine-gun fire. They had even counterattacked, forcing their way through to the German trenches. They had used up all their cartridges. Then enemy infantry began trying to encircle them, and cavalry might be wheeling around to take them in the rear (though they couldn't be sure of that). There wouldn't be so much crashing and banging on doomsday, old soldiers had never heard the like. Maybe three thousand of their regiment had been wiped out. They couldn't find words to describe it.

It was his fault. All his fault. He had heard the firing yesterday and had meant to ride over that morning. Why hadn't he? He had been wrong to wait there for them, he should have sought them out in their hour of need. There was more to it than that. A thought which simply hadn't occurred to him in the dim Landrat chamber burst through now: only yesterday, he had sent them written orders for today, on the advice of this same irrepressible general, telling them which highroad to cut so as to hold up the Germans; even as the crow flies they would have had twenty versts to go. And then he had sent them into the hottest spot, the only place where Germans had been spotted, standing their ground and fighting. Today he had ordered the shattered remnants of those regiments to "hold on whatever the cost . . ."

While they were talking more soldiers came and stood at the back. A flag on a pole arrived, with a St. George's Cross mounted on the knob and with jubilee ribbons. The standard-bearer came closer and stood silent on the left flank, with a handful of soldiers around him—wounded, bedraggled, and without weapons.

Samsonov had been speaking in a quiet, measured voice which everybody had been able to hear. He raised it a little so that the new arrivals could hear too.

"Men of the Reval Regiment, how many of you are there?"

The sergeant major trumpeted back, "The color guard. And one platoon."

Without asking permission somebody called out from the rear rank of the Estland Regiment in a hoarse, impatient voice, "Your Excellency! We haven't had so much as a rusk for three days now."

"What's that?"

The commander looked around in amazement, his face darkening. All day yesterday, advancing over oven-hot ground, under withering artillery fire, hurled into sudden bayonet charges, every tenth man seeing nine of his comrades die . . .

"No rusks, you say?"

"Not one," they assured him in a ragged chorus.

They saw the commander's bulk sway. His adjutant rushed to support him, but he regained his balance unaided.

It would have given him relief to crash to the ground and cry out, "I am guilty! I have destroyed you, my brothers!" It would have eased his heart to take all the blame on himself and rise from the ground commander no longer.

Instead, he gave a quiet order: "See that they get something to eat and find them a place to rest."

And his heart was as heavy as ever.

He walked off toward the town, stumbling like a man under a curse.

Just then several horsemen escorted by a staff officer rounded the Bismarck monument. The officer pointed to Samsonov, and the newcomers dismounted and walked toward him, lengthening their rolling cavalry gait—a cavalry general, a colonel of dragoons, and a Cossack colonel.

Major General Shtempel (Samsonov wrinkled his brow—there were so many generals in his army: yes, of course, one of Ropp's brigade commanders) reported that he had brought a combined force consisting of a dragoon regiment, three and a half squadrons of the 6th Don Regiment, and a mounted battery. The force had been formed by Colonel Krymov with the authorization of the Army Commander, with orders to reestablish live communications between the 1st and 23rd corps, which had been cut.

Samsonov could still see the Estland and Reval regiments, thoughts of their misery and his guilt were still chasing each other through his head, and at the back of his mind was the thought that temporary formations, detachments from one command and reassignments to another, are always a sign that things are going badly. But time wouldn't stand still, he must get at the facts and make sense of them.

"So. Right then . . . That's good . . . Between the two corps . . . Yes indeed . . ."

He shook hands with all three. Of course! The Cossack colonel he knew! He had recognized those rough homely features, that close-cropped gray hair, that bristly gray beard as soon as he saw the man. He had met him at Novocherkassk. "Isaev, isn't it? Aleksei Nikolaevich?"

He was getting on for seventy, but was as alert as ever. "The same, Your Excellency!"

"Why three and a half squadrons, though?" Samsonov asked with a faint smile.

Isaev, glad of an opportunity to complain (perhaps he would get his regiment together again), told him, but gave Samsonov a strange look as he did so.

Shtempel also looked askance. He and Isaev exchanged glances.

"Nobody pins medals on the bringer of bad news," bluff Isaev said, showing embarrassment.

Samsonov felt a pang. "What is it now?"

The skinny major general stood to attention and held out an envelope as though he expected to be shot for it. "A special messenger from Colonel Krymov caught up with us. He asked us to give you this."

"What's in it?" Samsonov asked, as though it would be less painful by word of mouth. But his fingers were already unfolding a sheet covered with Krymov's intricate handwriting.

"Your Excellency, Aleksandr Vasilievich! General Artamonov is a fool, a coward, and a liar. Acting on his misconceived orders, the corps has been retreating in disarray since midday. This is being kept from you. The splendid counterattack made by the Petrov and Neuschlott regiments and the Rifles has not been followed up. Usdau has been surrendered, and it is doubtful whether we shall manage to hold Soldau till nightfall . . ."

If he had been told this by word of mouth, even under oath, it would have been incredible. But Krymov would not have written it if it were not so.

Samsonov reared up, turned crimson, trembled violently; his chest heaved like a bellows. He had been dragging himself along, feeling drained and guilty, but now he had discovered a bigger villain than himself. Strong and righteous again, he bellowed over the crossroads, "I'm relieving the scoundrel of his command!"

He rested his raised hand on the rough rock of the Bismarck monument.

"You there! Communications with Soldau must be restored immediately. I relieve General Artamonov of his command. General Dushkevich is to take his place. Inform the 1st Corps and Army Group HQ."

He leaned against the monument as though it were a cliff, supporting himself with his left hand, or so he thought. But he no longer had a left arm.

They had cut that one off as well.

[2 9]

Only the day before, they had rushed the Narva and Koporye regiments northward, running them off their feet, denying them even a short pause by a well, driving them on and on though night was falling, calling a halt only in the pitch dark. There was a rumor that bread would be baked and distributed next day in Allenstein. But on the morning of the 27th, after the usual dithering and dawdling, waiting for orders unborn or stillborn, while the battalions were taking root, knowing all the while that their legs would have to pay for these delays, orders came for the Narva and Koporye regiments to go back leftward, away from Allenstein, returning versts to the invisible enemy as fast as their forced march had denied them to him yesterday, and rush to the aid of their neighbors, just as those very same regiments had done three days earlier, all to no purpose.

Perhaps the Brigade Commander was given some sort of explanation with this order. Perhaps some crumbs of information were strewn before regimental commanders even. But officers at battalion level received no explanation, and even the most trusting found it difficult to see who but a fool or a malicious joker would follow up yesterday's march with today's. As for the rankers, what could they think? Yaroslav Kharitonov was ashamed to face his men, whose bodies had suffered the torments of these traipsings, as though he were the sadistic traitor at HQ who the soldiers suspected must be responsible for it all.

But an unexpected recompense for two weeks of hunger and exhaustion on the march awaited their regiments. At noon, in bright sunshine, with a steady breeze blowing, and fluffy clouds sailing merrily up above, there in the spacious view from the Griesslinnen heights was the first town they had seen. Within an hour they were entering it without opposition—the little town of Hohenstein, one kilometer square, astonished by the steeply pitched roofs huddled so close together and by its emptiness. This indeed made it frightening for a minute or so. No Russian soldiers, no civilians, not a single old man, woman, child, or even a dog, just a wary cat or two. Some shutters had been smashed in, the window frames had been torn from their hinges and the panes shattered. The leading regiment could not believe it at first. They had expected to have to fight for the town, had posted reserves, and sent out scouts. Some little way ahead artillery was thundering and machine guns chattering, but by some caprice of war the sharp-roofed town itself was empty—and undamaged!—and whoever had got there before them must also have occupied an empty town without a battle, and abandoned it.

The regiments flowed in from the Allenstein highway still eager to do battle, ready to march right through the town and carry on to wherever they were ordered; but just as the hero in a fairy tale feels his strength draining away as soon as he steps into the enchanted circle, drops his sword, lance, and shield, and is suddenly completely in the power of the enchanter, here, too, the very first clusters of houses enveloped the battalions in some mysterious force as they entered. Feet were suddenly out of step, heads swung this way and that, the impetus which had carried them toward the noise of battle flagged and foundered, brigade and regimental commanders somehow no longer held sway over them, there was no one to urge the men on, no dispatch riders came galloping up with fresh orders. So the battalions began to break away to right or left, each searching the town for living space of its own; then, as the collective will of the battalion was paralyzed, companies acquired a life of their own until they in turn disintegrated into platoons. The surprising thing was that nobody was surprised. The enchantment in the air sapped their strength like an enervating ill wind.

Yaroslav tried, in spite of it all, not to forget for a moment that this was not how things should be, that their help was needed and expected up ahead. But his authority went no further than his own platoon. And next, platoons began noiselessly, imperceptibly dribbling, seeping into their surroundings like water finding its way around obstructions to settle in empty hollows. Kharitonov's platoon, though it was made up of the best and most disciplined soldiers, could not stand out in the sun alone, weighed down by weapons. His men had earned the right to rest.

And to food? After so many debilitating days on short rations, was it really so very bad if his soldiers too, feeling the pinch of hunger, began drifting off in twos and threes, some asking permission, like noble Kramchatkin, who stamped up to him, eyes rolling, as though his life depended on his commanding officer's answer: "Permission to speak, Your Honor! Can I have leave to look for something in the way of provisions?" Others just slunk behind a wall and came straight back with sugar and biscuits in colored packets, dropping things in their haste and their eagerness not to be seen by the platoon commander. Was it wrong? Ought he to punish them? After all, they were hungry, and if they were not fed they could not fight. Why should he concern himself with abandoned property, there for the taking? He wanted to consult other officers, but there seemed to be none in sight. Anyway, why should he need to ask anyone else? He was an adult person and an officer. He ought to decide for himself.

Now they were bringing macaroni, something Russian peasants had never seen in their lives. More amazing yet, veal, ready roasted, in glass jars. Naberkin, a restless little man with shining eyes, brought his lieutenant some, eager to please. "Sir, don't turn your nose up at it. Try some. It's really clever, the way they've done it!"

No, there was no crime here. The soldiers could eat it with a clear conscience. They had earned it. Something to stew. Something to warm up in a house, or outside, over a fire between bricks. Here was something still more interesting, something new and strange even to the officers—the way the Germans preserved eggs, putting them in whitish water, obviously with lime in it, and they would still be as though newly laid after who knows how many months.

The Germans didn't have heavy locks on their storehouses. They seemed to have the stupid notion that nothing would be stolen as long as there was some sort of lock. Word was going around that there had been large stockpiles in the town and that other battalions had got at them first.

No, Yaroslav didn't like it. It was wrong. He had to forbid it! He must line them up and explain . . .

Just then the keen and efficient sergeant, Yaroslav's right-hand man in the platoon, reported that there was a barracks on the edge of town and a lot of maps in the office there. Yaroslav suddenly felt an urgent need to cast an eye on those maps before they went any farther. The soldiers in his platoon were good lads, really. He left the sergeant behind with strict instructions, told a reluctant soldier to accompany him, and hurried off.

A few scavengers were scouring the barracks, but no one seemed to fancy German uniforms or sergeant major gear. The office door was wide open, and inside, sure enough, there was a pile of German maps of East Prussia, on a scale of one kilometer to a centimeter, and very clearly printed, much more legible than those which the Narva Regiment had distributed, one to each battalion. Yaroslav set the soldier to work handing him maps and putting them away tidily once Yaroslav had scanned them, looking for the places they had passed through and those in which they might find themselves next. War takes on a different complexion when you have a full set of maps! He scanned maps of the route to the Vistula eagerly; there is an irresistible fascination in a topographical map of a place in which you may soon set foot for the first time. Kharitonov assembled one big set for the Vistula crossing, and three separate sets showing the immediate neighborhood (he must present Grokholets with one of them!).

Eagerly, methodically, quickly Yaroslav sorted his maps and just as quickly his spirits sank. His pleasure in the maps was incomplete, somehow unreal, but there was nothing unreal about the gray disquiet stealing over him—or was it fear? Fear of getting back too late and finding the regiment gone? No, a different fear, a presentiment of disaster perhaps? And although what he was doing was very important, he wanted to drop it and hurry off. He would not be at ease until he was back with the regiment again! There wasn't even time to inspect the accommodation provided in German barracks for private soldiers—better than Russian junior officers got, no doubt. He grew more tense and anxious with every moment of delay; he had had enough of sorting and scanning—all he wanted was to get back to his comrades.

The soldier carried the maps, tied in a bundle, and Yaroslav hurried back to his platoon. He saw as he went how much the town had changed in a single hour: it had been an alien, an eerie place, but now it had begun to look like home. Soldiers with itchy fingers roamed the streets finding their way as easily as they would in their native villages. Their own officers did not shout at them, so it was not for Kharitonov to interfere. A barrel of beer was rolled down the street. They had found poultry in the town, and bloody feathers fluttered in the roadway, stirred by the breeze, among the rustling colored wrappings and empty packets. Litter and broken glass crackled and crunched underfoot. Through a gaping window space he saw a ransacked apartment: drawers had been wrenched out, tablecloths, women's hats, linen were scattered about the floor, but amid the wreckage you could still see how neat and tidy a loving hand had kept this place.

He felt more tense than ever. What about *his* platoon? Surely his platoon couldn't have . . . ?

Two soldiers were standing by the door of a shop, apparently on guard, barring the way to other ranks but standing aside to admit officers. An officer Kharitonov knew went in, and he for some reason followed. It was a clothes shop. Rankers were bustling about in the sales area, by the front window—Yaroslav recognized Kozeko's orderly—while in the back room officers were quietly and methodically trying on waterproof capes, knitted sweaters, warm underwear, gaiters, gloves, supporting themselves on chair backs or their orderlies' shoulders in the confined space, or else inspecting rugs and women's coats from all angles.

Kozeko, in yellowy-brown winter underpants, was delighted to find Kharitonov at his side. "Kharitonov, Kharitonov! Make the most of this opportunity! Help yourself to some warm clothes! It'll be getting cold soon—the nights are bad enough already. A man can't be thinking about death all the time. There are other things to worry about . . ."

Yaroslav couldn't make out who else was there. Some of them might be people he knew. There were men between him and the only window. He stood there half blind, not really seeing even Kozeko, or seeing not so much his face and his wiry figure as those warm, fleecy yellow drawers. It was Kozeko he spoke to, but perhaps loudly enough for others to hear: "You ought to be ashamed of yourself."

Kozeko started, advanced on Yaroslav, and even gripped him by his chest strap so that he could not escape and would have to listen. "What on earth is there to be ashamed of, Kharitonov? Just think a bit. You and I have no warm things, and who knows when they'll get around to issuing any? You know the Russian quartermaster service as well as I do. You and I will be freezing, we shall be sleeping on the bare ground in our greatcoats. We shall catch our death of cold. The nights are getting chilly. It has to be done, not so much for you and me personally, but for the army's sake. We shall fight better that way. Here, have this sweater."

Yaroslav's annoyance, his hasty impulse to put things right, were spent. They gave way to a marble heaviness in his legs, his eyes, his soul.

He wished, oh how he wished, that he did not have to walk any farther, see any more; that this wealthy town would sink into the earth. He wished that they were still trudging through the sand as they had for so many days. Material things had become loathsome, all of them. It was so easy to do without them!

"This isn't the way, though . . ." Kharitonov pushed the sweater away, wearily, weakly. He tried to remove Kozeko's hand from his strap, but it was not easy to loosen that grip.

"What is the right way, then? What should we do? Buy the stuff? We came in to buy—but where do we pay? The proprietor has run away. We could leave the money, I suppose, but who would get it? Anyway, you can't buy a lot with what we're paid."

"Well, I just don't know." Yaroslav had no ready answer. But his disgust was choking him. He freed himself and made for the door with Kozeko striding behind him, still gripping his shoulder, his face puckered as though he were crying. "Well, I agree that it's wrong," he said quietly, almost in Kharitonov's ear. "If you stop to think the front may be rolled back as far as Vilna, and the enemy may force his way into my little nest, with my little wife in it, and wreck it, like we've wrecked other people's delightful little homes . . . I don't want anything for myself. I don't want any medals, you know that!" His pleas were almost tearful. "But they won't let me go home till I get an arm or a leg torn off. So my advice is dress as warmly as you can, there's a winter campaign ahead, Kharitonov! Take some of these underclothes! And a sweater!"

Yaroslav still had faith in his platoon. He must get back to them. He had no more interest in food and drink, let alone things to wear . . .

The premonition of disaster was growing.

There was a fire somewhere in the town—big flames leapt high in the air with a steady roar. Other fires might easily break out: smoke was rising from campfires and field ovens. Soldiers wandered among them, looking like gypsies, dragging things around. How the Narva Regiment had changed in two hours!

Men were tying a bicycle onto a cart, on top of a wooden box full of perfumes and other stolen goods.

Some of the officers in the regiment had succumbed! But his soldiers had the common people's strong sense of right and wrong. They would understand at once if only somebody explained to them. Yaroslav felt that he himself was to blame. He had tried the potted meat and praised it. That was how it had all begun. He had felt impotent, felt that a beardless boy had no right to teach peasants, married men with families, the basic rules of life—but it was his duty to do so, if his epaulets meant anything.

He lost his way and had to make a detour. He still didn't recognize the place until he saw lanky, ladder-backed Vyushkov carrying something wrapped in a sheet over his shoulder.

Was it Vyushkov, though? Perhaps it wasn't Vyushkov . . . He caught up with him and yelled, "Vyushkov!"

It was a despairing wail, shrill enough to make Vyushkov drop his bundle and look as though he meant to run. But instead he turned around, lowering. He averted his head, avoiding Yaroslav's eyes.

Could this be the nimble-tongued storyteller with the winning smile, the spirit of old Smolensk? How hangdog and sullen and shifty he looked now. What a wretched fellow he had turned out to be.

Yaroslav's reprimand was a rain of hammer blows. "What are you doing? Where are you going? Where are you taking that to? We shall be under fire soon. We may be dead tomorrow . . . have you lost all decency . . . have you gone crazy?" But he added hopefully, pathetically, "What's come over you, Vyushkov?"

Vyushkov, eyes down, avoided his gaze. "Sorry, sir, the devil got into me."

"Well, come with me. Come on!"

Vyushkov's legs seemed to have taken root. They would not move away from the bundle.

Who was this coming toward them? Kramchatkin, the best soldier in the platoon—it couldn't be Kramchatkin—red in the face, staggering, humming or muttering to himself. It was Kramchatkin all right. His eyes fell upon his officer, he pulled himself together, took a step, even tried to stamp his feet smartly on the smooth flagstones, but why did the toe of one boot catch the heel of the other, why that wild, pop-eyed glare? Still, his hand shot up in a correct salute.

"Sir . . . sir, sir . . . permission to speak . . . Private Kramchatkin, Ivan Feofanovich, returning . . ."

But the oblique impetus of his salute swung him in an arc, and his cap fell off as he flopped with a heavy thud on the pavement.

My little brother! Ivan Feofanovich, of whom I was so proud!

Horrified, but angry too, Yaroslav hurried on. There had been warnings enough: looters could expect corporal punishment, they would be flogged unmercifully. But that was when looters were people you didn't know, remote evildoers, not men from your own Narva Regiment, your own platoon.

He would parade them at once, under the baking sun, with all their arms and equipment, and give them such a dressing-down as they had never had before! Find out exactly who had taken what. Make every one of them drop what he had stolen . . .

There was the house. The gates were wide open, and he could see a smoke-blackened pot suspended from poles, and lapped by flame from blazing coals. Fifteen men from his platoon were sitting around the fire on piles of bricks or boxes, on whatever they could find. The ground around their feet was strewn with cans and food of all sorts. They picked at it from time to time, but were more interested in drinking, dipping their mugs and mess tins into the pot over the fire.

They were all tipsy. The stuff they were ladling out must be—could it be?—alcoholic. But why was it over the fire?

No, the look on their faces was not one of drunken euphoria—it was the contented, benevolent look of men breaking their fast after Lent, smiling, chatting, telling stories with the relaxed and peaceable air of friends at table. Their unneeded rifles stood on one side, neatly arranged in pyramids.

They showed no alarm when Yaroslav appeared. They brightened, seemed glad to see him, made room for him.

"Your Honor! Come and sit down, Your Honor! Come and sit with us!" Two of them got busy with mugs—one rinsing his first, the other not bothering, racing each other to dip them in the pot and offer them, hot and brimming, with Easter smiles.

"You must try this coco-a, sir."

Naberkin, a rotund little man but quick on his feet, got there first, and said in his squeaky voice, "Have a drink of coco-a, sir! This is what Jerry keeps his strength up with, the bastard!"

He couldn't shout. Couldn't tell them off. Couldn't line them up and punish them. Couldn't even decline what was offered.

Kharitonov swallowed hard. Then swallowed some cocoa.

The back wall of the yard was not very high. There was an open space beyond it, and beyond that a two-story house with a mansard roof was on fire.

Those were not pistol shots but tiles cracking in the flames. Thick black smoke poured from the roof, then pink tongues of fire thrust their way through, burning vigorously and steadily.

They saw it, but no one ran to put it out.

It was not their property, not their labor, that smoke and crackling flame were flinging into the air. They had no use for it. Fiery voices whispered hoarsely, groaned that this was the end, that there could be no reconciliation now, that life would never be the same again.

[3 0]

Blagoveshchensky, after retreating twenty-five versts from Bischofsburg, covered by the reconstituted rear guard under Nechvolodov (who else?), halted, badly shaken, on the morning of 27 August in the little town of Mensguth, where neither he nor anyone on his staff issued any orders to the corps all day long. The rear guard remained in position for as long as it thought necessary. Some units of the infantry and cavalry divisions, finding it convenient to do so, withdrew without asking or informing Corps HQ. General of infantry Blagoveshchensky had never led so much as a company into action, and all at once he was commanding a corps. He had in his time been in charge of troop trains, he had been Chief of Army Signals, and in the Japanese war he had been a general on the staff, issuing rail-travel permits and composing a scientific manual on entitlement to such warrants. Yesterday he had suffered a crushing blow—and the general needed peace and quiet to gather and piece together the fragments of his shattered life.

It was, in fact, quiet all day: they had withdrawn too far during the night for the Germans to put any pressure on them. But a lull never lasts long in wartime. They weren't allowed even twenty-four hours' rest. At six in the evening they heard the first sounds of fighting to the north, where they had left the rear guard. Shells from distant German guns were soon winging in the direction of Mensguth. Anxiety muddied Blagoveshchensky's mind again, and his staff looked somber.

Then—that was all they needed!—a rider galloped in with a report from quite a different quarter, from the Don Cossack squadron posted to protect their flank. He had a written report describing how the squadron had clashed with the enemy fifteen versts away, but he was bursting to tell the story for himself. He had been there too, he too, once upon a time, had fought the Germans! So, when he caught sight of another squadron of his own regiment on the outskirts of Mensguth . . .

SCREEN

The dashing Cossack reins in his horse,
flourishes the dispatch,
points back over his shoulder as much as to say, "We've been fighting back there," and calls out to his fellow Cossacks the glad tidings:
"The Germans are here! The Germans!"
And gallops off—no time to lose, must get this dispatch to headquarters!
= While his brother Cossacks, in a spacious yard, behind a fence, look around in amazement. Germans? Is it the Germans? Lord love us! We aren't even saddled!
They spring to it, saddle up,
lead their horses from the stable at a run,
fasten the saddle bow straps,
leap into the saddle—
and off they go, out of the yard!
Clatter of hooves.
= Here they come! The whole squadron almost to a man galloping along the street!
Clatter of hooves
along the street.
= A Cossack lieutenant sees them from a side street, at a distance (his own regiment—same insignia).
= The cavalry's going through! They're going through!
= Back he runs, runs as fast as he can.
HQ isn't far away.
He finds a colonel of dragoons. The colonel is just reading the dispatch brought by the first Cossack.
The Cossack lieutenant, breathlessly:
"Sir, sir, beg to report, sir! German cavalry in the next street—squadron strength!"
He is not the least alarmed, the lieutenant:
"Permission to turn out the guard to protect headquarters against the cavalry."
The colonel of dragoons, wasting no time, shouts his orders:
"Duty officer! Turn out the guard—with rifles!"
= There's readiness for you! The infantry are already doubling out of their quarters, rifles in hand.
What a lot of them! Must be two companies!

Their own gallant officers don't put a foot wrong:
"Line up by platoons! Sort yourselves out!"
No time for any of that. They're already running at the double through the open gates, wheeling at once
as the Cossack lieutenant directs them:
"They went that way! That's the way!"
= Inside, the colonel of dragoons reports to a gray-headed general who looks limp with exhaustion and sinks deeper into impotence at every word:
"Your Excellency! Enemy cavalry has forced its way into the township of Mensguth! I have taken steps . . ."
What torment it all is to a sick old man! This was the horror he had been expecting. He is sick. He is in torment, a sickbed general . . . he must get to the doctors! . . . to the peace and quiet of a hospital! Even his lips sag and his mouth loses its shape:
"To Ortelsburg . . . To Ortelsburg."
= The colonel of dragoons gives brisk orders:
We're loading up! We're moving out!
= The staff had been about to hang a map on the wall.
Just as well they hadn't got around to it. Roll it up again!
The staff are soon ready. Everybody knows what to carry, and moves at the double.
= The car's outside waiting.
The general does his best to hurry, they give him a helping hand.
Now the car is full! They're off!
With an escort of Cossacks, naturally,
then come officers in carriages, officers in two-wheelers, officers in whatever they can find—
through the gates! Keep going! Move! Faster, faster!
= The highroad.
It isn't a highroad, it's a torrent of running men.
No, not running—they're too tightly packed—flowing. Each and every one of them wants, so wants to live, so wants not to be taken prisoner.
The poor bloody infantry,
the men on the limbers,
the men on the big guns. Everyone else is retreating—why shouldn't we?
The cook with the field kitchen, its chimney lowered.
The wagon drivers too! The wagon drivers more than anybody! They're supposed to lead a retreat—and they find their way blocked!

Confused noise of men and wagons on the move.

How can the Corps Commander's car navigate this river of humanity,

how can he tack past all the rest and outstrip them? He must go faster than any of them, his life is most precious of all!

Try sounding the horn?

It doesn't help.

Ah, look, the Cossacks up front

are clearing a path.

Get over on the verge, can't you, you horrible little man!

The car glides into the space they've cleared,

and the crowd closes in behind again.

The general's head can't take much more of it. He no longer cares—just get me out of here!

= The sun is setting.

Long shot

Visibility is getting poorer. A gray, rolling mass of . . .

Wait—there's a fire up ahead there.

Larger scale

A big fire.

Still larger—a close-up

It's Ortelsburg. And it's burning.

It's one great conflagration.

There is a rapid and incessant crackle of bursting tiles.

As seen from the head of the column

= That way's no good—we can't get through the town.

= Section after section, the column comes to a halt.

Only the Corps Commander's car tries to push on, with the aid of Cossacks brandishing their swords:

"Move, you blockheads! Get out of the way!"

The car triumphs over the last few meters of the jam, and turns off to make a detour.

It speeds on, swaying over the bumps,

showing the way around the town. Others set off behind it (their way lit by the burning town).

Behind them it is already dark.

And there, behind them, in the distance, something is moving. Moving with alarming rapidity—in their direction.

Piercing cries!

"Cavalry!"

"They're surrounding us!"

= Commotion! How to get off the highroad? The way is blocked!

Fear and horror on faces lit by the conflagration.

Hell, what's the difference? A two-wheeler leaves the road,

crosses a ditch, bumps over rough ground.
It turns over!
= It makes no difference! Everyone who can turns off the road!

Rifle shots.

Ours. Fired from the column. Aiming behind them, at the cavalry!
The cavalry cannot be seen. Just shadowy figures, vanishing into the night.
= A horse bolts.
Someone is knocked down and falls under its hooves.
A scream.

Farther on, cries of "*Hurrah!*" The bullets fly thicker.

You can't tell who is firing. Sowing the void.
"*Company! Single file! Lie down!*"
Figures lying down on both sides of the road. Spurts of flame as bullets strike the ground.
= Some horses are wounded. They bolt with a limber!
There are people in the way! They are trampled.
"*Hurrah*"? No. "*Aah-aah-aah!*"
The supply troops have lost their heads! People jump out of the way, run off the road, dropping whatever they have in their hands.
= A runaway cannon. It has smashed a cart!
And another!

Shafts snap with a loud report.

= Over there, men cut the traces, tip the cart into the ditch, and jump onto the horses.
All this is seen against the glare of the burning town, or in the reflected light it casts.
= A limber out of control—people jump out of its path.
The road is clear of people . . .
only horses trampling the litter of abandoned gear . . .
wheels bouncing over it and falling off . . .
A field ambulance—at full tilt!
Suddenly a wheel comes off while it is in motion,
rolls on by itself, overtakes it!
The wheel for some reason gets bigger and bigger.
Until it fills the screen!
THE WHEEL rolls on, lit by the great fire!
A law unto itself.
Unstoppable.
Crushing all in its path!

Hysterical firing, frenzied volleys from rifles and machine guns! Salvos from big guns!

The wheel rolls on, reddened by the flames!
The exultant flames!
A crimson wheel!
= And the faces of frightened little people, wondering why it rolls on by itself, why it is so huge.
= No, it isn't any longer. It's getting smaller.
Yes, it's smaller all the time.
It is just an ordinary wheel from a field ambulance, and it is already faltering. It has collapsed.
= While the ambulance speeds on, one wheel short, its axle scoring the ground . . .
and behind it the field kitchen, with its chimney broken, ready to fall off.

Firing.
= The column lies there, firing to the rear.
= From behind there, out of the darkness, men come galloping along the roadside . . .
Yes, cavalry charging at us!
We're done for—nothing can save us! But they're shouting!
It's our own dragoons shouting:
"We're Russians! Russians, blast you! Hold your fire!"

[3 1]

Through the mist and the buzzing that had muffled Samsonov's thoughts these past few days, and today more than ever, something quite irrelevant suddenly forced its way and floated to the surface—something from his school days, a single phrase from his German reader: *"Es war die höchste Zeit sich zu retten."*

It was a passage about Napoleon and the burning of Moscow. He remembered nothing else about it, but this one sentence had remained in his mind because of that strange combination of words, *"höchste,"* "highest," and *"Zeit,"* "time"—"the highest time."

Whether or not Napoleon had been in such danger in Moscow, whether or not it had really been "now or never," the Army Commander's heart was gripped by gloomy foreboding that for him *"die höchste Zeit"* had indeed arrived. Only he could not understand where the danger lay and where he must apply pressure. He had no clear grasp of the position of the army as a whole and could not order decisive action.

As a result of Artamonov's treason the whole left flank of the army was helplessly exposed. Should he then change the orders drafted that afternoon? Change what in them? The central corps were to wheel left and attack. Wasn't that obviously necessary? What ought he to change? Should he perhaps delay the attack by the central corps altogether? But he would be blamed for that more than for anything. Three days ago Zhilinsky had branded him a coward and he had been suffering torment ever since. Should he compel the flanking corps to take the offensive? That would be a very good thing—but just at present it was impracticable.

None of his staff officers came to ask for definite changes.

He remembered how in the Japanese war he had held out tenaciously at the Yantai mines with a Cossack division—Ussuri and Siberian Cossacks—doggedly covering the left flank of Kuropatkin's army (Rennenkampf was there too, on the right), and had even suggested to Kuropatkin that he should turn the Japanese flank. Kuropatkin, however, got cold feet quite unnecessarily, gave the order to withdraw, and so lost the Battle of Liaoyang.

Timidity never pays. The great lesson of military history is that a single daring stroke can save a hopeless situation.

This was no time to repeat Kuropatkin's vacillation—he must attack boldly and decisively with his central corps.

The telegraph was working again. A belated dispatch from Artamonov had crossed Samsonov's telegram relieving him of his command: "After heavy fighting and under heavy enemy pressure I have withdrawn in the direction of Soldau." Given the general's difficulty with the truth, it seemed likely that Soldau too had already been surrendered. But no—the telegraph via Soldau went on working throughout the evening.

They reported that General Dushkevich was up front, and that General Prince Masalsky, the Corps Artillery Commander, had taken the corps over for the present.

Army HQ itself did not immediately inform Army Group HQ by telegram of Artamonov's demotion. His corps had been attached to Samsonov's army only provisionally, and the order might not be confirmed.

There was no word from Zhilinsky and Oranovsky. No word from anyone, in fact. It was as though there had been no fighting of any significance that day and none were expected on the morrow.

Looking gloomy and careworn, the commander left the staff offices and went to his quarters to rest. No one would have guessed it from his face, but he was aware of it: a layer of his soul had been shaken loose and was slowly, gradually slipping, coming adrift.

Samsonov strained to hear its inaudible movement.

His room had been cool in the afternoon, but now toward evening it was stuffy although the window was half open and the fine-wire screen in place.

Samsonov took his boots off and lay down.

In the gathering dusk he could still see from his pillow a big print mocking him from the wall: Frederick the Great surrounded by his generals, fine stalwart fellows all of them, with twirled mustaches, invincible.

How strange. It had all happened only a few hours ago, yet he no longer felt angry either with Blagoveshchensky or with Artamonov for lying and retreating. They would never have done such things if they had not been under unbearable pressure, if they had not been going through hell. His anger was misdirected. How could he be angry with them when he himself was so much at fault? Putting himself in their place, Samsonov could even find excuses for them: when the action was scattered over such a huge area a corps commander had no more hope of dominating events than his superior.

But if the mistakes of his subordinates were to be excused, where did that leave the general?

Never in his army career had Samsonov imagined that everything could go so badly wrong at once.

When sunflower oil is shaken and becomes cloudy the bottle must stand for a while so that the liquid can regain its golden transparency, as the sediment sinks to the bottom and the air bubbles rise to the surface. The Army Commander's troubled soul needed stillness to regain clarity. He knew what he must do: pray.

Perfunctory prayers, mumbled morning and evening as a matter of habit, while your thoughts stray to mundane affairs, are like washing fully dressed and with one hand: you are very slightly cleaner, but you hardly feel it. But if you pray with concentration, surrender to it completely, pray as if you were slaking your thirst, when you cannot bear not to pray and nothing else will do—prayer like that, Samsonov remembered, always transforms and strengthens.

Instead of calling his orderly, Kupchik, he rose, felt for the matches, lit the cut-glass table lamp without turning up the wick, and latched the door. He did not pull the window shut—the building opposite had no upper story.

He had a portable icon made of Britannia metal—the sort Cossacks take on campaign with them. He opened it out and arranged its panels so that it stood upright on the table. He knelt clumsily without stopping to check whether the floor was clean.

Supporting his ungainly bulk hurt his knees, but the pain gave him satisfaction as he knelt with his eyes fixed on the crucifixion and the two side panels, St. George Bringer of Victory and St. Nicholas Man of God, and began to pray.

First, two or three well-known prayers—"God shall rise again," "A speedy helper He"—then that fluid prayerful silence, a wordless, soundless prayer put together by his unconscious, only occasionally attached to firm supports retained by his memory: ". . . the radiance of Thy countenance, O Giver of Life," "Mother of God, abundantly merciful"; and again prayers without words, wreathed in clouds of smoke, in mist, moving like ice floes in the spring thaw.

What most weighed on him found its truest and most helpful expression, not in ready-made prayers, or in his own words, but in kneeling on his aching knees until he ceased to feel them, in looking fixedly at the icon in oblivious muteness. For him this was the readiest way to lay his whole life, and the day's suffering, before God. God knew anyway that neither honors and awards nor the enjoyment of power were Samsonov's reasons for serving, for decking himself with medals. He was begging God now to send his armies victories, not in order to save his own name, but for the sake of Russia's might, because this opening battle could largely determine her fate.

He prayed that the casualties might not be in vain. Those whose bodies were so suddenly pierced by lead or steel that they had no time even to cross themselves as they died—let them not have perished in vain! He prayed that clarity might descend upon his exhausted mind so that at the very peak of his "highest time" he might make the correct decision, and so himself embody God's will that these sacrifices should not be in vain.

He knelt there, his whole weight pressing into the floor, gazing on the icon at eye level before him, whispering, praying, and the weight of his hand seemed to grow less each time he crossed himself, his body less cumbersome, his soul less dark: all the weight and darkness soundlessly and invisibly fell away from him, evaporated, were drawn heavenward. God who could assume all burdens was taking this burden to Himself.

Awareness of his rank, awareness of the town of Neidenburg, and of Army HQ two steps from him, seemed to fly away from the commander—he soared to make contact with the powers above and surrender to their will. Strategy and tactics, supply, communications, intelligence—was it not all like the busy scurrying of ants compared with the will of God? If God graciously decided to intervene in the battle—it had happened many times of old, so tradition said—victory might be miraculously won in spite of all faults and failings.

A vivid, dark moth was beating its wings against the fine mesh of the window screen, so big and noisy that it might almost have been a bird.

Perhaps its unusual size and sinister coloring were a bad omen?

Wiping the perspiration from his brow, Samsonov rose from his prayers. No one had come to look for him in need of instructions or with news good or bad. The scattered battles between tens of thousands of men were taking their course, without impinging on the commander. Or perhaps they did not want to disturb his rest. He had better go and find out.

First of all he went out of the building, past the sentries. It was pleasantly cool and dark (the power station had been damaged and the streets were unlit). The noise of battle was distant and muffled, as if the Russian forces had flung the enemy back farther and farther. (Perhaps the miracle had already begun to happen.)

Paraffin lamps and candles had been carried into HQ, making the rooms hotter and stuffier than ever. His staff were all in their places, all at work. The report to Army Group HQ on the past day's events was being drafted.

They brought in a newly arrived late-afternoon telegram from Artamonov, nervously hurried past Samsonov, then handed it to him after all.

"After heavy fighting I have held Soldau . . ."

(What fine writers they were! What nimble pens! It was a wonder he hadn't said that he had held Warsaw—he would have been recommended for the St. Andrew's Cross!)

". . . All our communications cut. Losses enormous, especially officers. Morale of troops good"(?!). "Troops obedient . . ."

(But near the end of their tether.)

". . . Holding the town with advance guard formed from remnants of various regiments . . ."

(He even called his rear guard an advance guard. Such diction!)

". . . To go over to the offensive injection of new forces essential, all now present have suffered heavy losses. Shall put all units of corps in order during the night and go over to the offensive . . ."

(Without any "injection of new forces" then? What a stupendous scoundrel! And why in any case had he put his name to this telegram? How dare he disobey the order replacing him? He was relying on his connections in high places.)

Still, the relief brought by prayer prevented Samsonov from getting very angry. And his staff were working splendidly. Here came the Chief of Staff, ambling in with the twice redrafted telegraph report to Army Group HQ for the past twenty-four hours: "For two days now the army has been in action along the whole front. Interrogation of prisoners shows . . ." (perhaps it did, and perhaps it didn't). "On the left flank the 1st Corps held its positions for some time, but was then withdrawn without sufficient cause" (not the place to give your tongue free rein), "for which reason I have relieved General Artamonov of his command. In the center Mingin's division has suffered big losses, but the valiant Libau Regiment has held its position. The Reval Regiment has been almost annihilated."

Samsonov pointed. "Insert 'Color guard and one platoon survive.' "

". . . The Estland Regiment has withdrawn in great disorder in the direction of Neidenburg . . . The 15th Corps . . . attack crowned with success . . . The 13th has taken Allenstein . . . Latest information about the 6th . . . stood up to fierce fighting at Bischofsburg . . ."

Altogether, the report was not at all disheartening. In fact, it was a victor's report. And it was, come to think of it, all more or less true. Blagoveshchensky? He hadn't retreated all that far. He was holding Mensguth, and would shortly move on Allenstein. So perhaps things weren't really so bad after all.

Just as long as Zhilinsky realized tomorrow morning that the Germans were not fleeing beyond the Vistula, but leaning their whole bulk on the 2nd Army.

It was eleven-thirty. All he had to do was sign, and then he might as well go to bed.

There was one other thing . . . an important correction he must make to his orders for tomorrow. One supremely important instruction was missing—find it, and the whole tiresome tangle would be cut, and peace of mind would return.

But his mind was still befogged.

Hanging his head, the commander went away to sleep.

He caught another glimpse of Frederick's proud heroes before Kupchik (a trumpeter from a Cossack horse artillery unit) blew out the light.

Samsonov thought that he would fall asleep at once: it was dark, it was quiet, all that he could accomplish had been done, and he was, he really was, so very tired. While he was compelled to move around and act he had felt an urge to lie down and turn to stone. Now that he had undressed and was lying in a comfortable bed the pillow was a stone under his head, the muscles of his arms and legs ached with the need for action, and he began tossing and turning.

He had racked his brains for days on end, until he was stupefied and could stand it no longer. Nor could he bear any more apprehensive hovering over the telegraph waiting for the speechless ribbon to wriggle out like a white snake, wondering where it would sting him next and what insult or humiliation it had in store for him. Samsonov probably now hated the telegraph more than anything. The direct line to Zhilinsky was nothing but a rope around his neck.

As always when a man cannot sleep, the time went by with merciless speed. Yet, between glances at his watch, time stood still in his mind at the hour he had last seen. Snapping his watch open with a fingernail, Samsonov peered glumly at the illuminated dial: quarter past one, five minutes to two, half past two . . .

At four it would start getting light.

To help himself fall asleep Samsonov said his prayers again—several "Our Father"s and "Hail Mary"s.

He could see nothing. But he heard clearly what sounded like a prophetic voice breathing lightly in his ear: "You are going . . . You are going . . ."

It was repeated several times.

Samsonov turned ice-cold with terror. It was a knowing, a prophetic voice, a voice perhaps with power over the future, but he could not understand its meaning.

"Going to pull through?" he asked hopefully.

"No, you are going." The voice was adamant.

"Going to sleep?" his soul suggested.

"No, to fall asleep," the inexorable angel replied.

Utterly incomprehensible. Still straining to understand, the commander woke up.

The window was uncurtained and it was already light in the room. As he saw it, light filled his mind and the meaning of what he had heard shone out bright and clear. He would "fall asleep" in the sleep of death.

He tried to focus his mind. We are in Prussia. Today is a day in August. Today is 28 August [15 August Old Style].

A chill at the bone. His flesh crawled. Today was the Feast of the Assumption, the Falling Asleep of the Blessed Virgin, Protectress of Russia. That was it.

I have been told that I shall die. Today.

Terror lifted Samsonov from his bed. He sat in his underwear, with bare feet and folded arms.

The distant but by now uninterrupted mutter of guns could be clearly heard.

The rumble of the bombardment restored Samsonov's courage and his clarity of thought.

Soldiers were dying already—and their commander was afraid.

In a deep, resonant voice Samsonov called out to Kupchik in the anteroom. Time to get up!

It took him a minute to collect himself, dress, and bring in the jug and bowl for the commander to wash.

With cold water on his face, white light flooding the room, and the relentless bombardment in his ear, the commander realized in a flash what he must do—he must move! Move out! Move his HQ up closer to the troops! He must go there himself—into hell! He must get into the saddle, like a soldier! He was ataman of the Don Cossacks and the Semirechye Cossacks—why was he not on horseback? If only he could ride right now in a cavalry charge, swoop and capture an enemy battery in a raid. That would set the blood racing through his veins! That was the sort of war for him! The Turkish war—that was the one!

He was like a bear rising from his den. Shirtless, large-bodied, hairy, he went to the window and flung it open. There was a cheerful current of cool air. The little town was draped with a festal garment of mist, like a bridal veil. Domes, towers, spires, steep roofs with ornamented gables rode above the mist like floating islands greeting the rising sun.

Things might yet turn out well. It would be such a liberation, instead of imprisonment in HQ with the telegraph for company, to ride forward and to act. He should have done it yesterday. Such an obvious solution! He would get away from Knox at the same time.

He gave orders for the staff to be awakened. There were no early risers in Bialystok. By the time the Living Corpse woke up—hey presto, no telegraphic link, no Samsonov, nobody to lecture!

Liberation!

But they were as slow as a lot of old women getting ready. Another two hours they took over it. His staff officers were slower rising than the commander himself and had more of a struggle collecting their wits.

The staff was divided in two. All administrative, auxiliary, and clerical personnel were dispatched twenty-five versts to the rear, beyond the Russian frontier, to the safety of Janow. The operations section (seven officers) would ride forward with the commander.

Those who were to withdraw accepted the decision without demur. Those who were to go forward looked sullen and resentful. Samsonov had eaten hardly anything, but invigorated by the cheerful morning, he strode around briskly, hurrying everybody along. The telegram sent from Bialystok at 1 a.m. and just this moment handed to him made him feel more lighthearted still—and more forgiving toward his ill-wishers: "To General Samsonov. Valiant units of the army entrusted to you have honorably performed their difficult task in the battles on 25, 26, and 27 August. I have ordered General Rennenkampf's cavalry to make contact with you. I hope that with the combined forces of all the central corps you will this day throw back the enemy. Zhilinsky."

His prayer was in part answered. We're all Russians, we can always make peace with one another! We can forgive past wrongs. He had made the right decision—to join the central corps. Rennenkampf would gallop in sometime during the day. United, joined in fellowship, surely we shall prevail!

This made the unanimous discontent of the seven he was taking with him even more of an affront and a nuisance. He called them together for a conference, standing up. "Have you anything on your minds, gentlemen? If so, please speak out."

Postovsky didn't dare. He naturally thought it would be more sensible for him to go to Janow and take charge there. But he had no wish to argue with the commander. The position of all the others was just as weak: the designation "staff officer" meant, so they told themselves, that they should be going to the rear, not forward. They waited uneasily. Filimonov, who could never reconcile himself to any decision not his own, looked grimmest of all.

"With your permission, Aleksandr Vasilievich. Neidenburg is now just as much in the front line as Nadrau, where you wish to go. The enemy is in the immediate vicinity of Neidenburg. Therefore HQ staff as a whole should move to Janow. Martos is managing splendidly—what is the point of joining him?"

One of the colonels spoke: "Your Excellency! You are responsible for every corps in the army, not just for those which are at present getting the worst of it. If you move up forward you are neglecting your duties as commander of the whole army. By breaking communications with Army Group HQ you simultaneously break communication with each of the corps."

How good they were at complicating the clearest and simplest matters, at finding excuses for any evasion of action. Samsonov felt clearheaded and untroubled in his soul for the first time in a week, full of the strength and courage his decision had brought, and right away they wanted to tie him hand and foot and render him helpless. They were too late. He could do no other.

"Thank you, gentlemen. We leave on horseback for Nadrau in ten minutes. The car will take Colonel Knox to Janow."

Ah, but Colonel Knox wanted to go forward with the commander! Colonel Knox had done his exercises, breakfasted, and now advanced with an athletic stride, dressed for action and ready to ride forward. He agreed to send his traveling bag to the rear. Samsonov indicated the car. "Bad news?" Knox asked in surprise. Samsonov took him to one side, without the interpreter, and made an effort to string a few sentences together in English. "The position of the army is critical. I cannot predict what the next few hours will bring. My place is with the troops, and you must go back before it is too late."

Eight Cossacks gave their own horses to the eight officers. They were escorted by a squadron and a half—a lively time was expected up ahead.

At five minutes after seven the cavalcade moved off at a gentle trot, clip-clopping over the smooth cobbles of Neidenburg's streets. Toward the northern exit from the town they looked around in the cheerful sunshine at the old castle of the Teutonic Knights.

At the commander's wish it was only at seven-fifteen, after his departure and immediately before the telegraph was silenced, that his last telegram was sent to Army Group HQ: "I am moving up to 15th Corps HQ at Nadrau to take command of the attacking armies. I am disconnecting the Hughes instrument and shall temporarily lose contact with you. Samsonov."

* * *

FATE SEEKS NO MAN'S HEAD—
EACH MAN'S HEAD GOES TO MEET ITS FATE

* * *

[3 2]

(27 AUGUST)

Day after day the German army did battle as an integrated whole, and the breakdown of communications with Mackensen's distant corps for just a few hours was felt to be an extremely serious lapse: planes were sent up right away, and immediate efforts were made to reestablish the telephone linkup by some roundabout route. Whereas the Russian army's operations disintegrated from day to day into individual actions by each corps: corps commanders ceased to feel themselves members of a larger whole and each of them waged (or sometimes did not wage) his own private war. At Soldau the collapse went still further. The city was not defended by a corps, but only by those smaller units which chose not to withdraw.

Nonetheless, the Germans needlessly gave the Russians a whole day to pull themselves together. Although General von François had to his surprise found Usdau abandoned and occupied it before noon, and although the road to Neidenburg was open, he had not felt it safe to content himself with a light defensive screen on the Soldau side of the town, but had begun entrenching himself that same evening in expectation of a counterattack. His orders from Army HQ for the following day were to the same effect: he was to refrain from advancing toward Neidenburg, and try to throw the Russians back beyond Soldau.

The reason why Hindenburg was particularly anxious about his southern flank was that when he returned to Army HQ on the evening of the 27th, after his far from enjoyable duty trip to Scholtz's corps, he was informed that François's corps had been almost totally destroyed and that its remnants were arriving at a railway station twenty-five kilometers from Usdau. Hindenburg immediately telephoned the stationmaster, who confirmed it. (It was night before they learned the truth: a battalion of grenadiers attacked by the Petrov Regiment had fled in panic and infected wagon trains with their terror along the way. The drivers had hurtled all the way to Army HQ.)

Scholtz's enlarged corps was only half a division smaller than all Samsonov's central corps together, and had superior artillery support, yet it was kept on the defensive on the Mühlen line throughout the day by heavy pressure from Martos. At one time it was thought that Martos was making a detour via Hohenstein, at another that he had taken Mühlen—and a division was diverted from the counterattack, was ordered to shed its packs and rush there, only to find that it was not needed.

In the course of the day came the news that the Russians had occupied Allenstein, which meant that the Germans had to switch in that direction: Below's corps, already in place on the other claw of the pincer, and Mackensen, already marching along the broad corridor (twice as wide as he needed) opened up for him by Blagoveshchensky.

Excessive caution blinded the Prussian High Command to the gap yawning south of Scholtz, where the front had collapsed: a quarter of the incomplete 23rd Corps was holding on with difficulty, and Shtempel's cavalry brigade was trotting around—and that was all. Hindenburg, however, supposed that there were two Russian corps in the area, and saw no way of encircling them. The day seemed to have gone badly, and the High Command could not order its troops to outflank the Russian army in depth, let alone go all out for a second Cannae. The Prussian High Command's one idea was to draw its scattered thirteen divisions closer together. In the overnight orders for 28 August the encirclement plan was whittled down still further: it was only Martos's corps, the most mettlesome and troublesome, that was to be surrounded.

The Germans naturally could not suppose that the proud Russian Empire would have fossilized generals totally incapable of managing bodies of men hundreds of thousands strong. There must be some cunning plan behind Samsonov's puzzling deployment of his corps like the fingers of a spatulate hand. There was probably some plan also in Rennenkampf's enigmatic immobility, while his hammer was poised over the head of the overextended Prussian army. Earlier that day Rennenkampf would still have had time to intervene in the main battle with the full might of his cavalry and snuff out the German scheme, but he did not take advantage of the twenty-four hours which the Germans had thrown away.

They planned to surround Martos by striking at Hohenstein from three sides and moving Sontag's division, the least depleted in Scholtz's corps, around Lake Mühlen as soon as it was light to occupy the village of Waplitz and the high ground nearby.

These orders reached the division shortly before midnight. The troops had just spent several hours digging in, preparing to defend the position; they had received their day's bread ration late, and had only just settled down to sleep. General von Sontag decided not to wait for daylight, but to make a surprise attack in the dark. The division was roused there and then, before midnight, and told to get ready to move. The hilly terrain and unpaved, sandy paths made it difficult for them to get their bearings. They blundered around, groping their way to their assembly points. The advance guard strayed to the right of the appointed line, the head of the main force to the left of it, while its trunk became the middle column. The division was unaware that the dragoons had entered Waplitz unopposed by the Russians, and settled in cheek by jowl with the Poltava Infantry Regiment, until a Russian patrol recognized them, whereupon the German cavalry withdrew at full gallop, in a hail of random bullets. Still in the dark, a Russian outpost near Waplitz noticed a German advance party approaching and retired, firing as it went. Before dawn, screened by a thick, milky fog, a German regiment attacked Waplitz on a broad front but ran into ferocious rifle and machine-gun fire. Soldiers are always particularly jumpy and vicious when they are first wakened.

Then the artillery on both sides opened up.

[33]

Happily—or more often unhappily—Martos was by nature easily roused and slow to calm down again. So many things had happened in those last few days, and especially that last day, to wind him up—the changing fortunes of the daylong battle, his altercations with Postovsky, chaos in Hohenstein instead of help from the brigade sent by Klyuev, the strain of trying to anticipate German moves.

He usually succumbed to fatigue in the evening whatever happened and woke a little later, so that his night was ruined. But on this occasion he had been so shaken up that he even missed his evening nap. He left the farmhouse while it was still pitch-dark to sit and smoke on a bench, very much as people around Poltava sit outside on mounds of earth around their houses to enjoy the gathering darkness; except that there the evenings are warm even in September, whereas here it was already a little chilly. Martos draped his greatcoat around his shoulders, but sat without his cap, cooling his head and massaging it from his temples backward to disperse the shooting pains. He also took a pill. He would sit like that for an hour, say, to compose himself, then collapse on his bed and sleep like a log.

He was waiting for Klyuev, now his subordinate. It was no good expecting the corps to arrive in the night, but he must hope that it would be there by dawn. The fighting next day promised to be heavier than all that had gone before. He was now at the center of the biggest battle anywhere in East Prussia—and he badly needed to double his forces by morning!

By midnight the firing had died away completely and there were no more sudden spurts of flame. Occasional points of light glimmered soundlessly and quickly died. The starry sky promised another fine day. With the army so widely scattered that was just as well.

For the past several days Martos could be said to be winning all along the line. Not once had he left the enemy in possession of the field; he had attacked incessantly and pressed hard at all points, although his artillery was conspicuously weaker and although even shells, not to mention provisions and fodder, were not delivered regularly. But Martos could not for the life of him see this unbroken series of successes adding up to one big victory. All his victories seemed somehow futile.

He needed to double his forces immediately if all his victories were to merge in a single decisive one.

But Klyuev's corps was still nowhere to be seen. There wasn't even a messenger from him, until a party of Cossacks galloped in in the dead of night.

Martos was handed a letter by someone who might have been an ensign, and anxiously went inside into the light with it.

Who would ever have thought that this was a letter from a general at war! More like a gouty old man writing to a friend two streets away to say that he could not come over for a game of cards. Martos had been hoping that Klyuev himself would come to his aid. Not a chance! Although now Martos's subordinate, he replied that he could not possibly get his corps moving by night. It would march early on the morning of the 28th, but even that would make sense only if General Martos could guarantee to hold his present position for another twenty-four hours, till the morning of the 29th.

This was murder! The man was an idiot, not a general!

What was there left to do?

Go on fighting . . .

At the Battle of Kulikovo an earlier Martos, one of the Prince of Bryansk's warrior knights, had rescued Grand Prince Dmitri Ioannovich from a band of Tatars.

Withdraw? Leaving the battlefield was now more difficult than continuing to attack.

He must continue doggedly, just as an experienced actor carries on when he sees that his fellows have lost the thread and are making nonsense of the play, that the heroine's wig has come unstuck, that one panel of the set has fallen down, that there is a terrible draft, that the audience is murmuring and for some reason edging toward the exits. He must carry on acting (fighting) with the lightheartedness of despair. Just as long as *he* did not ruin the show it might yet be salvaged.

With all heavy tasks the difficult thing is to make a start. Once the horse collar is around your neck you soon begin to accept it as your natural wear and stop feeling strange in it.

Out into the dark again.

There was still some shooting over to the left, after all. Beyond Waplitz somewhere.

Somebody over there was still restless.

Tomorrow was the 28th [the 15th Old Style]. That had always been an important date in Martos's life, as was the "twice 15th," the 30th. Many fateful or simply memorable things, good or bad, had happened to him on those dates. Moreover, when he had commanded a division it had been the 15th, and now he had the 15th Corps, including the 30th Regiment, which was of course the Poltava Regiment, from his own native place. So tomorrow, of all days, he must be wide awake.

The firing continued with no letup. Yes, it was between Waplitz and Wittmannsdorf. There was a deep ravine there. An awkward spot.

So many had been killed in the last few days. And those who had not been killed or wounded were very tired. So many splendid officers had fallen. Martos knew them all. He had known them for years—and one week of war had wiped them all out. They wouldn't be replaced in a hurry. How can you replace real professional officers, if you send them all to the front in the first few days instead of dividing them between front-line and reserve regiments? At that rate, Russia could perhaps carry on fighting for two or three months. But what if the war lasted longer?

The shooting went on and on. To an inexperienced ear, it might simply mean that the enemy was still restless, that he kept imagining something was afoot under cover of night. But Martos's ear knew the difference. There was nothing random about it. This sort of thing happened when large bodies of men were stirring in the dark. Russian troops might be doing some of the shooting, but the Germans were up to something.

He put himself in Scholtz's place, going over yesterday's situation in his mind. Yes, he was conveniently placed to turn Martos's flank. And this was as good a time as any. Martos could almost *see* the Germans attacking by night from that direction.

That was the moment when the general's organism was ready at last to collapse and sleep. But a warning signal had lit up in his mind, and he went inside to rouse reluctant and drowsy subordinates, make telephone calls, and send out messengers.

He gave orders for the corps reserve to be alerted, marched to that hollow, and stationed across it, promising to join them shortly. His orders to the artillery were that two batteries should take up new positions, and the others get ready to change their line of fire.

He sent a messenger to the left flank, to warn Mingin's two surviving (though greatly weakened) regiments—the Kaluga and the Libau—and another to Waplitz itself, to order the officer in command of the Poltava Regiment to be ready for a possible night attack.

By now his staff were on their feet, hating this wasp-waisted pest of a general. The regiments and batteries disturbed from their rest and moved around in the dark cursed him still more heartily. Exhausted and half asleep, the men could see nothing but senseless bullying in these nocturnal maneuvers.

Martos was smoking again, ranging the brightly lit staff rooms with his elastic step, ignoring resentful looks and receiving progress reports. Of course, it might just be that his ears were too suspicious, with the terrain around Waplitz so full of lurking threats, but his corps had not spent ten days getting there and the next five fighting only to wake up and find themselves defeated. By now the general would sooner see the Germans attack than day dawn peacefully.

Suddenly hundreds of rifles began barking furiously in Waplitz itself. Martos rushed up to his attic in time to see sporadic crimson flashes slowly dying away.

That was it! He had not been wrong! He called for his horse and rode off to join the reserve in the ravine.

The company in which Sasha Lenartovich commanded a platoon had been one of the first into Neidenburg. It went in firing and in battle order, but there was no one to fight. Garrison duty in Neidenburg meant that they had then missed the fighting at Orlau, arriving only in time to bury the dead there. Not until after the midday meal on the 27th had they caught up with their own Chernigov Regiment—and then their brigade was diverted to the corps reserve. However, by evening there were rumbles to every side of them, and a never-ending straggle of wounded, on foot or in vehicles. It was obviously their turn to go through the mincer on the following day. To tear a company or a platoon to strips, to mutilate a man, doesn't take a whole war, a campaign, a month, a week, or even a day; a quarter hour is quite enough.

The night of 27–28 August was a cold one, but Lenartovich's platoon slept in a barn, and if you burrowed into the straw you might even be too warm. The soldiers appeared to be enjoying a sound sleep, untroubled by thoughts of the day ahead. Theoretically, Sasha should have been pleased to be spending the night in this democratic way, but for days on end, while they were busy with fast-decaying corpses, he had not washed or undressed. He was sickened by filth and discomfort. His skin itched all over, and there was a sort of dull ache in his nerve endings. After tossing and turning in the hot hay he went outside to cool off.

What prevented him from sleeping was not so much that death might be close, but that it would be so irrelevant. Sasha was ready to die at any moment for some great and glorious cause. He had not even been an adolescent but a small child when his heart began to beat faster in expectation of some extraordinarily important and joyful happening, *something* (he knew not what) which with its sudden radiance would illuminate and transform life in his own land and throughout the whole earth. Sasha was rather more than a child when a sudden burst of light for a while illuminated the world—they had lived to see the day!—but it was trampled on and extinguished. Sasha was ready to break iron chains not just with his bare fist but with his own head. What made his flesh crawl even more than his dirty clothing, what gnawed at him and gave him no peace, was that he was in the wrong place, and that it would be absurdly easy to die for the wrong reason. He could not have got into a more ridiculous situation. To die for the autocracy at twenty-four! To have been lucky enough to discover the truth so young, to set out on the right road, so that the rest of his life would have been spent not in blind searching, not in Hamlet-like doubt, but in deeds—and then to perish in someone else's orgy of bloodletting, a pathetic pawn in the hands of professional bullies!

How unlucky Sasha had been never to have been jailed or exiled: he would have been among his own kind, his goal would have been clear, he would beyond doubt have been preserved for the coming revolution. All decent revolutionaries were there, if they had not emigrated. He had been detained three times—for taking part in a student meeting, for a demonstration, for disseminating leaflets—and each time they had released him, letting him off lightly because of his youth, preventing him from becoming a man! All was not yet lost, of course. If he could just scrape through these next few days of hacking and pounding, pounding and hacking, he must find a sure way out of the army, best of all by getting put on trial, but not for a military crime—for agitation, say.

Agitation in fact would have given some real sense to his time in the army. He had tried it, but to no effect. Not only were the soldiers in his platoon remote to a man from the ideology of the proletariat, devoid even of an embryonic class consciousness, they could not get economic slogans into their heads, even the simplest and most immediately advantageous to them. Their obtuseness and meek subservience drove him to despair.

How complicated were the twists and turns of history! Instead of marching straight ahead to revolution, it took a side road that led to war, and you were powerless, everyone was powerless, to do anything about it.

Late in the night there was a lull, but when Sasha began at last to doze, rifle shots holed his sleep like nails. Then there was shouting nearby, the tramp of feet, somebody was looking for somebody else—oh, how desperately he hoped that it would pass them by, he wanted only to lie low, to hug the ground, let the bullets whiz over his head, he didn't want to get up—but all the same the order rolled along the line and reached their company: "To ar-ar-arms!"

Blasted army regulations! Idiots thought them up, they had neither rhyme nor reason, but you had to obey. You had to wriggle out of the cozy warm straw, drag your stiff legs outside into the damp and the darkness, with bullets flying, and not only get out there yourself, hampered by your ludicrous sword, but speak to the men with false heartiness, pretend that it was very important to you to lead out your platoon and line them up with full ammunition and hear from the sergeant and rankers their nauseating slave talk: "Certainly, Your Honor!" "Yes, sir, yes, Your Honor!"

Then it was "Right face! Forward march!" They had left their warm barn, and now, in complete darkness, stumbling, bumping into each other, almost hand in hand, they wandered off they knew not where.

Some said that they were going to the rescue of the Poltava Regiment. To hell with it—if they hadn't stuck their necks out they wouldn't need rescuing.

They crossed the railway line, stepping carefully, but still catching their feet on the switches, until they came up against a blank wall. This was Waplitz station, now out of action—they had seen it in the daytime. Stumbling over the uneven ground, they took a crooked path and came out on a smooth highway. The order was given to form fours. Sasha passed it on, and made his own men do it. Their whole battalion and some other troops assembled out on the highway, and they set off en masse deeper into the darkness, but at least over a smooth surface.

They went over a bridge. Then the word was passed along the line: "Careful, there's a sharp drop on the left!" It was too dark to see anything.

Suddenly there was heavy fire up ahead, desperate, hysterical, deafening firing. Even in the daytime it would have been terrifying, but now, at night . . . ! Was it meant for them? No, it was not meant for them. No one fell, no bullets whistled by, and for some reason there weren't even any flashes, but somewhere close in front, right nearby, they were going to bump into it.

There was a strange trembling in his kneecaps, which seemed to be jerking themselves along, taking big jumps, with no help from his feet. In daylight he might have been ashamed, but it was too dark for a man to see even himself.

There were loud, peremptory orders to spread out, some to the right, some to the left. They blundered down the steep embankment, squelched blindly over boggy ground, their boots letting in cold water, over mounds and into potholes and through an orchard (was it?)—and just when they were ready to lie down the firing up ahead ceased completely. Once again, orders rang out to reassemble on the road and form up in reserve order. Once again they stumbled around, falling into the ditch, squelching through the same wet patch, and scrambled back onto the highway.

His knees were still jumping, jerking uncontrollably, all by themselves.

Once more they were a long time numbering, sorting themselves out, lining up. Then they marched on. Dark as it was they could see that the road led into a wood. They went through it. That was the explanation—it was because of the wood that they had seen no flashes.

All the battalions went on along the highway; then they were made to descend the slope again, this time to cross the river by a mill dam. Once across, they climbed and climbed, on firm ground over open fields. As before, there was not much gunfire, and Sasha, as before, decided that they were being marched for the sake of it, to wear their legs out. His knees had stopped trembling. Anyway, it wasn't from fear. He wasn't frightened at all. He just felt that this was not *it*, that this was not the place, that this was most certainly not where he should be laying down his life.

It seemed to be getting lighter, yet the visibility was not improving at all: even here, on high ground, darkness was replaced by thick mist.

Then they were hurried on either by poor field paths or by no path at all, whatever was growing there clung to their boots, but the worst of it was that the terrain was all knolls and gullies and sudden drops and boulders: the soldiers said that devils had churned it up playing ninepins.

Then furious firing started again quite nearby, perhaps a verst away to their right, from several hundred rifle barrels. Machine guns joined in. Still, nothing was coming their way as yet; the fighting was lower down and to the right, and they had to get to higher ground, as quickly as they could! Suddenly artillery began belching and pounding, pounding and belching puffs of smoky flame. Russian guns! The shells flew over their heads—take that! and that! Shrapnel gleamed dully in the milky mist.

The German guns struck up in reply, their shells bursting a little way off to the right.

Although he had no desire for victory and would make no effort toward it, Lenartovich was gratified to note that the Germans were outgunned. This, of course, contradicted the maxim "The worse, the better" but offered some hope that he would not be drilled by a splinter. In all that pandemonium the noise of the Russian guns had an undeniable sinister beauty.

As it got lighter, so the milky mist thickened. At three paces there was nothing but mist, and the flashes were fainter all the time. Now they were being rushed at the double through this curdled milk, over the leg-breaking gullies, rifles at the ready; evidently they were late in arriving somewhere. They ran uphill panting, then down, up another hill, down again. It was safer running with your head well down, but if you did you found yourself staggering. So they ran erect. There were shrapnel bursts overhead, but high up and to one side, so that when the bullets fell they were as harmless as dried peas.

They were ordered to open out and fire from the hip. They began firing, though they could not see at whom or what, and ran on. (Sasha did not give the order to adjust sights, and did not remember to do it himself.) No Russian had as yet been killed or wounded. This must be some roundabout route. The ground continued rising steadily. There was a hammering and a tightness in his chest, he could run no more, certainly not in that wet mist.

It was quite light by now, the sun was probably already up, but no dim disk could be seen in the mist smothering the whole world.

Then, as the ground began to fall, the invisible enemy struck—though they were just as invisible to him. The gun flashes were the merest flicker, but the bullets whizzed close, and one of them struck bright sparks from a stone.

Their sleepless night, their reluctant rambles, their wet feet, even the breathless stitch in their sides, were long forgotten—it was now a matter of minutes . . . shall we knock them down or they us? Shall we succeed or shan't we? It's kill or be killed. The soldiers all knew it, and were beginning to enjoy themselves, and so was Sasha. Their cartridge pouches were full, and they fired rapidly, excitedly, till their ears were splitting with the noise of their own firing and they could not breathe for their own powder smoke, and flame after flame rent the milky mist. Just as long as they didn't shoot their own comrades. Sasha corrected those he could. He found himself firing his revolver, although there was no point in it. Now they were jumping over a ditch, now they were hurling themselves over a hedge, now they were leaping over bodies—German bodies, not Russian! They thrilled with fear and pride. We're getting there! We've got the strength, say what you like!

By now they were fighting in the village, taking cover behind houses, peering out cautiously before going around corners. The soldiers were borne along with bayonets fixed, there was no holding them, and Sasha too blazed away with a strange enjoyment, wounding one German, who was immediately taken prisoner.

All this time a red sphere had been growing hotter and hotter to their left—and here it came at last, breaking through the fog: the sun! The whole world was still lapped in fog, but gradually objects began to stand out separate and clear. You could see the big beads of moisture on rifle butts and bayonets (some of them bloodied). The fog was drifting down in tatters from their height and faces could be clearly seen, glowing with the unholy glee of battle. Lenartovich felt it too. The grass was jeweled with blue, red, and orange glints and the victors were warmed by the yellowing sun of a new day.

It all ended very smoothly. No loud congratulations, no creeping rumor—a convoy from their own battalion escorted some three hundred prisoners back through the village together with a dozen or so officers, squinting miserably into the sunlight, some of them without their Jäger caps, some without carbines. Whereas on the Russian side when the roll was called the whole battalion had lost three men killed and a dozen wounded. One of the wounded was in Sasha's platoon, and he remained in the ranks cheerfully walking around and telling his story.

Meanwhile, it was as though the departing mist were gradually revealing a grandiose stage set: the view took on height, depth, and perspective, and objects as far down as the bottom of the ravine, creatures living and dead, acquired sharp outlines, zones of sunlight and shadowy hollows took their places, and the colors of plantations and vegetation stood out brightly—and looking down the slope from the Wittmannsdorf heights, they could see clearly a column of men in spiked helmets, several hundred strong, being led along the bottom of the ravine, and lower down still the heaps of bodies killed by Russian case shot.

There was no hurry now, no need to run, nothing to fear, and Lenartovich contemplated it all from a bench behind the orchard where he had sat down to rest. He was bursting with a strange feeling of triumph: his first victory not in debate, but won with his body, with his arms and legs. He sat there as though he himself were the Supreme Commander for whose eyes the triumphal procession below was meant. The soldiers were not allowed to rest: a shout went up that they were to dig in on the edge of the village. Lenartovich was forced to relay the command, but he himself did not have to dig and could sit for a while on the bench watching the theatrical representation of conquest, the deep blue valley, and savoring his happiness in the suddenly silent world—there was no shooting nearby now—and analyzing his new and unexpected feelings.

How easy everything now seemed! The cup of hope was running over. He would survive this war! How precious life was! Just to sit and look at such a morning, or to run in chilly air, or ride a bicycle along that tree-lined road over there, with the wind whistling by, or to feel soft, tawny apricots from the south melting in your mouth. All the books still to be read! So many things not even started! But through the piles of books and notes and even *literature* (real literature, underground literature), through the vision of hours, years, months sitting in the public library, there stirred, thrusting upward and pointing heavenward like an obelisk, a keen regret. What of women? Why had he let women pass him by all those years? Were they not every man's main reason for continuing to live?

It was not a very lofty thought, but he could think of nothing else. Half an hour earlier Sasha might have lost everything—the knowledge he had accumulated, his beliefs, his circulatory system. But the memory of a woman's love would, he thought, have remained on earth as something concrete, imperishable. Bullets were powerless against it.

Now it was clear that this joy would be his. In the past few days Sasha had been going around like a man with a burning open wound; the slightest touch was painful and he had bumped into things when he least expected it. While he had been arguing passionately with the doctor on the hospital steps a nurse had come out—a well-built woman with large breasts. She had not said a word to him and he would never see her again: it was as though she had slapped his open wound with a towel and then gone away. Many such memories from years past had crept upon him and stung his wound these last few days.

Most haunting of all—in Petersburg, a little while back, during his last visit: Yelya, Veronika's classmate. He had seen her only a few times. They had gone boating with friends, had met at a student party, but had not spent a single evening alone together. When they were boating he had been bad-tempered, he was sick of the white nights and those who thought them fun—and he was short with everybody, while Yelya sat slender and silent at the prow of the boat like one of those female figures with which the Vikings adorned the prows of their ships. At the party, though, Sasha had let himself go—on such occasions he could be witty, quick, and irresistible, everybody listened to him. Yelya listened attentively, but with the air she always wore in company. All the girls in their circle talked freely, had opinions of their own and could defend them, but Yelya just watched with her dark eyes and remained enigmatically silent through all the stories and arguments. It was impossible to say whether she was agreeing or demurring, but her silence provoked him to argue. She had a narrow little face and childishly full, soft lips—lips it was easy to remember: once, in passing, they had exchanged a joking kiss.

But in Petersburg his feelings had not ripened, he had made no effort to be alone with her. His days had been too full, and he was not anticipating war but his discharge in the near future. Her views, which were unusual in their circle, were another reason for his casualness toward her.

From the first day of the war she had filled the forefront of his mind—Yelya! Yelenka! Yolochka! He was consumed with regret, longed for the sweet sting he had missed because of his own stupidity in Petersburg that June. How could he have failed to understand and be drawn to her? She was all hesitancy. What would have been the gravest of faults in a man was the essence of her femininity: the puzzled twitch of her eyebrows, the uneasy movements of her head, the doubtful inclination of her neck, the restlessness of her shoulders, most of all the sudden stops and starts of her neat slender figure when she quickened her pace and broke into a comic little run.

Just as a treacherously gentle swell steals upon ships to rock and toss them, so did Yelenka's waverings threaten to pull Sasha and this life of great deeds he had planned off course and into her wake. He realized now that he must, that he needed to, could not fail to, put an end to these vacillations, with his own hands. He must still her in his arms, and only then would he be at peace himself.

But at the time he had not even had the sense to ask her for a photograph, and the letters in which he had begged her for one went through the censorship at tortoise pace, and all he had received from her was two lighthearted lines by way of a postscript to one of Veronika's letters.

For the present he had to defend his ghastly "fatherland."

[3 4]

The Russian town commandant of Neidenburg, Colonel Dovatur, discovered only accidentally from a telegraphist that Army HQ had left the town—the last of the staff were just on their way out—and that telegraphic communications had been suspended. Nobody had thought of leaving him instructions. They were so preoccupied with strategic matters that they had forgotten all about him. He rushed off to see the staff officers still in the town, but they were hastily packing the last of their boxes to send them by cart to Janow, and they merely shrugged their shoulders.

At that point an ensign from the 6th Don Regiment arrived with a report for the Army Commander from the commander of the combined cavalry brigade—and the commandant did not know where to send it and could not accept it himself. He had heard with half an ear sometime in the night that the brigade had been put under General Kondratovich's command, but where Kondratovich was, and where his HQ was, nobody had the least idea. At that same moment another courier surfaced: he had been galloping all night from Mlawa bringing the mail from Warsaw, among it, he stressed repeatedly, a letter to General Samsonov from his wife. These couriers were no concern of his, and the commandant had no advice to give them, just as the staff officers had no business with him and could be of no help to him.

Yesterday evening they had succeeded at last in extinguishing all the fires and clearing the streets. Six days after their entry, when the shops could open again and the town begin to look normal, the staff had left as though that was all they had been waiting for. Supply wagons and infantry, not in marching order but in straggling groups, and even individual soldiers had begun filtering through the streets from the north, all asking "the way to Russia."

Two wagons abreast and any Neidenburg street was blocked. Stop your lead horses on the town-hall square and the whole place was at a standstill. Rankers, with no officer in sight, yelled to each other to pull back, wagons got hooked on to each other, harnesses snapped, soldiers started fighting, and an officer who came up and spoke politely to them received an insolent reply. All this was watched closely and with malicious glee by German women peeping from behind their curtains. Order somehow had to be maintained in the town by means of the forces at the commandant's disposal (less than a company and some of them were posted as sentries) and through the good offices of the weighty burgomaster.

The commandant used his small forces to man roadblocks at the two northern entrances, with orders to make all units take the long way around. This might have worked, but the commandant looked in on the divisional sick quarters and the hospital and changed his orders: all wagons should be examined as they arrived, small loads should be thrown out, and the vehicles used to evacuate the wounded. He visited one roadblock himself, and told the platoon to be ready to use their weapons on anyone who refused to obey.

At the hospital the doctors were discussing the situation. An hour or two after the departure of Army HQ there was a whiff of surrender in the air. The war was only just beginning, and there was no knowing for certain how strictly the 1864 Geneva Convention on treatment of the wounded would be observed. It laid down that hospitals were to be regarded as neutral, would not be fired on, and must accept wounded men from both sides. Their personnel enjoyed immunity, could not be taken prisoner, and were free to leave whenever they pleased. The wounded would be repatriated as they recovered, after giving their word not to take up arms again. Any private house that took in a wounded man came under the protection of the Convention. There was no reason to suppose in advance that war had become more ruthless half a century after the conclusion of the Convention, but the newspapers averred that the Germans had, and the doctors had seen for themselves that with so many wounded and such a shortage of beds it was impossible to treat your own side and the other impartially. So as they prepared the hospital for evacuation it was impossible to predict what was in store for those left behind. The doctors were divided into two groups—those who would go and those who would stay. So were the nurses. The older women from the Red Cross societies, with good nursing experience, were to be kept back. Young volunteers, who had slipped through to the front in the confusion of mobilization, were to be sent to the rear. They varied greatly in learning capacity, but none of them was as yet of much practical use. They giggled a lot, and one madcap knocked a pharmacist down riding a bicycle along a corridor. Fedonin was, however, insistent that the chief medical officer should allow Tanya Belobragina to stay behind. She was by no means fully trained but she took her work very seriously, and in addition to her general ward duties showed a special interest in face and neck wounds. She herself would not ask to be evacuated.

Altogether, work was scamped while they were waiting for the order to evacuate. It was in any case impossible to operate with so many hundreds of bedridden patients and all they could do was dress wounds. They began selecting the men to be evacuated. How should they divide patients? Even in a stationary hospital there were no certain means of combating gangrene—what would it be like on a grueling journey?

They tried to keep it from the wounded until the time came, but the men themselves felt that there was something unusual about the rounds of inspection and became uneasy. All those who were conscious and at all capable of moving wanted to go. Perhaps because they could all see each other lying around, they seemed to feel that there would be something dishonorable in taking their ease while their fellow countrymen were fighting.

An orderly reported that some colonel was asking to see one of the doctors quickly. "Will you come down, Valeryan Akimich?"

Fedonin went quickly to the exit. Empty wagons were already gathering on the triangular forecourt, almost blocking it. On the stone porch a sunburned and crumpled colonel with a tear in the tunic over his raised shoulder was studying a map and questioning one of the walking wounded, a sergeant. He turned eagerly to meet Fedonin.

"Are you a doctor? How do you do. Colonel Vorotyntsev, from GHQ." A rapid squeeze of the hand. "Tell me, have any wounded come in from forward positions recently, and are any of them conscious? May I question them? Are there any officers among them?"

The doctors themselves were hardly dawdlers, but this solidly built yet agile colonel set a still faster pace. Fedonin readily complied and searched his memory.

"Yes. Some came in overnight. And more this morning. There's a second lieutenant from the 13th Corps. He was badly concussed, but he's come around and is quite conscious now."

The colonel pricked up his ears. "The 13th? That's interesting." He seemed surprised, and in even more of a hurry. A strong hand on Fedonin's elbow propelled him toward the wards. "You're 15th Corps—where does the 13th come in?"

There wasn't far to go—upstairs, along a corridor, through two wards—so Fedonin too wasted no time. "Tell me, what's going to happen to the town?"

The colonel's clear eyes glanced briefly at the doctor, seeing him for the first time as something more than a source of information. He looked cautiously to right and left, and said quietly, "If we can organize our defenses we can still hang on a bit."

"Organize?" Fedonin seized on the word. "You don't mean . . . ? What's Army HQ doing?"

The colonel made a contemptuous noise with his lips. "They're west of here somewhere . . ."

They were entering a ward and, prepared though he was for it, the colonel was rocked on his heels when it hit him—he frowned and looked somber as he crossed the boundary of that concentrated smell of medicines, blood, and pus.

In the first ward a priest was administering the last rites, covering the dying man's face with his stole.

"I believe, O Lord, and I confess my sins . . ." How many times in the last few days had he intoned these words in a hushed voice, yet always as though for the first time, with no trace of boredom.

They found the second lieutenant by the window in the second ward, and as it happened Tanya Belobragina was sitting on his bed. She rose as they approached and stood by the wall between the windows, hands behind her back, motionless, with her grave dark eyes on them.

The second lieutenant had a bandage around his brow, but his eyes had regained their boyish quickness and keenness and he made a special effort for the newcomers, greeting them cheerfully.

Fedonin touched his cheeks and felt his pulse. "Are you feeling a little better?"

"Yes, indeed," the freckled lieutenant happily assured them, raising himself upon his pillows and wondering how he could make himself useful.

"Is it difficult for you to talk and answer questions?"

Tanya, blushing, said, "We've been talking a bit. We're from the same place."

Nobody would have suspected her of talking much.

"What's your regiment?" The colonel was already sitting on the bed and unfolding his map. "Are you really with the 13th Corps? When did you join it? What was your position? Where were you wounded? What units were alongside you? . . ."

The second lieutenant, sitting up against his pillows, gazed lovingly at the colonel, and behaved as though it were an enjoyable examination, proud that he could answer all the questions, and could have dealt with others. He was radiant with that chivalrous adoration which young men may feel even before a woman becomes the object of their devotion. There was a buzz in his ears, his head was weak, he had difficulty in speaking, but he did his best to answer as precisely as possible. His finger moved over the map, unhesitatingly showing the route by which they had been marched out of Hohenstein the day before, toward the fighting not far off to the west (thinking to himself what an effort it had cost assembling them all, making all the arrangements by telephone and messenger, marching the men out of the town), and how they had been recalled yet again before they could get their regiment into the firing line. Then they had been sent back to Hohenstein for some reason, by a roundabout route because the roads were so bad (and then there was that fit of panic in the evening, when they had opened fire on Russian troops, but never mind that), and from Hohenstein (again with some difficulty) they had marched to the edge of the battle area . . . and that was when . . . (But the rest he would save for his mother, he couldn't tell the colonel: something had exploded so close that you couldn't find words for it and all you could think was, I'm dying! I must cross myself! Goodbye, Mother! The next explosion you didn't even hear . . .)

"What's wrong with your shoulder?" Fedonin asked.

The colonel himself had forgotten about it till then. "Will you take a look? A splinter must have grazed it yesterday."

The surgeon felt it. "Does it hurt to move it?"

"It's a bit uncomfortable."

"Go along to my room, it's on this floor. The nurse here will show you." He turned to Tanya. "The senior doctor is willing to keep you on. Have you any objection? You might be stuck here for quite a while."

Her sad, brooding look did not change. There was not even a flicker of interest.

"Somebody must stay. Of course."

She was waiting to show the colonel the way. When he turned his head quickly all his resolution seemed to be in his close-trimmed but full beard, which covered so much of his face that his mustache was hardly noticeable. It did not stick out, did not droop, was not curled, it was only there hiding his upper lip because an officer was required to wear a mustache.

The lieutenant, though, had neither mustache nor beard, and as yet his lips lacked character, showed nothing but extreme youth and good nature. He had the innocence and good manners of one brought up in a female household. He still knew nothing, absolutely nothing about life. Tanya was only a year older, but she felt herself ten years wiser.

What if she were taken prisoner? Tanya was ready for anything. Capture, wounds—nothing could stir any feeling in her. If she could be killed quickly that would be best of all. It was in the hope of dying without sin, without taking her own life, that she had hastened to the front. Whatever happened to her now could not be worse than what had gone before.

Through the window she could see the hurly-burly and the growing confusion in the narrow lane below. Soldiers were pushing their way around in disorderly groups or individually. Some halted in the shade, mopping their brows, lightened their sacks, shed spades, axes, boxes of cartridges, then moved quickly on. Nobody tried to stop them. Two Cossacks, on the other hand, were strapping something to their saddles.

. . . They had read together. Taken walks together, hand in hand. From one conversation to the next they had traveled the path every step of which is precious, to be remembered for life. Their love was growing like a plant. All things have their season—leaf, bud, blossom. Could not Tanya have hurried it along? That was not a woman's part, that would not have been right. But *she*—no better, no more beautiful, no more faithful than Tanya—*she* had swooped, seized him, snatched him away. There was no court to try such dishonest behavior. As for men, they might be staunch in war, but in nothing else.

What clever officers the army could produce in two years—and how good it was at ruining them in the next twenty. Such eagerness to serve, to do whatever was asked of him, such anxious concern for the army and its operations, was written on that boyish brow.

"Sir!" The lieutenant held Vorotyntsev by his sleeve, looking at him hopefully and struggling with his difficulty in speaking. "I've heard that there is to be a partial evacuation. I just can't stay behind. It would mean disgrace. I can't begin my army life in prison camp!" His eyes were bright with tears. "Tell them to be sure and take me out."

"Very well." The colonel shook his hand heartily, and turned away quickly. "Right, Nurse!"

Tanya briskly turned her back on the window, leaving there all the things she had been thinking of and showing the world that face which is so often seen among Russian girls—alert, ingenuous, and anxious to help.

Such a dark flame burned in her eyes, there was such firmness in her features. Perhaps it was because her headscarf was tied so low, hiding forehead, neck, and ears.

"Nurse, I shall urge the doctor to see that Lieutenant Kharitonov is not left behind, and you will follow it up." She looked anything but featherheaded. No need of threats there. For some reason he wagged an admonitory finger, but his lips were smiling. "Take care—you can't escape me! Where do you come from?"

"Novocherkassk."

"You won't be safe even there." He nodded, and walked off quickly between the beds.

In each bed lay a closed world, a unique struggle was going on in each unique body. Shall I live or shall I not? Will they leave me my arm or won't they? For them the whole war and all the maneuvering of corps and armies had receded into insignificance. An elderly but wide-awake peasant soldier, probably a sergeant recalled from the reserve, peered out at the world from under his sheet with suspicion in his intelligent eyes. Another man rolled his head from side to side on his pillow, uttering hoarse cries.

Vorotyntsev was in a hurry to get away from the oppressive stench in the ward and to breathe again. The nurse led the way.

When she got back and went after a while to the window, the lieutenant had sunk lower in bed and looked weak and pale, but he still found a smile for Tanya.

"What about you, fellow townswoman? Are you staying on? Write a letter for your family, and I'll make sure it's posted. Who's waiting for you there?"

Tanya's grave face turned deathly white. Her head jerked to right and left. She wouldn't write. Not to anyone.

There was no one.

She didn't care where she went after the war as long as it wasn't Novocherkassk.

Vorotyntsev would have been in Neidenburg early that morning in time to catch Samsonov had he not repeatedly turned off the road to see who was holding the front, and found no one. He had also hunted the fugitive Kondratovich, and not found him either. Missing Samsonov completed the tale.

There was a gaping hole in the left flank of the front line, and it ached as though it were in his own side, but no one was sending troops to fill it. There were in fact no troops except the Kexholm Regiment, which had replaced the Estland and Reval regiments, and which took its instructions from General Sirelius, who was also going around in baffling circles somewhere, without ever reaching the front.

Samsonov's departure was another cause for wonder. Why had he not given orders to strengthen Neidenburg's northwestern defenses? Why had he gone off along the overextended front instead of tightening it up?

The way in which the Estland and Reval regiments were behaving in Neidenburg amounted almost to mutiny, but Vorotyntsev had no time to deal with them. He had left the horses with Arseni and after an hour and a half darting around several districts of the city he had discovered what had become of Army HQ; persuaded a cornet delivering the cavalry brigade's report to let him see it and to wait a while before riding on; obtained, with the help of various people, particularly the wounded, a pretty good sketch map of the position in the army center; and learned from Kharitonov how things were at Hohenstein, though what had become of the rest of the 13th Corps was shrouded in a mysterious silence—it was still harder to make out whether there was any hope of a supporting attack by Blagoveshchensky and Rennenkampf. He would have galloped off there like the wind, but the gaping hole on the left also demanded his attention. When he rode away from the hospital Vorotyntsev had his plan more or less ready.

Even last night's withdrawal to Soldau was not the final catastrophe, if the mistake was corrected in the next few hours.

He had arranged to meet the cornet by that conspicuous landmark, the Bismarck monument.

In Bismarck's day the League of the Three Emperors had allowed Eastern Europe to live in peace for half a century. Peace with Germany was more beneficial to Russia than daredevil displays with Paris circus artists.

The horses were waiting, tethered to a tree. Arseni was sitting behind the rock in the shade. He rose in a hurry, but only halfway, and said in a hushed voice, "Sir, it's time we had a bite."

There was something in his mess tin.

"You nearly ruined everything yesterday with your rusks . . . What about the horses? Fed them?"

"Of course I have!" Arseni was indignant. He stretched his wide mouth in a still wider grin. "In the cemetery—there's good grazing there."

Two boulders formed a bench behind the monolith, and the handle of a spoon stuck out conveniently to hand.

"What about you?"

"After you," Arseni parried. The newly acquired formula of respect came automatically.

"No, we'll eat together."

"Together it is then," said Blagodarev readily. He sank to his knees before the mess tin and began helping himself.

Vorotyntsev also helped himself, with his left hand, eating greedily and absentmindedly by turns, and unaware what the food was. With his right hand he wrote a letter, resting the paper on the stiff smooth leather of his map case supported on his raised knee, and hurrying so as not to keep the cornet waiting.

Your Excellency! One-third of your army is on the left flank, which is under heavy pressure, but has not been broken. (They had the battle won—and then retreated because of some stupid misunderstanding!) But there are at present three corps commanders in the sector (Artamonov, Masalsky, and Dushkevich) and no single will. If you yourself found it possible to come here (the 6th Don Regiment would escort you here safely in two or three hours), you could correct the whole position of the army by an energetic offensive: you would tie down and overthrow General von François, whose present intention is to cut you off. Krymov and I urgently beg you to opt for this step. Colonel Krymov has now replaced the Chief of Staff of the 1st Corps.

I shall be somewhere west of Neidenburg, which because of the gap in the line is virtually undefended. Colonel Vorotyntsev.

He should also have advised Samsonov to pull the central corps back, but he dared not suggest it directly. Samsonov must think of it for himself.

The cornet rode up. Vorotyntsev warned him to burn the dispatch or swallow it rather than let it fall into enemy hands.

The other courier, from Warsaw, had got lost somewhere, and the commander was fated never to receive his wife's letter.

[3 5]

It was many days since Samsonov had felt so clearheaded and so sure of himself. He had ridden out of Neidenburg in high spirits at the head of his downcast staff, with his horse trotting spiritedly under him. He felt fresh although his sleep had been short. The damp August morning was still more refreshing, with the sun triumphantly rending the fog patches that had shrouded the sky at dawn.

How splendid it was to rise early in the morning! How gloriously easy it was to think and to act in the morning! In the cool morning air he felt reassured that the battle was going well! A man of fifty-five might have many such beautiful mornings ahead of him.

He had not chosen the route himself and they took him by a roundabout way, making a detour to the east, through the village of Grünfliess and a corner of the Grünfliess Forest. The commander of the Cossack escort and his own staff assured him that the short route to Nadrau was unsafe, that a German raiding party might break through, that they might be ambushed and fired on. Nevertheless, when they were halfway along they saw horsemen approaching in a cloud of dust. The convoy prepared to make a fight of it, and sent out a scouting party.

The troops proved to be Russian, a platoon of dragoons from the 6th Corps, escorting in platoon strength a piece of paper (Blagoveshchensky's dispatch) over some fifty versts of half-deserted no-man's-land. If HQ staff had not taken a circular route they would never have met them.

It was now eight-thirty and Blagoveshchensky's dispatch—signed between midnight and one o'clock, twenty-four hours after its predecessor—was a normal, detailed late-night twenty-four-hour report. It was as though nothing important had happened in the meantime. Well, was he or wasn't he going to Klyuev's rescue? Had he covered the rear of the central units? Had he occupied firm defensive positions?

". . . I have pulled back toward Ortelsburg . . ."

Without dismounting, Samsonov called for a map. Yesterday Blagoveshchensky had inexplicably withdrawn in the direction of Mensguth, and that was alarming enough. But today—if only he had stayed at Mensguth! Instead, he had slid back another twenty versts, taking the familiar route, the quickest way home to Russia . . .

The cornet of dragoons seemed eager to say more about this backsliding, but the commander checked him, to save his own face and to keep up the outward appearance of solid self-assurance which he had assumed for the benefit of those around him.

Of course, in the seven hours the dragoons had been in the saddle, Blagoveshchensky might already have abandoned Ortelsburg too. Perhaps he was already back in Russia.

What orders could he give now? . . . Hold Ortelsburg whatever the cost? . . . *Whatever the cost* . . . The steadiness of your corps will determine . . .

The cornet galloped back the way he had come, with his platoon and another piece of paper, to be delivered after midday.

The staff officers passed Blagoveshchensky's dispatch from hand to hand. Should Klyuev be informed? If so, how? He was on his way to join Martos anyway. And so were they.

There was one thing to be done, though: the Living Corpse ought to know about it. His feeble hands might be galvanized into action for once to put things right. Riders must take a message to Janow immediately, and it could be telegraphed from there.

Resting his big map case on his horse's head as before, he wrote in his bold scrawl: "The 6th Corps has withdrawn to a position south of Ortelsburg—in disorder according to an officer eyewitness. The corps has suffered great losses, and is greatly weakened physically and in morale. I am going to Nadrau, where I shall decide which corps are to take part in the offensive . . ."

He wrote "shall decide" as though his decision were not already made: the center would attack. But now that Blagoveshchensky had rolled back so far, ought he not to stop them? Call off the central corps? There was nothing he wanted less! The battered wings of the army were drooping more and more helplessly . . . But, oh, how Samsonov was loving that morning gallop which made him while it lasted a dashing young soldier again! "I shall make my decision"—he urged on his horse in the same direction.

His staff officers, grumbling in undertones, moved off behind him. (Postovsky, that great expert on filling out forms, consoled himself with the thought that even a few hours spent in the proximity of enemy artillery fire could be advantageously recorded in his service book and count toward a medal.)

From one hilltop they had a broad view of Maransen, an elongated lake that seemed to have no end to it. The sun was still low, and there was no reflected light from the unruffled, dark water. Thick forest stood around the shores. Lifeless farmhouses, their tiles glowing red, lay scattered about the hill slopes.

Samsonov forgot his cares as he drank in this soothing vision of a world without men. "Beautiful country, gentlemen! . . . Who would have thought they had all these hills, these wonderful views?"

A wagon train carrying wounded men (many of them with bayonet wounds) lumbered uphill toward them. Some could only groan, but others spoke out boldly, and all the more boldly when they saw the three generals. There had been a battle in the night, both sides using bayonets, outside a village ten versts away. A victorious battle. "We won!" they all said in unison.

There were still rumbles to be heard somewhere not very far to the left. God is our Protector, God and the Mother of God. On, then, gentlemen, faster, we still know nothing.

Martos's command point was called Nadrau after the nearest little village, but was in fact on the high ground to its left, half encircled by forest, an excellent spot with a wide view. The front line had receded, the place was no longer within range, and some officers were standing without cover on the hillside, in hot sunshine already, passing a pair of binoculars around.

Down below, a column was proceeding slowly along the road, to the railway line and over it—no, it was a column of prisoners, marching under escort! Yes, at least a thousand of them! Martos, short and narrow-shouldered, was sitting on a chair and also looking through binoculars. No one had told them that Army HQ was moving, or when. They looked around and with the sun in their eyes they did not at first recognize the riders.

Martos, though far from young, sprang to his feet with youthful ease, transferring to his left hand the short swagger stick which he liked to swish as he walked. He stood to attention and saluted his commander, squinting in the bright sunlight at the bulky figure on horseback.

"Your Excellency! The enemy attempted to attack by night in division strength, using the valley approach to the village of Waplitz. Their plan was discovered in time, and frustrated, in fact their whole operation was out of control in the end, and they were destroying their own troops by artillery fire at Waplitz cemetery, obviously computing the range without direct observation. The division which attempted to attack was smashed and thrown back, and we are holding the vital Wittmannsdorf heights. We have taken two thousand two hundred prisoners, including perhaps a hundred officers, and twelve artillery pieces. Although much depleted, the Kaluga and Libau regiments attacked the enemy in the rear and contributed to our victory."

Martos had no wish to rob his neighbors of their share in the credit for his success.

It was all there, plain to see: the prisoners were being marched past, and a small group of officers was diverted toward the top of the hill.

This was the moment of triumph which the commander had foreseen! For this he had torn out of Neidenburg that morning. His journey had not been in vain.

Samsonov remained in the saddle while the Corps Commander was reporting, but as soon as he had finished, dismounted, heavily but steadily, surrendered the reins, and without stopping to ease his stiff limbs, swooped on spry little Martos, clasped those narrow shoulders in his thick arms, and kissed him. "You'll do it alone! You, my dear fellow, are our salvation."

He leaned back and gazed at Martos as though he would like to bestow a quarter of his kingdom on him, seeing the order which should adorn that narrow chest but for the rules of seniority governing the award of honors.

Nothing more was heard of Postovsky's ridiculous suggestion that they should go to Allenstein. But perhaps the time had come to turn the 15th Corps sharply to the left and deal the enemy a heavy blow in the rear? Perhaps this was the moment for the sidestepping attack mentioned in last night's order to the army? Who should be heard first if not the victor?

"I should be grateful for your opinion, Nikolai Nikolaevich."

Martos held his brave head steady, his eyes flashed. He did not pretend that he needed time to think, did not wrinkle his brow in agonized thought. Shoulders effortlessly squared, mustache neatly twirled, he answered quick as a flash and fearlessly: "With your permission, sir, we should withdraw without delay!"

Though no one had informed him that Artamonov and Blagoveshchensky had retreated, he sensed instinctively that his corps should not stay there, but should pull back, and quickly. He felt the growing tension, just as snails or birds sense the coming of a storm because of atmospheric pressure or astral currents.

But the commander—was it possible?—had not understood. Withdraw? Why, for heaven's sake?

Postovsky, cautiously dismounting with the aid of a Cossack, approached him, and seeing that his commander did not agree, said to Martos, "What's this, then? Giving in to panic? Are your nerves playing up, eh? The Kexholm Regiment will move up on your left very shortly. One of the 13th Corps' brigades has been detached to reinforce your right wing. The 13th itself"—Postovsky looked around as though he expected to see the corps, but saw only a wall of trees—"will be here any minute now, all of it. And there's Rennenkampf's cavalry as well. How can you possibly ask permission to retreat?"

If there was one thing Martos had never learned it was indecision. He rapped out his reply: "The corps has been fighting for three days running, and five out of the last six. We have lost some of our best and bravest officers and several thousand other ranks. The corps is getting weaker and weaker and is no longer capable of positive action. I have no cavalry, and have to act blindly. Our shells are running out, and we are getting no supplies. We're short of cartridges too. Our continual attacks are of no advantage to the army, they only complicate its situation. We must retreat—immediately."

The plan which had seemed so trim and tight that morning was swept away by Martos's crushing logic. Not a line in it could be salvaged. The exhilarating attack, to which the Army Commander would gallop or send his aide, was no more. All the winning, planning, suggesting, and losing there was to be done had been done without him.

And Martos did not know as yet that the corps on both wings had withdrawn.

Samsonov blinked heavily as though fighting against sleep. He removed his cap as though it were suddenly too tight for his graying head. He mopped his brow.

His brow looked bigger and more defenseless than ever: a white target over a defenseless face.

[3 6]

In the heat and haste of the moment Vorotyntsev had slipped up: having begun the morning searching for Kondratovich, he should not have left the trail until he had found the elusive general and shamed him or threatened him with the wrath of GHQ. There was still time to station west of Neidenburg all of the 23rd Corps with any fight left in it.

General Kondratovich, who had—luckily, he perhaps thought—seen his corps dismembered and so been able to take leisurely train rides between Warsaw and Vilna on the pretense of reassembling it—General Kondratovich had certainly been in the vicinity that morning, he wasn't a disembodied spirit: he had come close to the front line for the very first time, and been seen in one place an hour, in another half an hour, before Vorotyntsev got there. But Vorotyntsev lacked the patience to gallop after him, and while he was gathering information from the wounded, Kondratovich had sped to Neidenburg. Finding there no one superior to himself in rank, he had given his orders: the commander of the Estland Regiment with six companies and a machine-gun detachment would withdraw eastward along the highway, escorting and guarding—General Kondratovich. He evidently calculated that since one bedraggled division of his half-formed corps was now under Martos's command, since the Kexholm Regiment had taken up its position and could hold out unaided, since the other Guards regiments would not get so far anyway, he himself, the Corps Commander, had nothing to do and would be safer beyond the Russian border awaiting the outcome.

Vorotyntsev learned all this belatedly after sending off his note to Samsonov.

Early that morning Neidenburg had been the seat of Army HQ, the nerve center of transport and communications, yet by noon there was not a single general left there, no one senior in rank to Vorotyntsev, no link with any of the corps or with Army Group HQ, and all those abandoned had to act as mind and conscience dictated.

Vorotyntsev's state, however, was unchanged; freed from any physical needs, any desires, any thoughts of his own, he was merely a mobile contrivance for saving what could still be saved. When he thought of the gap torn in the army's left side and the draft blowing through it, his heart pounded in his breast. He knew one thing only: the hole must be plugged for the few hours it would take the Army Commander to reach the 1st Corps.

In the blocked and apprehensive streets of Neidenburg he had come upon Lieutenant Colonel Dunin, a battalion commander in the Estland Regiment: his four companies, sadly thinned, had remained in the town overnight to recover, and the lieutenant colonel could not make up his mind what to do. Five more companies of the same regiment arrived from the north under another lieutenant colonel—companies scarcely larger than platoons. They had been in the line all night and the Kexholm Regiment had relieved them that morning.

Vorotyntsev briefly explained to these two lieutenant colonels and half of the surviving company commanders the situation of the town, the position of the army, the fact that other companies in their regiment had withdrawn to Russia together with the regimental commander, and what was required of those who remained.

As he spoke he looked into their faces. It was as though he were looking at his own face many times over. They were all, in some decisive respect, very much alike, the product of army tradition and years of garrison service in an isolated world, estranged from a society which treated them with contempt, ridiculed by progressive writers, their minds blunted or dimmed by the prohibition from on high against thinking about politics or reading political literature, constantly short of money. Yet in spite of all this they represented, in refined and concentrated form, the vitality and courage of the nation. This was their moment, and Vorotyntsev had no doubt of their response.

They would do what must be done. The lieutenant colonels agreed to put themselves under Vorotyntsev's command, but declared that their soldiers could no longer stand and fight: they had been particularly badly shaken by the German heavy shells which they had endured without the protection of trenches. Vorotyntsev asked them at least to have all their men fall in by the western exit from the town, on the road to Usdau.

While the companies were being assembled and marched back out of the town, shuffling sullenly along, bellyaching, and glowering at everything around them, Vorotyntsev found time to see Dovatur, the town commandant—a plump man with a paunch, very polite and obliging—reached agreement with him about cartridges and carts to transport them, and indicated the place west of the town to which he should send a message as soon as it was free of supply wagons and retreating troops.

The soldiers were drawn up in the shade in six ranks, in close order, so that there was no need to shout. In the few minutes while they were being lined up Vorotyntsev stood with his hands behind his back, feet planted firmly apart, surveying the force of which he found himself so unexpectedly in command and noticing particularly the right marker, a dark, lanky old veteran.

In the two days and nights while their regiment was going through the mill the survivors had grown old: they had begun to behave with the unhurried dignity of dying men, no one carried out orders with alacrity, no one threw out his chest and exerted himself. There was not a single carefree face, no one made a show of cheerful confidence. In their brush with death back there, dutiful habits had begun to peel away; but not, as yet, to the extent that orders had lost all power over them. A simple word of command would suffice even now to send them into the line—but they would probably run away as soon as they got there.

What was he to say to them now? Their ears were still deafened, they had not yet got their breath, they had narrowly escaped death, and along comes some unknown colonel telling them to go straight back. *He* wasn't aiming to die with them, of course, *he* would fade as soon as he had driven them into action.

Should he speak of "honor"? Of course not—that was an incomprehensible notion, all very well for the gentry. "Obligations to our allies"? Hardly. (Vorotyntsev was not too fond of "our allies" himself.) Call upon them to sacrifice their lives for their Little Father the Tsar? That was something they would respond to—the Tsar as a nameless, faceless, timeless symbol. But Vorotyntsev was ashamed of the present Tsar, and invoking his name would be hypocritical.

God then? God's name would move them if anything could. But Vorotyntsev himself could not have borne the sacrilege and the falsity of it—invoking the name of God at such a moment, as though it were supremely important to the Almighty to save the German town of Neidenburg from the Germans. Every soldier there was capable of realizing for himself that God would not take sides in that way. Why treat them as fools?

That left Russia. The fatherland. And that, for Vorotyntsev, was the true cause. That was what he understood. He also knew that the soldiers didn't understand it very well. Their fatherland did not extend far beyond their native villages, so that his voice would have the cracked ring of uncertainty, insincerity, ludicrous sentimentality, and he would only make things worse. "Fatherland" was another word he couldn't bring himself to use.

He just couldn't make up a speech.

He looked at those sullen, tired, somber faces; he made an effort to feel as they felt under those sweat-soaked blanket rolls and sweat-soaked shirts, under the straps that galled their shoulders, in boots red-hot from the unwashed feet inside; and having called them to attention and stood them at ease, he spoke, not in a brisk, ringing voice or a parade-ground bark, but as though he felt as tired and limp as they did, as though he still hadn't fully made up his own mind.

"Men of the Estland Regiment! Yesterday and the day before you took a hiding. Some of you have had a rest, others haven't. But look at it this way: half of your number have laid down their lives. War is always unfair—it wouldn't be war if it weren't. We shouldn't be wondering how we can get off lightly. We should be thinking about how to avoid letting our comrades down."

He saw now the easiest way to do it: tell them, simply and openly, how things really were, and explain the military objective to them—just what you weren't supposed to do according to army regulations but the only thing to do in actual fact. He couldn't be entirely straightforward, couldn't say, "Our central corps are doomed! The generals have bungled, they're all fools or cowards, now it's up to you ordinary Russian men to save the day!" Again he imagined himself burdened with one of those packs, galled by those shoulder straps.

"Brothers!" He opened his arms wide and stood rooted to the ground. The ranks saw and were impressed by his breadth and his solidity. "We shall gain nothing by trying to save ourselves at the expense of others. Russia is not far away, we can withdraw—but if we do, the neighboring regiments will be wiped out. The Germans will catch up with us next and we shan't escape anyway . . . I can see that every step you take is a terrible effort for you, but right now there's a gap in the front not far from here and nobody else to fill it. It has to be plugged until the wounded are removed from the town and the supply wagons get away. It must be held till evening! There's nobody to do it but you." He was not ordering them, not threatening them, just explaining.

When he saw those generous smiles break through, heard that low murmur of assent, the colonel dropped his arms and snapped to attention. He had resumed his authority, and called out in a loud, commanding voice, "Volunteers only! First rank! Those who want to go—three steps forward!"

The whole rank stepped forward.

Still more confidently, almost triumphantly, he shouted, "Second rank! Those willing to go—three steps forward!"

The second rank moved forward.

So did the third.

All six ranks stepped forward to a man, with cheerless faces and unsteady steps—but still they took the three steps forward.

Although he knew that there was nothing much to be glad about, that it was improper and out of place, Vorotyntsev could not help shouting, "Well done, Estland Regiment! Mother Russia still has stout sons left!"

For once "Mother Russia" sounded right.

* * *

THE HORSERADISH DOESN'T LIKE THE GRATER,
BUT THEY DANCE A MERRY JIG TOGETHER

* * *

[37]

There was no time to lose. He must run to his mounted escort—Arseni and the three Cossacks from the 6th Don Regiment who had attached themselves to him. The Cossacks were true to type—one had a topknot, one looked out from a thicket of whiskers, one was a touslehead, and all were tigers on horseback. But . . .

"As for you, Arseni, you're a disgrace. Didn't you say you could sit a horse?"

"So I can, only bareback, without a saddle. That's how everybody rides back home in Kamenka. A saddle is a gentleman's toy."

In his haste the day before, Blagodarev had ridden with a saddle and blistered his seat. Now he had thrown the saddle away and was riding sloppily. When the colonel reproached him he had the ingenious idea of attaching a feather pillow to the horse's back by means of ropes tied under its belly, and sat there complacently with his legs dangling, jeering back at the guffawing Cossacks.

"Does it look bad, sir?" he asked, showing that he was ready to untie the pillow at once, but making no move to do so. "I could ride all the way to Turkey like this." He puffed out his cheeks.

"Turkey's the right place for it . . ."

They slung their rifles slantwise behind them, cavalry fashion, and galloped off.

As soon as one worry was out of the way another loomed. A little while ago Vorotyntsev had been anxiously wondering whether he could persuade the soldiers to go back into that hell. Now he was worried because he had promised that it would be only till evening. If it had to be longer who would there be to relieve them? And, anyway, would he be able to hold them till the evening? And if he did, would anything be gained by their sacrifice, or had he deceived them? There was nothing he could do about the rest of the army. Anything might happen. It was quite enough for one little brain to decide where and how to position this combined but still weak force of five companies. How to make them stretch from the Kexholm Regiment in the north to the Usdau highroad in the south? They were too few to cover so many versts—but the whole idea was to hold an unbroken front.

Vorotyntsev's party rode for several versts along a byroad, not westward, but a little farther to the right, toward the hole which he had detected. They found that there was indeed a hole, an empty space with not a human being in sight, neither friend nor enemy, no local inhabitants, no stray horses or dogs, no corpses, no poultry. It was like the eye of a cyclone: howling, whirling darkness all around, but here in the middle halcyon calm.

Here, and not a step farther on, was the place to wait for the Estland Regiment and position them. Vorotyntsev left one of the Cossacks as a marker and took the rest with him to locate the flank of his neighbor to the left. It was a matter of urgency, and he would not come back till he had done so.

The sun, unscreened by clouds, poured down unmitigated heat, the open countryside was baking hot, deserted, dead, there seemed no likelihood of meeting anyone there.

There was a hill ahead of them covered with pine saplings, and Vorotyntsev decided to take a look around from it. The sturdy horses took the hill easily. The going was soft. They could see nothing for the pines, so that a strange growling noise as they neared the top took them by surprise. It stopped as soon as they heard it, but when they rode out onto the brow of the hill—Germans! A car! Right in front of them! Ten paces away! It had obviously just climbed up there and switched off.

The four Germans sitting in the car were no less astounded than the four Russian horsemen.

At first they all froze.

Then the Cossacks drew their swords with a resounding swish.

The officer behind the general pulled out a revolver and held it at eye level. After something of a struggle the occupant of the back seat thrust the barrel of a light machine gun through the window.

Blagodarev effortlessly unslung his rifle and chambered a cartridge.

It was a miracle that guns did not start firing, swords slashing, of themselves. That would have been the end of all of them. But the Cossacks awaited the word of command. And so, needless to say, did the Germans.

The diminutive general, however, did not draw his revolver or give the command. His head turned sharply this way and that, his sharp eyes looked in amazement at this rare and amusing sight: Don't scare them away, whatever you do!

Vorotyntsev read his thoughts, and only kept his hand on the hilt of his sword. (It would have taken too long to unsling his rifle, he wasn't used to it.)

The car engine was off, the horses had not whinnied, and there was dead silence in the space between them. Nothing disturbed the pine-scented air on the sun-baked hilltop except the breathing of horses and the buzz of a gadfly or a bluebottle.

All eight of them, when they had passed, without a shot being fired, through that moment of silence in which nothing existed except hot sunshine and the buzz of a solitary insect, had risen above death.

Swiveling his head, the general ("same one as yesterday, Your Honor") continued to peer at them with great curiosity, apparently discounting the idea that he might be shot or cut to pieces. His ears were flat against his head like those of a frightened animal, but he was not, in fact, the least bit frightened. His face had a comical look—perhaps because of the bristly mustache curling upward at the ends. Or perhaps he just had a sense of humor. He was not slow to demonstrate it, laughingly chiding Vorotyntsev: "*Herr Oberst, ich hatte Sie gefangennehmen sollen.*"*

Vorotyntsev was not sure yet what to make of this meeting and how he could take advantage of it, but François's gentle teasing was infectious. Responding only to the general's tone, he answered more merrily still, with a flash of his even teeth: "*Nein, Exzellenz, das bin ich, der Sie gefangennehmen soll.*"†

The light machine gun was cautiously lowered. Then the revolver. Then the swords.

"*Sie sind ja auf unserem Boden,*"‡ the general said argumentatively.

Entering into the spirit of it, Vorotyntsev went one better: "*Diese*

* "Herr Colonel, I ought to take you prisoner!"
† "No, Excellency, it is I who ought to take you prisoner."
‡ "But you are on our territory."

Gegend ist in unserer Hand." This was empty boasting, but he had to make the best of a bad job: for all they knew there might be Russian infantry over the hill there. He added, more sternly: "*Und ich wage einen Ratschlag, Herr General, lieber entfernen Sie sich.*"*

It was! Arseni had been right when he whispered that it was yesterday's general, the one they had seen jumping into the car as sprightly as any youngster, though he was no younger than Samsonov.

The general would not, indeed could not, be drawn. "*Bitte, Ihren Namen, Oberst.*"†

No secret about that, Vorotyntsev supposed. "*Oberst Worotynzeff.*"‡

Whether because he realized that the colonel was too shy to ask the name of a full general or because he was enjoying the conversation, he introduced himself, with the same humorous twinkle in his eyes: "*Und ich bin General von François.*"**

Oho! The commander of the German 1st Corps! Practically in their hands—perhaps they could take him captive?

Somebody was practically in somebody's hands—but who, and in whose?

In any case it was easy enough to shoot or cut up people you didn't know, but after you had introduced yourselves it was somehow unnatural.

"*Aha! Ich erkenne Sie!*" Vorotyntsev exclaimed with cheerful unconcern. "*War es gestern Ihr Automobil, das wir beinahe abgeschossen haben? Was suchten Sie denn in Usdau?*"††

The general nodded and laughed out loud. "*Es wurde gemeldet—meine Truppen seien schon drin.*"‡‡

He looked Vorotyntsev up and down, eyes narrowed in appraisal. War had its funny side for those who could appreciate it.

The Cossacks could. They understood the tone of these exchanges. Grinning, they sheathed their swords, making a sound like a sigh of relief—both Kasyan Chertikhin, the cross-eyed one with the topknot, and the crafty, unkempt Artyukha Serga.

By now the German officer's revolver had vanished from sight completely. The light machine gun was barely visible behind the driver's back. Blagodarev too had slung his rifle. He whispered to Vorotyntsev, not for the first time, "Sir, sir . . . The lion, look! They've pinched our lion!"

Till then Vorotyntsev had not taken his eyes off the general and the

* "This locality is in our hands. . . . And if I may offer you some advice you would do better to withdraw."

† "What is your name, please, Colonel?"

‡ "Colonel Vorotyntsev."

** "And I am General von François."

†† "Aha! I recognize you! . . . Wasn't it your car we nearly knocked out yesterday? What did you want in Usdau?"

‡‡ "I got a report that my troops were already there."

light machine gun and so had not noticed, attached to the radiator of the car, the very same toy lion that had kept up the spirits of the men in their trench at Usdau . . . how long ago was it now? The remarkable thing was that the lion was quite undamaged.

The Germans also had noticed something and were whispering and laughing together.

"*Wer sind Sie aber, ein Russe?*"* François asked, eyeing him again. He apparently wanted to go on talking. Confident of his irresistibility, he was obviously out to charm even this enemy officer.

"*Ein Russe, ja,*"† Vorotyntsev said with a smile, more or less understanding what this question meant from a European.

He finally decided: We'd better part company. The general had probably believed that there were Russian forces nearby. He must get the Estland Regiment into position quickly. He raised his hand to the peak of his cap, looking apologetic.

"*Pardon, Exzellenz, es tut mir leid, aber ich muss mich beeilen!*" He looked into the general's eyes again, and glanced fleetingly at the light machine gun. Surely they won't shoot us in the back? Never! "*Leben Sie wohl, Exzellenz!*"‡

The general answered with the same mocking politeness, but with a hint of regret, fluttering three small fingers. "*Adieu, adieu!*"

The Cossacks understood his gesture, turned their horses sharply, and galloped full tilt downhill, following the colonel, with shrill cries of satisfaction. Blagodarev did his best to keep up, his long legs dangling loosely because he had no stirrups.

There was an explosion of laughter from the Germans. Vorotyntsev heard it and understood. For the first time he was angry with Blagodarev.

"They're laughing at your pillow! You're disgracing the whole Russian army!"

Blagodarev rode on as smoothly as any steppe warrior, but with a resentful scowl on his face.

The German with the light machine gun still had time to shoot the lot of them. But that was impossible after their exchange of courtesies. And it would have been altogether unworthy of a commander who was about to enter the pages of history.

* "You're Russian, then?"
† "Yes, I'm Russian."
‡ "Excuse me, Excellency, unfortunately I must hurry. . . . Goodbye, Excellency."

[38]

A military leader of the first class cannot be content merely to win: he must also fight elegantly. History will not overlook his least little gesture, the minutest detail of his generalship. Historians will either improve his image by judicious chiseling and polishing or else represent him as a lucky deadhead and nothing more.

On the evening of 27 August, General von François had still been in no position to issue orders for the 28th: his heart yearned for Neidenburg, but the situation held an implicit threat of counterattack from Soldau, and that was the direction in which army command was pushing him. In such a situation a mediocre general spends the whole night fretting himself and worrying his staff, waiting for something to come up, so that the pens can scratch away, copying out instructions. But Hermann von François had written laconically: "Divisions will remain in their own sectors and prepare for an offensive. The nature and timing of the offensive will be made known at 0600 hours on Hill 202 near Usdau. Officers will kindly be present to receive their orders . . ." and then gone to bed under an eiderdown with a pink cover in one of Usdau's undamaged houses. After his gesture the commanders of divisions and of subordinate units would not dare suppose that there would be no offensive the next day, or that the Corps Commander did not know his own intentions.

An important contributory gesture was the choice of rendezvous for the commanders. François, in fact, would have chosen not Hill 202 but the hill with the windmill outside Usdau if his troops had not advanced so fast and so far. It had been the most picturesque and conspicuous landmark in the area, especially yesterday, when the mill was still undamaged and François had made his misconceived and unsuccessful but enjoyable attempt to take it. Yesterday, half of his artillery, using the "saturation" method first introduced in this war, had worked to churn up the hill and destroy the regiment in possession of it. And yesterday, by the afternoon, General von François had been able to see the sprawled heaps of Russians, dead or half dead, in the trenches and on the hill slopes, the first time in all his military experience that artillery had produced such results. (True, when they came to pick up the dead there were many Germans among them—because they had attacked prematurely.)

As he went up to the top of the hill, where the remains of the mill were still smoldering (the damp night air and the mist would put them out), François had been conscious of making history with every step he took. Here he was at the beginning of the Neidenburg road by which he was to make his historic leap forward. His sharp eye had not missed the yellow spot in the banked earth protecting a trench, and his drivers triumphantly retrieved the exquisite yellow lion, which had survived the murderous bombardment intact. They took it into their heads to attach the lion to the radiator of one of the cars and promote him to sergeant major to mark the capture of Usdau, in anticipation of a long procession of victories which would raise him to the rank of field marshal.

It would have been better to assemble the commanders nearer to the front line. Thick mist shrouded even the high ground, blurring the details. François was there before the appointed time, pacing back and forth with his arms folded. His lonely greatness was emphasized by his persistence, for ten days now, in ignoring his Chief of Staff, denying the traitor any part in what needed to be done.

François had decided early that morning to use three of the divisions under his command to launch an attack on Soldau, as his superiors demanded, and to keep the other half back for a surprise dash to Neidenburg (concentrating in advance a flying column comprising motorcyclists, cyclists, an Uhlan regiment, and a battery of horse artillery at the head of the highroad). The silence of the Russians in Soldau and their lack of concern assured him that there was nothing to be feared from that quarter. The Russians there were preoccupied only with their withdrawal across the river.

When the great moment comes, its first knock at the door may be no louder than a heartbeat, and only the ear of the chosen one can distinguish it. Although he could only guess what was happening at Soldau, although an unexpected bombardment had started up in the night in Scholtz's sector, on the left, and continued into the morning, General von François was confident that he could hear fate's muted signal. At his own risk he launched the flying column at Neidenburg but ordered a detour to the south, to capture the Russian supply wagons, which by now were probably pouring southward. The direct route he reserved for his main force, which he himself would shortly lead into action.

The situation at Soldau looked promising—answering fire from the Russians was halfhearted, they were abandoning the city without attempting a counterattack. But the worrying bombardment in Scholtz's sector went on, and between 9 and 10 a.m. François's plans were ruined by the arrival of a car with urgent orders from Army HQ that he was to refrain from unauthorized action: "General von Sontag's division has been pushed back from the village of Waplitz by the enemy and is still retreating. Your corps must concentrate its reserves and send them to his aid immediately. *This action must take the form of an attack. Begin at once.* The situation calls for haste. Report when you make your move."

Alas, they were not cut out to be commanders in the field, neither Ludendorff nor Hindenburg! Fate was knocking at the door, but they had no ears for it. The least little sign of life from the enemy terrified them. A trickling leak made them fear that the bottom had been knocked out. What an unimaginative, what a craven order—rushing his corps into a head-on attack on an objective fifteen kilometers away when the most beautiful of encircling operations was begging to be carried out! But now that François's reputation for insolent defiance of his superiors had reached the Kaiser himself he could not refuse to obey.

Nor, however, could he knuckle under to fainthearted mediocrities.

Compromise in war is seldom wise and often disastrous. But in this case compromise was the only way out: François dispatched one division of the reserve to help Sontag as ordered. He himself stayed where he was, with a strong brigade, poised for the dash at Neidenburg. As soon as Soldau was taken, toward noon, the division dribbled back from that sector to replenish the Corps Commander's reserve.

He knew that no order from Ludendorff would stand for long—and sure enough, just before 1 p.m. another liaison officer turned up with a new one: to send help to Sontag by a different route, more to the east and lower-lying.

No, Ludendorff was no war leader! The commander of armies should not keep changing his mind like a capricious grande dame. You cannot start a movement "in the form of an attack," and then swing it onto "a lower-lying route." Ludendorff did not know himself what he wanted, beyond preserving his prestige in all circumstances, without ever taking a risk.

François regretted doing anything about the first order—it would have canceled itself out.

"The whole outcome of the operation depends henceforward on your corps."

It had depended on François's corps from first to last!

He dispatched the brigade he had ready, together with a Jäger regiment, along the Usdau–Neidenburg road. They would take the town and continue their advance. Leaving only a dotted line of patrols and checkpoints, they would then extend their claw of the pincer as rapidly as possible along the same road in the direction of Willenberg. Field kitchens would catch up with these units without delay and feed them. (A commander must think about his soldiers' stomachs.)

No longer attaching much importance to telephone communication with HQ, he rushed off with two carloads of officers to inspect and guide the units as they left.

That was when he had had his amusing encounter with the Russian horsemen among the half-grown pines on the lonely hilltop.

The division sent to help Scholtz had joined battle with a Russian Guards regiment en route when a third order overtook General von François toward 3 p.m.: previous orders were canceled, and there was no need to send Sontag any help. The objective of François's corps as the High Command now saw it was "to cut off the enemy's retreat to the south by occupying Neidenburg this day and moving on toward Willenberg at dawn tomorrow."

See what great strategists they were—if only you could wait long enough for them to see the light! He shouldn't have allowed his forces to be split that morning! How many additional Russian supply wagons he would have taken! In war compromise is *always* a mistake. Changing orders and shifting assessments, hopes raised only to be dashed and dashed only to be raised again, had so preoccupied François that the long summer's day had gone by before he noticed it. Around 5 p.m. the Jäger regiment entered Neidenburg unresisted and found there no Russian fighting units, only auxiliary and supply services. Only the thin line of infantry strung out northward from the highroad put up any resistance (opening fire from a potato field on François himself). The general was surprised how little understanding the Russians had of the situation if they didn't even propose to defend this key town! How could they possibly hope to win the war? How had they dared put themselves in such danger?

Russian supply troops were the main obstacle to the advance of François's corps. The flying column sent out in the morning had created traffic jams of supply wagons on the roads to the south of Neidenburg. The booty included even a field paymaster's office with a third of a million rubles. Russian wagons blocking the streets made it still more difficult to pass through Neidenburg. François and his staff rode in just before dusk, and their cars were brought to a halt immediately. They had to make their way on foot to the hotel on the market square.

A squad of policemen and a battalion of grenadiers (they had retreated twenty-five kilometers from Usdau the day before, and their major was trying to repair his damaged reputation by a show of zeal) were searching houses from cellar to attic, flushing Russian soldiers from their hiding places and marching them off under escort, all this with hardly a shot fired.

Outside the hotel two personages presented themselves to the general side by side—the German burgomaster and the Russian commandant. The commandant, laying down his responsibilities, reported on the state of the hospitals, the stores of (German) equipment, and the arrangements made for prisoners of war. The burgomaster expressed his great appreciation of the commandant's efforts to keep order in the city and protect the lives and property of its inhabitants. The general thanked the commandant, and asked him to choose a room to which he would confine himself as a prisoner of war. He also asked the commandant's name again.

"Dovatur," the pudgy, dark-haired colonel informed him.

François acknowledged it with a twitch of his eyebrows. "And your first name?"

"Ivan," the colonel said, smiling.

Hermann von François's eyebrows arched still more expressively, and a reflective smile formed on his lips.

Two descendants of French aristocratic families, dispersed at different unhappy moments in their country's history—one Huguenot, the other royalist—had met for a minute on the outer edge of Europe, for one to give an account of himself and the other to dismiss him under arrest.

By now a room had been made ready in the hotel for General von François. It was getting dark. The town rang with shouted orders, carts creaked, horses neighed. The town was sinking into night in a state of chaos.

The brigade sent on ahead together with the Jäger regiment was already moving on along the road beyond Neidenburg in the gathering dusk—eastward, to form the other half-circle of the closing ring.

* * *

Jerry, Jerry, silly-billy,
We don't give a damn for Willy!
As for daft old Emperor Franz,
We'll knock him down and pinch his pants!

[39]

On the rise behind Martos's command post stood a copse of beech and pine and beyond that again two farms. There for the time being Samsonov's mobile HQ and the Cossack squadron escorting it were installed.

No retreat? What then? The staff officers walked around restlessly, grumbling: what point was there, what sense, in ramming them into a tight spot on the front line with no means of communication by telephone, telegraph, or even dispatch rider? German shells were crashing and Russian guns growling nearby; machine guns beat a tattoo. The Mühlen line, which the Germans had held yesterday and the day before, was beginning to crack: the division's flanks were exposed and it was squeezed tighter from one hour to the next. Nor would the Poltava Regiment be able to hold until nightfall the positions it had won at Waplitz. The Army Commander had refused to authorize withdrawal, but suggested no way out of this cramping situation. The retreat began spontaneously just as hard metal becomes fluid, without permission from anyone or anything except its melting point.

The staff officers were denied the right to complain openly, but they prudently decided not to wait for his slow brain to take in and analyze the situation. They now began enthusiastically drawing up a minutely detailed plan of retreat (without, however, using that word, which the farsighted Postovsky feared might be a blot on their record). A map lay on a table planted in the ground under an apple tree. Filimonov's hand moved confidently over it, and the staff officers buzzed around him. If they were to escape subsequent censure, the complicated plan for a "sliding shield" had to be a superb staff-college exercise. The rear units were to advance southward, as smoothly and continuously as an endless belt passing over its pulleys, ensuring that the western defensive wall remained intact. The supply troops would be first to withdraw under the protection of the wall, then the 13th Corps (only it hadn't moved up into line yet—that was the snag), while the 15th Corps (this would be its seventh day of fighting) together with the remnants of the 23rd Corps would hold the front. Afterward, the 15th Corps too was to slip leftward, leaving the Poltava and Chernigov regiments behind as rearguard. (How unwieldy, how big and clumsy a corps seems when it has to retreat!) As soon as the 15th had pulled back as far as Orlau, the scene of its first victory, it would hold the front line again, this time facing southwest, toward Neidenburg, while the remnants of the 23rd slipped past behind it. In the meantime the 13th Corps, which had been moving back throughout the previous day (at the rate of forty versts in twenty-four hours), would take up position to the left of all the others—and so enable them to retire over the Russian frontier.

The commander sat apart, on a broad, rough-hewn peasant bench with no back. Everybody could see him, but he might just as well have been in his private office. His gold-hilted sword and his map case lay beside him on the bench, his cap was off, and he mopped his lofty brow from time to time with a handkerchief, although he could hardly have felt hot in the shade, with a breeze freshening the August air. Samsonov had reduced his staff to despair by sitting like that for hours on end, barely moving, his eyes blank, answering politely as always when he was spoken to, but in monosyllables. Only his neck showed the strain he was under. Was he thinking up a way of escape for all of them? Or had he stopped thinking, forgotten that he had a whole army under his command? He could sit like that, with his huge hands at his sides flat against the bench, motionlessly gazing at the ground, for half an hour at a time. He was not sleeping, not resting, not even merely idling while he waited for news—he was thinking and suffering torment. It was as though his thought was a great boulder poised on his motionless head. That was what made him wipe his sweating brow.

What could he be waiting for? Could he be hoping to see Klyuev's columns advancing from the north—the direction in which he was facing—in a thick cloud of dust? Or the lances of Rennenkampf's cavalry?

Perhaps he saw nothing and was looking for nothing, just listening to what was going on inside him: the stealthy sounds of a world taking shape, or the clangor of a world collapsing?

On the side where he was sitting the hill fell away to a peaty bog and beyond it, not more than a verst away, the road from Hohenstein to Nadrau could be clearly seen, rising from left to right up the slope of another hill. There had been little traffic—mostly ambulances—along that road all day. It was not a lateral route, and so of little help to the 15th Corps. But sometime in the afternoon supply and ammunition wagons and limbers (but not a single cannon) came streaming from the direction of Hohenstein in total disorder, with infantry straggling among them. The sun was behind the staff officers, and they could clearly see that these soldiers not only had strayed from their units but, if they had not already done so, were throwing their rifles away and shedding their equipment as they went along.

Samsonov, motionless in the shade and apparently with eyes for nothing, was one of the first to notice this disorderly flight. He jumped up on his sturdy legs and yelled to his officers to head them off, halt them, and restore order.

Whether they had grumbled at the commander or not, colonels and captains alike jumped to it, hastily picking up a Cossack as escort or drawing a previously undischarged staff revolver, and dashed down a grassy path to the bottom of the hill, then along the wire fence between a pasture and a stone dike beyond which lay a marsh, then uphill again. They could be seen brandishing their revolvers and waving their arms. The milling crowd on the road was dammed. Those at the back were still throwing their equipment away, but those in front were being made to pick it up again. Liaison officers galloped over there and back again to report: they told Samsonov that these were the Narva and Koporye regiments fleeing from Hohenstein in disorder and leaving an unprotected artillery battalion behind them; that the machine-gun detachment had also run away; that the commander of the Koporye Regiment had behaved disgracefully; that the retreating troops were frightened out of their wits and sure that all was lost; but that thanks to action taken by his staff officers . . .

Then back they went again with orders from the commander: they were to sort out the runaways and group them by units along the roadside; question the senior officers further about the circumstances of the flight; send as many as possible back to Hohenstein; and line up a battalion of each of the offending regiments under its regimental colors.

Samsonov came to life again and strode here and there, looking through his field glasses. The thoughtfully narrowed eyes over the dark, heavily mustached and bearded lower face promised calm leadership and a wise solution: nothing was lost, no one was lost, the commander would save them all. He had found at last the elusive task he had to perform—the reason, perhaps, why he had ridden there that morning! With every day that went by he had felt more powerfully drawn toward the foremost sector of the front, and now the front had swept toward him and was in sight only a verst away.

The commander's horse was saddled and waiting, but it took a long time to sort out the muddle, to get the two battalions together and parade them outside Nadrau. Meanwhile, hundreds of shells had burst over Martos's sector of the front, and a probably unhelpful reshuffling of units had taken place. The sun had shifted from its early-afternoon to its early-evening position before the commander could ride over to where the guilty battalions were lined up waiting. He swung easily into the saddle and rode off confidently.

The two battalions stood waiting for the general to pass judgment on them, each with its regimental flag unfurled to the right of the front rank. The mounted commander with his powerful frame and his godlike superiority approached to inspire them to a martial miracle. His massive head sat firmly on his solid body. His voice boomed out, a rich, effortlessly powerful bass, somewhat resembling the tolling of a Russian church bell, echoing down the ranks and over the hillside: "Soldiers of the Narva Regiment, Field Marshal Golitsyn's Own! Soldiers of the Koporye Regiment, General Konovnitsyn's Own! Shame on you! You swore allegiance to your colors. Look upon them! Remember the famous battles for which your flagpoles are crowned with eagles—and with the St. George's Cross!"

There could be no harsher rebuke. He could not abuse and curse them—these were noble Russians, and it was to their noble nature that he was appealing.

But the mighty voice floated over their heads and was lost, and the strength which the commander's self-assurance had given him ebbed with its sound. A little while ago he had known just what to say, how to bring about the miracle, how to turn these battalions, the regiments to which they belonged, and each of the central corps back the way they had come; then, all at once, his train of thought had snapped, he had lost the right words to say next, and another incident in his life had floated into his confused mind. It was as though it had all happened before. Then, too, fleeing soldiers had been halted with difficulty and lined up before him—only shirts had been even more ragged, rifles and mess tins even fewer, faces still more distorted and powder-blackened. That time . . . What had happened that time?

A commander's words must strike home. Military history is made by such words. At a difficult moment the commander appeals to his troops in person, and they, inspired by his words . . .

"So be once again the brave soldiers you were! Be faithful to your colors and the famous names borne . . ."

It was no good—he had lost the words he needed. He could only ask yet again: how could they have done it, how could they have brought such shame on themselves?

A commander's word is of a special kind, it exhorts his hearers to act in a certain way and no other, it brooks no objection, it invites no debate. Samsonov had asked them how they could have behaved so, but he had not asked how hard a time each officer and man standing there had had.

Yet Staff Captain Grokholets, he of the fierce mustache, a dashing soldier even on this shaming parade, could have explained in his harsh, spluttering voice how they had spent a fairly quiet night standing guard on the other side of Hohenstein, how on Martos's orders they had launched an attack the next morning and prevented the enemy from completing his encircling movement on the flank of the 15th Corps, but had then come under fire from more than a dozen batteries, a bombardment the like of which the commander himself had probably never experienced. They were held in fiery claws on three sides and they had only three batteries of their own and were short of shells; so they had retreated into the town and held it—but by then they were even running out of cartridges, and the promised help from the rest of the 13th Corps was not forthcoming. Then the enemy had exerted pressure from three sides, on an arc running from southwest to due east of Hohenstein. Enemy cavalry had tried to break through to cut off their retreat but they had stood their ground and were saved by a Russian machine gun which opened fire on the advancing Germans from the tower of the town hall. Then the dust cloud they had been expecting rose in the northeast, only it was not Klyuev coming but the enemy. Only then had the battalion taken flight . . .

Or again, Kozeko, blinking away there in the rear rank, would have found complaints aplenty, for the Army Commander's ear only—told him how the whole thing was bound to end in flight from Hohenstein, what a tough time they had had, and how frightening it was to imagine yourself lying weltering in your blood, or torn to pieces, or pierced through the eye by a bayonet; how terrified your dear little wife would be by your disappearance, even if you were only taken prisoner . . . They had seen far too many corpses that day, they had taken no pleasure in seeing the German dead, and today they couldn't keep count of all the Russian casualties. How many had fallen? And for what? What had they gained by it?

Private Vyushkov, peering with one eye from behind another man's head, was thinking: You're put there to preach to us, but we have heads to tell us better.

Naberkin, on his short legs: They're such terrible fast fighters, Your Excellency! We're none of us used to anything this fast!

Kramchatkin, in the front rank, right in front of the general, head thrown back, every sinew taut as a bowstring, devouring the general with beaming, bulging eyes: I've done what I could do, I can't do more than that.

The general could not help noticing this worthy warrior silently exhibiting his loyalty and his readiness to serve, and drew strength from him. "I am relieving the commander of the Koporye Regiment of his duties. A new commander will lead the regiment into battle—Colonel Zhiltsov there! I know him from the Japanese war, he's a gallant soldier. Follow him bravely and be worthy of him."

The big general sat his big horse well. He looked like an equestrian monument. He raised his hand toward Hohenstein. The song leader's voice soared hawklike at the sign into the opening bars of a marching tune. The battalions turned and stumbled back along the road down which they had fled. (The Army Commander had made Zhiltsov give his word that he would not retreat unless ordered.) After this Samsonov also turned around, and set off for HQ.

But there was something he had forgotten to say. He was dissatisfied with his speech. He felt sure that he had made better ones. The most important effort of the day had somehow misfired.

Samsonov slumped limply in his saddle. As he rode to the top of the hill and saw Martos riding out of a copse, lithe as ever though he must be tired too, the decision which he could not take that morning suddenly ripened in the commander's mind. When he had raised his arm ten minutes ago, what order had he given to the battalions? Not to retreat, obviously! But now, shielded from the setting sun in the gray shade of the copse, he looked into Martos's red, weary eyes and suddenly he yielded—without waiting for Martos to tell him that the regiments were drifting away, the command points giving ground, the telephones falling silent, that this or that fine commander had been killed in the past hour or so. He had harangued the runaway battalions—and now he was on their side.

The biggest decision of his life was taken in a single minute and seemed to require no effort of will. But when had everything turned upside down? When had all those movements and maneuvers, which had seemed so purposeful and coherent on the maps these last two weeks, suddenly begun to work against him? It was as though north had become south, east west, as though the whole sky had swiveled around on the tops of those pines. When and how had Samsonov lost the battle? When and how? He hadn't noticed.

Now they were offering for his approval this neat and rational plan for a "sliding shield"—another rotatory movement, reflecting the revolution of the sky.

Seeking some firm support in this dizzy whirl, Samsonov rested his heavy paws trustingly on the shoulders of the man whom he had so undervalued in the first days of the war and who was now his favorite corps commander. "Nikolai Nikolaevich! According to the plan your corps will take its stand at Neidenburg tomorrow. The whole issue will be decided there. Kondratovich should be there somewhere. So should the Kexholm Regiment. After you've given your order to the corps, ride on ahead to assess the situation and choose the best positions for a stubborn defense of the town."

The Army Commander had shown his supreme confidence in Martos: once again, he was the keystone.

Martos, though, did not understand. Was he being relieved of his command? Why must he leave his corps? Why must he go on without it? Just because the Army Commander had the right to send people where he liked? But did the Army Commander know what he was doing?

"And be quick about it, my dear fellow. The issue will be decided there tomorrow. We shall go there as well."

Neidenburg, abandoned that morning as a useless burden, had now come to look like the key to their deliverance.

Samsonov affectionately embraced Martos to speed him on his way. And broke his will. The fierce energy that had bubbled in Martos for days past suddenly dried up. He had been a steel rod, now he was a reed. One word and he had abandoned his corps and was going where he was told.

It was getting dark by now. The orders were sent out. (A captain went to instruct the 1st Corps to advance on Neidenburg immediately. The 6th Corps . . . well, the 6th was to hang on whatever the . . . And the missing 13th? It was no longer subordinate to Martos.) The staff officers were not behindhand. They tried to persuade the Army Commander to go to Janow. Neidenburg, said Samsonov, and nowhere else.

Intolerable that morning, the town now lured him irresistibly, even if he was to die outside its walls.

The staff officers pressed in on him, telling him that their route that morning had not been circuitous enough and they must go a longer way around.

Enemy shrapnel shells were bursting almost over their heads and fiery flashes were now clearly visible in the twilight. In Nadrau too, which they could not avoid, flares had set two houses on fire. Machine guns began chattering—who was firing, and at whom?—in a town seething with the confusion of a disastrous day. In the light of the burning houses men could be seen running to new positions—or running away?

Then the firing ceased. No one tried to put out the leaping flames. Dogs, unseen in the daytime, now started howling.

The Feast of the Assumption was over, and in spite of his incomprehensible dream Samsonov was not dead but alive.

General Samsonov was alive, but his army was dead.

[4 0]

Who can confidently point to the decisive battle in a war that dragged on for three years and left a nation spiritually wrecked? There were innumerable battles, more of them inglorious than glorious, devouring our strength and our faith in ourselves, dismally and uselessly picking off the bravest and strongest among us, carefully leaving behind the feebler. Nonetheless, it can be said that Russia's first defeat in East Prussia was in some sense a continuation of those she had suffered at the hands of Japan, and a warning that the war just beginning would follow the same pattern: we had begun the first battle without waiting to muster our forces in a sensible fashion, and we would never afterward succeed in mustering them. We never lost bad habits, contracted right at the start, of throwing in untrained troops as soon they reached the front, of trying to stop up every hole and every leak, of straining frantically to recover every inch of lost ground, never pausing to think whether there was any point in it, never counting our losses. Our morale was crushed from the first and we never regained our old self-assurance. From the first our enemies and our allies alike sneered at our military prowess and, branded with their scorn, we had to fight on until we collapsed. From the very first the seed of doubt was planted in our minds too: had we the right generals, did they know their job?

We shall permit ourselves no flourish of fantasy. We shall collect the most precise information we can, stick close to the historians and steer clear of the novelists—and even so we shall throw up our hands and admit once and for all that no one would ever dare to invent anything so unrelievedly black, that for the sake of verisimilitude any novelist would distribute light and shade more evenly. But from the very first battle our general's badges of rank began to look like badges of incompetence, and the higher the rank, the more hopeless its holder. Hardly a single one of them deserves a grateful glance except Martos. (We might look for consolation to Tolstoy's belief that armies are not led by generals, ships are not steered by captains, states and parties are not run by presidents and politicians—but the twentieth century has shown us only too often that they are.)

If you had read in a novel that General Klyuev, who led his central corps deeper into Prussia than any of the others, had never seen action before, would you have believed it? There is no reason to suppose that Klyuev was stupid. He had a certain skill, a certain adroitness. In his dispatches he was clever enough to present his divisions' belated and futile dash to Orlau in such a light that, when Army Group HQ reported to the Supreme Commander and to the Emperor, he and not Martos emerged as the victor: he it was who had compelled the enemy to withdraw by threatening to outflank him. In the memoirs he wrote in captivity he went on trimming and embroidering and tricking out his tale, putting the blame on everyone in sight except Klyuev. We have no direct information that Klyuev was a worthless character, and experience of many similar cases leaves us in no doubt that reliable mitigating evidence would show him to be a good family man, a lover of children (especially his own), an agreeable conversationalist, and perhaps even a man of jest on convivial occasions. Alas, no virtues can shield and excuse the man who assumes the leadership of thousands and leads them badly. We can pity the novice soldier trapped in a cruel war, with bullets flying and shells bursting around him for the first time, but the novice general, however dazed and however queasy he feels, we cannot pity, we cannot excuse.

Consider the deeds of General Klyuev. Present with his corps in Allenstein at the extreme tip of Samsonov's army for almost the whole of the 27th, he made no effort to discover by reconnaissance whether there were enemy forces to the right, to the left, or ahead of him, and in what strength, but requested Army HQ to supply all this information from Neidenburg. His own staff failed to decipher Blagoveshchensky's coded telegraph message. Certain that no one except Blagoveshchensky could approach him from the east, Klyuev dispatched a plane in that direction with an uncoded message that he would advance westward in the direction of Hohenstein on the 28th. The pilot unsuspectingly flew low over a German column and was shot down, so that Below already knew Klyuev's intentions on the 27th. However, Klyuev and his men had made themselves so much at home in Allenstein, and the war seemed so far off, that on the night of the 27th–28th he disobeyed a direct order to move up to Martos's assistance. Because he did not want to sacrifice his soldiers? No, because he did not want his night's rest spoiled, or the additional risk of moving in the dark. Nor did he set off when the summer's day dawned, as he had promised Martos he would, but only at 10 a.m. As he left Allenstein he announced the fact in an uncoded wireless telegram, simultaneously informing his own side and the other of his line of march, the staging points, and the timetable for his dash to help Martos. Klyuev had six regiments left, and he was recklessly generous with them. He left behind two thousand (doomed) men, a battalion of the Dorogobuzh Regiment and a battalion of the Mozhaisk Regiment, to defend Allenstein "till Blagoveshchensky comes." Stringing his corps out in a long column southwestward along the highroad to Hohenstein, he quickly left the rest of the Dorogobuzh Regiment to face death guarding his rear when he discovered that for some reason he was being pursued. (The reason was his own wireless telegram, intercepted by the Germans at 8 a.m. The Germans launched a pursuing force in a great hurry; still unused to the idea that the Russians were always late, they did not realize that if Klyuev threatened to be somewhere at midday he would not totter in before evening.) When Klyuev came in sight of Hohenstein from the Griesslinnen heights—this, remember, was the railway junction and the town which he was supposed to hold so as to help Martos, and in which his own Narva and Koporye regiments were now kicking their heels—he stopped and waited. Was he waiting for the rest of the column to close up? Couldn't he make up his mind who exactly was in Hohenstein four versts away? (Hohenstein stands in a hollow and the Narva and Koporye regiments mistook their own corps up on the hills for a steadily growing German force.) When another (German) formation took up position between himself and Hohenstein, Klyuev did not try to hinder it. Was he waiting for something more definite to happen? Or for fresh orders?

The only decision he took was to send his leading regiment off at a tangent for a whole day of unnecessary fighting in the dense Kämmereiwald. Pervushin, who was in any case unfit to fight, led his Neva Regiment with no artillery support, nothing but a machine-gun company, into one of those forest battles that are unlike all others: you cannot see more than twenty paces ahead or to either side, you cannot make out where the shooting is coming from, and it sounds louder and more ominous than usual—a shrapnel burst is like a hurricane crashing through the treetops; bullets splinter trees as though they were dumdums, and ricochet as though fired afresh; men are wounded by the tree splinters and by falling trunks; men shoot over each other's heads and are killed by their comrades' bullets, so that even brave soldiers are unnerved and the whole force huddles together in confusion. Yet the Neva Regiment harried hour after hour a force which gradually swelled to divisional strength, dispersed the German division's HQ staff, leaving the general with an escort of eight ordinary soldiers, pushed its way through several versts of thick forest, and reached the western edge victorious toward nightfall. But the victory was an empty one; the forest was of no use to the Russians, and the regiment was ordered to withdraw.

In the morning the march of the 13th corps could have been seen as the vector of an offensive. But when it had marked time for half a day on the Griesslinnen heights, without firing a shot or achieving anything, the corps turned by imperceptible degrees into a heap of junk. It needed to be on the move quickly—whether to help Martos (he was nearby and sent an officer to fetch them) or simply to escape southward without an hour's delay while there was still free passage between the lakes. Instead, Klyuev dithered all through the Feast of the Assumption, and was still there when night fell.

While he was dithering the Narva and Koporye regiments abandoned Hohenstein to the Germans and ran for it southward. While he was dithering, the two battalions of the marooned regiment were caught in Allenstein and cut down by cavalry or shot (townspeople also fired on them from their windows, and a machine gun opened up from the LUNATIC ASYLUM. PLEASE DO NOT DISTURB). During the same period, the corps' supply wagons, sensibly dispatched to safety by a route well in the rear that morning, were seized and their convoy massacred. The Neva Regiment was being thrashed in the forest battle so that the corps could continue its pointless hovering. But it was above all his abandoned rear guard, the Dorogobuzh Regiment, ten versts behind him, that made it safe for Klyuev—not to withdraw, not to escape, but to go on dithering.

The Dorogobuzh Regiment found itself fighting rear-guard actions with three depleted battalions shortly after the withdrawal from Allenstein. Corps HQ had given Colonel Kabanov no instructions as to his timetable or his precise area of operations, only told him to continue rear-guard action until he was called off. Colonel Kabanov most probably viewed Lieutenant General Klyuev, his orders and his tactics, rather coldly, but he did not let that affect the way in which he did his duty that day. His only concern was to decide where and how he could hold up the persistently attacking enemy longest.

We, who in our everyday lives are always governed by the dictates of self-preservation, shall not try to explain the mysterious power of their sense of duty over professional soldiers and certain others. Trained in the same hard school, we might be like them ourselves, might show the same unnatural willingness to die, however premature and unnecessary death may seem. How can a human being cease resisting death? In every army there are officers in whom manly fortitude is found in an astonishingly high concentration. But on that Feast of the Assumption a man like Kabanov would have more important things in his mind then self-doubt and its resolution. He would of course have given his own life there and then without hesitation, if by doing so he could hold up the enemy; but it would take all his soldiers—and they would still be too few, because a whole enemy division was pressing hard on them. If any doubt entered Kabanov's heart at all, it could only be this: Ought he to sacrifice the regiment he loved, the regiment entrusted to his care, in order to save the main body of the corps? Or ought he to try to save the regiment itself? The cruel thing was that the commander had to assume for his regiment the role of Fate. It was he who would have to pronounce the sentence of death on it. He had been left without artillery. His ammunition wagons had vanished somewhere along the way. There was such a shortage of ammunition that only one machine gun out of four was usable, and there would soon be none for the rifles either. In the fourteenth year of the twentieth century the Dorogobuzh Regiment was reduced to facing German artillery with the Russian bayonet. The regiment was clearly doomed, and that death sentence on each and every one of his soldiers lay heavy on the commander's conscience—but did not interfere with his powers of clear decision: where to draw his boundary lines, where to locate strong points for close bayonet charges, how to sell Russian lives most dearly, and gain the most time.

Kabanov chose Darethen as one such boundary. The rising ground was helpful, a big lake screened one flank, and a chain of small lakes the other. There the Dorogobuzh Regiment took their stand and held out all through the sunny second half of the day and the radiant evening. There they finally ran out of cartridges, and there the whole regiment counterattacked three times with the bayonet. Colonel Kabanov (aged fifty-three) was killed and fewer than one in twenty survived in any company.

Here was a miracle greater than the fortitude of the officers: soldiers, half of them reservists, peasants who had reported for duty only a month ago in birchbark clogs, their minds still on the sights and sounds of home, their fields, their prospects, their families, totally ignorant of European politics, the war, the East Prussian campaign, the objectives of their corps or even its number, did not flee, or slink into the bushes, or hang back, but, possessed by some unknown force, passed the dividing line beyond which love of self and of family and even the instinct of self-preservation cease to exist, and, belonging now not to themselves but to their cruel duty, rose up three times and advanced into gunfire with their noiseless bayonets. Put them in the Narva Regiment's place in rich and empty Hohenstein and they would, of course, have looted and junketed just the same (just a week earlier they had, in fact, swilled and spilled alcohol in Willenberg). And put the Narva Regiment in their place on that pitiless line (but, *pace* Tolstoy, give them Kabanov and his battalion commanders) and they would have risen to heights at which we begin to see what heroes simple soldiers can be.

We are cut off: others, men just like us, are withdrawing, will escape, will go home, and we who owe them nothing, are not their kin, not their blood brothers, remain here to die so that they can live after us.

What did the doomed men think of, that day, looking at the blue but alien sky, the alien lakes, the alien forests? Whatever it was remained there with them, buried in the Russian communal graves which survived near Darethen into the Second World War.

What did Colonel Kabanov look like? Because few knew of his heroic feat, or because it was difficult to obtain a photograph, none appeared in the press. As for the common soldiers, it was not the practice of newspapers and magazines to show pictures of them, and anyway it would have been an unmanageable task because of their numbers, which were always so inconvenient except when they were called on to fight to the death. The press left out "the gray heroes" completely—and made a mistake. There are no photographs of them, and this is all the more regrettable because since then the composition of our nation has changed, faces have changed and no lens will ever rediscover those honest beards, those good-natured eyes, those relaxed and unselfish expressions.

No one sent word that the regiment's task was completed and that it could withdraw. The Dorogobuzh Regiment perished; very few got out alive. Ten soldiers carried back their dead colonel and the regimental flag. It is well attested that late that night, when the time came for hard-earned sleep, the Germans attacking from Allenstein had made no progress.

There is no knowing how long Klyuev would have stayed there, but near midnight an order from Army HQ arrived to the sound of hoofbeats: "To facilitate the more effective concentration of army units and ease the supply situation the 13th Corps will withdraw in the course of the night to the region of . . . using the following route between the lakes . . ." (The order then mentioned a route which had been overlooked the day before and to which there could now be no return.)

No mention, thank God, of any of yesterday's assignments, or those of preceding days. Postovsky's hand at work there, keeping things tidy, behaving as though it were all a matter of comfortable peacetime routine. "To ease the supply situation" would the 13th Corps find it convenient to make a short jump of twenty versts over seven lakes, arriving overnight at a tiny village of perhaps a dozen houses, where it would find all that it required?

The corps was certainly in need of provisions. The men had eaten nothing since leaving Allenstein the day before.

Escape! The time had come, and Klyuev was quick to see that the order from Army HQ gave them the right to escape.

So, by whatever roads and byroads he could find, almost rubbing shoulders at times with the enemy, Klyuev noiselessly hurried his corps along—a corps no longer, only three regiments out of eight. The rest had been thrown away. The Kashir Regiment, with sixteen guns, Klyuev had left at Hohenstein; yet another rear-guard action, yet another regiment for annihilation. The Neva Regiment now had to abandon the position it had conquered and struggle back by night through the forest it had won by day. As for the sapper company, Corps HQ simply forgot it. When it awoke it would see that it was alone (no one had left word where it should go) and that the enemy was all around. After that it would see little else.

*

* *

Neigh then, my horse,
Make all the noise you can,
Maybe he'll hear you,
My own dear daddy,

Maybe he'll tell her,
Tell my dear mommy;
Tell her to go down,
Where the blue sea shines,
Scoop up some sea sand,
From the sea bottom,
Plant it on gravel
In her green orchard;
And when that sea sand
Puts out shoots in the springtime,
Then that dear son of hers
Will surely come home again.

[4 1]

(28 AUGUST)

General Yuri Danilov, Quartermaster General on the Supreme Commander's staff, nominally the third-highest-ranking officer in the Russian army, but the most important in the conduct of affairs, had been working diligently on a number of momentous problems in the past few days. He was drawing up plans for the immediate conversion of East Prussia into a separate governor-generalship (with the renowned General Kurlov, of whom we shall have more to say, as a possible governor-general), the speedy termination of hostilities in the area, and the projection of Rennenkampf's army, once free, across the Vistula, to move on Berlin. For this purpose Danilov requested the Northwestern Army Group HQ to turn its mind at once to transferring one corps from Rennenkampf to Warsaw.

Oranovsky, Chief of Staff on the northwestern front, could not protest against this too vociferously, because any objection from down below always damages the position and prospects of the protester. So he immediately gave instructions for the corps in question to return to the railhead. (Rennenkampf, misinterpreting the order of the previous night to give Samsonov what help he could, would plunge the corps deep into Prussia and receive a serious reprimand for this insubordination.) Oranovsky did not dare emphasize in reports to his superiors the growing anxiety at Northwestern Army Group HQ. He did report that the 1st Corps was hard pressed at Soldau and in some disorder, and that two German corps (François's and Mackensen's), which had vanished from Rennenkampf's sector, had suddenly turned up in the path of the 2nd Army, but Supreme Headquarters was not at all concerned, and on the night of 28–29 August, Danilov had a lengthy telephone conversation with Oranovsky, insisting that the Guards corps should in accordance with his latest plan be transferred as soon as possible from the Warsaw region to the Austrian front, airily remarking that Samsonov had nearly five corps and would get by.

Zhilinsky and Oranovsky would have taken out the anxieties of that day on Samsonov, but to their annoyance (and also somewhat to their relief—it was all his fault now!) he had cut communications. They stopped fussing. Army Group HQ had cavalry, cars, flying machines, but it made no attempt to find the missing units, or to take over Blagoveshchensky's corps and what had been Artamonov's and rush them to the aid of the main body of the 2nd Army: that would have cost far too much trouble, and some loss of face since it was not part of their official duty anyway.

Meanwhile out on the right flank Blagoveshchensky's corps was living an independent life, as though it had no responsibility to any larger body. Consulting no one and stopping for no one, it rolled back almost to the Russian frontier, where it was in no one's way, never raised a finger against anyone, and had in effect pulled out of the war for the time being.

It was only by good fortune that General Blagoveshchensky had not been relieved of his corps twenty-four hours before Artamonov (he owed his survival to his skill in drafting and his delay in sending dispatches). After the fright he had been given on 26 August, when he had collided with the Germans without prior warning from the High Command, after those moments of fear when he might have been taken prisoner at Bischofsburg or killed at Mensguth, after those nightmarish retreats from one hopeless position to another on 27 August and again at dawn on the 28th, when a tidal wave of panic had seized the corps and swept it away—after all this General Blagoveshchensky's nerves needed time to recover, and anyway, at the age of sixty, he could live very well without exasperating orders from outside and without wasting his strength drafting orders of his own. With no one pursuing him, and cut off from telephone and telegraph, he now, praise God, had time to regain his composure and let the corps do the same. He did not order them to hang on to Ortelsburg, which was a road and rail junction, but had them bypass the burning town, abandon it without a fight, and continue the withdrawal, avoiding the roads, into inaccessible country.

Blagoveshchensky very much hoped that the dragoons he had sent in the night with a dispatch to Samsonov would not return. He didn't want them to be killed, of course, just detained at Army HQ and attached to another unit. He wouldn't really mind if they did return for orders in a day or two, but not today, so that he could have his sleep and recover his strength in a quiet corner. His hopes were vain, alas! The tireless dragoons struggled back over fifty versts of enemy territory to arrive at noon on 28 August bringing a message in the Army Commander's own bold scrawl: "Hold out whatever the cost in the region of Ortelsburg. On the steadfastness of your corps depends . . ."

Blagoveshchensky couldn't quite see it. Ortelsburg was twenty versts away by now! Resentfully he read the message, reread it, reread it again, then summoned his staff and went very thoroughly over the reasons why it was absolutely impossible to carry out this unwelcome order.

After which he decided for the welfare of the corps entrusted to him (and to the relief of many of his subordinates) to amend the Army Commander's instructions: not only would the whole corps stay just where it was that day, but the next day also was declared a rest day. No one except Blagoveshchensky need exert himself: he had to compose a respectable and convincing dispatch explaining why Ortelsburg had been abandoned and why it could not have been otherwise . . . "Approaching Ortelsburg we discovered that the whole town was burning, set afire by the inhabitants. This, of course, was a trap set for us. I realized that it was impossible to stay on the hills nearby and withdrew the corps to the south." He even added that "the men are tired, and I request permission to give them a rest." His next clever idea was not to send the message off at once (by dispatch rider to a Russian town, from which it would be telegraphed) but to wait until the next morning, when the day of rest would have begun.

As for the 1st Corps on the Russian left flank, Masalsky nervously took over for twenty-four hours from Artamonov, who though demoted was still a powerful presence, until Dushkevich caught up with them and assumed command. This corps, with no single will directing it, and demoralized by its retreat, rolled back though none pursued, drawn by inertia beyond the Russian frontier to Mlawa. The frontier, of course, was not a line of fortresses, or even of trenches, but only a symbolic line on the ground, yet it seemed to offer some protection against the Germans. The corps knew that Neidenburg was now in German hands. But not one of the dozen generals hanging around Corps HQ with no firm orders to take decisive action was capable of using his initiative.

So then, on 28 August, everything necessary had been done on the Russian side to ensure the enemy's triumph and his revenge at Tannenberg for his defeat there long ago. Only the two doomed central corps showed any spirit. The Kexholm Regiment, which reached the front line halfway through the day, had lost more than half of its complement by evening. The fighting at Waplitz wrecked the German plan for a "tight" encirclement at Hohenstein. Every encounter in the central sector that day was won by the Russians, or at any rate not won by the Germans. But in the ups and downs of battle the face of war changes rapidly and what crack regiments win is soon frittered away by incompetent corps and armies. With every tactical victory they won in the center, the Russians came one step nearer to losing the day, and were pushed one step closer to destruction.

This, however, was not yet so clearly visible from the German side. Scholtz's sanguinary attacks ended in absurd failure, with nothing working out as expected. More than once, his wheeling squadrons were mistaken by his own infantry for Russian cavalry, fired upon, and scattered. His own artillery opened fire on his infantry. His troops reeled back when Russian infantry raked their flank. After a day's fighting the Germans were little or no farther forward. The setback at Waplitz that morning checked the impetus of almost all German units. One of Scholtz's divisions was mislaid in the morning mist, and it was hours before they found it. Another German division, together with its HQ staff, was badly mauled in the Kämmereiwald by the Nevsky Regiment. Hindenburg and Ludendorff themselves, driving in the vicinity of Mühlen, were caught up in a momentary panic caused by Russian prisoners: some medical units and artillery ammunition wagons sped past shouting, "Russians coming!" The thought that Klyuev might link up with Martos had kept them shaking in their shoes all day. They had ordered General von François not to attempt encirclement, but to go to the rescue in the central sector. While two corps commanders, Below and Mackensen, had been unable all day long to agree on which of them should proceed to Hohenstein and which move south, Mackensen, the senior in rank, had ordered Below to leave the road clear for his corps. Below had ignored the order. A plane was sent off to get HQ to settle the argument, whereupon

Mackensen stopped moving altogether and granted his corps a day's rest. It was almost 4 p.m. when Hindenburg managed to get through to Mackensen by telephone and order him southward, to encircle the enemy. Less than an hour after his telephone call, the idea of encircling the Russians had to be abandoned, and both Mackensen and Below were diverted to deal with Rennenkampf. Information (false as it happened) had been received that Rennenkampf, with three corps and some cavalry, was moving west. The German corps were all in disarray and had their backs to this new danger. ("Rennenkampf only had to come a bit closer and we should have been defeated," Ludendorff writes.)

In actual fact, Zhilinsky's main order to Rennenkampf that day was to blockade and observe Königsberg. However, Zhilinsky and Oranovsky had begun to feel vaguely perturbed on the night of the 27th–28th by their inability to understand what was happening on Samsonov's front, and by the appearance there of one additional German corps after another, and they ordered Rennenkampf by telegram to turn leftward in Samsonov's direction and send his cavalry ahead. Rennenkampf's slumbers were sacrosanct and he was given the telegram only at 6 a.m. He sent out his orders, but the main cavalry force, under the Khan of Nakhichevan, was unable to bestir itself before the evening of the 28th. General Gurko was closer to the field of battle, but even he did not make contact: his deep but belated sally as far as Allenstein only showed how easily Rennenkampf could have changed the whole course of the battle had he intervened earlier.

At Prussian Army HQ, meanwhile, the order for the 29th was being redrafted. Ludendorff makes no mention of this order in his memoirs, though Golovin considers it an excellent piece of work, a model of strategic thinking: a new front against Rennenkampf would be created by minimal redeployment of the two corps commanded by Mackensen and Below while François's corps and Scholtz's corps would pursue and outflank Samsonov and simultaneously lay the dragnet into which Rennenkampf's advance would carry him as into the open mouth of a sack. In this order there was nothing about encircling Samsonov's army.

The High Command in Prussia had said goodbye to its dream of a Cannae when it reported to GHQ that evening: "The battle is won, and pursuit will be renewed tomorrow. The encirclement of Russian units in the north may prove no longer possible."

Hindenburg's and Ludendorff's decision represented the triumph of mediocrity. They showed not the slightest glimmer of intuition!

That intuition shone brightly in the actions of the wayward François, who was probably ignorant of Tolstoy's advice that "it makes no sense to stand in the way of people concentrating their whole energy on flight." François went beyond his orders and pushed his Uhlans, his bicyclists, and his armored cars as fast as he could through Neidenburg, and beyond, eastward toward Willenberg. The refractory Mackensen, equally exasperated by Army HQ's chopping and changing orders, and smarting from the ruling in Below's favor, took off as though he had not received his latest orders, and once out of earshot of his superior officers' second thoughts, hurtled southward, also in the direction of Willenberg!

Nor should we forget that the German supply services operated without interruption, so that, however rapid and unpredictable its movements, no German unit lacked for anything: they were always adequately fed, equipped, and armed.

[4 2]

To go around Moscow saying goodbye even to the most notable parts overtaxes even tireless young legs. At every crossroads there are choices to be made, every street unentered is an itinerary lost. They visited the offices of the Aleksandrov Military School early in the morning and were given an appointment for later in the day, then went to the University for the last time, and their business was all done. Only the farewell tour remained! They would follow no predetermined route. They would go where the heart directed. They weren't even real Muscovites, mere immigrants, but . . . the heart aches, the head spins! . . . Mos-co-ow! . . . How can I leave you! . . . Parting is too painful. The spacious square by the Church of Christ the Saviour was the traditional place for first making the city's acquaintance and for saying farewell to it. Looking along the embankment you saw twenty or thirty conical projections at once—tops of tall buildings, belfries, the Kremlin towers. Their legs carried them unbidden along embankments—a hundred paces wide, so that the views from near the buildings and from the parapet were quite different. Bridges invited them to turn right to the Tretyakov Gallery, but much as they longed to there was no time, even to run a hand over its patterned wall. Instead—through the Kremlin!—there's no walk like it, and they had always been too busy, always hurried past—but today, of all days . . . ! The Kremlin is a city within a city, and so is Kitaigorod. Then there were Varvarka, Ilinka, and Nikolskaya streets with their tight rows of curved and stuccoed façades, and a church at every bend in the road, every one of them crowded for the Feast of the Assumption, and on every street two monasteries, boyars' palaces, or cramped merchant houses.

Perhaps it is a good thing after all that the city was not built to a plan, that everyone raised his walls where he thought best, that no corner is like any other—that is what gives Moscow its special character.

It would be nice to go on to the boulevards, we still have the ponds to see, we ought to pay our respects to the Art Theater, we could fill our bellies in Okhotny Ryad on the way—but have we got time, do you think? We have to go to Znamenka again for our posting orders. How can we fail to visit Pushkin on Strastnaya? Shall we take a tram? No, thank you—that's no way to say goodbye to your student past. Is it all in the past? Shall we never return? Of course we will, we will return! (Some won't come back, but we certainly shall.) Will we finish our studies? Of course we shall, why shouldn't we?

What a marvelous thing it was to be a student in Russia! Everybody seemed to admire you, everyone had a welcome for you, all paths in life were open to you!

But that was all over. This was their last day.

Those dear stones would be there when they were gone. Pavements and roadways became softer to departing feet, as though they trod with less than their full weight. It was not long since Sanya and Kotya had stepped out onto the square in front of a Moscow station for the first time, two shy lads from the south, but in two years they had come to know and love the city. In some respects they had indeed outgrown it, but their feeling of superiority made them love it still more generously that day.

Another thought colored their sightseeing: Moscow did not seem to be very much aware of the war, did not realize that it might decide her fate. If you hadn't heard about the war, if you didn't peer closely at the posters pasted up here and there, if you didn't notice the party of reservists marching to the bathhouse, you would never guess that Russia had already been at war for four weeks: there were as many people and as many carriages as ever on Moscow's streets, faces and garments were no more somber than before, trade was as cheerfully noisy, shop windows as alluring, nothing had changed except that there were more soldiers around, and in some places flags and portraits put up for the Tsar's recent ceremonial visit had not yet been taken down. Kotya and Sanya eagerly shared these observations with each other, but did not put into words the uneasy surmise, the doubt burrowing into their minds. Had they been headstrong and hasty? Why were they in such a hurry to exclude themselves from the teeming and still tearless life of this city? It would have seemed more natural to be setting out for the front from a weeping, a funereal, an angry Moscow—but should they be rushing away from this cheerful and lively scene? As long as this doubt stirred mutely and hesitantly deep inside them it did not yet exist. But if either of them put it into words he would help it to grow, and would give pain to his friend, who was of course too noble for such thoughts. Kotya in particular could not express his doubt because it would sound like a reproach to Sanya for coming to see him in Rostov and suggesting that they should volunteer. It had, after all, been Sanya's idea. Never mind that Kotya had said, "Right, let's go," before the words were out of Sanya's mouth. Till Sanya arrived he honestly hadn't thought of it, but he had realized in a flash that Sanya was right; of course they must join up—let's go, let's go, Mama will be dead set against it, but let's go just the same. (She was so much against it that there were twelve solid hours of nerve-racking, tearful recriminations, and Kotya left his robust and strong-minded mother swooning.) Even that morning in the offices of the Military School it would not have been too late to withdraw (but for his friend's presence) but now it was too late, much too late.

So the two friends exchanged all their thoughts, except one, more lightheartedly than usual, and laughed a great deal.

On their second visit to the office they were given their papers for the

Sergievsky Heavy Artillery School, which was what they wanted, and told at what time in the morning to report, and what they should and should not take with them. By then the evening chimes were ringing out from church to church as they went across Arbat Square toward Nikitsky Boulevard with their feet pleasantly tingling from so much walking. They came to the strait between those two islets, Blank's pet shop, a place of pilgrimage for all small boys, and the Church of SS. Boris and Gleb. A tramcar miraculously threaded its way through the narrow passage though there was scarcely room for two drunks enlaced, and turned on to Vozdvizhenka, insinuating its warning clang into the clamor of the church bells up above and the general hubbub of the Arbat: the clip-clop of cab horses, the clatter of heavier hooves, the rumble of carts over cobbles, the cries of newspaper sellers, the solicitations of hawkers. Here, a cabby yells at a pedestrian: "Get out of the way, can't you!" Over yonder a wheel has caught on the curbstone and the driver whips his horse: "Gee up there!"

The young men had become more aware of the pungent smells borne on the evening air—from a confectioner's, from a cookshop, and from freshly baked bread. They began to think of eating in a tavern before continuing their stroll.

They saw walking in front of them on the Nikitsky Boulevard a long lath of a man with gray hair and a loose bundle of books clutched awkwardly under one arm. They recognized him at once: they were used to seeing his back for hours on end in the Rumyantsev Library. Kotya nudged Sanya and said, "Look, it's the Stargazer!"

Sanya, irritated, caught his arm. Kotya never realized how far his voice carried and had never learned to speak quietly. It would be very embarrassing if the Stargazer heard and looked around. It wasn't as if they really knew him, they had never exchanged names or got into conversation with him. Once, in the reading room, he had glanced reprovingly in their direction when they were whispering loudly, and they had stopped. On another occasion they had come upon him in the corridor. He was carrying a dozen books under his arm, as he was now, and had dropped them. The boys rushed to his aid, one on either side, and picked them up. After that although they remained, strictly speaking, unacquainted they would nod and half smile when they met. They often saw him at his desk in the reading room. The Stargazer stood out even among the awesome intellectuals who used the Rumyantsev Library, whether because of his eyes darkly shining from cavernous hollows, which made his face look profoundly serious at all times, or because his whole figure, head as well, seemed to be pinched in at the sides, or because of his strange behavior when he was sunk in thought, elbows on the desk, forearms raised, fingers plaited to form a wigwam, with the extreme ends of his beard lightly brushing them, staring stubbornly over all those heads at the upper shelves and the galleries. It was at some such moment that Kotya had named him "the Stargazer." They had no idea what he was studying and were too diffident to speak first. Now they both spoke at once. "Shall we say hello to him?" They were taking leave of Moscow and could rise above its restraints. They had nothing to lose. They overtook him, both on the same side of him this time, apologizing by the tone of their voices for their discourtesy in addressing him without knowing his name.

"Good day."

"Good day."

The old man wasn't startled. He turned his withdrawn gaze on the young men. He wasn't looking down at them—only his gauntness made him seem so tall—and he recognized them.

"Ah, my young friends! How nice to see you." He straightened the books under his left arm and held out his free right hand. The wrist emerging from his sleeve was a slender one, but his hand was as broad and heavy as any workman's.

"My name's Varsonofiev."

They told him their names, and stood awkwardly before him in their spotless linen shirts, their narrow belts, and their student caps, until Kotya tapped his cap and loudly announced, "We've finished with all this. Today's our last day. We go into the army tomorrow. We've volunteered."

He wasn't showing off. He was always the same: the happiness within him demanded expression, his broad, high-cheekboned face shone with enthusiasm, his hands marveled restlessly at the richness of life.

Pavel Ivanovich Varsonofiev allowed a slight gap to appear between his close-cropped, stiff graying beard and the curve of his luxuriant graying mustache. He was evidently smiling, although his lips were hardly visible.

"You have, eh?" He looked closely at each in turn. "Hmmm." His voice also seemed to boom out from the depths of a cave. He scrutinized them again. "Aren't you afraid your fellow students may jeer at your patriotism?"

"They will, of course," Sanya said. "But we *are* patriots of some sort."

"What's wrong with being patriotic?" Kotya sputtered indignantly. "We aren't the aggressors after all. *They* attacked Serbia."

Head bent, the old man studied them. "True enough. Still, until a week or two ago the word 'patriot' meant more or less the same as 'Black Hundreder' to people around here. Hence my question."

Kotya asked pressingly, "What do you think? Is what we are doing right?"

This opportunity was too good to waste. He could test his decision yet again without upsetting his friend. The old fellow might come out with something worth thinking about.

Varsonofiev raised one eyebrow. "To decide whether you're right or wrong we should have to start from your beliefs." His dark, brooding eyes twinkled. "I daresay you are socialists?"

Sanya shyly shook his head.

Kotya smacked his lips loudly to express regret.

"Really? You aren't? I expect you have anarchist views, then?"

No, there was no nod of assent from the boys.

But they could see that the old man was not making fun of them. Indeed, a mocking smile was unimaginable on his terribly serious face, and if his lips parted at all the merging of beard and mustache almost completely obscured them. There was, however, a cheerful gleam in his eye.

"If you really want to know, I'm a Hegelian," Kotya told the old man firmly and solemnly. He had a forthright way of speaking, jaw firm and chin jutting.

The old man looked surprised. "A pure Hegelian? That's most unusual!"

"Yes indeed, a pure Hegelian," Kotya proudly and uncompromisingly confirmed. "And he"—poking Sanya's chest—"is a Tolstoyan."

Meanwhile they had started walking again, and all three went on toward the Nikitsky Gate.

"A Tol-stoy-an?" The old man looked sideways in amazement, sizing up the shy and diffident Isaaki. "Great heavens! Why then are you going to war?"

He saw, however, that Sanya was excruciatingly aware of the muddle in his mind. Sanya looked pitifully at Varsonofiev, smoothing the soft, corn-colored hair back from his forehead.

"I'm not a *pure* Tolstoyan anymore."

"I should think not!" Kotya trumpeted. He felt more and more at ease with this splendid old man. "At one time he wouldn't even eat meat. Imagine what it would be like for him in the army. There's no picking and choosing there, everybody gets the same!"

Between friends this was harmless teasing. But in spite of his faint smile Sanya was displeased with himself.

The old man looked kindly from one to the other. "I tell you what, young men, if you're not hurrying off to see your young ladies why don't we go for a beer somewhere? I daresay you're starving too?"

No, they weren't hurrying off to any young ladies. They hardly needed to look at each other—the answer was yes. Getting to know the old man would be an interesting way of spending what was left of their last day in Moscow.

"Right, wait here a minute while I pop into the pharmacist's."

They had reached the rear wall of the Nikitsky Gate pharmacy. Varsonofiev went around the corner. He walked with a slight stoop.

"Hey!" Kotya had a sudden thought. "We should have offered to hold his books for him and taken a look at them. We didn't that time we picked them up off the floor. Listen, don't go on too much about Tolstoy. There's nothing new to be said about him."

Sanya smiled acquiescence. "It was you who started it."

"I'd sooner hear what he thinks about us going into the army. And then we'll try and get him onto some historical theme—you know, his general ideas on East and West, something of that sort."

Tramcars hissed and clanged by. Cabs rolled past, dawdling or hurrying to suit the passenger. People sauntered along the boulevard as though they had never heard of the war. A little girl with long plaits was carrying her practice piece to a music lesson, a slovenly waiter with grease stains on his white coat darted across the road with somebody's supper in covered dishes. A policeman in black and white stood at the crossroads by the semicircular structure with the jolly advertisement for Uncle Kostya cigarettes, surveying the impeccable order which his presence ensured. A variety of other advertisements went by, fixed to the tops of trams. The long succession of shop signs, which had brought them to this place, with the names of tradesmen—as though they were immortal artists themselves—in ornate lettering, stenciled or embossed, plain or convoluted, affirmed the solidity and durability of this city—but at the same time it was quite unreal, because tomorrow the two boys would no longer be there. Only the Union cinema declared its sympathy with them, advertising: *IN DEFENSE OF OUR BROTHER SLAVS, Sensational Pictorial Record of the Tremendous Historical Events Through Which We Are All Living*. Otherwise, the city stood still and was in flux, it changed and remained the same, unaware in its unfeeling immensity what a great and awesome day this their last day was, what an important frontier they were crossing so boldly. They were leaving the city behind, forsaking it, but there was no pain in their breasts, because whatever good they had received from the city, and all they had brought to it, they were taking away with them.

Sanya "felt a sneeze coming on"—that was how they described the way he had of tilting his head backward, half closing his eyes, putting both hands on his friend's shoulders, and musing aloud.

"Listen . . . it's all so . . . all so . . ." He looked around for the word to describe it all, but it eluded him. Anyway, they were thinking the same thing—no two people could have understood each other better. "Let's come back here after the war to this very spot, shall we? What do you say?"

"Of course, of course!" Konstantin said heartily, hugging Sanya and briefly lifting him off his feet. He was as strong as the wrestler Ivan Poddubny.

Their lightheartedness carried them up above the garish, jingling, clattering city. A fierce joy was hurtling them into the future. Perhaps disaster had already struck, perhaps the catastrophe was already being enacted, but—a discovery!—you could pass unharmed through the midst of disaster, conscious of its fearsome beauty.

Varsonofiev came out of the pharmacy and beckoned them toward the Union. No, he wasn't stoop-shouldered, it was just that he held his bare head, with its close-cropped silver-gray hair, forward a little, as though straining to hear or see something.

"There's a very decent beer hall, with very respectable customers, here below the Union."

Not such an otherworldly old man. He obviously knew a thing or two.

Inside they were met first by warm, savory, cheering food smells, mingled with the heavy fumes of beer. There were three communicating dining rooms, one of them looking out on Nikitsky Boulevard, and another, into which they turned, on a walled yard. Kotya dug Sanya in the ribs: a famous professor from the Moscow University Natural Science Faculty was sitting over beer and dried roach with his students around him. There was a sprinkling of officers and what looked like lawyers. And not a woman in sight. A sanctuary for the male at leisure. It was obvious from the bottles left on the tables for the reckoning that people sat there for hours on end, unburdening themselves. Some were reading newspapers and magazines. Kotya picked up *Field* and Sanya *Russian Word* in passing. They chose a table by the window, looking out on a huge stack of beer crates.

"Things are going pretty well so far," Sanya said, scanning his paper. "We're advancing in Austria and in Prussia, winning all along the line."

"Listen to this!" Kotya called out loudly. "Order to the troops from Lord Kitchener, Minister of War: 'Treat women with courtesy, but avoid close relations with them.' Good, eh? They must need something to worry about!"

He gave a deafening guffaw. But it *was* pretty funny. There was noise and laughter all around. The beer hall was no place to come to for quiet. They were very hungry, and the smells had tickled their palates. They were ready for a drink too.

"Well, young men, what is it to be? Hot pot? Rissoles?" the old man asked hospitably. "Do you still object to meat?" he asked Sanya solicitously.

"Hot pot for both of us," Kotya decided.

Steam with a rich, tantalizing aroma rose from a tureen as it was carried past.

Varsonofiev ordered for two.

"What about you, Pavel Ivanovich?"

Varsonofiev held up a long white finger like a candle. "At your age eating is a pleasure, at mine the pleasure is in abstinence."

"How old are you, Pavel Ivanovich?"

"Say fifty-five in round figures."

Judging by his gray hair and sunken cheeks they had expected him to be older. But fifty-five was old enough and they didn't question it. For his part, Pavel Ivanovich enjoyed himself giving their order, pouring out beer, and nibbling salt peas between sips.

"How did you and Count Tolstoy come to part company?" he asked Sanya.

Sanya did not answer immediately. He wanted to get it right. And he was never in a hurry to speak. Kotya unhesitatingly spoke for him.

"It was the cart!"

"The cart?"

Sanya thought a bit and nodded. "Yes . . . some literate peasant wrote to Tolstoy. The Russian state, he said, was like an overturned cart, and it was very hard going, very awkward dragging it along—how long, he wondered, would working people have to go on doing it? Wasn't it time to get it back on its wheels? And Tolstoy answered: Get it back on its wheels and those who turned it over will jump in and make you pull them, and you'll be no better off. What, then, were they to do?"

Sanya looked apologetic: was he talking too much? No, Pavel Ivanovich was listening, and showed no sign of boredom.

"Well, what Tolstoy told them was: Let the wretched cart look after itself! Just ignore it altogether! Unharness yourselves, and go each his own way, in freedom. Then your lives will be easier." He looked at Pavel Ivanovich, on the defensive. "Well, I'm a peasant myself, and I most emphatically cannot take Tolstoy's advice. I wouldn't just abandon even the most broken-down cart on my father's farm. I would be bound to put it back on its wheels, and if necessary haul it out of the ditch without oxen or horses, putting myself in the shafts." He looked again to see whether they were bored. "And if the cart stands for the Russian state, how can we possibly leave it overturned? It's just another way of saying every man for himself. Walking away is always easiest. Righting the cart is a lot harder, righting it and getting it rolling. And keeping the rabble from jumping on it. Tolstoy's solution is simply irresponsible and, in my view, I'm afraid, dishonest."

His manner was apologetic: these were strong words from a nobody like himself. "This refusal to help everybody else haul the cart was what first turned me against Tolstoy. His hasty oversimplification . . ."

"And what else?"

"This, for example: if you read Tolstoy carefully you find that he sees love as merely the result of clear and sound thinking. Thus he claims that Christ's teaching is based on reason, and is therefore of immediate practical advantage to us. Now that's quite wrong. In a worldly sense Christianity is not at all reasonable, in fact it is quite irrational. That is in its nature. And it puts righteousness above all earthly considerations."

There was a gleam of acquiescence from the cavernous hollows. But the old man spoke jestingly: "Ye-e-es . . . so you've strayed from the straight and narrow. That's always the hardest thing in this life—sticking to a doctrine in its purest form, as your friend sticks to his Hegelianism. A mixture is always easier to swallow, anybody can manage it—even a toothless man can manage hot pot."

It arrived as he mentioned it. Kotya, who had no patience at all with Tolstoy, eagerly defended his friend.

"He was never so much of a Tolstoyan as all that. You mustn't be hard on him. Not altogether a Tolstoyan anyway. Back in the village they used to call him a populist."

Varsonofiev puffed out his mustache. "Fine company I've got myself into!"

He ordered four more bottles of beer.

Varsonofiev learned that they had each done three courses in the Faculty of History and Literature. Kotya was more of a historian, Sanya leaned more toward literature. Next he resumed his questioning of Kotya, with respectful interest.

"May I ask which of Hegel's ideas is your favorite? Just tell me the first thing that comes into your head."

Kotya's face with its prominent cheekbones and the wide arc from temple to temple could smile broadly and look thoughtful all at once. He could think of many splendid things—the self-unfolding of the absolute, the preservation of an unproven principle until it reveals its potential . . . But best of all? "The 'dialectical leap,' perhaps!"

There was something very alluring in those "leaps."

Varsonofiev settled down to enjoy himself, fingers interlaced on the table. "But if you are a Hegelian you must take a positive view of the state."

"Well, I . . . I suppose I do," Kotya agreed with some hesitation.

"But the state does not like sharp breaks with the past. Gradualness is what it likes. Sudden breaks, 'leaps,' are fatal to it."

They ate. They drank beer just cold enough and just strong enough. Varsonofiev chewed salted rusks. His teeth were white, strong, and even.

"Pavel Ivanovich," Kotya trumpeted, "am I allowed to ask you what *you* are studying? We were trying to guess just now . . ."

"Well, what can I tell you? I read certain books and write others . . . I read thick ones and write thin ones."

"That's a bit vague."

"When things are too clear they cease to be interesting."

Kotya had this way of blurting out his thoughts with no regard for politeness, and Sanya suffered when he did it. He joined in to cut the interrogation short.

"Do you really mean that?"

"You must know that the more important a particular aspect of life is to us, the more obscure it seems. Only the most banal things are ever completely clear. The best poetry is found in riddles. Have you ever noticed how subtle and intricate the thought behind a riddle can be?"

"I have two ends, I have two rings, I have a nail through the middle," Kotya chanted, exaggerating the stresses as though it were a counting rhyme. He burst out laughing. His loudness made no impact on the general hubbub. Within that circular wall of noise they could hear each other as clearly as if the room was silent.

"Here's a better one. In the evening the little white hare frisked merry and free, but when midnight came she was dished up for me."

He intoned the words of the riddle in a deep singsong, different from his usual voice, and still more unlike the carnivorous and beery voices around them.

"Well, what is it?" Kotya asked eagerly.

In the same unearthly voice he emitted from between beard and mustache: "A bride."

"On a dish?"

"If she was on a bed there'd be no riddle. It's a poetic figure of speech. She's on a dish because she is offered up like a sacrificial victim, helpless, spread-eagled."

Was Sanya blushing slightly? No, he was thinking about it.

They ate and drank.

Varsonofiev puffed out his mustache.

"Words get worn out and often obscure meaning. What does it mean nowadays—being a populist?"

Sanya concentrated, forgetting the things on the table. In spite of his sturdiness and his steppe dweller's tan, conspicuous as ever in the poor light from the small windows of the beer hall, his face was soft and gentle. In the mild blue eyes below the sun-bleached hair you could see that his mind was working all the time, leaving him little wish to talk, and when he did, he was always ready to give way.

"Well . . . a populist is somebody who loves the people. Believes in their spiritual strength. Puts their eternal interests higher than his own petty, short-term advantage. Lives not for himself, but for the people and their happiness."

"Happiness?"

"Why yes, their happiness."

Varsonofiev's eyes bored into him like searchlights from under the protective covering of his sweeping eyebrows.

"For the majority of the people happiness means being well fed, well clad, generally well off, the full satisfaction of all their needs, doesn't it? But if you think of it, it will take a whole century to feed and clothe everybody. A century before you even think of their eternal interests—because poverty, slavery, ignorance, and inefficient government stand in the way. To abolish or reform all these things, all this will take how many—three generations of populists?"

"Well . . . it might, I suppose."

Varsonofiev could stare without blinking, never taking his eyes off the object of his scrutiny.

"And all these populists—for whom nothing will do but to save the whole people all at once—will do nothing to save themselves in the meantime. And they feel compelled, don't they, to dismiss as worthless anyone who does not sacrifice himself for the people—anyone, that is, who practices one of the arts, or inquires into the ultimate meaning of life, or, worse still, turns to religion and the salvation of his own soul."

Sasha listened with agonized attention. He raised one hand, one finger, to say something he might forget later. "Can't a man's soul save itself in the course of struggle for the people?"

"But suppose the sacrifice is futile? And tell me, do the people themselves have obligations? Or only rights? Can they just sit and wait for us to give them happiness, after which they can think of their eternal interests? What if they are not ready for change themselves? In that case neither a full belly, nor education, nor institutional reform will help."

Sanya rubbed his forehead. He did not take his eyes off Varsonofiev. He seemed to be trying to read his mind. "Not ready in what respect? Aren't they on a high enough moral level? If they are not, who is?"

"That's just it . . . Maybe your high moral level existed before the Mongol invasion. But since they started stirring the people up with the devil's mixer—you can date it from Ivan the Terrible, or Peter, or Pugachev, it doesn't matter when it began, it's gone on ever since, right down to our time, with its Black Hundreder tavernkeepers, and be sure not to leave out 1905—what is written on the people's invisible face and in their hidden heart? Take our waiter now—there's a pretty unprepossessing physiognomy for you. Up above us is the Union cinema, a temple for the Antichrist of the arts, with a pianist playing in the dark—what, I wonder, is in his soul? I wonder what sort of bestial face will leer out from the Union one of these days? Why should we be expected to sacrifice ourselves for them all the time?"

"Cinema pianists and beerhouse waiters aren't exactly 'the people,' " Kotya declared.

"Where are they then?" Varsonofiev's close-cropped, silver-gray hair gleamed as the narrow head turned toward Kotya. "How long will you go on saying that only the peasant counts? Millions have drifted away from the land. Where have they got to?"

"What we need is a strict scientific definition of the people."

"Yes, we all like to look scientific, but nobody has ever defined what, precisely, is meant by 'the people.' In any case 'the people' don't just comprise the peasant mass. For one thing, you can't exclude the intelligentsia."

Kotya broke in boisterously. "The intelligentsia also has to be defined!"

"Nobody seems capable of that either. We would never think of the clergy, for instance, as part of the intelligentsia, would we?" He took Kotya's snort as a sign of assent. "And nobody with what are called 'retrograde' views is considered an intellectual, even if he's the greatest philosopher of his time. But all students are automatically intellectuals, even those who fail their exams, or take twice as long to finish the course, or have to rely on cribs . . ."

He evidently felt that he had become too serious, and beard parted from mustache in an indubitable smile. Beer froth clung to his mustache. He gestured to the unprepossessing waiter: "Two more, please."

Seriousness was on the decline around the table, but Sanya was still in its grip. Something in that short discussion had been left unsettled. It had set him thinking, and it had also depressed him.

"If it is not an impertinent question, I should like to ask you young men who and what your parents are. What stratum of society do you belong to?"

Kotya reddened and became quieter. "My father is dead," he said hoarsely, and was heard in silence.

He poured out some beer.

But Sanya knew Kotya's weak spot: he was ashamed that his mother had a stall in the market, and avoided mentioning it whenever he could. He tore himself away from his unfinished thoughts to shield his friend.

"His grandfather was a Don fisherman. And my parents are peasants. I'm the first in the family to go to a university."

Varsonofiev twined and untwined his fingers complacently. "There you are, you see. You are from the soil—and you're students of Moscow University. You're the people—and you're also the intelligentsia. You are populists—and you are going to the front as volunteers."

True enough, it was a tricky choice to have to make. Where did they belong?

Kotya tore at some dried fish as though rending his own breast. "I'm beginning to think that you are no enthusiast for people's power."

Varsonofiev gave him a sideways look.

"However did you guess?"

"So you don't think that the rule of the people is the best form of government?"

"No, I do not," Varsonofiev said quietly but weightily.

"What form of government do you propose then?" Kotya had recovered his almost childish high spirits.

"Propose? I wouldn't presume to do that." The dark eyes gleamed at Kotya, and at Sanya, from the cavernous depths. "Who is so rash as to believe that he can invent ideal institutions? Only those who suppose that nothing valuable existed until the present generation came along, who imagine that whatever matters is only just beginning, that the truth is known only to our idols and to ourselves, and that anyone who doesn't agree with us is a fool or a scoundrel." He seemed to be getting angry, but immediately took himself in hand. "Still, we mustn't blame our Russian youngsters in particular, it's a universal law: arrogance is the main symptom of immaturity. The immature are arrogant, the fully mature become humble."

Sanya couldn't keep up with the conversation. He wanted to hear these new ideas, but was still thinking over what had been said before. They had picked at so many subjects, dropped them, and moved on. He had lost all hope of catching up. Instead he rose to Varsonofiev's last remarks.

"Anyway, can there be such a thing as an ideal social order?"

Varsonofiev looked at him affectionately. Yes, that unwavering stare could express affection. So could his voice. He answered quietly, pausing now and then.

"You speak of ordering and perfecting society. But nothing is more precious to a man than the order in his own soul, not even the welfare of remote generations."

Now they were getting somewhere. That was what Sanya had been trying to pin down: you had to choose! But wasn't that just what Tolstoy said? What then of "the people's happiness"? Deep wrinkles creased his brow.

"That is our whole vocation," Varsonofiev went on, "to perfect the order in our souls."

"What do you mean, vocation?" Kotya interrupted.

Varsonofiev checked him with one finger. "It's an enigma. But you must beware that worshipping the people as you do and sacrificing everything for them, you do not tread your own souls into the dust. What if one of you is destined to hear some great truth about the order of the universe?"

He looked from one to the other, lowered his eyes, took a sip, wiped the froth from his mustache yet again. Had he gone too far? No—the gleam in their eyes showed that the young men were intrigued, asking themselves whether that might be their destiny.

"But what about the social order?" They still wanted to know.

"The social order?" Varsonofiev, clearly much less interested in that, helped himself to salt peas. "The social order? One social system must be better than the rest. In fact one of them may be the height of perfection. The only thing is, my friends, we cannot by our own deliberate efforts devise this best of social systems. Nor, though we are so very scientific, can we construct it by scientific methods. Don't get carried away with the idea that you can invent a model society and then twist your beloved people into the right shape to fit it. History," he said, "is not governed by reason."

More wisdom! Sanya drank it in, folding his arms to help him concentrate.

"What is history governed by then?"

By goodness? By love? If only Pavel Ivanovich would say something like that, thoughts heard from different people in different places could all be tied together. It was nice when things fitted so neatly!

But Varsonofiev's abrupt reply made things no easier for him. "History is irrational, young men. It has its own organic fabric which may be beyond our understanding."

He said it despondently. Until then he had sat erect, but now he bowed his head and slumped against the back of his chair. He looked neither at Sanya nor at Kotya but stared at the table or at the distorted world seen through the muddy green glass of the beer bottles. Without pausing for their reactions he started speaking in a more sonorous voice, leaving no loose ends in his argument. He must have given lectures in his time.

"History grows like a living tree. Reason is to history what an ax is to a tree. It will not make it grow. Or, if you prefer, history is a river, it has its own laws which govern its currents, its twists and turns, its eddies. But wiseacres come along and say that it is a stagnant pond, and that it must be drained off into another and better channel, that it is just a matter of choosing the right place to dig the ditch. But you cannot interrupt a river, a stream. Disrupt its flow by a few centimeters—and there is no living stream. And here we are being asked to make a break of thousands of meters. The bonds between generations, institutions, traditions, customs, are what keep the stream flowing uninterruptedly."

"So, it's no good proposing any change?" Kotya sighed. He was tired.

Sanya laid his hand gently on Varsonofiev's sleeve. "Where should we look for the laws that govern the stream?"

Varsonofiev had no cheer to offer. He sighed in his turn. "Another riddle. They may not be accessible to us at all. They certainly aren't to be found on the surface, for every hothead to snap up." He raised his big finger again, like a candle. "The laws for constructing the best social order must be inherent in the structure of the world as a whole. In the design behind the universe and in man's destiny."

He was silent, frozen in his library posture, elbows on the table, hands raised, clasped to form a wigwam, his neatly trimmed spade beard brushing, brushing his interlaced fingers.

Perhaps he ought not to be saying all this to them. But they were not altogether ordinary students.

Kotya sipped his beer glumly. A vein stood out in his forehead from the strain of thinking. "So there's nothing we can do? Except stand by and watch?"

"The true path is always difficult," Varsonofiev answered, his chin resting on his hands. "And almost invisible."

Kotya came to life. "Are we doing the right thing in joining up?"

"I am bound to say that I think you are," Varsonofiev said emphatically, nodding approval.

Kotya had decided to be stubborn about it although he had his posting orders in his pocket. "Why, though? How can anybody be sure?"

Varsonofiev spread his hands, fingers apart. He would treat them as equals and speak candidly. "I can't prove anything, but I feel it. When the bugle sounds, a man must be a man—if only for his own sake. That's another thing you can't put into words. I don't know why, but Russia's back mustn't be broken. And to prevent it young men must go to war."

Sanya had not heard these last remarks. He was thinking that the path or bridge must be invisible, or visible to very few. Otherwise mankind would have crossed that bridge long ago.

Nonetheless he challenged Varsonofiev. "What about justice?" That was something he hadn't mentioned. "Surely justice is an adequate principle for the construction of a good society."

"Yes indeed!" Varsonofiev turned the two brilliantly lit caverns toward him. "But not the justice we devise for ourselves, to create a comfortable earthly paradise. Another kind of justice, which existed before us, without us, and for its own sake. What we have to do is solve the riddle."

Kotya breathed out heavily. "You're full of riddles, Pavel Ivanovich, and all of them hard ones. I wish you'd ask us something easier."

Pavel Ivanovich's lips curled mischievously.

"Right, here's one for you:

If I stood up high, I'd reach the sky.
If I'd arms and legs, a thief I'd tie.
If I'd mouth and eyes,
I'd tell all without lies.

Kotya, a little tipsy by now, was happy that Varsonofiev approved of their going.

"Come, come, Pavel Ivanovich," he said playfully, tapping his plate with a fish tail. "I've got a feeling we shall never get around to asking you the most important question. When we get to the front we shall regret it."

Varsonofiev softened, smiled, and relaxed. "The most important questions always get circular answers. The most important questions of all no one will ever answer."

* * *

THE ANSWER TO A RIDDLE IS SHORT,
BUT THERE ARE SEVEN VERSTS OF TRUTH IN IT

* * *

[4 3]

Terenti Chernega barely remembered his father. He had been brought up by his heavy-handed stepmother, then a stepfather came along and Terenti left home. He had picked up very little from any of them. Nor was there much to be gained from the two-year village school and the one-year trade school he attended. But a man has no need of learning and books if he faces life with a pair of true eyes and a pair of true ears. When it was worth his while Chernega's nimble mind could keep up with the conversation of educated people, even officers.

Chernega had heard the Brigade Commander, Colonel Khristinich, talking to his battery commander, Lieutenant Colonel Venetsky, about the general state of affairs in the artillery: about the waste of horsepower, and the number of guns out of service because in the Russian army there were eight to a battery, whereas with the Germans it was six or four, and the government lacked funds to convert six eight-gun batteries into eight six-gun batteries. It was cheaper to carry guns around without ever firing them. Then again, battery commanders were bogged down in routine chores, so busy maintaining and cleaning spare equipment that they had no time for firing practice or for reading gunnery manuals, which were all out of date anyway—the latest ones hadn't reached them because of the war.

This further confirmed Chernega's belief that the man who matters in the artillery is the battery sergeant major. Who, if not he, was responsible for all that equipment? During his year in the regular army before the war Chernega had worked his way up from trailman to number one and then to gun commander. He had been recalled on the first day of the war, and joined his unit in Smolensk on the third. There he had caught the Brigade Commander's eye: Colonel Khristinich turned his shaggy gray head as he walked by and told Venetsky that it was "a sin for a stout fellow like that to stay a sergeant—make him a sergeant major."

The colonel had shown how shrewd he was. Chernega himself had known all along that he would be an excellent sergeant major. When he got to know Lieutenant Colonel Venetsky he surmised that Khristinich would not have advised every battery commander on his choice of sergeant major. Venetsky knew all about range-finding, gunsights, distances, but he was too soft a master, he addressed his men apologetically, and gave his orders as though they were requests. There would have been no one in the battery to clench a fist if Chernega had not been made sergeant major. From his very first screaming bellow he took to his new duties as though born to them, and the whole battery immediately acknowledged his authority. The way the war had gone so far, the sergeant major was certainly the most important man in the battery. For two weeks the guns were never unlimbered or emplaced, and whether or not gentlemen officers had the contents of military manuals in their heads was of no moment whatsoever. They, of course, pointed out the roads to be taken—but that was obvious anyway, from the movement of the division as a whole. They also, of course, wrote dispatches. But who led the battery, looked after its food and drink, allocated sleeping places, watched over the horses, kept the shells safe and ready? Chernega, of course: the whole battery acknowledged him as first among them, and the twitching of the horses' ears showed that this man understood them. (Horses responded to Chernega from the very first pat on the neck. He knew them through and through, he had bought and sold so many of them, not for profit, but for the enjoyment of it. Chernega lusted more after horses than after women.)

Terenti could carry an outsize barrel of sauerkraut on his shoulder, bend horseshoes and coins, win prizes for wielding the hammer at fairs, do all the feats in which Russians with leisure and strength to spare liked to vie with each other. He was like a great tub. He was not as tall as he could wish, but nonetheless strong for that. Except in fire or flood, he had probably never been called on to exert himself to the full. He got all he wanted from life using half his strength. He had many skills and wiles too, and a skill is not a yoke, it doesn't hurt your shoulders, so he kept his physical power in reserve. Nor had Chernega as yet shown his full strength in the field. He could get by without it. He gave his orders half dozing and half joking. The war had burst in on him when he least needed it, he was thirty-two, in his prime, and he thought, as everyone always thinks at that age, that everything was his for the taking. His object now was to barge through the war without wearing himself out.

But when the alarm was sounded in the middle of the night, and the anxiety which the men had suffered all that week, not knowing what was happening, seeing no other soul, feeling trapped, was suddenly dispelled by a clear order, or rather authorization—"Off you go, boys, run for it"—it took Chernega two heartbeats to unleash all the strength that lay dormant in him and rush to the lieutenant colonel's side.

"Just tell me what you want me to do, Your Honor."

Lieutenant Colonel Venetsky, sitting in his tent by candlelight, seized Chernega's muscular forearm. "We've got to get across this stream, Chernega." A lock of white hair fell over his forehead, his finger moved more quickly than usual over the map spread out on the camp bed (soon to be abandoned forever) and for once he did not mumble.

"We don't want to come out on the main road or make a big detour, and anyway the Germans are all over the place. There is some sort of bridge over the stream here, it may have been damaged, it may be rotten, and the approaches to it are marshy, but all the same we must get across it! We shall save ten versts and miss the Germans. Then we must get onto this isthmus here, Schlage M."

Chernega looked at the map, but there was not much to be learned from it. Green, black, blue . . . lakes, lakes, and more lakes—no legroom between them. He took it all in quickly with his round eyes, more quickly than he was supposed to, but one thing puzzled him.

"Schlage M—what's that mean?"

(*Schlage* means a big hammer, and there's a Polish saying: *Niech szlag trafi*, meaning "Drop dead," "May you have a stroke.")

"It's obviously the name for a dam—either a mill dam or the dike outside Mörken village. We can bypass Mörken, but we've got to get across the dike. If we do, we shall come out alive, whereas here . . ."

If we stay here, we're finished! Chernega took the lieutenant colonel by the shoulder, taking care not to crush it. "Consider it done, Your Honor! Send the officers ahead to study the route and we'll see to the guns!"

"And the shells . . . understand, Chernega?"

"Of course."

Chernega was already diving out of the tent. "If we have to we'll unscrew our arms and leave them behind, but not the shells."

Fire and flood were about to submerge them and at such moments officers have no hands—the sergeant major's the man. All officers can do is cough apologetically and dither as they have for two hundred years . . . someday they'd be told where to go! If Chernega made up his mind not to take the shells, they could order him to a hundred times and they would still be left behind. What galled him was that there weren't enough shells, and every shell could save five soldiers' lives, if not twenty.

So Chernega roared at his men like a lion, drowning out all other commands, the muttering of the men, the neighing of horses, the clanking and the clatter. The battery knew its sergeant major, yet did not know him until that night when the war came to them. That lion's roar told them that not a hamstring must slacken, that if the horses balked they would carry the cannon on their own backs. (It could only be called a roar, but it was a muted roar: sound carried a long way in the night, and they didn't want the Germans to divine that they were on the move and in what direction.) The night was fine and quiet, but full of confusion and foreboding, with only a few tiny stars showing after the moon went down. No announcement had been made but the rumor sped around, and was accepted unquestioningly, that there was a bridge somewhere, that they had to get there quickly, and that if it had been destroyed they were done for. Chernega ran backward and forward along the column without pausing to draw breath, always where he was wanted, always on the spot to sort out every problem. The men stooped and strained as though they were advancing into driving rain, as though under fire, never stopping for a breather. The field path meandered and crossed other paths. Beacons lit by the advance party of officers waited at forks in the road. As they got closer to the stream Chernega tested the ground with his foot to find where the boggy patches were. It was hard work getting to the bridge. Stumbling, and sinking into the mud, they unharnessed the limbers and tugged and heaved the guns toward the bridge, everybody putting a hand to the load. There was hard work to be done on the bridge too: at the last farm they came to they had dismantled a barn, and they now used the timber to replace missing planks. They watered the horses. Once across the bridge they struggled on over low ground, unharnessing the limbers again so as not to get stuck. Then the ground turned sharply uphill, so the teams were harnessed up, and the crews pushed at the wheels again until they came out at last on firm ground. That is war for you: rudely awakened at midnight, they achieved feats in the dark hours which would have been too much for them in the daytime. It had taken the whole of the short night. At first light the battery noiselessly pulled itself up onto the highway, under cover of a wood to their right, and left the bridge and the dark dirt path to the rest of the regiment. Nobody shot at them, nobody tried to bar their way, the Germans seemed to have had enough shooting in the past few days. The night was as quiet as though there were no war.

The battery was halted in the shelter of the wood at the edge of the road. They were the first to arrive. Their detour must have taken the others a long way around, and some regiments might have gone astray. Visibility was quite good by now, though it was not yet broad daylight. The village of Mörken, which had become so important, was on high ground to the right, one verst away from the road. Along the road to their left, no more than six hundred meters away, the magical Schlage M awaited them, and if the scouts did not draw fire the battery would be over it in fifteen minutes. True, the commander of the first platoon had said that there was another bottleneck five versts farther on. But once they jumped over that one they would be back where they had been a little less than three days ago.

They had struggled along for three days with all their guns, equipment, supply wagons, without ever launching a single shell; they had made a forty-verst detour, and now there they were, sweating and fretting to get back to where they had started.

Chernega perched on a broad tree stump on the fringe of the wood. He let his arms dangle and eased his legs: they were aching. He had stopped feeling hunger or fatigue.

They could hear the rumble of wheels, and people talking from the village. Russian troops were approaching along the highway. The enemy would be on top of them soon—they must hurry to get there first.

The scouts were back: Schlage M was unoccupied! Nobody there! A miniature dam four meters wide but unoccupied? Four meters? Lord help us!

Loud voices (no more need for concealment) rang out, ordering them to be ready: "To horse! Wagon drivers in their seats." And the battery wheeled onto the highway and began the descent to Schlage M.

Then suddenly German guns opened fire on Mörken. A house went up in flame. Machine guns struck up from the German side—but where *was* the German side? There were Russians as well as Germans over there, more Russians than Germans—a whole corps of them was still wandering aimlessly around. Down in the dip fiery flashes were glimpsed on all sides—to the left of the village, to the right of the village, and beyond it. Only one quarter was safe and sure. Right there down the slope Schlage M was unoccupied. They had churned up the bog, torn their nails till they bled, overdriven their horses till they dropped, just to get there. If they occupied the road quickly and went down to the causeway they could still get there before the wagons fleeing from Mörken and the bombardment rushed through at a gallop—they could hear the rumble of wheels already. And there came the infantry, running along the verges.

These were the crucial moments in which every man, every body of men, ceases to think, in which no voice can be heard, the commander cannot be seen, and you must make all the decisions for yourself, yet make none because there is no time to think, and everything is decided before you know it.

The guns had drawn up behind them. They couldn't wish for a better position. Should they go down the slope? They wouldn't be able to shoot from there. Chernega jumped up and with a sweep of his arm as though he were flinging a thousand rubles to the wind showed the first gun, then the second, where to turn.

They need not have obeyed. Why take orders from the sergeant major? Where's the commanding officer? Down below, the causeway, their way home to Russia, awaited. After a night of stumbling and sweating and heaving they had every right to be first home!

But Chernega's reckless generosity was catching. The drivers followed their drill and swung the guns into position, and Kolomyka, with the homely features and the high cheekbones, was soon unlimbering his. The staff captain ran up waving his arms frantically. What was he trying to say? Don't do that? Cut it out? No! He was saying, "Carry on! That's the idea! Good going!"

Tall, thin Lieutenant Colonel Venetsky emerged from the forest, steadying his sword and pouch with his hand as he ran onto the high ground overlooking the village. Signalers running behind him reeled out telephone wire.

It was broad daylight by now, though the rising sun was hidden by the wood behind them. The rumble of gunfire was spreading along the bare hillsides and beyond the hills in all directions. The 13th Corps had not made good its escape as it had intended during the night, and now it was caught.

The four guns of Chernega's battery swung into line on the near side of the road. Their limbers drove back to a spot in the forest, from which ammunition could be brought up—you couldn't imagine a better position. The first fear-crazed carts charged by, tangling as they tried to overtake each other. If it was like that on the road what would it be like on the causeway? Guns five, six, and seven blocked their flight to cross the road and take up position on the other side.

Then infantry came running. Wherever did they find such sprinters?

"What's your unit?" Chernega roared at them over his gun shield. "Who do you belong to? What are you supposed to be doing?"

"Zvenigorod Regiment," they answered.

Chernega looked like a maddened bull. "Rotten bastards! Stampeding to save your lousy Zvenigorod hides while we keep the enemy off! Turn back, I tell you, and give us some cover!"

The gunners around Chernega ran down the hill and by shoving and punching, more than by shouting, tried to stop the runaways. With much jostling and wrestling the milling crowd was turned. The first wave began to roll back, but might easily turn again. A little late—as so often in the Russian army—one of their officers appeared, and instead of urging them on toward the causeway led them off the road and showed them where to station themselves.

The sun had still not risen from behind the forest, but the sky was reddening. The men of the Zvenigorod Regiment were digging themselves in on the slope ahead, while the gunners erected ramparts around their positions and stacked the shells in a bunker dug into a hillock. Schlage M had acquired the defenses not provided for by the commander of the corps, which was now following its nose in rapid flight.

The battery did not join in the firing immediately: within a radius of a few versts the two sides were blazing away wildly, sweeping the periphery from the center, stabbing at the center from the circumference. The Russians began falling back, running toward the path along which Chernega's battery had dragged itself. Then, from the edge of the wood, just where the battery had emerged, two battalions of the Neva Regiment came marching in, led by the tall, fierce-looking Colonel Pervushin, whom the gunners and the whole division knew well. They gathered in a gully by the roadside to get their breath and bandage wounds. They told how as they came out of a distant wood that night two of their battalions had wandered off in the direction of the town and had not been seen since. They themselves had been caught in cross fire between Germans and Russians, and barely escaped. It was the Zvenigorod Regiment that had fired on them.

The Russian and the German lines were more clearly defined by now. The Germans were bearing down from the right—on their present position, on the village, and on the town of Hohenstein. As soon as the sunlight began pouring down from over the pines, tiled roofs and chimneys became visible from the depression in which they stood—Hohenstein, the town to which they had been marching throughout the previous day, never to reach it. There were obviously Russian troops in the town, but they were in a sack and the drawstring was tightening.

Venetsky had begun giving orders: "Number one gun! Elevation . . . range . . . shrapnel . . . fuse . . . fire!" Number one gun belched, and the whole battery echoed it.

Shrapnel mows beautifully. A battalion in line of march can cease to exist in three minutes.

The Germans opened up in reply, and their rounds were closer every time, but with the sun in their eyes they could not find the Russian battery.

The Sofia Regiment was through.

Batteries went by with all their vehicles.

The Mozhaisk Regiment marched past.

Chernega's battery counted not the minutes, not the shells, not their own wounded, but the columns marching past. How many would dive past to safety? How many would be cut off? A gunlayer was knocked out and Chernega took his place.

The village was burning in several places, smoke billowed up, and Russian troops poured out of it, riding, walking, running—there was no end of them: two battalions of the Zvenigorod Regiment, the remnants of units fragmented and remixed, a handful of the Dorogobuzh Regiment from somewhere, then their own lord and master, Colonel Khristinich, with the laggard half-battery.

He had recognized them. He flapped his arms: "Well done, boys, great stuff!" They waved and shouted in reply. He dismounted and embraced the staff captain. They both dived into the ditch—not the best time for leisurely embraces! The Germans had begun landing shells accurately on the road itself, and those who were not flattened hastily left it. The road emptied. Retreat was cut off. No more would get through.

This was all that Pervushin had been waiting for. He took the men of the Neva Regiment with him down the slope toward the open causeway.

The men of the Zvenigorod Regiment broke cover and ran for it.

It was Khristinich's turn to give the order. "One at a time, limber up!" As soon as the horses were harnessed to the gun they were driven off at a canter toward the causeway.

What of Venetsky? Would he be left behind? A pity, that would be. He was a considerate master. But no, they came running like hares, Venetsky and the signalers. The Germans could reel in the wires for their own use if they liked.

Two of the guns were belching their last.
We've done what we could, brothers! Remember us kindly!
For those left in Hohenstein the end had come.

Document No. 5

29 August

From the Headquarters of the Supreme Commander.

On 25, 26, and 27 August stubborn fighting continued on the East Prussian front in the Soldau-Allenstein-Bischofsburg area, where the enemy had concentrated all the corps retreating from Gumbinnen together with fresh forces. Allenstein is held by Russian troops. The Germans suffered particularly heavy losses near Mühlen, where they are now in full flight . . .

Our vigorous offensive continues.

[4 4]

We are told that Abgar, Prince of Edessa, who was covered with the sores of leprosy, heard of a prophet in Judea, believed him to be the Messiah, and sent a message inviting him to his principality, where he would be made welcome. Or, if that was impossible, he could get an artist to make a likeness and send that instead. So while Christ was teaching the people, the artist tried as best he could to record his features. But they changed so often and so wondrously that his labor was in vain, and his hand failed him: to portray Christ was beyond the power of mortal man. Then Christ, seeing the artist's despair, washed his face and pressed it to a towel, and the water turned into paint. Thus was made the Miraculous Image of Christ, and Abgar was cured of leprosy by that towel. Afterward, it hung on the gate of the city, protecting it from raiders, and the ancient Russian princes adopted the divinely made icon of the Saviour as the standard of their warrior bands.

Samsonov had heard this story from the dean of the Cathedral of the Don Army at Novocherkassk. Beginning with the little village church of his childhood in Yekaterinoslav province, Samsonov had stood through hundreds of vigils, liturgies, thanksgiving services, requiems: all those hours added up to months and months of prayer, meditation, and spiritual exaltation. In many churches he had been vouchsafed a vision of the Comforter descending in dove-gray clouds of incense. In many churches a tilt of the head had shown him things to marvel at. But nowhere had

Samsonov ever felt so much at home, and spiritually so much at ease, as in the huge, steep-shouldered cathedral at Novocherkassk, which was as much a part of the Don Army as of the town. Novocherkassk and Samsonov were built to much the same pattern. It was a steep, precipitous, rock-solid town, sprawling over the hillside, with three great thoroughfares scarcely less wide than those of St. Petersburg, a market hall to rival that of St. Petersburg, and a cathedral square on which ten regiments could parade with room to spare. Samsonov's two years in Novocherkassk had been among the happiest in his life and they were what he now remembered sadly and affectionately during his sleepless night. He remembered particularly the August services in the cathedral.

At midnight this year, between the Feast of the Assumption and the Feast of the Miraculous Image, Samsonov was in the saddle retreating. The last minutes of the Feast of the Assumption trickled away, vanished, sank into oblivion, and the Mother of God had still not reached out her compassionate hand to the Russian army. It began to seem unlikely that Christ Himself would do so.

It was as though Christ and His Mother had disowned Russia.

At the darkest time of night, around 2 a.m., traveling by roundabout and little-trodden ways, the Army HQ party struggled through to a hamlet of six houses near Orlau—a name which the first battle had made glorious but which now had a mocking ring. And there as they stumbled and blundered and fumbled, finding their way by ear rather than by eye, they learned from a squadron of the same 6th Don Regiment, and from a supply train of the Kaluga Regiment, that there was now no cover to the west as envisaged by the "sliding shield" plan; that the Kaluga and Libau regiments (having performed feats beyond human strength) had the night before withdrawn from the lines which they had been told to hold for another whole day, and that the front line was just out there in the dark, very near to them, perhaps only three versts away. In Orlau the streets were blocked: two wagon trains had tangled and their drivers were fighting for the right-of-way.

Two army corps were still up there to the north, in an overturned pitcher the neck of which was narrowing. Neidenburg, too, they loudly agreed—and it was difficult to read anything different into the map—was in German hands already.

This made the staff officers all the more stridently impatient to move on. It showed how right they had been when they warned Samsonov not to go to Neidenburg, but to head straight for Janow. The commander, alas, no longer understood or even heard them. He seemed to have forgotten his position and his duties. Instead of thinking about the army as a whole he had started supervising battalion commanders.

Samsonov, in fact, felt more confident and more independent of his advisers with every hour that went by. The army staff had ceased to exist for him—they were a bunch of superfluous noncombatants hanging around for no known reason. By the light of a paraffin lamp in a room cleared of sleeping men Samsonov sat at a table, his big head bare, his brow furrowed, giving instructions with the help of a map to officers he had sent for. He told them how to get the Kaluga and Libau regiments back to their former positions, what artillery support they would have, which roads were to be checked and cleared for the approaching wagons of the 15th Corps. He explained things in detail, listened patiently to objections, keeping his temper and speaking cordially—"My dear fellow," "Would you be so good as to . . ."

By now dawn was whitening the sky, morning was ripening, dimming the lamplight. Samsonov, in no hurry at all, sat on over his map (he was still banking on the 6th Corps' moving up), slowly smoothing his coarse-combed beard with gentle curving strokes to right and left, and feeling his close-cropped side-whiskers. His big, wide-open eyes seemed to have no need of sleep.

Surely he would now, at long last, evacuate his staff? Alas, he had lost all sense of his responsibilities, and the staff officers, shrugging their shoulders and hunched with cold, had to clamber onto their horses and ride for no obvious reason along the front line as far as Orlau.

The rough forest road, a dotted line on the map, had been driven over and flattened by a succession of carts, two-wheelers and wagons, carrying away the ammunition shells needed right there on the spot. If a single two-horse cart pulled up everybody had to stop. There was no way around and it was easy to imagine the agonized frustration of two whole corps trapped on roads like this. The party of staff officers and Cossacks rode around the carts in single file, bending back branches.

The forest narrowed until it was the thin end of a wedge. Till then the sun had brightened only the tops of the pines, but now the road led them from the half-darkness into a clearing flooded with red light from a sun which had just sailed up over the twenty-verst expanse of the dense, dark Grünfliess Forest, somberly awaiting the retreating Russian army. The four hundred or so meters between them and this other forest was a steep drop to low-lying water meadows, and the depression was full of writhing fog, thinning to steam as it rose.

Samsonov shuddered, looking at the mist and at the red sun as though he were seeing such things for the first time.

This floating splendor shed light on many things—more than he had understood in the past day and night, which had not been poor in thoughts.

The cavalcade descended through the steaming mist to a damaged mill dam and went uphill again toward Orlau. This was the field of the recent battle, with its furious charges and heavy losses and the tussle for the Chernigov Regiment's flag. If they rode around looking they would surely find the graves of many brothers awaiting their visit. The foul stench wafted to them from time to time meant that not all the dead had been buried. But nobody except the Army Commander spared a thought for the battlefield—their minds were on the crossroads, where the wagon jam had still not been unscrambled and more and more vehicles were barging in from the west.

That was where they spent the morning. All communications were cut, and five infantry divisions, five artillery brigades, cavalry, and sappers were scattered far and wide in a strange country and in unexpected and extremely difficult situations. But news still came through—all of it bad—borne by whoever chanced to pass, more swiftly and surely than any chief signals officer could have contrived.

They were told that Colonel Kabanov had been killed and the Dorogobuzh Regiment put out of action. They were told that the Koporye Regiment after its return to Hohenstein yesterday had stood its ground for less than an hour and then fled again, and that Zhiltsov, the newly promoted regimental commander, had planted the regimental flag in the ground, knelt before it, and shot himself. They were told something still worse: Cossacks from Martos's escort had reliably reported that the general had been killed.

These three items of news were relayed to Samsonov. Three times he doffed his cap and crossed himself. (Zhiltsov—I put him there yesterday. Martos—he died where I sent him.) But even this could not disturb his new look of quiet sadness and late-won understanding.

Samsonov seemed to be listening to something. Not to the din around him. Not to the noise of guns in the distance. To something beyond.

He had abandoned and perhaps even forgotten his guiding thought—of going to defend Neidenburg. Instead, he left his staff in Orlau and rode up front with a small escort, to the Kaluga Regiment. As he approached he found a battalion commander in a hollow, wielding his stick and trying to drive soldiers who had left their posts out of the bushes—whereupon he gave up his original aim of reinforcing the position and took this lieutenant colonel aside for a talk.

Meanwhile, Army HQ staff hung around in Orlau, ashen with anger. They had nothing to do, but dared not leave without the Army Commander. But then certain more cheerful things happened. General Pestich, Chief of Staff, 13th Corps, arrived to report and ask for instructions. The corps, it seemed, was still in being and on its way, but did not know the situation and had no orders. Regiments belonging to the 15th Corps also started appearing outside Orlau. They reported the glorious rearguard action of the Kremenchug and Aleksopol regiments at Kunchenguth: they had managed to measure off the right intervals in the twilight, find safe places for their machine gunners and riflemen, and ambush a German column consisting of three kinds of troops. The Germans, pursuing in strength, were caught in a hail of bullets in the dark and thrown back. The regiments were still in good spirits, and all the senior officers believed that at any moment, and certainly that day, help would arrive from the two flanking corps, the 6th and the 1st.

The staff officers took heart: just reinstall the sliding shield and all would yet be well! They sat down to draft a modified plan. The 13th Corps would withdraw by forced marches (it was hardly dawdling as things were) . . . in such and such a direction . . . with the object of . . . the 15th Corps and the remnants of the 23rd Corps were to hold the line at . . . The difficulty with all this was that there were not enough corps and divisional commanders. If only they could scrape enough together and deploy them correctly HQ staff would be free to retire to Russian territory! They thought of a way to do it: appoint a single officer to command all the units threatened with disaster. Yesterday Martos would have been the man, but Martos had been killed. Kondratovich would have been ideal, but nobody had seen him lately. So naturally they decided to give command of the general withdrawal to Klyuev, although he was in the rear of all the others; Pestich in person would take the order to him. One question remained: Would Samsonov sign an order to this effect?

At this point firm information arrived that the whole Kashir Regiment had fallen at the village of Mörken that morning, and that its colonel, Kakhovskoy, had been killed in the final attack, defending the colors.

Meanwhile Orlau, or rather a field outside Orlau, was inundated with units, intact or mixed, awaiting orders. Supply trains and ammunition wagons were leaving all the time, carrying the wounded away, but the congestion was not reduced. The site was exposed, and though it was not yet noon the sun was baking hot. There was not enough water to go around, and there was no food to be had at all. The smell from corpses left by the fighting six days ago lingered in the air. The ever denser crowd was more like a confused and defenseless gypsy camp than an army.

After five days of uproar the fighting had slackened. It was as though the Germans, soft and forgiving, no longer cared whether they caught up with the Russians and drove them out.

A plane flew over the gypsy camp, and no one managed to take a shot at it.

It was nearly noon when Samsonov returned from the forward positions, but instead of following the bend in the road toward the house in which he had left the staff, he rode straight on over the stubble, up the hillside, right up to the gypsy camp, and into the thick of it.

It was an extraordinary thing, this melee of units drawn up higgledy-piggledy with no one to tell them what to do or where to go. Extraordinary too was the general's approach, with no one shouting orders to fall in and dress by the right, while two hundred voices yelled in response. More extraordinary still was the general himself, his heavy body slumped wearily in the saddle, his cap held in his dangling hand, his head bared to the burning sun, the look on his face one not of authority, but of sadness and compassion. He wore a greatcoat with the dark blue facings of the ataman's Life Guards and the ribbon of the St. George's Cross in his buttonhole, but, contrary to regulations, it was unbuttoned. It was like a church fete, but a strange one, with no bells ringing and no women in gay headscarves. A crowd of sullen peasants from neighboring villages had gathered on this hillside, and their landlord, or a priest on horseback, was riding slowly around the gathering promising them land, or more likely bliss in Paradise, for their sufferings in this world.

The Army Commander did not scold the soldiers for leaving the front line, he did not try to make them go anywhere, he made no demands on them. He addressed the nearest of them quietly and kindly: "What unit do you belong to, boys?" (They answered.) "Were your losses heavy?" (They answered.) He crossed himself in memory of the fallen. "Thank you for doing your duty! Thank you for doing your duty!" He nodded to this side and that. The men did not know what to say—their response to the general was a sigh or a muted groan vaguely resembling the usual "Very good, sir!" At which the commander rode on . . . and was heard again, more faintly this time, asking, "What's your unit, boys?" . . . "Were your losses very heavy?" . . . and saying, "You did your duty—thank you!"

At the very moment when the general began his valedictory ride around the gypsy camp two men on horseback—a colonel and a ranker whose long legs dangled without stirrups—approached by another field path, at an angle to the first. At some other time the colonel meant to present this soldier to the commander and recommend him for the St. George's Cross. But for the present he left him on the fringe of the crowd and forced a path through to Samsonov, but when he began to speak the general, whose mind was far away, did not even notice him. The colonel accompanied him at a short distance.

The commander's voice was kindly, and equally friendly were the looks that followed him as he rode on after thanking the men and wishing them well. There was not a hostile glare to be seen. The bared head and the solemn grief, the unmistakable Russianness, the unalloyed Russianness of his face, with its bushy black beard and its homely features—big ears, big nose—the heroic shoulders bowed by an invisible burden, the slow, majestic progress, like that of some old Muscovite Tsar, disarmed those who might have cursed him.

Only now did Vorotyntsev notice (how could he have failed to see it at their first meeting? It could not be a momentary expression) the doomed look imprinted on Samsonov's face from birth: this was a seven-pud sacrificial lamb led to the slaughter. He kept raising his eyes to something slightly, just slightly above his head as though he were expecting a great club to descend on his meekly upturned bulging brow. All his life, perhaps, he had been expecting this, without knowing it. Now he was resigned to it.

In the days since they had seen each other Vorotyntsev had done his best to think well of the general. Confronted with so many reasons for blaming him, Vorotyntsev had sought excuses and anxiously hoped that he would act in time and decisively. That first evening he had felt that he himself might exert a powerful corrective influence at the crucial moment. He had indeed been half inclined to stay on at Army HQ, where he was nobody, nothing, an unwelcome prying intruder, an all-around nuisance. In the last few days he had felt an urge to go back and see Samsonov, warn him, help him to avoid the false step which, he now realized, he had expected from the first.

The catastrophe which had befallen the 2nd Army, indeed the Russian army as a whole, could have been prevented at some time in the last four and a half days, if only they had . . . (here he glanced at Samsonov's solemnly forgiving face) . . . and if only they had not (that pre-Petrine, pre-Muscovite valediction) . . . and if only they had altogether avoided . . .

What *could* he tell Samsonov now that he had found him? That although they had been retreating since yesterday there was still resistance in places, the remnants of the Estland Regiment were holding on, for instance, on exposed ground, with a single machine gun and a few last rounds—and to what purpose? Why had the commander not gone over to the 1st Corps? And why, in a protected spot like this, had the troops become a gypsy rabble? Why were they trickling away in ineffectual little groups? They might at least stay where they were for twelve hours or so, form a wedge with some striking power, and then try to break out. But these things, undoubtedly so important for Samsonov to know, were somehow not important to him at all.

"Your Excellency!"

Samsonov turned to look at the sunburned, dust-stained colonel with the bandaged shoulder and the bruised jaw, and nodded benevolently, but with no clear recollection of who he was. Vorotyntsev too had been forgiven, and thanked for doing his duty.

"Your Excellency! Did you receive my note from Neidenburg yesterday?"

A shadow of guilt flitted across Samsonov's brow. Perhaps half recognizing him, perhaps unthinkingly, he answered, "No, I did not."

What was there left to do? Now whom could he tell what it had been like at Usdau? And at Neidenburg only yesterday evening?

It was too late, and no use. Samsonov was soaring at such a height that he had no more use for such things, he was no longer surrounded by terrestrial enemies, no longer threatened, he had outsoared all dangers. No, it was not guilt but a sense of unappreciated greatness that had shadowed the commander's brow: perhaps seen from the outside he had done things that contradicted ordinary earthly ideas on strategy and tactics, but from his new point of view every action of his had been profoundly correct.

"I'm Colonel Vorotyntsev! From GHQ."

The commander, not so much riding as floating above the gypsy tribe, the whole battlefield, felt no need to recall past encounters and the affairs of this world.

Why was he saying goodbye? Where was he going? Yesterday morning he had ridden out to visit the central corps—in whose care was he leaving them today? Why was he not organizing a breakthrough group? Was his own revolver loaded?

It was no use. His age and his long years of service as a cavalry general would have made him impervious to good advice from a colonel, even if he had not been in the clouds. Rising so high had left him defenseless.

Their horses' heads were side by side. Suddenly Samsonov smiled unaffectedly at Vorotyntsev and said simply, "All that's left for me now is an existence like Kuropatkin's."

Had he recognized Vorotyntsev after all?

He signed the order of the day as it was presented, without question.

All at once he looked limp and hollow. When the Army HQ staff rode out of Orlau in the early afternoon General Samsonov was still able to sit his horse. But somewhere along the way they got hold of a cart, and Samsonov and Postovsky sat in it side by side, shoulder to shoulder, swaying together as they went along.

[4 5]

Only that morning Sasha Lenartovich had experienced that wildly joyous, bestially joyous sensation of victory. Victory over whom? Victory for what? It would have been a long time before he forgave himself that animal feeling, if it had not evaporated in an hour or so.

What had victory—the captured guns, the column of prisoners fifteen hundred strong, which they now had to drag along after them—done for the regiment? Nothing. It could do nothing. It had only prolonged the suffering, multiplied the casualties. The fighting had not ceased as a result of their victory, and the past day had been harder rather than easier. The German artillery had bombarded them furiously all day long. The Germans were not wasting men on counterattacks, just blazing away relentlessly with their big guns. Their calibers were so much larger, and they were so much better off for shells. The morning's victors had spent the rest of the day as sitting targets, more than once expecting certain death, digging themselves in deeper, throwing out the earth with shells falling around them, pulling back, while the wounded crawled, walked, or were carried away.

The bombardment was never a light one, but at times it became a hurricane. Emptied of all feeling, mentally exhausted, limp and dazed, Sasha despaired at times of reaching the evening. He sat hunched up in a shallow foxhole, despising himself for being cannon fodder, despising the cannon fodder in his own person. What could you expect of uneducated and illiterate men if he, a man in the habit of using his mind, could think of no way of resisting, and just sat in that little hole with his head wedged between his knees for safety, waiting all day long for one thing only, to see whether he would be pulped, waiting passively, will-less and lifeless? He tried to concentrate his thoughts on something intelligent and interesting, but nothing came into his head: it was an empty box of bone, hanging down from his neck, waiting to see whether or not it would be hit.

Where you had universal conscription war could never be different, it would always be as senseless as this one. Men were driven forcibly against other men unknown to them, but just as miserable as themselves, men whom they were not even required to hate. Such a war had no justification. Quite different was war waged voluntarily against your real enemy, the age-old class enemy: you did not fear death at the hands of an enemy you knew, an enemy you had chosen for yourself, an enemy you really wanted to destroy.

Spend a tenth of those lives, a tenth of that endurance, and half as many shells on revolution—and what a happy life you could build afterward.

One such day under fire made an old man of you. This was the last such day he would live through—he must make a change. Sasha knew for sure he had to make a change. That very night, as soon as the shelling died down.

But how could he change things? It was not in Sasha's power to stop the whole war for his own sake. What then could he do to help himself? The most sensible thing would have been to emigrate but he had let that blessed opportunity slip when many of his friends had taken it. Out there, in Switzerland and France, party politics, the exchange of ideas, the serious business of life, went on unhindered in spite of the war. But from where he was, in a foxhole in East Prussia, there was only one way to emigrate: by crossing the lines. In other words, by letting himself be taken prisoner.

Why not? It was quite possible and it would be sensible to give himself up. All that really mattered—his life, his knowledge, his social skills—

would be preserved. It could be done, but it was difficult. You couldn't just walk over there while the shells were falling. And if you went at night you might get lost, be trapped, get killed. Surrender was easy when by some happy chance the armies were thoroughly mixed up. But what if you did surrender? How could you be sure that the Germans would believe you and recognize you as a socialist? Would an ordinary officer in the Kaiser's army know one Russian from another? And did they want socialists anyway? They shoved their own socialists into the army. They wouldn't let him go on to Switzerland, they'd send him to a prisoner-of-war camp. Still, he would save his life. But how could he cross over? . . .

All this logical thinking was not easy for a head that felt as though it were about to burst. Would the day never end? The bombardment—would it never end? How had the Germans come by all those guns, all those shells? How had the brainless Russian idiots dared to start a war on such unequal terms?

Mercifully, the sun was going down behind the backs of the Germans, and 28 August, impossible as it had seemed, was over. The bombardment was over. Not altogether, though. It was some time before the chatter of machine guns ceased tearing the darkness. Still, night had come. And Sasha was still alive.

The night air gradually freshened. The field kitchens came in and fed them. There were platoon chores to be done—roll call, listing the property of men killed. Sasha left all this to the sergeant. The men gradually straightened their backs and got their legs working. Voices became louder. They went over all that had happened since last night, who had been wounded, who killed, how it had happened—and yes! now and then there was laughter. An incorrigible people! They were in no hurry to go to sleep. They wanted to get their breath, to enjoy the night air. The officers paid calls on each other.

An hour went by, two hours, and Sasha had still made no move. After supper he sat on a stump by a smashed fence doing nothing. He found it difficult to pull himself together and get started. Yet all he need do was walk away. It was dangerous, but no more dangerous than when they had charged the enemy at dawn the day before.

The power of rumor—no order was given, no announcement made, the regiment was lost in the night, yet from somewhere the whispers filtered through to officers and men: We have begun retreating. The Kremenchug Regiment has already received the order . . . The Murom and Nizhni Novgorod regiments are also getting ready . . . General Martos has gone . . . Torklus is nowhere to be found . . . it will be our turn soon . . .

The feeling that something was missing trickled down from above. The army's leaders were on the run! No longer there!

How could anyone be sure that they had run away? Perhaps they had been killed or taken prisoner? No, the rumor spread like a plague: The top brass are on the run! It's our turn soon.

Sasha's heart beat furiously. This is the moment! Right now! Don't wait for the order to retreat! When they led the regiment out they would subject it to another bombardment just as bad, only one village farther on. He must leave alone. What was good enough for Torklus was good enough for Sasha. The situation had become so chaotic that he would have no difficulty in explaining himself.

It did not enter his head to take anyone else with him. Lenartovich had made little use of his orderly. The soldiers in his platoon were, as a rule, withdrawn, cowed, there was no way of getting through to them. If you made a joke of it—what say we leave the top brass to it?—even the least prim of them would purse his lips and say nothing.

Lenartovich had no map. He borrowed one from the staff captain on some excuse and back in his quarters studied it by candlelight, trying to memorize it. Wittmannsdorf's main street led into the main road to the east. Three versts farther on you crossed the railway, another two and you turned off toward the church . . . farther on the road forked and if you took one of the three ways you might land back in the front line . . . another of them led to a river . . . the third to Orlau. The name seemed familiar.

Lenartovich mastered all this and went outside.

He had in fact nothing more to do—the sergeant knew how to look after the platoon. His most precious possession—the notebook in which he jotted down his thoughts—was in his pocket. His sword was of no more use than a silly stick, and he would throw it away the moment he got onto the road. His revolver too—Sasha was not much of a shot.

It was quite quiet by now, almost peaceful: after the machine guns the occasional rifle shot was reassuring rather than alarming. It was dark but the road was full of life: wheels creaked, hooves clattered, whips cracked, men swore at horses. Some people were losing no time in leaving.

Instead of returning to his platoon Lenartovich strode off with a lighter step in the same direction. With no platoon and no wheels to hinder him he easily outdistanced the human stream. He had excuses ready in case anyone stopped him.

But no one was checking the traffic on the road. It flowed freely wherever it pleased. Heavy field ambulances crawled along. Ammunition wagons rattled by, traces jingling. They moved at first in a single line, then, as others joined the stream from side roads, formed two lines and occupied the whole road. If anything came from the opposite direction they showered it with obscenities and closed up to prevent it from passing. In the column itself there was peace and harmony. Drivers walked beside vehicles conversing, cigarettes glowed in the darkness.

Nobody was checking, and the ensign's legs carried him happily along.

There was still time to turn back, no one would have noticed his absence yet, but he had decided that he had no right to lay down his life for an alien cause. He brought his feet down hard on the hard road, steeling himself in his conviction that he deserved to be something better than cannon fodder.

His route, however, was less simple than the map had made it seem. There were steep rises and dips, bridges, a dike, none of which he had noticed. He found the church, but there were more houses beyond it, and Sasha had forgotten how far it was to the main fork in the road. He came to one fork, but the road leading from it was tree-lined and he had been expecting a field path.

He didn't want to ask anyone, and it was quite dark. Weariness came over him. A day and a night of overexertion had begun to tell on him. Sasha left the road and lay down on a heap of straw. He was very thirsty but had no flask with him, and did not know where to look for water.

He woke at dawn, chilled to the bone in spite of the straw. He collected himself and went back to the road, but seeing some Cossacks riding along slowly, several small bands of them at intervals, he returned to his straw pile. It was stronger than reason, something inborn. Since childhood he had felt every Cossack to be his enemy, and Cossacks in general an obtuse and intractable force. Even dressed up as an officer (people said the uniform suited him) Sasha still felt like a student in their presence.

The Cossacks passed him, a long wagon train rolled by, and Sasha stepped out onto the road. He came upon a pile of what turned out to be jettisoned loaves, bread from an army bakery, stale and some of it already moldy. The troops had been without bread during the attack, and here bread had been thrown away to make room in a cart for something else.

He was hungry too. But an officer with a loaf under his arm would be a strange sight. He cut one loaf up with his sword, stowed slices away, chewed a bit, and walked on.

The sun was up. Still no one tried to stop anyone, no questions were asked. There was something new about those who were walking or riding along, something he couldn't put a name to at first. They still for the most part had their weapons and ammunition, still behaved as though they were carrying out an assignment or were part of a unit, as though this were not yet desertion, as though they were still an army subordinate to its commanders, but there was a difference—that was it, the expression on their faces when an officer addressed them, a look that said each had worries enough of his own, and no thought for the common cause.

Splendid! That made it all the safer for Sasha.

It was the right road, the road to Orlau, after all. It ran downhill to a mill dam, and at that point another road from the wood merged with it. So many guns, ammunition wagons, carts, riders, and men on foot had collected on the two roads that it was difficult either to squeeze past or to stand and wait your turn. Horses collapsed, exhausted, and were shot and dragged clear. Nearer to the dam the crush of snarled carts was worse still. An ammunition wagon had rolled downhill, rammed the team in front with a shaft, and killed one of the horses. Men were unhitching horses, yelling at each other, almost ready to come to blows. Officers and rankers alike gave vent to their exasperation. A little staff captain with a bandage around his head was raging at a tall battery commander: "I won't let you through if I have to hold you back with bayonets," and the battery commander waved a long arm at him: "I'll run your infantry over if you aren't careful."

Everybody was doing his best to let his comrades through and nobody else. Then two planks on the dam broke and voices called for someone to repair it. Volunteer carpenters came forward. From higher up the road you could see officers crowding around, each of them pointing and giving instructions, but the senior carpenter, a burly old man with a luxuriant gray mustache, shirt outside his trousers, unbelted, brushed off his advisers, officers and rankers alike, and did it his way.

By now the sun was overhead and scorching the dense crowd. The stream was not very wide and only breast high. They began watering the horses and bathing until the stream was aswirl with mud—at first only the rankers, but then officers as well.

The slope and the high ground beyond the stream were the site of the famous battle. This was the very place where they had suffered their first casualties, several thousand of them, and packed the hospitals of Neidenburg. It should have made the war seem all the more senseless: thousands had fallen just to push the Germans a little farther north. And now here they were, helplessly jammed together all in a heap, hungry, angry, lashing each other's horses, punching each other's noses, all because the Germans were pushing them southward over the same ground.

But no hardships, no amount of bloodshed, can jolt Russians out of their habit of passive acceptance. Not one of the fifteen hundred or so thronging the approach to the dam understood or was capable of understanding the senselessness of it.

Lenartovich had heard from more than one person that Neidenburg had been surrendered in the night. Why then was this great mass of men streaming there, and what was he himself hoping for? He did not really know. He had planned his journey as far as Orlau; he hadn't thought any further.

Up the hill, to one side of the road, field ambulances stood waiting their turn to cross the stream, and in one of them an amiable lieutenant colonel lay wounded. They got talking. The lieutenant colonel produced a map, they spread it out on top of him and looked at it together. Sasha told him some sort of tale about a mission he had been sent on, but all the time he was busily calculating: that great tongue of forest now . . . if you took the path through it . . . there was the village of Grünfliess, on the way to Neidenburg . . . Should he go to ground in the forest and wait for the Germans? But by now he was less keen on the idea of being taken prisoner. In the present chaos he might get clean away. Would he, though? There was an immense green expanse in the path of the retreating army, and beyond it, more likely than not, machine guns. "They're surrounding us"—somehow everybody took it for granted.

Sasha wasted a lot of time at the dam—he did not feel like undressing and fording the muddy stream.

A disorderly conglomeration of troops was waiting for something or other in the fields outside Orlau. Men were digging up and eating turnips and carrots or whatever else they could find in the gardens. Sasha had to go through this rabble to reach the forest which was his goal. But he no longer felt afraid as he forced his way through them. He felt sure that in the general muddle and confusion nobody would challenge him or detain him.

He found that he was wrong. A rabble it might be, but someone was treating it as a parade, inspecting the men on horseback, greeting them, talking to them. Lenartovich recognized the Army Commander (he had seen him at close quarters in Neidenburg).

Yes, it was General Samsonov! A big man on a big horse, looking like an ancient Russian hero in an oleograph, he rode slowly around the gypsy tribe, apparently not noticing how disgracefully unlike troops on parade they were. Nobody called the men to attention, he told no one to stand at ease. Occasionally he lifted his hand to the peak of his cap, not to salute, but to bare his head in a humble gesture of farewell. He was pensive, absent, and he was not wearing that air of menace in which a commander's authority chiefly resides.

By now he was quite near, but Ensign Lenartovich did not hurry to get out of his way. He could not tear his eyes away from this spectacle. You had this coming to you! What a nice old thing you've become all of a sudden. A good sharp bang on the head, that's what you all need to soften you up, you graven images. Just wait a bit—there's more to come!

As he stood staring with fascinated hatred the commander rode straight at him and spoke, not addressing him by his rank, looking straight into the ensign's eyes with his own docile, dreamy, bovine ones. Spoke to him like a father: "Whom have we here? Who are you?"

What a blunder. There was no time to think, he couldn't walk away, all those around were waiting for him to say something—but what could he say? Tell a lot of lies? He couldn't do that either . . . Rap it out as sharply as you can then.

"Twenty-ninth Chernigov Regiment, Your Excellency." His hand moved vaguely, like a fish's fin, by way of a salute. (This would be something to tell Veronika and the others in St. Petersburg if he survived.)

Samsonov showed no surprise. He did not wonder what the Chernigov Regiment was doing where it was not supposed to be. No, he just smiled, and his face lit up with warm memories. "Ah, the glorious Chernigov Regiment—"

(I've put my foot in it now! What if he starts asking questions?)

"—a special thank-you to you, men of the Chernigov Regiment."

He nodded, forgivingly, understandingly, gratefully, and rode slowly on.

His horse also seemed to nod, bending its neck low.

Seen from behind, the broad-backed commander was still more like a hero in an old legend, despondently reaching the parting of the ways: "If you go right . . . If you go left . . ."

[4 6]

Somebody might have been deliberately playing tricks on the 13th Corps, pushing it in so far that withdrawal would be extremely awkward. The lakes were so placed that the corps could not slip along the only escape route. It had to move away obliquely to the southeast, but waiting for it was Lake Plautziger, seven versts long, extending two creeks like two restraining arms, and the angry sparkle of its deep blue water seemed to say, "I shall not let you go!" Near the top of the left arm its waters lapped against the four-meter dam, Schlage M, and then the hostile Prussian waters barred the corps' way with a chain of small lakes and Lake Maransen spreading its six-verst wings.

The corps paid a heavy price for Schlage M, but in the end broke through toward the southeast. Once again, it had only one loophole, at Schwedrich—a bridge and a dike, across which it had to thread its way in a narrow column. Having crossed, instead of finding space for its oblique maneuver, it was wedged into the north-south corridor between two watery barriers: behind, the chain of lakes it had already passed, ahead the ten-verst Lake Lansker, together with a string of smaller lakes threaded onto the marshy river Alle. Once past this second barrier the corps ran into a third watery embrace—the forbiddingly outspread wings, tail, and talons of Lake Omulew, six versts long. Try as it would the corps could not go the way it wanted, but had to sidle sheepishly southward, where it was likely to collide with the neighboring 15th Corps, and where a little farther on the enemy would by now have blocked the roads. Even when it had rounded Lake Omulew it landed in the boundless Grünfliess Forest, at a point where the only direct, paved road between

Grünfliess and Kaltenborn ran athwart its path, and it had to make its way by winding forest paths.

This ill-fated 13th Corps had already marched farther than any of the others, and now its fate was to cover the seventy versts from Allenstein in forty hours without so much as a dry crust for the men, and no chance to feed or unharness the horses.

Horses are perhaps the only ones who do not understand the special character of this military operation—a retreat. To send the lower ranks into an attack, those higher up have to find slogans, persuasive words, they have to offer rewards and utter threats, and they must often lead the way themselves. But everybody from the highest to the lowest understands in a flash, and unquestioningly, what must be done in a retreat, and the lower ranks are permeated with a still sterner sense of duty than is their corps commander. Suddenly awakened after three days without food, ill shod, marched off his feet, unarmed, sick, wounded, dazed, the soldier responds with alacrity, and only those beyond rousing remain indifferent. At night or in pouring rain, this is the one idea that is quickly grasped by all, and all are ready to make sacrifices without asking any reward.

Only the night before, the 13th had been unable to go to the rescue of the 15th because it was exhausted and its supplies had not been brought up in time. But the following night nobody grumbled about the laggard field kitchens, nobody asked when the next rest day would be—instead the corps hauled its swollen body at extraordinary speed clear of strange forests and corridors between lakes.

Except for the rear guard.

In the Russian army in 1914 no rear guard ever saved itself by surrender. Rear guards died.

In the Hohenstein depression the Kashir Regiment and two battalions of the Neva Regiment, which had fallen behind, were attacked on all sides by Below's corps, and two small Russian batteries were overwhelmed by sixteen heavy German guns. But the Kashir Regiment fought on without artillery until 2 p.m., even counterattacking the railway station, and individuals held out in the buildings until evening. Colonel Kakhovskoy, who was killed defending the flag, had gained time, as ordered.

The Sofia Regiment, until then the least damaged of all, dug itself in where the passage between the lakes narrowed at Schwedrich, and fought on with great loss of life until 3 p.m., thus purging its guilt of two years' standing. It had not been paraded on ceremonial occasions since it had stained its reputation in 1912: at the centenary celebration, on the battlefield at Borodino, a private in the Sofia Regiment had broken ranks to present a petition to the Tsar. Now every three companies of the regiment were merged into one, and still there were fewer than a hundred men in each. But the pursuers too had dropped behind.

The 13th Corps was clear at last of all those distant and dangerous places.

However, the gallantry of its rear guard was of no avail: the corps could still not deploy itself over a wide front, and 29 August was drawing to a close. The 13th needed to slip past in the rear of the 15th overnight, but the 15th itself was under heavy pressure and sliding back onto the same roads. Moreover, the 13th Corps was a corps no longer, few of its regiments were regiments, and none had a full complement in more than a few companies. True, it still had a hundred guns, and the ammunition wagons had not dropped behind, so there were shells for them. Then, around noon, the 40th Don Regiment, newly arrived from Russia, reported to General Klyuev more or less intact, in good spirits and in excellent shape. This was just the sort of cavalry force which the corps had missed so sorely during all the fighting.

General Klyuev was not at all glad of this new encumbrance, and could not think what to do with it. He was still less pleased with the letter brought by Pestich, ordering him to take command of all three corps. The artful beggars were running for it themselves and leaving Klyuev to perish in a blind alley. And how was he supposed to find those other corps, when he couldn't even account for the whole of his own?

There was only one advantage: until then, Klyuev had supposed that the more convenient western roads had been assigned to Martos, and that he was meant to make his own retreat by back roads through the forest. Now he could issue different instructions.

Toward evening, without reconnoitering to see who else was on the road, he turned his whole corps to the right from Lake Omulew instead of to the left as ordered. And rammed the rear of the 15th Corps.

The 15th Corps had worn the enemy down so much during the preceding days that it had ensured itself a comparatively unhindered withdrawal: the Germans fired a few rounds after it, occupied places which it had just left, and that was all. But the corps was not withdrawing intact—it was minus its staff, several of its senior officers had been killed or had vanished, and the withdrawal had begun half a day earlier than the "sliding shield" plan envisaged, thereby ruining it: the forces meant to hold the Germans up in the west were melting way. Only the remnants of the 23rd Corps were trying to hold the shield in place when darkness fell, at what cost in blood no one knows, while the 15th Corps, once the Germans had cut the roads near Neidenburg, was drawn farther and farther into the immense Grünfliess Forest, which was already eerily dark before dusk.

It was then that the two corps collided at a right angle at the fateful crossroads in the by now impenetrable gloom of the forest night. In this place, where four carts had not been able to scrape past each other in the daytime, two whole corps were supposed to pass *through* each other by night. Till then the Russian 2nd Army still had some sort of existence—after the crossroads it ceased to exist. The hysterically screamed oaths, the seizing of harness and shafts to drag vehicles aside, the beating of horses about the head, the jostling and shoving, the snapping of branches, only those who have been in a similar situation at the front can imagine. There were, needless to say, no senior officers at the head of the columns, and it was some time before the junior ones who were there could make themselves heard, identify each other, and think of a plan. They stood at the crossroads, rooted to the spot, grabbed every soldier they could by the shoulders, asked him what unit he belonged to, and directed all those from the 13th Corps eastward toward Kaltenborn, all those from the 15th and the 23rd southward. In other words, they would manually divert every man so that the two corps would move again and not cut across each other's paths.

That crossing in the forest, into which by day the peaceful sun would be shining through the peaceful pines, was now a chink in the roof of hell. When he had exercised his tonsils at the crossroads sufficiently, without getting at all hoarse, Chernega contented himself with silently counting wheels to make sure that the whole battery turned around—and did not realize that this was the very crossroads where five days earlier Kharitonov, the obliging second lieutenant with the freckles, and his footsloggers had given them a push. Nor did he recognize in the yawning blackness through which they were now filing the road which had been cool even in the heat of day when they had traveled along it on their way from and then back to Omulefoffen.

The two bodies of men went their separate ways, meandering through the forest, feeling their way, stopping every now and then. The soldiers stumbling along had not eaten for two days, they had no water in their flasks, and their mouths were so dry that they could have sucked mud. They had lost all faith in their generals and no longer believed that there was any rhyme or reason in all this forced marching. By now, some of them were hiding their company insignia so that they could not be picked on, or were simply falling out and going to sleep on the ground.

But the cavalry, whose nobility and speed had been irrelevant until then, at last made use of its capabilities. Cavalryman closed up with cavalryman, especially if it was one Don Cossack and another; whoever saw and recognized his comrades, and was quick enough, joined this gathering column. They could see for themselves the irremediable dislocation of units and the dislocation in men's minds, and they knew that the army could not be reestablished. So the cavalry set out for the place where, so they thought, there was still a way out—the very mouth of the sack. They had bypassed the fatal crossroads, where all was confusion, while it was still light. Before the Germans got there they were through the villages where, at dawn and all the next day, the Russian infantry would have to fight. Tomorrow, the infantry would find the twenty versts of forest road to Willenberg as interminable as the road to heaven; but tonight the horses covered them briskly. On the way the Don Cossacks picked up the legendary Torklus, whom his own division had not been able to find, and the dragoons picked up the 2nd Army staff. Willenberg was already in German hands, so they turned aside again, broke out by way of the forest, left a rear guard at Chorzele, and continued their withdrawal.

This was quite an achievement. This way, gunners! This way, ammunition wagons! This way, infantry! Fight your way through, we're waiting, we're holding the door open for you.

But for some reason the lads didn't come marching and rolling in. Not until daylight would they extricate themselves from the forest, after which the Germans would craftily let them advance one kilometer into the bare plain, then mow them down, every last man, with cannon and machine guns.

By the evening of the 29th the 2nd Army no longer existed. In its place there was a confused and leaderless mob. On the morning of the 29th, the Don Cossacks had been a loyal unit of the Russian army, but by evening they had got the point and decided that charity begins at home.

Why should they go down with Mother Russia? The Don Cossacks have their own destiny, so—gee up! Let's break out, my Cossack brothers!

Nobody could reproach them for it. They hadn't started it.

In much the same way a tremendous storm in the heavens announces its imminence in a spark from a magnetic coil in a school laboratory.

* * *

TSAR AND COMMONER—
THE GRAVE AWAITS THEM

* * *

[4 7]

A feeling of purification flooded gently through his resting body. He was not aware of falling asleep, and he was not aware of waking up, if indeed he was awake. He had just enough strength to raise his eyelids and see immediately before his eyes the grass, untrodden and silky, from which the feeling of purity had flooded into his body. He might have been aware that he was lying on his side, might have dimly seen a corner of the glade, but the grass occupied his dreamy and unfocused attention completely.

The sort of grass he had known in childhood. Grass that looked as though it had been sown, with an admixture of mallow, grew in the neglected yard of the manor house at Zastruzhe, and more of it along the wide village street: thick, vigorous, but too short for the scythe. There were not many homesteads in Zastruzhe, cattle were not driven through the street to pasture, and so rarely did anyone ride along it that there was no longer either roadway or ruts in the grass, but unbroken turf, on which he had played with the village children.

He found strength to move the fingers of his lower hand just enough to touch the grass. Yes, it was the same.

He had strength for nothing else. Mercifully, salutarily he had not even the strength to remember the date, where he was and why, and why it was so quiet. His memory glided from the grass to other things.

To the chapel. The little stone chapel on the same village street, behind a fence of its own. It was hardly a chapel at all—no one who went into it could stand up straight. It was more like a wayside shrine under a roof.

To the services. They were held both before the chapel and out in the fields, when worshipers came in procession from the parish church five versts away on the Feast of the Assumption, which may have been chosen because in the Kostroma summer it was a convenient time to end the harvest.

The Feast of the Assumption—when was it? Had it gone by? Was it still in the future? He could not remember. His mind shut out everything that might recall him to reality and awaken him.

The venerable, gray-haired priest never came in his tarantass, but always on foot, bareheaded. Two icons were carried in procession, each by two women. But the procession was made up mainly of youths. Two or three of the older ones carried banners, looking solemn and intense, lads with big, clean-shaven heads, black and white shirts belted at the waist, peaked caps in their hands. They never laughed or played the fool. The girls were always in long, ankle-length skirts, and even the littlest one wore a kerchief: no female head must be left uncovered. Peasants arrived in bast shoes or barefoot, but always in clean clothes, and there was so much simple trust and commitment, so much pure faith in their faces. Meek contentment obliterated the lines of mischief and defiance. The two solitary banners brought a holiday air to the whole countryside.

Memories of the place in which you grew up are always poignant. To others it may seem uninteresting, no different from anywhere else, but to you it will always be the best place on earth. Nothing can stir such regrets for days gone by as the bends in the field path around the boundary posts. The lopsided carriage house. The sundial in the yard. The unfenced and untended tennis court with the ridge in the middle. The roofless summerhouse of plaited birch splits.

When their grandfather's decayed estate was divided among his five children Vorotyntsev's father had given up his share in everything else in return for Zastruzhe—for his soul's sake, and for the solitary walks he could take to contemplate his wasted life, and because there was nothing that could be profitably farmed, just enough arable land to feed the bailiff's family (he was also the stableman), and all the proprietors in Moscow ever got was two or three turkeys and a tub of butter at Easter and Christmas. Their austere mid-eighteenth-century, two-storied stone house had been built by Yegor Vorotyntsev, lieutenant in the horse guards, whose discharge, in copperplate, signed by the Empress Elizaveta, was preserved in their Moscow apartment.

The life of the present Georgi Vorotyntsev was a continuation of the horse guards lieutenant's career. After two generations of civilians he had gone back into the army. (He cherished a hazy belief in something more: that his family were indirectly descended from the extinct boyar line of the Vorotynskys on the Ugra, one of whom was the glorious voivode Mikhail Vorotynsky, burned at the stake by Ivan the Terrible, who saw in him a rival for the throne. But there were too many missing links, and it was unprovable.)

His eyes were now wide open and he could see the whole of the glade—where a few oaks were dotted about in the closed sea of coppery pines—and the late-afternoon light, when suddenly his ears were unstopped and he caught the growl of guns, neither few nor distant.

The sound shattered his enfeebled calm. The empty boiler of his mind roared and the words were beaten out red-hot on the anvil of his mind: Samsonov had been saying farewell to the army! That day, a few versts from there. All was lost, there was nothing to be done.

And his Estland Regiment was no longer with him. Had he persuaded them to return to their doom, all for nothing?

He no longer had his horse either. Horses, rather—there had been two. Where was Arseni?

Vorotyntsev raised his aching body on one elbow and looked to the right and the left. No Arseni.

He craned his neck to look behind him—it was painful to his shoulder and his jaw. There he was, lying full length on his back, with his head on a log. He might be sleeping, but his eyes were only half closed. No, he wasn't asleep, he was looking at something, but his face was as peaceful as a sleeping man's.

This was the only man left to his care. Vorotyntsev had rushed impetuously to exert his influence, to help a whole army. And now he was left with one soldier.

"Have we been sleeping?" he asked, anxious to hear Arseni's voice.

Arseni's lips parted lazily, and he said in a slow, unmilitary way, "A-ha."

"How did that happen? We shouldn't have been sleeping!" Vorotyntsev said in surprise, but he was still not quite strong enough to jump up, and all he could do was roll over onto his other side and face Arseni. He took out his watch, but looking at it still did not help him to think precisely.

The body has its own rhythm, its own authorized tempo. However quickly regiments and divisions were sucked spinning into the abyss of defeat, the clod that was his body could not begin its struggle to resist that whirling motion until what had gone before had been shut off and annulled by motionless sleep and lazy contemplation of the blades of grass under his eyes. The body needed an interval of torpor, of withdrawal, before it could gear itself to some new purpose.

How could he have slept? It must be nearly four o'clock. They had lain down for five minutes. The army was perishing, he could have been leading some of them to safety, doing something—and he had been asleep!

"Why didn't you wake me up? Didn't you know I shouldn't be sleeping?"

Arseni smacked his lips, sighed, yawned. "Well, I was asleep myself. Your . . . I've been without sleep for three nights. And this is your fifth. Where should we be going?"

Of course he was right. They had had to sleep. His body lay gratefully hugging the ground, still unable to rise immediately. But the ranker did not know that it wasn't fatigue that had felled the colonel. Since leaving Ostrolenka he had been riding, exhorting the men, urging them on for five days, and now he had collapsed, in despair. Despair was something he had never experienced before, and it was unforgivable. He had lain there sluggishly, remembering the past—something you don't do when things are going well.

His dazed mind was clearing, but Vorotyntsev could still not grasp the full dimensions of the catastrophe—it was immeasurable. There was no possibility now of saving much of anything from the wreck. But surely he could save something? There must be something he could do. Ah—now he had remembered. His map was gone. The map was with the horse. So now he was blind.

Vorotyntsev groaned and struck his forehead with his fist. Fighting against the languor of his body (it was grateful, so grateful for this rest), he drew up his knees and hugged them. If only he had a map! If only he had a map!

He still had his head, and still had in his head a rough idea of the lie of the land, but that was not enough.

He turned around to get a better view of Arseni, who reluctantly raised himself under the colonel's scrutiny and sat with his hands on the ground behind him supporting his trunk, without moving his long legs at all. His cap had slipped off and lay on the ground, his hair was tousled and his face morose, as though he were recovering from a drinking bout. He blinked.

"I've got you into a jam," Vorotyntsev said. "You should have stayed where you were, you weren't surrounded."

Arseni lolled backward. "Who knows, I might have had no head by now."

Vorotyntsev marveled again at this soldier's self-possessed dignity, his ability to remain his own man without insubordination. With no trace of a superior officer's condescension, speaking as he would to one of his own circle, Vorotyntsev said quietly, "We shall get out of it somehow, though, don't you worry."

Arseni's fleshy lips parted in a grin. "I should say so! This forest will be a big help!"

"Anyway, I don't think it goes anywhere near the main road. And that's where the Germans are."

"So let's spend the autumn here. Until they remove the cordon."

"What do you mean, spend the autumn?"

"We can make a cabin out of branches and hole up in it till winter. We can always live on roots and berries."

"For three months?"

Blagodarev screwed up his eyes as though looking at something far off. "People have done it. For years, even."

"What people?"

"Hermits, say."

"You and I aren't hermits. We would soon starve to death."

Blagodarev, still propped up on his elbows, turned a knowing eye on the colonel. "When you have to you can do anything."

"But we're soldiers, not monks. We shall break out. And do it as quickly as we can, while we still have the strength. I expect you feel hungry?"

"I'm too hungry to feel anything," Arseni said, chewing empty air.

Their sleep side by side had restored their strength. No more trying to rally the battalions. What they had to do now was break out themselves. He, Vorotyntsev, must get through to GHQ, discover the truth, and see that the truth was known. If he did, the journey would not have been entirely in vain. That was his duty—and his alone in the whole encircled army. There were officers besides himself to collect the battalions.

Once again it was as though his ears had been opened. And what Vorotyntsev heard was silence. The artillery was no longer firing. There was an occasional distant shot, or a volley from two or three rifles.

This could mean that all was over.

He braced himself to spring up, but he couldn't use that hand—a searing pain shot through his shoulder. Because of it, he was slower to prick up his ears than Arseni, who had cast off his torpor and was staring intently into the trees.

The crackling of pine needles told them that somebody was coming. One man. Unsteadily.

"One of ours," Arseni decided.

If he was alone it could not be otherwise.

But they stayed on the ground.

The other man came toward them. Staggered into the clearing. An officer. Haggard-looking. You wouldn't call him a young man, just a boy. Was he wounded? His sword seemed too heavy for him. He was somehow familiar.

Vorotyntsev recognized him, raised himself, and shouted, "You're the second lieutenant from the Rostov Regiment, aren't you?" The boyish, mustacheless lieutenant started, but alarm quickly gave way to joy.

"Oh, it's you, Colonel!"

"So you weren't evacuated? Have you come all the way from the hospital on foot?" Then, without waiting for an answer: "You haven't a map by any chance, have you?"

The second lieutenant had no sword belt, but the buckled vertical straps from shoulder to waist were straight, and slim as he was he was carrying an officer's pack, large-sized and full.

"Indeed I have." The pale young man's smile broadened as he unbuckled his pack. "It's a very detailed one too," he said, eager for praise. "A German one. I found it in Hohenstein. It was torn, but I glued it together while I was in the hospital."

It cost him an effort to speak, and to stand. Was he feeling faint, did he want to lie down?

"Good lad," Vorotyntsev said, patting his shoulder. "Well done! Where's your wound? You're concussed. I can see that. Your head, is it? It's getting better, though, isn't it? Look, put your greatcoat down here and lie down a bit. You look pale . . . I said lie down."

He was already unfolding the map and opening it out on the grass—two sections, then four, then eight.

He hung over it like a hawk hovering over its prey. It was impossible to imagine that he had been sleeping half an hour ago, or that he was capable of lying down and resting at all.

"Arseni, bring me some sticks to hold the corners down. Right, now–Second Lieutenant, tell me which way you came."

Vorotyntsev knelt before the map, and Kharitonov lay on his belly, holding his greatcoat bunched up under his chest to support him. He paused for breath from time to time, or half closed his eyes; he tried to speak without breaks, precisely and crisply. Pointing to the map, he told them how he had left Neidenburg the evening before, when the main road had already been cut, how he had kept getting closer to the road and moving away again, where he had spent the night. Today he had made for the village of Grünfliess, but—

"What, Grünfliess as well? When did they get there?"

"Let's see . . . I should say about three hours ago."

While he and Arseni had been sleeping.

—he had expected to find his regiment with the 15th Corps—

"And where do you suppose we are now?"

"Right here. If we go on farther there ought to be a cutting on the right, then the forest ends and Orlau should be visible."

"Correct. We came this way—you're quite right. Only you're too late to find your regiment."

They had a map and they had a starting point. For the rest, he must rely on his eye and his brain. His thoughts rallied quickly to the task, like a gun crew springing to their gun, like an infantry company at the call "To arms." All the Russian units will be rushing toward the mouth of the big sack—perhaps it had not yet been tied. They will all be trying to get as far as possible from the German western wall, so we shall go as close as possible. The Germans weren't hanging about there either, they were in a hurry to close up the ring. Where Vorotyntsev and his companions were now there were no roads for vehicles, which made it all the better for a small group. The forest paths ran southeastward, which was just as it should be. They had only to make a loop of three versts to get around the treeless Grünfliess triangle, then keep to the woods and keep going. The railway line ran through dense forest and there would be no one on it. Then by forest paths again. There was just one little spot, near the village of Modlken, where the forest came right up to the road twice within half a verst. That was the place to cross! Keep the number of versts down as much as possible. The fewer versts, the less they would tax their strength, the quicker they would be out of it. Sitting it out in the forest and waiting for everybody to leave the highroad was a bad plan. The Germans might have erected barbed-wire barricades. No, the quicker, the better! But they wouldn't get across that night. It would have to be tomorrow night. Which meant that they had twenty-four hours to reach the road. Right—route, time, place, plan all ready.

On the map spread out before him the green expanse of the forest, though enormous, was neatly ruled off into two hundred and fifty numbered rectangular sections: every meter of it had been inventoried, patrolled, and tamed by the fugitive foresters—why should it not yield to Vorotyntsev?

Some of this he thought aloud for Kharitonov's benefit. The concussed second lieutenant was their weak spot. But he was so unflinchingly eager to serve, he listened to his senior officer's plan with such a bright and open look, collecting his strength even while he was still lying on the ground, that it was certain that he would not let them down.

"Which training school did you go to, Lieutenant?"

"The Aleksandrov."

"We're schoolmates, then."

They were both delighted. But there was no time to exchange reminiscences.

Blagodarev stood upright beside them. He looked down as if from an airplane on the whole of East Prussia spread out before him—it was now theirs to do what they liked with it.

A few hours earlier Vorotyntsev had collapsed on that spot in a stupor of despair and exhaustion. An hour ago he had not had the strength to think what to do. Now a luminous and confident plan had taken shape and he could not bear the thought of wasting a minute: the decompressed springs were propelling him—quicker, quicker!

"Here, Arseni, take hold of these two corners."

They swiveled the map around to get their compass bearings and fit their little clearing into the neat pattern of the forest. A cross path showed them which way to set out.

"What about it, boys?" Vorotyntsev said impatiently. "Shall we go?" He looked anxiously at the second lieutenant. "Still feeling weak? Want to lie there a bit longer?"

He did, but . . .

"No, I'm ready, quite ready, Colonel!"

Arseni smacked his lips loudly and started putting his shoes on.

Vorotyntsev carefully folded the map so that the sections he would need first were handy, making new creases to spare the well-worn older ones.

Immediately to the west they came to an open space, but the sun had gone down so low beyond the forest that no light reached them even there. The bronze-scaled trunks were a dark wall, and only the needly foliage twenty meters or so up was still touched with gold.

"Right!" said Vorotyntsev, looking around at the injured lieutenant's awkwardly wobbling sword. "Throw that away!"

Kharitonov didn't understand. "What?" he said in surprise. "What did you say?"

"Chuck it away!" Vorotyntsev commanded. "That's an order! I take the responsibility. I shall throw my own away shortly."

Not yet, though.

"Shall I . . . shall I break it first, Colonel?"

"You haven't the strength to break it. Arseni, you'll be last. Take the second lieutenant's greatcoat." A raised finger greeted Kharitonov's protest.

They went on in single file, the skinny youth, burdened now only by his pouch and the revolver in his breastband, walking carefully straight ahead, his head held high, with the sturdy, light-footed colonel in front and the loose-limbed soldier ambling behind. In addition to two greatcoats, two rifles, a knapsack, a cooking pot, and a water bottle, Blagodarev was also carrying an unbroached lead cartridge box, and a trenching tool was slapping his thigh. He still contrived to somehow look as though he were traveling light.

They walked through three of the sections marked on the map, turned into a fourth and went halfway through it. The moon's slender sickle had also sunk, darkness had fallen prematurely in the forest, but Arseni noticed a man sitting on a tree stump at a little distance from the path, ten trees away.

"Hey, look! Somebody's sitting there!" His voice echoed as though he were yelling into a barrel.

It was suddenly a forest in which every bush might come to life.

The officers too stared hard at the man. He just sat there—didn't shoot, didn't run off, didn't try to hide, but didn't run to meet his fellow countrymen either.

He rose and walked slowly toward them.

There was still enough light on the path to see that everything he wore was muddied, and his austere and defiant face dirty. An ensign, also without a sword. He saw the colonel's epaulets, and was of two minds about saluting. He didn't salute and didn't make much of an effort to stand straight. Well, it was a forest, not a parade ground. He frowned, thinking hard or feeling a pain in his chest, and said grudgingly, "Ensign Lenartovich, Chernigov Regiment." Vorotyntsev had already spotted the university badge on his chest under the unbuttoned greatcoat and sized him up, as he always did every officer or ranker in his regiment. He had also supplied the missing words: (the Chernigov Regiment) "which is, to be sure, nowhere in this vicinity." Though, with things in such confusion . . .

"Are you wounded?"

"No." He spoke morosely and with no trace of deference. "I nearly got killed, though."

"I don't understand," Vorotyntsev retorted sharply.

Most people had "nearly got killed." And most people saved the news for their wives after the war.

Lenartovich pointed back over his shoulder. "I meant to come out at the village, but the Germans are there already. They pinned me down in a potato field with a machine gun. I don't know how I managed to crawl away."

"Where is your platoon?" Vorotyntsev asked hurriedly. They must not waste the night. A band of lumpy, pewter-colored clouds stretched across the sky, but did not threaten a storm. He made no comment on what the ensign said and probably disbelieved his explanation, but more important things were at risk than this man's fate. Vorotyntsev would not have wanted him in his regiment, but something told him that even this student with his contempt for military service could with proper training be turned into an excellent soldier. He was well built and held his head high.

"Are you staying here?" he asked quickly. "Or coming with us? We're going to break out."

There was a moment of hesitation, but Lenartovich answered more briskly than before, and quite firmly: "If I may."

"I warn you," the colonel said roughly, "we shall all have to do whatever jobs are necessary irrespective of rank. The only distinction made will be between the fit and the wounded."

"Of course, of course," Lenartovich quickly assented.

Wasn't he in fact a democrat, and weren't all distinctions between "higher" and "lower" particularly painful to him?

Vorotyntsev nodded to his men. "Forward march!"

And off they went.

Lenartovich was truly glad that he had fallen into what were obviously safe hands. A little while ago he had had his mouth full of the crumbly soil between the potato plants. Showered with clods torn up by uncomfortably close bullets, he had said goodbye to a life unfulfilled, indeed scarce begun—his oh so precious life! He had wriggled backward wormlike out of the interminable furrow without ever raising his head from the ground, then wandered dazed through the forest, his scratched hands trembling and one finger sprained, spitting out the last of the soil and picking it from his nose and ears.

Trying to give himself up had proved even more dangerous than fighting to the last. That was war for you—you couldn't even quit it, couldn't even cut loose from it. And if these new companions didn't suspect, didn't reprove him, but promised to get him out of it, the best thing he could do was go with them, shoot, fight. If someone had tried to kill you, and very nearly done it, you had a right to reply in kind.

He had noticed Blagodarev's water bottle: his throat was parched, cracked with thirst, but for some reason he could not bring himself to ask for a drink.

[48]

They led him, carried him. His body was moved by others. He himself could only meditate. The shifting strata had finally collapsed. The dust had settled. The veil was rent. The air was cleared. All vague and uncertain movements were over. The world as it was now, and the world as it had been in times past, stood out clearly.

The tight blindfold was removed from his reason, and his heart had shed a great burden. From the time when he had inspected the troops at Orlau, thanked them, and taken his leave of them, the weight had disappeared of itself and his mind had been easier. Although the handful of soldiers on the hill at Orlau could not speak for the whole army or all Russia, it was their forgiveness his soul had thirsted for. He gave little thought to a possible trial for dereliction of duty: those who are highly placed are not put on trial, they are reprimanded, kept on the reserve for a while, given a fresh command. "Shame doesn't eat your eyes out." They might, of course, appoint a commission of inquiry, but it would search in vain—no one would ever be able to disentangle the facts, it was too late already. What had happened was part of God's plan and men were not meant to understand it, or not yet.

No longer a proud horseman, but a rider in a cart, jolting over roots and tussocks, bumping shoulders with Postovsky, but exchanging never a word with him, in fact forgetting him altogether, Samsonov thought his long thoughts.

He did not think about Army Group HQ and Zhilinsky, did not dwell on the insults and humiliation which had tried him so sorely in the past few days. He made no effort to think up proofs that Zhilinsky was more to blame for all that had happened than he was himself. His resentment had cooled to a hard bright realization that Zhilinsky would wriggle out of it, get off scot-free. It no longer galled him. It was strange that an accusation of treachery from that contemptible person had been so hurtful just a little while ago, and had affected his handling of whole corps.

He was thinking rather of something else: how hard it was for the Emperor to choose himself worthy helpers. Self-seeking mediocrities are more pushy than the good and loyal, they acquire great ingenuity in flaunting their specious loyalty and their specious talents. Nobody ever sees as many liars and deceivers as the Tsar does—and how could he, a mere human, acquire the godlike perspicacity to penetrate the darkness of other men's souls? So he became the victim of wrong choices, and these self-seekers were sapping the Russian state like worms gnawing at a mighty tree.

These were thoughts for a man on horseback, not one jolting and rocking in a cart.

Samsonov's reflections, calm and detached, had no relevance to the object of the staff group's journey, which was to find a chink in the encircling forces and slip through it. When his musings were interrupted he did not immediately understand what people were telling him: that the road to Janow, by which they were traveling, had been cut, that there were Germans on the road ahead of them, and that the way out of the forest was under fire. His staff officers suggested changing direction from south to east, making a detour all the way around to Willenberg. Willenberg at least ought to be in Russian hands (Blagoveshchensky's). Samsonov nodded—Samsonov had no objection.

They had to go back the way they had come, losing versts and time, then turn into a convenient path to the east. Samsonov took no interest in any of it—the choice of path, or the loss of time and distance. A protective shutter in his mind barred the way to all possible unpleasantnesses and annoyances from the outside world. The faster and more irremediably external events flowed, the slower the motions in Samsonov's own body, the more deliberate his thoughts.

He had meant well and the results were extremely bad, as bad as they possibly could be. But if he with the best intentions could be left without a stitch to cover his nakedness, what would the actions of the selfish lead to in this war? And if Russia's defeats were repeated, would there not be another upheaval like the one that followed the Japanese war?

It was painful and terrifying to think that he, General Samsonov, had served his Emperor and Russia so ill.

It was getting on toward evening. The sun was quite low. The majority opinion among the staff officers favored an attempt to turn south again and look for a way through there. The commander nodded agreement to everything they said, without really trying to understand.

The terrain had become forbidding: they had left the dry elevation with its reddened pines and were riding over low-lying ground overgrown with bushes, along paths where the wheels were slowed by tacky sand, fording too many unexpected streams and drainage channels.

On a number of occasions the Cossack scouts rode forward, but the chatter of machine guns was shortly heard and they returned—occupied territory ahead.

What sort of Cossacks were they anyway, this squadron escorting HQ staff? Second- or third-rate, flimsy fellows, timidly diving into the bushes as soon as the firing started. It almost seemed that Russia's supply of Cossacks had dried up too. The ataman of the Semirechye and Don Cossacks hadn't a single good squadron to his name!

He needed to think, to do a lot more thinking before the day was out. Postovsky or Filimonov ought to be able to deputize for him to the extent of leading the little staff group, but they had both gone soft. The greedy, predatory look had been wiped from Filimonov's face and he was puffing and sniffling as though he had influenza. Near the village of Saddek, no more than four versts from the highway, the younger staff officers asked permission from the commander himself to attack with the Cossack squadron and try to break through. As they emerged from the forest there was more than a verst between them and the higher ground along the road, and the treeless terrain gave little prospect of success, but the officers were so insistent on making one try at least that Samsonov consented, as though in a dream, without really thinking about it.

Colonel Vyalov tried to talk the Cossacks into attacking. They jibbed, didn't want to leave the forest, objected that their horses were exhausted, whereupon Staff Captain Ducimetière cried, "Hurrah!" and galloped off alone with drawn sword in the direction of the machine gun. Vyalov and two other officers followed, and only then did the Cossacks stir. They charged in disorder, firing randomly into the air, whooping and yelping, not so much to scare the enemy as to give themselves courage. However, three of them were unhorsed, and fifty paces from the machine gun the others turned off into the trees. Seeing this disgraceful conduct restored Samsonov's powers of action and decision. He called them all off, forbade the officers to try a second attack, on foot this time, and ordered them all to retrace their steps northward and then turn east again toward Willenberg.

Once more they rode into the pine wood, darker now, scrambled onto the stony track, and moved quickly and unhindered in the direction of Willenberg. But as they emerged into the twilight three versts from the town they met a Polish peasant and asked him whether there were many Russian soldiers there.

He scratched his head. "*Nie, panowie, tam wcale niema Rosjan, tylko Niemcy, dużo Niemców dziś przyszło.*"*

The staff officers drooped. They sat and despaired. Where could Blagoveshchensky and his corps be?

Samsonov seated himself on a tree stump, and his head sank onto his chest. If even the army staff was too late to break out, what must await the army as a whole the next day?

The staff officers discussed the situation: they would have to steal through somewhere during the night, that very night. It was their last chance.

Samsonov saw the hand of God in it. Who had darkened his mind and made him leave his army? Yes, the hand of God was in it! He steeled himself and announced: "You all have my permission to leave, gentlemen. General Postovsky, take charge of the breakthrough of HQ staff. I am returning to the 15th Corps."

(The 15th Corps or the 13th, it made no difference—in those twilight minutes twenty-five versts to Samsonov's rear the two corps were inextricably entangled at the fatal forest crossroads, and were rapidly ceasing to exist as separate units.)

However, the staff officers, irrespective of rank, rushed as one man to surround the commander and urge on him, speaking all at once but each with arguments of his own, the impossibility, the error, the absurdity,

* No, there are no Russians there at all, only Germans. A lot of Germans arrived today.

the impermissibility, the wrongheadedness of his decision. He was in command of the whole army . . . his duty to the flanking corps . . . his duty to the Northwestern Army Group . . . were just as important . . . he and only he could reunite the forces remaining to them in a matter of hours and so save Russia from invasion by the enemy . . .

Yesterday, when they objected to leaving Neidenburg for Nadrau, they had not dared to protest so emphatically. But a great deal had happened in the hours between.

Samsonov sat on the low throne which the forest had grown for him, listened to them, and closed his eyes. He was thinking how uncongenial to him his staff officers all were: they had been brought together by chance, yet all of them, in heart and mind, were alien. He felt some kinship only with Krymov, whom he had sent away.

The staff officers' arguments were solidly built, but to Samsonov they had a hollow ring. He did not reproach them with it but he could tell from their voices that their concern was not for him or for the army but for themselves. None of them wanted to go back with him, but army discipline made it impossible for them to escape without him.

Yet Samsonov no longer had the strength to argue with a dozen importunate subordinates; worse still, he no longer had the strength to set off into the dark distance with only his orderly, Kupchik, for company.

There was a third possibility—to summon all the fighting units to this place and try to fight their way out—that no one suggested. It occurred to no one. The question was: how to escape? "We won't get out of it with that gang"—looking at the Cossack squadron, every man of them had the same thought. The Cossacks were dismissed, to make their way out as best they could while the staff officers continued on foot. It seemed sensible to suppose that, in the night and on bad roads, they would have a better chance without horses. The local inhabitants were Poles, and sympathetic.

Samsonov sat on his stump, beard on chest, oblivious. The defeated general was calmer than any of his staff.

He was waiting for the fuss, which distracted him from his thoughts, to end, waiting for the smooth motion to begin again so that he could think calmly.

But even when they were rid of the Cossacks, even after unbridling and releasing the horses, the staff officers were still not ready for the night march, still found things to fuss about. In the fading gray light, with a glimmer of moonlight showing, Samsonov could dimly see that a hole was being dug and the officers laying in it something from their pockets. He saw it, but attached no importance to it. He was commander no longer, he had ceased ordering them to do this and not to do that. He was waiting, endlessly it seemed, to be led away.

Postovsky, polite but insistent, approached and loomed over him.

"Your Excellency! Permit me to remark. We don't know what may happen to us . . . If we should fall into the hands of the enemy . . . there may be documents or badges they shouldn't get . . . Why present them with a prize like that?"

Prize? Badges? Samsonov did not understand.

"Aleksandr Vasilievich, we're burying everything we don't need . . . marking the spot . . . We shall come back later, or send somebody . . . If you've got any documents . . . anything that gives away names . . ."

From the eminence that Samsonov had reached in that long day these worries seemed piffling. But here came the younger officers, strutting up to tell him earnestly that he must not let the enemy know who their prisoner was—let them think that he had slipped through their fingers: after all, if a regimental flag couldn't be carried away safely, it was cut up or burned or buried, but never surrendered . . .

How quickly things had changed. A quarter of an hour ago he could have consented or refused to go with them. They had implored him to go, it was all-important to them. Now, they didn't much care what he thought they should do. He was like a golden idol, the god of a savage tribe—if they brought him back safely the curse would not fall on their heads.

Not on theirs. But on his.

Now they were moving, in single file, with Samsonov somewhere in the middle and Kupchik behind him carrying the saddlecloth from his abandoned horse. The faint light of the moon filtering into the less dense parts of the forest made it possible to distinguish tree trunks, thickets, piles of brushwood, and clearings, but only very close up. And they could see each other only at a very short distance. Then there was no moon, and those in the lead almost groped their way along, stopping to consult a luminous compass. When they did so all the others stopped too. It was quite impossible to go straight ahead: they had to get around holes in the ground, boggy patches, thickets, and every time they had to make sure of their direction again.

General Samsonov was at liberty to resume his meditations. There was no more talk, nothing at all to prevent him from thinking his thoughts through.

Only he found that there was nothing more for him to think about. Nothing at all. All the thinking had been done, all the decisions made. The room was swept and garnished. All that was left was remembrance.

The memories that came to him were not of his rural childhood in Yekaterinoslav, not of his cadet school, not of the cavalry training establishment, not of the many, many places in which he had served, his eventful career, those who had served with him. Shutting out all else, the Cossack cathedral on the hill loomed in his mind again; huge, menacing, with its intricately patterned brickwork. He was born in Little Russia, had been in Moscow, lived in St. Petersburg, in Warsaw, in Turkestan, and beyond the Amur River, yet—though he was no son of the Don by birth—he was carried irresistibly to the broad-browed hill at Novocherkassk. Not to the upper part, where Yermak's monument rears up, but downhill toward the Kreshchensky descent, where, on a granite plinth raised only slightly above the cobblestones, lie a Caucasian cloak and a tall Caucasian cap in bronze, as though their owner, Baklanov, had carelessly flung them down and just left.

Left for his grave, in the vaults of the church.

For a soldier's burial.

With victories to be carved in granite.

Walking was difficult. His legs had lost the habit, and worse still was his shortness of breath: just walking, with nothing to carry, made him wheeze and pant as though he had asthma.

When a man loses his position of superiority, his means of locomotion, and his means of protection, his body is put to the test, and he finds that the truth about him is expressed, not by his general's tabs, but by a flagging heart, lungs that refuse to expand fully, as though they were two-thirds blocked, weak legs, and unreliable feet that tread awkwardly, stub the ground, stumble over tussocks, moss beds, and fallen branches. If anything can give him pleasure it is not that he is making progress, not the thought that he may yet scrape through, but the holdups ahead, when everybody has to stop and he can lean against a trunk and try to get his breath.

Samsonov was ashamed to ask for a rest, but out of consideration for him they stopped every hour and sat down. Kupchik always spread the horse blanket with alacrity for the commander, whose aching legs were grateful for a chance to stretch out and rest.

But they could not sit for long. The short night and their last chance were hurrying away. Around midnight the stars were obscured and it was too dark to see anything at all. The little group plodded on, single file, informed of each other's whereabouts only by the snapping of twigs, heavy breathing, or the occasional touch of a hand. The path got worse—at one moment boggy ground squelched underfoot, at the next unthinned bushes or dense clusters of young trees barred the way. They assumed that it would be dangerous to stray in the direction of Willenberg. But there were other dangers—they might bump into a German patrol, or get lost altogether. They clung together, called to each other in whispers. There were no more stops for rest. When they came to a ditch Kupchik and the Cossack captain helped Samsonov across, almost dragging him.

Samsonov was oppressed by the burden of his body. Only his body was pulling him on to more pain and suffering, more shame and disgrace. To escape from the disgrace, the pain, the heaviness he had only to release himself from his body. It would be a blissful liberation, it would be like taking the first deep breath after the lungs have been congested.

Only yesterday he had been an idol to whom his staff officers looked for redemption. Since midnight he had been a fallen idol, a millstone around their necks.

Slipping away from Kupchik was the one difficulty. The Cossack orderly kept close behind his general, touching his back or his hand from time to time. But Samsonov tricked him: as they went around a thicket of bushes he stepped aside and stood hidden.

The heavy steps, the crackling, the snapping, passed him by, grew distant, then he could no longer hear them.

There was silence. The perfect silence of peacetime, with no reminders of battle. The only sound was that of the fresh night breeze sighing in the treetops. This was not an enemy forest, it was neither German nor Russian. It was God's forest, giving shelter to any of His creatures.

Samsonov rested his weight against a tree trunk and listened to the forest—close to his ear, the rustle of peeling pine bark; closer to the sky, the cleansing wind.

He felt more and more at peace with himself. He had served long years in the army, had accepted danger and sudden death as his fate, had faced death and been ready for it, yet had never known that it could be as easy as shedding a burden.

But suicide was accounted a sin.

A faint sound—his revolver cocked itself. Samsonov laid his upturned cap on the ground with the revolver in it. He took off his sword and kissed it. He fumbled for the locket with his wife's picture and kissed it.

He took a few steps to an open space. The sky had clouded over. Only one star was visible—obscured for a while, it peered out again. He sank to his knees on the warm pine needles. Not knowing where the east was, he looked up at the star as he prayed.

At first he prayed in remembered words, then without words, kneeling, gazing at the sky, breathing. Then he groaned aloud, shamelessly, like a dying forest creature.

"O Lord, forgive me if Thou canst, and take me into Thy rest. Thou seest that I could do no other, and can do no other."

[4 9]

(REVIEW OF OPERATIONS ON 29–30 AUGUST)

The highroad from Neidenburg to Willenberg might have been laid and rolled smooth for François's mobile units to race along it and link up with Mackensen. The central Russian corps had crossed this highway some days earlier without foreboding, but now it had turned into a wall, a weir, a moat at their backs. François's forward units cut their night's rest short and hurried on toward Willenberg before daybreak, smashing Russian transports and any other stray force they came across. There was no opposition and they occupied Willenberg toward evening. True, only sparsely scattered roadblocks and patrols had been left behind on the forty kilometers of road covered: the encirclement was for the time being a dotted line. It would take another twenty-four hours for one of François's divisions to pour along the road and occupy it.

Mackensen's leading brigade also rushed ahead, making the best of much worse roads by slinging their packs onto farm carts and occasionally taking a ride themselves. Mackensen himself hovered to the north of the highway, posting detachments on both sides of the main body—toward Ortelsburg and deep in the forest, pointing at the encircled center.

Though the two claws of the pincer movement had not quite closed their grip by the evening of the 29th, there were only ten versts or so of impassable forest between them, too far away for the Russians to realize it and get there in time. All the same, Hindenburg could not be sure that the encirclement was a success when he signed his overnight orders for the 30th. Fighting had slackened in other segments of the half-circle where it had been so fierce the day before. A few skirmishes in the corridors between the lakes were enough to hold up pursuers. They would have had no forces to defend themselves if the Russians had broken the ring from outside on the 29th.

But they did not even try.

Samsonov's last dispatch burst through the dotted line of encircling troops on the evening of the 28th and reached Bialystok on the morning of the 29th, just as Zhilinsky was about to have breakfast with Oranovsky. The hapless Samsonov was as mulish as ever in the hour of failure. He reported that he had ordered the whole army to fall back to the Ortelsburg-Mlawa line—that is, almost to the Russian frontier. He had deserved all that had befallen him, it was always to be expected, and it was a very good thing that he had taken the initiative and disgraced himself by ordering a retreat without consulting Army Group HQ. At breakfast on that auspicious morning (with the doomed Kashir Regiment already surrounded in Hohenstein) Zhilinsky and Oranovsky decided that they had been wasting their time yesterday when they forced Rennenkampf to advance into what they now saw was an empty space from which Samsonov had already withdrawn. They telegraphed immediately: "2nd Army withdrawn toward frontier. Halt all corps moving up to support."

Rennenkampf had not set out until after dinner on the day before. His corps were a hundred versts away from today's fighting as the crow flies, and the cavalry seventy. He was only too happy to give the order at noon: All corps halt and prepare to withdraw tomorrow.

But a new cause of alarm slipped into Bialystok to trouble Zhilinsky and Oranovsky, and at 2 p.m. they sent Rennenkampf another telegram, contradicting the first: "In view of the heavy fighting in which the 2nd Army is engaged, direct the deployed corps and the cavalry to Allenstein." (Why Allenstein? How could anyone in his right mind send *eight divisions* to a place where it was certain that nobody had needed them for nearly two days?)

Anyone with military experience can judge how helpful this hourly switching of orders was to forces on the move.

Disposing of such huge masses far from the field of battle, Zhilinsky and Oranovsky no longer troubled their heads about the deployment of the flanking corps near to the fighting, nor indeed was it in order for them to interfere there, bypassing the commander of the 2nd Army. Especially as Blagoveshchensky was taking a day's rest. The most they could ask was for a cavalry division of his to attack somebody or other for the sake of appearances.

So Tolpygo's cavalry division found itself riding out in the middle of the day. Its route led past the bewitched town of Ortelsburg. It had been empty the day before (when Samsonov had given orders that it was to be held whatever the cost), but today there had been occasional shots fired from the town since dawn. So the cavalry division skirted the town and advanced cautiously through deserted countryside in the direction it had for reasons unknown been ordered to take until the enemy appeared again.

The gathering darkness, however, and the wooded terrain were unhelpful to cavalry, and General Tolpygo considered it best to return to his corps. Turning about by night was not easy or safe, but they were back toward morning. One amusing thing happened on this expedition: they flushed a German general, a division commander. He shot off in his car, but left his greatcoat behind with a map in the pocket. Marks on the map showed how Mackensen was surrounding the central Russian corps. For the sake of a quiet life *this map was allowed to go no further*!

The 1st Corps, unlike Blagoveshchensky, enjoyed no peace and quiet. It rolled back as fast as it could, but not too far for a captain with orders from Samsonov to catch up with it on the night of 28–29 August: it must ease the situation of the encircled center by advancing on Neidenburg immediately.

(If the corps and a half present there had indeed moved against Neidenburg immediately, they would, given their overwhelming superiority, have entered the town unopposed in the middle of 29 August, and not only would the encirclement have caved in but, as easily happens in wars of maneuver, François's corps would have been caught in tight pincers and in danger of encirclement in its turn.)

But now that they had clear orders, the generals—a dozen of them, from various divisions or unattached units—still found it difficult to concert their efforts and carry them out.

Colonel Krymov, whom Dushkevich had chosen as his Chief of Staff, could not unite the generals. The order would obviously have to be carried out by somebody—but by whom? In the absence of a general incontestably senior to the rest, each of them could insist that whichever unit went it would not be his own, or under his command. Haggling between the generals went on in Mlawa *throughout* 29 *August*: who should contribute what to the joint expeditionary force and who would lead it? It turned out that the only untouched regiment was the Petrograd Life Guards (part of the dismantled Guards division). The other battalions, squadrons, and batteries would be auxiliary to it, so that the task of leading the whole force into this desperate enterprise fell to Sirelius, the Petersburg general, commander of the Guards in Warsaw.

After all the wrangling and ready-making Sirelius moved out at 6 p.m., and even then only with the spearhead of the expeditionary force, on the understanding that the other units would follow one by one. In the course of the evening and the night that followed

Sirelius's force covered its thirty versts, clashing with the German covering force for the first time early in the morning of the 30th, five versts from Neidenburg.

A German plane looked down on the skirmish.

General von François had now passed two nights in Neidenburg and chuckled over two sets of late-night instructions from Ludendorff. Ludendorff still hadn't divined that the encirclement was nearly complete; he was still preoccupied with preparations against Rennenkampf. During the night of the 29th–30th François was, on his own orders, not allowed to sleep: captured Russian guns, an endless procession of them, were being towed in for exhibition on the market square. François dozed from time to time and woke up to jot down some felicitous phrase for his memoirs. On the morning of the "most beautiful and proudest day" in his life he jumped out of bed fresh and eager, had a good breakfast, listened to reports, sent a telegram to Ludendorff, and—in his own mind already famous throughout Germany, no, throughout Europe, as the victor of this new Cannae—went out on the porch to view the booty. But there was the drone of an engine in the sky. The reconnaissance plane sent to observe the Russian retreat was back. The pilot did not keep the general on tenterhooks, he dropped a packet on the roadway, exactly in front of the hotel. François smilingly commended him. His adjutant rushed to pick the packet up and hand it to the general. They unsealed it: "Machine No. . . . Lieutenant . . . Route . . . dropped . . . Columns of troops of all kinds . . . Head 5 kilometers south of Neidenburg, tail 1 kilometer north of Mlawa . . ."

As though he were playing snakes and ladders and an unlucky throw of the dice had plunged him from the top line back to the starting point, the radiant victor immediately assumed the grave look of a novice who still has everything to do. He tossed the report to his staff officers, but even without their calculations he knew that a column thirty kilometers long was a corps. A shell burst of decisions followed—oral instructions only, no time to put anything on paper. Two battalions in reserve? Advance and engage the enemy! Another battalion on guard? Stand it down! Not a single German battery south of the town and two to the north? Move one of them south! Don't take anybody off the highroad, the encircling force must stay in place! There are Russian prisoners in the town? Move them north. You say there's still a Landwehr brigade at Soldau? Get it here in a hurry! Is there anything else we can take over? Report by telephone to Army HQ. No, shells falling, communications cut. Never mind. Plenty of cars, we can use them for liaison. Bursts of Russian shrapnel over the town. Fougasse bombs falling. This is no longer the place for Corps HQ. Retreat? Certainly not—attack! Along the road to Willenberg.

The yellow lion is still on the radiator. The younger François records the general's thoughts. They meet a car carrying a Russian general captured at dawn. The car stops, the Russian is brought over to them. He is exhausted, his uniform torn by underbrush and bullets, his lips parched. He looks about sixty, but holds himself well and moves easily—not at all what they expect in a Russian general. His hand still clutches a useless staff. A full general, then, and it is easy to guess which corps he commands: the one that has been trouncing Scholtz all this week. Get out, go over, shake his hand, say a few words of praise and consolation: a brave general is never insured against capture.

Martos, dispatched to Neidenburg as a quite unnecessary messenger, had spent a day and a night roaming on the verge of the Grünfliess Forest, with no troops to attack the town he had taken only a week ago. His Cossack escort had taken flight, shrapnel from guns not more than two thousand meters away had started falling around him, and in the night a searchlight had picked him out by the roadside. Rifle fire point-blank—the corps Chief of Staff was killed. Martos's sword had been broken, and the pieces handed to a German officer.

Now Martos pricked up his ears, surprised and hopeful; that was Russian artillery bombarding Neidenburg from the south. So it still wasn't certain who was encircling whom? He noticed with satisfaction the disorder in the German support column and the nervousness of the infantry.

François: "Tell me, General, what is the name of the Corps Commander heading this way? I want to call on him to surrender. Or perhaps you would be willing to go and suggest that he lay down his arms?"

Martos jumped at the chance. "Yes, I'll go!"

François sobered up. "No, it won't be necessary."

Martos was seated in a car between two Mausers and whisked along the road through Mühlen, the town he hadn't quite managed to take. At the little hotel in Osterode, Ludendorff came out to meet him.

"Tell me, what were your General Samsonov's strategic intentions when he invaded East Prussia?"

"As a corps commander I made only operational decisions."

"Yes, but now you are all beaten, and the Russian frontiers are wide open, and we can advance to Grodno and Warsaw."

"When my forces equaled yours I got the better of you in battle and took many prisoners and guns."

Hindenburg came in. He saw that Martos was distraught, and held both his hands for some time, urging him to compose himself. "You are a worthy opponent, and I shall return your gold-hilted weapon; it will be brought to you."

It was not. Martos was driven under escort to Germany and kept prisoner until the war ended.

Ludendorff held out until the morning of the 30th, and then reported to GHQ that a tremendous operation to encircle the Russian armies had been successfully completed. That was just half an hour before François howled for help, after which the line was cut. Three divisions were immediately detached from Scholtz's pursuit force and sent twenty, twenty-one, and thirty kilometers respectively to help at Neidenburg. Within the next few hours a report came in that some of Rennenkampf's cavalry divisions were advancing deeper into East Prussia. And a second reconnaissance plane reported a Russian force advancing on Willenberg.

The encirclement was coming apart at the seams.

General Sirelius stood up to eight companies of garrison troops for ten hours, waiting for the whole corps to join him. By the evening of the 30th he had pushed the Germans out of Neidenburg, but it was too late for him to break through to other Russian forces a few versts farther on: by then a hundred guns were trained on him, and German reinforcements were moving up from all sides.

In far-off Bialystok, Zhilinsky and Oranovsky learned of these happenings, not from their pilots, not from their scouts, not from the commanders of units in the field, but from the deserter general Kondratovich. As early as the 28th he had pulled half a dozen companies out of the front line to protect his person and fled across the Russian frontier at Chorzele, where he spent the whole of the 29th anxiously waiting for orderlies to ride in and tell him whether the Russians or the Germans had the upper hand. When on the night of 29–30 August it became clear to him that the Germans had won he made an ingenious attempt to conceal his desertion, telegraphing as though he had just arrived and supplying a grateful Army Group HQ with information about the central corps which it had been unable to obtain elsewhere.

Zhilinsky and Oranovsky were raised from their beds at that unearthly hour (perhaps almost as Samsonov was cocking his revolver to shoot himself), and after an undisturbed day found themselves lumbered with night duty. They had to salvage what they could, make decisions, find some way out of the mess! They had imagined last night that responsibility for the failure of the operation and the retreat of the 2nd Army would rest with Samsonov: after all, the order to retreat was his. But it was now beginning to look as though Zhilinsky had been late in ordering the 2nd Army to retreat, and he feared that some part of the blame would fall on him. Was there any way out? Better draft a telegram—"The Commander-in-Chief has ordered the withdrawal of the 2nd Army to the Ortelsburg-Mlawa line"—with no indication of the precise time, and pretend that it had been sent to Samsonov . . . We can't help it if the line doesn't go that far.

Next, another message to Rennenkampf: "Organize cavalry search to determine General Samsonov's whereabouts." One to Blagoveshchensky: "Concentrate your forces in the region of Willenberg" (better not say "*take* Willenberg"). One to Kondratovich: "Group the forces at your disposal" (his bodyguard!) "in the region of Chorzele" (since he was there already!) "and act *as circumstances require* in conjunction with Blagoveshchensky." To the airmen: "Look for Army HQ and for the 13th and 15th corps, somewhere between Hohenstein and Neidenburg." Transmit all these orders by word of mouth, and on no account on paper. Finally, tell the 1st Corps to *try to occupy* Neidenburg.

Just as long as the 1st Corps didn't land him in more trouble! The Supreme Commander had authorized him to move it up to Soldau on 21 August, and he might be blamed for failing to act on the order.

[5 0]

But for the ruler-drawn paths it would have been quite impossible to move by night in such a forest. The paths, however, coincided exactly with what was shown on the German map. Vorotyntsev struck a match from time to time to consult it, took a few extra steps to make sure of his direction, and led his little party around the unwooded triangle exactly to the isolated building which he had picked out on the map.

It was not a forester's hut, and in the dark they could not be sure what it was. They stumbled over soft yet stiff flatly folded objects. Only afterward, when they had found a lamp and lit it, did they see that their trousers, boots, and hands were bloodstained. The objects on the floor were cowhides. They were in a slaughterhouse. At least there was a well—they could drink their fill, wash, and drink again. There was also dried and smoked meat, more than they could eat or carry away, a little bread, and a kitchen garden. Blagodarev found a set of cleavers and butcher's knives with unbendable blades. He took his pick. Vorotyntsev also tucked a neat little chopper inside his belt. When they had rummaged around, moving cautiously with the lamp, and taken all they wanted, they slumped on the floor and slept a little. At least the other three slept while Vorotyntsev kept watch. Being the man he was, he could not have slept. The escape plan, his hopes and calculations, had bored so deeply into him that he could not let himself weaken and sleep until it was all over. His thoughts raced on beyond that to what he would have to say at GHQ, if they did get away, and what effect it would have.

He had to make an effort, not to keep awake, but to control his impatience. He strode around a spacious grassy yard hemmed in by a dark oval wall of close-set trees. It left a view of a larger oval of starry sky above the clearing. A straggle of light puffy clouds drifted over it, lit from some invisible source and shedding a gentle diffused light in which the tops of the nearest tall trees stood out clearly. The small, unhurried clouds held no threat of bad weather—something to be thankful for! Around midnight the whole sky clouded over, but later on it began to clear again. The night grew chillier, but there was not much dew.

Nearby a whole army was falling apart, regiments and divisions were perishing, but there was no loud noise. He heard not a single shot from Neidenburg, or from anywhere along the German lines to the west: perhaps the Germans were satisfied, gorged with success, and had no thought of pursuit.

There were fewer stars now. The sky, black at midnight, was turning gray, and but for the stars it would have been completely overcast. The hour was approaching when there would be no color at all in the world, just a gray sky and elsewhere unrelieved blackness. Anyone who had never seen the color green, say, would not have been able to imagine it from the trees or the grass.

He mustn't wait any longer. Time to awaken them. Kharitonov woke up easily, as though he had not been sleeping at all, just waiting to hear footsteps. Lenartovich jumped as though he had been struck, but rose without delay. Arseni moaned, mumbled a protest, had to be shaken twice before he was awake, then lay there breathing hard.

They set off again in single file, more heavily burdened than before, with the meat and the butcher's tools. Branches, bodies, tree trunks could be seen when light shone through from the sky. Everything else was a featureless blur.

Yaroslav had not been allowed to sleep long, but his mind was clearer and steadier than yesterday. He was getting better all the time, though he still felt as though his eardrums were dented, so that the forest was either dumb or raucous—gentle stirrings were inaudible to him. Back in the hospital he had envied those who served under this brisk, quick-thinking colonel with the bright, darting eyes. He had felt such relief, such joy, when he stumbled upon him again in the forest and was able to help with the map. The army and his own regiment were in a bad way, he had lost his platoon, but he himself could not have fallen into better hands if he hoped to carry on with his one and only, dearly loved, irreplaceable life.

They went through two sections of the forest, deserted but watchful in the growing light, checking the intersections on the map, and turned along another path which led to a wider, irregular clearing.

It was getting light quickly; visibility increased to a quarter, then to a half verst, and suddenly they saw people walking in the clearing ahead of them. Soldiers—in caps, not helmets. Russians. Moving slowly. Weighed down. Carrying something heavy on their shoulders.

There was no other road. Might as well catch up. The others spotted them. Two fell back and stood on opposite sides of the clearing, rifles at the ready. Vorotyntsev raised his cap and waved it. Recognized as friends, the four quickly came abreast. The eight carriers lowered two stretchers to the ground.

The stretchers were made of withes plaited between two poles, and little blocks of wood served as legs. Only quick peasant hands and quick peasant axes could have improvised them out in the forest. Yaroslav would never have thought it possible.

On the rear stretcher lay a dead body—a burly man, his face hidden by a white handkerchief knotted at the corners. He wore a colonel's epaulets. The other stretcher was occupied by a lieutenant with one trouser leg cut away and a heavily bandaged knee. The ten who could walk were all rankers, not a sergeant among them, and almost all of an age, reservists. By now their faces could be seen in the gray-blue dawn light, pinched and haggard, some caked with dried blood. They were all dirty and bedraggled. The eight stretcher-bearers had not shed other burdens. They all had their rifles and bulging pouches at their belts—some more than one. The two sentries were even more heavily laden.

Where had they come from? Who were they? Vorotyntsev and Lieutenant Ofrosimov exchanged greetings. The lieutenant's arms and the whole upper part of his body were uninjured, he could give orders, he could shoot, he could do everything except walk. He was a rough-looking fellow with a pitch-black woolly mop. He spoke hoarsely, not altogether coherently, and rather reluctantly, as though he was tired of telling his story, as though his party had been repeatedly halted and made to account for themselves on their way through the forest. He propped himself up on his elbow but was still too close to the ground, and Vorotyntsev squatted down beside him. Not one of Ofrosimov's soldiers moved aside as they should have done while the officers talked. They stood or sat in a tight circle around them, like equal partners, and even put a word in here and there. (Quite right, Yaroslav thought. That was how it should be among soldiers. They shared the risk of death equally. They should share everything else.)

They all belonged to the Dorogobuzh Regiment, which had been left behind to cover the rear of its corps two days earlier. They had held the enemy back till darkness fell, with bayonets mainly—they were short of cartridges. (They knew now that cartridges are more precious even than bread and had loaded themselves with ammunition dropped along the way.) Most of the regiment had met their end there. Perhaps a dozen men to a company had survived. Perhaps fewer.

They had vowed to carry their regimental commander, Colonel Kabanov, home to Russia and bury him there.

They had nothing more to say, neither the morose lieutenant on the stretcher nor his soldiers. The lieutenant was the sort of officer Yaroslav disliked: a gambler, a foulmouth, a teller of unfunny dirty jokes—one look at him told you everything. But how those soldiers must love him, to stagger along wheezing under their load, stopping now and then to get their breath. What heroes they were! What a fight it must have been—bayonets against machine guns and cannon! Yaroslav found it too much for his imagination.

They had said all they meant to say. They stood or sat a minute longer in a silent huddle, then took up their positions to carry the stretchers. But instead of going their own way they lingered hopefully for one more minute. Yaroslav was longing for his beloved colonel to take these men of the Dorogobuzh Regiment under his wing too. They would never manage alone; and what would it cost him?

Vorotyntsev, who had a bloody scratch on his own jaw, was affected less by their trusting looks than by the hope that they had more to tell him about the battle. He unfolded the map on the pine needles and cones, and his hands and thoughts groped for the unknown regiment which had perished far away.

"Is that where you made your stand? Which way did you come? How many versts from here?"

The soldiers answered before the lieutenant could speak: "Could be forty . . ." "Might be more." (Forty versts! Carrying their two officers! Surely their faith and their strength deserved encouragement!)

The lieutenant couldn't make much of the map, he had been without one for so long. He had known only where Darethen lay, and moved southward from it with the aid of his compass, making for the narrow passage between the lakes through which they had advanced earlier. The soldiers' interpolations helped: they had come through a mixed oak and pine forest, all hillocks; after they had crossed "the line," there was a ruined farmhouse, a long wood, a neck of land all overgrown, a village with a church, a river, which they had forded. Farther on, Russian troops had crossed their path, thousands and thousands—the place was black with them; only . . .

Only these men from the dead Dorogobuzh Regiment no longer felt that they had anything to do with their corps: they had discharged their debt to it for the rest of the war. On that Feast of the Assumption they had already sojourned in the land of the dead, and those whose legs were still working were free to depart whenever they pleased. They had covered the withdrawal of all the others with their unarmored bodies once already and owed them nothing more. They did not say it in so many words, perhaps they hadn't consciously thought it, but it stood out in the words they spoke, and in those they kept back, in their surprising readiness to discuss things with a strange colonel over their lieutenant's head, and in the way they had carried those two stretchers without a murmur through forty versts of bristling backwoods (thirty as the crow flies, but more than forty with all the twists and turns). So they had not merged with their former corps, but evidently crossed its route surreptitiously and continued through the forest according to their own separate plan, with no one giving orders and no sergeant to chivvy them along, certainly not on Ofrosimov's orders, because he would not have ordered them to carry him, disabled as he was, forty versts on their shoulders. Whatever might have passed between them before the last three days—mutual recriminations, resentment, antipathy—had been cauterized by that deadly day.

They had kept their secret until then (from whom were they concealing it?). They were also carrying the colors of the Dorogobuzh Regiment. Wrapped around the lieutenant's body.

Yaroslav felt a lump in his throat. He envied Ofrosimov: there was a man who knew how to merge with the people! That was what he had hoped to do himself when he joined the army. But his crack soldier Kramchatkin had proved to be an idiot and a hopeless shot, while Vyushkov was a rogue and a thief. If he had dared, Yaroslav would have plucked the colonel's sleeve and whispered there and then, "Let's take them with us! What noble hearts they have!"

The colonel apparently needed no prompting. He folded the map and asked loudly, "When did you eat last, boys? Want a bite?"

They mumbled yes.

"That's fine. Less for us to carry. Get over there, under the trees, all of you, and take the lieutenant, you can't stay out in the open. Arseni!

Divide up the meat, all of it." Blagodarev looked at him, arched his eyebrows, coughed, wondering if he had heard correctly. He dragged his gypsy bundle to one side, knelt beside it, untied it, and began hacking off pieces of meat with his slaughterer's knife and handing them around.

"You've had a rough time of it, pals. I can see that!"

The Dorogobuzh party were ravenously hungry; a shoulder of beef wouldn't have made them a breakfast. Luckily there was more.

Meanwhile Vorotyntsev left them and lifted the handkerchief from the dead man's face. Yaroslav also felt an urge to go over and look: the hero was so remote now from all living things, but his face still perhaps bore traces of what he had felt as he rallied the Dorogobuzh Regiment for its last attack. But he was too shy to intrude.

The sky above the pines was turning blue, and the lingering wisps of cloud were touched with pink. Another serene and sunny morning, innocent of war. No shooting could be heard nearby, only a vague rumble in the distance.

"I've got a feeling you're from somewhere around Tambov," a middle-aged man with a bristly beard and a thoughtful expression said to Arseni. "Which district?"

"Central," Arseni, still kneeling, replied with his usual readiness.

The beard expressed surprise, as far as decorum allowed—his manner was that of a literate person.

"Which canton? Which village?"

"I'm from Kamenka," Arseni said happily.

"From Kamenka? Whose boy are you?"

"Blagodarev's."

"Which Blagodarev? Not Yelisei Nikiforovich?"

"The same! I'm his youngest," Arseni said with a grin.

"Well, well." Arseni's older compatriot looked at him approvingly, stroking his beard in a dignified fashion, forgetting that he was a common soldier.

"I know you, then. Do you know Grigori Naumovich Pluzhnikov?"

"I should say I do!" Arseni sounded almost offended. " 'Dad' we all call him—he's a clever one! Where are you from?"

"I'm from Tugoluki."

"Tugoluki!" Arseni threw his arms out, inviting all who heard to marvel. "Always get good horses there. We know, we've bought a few."

"My name's Luntsov, Kornei Luntsov."

"You've got five hundred households in Tugoluki, so I don't know everybody."

The soldiers all smiled, delighted that the two groups had suddenly become blood brothers. If you come from neighboring villages it doesn't matter a bit that you belong to different regiments.

"There's another fellow from Tambov with us—Kachkin over there."

Luntsov pointed to a morose hog of a man who looked about thirty. His head was broad, his shoulders excessively wide, his chest and back seen sideways looked like a cartwheel. Fieldwork had rounded his breast. There was nothing womanish about him, though—put him to the plow and you would need no horse.

"Only he's from the other end, from Inokovo."

Arseni didn't mind even Inokovo. "You get there through Vorona, don't you?"

"Hey, Averyan, here's a lad from the next canton."

Kachkin frowned even to express approval.

"He's what I call a neighbor," he said. "I like his grub." He screwed up his eyes, which were small enough to begin with, but sharp. "Chuck me your knife."

"What for?"

"To carve a few Germans up."

"That's what I want it for."

"You've got more than one."

True, Arseni had brought some spares along. But ought he to give them to soldiers of another unit? He turned toward his colonel.

Vorotyntsev took one look at Kachkin's wheel-like chest and back and said, "Give it to him."

Arseni didn't stand up to hand it over, didn't hold it out to him. He remained on his knees some eight steps from Kachkin, brandished the knife, and flung it so that it narrowly missed another man's shoulder, grazed a protruding pine root, and stood upright in the ground near Kachkin's foot.

Kachkin kept still, and didn't move his foot.

"You'll do," he said as he pulled the knife out of the ground. "You could pass for a Tambov boy anywhere."

He held the knife up to the light, looking along the blade from the point.

"Anybody here from Kostroma?" Vorotyntsev asked.

No one. One from Voronezh. Two from Novgorod.

The colonel scanned their faces, lingering on each one. The man who looked like a huffy gander was no use. But that keen, friendly-looking chap was obviously eager to stand up, tell all he knew, and answer questions.

"Where are you from?"

He jumped up, beaming.

"Archangel, sir, Pinega district. Near where the monastery of Artemi Pravedny is—maybe you've heard of it?"

"Sit down, sit down." He looked around again, and saw a reservist with enormous eyes and the sort of beard you comb with a harrow. "What about you?"

The man answered without rising, as though it were a casual conversation between equals. "From Olonets." He chewed as deliberately as he spoke, gazing calmly about him.

Vorotyntsev seemed preoccupied. "Finished eating? There's water farther on, a pool. How are your feet?" They answered, but his mind was on something else. "If you want to, you can come with us," he said noncommittally.

Kharitonov smiled happily. It had to be that way, of course!

"We shall have to get out by night," Vorotyntsev explained, looking more and more preoccupied. His eyes avoided the lieutenant—they were busy examining the soldiers' faces: the man from Olonets, Luntsov, Kachkin. "And it'll have to be tonight. We need to cross the highroad. That's going to be complicated. And once across we shall probably have to run for it."

Lenartovich was sitting on a log at some distance, his mind working busily, looking at Vorotyntsev in alarm. He had made up his mind too quickly that this was an intelligent man. Had he taken leave of his senses? How could they run for it on the other side of the highroad carrying this lieutenant on the stretcher? And why lug that corpse around, as though they were performing some idiotic ritual? They'd be shot, the whole lot of them. Why sacrifice the living for a dead man? Surely he wouldn't take them along just as they were?

Yaroslav, on the contrary, was delighted with it all, deeply moved by their unreasoning obstinacy, their determination to carry the dead man with them, not to leave their regimental commander behind on foreign soil, even in death.

Yaroslav understood too why the colonel had hesitated: they were a strange group, somehow not altogether soldierly; mutual trust seemed to have taken the place of discipline among them. The group was not commanded by Lieutenant Ofrosimov, it somehow commanded itself, which was why the soldiers, not their officer, had to be asked.

Vorotyntsev looked at them all in turn. The soldiers were silent.

Of course, thought Lenartovich, that was the difficulty! The lieutenant couldn't tell them to ditch the colonel while they were carrying *him* all that way. If he'd undermined their naïve idea of what was right they might have left him behind as well. But Vorotyntsev was free to make them bury the dead man, and then they could all think again about carrying the lieutenant. The men of the Dorogobuzh Regiment sat higgledy-piggledy, some on tree stumps, some on the ground, some on greatcoat rolls; it would have looked like a village assembly but for the pyramid of rifles. While Vorotyntsev, the efficient, self-confident, inflexible colonel, stood dithering, feet wide apart, arms folded, peering from under the peak of his cap. Peering at the Dorogobuzh men. Saying nothing.

The soldiers were also silent. Some of them looked, not at the colonel, but at the ground or at the stretchers some distance away.

When the colonel had studied all those faces, once more his eyes rested on Kornei Luntsov, who stroked as much of his bristly gray beard as one hand could cover and asked earnestly, "How many more versts is it to Russia, Your Honor?"

Dolts! They seemed to think the Germans couldn't get at their precious Russia! They didn't think about machine guns, only versts. If the colonel gives in to them, thought Sasha, I shall have to leave this bunch.

Kachkin was tossing a crooked bit of root from hand to hand. Do we, don't we, do we, don't we . . . ?

Vorotyntsev again searched the eyes of the man from Olonets—they were like still pools—and snapped out of his indecision.

"Right, off we go!" he ordered crisply. "Ensign!" He looked quizzically at Lenartovich's arrogantly held head. "You and I will relieve two of the dead man's stretcher-bearers."

Sasha was transfixed. A nonsensical game, but there was no way out of it, it was no good arguing. He shook his head incredulously. He shrugged his shoulders. He rose slowly, plodded reluctantly to the stretchers. These idiots and their funeral cortege!

Kharitonov sprang anxiously to attention. "Let me help, Colonel!" But Vorotyntsev made a gesture of refusal.

He and Lenartovich took hold of the poles at the front and lifted the stretcher, more or less in unison with those behind. They were of the same height, and they fell into step with the others as they moved off so as not to rock the stretchers. It was not a heavy load for four men, but an awkward one, and it would be easy to stumble.

Although the colonel had given him an unfriendly welcome the day before and was obviously suspicious of him, Sasha himself had decided overnight that meeting these companions was a piece of luck. This could well be the man to get him back safely. He had been having such an exhausting time of it, continually on the move and in constant danger. He had reached the limit of his endurance. Now, in the hands of this strong and clever man, he was cushioned against alarming reality. No need to plan, no need to worry, just do what, and go where, he was told. Besides, Sasha saw at once that this colonel with the high forehead was a very unusual army officer: he appeared to be a genuinely intelligent and educated man. But if that was so, why had he not used his authority instead of giving in to the ignorant, unspoken behest of these barbarous reservists from the uncouth backwoods of Russia? Carrying the regimental colors home—a bit of rag from the quartermaster's store, utterly useless, just a joke nowadays—was one thing, at least they weighed nothing; though really of course it was just a good excuse for Ofrosimov to make them carry *him*—but . . .

"Colonel, sir! Why should we carry a dead man? It's simply absurd."

They were in front, and even a third person immediately behind would have had to bend his head low and sway in time with them to hear.

Vorotyntsev did not contradict him, and Sasha grew bolder.

"Surely there's no place for this sort of thing in a modern war?"

He had clever, quick eyes which would see through any stupid conventional army formula. Vorotyntsev, though, had a tone of voice to make even those eyes blink.

"Modern warfare will be waiting for us on the highroad, Ensign. You'd better make up your mind in advance what you're going to shoot with. You won't kill many with that popgun."

Perhaps he was right, but it was still an evasion. Sasha tried to bring him back to the point.

"You're making me carry this corpse, and later on you'll order me to carry that lieutenant, who is certainly a Black Hundreder—I can see it in his face."

Sasha expected the colonel to get angry. He didn't. He answered as abruptly as before, and as though he was thinking of something else. "Yes, I shall, Ensign. Political differences are just ripples on a pond."

Sasha, astonished, stumbled and shifted his shoulder to steady the pole. Two or three lines of argument were open to him, but attack was the best plan. "What about national differences, then? Aren't they ripples on the water? Aren't we fighting because of them? What sorts of differences do you consider important?"

"The difference between decency and indecency, Ensign," Vorotyntsev returned, still more abruptly. He raised his map case with his free, outside hand, undid it, and walked on, looking now at the ground, now at the map.

It wasn't just a matter of principle, in fact it wasn't that at all; carrying the stretcher wasn't at all easy, it was really hard work, it felt as though two men were lying on top there, the pole cut into your shoulder and made you want to stoop . . . One of the soldiers at the rear called out to him, "Keep it higher, sir."

Sasha had spent his whole life developing his mind, which was what really mattered, and had had no time for his body. He had become feebler than ever in the last few days. Clenching his teeth, he picked out a tree, told himself that he would carry his load just so far and ask to be relieved. Then he added another length.

Meanwhile, they found themselves on the edge of a clearing to their left, and the sun blazed down on them almost unhindered from over the distant treetops. They turned into another cutting, dark between close walls of pine trees. The path began to rise steadily, it was harder all the time to carry the stretcher, Sasha's heart was pounding, but the colonel steered away from the path up a still steeper incline and through the pines. True, the forest was rather thinner here, brushwood and undergrowth had been cleared away, and the going was easy over a soft carpet of needles, in which pine cones were the only bumps. Sasha endured it a bit longer—he couldn't very well give up while they were climbing. When they reached the top the colonel just beat him to it.

"Halt! Lower the stretcher."

They were on an exposed ridge in the depths of the forest, obliquely lit by the morning sun. The pines were more widely spaced here, and chinks of sky showed through the caps of heavy foliage held aloft on spreading branches by the red-brown trunks.

The early sun was already warming the trunks, and it would not leave this spot until it finished its full round in late evening. Squirrels must love the place, and small animals would make their way there when the world was first drying out in the spring: the snow would disappear very quickly here, there would never be puddles. Behind them, in the direction from which they had come, the ground fell away in a broad, gradual slope down to a hollow no less spacious: if you wanted to you could lie on your side and roll all the way downhill over clean pine needles between the clean pines.

An isolated hillock stood out from the ridge, and that was where they carried the stretchers.

Vorotyntsev gazed around without a word, and gave the others time to do the same. Then he addressed the men of the Dorogobuzh Regiment, no longer diffidently asking them but telling them firmly what must be done.

"Men! We shall bury Colonel Kabanov here. We shall never find a better place. And the Germans aren't heathens."

He looked at them all in turn, looked again, and quietly added, "It has to be done. Otherwise we won't get out of this."

He could not have said it and they would not have accepted it when they first met in the clearing by the gray light of dawn, but here, on this cheerful eminence caressed by the morning sun, with the fresh scent of warmed resin in their nostrils, and from one who had helped to carry the dead man, it found acceptance, it suddenly seemed right. This unknown colonel had dispelled the brooding shadow from their faces—the shadow of guilt? Guilt for what? Not dying when so many others had? They showed no sign of resistance.

The man from Olonets took off his cap; he turned to the east and crossed himself devoutly; he bowed low till he was bent double, and said with a heavy sigh, "God will forgive us." Some of the others also crossed themselves.

Vorotyntsev did not hesitate for a moment. "Arseni!" he called. "Where's your spade? Get started. Right here." He pointed at the hillock.

Blagodarev, who was equipped for everything and had every skill, uncomplainingly unstrapped his trenching tool and climbed the hillock (there would be room for them all to gather on top) as though he had come so far just to do this very job, knelt down—with his long legs he would have been uncomfortable standing up—and dug in at a spot free of roots.

The Dorogobuzh men also produced two spades. Lumpish Kachkin, who had been ready for action before any of them, bowled himself uphill and began, also kneeling, to dig and throw out soil with furious energy, never pausing for breath.

"Good man, Kachkin, that's digging!" Vorotyntsev remarked.

Kachkin paused and knelt there, grinning. "Kachkin knows all the tricks, sir. I could do it this way if I wanted." And suddenly he was clumsy, fat, feeble, breathless, scarcely able to scrape the ground and lift a dribble of soil on the tip of his shovel. "And nobody would ever catch on!" His wild boar eyes flashed. Then he was himself again, furiously gouging, and the soil flew through the air as though from the magic shovel that erects palaces overnight all by itself.

Yes, Kachkin could do it either way.

Meanwhile Luntsov and a mate went off to cut branches and plait a lid for the stretcher so that it could serve as a coffin.

The forest was so big and so dense that the war raging all around it had not so much as peeped into its depths all that week: not a trench slit, not a shell hole, not a wheel track, not an empty cartridge case to be seen. The peaceful morning was brighter and hotter now, the warm pine scent was growing stronger, the birds, taking their August rest, called to each other in muted voices or flew silently from tree to tree. The men too were wrapped in a feeling of ease and security, as though there were no encirclement and once the burial was over they would go their different ways home.

The grave was ready, and so was the coffin lid. But should there not be some form of burial service? Some scrap of requiem? Vorotyntsev had heard many of them, but he could not repeat the prayers or tell anyone else what to say. That was the business of priests not of officers, and the words had not stayed with him.

Arseni, who was at the colonel's side, stretching to ease his aching back, caught his hesitant look and read it correctly: he had a remarkably quick understanding which owed nothing to education. Moreover, a tacit division of rights and responsibilities had been established between the two of them in the past three impossibly full days such as would normally be unthinkable between a colonel and a ranker, especially given the difference in their ages.

Not a word was spoken, nobody ordered him to do it and he did not offer to, but Arseni, who had already appeared in so many different roles and seemed at home in all of them, now undertook another. He straightened up and an austere dignity borrowed from who knows where appeared in his face and his voice.

He took off his cap and flung it behind him without looking. Frowning imperiously and addressing no one in particular, he asked in a voice unrecognizably solemn, "What was the name of the departed?"

The soldiers, of course, couldn't tell him—"Your Honor, sir" was supposed to be enough for them. But for Ofrosimov they would never have known. From his stretcher down on the ground he answered the mysteriously exalted ranker, "His name was Vladimir Vasilievich."

At this Blagodarev strode over to the dead man, bent down, and removed the handkerchief from his face, something he would not have dared to do five minutes earlier. Throwing out his chest and holding his head high, he turned toward the east, toward the sun, and intoned in the manner of a church deacon, in a strong, clear voice that rose to the tops of the lofty pines: "Let–us–pray–unto–the–Lord!"

He played his ecclesiastical part with such authority, such power, and such precision that they needed no second invitation. The man from Olonets, Luntsov, and two others understood immediately, crossed themselves, bowed to the east, each where he stood, and gave the response: "Lord have mer-er-er-ercy!"

Arseni joined in, singing loudest of all, abandoning his role of deacon for that of choir leader. Then the deacon's sonorous boom again. Rhythm, intonation, recitative were all astonishingly correct. Vorotyntsev could not join in, but he recognized the words beyond doubt.

". . . for God's servant Vladimir, newly departed this life, for his repose, his peace, for his blessed memory, let us pray unto the Lord!"

By now they were all under the spell, officers and men, and gathering around the dead man, they bared their heads, faced east and sang: "Lord have mer-er-er-ercy!"

Every man has so much more in him than meets the eye. This young peasant, for instance, from the dark recesses of Tambov; you risked death together for three days, and but for this curious chance you might have lost sight of him forever without ever being told, without ever guessing, without ever considering the possibility that he had sung in a church choir, perhaps for many years, that his ear was attuned to the liturgy, that it was an important part of his life, that he loved it and knew it by heart. Every note and every pause was accurate, every word was given its full weight, every intonation was true. "Let us pray unto the Lord for those who are called to stand before the dread throne of His glory . . ."

They had brought Ofrosimov closer, setting him down with his face to the east. He was able to cross himself and join in the singing. Kharitonov too, who had now seen the hidden face of the hero, sang with them and felt the tears welling up, liberating tears: "Lord have mer-cy upo-o-on them!"

Again the deacon's voice boomed out powerfully, unawed by the alien forest: "That the Lord our God may establish his soul in the place of light, the place of plenty, the place of peace, the dwelling place of all the just, let us pray unto the Lord!"

That prayer had been partly granted already: a place of light and peace had been made ready for the body.

They were all facing east, each man could see only the backs of those in front of him. One man at the rear was invisible to all of them—Lenartovich. He did not once join in the responses, he wore a wry smile, but he had bared his head. In front of them all Blagodarev alternately bent and straightened his strong, supple back, a broad back you would have said if it had not been so long. He crossed himself fervently with bold, sweeping movements of the long powerful arm which was as ready to fight for his life in the middle of the night as it was for his day's work.

"Praying that he and all of us may obtain God's mercy, the Kingdom of Heaven, and the remission of all our sins, let us dedicate one another and our lives wholly unto Christ our God!"

And soaring above the sky, beyond the sun, straight to the throne of the All-Highest, from the breasts of fourteen men, their voices now effortlessly blending, rose—not their petition, but their act of sacrifice, of self-abnegation.

"Unto Thee, O Lord . . ."

[5 1]

Though they had lost their High Command, and troops of all branches had merged in a confused mass, blocking the forest roads and spilling over the verges, the Russians could still move freely in the depths of the forest. But as soon as they showed themselves in a large clearing or near a village they were fired upon. Every volley provoked a reply. Sometimes Russians took other Russians for Germans and opened fire on them.

At dawn on 30 August the head of the disorderly column, all that was left of yesterday's 13th Corps, ran into cannon and machine-gun fire as it was about to leave the forest five hundred meters from Kaltenborn. There was no agreed joint command, but Colonel Pervushin happened to be up in front, and helped by a motley assortment of volunteers, he lined up the first guns to hand on the fringe of the forest. They opened fire and he advanced on the village with a mixed company flying the flag of the Neva Regiment. The Germans fled, leaving four fieldpieces behind.

Conquered Kaltenborn, however, was a clearing one square verst in area, and the Russians had to plunge into the forest again. Two versts farther on they emerged near another village and were fired on this time by enemy troops commanding all the roads and forest paths. Pervushin's soldierly qualities had survived long years of service, and he it was who inspired the next breakthrough. He and his men were so much part of each other that he could never lead them into an impossible venture, and where he led they could not but follow. In the van with Pervushin was a mixed bunch of men from the Neva, Narva, Koporye, and Zvenigorod regiments. Two depleted batteries followed, with Chernega somewhere among them.

Once again, they positioned their handful of machine guns and cannon, raked the enemy with a sudden burst, and charged as they had at Kaltenborn. Pervushin, in the lead again, received a bayonet wound. Once again the sudden Russian thrust was so powerful that the German covering force, which was in regimental strength, fled precipitately, leaving behind many machine guns and twenty field guns, some complete with carriages.

Pervushin's advance guard spent the whole day in "toilsome fray," as our ancestors used to call it. The road to safety was still a long one, through many versts of forest, with German covering forces, roadblocks, and barbed wire at every turn; machine guns along the cuttings and cannon at intersections lay in wait for the disorderly rabble of helpless victims. As soon as they showed themselves the Germans showered them with every kind of projectile. Each little success seemed only to make things worse for the Russians. Their strength was ebbing, they were getting hungrier, thirstier (the wells had been blocked), their ammunition was running out, they had more wounded on their hands, the ambushing forces were stronger all the time. Their only hope was a bayonet charge. It was now well past noon. The column, dense in the morning, was melting fast. Men were losing all hope, all reason for acting. Before the last desperate dash, Pervushin, bayoneted twice already, called out to . . .

S C R E E N

= an ensign carrying the regimental colors, furled.
A man who would fall with the flag sooner than yield.

= Pervushin, with one wound bandaged and the other not, waves his uninjured arm: remove the colors!

Gunfire. Shells burst nearby.

= The standard is adorned with a St. George's Cross, fixed in a notch at the tip of the pole.

= The standard-bearer is reluctant. His heart aches. He crosses himself.
He detaches the colors and hands the pole
to a helper. The helper breaks off the top.
What is left is just a stick, and he throws it away.
= They walk off, downcast, carrying a shovel.
= They start digging. Dig a hole.
Look around for landmarks, memorable trees.
The treetops shudder
as shells explode round about. A tremendous din. Listening to this music,
= Pervushin sits on a tree stump.
Just sits there, thinking.

Close-up. We see

= Pervushin, moving cautiously because of his wounds. The blood on his face, his neck, his tunic.
The hole in his cap. His cap is tilted, not at the regulation angle.
His fierce mustaches are drooping. There is no defiance and no humor now in his wide-eyed stare, only desperation.
He speaks to no one, and no one comes near him. These few minutes of reflection may be the last in his fifty-four years of life.

Explosions. Guns rumble.
He turns his head
to look at the standard-bearer. Who reports that he has carried out his orders. Buried the colors. Buried a piece of his own heart.
= With an effort (having to rally *himself* is something new to him) Pervushin calls:
"Staff Captain! Staff Captain Grokholets!"
= And here is Grokholets, already known to us, capless, so that we now see how bald he is—quite hairless except for a close-cropped island on his crown and two at his temples. He is obviously not at all young, but surprisingly agile and keen. These lean men are often like that. His mustaches are as tightly twirled as ever—but perhaps in despair.
Pervushin speaks to him:
"Right, shall we give it a try? Collect all those who can hold a rifle. Give the order to the machine gunners."
Grokholets:
"Right. Let's do it. Now. Nothing to it. We can manage."
Pervushin rises. He is no mean height.
And he looks awesome, a father figure! They will follow him!

He flourishes his cap—twice—
= to the gunners. There are two cannon ready for battle,
but drawn well back behind the trees. Enlarged crews cluster around to roll them out.
We see Chernega among them, stripped to the waist. His shoulder muscles are snaky patterns molded in his flesh.
His head still looks like a cheese with a clipped mustache, but his expression is ferocious:
"Get a good grip, boys! Let 'em roll!"
And roll they do.
Guns, feet, crash, crunch, stamp through the undergrowth. A desperate voice—his own, yet not his:
"Volley . . . fire!"
They fire! Russian machine guns join in from somewhere nearby. Such as are left let loose with everything they have.

Rear view

= We see through the trees at the edge of the forest Russian troops charging, threading the pine saplings, trampling the underbrush.
The subalterns, of course, are in the van, their dress swords held quivering overhead,
a desperate gesture, which holds no threat for the enemy, but is meant for their own men: Don't drop behind, boys, we're all in this together!

Now we are at their side, running with them

= Not charging, stumbling.
They raise a cheer:
"*Ah-ah-ah*"—the ghost of a "*hurrah.*"
They carry rifles with fixed bayonets but can scarcely heave them along, let alone stick them in anybody.
One goes head over heels.
Killed? No, lying down for a rest behind the stripling pines: Go on, leave me here, I'm finished, I'll await my fate where I am.
Even the officers' swords tremble as though some force were pressing them earthward—any moment now they will drop.
Rattle of machine guns.
= Our men are falling! Dropping their rifles and falling. Look, one rifle has plunged bayonet first into the ground and stands upright, butt swaying.
= Grokholets, running. An endearingly comic figure. We recognize him from the rear by his baldness.
Will they bring him down? He's still running!

= Out in front Pervushin's tall figure has overtaken all the rest.
He is his menacing self again.

Back me up!

With his fierce mustaches
and his rifle at the ready. Bayonet fixed.
Now he has stumbled
over a wire, too close to the ground to be visible.
= And out of concealment, out of his foxhole,
a sturdy German confronts him, plants his
bayonet in the towering, the terrible colonel!
Stabs three times! It takes that much.
Colonel Pervushin crashes to the ground.

Machine guns, relentless machine guns
= thin,
halt,
turn
the Russian attack.
= On the fringe of the forest ferocious Chernega, Chernega of the bulging muscles, sees that the time has come to stop firing and fade.
Jumping up on the wheel of a cannon,
he unscrews the sights, and at a sign from him
the crews remove the locks from the guns
= and run, carrying them,
into the forest,
deep into the forest! Back the way they came.

[52]

General Klyuev himself was neither at the head of the corps with Pervushin nor among the rear guard, where the Sofia Regiment was holding its own in the battle among the trees. He kept to the middle of the column, creating confusion, darting from place to place, wasting the men's strength by swinging them around every German blockade. Since the German ring seemed to him unbreakable, there was no one to rally that half of the corps for a breakthrough.

The remnants of the Russian artillery operated independently, changing position, firing over open sights whenever they spotted the enemy, then lugging their guns away or abandoning them as they fled. When the Grünfliess Forest relaxed its hold, a strip of bogland, with many drainage ditches running down to a river, barred the way of the Russians. Artillery and supply wagons sank into the low-lying bog, and although the road was now within sight straight ahead, only three versts away, the troops veered eastward again in the direction of the elusive Willenberg, hoping to cross dry-shod. The stream of retreating men dwindled as hundreds, thousands, vanished from one hour to the next. The disorderly crowd around Klyuev spilled out into the clearing near Saddek, came under shrapnel fire, and reeled back into the forest.

This was too much for the commander of the encircled central corps. *To avoid unnecessary bloodshed*, General Klyuev—with twenty batteries that had been hauled and mauled all over Prussia—General Klyuev—with tens of thousands of men scattered about the forest, against six German battalions in that neighborhood—General Klyuev ordered white flags to be shown.

Golden words, those—"to avoid bloodshed." Any human action can be wrapped in golden phrases. "To avoid bloodshed"—so noble, so humane! What could anyone possibly say against it? Only, perhaps, that if your object is to avoid bloodshed you should have the foresight not to become a general.

There were no white flags anyway. They are not part of normal issue—to complement regimental colors.

This happened in a clearing, near the edge of the forest.

SCREEN

= The clearing is choked with every imaginable wheeled vehicle—supply wagons, gun carriages, ambulances, in no sort of order, all pointed nowhere.

Two-wheelers and vans carrying wounded men,
nurses, and doctors.

Carts piled with anything and everything—weapons, ammunition, clothes, some of them probably looted from the Germans.

Infantrymen standing, sitting, changing their boots, adjusting their equipment.

Tight knots of mounted Cossacks.

Fieldpieces separated from their batteries.

= A rabble army, and doomed.

= Now we see a group of generals on horseback,
escorted by Cossacks.

= General Klyuev, struggling to preserve his dignity. General Klyuev's imperious stare, the awesome lift of his eyebrows. (Without which the men might stop obeying him!)

"Sergeant Major! Take off your shirt!

Put your undershirt on a lance and ride slowly toward the enemy."

= The sergeant major does as he is told. Gives his lance to his neighbor, removes his shirt, his undershirt . . .

= Now he is dressed again, and his undershirt is a white flag at the end of a lance. Will he ride?

But what is that buzz?

= The Cossacks are muttering.

= The sergeant major looks at them and stays where he is.

Klyuev also turns to look.

The buzz dies down.

Klyuev waves his hand,

and the sergeant major rides off with the white flag.

The buzz grows louder.

= From another group of Cossacks a little farther off we hear:

"We could stick it out! Of course we could!"

"Who ever heard of Cossacks surrendering?"

It could be the rogue and ruffian Serga Artyukha, a rotund fellow with his cap awry, who yells from behind somebody's back in an insolent voice meant to carry:

"Stop shilly-shallying!"

= Klyuev in an earsplitting voice, but obviously unsure of himself:

"Who is in charge there?"

= A lithe, well-built officer wearing captain's epaulets without stars rides out, swaying in his saddle. In his set face, his black eyes, there is no sign of respect. He sits motionless. Now he leans sideways, his fingers are on the hilt of his saber:

"Vedernikov, Captain, 40th Don Cossacks!"

He looks at the general, as if wondering whether to add anything.

He doesn't.

More rumblings, more exclamations.

= Klyuev looks around, helplessly—

at the infantry, at the disorderly throng.

Some don't care, some are weak, some quite happy to surrender,

but one soldier cries out, clutching his head—his cap is slipping off (what has become of discipline? what has become of dress?):

"What are you telling us? To give ourselves up? We'll never agree to it!"

A murmur of support

from soldiers near him.

Their lieutenant colonel pushes through the crowd and walks around the carts
toward the mounted general.

He turns

= to look up at Klyuev, like an assassin about to shoot a Tsar. Any moment now he will whip out his pistol. His hand jerks upward.

No—he is only saluting:

"Lieutenant Colonel Sukhachevsky, Aleksopol Regiment! You have taken the 15th Corps under your command! It is your duty to lead us out . . . General."

Looking up at him, through him rather, with a contemptuous, piercing gaze.

= He does not even say "Your Excellency." But Klyuev is not man enough to protest. His head is swimming. He shuts his eyes and opens them again,

Sukhachevsky has not vanished. Hasn't budged an inch.

They must think I don't understand. Must think it's easy for me. All I want is to avoid bloodshed . . .

Well, I'm not going to force them.

"Very well," he says weakly, "those who want to can try to get away. As best they can."

He takes out his handkerchief. Mops his brow. Gazes at the handkerchief.

= A white handkerchief! A large one! A general's handkerchief!

= Taking it by one corner and waving it as a precaution, he urges his horse down the slope at walking pace, to get away from all this unpleasantness with his subordinates,

to surrender,

riding behind the sergeant major with the white shirt.

= His whole staff troop after him, and all those who want a quick end to it trail behind.

Enough is enough! Let's get it over with!

= Near a field hospital

a doctor on horseback calls out an order:

"Attention! The Corps Commander has called on us to surrender. Everybody anywhere near this hospital will lay down his arms at once!"

= A slightly built soldier cradling his rifle asks in bewilderment,

"Where are we supposed to put them?"

"Throw them down under the trees, over there!"

A wounded man in his underwear and heavily bandaged struggles out from under the canopy of a covered wagon:

"Not on your life! Give me your rifle, neighbor."
He wrests the rifle from his startled comrade
and strides off in his underwear, carrying it.
= Others, though, throw their rifles onto
a growing pile under the trees.
= Soldiers' faces—
The faces of the wounded.
A ringing, martial voice:
"Hey, you, Cossacks!"
= It is Captain Vedernikov, twisting his horse's head around toward his men:
"This is no place for us!"
= His Don Cossacks stand up fast! They will not surrender!
A hum of belligerent approval.
Serga Artyukha bares his teeth. We can't help liking him. When shall we see him next?
= Vedernikov gives his orders:
"To horse—everybody! By the right in columns of three, at the gallop—forward!"
He waves his hand and rides off. After him,
forming threes as they go, ride the Cossacks.
= Lieutenant Colonel Sukhachevsky is rather short, and he cannot see comfortably over all those heads, but he too calls out:
"Aleksopol Regiment! . . . Do we surrender? Or do we fight out way out?"
= His men shout back:
"Fight our way out!"
Perhaps they didn't all shout, but the response was firm enough.
Sukhachevsky:
"I'm not forcing anybody. Those who want to go" (he points) *"form fours over there!"*
Soldiers push to the front and fall in.
Some might prefer to stay.
Some are on their last legs.
But they want to be with their comrades.
= Other soldiers crowd around:
"Can we come, Your Honor—Kremenchug Regiment?"
Sukhachevsky, gruff and happy, says,
"Come on then, boys! Fall in, men of the Kremenchug Regiment!"

General Klyuev made a present of thirty thousand prisoners to the enemy, most of them not wounded, but many, it is true, noncombatants.

Lieutenant Colonel Sukhachevsky led twenty-five hundred to safety.

Captain Vedernikov's party fought their way out, taking two German guns in a cavalry skirmish.

[53]

General Blagoveshchensky had read *War and Peace* and, being sixty years old, gray-haired, corpulent, and lethargic, saw himself as a second Kutuzov, only with two good eyes. Like Kutuzov, he was circumspect, cautious, cunning. And like Tolstoy's Kutuzov, he knew that one must never take any abrupt and decisive steps of one's own; that nothing but muddle could ever come of a battle begun before it wants to begin; that warfare always goes its own way, always goes as it must go, irrespective of the plans of mere men; that events follow their inevitable course, and that the best general is the one who refuses to interfere with them. His whole long military career had convinced the general that Tolstoy's views on this subject were correct: nothing was worse than charging in with one's own decisions—people who do that always come to grief.

For the third day and night running, the corps had managed to hold out in a quiet, deserted corner right on the Russian frontier. The Corps Commander had his own little cottage away from his staff, and he found these cramped quarters cozy and reassuring.

Only occasionally did he hear indistinctly the low grumble of distant guns, and he could reasonably hope that the great happenings in Prussia would run their course with no assistance from General Blagoveshchensky and his corps.

His men took their rest unaware that they owed their happy state to their commander's skill in drafting reports. Indeed, Tolstoy himself forgot to mention that a general who refrains from giving orders must be particularly adept at drafting reports; that without positive reports carefully contrived to make peaceful immobility look like hard fighting, battered troops cannot be saved; that without such reports a general cannot be saved; that without such reports a general cannot, like Tolstoy's Kutuzov, *direct his efforts not to killing and destroying people but to saving lives and reducing suffering*.

So it was that in his report for 29 August Blagoveshchensky spoke as if Rikhter's division, reinforced at last by the regiment previously held back, was moving up the next day to take possession of Ortelsburg (abandoned in a panic two days earlier to nobody in particular), where there were large enemy forces, at least one division (there were in fact two companies and two squadrons), while Komarov's division would hold its ground to the left in echelon formation (an important term much in vogue with Russian strategists—no military document looked professional without it). The report also put a high gloss on the perambulations of Tolpygo's cavalry division. Blagoveshchensky could confidently count on getting through 30 August without unwelcome excitement.

On the morning of the 30th Rikhter's division, which had not so far tasted battle, moved on half-deserted Ortelsburg, observing all the rules in the tactical manuals, began their preparatory bombardment, and were already closing in for the attack (they would certainly have taken the town) when suddenly at eleven o'clock, five hours late, the early-morning order from Army Group HQ hit them: Blagoveshchensky's corps must go to the rescue of others now threatened with destruction, and for this purpose move not on Ortelsburg, almost due north, but toward Willenberg, almost due west. "The Commander-in-Chief expects you to carry out energetically the task assigned and to make contact as soon as possible with General Samsonov."

Just what Blagoveshchensky had feared all along! The tornado had touched them as it blew itself out—but even at the last moment it might be lethal.

Still, his operational instructions could be interpreted freely. Deployed as they were at present, it was as though his troops had been approaching Moscow from Ryazan and were ordered to go to Kaluga instead. What more convenient plan than to withdraw toward Ryazan first and make for Kaluga later? Blagoveshchensky therefore ordered Rikhter's victorious division, which was already entering Ortelsburg, to abandon the captured town, and instead of moving leftward toward Willenberg, to withdraw fifteen versts to the right so that it would have a long run-up for its jump at the place.

Even before these maneuvers Blagoveshchensky had sent a vigorous dispatch to Army Group HQ: "A mounted patrol has been sent to Neidenburg to locate General Samsonov, and another to Chorzele to make contact with the 23rd Corps. No information available as yet. Am engaging the enemy at Ortelsburg, with the object of withdrawing to a line . . . with my HQ at . . . (HQ staff, of course, would draw farther back) *in order to* (!) operate in the direction of Willenberg."

Tolpygo's cavalry division would naturally be part of the attacking force used—it must at least be moved back to the place from which it had returned without authorization that morning. But General Tolpygo explained in a no less lengthy and skillful report of his own that his division was tired and had only just unsaddled its horses and could not "at present return to that difficult task." Blagoveshchensky issued another order in writing, which Tolpygo, also in writing, again refused to obey. Only the third order, accompanied this time by threats, was accepted, and they began saddling up.

Now that the complicated part of the maneuver was safely under way somebody had to be sent directly to Willenberg, for the sake of appearances. The combined force under Nechvolodov seemed very suitable for this purpose. Blagoveshchensky had previously condemned Nechvolodov's bad habit of sticking his neck out—only yesterday he had disturbed the day of rest by begging permission to make such a swoop, but had been told to await orders. This was the sort of subordinate Blagoveshchensky found most intolerable, and he did his best to punish such people by laying heavier duties on them. To make things worse, Nechvolodov was *a writer*, ever ready to interfere and pronounce on matters that were none of his business. Obviously he was ideally suited to the dangerous task of leading the advance party.

Nechvolodov was dispatched with the Ladoga Regiment and two batteries after midday on 30 August. His orders were to make haste, in the knowledge that the main body of the division would set out later.

[54]

Nechvolodov's prime characteristic was not speed but doggedness. He had often found that the dogged man arrives before the erratic fast mover who is tempted by side roads.

His ambition was not a personal one, not a selfish one. At fifty he was a bachelor, with an adopted son whom he was setting up in life with no great strain. He had both the leisure and the personal freedom to pursue an external, suprapersonal ambition, and no land or other property to hinder him. Ever since boyish enthusiasm had led him to cadet school, ever since he had taken the oath as a senior cadet in the year when the Tsar Liberator was vilely murdered, his object had been to serve the Russian throne and Russia. Forty years later this vision of his remained the same—undimmed, undivided, unwavering: nothing had changed except the tempo at which he pursued it. In his youth he had been in a hurry to move mountains single-handed. The routine of a regular officer's training was too slow for him, and he was hardly out of the academy when he put forward a plan for the reform of the General Staff and the War Ministry. That was where his unusually rapid ascent was cut short. That was his first collision with the concerted hostility of his own superiors, the generals, and the Guards. Nechvolodov had taken it for granted that they would make sacrifices to reinforce the Russian army and through it, of course, the Russian throne. He found that even in their circle, though ringing declarations of enthusiasm for the monarchy were customary, genuine devotion to it was unrespectable. Almost to a man, they burned with the fever of self-interest, not the flame of patriotism. The higher you looked, the fewer exceptions you found. They served the Tsar not as God's Anointed but as the giver of gifts. Before Nechvolodov realized this, they had seen through him: he was an alien being in their midst, dangerous precisely because he sought no advantage for himself, and for that reason his activities might be disastrous for his fellow officers. Ever since, they had seen to it that Nechvolodov crawled from rank to rank only by seniority, that he was slowed down by unfavorable reports, and that he carried out orders without modifying them to suit himself. Thus he could not serve the throne by speed, but only by staunchness and, should opportunity arise, by bravery.

In an effort to find some application for his pent-up energy, Nechvolodov took up his unfortunate history of Russia for the common people. He did not feel that Russian history was something separate from his army service, but rather was a shared tradition outside of which his own present service as an officer would be meaningless. He sought inspiration and refreshment for himself in other times, when Russians had a different attitude toward their monarchs, and what he wanted for his readers was to reconvert them to older habits of mind, and so bring his unchanging aim more surely within his grasp. But although his history was noticed in high places, and recommended to both public and army libraries, the author did not see the general public eagerly devouring the book and changing their way of thinking. If Nechvolodov's devotion to the monarchy had seemed extravagant to the generals and alarmed them, it now incurred the ridicule of the educated, who held that Russian history could only arouse derision and disgust—if, of course, it could be said ever to have existed. Nechvolodov's belief that the monarchy was not Russia's ball and chain but her mainstay, that it did not fetter Russia but prevented her from plunging into the abyss, they found utterly absurd. His devotion to the dynasty also rendered him powerless to argue with his critics: whatever happened in the country, he would never venture to condemn the Emperor or those near to him, he could only defend them and explain why what "society" thought bad was in fact good. Years of patient silence had left him more doggedly determined than ever. If he had a soft spot for his Ladoga Regiment, it was because it had shored up the throne during the Moscow rising. Nechvolodov had never served with the regiment himself, and its personnel had changed almost completely since 1905, but he knew some of the veterans and made much of them.

To hold his tongue and be patient was all that Nechvolodov had been able to do in the last two quiet days of the 6th Corps' life. His stubbornness in rear-guard actions had not proved infectious, and now he had been made to endure the misery of inactivity while a major battle was being fought only twenty-five versts away and evidently going badly. The general had ridden more than once to the top of a hill two or three versts away, listened to the rumble of guns, and stared aimlessly through his field glasses.

Now with two wasted days and nights behind him Nechvolodov was ordered to make haste. He did nothing of the kind, but moved off at a normal pace. All his preparations had been made two days earlier. Why should his soldiers have to make up for the dilatoriness of his superiors with forced marches? And who knew how long the main body would take to drag themselves after him? He sent off all his cavalry in a hurry—half a squadron under Cornet Zhukovsky—and that was all.

During the two days before he was let off the leash Nechvolodov had felt unwell, languid, dull. But as soon as he had orders to take the field he started feeling better from one minute to the next. He smiled at his Ladoga Regiment, the only men in the whole corps allowed to fight, and shouted encouragement to the gunners, telling them that they were going to rescue their comrades. Knowing this turned one regiment into two, and two batteries into four. Only their shells were not multiplied. But they no longer had limp generals on their backs, their hands were free, their heads clearer.

Nechvolodov, gangling and silent, on his tall stallion again, feet low in the stirrups, rode at the head of his combined force, which was now the advance guard. One length behind and to one side rode Roshko, his cheerful adjutant: his face was as round and plump as the dumplings he was reared on and shone like a burnished copper kettle.

As they approached Willenberg their road entered a mature pine wood: trees twenty meters high with red-brown trunks, their tops gently swaying against the serene summer sky.

After ten versts or so the firing grew louder—mostly rifles and machine guns, but occasionally a field gun could be heard. What could it mean? Russian troops must be trying to break through under fire. Willenberg was obviously the outer pivotal point of the encircling force, and there might be, must be, Russian troops immediately beyond it. The general's stallion quickened its pace, leaving the foot soldiers behind.

The forest screened Nechvolodov's advance almost as far as Willenberg. There were no Germans around anyway. They were so sure of themselves, so relaxed, that they had posted no troops on the approaches. As they neared the edge of the forest Nechvolodov ordered his men to spread out and sit down while he rode on almost into the open. The cornet and his reconnaissance party had left their horses there with holders and crossed the river on foot. The sun was setting over Willenberg, flooding the spot where Nechvolodov stood with blinding yellow light. He could still see, though, the water meadow in a dip ahead of him, the little river, and beside it a single elevated road, a clear straight road leading to a bridge. An undamaged bridge! The Germans hadn't had the heart to blow up their own property. And there was no guard post this side of the bridge. Did the Germans take their enemy for fools?

The cornet and his scouts had already installed themselves in the first scattered houses on the outskirts and were shooting. Nechvolodov quickly sent a detail with two machine guns over the bridge to join them.

Farther on the houses were closer together, then came the railway station, and immediately beyond it the town proper. There was no way around it to the right—nothing but waterlogged meadows. The way around to the left was cut off by another river, a tributary of the first. But in an hour's time the whole regiment could cross the bridge openly in column of route, with no need to fear enemy fire, and then take up position to attack the town.

Nechvolodov ordered both batteries to take up position on the edge of the forest, to the right and left of the road.

There was shooting on the outskirts of the town nearby. There was shooting on the other side of the town also. The Germans evidently had no firm footing there. It was worse than being caught in pincers. Their pursuit force was facing west and scattered over a big area, little suspecting that they were about to be taken in the rear from the east.

The general's heart thumped with joyous anticipation, and his dour face lit up: a quick and easy victory was within his grasp. He summoned the battalion and battery commanders, and they discussed how they should cross the bridge and who would do what once they were over.

At that point a dragoon came running up with a message from Cornet Zhukovsky. He reported that seven Russian soldiers had broken through from the other side of the town to join him: two strays from the 6th Dragoons, four from the Poltava Infantry Regiment, and one Cossack from the Army Commander's escort. The Cossack asserted that General Samsonov had been killed in an exchange of fire.

Nechvolodov postponed consideration of this news, which might only be a rumor, and seized on the main point: individual soldiers could walk through Willenberg, the place was a sieve! He had only to reach out and take it. The moment had come to smite the leaky barrel with a battering ram! The quicker, the better—the whole front must be in a state of disastrous confusion if soldiers from the Poltava Regiment, which belonged on the opposite flank of the army, had gone so far astray.

He sent the message around the companies: Look, our brothers are breaking through! They are here already! Then he sat down to write to Division HQ, reporting that he was about to begin the battle for the town and asking the commander of the main body to help by sending more shells in a hurry together with at least one more battery.

The sun had set, but darkness was still a long way off. He could see two houses on fire, near where the cornet was fighting. "1st Battalion—follow me to the bridge. 2nd Battalion—follow after an interval."

The 1st got across without a hitch. It was not fired upon, but it was spotted, and a battery concealed in a copse beyond the river to the left began pounding the 2nd Battalion. The Russian artillery replied. Another German battery joined in. In the meantime the 2nd Battalion had dashed across the bridge, a company at a time.

The light was fading. The fires in the town stood out more vividly.

Nechvolodov reached Cornet Zhukovsky and saw the men from the Poltava Regiment and the shifty-looking Cossack from Samsonov's escort for himself. He drew up the 1st Battalion opposite the station, from which the Germans were shooting more persistently, and waited for the rest of the Ladoga Regiment. The 3rd and 4th Battalions should be able to get across more easily in the dark.

The artillery had quieted down in the gathering gloom. There was a crimson glow from the burning houses, but apart from a few dim lights no other illumination in the town. The electricity supply had been damaged.

There was just enough light from the crescent moon to their left and the burning houses for the attackers to keep each other in sight and not fall into confusion if attacked, but not enough for them to be seen from a distance. Everything was in their favor. In an hour's time the battalions would take up position, make ready, then the 1st and 2nd would advance on the town, bent double, without firing a shot; the 3rd would make a detour to the sawmill; and the 4th would remain in reserve. In the meantime Nechvolodov, slinking like a wolf, together with Roshko and a few other officers, ranged over the hard, dry pasture which sloped leftward down to the river. He showed them where to take their battalions.

There was still firing on the other side of the town, though it was less frequent. There were three or four versts between Nechvolodov's men and their comrades, but on one side the feeling was "We are together," on the other "We are cut off, surrounded, doomed, there are no other Russian troops left in the world."

Nechvolodov was now walking about boldly in the reddened night at his full towering height, waving his long arms as he gave orders.

He was sure of victory. His forces sufficed for a night attack on the town, and when the main column came up in the morning the German ring would be broken. If he could hold the breach open for a day the news would travel around the encircled army and they would all pour into it.

Nechvolodov was filled with a tremulous, aching joy. He could not remember feeling so happy in all those weeks of war, or in all the years of peace before.

There was ten minutes to go before the planned attack.

He went back to the road.

Someone had been looking for him—an orderly from Division HQ.

Nechvolodov took his usual long, thin, infallible flashlight from his greatcoat pocket and shone it on the paper, screening the light behind a telegraph post.

To Major General Nechvolodov, Officer Commanding the Advance Guard:
In view of the absence of any significant enemy forces, the main column has been recalled. Do not give battle at Willenberg; we shall not support you, especially in view of the fact that the withdrawal of the whole corps to Russian territory is expected. Await further instructions.

Colonel Serbinovich

Roshko cried out; his general bellowed as though stabbed between the ribs, staggered against the telegraph post, and tore with his teeth at the sun-baked, splintery wood.

[55]

In the end there had been no change of plan on the ridge where they had buried Colonel Kabanov. Gunfire had been heard from the direction of dormant Neidenburg; obviously Russian artillery was firing *from outside* the town and the Germans were unable to reply. Vorotyntsev had thought for a while of making for it, but the noise stopped except for halfhearted rifle shots.

Ready-made plan or not, every quarter of an hour demanded that Vorotyntsev use his ears, his eyes, look at the map, the terrain, his men and their feet, make decisions, and give orders. It might be supposed that military preoccupations would leave no interval for other thoughts, but it was as though there were two corridors in his head running side by side, with a glass wall between them: each was visible to the other, but undisturbed by sounds from it. Along one corridor raced thoughts about the immediate practical problem—how were the fourteen of them to fight their way out, carrying a wounded man? Along the other, at their own pace, drifted unforced, autonomous, and not even logically connected thoughts about the past in general, about all that he had missed in life and all the mistakes he had made. The first set of thoughts were in a hurry to break through into life. The second looked around for a chance to die.

He thought again of the Estland Regiment: they would not let him alone, they demanded their due. (And this was in the first twenty-four hours. Would not his remorse be still more acute later on?)

Such a short time ago, and so irremediable: those who were going to be taken prisoner had been by now, those who were going to escape would escape by their own efforts, those who were to die had already fallen.

Thinking about it did not help. And anyway, Vorotyntsev had not cheated them. This, though, was the reproach on their lips as they filed through the soundless second corridor, dressing to the right by the dark fellow with the crooked face. He had not cheated them, but would they ever cease to reproach him? He had not deceived them—he had honestly told them the whole truth, they had held a crucial sector for twenty hours, and that would have helped the whole army if others had acted correctly. But others had ruined it all.

So that he had in fact deceived them.

What was the right thing to do? Not to make an effort, not to exercise ingenuity, not to struggle to the limit of one's powers and beyond? If so, there was no point in serving, or even in living. But whenever you had a good idea, whenever you constructed something, some blind, blundering, flat-footed fool up above would upset it and crush it.

When all around is collapsing, what is the best thing to do? To act? Or not to act?

The thoughts in the second corridor did not interfere with those in the first, did not crowd them: they had space enough of their own. There was space for memories. Space too for regrets.

He felt a pang of pity for Alina, imagining her as a widow, in despair, rushing around helplessly lost and friendless, sobbing till her slender throat ached. It might be many, many years before she could start life afresh.

He remembered how skillfully she removed every speck of dust from his cluttered desk in St. Petersburg without displacing a single pencil. How she could keep quiet for hours, passing his study door noiselessly, when he particularly needed silence. How, much as she loved parties and public places, she would refuse invitations and refrain from asking to be taken out so that he would not have to join in activities which to him were irksome. Happy, yet unhappy in her husband, she knew how to make sacrifices. What had life with him brought her? They never paid visits, never traveled, never went to see anything.

Things would have to be very different after the war. All things passed, and nothing was unchangeable unless he died. And, as he told Kharitonov with a laugh: "I'm in no danger. My survival is guaranteed." They were lying prone, side by side, on the same greatcoat.

"Oh? Why?" The boy with the freckles took him seriously, and looked glad.

"An old Chinese told my fortune in Manchuria."

"What did he say?" asked Yaroslav, gazing lovingly at the colonel.

"He forecast that I should not be killed in that war or in any other, however many I fought in, but that I should die a soldier's death all the same, at the age of sixty-nine. A happy prophecy for a professional officer, wouldn't you say?"

"Splendid! But wait a minute—what year will that be?"

"It's quite a mouthful—the year one thousand nine hundred and forty-five."

A year out of H. G. Wells.

They were lying among closely planted green-tufted pine saplings, the sort of place in which hares love to play on sunny winter mornings. Vorotyntsev had chosen it because anyone could walk by five steps away and not notice people lying there. They were now a verst and a half from the highroad, and could hear already the unmistakable noise of cars and motorcycles traveling in both directions. If the Germans had had men to spare they would have sent patrols to comb this part of the woods. They obviously had not, so that it was possible to lie there without worrying until nightfall. They could not, however, move any farther forward before the time came: there was only a narrow promontory of forest ahead of them. Other Russian units might be gathering there, and the Germans too might come that way from the neighboring village of Modlken before it was time for Vorotyntsev's party to make their move. Vorotyntsev had posted six lookouts—two to the left, two to the right, two to the rear—and the rest of the party lay in the middle. They had arrived in the heat of midafternoon, and the baked air hung heavy, draining their strength, burning them, parching them—not all of them had water bottles.

"Never mind," Vorotyntsev said, trying to cheer them up. "As long as you're in daylight there are worse things than a hot day. Take Liaoyang, for instance, on 31 August—it's the 31st tomorrow. It was just as hot as this, we had to retreat toward evening, the Japanese were shelling us, we were shelling them, and to top it all there was such a strong wind, full of dust, such a black sky, such a furious storm, the sky was torn into a thousand pieces, there was a tropical downpour, the Japanese kept pounding away and you couldn't tell thunderclaps from gunfire."

It was stifling lying there, but they had no wish at all to draw back. Getting so far had not been easy. It had meant crossing the exposed railway line, which the Germans could easily have raked with fire from handcars; but obviously they had no forces to spare—something had been going on all day at Neidenburg, firing had flared up and died down again without getting any nearer. This was the day to attempt a breakout. Tomorrow would be too late.

Vorotyntsev was devastated by the catastrophe that had befallen the army. How had the battle at Neidenburg ended? How much was left of the 1st Corps? Where was Krymov? These questions troubled him more than his own group's chances of escape. Nonetheless, he kept the map open before him for hours on end, forcing himself not to look at the whole area but to memorize while it was still light every twist and turn in the contours of the forest so that he would have a clear picture of all the distances, wherever they got to in the darkness—otherwise he would be bound to overlook some detail, or doubt his memory and have to strike matches to examine the map under his greatcoat.

If Vorotyntsev had followed the rules, he would have laid his final plan before officers only, but his men were as much like partisans as regular soldiers, and it was they who would have to carry it out. So he explained it all to Blagodarev and Kachkin; to the two best shots in the Dorogobuzh contingent (named by their comrades)—the sturdy, slow-moving volunteer from Vyatka and Yevgrafov, the young draper's assistant from Ryazan; and to Second Lieutenant Kharitonov, who turned out to have been one of the best shots in his class and asked to be given the most distant targets. Vorotyntsev beckoned to these five and they crawled over the sand to sit with him under the low branches of the saplings, six heads together, six pairs of legs splayed outward. They were also within hearing of Lieutenant Ofrosimov on his stretcher. He had a fever and his wound was aching badly. He could not help, but something he alone could say would make things easier, and Vorotyntsev was giving him that opportunity.

They had to start moving as soon as night fell, by moonlight—bent double to begin with, and crawling as soon as they reached the danger zone. Blagodarev and Kachkin would take the lead, armed with knives. They would steal forward without hurry, taking care not to snap twigs: they had half the night in hand—the attempt to cross would be made somewhere toward dawn because the Germans were more on their guard in the evening. When they had crawled two hundred meters without mishap they would come back to fetch the second group, the marksmen. They in their turn would go forward two hundred meters and send back a messenger to fetch the third group—the rest of the party, together with the stretcher. If the first two ran up against a German outpost they would kill the sentries silently with their knives.

"All right?" he asked, looking hard at loose-lipped Blagodarev and barrel-chested, shaven-headed Kachkin.

"Lord, yes!" Arseni breathed out like a blacksmith's bellows. "They're in our way and we want to go home!"

"I do the slaughtering for half the village," Kachkin said with a twitch of his dark, bristly cheek.

There would be four marksmen, including Vorotyntsev. The second lieutenant would take Blagodarev's rifle, which had already been tried out. They had three small pouchfuls of cartridges each. It was unlikely that they would have to open fire in the forest, but as they left it and moved across the road they might—and afterward, from the other side of the road, to cover the flight of their comrades.

He told them how to shoot at different targets—when they should use volley fire and when to shoot singly. At this point Lieutenant Ofrosimov showed that he knew his duty. His dark, unshaven face distorted with pain, his eyes wandering, he raised himself on one elbow on his odious stretcher.

"Permission to speak, Colonel! Please do not think that you have to carry me with you whatever happens . . . if there should be . . . circumstances . . . We'll unwind the flag now and I'll hand it over. Just put me down in a convenient place with plenty of cartridges."

"Agreed," Vorotyntsev replied at once. "Thank you, Lieutenant. Yevgrafov, you'll take the flag."

Quick-witted Yevgrafov and Kachkin were the first of the Dorogobuzh men to recover from their dismay. Yevgrafov was jumping up even as he spoke.

"Yes, sir! Will you help me to wrap it?"

"You lie down for now!"

As things had worked out, Lenartovich alone of the officers had not been invited to the council of war. Whether or not he was offended, he moved closer to sit by Ofrosimov and listen.

"Would you mind telling me, Colonel, what happens if it is simply impossible to cross the road?"

"Impossible? What does that mean?" Vorotyntsev looked at him sternly, pityingly: something might yet be made of him, but time was short. "They aren't standing elbow to elbow. A fox could dart across, couldn't it? Right, so shall we. Have you thought what it's like for them on the road there? They're strung out in a thin line. They're more frightened than we are: they don't know where and when our forces may come pouring out of the forest."

Ofrosimov added a rebuke of his own: "There's no such thing as impossible in the army. In the army all things are possible."

Lenartovich did not answer, but thought: That's just the trouble, you've got used to thinking there's nothing you can't do. That's why all the armies in the world must be disbanded.

The council of war was at an end. The flag and the cartridges were handed over. Vorotyntsev pressed his ax on Lenartovich. "You're barehanded, you must have a weapon of some sort." He could see Lenartovich hesitating, afraid that he was being made fun of. "Take it, take it. It's the best of weapons, an ax!"

The colonel took time to tell the men with knives and the marksmen at length what the road ahead was like and what to expect every few paces or so. He made them repeat it and draw diagrams in the sand to show that they had understood.

All they could do then was lie down, cradling their heads in their hands, faces downward in the sand, and wait anxiously. They all wished the night would come quickly: these last few hours were not their own anyway. Nobody said anything about war or fighting. The older of the Dorogobuzh men talked about cattle feed, about the black-and-white cows in these parts, about their own cows at home. After a while nobody said anything.

The sun was sinking and fading, but the deep crimson glow from behind the main forest shone through to their plantation. Scattered clouds caught the sun's last rays, turning pink at first, then darkening to dove-gray and mauve—did they herald a change in the fine weather that had witnessed both the arrival and the destruction of the Russian army?

Sasha had never before suffered such suspense. Would he live to see morning? Was this his last sunset? Would he be in this world or the next by tomorrow? Sprawled on the sand, arms flung out? Marching under escort to a prison camp? Or eagerly scribbling on a scrap of paper, "Dear all, I got out! I've survived!" and "Veronika my dear, give Yelya a kiss for me"? From this place it wouldn't seem too familiar, in bad taste. Just affectionate.

He handled the ax tied to his belt. It was small and light, but honed so sharp that he could imagine how easily it would sink into a skull. But could he really strike a fellow man with it? Sasha wasn't sure that he could bring himself to do it. It was obscene. It was murder. Logically considered, though, was a bullet any better? People had been trying to kill Sasha yesterday, and had come very close to it. If there was no other way, if Kachkin and Blagodarev quietly knifed a few Germans that night, or that pup of a second lieutenant put bullets in them, he would feel no regrets. But to do it himself, with an ax, looking into a living face—no, he didn't like the idea.

How hopelessly topsy-turvy things were. The Germans were buzzing up and down the highroad. There were Social Democrats among them too, brutally herded into this slaughterhouse. In other circumstances Sasha would have been glad to shake them by the hand, to welcome them at a political meeting. But now his only hope of living lay with this second father, this colonel, this servant of the throne.

Dusk was closing in. The whole forest was dark, but the young crescent moon shed a glimmer of light on the young pines. Elongated clouds like dark sleeves were stealing toward it from the west, threatening to hide it.

Vorotyntsev gave the order to start moving and not to shake the treetops.

They moved into the forest. It was much darker here, but there was still a faint light from the moon. The men with knives set off. The marksmen got ready. Then suddenly there was a terrible brightness, glaring, phosphorescent. Taken aback, they looked in alarm toward the little plantation. It was a searchlight, somewhere very close at hand, near the road and the village. The beam was not aimed at them. It swept the road from right to left, and only diffused rays reached them from the narrow source of light.

So much for their hopes of getting across! In war, the best-laid plans . . .

"That's it, then!" Sasha burst out. "If only it had been a bit farther on, not right where we are."

"No, it's a good thing it's close," Vorotyntsev reflected. "Let's just hope there isn't a second one. Close up we can shoot at it, it's an easy target."

The marksmen set off.

The moon was veiled. The beam did not move. Its wavering outer edge only heightened the blackness on its borders. Nothing happened. There were only noises—occasional bursts of machine-gun fire down by the road, whether as a warning or because Russian troops were sticking their heads out, and a rustling, which came nearer and might have been the enemy but was in fact the messenger from their sharpshooters: they could go forward. They carried Ofrosimov with their hands lowered, stepping softly, as though he was asleep, holding the stretcher so long that they felt their arms were being pulled out. The forest floor looked even enough, but from time to time they came upon piled cones (the Germans were as tidy in the forest as in their own homes) or a ditch or a hole. They moved forward twice, then there was a long wait for the call to go on and they began to think that everything had gone wrong.

They learned later that the men ahead had lost their compass and were looking for it in the dark. Ofrosimov, by way of a change, interrupted his groaning to whisper curses into the blackness. Sasha asked him to stop it—it could be dangerous; they had already heard voices from somewhere not far away to one side, certainly not from their own group. They didn't know who it was, couldn't even tell what language. They froze, fixed bayonets.

Nothing happened. They caught what sounded like the growl of a dog. There was no dog. Nothing happened. They had probably dragged themselves along like this for a verst or more. When there was a rumble, or a burst of firing on the road, it sounded very near now. It had got lighter too, because their path impinged more and more often on the oblique beam of the searchlight, still happily stationary. Something like three hours must have gone by in this way. There had been no change to their advantage, and they could easily have blundered into a trap from which there was no way out to the rear or ahead of them: the Germans would only have to swivel the searchlight and close in on them. Sasha wasn't exactly frightened, but he felt depressed and hopeless. He clutched the handle of the ax. He would, if he had to, bash somebody's skull in.

Suddenly there was rifle fire over to the right. The four marksmen had opened up, not with a volley, but in rapid succession, as though competing in speed. At the tenth shot or so, the searchlight went out. It was out! The whole world was in darkness, total darkness! And the marksmen had fallen silent too.

What to do? Where to go? . . .

Right then a machine gun—no, two of them—struck up from the road. At random, though, firing wildly, at no matter what.

Something crashed like a wild boar through the undergrowth ahead of them. What was it? Who was it? In charged Kachkin: "Where's the lieutenant? Leave the stretcher, I'm carrying him on my back. Awkward squad, fall in behind!"

[5 6]

On the morning of the 30th guns to the south of Neidenburg suddenly opened fire on the town and the Russian wounded took courage, rolling onto their sides to look out of the windows while the nurses rushed out to gaze up delightedly at clusters of Russian shrapnel and cascading Russian shell splinters as though no Russian could meet his death from them. The German doctor and medical orderlies chuckled to themselves, certain that their troops had not withdrawn. There was shooting around about all day long, but no battle: there were hardly any German troops on hand, yet the Russians did not enter the town. It was not until evening that the German sentries left the hospital, leaving behind wards full of German wounded. The new authorities were in no hurry to make their presence felt, inspect the hospital, and evacuate their wounded.

It was dark when Russian vehicles began rolling through the town and troops rode or marched by. Buildings set on fire in daylight shed a sinister glare on the otherwise unlit town when darkness came. One of the windows in Tanya's ward gave a view of the fires and the whole town, and she stood by the open casement staring, staring and occasionally answering questions from patients. The peculiar features of the foreign buildings stood out sharply against the diffused red glow from the fires—ornamental pediments over the façades, lacy or jagged patterns in the brickwork, elaborately decorated balconies.

To Tanya, in her present state of mind, the shooting, the fires, the withdrawal of one side and the arrival of the other, were not frightening but a relief. She found refreshment in the stuffy wards and the scorched smell of gun smoke and burning buildings, and felt nothing at all resembling ordinary human fear. On the contrary, it all made her heart feel lighter and eased her pain. What was happening was, she knew, dreadful, but she refused to look at it squarely. She felt more cheerful and stronger than usual, she hardly needed to sleep or eat. She simply did whatever she was told.

The hospital had no reliable information and was running out of rumors. Even while the Germans held the town its numbers were swelled from time to time by Russian wounded from various units, bringing stories that all the senior commanders had been killed, that all Russian units had collapsed into a single formless mass, and that the Germans were bombarding it from all sides, dissecting it and taking prisoners. One of those who turned up in Tanya's ward was a Cossack lieutenant with a forelock, one of Martos's bodyguard (he took the corner bed vacated by the second lieutenant from Rostov, who had left on foot at the last minute). He was not badly wounded but in a highly excitable state, disturbing everyone with his loud ramblings about the destruction of his corps and the death of its general. He spoke of these things with uncontrollable eagerness, as if he took pleasure in the thought that things were very bad and that all those men had perished. News of this lieutenant had gone around the hospital and doctors came along to hear him.

As night fell they were waiting for wagons to evacuate the wounded and for a visit from HQ. Sure enough, at midnight by the dull red glow from a burning building they saw a car drive into the square in front of the hospital and the head of medical services, followed by a general and an adjutant, step out. In two minutes they were in Tanya's ward, making for the Cossack lieutenant. Tanya took the paraffin lamp from the table and carried it over to his corner.

There, the disheveled man with the forelock almost jumped for joy as the general approached his bed: this, it seemed, was the audience he had been waiting for all along. The general—a St. Petersburg dandy with an unnaturally white, carefully tended complexion, a carefully trained mustache, and no trace of affability in his manner—seemed just as eager to meet the lieutenant. This was to be no cursory interrogation. He sat down on the soiled bedcover, fixed the lieutenant with the eye of authority, and ordered the adjutant to take his statement down in full, beginning with name, rank, and unit.

Tanya's steady hand held the tall lamp, with its greenish-yellow glass chimney, over the adjutant's notes and between the two heads, the general's and the lieutenant's. She gazed from face to face curiously and with growing enlightenment.

The lieutenant repeated his whole story for the two-dozenth time, embellishing it with fresh details, but not seriously contradicting earlier versions. He told them that the rest of the corps had stayed put when the Army Commander, Samsonov, had sent Martos to occupy Neidenburg. Martos and his force had been riding toward Neidenburg yesterday morning when dragoons sent out to reconnoiter had reported that it was already in German hands. They had ridden on looking for a new position, and run into a hail of case shot from six or seven hundred meters away. The corps' Chief of Staff, division commander General Torklus, and many Cossacks had been killed. He himself and others who remained loyal had retreated into the forest with Martos. Martos's adjutant had vanished with their food, tobacco, compass, and maps in his saddlebag, so that the general was left hungry and didn't know which way to go. Their horses had been killed under them and they had wandered around the forest on foot, but whichever way they tried to go there were Germans everywhere. Martos had ordered this very lieutenant to break through to the town and report the debacle, embracing him as he left, and then shooting himself before the lieutenant's eyes because he could not stand the disgrace.

The general nodded his white-skinned, elliptical, egglike head and asked the lieutenant to repeat the last bit: "You confirm, then, that General Martos shot himself in your presence?"

"As God is in heaven, Your Excellency!"

The adjutant wrote it down.

The general—a Guardsman—nodded, looking stern and rueful but not really surprised: it was no more than he had expected, it was exactly as he had foreseen. He *was* surprised and put out, though, by the look on the nurse's face: there was something unpleasant in the dark burning gaze fixed questioningly on him from beyond the lamp. He tried not to look at her.

Tanya herself felt as if she had just woken up. This was the first time in weeks, ever since her fiancé had jilted her, that she had given her undivided attention to events in the world outside herself, but now she was absorbed in what was happening less than a meter from the bright, unsmoking lamp with the spotless glass chimney.

Tanya could not have given her reasons, but her unblinking gaze saw through the lieutenant's garrulity, his overexcitement, his passionate efforts to convince his hearers: he needed to conceal some sin, perhaps that of running away and abandoning General Martos when he was in danger. She knew too why this glossy, self-important general was so ready to believe it all, why he made no effort to probe the lieutenant's story and catch him out: for some reason he wanted it that way.

Like the Lady with the Lamp, she had shone her light into the dark triangle of heads and fearlessly shown up their secret.

Until then she had thought of war as something inevitable and elemental, in which fighting men were condemned to be wounded and to die. Man was powerless in the face of that elemental disaster. Even while she was assuaging the sufferings of the wounded men around her she had never for a moment supposed that her own emotional wounds, her own humiliation, her feeling that she had been defrauded were less painful: now all at once she discovered that hers were not the gravest hurts in the world, and indeed were quite petty.

Stubbornly, defiantly she held the light of truth aloft, seeing how it hurt the general's eyes and how unwelcome it was to him.

The loquacious lieutenant, whose boldness now knew no bounds, had some advice for the general: "Your Excellency! The enemy knew what he was doing when he let you into this town. It is a trap. They've got a lot of free troops now, and they're all gathering around you. Mind they don't slam the door!"

Of course, of course! That was just what General Sirelius had feared. He had in fact been surprised that the Germans had abandoned this key town to him so easily. They were stronger than he was—why had they let the town go? The longer his division remained there in isolation, the greater the danger. There was no knowing when the reinforcements strung out along the road from Mlawa would come up, and the trap might be sprung at any hour of day or night—most probably at daybreak. He probably hadn't much farther to go to join up with the encircled Russian units, ten versts perhaps, but he wasn't going to walk into the unknown, perhaps into the thick of the Germans, in the middle of the night. Anyway, what condition would he find the troops in?

Eyewitnesses confirmed that all the generals had been killed and their units scattered. They were all done for anyway, and it would not be right to aggravate the defeat with yet another sacrifice—Sirelius's Guardsmen. Besides, the orders on which his force was acting were of dubious validity: Sirelius belonged to the 23rd Corps and as a senior Guards officer was not obliged to obey the mere line officers commanding the 1st Corps. This lieutenant's firsthand evidence gave him a good excuse for reconsidering their orders.

He rose, with a gooselike wiggle of his neck, evading the inquisitorial and frankly hostile gaze of the stately, dark-eyed nurse as he passed her lamp and went out with his adjutant.

Shortly afterward his car started up noisily and left the square.

No one had been told what the general had in mind. But all those in the ward who had been conscious and listening knew; knew that they would not be taken anywhere, that they were prisoners again.

Tanya almost ran to look for Valeryan Akimich, who had disbelieved the lieutenant's story to begin with. But what could he do? Should she tell the senior doctor? He was their senior, but an insignificant little man to the general and his like. Besides, she had only what her heart told her to go on.

She wanted as never before to make herself useful—and didn't know how.

For so many weeks she had exalted her suffering above that of others, and now she was ashamed.

There was no gunfire all night long. The fires were burning out, though no one had tried to extinguish them. Guns rolled by, retracing their route of the night before. The infantry was returning by a different street.

At first light the town was quiet and deserted. But people began to show themselves earlier than usual, before the sun was up—they too had been wide awake behind their windows. They started walking about the streets, noiselessly at first. But before long there was a cheerful hubbub; they shouted, congratulated one another, greeted the first German soldiers to enter the town.

The wounded lay still, holding their heads. The nurses walked about with tears in their eyes.

German sentries arrived and took their stand in all the corridors.

It was shortly after this that an elderly, fussy, snub-nosed nurse ran in from the abdominal-wounds ward and whispered breathlessly to Tanya, "Tanya dear! A new patient has just wandered in. I've got him in bed. He only just made it, he may die any minute. He's carrying the Libau Regiment's flag wound around his chest. What shall we do?"

Tanya's eyes flashed. "Come on!" she said, without a moment's hesitation. "I'll wrap it around myself."

"Yes, but there are Germans in the corridor," the snub-nosed nurse clucked. "You'll have to do it in the ward and quickly."

"In the ward, then." Tanya had already left her companion behind and was resolutely on her way there.

She had always avoided undressing in the presence of other people, even women, ashamed of her breasts, which were big and heavy even for a woman of her build. In adolescence she used to cry over what seemed to her a disfigurement.

"Shall we pin it on?"

"No, sew it! Where is it? One of us can wind it and stitch it up while the other stands at the door to keep the Germans out."

[57]

(31 AUGUST)

Still, even if Sirelius had not got cold feet on the night of 30–31 August he could not have held Neidenburg. He had been too long getting there, and his troops were overextended. The Germans were as resilient and quick to react as ever. François had three divisions outside the town and two more on the way before the night was out. He himself was poised like a tightrope walker on the ribbon of road through the village of Modlken, with no other support, groups of Russians were breaking through from the north, one of them had put his searchlight out of action with rifle fire just outside the village, and they might even force their way through to his headquarters, but he gave the five divisions detailed written instructions as to how they should form circles around Neidenburg and take it. Meanwhile the High Command of the Russian northwestern front was as bonelessly pliant as ever, and it was on the evening of the 30th, just when Nechvolodov and Sirelius were at the height of their success, when many powerful Russian groups (that around Willenberg was fifteen thousand strong) were still getting ready to try to break through the ring during the night or early in the morning, that Zhilinsky and Oranovsky ordered the corps on both wings not to try to rescue the encircled forces but to retreat.

And to make a good job of it Blagoveshchensky was to withdraw twenty versts if he was not under pressure from the enemy, and all the way to Ostrolenka (another thirty-five versts) if he was "under pressure"! Dushkevich would withdraw thirty versts, or possibly as far as Novogeorgievsk (another sixty). The sagacious Kondratovich had got it exactly right—he had fled to the new line without awaiting instructions.

In the night watches the eyes of fear grew bigger still.

Postovsky had hared off on the 31st to install Army HQ (saved by dragoons) forty versts to the rear of its previous location at Ostrolenka, and Army Group HQ's permission—"Your move agreed"—caught up with him later. Normal telephone and telegraph links with Army HQ were now conveniently restored and dispatches exchanged. Army Group HQ at last gave HQ 2nd Army written permission to move the 1st Corps beyond Soldau if necessary.

What of Rennenkampf? "General Samsonov has failed completely and there is now nothing to stop the enemy from turning against you." After all its shilly-shallying his cavalry chose this moment to penetrate more deeply. Suddenly the Khan of Nakhichevan's cavalry corps was poised to strike at Allenstein! General Gurko's cavalry division was moving up to breach the eastern arc (the weakest) of the ring; 31 August was the day when General Gurko entered without difficulty the unlucky town of Allenstein, from which all the misfortunes of the 13th Corps had flowed. If there were Germans anywhere around they had their backs to him, and his horsemen could have cut an even bigger hole in the German encirclement with little further effort. This was the *third* place in twenty-four hours at which the Russians had cut through the German ring.

But for Army Group HQ this was all too risky, all highly dangerous! "The forward cavalry units are to close up with the main body of the army." (Drafted so as to avoid the words "pull back.") And the whole 1st Army was to begin withdrawing.

(Again Rennenkampf would move rather slowly—perhaps pride played a part this time—and a week later his army would have to make a marathon run—its *Rennen ohne Kampf,** as the Germans would call it—to escape encirclement itself.)

One more thing: as a fitting successor to the late Samsonov, Army Group HQ would send General Sheideman, previously a corps commander.

And a Bolshevik to be.

Document No. 6

31 August

Démenti from the Chief Administration of the General Staff

In their communiqués on the situation in their respective theaters of military operations, the German and Austrian General Staffs continue to adhere to their usual methods: according to telegraph messages from the Wolff Agency the German army

* "Run without fighting."

"has won a complete victory over the Russian armies in East Prussia and flung them back beyond the frontier . . ."

The veracity and value of such communiqués require no commentary.

* * *

YOU CAN'T HIDE FIRE UNDER YOUR COATTAILS!

* * *

[58]

SCREEN

= A horse's head.
Not a thoroughbred. A bay horse. A Russian peasant's horse.
A defenseless, unresentful face.
As well able as any human face to express despair: What is happening to me? What have I come to? So many deaths I have seen! And now I am going to die myself.
Its collar has not been removed. Or even eased.
It is exhausted, its legs can scarcely support it. It has not been fed, not been unharnessed, only flogged unmercifully—Pull harder! Save us—until it snapped the traces and broke loose itself.
Twitching one ear, then the other, it wanders away, hopelessly, to some place
where its foot sticks fast in
the squelching
quagmire.
It bucks, frees itself with an effort from the treacherous spot,
wanders off again, catching its feet in the traces, which trail along the ground,
its head is bent low, but it is not looking for grass, there is none.
Fearfully, it steps around
the corpses of horses with distended bellies and all four legs in the air like posts.
How swollen they are! Extraordinary how much bigger a horse becomes when it dies.
Whereas a man becomes smaller. As he lies face down, crumpled, small, you would never believe that he was the cause

of all that thunder, all that gunfire, all the marching and countermarching of masses of men
now abandoned, laid low. A cart on its side in a ditch,
its upper wheel looks like a steering wheel . . .
A wagon, on its back, holds up its shafts in horror . . .
a frenzied cart rears up on its hind wheels . . .
a harness, tangled and torn, litters the field . . .
a whip . . .
rifles, bayonets broken off from guns, and gunstocks knocked off . . .
first-aid kits . . .
officers' chests . . .
forage caps . . . belts . . . boots . . . swords . . . officers' field pouches . . .
soldiers' kit bags—sometimes on dead men . . .
barrels—undamaged or holed or empty . . .
sacks, full or half full, tied up or untied . . .
a German bicycle intercepted on its journey to Russia . . .
abandoned newspapers . . . *Russian Word* . . .
documents from regimental offices flutter in the breeze.
The corpses of those two-legged creatures who harness us, drive us, flog us . . .
and more of our own kind, more dead horses.
If a horse is disemboweled—

Close-up

—flies, gadflies, gnats hum greedily over the protruding and rotting entrails.

While higher and higher still

birds circle, swoop toward the carrion,
and screech in dozens of different voices.

= Our horse will never forget this. Nor is it
= alone here! There are so many of them wandering over the battlefield,
on the low-lying, marshy ground, the accursed place
where all these things have been abandoned, dropped, overturned,
among corpses, corpses, corpses.

= Horses roam the field in dozens and hundreds,
bunch together in herds,
or in twos or threes,
lost, exhausted, mere skin and bones, still just about alive, some of them have succeeded in struggling free of a dead team,
others are still in harness, like our horse,

or trail broken shafts around
or—here are two, with a snapped-off center pole dragging between them . . .
there are wounded horses too . . .
the heroes, undecorated, unmentioned in dispatches of this battle, who have lugged over a distance of one hundred or two hundred versts
all this artillery, dead now and drowned in the bog . . .
all this gun fodder, these shell boxes slung from chains—try hauling them!
= Those who did not free themselves—this is their fate: two teams, every horse dead, sprawl across each other . . .
seem to trample and crush each other, though they are dead.
Or perhaps they are not all dead, but there is no one to unharness and save them.
= Look again—dead teams, caught in a bombardment as they were approaching to move a battery to a new position. The battery fought to the last man; shattered guns,
dead gunners all around.
The colonel, a crooked bean pole of a man, had obviously taken over from the sergeant bombardier . . .
But there are dead Germans too, killed in the attack, lying in heaps on the field in front of the battery.
= Back to the horses. People chase us, grab at us, try to catch us . . .
We horses shy away from them . . .
they try again, they tie us up . . .
They are German soldiers,
their unenviable orders are to chase the horses,
mustn't let the spoils of war, all those thousands of horses, go to waste.
= But it is not only horses they chase. Look there—on the edge of the forest they are lining up
a column of Russian prisoners,
some of them with undressed wounds.
Deeper in the forest, deeper,
there are still many men lying on the ground, in a state of collapse, or sleeping,
or wounded,
and the Germans are combing the forest,
and when they find them, when they track them down
like wild beasts,
they make them stand up—
and if a man is badly wounded . . .

A shot.

. . . they finish him off.

= Now see the column of prisoners shuffling along, almost unguarded.

Prisoners' faces. It is a cruel fate—those who have experienced it know.

Prisoners' faces. Captivity is not escape from death, it is the point at which suffering begins.

They are bent already, they stumble.

It is especially hard on those with leg wounds.

The only hope is that a loyal comrade will help you along if you put your arm around his neck, half carrying you.

= Other prisoners are still worse off; not traveling light, but harnessed like horses to haul and maul

their own Russian cannon, German booty now,

to the highroad for the victors, where armored cars are driving around,

and there are armed bicyclists,

and machine gunners sit at their guns, ready to shoot.

= Rows and rows of Russian cannon, howitzers, and machine guns are already drawn up there.

= And here is something else, hefty cart horses are drawing a huge farm wagon with a hayrack along the road. It is carrying something else, though—

Close-up

Russian generals!

Generals to a man! Nine all told.

Sitting quietly on the straw with their legs tucked under them.

Their heads all turned in the same direction, looking humbly homeward, humbly submitting to their fate.

Some look black, but others are very calm: their war is over, and most of their troubles.

= The wagon is stopped by a German general standing by his car, a shortish, sharp-eyed man, rather jumpy, overexcited perhaps by his triumph.

General von François, wearing a victor's frown,

feels no pity for these generals, but is disgusted by their wretched circumstances. He gestures:

Get out! Why on earth are you on that cart? We have plenty of cars for generals—get into those four over there.

= Stretching their numbed legs, the Russian generals get down from the hay wagon

and take their seats in the German cars

looking sheepish, yet quite pleased to be treated with such respect.

= The column of footsloggers is marched into
a compound with a temporary, almost a token
fence of barbed wire
stretched between temporary poles in the open field.
The prisoners scatter to lie or sit on the bare ground, holding their heads,
or stand or walk around,
exhausted, bedraggled, bandaged, with bruises or open wounds.
Some, for whatever reason, in their underwear,
others without shoes,
and all, of course, unfed.
They stare at us through the barbed wire, forlorn and sad.
= A novel idea! To keep so many people
in an open field, and make sure they don't run away!
Where else could you put them?
= A novel solution! The con-cen-tra-tion camp!
The fate of future decades!
The harbinger of the twentieth century!

Document No. 7

1 September 1914

FROM THE HEADQUARTERS OF THE SUPREME COMMANDER

Following a buildup of reinforcements drawn from the whole front thanks to the highly developed rail network, superior German forces fell upon Russian forces of about two corps, which were subjected to extremely heavy bombardment by heavy artillery, as a result of which we suffered great losses. Information received shows that our troops fought heroically; Generals Samsonov, Martos, Pestich, and several staff officers fell in battle. All measures necessary to counter this lamentable event are being taken with the utmost vigor and determination. The Supreme Commander still firmly believes that God will help us to carry them out successfully.

[5 9]

Some children adopt our ways and our opinions with a readiness that leaves nothing to be desired. Others, though not openly disobedient, though guided in the right direction at every step their infant feet take, persist in growing up to be themselves and not what we would have them be.

Adalia Martynovna had learned both these truths when first her brother's wife and then her older brother died, and she took on the task of bringing up Sasha, age eleven, and Veronika, age six. Her sister, Agnessa, when she came home from Siberia some years later under the amnesty for participants in the 1905 revolution, had to learn the same lesson, for all her revolutionary ardor and drive.

It was not, of course, only a question of character. Sasha was sixteen when Uncle Anton was executed, had known him long enough to acquire much of his philosophy, and if the older man had given the word would have been ready to join him in an "action." Sasha had not lost the impetus his uncle had given him, and he could not imagine a life or any sort of career in which the people's needs and the people's wrongs were not his first concern. Sasha judged people, books, events by one all-important criterion—whether they furthered the liberation of the downtrodden or reinforced the government.

Veronika had little memory of her uncle alive, but she had his portrait continually before her eyes, on the drawing-room wall like an icon. Perhaps girls should not be expected to be as deeply committed as boys? Well, in *their* time, when Adalia and Agnessa were young, there was no shortage of what might be called "nuns of the revolution," heroines of the populist movement who looked everyone (and everything) in the face, made no attempt to be amusing, and had one concern only, to serve society, to perform heroic deeds and sacrifice themselves for the people. They concealed their beauty, if beautiful they were, so that it would not distract others, wearing coarse brown dresses and kerchiefs like peasant women. Adalia and Agnessa had both been more or less like this, and the flame that still burned in them might have had a decisive influence on Veronika. But it had not.

When Veronika was ten she had looked so plain and artless, with her hair parted down the middle, her two plaits, her clear gaze, her prim lips, that Agnessa, newly arrived from Siberia, had confidently declared, "She's growing straight and true—she's one of us." The two aunts were of different political persuasions. Adalia belonged to no party, but was more or less a populist at heart, certainly to the left of the Kadets, roughly at the same point on the political map as the populist socialists. Agnessa, on the other hand, wavered between anarchism and maximalism. But the factional divisions of the Russian intelligentsia were of little real importance. The whole intelligentsia was ultimately a single tendency, a single party, one and indivisible in its hatred of the autocracy, its contempt for the police, and its yearning to bestow democratic freedoms on an imprisoned people. The sisters had no common political program, but they were almost of an age, they had grown closer over the years, they were fond of each other, they both venerated the lost brother who had been ten years their junior, and were almost always at one in their enthusiasms, their aversions, their anxieties, and their hopes.

But as time went on Veronika's eyes became somehow more knowing, the line of her lips softened, her smile took on a new meaning—and her aunts began to worry: they would have to take her education in hand! The sisters also differed somewhat in their knowledge of the world. Adalia had been detained only once, for a day and a half, had always lived a normal life, had been married and widowed, while Agnessa had been in prison on and off and in Siberia, had devoted herself in the intervals entirely to revolutionary politics, and had never married although she was quite good-looking. But where Veronika was concerned they were at one—determined to make her see that character was so much more important than beauty. Beauty, they told her, was as dangerous to a woman as excessive cleverness was to a man: its consequences were self-infatuation, irresponsibility, narrow egoism. At first the aunts were happy to suppose that Veronika's temperament was their ally. Her natural placidity, her cautious responses to the world around her, the air of purity that clung to her, forced her admirers to content themselves with friendship and serious conversation, even on jaunts through St. Petersburg on white nights. It had been instilled in her that she must try to bring out the best in people, and that was what she did.

Yet these same qualities, this very temperament of hers, also thwarted her mentors. Veronika was sincerely moved by suffering, everybody's suffering, but sympathy never looked like hardening into an appetite for struggle, into hatred of the oppressors. In her diffuse and boundless compassion there was no sharp dividing line between victims of social oppression and victims of congenital deformity, of their own character defects, of misplaced affection, or even of toothache. (For the same reason Veronika had eyes only for the simplest and most superficial fact about the war that had now broken out: that men would be killed or reported missing, that there would be widows and orphans. Her thoughts did not rise above that.)

Then there was the effect of those unbearable years after 1907, after the burst of crimson flame had been extinguished and life became grimmer and harder than before the revolution. A renegade age, an age without horizons, a reptilian age. Gone was the dazzling epoch described by the poet:

Come, friends, come, brothers, raise your voices,
Hymn destruction's wondrous feast!

Now the warriors were gasping for air, and another poet's words rang true:

Times were often worse
But never baser.

Previously, Sasha had had a very good influence on Veronika, more influence indeed than her aunts. He was five years (half a school career, then a whole degree course) older than his sister, he had decided views on everything, he was incapable of leaving any objection unrefuted, unquashed, so not surprisingly he had so much intellectual and moral authority over Veronika that she shamefacedly confessed her errors to him and tried to purge herself of them, or at least to mask them, so as to be worthy of her brother. But a year had passed since the voracious army machine had swallowed Sasha, and it had been a very important year for his sister, her first at the university.

The dominant group in student circles ten or twenty years earlier would probably have turned Veronika's compassion and her hatred in the right direction. However—and this was something possible only in that long-suffering servile land—the post-revolutionary oppression did not toughen the student body, temper them for the struggle; instead they succumbed to the general fatigue, the doubts, the incantations of murky prophets. Student youth seemed to have forgotten the behests of the great teachers, and even to have forgotten the people. It was fashionable to speak cynically of the noblest revolutionary deeds. After several self-immolating generations the decadent young people who now seeped into the lecture halls in an evil-smelling stream were the very opposite of all that the words "Russian student" had once meant. This new student body made it clear, indeed boasted of the fact that the sacred names of Chernyshevsky, Mikhailovsky, and Kropotkin meant nothing at all to it, that it despised them without ever having read a line written by them, let alone by boring old Marx. If this went on a few years longer, the great tradition of half a century, the sacred, freedom-loving tradition, would collapse in inglorious ruins. Why did Veronika have to grow up and develop in such a loathsome time?

Even in that milieu she might have found herself better friends, but no, the creature who attached herself to Veronika in her first year, Likonya, or Yelya as she called herself (short for the impossibly lower-middle-class name Yelikonda), was a concentrated dose of the poison of the times. She was a girl from an entirely different world, forever coquettishly adjusting her shawl, stuffed with symbolist nonsense, changing her role from time to time—by turns world-weary and blasé, mystically intense, or ethereal and expiring. Now and again she would declaim, relevantly or irrelevantly, the nebulous ravings of her fashionable poets:

He who would build a tower to the sky
Shall hurtle down in fearsome flight
In a world-deep well to lie,
Curse his madness, moan his plight.

She made great play with her voice, and even more with her eyelashes. Her eyes were the first thing you noticed about her—their beauty and the way they flashed mysteriously meaningful glances, as though in what was going on around her she saw much more than did others. The hesitant, wondering turn of her head and the thick black hair falling loosely to her shoulders would have done credit to a beauty of great experience. She sometimes had a ribbon in her hair, and always wore a shawl, fidgeting with it to show off her narrow body: she seemed to have no hips, but skinniness was in fashion at the time and she wore straight, narrow, smooth, unwaisted dresses to accentuate her slender lines.

This young person was doubly poisonous; not only did she and Veronika become inseparable friends, but when Sasha came home on leave she bewitched him too. He devoured her with his eyes and became stupid—lost that air of proud independence which was so reminiscent, not of his father, a cautious barrister, but of his uncle, the heroic Anton. (Sasha was approaching the age at which Anton was hanged, and looked like Anton come to life again.)

What, though, could be in the head of this slip of a girl, so solemn and enigmatic in her ways? At the tea table, and at other odd moments, the clever, sharp-eyed sisters used every opportunity to question her and argue with her, trying to discover whether there was anything in the small head under that cascading hair. She obviously didn't live by the light of reason!

"Tell me, girls, what *do* you want to achieve in life? What is your ambition?"

The girls exchanged cautionary coughs. Likonya, taking care to purse her bee-stung lips beautifully, vouchsafed a reply: "To live."

"What do you mean—to live? Just to live? *How* do you mean to live?"

They exchanged glances, and tried to avoid answering. But Veronika if pressed would begin speaking as though for the edification of people younger than herself.

"My dear aunts, are you trying to inflict *progress* on us? Unfortunately, politically progressive generally means culturally retrograde."

Agnessa puffed out an impatient reply with her cigarette smoke: "The answer to that is very simple: our object, the main object common to all of us, is the struggle with autocracy."

Two little noses, the broader one and the narrower one, wrinkled skeptically.

"And afterward?"

"When the present order collapses and the chains of oppression fall away, all sorts of opportunities will open up—in the cultural sphere as in others."

Likonya darted frightened glances—probably a well-rehearsed trick.

"What if they don't?"

"Don't what?"

"If these opportunities don't open up?"

"But they will!" the aunts answered in unison. "The guarantee is that we have a healthy intelligentsia, and its upsurge promises a glorious recovery for our sick country. Russia's past may have been pitiful, its present may be contemptible, but its future will be magnificent."

"Aunts, aunts!" Veronika sighed in good-natured exasperation. "I wonder whether your generation understood what *culture* is? The cultural life of the nineteenth century was very humdrum."

They were lost for words. They could only splutter: "Humdrum? Our century? Ours? You just . . . don't . . ."

The girls seemed almost sorry to have to say it, but: "Of course it was. Political ideas are inevitably narrow. All that stuff floating around in the sixties. What was on offer? Politics, socialism, every book that was written was overseasoned with social significance, every picture painted was ruined by it. Culture did not exist in its own right . . ."

"If only you could rise to the level of the sixties! You are the real nihilists! What is it your idol says?

To good or evil
There are two paths,
Take one, no matter which . . .

"The real nihilists aren't the glorious pioneers vilely misrepresented by the world of the gentry and the landowner litterateurs, but those people of yours with their *Apollos* and their *Golden Fleeces*."

Likonya wrinkled her pretty brow: "We have to be citizens of the universe."

If the argument looked like dragging on, Veronika would say with a wistful sigh, "We know nothing about Scandinavian literature or the French Symbolists, and yet we think we're entitled to sit in judgment!"

By "we" Veronika meant her aunts—she and Likonya knew all right!

If the aunts pressed too hard the girls would wriggle out of it with some such remark as "Well, it's better to go your own way even if you get lost than to repeat hackneyed clichés."

Sometimes, though, the aunts attacked them not on the peripheral ground of politics but in their innermost fastness. How exalted was their idea of love? To test this, they asked one of the questions that had so agitated yesterday's intellectuals: Was jealousy compatible with true love?

The girls, all eyelids and lashes, would say something like "It's best to avoid the word 'love' altogether. Just using the word makes love seem dirty and dead."

By herself, and at home, Veronika was manifestly much more mature, but in Likonya's presence she became more stupid, and it was hopeless trying to keep them apart.

It was just the same in the first days of the war. (Agnessa was superstitious about dates: "Have any of you noticed on what day the war began? The day the Sveaborg rising was put down. History is exacting retribution!") Now war had begun, and against all expectations a horrifying epidemic of patriotism had suddenly swept over and intoxicated even the working class on the Vyborg side, interrupted its splendid strikes, and sent it marching tamely with loyalist banners (red flags furled and put away) to the mobilization centers instead of rebelling and refusing to answer the call-up. More terrible still was the shameful, servile scene on Palace Square (the very same square, still caked with blood shed in the massacre of 22 January). There were tens of thousands of them, free people, under no compulsion. Who could have made them do it? Who had brought them together there? What power had hamstrung them? Tens of thousands of people sank to their knees before the ludicrous toy Emperor standing on the balcony of the vulgar, jerry-built palace, and not just shopkeepers, not just the lower middle class, there were intellectuals kneeling there, students kneeling there, and in a unanimous, ecstatic outburst singing, "God save the Tsar," shouting, "Our great Emperor," "Our great people." Was there any difference between them and the Black Hundreds? Then for several days afterward an insensate crowd paraded around the city singing hymns. What had come over them all? A hopeless people. A hopeless country. How could they forget so easily the executions, the "Stolypin neckties,"* the insulting encroachment on the freedom of the press, the Beilis trial—and kneel down singing hymns? No, this country deserved to be enslaved—by the Tsar, the Tatars, the Khazars, by anybody and everybody—it was no sort of country, no sort of people. But the intelligentsia? What could have inspired that telegram to the Tsar from his "most loyal subjects" (the very words were enough to turn your stomach—had they no ears?), the Council of St. Petersburg University: "Be assured, great Emperor, that *your* university is fired with the ambition to dedicate its forces to serving you and the fatherland." Couldn't they have done without this toadyism?

"What do you think of that, girls? Veronika—what do you think of it?"

Veronika's gaze was as calm and dignified as ever. "It's in bad taste, of course." As though that was the worst of it!

"Taste! 'Great Emperor'—don't you realize that's the language of the Black Hundreds? If your institute had sent a telegram like that, wouldn't you have protested? Wouldn't your friends?"

* Stolypin necktie: the Kadet deputy Rodichev's name for the noose used to hang terrorists summarily tried by Stolypin's field courts-martial. [*Trans.*]

Veronika shrugged off this impossible suggestion. "Well, all these protests and resignations are in even worse taste. It's just herd behavior!"

That was the tragic thing—they didn't react at all to what was going on. Their latter-day nihilism showed itself in their insensitivity to dirty tricks and betrayals. Their ears were blocked to urgent social concerns, whereas something as silly as the *World of Art* exhibition seemed like a revelation to them. What had become of the Russian student's spiritual fire? Some sort of debilitating sickness had come upon the young.

But what could you expect of the young when the State Duma damned itself in a tragicomic one-day session that swelled the rousing choruses of musical-comedy patriotism. To come together for a single day, hymn the praises of imperialism, and immediately disperse—was that a fitting way for a parliament to behave? Though it had to be acknowledged that the socialist deputies weren't letting anybody pull the wool over their eyes. Khaustov promised that the socialist forces of all lands would succeed in converting the present war into the last splutter of capitalism. And the scintillating Kerensky had managed in a bold speech to bombard the regime with reproaches: it was gagging democracy, it refused even now to grant an amnesty to political fighters, it showed no desire for reconciliation with the oppressed nationalities of the Empire, the burden of military expenditure was being laid upon the toiling people. The brave fellow managed to say all this undeterred by the patriotic uproar around him; he did not omit to mention the regime's "inexpiable responsibility" for the war and his ringing peroration was a subtle hint of the revolution to come: "Peasants and workers, first defend your country, then set it free!" In the Duma record there was a fraudulent "mistake": "Peasants and workers, defend your country and set it free!"—as though he had meant set it free from the Germans. Only in Russia could thoughts be so distorted with impunity!

But this had no impact at all on the girls. They did not raise an eyebrow. Nor were they affected by the politically encouraging news of the Russian army's defeat now filtering through. They listened indifferently when they could not avoid it, Veronika mildly resistant, Likonya absentminded and uninterested, as they finished eating their jam with one eye on the clock. They made no attempt to argue. They would have thought it beneath them. They only sniffed at the aunts' old-fashioned notions. They were always hurrying off somewhere from the house on the out-of-the-way corner where the 21st line met the Nikolai Embankment—not of course to a workers' school, not to bring enlightenment to the people, but to sample and consume: at the theater, at an evening of poetry, at a lecture on "the value of life" or a debate on "problems of sex."

It was sometimes even more offensive when they stayed at home. In the dining room, where a large portrait of Mikhailovsky hung on the wall, and not far from a picture of Uncle Anton with the foreboding of doom on his face, Veronika sat solidly on the couch with her legs tucked under her, her hair piled high over her stubborn brow, a look of specious profundity in her eyes; while little Likonya leaned back against the wall, supporting herself with the tips of her fingers twined in her shawl, swaying her head and her body, pouting like a puzzled child, and expressing her feelings in someone else's blasphemous words:

He who would destroy the shrine
Shall lie crushed beneath its stones,
Abandoned by the love divine
With none to hear his dying groans.

[6 0]

Her aunts could no longer bear to watch Veronika abandoning the family tradition. Her uncle's niece must not be allowed to grow up indifferent to social questions—that would look like a betrayal. Even Sasha would see no excuse for their neglect. Silly girls like Yelikonda, the aunts thought, can do what they like, their families are tradesmen or moneygrubbers of some sort, we know nothing of their traditions, but our Veronika must be yanked out of this quagmire, after all her heart is not closed to noble feelings, she can be saved by suggestion, by admonition, by shining example.

Shining example is the decisive thing. In our day, girls used to be blessed—you were, Nesa!—with Vera Figner's portrait, as though it was an icon. And that determined your whole future life, didn't it? Vera Figner was always before your eyes, leading you like a pillar of fire!

Only we must find lots of examples, and make sure they are truly heroic! We've seen them for ourselves, lots of them, and heard of lots more, and yet we're tongue-tied with these chits of girls, we're at a loss for names and stories, we talk in generalities. So many young lives rich in promise were condemned to rot in solitary confinement. So much youthful talent and energy was sapped by the harsh climate in remote places of banishment. And so many less strong-willed characters, alas, cracked under the strain, lost their faith, and ambled along with the herd . . . Surely everybody must want his motherland to be free and enlightened? Could anyone refuse to serve his country with all his strength and, if the end should be imprisonment, to raise the coveted cup to his lips with tremulous joy? No, Veronika cannot be so unfeeling. And since it's beauty she is drawn to—that's the place to begin!

The aunts took their time preparing for their talk with her, reminding each other of names and events, going over their arguments. They waited patiently until they could be sure that Veronika would be at home without her friend all evening. They did not, of course, solemnly announce that this was to be the decisive discussion. They did not both swoop down on her like a whirlwind. They had preconcerted what seemed to be a casual conversation but was really a cunning sequence of interlocking ideas.

"Look, Veronika dear, you're always repeating the word 'Beauty.' In our day too we aspired to Beauty—it's natural for human beings to do so. But our generation didn't divorce it from Truth and Justice, the three things all went together. The Beauty-to-be was a beacon constantly before us—in the Kingdom of the Future, Nobility and Justice would reign unchallenged."

Veronika listened in a daze, but a good-humored daze.

"But the radiant, wise, and beautiful life of the future is for the present hidden in darkness, is only ripening—and our duty, as we saw it, was to make it burn with a bright flame. And we can't understand, Veronika"—Adalia was always the softer speaker, there was something maternal in her voice—"your aunt and I can't understand how you can ignore the great, the sacred tradition that goes all the way back to the Decembrists. How can you break with the revolutionary movement?"

A faint smile hovered on Veronika's pretty lips: she wanted with all her heart to please her aunts. "But those who are vulgarly described as decadents, and who represent art in our day, *are* revolutionaries, aunts! They are revolutionizing feeling. You can't contemptuously turn your backs on that either!"

"My dear girl!" Aunt Agnessa gripped her cigarette between her teeth—she very rarely let go of it. "Nobody wants you to give up art. Art is also a means of beautifying life, but it is very far from being the most important. The greatest beauty lies in the struggle for an idea, the greatest joy in combining the Good with the Beautiful. Have you no ears? Brute force is triumphant everywhere, and Russia's woes cry out to be avenged. How can you remain insensitive to that call? It is time for you too to return to the people and give them your love. Tell me, have you ever heard about a single "action"? Vera Zasulich's action, let's say. You remember the name, but the deed escapes you? Well, I think that's quite shameful!"

But it was they themselves who had failed. They had thought either that it was too soon, that there was plenty of time, or else that she would pick up these things from the family atmosphere, but in any case they didn't inculcate it systematically, didn't keep a close watch on her development, and so she had slipped away from them.

. . . Vera first got into trouble as a young girl, over Nechaev. She helped to transmit clandestine letters to him, and for that she spent two years in various jails, and was then exiled and lived under police supervision. Ten years of hardship followed. She wanted to get away from midwifery and become a schoolteacher, but could not. You might think that she would get tired and give it all up. But in the summer of 1877 she read in the newspapers in Saratov that Bogolyubov—a student!—had been given twenty-five strokes of the birch (twenty-five!) in the St. Petersburg preliminary detention center for a breach of prison regulations. And care had been taken that the whole turbulent prison should see the preparations and hear the groans. Vera Zasulich waited to see whether anyone would exact vengeance from Trepov, the St. Petersburg police chief who had ordered the birching. But months went by and nobody did. So she went to St. Petersburg, and asked somebody to buy her a pistol of the largest possible caliber, almost as big as those used by bear hunters, because it was essential that she should not miss. Then she went to Trepov with a request to be allowed to work as a family governess, and fired at him point-blank from under her cloak, wounding him but not fatally. Terrorism in Russia really got going with this action by the glorious Vera Ivanovna.

Zasulich's trial was a still more glorious moment in Russian revolutionary history than her pistol shot. Vera had, so she declared, set out to show, at the cost of her own destruction, that those who failed to respect the rights of the individual could not be sure of immunity. Her counsel gave one of the best speeches in the history of the Russian courts. To believe him, Russia more or less owed its greatness to the birch! A crime against the state became in his version merely a prematurely promulgated doctrine of reform. Could anyone who considered the motives for Zasulich's shot fail to see it as an honorable and noble impulse? It was an act of reckless self-sacrifice: what she wanted was not Trepov's life but an opportunity to appear in court. Any sentence you pass, he told the court, can mean little additional suffering to one whose life is already in pieces. There have been women who revenged themselves on unfaithful lovers and walked out of here not guilty! Even judges with stars on their breasts applauded this advocate, and the jury returned a verdict of not guilty—not guilty of anything at all. A bright moment in Russian history. At the corner of Shpalernaya Street and Liteiny Prospect a crowd of thousands carried the acquitted woman to safety.

Vera's first reaction to her acquittal—utter surprise—was followed by a feeling of sadness. The moment she was free she was burdened with a compulsion to do something else. Getting away so lightly with her heroic deed gave her no satisfaction and now she was ready for new sacrifices. Alas, her lot was many years of emigration and black ennui by Lake Geneva.

But Zasulich did not long remain a lone star. The Russian sky was soon thick with them, a long and brilliant succession of women, members of the People's Will Party, entered the revolution: Sofia Perovskaya,

Galina Chernyavskaya, Olga Lubatovich, Jessie Helfman, Vera Figner. Each of these lives was a lofty and enthralling story of heroism. To appreciate any one of these lives you would have to give a year of your own. But Iron Sofia perhaps eclipsed the rest of them.

She came from a great family—the Razumovsky-Perovskys. She was the niece of the governor-general of Orenburg, and the daughter of that vice-governor of St. Petersburg who had let Karakozov in. The final mishap in her father's career was also the first intimation of his daughter's future. Nothing in her own circle gave her any joy. It was almost as though the little girl had a presentiment that her childhood playmate would be the prosecutor when she and her friends of 13 March* were tried. The milieu was hateful to her, she revolted against it, would not go to high school, would not learn her Scripture, and in the end ran away from home. She read Pisarev avidly, trained as a medical orderly, and would have become a schoolteacher had her way of life permitted. She seems to have grown up with an awareness of her extraordinary destiny, of the enormous tasks ahead of her (one of her childhood dreams was of becoming a queen). She always treated men with reserve and respected women more: her heart was armor-plated and her strongest expression of contempt was "ladies' man." She was an admirer of the great Rakhmetov, and sometimes slept on bare boards. She had been secretive all her life, a born conspirator, she had a cool temperament and could not forgive her comrades their emotional lapses. She belonged to the first St. Petersburg student communes and at the age of seventeen was in Mark Natanson's circle, which admitted no one who had a weakness for starched shirts, a liking for strong drink, or a frivolous attitude toward women. The circle dreamed of a socialist uprising in which the monarchy and the dynasty would perish as in a great storm. Then came her early arrests. She was acquitted in the Trial of the 193, as were most of the women defendants. She did not escape the romantic experience of visiting an incarcerated hero as his supposed bride-to-be, never of course guessing that Tikhomirov, the prisoner in question, would end as a renegade. She helped Kropotkin to escape. At twenty-three she was in Natanson's Land and Freedom Party.

No one need aspire to this way of life who does not possess remarkable single-mindedness and a capacity for great sacrifices. Try to imagine in advance what it feels like: the revolutionary is a condemned man, with no interests, no attachments, no property, and sometimes not even a name of his own. His whole being is swallowed up by a single thought, a single passion—the revolution. The revolutionary despises conventional morality and society's views on what is important or unimportant, good or evil.

* 13 March (1 March Old Style) 1881, the date of the assassination of Aleksandr II by the People's Will Party. [*Trans.*]

From the age of twenty-four Sofia was always underground. She was twenty-six when the Land and Freedom Party split, at the Lipetsk and Voronezh congresses, into the futile "Rustics," who rejected terrorism and did not even accept that the struggle with the government should be the main objective, and the People's Will group. Sofia was for terror as a means to arouse the masses, for the assassination of Aleksandr II as the signal for a mass uprising, and even if no political freedoms were gained by terror she was for it as a weapon of revenge. So we find her on the Executive Committee of People's Will; and in August of the same year, 1879, in a St. Petersburg suburb, the Executive Committee sentences the reigning Emperor to death! That is the beginning of a great drama, with all Russia looking on, in which all the movements of the avengers are concealed and only the series of unsuccessful pistol shots and explosions, six in all, chart the position of the players for the spectators. As soon as the sentence is passed, Perovskaya and nine others dash off to set a mine under the Kursk railway beyond the Rogozhsk crossing. Sofia played, skillfully and proudly, the part of an ordinary housewife—she was always good at that—and at one point saved the tunneling operation by popping up with an icon and putting on a religious act for the benefit of some Old Believers. When the Tsar's train came in sight it was Perovskaya again who gave the signal for the explosion, but a butterfingers couldn't close the circuit in time and some sixty pounds of dynamite blew up unproductively in the wake of the train. Never mind—Perovskaya and Figner hurried to Odessa, and in three months' time they had finished another tunnel, under the street from a shop. The Tsar, however, did not go south that spring.

The tempo quickened. The Tsar hurriedly issued a fraudulent constitution, and the People's Will Party hurriedly prepared to execute the Tsar. There were fewer of them all the time. Hartman fled abroad, Zundelevich, Goldenberg, and Kwiatkowski were arrested, then more and more were arrested, singly or five at a time, thinning the ranks before the seventh and last attempt.

It is not true that the revolutionary has no feelings. His heart is as tender as anyone's, but he gives his feelings free play only when they are compatible with the revolution. (The love of a revolutionary is all the more sublime, all the more lustrous for that.) At the age of twenty-seven Perovskaya the man-hater yields to Zhelyabov, and they are lovers in those final nerve-racking months as they close in on their quarry. So much is crammed into those mad months—contacting Nechaev in the Peter and Paul Fortress, planning his escape (he had brainwashed his guards, and Sofia had the addresses of their mistresses in code), the staking-out of the ambush so that the bear could not possibly break out: there would be an explosion in a tunnel under the street from a cheese shop, four patrolling bomb throwers, and if none of that did the trick Zhelyabov himself would use his dagger. The nearer they got to the attempt, the more helplessly drawn along they were, the harder the waiting got, and although none of them any longer expected to change the political order by killing the Tsar, they could not weaken in their intention.

Posterity cannot easily appreciate the excruciating nervous strain of this unequal duel.

On the evening of 11 March Zhelyabov too was arrested. The valiant few were threatened with disaster—and to save the common cause and that of her lover, Perovskaya now took the leadership into her own little hands, treating her comrades with masculine severity and her enemies pitilessly. (As Kibalchich said, "Our women are harder than we are.") But for Perovskaya there would have been no 13 March. Now that Zhelyabov's dagger was no longer available, Sofia wanted to be one of the bomb throwers herself, but there had been no time to make a fifth bomb. She stalked the Tsar's carriage, and the bomb throwers changed position according to her signals. The men had lost their nerve in those feverish days: Timofei Mikhailov deserted his post altogether and refused to throw, Yemelyanov became so flustered that he rushed to the aid of the wounded Emperor with a bomb under his arm, an hour after the event Rysakov went to pieces under interrogation, Tyrkov's tears choked him—only Perovskaya ran up to assess the results of Grinevitsky's bomb and then walked sedately to meet the survivors. In the days that followed she narrowly escaped arrest several times, hurriedly composed a proclamation to the Russian people and a letter to the new Tsar, Aleksandr III, and tried to drum up a team to free Zhelyabov. Only when she heard that Zhelyabov was to be executed did her nerve fail her. In a state of collapse she implored those of their friends who were still left to save their leader. She now ceased to think clearly, with fatal results for others and for herself: forgetting the first rule of the revolutionary code, she was arrested with a list of the prison guards' women friends on her. But she was herself again—impervious, a woman of iron—as she rode to the scaffold in a black smock with a board bearing the inscription "Regicide" on her breast.

You rebelled and you killed
Because you were filled
With fear for the land you loved best.
A ruthless state,
A tyrant's hate
Extinguished the life in your breast.

Sofia, Vera, Lubov . . .

Vera Figner and her struggle to resurrect People's Will after 13 March need an epic of their own.

What women they were! The glory of Russia! The aging Turgenev was thrilled: "Saintly one, enter in . . ."

Alas, as they had foreseen on the scaffold, 13 March did not transform Russia, did not provoke a national uprising. Russia drifted into a gray period of gloom and despair, the Chekhov age . . . When Adalia and I were girls . . . and young women, Nesa . . . You needed such faith to realize that you were not in a blind alley, not in a dungeon, but in a long tunnel that would suddenly open into daylight!

Figner landed in Schlüsselburg. They all got twenty-five years. Nobody ever imagined that they could actually serve the whole sentence, that the human heart could stand so much.

We mustn't forget Ivanovskaya. She was sentenced with other People's Will members and served more than twenty years. When she got back to St. Petersburg she was by no means a young woman, but she joined the terrorists again. There's a great heart for you!

There were other names too, women who had been brave and strong in their own way—a less thrilling way, perhaps, but not an easier one. The indomitable champions of female equality, for instance—Filosofova . . . Konradi . . . Stasova.

And what of Tsebrikova? Not many people remember the name now, but in the nineties we pronounced it as reverently as the name of Chernyshevsky was whispered in the seventies: her celebrated letter to Aleksandr III branded the autocratic regime with such fiery force . . . she had no fear of rough justice . . . and she was bundled off to Smolensk province. Handwritten copies of the letter circulated among the young. New hands held it, new eyes read it.

How enthusiastically we greeted the twentieth century! How brightly the torch of hope burned! Nor were our hopes disappointed. History seemed to have been awaiting this human landmark, and in the first years of the century it released the student crowds on the Cathedral of Our Lady of Kazan and terror vaulted into the arena as Gershuni threw his bomb. Very soon not a month went by without splendid actions, and erstwhile Populists were reborn as Socialist Revolutionaries.

Against the background of their glorious predecessors it was difficult to believe in the merits of the young, but what a brilliant new constellation they were! And as for the women, what women they were! And we aren't talking about hoary antiquity—they were all active in your childhood, you were already seven or ten or twelve when their star shone out, and those who haven't been executed or lost their minds are in Siberia or living abroad to this day.

One of the greatest, of course, was Dora Brilliant—she's ten years younger than you, Dalya. She was a Kiev student, and her big black eyes shone with the holy joy of terrorism. She was eager to sacrifice herself, she dreamed of dying—and taking life was torture to her, yet she pleaded with her comrades to let her throw a bomb herself. But she was only allowed to make bombs. She went mad in the Peter and Paul Fortress.

Ah, but Maria Spiridonova—she really was one of the greatest. She had no revolutionary training at all and wasn't a member of any party, but the idea of holy vengeance was in the air, and young hearts responded to it, could not help responding to it! She was still a schoolgirl when she went onto the platform at Borisoglebsk station with a revolver in her muff to meet a general who had put down peasant disorders and, to avenge those he had flogged, shot him dead. Before she got anywhere near a court she was the victim of Cossack justice—a whole platoon of them took turns raping her.

You have endured, Maria,
All the torturers' cruel spite.
Yours is the icon I pray to, Maria,
In the silence of the night.

Voloshin puts it even better:

The whip has raised a weal on that pure body,
And there's blood upon the alabaster brow.
The proud white seabird, freedom's emblem,
Limps earthbound, broken-winged, now.

Then there was Bitsenko-Kameristaya. Hers was one of the most remarkable acts performed by a woman single-handed. And she staged it so imaginatively! She visited Sakharov with a petition, as Zasulich had visited Trepov, but she went one better: the "petition" was his death sentence. She let him read a few lines, realize what it was, and look up in surprise—only then did she shoot! All strictly correct. Sentence pronounced—and carried out! Her counsel's first action was to send a big bouquet to her cell.

Profound belief in a sacred cause—that is what inspired them all. As Barannikov wrote while awaiting execution: "One last effort and the government will cease to exist. Live and triumph! We are triumphant in death!"

The beauty of terror and its philosophy were well understood by Zhenya Grigorovich. And do you know—she was another general's daughter, and the general practically shared her views! Another sign of the times! He helped her to save revolutionaries from arrest, concealed women conspirators in his house, found out for her the times at which persons marked down for assassination rode through the streets to and from their offices and made themselves accessible. When Zhenya was planning her attempt on Trepov a friend of her father helped her to find accommodation in Peterhof, right by the Tsar, which was no easy feat. Suddenly Nikolai and Alisa go riding by, three steps away from her, in a barouche, but Zhenya has no weapon with her, and no plans have been made for such a contingency. She tells us how she eyed the royal couple like a cat watching fish through the glass wall of an aquarium. She lived an active social life and dabbled in painting to divert suspicion, but always kept a capsule of cyanide with her although the Party forbade suicide. She looked forward to the action as though it were a festival, enjoying herself with a friend, and practicing her marksmanship in a wood, using a piece of paper inscribed "Trepov" as her target. She slept late on the day of the attempt, ate a hearty lunch, received a specially ordered theater frock from her dressmaker, laughed and was merry, and went off in high spirits to see Ksheshinskaya dance. That's how real revolutionaries go to sacrifice themselves and die. Unfortunately, for some reason, Trepov did not appear in the theater, and Zhenya immediately became bored and disgusted with the stupid jigging on the stage, the backs of well-groomed heads in the stalls, and the inane chatter in the gallery. All at once she saw the impossibility of victory, and the impossibility of destroying herself. All she could do was leave for Italy.

Or take Kalyaev. Now there was a great man, and a born poet—that's what they called him, the Poet. But he sacrificed his gift and converted it into "actions." The things he found himself doing while he was stalking Pleve! What a splendid performance! His appearance was normally elegant, exquisite, but he went around in a filthy patched jacket, down-at-heel boots discolored with age, and with his cap on one side. He chewed sunflower seeds, swore at people in the streets, hobnobbed with yardmen and cabmen, and went to church on Sunday with his landlord wearing a red shirt, crossed himself devoutly, and fell flat on his face at the moment of consecration. So that he could keep watch in the streets more easily, he acted the part of a peddler, hauled around a heavy chest, and sold cigarettes, postcards with pictures of heroes in the war against Japan, and miscellaneous rubbish. "I hate those pictures," he said. "The artist in me suffers agonies, but some ass or other will give his last five-kopeck piece for them. Heroes of the *Varyag*, heroes of Chemulpo, sticking their chests out and sneering all over their ugly mugs! The pride and joy of their fatherland! Patriotism is an epidemic form of stupidity. Just you wait, you morons, the Japanese will knock some of the swank out of you."

"Action" did not always mean assassination. There were grandiose schemes intended to leave all Russia dumbfounded: like the plan to seize the whole State Council while it was in session (also at Peterhof). Imagine what a fit the distinguished old graybeards would have! Our own people, the Maximalists, led by Mikhail Sokolov, thought that one up. Their plan was to burst in on the meeting, bombs in hand, take them all as hostages, and make some demand to the government—exactly what they'd decide later. If the demand was refused, they would blow the whole State Council up, and themselves with it! What words could describe it?

Agnessa had known Sokolov well. A giant, not a man! He had been the first to think of terrorist action against ordinary landowners, making life on their estates unlivable for them, *and* of terrorist acts in factories, *and* of "expropriating" sums of money. The moment the Moscow rising began he rushed to Presnya to lead a strike force. He had founded Maximalism when he split off from the Socialist Revolutionaries because of their bureaucratic habits, their lack of imagination, their excessive caution. Uncle Anton had Sokolov's approval for his own "action." One of Sokolov's plans was to crash through the Tsar's entourage in a car packed with dynamite and blow up the whole dog pack. The celebrated bank raid in Fonarny Lane was also his doing—six hundred thousand rubles were seized in one go. Yet for all his toughness what a sensitive soul he was! When they were planning an action Sokolov would get someone to play the piano and would hum the tunes. He was arrested because a detective recognized him as he turned around to give a beggar money in a Petersburg street. He was executed a day later. He shouted, "Hands off!" when the executioner went to put the noose around his neck—and did it himself.

Ah, but Natasha Klimova! The fine flower of the Maximalists! She found her boring, pampered existence in a Ryazan gentry family suffocating; life in her own circle had no meaning. She too looked for truth in beauty to begin with, just like you. But then she sought it in the service of others, and that led her into terrorism. Where can you expect to find happiness in this life, Veronika dear, except in bold action for a just cause? She was Sokolov's partner in planning the seizure of the State Council, and when they blew up Stolypin's house on Aptekarsky Island, Natasha was the "lady in the phaeton." Sokolov and Klimova acted the parts of husband and wife when the servants were around. Sokolov was dressed up as a gentleman and affected an upper-class laugh, while Natasha bought herself some fake jewelry. Being alone together was rather embarrassing—they never undressed when they went to bed. What a talented creature she was! She often said to me that all nature is a miracle, the sunset is a miracle, every little detail in the natural world is a miracle. Constant closeness to death gives you insights of which you would be incapable in a normal life. It is worth sacrificing years of tame comfort and security to live so intensely for a few weeks. And for eloquence and power of persuasion she was a second Nechaev. She succeeded in converting the prison matrons to her beliefs and organizing the famous breakout from the Novinskaya prison.

Yes, art was sometimes the entrée: girls from well-off families were sometimes sent abroad to study art, and there came into contact with the best of their generation, acquired a conscience, and joined the revolutionary ranks.

Tanya Leontieva, an aristocrat with bright blue eyes and exquisite manners, and incidentally a niece of that same Trepov, was intended to be a lady-in-waiting to the Empress. (Her finest scheme was to kill the Tsar at a court ball while presenting a bouquet.) She was the daughter of a vice-governor but found high society and the company of unpleasant people irksome. She moved in the most exclusive circles in Petersburg and was able to provide the revolutionaries with extremely valuable information. She also concealed dynamite in her quarters. Her family's position made a police search most unlikely. When she was nevertheless arrested in possession of dynamite, her relatives contrived to have her certified mentally ill, got her out of the Peter and Paul Fortress, and sent her off to Switzerland, where she joined the Maximalists. But she was remarkably unlucky: in the hospital of the Lefortovo prison on one occasion she was given the task of finishing off an already wounded spy—and failed. In Switzerland she took an elderly local inhabitant for Durnovo. There was some resemblance, and the man was called Karl Müller—a name Durnovo had used when traveling incognito. She discovered too late that she had shot the wrong man. She always took things so much to heart—when Kalyaev was executed she couldn't stop crying.

Sometimes the nervous strain was too much. Tamara Prints, another general's daughter, could not bring herself to kill her father's friend, also a general. Three times she left home in her black silk dress, the classic uniform of the woman terrorist, intending to kill him. The first time she just couldn't do it. The second time she became hysterical, screamed out the whole story, and was arrested. When they let her out she made a third attempt, this time carrying both a Browning and a bomb. She dropped the bomb in the street, there was a small explosion (just the detonator), Tamara's nerve failed her completely, and she ran all the way back to her hotel and committed suicide.

There is no need to be sorry for those who perished or were captured after a successful action: they fulfilled themselves. Infinitely pitiable are those who are halted on the road to victory—like Zilberberg and Sulyatitsky, with their daring plan to shoot Stolypin during the religious ceremony at the opening of the Medical Institute. Similarly, Maks Shweitser was supposed to set off a bomb at a memorial service for Aleksandr II—this would have been on the anniversary of the assassination, 13 March, and Bulygin, Trepov, and Durnovo would all have been blown sky-high, but instead the poor fellow blew himself up in his hotel while he was getting ready. Sinyavsky, Naumov, and Nikitenko were all hanged before they could carry out their plan to blow up the Tsar in his palace at Peterhof. So was Solomon Ryss before he could get around to it . . .

Many of the women did not shoot or throw bombs themselves. They made the bombs. Maria Benevskaya had her arm blown off—but they showed her no mercy and sent her to Siberia. Her partner followed the one-armed girl there and married her. She came from a family of landed gentry and soldiers and had derived her belief that violence can be used in the struggle for good from the New Testament. She always insisted that terror requires a moral justification.

Manya Shkolnik, a dressmaker from a shtetl, wanted nothing in the world more than to throw bombs herself, although she was temperamentally better equipped to be a propagandist—she was a very passionate speaker. Her husband, Aron, did his best to hold her back, but it was her bomb, not his, that wounded the governor-general of Chernigov.

These heroines were all members of People's Will, anarchists, Socialist Revolutionaries, or Maximalists. For purposes of camouflage they would sometimes wear dowdy clothes like Social Democrats and carry *Das Kapital* under their arm—that way they could move about freely without interference from the police. Social Democratic women did not need to dress well and make themselves look attractive, did not need to "infiltrate," or even to wear a little mirror on a chain to check whether or not they were being followed.

Then there was Yevlalia Rogozinnikova. Another of the queens of terror! Her hope was to take as many as possible with her. After shooting the chief of the prison administration she was supposed to throw her Browning out through the ventilation pane as a signal to her comrades to go and kill Shcheglovitov and others. When the showdown began she intended to blow herself up, together with a number of senior officials and the whole administration block, which also contained private quarters for the staff on several of its floors. Unluckily for her, she was not interrogated by senior officers. Instead, they sent jailers' wives to search her, and called in an artillery colonel to disconnect the wires leading to Yevlalia's bodice—which was packed with thirteen pounds of dynamite—while she was spread-eagled on the floor.

What desperate militancy, what fanatical zeal for justice! To turn yourself into a walking human bomb!

Remember what Zhenya Yemelyanova used to say? Make a start, and hang the consequences!

Think of the righteous hatred that moved these young girls, these brides-never-to-be!

How can anyone live an easygoing, trivial life—exhibitions, lectures, theater—and forget these heroines? How can anyone contemplate their sacrifices without a burning sense of obligation to them?

But why look so far for examples? Surely you must feel some responsibility toward your own uncle, Veronika!

[6 1]

Any fresh eye looking at Uncle Anton's portrait for the first time was bound to notice above all the yearning in his face. Here was a young man who had plainly not found his niche in life, and had no interest in doing so: his one wish was to seek the truth and serve it. You could see it in his eyes, gazing from under lowered lids at a spot somewhere above the camera; in his brow, from which the creases of anxious thought were never smoothed away; in the way in which he inclined his head instead of striking a conventionally challenging pose; in the slender neck, which you could almost see trembling in the photograph.

The aunts took one hand each and led Veronika to the portrait, where she stood like an older and larger sister between fragile Aunt Adalia and dumpy Aunt Agnessa.

Anton was infinitely dear to the Lenartoviches as their brother and uncle, but a more generalized kinship undoubtedly shone from his portrait, the unique, the incomparable, selfless kinship that binds together all the intelligentsia, so that they recognize each other at first glance as kindred souls and allies.

Features bearing the stamp of talent. A lean energetic body. That sad droop of the head, as though the young idealist was already disillusioned with people.

Indeed, Anton had worn the look of a doomed man from the day he was born, and had seemed to realize that he was doomed when scarcely more than a boy. Even as a small child he was strangely upset by the expression "to die of St. Anthony's fire," and kept asking, "What's Anton's fire, and why do people die of it?"

Of course, any face with such a vulnerably innocent expression inclines us to think that its possessor is doomed.

If it is true that the stars in the sky leave their mark on the newborn babe, Anton must have been marked by that spring day, that cheerful break in the gloom, when the tyrant was executed and he himself was born, when the people, not understanding where their happiness lay, wept in the thousands at requiem services. Not only did they not understand that this blow had been struck to set them free, they ascribed the assassination to the corruption of Petersburg and the malice of landowners upset by the abolition of serfdom. Instead of drunkenly rejoicing in taverns and pubs the long-faced populace shunned them. There were no drunks on the streets. Only students made merry, in their lodgings, and taunted the university watchmen: "Say, 'Thank God, thank God.' Rejoice, your Tsar has been killed."

The corpses of the martyrs—once more, as with the Decembrists, five of them were hanged—had swung over Anton's cradle.

Happily for them, the five valiant warriors were strangled without suffering disillusionment: they had no inkling that the assassination would provoke only bitter hostility among the obtuse citizenry, the benighted masses, toward their saviors, the student youth. The execution of the Tsar, which had been thought of as the high point of the struggle for freedom, the signal for a general uprising and the massacre of landowners, proved to be only the first peak in the arduous and dizzy ascent, only the beginning of a long and costly crusade.

"You might say that Uncle Anton grew up under the aegis of the terrorist movement. He heard revolutionary talk in the house, and it did not affect him as it affects you. He began to understand it all at a very early age. And just as he reached his twenties the great actions began. He decided immediately that this was the only path for him."

"He prepared himself thoroughly. He used to say that no one should knock on the door of the Combat Organization until he had made sure that he was worthy, made sure that his motives were pure. You must remove your shoes to enter the sanctuary."

"Do you remember, Nesa, how young he was when he started hating all the Petersburg palaces? He used to say, 'That's what we're fighting against! I feel my fists clenching whenever I see a palace—they look so brazen and boastful. It won't be long now! You've got a terrible shock coming, you and your inmates!' "

"He knew Kalyaev, in fact he was Kalyaev's pupil. That's where he got the idea . . . that he very much wanted to perish on the spot, in the act, to flare up and burn away completely! An intoxicatingly happy death that would be!"

Aunt Agnessa was excited. In spite of her forty-two years she obviously still shared Anton's idea—perhaps she was Kalyaev's pupil too. From the mauve cloud—her smoke-clad self—her eyes flashed like signal lights.

"But! But! There is a still greater happiness—to die on the scaffold! Death in the act somehow leaves the act incomplete. Whereas between the act and the scaffold there is a whole eternity, and it can be the greatest time in a man's life. It's only then, he used to say, that you experience fully the beauty of the idea, that you feel yourself mystically wedded to the idea. The sweetest of all pleasures is to die, as it were, twice: at the moment of the act and on the scaffold. Then again, how delightful it is to stand trial! If you die committing the act you take your hatred with you, without ever putting it into words. But in court you can heap contempt on your judges, show them how little you care for their show of judicial correctness, pour out upon them all the indignation boiling inside you, pillory autocratic Russia, whoremonger to the world at large."

It cannot be said that Veronika was fired by the great terrorist's revelation—her aunts knew that she was too phlegmatic for that—but she was warmed by it. She looked at the portrait with wonder in her big, dark eyes. That would do for a start, the soil had been loosened.

But every age presents its children with new tasks and new means of carrying them out. When Uncle Anton reached maturity and was ready to give himself entirely to action, the 1905 revolution was in full swing, things were moving very quickly, the situation changed from one month to the next, there were revolts here, there, and everywhere, then finally came the Moscow rising—and in that year Anton was one of many who rejected individual terror and plumped for armed uprising. Armed uprising was everywhere desirable, but the one in Petersburg would be decisive. Anton was one of the first to raise the question of the navy: young, politically conscious Petersburgers found themselves in the navy, with friendly Finland, always hostile to the Tsar, nearby. The cannon of the Baltic fleet, and especially Kronstadt, could bring the Tsar down almost without opening fire. Anton was one of the first to pore over lists of seamen supplied by revolutionary officers. He got to know the men, and had supporters everywhere. The navy's defeats in the war with Japan and the damage they did to morale were a great help.

But the rising in Petersburg hung fire, and the flare-up came in Moscow. Anton was nobly envious, but did not abandon his own patch to rush there. When the Moscow rising was suppressed he was sure that Petersburg would exact vengeance. But even when the Duma was dissolved Petersburg shamefully pretended to have lost its voice. Suppose the navy *still* refused to mutiny?

"How did we manage not to win in 1905? The government was at its wits' end, the city police were unarmed, the factories were packed with youngsters—they weren't being sent to fight the Japanese . . ."

"The simple fact is that the people still drew a line between themselves and the revolutionaries."

In the hectic days immediately after the dismissal of the First Duma a prompt response was essential. There were plans to bring about simultaneous mutinies at Sevastopol, Kronstadt, Sveaborg, throughout the fleet, and to finish Tsarism off with a single blow. The Organization sent Anton to Sveaborg, the main base of the Baltic fleet.

"I don't suppose you know anything about Sveaborg?"

Veronika could only blink in reply, looking by now just a little guilty.

At Sveaborg agitators had long enjoyed a free run and greatly widened the horizons of the discontented. Two or three progressive officers had themselves distributed pamphlets among their subordinates. No sooner did the command satisfy one set of demands than others were put forward in the name of the masses—the ferment had to be kept going. The important thing was to waste no time in bringing about a rising, and meanwhile to keep in touch with the dispersed Duma. But there was no concrete plan, and no date had been fixed. The men had not been alerted in time and preparations were still incomplete when the agreed signal for the rising, a single cannon shot, was given. On one of the islands the gunners mutinied, but the infantry, mentally crippled by barracks discipline, took sides against the people and put up a bloody resistance. In places men had to be compelled to join the cause. Some of the islands mutinied and arrested their officers; others, including the main fortress, did not; and the rising degenerated into a war between artillery and infantry. The mutineers pounded the fortress with their big guns, but the infantry, although they had only small cannon, put up such a heavy barrage of case shot that the whole area was ablaze. Anton was one of a group of volunteer agitators who arrived belatedly with Staff Captain Seryozha Tsion to direct the uprising. Tsion became its leader. But to their great disappointment the fleet would not rally to their slogan—"Let us replace the robber government with a Constituent Assembly!" Not a single ship joined in the rising, although hopes had run high after the *Potemkin* and *Ochakov* mutinies. Obviously, the agitators had been too thin on the ground. Battleships appeared on the horizon and someone had the brilliant idea of sending a rebel officer in a launch to meet them with faked orders from the commanding officer to fire on the fortress, but he was recognized and arrested. The fleet, like the Sveaborg infantry, behaved like traitors. Though the sympathies of many soldiers and sailors were undoubtedly with it, the rising was a miserable failure. True, the Finnish Red Guard came to the aid of the mutineers—there were only two hundred of them, but they brought in arms. The leaders conferred three times, trying to decide whether to explode the minelayers' pyroxylin stores. If they did, the central fortress held by the government would be blown up, but so would many of their own men, and Helsinki's seafront would be wiped out. There were no experts on hand to calculate the force of the explosion, and they decided against it, not sure whether their own losses would not be greater. Another of their magazines was blown up, and sixty men killed, as a result of hasty and careless firing. Nothing was going right. On the second night of the rising Tsion and Anton, with a handpicked team, themselves dragged their dead down to the sea so that the sight of them would not sap the morale of the others.

Anton could stomach a great deal, but that bloody mess of mangled flesh was too much for him and he fell ill. Then the fleet began firing from a safe distance, placing shells closer and closer to the pyroxylin stores. Tsion disappeared and the wounded Second Lieutenant Yemelyanov and a council of representatives decided to raise the white flag. The representatives themselves would have to flee from the islands: anyone found in the fortress in civilian dress was likely to be executed. They concealed themselves on civilian craft (some of the boats had mounted machine guns) and broke through to the city singly. Anton, miraculously, escaped—with the rebel son of one of those defending the fortress, a lieutenant colonel. The wounded had to be left behind to be taken prisoner, and not many of the uninjured got away either. Several hundred men had been killed.

No one who had experienced such a heavy defeat could possibly think of a second attempt. The idea of a general uprising had foundered. When all Russia was turned into one great prison, daring strokes by individuals were the only possibility. To exact vengeance, over and over again, was the only course. Anton returned to his old religion—terror.

"You don't remember and you can't easily imagine what a black time that was, when the dark night of reaction once again enveloped us! Even seasoned revolutionaries were discouraged by the thought that their sufferings and sacrifices were senseless and would never benefit anyone. They were completely disheartened, everything, absolutely everything seemed crass and stupid and nasty and futile. This second spell underground, after the freedom of 1905, was much, much harder to bear than the first; I can't tell you how many fine spirits it wrecked!

"Only rare proud heroes still saw undimmed the stars that heralded renewal. Anton was one of them. For him every setback was not so much a setback as a crime, and if it could not be put right the only way out was hara-kiri. His chosen target was now Dubasov, who had crushed the Moscow rising. Anton sought revenge for Moscow and for Sveaborg both at once. The old admiral—who had already eluded several would-be executioners, including Savinkov himself—was in the habit of strolling in the Tauride Gardens, and Anton went hunting for him there."

"This was the first major 'action' after that in Fonarny Lane. Anton wanted to fire a salute on the anniversary of Sokolov's execution! As a result they were in too much of a hurry and failed yet again. Dubasov survived.

"Anton completed the cycle as he had planned and desired—'action,' trial, scaffold. And of course he poured out his contempt and hatred upon the judges. But there was no one to witness the trial or the execution. Moreover, his activities were such a close conspiratorial secret that Anton sacrificed his life without achieving fame and entering the pantheon of laureled heroes. Accompanied by his partner, Vorobyev, he fired his shot, he was arrested, tried, and hanged—all incognito: he saw no need to reveal his identity to the judges, and because a yardman involved with him had got his name wrong he appeared in the trial list as Beryozin.

"Hanged! This is the very apartment, the very room our heroic young brother left to be strangled by a length of government-issue rope. Can his own niece, the next generation of his family, feel free not to remember him? Free from any moral obligation?"

Confronted with the portrait of the uncle who had died so young, Veronika, of course, could offer no defense for herself. Who would not be touched, who would not be humbled by a young man's unquestioning sacrifice of his life? Are young people naturally so eager to die? Veronika fumbled for words, turning her unwaveringly attentive eyes from aunt to aunt. She herself did not understand how she could have strayed so far from the family traditions . . . but . . . but . . .

"Dear aunts . . . We all love Uncle Anton, I as much as you. But all the same, if I may say so, he wasn't a saint, he wasn't an innocent little lamb. Wasn't it he who started killing first?"

The aunts gasped. "Started first? Who started oppressing the people? Who first blocked all other roads to freedom? Who started executing those who took a single step toward freedom?"

"Well, the People's Will Party started killing people, didn't they?"

"They did not!" Adalia retorted. Whenever the Populists were mentioned her face hardened and glowed like her sister's. "The Populists set out to stir up some sort of social action, some awareness of their civic rights among the common people. If no one had interfered with them they would not have started setting off bombs. It was the government that forced them to deviate from pure socialism."

"But, aunts!" Veronika's fine eyes looked almost imploringly from under her delicately arched dark brows. "Does anyone have the right . . . to take the path of violence?"

"We do!" Aunt Agnessa erupted like a smoke-wreathed volcano. Aunt Adalia could be trusted to explain things up to a point, but here Aunt Agnessa's passionate certainty was needed. "That's the meaning of the word 'revolutionary.' Revolutionaries are the knights-errant of the spirit. They want to bring down to earth an ideal already visible in the kingdom of God, which is within them. But what are they to do if that ideal is still beyond the grasp of the majority? The ground has to be cleared for the new world—so away with all the old garbage, beginning with the autocracy! Revolutionaries are not to be judged by the yardstick of old-fashioned morality. To a revolutionary, everything that contributes to the triumph of the revolution is moral, and everything that hinders it is immoral. Revolution is a great new birth, the transition from arbitrary rule to a superior law and a superior justice, to a higher truth. The man who truly values life for its own sake, yet dedicates his own life to death, the man who knows what he is sacrificing and what he is taking away from others—that man has the right to take another's life." Aunt Agnessa made this pronouncement with such fervor that she seemed capable of leaving the room that moment to carry out an "action." "Violence is most certainly permissible as a method of social struggle. But it must be used in carefully measured quantities, to avoid greater injustices than those against which you are struggling."

"And how can you measure them?"

"It's always obvious. When the struggle is against the autocracy there can be no mistake: it is impossible to imagine a greater evil than autocracy."

Veronika stood her ground, argumentatively shrugging her shapely shoulders. "A rising I can understand. At least if it's a spontaneous popular rising, not one in which people are forced to join under threat. But—individual murder?"

"It isn't murder!" Aunt Agnessa stamped her foot. She was beginning to get irritated. "We have been left with no hope of breaking through to freedom except by way of violence. In the long run what we need is a general revolution, of course. But terror, and only terror, leads revolution by the hand! Without terror to guide it revolution would simply get bogged down in the Russian mud and clay. Only the winged horse of terror can drag it out. You must look not at terror itself but at its lofty aims. Terrorists do not kill this or that individual—in his person they are endeavoring to kill evil itself!"

"The aims are lofty, I know that." Veronika spoke gently, looking from aunt to aunt. No, she was not beyond redemption, not yet hopelessly debauched by nihilist indifferentism. Even now, in spite of what she was saying, her aunts could see in her face an honest willingness to surrender to her feelings and believe. "And no one can help sympathizing with the idea of liberating the people. You can't suspect me of feeling differently. But you yourselves have told me about the spurious love letter sent by Gershuni and Kochura to the governor of Kharkov. Didn't it occur to them that they might compromise the woman whose name they forged? And why was that woman and her private life so much less important than 'the interests of the people'?"

Back into the quagmire! Veronika hastened to improve matters. "What I mean is that when he goes in for terror even the most high-minded and purehearted of men must do some not very pretty things . . . before he ever fires a shot or explodes a bomb. He may have to forge a letter, say, lie, pretend to be what he isn't, or abuse someone's simple trust in his fellows in order to murder him. I'm thinking of all those callers with a petition in one hand and a revolver in the other. Rogozinnikova even turned up in the evening, outside office hours, bluffed her way in with tears, played the cruelly wronged woman, and all the time she had not only a Browning but a pud of dynamite on her. That way people could lose all trust in one another—lose something that may be more important even than the liberation of the people."

Now she had gone too far! The unfeeling girl was equating the oppressors of the people and its liberators, speaking as though they had the same moral rights! Her aunts steered her back to the couch, pinned her between them, and began urgently and anxiously—Agnessa particularly, with fiery and smoky passion—to expound the credo by which they had lived all their lives.

"My child, there's no need for rhetorical abstractions. This is not an attempt at pharisaical self-justification. Needless to say, nobody insists on the *absolute* moral purity of the revolutionary. Anyway, absolute moral purity is imaginable only in the world of angels. Human beings are *too* human to be so radiantly pure. The conditions in which we live together on earth are too vile as yet, and Russian life is particularly nasty, so that we cannot help soiling at least the hems of our garments. The revolutionary is no exception—we cannot speak of absolute purity in his case either, only of purity *where and insofar as it is possible.* Just as long as he is disciplined by his pure intentions, as Uncle Anton was. As long as his political, social, and moral ideals are in harmony. As long as he lets himself be drawn down morally dangerous roads only where it is unavoidable. Let him lie—as long as it is for the sake of truth! Let him kill—but only for the sake of love! The Party takes all the blame upon itself—so that terror is no longer murder, expropriation is no longer robbery. Just as long as the revolutionary does not commit the sin against the Holy Ghost, against his own party. All the rest will be forgiven him! I'll give you some more examples. Revolutionaries sometimes have to behave for brief periods like police agents, though no one could ever feel such ferocious aversion as they do for gendarmes and provocateurs—foul creatures! Yes, there have been cases when suspect comrades have been put under surveillance, and their quarters searched surreptitiously or forcibly, to verify suspicion. Yes, revolutionaries have resorted to all these things any number of times—violence against the person, false pretenses, forgery, fraud—but always for a pure purpose. The unhappy Sazonov, who killed Pleve, suffered torments in prison: 'God have mercy on me, a sinner!' The tragedy of terrorism is the tragedy of the man who has dared to strike a blow for freedom, the tragedy of the man who has voluntarily shouldered a burden too heavy for any man, who has gone to meet his own death of his own free choice and assumed responsibility for all the consequences. Yet there is in this proximity to death a cleansing power. 'Go, fight, die!'—the revolutionary's whole life is in those three words. And the man who voluntarily goes to his death is politically to the left of everybody else and morally more right than all the others! I shouldn't have to say all this. The whole Russian intelligentsia, with its unerring insight, has always understood these things, always accepted them! It is not the terrorist who is heartless. The heartless ones are those who have the audacity to execute these splendid people after the event!

"In Anton's case this was even more evident: they didn't, after all, kill the bloodstained bigwig, only shook him up. (It was rumored at first that they had killed him—and both capitals, and the newspapers, rejoiced to hear it.) Why, then, were they so heartlessly hanged?! Even if they had killed him, how can you compare, how can you equate the lives of those two self-sacrificing boys with that of a sottish butcher of revolutionaries? Who was more of a murderer than Dubasov, who choked Presnya, choked Moscow into silence?"

"We know for sure, though"—Aunt Adalia swallowed painfully—"that Dubasov himself begged for clemency for his assailants."

Agnessa spluttered. "Come on now, nobody can know *for sure*, we haven't read the documents. Hangmen like to adorn themselves with legends."

"It comes from the very best sources. Even Dubasov forgave them. It was Stolypin who refused to forgive them." Aunt Adalia laid her weightless hand on her niece's shoulder. "So you can take it that it was Stolypin who hanged your uncle."

Sto-ly-pin! What a menacing ring the name had. It fell across the history of Russia like a dark shadow.

"If we still have no freedom to this day, it is because Stolypin, and no other, has taken it from us."

For it had once been within their grasp!

Aunt Agnessa's eyes, which were gray with a twinkle in them, lit up. "But our Maximalists gave him the shock of his life on Aptekarsky Island! Now *there's* an action for you! Monumental!"

She herself had just been amnestied and returned from Siberia at the time, so they had let her rest and not taken her along.

"It was a tremendous scheme—and only one trivial detail let them down. Their technique was faultless: three of them had Brownings in their pockets in case they succeeded in getting close (one was disguised as a general and should have got through easily enough), and in reserve they had immensely powerful bombs in their briefcases—if everybody got killed that would be just fine! What let them down was a finer technical point. Two of the terrorists were disguised as gendarmes, but you can't keep up with everything and they didn't know that the gendarmes' regulation helmets had been modified two weeks earlier, and because of those damned helmets the general on duty and a dog of a doorman rushed to stop them as they arrived. (They had their briefcases under their arms and may also have aroused suspicion by carrying them too carefully.) The best they could do was to dash into the anteroom and drop the bombs on the floor, just where they were. The bombs went off beautifully. They weren't laboratory-made, those bombs; the days of amateur craftsmen like Kibalchich and Dora Brilliant, who put bombs together in their own apartments, are over. Nowadays explosives, beautifully packaged and fully guaranteed, can be bought from Western European firms. The explosion was so powerful that it shattered windows in a factory on the other side of the Neva, which is quite wide at that point. But the butcher was lucky—not even scratched. All the same, Sokolov considered it a success. All Russia heard the bang—dozens of people were killed or wounded. And the important thing about terror is to daunt the enemy, to let them know that relentless planning is going on, that we shall be back! We shall get you yet! Make them realize that they are up against a powerful foe. What matters is not so much eliminating as intimidating.

"But another five years went by, and many other attempts were defeated; the daring divers under the huge overhanging prow of the good ship

Russia were near despair—it sailed steadily on. Russia was drunk on crass prosperity, it looked as though the happy days of battle were over—when Bogrov's historic shot rang out!"

"Now, now, Nesa, choose your words more carefully!"

[6 2]

"Of course it was historic: in its results, its consequences, the act of 14 September surpasses all other acts, it is the crowning achievement of Russian terrorism! There is nothing to equal it except the bomb of 13 March. And as an act of retribution . . ."

Aunt Adalia shook her head doubtfully. "You know, I somehow feel that Bogrov's action owes nothing to us. The public is not so wholeheartedly enthusiastic about 14 September as about 13 March. The action on 13 March was carried out by our own hands, and People's Will took responsibility for it. Whereas that of 14 September was carried out by an ambiguous figure, an alien soul, a creature of the shadows. And nobody claimed responsibility for it, then or later."

"And that is a disgrace to the revolutionary parties! Bogrov's action was a *tremendous* event! In three respects, you might say. It was carried out in the year when terrorism was supposed to have been crushed once and for all. It was organized by a single person. And the victim was the biggest and most dangerous bull in the reactionary herd."

Aunt Adalia drew in her bony little elbows with a shiver. "You're wrong, I tell you. Honor is more important than all else! You have been arguing that a terrorist can be forgiven for many things, and I agree. But there is one sin for which no court of honor will ever forgive a revolutionary, and that is collaboration with the security services."

"Only it wasn't collaboration! You have to distinguish between collaboration and involuntary contact in the course of an operation, between working for them and using them for the sake of the revolution."

"So according to you Azefism is bad but Bogrovism is good?"

"Bogrovism! I don't know how you dare coin such a word!" The sparks in Agnessa's gray eyes flared up. "Azefism is the only such thing. Azef was a werewolf!"

Veronika knew that "Azef" stood for some sort of terrible, loathsome treachery than which there was nothing worse. And that was all—she wasn't even sure whether Azef was a real name or a revolutionary nom de guerre.

"What makes him a werewolf? He simply served the security services conscientiously instead of the revolution."

"How can you say that? He became one of the party leaders and was involved in terrorist operations."

"What actions was he involved in? Name them. Pleve was killed in the summer of 1904, the Grand Duke Sergei Aleksandrovich in the winter of 1905, and throughout that period only the Combat Organization was active. The Central Committee of the Socialist Revolutionary Party was not allowed by its statutes to direct terrorist actions or even to know about them—Mikhail Gotz was perhaps the exception, but even he never knew the details. Azef was the Central Committee member in charge of printing—and he saw to it that the presses were promptly put out of action. That's all he did."

Agnessa was not a Socialist Revolutionary, but still . . . "People like Savinkov, Chernov, and Argunov could not lie!"

"When Lopukhin exposed Azef to Burtsev it was as an informer, and even Burtsev didn't immediately identify him as a double agent of genius. But by the time those three went to see Lopukhin in London they had invented the whole story."

"Why should they do that?"

"Oh-ho! It made very good sense! It was the excuse they gave to younger Socialist Revolutionaries for their failures. If the government too was confused, if the government had been killing some of its own members in order to smash the Socialist Revolutionaries, the whole picture looked different. Why do you think Gershuni, the tiger of the revolution, defended Azef before he died? Just think. He knew better than anybody that Azef had no connection with the Combat Organization! In fact, no one else has ever produced any real evidence against Azef."

"I admit that there is no proof in particular instances, but logically Azef was bound to deceive the police too, and assist the Socialist Revolutionaries honestly at times, otherwise how would he ever have risen to be a member of the Central Committee? And once on the Central Committee how could he have remained inactive?"

Name after name was dropped, all of them supposedly world-famous, and Veronika caught a glimpse of a whole unwritten and controversial chapter of history which she had no real wish to know. But still, as she was there to listen . . .

"Dear aunts, tell me, what *was* the Combat Organization?"

"The kernel of the whole terrorist movement. And at all events Azef was certainly at the center of the Organization after Savinkov's arrest in 1906."

"Yes, and that was the end of actions organized from the center. Those that were carried out had nothing to do with the Socialist Revolutionary Party's Central Committee—Anton's act, for instance."

"Anyway, it was you who dragged Azef into it—I didn't even mention him. I was going to compare Bogrov with Voskresensky, if anybody."

"Who is Voskresensky, Aunt?"

"Surely you remember Voskresensky? Alias Petrov. It's no more than five years ago, right here in Petersburg, and you were no longer a child—do you really not remember? What can have driven these things out of your head?"

They explained. He was a teacher from Kazan, a Socialist Revolutionary activist; he had been sent to prison, and from there, obviously influenced by the Azef story, had written to the security police offering his services in return for his release and that of his partner. The security police did release Voskresensky and put him on their payroll, but he promptly made a clean breast of it to the Central Committee, and they ordered him by way of expiation to blow up a number of senior police officials. He did his best to catch two or three of the most important at once, but Colonel Karpov was the only one to cross his path. Voskresensky blew him up on Astrakhan Street.

Aunt Adalia was unmoved. "What difference does any of that make?" she asked, tossing her neat, graying head. "In the court of revolutionary ethics there can be *no* justification for dealings with the security police whatever the purpose—and that includes Voskresensky."

Aunt Agnessa seemed astonished. "This ultrarationalism of yours! At that rate it would be impossible ever to do anything, impossible to act at all! Why shouldn't the security police be used against themselves? If the security police are deceived, discredited, and punished, do you say that's wrong? That really is taking puritanism too far. What matters is not what a man pretends to be, but which cause he truly serves. Voskresensky decided to fight the security police with their own weapons. He risked his honor as a revolutionary—and saved it by sacrificing his life."

"Under our Populist rules it's still not allowed."

"Yes, but he hadn't betrayed anybody. He went and owned up to his comrades of his own free will."

"So where do you find any resemblance between him and Bogrov? Bogrov really did work for the police and betray people."

"That has yet to be proved," Aunt Agnessa said heatedly. "All the information comes from the police themselves. That's the fate of the lonely idealist—on top of everything else posterity is given a mendacious picture of him. Voskresensky didn't have an easy time of it, he died trying to redeem his errors in the eyes of the Party. Even on the scaffold he thought of himself as an emissary of the revolutionary center. His was an entirely different case. Whereas Bogrov, in a period of general disillusionment and degeneracy, a lonely man with no one to confide in, had the strength of character to follow his own inflexible line—and he was so solitary, so secretive, so proud that only now, after three years, are the details beginning to emerge and receive some sort of explanation."

"Where from, Aunt Agnessa?" Whatever else, there was no denying that passions ran high in this strange, secret world.

"There you are—you never read anything except *World of Art* and stuff of that sort. Two books about him came out just recently. One a fine, honest book from the emigration, the other from the security police sewer."

Aunt Adalia dismissed them both. "They left things no clearer than they were before."

"Only because the Anarcho-Communist group with which Bogrov was ideologically in sympathy has for reasons of political caution been unwilling so far to certify in public his revolutionary purity. That is obviously thought detrimental to the Party's aims. So all the mud still sticks to the dead hero. He was an enigma when he left us—and for three years no one has attempted to explain how Bogrov came to perform his great deed. The cowardly government, of course, had its own reasons for hushing up and burying the Bogrov affair. And then Russia's attention was distracted by the Beilis trial. There seemed to be a general conspiracy against a single, isolated individual. Absolutely everybody found it convenient either to lie, or to accept a lie as the truth, or if he knew too much to remain silent. Even Bogrov's personal friends are silent. He is naturally hated by the reactionaries. But some revolutionaries also are too sure of their own immaculacy and ready to attack him. The educated public and the press have found some political advantage in accepting the police slander as God's truth: if Bogrov was a loyal agent, that makes it all the easier for them to condemn the security system. What do they care about one man's reputation? The pathetic liberals see in it a useful opportunity for distancing themselves from the terrorists. They've fallen out of love with terror and are ready to proclaim themselves loyal goody-goodies. It suits the liberals best to regard Bogrov as a provocateur and blame the government for trying to hide the rottenness of its own system. It suits the liberals best to see the Okhrana's hand, and nobody else's, in this murder. The Social Democrats too, who don't know how to hold a revolver, who can't tell the handle from the barrel, were overjoyed: the blame couldn't be shifted onto the revolutionaries, or onto the Jews, it couldn't be made an excuse for persecution. Chickenhearted creatures! The newspapers cooked up all sorts of suspicious reports, anything for the sake of sensation. The newspapers are the origin of this mass hypnosis. A hero has been consigned to oblivion in a dirty political game, and a feat of the highest heroism has been robbed of its moral enchantment. They kick a man when he's down, and there's no one to speak up for him. Kick him—the state has killed him, he can no longer defend himself! They sling mud at a man barely cut down from the gallows. And you, Dalya, lend yourself to this foul liberal slander!"

In passionate argument, whether attacking or defending herself, Aunt Agnessa could become a pink-and-gray panther, the pink spots on her cheeks contrasting with her graying hair. She was rather frightening. Her paw was raised to strike—sparing no one, fearing no one.

But she made a thrilling picture, bravely standing alone against a general conspiracy of the unjust.

At moments like this, when Aunt Agnessa was even more heated than usual, Aunt Adalia, looking like a nun in her dark-gray or rusty-black dress, tried to score as heavily as possible by keeping cool, her hands locked fast over her narrow chest and the eloquent curve of her thin lips betraying her skepticism.

"Hm, hm. But somehow it seems too much of a coincidence that people who never agree about anything else, absolutely everybody from the extreme left to the extreme right, should suddenly find some advantage in regarding Bogrov as a police agent. Wouldn't you say that makes it look like an irrefutable fact?"

"No, I wouldn't," Agnessa snapped back. "Fatal coincidences of that sort have happened in history. The government blurted out a promise in the Duma to 'shed the brightest light possible' on the affair—and went no further."

"Ah, but why?" Adalia's almost sarcastic self-assurance showed in the way she kept the thin fingers of her aging hands under arrest. "Does it really not seem strange to you that when Stolypin's supporters got together to shed a tear or two over the precious remains, when the memorial was unveiled with so much ceremony the other day and they were all praising the dear departed to the skies, not one of them came forward and said simply and clearly who killed him and why. What reason could they possibly have for concealment? The whole truth about Bogrov is in the police department, in the Okhrana files—but they won't release it. Why?"

"Because the government and the entire ruling class are afraid of the truth about Bogrov!" Agnessa, pinker all the time, strode about the room trailing cigarette smoke.

"Because," Adalia said, quiet and caustic, keeping her seat, "the government could not admit that the Chairman of the Council of Ministers had been killed by a government agent. It would be Azef all over again."

"No! *Because* the government is ashamed to admit that the whole might of its renowned security service was made to look foolish by a single clever revolutionary. What price their whole police department after that? What respect would anyone have for the state? So the government put its stamp on Kulyabko's desperate fabrication. Trusevich, and subsequent investigators, sensed which way the wind was blowing up top, and accepted the story that Bogrov was a secret agent before they had even started looking into the case. And so the slander started by Kulyabko to save his own fat carcass, his own lazy hide, was adopted unanimously and without verification by the police establishment, by the judges, and—alas—by the educated public, for its own selfish reasons."

Veronika had made no progress at all toward understanding Bogrov, and now there was this Kulyabko. "Who was he?"

"Head of security in Kiev," Agnessa said impatiently. "He started the story that Bogrov was an agent. No other version could have saved him and the Okhrana. Without it he would have gone to Siberia. It was safer for him to be implicated with Bogrov, representing him as a 'loyal collaborator of long standing.' It was safer for all the top brass to reduce the whole thing to a breach of one clause in standing orders. It was especially useful to pretend that Bogrov had been recruited much earlier, and had been a very successful agent. They even spread a lying tale that Spiridovich had recruited him when he was in the fourth class at high school. There was no end to the lies infiltrated into the press. That Bogrov had had accomplices, for instance, who had been rounded up. Whereas he had gone to his death alone, with no thought of saving himself! Who was the only witness against Bogrov at his trial? Kulyabko again! And who supplied the investigators with the only evidence that Bogrov was an agent of long standing? Kulyabko, of course. There's only his word for any of it."

"Only his word?" Adalia asked with insidious sweetness. "Bogrov vanished from the Okhrana scene for eighteen months, then suddenly turned up at a critical moment and was immediately accepted as fully trustworthy. There have to be good reasons in the past for the Kulyabkos of this world to show a man such blind confidence."

"A clear case of the superiority of a brilliant mind. Bogrov outwitted the Okhrana, made fools of them, and opened all the doors marked NO ENTRY!"

"And who handed Bogrov a ticket for a performance which some generals couldn't get into? And why? No one gets a ticket on such an occasion without good reason."

The aunts had quite forgotten their niece. When they started arguing on matters of crucial importance they forgot that something might boil over or burn on the stove, lost their sense of smell, didn't see smoke. Several saucepans had perished in the heat of their encounters.

"Now, Dalya, it isn't Bogrov's fault that you and I can't explain how he got his ticket for the theater. There are lots of things we won't understand until the time comes. Bogrov carried the truth to the grave with him, but that doesn't absolve us from trying to discover it."

"And what have you discovered so far? What if Bogrov was given his ticket to help the police department get rid of Stolypin, as the nationalists claim?"

"Try to remember that all the information anybody has comes from Kulyabko. And *he* may not have been the one who gave Bogrov his ticket. Detective stories can be more complicated than that. There was a fleeting mention in the papers that he might have got the ticket from some café entertainer called Regina with a highly placed protector."

"That's too farfetched. Another Okhrana invention."

"No more farfetched than Kulyabko's lying tales that Bogrov had performed 'valuable services' on a number of occasions from 1907 on, and participated in the liquidation of anarchist groups. Trusevich called for the files on anarchists previously tried, and for whatever reason found no evidence to quote in his report."

"Really, Nesa! Of course they can't publish secret-police archives!"

"And they take advantage of that to tell enormous lies. The Trusevich report 'knows' that Bogrov betrayed anarchists, but gets mixed up about his party and puts him down as a Socialist Revolutionary."

"And you think you've caught them out! Don't make me laugh! We all know bureaucrats make stupid mistakes. Besides, nobody knows what Bogrov's views really were—he was always shifting his ground. Anyway, how do you explain his dissipated life in high society? His cardplaying, his betting on horse races, his bourgeois clubs? Would any decent revolutionary go in for such things?"

"Dalya, the newspapers were given false information, and the facts have never come out. Perhaps there never was any betting on horses, or perhaps it was a subtle form of camouflage. Why, he's even been accused of selling himself for money—with a father as rich as his . . . He could have lived in luxury and had a most brilliant career . . ."

"You mean, then, that he served the police for purely idealistic reasons? So much the worse! There was a wave of arrests in Kiev—and he survived. He was the only one not arrested over the Sandomirsky affair . . ."

"That was because he went to Baku for three months to lie low while things were really hot."

"They didn't touch him for six months. In the course of which he was running guns to Borisoglebsk, and there were arrests . . ."

"He can't be held responsible for that."

"But in September they did finally arrest him, and a whole group of others with him. Someone put a stop to the breakout from Lukyanovka prison, and the attempt on the commander of the Kiev Military District . . . The rest were all held and tried, but he was released after two weeks!"

"Let me tell you the reason: his father's connections, no more and no less."

"Whatever connections he had, it looked very, very strange: all his comrades in jail or in Siberia, only Bogrov at liberty. There was no getting away from the rumors."

"That's the tragic aspect of the situation: rumors fly around, all his senior comrades are in jail, they can't vindicate him, and new recruits believe what they hear."

Veronika listened eagerly, and suddenly felt herself succumbing. Fascinated by the flash and clash of arguments, she really wanted to know the truth about Bogrov. But there was more than that: through her aunts' quarrel she sensed the precariousness and poignancy of life in the underground, a life that really was a succession of thrilling experiences. Her uncle had been true to that way of life, and Sasha was true to it today. How could she have lost the taste for it, dropped out, betrayed it? While they had all taken risks and striven for the common cause, for the people!

"He was slandered by Rafail Chorny after his visit to the Maximalists in Voronezh!"

"So you even forgive him for the Maximalists?"

"The Voronezh Maximalists were unworthy of the name. Their trial was the dirtiest in the history of the Russian revolutionary movement, they all told tales about each other, accused each other of provocation—just a gang of petty criminals . . . Chorny accused Bogrov of embezzling party funds, two thousand rubles—ridiculous, he could easily have got such a sum from his father. Then they started attributing Behemoth's betrayals to Bogrov, Behemoth was killed in Geneva—and yet again he had no way of clearing himself. Even if he had wanted to, how could a rank-and-file anarchist, a mere beginner, have betrayed on such a scale? Betrayed the whole south? The southwest? Wrecked the northern network? And those in the Baltic provinces? He was in fact cleared by an anarchist comrades' court! After that there was no anarchist activity in Kiev at all, and there were no arrests."

Adalia had never been sent to Siberia, had never been a revolutionary herself, but who in Russia is not interested in conspiratorial activity? The whole intelligentsia considers it a matter of honor to know the rules.

"According to *the rules*, anyone released from prison must disappear from the place in which he is released. Why did Bogrov stay around?"

"Precisely so that his comrades still in jail could clear his name—it worried him terribly."

"And not because he was sure that he was safe? He was watched, of course. If you are right about him he could not have met anybody without putting a noose around his neck. No, no—rules are rules! Then there was Petersburg. Didn't Bogrov go to see von Kotten with a letter of recommendation?"

"Heavens—another new name!" Veronika cried in despair. Just when she thought that she was beginning to understand some of it.

"Head of the Petersburg Okhrana at the time, child. After Karpov was killed."

"That's a myth! How is it that none of the investigating commissions could find the letter?"

"I tell you, Nesa, they can't publish such things! Do you think they want to put themselves out of business? If Bogrov had no connection with the Petersburg security department, would he have dared refer his questioners to it after he had killed Stolypin? He knew, of course, that they would send someone to check, and they did in fact ask questions about Kalmanovich and Lazarev, but they didn't even ask von Kotten about Bogrov. Why?"

"No mystery! The wondrous workings of bureaucracy! Departments of the Okhrana keep to themselves, and don't like sharing their prey. There's too much rivalry between them."

"No!" Aunt Adalia's firmly rounded lips pressed the word into an uncompromising shape. "No, I say. They knew very well that it was just as he said. There was no need to check."

"Look—Kulyabko was surprised himself when von Kotten cropped up in Bogrov's note. Kulyabko went in to dinner, and when he came back with Spiridovich, von Kotten's name had been written in. He had to play along. And what was it that von Kotten told the investigating commissions later on? That Bogrov had performed no services for him and had gone abroad soon after—that's how valuable a collaborator he was!"

"Von Kotten was a hopeless bungler anyway. They asked him about Lazarev the day before the assassination, and he didn't get around to telling them that the man wasn't in Petersburg—his banishment to Siberia had been commuted to exile, and he was in Switzerland, so that he could not be planning an action with Nikolai Yakovlevich or anybody else."

Veronika had let many names pass her by, but she was quick enough to ask about Nikolai Yakovlevich.

"My dear child, he was Bogrov's most brilliant invention!"

"So then, von Kotten could have exposed all his trickery on the last day! How could Bogrov risk lying so outrageously?"

"He got away with it, didn't he? Obviously he could risk it. It was a calculated risk. And victors aren't called to account."

"Very well. But don't you admit the possibility that the anarchists *sent* Bogrov to kill Stolypin and so make amends for his offense? As Voskresensky and Degaev were sent?"

"There is no comparison. Voskresensky confessed, and asked to be sent to expiate his guilt. Degaev repented, and was coerced into killing Sudeikin. The idea was to make the two reptiles destroy each other. What do these people have in common with Bogrov?"

Adalia squeezed out a reply through thin lips. "Burtsev is still almost sure that Bogrov was a provocateur."

"*Almost!* Even Burtsev isn't clairvoyant. It wasn't in Bogrov's nature to do anything base. His choice of means to the end was as well judged morally as anybody's. His lies were righteous lies, his deceptions justified deceptions! I cannot see anything contrary to morality in any action of his. The one exception perhaps is that he was rather careless in his use of Kalmanovich's and Lazarev's names, thinking they were known to the police anyway. But he didn't in fact do them any harm."

"No, really . . . no, really . . ." Adalia saw it all clearly. "If he had never worked for Kulyabko, would he have risked bringing the Okhrana into his 'action'? Could he ever have hoped that they would believe his fantastic cock-and-bull story?"

Aunt Agnessa glowed youthfully through the cloud from a fresh cigarette as she remembered her own fighting days.

"Of course it was a risk! A desperate risk! That's what makes him a hero. Of course there were flaws in his plan, that's unavoidable, but it's daring that takes cities—and it did! He rightly relied on his dazzling personal charm. He really had that! However funny it may seem, they all believed him, even that old dog Kurlov. Bogrov captivated them all with his carefully rehearsed behavior, and they all swallowed the hook he had baited with hopes of a coup and rewards."

"It's hard to believe that even policemen could be such idiots! Why should they have trusted an informer who had never previously collaborated, or not for the past eighteen months?"

"That's what I'm trying to tell you. He bewitched them! He had no crude ready-made plan—he went along pretending to be in doubt and difficulty, asking for advice on how to deal with his former comrades. Anyway, Kulyabko would have had less faith in a dreary regular agent than in this brilliant volunteer from out of the blue. The reason they believed so readily is that a true revolutionary stood before them!"

"That's what you say!" Aunt Adalia threw up her hands as if this were a street argument or a family row. Unlike Aunt Agnessa, she was apt to lower the tone of a debate. "You are crediting Kulyabko with your own judgments. To you Bogrov is a man of worth. To Kulyabko, if you are right, he was an enemy, and unknown. Why should he believe him? Especially when he contradicted himself at every turn. Nikolai Yakovlevich was supposed to have appeared at the beginning of August—why then did Bogrov go to the Okhrana only at the beginning of September? Why did he delay for a month?"

"His story was that he didn't want to turn up empty-handed, that he wanted to gather more information first. Ordinary agents can and must go along and report every little thing. A new man has to bring them a lot of valuable information at once, otherwise they won't believe him."

"But if he had committed himself to assisting Nikolai Yakovlevich so actively, why had he got so little information out of him?"

"Because the other man was an experienced terrorist. That seems likely enough."

"Well, why did he turn up on 8 September with information a month out of date? Why didn't he wait to learn more?"

"Because the celebrations were getting close and further postponement was impossible. The naïve young man alarmed by an imminent threat to very important persons—that was his role. And he was irresistible in it."

"But if your naïve young man was new to the game, how did he contrive to take his story straight to the chief sneak?"

"He was very resourceful."

"And the chief sneak immediately believed a complete stranger who walked in from the street. Kulyabko, remember, didn't invite him to the Okhrana office but to his own house."

"He just happened to be there when he heard that Bogrov had an extraordinarily important message to give him."

"Why, though, didn't Kulyabko put this volunteer under surveillance immediately *afterward*?"

"So as not to compromise him in the eyes of the revolutionaries. Of course! To keep the revelations coming."

"It's like three Jules Vernes and five H. G. Wellses rolled into one!"

"I'm shocked, Dalya, to find how little revolutionary feel you have. How incapable you are of distinguishing the genuine from the bogus."

"You've just created an image to worship, and you want it to be absolutely honorable."

" 'Absolutely' is not my word. As with any revolutionary, it depends how you look at him. But a revolutionary does have a right to an unsullied name."

"Well, I'm not saying that he was a hundred percent Okhrana agent."

Agnessa, tired of pacing, was standing now with her back to the wall of the stove, wreathed in smoke, which seemed to be pouring through cracks between the tiles.

"What we have to assess is not Bogrov but the action of 14 September in itself. When there was general public apathy . . . the years of high excitement were behind us . . . the revolution had collapsed . . . the revolutionary parties were impotent . . . the moral atmosphere was one of insufferable decadence . . . the stench of treachery and provocation filled the air—one man turned his gun on the wretch who had brought all this about. Can anyone with an uncorrupted revolutionary soul accept that any form of action is closed to him? It could be done only by one man, acting alone. Bind yourself to any Central Committee and you will fail utterly; act alone and you may be victorious. Single-handed, at one stroke, you may clear the foul air and save the whole country! But by the same token you are condemned to remain unknown, misunderstood, maligned, the victim of slander—just because you dared go into battle alone, with no party to help you. Veronika! Do you really not understand the beauty and power of such a feat?"

Veronika was sitting on a low cushioned stool in a corner. She had been following the debate, the loosely connected scraps of argument which her aunts were in too much of a hurry to elucidate, with growing interest and respect. There was no doubting the explosive strength of their feelings. They were not something you kept in a chest with mothballs, as she and Likonya had supposed. Her aunts argued as though they might bring the roof down at any moment. Veronika suddenly saw that she and her friends really might be in some way lacking, that perhaps some finer way of life really had passed them by. Heroism—for all generations and all nations—is always heroism. And the lonely hero, keeping his secret, putting his trust in no one, having nothing to do with parties, intrigues, elections, co-optations, resolutions—the daring individual challenging Leviathan with a lance . . . what heart could remain unmoved by him? Perhaps Likonya and she had failed to see something very important.

Agnessa saw from Veronika's face that she was thinking it over, that perhaps she could be won. Agnessa leaned her shoulder blades against the white tiles and stared ecstatically into the upward-curling smoke: "For that one blow, let his name live forever! We dare not be ungrateful: he ascended the scaffold and died the death of a titan! We squander people, but there is always a shortage of *real* people in Russia. A man dares the most heroic of deeds, and we run to sling mud at him just because no political party has claimed his feat for itself. Bogrov has carved himself a large niche in the history of our time. In the free Russia of the future Bogrov's honor will be vindicated. He will become one of the nation's best-loved heroes, and monuments to him will be erected in city squares. The triumph of reaction in Russia seemed complete. All hope had, it seemed, been suppressed for a thousand years to come. And then he raised his black Browning . . . and . . ."

FROM PREVIOUS KNOTS

September 1911

June 1907

July 1906

October 1905

January 1905

Autumn 1904

Summer 1903

1901

1899

[6 3]

He was born on the day on which Pushkin died. The very day, only exactly fifty years later, when the century had turned half-circle. And in Kiev.

His paternal great-grandfather and maternal grandfather had been licensed distillers. His paternal grandfather had also been employed in the drink trade, but turned out to be a writer of some talent: Bogrov's *Memoirs of a Jew*, published by Nekrasov, was favorably received in the 1870s, though it provoked attacks from Jewish readers by exhibiting the less pleasant sides of Jewish life. Quite late in life this grandfather was baptized so that he could marry an Orthodox Christian girl. He abandoned his first family and died in the depths of the Russian countryside before his grandson was born. The son of his first marriage, Gersh Bogrov, remained loyal to the Jewish faith, inherited money from his mother's family, and became an influential lawyer and a millionaire (he could donate eighty-five thousand rubles to a hospital in a single gift). He received a considerable further income from a house he owned on Bibikov Boulevard (the second one around the corner from the Kreshchatik*). He was a prominent member of the Kiev Nobles Club, chairman of the Senior Members of the Concordia Club, and well known as an extremely lucky gambler. Distinguished members of Kiev society met around the card table in his house. The family frequently went abroad, and lived like Russian aristocrats. The two sons had a Fräulein each to teach them foreign languages. The younger of the two, from early adolescence to the end of his days, was addressed by the servants as "master." To make life easier the young man's apartment had its own front entrance. Visitors were shown in by a maidservant.

High School No. 1, a few doors away from his home, made no difficulty about admitting him. Like all high school pupils at that time, he immersed himself in the teachings of liberals and revolutionaries. Sympathy for revolution and hatred for reaction hardened into a fixed habit of mind in him, as in all young people in Russian schools and universities. As a schoolboy in the fifth class Bogrov was already attending self-education circles, reading the *literature*, and engaging in political agitation on his own account—among bakers and coachbuilders. He decided very early to despise the halfhearted Social Democrats and approved of "exes" and other terrorist acts. He changed around, sympathizing at various times with the Socialist Revolutionaries, the Maxi-

* Kreshchatik: the main street of Kiev. [*Trans.*]

malists, the anarchists. In argument with his father, who preferred the evolutionary course of development, the boy would desperately defend not only revolutionary means of changing the existing system but the complete destruction of the foundations of the state as such. On a trip to a European spa with his parents, the young Bogrov was searched by police at the frontier—and his parents first beheld the halo of outlawry around their son's head.

In the spring of that very remarkable year 1905 he graduated from high school with distinction, and that same autumn he entered Kiev University. But the revolutionary phase had already set in, and his parents removed him and his older brother to Munich University. It was a long time before he forgave himself for giving in to this: his contemporaries in Kiev were holding meetings on the Kreshchatik, tearing down the imperial crown from the City Duma's balcony, slashing pictures of the Tsar, shooting, while the Bogrov brothers were kept in Munich for their own safety. Immediately after the Manifesto of 30 October came the Kiev pogrom, news of which made Bogrov desperately anxious to return. "I cannot remain idle abroad while people are being killed in Russia!" But his parents would not let him have a separate passport, although he was nineteen years old.

While in Munich he read great quantities of revolutionary literature and renounced the individualist anarchism he had previously favored, because it exalted the individual as such and led toward a bourgeois ideal. He read Kropotkin, Reclus, Bakunin, and was converted to anarcho-communism. That doctrine is hostile to the state, private property, the Church, public morality, and all established traditions and conventions; without any of these every member of society can be sure of receiving a sufficient quantity of the goods he needs; man is not by nature greedy or slothful, and no one would want to avoid work since the tendency toward mutual aid is deeper-seated in human beings than that toward egoistic individualism.

But he was tortured all the time by the knowledge that he had turned his back on the stark struggle in that hard year, and at the end of 1906 he went home to Kiev.

He reached manhood with a disciplined mind and the strength of character necessary for systematic action. One of his striking traits was his unwavering concentration, his watchful, cautious, indeed excessively intense manner. Another conspicuous peculiarity was that he never took his opinions from anyone else but always had his own. There is a description of him at a mass meeting in the Darnitsky Forest: he was withdrawn, unsociable, uncommunicative and, when he made his speech, precise and peremptory. He was naturally aloof, he needed to be alone a great deal, to commune with himself, he preferred strictly businesslike relationships, and kept would-be friends at arm's length with irony, mockery, and cold indifference. Mockery seemed to stream from his piercing eyes, his protruding lips. It cost him an effort not to express himself caustically. But sometimes he found it in himself to spend a little time in company, with a stock of ready-made small talk, and he earned a short-lived reputation as "a jolly fellow, a great joker."

His gaze, now always from behind a metal- or horn-rimmed pince-nez, was pensive, with a suggestion of melancholy and irony. There was nothing at all revolutionary in his appearance—on the contrary, with his narrow breeches, clean collar, and black tie he looked a typical upper-class exquisite. His clothes were usually elegant, and his manners matched them. He was rather tall, thin, always either pale or unhealthily flushed, and unnaturally youthful-looking, with no trace of a beard at almost twenty. He always seemed exhausted, perplexed, out of spirits. His voice was cracked, and sometimes quavery, like that of someone with lung trouble. If Bogrov ever smiled, his smile was a mechanical addition to his face, it did not sink into his features. He had no muscular strength at all, though he tried hard to acquire it with the help of the gymnastic fittings in his luxurious apartment.

His police shadows nicknamed him "Pretty Paws," which aptly described his appearance and his manner.

At an early age he had seen a good deal of high life—in the clubs of Kiev, at theaters, races, foreign resorts. He used to bet on horses, play cards and roulette, gamble recklessly and enjoy it. His father never kept him short of money.

It was not what Bogrov regarded as the ideal way of life, but he could not give it up. His pampered body was used to luxuries and shrank from any harsh demands made on it, however briefly. He felt himself that his penchant for the comforts of life was a weakness, a form of corruption. A man could enjoy those comforts without a bad conscience only if he had another, secret and meaningful life. Only the life of the revolutionary was that. His own instincts and the mood of society alike impelled Bogrov in the same direction. He set out to make acquaintances in revolutionary circles.

At one time he went to the university with a Browning in his pocket, because he hated official brutality and had a duty to fight it should he suddenly encounter it. The Browning in his pocket was a demand for freedom. Yet Bogrov disdained the futile fussing of student organizations: you went to the university to pass examinations, and no self-respecting conspirator would speak in an ordinary student gathering.

Choosing his party was the most important decision of a man's life. Bogrov wobbled between the uncompromising Maximalists and the anarchists. Among the anarchists, some of them in their twenties, some not yet that old—Naum Tysh, the Gorodetsky brothers, Saul Ashkenazy, Yankel Shteiner, Rosa No. 1 (Mikhelson), and Rosa No. 2—Bogrov had in 1907 a reputation as a skillful and daring militant, although he had not as yet personally participated in a single "ex," a single "action," or a frontal assault on anyone. All he had done was fight back bravely when a meeting of the Literary and Dramatic Society was broken up, and disseminate propaganda among the workers in the Arsenal. But his comrades appreciated Bogrov's pungent pronouncements, the soundness of his views, and his ability to keep cool when concealing or distributing weapons. He managed the party funds and furnished the money to equip an explosives lab and buy weapons and transport them to points in the south and also to Tambov and Borisoglebsk. True, there were some, like Leonid Taratuta, Yuda Grossman, and Dubinsky, who did not much like Bogrov because of his wealthy background. Everybody called him "bourgeois Mitka," but nonetheless he became a certified hero, especially to girls like Hanna Budyanskaya and Ksenia Ternovets, who would hardly have found him irresistible in any context except that of party business. Soon his standing among the Kiev anarchists was such that when Burtsev spent five days in the city after escaping from Siberia, Bogrov was the only one of them who knew where he was hiding and went to see him.

He also showed himself superior to many of his comrades as a theorist. He argued that the prerequisite for broad mass movements and great social upheavals was highly organized party activity of a sort which did not and could not exist where people were so inefficient as conspirators and so incapable of holding their tongues. Neglect of the conspiratorial code enraged him. The easiest methods to apply, which always produced spectacular results, were those of terrorism. The bourgeois social order was sufficient justification for any kind of revolutionary terrorist act. All you needed to know was whether it served the interests of the oppressed class at that particular time. Thus, he took the view that the proper targets for the terrorist were not members of the high bourgeoisie but servants of the autocratic government, and that *central terror*—killing the most important officials, not their underlings—was the correct policy. In response to discrimination against the Jews and to a number of events affecting them in Kiev after the Second Duma had been dissolved in its turn, Bogrov declared repeatedly, and to various people, that it was time to switch to terrorist action against the state, and recommended the elimination of the head of the Kiev security police, the senior gendarme officer, and the commander of the Kiev Military District, Sukhomlinov. In the same year he stated more than once his intention of killing some high-placed person himself. This theme subsequently disappeared from his talk.

Various groups of Russian anarchists expressed their wild beliefs in three émigré journals: *The Anarchist*, *The Rebel*, and *The Stormbird*. Bogrov once wrote a theoretical article for one of them. In it he condemned *economic terror*: the killing of factory foremen did no very serious damage to the existing order and could sometimes turn workers against anarchism. He also condemned trade unions: the struggle to improve the terms of sale of labor had no place at all in the violent struggle of a revolutionary working class. But the most important question for the practicing revolutionary was his attitude toward expropriations. The point was that the anarchist leaders had begun to look tolerantly on the sharing out of money obtained by expropriations to cover the personal needs of anarchists. But expropriation on these terms could have no real revolutionary significance, because the money in effect merely passed from one proprietor to another. The Kiev group, Bogrov assured his readers, had rejected the distribution of money so acquired among individuals.

If they had rejected the practice completely, or rejected it some time earlier, Bogrov would have had no opportunity to observe it. In fact, it was all the rage, and Bogrov was more and more perturbed by it. In letters and conversations at the time he did not hesitate to express his disgust with their greed. "It's all right for a bourgeois like you," his brother anarchists replied. "You can get it from Daddy!"—and he was stumped. That was the beginning of ideological friction between them. Revolutionaries had always been supposed to talk only about the oppressed proletariat, on the assumption that the well-off, self-employed, and educated strata did not deserve to be defended or to enjoy a freer and better life.

Bogrov even began to think that the similarities between all these revolutionary parties and groups were greater than the differences, and that it didn't matter all that much which you chose. Or whether you chose one at all. No *Party member* could achieve anything of great importance, only a talented individual acting alone could do that.

His father took none of it very seriously. He respected his clever son and had no doubt at all that he would come to his senses. In Russia no decent person could help having some slight contact—and a great deal of sympathy—with the revolutionary movement.

All at once the whole movement subsided, fell flat, showed how ineffectual and insubstantial it was. No steppe fire of mutinies and strikes flared up in reply to the dismissal of *this* Duma, as had happened in 1906. The banners were down, the shouting and the explosions died away. The trick so nearly taken had been clumsily lost. In the end revolution did not, and the autocracy did, have forces it could rely on.

With the rabble Bogrov had seen, that victory would have been a miracle. The iron legions of the revolution could never be recruited from them. What is more, it would be frightening to win with such help: those ruffians hungered only for plunder to divide among themselves. Once victorious, they would emerge as the destroyers of freedom and independence.

Bogrov felt a physical loathing for this riffraff, a squeamish need to cleanse himself, to shake off his ties with the underground and return to his privileged and secure way of life. Not in order to vegetate happily: he needed leisure and space to reflect on the humiliating defeat. It was Bogrov's circle, Bogrov's stratum, the enlightened section of society, that had suffered defeat and had freedom snatched from its hands.

To shake off old ties was not, however, all that easy: all his anarchist brothers and sisters sank their claws into him and held tight. In the harsh times ahead they might, they were sure to destroy him with their amateurish bumbling and their indiscretions. The whole lot of them together were incapable of effective action. On grounds of elementary hygiene this filthy crowd deserved to be wiped off the streets of Kiev. The withdrawal process must inevitably become an exercise in disinfection. The really tiresome thing was that Bogrov had dirtied himself without achieving a thing, and could make no further move because he was already under suspicion and in the Okhrana's bad books.

He wanted to withdraw from the Party but not from revolutionary activity. He no longer needed, at least for the present, any party or organization, and he knew no individual with whom he would wish to share his plans or collaborate. Lonely and vulnerable, he needed to get over his anguish by himself, to find, however long it took, some way to replay the lost game—he could not reconcile himself to that crushing defeat.

But wherever he looked he saw the Okhrana barring his way.

He had somehow to divert their attention—if it was secretly fixed on him—but not by an excruciatingly long period of keeping quiet and behaving himself. On the contrary, he would go to them, look the watchers in the face, and *know*. You *must* know your enemy. Why not introduce yourself to the lion and tickle his whiskers? Another exciting game, a gamble for higher stakes. It would be worthwhile.

It wouldn't even contradict what he had been doing a little while back. Anarchists are not under party discipline; their doctrine allows every member to choose his line of conduct as he thinks fit.

Once he got to know the enemy it would be easier to see how to lead him by the nose. The legal journal *Times Past*, an authorized publication, had shed light on some fine points of the Okhrana's procedures. He would have to learn the rest from personal experience.

If he meant to act at all no other course was open to him.

When he reached this decision Bogrov had spent just half a year (the six months since his arrival from Munich) in the turbulent atmosphere of the anarchist movement in Kiev. He went next to the Kiev division of the Okhrana and offered his services as a secret informant. For a student, and especially one belonging to such a respectable family, and still more especially one of such formidable intelligence, to approach the secret police voluntarily was a rare occurrence, which gave great joy to

Captain Kulyabko, the officer who controlled secret agents in the Kiev division. (Bogrov had made inquiries in advance and discovered without difficulty that Kulyabko was not one of the brightest stars of the security service, that he had been discharged from the Moscow police for incompetence, that he had started in Kiev as a clerk and owed his promotion to the patronage of a brother-in-law who had also gone up in the world.)

This new friendship could not, however, stop at smiles and agreeable conversation. Quite obviously names, events, and plans would have to be mentioned. Bogrov had considered his tactics in advance and, looking at Kulyabko's foolish, eager face, he could no longer doubt that he was safe in his superiority. Kulyabko was an incomparable ass, staggeringly ill-informed, glad of every trivial scrap of information, and quite incapable of determining its worth. (And not so long ago Bogrov had been thinking of assassinating this blockhead!) In this situation there was no need to give a great deal away at a time. He could trick Kulyabko by making the results of earlier police roundups look like confidential information. He could present information of no consequence, even theoretical arguments in party circles, in an intriguing form. Or he could draw attention to crimes which they already knew about without mentioning names. Or mention the names of anarchists known to the police, leaving out their criminal acts. Feeling ten times cleverer than his victim, Bogrov began playing all these games with ease, and bumbling, stupid, greedy Kulyabko was radiant with the joy of inside knowledge. Bogrov, to him, was a luminary, he had never worked with anyone like him. Bogrov sometimes had to provide a weightier catch, but he did not mind sacrificing a few of the animals who merely fouled the banner of the revolution: why not tell him somebody's address, or what sort of forged papers a man had, or the route used for somebody's (not very important) correspondence, or *The Stormbird*'s delivery point? Why not inform on the swinish Maximalist group at Borisoglebsk? Or the individualist-anarchist group? (There perhaps he had gone a little too far.) Why not help to prevent an expropriation at the Polytechnic Institute? (They would only have divided the money up among themselves.) On another occasion he "cleared up" the difficult case of Yulia Merzheevskaya, a neurotic or possibly insane young woman who had by the merest chance failed to reach Sevastopol in time to kill the Tsar (she had missed her train), but had subsequently blurted out the story of her attempt, and was doomed anyway. Bogrov got into her confidence, picked up letters from her for secret transmission, and took them straight to the Okhrana. (There were no limits to Kulyabko's trust in him after that.) When, however, Sandomirsky's group was broken up Bogrov did not hand over the very important documents in his possession.

To make himself more convincing Bogrov had to put up with a search at home, which upset his parents, then go away to Baku until the end of 1907 while the roundup was at its height. When he got back he could resume his weekly visits to the Okhrana with still less anxiety than before.

All this provided the cool, perceptive young man with amusing material for reflection. He observed the limitations, the naked personal ambitions, the feeble methods, the blindness of these officials, and wondered what kept the Okhrana in business, or whether it existed in Russia at all. In effect they had no firm knowledge of anything important except what clandestine informants could bring them. Kulyabko himself Bogrov could see only as a comic figure. Fooling this goose presented no difficulty to one who had deceived so many mistrustful revolutionary friends.

To make himself believable Bogrov, of course, also complained that his father was stingy and that he had difficulty in paying his gambling debts. The Okhrana paid him a hundred and sometimes a hundred and fifty rubles a month, and it amused him that they thought loyalty could be bought so cheaply.

His suggestion to his anarchist friends in 1908 that the whole anarchist network in Russia should be reorganized, with only the conspiratorial center and the laboratories remaining in Kiev, and the rest of the country becoming the scene of terrorist action, made practical sense, but it may also have amused him to think that he and Kulyabko would have a quieter life.

In addition, Bogrov took a great interest in prison escapes and helped to arrange them, but betrayed two important attempts—those of his comrades Edgar Horn and the Tysh group from Lukyanovka. To damp down suspicion he had to get arrested himself—and was, in the autumn of 1908. (As though fate was giving advance warning, this was on a September night outside the Opera House!)

His arrest was Bogrov's own suggestion to Kulyabko, but at the decisive moment he got cold feet: his spoiled body protested against being plunged into the stifling common cell in Lukyanovka. He had a physical dread of prison, so Kulyabko arranged for him to sit it out in a police station, in a decent room furnished for the use of officials. But he could not bear to remain a prisoner even under such privileged conditions, and made the rash decision to seek release after fifteen days.

His speedy release, of course, aroused suspicion, and even provoked rumors that he was a provocateur. Bogrov explained it by the intercession of his influential father. (The efforts of Bogrov senior were made in good faith, and indeed with the support of the governor of Kiev.) But this all happened just as the revolutionaries took their revenge in Geneva on Boris Londonsky (alias Behemoth, alias Karl Ivanovich Jost)—an undoubted provocateur who had betrayed the whole powerful Southern International Combat Group of Anarcho-Communists and the star of the anarchist movement, Taratuta, and had driven one of the Grossmans into a position from which suicide was the only escape. Other suspicions now fell on the victim of revolutionary justice and Bogrov was cleared.

The biggest shock was that the murder took place under the blue skies of free Geneva. Not even in those lovely Western cities, those halcyon health resorts, not even in Munich University, then, could anyone suspected by his comrades live in peace. After his release Bogrov obtained a passport to travel abroad and went to Merano for his health, then to Leipzig and Paris for a while, visiting foreign anarchist centers while he was at it. (The Okhrana paid for some of these trips, and he would come back with something new to keep Kulyabko amused. The Tsar's servants, of course, all had links with one another and Bogrov was privately commissioned by Kulyabko to visit one Butovich, a Russian landowner in Nice, inviting him to surrender his wife voluntarily to General Sukhomlinov, who had escaped assassination after all and was obviously not worth killing anyway.) But however honestly he worked, suspicion of him lingered and festered, rumors were repeated. He could not let them go unanswered. He returned to Kiev, and in 1908 obtained a declaration of his innocence from a comrades' court in Lukyanovka prison. He went to Paris again in 1909 with this letter of rehabilitation and asked the émigré press to publish it. The anarchists at the center dissuaded him—it would only increase the attacks on his honor.

Now that most of the comrades had gone off to jail or Siberia, Bogrov became a conspicuous figure, one of the few "old activists" to have survived the wreck and to have reliable connections abroad. He was the only one of his kind in Kiev, and he could be sure that whenever the anarchists wanted to try something in Russia they would be in touch with him.

But ambition had never been one of his more powerful motives, and this new responsibility was unwanted. The nervous strain of his double role was much more acute than anything he had experienced playing roulette or betting on the horses. He went on from day to day in lonely secrecy (he could not confide in his father or his brother, and he had no sweetheart), he could only take solitary pleasure in his own artistry—his success in wriggling noiselessly, invisibly, between the revolutionary and the police lines, finding himself a niche and fitting snugly into it. No one else in Russia would ever have thought of it.

Then, suddenly, still in January 1909, he read in the émigré newspapers in which he had hoped to see his rehabilitation published, and a few days later in the Russian press, about Azef. This hurt him badly, and in two ways: he found that he was not, as he had supposed, unique in his cleverness and his ingenuity, that there was someone better at the game than himself, and he also saw that Azef's double-dealing had ended in public exposure. He followed every detail in the newspapers, and even went to the offices of one Kiev paper to ask for further information. When thick glass is broken the snakelike cracks run in all directions, and it was impossible to count and trace the conclusions to be drawn from Azef's downfall. The revolutionaries would be much more suspicious. If Bogrov was not the only one of his kind in Russia, who was to say that he and Azef were the only two? Perhaps there were many such, like reflections in facing mirrors; perhaps those with whom he so blithely played were really playing with him. He found that he had much less time and much less freedom of action than he had thought.

And still he had not taken a single step toward his great objective. It was four years ago now and still he had not exacted revenge for the Kiev pogrom of November 1905, from which he had allowed himself to be carried to safety—which meant, since he was a ripe eighteen at the time, that he had run away.

As though seeking support for his efforts to justify himself, he quite needlessly broke cover in Paris that winter and confided to the editor of *The Anarchist* his never abandoned, carefully nurtured, and ever more positive belief in central terror. "Our task," he said, "is to eliminate the enemies of freedom, strike fear and confusion into ruling circles, force them to realize that the autocratic system cannot be preserved. That goes without saying. But killing governors, admirals, and army commanders is no way to do it: we must kill either Nikolai II or Stolypin."

The words we say out loud, and with which people connect us, are absorbed into our system of beliefs as objective realities and reinforce them. It was a simple theoretical calculation; only terror at the center, not terror at the provincial level, could change the course of such a huge country. It was obvious from afar that Stolypin was entirely responsible for the surprising strength of a state which two years ago no one could possibly have expected to recover. Stolypin, and no one else, was the strongman of unbridled reaction. Stolypin was the most dangerous and pernicious man in Russia (he was often mentioned with hostility in Bogrov's father's circle). Who, if not Stolypin, had broken the back of the revolution? Against all the odds, the regime had been lucky enough to find a man of talent. He was changing Russia irreversibly, but not in a European direction. That was an illusion. He was strengthening the backbone of the medieval autocratic system so that it could last and last and no genuine liberation movement would be able to spread. Intelligent, strong, persistent, unbudging—he was the obvious target for the terrorist.

Some might say that Stolypin had introduced no anti-Jewish measures. No, but he had created the general atmosphere of depression. It was under Stolypin, and with the election of his Third Duma, that the Jews had begun to give in to despondency, to despair of ever obtaining the right to exist as normal human beings in Russia. Stolypin had done nothing directly against the Jews, he had even made their lives easier in some ways, but it did not come from the heart. To decide whether or not a man is the enemy of the Jews you must look beneath the surface.

Stolypin boosted *Russian* national interests too blatantly and too insistently—the *Russianness* of the Duma as a representative body, the *Russianness* of the state. He was trying to build, not a country in which all were free, but a nationalist monarchy. So that the future of the Jews in Russia was not affected by his goodwill toward them. The development of the country along Stolypin's lines promised no golden age for the Jews.

Bogrov might or might not take part in revolutionary activity, might associate with the Maximalists, with the Anarcho-Communists, or with no one, might change his party allegiance and change his character many times over—but one thing was beyond doubt: his exceptionally talented people must gain the fullest opportunity to develop unimpeded in Russia.

Life, however, finds ways of obstructing a man's most cherished schemes. The time to finish his university course was approaching—he needed a Russian diploma. It might be best to see as little as possible of the surviving anarchists, to let his former friendships go cold. He could fob Kulyabko off with any silly nonsense. If casual acquaintances who showed intelligence mentioned politics Bogrov would say that it no longer interested him. On the other hand he was often seen, a young man-about-town with faultless manners, at the card tables in the Commercial Club, the House Owners' Club, and the Huntsmen's Club.

But none of that gives a twenty-two-year-old much joy. He decided that in the last analysis life is no more than a dismal obligation to eat an endless series of rissoles. His deepest disappointment, perhaps, was that he found no woman to love him. It shines out from his picture: the face is that of a plaster saint, but with pouting lips. In conversation and in his letters he hinted at personal difficulties which were driving him crazy. (Suspicion of him lingered.) Like all of us in that sort of situation, he was disgusted above all with the place he lived in—with Kiev—which he could not leave because of the examinations ahead of him, with his unaccommodating country as a whole, with his barren life. The best thing would be to go abroad again, to the Riviera perhaps, but his hands were tied. Before him lay examinations and yet more examinations.

He graduated at last in January 1910 and was now "a useless member of the lawyer caste." As a Jew he could not immediately become a practicing attorney. His father offered him a large sum of money to set up in business, but he refused it. Certified politically reliable by the Governor's Chancery, he was taken on as an assistant by a Kiev lawyer named Goldenweiser, his father's friend. He still wanted to leave Kiev as soon as he could, partly because he disliked his work, but also because the suspicions of his revolutionary comrades weighed heavily on him. Kulyabko also advised him to go. But go where? Where could he find rest in that joyless land? Certainly not in some provincial hole in European Russia, that slapdash amalgam of bogland and ignorance. Perhaps among the exiles in freedom-loving, intellectual Irkutsk? With his university diploma he could now live where he pleased. This right had previously been denied him, because like his father he refused to change his religion for the sake of privilege. His first name is always given as Mordko in official documents.

Compulsory military service was another set of shackles. Even university graduates still had to serve their time. He was lucky enough to obtain a certificate of exemption (there is no knowing whether his father helped with this too or whether the doctor provided it honestly): "This young man is unfit for military service because of his eyesight—*he is incapable of taking aim and shooting at a target.*"

During his last months at the university the big bang on Astrakhan Street in Petersburg exposed, posthumously, yet another double-dealer, Petrov-Voskresensky. How many of us are there? he wondered. One after another was exposed to the public gaze, and the blaze of their destruction illuminated each of them at a different stage in his breakneck career, and in a different pose—this one abjectly cowering, this other challenging high heaven.

The full story of Petrov-Voskresensky never came to light, but as far as anyone could understand he had gone a stage beyond any other terrorist in inventiveness. He had played a complicated game of his own with the Socialist Revolutionaries and the Okhrana, devising and carrying through all the moves himself. He had made himself indispensable to the Okhrana, and was casting his net to kill several of the most important police officials simultaneously, including Kurlov, the Vice-Minister, but as chance would have it only Karpov was blown up.

There was a lesson here: Do not give yourself away by following the stupid instructions of an underground gang. Bogrov's intentions were quite different. He felt within himself the concentrated will to engage the whole state in single combat and strike at its heart. Once free of the university and the army, he left Kiev in a rush and without regret, not of course for Irkutsk but for Petersburg. He would have a clearer view of things there.

Petersburg was not a center of free thought, but a Jewish lawyer's position was more comfortable there than in any other city. Besides, his brother, Lev, also an attorney's assistant, lived there (the Bogrov family, following the fashion of the time, were all going in for law). Strings were pulled and the well-known attorney Kalmanovich readily took Bogrov on. He did not have time to acquire a clientele, and earned nothing, but other patrons found another part-time job for him with the Society for Combating the Adulteration of Foodstuffs. He became an habitué of Petersburg clubs.

The break with the Kiev Okhrana division seems to have come as a relief, but he providently asked Kulyabko to write recommending him to von Kotten, Karpov's successor as head of the Petersburg branch of the

Okhrana. He made no approach until June, when he arranged to meet von Kotten in a restaurant.

Von Kotten, perhaps because his predecessor had so carelessly got himself killed, was mistrustful, unforthcoming, and also more intelligent than Kulyabko. He seems, moreover, to have taken a dislike to Bogrov. Still, he gave the newcomer the job of keeping an eye on the Petersburg anarchists and offered him one hundred and fifty rubles a month, as before. At their second meeting Bogrov announced that there were no anarchists in Petersburg, and was told to watch Socialist Revolutionaries instead. In beginning this game all over again Bogrov had no clear end in view and no serious intention of throwing light on anything. Nor did he regard von Kotten with the humorous condescension he had felt toward Kulyabko. He seems to have given some sort of information, but at very irregular intervals. Okhrana divisions were so ill-informed that his reports may have looked serious, but there was nothing important in them. The Okhrana was no better off for knowing that the Socialist Revolutionaries abroad were up in arms against Burtsev after his hasty and sensational revelation of Petrov's party affiliation. The biggest item was the following episode: A woman who happened to be returning from Paris had brought letters from the Central Committee of the Socialist Revolutionary Party and was supposed to pass them on via Kalmanovich (this would do him some slight damage, but he was in a strong position) or via Yegor Lazarev to the editorial offices on the Nevsky, but the Socialist Revolutionaries had forgotten that everything would be closed and everybody would be on holiday for three days for the Feast of the Holy Trinity. The job of looking after the letters went to Bogrov, and he was able to show them to von Kotten. There was in fact nothing concrete or of much interest in them, which of course is why Bogrov felt he could show them. He could tell himself that he was not working for the Okhrana; he was, so to speak, continuing his study of an Okhrana division, this time that of the capital. He was not much more favorably impressed than he had been by the Kiev branch. Why, even Petrov had managed pretty well in Petersburg.

Petrov was like one of those serial reflections in double mirrors, showing Bogrov his own image and what the possibilities were (there were many more than the other man had seen).

But it was hard to steel his will for the sacrificial act, enfeebled as it was by his bourgeois existence—just as it had once been too hard for him to face imprisonment in Lukyanovka.

Then something startling happened. That June, Bogrov was sent incognito by the Society for Combating Adulteration to check the filtering plant at the city waterworks. While he was there someone suddenly pushed past him. There was no bodyguard, no sign of security precautions, and the man was accompanied only by a group of engineers—but when he stopped a few steps away Bogrov saw . . . Stolypin!

The robust figure, the deep voice, the firm step, the decisive manner reinforced the impression of strength, unshakable determination, and health which could be picked up in newspaper reports from remote parts of the All-Russian amphitheater. About his strength there had never been any doubt: he alone had rescued his immense country from that dreadful situation. At that distance Bogrov felt the magnetic pull of his triumphant hostile strength.

But his Browning was not in his pocket. He had lost the habit of carrying it.

And if it had been, would he have had the strength of purpose to do the deed? Theoretically, he had it all worked out—but doing it just like that and . . . then . . . and then?

This encounter laid bare Bogrov's impotence and plunged him into gloom. An improbable opportunity had come his way and passed him by, and he could not expect it to happen again.

Petersburg had brought him no closer to achieving anything . . .

But Stolypin, in his speech about Azef, which Bogrov read with the keen eye of hatred, straightforwardly endorsed his plan, confirming in effect that no "action" of any importance had ever succeeded if it was connected with a large organization. Among thousands of careless readers Stolypin had one—Bogrov—who carefully noted the statement that from 1906 on actions organized by the Central Committee of the Socialist Revolutionary Party had invariably failed. There was obviously no point in working with them. The explosion on Aptekarsky Island, the "ex" on Fonarny Lane, the killing of Min, Pavlov, Count Ignatiev, Launits, Maksimovsky—all these actions had been successfully carried out only because they were the work of autonomous groups, flying squads, unconnected with the Central Committee.

Central terror was essential, and it could not be, it surely was not impracticable even in an epoch of general enfeeblement. But it could only be carried out by individuals!

Bogrov became keenly interested in criminal law. He sometimes sat through the proceedings in a criminal court as an ordinary spectator. He wrote from Petersburg: "I have looked into millions of different confidence tricks. Someday it will be *something special*, as we used to say."

He went around Petersburg silent, polite, aloof. He never exchanged a word even with his landlady.

The unimportant affair of the SR letters from Paris gave Bogrov the occasion to call on Yegor Lazarev. Lazarev was well known as a member of the SR Party, an enemy of the regime, a supporter of murderous terrorism, but at that particular time no criminal charges could be brought against him and he had never been banished from Petersburg, but worked undisturbed in an editorial office on the Nevsky Prospect.

After his first unimportant visit Bogrov, in a state of high excitement, asked to be allowed to make a second. He was excited because the Socialist

Revolutionary Party was incomparably superior to the anarchists when it came to central terror and because Lazarev was quite a major figure. For the first and last time Bogrov brought himself to give someone else a glimpse of his maturing plan. (But how could he be sure of convincing the man?)

The famous Socialist Revolutionary's caller was a beardless youth wearing a pince-nez, looking rather ill and very tired. His upper incisors were too long and stuck out when his upper lip rose as he spoke.

"I have decided," he announced in a cracked voice, "to kill Stolypin. I have no suitable partners in mind but I don't in fact need them. My decision is a firm one."

(Was it so very firm, though? Quite irreversible? We sometimes try out desperate thoughts as a sort of game: What if I jumped from the train this very moment?)

Lazarev could not conceal a smile. "Why are you starting right at the top?"

Bogrov's answer to that had been ready long ago. "In Russian conditions only systematic revolutionary struggle with members of the central ruling group can have any effect. In Russia the system is personified by the ruling few. We must kill them one after another, as they step into key positions. Give them no chance to settle down. They will have to give in. That's when we shall change Russia."

"But why start with Stolypin?" Lazarev asked teasingly, as though he were talking to a little boy. "How did you conclude that it had to be him?"

Well, he had considered the pros and cons very carefully indeed: "We have to strike right at the nerve center so as to paralyze the whole state with a single blow. And for as long as possible. Only a blow aimed at Stolypin can have that sort of effect. He is the most noxious personage, the kingpin of this regime. By standing up to the attacks of the opposition he gives the regime an unnatural appearance of solidity, when it is not really solid at all. His policies are exceptionally harmful to the people's interests. The most dreadful thing he has brought about is the incredible decline in the people's interest in politics. The people no longer have any enthusiasm for political reform. As things are going 1905 will soon be forgotten! People are beginning to feel at home with the changes Stolypin has made and the very memory of the Liberation movement is fading, as though the Decembrists and Herzen and the nihilists and the People's Will Party and the ferment in the early years of this century had never been. Stolypin is repressing Finland, Poland, and all the non-Russian peoples of the Empire. We must put an end to all this with a single swift blow."

"Listen, young man," Lazarev said more sympathetically. "So many activists have thirsted for Stolypin's blood—but nobody has had any success."

A young man in a pince-nez, with puny arms, and a stoop, as though his growth had been stunted. Weak and sickly in appearance. But his manner was imperturbably calm and businesslike. "Excuse me. I have planned Stolypin's murder with great care and am determined to carry out my plan at all costs. He is—if I may put it that way—too good for this country. I have decided to eject him from the political arena for my own private ideological reasons. Besides, killing ministers of the interior is an excellent tradition. Whoever holds the post must be made to feel that it's too hot for him."

Bogrov's composure and his ready answers had made something of an impression and given Lazarev a lot to think about. But he still knew too little about this youth.

"But you are a Jew. Have you considered carefully what the consequences could be?"

He had considered everything. His automatic response was even prompter than before.

"Precisely because I am a Jew I can't bear the knowledge that we are still living—if I may remind you—under the heavy hand of the Black Hundred leaders. The Jews will never forget the Krushevans, Dubrovins, and Purishkeviches. Remember what happened to Herzenstein. And Iollos. What of the thousands of Jews savagely done to death? The chief culprits always go unpunished. Well, I shall punish them."

"Then why not go straight for the Tsar?" Lazarev asked with a smile.

"I've thought it over carefully. If Nikolai is killed there will be a pogrom. But there will be no pogrom for Stolypin. Anyway, Nikolai is only Stolypin's puppet. Moreover, killing the Tsar would do no good. Stolypin would continue his present policies with still greater assurance under Nikolai's successor."

Bogrov's intelligence made a powerful impression, as always. But his physical appearance was so unimpressive. Lazarev was still uncertain and shook his head slowly. "But why exactly did you decide to tell me all this? Is there something I can do to help you?"

Bogrov risked a little fib. "My real reason for coming to Petersburg was simply to see you."

He was quick to explain that he had certainly not come to seek material or technical aid from the mighty SR Party, or a training course on the assassination of prime ministers of great states. No, he could plan it and do it all himself. What he wanted was a little advice: in whose name should he act? He was asking permission to do it in the name of the SR Party, that was all. "I shall do what I have made up my mind to do. But I am haunted by the thought that my action will be misrepresented, and so lose its political significance. If it is to have its proper educational effect, there must be people, preferably a political party, to explain my behavior correctly when I am gone."

Lazarev listened to Bogrov's assurances that it was all irrevocably decided, but he also heard the reedy voice, he saw out of the corner of his eye the slack, sickly face, the puny, pampered body softened by self-indulgence—and was unpersuaded. It was too easy to imagine the young man's strength failing him when he came to throw his bomb, too easy to see him dropping his pince-nez while he was taking aim. Or else he would be grabbed by the police, flop into the mire, and leave a nasty stain on the reputation of the SR Party. (And there was always the possibility that the whole thing was a provocation.) So he passed it off with another joke.

"What I don't understand is how you can be such a pessimist at your young age? Disappointed in love maybe? You'll get over it."

Bogrov insisted that his decision was absolutely final. (Having to insist so much reinforced it further.) Surely the SR Party would not refuse the honor of associating itself with such an act? What weighed on his mind was the thought that an individual act planned in secret and explained to no one would be subject to malicious misinterpretation. Well, he was asking the SR Party to sanction the act only after his arrest, interrogation, trial, and execution—only if he died worthily! But he had to go to his death with the assurance that he would be supported and explained.

He did not carry conviction. Lazarev refused outright even to submit Bogrov's proposal to the SR Central Committee. He gave him one piece of advice: that if his present state of mind was not just temporary he should confide in no one else.

Bogrov could see that he was doomed to remain isolated.

"Very well, but what if . . . Maybe I could write to you sometime?"

"Write if you want to. To the office. Address it to Nikolai Yakovlevich."

Bogrov had not expected to be turned down like that. His supports had collapsed under him. His hopes and expectations were left in the air. The assassination plan became a hazy notion of dubious value.

It was quite hopeless trying the Social Democrats. Secretly they would be glad of the murder, but publicly they would dissociate themselves from it and feign indignation.

If only the Petersburg climate were not so rotten! Eight months there had ruined his health. If it wasn't backache, it was stomach trouble. He was lonely and bored, he lost all interest in life. So the doctors sent the exhausted young man to Nice to rest and recover from nervous strain. His legal career was over before it had begun. And the whole idea of the assassination had receded into the mists.

In December 1910 he was on the Riviera. He spent the whole winter in the south of France instead of in dank, dark Petersburg, and his parents, who also liked a winter holiday by the Mediterranean, joined him there.

On this occasion he had no contact with émigré revolutionaries. But, to keep his hand in, he wrote to von Kotten giving him trivial snippets of information about the SRs abroad and asking for money. Von Kotten sent him some, but Bogrov did not even collect the last remittance from the post office.

He played roulette in Monte Carlo, played cards, and felt his depression gradually lifting. From the plate-glass windows of his hotel he could see blue bays. What strange mirage had he pursued so doggedly? Something to do with an assassination? Life was so beautiful without all that.

But every idyll must come to an end. In March he returned to Kiev and registered again as a junior barrister. But, as before, he did not practice. He never had occasion to speak in court or to turn the celebrated Goldenweiser's patronage to good account. Nor did he call on Kulyabko. He had not in fact done so since leaving for Petersburg. He had given that game up.

He was racked by a feeling of spiritual unfulfillment, an indefinable anxiety. After his promising university career he found his present life empty, and all his luxuries, his advantages, his amusements meant nothing to him. No woman struck a spark in him, and no one fell in love with him. He was soon sick of Kiev again. He had had one taste of Petersburg and that was enough. As for jingoistic Moscow, he never even thought of going there. The time itself had palled on him: a time in which everybody else was so busy living and experiencing to him was a meaningless succession of empty hours, a blank age.

When he returned to Russia that March he had suffered another soul-sickening blow: a government decision extended the Jewish *numerus clausus* to external-degree students. This did not immediately affect either Bogrov or his relations, but it was like a punch in the solar plexus. It jolted him out of his torpor. Until then a Jew could get around the *numerus clausus*, if his family was at all well-off, by enrolling as an external student. Now even that road was closed.

Still in March, some boy or other was murdered in Kiev. There were allegations that it was a Jewish ritual murder, and a Jewish shop assistant who lived near the child's home was charged with it.

The country was incorrigible, and so was its cocksure Prime Minister, whom Bogrov read like a book. Only a powerful explosion would cut that benighted epoch short. But bomb throwing was beyond his powers. It would have to be the right bullet in the right chest.

Bogrov always kept several revolvers in his apartment. He could permit himself this because of his father's position and his friendship with Kulyabko.

But what good were they now? His boasts to Lazarev had been idle: how could he ever get close enough to Stolypin? The most experienced terrorists had failed. There would never be a second chance like that at the waterworks.

That spring the newspapers suddenly started clamoring about Stolypin's fall, his impending retirement. Was it too late? Would he fall without being pushed?

Stolypin kept his footing. But his prestige with the public was much shaken. Now was the time to finish him off . . .

Rumors went around Kiev, followed shortly by crude preparations for a ceremonial visit by the Tsar in September. What was it all about? A memorial to Aleksandr II on the fiftieth anniversary of the emancipation of the serfs, a memorial to Princess Olga, but above all they wanted an excuse to plant the autocratic heel firmly on Kiev, to make it a bulwark of Russian nationalism—another of Stolypin's ideas.

What luck! No need to seek out Russia's "central" figures in Petersburg—they were bound for Kiev!

The Tsar would be there with his dog pack of courtiers, but would Stolypin?

This brazen junketing must surely ignite the flame of hatred in any heart touched by revolution. He could not, would not refrain from spoiling his enemies' fete and making them ridiculous.

In June his parents went to their summer place near Kremenchug and he went with them. He took solitary walks along the Dniepr, thinking things over. The steppe air failed to soothe his torn and tormented breast.

Bogrov's brother also came to stay, with his wife. But neither his brother nor his father was given any inkling of what was in his mind.

They returned to Kiev in August. His parents then left to continue their holiday in Europe, while his brother went back to Petersburg. The younger Bogrov was left behind in their multistoried house with nothing to do except keep an eye on the lodgers, and all alone unless you counted an old aunt, a maid, a cook, and a few other servants.

Alone.

It was a great relief to heart and mind. He need no longer pretend, no longer conceal things, no one would question him about his comings and goings. He could live in silence. Live within himself.

Meanwhile, police invaders from Petersburg and Moscow had started accosting even people of respectable appearance on the streets and asking to see their documents. Political undesirables were temporarily banished from Kiev. Apartments, garrets, and cellars were being inspected along all the routes which the royal procession might follow. Searches were made here and there.

Get on with it, you dogs! Get ready for what's coming!

All this time Bogrov never once lost his self-possession. He was blessed with a rare characteristic: the closer the danger, the more self-possessed he was. He wrote detailed business letters to his father (he would have been perfectly capable of running a successful business!) recommending a bribe to an engineer to get someone a profitable order from the city council, suggesting precautions to make both sides feel safe and ensure that the bribe would not slip through the giver's fingers with nothing in return. "I hope you will trust my experience, Papa."

If doubt, anxiety, despair preyed on him none of this showed on the surface.

In every man's life there is, sooner or later, a supreme moment. For Bogrov the moment was approaching.

[6 4]

The streets and buildings of Kiev were decked with flags, pictures of the royal couple, the royal monogram. Many balconies were draped with fine rugs or tapestries and adorned with flowers, and some houses were lit up. The populace awaited the promised spectacle openmouthed. For their information (and for Bogrov's) a detailed program of the festivities which were to begin on 11 September and end on 19 September was made public.

Bogrov spent a lot of time at home alone, waiting, achingly expectant, sitting, lying down, wandering from room to room, daydreaming, going over and over his plan, examining it from all angles and eliminating whatever should not be there.

It was like a colossal circus with all Kiev, all Russia, indeed the whole world as the invited audience. Hundreds of thousands of spectators goggled from the amphitheater at two performers on a platform high up under the big top—the crowned idiot and Stolypin. To strike a mortal blow at one of them little Bogrov had to get very close, rise to a great height, and since he could not fly, he had to climb, but without a ladder, and with thousands of policemen there to stop him.

When you visualize a circus the first thing you see is the center pole supporting the big top. He had to hoist himself up such a pole, smooth and slippery, without a notch or a knot in the wood, with nothing but the polished surface to cling to, with no one supporting him and everybody willing him to fall.

An impossible task if ever there was one.

But look more closely. Perhaps at least one of the terms of the problem could be changed? Could he give himself wings? Nature forbade it. Should he go around the various Central Committees looking for helpers? He had already rejected the idea. Shorten the pole? Its height was not one of the variables. Make the pole rougher? His own tender skin would suffer most. Or maybe, once on the pole, you could somehow neutralize the resistance of the Okhrana? He must try. Otherwise, what had been the point of those past few years of pretended collaboration?

If the Okhrana turned out to be clever after all, the game would be up. But experience suggested that they wouldn't be.

He lay around, paced the room, lolled in his rocking chair, did exercises with dumbbells. Indulged in daydreams. Reviewed his plans.

It was stuffy and the windows were wide open. Ice cream was served at lunch, and there was ice with the drinks. He faced his aunt across the spacious table, at lunch and at dinner, in a dream. He did not go to his clubs, did not play cards. His purpose demanded total mental and physical concentration.

The program for the royal festivities lay before him. The convenient midpoint was obviously 13 September, in the Merchants' Garden on the bank of the Dniepr.

But if it was done there, by the river, why not try to slip away after? Find a motorboat, run to it, jump in?

He started wandering along the embankments, onto the quays, along the shore.

But it was easier to invent the unimaginable—a way of getting through to the chairman of the Council of Ministers—than to find a way, and a language, to approach the rough, strange, incomprehensible Dniepr boatmen, to inspire confidence at such a suspicious time, and to let someone else take a peek at his secret. He could pay whatever might be asked for the motorboat. What he could not do was spin a plausible yarn. To him those boatmen were creatures from another planet.

On 8 September he called on some reliable acquaintances and left letters with them—one to his parents and two for the newspapers.

Then he telephoned the Okhrana from home, gave his name, and asked whether "the boss" was in.

He was out of luck. He had missed Kulyabko. But he knew everybody there and proposed an early meeting with Samson Demidyuk, who was in charge of outdoor surveillance.

They met in a doorway in Georgievsky Lane, and Bogrov solemnly informed Demidyuk that "there are plans to make an attempt on the lives of extremely important people in the course of the celebrations."

This one tremendous sentence would have sufficed to send Demidyuk running to Kulyabko. But Bogrov did not begrudge him a few details. The assassination team was coming from Petersburg, bringing its weapons. It was looking for a safe way to enter Kiev and establish itself there. Bogrov would be given his instructions.

His inspiration was as brilliant as it was daring: he would proceed *almost* straightforwardly, speak *almost* the truth. Insistently warning the police that the murder would take place was an important part of his plan. Had anyone ever done it that way before?

At the very least it gave him a toehold. It was an official impossibility for them to ignore such a sensational piece of information.

He went home and paced the room nervously. Making a start was what mattered: discovering whether you could shinny up the pole a little way or whether you would slip back immediately.

He rang the Okhrana office again, and this time Kulyabko was in. The stupid bleating voice expressed pleasure! Not a word from his favorite informer for eighteen months—and suddenly he turns up again with such sensational news! Kulyabko believed him, Kulyabko was hooked—so far, so good. He had climbed the first couple of meters, he was holding on, he wasn't sliding back.

What happened next was something new. Kulyabko invited him not to the Okhrana offices but to his home. That had never happened before. Why the change? Was it a trap? Kulyabko's explanation seemed honest enough: he had dinner guests and could not put them off. This confession of human weakness, and his cordial tone, reassured Bogrov that he was trusted completely. All the same, he went along with the Browning in his pocket. (He had made his plans when he thought he would be going to the Okhrana offices: if his story was not accepted, if he was seen through immediately, he would shoot Kulyabko and the others, run for it, and maybe shoot himself. On Kulyabko's hearth the gun was probably superfluous, but it might not be. He didn't know the house, the ways in and out of it. Besides, in Kulyabko's own home there would be no body search. Right, take it.)

There was not a single toehold of fact, nothing real to cling to, in Bogrov's communication. One slip and he would break every bone in his body. There was no retreat. The gun was in his pocket.

Demidyuk led him along Zolotovorotskaya Street and by the back entrance to Kulyabko's apartment. The master of the house (Lieutenant Colonel Kulyabko now) met him in the anteroom at the rear and, showing his trust, led him to the study by way of . . . the bathroom! There was no other way in.

The lively after-dinner conversation in the dining room was quite audible from there. Kulyabko had not wiped the grease from his lips. There was still dessert to come, and how he would enjoy it with this visitor to boast about when he returned to his guests. He looked so cordial, so jolly, so trusting—as though he would have liked to invite Bogrov to join the dinner party if etiquette permitted.

Bogrov started going over it point by point, developing the theme, but Kulyabko wanted to get back to his food and his guests: "You sit there and write it all down, my dear fellow!" He left Bogrov in the study (the explosion on Astrakhan Street had taught him nothing!) and went back to finish his dinner.

Write it down? What if it turned out to be true, and the terrorists were right behind him? In that case, putting it in writing would be suicide. What did Kulyabko expect him to do with a pen? Chew what was left of the quill?

Events which at the time seem trivial sometimes prove surprisingly useful later on. Instinct told Bogrov to retrieve such plausible details from the past as he could, to tell the truth wherever it no longer mattered. For some days past he had been dredging insignificant fragments from the depths of his memory: for instance, the woman who had arrived from Paris on the Feast of the Holy Trinity in 1910, a friend of Kalmanovich's daughter if he remembered rightly. For some reason she was the intermediary for less important letters from the Central Committee of the Socialist Revolutionary Party . . . When Kalmanovich went away himself he had left his assistant Bogrov to pass on all correspondence. Bogrov had showed the letters to von Kotten . . . then passed them on to Yegor Lazarev (Bogrov knew that Stolypin had commuted Lazarev's sentence of Siberian exile to exile abroad, so that he was in no danger) and . . . there had been two other letters . . . One to a young revolutionary . . . let's call him Nikolai Yakovlevich. (Lazarev had mentioned this name in his office. It was all grist for the mill.)

The plot was thickening! Get on with it! Yes, well, this Nikolai Yakovlevich had suddenly written in early summer to ask whether Bogrov's views had changed. You have to be on your guard with revolutionaries: saying nothing is as dangerous as telling the truth. So he had said no, they haven't changed. And all at once who should turn up in July, at the Bogrovs'dacha near Kremenchug (when he was there he had wandered around bored and apathetic, little knowing how useful his holiday would prove in his catalogue of plausible coincidences), who should turn up but Nikolai Yakovlevich in person! Who had then revealed . . .

(But if Nikolai Yakovlevich was a serious terrorist, and committed to such a great enterprise, would he, on the strength of a single sentence in a letter, immediately set off to see the suspect and no longer active anarchist Bogrov, and expose himself and all his secrets? Oh, what a smooth and slippery pole it was! He must embrace its thin body more tightly, use all the friction of his own body to ease his way over the improbabilities.)

. . . who had then revealed that his terrorist group—three comrades from different places—was on its way to Kiev to carry out an action during the festivities. He had heard that papers were strictly examined at the railway station and the quay, and wondered whether Bogrov would help by getting them into Kiev immediately before the festivities—say, by motorboat from Kremenchug. (Kremenchug had come in very handy—like the woman from Paris. The motorboat too had bounced into the picture. It was all fitting together beautifully, without his help.) Would he get them a motorboat, and also a hideout for three in Kiev? Nikolai Yakovlevich had then left.

The diners appeared, cheerful, tipsy, unsteady. First Kulyabko, like a fat drake. Then Colonel Spiridovich, a handsome, well-educated, sharp-witted martinet with spiky mustaches. There was also a pale, sickly-looking civilian—Verigin, a state councillor. Bogrov's story had evidently been told at dinner—and now, gentlemen, here he is, the interesting character who worked for me for some years and always gave accurate information. What has he got for us this time?

They took the sheet of paper in their warm fingers, greedy for novelty, read it with half-drunk eyes, turned it this way and that, passed it around, exchanged significant looks. If we can catch a team like this, when everybody imagines that terror has died down, it will be medals and promotion all around. And the terrorists are walking straight into the net!

Yes, he had baited the hook cleverly. He knew their sordid little souls, Bogrov did! Would any of the stuff he had written convince a sober man? That bulge in his pocket was the Browning. (He cursed himself for bringing it, but their six eyes somehow couldn't see it. What if they did, though? Asked what it was? Would he shoot? There were three of them—he would never get out of the apartment . . .)

They were, however, policemen and did not forget to frown at him and fire awkward questions: "How did Nikolai Yakovlevich know your address in the country?"

"He went to my house in Kiev first and one of the household told him."

"Right, but . . . why didn't you bring us this important information immediately?"

(It didn't occur to them to ask why he had come at all: it was everyone's duty to report, of course. Kulyabko had never once wondered in those four years why Bogrov was so eager to serve or what sort of man he was.)

The young intellectual with the narrow head always held a little to one side, and the invariably parted lips, gazed trustingly at the experienced police officers through his pince-nez. He was obviously incapable of hiding anything. "Well," he told them, "Nikolai Yakovlevich went off immediately and I was left empty-handed and I would have felt awkward coming to you with nothing. I've been waiting all this time for him to put in an appearance. But time is going by, the celebrations are getting close. Then in one of the papers"—it had in fact been in one of those right-wing papers that lawyers devoured so eagerly—"there was some mention of a possible assassination attempt. I was in such a state I didn't know what to do. If they dropped on me now and asked me to help, they would keep me under observation and I would never get to you to ask whether I ought to buy them a boat or find an apartment for them . . ."

Spiridovich sternly vetoed the motorboat. What about the apartment? Why not? In order to know where they were and take them more easily. Kulyabko thought it was all right, and even knew the right house—it belonged to the former wife of one of his clerks.

(That didn't suit Bogrov at all. You can't billet phantoms on a real live landlady!)

He demurred. He was afraid they would smell a rat. If the landlady aroused their suspicions the whole operation would collapse.

"Whose apartment would you suggest, then?"

"Well, a woman I know has gone abroad. Or, if you agree, they could even have mine. My parents have gone away."

"Well, perhaps that would be the best thing." (It would be easier to keep an eye on them through Bogrov.)

(He was holding on!)

He would move even closer to the truth, make it even more natural.

"As I understand it, the action will take place not at the beginning of the celebrations but toward the end, when security is getting slacker." (That was indeed how it would be—so tell them straight! Warn the Okhrana directly—there's daring for you!)

Spiridovich was the most professional of them, and the only intelligent one. "Why," he asked, "did Nikolai Yakovlevich confide in you so readily and tell you all the details?"

"Well, I told Nikolai Yakovlevich that I didn't want to be a pawn in their hands, that I would help only on the condition that I was made privy to all their plans." (See, I'm not such a little fish! I mean to know everything! Just trust me! Just hang on to me!)

It sounded convincing.

Still, Spiridovich's eyes, as sharp as the points of his mustaches, bored away.

"Well then, if you know the whole plan, who is it to be? His Imperial Majesty?"

No! (Not only because that *was* the correct answer—as nobody could know better than Bogrov—but to make sure that nobody would entertain the thought. If he let them think that it was even a possibility they would become far too active.) "Oh no. They're afraid that there would be a pogrom. So they plan to make attempts on two ministers—Stolypin" (right out with it!) "and Kasso" (very realistic—the Minister of Education was violently hated by progressive students; it would also divide the Okhrana's attention).

Spiridovich's wariness was evidently giving way again to a blissful state of postprandial repletion.

(He was holding on! How clever he had been!)

They asked him next to describe Nikolai Yakovlevich. He would do his best, though he hadn't got to know the man very well yet. He spoke without hesitation, but the description was somewhat vague: jet-black hair, medium long, a black mustache, neither big nor small, an intellectual face, attractive eyes . . .

They took it all in. Jotted it down. "Must send this to Kremenchug."

The state councillor said, "Just sign these notes, if you please."

Bogrov only grinned to see what a novice the state councillor was, and what a ninny. "Oh no! That would be too dangerous for me. There may be traitors on your staff."

(Also quite plausible. I've scored again!)

They had run out of questions. Neither the lieutenant colonel nor the colonel had any more doubts . . .

(This was just as Bogrov had hoped. He knew, and other people acknowledged, that he was an unusually convincing storyteller: when he wanted to he could stick out his neck and warble like an exotic bird, enchanting his hearers. Even his enemies were charmed by him at such moments.)

He grew bolder, cheekier, and hoisted himself a little higher still. No one outside the world of officialdom could possibly grasp the importance of this latest move. He did not realize himself what a staggering stroke it was. He only wanted to slip a drop of poison into relations between the three and weaken them.

"Nikolai Yakovlevich says that they even have connections among the staff of the police department and in the Petersburg Okhrana division. They are sure that they will succeed."

(Why, then, need they come to Kiev? Had he gone too far this time?)

No, he hadn't overdone it. They were all allies here, all on the same side, what one of them said all four thought. Kulyabko went over to a packet conveniently lying there: courtesy tickets to the gala performance at the opera, and also to the garden party in the Merchants' Garden on 13 September. He offered one of each to Bogrov—"I'll just write your name in." (Out of gratitude? Or with what object? Or was it just that he had to be fussing and bustling? Bogrov couldn't understand it. Silly fellow with his silly blond hair plastered flat—made him even more like an old drake. Bogrov had always known that Kulyabko was stupid, but he had not expected things to be as easy as this!)

The daring acrobat saw himself already halfway up the pole—no, more than halfway: the impotent ants from among whom he had begun his upward crawl three hours ago now looked very tiny. The longed-for platform was not so very far above him! With no one to vouch for him, how had he hauled himself so far up the slippery pole of improbabilities? What was holding him there?

The very thing he needed! A ticket for a closed performance at which Stolypin would be present and wide open . . . and so, incidentally, would that . . . Emperor of theirs. The theater ticket was floating toward his gun hand, scorching it. What a stroke of luck! What a victory! And at his first attempt!

Any other young man would have grabbed the ticket, but Bogrov was too wise for that. Never accept victories too easily won! The trust he had established was worth more than the ticket. (Besides, the performance was six days away. They might come to their senses and take the ticket back.)

And so he declined the enticing crimson ticket with a gesture of languid disinterest and his head slightly on one side, meaning: I don't want to make myself conspicuous.

Very well. His instructions were to go on observing the terrorists. In case of need Demidyuk was at his disposal. With that, they said goodbye, leaving Bogrov free to act as he pleased, with no obligations and no arrangement about future contacts or the next meeting.

Astounded by a success beyond all his expectations, borne along by the joy of victory, a merry Bogrov went to recover from his friends the letters explaining the shooting which might have taken place that day but had proved unnecessary.

O happiness! Had he really neutralized the enemy? Better than that—he had made the police his helpers, instead of the SRs! What a splendid joke! Though there was no one to share it with and he could not be sure that anyone would ever appreciate it.

The conditions of the enterprise had changed drastically. No longer was everything against him. He just had to take care not to let go of what he had already won.

Stop! Perhaps they had put him under surveillance. He checked. No, his movements were unobserved.

The idiots! The blockheads!

O happiness! Somewhere in the future was the shot he would fire—and his doom. Today, though, was a day of victory and freedom, in a Kiev summer with the chestnuts fast ripening. Ahead of him lay another week of freedom.

He was, in fact, entirely free. He had put himself under no obligation. He had signed nothing. Quite possibly "Nikolai Yakovlevich" would think better of it and stay away. Then the only consequence would be his pay envelope from Kulyabko.

That and the loneliness.

The nagging thoughts.

The mounting tension.

9 September.

Whereas if the deed was done, he would be free at once and forever of all suspicions and accusations. Once he had killed, he would be clean forever.

10 September.

You can play cards with a pack of fifty-two, thirty-six, or fewer. The elements in his game were fewer, but harder to read. Kulyabko had, it was true, taken shape as a fat duffer, a king of diamonds. But he could not picture Nikolai Yakovlevich in the flesh. His imagination failed him.

They would have sent a whole squad of detectives to Kremenchug. All the better, there would be fewer knocking around in Kiev. Kremenchug and the motorboat had gone down beautifully. There was an air of probability about it.

The elements were simple but not sharply defined. They blurred, ran into one another; the permutations multiplied. Which of them should he commit himself to next?

He would bait his hook so as to tantalize them with the hope of taking the terrorists in the act and scoring a resounding professional success. Play them till the last moment, or even beyond, by never bringing anything to a conclusion.

If that was the way, it would be best to avoid haste, to drag it out, not to see the Okhrana too often.

Another thing—if he didn't see too much of them they might not foist that police apartment on him.

Shut up in his airless room, he paced restlessly, sat down again, rocked, and thought and thought. The few necessary drops for the fatal moment had to accumulate. In his brain? In his craw? In a tooth?

11 September.

For three days his plan had been maturing in a dizzy whirl of thoughts. He had filed every component to a perfect fit. He had gone over all the possible variants—the treacherously splintering contingencies. Worst of all was the worry that at the crucial moment his quick-wittedness would desert him. Or his powers of observation. Or his memory. Or his courage.

The great surprise was that the Okhrana seemed unconcerned, asked no questions, did not telephone. Apparently a trivial matter like a group of terrorists in the city at the same time as the Tsar didn't worry them. They tactfully refrained from troubling him with questions—and did not even keep him under observation. He was never followed! There was just one man discreetly watching his door in case the unmistakable Nikolai Yakovlevich arrived.

Nothing could have been more helpful to Bogrov: his plan was to leave the Okhrana as little time as possible to think over their countermeasures.

It was maddeningly difficult to refrain from doing more than he should, and so tumble from the height he had reached. The hours of loneliness dragged unbearably. He felt sure that he had overlooked some contingencies. (But the detectives' notebooks do not record that Bogrov left the house in all that time.)

To be precise: he dined each day with his aunt, he was visited by unavoidable friends—Feldzer senior and Feldzer junior—at certain times he went to Goldenweiser's office. On 11 September he posted a very businesslike letter to his father abroad—about a poor repair job on the floor, and the insurance. Then at 11 p.m. another friend, Sklovsky, called with his lady friend, and the three of them had a few drinks.

Around 1 a.m. Bogrov went out to see them off, and was able to reassure himself yet again that he was not under surveillance at all, which meant that Kulyabko trusted him implicitly. There was a special piquancy, a special excitement in tippling with people who had not the remotest idea of the feat he was to perform and the successes he had already scored: all that remained an unshared happiness while he chattered merrily about trivialities.

There on the corner of Vladimir Street stood his old high school, the nursery of all his youthful hopes. What former pupil, even with gray hair, even in the empty night hours, will pass without a quickening of the heart the unforgettable building where he and his contemporaries shared their dreams of success and fame? The high school was, as it happened, looking forward to its centenary that month, when the celebrations would be in full swing. Little did the school suspect what sort of birthday salute awaited it.

Bogrov held out until 13 September, and even then it was not until the afternoon that he picked up the receiver at home and asked the exchange to connect him with the Okhrana.

One (not the only) disadvantage of the telephone was that the operator might overhear his conversation. Still there were no operators clever enough to understand and get curious.

The telephone was answered by the duty clerk, Sabaev, whom Bogrov knew well. He dropped in unannounced almost daily to see, not Bogrov's parents, but their cook. "Lieutenant Colonel Kulyabko? Not in."

An indirect message might cost him something. Weaken the effect. Increase the risk. Still—"Please tell the lieutenant colonel that Nikolai Yakovlevich has arrived, that he has the goods with him and is staying with me. And that I need a ticket for the Merchants' Garden today."

An excruciating wait—several hours of it. Kulyabko wasn't responding.

Now he regretted keenly not taking the ticket. He had overplayed his hand.

Doesn't he trust me anymore? Has he found me out? . . . Have I failed?

Overplayed. Overfinessed.

Too clever, I've been. The ticket was there for the taking.

Only a few hours to go before the garden party—and the telephone was silent.

Would anyone ever appreciate his tactical skill and daring in bringing his own home and himself under surveillance immediately before the action? And with the Sabaev coincidence threatening destruction! It was no good telling the maid not to let Sabaev in, and he could so easily come along in person and find out from the cook that nobody new had appeared in the house.

Another possibility—perhaps they had already cordoned off the house and would rush in to seize Nikolai Yakovlevich without waiting for the other conspirators to turn up. It had not been a good idea to say, "He has the goods." If they could catch him with a bomb, what more would they want?

He went out more than once onto the balcony. He surveyed Bibikov Boulevard with a practiced eye. No, no cordon. Just one bored detective on duty.

No, they wouldn't charge in to make an arrest. Supposing they did catch one solitary individual with a weapon, what proof would there be that he had been planning an attempt on any state dignitary? Who would be impressed? If they pounced too soon they would have proved nothing.

Why then no telephone call? It was maddening.

Too bad that he hadn't got on to Kulyabko, to hear his reaction and draw encouragement from his splutterings.

No! Here it came! Sure enough, a ring, a delighted Kulyabko spluttering excitedly into the telephone. "He's come, has he?"

To make it more convincing he spoke in a discreetly hushed voice (somebody in the next room, of course), made it sound as if he was reluctant to talk about top-secret matters on the telephone but felt bound to say something: "Yes, there's one of them here now, there will be others. I've refused to take an active part, but I've been given little jobs to do, and they'll check up on me. To avoid being caught out I have to be in the Merchants' Garden today."

He'll never believe it. Too crude by half!

A numbing chill stole over the whole length of his body: any minute now he would fall straight to the ground. The fall would be too painful, he should never have started climbing.

Kulyabko, however, did not even stop to think; did not even ask why exactly Bogrov wanted the ticket. To the Merchants' Garden—when even the best families in Kiev couldn't get in! Fine, send somebody to pick it up!

Another success! He had stretched his length and swung himself upward with a spiral motion—and still he had risen!

No sooner had he put the phone down than it rang again. An acquaintance, Pevsner. He begged forgiveness, he had rung Bogrov two minutes earlier and the operator had plugged him in by mistake before he had finished his previous call.

Bogrov turned to ice.

Pevsner was very, very sorry, but he couldn't help hearing how readily they had promised Bogrov a ticket to the Merchants' Garden. It would be very interesting to be there. Could Bogrov possibly arrange a ticket for him too . . .?

That idiotic operator! And what an unlikely coincidence! Didn't happen once in two hundred calls!

He interrupted sharply. He was in no mood for conversation; his tongue refused. “I hope this is between ourselves?” was all he could say.

Anxiety clawed at his chest, lacerated him. How much *had* Pevsner heard? All of it perhaps?

How is it that our false steps, our slips, our tumbles always seem to come, not when we are gliding smoothly along, but in the steepest and most dangerous spots?

How is it that time so often dawdles and dozes, and then suddenly tightens into a cutting noose?

Thoughts, plans, dangers, dodges . . . His brain was in a whirl. The messenger had been sent for and gone off and—

Maybe this is your last hour of life?

“My dear, my beloved papa and mama!” (Looking at it through their eyes, imagining their feelings made him sorrier for himself) . . . “You will be terribly distressed by the blow I am inflicting on you, but I can do no other. You know that I have been trying for two years now to give up my old ways . . .” (His letter *zh* had a broken paw, his *ya* dipped below the line like a carrot.) “But even if I had made a success of my career, I would still have ended up the way I am ending now.”

He also wrote another letter, to a friend.

(Nobody was watching him!)

The messenger came back with the precious ticket. With his Browning in his pocket, he squeezed his way unhurriedly through the insanely bright streets past buildings rimmed with a blaze of light, past mountains of fire, past the monument to Aleksandr II unveiled the day before at the entrance to the Garden (an Italianate object in bronze, with a frieze of crude folksy figures and the legend TO THE TSAR LIBERATOR FROM THE GRATEFUL SOUTHWESTERN TERRITORY), past the police at the gate, flourishing the lucky ticket, into the forbidden Garden.

(Still no one watching!)

Through the crush in the Garden, which was still more madly illuminated. Rainbow-colored fountains. Sheaves with dazzling bulbs for ears. Bouquets that spilled their petals in a rain of stars. Some way to the left through the dense trees, St. Vladimir’s cross, outlined in fairy lights, seemed to hang in midair. There was a symphony orchestra near the Tsar’s box. A peasant choir. Russian and Ukrainian folk ensembles.

Past the orchestras, the choirs, the dancers’ platforms. How plaintive those violins were! Perhaps he should surrender to the music, the illuminations, the caressing warmth of the southern night, and give the whole thing up? He had made no promises, nobody was expecting anything from him, nobody would rebuke him.

How often he had touched life with unfeeling fingers, taken it between numb lips, and told himself that it was not worth clinging to, and now, suddenly, he felt such poignant regret. He was only twenty-four, after all. He could live another half century! He might live to see what would happen in 1960! Your life, he told himself, is still fully yours, all hope and expectancy, buoyant on the waves of this music! Somewhere there are women who may bring themselves to love you. (And perhaps, somewhere, fearless ones lurking with revolvers, heroes whom you can save with your brilliant speeches—and leave the courtroom to applause.) But if you yourself press a trigger just once, the bang will be that of your whole world crashing in ruins.

He loved himself. And he despised himself.

A pity he hadn't got hold of that motorboat.

Now he was on lawns flooded with electric light . . . in the green gloom of the avenues . . . among the first few rows of the crowd near the Tsar's marquee.

The marquee was pitched on the steep bank of the Dniepr, to give a view of the fireworks. It was made of dark blue cloth embroidered with golden eagles and surmounted by the crown of Monomakh in blue and white lights. Looking down from the steep bank you saw the twinkling lights on the quays—one quay white, the next green—the huge Brodsky mill, the imperial monograms blazing on Trukhanov Island, a boat transformed by lights into a swan slowly floating down the Dniepr, its shape reflected in the water. The dimmest light was that of the moon from beyond the river. Clusters of rockets burst and the crowded banks could be seen as clearly as by daylight. Bands on both sides struck up the national anthem.

He did not see the Tsar by the marquee. But near the Ukrainian choir's platform he suddenly appeared, squeezing past, two—not three, just two—steps away! Bogrov, slightly behind him, saw the side, then the close-cropped back of his head under his service cap. He had a clear view—he could aim so as to miss the heads of his entourage and hit the Tsar. He had his Browning ready with the first bullet in the chamber. All he need do was feel in his pocket, lift the safety catch, whip the gun out, and fire.

Blow their glittering fete to bits!

Bogrov trembled with sweet longing. How often he had rejected the thought of killing the Tsar. But when it could be done so easily—nothing to it!

The sense of power made his head spin. A gentle squeeze with his index finger—and yet another Russian Tsar would be no more. He might even extinguish the whole dynasty, all the Romanovs, with that one slight movement. An event of world-historical importance!

But—with an effort—he cooled down. This Tsar was a title, and no more. Not a worthwhile target. An object of public ridicule, the utter nonentity this wretched country deserved. Why shoot him? No successor would ever weaken his country more than this Tsar had. For ten years past people had been killing ministers and generals but no one had touched the Tsar. They knew better.

On the other hand, the vengeance exacted if he was killed or wounded would defeat Bogrov's ends. If the Tsar was done away with anywhere else, it might not be too bad. But if it was done in Kiev, and by him, it would mean a terrible pogrom. The mindless mob would rise up in a rage. The Jews of Kiev were his own flesh and blood. The thing Bogrov would most want to prevent on this earth . . . Kiev must never become the scene of mass outrages against the Jews, this or any other September.

He heard the still, sure voice from three thousand years back.

He smothered his excitement—this was not his quarry. Let himself be pushed aside. Walked on.

Stolypin, though, he was determined to kill there and then. Nothing would save Prime Minister Stolypin that evening—no defending hand, no interposed body. As for the mob, they did not know him, and would not riot for him.

Only Bogrov did not encounter him. Did not catch a glimpse of him. Perhaps because he was nearsighted.

He did once think that he could see Stolypin dimly, some way off. He set off in pursuit, pushing through the crowd, but lost the man.

Perhaps, though, he hadn't searched as hard as he could have?

He loved himself. And he despised himself.

He didn't meet Stolypin. Couldn't find him.

The garden party had ended.

A chance missed.

Once out of the Garden, among the carriages driving away at the mouth of the Kreshchatik, which was cordoned off at Mikhailovskaya Street by policemen and Cossacks to prevent the curious crowds from flooding in to watch, he got over his fit of feebleness and felt a griping anguish.

Those boneheaded thugs were *his* bodyguard! There he was, pierced to the heart already, carrying the fatal sting in him! But Bogrov's presence of mind failed him, he was too late.

You can't escape yourself. Before his cab reached Bibikov Boulevard, Bogrov knew that he must somehow get hold of the other ticket.

Tomorrow perhaps? Get a night's sleep first?

No, there was no more sleep for him.

But Kulyabko?! All this time he had seemed unconcerned, never once asked whether the terrorists had come or not, what had happened in the Merchants' Garden, and why Bogrov needed so much to go there. Nikolai Yakovlevich *had the goods with him*—and Kulyabko wasn't at all worried! What bliss to be so thick-skinned! With all his knowledge of security police officials Bogrov hadn't expected this. Who appointed them? How did they make their way up the ladder? It must all be done by pulling strings and toadying.

Perhaps he was wrong, though. Perhaps they had guessed the truth? Perhaps they would come and arrest him shortly? Perhaps he'd been watched in the Garden?

It seemed quite likely. More likely than not! He turned cold.

Midnight. One a.m. Should he start undressing? No, there was no hope at all of sleeping. With every hour of inaction he was losing ground.

How could he have been so weak in the Merchants' Garden, how could he have wasted his chance? He should have hurried around searching instead of listening to violins.

Kulyabko would not be in again next morning. Tomorrow afternoon there was a continuous program of ceremonies. He might miss the theater.

He must try to get the ticket right now, this very moment. He could not risk postponement.

You get so used to your own deceptions that you begin to experience a double reality. "Nikolai Yakovlevich" is sitting in the next room there. What will he think if he hears his dubious host go out into the night? What excuse shall I give him? How can I anticipate his plans for tomorrow? What can I tell Kulyabko? Will Kulyabko believe me? Will Nikolai Yakovlevich believe me? Just as long as I keep my wits about me, don't lose my skill at improvisation.

Let's rehearse the story. Put it all down clearly on paper. Anyway, I can't get in to see Kulyabko in the middle of the night without some sort of note.

Here goes. Nikolai Yakovlevich is spending the night in my house. He has two Brownings in his luggage . . . (Keep as close as you can to the truth and you won't slip. The nearer to the truth, the more convincingly you play the part, the less you will have to rack your brains.) "Nina Aleksandrovna" has also arrived . . . (He had once met a bewitching young woman with that combination of names.) I haven't seen her. She has a bomb. (Without which he would be saying nothing new, and would make no impact on the Okhrana.) She's staying in a different apartment. (A splendid tactical invention, that: if the terrorists aren't all here in my place it's no good raiding—it would only frighten the rest away. But he must also give them something to look forward to. And not keep them waiting too long.) . . . She'll come to my apartment between noon and one o'clock tomorrow. (He dared not look down! It would make his head spin! He was at such a dizzy height!) My impression that Stolypin and Kasso are the intended victims is confirmed.

All was now revealed! They knew it all, from start to finish! He had informed on himself in advance! Would Lazarev unravel it someday? Would he appreciate it?

Nikolai Yakovlevich considers their success assured. (Kulyabko had to be shaken up a bit. Mustn't alarm them too much.) But he has hinted yet again at mysterious protectors in high places. (My tired head can't invent any new themes.) . . . I have promised full cooperation. I await instructions.

He was enchanted by the malicious irony of it, the sheer impudence of telling them just what was to happen. Kulyabko would surely be dumbfounded, and meekly obey.

All the same, he just could not understand why they seemed so unexcited.

Nina's bomb would blow Kulyabko's complacency sky-high! But the names of the intended victims (mere ministers) would have a soothing effect. And protectors in high places would paralyze him, sting him to the heart. If that was what these high-placed persons wanted, why should Kulyabko make any special effort?

At 2 a.m. a well-dressed gentleman approached the policeman at the main door of the Okhrana offices and asked permission to report to the officer in charge. Sabaev was still duty clerk—he had not been relieved. (When he is, though, he may be going to see our cook—just when she ought to be getting Nikolai Yakovlevich's breakfast!) Sabaev invited Bogrov into the waiting room and started phoning the lieutenant colonel's apartment, trying to wake him up. (Bogrov couldn't have made himself more of a nuisance if he personally, and not the Prime Minister, had been under threat.) Kulyabko, of course, was terribly reluctant to break up the night. "What's the hurry all of a sudden? . . . All right, tell him to put it in writing." "He's got it written down already. It's right here." "Send it to Demidyuk, then. He can look into it." "No, he insists on giving it to you personally."

They took the note to Kulyabko. The night was going by, with intervals of sleeplessness and fitful dozing. Bogrov sat with Sabaev. Sabaev kept nodding off. Kulyabko, no doubt, had gone back to bed for the quarter of an hour it would take the messenger to reach him. Would he come to the office when Nina Aleksandrovna's bomb went off under him? No, of course not. He called and gave orders for Bogrov to be brought to his apartment.

A second interview! *Chez* Kulyabko once again! It was working!

This was just what he needed! A man fired with an ambition is incomparably stronger than the man who only wants a quiet life. A man who has not been to bed is always superior to a man rudely torn from his rest. Following up his carefully drafted note, Bogrov, cool and collected, appeared on the scene in person, to hypnotize Kulyabko, whose resistance was sapped in advance.

Kulyabko had resumed his slumbers during the second quarter-hour interval, after his call to send for Bogrov. He emerged to receive his guest with typical Russian lack of ceremony, yawning uncontrollably, waddling like a drake in his claret-colored dressing gown—he had not troubled to dress because he would be going straight back to bed.

"Why are you in such a state, my dear boy?" He sounded sorry for himself and for Bogrov, his comrade in misfortune.

He isn't all that old, you know. Not forty yet. Fat, though. A man in a dressing gown, loosely wrapped around him, is no match at all for a man in a suit. We are costumed for the climactic scene in the drama.

All Bogrov wanted was one theater ticket for tomorrow night. They were lying there, in the study, a thick wad of them. But to come right out with it might be dangerous even now. (The strain of deliberate delay made him ache all over. His whole body was in pain.)

Kulyabko received him with sleepy cordiality. He did not seem greatly shaken by Nina's bomb, or paralyzed by the protectors in high places—and Bogrov patiently gave his friend the lieutenant colonel the details which he could not mention over the telephone earlier: the terrorists had commissioned him to discover how they could identify Stolypin and Kasso. (Their pictures were in all the illustrated magazines, but sleepy Kulyabko wouldn't think of that.) That was why he had had to go to the Merchants' Garden. Not to go would have been unthinkable. The terrorists were, of course, watching to see whether he was carrying out instructions.

The pole seemed safe enough, firmly planted, but how it swayed toward the top, high under the dome! He would be shaken off! Hanging on you know not how, you become helpless, you make the most absurd movements. Where had he said the terrorists were watching him? In the Garden. So they could have identified the ministers for themselves and made the big bang there and then . . . And if they couldn't trust him to go to the Garden, how was it they trusted him with all their secrets, their plans, their very lives?

He ought to tie up the loose ends, but his weary mind wasn't up to it.

Sleepy Kulyabko's mind, however, was still less active. The stupidity in Kulyabko's face was not just an individual trait, it was characteristic of his type, perhaps of his race. He scratched and pulled his dressing gown around him. He had noticed nothing. Everything was as it should be. Slee-ee-eep was what he wanted! He was like a triple feather bolster himself.

Grinding the contents of the note still finer, Bogrov said that he hadn't seen Stolypin, and so couldn't provide a description as instructed. But Nikolai Yakovlevich was insistent . . . (He was hinting that he would need the theater ticket. But he mustn't accept it right away. Keeping Kulyabko's confidence was more important. He might hand over a ticket but put three sleuths on Bogrov's tail.)

But no attempt would be made on the Emperor?

No, no.

Kulyabko was becoming less worried all the time. In fact Kulyabko didn't know why he had been woken up at all.

Oh yes! He had just remembered, there was a complaint from Kremenchug: the description of Nikolai Yakovlevich was too vague. With so little to go on, it was no good looking. "Can't you be more precise, dear boy?"

Idiot! Why was he worrying about Kremenchug?

"Yes, of course I can." (He was caught off guard, though.) "Ready? Above average height . . . quite well built . . . dark hair . . . small mustache" (what had he said about it last time?) ". . . closely trimmed beard . . . sandy-colored English overcoat . . . bowler hat . . . dark gloves."

The dark gloves would seem especially convincing to a true-believing gendarme: terrorists have claws to hide, of course.

Kulyabko went to bed, and Bogrov walked through the empty streets to get some fresh air.

He reassured himself yet again that the house was not watched at night. The detectives had been taken off the door. Or else gone to bed without asking permission.

He was wriggling—higher, higher. Such artistry! His presence of mind, his sense of purpose had not failed him.

But . . . in the morning? When Kulyabko came to in the morning he would presumably have to report. How high up? To Stolypin himself? On a matter of such importance he could not fail to report.

Had the dagger of truth sunk too deep, then?

Again, they might have reported earlier. They should have done so. Yet nothing had happened.

Had he carried frankness too far? . . . Still, if he had mentioned only Kasso they wouldn't have given him the ticket.

In this game of truth and dare there was one monstrous imponderable. If they told the Prime Minister that there were plans to assassinate him he would take precautions, perhaps not even go to the theater.

No. He wouldn't hide. He would go.

Bogrov had studied his intended victim no less carefully than that lard cake Kulyabko. Challenged by a pilot who belonged to the SR Party, Stolypin had gone up in a biplane with him. It was not in Stolypin's character to shrink from danger. Which was why he would go to meet certain death.

The trap had been beautifully baited. The terrorists would be assembling, but not before noon. Until then there was no hope of catching them. No reason to descend on Bogrov's apartment with a warrant. (Just as long as they hadn't checked up through Sabaev!) But it meant also that he could not ask for the ticket any earlier: obviously, he could not yet know what the terrorists would decide to do, and what orders they would give him.

Though he had slept so little, he felt cheerful the next morning as he ground his coffee. He rejoiced in the thought that he had outwitted them, that he had triumphed, that he had drawn close to his victim, and that the moment for which he had waited all his life was approaching.

He had hardly slept, but his head was always clearer in the morning. He had made no mistakes in his nocturnal interview with Kulyabko. But nothing had been decided either.

He had to build on what he had achieved there. Deepen the impression made then.

So before noon, when the critical meeting of the terrorists was still an hour away, the tenant of the apartment went out on foot. (The shadows stood and watched but did not follow him. He was still trusted.)

He turned onto the Kreshchatik and in the broad light of a sunny day walked boldly into the Yevropeiskaya Hotel, where he knew that he would find Kulyabko, where, as all Kiev knew, many visiting notables had settled in to make merry during the days of high festival. (What extraordinary courage! The terrorists are keeping him under observation—but is he afraid of them? No more than yesterday, when he telephoned the Okhrana directly from his home and sent a messenger for the ticket . . . These extraordinarily patient terrorists would put up with anything, nothing seemed to worry them! It was all a bit thin, and he shivered in the warm light of the southern day!)

Kulyabko received him in the room of the state councillor he had seen before. Verigin.

Two of them. (But the third was not there—that was good.)

Careful! Every word he used must be irreproachable. No, what mattered most was the hypnotic spell he cast—not what he said but how he looked. He could rehash the same old stuff. (*They* hadn't changed.) Just one modification: the terrorists would not be meeting that afternoon. (How, though, did each of them find out exactly what the others were doing? How did they concert their plans?) They had changed the time and place to 8 p.m. on the corner of Bibikov Boulevard and Vladimir Street. (An hour before the performance.)

So they'd postponed their meeting—did that mean they'd canceled the *action*?

Oh no! Bogrov boldly reassured them, never once taking his honest eyes off them.

He was getting through to them. They asked both at once *where* it was likely to happen.

The truth, the whole truth, and nothing but the truth! Most probably . . . *by* the theater.

The blotting pad of a state councillor, anxious to show off his detective skills, asked how they would recognize the terrorists on a crowded street, and how would they know whether the terrorists were going through with the action or were postponing it again? (If it's postponed we'll take our time arresting them—was that what he meant?)

Kulyabko said that if the terrorists intended to act Bogrov could give the signal by smoking a cigarette.

(It was all coming apart at the seams. If he had to be on the boulevard sitting on an empty bench, how would he get into the theater? His plan was falling apart, and he had no arguments to stick it together again.)

All he could do was gaze at them seductively, with his head to one side, such a sweet boy, you wanted to believe him, you couldn't help believing him, you had to believe him.

He agreed to everything of course, cigarette included. But he couldn't stand the thought that the terrorists might involve him in their violent action. He had in fact intended to isolate himself, to avoid their company at that hour, and of course he didn't want to be arrested with them. He would like to keep clear of the bomb throwers.

On what excuse, though?

As it happened, he had a good one. He had failed to put together a description of Stolypin at the Merchants' Garden yesterday. Nikolai Yakovlevich had been displeased, and was still asking for it. That could be his excuse for going to the theater—to reconnoiter.

(In the harsh daylight the whole bluff looked so unreal, he was so obviously clinging unnaturally to the pole where he should not be at all. The whole thing was coming unstuck. Why should he want to get into the theater if the terrorists were meeting on the boulevard and the action was to take place outside? How could he signal what the terrorists were up to if he isolated himself from them? And would they still be asking for descriptions of their victims at this late hour? But miraculously his scheme held together, welded by mesmeric wave force.

Perhaps they would swallow this one: if he was in the theater he could spoil the terrorists' plan by giving them a misleading signal.

It worked.

In the festive bustle (they were hurrying off to another champagne lunch, sure of their coup and their rewards), it held up.

"How will you explain, though, where you got the ticket?"

"Easy! Through Regina, the singer. She got it from her aristocratic protector."

Another problem: Bogrov wouldn't be there to point out the terrorists on the boulevard.

Well, the detectives could easily follow Nikolai Yakovlevich from Bogrov's house. He himself might possibly be of more use in the theater.

Just possibly . . .

But how could the terrorists penetrate into the theater?

(Things were getting very mixed up.)

Ah-ha! That was where their high-placed protectors came in.

Spellbinding.

Kulyabko and Verigin discussed other difficult situations in which the terrorists might put their collaborator.

Gently—but with growing confidence—he broke it to them that he must have a seat in the stalls where he could be seen. "They may be watching to make sure I'm there."

He was obviously strictly monitored by the terrorists. Every move he made would be scrutinized.

Verigin: The front rows are absolutely impossible. Only generals and other bigwigs have seats there.

Kulyabko: We'll put you in the stalls, but farther back. I'll send the ticket, unless the terrorists change their plans again. They seem to keep changing all the time.

Had the ticket eluded him? Perhaps not. He mustn't press too hard. (His body was getting weak, his muscles slackening, his tongue was tired, he couldn't keep his eyes open. Any moment now he might fall like a dead weight from the pole.)

Home by cab. He felt weak, and he wanted to make it seem that he was hurrying back into the jealous company of Nikolai Yakovlevich, whose suspicions might be aroused by his absence.

Home in fact to his own claustrophobic company. He had spun a wonderful yarn. He had climbed so skillfully. Was he to lose his footing now? Tomorrow the whole royal gang would leave for other cities, and he would have to move his counters, Nikolai Yakovlevich and Nina Aleksandrovna, to other squares, invent new dramatis personae, new plots, new faces. His head could no longer hold it all. He was beginning to slip.

He was tired . . . Superior people like myself squander so much energy and skill on . . . on what? Damn them all! They turn us into sneaks like themselves.

Then came hours, lonely hours at the end of a cul-de-sac, shuffling and redealing the possibilities like cards in an insoluble game of patience. Lunch with his aunt. He could swallow nothing. He started talking to her too freely and let slip that he had been in the Merchants' Garden the night before. She was astonished. How had he got in? Friends from Petersburg had helped him.

How could he have missed his chance at the Merchants' Garden? Such strokes of luck do not repeat themselves.

Another thing he had forgotten—the doorman. They would simply go and check with him whether anyone answering a certain description had, even just once, passed through his front door.

There, pressed and hung ready for him by the maid, were his frock coat and vest. The coat had been made for his first appearance in court, which had never taken place.

Hours of dreadful suspense. If only it were over! Just to be done with it would be reward enough. No more hiding. We'll meet face to face and see who blanches. I must end it. I must shoot soon. Stolypin is shutting out my light.

Suddenly a knock at the door of his room. One he didn't recognize. His revolver was on the table. For some reason he rushed to the door without stopping to conceal it.

A policeman!

Sabaev.

Had they found out? Was it all over? Had Sabaev gone through all the rooms and found no Nikolai Yakovlevich? Was the police detail cooling its heels in the entrance hall?

Sabaev asked politely whether he could use Bogrov's phone to ring headquarters.

No, he could not!

(Could be a trap. Could he be asking for reinforcements?)

Sabaev was surprised.

"You must understand, in my position I can't afford to let *anyone* use it. It might attract attention."

It was all right. He had got away with it. Sabaev was only visiting the cook. Things were fine where he had come from.

More pacing, more waiting, more anguish. He tried to lie down, and couldn't. He tried standing, but couldn't walk.

Would he get the ticket?

The hands of the clock crawled around somehow. Closer. Closer. Nearly seven. He couldn't wait till the hand was on the hour. He rang Kulyabko. For once he had taken the initiative.

In a hushed voice (Nikolai Yakovlevich mustn't overhear!) he said that there had been no change of plan and asked Kulyabko to send the ticket.

"Very well. Demidyuk will leave it with the doorman himself and say it's from Regina."

Kulyabko's voice was his ordinary voice.

But twenty minutes went by, then thirty—and nothing came.

By now he had his frock coat on. It was tight and hot. He had the Browning in a trouser pocket. He walked around, getting used to it. It was a big gun, and the bulge showed. He must cover it somehow.

No messenger. With a note in his pocket just in case, explaining why he had left home ahead of plan and why the terrorists were delayed, he went out into the street.

"Nikolai Yakovlevich," he had written, "is very worried . . . Your surveillance was too obvious, and he can see the watchers through binoculars from the window . . . But I haven't been found out yet."

Eight p.m.! They're on the boulevard now!
Bogrov went out into the street himself.
To perform the first "action" in his life.
It was quite dark by now. The detectives were in place. Nikolai Yakovlevich mustn't get through . . .
Ah, there was Demidyuk. To avoid being seen by a terrorist from his own window Bogrov signaled to Demidyuk to follow him into Fundukleev Street.
Now he had the ticket in his hand.
Keep calm. Fold it again. Pocket it.
On that ticket depends the fate of the government. The fate of the country.
And the fate of my people.
Along Fundukleev Street, along Vladimir Street, and on to Theater Square there was hardly a break in the crowd. Thousands of stupid people hoping to catch a glimpse of their stupid Tsar riding by.
Cars and carriages with fine people in fine clothes arrived every minute. There was an hour to go until the performance, but the theater was full.
(But it was after eight already, and the terrorists had not gathered on the boulevard. Had they put it off again? How could they keep switching gears? By telephone? Someone might overhear them—remember Pevsner. Perhaps the police had thought of tapping it? If they had put it off, if there was to be no attempt, what was Bogrov doing there? Of course—he was there to get a good look at Stolypin and to give a false signal . . . What signal? To whom? Signal for what? And to prevent the attack unarmed and single-handed?)
A policeman stood by every usher. How proud Bogrov felt to have a genuine, valid ticket made out in his own name. His frock coat and his impeccable manners made him all the more obviously one of that select assembly.
(Suppose they suddenly felt his pockets? They would easily find the Browning and his eight cartridges. For a terrible moment he expected to be searched. It would be only natural.)
Kulyabko was strutting about the vestibule waiting for news—that was something. Ready there and then, uniformed and bemedaled and with everyone watching, to talk to his favorite.
Poor, stupid old drake. You felt sorry for him sometimes. Since he had provided the ticket Bogrov had begun to sympathize with him.
"Come behind this pillar. Look, I'm being watched from two angles, it's very dangerous for us to talk where we can be seen."
"Do you think they have agents in the theater?"
"Indeed they have! With their connections . . ."
(Might even have to fight them! Might have to ruin my own relations with them.)

"What about the rendezvous on the boulevard?"

"Canceled."

"What, again?"

"Relocated to a private apartment. I don't know where. Nikolai Yakovlevich will be moving there after eleven o'clock."

Kulyabko broke into a sweat and wiped his neck under his tunic collar. Had they worked so hard to bring their quarry to bay all for nothing? Would the terrorists trickle through their fingers? Slip away? Taking Kulyabko's decoration with them?

"Well then—go and see if he's still at home."

(Overdid it again! Striking the right balance—that was the most difficult thing.)

"Well, I've only just come out and he was at home then."

"No, no—go back and check right away!"

"But I'm here in the theater on his behalf—how can I go back?"

"Say you forgot your gloves."

The fat man was shivering and sweating.

How could I have felt the slightest twinge of pity for him? I've climbed to this inaccessible, this incredible height—for what? To slither back down again? The ticket in my pocket might as well not be there.

"Away you go, dear boy!" Kulyabko shooed him off with his usual fidgety impetuosity. "Go and check—and when you get back you'll report to me."

Slithering down, down the smooth-planed pole. No splinters, at least. Sliding down was not really easier than climbing up. How tired his lumbar muscles were.

Should he go home? It was silly. He would never get through the crowd and be back in time for the curtain. Not go home, then? The sleuths would report that he hadn't.

But that would be *afterward* . . .

He crossed to the other side of Vladimir Street. Hung around the Café François for fifteen minutes or so. Was he being followed now? Perhaps it was all up? You wouldn't spot a tail in this crowd.

He went back to the theater, to a different usher. The policeman standing by wouldn't let him pass because his ticket had been used already.

But sharp-eyed Kulyabko saw it and hurried to the rescue. "You can let this man in! I know him personally! Well, what's the news?"

"He's at home, having supper. But he's noticed that the house is being watched. They're pretty crude about it. He's very alarmed." (Should have said that before! I forgot—and all the while I had the note in my pocket.)

So Nikolai Yakovlevich wouldn't be going anywhere. So it was time Kulyabko stopped worrying.

Would the performance never begin? The audience was still crowding the foyer, the buffet, the corridors, strutting around in their finery to see and be seen. The Kiev Opera House had not known such a gathering for decades past. Many of them were Petersburgers.

They were *his* audience! They thought they were there to see *The Tale of Tsar Saltan*, and admire the Tsar's daughters' necklaces—but they would see something Russia had never seen before, and every one of them would tell his grandchildren: "I was there when Stolypin was killed, let me tell you about it . . ." This audience had not watched him clambering up into the dome, onto the high platform—they would see only the *final* stunt.

He had found that by holding his program at waist level he could make the bulging revolver less conspicuous.

Bells were ringing. Ladies in bright dresses went by, buffeting him with their perfume. There were men in military uniforms everywhere. The Tsar and a couple of his daughters were in the governor-general's box, to the left of the hall, high above the orchestra. The Tsaritsa was nowhere to be seen.

Stolypin was somewhere among the dignitaries at the Tsar's feet, but Bogrov was too far away to distinguish him from behind. That was where he must be, though. That was where the theater was different from the garden party: places were assigned according to rank.

The lights went down. The overture was played. The curtain parted. In an idiotic peasant cottage silly wenches in exaggeratedly "Russian" dress twittered away while a ludicrous Tsar eavesdropped and wondered which of them he'd like to marry.

Another thought kept occurring to him. Why must he assume that he was doomed? Why not run away after he had fired his shot? Everybody would be so flummoxed that he might be able to dash out of the theater and grab a cab.

He had to be sure that he was not being watched. That wouldn't be like Kulyabko—but still. If he was under surveillance he could do nothing—they might seize his arm as he took aim.

This meant that it was no good trying anything in the first intermission. He would use the time to check whether he was being watched or not: a quick visit to the lavatory before anyone else got there, a quick trip up and down the stairs. Right. Postpone the action, then, until the next intermission.

Or put it off altogether . . . ?

In his fevered calculations the one thing he had scarcely stopped to ask himself was whether it must inevitably be done, and by him.

By now too many lucky circumstances favored it. It was like throwing three dice and getting three sixes.

Who else could ever have managed it?

Intermission. Hurry out to check.

No, nobody watching him.

He scanned the hall from various vantage points with his rented opera glasses. Where was Stolypin? How many guards had he?

Look up in front . . . There were no obvious security men at the foot of the royal box. If special people had been planted here and there they were undetectable. Up front there, somewhere.

Yes! Stolypin, in a white coat, was sitting in the front row under the royal box, almost by the aisle.

Apparently without a bodyguard. Just chatting to people he knew.

Was this it? Time to attack?

The hot blood pounded in his veins.

No, he wasn't quite ready. Still some reconnaissance to be carried out. Anyway, there were three intermissions, and there would be another chance when people were waiting outside for carriages.

The pit of the theater was an extraordinary sight: epaulets, more epaulets, stars on ministerial breasts, courtiers with stars and ribbons, ladies wearing diamonds. A performance for the people, as announced.

He suddenly noticed something that made him sweat. The men were nearly all wearing uniforms, military or departmental, but because of the heat the few in civilian clothes were wearing light summer suits, not evening dress.

He was almost the only black spot among them. Much too conspicuous. An oversight.

Kulyabko again. He came indecently close, drew Bogrov into a corner. He had nothing new to say, he just wanted another chat about Nikolai Yakovlevich.

Bogrov detached himself only as the second act was beginning. He sat through the whole of it motionless, hunched up, with his opera glasses trained, from the eighteenth row, not on the stage but on what he took to be the back of Stolypin's head in the front row.

Hatred was so strong in him he felt he could stab the man with his eyes through the glasses.

Second intermission. Most of the audience wandered out. And there Kulyabko was again. A nod—come over here where it's quiet.

He had never been on the boil like this before. An hour and a half had gone by and still no sign of Nikolai Yakovlevich. Has he slipped past the detectives? There's nothing of importance for you to do in the theater. No need for you to stay on. Go home and keep an eye on Nikolai Yakovlevich.

The tiresome creature didn't catch me out when all he had to do was have me watched. Now he's going to spoil everything with his silly fussing. Won't let me hang on for the third intermission. If I don't agree he'll give me no peace. And if I leave the theater now that's the end of it.

He answered immediately to avoid arousing suspicion: "I'm on my way." And off he went, knowing that he would never have such an opportunity again. And—worse—his deception would be discovered within a few hours. This was the very last chance.

So he hid from Kulyabko in the corridor, then turned back and went into the hall, risking another encounter. (Well, he could say he'd forgotten his opera glasses . . . or his gloves!)

No Kulyabko.

Perhaps, though, Stolypin would not be in his place at this, the only possible moment. He was! Standing there so boldly, with no attempt at concealment, dazzling white in his summer suit, with his chest out, he looked like a specially mounted target, at the very end of the left-hand aisle, leaning back against the orchestra rail, talking to somebody.

Bogrov met hardly anyone in the aisle, and the hall was four-fifths empty. He forgot everything else—he did not even cast a glance at the Tsar's box to see whether there was anyone there.

Looking as casual as he could, he sauntered down the aisle, holding his program over the bulging pocket . . . nearer . . . nearer . . . nearer!

He had to be very near. He had been excused from military service because he was too nearsighted to use a gun.

Nobody tried to bar his way to the Prime Minister.

He saw at once that there was no one, sitting or standing, nearby or farther away, on guard. All those soldiers in the theater—and not one of them guarding him. He saw it at once, but had no time to think about it. He had told them straight, and repeatedly, that there would be an attempt on Stolypin! The whole town, the whole theater was ringed and double-ringed with guards—yet Stolypin had not a single man near him.

Nobody hurried after Bogrov, nobody clutched at his shoulder or his elbow.

Now you will hear what *we* have to say—and remember it forever!

Four steps away from the white breast with the big star he let his program fall, whipped out his Browning, took another step, and, seeing Stolypin about to grapple with him, fired! And fired again! Point-blank!

[6 5]

(PYOTR ARKADIEVICH STOLYPIN)

In men of high purpose the seed of all their future endeavors is sown in their earliest years, and often germinates without their knowing it. Later, circumstances often conspire to feed and foster it as much as any deliberate intent of their own.

Pyotr Stolypin's central concern developed very early in his childhood at Serednikovo outside Moscow: he was preoccupied with the Russian peasant and the Russian land, with ways of ensuring that the peasant owned the land and worked it for his own benefit and that of the land itself.

This keen feeling for the land, for the upturned soil, for seedtime and harvest, easily understandable in a peasant boy, is something one would not expect to find in the son of an adjutant general and great-grandson of a senator. (He was a descendant of Suvorov and related to Lermontov.) It was not a question of knowledge, or conscious thought, or intent; it was just a persistent and poignant feeling that the Russian land and the Russian peasant were inseparable, that both were inseparable from Russia, and that away from the land there was no Russia. He had a constant anxious awareness of all Russia as though it were there in his breast. Unsleeping compassion, a love that nothing could alter. But though his love was all gentleness and tenderness, when anything threatened the things that mattered to him he was as unyielding as an oak. All his life he was like that.

This feeling for the land had come to the surface in his horseguardsman grandfather: from him came the knowledge, sure as holy writ, that the Russian peasant would never prosper while he was shackled by the commune and collective liability, the responsibility of each for all, compulsory egalitarianism, while disheartening redivisions of the land made any improvement senseless, made it impossible for the peasant and his land to grow together, perpetuated holdings each consisting of widely separated, long, narrow strips of arable land and meadow. Travelers from quite nearby, from the Belorussian or Ukrainian lands, say, looked aghast at the excruciatingly wasteful Great Russian strip-farming system, though they might admire the age-old skill of the peasants in parceling into equal portions land that was uneven, intractable, and variable in quality.

Stolypin's idea was one of shining simplicity—yet too complicated to be grasped or accepted. The repartitional commune reduced the fertility of the land, took from nature what it did not return, and denied the peasant both freedom and prosperity. The peasant's allotment must become his permanent property. Perhaps, though, in this self-denial, this harmonization of the will of the individual with that of the commune, this mutual aid and curbing of wild willfulness, there lay something more valuable than harvests and material well-being? Perhaps the people could look forward to something better than the development of private property? Perhaps the commune was not just a system of paternalistic constraints, cramping the freedom of the individual, perhaps it reflected the people's philosophy of life, its faith? Perhaps there was a paradox here which went beyond the commune, indeed beyond Russia itself: freedom of action and prosperity are necessary if man is to stand up to his full height on this earth, but spiritual greatness dwells in eternal subordination, in awareness of oneself as an insignificant particle.

Thinking that way makes action impossible. Stolypin was always a realist. With him, thought and action were one. No one can ask the people to behave like angels. We have to live with property as we live with all the temptations of this life. And in any case, the commune created a good deal of discord among the peasants.

(Although the necessary outline of Stolypin's life and work which follows will be as succinctly factual as the author can make it, he suggests that only the most indefatigably curious readers immerse themselves in these details. Others can easily go straight on to the next section in larger print. The author would not permit himself such a crude distortion of the novel form if Russia's whole history, her very memory, had not been so distorted in the past, and her historians silenced.)

People will often cling to hastily formed pet theories instead of taking the trouble to study a subject. We are told, for instance, that the Russian agrarian commune was the finest creation of the Russian spirit, that it existed from the days of Rurik and Gostomysl, and will exist as long as the Russian people lives, amen! You have to peer very hard to see through the mists of romance: the commune did indeed exist in Russia from of old, but as late as the seventeenth century there was no compulsory equalization of landholdings. The commune was a parish; it maintained the parish church, it chose the priest and good men to collect taxes and to see justice done, it dispensed aid to widows and orphans. What it did not do was force men to redivide and equalize their holdings: wherever its ax, plow, and scythe had gone, a peasant household owned the land by squatter's right, could sell it and bequeath it.

From the time of the first Romanovs, however, the freedom of the Tsar to make grants was more and more boldly asserted over wider and wider areas of peasant landholding, so that land under the peasant plow and scythe was gradually converted into land held by the Tsar's servitors. Then Peter the Great imposed his cruel poll tax and made the landlords responsible for exacting it. To ensure that it was paid in full it became necessary to adjust landholdings to dues, which in turn meant periodic redistribution. This was how the repartitional commune came into being—in Great Russia alone. This was the origin of that "primal creation of the national spirit" which has since found favor in such various quarters for very different reasons: with the state bureaucracy, because it was a convenient instrument for collecting taxes and keeping order in the village; with the Land and Freedom Party, the populists, and the socialists, because they thought they saw something like ready-made socialism in the Russian village—just one step further, to cultivation of the land and use of its produce in common, and today's commune, that sacred anachronism, would grow up into the devoutly longed-for All-Russian Agrarian Commune of the future.

The peasants were freed, but the village declined instead of flourishing. A period of stagnation followed the Emancipation. The peasants' land remained what it had been, it did not expand, but the population grew rapidly and average holdings decreased. People bewailed the impoverishment of the central Russian provinces, the intolerable congestion on the land, yet the Russian peasant had four times as much workable land as the British, three and a half times as much as the German, and two and a half times as much as the French peasant. Only he cultivated it badly, feeling no commitment to those scattered strips which he could not leave to his heir, and where a yield of eighty puds a desyatin was possible, he reaped forty. The commune defended no one, and weakened everyone. No peasant could indulge his preference for a particular branch of husbandry, all had to farm in the same way. What we call "the commune" ought to be called "a system of three-field strip farming in which the individual has no right to choose his crop or even his sowing and harvesting times." Because there is no individual incentive you must never invest too much labor or fertilizer in a particular plot—repartition will soon come around and you will have to hand it over, perhaps to some good-for-nothing loafer. Shortage of land should, I hear you say, make for intensive cultivation. Instead, it encourages negligence and drunkenness. The peasant has no heart to improve the land he already holds—he yearns for more instead. He has land, yet he is landless: of all his appetites the sharpest and fiercest is for that extra patch of dirt he must get his hands on somewhere.

But when the land ceases to feed those who dwell on it, surely things must be rearranged so that it will do so? You cannot reduce people to a less than human level of existence.

It was because of his links with the land and what grows on it that Pyotr Stolypin chose to study science (at Petersburg University). For the same reason, he resisted the lure of student political activity and entered government service upon graduation, joining the agricultural department in time to work on one of the commissions administering the peasant reforms of Aleksandr II. (And to see at first hand Aleksandr III's efforts to halt the reforms.) His subsequent career took him—as district marshal of the nobility, then provincial marshal, then provincial governor—to the western provinces, where peasant land was as a rule held by each household separately. Pyotr Arkadievich saw how much more productive this system was. In some places where the commune did exist, he persuaded the peasants to establish separate homesteads, each with its permanent allotment, with good results. Everywhere he went he took a passionate interest in the agricultural machinery depot, the local agricultural society, sowing, mowing, planting, horses—he was never happier than when he was breaking in trotting horses or striding over soggy autumn fields in high boots and waterproof jacket, at that special time when the land speaks only to those who work it and is shunned by and inhospitable to picnickers.

He was forty and the youngest provincial governor in Russia when the revolutionaries killed yet another minister of the interior—Pleve. In the general reshuffle which followed, Stolypin was suddenly transferred to Saratov, an important province and one of the most turbulent. The left-wing parties there were wealthy (thanks to contributions from rich people) and spent lavishly on newspapers and handbills. The general attitude toward authority was one of white-hot hostility, so much so that even at a symphony concert intellectuals would bang their seats and walk out of the hall if the governor appeared in his box. Before Stolypin's arrival it was becoming the rule for senior officials to desert Saratov and take to the countryside as soon as any disturbance began, leaving an illusory authority in the hands of their juniors. (Indeed, some of the seniors, much decorated by His Imperial Majesty's government, flaunted oppositionist views of their own.)

Saratov "society" had a keener sense of its own unquestionable rightness and expressed it more loudly than many other communities in Russia. The authorities might deploy troops in reply, but not arguments, apparently reconciling themselves to their presumed guilt. The new governor came as a surprise. He was erect and well built, his movements were assured, his manner masterful—he was obviously not one of those who lay sleepless and trembling at night in their gubernatorial palaces. He could ride out without escort to face a furious mob on the city square, toss his greatcoat—"Hold that!"—to a hefty fellow advancing on him with a cudgel, and with a confident speech delivered in a ringing voice persuade the crowd to disperse. Conversely, when another crowd, moved by patriotic outrage, besieged a building at Balashov, Stolypin intervened personally, pushed through the crowd to save the intellectuals inside who were discussing political revolution, and suffered further damage to his congenitally weak right arm from a cobblestone flung by a murderous hooligan.

In the first three years of this century, 1901, 1902, 1903, Russia was in the grip of a chill which would soon be a raging fever. Everything pointed to the need for sustained and methodical treatment of her disease. Instead, her rulers plunged her into the war with Japan, which was like pushing a consumptive through a hole in the ice.

Loyalty to the monarchic principle, as well as to the service of which he is part, can stiffen discipline and force a man to suppress his doubts and misgivings, to put on a bold front even though he feels the ground slipping from under him. The origins of the war were obscure, its historical inevitability for Russia unobvious. This made it difficult for him to summon up the will to make sacrifices himself, let alone to awaken enthusiasm for them in others. "But when the Tsar calls, no son of the fatherland has the right to . . ." (Delivering thankless speeches of this sort developed his skill as a speaker and his faith in his oratorical powers.)

Saratov, that progressive province, was not behind in terrorist actions. In the stormy autumn of 1905 Adjutant General Sakharov, who had been sent to crush the local rebels, was blown to bits by a bomb in Stolypin's Saratov home. (These bombs were delivered in the simplest way imaginable—by some woman who turned up with a woebegone look and a petition. Any petitioner had access, unsearched, to those in charge of the punitive operation even in their off-duty hours.)

The first attempt on Pyotr Arkadievich was made that summer in a village street while he was on a tour of inspection: two shots were fired at him (just as two shots would be fired in the final and successful attempt made by Bogrov). Stolypin himself rushed after the would-be assassin, who, however, escaped his pursuers. The second attempt was made on the theater square, which was packed by an excited and hostile crowd: a bomb fell at his feet from the second story, killing several people, but the governor was unhurt, and indeed succeeded in persuading the crowd to disperse. The third time (and the last time would be just the same), the assassin leveled his revolver point-blank at his intended victim, once again in the presence of a crowd, but dropped his weapon when Stolypin undid his overcoat and called out, "Go ahead—shoot!" When they had repeatedly failed to kill him, anonymous letters began to arrive (as revolutionary protocol demanded): your two-year-old son will be poisoned—prepare yourself! (His one and only son—after five daughters.)

But all these attempts on his life could not make Stolypin cautious or change his habits:

he continued his tours of the province, more obstinately than ever, making a point of visiting the very places where the ferment was most serious and the leftists most daring and of plunging unarmed into angry crowds. He became adept at controlling his voice and his temper, and could always pacify a crowd by reasoning with them, never shouting or uttering threats. His whole life revolved around a single idea, and when he was talking to peasants he could not help expounding it. There was nothing he loved more than looking them straight in the eye and patiently *explaining* things—a method which Russian administrators had long forgotten. "So you want to share out landlords' land? There isn't enough to go around: if you shared out all of it you wouldn't be much better off—and without the Tsar you'd all be reduced to beggary." It was with peasants that he was most successful: they gave him a fair hearing, and there were occasions when a rebellious village meeting sent for the priest to lead them in prayers for the Tsar.

The more the young governor of Saratov thought about it, the more certain he was that the greatest danger to Russia was neither demonstrations by the educated class, nor student disorders, nor the bombs of revolutionaries, nor striking workers, nor even the risings on the outskirts of some cities. The great menace to Russia was the brushfire of peasant unrest, the wave of mob violence which swept through the countryside so irresistibly that you could stand by one burning manor house and without straining your eyes see the next. Saratov province too was one of those in which there was no lack of fire-raisers in 1905: arson spread like a plague, and the bigger landowners gave up visiting their estates altogether. An undeclared revolutionary war by fire was being waged over the far-flung farmlands. At the same time, these happenings were not, as far as the compassionate observer could see, the effect of revolutionary ideas on the mind of the people, they were explosions of despair caused by a deep-seated fault in the structure of peasant life.

Even after the bumper harvest of 1904 the peasant's earnings did not serve to improve his situation but were squandered for the most part in drink shops. Something always blocked hopes of improvement, of consolidating the peasant's position. What barred the way was the impossibility of truly owning the land which the peasant loved and longed for. Communal land tenure was an insurmountable barrier, an entanglement in which the peasant was helplessly caught. Russia's future, Russia's salvation depended on pacifying the exasperated peasants and halting the destruction of landowners' estates. But punitive action by troops would not do it. A way must be cleared for the peasant to use his land freely and skillfully, so that it would feed him amply and satisfy his need to see some reward for his labor. The only way was to improve methods of cultivation.

At the end of each year governors were required to send a routine report to the Emperor on the state of their provinces. Each year Stolypin succumbed to the temptation to include some of his long-cherished thoughts on the peasantry and the land. But at the end of 1904 the governor of Saratov overstepped the bounds of a bureaucratic missive to express his ideas and sympathy for the peasants more fully, in the hope of persuading his reader (in his imagination the Emperor himself) that the doors of the commune must be thrown open so that peasants could become independent and prosperous farmers. Firmly established representatives of the land would become a prop for the throne and for stable government, creating a strong agrarian party to stand up against town-based hothead theorists and their destructive propaganda.

The seed he had cherished all his life was sure to germinate at last—and its vigorous shoot even broke through the thick crust of bureaucratic prose. But as many as a hundred such provincial reports, beautifully bound but futile, accumulated annually at Peterhof, not all of them destined to feel the Tsar's touch, let alone to be flipped through or (most unlikely of all) read carefully. It is one of the miracles of Russian history that those particular pages were perused (on whose advice we shall never know) by a monarch not noted for his assiduity as a reader or thinker. Stolypin's message found its way to his heart, which was never unfeeling, but full of dreams, anguished and perplexed, of making his people happy—all he lacked was stamina. The velvet all about him blurred the Emperor's vision and hampered his movements. (Stolypin may have had in mind his quick response on this occasion when he wrote three years later: ". . . at a moment when belief in Russia's future was tottering, when the convictions of many were gravely weakened, only the Tsar's faith in the strength of the Russian peasant remained undamaged.")

In April 1906 a telegram urgently summoned Stolypin from Saratov to Petersburg. The Emperor received him cordially, said that he had been watching his work as governor for some time, regarded him as an exceptionally able administrator, and was appointing him Minister of the Interior.

Among hundreds of nominations to governmental posts, nearly all of them pernicious, shortsighted, or merely ludicrous, Stolypin's appointment to the first cabinet which would, very shortly, have to deal with a Duma, three days after the promulgation of the first Russian constitution and on the brink of a new period in Russian history, was another historical miracle. The Duma was on its way—and the government had the man to deal with it.

Stolypin was taken aback. He had never foreseen such advancement, he had not prepared himself for so much responsibility and such authority. He was confident of his strength, of course, he knew himself to be a born leader, and his thoughts rose far above the provincial level, but . . .

"It would go against my conscience, Your Majesty. Your favor to me is greatly in excess of my abilities. If you would graciously consent to appoint me Deputy Minister . . . I know nothing about Petersburg and its hidden currents and influences . . ."

For once the Tsar did not waver.

It was, however, a poisoned gift: two of Stolypin's predecessors in the post had been assassinated.

His thoughts rose above the provincial level—he knew that the monarchy would perish unless a savior with a strong hand and a strong head appeared. Still, he took office in Petersburg not as a metropolitan official but as an iron-willed envoy of provincial Russia. (In cabinet other ministers raised their eyebrows at his provincial ways.)

There are two routes to the post of Minister of the Interior: the police ladder and the administrative ladder. The route by which he arrives may decide whether the minister gives more thought to police or to administrative activity. Stolypin's thoughts were those of a statesman. But his first task, a strange one to him, was to lead the police into battle—such a battle as Russia's revolutionaries had never encountered or expected.

The First Duma assembled, sure of itself, loud and peremptory, still hotly exulting in its narrowly won victory. The Duma assembled to fight against any legislative proposal, no matter what, put forward by *that* government. When the number of terrorist killings in different parts of the country was read out from the government benches there were cries of "Not enough!" from some deputies. The Duma assembled in a mood harsher and more uncompromising than that of Russia itself—not to do boring spadework on legislative commissions, not to amend and approve bills and budgets, but by its combined lung power to huff and puff the government and the monarch off their pedestals, to usher in a brilliant epoch in which republican Russia would be governed by the best minds to be found in the academic and tub-thumping circles presided over by the noble, silvery mane of Professor Muromtsev. In its very first resolution this Duma demanded the sequestration and redivision of privately owned land (!), the abolition of the second chamber, the State Council (to give itself more latitude), and—wait for it! but of course!—the resignation of the government. The Duma began its legislative existence by calling for amendments to the constitution (to do so outside those walls was considered a criminal act), in effect promising society a continuation of revolution by other means! Sitting (when they were not leaping to their feet) in the Duma were barely disguised Socialist Revolutionaries, barely disguised terrorists, legal representatives of illegal parties, and—first and foremost—Constitutional Democrats, the fine flower of the intelligentsia from both capitals and a dozen other particularly loquacious towns, all reveling in their intellectual superiority to an obtuse and decrepit government which had never, as far as anyone could remember, produced an orator, a thinker, or a statesman.

It was like a blow in the face when they were suddenly confronted by the unknown Stolypin. Not a general, not a metropolitan bureaucrat, but a man without a single imperial decoration; not a doddering old wreck, as custom demanded, but indecently young for a Russian minister, he ascended the rostrum with a firm step. He was strongly built, a fine figure of a man, with a rich, deep voice, a match for the most eloquent speakers in the opposition, expressing ideas which were at once fresh and effectively argued, with an assurance that neither years in high office nor a furtively consulted text could have conferred. An assurance that could not be shaken, or ridiculed, or simply rebuffed, a conviction that no sensible person could fail to agree with him—and the leftists were shaken, outraged, jumped up and down, roaring, stamping their feet, banging the lids of their desks. "Resign!"

Stolypin stood unbowed, defiantly calm. He was perhaps as surprised by the Duma as it was by him: the population figures might have led him to expect a peasant Duma, but since it was what it was, he nonetheless addressed it completely seriously, refusing to let its manners affect his own. Unashamedly accepting the abusive label "patriot," hoping to win over even these people, he called on the deputies to join in patient work for the fatherland—but they had assembled only to thunder out their summons to revolt. Rebellion had misfired in the main cities; learned professors could not sustain it unaided. They could, however, still fan the flames via the countryside, incite the peasants to seize private lands, then stand aside while the fires flared up everywhere, and roaring mobs rampaged, until the throne was overturned and Russia became a happy democracy. On this rustic road, though, a solid figure loomed, stubbornly blocking the Duma's way—Stolypin again: there would be no free handouts of land, no anarchic redistribution. Like many a long-overdue historical act, the reform of communal land tenure had been considered in high places before Stolypin, but he was the first to devote his will, his faith, his whole future to it. In the heat of revolution this reform had become even more urgently necessary. Stolypin insisted in the Duma that no repartition could make Russia as a whole richer, it would only lead to the ruin of the best farms and a reduction of the harvest. He quoted agrarian statistics quite unknown to the uninstructed peasant (none of whose rulers had ever felt inspired to leave his snug estate and explain such things to the common people), but also so unpalatable to the Kadets that they refused to accept and digest them. The country, said Stolypin, had 140 million desyatins of state land, but most of that was tundra or desert, and the rest was already allotted to peasants. The peasants had, altogether, 160 million desyatins, the gentry a third of that, 53 million, much of it forest, so that if the last scrap was redistributed it would not make the peasants rich. So then, handing out land left and right, seeking to pacify rebellious peasants by almsgiving, was useless. Instead of trying to grab more land from others everyone should till his own holding differently, learn to get eighty or a hundred puds from a desyatin, as the most efficient farmers did, instead of thirty-five.

But, inside and outside the Duma, the left stopped its ears to Stolypin's arguments:

> The government wishes to see the peasant rich and self-sufficient, and with prosperity come enlightenment and real freedom. To this end the able and hardworking Russian peasant, salt of the earth, must be given the opportunity to free himself from his present trammels. We must deliver him from slavery to the obsolete commune, give him control over his land.

While the right stopped its ears to this:

> Landowners surely wish to have as neighbors peaceable and contented people, not hungry and lawless hooligans. It is the peasant's lack of land of his own that undermines his respect for other people's property.

(He hoped that their own proprietorial sense would help them to understand the peasant's need.)

Town dwellers of all parties, and the Kadets to a man, defended the commune—even those who found it irrelevant, incomprehensible, and strange—either for their own private reasons or as part of their political game.

Early in July the government appealed to the people, trying to explain something of the real situation; and a little later the Duma resolved to address the people directly, over the government's head, assuring them that it would never retreat and would not let itself be swayed from the principle of compulsory alienation of private lands.

The Duma had molded its own fate! The legislative assembly might just as well have uttered the rallying cry: "Peasants, seize the land, kill the landowners, start the general repartition!" But the politicians' calendar and nature's calendar did not coincide: the crop was still standing. Ah, but just let them get the harvest over and everything would go up in flames!

What could be done with such a reckless Duma? Stolypin was one of those summoned for consultation to Peterhof, where the Tsar had shut himself away from the revolution, and he saw for himself that those nearest to the throne had no grasp of the situation at all. The Duma in their view had treated the government outrageously—but it was the *people's* Duma, wasn't it, so it could not help being loyal, indeed could not help feeling a family allegiance to its own, to the people's Tsar? The voice of the people demanded that the land be taken away from private owners—perhaps it should be heeded. There were secret negotiations with the leaders of the Kadet Party in the Duma, who readily agreed to take power without promising any concessions in return. Meanwhile, the wily but worn-out Goremykin, who had outlived the normal term of service, was losing his grip on the helm, very much wanted to surrender it, and strongly recommended Stolypin as his successor. (Such an appointment would be a tremendous shock, a thunderbolt to the Court.) The Tsar's First Minister was always appointed with due regard to each candidate's seniority, the number of decorations awarded to him, his proximity to the Tsar's intimates, and his record as an obliging or at least an inoffensive fellow. But Stolypin's program of decisive measures clashed with the starry-eyed proposals of another candidate for the premiership, Dmitri Shipov.

Love for the people takes different forms and can lead us in different directions. Shipov was a distinguished zemstvo man,* he was a man of the greatest integrity, and he had devoted his whole life to the service of God's chosen people. Shipov remained true to his noble ideas that all men are fundamentally good and that the people are good—it is just that we do not know how to make them happy. He refused to accept the post of Chairman of the Council of Ministers from the Tsar while the Kadets were the majority party in the Duma: they were the people's choice, and they should head the government. He was still more emphatic in his protests against dissolution—not because such an action might produce an explosion, but because the Duma, work-shy, incapable, and rebellious as it was, must, simply must, be allowed to make its own mistakes! No matter where it might lead Russia—that was the natural path of development, because the populace would know that the mistakes were those of its chosen representatives and would correct them at the next election.

Stolypin retorted that the whole cart would be upset before it passed that test. That nothing was more dangerous in Russia than showing weakness. That Russia must not copy Western institutions so slavishly, but must have the courage to follow its own, Russian, path. It was not enough to have the right ideas. One must have the strength of purpose to make them reality.

Shipov, in turn, argued that strength of purpose and efficiency in action were not everything: still more important was that profoundly moral view of the world which he accused Stolypin of lacking.

In the quiet of Peterhof in those July days yet another of those critical moments which were becoming so frequent in Russian history arose. Should they dissolve the Duma—and perhaps provoke a still worse revolutionary upheaval? Or not dissolve it—and slide more gradually in the same direction?

Stolypin had only the two or three days of the Peterhof consultations to make up his mind whether or not to accept the cruel burden of power. He knew very well what sort of legacy was being offered.

Stolypin's arguments prevailed with the Tsar (though he still vacillated: he had agreed to dissolution, and the announcement had been made, and still he hesitated to sign the

* Zemstvos: elected local government bodies established in some parts of the Russian Empire in 1864. [*Trans.*]

decree). Stolypin was named Chairman of the Council of Ministers—it would be for him to weather the storm dissolution would stir up. Two months earlier he had been a mere provincial governor, now he was Prime Minister.

The autumn before, in Saratov, Stolypin, like all the other provincial governors, like the provincial authorities generally, had been taken completely unawares by the Manifesto of 30 October 1905. Not only had there been no warning, but the Manifesto was promulgated in such a ludicrously inefficient way that the text (preceded by rumors) first reached some parts of the country by private rather than by official channels. In Saratov it was reproduced by a private printing firm and hung in the window of a Jewish pharmacy, to the scandal of the policemen on duty, the bafflement of the authorities, and the delight of the educated public. A crowd gathered to rattle the gates of the Saratov prison two and a half hours before the administration received orders to release the amnestied prisoners.

The Manifesto, which changed the historical course of a thousand years with a single oblique blow—was it wrested from the autocrat's hands by the whirlwind? He can hardly have had time to read it through twice himself. It was promulgated in such a hurry, with such catastrophic urgency (why? from Saratov, or Archangel, or Kostroma, it seemed incomprehensible) that no explanation was drafted and distributed for the benefit of local authorities. Everyone interpreted it to suit himself—the revolutionaries giving it the widest possible meaning—and there were clashes in some towns between crowds demonstrating for and against it. Worse still, the Manifesto itself contained not a single practical measure but only a muddle of promises, little more than slogans—first of all to guarantee freedom of speech and assembly, then to

> enable those classes of the population at present denied the vote to participate

in elections to the State Duma. Did that imply universal equal franchise? The question was simply evaded, although it could so easily have been answered. On the other hand, there was the precipitate promise to

> establish the unshakable principle that no law can take effect without the approval of the State Duma.

The task of preserving the future system unchanged was entrusted to a body still to be chosen, no one yet knew how. The authors of the Manifesto were in a hurry to put their necks into the noose and draw it tight. The electoral system itself came two months later, from a group of limp elder statesmen, and it too was hasty, ill considered, confusion ten times confounded. The drafters had opted neither for universal franchise, nor for class franchise, nor for property franchise, but they had, for instance, truckled to the workers by reserving seats for them in the Duma, thus reinforcing their sense of their own peculiar importance by separating them from the population as a whole.

Yet the electoral law was not merely the result of panic and haste. It was grounded in fundamental misconceptions. One was that enormous, unwieldy Russia, which was almost a continent in size, a sleeping giant of a country and obviously one of a kind, could find nothing more appropriate to itself than the institutions elaborated by a handful of small, highly civilized European countries with a unique history and an entirely different outlook on life. Another mistake was to suppose that the whole mass of the country's peasant, lower-middle-class, and merchant population needed the same things that small groups in some of the big cities, with no real support, were so vociferously demanding. The third mistake was to suppose that although there were such huge differences in education, way of life, and customs among the population, it was possible, and high time, to devise an electoral law under which the unpolished mass would send to the Duma its own unpolished deputies, truly representative of the character and spirit of the country, and not let itself be fobbed off with glib fly-by-nights and smart alecks who would usurp the right to make pronouncements in the name of all Russia. In the countryside the franchise was almost universal (and the secret ballot suited the Russian peasant as a saddle suits a cow), but two or three levels higher up delegates fell out and were replaced by others. Allegedly for the sake of simplicity there was no provision for district electoral meetings at which electors from the separate and isolated electoral colleges could meet, get to know each other, and send to the provincial level worthy and genuinely local representatives of the population as a whole, well known to their constituency, who would continue to work for local interests at the higher stage. Instead, the electors from the different district colleges went straight to the provincial electoral assembly and were swallowed up in a crowd of strangers. The peasants in particular had no experience of anything like the new system and were quite lost, so that it was easy for the educated Kadets to wear them down and run rings around them in provincial assemblies. In fact, they forgot all about districts and clubbed together according to class, which gave the loud-mouthed political bosses their opening. So that the support which the state expected to find in the peasantry was frittered away. This usurpation threatened to leave Russia unrepresented in its own parliament for decades to come. Its true representatives would be too shy; they needed time to acquire self-confidence, literacy, verbal facility, breadth of vision, and experience of state affairs. There was probably nothing more important for the future of Russia in public life than the development of the zemstvo organizations as working bodies at all levels, and especially, after forty years of delay, at the canton level.

As promised by the Manifesto a parliament was convened in Petersburg. But the proportion of the population living in the countryside—82 percent—was not reflected in its composition. The country's rulers were afraid of a parliament dominated by peasants. The "dark masses," who were still a long way from acquiring a sense of loyalty (why, then, this parliament?), would swallow the cultured and organic elements of society. The Russian state power, wedded as it was to the frightened landed gentry, showed the same distrust of the peasantry as in the previous reign, and stunted their development with this specious parliament. The rulers themselves had no faith in the essential Russia and the class in which all its hopes for the future lay.

The Manifesto of 30 October was not only hastily and carelessly drafted, it was also obscure and ambiguous. Embodied subsequently in the constitution of 6 May 1906 (described as the "Fundamental Laws" so as not to offend the Emperor's ear), it appeared to aim simultaneously at limiting the autocratic power and preserving it.

The Manifesto only opened the gates wider to revolution. The newly summoned Prime Minister was faced with the task of closing them, using only the lawful methods open to a lawful government. With hands tightly tied by the gaudy ribbons of the Manifesto, he had to drag Russia out of chaos alive.

But Stolypin knew when he accepted the post what he was undertaking and on what conditions. The constitution was in being and it divided a previously undivided authority; he must be the first to learn and to teach others how to live by it, and how to steer Russia along this new and strange middle channel. He intended to carry out these duties honestly and unswervingly, and took into his cabinet only ministers who sincerely accepted the new constitutional order. He knew that swarms of enemies would gather on both wings: the right extremists, who wished to scrap the Manifesto and return to irresponsible government, and the liberals, who were as immoderate as only Russian liberals could be, and who wished not to see the ship make headway, but to overturn it and crush their opponents.

Stolypin, as governor and Prime Minister, had a painfully clear picture of Russia reeling dangerously off balance. It was no longer the sturdy and stable country it had been. That is the way with revolutions: the old order is not easily budged, but once it is shaken the rocking becomes wilder and wilder, the props snap and you can see that they are rotten through and through; parts of the age-old structure splinter, slide loose, pile up in confusion.

The revolutionary's battle cry was no longer "Land and freedom" but "All the land and unlimited freedom": he insisted that since the Manifesto had tossed the people only scraps of freedom he and his friends would leave not a single scrap of land in the hands of its present owners.

There were supposed to be legal restrictions (much relaxed) on trade unions and professional associations, but some unions (engineers, lawyers, teachers) operated freely, without even trying to legalize themselves as they were politely invited to. The press was free, and did not ask the government to authorize its outpourings; inevitably persons hostile to the government made use of it to corrupt the people (which meant the army too!). To mention only the least of these abuses, the legitimate press "reproduced without comment" revolutionary appeals however wild and nonsensical, and the resolutions of illegal conferences whatever their character. Intellectuals harbored the whole Soviet of Workers' Deputies in private apartments and printed its destructive exhortations. The educated public was disposed to believe any lie or libel, so long as it was directed against the government, and newspapers had a predilection for printing such things and then not retracting them. The press had usurped a power greater than that of the government.

Stocks of revolutionary publications and weapons, "laboratories" producing bombs, illegal presses, and the headquarters of revolutionary organizations were concealed in educational institutions. But every time the police tried to lay a hand on them "the public" and the press raised a howl about their illegal interference in matters which did not concern them, while the educators, who could not quiet the rebellious young, sucked up to them and called into question the results of searches. At teachers' meetings caps and handbags were passed around labeled "For propaganda among the workers," "For arms," "In aid of the Socialist Revolutionary Committee."

Civil and military courts trying political cases were biased in favor of the offenders. Revolutionaries guilty of particularly heinous murders were released pending trial. Lenient sentences almost as good as acquittal were handed down to the plaudits of the crowd. Cases were regularly adjourned, and sometimes never heard at all.

The revolutionaries grew more brazen everywhere. They brought arms in from abroad in quantities which endangered the country. They coerced people to take part in riots or strikes. Where they could not provoke a strike they damaged bridges or railway beds, or tore up telegraph poles, hoping to disrupt the country totally even without a strike wave. Liquor shops everywhere were of course enthusiastically looted.

The local authorities were caught off balance—disunited, slack, and above all terrified that they might get hurt themselves. Officials who supported the Kadets went on claiming their salaries from the government while demonstrating their opposition to it: nominally in the service of the state, they secretly agitated against it or worked for revolutionary groups, sometimes because they genuinely sympathized, sometimes for fear of reprisals. The flabby representatives of authority were frightened into a state of bewildered inertia.

Those officials who actively opposed the forces of disorder were murdered by terrorists, who went unpunished.

The rulers were overcome by fear—that in itself was a defeat for them and a triumph in advance for the revolution.

The police too were either dormant or terrified. The lower ranks, and the men on the beat, who were on easy terms with the local population, ignored the growing ferment around them as long as they could—and when the explosion came it destroyed them first of all. The lower ranks have least defense against murderous attackers. Anyone can approach the man on the beat to ask for information, and the terrorists took advantage of this. The police in small towns often exhibited helpless weakness when confronted by a hostile mob, thereby inciting them to further excesses.

The countryside is still harder to keep under observation and control, and any agitator can sow the seeds of revolt over those broad expanses. Thus, three agitators from the city, one of them a girl, stirred up four hundred peasants to take their carts along and sack a sugar refinery. The city folk wore masks, and played the piano in the manager's quarters while the peasants were destroying the plant. Incendiaries from another district—not local peasants—slit open the bellies of a herd of purebred cattle, and dying bulls and cows bellowed at the sight of their own entrails. Peasants burned manor houses, libraries, pictures, chopped up antique furniture, smashed porcelain, trampled, broke, tore . . . They either saw to it that nothing was saved from a burning house or plundered it and carted off the contents. (One of the houses sacked belonged to a liberal landowner, who appealed to the governor for help.) The rural clergy, downtrodden for so long, were powerless to restrain their rebellious flock. (In the towns some priests acted against the government themselves.)

Large bodies of troops were dispatched to deal with the rural disorders—sometimes whole regiments. The entire contingent would be stupidly kept together in one place, so that areas under threat were left unprotected, or else broken up into tiny detachments, themselves an easy prey for agitators. The right to use troops in unusual places went to the heads of many civilian officials: they surrounded themselves with inordinately large escorts whenever they rode out, stationed large detachments with artillery outside their private quarters, and made rankers perform menial tasks for them—insulting the troops and demoralizing them as effectively as the agitators themselves.

The ferment in the country spread of course to the armed forces. Soldiers off duty went into town with a leave pass and stood with the schoolboys listening to political speeches. Out of barracks there was no discipline at all—soldiers could drink as much as they liked. Some newspapers told them that this was the time to forget everything else and mutiny. Agitators actually appeared in the barrack rooms. They had only to slip on a uniform, and they could bring in great piles of leaflets and spread the word without hindrance. There was by now a standard terminology: Russia was ruled by a gang of robbers, the army was commanded by enemies of the toiling people, everyone in the army (indeed in Russia) was trained not to answer back but to hunt down and punish those who did. The agitators took advantage of every weak spot, every oversight—slowness in releasing time-expired conscripts, delay in replacing uniforms, short rations, withholding of travel warrants. There was negligence everywhere, of course, because the country was backward, and because its development had been delayed by having to contend with these revolutionaries for several decades. There was plenty for agitators' tongues to wag about. No one kept an eye open for agitators in army units, and commanders made a habit of complacent reporting. The army command, like the civil authorities, was either boneheaded or too easily frightened: it suddenly authorized barrack-room meetings at which the soldiers could draw up lists of demands. Lists were indeed drawn up (by party agitators): "Tell them you want a reply within three days! An extra half pound of meat a day doesn't improve your allowances."

Soldiers ought to be paid more than twenty-two kopecks a month, and allowed to smoke in places other than the latrine, and not punished for not saluting by being made to stand as stiff and still as senseless posts. Like the peasants and like the workers, the army had been badly neglected. It was governed by fossilized tradition. Colonels and lieutenants alike believed that there was no need to trouble their heads, that things could be allowed to drift and drift and drift for another three hundred years.

Stolypin had very little time for reflection: should he seize the bridles of the runaway horses already pawing the abyss or watch the Russian chariot plunge to destruction? Should he take the insupportable burden of power at this insupportable moment?

Even while the Peterhof consultations were in progress our little terrorist friends managed to kill a general in Peterhof itself (misled by his uniform, they mistook Kozlov for Dmitri Trepov) and an admiral at Sevastopol.

The first decree drafted by Stolypin's mind and pen was placed before the Emperor for his signature:

> The elected representatives of the population, instead of working constructively, have strayed into a sphere which is not properly theirs, and acted in ways which are flagrantly illegal, as in their appeal to the population in the name of the Duma.

The dissolution of the Duma might seem, might look—did look—less like a last-minute grab at the bridle than another desperate shove toward the abyss! (The Tsar's entourage and Trepov were very apprehensive about it.) But it was a risk taken coolly; he had tightened his grip, and he would maintain it:

> May calm be restored to the Russian land and may the Almighty help us to accomplish the *most important* [Stolypin put the words in italics] of our monarchy's tasks—which is to raise the prosperity of the peasantry. To do

> so is our unbending will [as long as Stolypin was guiding it!], and where there is a shortage of land the Russian tiller of the soil will be given, without detriment to anyone else, a legitimate and honest means of expanding his holding.
>
> We believe that heroes of thought and deed will come forward and that by their self-sacrificing toil . . .

Battle had been joined already: now its objectives were defined. Both sides wanted to "raise" the peasantry: the radical intelligentsia wanted to "raise" them in rebellion, to see them burning, wrecking, and looting, to turn the life of Russia upside down, while the liberal-conservative Prime Minister wished to "raise" the level of the peasants' existence so as to strengthen the Russian land.

Expecting the revolutionaries to strike, Stolypin that same day declared a state of emergency in Petersburg province.

The Duma had been so eager to fly at the government's throat, had seemed so unrestrainable, so confident of victory that they had not for a moment anticipated a counterstroke. Now what? The blow had been struck, the moment had come to sound the call to revolution! But, surprisingly, no battle cry was let out. What *was* let out sounded more like the air escaping from a punctured balloon, loud at first, but immediately quieter: the Vyborg appeal.

There were, however, others in the dismissed Duma besides the suddenly timid Kadets. There were militant SRs (renamed "Laborites" for purposes of legal political activity) and there were spluttering Social Democrats. On 25 July these groups published in Petersburg a

> MANIFESTO TO THE ARMY AND NAVY
>
> Soldiers and sailors! We were elected to tell the Tsar about the people's grievances, and to win *land and freedom.* But the Tsar has listened to the richest landowners, who do not want to let go of their estates . . . to the generals who ran away from the Japanese in Manchuria and turned their guns on Moscow . . . Why should you defend the government? Is yours a good life? You are reduced to slavery as officers' servants . . . We intended to issue laws improving soldiers' pay and forbidding all forms of humiliating treatment.
>
> We, the lawfully elected representatives of the peasants and workers, declare to you that without the State Duma the government has no legal existence! You have taken the oath to defend your fatherland. Your fatherland is the cities and villages of Russia. Anyone who fires on the people is a criminal, a traitor, and an enemy. For such people there can be no return to their place of birth. *The government has entered into negotiations with the Austrian and German Emperors*—it wants German troops to invade our country. *For engaging in these negotiations we accuse the government of high treason!* It has put itself outside the law! Soldiers and sailors! It is your sacred duty to liberate the people from this traitorous government! Take arms for land and freedom!

Any sort of wild nonsense (even the tale about negotiations with Germany) can find a home in revolutionary proclamations—no need to check its credentials. But these people produced more than verbal explosions. Revolutionary couriers shuttled between Sevastopol, Kronstadt, and Sveaborg to bring about a concerted rising! (They did not even try to conceal their plan: they would touch off risings in the countryside as soon as the harvest was in, large numbers of troops would be rushed there, and that would be the moment for "progressive" garrisons to mutiny.) Once again they would crimson the air with the exhilarating flames of revolution!

We have caught two glimpses of Finland—Vyborg, where the Duma was able to promulgate its appeal, and Sveaborg, the main naval base on the islands just outside Helsingfors. There is a very good reason for this. The law had lost much of its force in Russia generally, but in Finland it hardly operated at all. The moment the Duma was dismissed, its deputies were summoned by a telegram from Staff Captain Tsion: "You will be under the protection of Sveaborg's guns!" It was to Helsingfors that revolutionaries came rushing, from abroad and from Russia itself. In the coffeehouses and squares of Helsingfors the best orators vociferated, while sailors and soldiers from the garrison sauntered unhindered from one street meeting to another, hearing that the government had committed treason and that the time had come to overthrow it. Not only did Finnish law preclude interference with such meetings, but armed detachments marched through the city in open support of the revolutionaries; the Fougasse publishing house continued to operate; and the Social Democratic *Barrack-Room Herald* appeared regularly, summoning soldiers and sailors to rise against the "terrorist government" and the "hangman of all the Russias."

Finland! Yet another of the sore spots in Russia's ailing body. For the sake of aggrandizement or adornment, or for some other supposed advantage, Russia had detached Finland from Sweden and incorporated it. Finland was given a constitution a hundred years before Russia, and a parliament sixty years earlier. Under Aleksandr I and Aleksandr II it obtained privileges which Russia's rulers dared not then or later concede to Russia herself. Finns were exempt from compulsory military service. The Finns had special rights anywhere within the territory of the Empire. The Finnish currency system was so devised that the Finns lived at Russia's expense. The relaxation of controls on two frontiers—that between Finland and Sweden and that between Finland and Russia—opened up an easy route for revolutionaries, revolutionary literature, and arms from Europe. Stolypin did not have the right at this stage to act as though these concessions had never been granted. Finland became a safer refuge for Russian revolutionaries than the neighboring European states, from which they might be deported under extradition treaties, whereas in Finland the local police did not keep track of them and the Russian government could not maintain its own network of agents. Finland became a legal reservation and bridgehead for all revolutionary conspirators, and manufacturers of bombs and forged papers could work there in safety and comfort. In Finland, a mere twenty-five versts from the capital of the Russian Empire, and there was no frontier to cross, dozens of revolutionary congresses and conferences were held, and terrorist acts against Russia were prepared. Terrorists exported to Finland the money they stole in Russia. When Russia's new time of troubles began, the Finns were permitted to establish their

"Red Guard"—supposedly a peaceful class organization—which conducted military training exercises and parades throughout Finland, even in sight of the Vyborg fortress, and attacked the police. Mighty Russia's only protection against this canker was the Beloostrov cordon.

In Finland again a savage mutiny broke out on 30 July at Sveaborg, beginning with fighting between mutinous artillerymen and nonmutinous infantry. Russian soldiers did battle with other Russian soldiers for three whole days. Men were forced to join the mutineers under threat of death, officers were arrested. (Some were shot, some bayoneted, some drowned, and one shot himself.) "Kill the officers!" was the battle cry with which they appealed to the infantry, but the infantry would not join in, and for three whole days it was pounded by big guns, defending itself as best it could with only its fieldpieces. Several hundred Russian soldiers were killed by Russian shells in this bombardment and later when the powder magazines were blown up because they could not manage them without officers. Several dozen crazed civilians rallied to the mutineers and incited them to continue this mutual destruction. During the last night of the mutiny Tsion and his friends slunk away, leaving the mutineers to their punishment. The Russian authorities could not muster enough troops in the whole of Finland to crush the mutiny. That had to wait for the fleet, which bombarded the place yet again. On the third day Kronstadt also rose, but the mutiny there lasted only six hours.

Finnish Red Guards had blown up bridges between Helsingfors and Petersburg, felled telegraph poles, been caught with weapons on the territory of the mutinous fortress, but under Finland's liberal laws there could be no thought of court-martialing them. That would have offended the Finnish sense of constitutional propriety, so they were all consigned to lenient civil courts for trial, while only Russians faced court-martial (the majority of those sentenced to death were later pardoned).

Stolypin told himself that the tougher he was to begin with, the fewer lives would be lost in the end. Excessive leniency at the beginning could only increase the number of victims later. He would use conciliatory methods where persuasion was possible. But the mad dogs would not be converted by persuasion—swift and relentless punishment was the only thing for them. What sort of government would it be (and where in the world would you find another?) that refused to defend the state order and forgave murderers and bomb throwers? The government was defending itself. Why should it, rather than the revolutionaries, retreat?

> If people force their way onto trains with bombs and rob peaceful citizens under the flag of social revolution, it is the government's duty to maintain order, ignoring the outcry against "reaction."

(In Russia at that time such a declaration was seen as blatantly reactionary. Seventy years later the world at large may understand it better.)

Armed revolutionaries seized printing presses and distributed exhortations to a general uprising and mass killings. They proclaimed local republics in some regions. The Baltic states were in flames. Regiments mutinied at Tambov, in the Caucasus, and at Brest Litovsk. There was unrest at Stavropol and Batum. The Caspian fleet, the Tula arms works, the whole southern industrial region, and all of Poland were on strike at one time or another. The measures taken had to be resolute, indeed harsh, but strictly in accordance with the law. The huge caches of weapons had to be confiscated. Strikers must be replaced by volunteers from patriotic organizations, who would have military protection but not weapons of their own or any right to fight other workers. The police must be staunchly supported—their lot was a particularly hard one. It was for the courts to make summary procedures unnecessary by prompt, firm, and just action. Feebleness in judicial retribution had a demoralizing effect on the whole population.

> Indulgence shown in some cases may give rise to the idea that in others too strict punishment is inappropriate—it comes to be seen as superfluous cruelty.

Moreover, the court machinery worked too slowly to make any impression on the masses or to reassure anybody. Field courts-martial were the only thing for it. The situation was one of civil war—so the laws of wartime must apply. Swift measures would elicit popular support, and that was the surest way to stop the revolutionaries.

> The resolve of right-thinking people to be seen defending order will in itself produce an impression calculated to daunt the "militants," whose insane daring thrives on the pusillanimity of those who prefer a quiet life.

These simple thoughts, however, were not only in advance of their time (outside or inside Russia) but too advanced for the Tsar. He had shrunk from the audacious step of dissolving the First Duma—and now he was asked to go farther along the fearsome road of repression.

The terrorists themselves brought matters to a head by their decision to cut short the life of the new Prime Minister after he had been in office for one month. They blew up his official out-of-town residence on Aptekarsky Island, at a time when he was receiving visitors. This was one of the revolution's most successful bombings: twenty-seven killed and thirty-two seriously injured! (Most of them were not members of Stolypin's household or officials.) Two regiments of soldiers and five teams of firefighters dug the wounded and the mangled dead out of the rubble. Many had had some part of the body—arm, leg, head—blown off. Half of the building was blown to bits. Walls and staircases collapsed. Stolypin's only son, aged three, and one of his daughters were catapulted from a balcony over a fence and some considerable distance onto the embankment. The boy's leg was broken, and the girl fell under the feet of the wounded and terrified horses harnessed to the phaeton in which the revolutionaries had arrived. One of the petitioners had a child in arms with her—both were killed. The revolutionaries too were torn to shreds, as were the general and the doorman who tried to stop them. Only one room in that house was completely undamaged—Pyotr Arkadievich's study. He was at his desk when the bomb went off. The blast caused a big bronze inkwell to fly over his head, spilling ink on him—and that was all the harm he suffered.

The Tsar's launch came and took Stolypin's family to the Winter Palace. As the launch passed under the bridges on that bright summer Saturday morning, a rowdy procession with red flags marched overhead. Stolypin's uninjured eight-year-old daughter was terrified and hid under a bench. Stolypin, who had just prevailed on the doctors not to amputate his injured daughter's legs (she would regain the use of them after two years of agonizing treatment, but would be lame all her life), told the other children, "We mustn't hide just because people shoot at us."

The whole left-wing press was full of hints that Stolypin should learn his lesson before it was too late ("His children's sufferings have affected his nerves") and retire, for his own safety and that of his children. (Noting simultaneously that the government was doomed: "Perhaps this has refreshed its realization that it cannot govern without the plenipotentiary representatives of the people.") But no! Stolypin was more determined than ever not to give in to the terrorist ringleaders. Let cowards resign—he would stay!

> Where bombs are used as arguments the natural answer is merciless punishment. To our grief and shame only the execution of a few can prevent the spilling of seas of blood.

That was the beginning of the notorious Stolypin terror—a phrase so persistently foisted on the Russian language and the Russian mind (abroad it was worse still!) that even now the image of a black era of cruel excesses is seared onto our eyeballs. Yet all the terror amounted to was the introduction of field courts-martial (which operated for eight months) to deal with especially serious (not all) cases of looting, murder, and attacks on the police, on the civil authorities, and on peaceful citizens, so as to bring trial and sentence closer to the time and place of the crime. (Urged to hold terrorists already under arrest hostage for the actions of others not yet captured, Stolypin of course rejected the idea.) Dissemination of subversive ideas in the army (previously practically unimpeded) was made a criminal offense. So was praise of terrorism (in which Duma deputies, the press, and indeed the general public had hitherto indulged unhindered). Bomb throwers were now subject to the death penalty, but those caught making bombs were not treated as actual murderers. Meetings organized by political parties and societies, provided they were not in public places and there were no outsiders present, or only outsiders belonging to the educated classes, did not require administrative supervision.

These draconian measures aroused the unanimous wrath of educated Russian society. There was a spate of newspaper articles, speeches, and letters (one from Lev Tolstoy) arguing that no one should ever dare to execute anyone, not even the most brutal of murderers, that field courts-martial could do nothing toward the moral rejuvenation of society (as though that was what terror was doing) but could only further brutalize it (something which terror did still more effectively). Guchkov, who had the temerity to support the introduction of field courts-martial openly (they were better, he said, than random shootings by exasperated policemen or soldiers), was assailed on all sides by leftist persecutors. Even telegrams of sympathy to officials hurt by revolutionaries were invariably greeted with indignation by the liberals. Anyone who did not loudly approve of revolutionary terror was regarded by Russian society as a hangman himself.

Yet, whether Stolypin was brutalizing Russia or not, terrorism declined from the moment the field courts-martial were introduced.

During these most crucial months, the Prime Minister and his family lived, at the Emperor's insistence, in the Winter Palace, that ornate and gloomy penitentiary in which the imperial family itself had long ceased to dwell. Doors and gateways were strictly guarded.

Pyotr Arkadievich, who loved horseback riding and strenuous solitary walks over open fields, now strolled from one great room to another in the palace, or went up on the roof, where there was a place for Tsars to stretch their legs. There, and only there, high above the very center of Petersburg, and concealed by pent roofs, the Prime Minister of Russia was not under threat. The country's Emperor had been lying low for well over a year on his little estate at Peterhof, and in all that time had not dared to show himself in public or travel the roads of his own country even under escort.

In whose hands was Russia, then? Had the revolutionaries already triumphed?

Only night lights burned in the halls of the Winter Palace, which made it gloomier than ever. The gilded frames of the innumerable portraits, the gilt and crystal of the unlit chandeliers had a sinister gleam in the half-dark. Dustcovers shrouded an endless profusion of superannuated furniture, which had taken so many supremely wise statesmen into its elegantly curved embraces and now stood strait-jacketed, its stiff arms locked around nothing.

The imperial throne was also under covers, as though it too had served its time.

A shudder ran over him. Was the Russian monarchy still alive? The dynasty that was about to celebrate its tercentenary? Or had it choked on that panicky Manifesto of 30 October?

Behind that lifeless furniture Stolypin sensed the presence of thousands of highly placed living corpses, a great throng of them closing their ranks to bring history to a halt, while around the palace prowled rabid young men with bombs, eager to blow history up and put a stop to it *their* way. Stolypin saw in his mind the only path, the natural path, though in earthquake conditions it looked improbable: a knife-edge path along a broken ridge. In the past reform had for some reason always signified a weakening and possibly the collapse of the regime, while stern measures to restore order were taken to indicate a renunciation of reform. He saw clearly that the two things must be combined! And, characteristically, what he saw and knew he felt able to carry through courageously. He had no time for public political wrangles, and none for empty show: his preference was for purposeful action. He saw the path forward, and set out on it. Even Witte's imbecilic Manifesto could be the starting point from which he could lead Russia onto a firm road. He would salvage the flimsy constitution which they had cobbled together in their panic.

But to spare the Emperor's feelings he would not risk using the words "constitution" or "constitutional order." As if serried ranks of ferocious enemies to left and right were not enough, the Prime Minister had to perform a nimble balancing act to avoid hurting the Tsar's tender feelings. Just as a believer can never do anything serious without saying and believing that it is not by his own power but through God's grace, so the monarchist can undertake no great deed for his country's sake if he ceases to respect his sovereign. In those few months Stolypin had measured himself against Russia's champion windbags—almost legendary figures, seen from the provinces—and decided that they were really neither strong nor clever. He had seen that he was more than a match for them. But having accepted the post of head of the Russian government, what he had to think about was not how to further his own independent designs, but how to make them fit in with his sovereign's will. Even though the sovereign's actions showed not strength of purpose but a mixture of timidity and obstinacy, obstinacy even in error, even though the sovereign's highest motivation was to avoid disquiet, he must nonetheless carefully seek out the dim spark of the sovereign's will, shelter it from drafts, tend it so that it would not flicker out, because for the foreseeable future Russia could not advance, or indeed survive, if its monarchic structure and character were demolished. He must not give in to an ordinary human judgment of the limp and somewhat sluggish man facing him across the desk and smoking, with a soft, unassuming smile between his unassuming mustache and beard. He must continue to believe sincerely in the golden-haloed image which had haunted him of old. The greatest of ministers was no substitute even for a weak hereditary monarch: Stolypin could never have chosen for himself the path of Bismarck, who had ruthlessly violated the will of the monarch in the interests of the monarchy.

There was no doubt that the Emperor was perplexed, unsure of himself, afraid to take decisive steps lest they aggravate the disorders. (His idea of ruling the country was typified by his instruction that "an exact count of the telegrams received by me from the Union of the Russian People is to be kept, and a summary presented later.") He undoubtedly needed a strong man to do everything for him ("The Council of Ministers has my permission to discuss my suggestion"), but in such a way that the people would see the Tsar's will at work and know that their own joys and sorrows were his close concern.

All this together stirred in Stolypin pain and pity, first for Russia, but then for his sovereign too, that weak but virtuous man, weaker than any former Romanov, who through no wish of his own had found himself wearing the crown of Monomakh in those most difficult years. He could not leave this Tsar in distress, he must instill in him his own resolve; not only because they would not otherwise be able to accomplish their work for Russia but because he pitied the man's fatal dilatoriness and indecision. (Although it needed no great foresight to see how easily this Tsar might recoil from his minister and betray him.)

He must follow the established form and cushion his swift and forceful decisions with the formulae of respect: I beg to submit for your gracious consideration . . . Your Majesty is right indeed, and so quick to see the solution . . . Forgive me, Sire, for presuming to express my candid opinion, as my duty and my oath of loyalty require, and please believe that there is nothing I want less than to interfere with your freedom of decision . . . All my endeavors are to spare you difficulty and unpleasantness.

Songbirds called to each other in many voices in the winter garden. And there were aged footmen on duty in all the halls and at all the doors, guarding, as they always had, hushed and decaying antiquity, and as unpleasantly startled by the living presence of the Prime Minister as they might have been by Hamlet's father's ghost. They shuffled their feet and held their peace, or answered questions reluctantly, all in a dutiful ritual way, and they showed animation only when they were asked about days long gone.

Stolypin found it stifling. Without an hour of brisk walking his normally inexhaustible capacity for work—he could finish at three in the morning and begin again at nine—might fail him. A single hour of brisk walking and thinking made things stand out boldly in their true proportions. Without it big decisions were impossible, he was doomed to drown in detail.

Little outings were invented for him, planned not by the Prime Minister but by his bodyguard. It was they who decided through which of all those splendid doors they would take him, where his carriage would be waiting, which streets they would ride through and where to. Once out of the city Pyotr Arkadievich would walk for a while, then leave it to the others to decide on the route back. He had promised not to interfere, and not to confuse the driver by giving him instructions. He waited on the Tsar with his reports under similar conditions—at Peterhof in summer and Tsarskoye Selo in winter. In the Tsar's timetable morning began about midday, so Stolypin always went to report in the evening and returned toward 1 a.m.

In spite of his secluded life the terrorists thought up schemes for finding and killing him. First they made use of his oldest daughter to introduce a terrorist student into the family as tutor to his younger daughters. This plan was uncovered in time. (The tutor had paid court to the older daughter and invited her to his apartment. She thought it dishonorable to disclose the address to her father, and he respected her decision.) Next, they insinuated a terrorist into Stolypin's bodyguard—and couldn't have hoped for better luck: on one occasion he was standing guard, revolver in his pocket, at the door from which Stolypin emerged, but he was taken by surprise, failed to shoot, and was unmasked soon afterward. On another occasion, the Socialist Revolutionaries, observing Stolypin's regular visits to his invalid sister, rented an apartment in the house opposite, intending to fire on him from their window and through hers. This too came to nothing. Another attempt was planned by the Zilberberg group for the opening ceremony at the Medical Institute, and yet another by Sulyatitsky, to be made as he drove to Peterhof for his audience with the Tsar. In the course of the year the police thwarted attempts on Stolypin's life planned by the Dobrzynski group, the "flying squad" of Rosa Rabinovich and Lea Lapina, Trauerberg's "flying squad," the Strogalshchikov group, Feiga Elkina's group, and Leiba Liberman's group.

Speaking of those months, Stolypin would tell his intimates, "I offer up a prayer every morning and think of the day ahead as my last. In the evening I thank God for granting me one more day of life. I realize that death is often the penalty to be paid for one's beliefs. And I feel strongly at times that the day will come when some murderer's plan will succeed. Still, you only die once."

Stolypin went to his desk on the very first evening of his enervating life in the Winter Palace, though he had barely recovered from the explosion, with two of his children injured and the others still terrified. He worked far into the night. The hour of greatest danger, when life is cruelly straitened, is when life's greatest tasks are often accomplished. Terrorists were straining at the leash to kill him, but Russia was on the edge of the abyss. Manor houses were burning, bombs were exploding, army units had mutinied, the field courts-martial were in being, but it was his duty to look far into the future and move forward along the only possible axis of a systematic reform program. While seeking to halt the disorders by physical force, it was all the more incumbent on the government to concentrate its moral strength on the renewal of the country, and in the first place on land reform.

> We shall be called to account by future generations. We shall have to answer to them if we fall into despondency, into a sort of senile impotence, and lose faith in the Russian people.

The village was the nodal point of Russia's destiny. To cure society's ills he had to begin not at the higher levels of society, where everyone was spoiled and corrupted: bureaucrats by the routine of office, landowners by their free and easy life, with no obligations to anyone or anything, the court itself . . . it was not proper for a monarchist to pass judgment on the court. A state needed above all strong legs, and the cure must begin below, with the peasants. Whether Russia would develop in a healthy way would be decided in the village and nowhere else. Stolypin's central idea was that it is impossible to introduce the rule of law until you have independent citizens, and in Russia those citizens would be peasants. "Citizens first, then civil rights." (Witte too used to say that emancipation of the peasants must precede the introduction of a constitution, but had then himself introduced a constitution in a moment of panic—and now Stolypin had to emancipate the peasants after the event.) The abstract right to freedom without real freedom for the peasants was "rouge on the corpse." Russia could not become a strong state until its main class had a vested interest in the existing order. As Stolypin put it:

> There is no limit to the assistance I am ready to give and the concessions I am willing to make to put the peasantry on the path of cultural development. If we fail to carry out this reform we should all be swept onto the rubbish heap.

The government had a moral duty to offer the peasant a way out of poverty,

> to enable every hardworking tiller of the soil to farm on his own account, applying his own labor without encroaching on the rights of others.

This was to be achieved first by immediately ceding to the peasants some state land, some appanage land, and some Church land. (Nine million desyatins from these sources were ceded immediately, under a decree signed on the day of the explosion on Aptekarsky Island, against the concerted opposition of the Grand Dukes, who did not want to give up all the appanage land, or give up any of it without compensation.) Second, by easing restrictions on the sale of land held in trust or entailed (Stolypin himself set an example by selling his Nizhni Novgorod estate to the Peasant Bank). Third, by reducing loan repayments and offering more generous credit. But the most important thing was freedom to leave the commune.

> The obligation for all to conform to a single pattern of farming can be tolerated no longer. It is intolerable for a peasant with initiative to invest his talents and efforts in land which is only temporarily his. Continual redistribution begets carelessness and indifference in the cultivator. Equal shares in the land mean equal shares in ruin. Egalitarian land use lowers agricultural standards and the general cultural level of the country at large.

When he raised his hand to destroy the commune Stolypin knew very well how many previous enactments had sought to weld it more tightly together, to freeze it. Even Tsar Nikolai I had consistently followed an agrarian program indistinguishable from the dream of the latter-day Socialist Revolutionaries: equal land endowment (by households, villages, cantons, counties, and even provinces) and periodic redistribution in accordance with census returns. Experiments at the end of his reign in resettling state peasants on family smallholdings were stopped under Aleksandr II. When the peasants were freed from their landlords it was obviously nonsensical to leave them dependent on the commune, but that was precisely what was done. (There was, theoretically, a way out: the peasant was free to leave after paying his full share of the commune's redemption dues, but hardly anyone was wealthy enough to buy himself out in this way, and at the end of Aleksandr III's reign the practice was forbidden, and remained so until redemption dues were canceled by a stroke of the Tsar's pen in 1905.) Russia's Tsars, one after another, nursed a distrust of the broadest and most hardworking class, the country's firm foundation. Aleksandr III, as distrustful as the others, forbade even the departure of grown-up sons from their father's household without the commune's permission, reminded the peasant in special decrees that allotment land was inalienable (this immediately after the 1891 famine, from which one might have expected the opposite conclusion to be drawn!), and further restricted the humble rights of the village assembly by introducing "land captains," with power to fine, arrest, and flog peasants.

That was Aleksandr III's mistake—visiting on the peasants the wrath aroused by rebel intellectuals.

The monarch now reigning had no faith in the peasants either. Only three years earlier he had insisted on the inviolability of the commune, even after the abolition of the unjust and intolerable system under which all its members were collectively responsible for the bad debts of individuals. And only a year ago it had been stressed once more in the name of the Tsar that allotment land could not be bought and sold. Pobedonostsev (whose power ran out only in the autumn of 1905) had also insisted on the retention of the commune.

The simple fact was that, consciously or unconsciously, the whole ruling caste was anxiously and greedily hanging on to its own land—the gentry, the Grand Dukes, the beneficiaries of appanage land. They feared that any movement of landed property, wherever it began, might sooner or later reach them. (And also that if the peasants acquired land of their own the supply of peasant labor would shrink.)

In the argument about gentry land the peasants' hereditary grievance was proof against the most eloquent statistics: You took the land away, not from the present generation, not from our fathers, our grandfathers, or even our great-grandfathers, but from distant ancestors of ours somewhere, and you gave nothing in return. You gave the land to the gentry and gave them whole villages of us along with it! The centuries had not cooled their burning resentment.

But the peasant's lack of land that was truly his, land that he felt to be his, was precisely what undermined *his* respect for everyone else's property. The mentality of the obsolete commune also fostered socialism, which was gathering strength throughout the world. In spite of the holy commune, the village had showed itself to be a powder magazine in 1905. The peasant's lack of legal rights could no longer be borne. He was enserfed to the commune. He must not be kept in leading strings any longer. His present position could not be reconciled with the existence of any other form of freedom in the state. "The desire for property is as natural as hunger, as the urge to continue one's kind, or as any other inborn characteristic of man," and it must be satisfied. Peasant ownership of land is a guarantee of order in the state. The peasant without land of his own lends a ready ear to false doctrine, and is susceptible to those who urge him to satisfy his desire for land by force. The solid peasant on land of his own is a barrier against all destructive movements, against any form of communism, which is why all socialists are so desperately anxious not to see the peasant released from the slavery of the commune, not to let him build up his strength. (And of course overcrowded villages make the work of agitators easier.) Land reform will make the incendiarism of the Socialist Revolutionaries a thing of the past.

Stolypin saw the key act in his agrarian legislation as part two of the reform of 1861. This was a true and full emancipation of the peasants, forty-five years late. (The Japanese war had precipitated this second reform, as the Crimean debacle had the first.)

Much of this was probably said, and urged on the Emperor, when Stolypin was received at Peterhof on summer and autumn nights in 1906—and it had its effect. The Emperor was sincerely and excitedly convinced that these were his own feelings, his own words: "The well-being of the peasant is the main object of our royal endeavors." Convinced that the plan to continue his grandfather's great work of liberating the peasants was his own, and that by good luck Stolypin was finding the terms in which to formulate it, the Emperor himself now insisted that the law should be enacted under Article 87 of the Fundamental Laws, bypassing the Duma, which might hold it up. Article 87 provided:

> In the intervals between convocations of the State Duma, the Council of Ministers may, if extraordinary circumstances make it necessary, submit a legislative measure directly to H.M. the Emperor.

(But a law not ratified by the State Duma two months after the resumption of its sittings or, of course, one not submitted for ratification, lost its validity.) This was the golden age in Stolypin's relations with the Emperor, and he hurried ahead with his practical tasks.

He made a number of unsuccessful attempts that summer to draw into his cabinet representatives of sections of the educated public not too far to the left—Guchkov, Shipov, Nikolai Lvov. His line of argument was that the present time was one for deeds and work, not party programs and resounding arguments. Deeds would carry conviction, would win people over sooner and more surely than words. There need be no hurry to convene another ineffectual Duma so that it could indulge in the same sort of irresponsible waffle, while its deputies carried on their subversive work under cover of parliamentary immunity. What could not wait were practical measures and reforms which were matters of urgent necessity to large sections of the population.

They must not mark time, must not look over their shoulders, but must move forward, keeping abreast of the age they lived in, yet taking care not to let the speed of movement blur the contours of the present situation. They must be able to discern what was best, and have the stamina to realize it in practice. That was a talent Stolypin himself possessed. He fought revolution as a statesman, not as the head of the police.

Alas! To the Russian "public," blissfully dazzled by the sun of Freedom, no disaster could detract from the joy of opining out loud. "Man of action" was regarded as a synonym for tyrant. None of the public figures invited would risk joining Stolypin's cabinet, though some of them sympathized with him.

On 18 October 1906 Stolypin obtained the Tsar's signature to the decree granting the peasants equality before the law with members of other classes: they acquired the status of "free rural inhabitants" promised to them in the act of 3 March 1861. They were given the right to change their place of residence freely, to choose their occupation freely, to obtain loans against security, and to join the civil service or enter higher educational establishments on the same basis as the gentry, and with no need to ask the commune or the land captain for permission. The last of the forms of punishment reserved for peasants only were now abolished. (The Second, Third, and Fourth Dumas all loved the people passionately and loved only the people, but never got around to ratifying this law! It was debated year after year, with rightists loudly encouraging left-wing speakers—and accusing Stolypin of revolutionary tendencies! When the Revolution broke out in the winter of 1917, the law was still unratified.)

He put through the decree on rural district zemstvo organizations—that is to say, local self-government by representatives of all classes—as a first step toward the decentralization of administration. (This law met the same fate: the people's freedom-loving defenders would suppress it right up to March 1917, objecting to it as insufficiently democratic, with the rightists happily supporting them. So the peasants were denied for all time the right to manage their own local affairs—finance, irrigation, roads, schools, culture.)

When the urban intellectuals made so much of the freedoms promised in the Manifesto—freedom of speech and of assembly—they tended to forget that there is also such a thing as freedom of worship. In the interval between Dumas Stolypin abolished various forms of discrimination, giving the Old Believers and the sectarians equal rights with the Orthodox. He removed restrictions on the use of buildings for worship and on the founding of religious communities.

He also spent a long time drafting and promoting a law granting equal rights to the Jews. He was acting in the spirit of the Manifesto, but also hoping to tear numbers of Jews away from the revolutionary cause. His law relieved the Jews of many of their disabilities (some alleviation of their position was already in progress). The cabinet submitted its resolution, but after hesitation no less prolonged Nikolai II rejected this law with what was for him quite unusual decisiveness. Stolypin was taken aback, but tried to ensure that the Tsar's refusal would not besmirch his reputation in the eyes of the Russian public. The indefinite postponement of the law on equal rights for the Jews gave the Duma an excellent excuse to delay the granting of equal rights to the peasants.

A number of other enactments affecting the peasants followed: on land tenure, on melioration, on improving land use, on subsidized credits.

They were crowned by the fundamental decree of 22 November 1906, giving the peasant the right to leave the commune, consolidate his allotment as a private holding, or separate himself completely from the village and set up a farm with a house of its own.

But these were only a small part of the legislative proposals prepared that autumn and winter with the historical reconstruction of Russia in mind—not the potential of the Second Duma, to which they would be submitted.

Elections to the Duma were absolutely free. The dismissal of the First Duma had generated a great deal of heat, and its successor met in a no less threatening mood. Petersburg seethed with rumors that the convocation of the Duma was a trick, and that it would be dissolved immediately. Not so. Stolypin convened it in order to work with it, and sincerely proposed that government and Duma should criticize each other's legislative projects in a spirit of equality.

The Duma was opened at the beginning of March 1907, but on 15 March the high ceiling of the Tauride Palace collapsed. Beams, chandeliers, laths, and plaster covered the whole central area of the hall, including three-quarters of the deputies' seats, the presidium, the rostrum, and the government box. If it had fallen a few hours later it would have buried three hundred deputies and seriously injured them, leaving only the extremists on the right and on the left unhurt. The Duma survived only because the cave-in occurred when it was not in session.

Left-wing deputies did not fail to see the event as a sign of "gross contempt for the people's representatives," and even as the result of a plot:

> If this is part of the reckoning, it is a cruel reckoning. We must safeguard our lives for the future.

One socialist loudmouth, the "worker" (proofreader) Aleksinsky, said:

> If the people learn that ceilings collapse on our heads, they will draw the appropriate conclusions.

(Completely credible explanations were subsequently put forward. Examination showed that, given the building methods used in Potemkin's day and the decay caused by the hothouse which had been there for so many years, the ceiling was bound to collapse. All the same, the incident inevitably made a great impression at the time: even materialists were tempted to see in it some sort of symbol—but a symbol of what? The fall of the Duma? Of Stolypin's government? Of Russia itself? Ten more years were to go by, ten years to the day, before the meaning of the symbol, and the significance of the date on which the ceiling collapsed, became clear.)

The Duma's sittings were transferred to the White Hall of the Gentry Assembly on Mikhailovskaya Street. There it was that the indestructible Stolypin appeared before yet another "Duma of the People's Wrath" (this time, though, there was no booing and whistling). He was as collected, as immovable, as direct as ever and he spoke with the same bold confidence in his cause, the same challenging gaze, as he read out the government's declaration. In his very first words he gave the assurance the Duma longed to hear:

> It is our sovereign ruler's will that the conversion of the fatherland into a state ruled by law shall continue, so that the rights and duties of Russian subjects are defined by written laws, not by the arbitrary decisions of individuals.

In other words, he declared that the state would be reconstructed in accordance with the Manifesto of 30 October (and even represented this process as one of accelerated national *growth*), and that to this end the whole body of legislation currently in force would be reviewed (to the rightists this was a revolutionary outrage no less than the explosion of an anarchist's bomb). Stolypin passed on immediately to arguments in favor of the agrarian law which meant so much to him:

> We cannot set aside the urgent requests of the peasants, who are being drained of their substance and increasingly impoverished by our clumsy system of land tenure; we must not be slow to prevent the total ruin of the most numerous part of Russia's population, which has become economically weak and no longer capable of ensuring for itself a decent existence by tilling the soil in the time-honored way.

As though Russia had long been a parliamentary state and the body before him were a parliament with traditions and experience, Stolypin spelled out to the newly convened

Duma a broad and detailed program to be implemented by stages—the fullest, most logical and craftsmanlike plan for the rebuilding of Russia ever presented in the country. Though all he had to offer was

> dull work day in and day out, in the knowledge that its hidden significance will shine forth in time.

He ranged through a detailed schedule of measures in every sector of public life, united by a single governing purpose. He would unify provincial and county administrations, abolishing the numerous redundant local offices. Abolish the land captains, who had become a nuisance to everybody. Abolish (yes!) the Corps of Gendarmes, introduce a new police system, and define precisely the limits of police powers. Rescind the regulations concerning administrative banishment. Give the courts the right to authorize or forbid arrests, house searches, and the interception of letters. (None of these measures, I think, has been implemented in Russia at any time in the twentieth century, though all of them remain as timely as ever they were.) He would set up local courts which would be easy of access, cheap, quick, and near at hand. Justices of the peace would be elected by the population, and their competence widened. State officials would be made answerable to the criminal and civil courts. People under investigation would be entitled to legal aid. A probationary and parole system would be introduced.

Measures to assist those unable to work and a state insurance scheme for the sick, disabled, and aged would be worked out. The state would interest itself generally in the welfare of the workers, and there would be no penalties for economic strikes. There should be a natural outlet for the worker's aspiration to improve his wages and conditions, and there should be no bureaucratic interference in relations between employers and workers. Medical facilities should be provided at places of employment. Women and children should not be allowed to work night shifts, and the working day should be shortened. Roads should be improved. The railway network must be extended. Waterways too. And the merchant marine. The Amur Railway (from Lake Baikal to Khabarovsk) would be built. The educational system would be reformed: at each stage (primary, secondary, higher) the syllabus would be complete in itself, but the three stages would be interconnected. The material conditions of teachers at all levels would be improved. Primary education must, after due preparation, be made first available and then compulsory throughout the Empire. More trade schools should be established. Finally, funds for all this must be provided through the budget, difficult as it was after an unsuccessful war. There was a need for strict economy. The tax burden must be equitably distributed over the whole population—income tax would be progressive, with relief for the less-well-off. Funds must be found for zemstvo organizations and towns.

Stolypin might reasonably have hoped that at least some of those present would appreciate the boldness and the logic of his program. If there were a few such deputies in that inexperienced body their voices were not heard. The perfervid orators of the Second Duma had not come together from all over the Empire to hear this sort of thing, least of all those from beyond the Caucasus. (The Duma was supposed to represent the whole population of Russia, but for some reason a succession of unbridled Caucasian Social Democrats flitted across the rostrum in rapid succession.) Did he think they were there to doze over the fine print of state revenue and expenditure? Were they expected to spend every evening in committee, working till midnight to finalize this unmanageable heap of draft bills? No, thank you! Weak beer of this sort could not whet the appetites of Duma deputies! The public would not appreciate such quantities of dull work with a hidden significance that would shine forth in time. Where could they direct the blood-red jets of their libertarian rhetoric? Stolypin's program, with its wealth of concrete proposals, including measures for the relief of the working class and the abolition of administrative banishment and the gendarmerie, could only be a sly, hypocritical dodge to prevent revolution. Why be inveigled into legislative pettifogging and unrelieved hard work when you can be loudly denouncing the government and prattling about freedom?

Tsereteli, socialism's paladin, immediately flung himself into the fray. The government, he said, was

> the government of courts-martial which has put the whole country in fetters and reduced the population to utter ruin.

(In the eight months of its existence, and no doubt by its laws giving peasants equal rights and allowing them to set up as independent smallholders.) Like all Russian socialists of his day, he went on and on with his catechism, as though he had heard nothing of what had been said and did not expect to achieve anything by taking part in that gathering. (Golovin, in the chair, thought it his duty to confirm that he saw no reason to call the speaker to order.)

Tsereteli:

> The government is organizing the execution of whole districts!

(Here the president had to call right-wing deputies to order.) Tsereteli whipped up the waves of anger:

> . . . in order to preserve serfdom! The draft bills curtail even those rights which the people have already wrested from the hands of their enemies. We shall examine these proposals in the light of the government's bloody deeds. May our accusing voice carry throughout the land and inspire to battle all who are not yet awakened. We appeal to the people's representatives to prepare the people's forces.

(For what? For an uprising? There was nothing else it could mean.)

> On the pretense of pacifying the country the government has taken steps to safeguard the interests of parasites of all kinds . . . It is selling land in the interests of the landowners . . . The Social Democratic faction in the Duma places all its hopes on *the movement of the people themselves.*

Aleksinsky:

> . . . these landowners who call themselves the government of Russia . . . The peasants want to obtain all the land without redemption payments, but they will never acquire it without *fighting* for it.

The Kadets preserved an ostentatious silence throughout this session. That was their way of expressing a degree of indignation too great to be put into words. But there was a trace of embarrassment in their silence. The Kadets could not help seeing—though they tried not to see, forbade themselves to see!—that Stolypin was putting forward a liberal, an emancipatory program, sketching for them a reformed state system, setting the correct pattern for the relationship between the executive and the legislative power, showing the Duma itself how it should behave. But all this was coming from the *regime*, from *the wrong hands*, and could lead too directly to stabilization, when what was needed was upheaval. The Kadets were silent, silently hating this parvenu. The constitutional party, to which concessions were being made, would have nothing of them, and panted for revolution.

All the Duma groups, from the Kadets to the far left, refused even to discuss the substance of the government program. Some benighted peasant deputies vainly called on the Duma

> above all to work, and work with the government. When Russia sent us here it commanded us to forget about revolutionary measures, and try by peaceful means to relieve the wants of the people, appease their hunger and give them light.

Dzhaparidze, on behalf of the Social Democrats, moved that the Duma pass on to other business:

> The State Duma, fully sharing the people's lack of faith in the government, intends to convert the people's will into law, *relying on their support*.

In other words, by an insurrection. Yet this intolerable minister of the Tsar did not take flight, did not seek refuge, refused to be annihilated under the hail of speeches from the left. In his tightly buttoned black coat, with his statuesque poise and his mystical self-assurance, he was intolerable above all because he was not a faded anachronism smelling of mothballs, not an ogre, not a cretin, but a fine figure of a man, and because, conscious of his strength and certain of victory though he stood alone against five hundred, he replied from the rostrum loudly and clearly:

> The language of hatred and malice cannot be that of partnership in work, and I shall not use it. The government had either to make way for the revolution, forgetting that the state power is the guardian of the Russian people's well-being, Russia's national integrity, or to defend what had been entrusted to it. I say to you that the government on its benches here is not in the dock. We shall answer to history for our actions at this historic moment, just as you will. The government will welcome any candid exposure of inefficiency and abuse. But when attacks on the government are intended to paralyze its will, and amount to no more than cries of "Hands up," we can reply with absolute calm and assurance that we are right: you will not succeed in frightening us!

His words imprinted themselves on the minds of friends and foes alike. For the first time in many years the opposition had come upon an opponent as brilliant as he was courageous.

His speech quickly became famous outside the Duma, and letters of congratulation with tens of thousands of signatures (including those of literate peasants) poured in. To some Muscovites, Stolypin (he had spent his childhood in Moscow) replied as follows:

> My hope is not in myself but in that collective spiritual strength which has so often emanated from Moscow and saved all Russia.

At that time many Russians were haunted (as they would be ten years later) by visions of the Time of Troubles: orators conjured them up, politicians were inspired by them, and it seemed that we were capable of turning them into reality once again.

Later Stolypin, firm and self-possessed as ever, a figure of epic presence, again came forward to reply:

> We have heard here that the government has blood on its hands, that the field courts-martial are a shame and a disgrace to Russia. But when the state is in danger it is obliged to adopt exceptional laws to save itself from disintegration. This principle is in the nature of man and the nature of the state. If a man is sick, he is sometimes treated with poison. If an assassin attacks you, you kill him. When the organism of the state is shaken to its roots, the government can suspend the operation of the law and all legal norms. There are fateful moments in the life of the state when we must choose whether certain theories or the state itself should be preserved intact. Such temporary measures cannot become permanent. But neither must bloody terrorism be allowed to rage unchecked—it must be forcibly resisted. Russia will know the difference between blood on the hands of a headsman and blood on the hands of a conscientious surgeon. The country expects a display of faith in itself, not a display of weakness. From you too we await the word that will bring peace in place of murderous madness.

And you can go on waiting! The left-wing deputies would have ceased to represent their parties if they had dared call for an end to terror. Wind up your field courts-martial, but we shall carry on with our terrorism! The Duma refused, of course, to condemn the glorification of terror in the press and anti-government propaganda in the army.

Needless to say, the Duma refrained from scrutinizing the budget (a good way of muddling government business, this), nor did it consider a twentieth part of Stolypin's constructive program. The word "constructive" meant nothing to it. The Duma commissions could not get down to work—work was a habit none of them had acquired. The Duma was not interested in Russia's historical progress but in the plaudits of the left-wing public. The government was showered with questions at every session, and speakers vied with each other in loudness and shrillness. Perhaps the Duma's supreme objective was to make its sessions as long as possible, to drag them out until the field courts-martial automatically ended. Once that happened, the left wing was in fact eager to see the Duma dismissed—to reinforce the legend of its strength and the government's weakness.

Since they remained unconfirmed by the Duma the law on equal rights for the peasants and all of Stolypin's agrarian enactments were also due to fall into abeyance. This Duma, like its predecessor, demanded instead the forcible transfer of land from the gentry (and members of the Duma writing in the press called on the people to take matters into their own hands). Stolypin took the floor again (the Duma called for a vote on whether he should be allowed to speak) and tried to make them see that

> if all the land is redistributed the state as a whole will not obtain a single extra ear of corn,

that the distribution of privately owned land would not be a statesmanlike act, that Russia would not achieve prosperity by ruining a hundred and thirty thousand efficiently run estates, while the peasants' holdings, although they would be somewhat larger as a result, would soon be reduced to dust by the rapid growth of the population and by the redivision which this would make necessary. In general,

> repartition, on whatever basis, is not progress—progress lies in the more effective application of labor.

If they once began repartitioning they would not be able to stop at gentry land but would of necessity go on to divide up the holdings of the more successful peasants, to fragment whatever was exceptionally good, divide it up and render it valueless.

> You cannot give strength to a sick body by feeding it lumps of flesh cut from itself. You must make nourishing juices flow to the affected part, and then the whole organism will help to overcome the sickness; all parts of the state must come to the help of the weakest: therein lies the justification of the state as a social whole.

The state would purchase private land offered for sale and add it to the common stock so that underendowed peasants could acquire it on preferential terms.

No! Such a drab and prosaic solution, with not a single estate sacked or burned, could not satisfy Russia's freedom lovers.

But Stolypin too was adamant:

> A government conscious of its duty to observe the behests of Russia's history, a stable and purely Russian government . . .

What did this loathsome allusion to *purely Russian* government mean? And what indeed were the behests of Russia's history? Who needed them?

> The opponents of statehood want to free themselves from Russia's historical past. In the midst of other powerful and stable nations they want us to reduce Russia to ruins, in order to build on those ruins a fatherland of which we know nothing.

And then, as he approached one of his famous phrases, his voice hardened, grew louder and clearer, to express its powerful simplicity.

> THEY WANT GREAT UPHEAVALS—WE WANT
> A GREAT RUSSIA!

Hated as he was by the Duma, by *progressive society*, and by the bomb-throwing socialists, the Prime Minister who is now stamped on Russia's historical memory as a grim hangman without a single rational idea indefatigably attended abusive sittings, eagerly took the floor at the very beginning of the debate, to set out the government's views firmly and precisely and to help the Duma reject the irrelevant.

(A decade later, in the last months before the February Revolution, when Russia was sickened and shamed by a rapid succession of worthless ministers, Stolypin's enemies, even Kerensky, would recall that *his* words were never an attempt to conceal vacuity:

> Do you remember Stolypin's first declaration? Remember the rapt attention with which the Duma received his every word, some deputies noisily approving, others showing their anger. They knew for sure that his words were not just a displacement of air but the decision of a powerful government possessing the enormous strength of will and authority necessary to carry out its promises.)

Stolypin's stand could have been, and looked like, the beginning of a new period in Russian history. It began to seem obvious that there would be no repetition of 1905–6. ("Another ten to fifteen years," Stolypin would tell his close collaborators, "and the revolutionaries won't have a chance.") Believing as he did in Russia, he sought to revive her belief in herself:

Russia is not about to collapse in the second millennium of her existence.

He took over the conduct of affairs in conditions of chaos and disarray, and set about rebuilding a Russia free from poverty, ignorance, and deprivation of rights.

He addressed the Second Duma repeatedly, hoping to make it see reason and save it so that it could do useful work. Accepting as an unavoidable legacy the fact that representative institutions were already in being, he persuaded himself, and tried to persuade Russia, that the epoch of constitutional government had begun. Indeed, he became a supporter of constitutional government and treated the Duma more seriously than the deputies themselves did, doing his best to believe that in the end he would manage to cooperate with this Second Duma (and even liberalizing the composition of his government for its benefit). Then again—why dismiss a bad Duma when it would be followed by a worse one?

But, as Stolypin admitted, "the First Duma was difficult to dismiss, the Second difficult to preserve."

As the inevitable conflagration drew nearer everything combustible was thrown into the flames. When the order for the next call-up to the army was submitted for ratification, Zurabov, a deputy from Tiflis, mounted the rostrum and in dreadful Russian began reviling the Russian army and everything to do with it, gloating over its defeats, saying that it had always been and always would be beaten and that the only thing it would ever be good at was making war on the people. The Duma noisily applauded Zurabov's insults, but beyond its walls broad sections of the public were incensed, and there was never a moment when dissolution would have been viewed more sympathetically.

Stolypin, however, kept up the struggle to preserve it, and the Zurabov incident had no further consequences.

When spring arrived the Stolypin family began to find their incarceration in the Winter Palace unbearable, and at the Emperor's invitation they moved to the Yelagin Palace for the summer. (Aleksandr III had enjoyed living there, but like the Winter Palace it had been uninhabited in recent years.) The palace grounds were surrounded with barbed-wire fences, with sentries patrolling outside and Okhrana agents inside, but the terrorists had not raised their siege and this was the only place where the Prime Minister of an immense state could take a walk or go rowing some two hundred meters along a backwater of the Neva with a prison fence of its own. (Stolypin's injured daughter had by now undergone several operations, but still could not walk.)

It was time to think again, and to decide on the future of the Russian constitution.

Perhaps the main reason why systems of government collapse is psychological: the circles accustomed to power do not—because they do not want to—keep up with changing times, are not quick enough to make sensible concessions while they still have a great advantage and in the most favorable circumstances. The wise man yields while still on his feet and armed, he does not wait to be laid on his back. But to begin making concessions—to give up absolute authority, power, titles, capital, land, automatic election while all these rights of yours are still bathed in sunlight and there is no warning of the storm to come—this is something that human nature finds difficult.

A beginning was made with sensible changes of this sort in the reign of Aleksandr I, but the Tsar and his ministers showed their lack of foresight by abandoning them: victory over Napoleon blinded them to other things, and the most propitious time for reform—immediately after the Fatherland War—was missed. The Decembrist rising jerked Russia off course. Nikolai I, who vanquished the Decembrists, did not draw the correct lesson from his victory (victors usually fail to do so, whereas defeat is an unsparing teacher). He interpreted victory as a sign that he could halt all progress for a long time and began preparing to move forward only at the end of his reign.

Aleksandr II was in a hurry to introduce reforms, but the country was not fated to get out of its rut and onto level ground. Herd instinct, or the urgings of the devil, told the terrorists that this was their last chance to use the gun, that only with bullets and bombs could they interrupt reform and go back to revolution. They succeeded beyond their expectations, forcing Aleksandr III also into isolation and unyielding resistance, though with his generous nature he was capable of making concessions, while with his love for Russia he would not have strayed from her true path. Over and over again the chance was missed.

Nikolai II was precipitated onto the throne before he was ready: neither his age nor his character fitted him for Russia's stormiest years now that her time had almost run out. The years 1901, 1902, 1903 sped by like crimson beacons, but he and his whole entourage failed to read the signs. He had supposed that endlessly docile Russia would be ruled eternally by the will of whoever occupied the Russian throne—and had let himself be dashed on the Japanese rocks. The trials that beset him in those years would have been too much for any Romanov except perhaps Peter the Great. Nikolai, at his wits' end, took shelter behind the Manifesto.

It was a rash and ill-considered act. It left him with no retreat and nothing in reserve. But done it was. And when those around the throne, and all the diehards for whom Russia was an inert mass incapable of developing, rejoiced in the idiocies and the disruption of two Dumas and nagged the Tsar to retract the Manifesto and return to the previous state of affairs, they were not only urging him to behave dishonorably but repeating the errors of the two previous periods of damaging stagnation.

There could be no backtracking. To give up the legislative institutions and withdraw concessions already made was no longer possible—that would only plunge the country into revolution. Russia could not return to the status quo before 1905. A constitution had been granted: the country had to learn to live by it.

But the present drift could not go on—that was as sure a way to revolution, and no slower. It was not Russia that Witte's electoral law had summoned to the Tauride Palace but a caricature of the country. That electoral law would never produce a Duma truly representative of Russia anyway: the country did not yet possess a mass electorate ready for universal equal franchise. So then—the electoral law had to be changed if the Duma itself was to be preserved. Such an amendment, even by imperial decree, was illegal after the Manifesto. But there was no other way of creating an effective Duma. Mere dissolution would only exacerbate the opposition—and the next Duma would be still more fatuously revolutionary. That was the paradox: only by illegally changing the electoral law could the electoral principle and national representation be saved. Any man called to act at one of history's most difficult moments treads between two abysses, and must keep his equilibrium on the knife-edge or fall into one of them. But this was the true path—between two revolutions, two warring mobs, two rival concentrations of mediocrity and philistinism.

That spring Stolypin had secret meetings with some of the not entirely hopeless Kadets (those who were jokingly called "Black Hundreders"): Maklakov, Chelnokov, Struve, and Bulgakov. He was trying to reach an understanding with them and form a government so perfectly poised that it could not be overthrown. Their meetings were kept secret from both the left and the right. These particular members of the Kadet Party trusted Stolypin: he impressed all who met him face-to-face with his directness, his candor, his calm, honest gaze, the precision of his statements, and the gleam of intelligence and determination in his eyes. But they were afraid even to disclose to their fellow Kadets what they were doing. There could be little hope of forming a government with such people.

This was the third attempt by the Russian government in less than two years to invite members of the educated public to share power. Each time they refused, so as not to sully their reputations. The role of outraged opponent was, as it always had been, easier. The Russian radicals had, it seemed, a dream: they would raze Russia to its foundations (without, however, sacrificing their Petersburg apartments or their servants), and then build an entirely new, totally free, marvelous regime such as Russia had never seen before. They did not realize how much they needed the monarchy. They did not know and refused to learn how to govern, but took a childish delight in explosions and conflagrations. What was more, Stolypin was immovably convinced by now that this Duma would never ratify his agrarian reforms.

The last secret meeting with the Kadet quartet took place in the Yelagin Palace on the eve of 16 June.

An incident in May was helpful: police had caught members of the Social Democratic group in the Duma conferring in a deputy's apartment with delegates from a revolutionary cell in the army. On that occasion the Duma deputies had been released.

On 14 June, Stolypin spoke in the Duma and unexpectedly—every major step of his always took "the public" by surprise—he proposed that the Duma should exclude the fifty-five members of the Social Democratic fraction for participating in a conspiracy against the government and agree to the arrest of the fifteen most deeply involved.

> Besides its duty to respect the immunity of deputies the government also has a duty to preserve public order, especially in a capital where so much has happened.

(The Social Democratic group in the Duma had unblushingly propagated subversive ideas in the Petersburg garrison. On 18 May a soldiers' delegation had gone to a deputy's apartment at No. 92 Nevsky Prospect, where deputies were waiting to receive their petition—and the police were keeping watch.)

The Duma was flabbergasted: for all their outcry against intolerable harassment they regarded parliamentary immunity as a license to do whatever they pleased, even to throw bombs. The president, Golovin, performed all sorts of contortions looking for a formula to avoid a vote, which would be fatal to the Duma, whether it sided with the subversives or disowned them. But the dodge did not work: on 16 June those of the fifteen who had not gone into hiding were arrested, the Duma was dissolved by decree, and a new electoral law was promulgated. The accompanying imperial manifesto (drafted by Stolypin) stressed that this was not a departure from the Manifesto of 30 October, that all the rights of the people remained intact, but that

> many of those sent to the Duma by the population had approached their task not with honorable intentions but in the hope of aggravating disorder and helping to bring about the breakdown of the state,

for which reason the electoral system itself was being modified so that those chosen would express the people's wishes more accurately.

Stolypin, needless to say, was still determined to push the interests of the peasants, but for the present he reduced their representation in the Duma (their representatives so far had reflected the peasant's inexperience, not his real wants) and strengthened the big landowners, particularly the experienced and cultured zemstvo men.

The dissolution of the Duma, and the accompanying explanation, might not have aroused such fury among the public and left such a deep scar if the royal manifesto had not sounded the patriotic note so intolerable to the liberal ear and so relentlessly characteristic of Stolypin:

> The State Duma must be Russian in spirit. The other nationalities which form part of Our Domain must have deputies in the Duma to represent their needs but they must not, and shall not, appear in numbers which give them the possibility of determining matters of purely Russian concern.

The franchise was restricted in the eastern borderlands, the number of deputies from the Caucasus and from Poland was reduced, and some towns were submerged in their provinces. It did no good for Stolypin to repeat that the object was not just to keep the country quiet by police methods but gradually and patiently to build a state ruled by law, something which neither he nor anyone else could achieve at a stroke—they shut their ears to him. The educated Russian public designated the bold step taken on 16 June a coup d'état, and the insufficiently leftish part of it, which accepted the change and subsequently cooperated with the government in its attempts to reconstruct Russia instead of tearing it apart as effectively as the terrorists with their bombs, became known as "sixteenth of June men."

(Several decades would go by before V. Maklakov, from his remote vantage point in emigration, could admit that

> the sixteenth of June has become for us a term with the same sort of pejorative and disgraceful connotations as the second of December in France. But, after all we have lived through, this judgment seems biased. The coup put an end to the violent period of bitter struggle between the old regime and progressive society, but it also initiated a short period of cooperation between the regime and society within the framework of the constitution. If Europe had not gone to war in 1914, Russia's recovery might have continued without upheavals. The coup of 16 June, in spite of its illegality, may have enabled

us at the time to avoid a complete collapse of government ten years before 1917 in conditions no less unfavorable to peaceful recovery.)

The whole "public" could only revile Stolypin for his reactionary behavior and his blasphemy against the constitution. No one could see that the sixteenth of June was the beginning of the great work of rebuilding Russia. In their exasperation they failed to see that while the law of 16 June curtailed some existing rights, it extended those of the zemstvos, which was obviously in the people's interests. As Stolypin saw it, the zemstvos were not an appendage to a centralized bureaucracy, but, in the spirit of old Russia and in the form given to them under Aleksandr II, should become the solid foundation of the whole state. Efficient, willing zemstvos, engaged not in feverishly baiting the government, not in politicking, but in making the life of the people more secure and richer, were Stolypin's ideal, and he hoped to raise the Duma to the same level.

He did not succeed in that, but the attitude of the zemstvos toward the Ministry of the Interior, and so toward the authorities generally, changed quickly and conspicuously under Stolypin. This was a response as much to his own dealings with zemstvo activists as to his legislation. At each stage in his ascent he had felt the need to learn more and more—about constitutional law, Russian and Western, about military and naval science. Each post he held was an obligation to work ten times harder. But he was all the more anxious to give zemstvo members the benefit of his understanding, his ready appreciation of another man's ideas, his capacious memory, and his practical skills. He met them frequently, inquired into their needs, collected information about the wishes of the zemstvos, and did his best to satisfy them. These men saw how different he was from his predecessors, with his precise and eager knowledge of the needs of the country as a whole and of particular regions, and they went away spiritually in thrall to him, wondering or not always bothering to wonder what excuse they could give their liberal friends for their sudden conversion.

Until Stolypin came along Ministers of the Interior and governors were forever complicating and hampering the work of the zemstvos, and the zemstvos often got bogged down in politics. This aberration was aggravated by the years of revolution. Stolypin, however, considered local self-government scarcely less of a blessing for Russia than the reorganization of peasant farming in smallholdings. In his first months in power he began energetically reviving the zemstvos. He reintroduced direct election of county electors by peasants at rural district meetings, which had been abolished under Aleksandr III, and so cleared a way for peasants into the county zemstvos. He abolished the provincial governors' right to audit zemstvos' budget estimates. He made the Ministry of Education give substantial annual grants for zemstvo schools (two years later he put through a law which would gradually make primary education in such schools available to all). Other subsidies poured into the zemstvos from the Chief Administration of Agriculture and Land Tenure, for the benefit of peasant farmers: the zemstvos were to maintain experimental fields, bases for combating erosion, veterinary stations, depots for hiring out agricultural machinery, and a whole army of surveyors, advisers on land use, and agronomists. Stolypin gave support to lending banks, agricultural cooperatives, and rural fire services, and convened national congresses of experts in all these fields. The character of zemstvo congresses changed under Stolypin—they became friendly to the government.

> I see the future of Russia in the close cooperation of the zemstvos and of municipal administrations with the government.

By expanding and improving the activity of the zemstvos Stolypin hoped, very reasonably, to raise the standards of peasant agriculture throughout Russia. Everything he did was designed to serve directly or indirectly one dearly cherished supreme ambition—to raise up peasant Russia.

At the opening session of the Third Duma in November 1907 he had no need to set out the government program in great detail: it remained much as it had been before. The Second Duma had scarcely touched it. One further proposal had ripened in the intervening months—the provision of "an insurance scheme and state medical care for sick and disabled workers." But while stubbornly carrying forward his program as a whole Stolypin just as persistently reverted to his leading idea:

> Improvements in administration will have no deep effect until the condition of the main class, the agricultural class, is improved. As long as the peasant remains poor, as long as he has no land of his own, as long as he is forcibly held in the grip of the commune—so long will he remain a slave.

Stolypin's presence left no one in doubt that nature, and destiny, had endowed him with invincible strength of character. This was what most impressed the opposition and the public at large. It was more conspicuous than ever on this occasion: it had found concrete expression in the speedy termination of bloody chaos and the convocation of the Third Duma, in the hope that it would get something done. The chariot had not plunged into the abyss, but swerved away from the brink. But was revolution the right word for what had happened?

> It is now obvious to everybody that the destructive movement created by the extreme left parties has turned into undisguised brigandage, and brought to the fore all sorts of criminal and antisocial elements, ruining honest toilers and debauching the younger generation.

But:

> a rebellion is extinguished by force, not by concessions. . . . To make a vision reality strength of will is needed. No government has any right to exist unless it possesses a mature political vision and a strong political will.

He came before the Duma stronger and more authoritative than ever, now that he had diverted Russia from the road to ruin onto that of recovery (a little while ago it would have seemed incredible, but it had happened!). After the sixteenth of June coup he no longer confronted them to answer charges of deviating from the constitutional path, but to proclaim

> the restoration of order and of a sound institutional structure appropriate to what the Russian people know to be their true self.

Over and over again he reiterated his dangerous determination to follow a specifically *Russian* line:

> If they are to bear fruit our reforms must draw strength from Russian national principles—from the development of the zemstvo system and local self-government, from the creation at the base of strong support from *people of the land*, closely linked with the central authority. The basic population

> means more than a hundred million people, and in them lies the whole strength of our country.

It was difficult not to be impressed by this obstinate repetition of thoughts ridiculed time and time again by liberals. How could an educated man have so little fear of "the public's" laughter?

> Peoples sometimes forget their national mission: but when they do they perish.

This from the Duma tribune. Transfixed by the pitiless gaze of hostile reporters, Stolypin, coolly and without a trace of irony, declared that

> the Russian state and the Christian Church are bound together by ties many centuries old. Devotion to Russia's historical principles is the counterweight to rootless socialism.

He even had the audacity to give Russia's most highly educated citizens, the ultralibertarian ultimate authorities on freedom, a lesson on the meaning of the word:

> Real freedom is made up of civil rights *plus* loyalty to the state and patriotism.

A few days earlier this Duma had rejected the word "autocrat" in its address to the Emperor, so Stolypin, with no inhibitions about appearing old-fashioned, ventured to give the people's elected representatives another little lesson, on—of all things—the merits of autocracy:

> The historic autocratic power and the unfettered will of the monarch are the most precious asset of the Russian state system, since that power and that will alone are destined to save Russia in her moments of disaster and danger, and to guide her onto the path of order and historic truth. There can be no Russia unless all her sons strive to preserve the Tsar's sovereign power, which welds Russia together and saves it from disintegration.

In spite of his (still premature) hope that "in Russia power cannot stand above the law," he saw that the path to parliamentarism could be neither simple nor quick:

> The Russian state has developed from roots of its own, and we cannot graft a foreign flower onto our Russian trunk.

This defiance could not be taken quietly by the left—the Kadets would have been Kadets no more. Rodichev, among others, reared up to retort—one of the nimblest tongues in the Kadet Party. Incapable of speaking calmly (if he tried to, his speech buckled and went to sleep under him), he always breathed fire and passion, and gave no one time to weigh what he was saying. His subject was "Russia so called":

> Russia never had a history—we do better not to speak of it. She has never in all her thousand years produced individuals. Autocracy was the reason for that. But without individuals there is no history.

It was very much the fashion at the time to assert that Russia, which teemed with them, had no capable people, and especially to deny the "people of the land" any merit. He launched into the Russian radicals' favorite tune:

> When people talk to me about truly Russian principles I always wonder which of them they have in mind. We too have patriotic feelings, which make us demand first and foremost that rights be made a reality. Can any

one of us be sure that his rights will not be infringed for the convenience of the state?

This is an age-old problem, unresolved to this day—the scales are forever going up and down: how can we obtain rights without assuming burdensome and even dangerous duties? Alternatively, how can we shackle our fellows with duties while granting them no rights? Is it perhaps possible to strike a precise balance between the two?

Did Rodichev feel that his speech was becoming academic, that it would not appease the rage of his party? He began speaking more angrily, got onto the field courts-martial, but still his speech would not have gone down in history had not his reckless passion for aphorisms, and the impelling sense that his party was unsatisfied, provoked him to mime the tightening of a noose with his fingers around his throat and to speak of "Stolypin neckties" (a variation on "Muraviev collars").

He paused for the applause to which leaders of the opposition had grown accustomed. But before he could bestow the usual tired but happy smile on the hall, Stolypin, white in the face, had left the government box, and a deafening noise filled the hall. Half of the Duma began banging the lids of their desks, yelling or charging the rostrum with the idea of pulling Rodichev off it. The noise was such that no one could hear himself speak, and the president adjourned the session simply by leaving the chamber, while another Kadet, a tall old man, covered Rodichev's retreat to the Catherine Hall. There he was overtaken by the Prime Minister's seconds, challenging him to a duel!

Some ministers when insulted seek legal redress, but not Stolypin. We see the whole man, the full stature of him, in his reply to wanton slander, to the prostitution of freedom of speech under cover of parliamentary immunity: to this twentieth-century abuse he made the only manly reply—a chivalrous challenge. Russia, led by his sure hand, was beginning to find peace after the years of criminal violence, but he had never imagined himself to be so uniquely valuable that he could overlook personal insults. In his inmost being, above and beyond his state duties, he was a *preux chevalier* ("with visor raised" was a favorite expression of his). He put the whole of himself—his mind, his heart, his life—into his task as a statesman but at such a moment he was ready to abandon everything, to fight the man who had wronged him, to face death the very next day. Only one whose life is especially precious is ever so ungrudgingly and selflessly willing to sacrifice it.

The son of General Stolypin of Sevastopol said, "I cannot allow my children to hear me called a hangman."

His behavior was all the more sensational because it was so archaic. Rodichev was stunned, as were all the Kadets: after all those years of slick eloquence they had forgotten that an insult may pull the trigger of a pistol. Scintillating mockery of everything uncongenial to them had become a habit—but they had forgotten that men must answer for their words, sometimes with their lives.

The Prime Minister, forty-five years old and the father of six children, did not hesitate to stake his life. The fifty-three-year-old deputy from Tver was not prepared for such a turn of events. So before the recess was over the crestfallen orator reluctantly betook himself to the ministerial rest room in the Duma to beg Stolypin's pardon. Stolypin looked Rodichev up and down, said contemptuously, "I forgive you," but did not offer his hand.

Eighteen months earlier he had been unknown to Russia, but now his strength was becoming more incontrovertibly clear every day. He stayed until the end of the session, and the Duma gave him an ovation. Rodichev had to take back his words and apologize to Stolypin from the rostrum, but was still suspended for fifteen sittings.

(Rhetoric had nevertheless done its work, and the phrase "Stolypin neckties" went down in history. In the twentieth century Stolypin was at a disadvantage. An age of unlimited civil freedom is also one of irresponsible accusations.)

Stolypin's family again spent the winter in the Winter Palace, lost in those dead, deserted halls. Nowhere could it have been more difficult to believe that the autocracy was capable of change. There was a trickle of anonymous threatening letters. The terrorists were as eager as ever to pierce the impenetrable minister with metal. One attempt was frustrated in the Duma itself: a Socialist Revolutionary carrying an Italian reporter's passport was going to take a shot from the press gallery.

Ever since Aptekarsky Island, Stolypin had had, not a foreboding, but a resigned awareness that he would not die a natural death. (Warriors do not expect to.) Every time he left home he mentally said goodbye forever to his loved ones. And he repeated his behest until there was no forgetting it: he wanted to be buried *where he was killed*.

Aleksandr Guchkov promised Stolypin the support of the Octobrist Party. Its support was uneven and conditional: sometimes hearteningly friendly and timely, at others more like competition or even confrontation. The law of 16 June had proved effective, though even the new Duma as time went by showed more and more interest in political maneuvering and less and less in practical work.

Guchkov's Octobrists outnumbered the Kadets, and the right wing was not strong enough to obstruct Stolypin's reforms from the other side. So this Duma offered some hope of that reconciliation between the regime and the moderate public which, as Stolypin saw it, was Russia's only salvation. With the Duma reinforced in this way he also had some hope of standing up to the always anonymous forces at court—those leeches on the body of the monarchy. But Stolypin was now to experience the drawbacks of parliamentary government. He counted on the support of the Octobrist majority, and he discovered that it was also capable of opposition. (Only the Russian nationalists invariably supported Stolypin.) It began early in 1908 with the debate on the building of four warships, a matter of the first importance to Russia at that time. Since the Tsushima debacle her best naval forces had been resting at the bottom of the Sea of Japan and Russia had been without a navy for three years. There were only single vessels, which did not add up to a coherent force, and coastal defenses. Overwhelmed by the defeat, neither the senior naval officers nor the government had dared put forward an ambitious naval program. They wanted just these four ships, which were what Russia could readily afford. No one argued that there was no need to rebuild the fleet, or that the funds requested were excessive. The public's objection, insistently voiced by Guchkov in the Duma, was:

> The Navy Department is in disarray, and must be reorganized before the navy itself. Our criticism has no malicious intent whatsoever. The atmosphere in this hall is heavy with patriotic mourning. My political friends and I find it extremely painful to refuse the government these credits after

> such a catastrophe. But the 1905 rescript contained a promise: "It is our moral duty to our country to reflect on our mistakes."

And what had been done in those three years? There was still the same empty show in the navy. Admiral Alekseev had criminally bungled the Japanese campaign—but had he been punished? No, he was in the State Council. The Octobrist majority in the Duma could not approve the credits until all the wreckage and rubbish had been cleared out of the naval staffs.

They were right, and Stolypin himself could not help sympathizing. It was the same old court circles who were hindering the clearing-out, and some forceful action to speed it up would be a good thing. But, taking a still deeper view, Russia's external enemies would not bide their time and Russia lay defenseless and inert. The years of peace he so badly wanted for her depended on a strong naval shield. Stolypin was tireless and astonishingly resourceful in debate—he rang changes on old arguments and found an inexhaustible supply of new ones. He appeared, urgent and optimistic, before three bodies—the Duma commission, the full Duma, and the State Council—facing a resistant majority in each of them, and leaving it shaken:

> If not to change a preconceived opinion, at least to show that a contrary view is possible and not insane.

Many a minister with much greater parliamentary experience could not have matched his energy and shown such respect for the forms of debate. Certainly no minister of the Tsar's had ever had the occasion, or the audience, for such a display of ingenuity and determination in debate, such a masterful deployment of arguments, such a dazzling cascade of comparisons, at times earning a laugh from opponents as well as allies:

> If a schoolboy fails an exam you don't punish him by taking away his textbooks.

He tried to make them see that their way would gravely weaken Russia. While all the countries of the world were reconstructing their navies, Russia would not be able even to defend its shores, the fleet would turn into a collection of old tubs, and without a real squadron the men could not be trained. He begged them not to relieve the government of its responsibility for the naval defense of Russia. All in vain.

A little later the Duma refused to make the necessary allocations for the construction of the Amur Railway—not because it had any answer to his warning that foreign influences were seeping into that distant region and that it would be lost to Russia, but simply because it thought that the debilitated country could not afford this expenditure, or rather because it was immature and as yet unused to forming statesmanlike opinions.

Stolypin usually succeeded in winning the Duma over, but not on these occasions. He abandoned his desperate attempts at persuasion for desperate action: he used the recesses between Duma sittings to enact his decisions under Article 87.

On these two occasions, the Duma when it reassembled could not bring itself to halt the building of either the warships or the Amur Railway. He used the same maneuver to put through the law on communities of Old Believers and on conversion from one religious denomination to another. But in this Stolypin was being dangerously short-sighted. He was not a courtier, he had not risen with court patronage, he had not depended for a single day on support from that quarter. He could never have performed his balancing act without the Duma. He felt a genuine need of it. He more than anyone had tried to persuade Russia that the epoch of constitutional government was there to stay and now, suddenly, he was unable to put urgently required measures through the Duma, and felt a need to bypass it.

Would any other form of government have enabled a leader so devoted to his country to take swift and energetic action for its own good? There was no country in which legislative bodies had begun functioning steadily and authoritatively overnight.

Even to this strengthened and far from mischievous Third Duma Stolypin had to defend restrictions on the press, the "mother of revolution":

> If anyone were mad enough to introduce unlimited political freedom into Russia by a stroke of the pen, a Soviet of Workers' Deputies would be meeting in Petersburg tomorrow, and within six months it would plunge Russia into the flames of Gehenna.

And emergency measures against terror (Guchkov with his middle-of-the-road majority supported them at first, then demanded that he put an end to them):

> Do not imagine, gentlemen, that our slowly recovering Russia needs only some artificial color on its cheeks—freedom in all its varieties—to become well again. We have to carry out our tasks between the bomb and the Browning. When the fever-racked and enfeebled body of the nation grows strong, the emergency measures will disappear automatically.

Stolypin's powers were exhibited in speech after speech: his instant understanding of remarks from the floor (a deputy would shout out a few deceptively simple words, and their meaning had to be guessed in a second); the ease with which he parried such interjections as they were made; the orderliness of his memory, and his skill in producing supporting arguments from its recesses to give his speech body and depth; his alertness to subtle distinctions when discussing concepts, definitions, or procedures, and his equally quick and skillful retrieval of the examples he needed from European constitutional law, which, with his fluent knowledge of three languages, he tirelessly studied; the almost unbroken flow of unexpected homely images, which were always illuminating and often very funny. In a country where the whole official hierarchy from the Emperor down to the village constable preferred to hide in silence behind printed instructions, this unique minister wore down and won over the opposition with speeches as neat and clean as his handwriting. He never skipped a session or a chance to speak, to advance his cause, to expound his beliefs. His was such an ardent nature that he could not refrain from speaking even when evasive silence might have helped.

That was how it was in February 1909, for instance, when the opposition asked for a statement on Azef. The Socialist Revolutionary leaders, smarting under that and other setbacks, had propagated a complicated fantasy about Azef's double-dealing, according to which the government had taken part in terrorist acts against itself: the government had created Azef and been willing to see even people in high places assassinated in order to disorganize the revolutionaries. This was a brilliant accusation against the government, and the Russian "public" eagerly seized on it, without asking for proof. It was noised abroad that the opposition would hurl a thunderbolt at question time on 24 February. Stolypin was not obliged by law to answer in person: he could have done it in writing, and taken a month over it. But he rushed to the session and listened to the speeches of the left, which were replete not with evidence or knowledge of the facts but insults to the government and the state. In a chamber full to overflowing the opposition speakers, Pokrovsky and Bulat, failed to reinforce their sensational hypothesis with a single fact. Stolypin rose in a rage and entered the fray. He made it glaringly obvious that the leaders of the left were peddling fables to save their own reputations. He refused to keep silent—and left us a speech without which it would not now be possible to get at the truth of the matter.

The strength of Stolypin's feelings may be partly explained by the fact that the former chief of police, Lopukhin, who gave Azef away to the revolutionaries and helped Burtsev to elaborate the Azef myth, was an old schoolfellow. He had displayed the weakness of character so common among educated Russians, and especially perhaps—that was the terrible thing—in officials close to the throne. The most prominent victims—Pleve and Grand Duke Sergei Aleksandrovich—had been assassinated during Lopukhin's tenure, and he had done nothing to prevent it—in fact, he had ignored warnings from Azef himself and taken no security measures. In an attempt to salvage his career he tried to shift the whole blame onto Azef, who had been put on the payroll by a predecessor (but had once saved Lopukhin's life). He had let his own superior, Pleve, be killed, and then found it in himself to meet the assassin, Savinkov, to concert their lying tales about Azef and the government. He even wrote to Stolypin protesting against an attempt to stop him from visiting terrorists in London, and sent a certified copy of the letter to SRs abroad, for publication in the Western press. Stolypin was appalled not so much by Lopukhin's own vileness as by a hardening suspicion that the ruling stratum in Russia included dozens (perhaps hundreds) of unscrupulous careerists like him.

Stolypin gave the Duma incontrovertible facts and dates. Azef had been a voluntary secret agent of the police from 1892 until just recently. (The Duma was not the place to describe how very reliable and productive he had been.) Until 1906, when Savinkov was arrested, Azef had taken no part at all in the terrorist activity of the SRs, but had passed on to the police every scrap of information he managed to obtain through his connections in the party. He had, for instance, given information about Gershuni's central role among the terrorists, frustrated an attempt on Pobedonostsev and one of the attempts on Pleve, given details of plans to assassinate Trepov and Durnovo.

He had given warning of another attempt on Pleve—the successful one in July 1904—even mentioning the assassin, Yegor Sazonov, by name. The accusations that Azef had taken part in the murder of Pleve and Sergei Aleksandrovich were clumsy fabrications which paid no attention to facts: on both occasions Azef had been abroad, whereas in SR practice those who inspired and directed assassination attempts were always on the spot to encourage the assassin. Gershuni, for instance, was on St. Isaac's Square when Sipyagin was killed, on the Nevsky Prospect when the attempt was made on Pobedonostsev, in Ufa when Bogdanovich was done to death, and had sat next to the assassin in the Tivoli at Kharkov, urging him on when he seemed to be wavering. Savinkov too had always been in attendance—at the murders of Pleve and Sergei Aleksandrovich, the attempt on Trepov, on Cathedral Square, and at Sevastopol. From 1906, when Azef was brought into the activities of the Combat Organization, every one of its "actions" had been skillfully sabotaged, so that the word "provocateur"—such a favorite with revolutionaries trying to explain away their failures—was in no way applicable to him. Only the instigator of a crime, not an agent and informant of the police, could be called that.

> This is a matter in which light can only help the government, and darkness is essential to the revolutionaries. Imagine, gentlemen, the horror of any young man or woman attracted by revolution and suddenly faced with the utter sordidness of its leaders. Obviously it is more profitable to spread monstrous rumors of crimes committed by the government, and to lay on the government all the criminal machinations, the demoralization and disarray of the revolutionaries

in the hope that

> the government will be naïve enough to help destroy obstacles in the way of the triumphant march of revolution

by ceasing to use secret agents altogether—although only they gave warning of murderers.

> Our whole police system is only a means to make it possible to live, work, and legislate. Criminal provocation the government does not and will not tolerate.

It was after midnight when he stepped down to the applause of the entire chamber.

The prophetic note made itself heard yet again in the speech on Azef:

> We are erecting the scaffolding for our work of construction. Our enemies condemn it as ugly and furiously try to chop it down. This scaffolding will surely tumble down someday, and we may be crushed in the wreckage—but let it happen when the main lines of the new building, the renovated free Russia, are already discernible.

The opposition was crushed by this. Stolypin made them realize that honesty was not on the side of the revolution. (All the same, the prevailing liberal wind ensured that—like the "Stolypin neckties" and the "Stolypin wagon"—the penny dreadful by Chernov and Burtsev, not the truth about Azef, would stick.)

More than once Stolypin found himself arguing with the Kadets about their empty concept of freedom:

> We cannot simply hang out the flags of so-called freedom on the heights—our task is to free our people from poverty, ignorance, and oppression.

Whatever the subject under discussion—domestic policy, foreign policy, administrative or constitutional matters—Stolypin was always conscious of his ties with the masses, the main support of the state:

> We must raise up our impoverished, our weak, our exhausted land. The land is the pledge of our future strength. The land *is* Russia!

Alas, improved though it was by the daring law of 16 June, the Duma had still not become a serious national assembly, responsive to the peasants' interests. In the Third Duma, as in its predecessors, agrarian reform fared worst of all. One year, two years went by after the decree promulgated under Article 87, bypassing the Second Duma, and still its successor was stewing over each and every article—demurring, protesting, demanding explanations. The Kadets, in their polemical ardor, had ceased to understand that Stolypin's program in the countryside was in fact one of liberal reform by legal means, and they rallied to the defense of the commune. So great was the aversion of educated society to this step—emancipation of peasant labor and the granting of independence to the peasant—that they picked at every comma when they saw a chance to delay the passing of the law. One bright idea the lawyers and professors had was that the head of a peasant household should not be allowed to dispose of his allotment as he pleased, but must have the agreement of other members of the family, women and children included, to everything he did with his property. Any one of these well-to-do, independent town dwellers and landed gentlemen would have thought it an affront if he were required to do things this way in his own family (and any European would have thought it a stupid joke). But the oppressed peasant, the *holy toiler,* whom they one and all so dearly loved, as Russia's writers bade them, the peasant whom they were there to serve exclusively in the national assembly (although they did not speak his language and were ignorant of his ideas)—that peasant they considered so incapable even in adult years and such an incorrigible drunkard that if he became the proprietor of his allotment he would immediately squander it on drink and reduce his family to beggary—so that if neither the landowner nor the commune had power over the holy toiler any longer, at least the authority of his family must be preserved. They drew from Stolypin the retort that you could not make the whole adult population wards of their own children, could not regard all the peasants as chronic weaklings and the whole Russian people as drunks:

> You cannot adjust a general law to fit an abnormal phenomenon. In drafting a law for the whole country we must consider the sensible and the strong, not the drunken and weak. Strong people of that sort are the majority in Russia.

Whereupon they dropped his last sentence, seized on the rest, inverted its meaning, and made of it an indelible slander with the skill that comes naturally to the many-headed faceless "public."

Stolypin, it seemed, had given himself away: his law was a wager on the *strong* peasantry, *meaning* the land-grabbing kulaks. The right chimed in: "Defense of the strong is a profoundly anti-national principle." (So that the image of the inflexible Prime Minister would imprint itself on the history of his century with this stigma as well as others. After his death enemies disfigured his memory with lie upon lie.)

Some of the clergy also opposed the reform on the ground that resettlement on separate farmsteads would weaken the Orthodox faith among the people.

In those two and a half years applications for permission to farm independently had flowed in from a million peasants, the land tenure commissions were already at work reorganizing communal land into consolidated individual lots, the government had sent its agents into rural areas to explain the law (what Stolypin did not know was that students followed on their heels contradicting their explanations—"Don't listen to them, don't move out; they'll trick you again!")—and after all this the Duma reluctantly condescended to ratify the law by a majority of a few votes.

It took a year longer for the law to get through a fractious and vacillating State Council.

When all the legislators had finally cast their votes the law still had months to wait for the Emperor's signature, during which Stolypin was the target of violent attacks from the right: they now accused him of clumsy bureaucratic tinkering, alleging that his underlings were forcing the peasants out of the commune, and that the dismantling of the commune was a particularly damaging idea of his which delivered the peasant into the hands of Jewish land sharks. (This although the law clearly stipulated that allotment land could not be disposed of to anyone except a peasant, could not be sold outright for cash, and could not be mortgaged except to the Peasant Bank.)

So there was yet another wait for the Emperor's signature. Would intrigue behind the scenes push him off course?

One of the Emperor's most disheartening characteristics was that just one agreeable visitor could in just one conversation change what had been for many years his firmly held opinion. Around the Tsar radiated and revolved individual luminaries and whole constellations, bejeweled with rank and titles: essentially they had nothing to do with Russia, yet on their conjunctions the fate of Russia depended more than on anything else.

In the space which these "spheres" occupied it was not they who were the unhealthy, the deviant, the abnormal phenomenon, but Stolypin himself, the little squire who had cut across their orbits to trespass near the zenith of power, a provincial parvenu without prescriptive right or friends in high places, a foreign body, yet now established. He had become the second person in the empire, though he had no kinship at all with the world of the court, that of high society, or that of the senior bureaucrats, and had never been trained to move in them. In the great Russia outside, Stolypin could try to construct a new code of laws, and his laws might even begin to operate throughout the length and breadth of the land, but in that inner space occupied by the court circles they exerted no influence at all.

Looked at more broadly: they all of them needed and used Stolypin while he was saving them from revolution, from incendiarism and rampaging mobs. From the summer of 1906 until the autumn of 1908 right-wing circles made no secret of their ill will toward him, yet allowed him to get on with the fight against revolution. When this battle had ended in a resounding victory for Stolypin, and Russia sailed out of the desperate turbulence of her Time of Troubles into the calmer waters of normal statehood, Stolypin's policy began to seem impossible, intolerable. Above all, the right could not understand why he had still not retracted the 30 October Manifesto, but continued to play the game of constitutionalism, parliamentary institutions, and the rule of law.

"All of them," as defined by Guchkov, meant three groups: the court camarilla, which under the new constitutional order was required only to fade away; the retired bureaucrats, failed rulers of Russia who formed a tight community of their own on the right of the State Council (it was populated by ineffectual elders who served to slow down the movement of vitally necessary measures, just as a senile organism slows down the circulation of the blood); and the diehards among the gentry, who thought they could dominate Russia for centuries to come without yielding an inch. We can add the Union of the Russian People to this list: as soon as they saw signs that the country was calming down they began abusing Stolypin for not being firm enough in his handling of revolutionaries, for mollycoddling the Duma, for his loyalty to the constitution, for his tacit concessions to the Jews, for his *liberalism*: where did he think he was taking Russia . . . ! Stolypin did not give way to them, any more than to any other party. He served Russia, not Petersburg—the pool in which all these currents converged. His actions were never at any time governed by self-interest.

Stolypin had no thought of retracting the Manifesto. Indeed, once he had crushed the revolution he earnestly went ahead with a series of intolerable reforms and tidying-up operations which would disturb the blissful repose of the spheres in their fixed orbits, and thereafter their very existence. They saw it before even he did, and some groups felt directly the menace of a wave of senatorial investigations.

Absorbed in his single combat with revolution, and with the usual optimistic self-assurance of the man of action, Stolypin underestimated the threat from the right. He advanced unswervingly, triumphantly promoting his laws, confident that he would be able to force them through and establish them firmly in the higher spheres, without ever adapting himself to any law of theirs. He looked for neither friends nor allies among them and never asked their opinion. (He was not one of their own bureaucratic kind, and they could not detect that wax coating which would have made him kin.)

Hating greedy careerists and bribe-takers above all, and already contemplating the reform of the police, he had appointed a commission to study the matter, yet failed to see how he and his plans would be hindered and endangered when in those very months, early in 1909, the rapacious polecat Kurlov was foisted on him as First Deputy Minister of the Interior. (With the Tsar's blessing and indeed at the wish of the Tsaritsa in person. This may already have been in preparation for his dismissal. Stolypin's own ministry began monitoring its chief's telephone calls.) Stolypin went his own way: the higher the circle he addressed, the more uncompromising his home truths. He appeared not to notice the Empress's hostility toward him (the statutes under which the Council of Ministers operated provided for no relationship between them, but the Tsar would often mention in argument that "the Sovereign Empress completely shares my point of view"). He had come to expect and was ready to parry at any moment the Emperor's sudden changes of mind: one minute he would agree to bold measures to be taken by the Ministry of Education, even at the risk of student disturbances, the next he would be promulgating orders to the contrary effect without consulting the minister concerned or the Prime Minister, which, to say the least, did not make for firm government. Whenever the Emperor gave his consent to something, it was as well to remember that this was probably not his last word.

The Emperor found it convenient to receive his Prime Minister only after ten in the evening, and never on Saturdays and Sundays, which were naturally set aside for his family and for recreation. Then there were months on end when Stolypin had to travel, not by carriage to Peterhof, but by train to the Crimea and back, a week's travel for two days of work with the Emperor. Then, once the danger of revolution was eliminated, the Emperor would retire to Germany for as long as four months at a time, for a holiday in his wife's homeland. Whenever he was received by the All-Highest, Stolypin, always ready for sudden changes of that unstable will, carried a letter of resignation, signed and bearing that day's date, in his briefcase, and on more than one occasion he submitted it.

When the "spheres" began bearing down heavily on Stolypin in the spring of 1909, his resignation, long imminent, almost became a reality. The issue was at first glance a trivial one—reduction of the Naval General Staff—but Stolypin, impatient as always to get things done, took the matter to the Duma and insisted on his own solution, while Witte was quick to point out in the State Council that the Prime Minister was creating a precedent by limiting the imperial prerogative in matters affecting the armed forces. The course of events was disrupted by Stolypin's sudden attack of pleurisy. The Emperor suggested that he should take a leave and convalesce at Livadia. "Leave" could only too easily be interpreted as the preliminary to retirement, and the imperial rescript dispatched to Livadia announcing that Stolypin had been awarded the Order of the White Eagle as an attempt to soften the blow. Stolypin returned to Petersburg in April with the warm air of the Crimea still in his lungs, hoping to find fresher air in the capital too. He hurried out to damp Yelagin, where the snow was still on the ground! All Petersburg was talking about his imminent replacement as Prime Minister by Kokovtsov, and as Minister of the Interior by Kurlov. The Emperor was indeed probably making up his mind at that time to dismiss him. But at the end of April a further rescript publicly reconfirmed his position. (He had, however, to leave full authority in military matters to the Emperor—and so began to lose the support of Guchkov and the Octobrists.)

His relations with the Emperor were his vulnerable point. They did not affect the direction of his work, but could make the difference between success and failure. How unmercifully "society" abused the Tsar! What a ludicrous stuffed dummy he was in the eyes of educated Russia. The almost unanimous view was that he was shortsighted, stupid, malicious, vengeful, callous. Stolypin, even when the Tsar was still remote and invisible, had never permitted himself such thoughts. When he entered into close contact with the Tsar and talked to him about the things that mattered most, he concluded that it was not at all true. The Tsar was morbidly insecure, easily hurt, repressed. Only excellent physical health made his hypersensitivity bearable. Far from being vengeful and malicious, he was kind and gentle, a true Christian on the throne, who loved his people with all his heart and had nothing but goodwill for the thousands with whom he was forced to have dealings. (Though he could bear a grudge, and go on bearing it to the end.) He sincerely wanted all his own subjects, and those of all other countries, to be happy. (Provided this did not demand sustained exertion on his part.) He could grasp the essentials of any argument, and there was no need to simplify ideas for him. (Provided that he was not called on to think too often and too tiringly.) The Emperor Nikolai Aleksandrovich diverged no farther from the mean of mediocrity than the average monarch, who is more likely to be congenitally mediocre than not, but in his goodness of heart he was abundantly, perhaps excessively, superior to the average. That made it even more inescapably the duty of a monarchist to learn to work with this Emperor.

The Emperor was sincerely convinced that the one aim which he kept before his eyes at all times was the well-being of his motherland, and that petty personal considerations faded in comparison. He often spoke of his terrible responsibility before God, but filled important posts at a whisper from the palace commandant or the head of his traveling chancery. The Emperor was sincerely aware of his terrible responsibility, and just as sincerely, just as ingenuously, interminably put off state business, however important, if it threatened to bore him, or canceled altogether disagreeable procedures like receiving the whole Duma in person. A good deal of the Third Duma's business might have gone differently if the reception had ever taken place, but for a lover of grandiose parades (where the participants of course were mute) or intimate chats at the dinner table (where the participants were all friends), nothing was more uncongenial than having to meet a dozen, a hundred, or maybe even five hundred educated people with views different from his own, none of them mute and none of them friends. The Tsar was so sensitive about his views, and especially about his ability to defend them, that he could not expose them to the winds of public opinion. He could only cherish in a sealed vessel his faith in his splendid people and in the splendid statesmen who would do all that was needed to make Russia educated, humane, free, and prosperous. For a long time he valued Stolypin as just such a splendid minister, who would realize those splendid aims and lead the people to a life of bliss—all he asked was that the Prime Minister should not fret his Emperor too much, and should not try to make him be unkind to some splendid fellow in court circles.

As a loyal servant Stolypin had no choice but to support the Emperor and do everything for his greater glory, but there was more to it than that. He felt a genuine affection for this man who for all his serious shortcomings as a ruler was good and honest. ("*J'aime le petit*"—"I like the little man"—he would tell his wife. He was a *little* Emperor, not a strong one, like some before him.) He made great efforts to help the Emperor overcome his faults and steel himself against his weaknesses. If his fixed aim was to reinforce Russia's historical foundations he must serve the present monarch with all his strength, patiently accepting his inadequacies, as a son learns to live with an ineffectual father. Stolypin never missed a chance to glorify the Emperor. He made him the centerpiece at national festivals (the bicentenary of Poltava, for instance). He never mentioned him except with the greatest reverence. He attributed his own inspirations, his own enactments to the Emperor ("His Majesty has turned his gaze upon the Russian peasantry"). He adjured his hearers to be loyal ("Russia is true to her Emperor"). Even with Guchkov, his ally in the parliamentary battle, with whose speeches Stolypin sympathized more than he could openly confess, and with whom he discussed plans to split the right wing of the Duma and draw off its more moderate members, even alone with Guchkov, who was ill disposed toward the royal couple, Stolypin never allowed himself to speak disapprovingly of the Emperor. The weaker the Emperor was, and the more stubborn (to reassure himself that he was really being strong), the more important it was for Stolypin to yield to his stubbornness, for fear that his illusion of strength would crumple. He would bolster the illusion, thank the Emperor for his gracious interest, excuse himself ("I have no wish to put Your Majesty in an awkward situation with an uncalled-for measure . . ."). There were times when he would have been disloyal to his monarchist principles if he had not given the monarch a lesson. He would then make it appear that the lesson was being given for his own good, or that it concerned some third person: "There is no greater sin in a statesman than pusillanimity."

Stolypin was extremely clear-sighted in his approach to the premiership. He knew his capacity to exercise authority. He knew how much this Tsar needed him. But the Tsar, of course, was unaware of the disproportion between his own and Stolypin's expenditure of intellectual effort and of energy on the government of Russia. He genuinely did not understand how much time and work had to be invested. For this reason he could not see how onerous it was for the Prime Minister to travel all the way from Petersburg to Livadia for an audience, or, when he had taken time off to inspect his favorite innovation, the new peasant farms in the province of Orel or Poltava, to have to hurry back for an imperial banquet in honor of the Danish royal couple.

The Emperor had forgotten, or perhaps had simply never understood, how nearly Russia had toppled over into the abyss in 1905–6. When, three years later, the Emperor was able for the first time to travel freely to Poltava, Stolypin informed him, with a certain pride:

> The revolution has been extirpated, Your Majesty, and you can now move about freely,

and the Emperor replied with obvious irritation:

> I do not understand what you mean by revolution. Such disorders as there were would never have taken place if power had been in the hands of braver and more energetic people, like Dumbadze, the police chief at Yalta.

Stolypin felt aggrieved. How quickly and easily the Emperor had forgotten the dangers to which he himself had been exposed. He seemed not to have noticed all that had been done to save the country.

In fact, the Tsar was very well disposed toward Stolypin in the first years, and keenly aware that here was his own, and his country's, savior. For safety's sake he offered the Prime Minister his own palaces to live in, and the imperial yacht to cruise among the Finnish islands, as he sometimes did himself.

On one such cruise in the summer of 1908 Stolypin spent some time incognito in Germany, where he enjoyed the happiness, which ordinary people seldom appreciate as much as they should, of walking the streets freely with no need to hide from assassins. Kaiser Wilhelm heard of his visit and asked to meet him, but Stolypin avoided him and slipped away. Wilhelm sent several ships in pursuit but could not catch him. (Their conversation had to wait a year, until the meeting of the two Emperors. Wilhelm was rudely inattentive to his imperial brother and his spouse, and completely absorbed in his conversation with Stolypin, who fascinated him. Even twenty years later the Kaiser often said that Stolypin was superior to Bismarck and more farsighted.)

In addition to domestic policy (and that—the patient reorganization and development of your own country—is all that really matters) there was foreign policy. Stolypin, who was Prime Minister and not merely Minister of the Interior, should presumably have given a lot of time to foreign policy. Not at all. He took no more interest in foreign policy than he was forced to take, ignored it, grudged whatever time he had to spend on it. International problems seemed to him extremely easy to deal with compared with those at home. There was not, in Russia's relations with other countries, the same history of neglect, the same centuries-old accumulation of absurdities and bungling. Above all, Russia was not confronted abroad by the same destructive hatred, or by such ferocious ideological foes, for whom life had no content except their enmity. As he saw it, he need exert only a quarter of his strength in foreign policy—like the fabled giant who moved mountains. The mountains and chasms in international relations were more apparent than real. He was convinced that a ruler of the most mediocre intelligence could prevent war between nations at any time.

The young and ambitious Minister of Foreign Affairs, Izvolsky, may have been inflicted on Stolypin's government as punishment for this inattentiveness of his. (Could the Russian government, however, be thought of as a government? They were only just beginning to get used to the idea that it was an integral body. Throughout those years the Minister of Foreign Affairs was not required to repeat to the Prime Minister the reports he made to the Tsar. Nor did the decision whether to dismiss the said Izvolsky or leave him at his post rest with the Prime Minister.) In his eagerness to dazzle the world with a diplomatic success and to obtain a free hand in his dealings with Turkey, Izvolsky stepped into a trap set by his Austro-Hungarian colleague, which enabled him to announce that the annexation of Bosnia and Herzegovina at the end of 1908 had the prior approval of Russia. This was an insolent exploitation of Russian weakness after the defeat by Japan. The Central Powers trod on Russia's toes and compelled her to smile. Germany demanded from Russia not just silence and neutrality but a humiliating public declaration of consent to the occupation: she must bend the knee and renounce her protection of the Balkan Slavs. The Russian public was outraged: there were hysterics in the press and in the Duma. But it was too late for any retort short of war. And war was the surest way of getting nowhere. A hard look at the War Ministry had reinforced the opinion which Stolypin had reached on general grounds that Russia simply could not go to war, and would not be ready to do so for a long time to come, that in her present state war would mean defeat, and that revolution would break out even before that happened. Though bitter enough, the conclusion was still not too hard for Stolypin to swallow: he had never thought of going to war in any case, and had certainly never been an ardent believer in Russia's Pan-Slav mission. A temporary dent in the national pride was nothing, in the context of his grandiose program of national reconstruction. Stolypin could not disclose his thinking publicly. He simply dissuaded the Tsar from acting on his decision to mobilize against Austria: that would mean war with Germany as well, and threaten the existence of the dynasty. ("Today I saved Russia," he told those closest to him.) He talked privately to the leaders of the enraged and bellicose Duma majority and calmed them down. The Kadets were for plunging into battle—not in person, of course, not bodily, but by proxy, and kept up their angry protests against the Potsdam meeting of the two Emperors in 1910 for some considerable time: why, they wanted to know, had Russia backed down? The French were disturbed by the demolition of four Russian forts in Poland. Stolypin's view was that the allies were not really allies at all—they would turn away from Russia if ever misfortune befell her. England was alarmed by Russia's international strength, and would like to see her disintegrate. There was no love or respect for Russia in France, only fear of Germany. No one in Europe, or indeed in the world at large, had any use for a strong, nationalist Russia.

The outcome confirmed Stolypin in his view that foreign policy was not worth prolonged and constant effort: all real threats had been eliminated without difficulty. If a strong state *did not want* war, no one could force it to fight. When Sazonov was appointed to succeed Izvolsky, Stolypin asked him just to avoid international complications—that was all the foreign policy he wanted. As far as Russia was concerned, war was absolutely unnecessary. She needed ten to twenty years of peace at home and abroad, whatever happened. Once the reforms were complete Russia would be unrecognizable, and would have no reason to fear any foreign enemy:

> Once the roots of the Russian state are healthy and strong, the words of the

> Russian government will have a different ring in the ears of Europe and of the whole world.

After the annexation of Bosnia and Herzegovina, he foresaw no circumstances in which Russia would be more strongly tempted to go to war.

They avoided war that time, and were none the worse for it: the light of the self-sufficient planet called Russia was not perceptibly dimmer. Nor did he feel that he had compromised Russia's honor, or behaved badly toward her disloyal British ally, when he and the Emperor promised at Potsdam in October 1910 not to join in British intrigues against Germany, in return for which Germany undertook not to support Austro-Hungarian aggression in the Balkans.

Russia and her people were becoming more energetic and purposeful in their normal activities from day to day now that the country had acquired a sensible structure.

For the fifth year in succession Stolypin was patiently taking his country down what he believed to be the right road. He had shown that to govern means to foresee. Shown it in the surest way—by results. By his own conduct. Loving Russia, he was indifferent to parties, did not side with any of them, remained free from party pressure, and rose above them all, so that while he was in office they lost their overbearing force. The space around him was weeded clear of petty politicking. He was above trivialities and so above petty ambition. People were attracted to him because he was so obviously disinterested. He radiated cheerful confidence. He grudged no effort when there was someone to be persuaded. Working with him was easy and enjoyable, and those who did acquired something of his imperturbability in the face of threats, and his almost artistic approach to his enormous tasks. He was in his prime and at the height of his powers and he infused the whole administration with his own youthful vigor. He hid nothing, stood where all Russia could see him, and left no dark patches where slander might flourish. He lived up to his name, the pillar (*stolp*) of the Russian state. He became the hub of Russian life as no Tsar had ever been. (His qualities were, in truth, kingly.)

A second Peter ruled Russia—a Peter as energetic and tireless as the first, as concerned for the productivity of the people's labor, as radical a reformer, but with ideas that distinguished him from Peter the Great.

> To reform our way of life, without damage to the vital foundation of our state—the soul of the people . . .

(Or to their character and beliefs.)

> The Russian state has been wedded for centuries to the Orthodox Church. You have all of you, believers and nonbelievers, been in a village church in the depths of the countryside. You have seen how devoutly our people pray, you cannot have failed to be affected by that atmosphere of cumulative devotion, cannot have failed to realize that for those worshippers the words that echo through the church are divine words.

(At about the same time he showed his awareness of the other side of the picture:

> Your Majesty knows how deeply I feel the decrepitude of our synod and our church.

The Chief Procurator of the Synod ought, he told the Tsar, to be a man strong both in intellect and in will.)

Stolypin's policy became the rallying point for all those educated people—as yet, alas, so few—in whom some unchilled remnant or some hesitant beginning of Russian national sentiment and Orthodox belief could be detected.

This spiritual process needed time to develop—for perhaps the same twenty untroubled years of which Stolypin had spoken.

By now he was so firm on his feet and so sure of his ground that he received the opposition's worn-out darts unmoved, and hurled them back with fine-sharpened points.

> After the trials she has gone through Russia naturally cannot be content. But she is discontented not only with the government but with the State Duma too. And with the State Council. With both the right-wing and the left-wing parties. She is discontented with herself. This discontent will pass once Russia's confidence in herself as a state is reinforced. Once Russia feels herself to be Russia again.

His law permitting peasants to leave the commune finally received the royal assent, after working its weary way through the two legislative chambers. Two million heads of household had applied to farm independently in the meantime. Foreseeing a glut of grain, Stolypin created throughout Russia a broad network of elevators belonging to the State Bank, and gave subsidies to the peasants who stored their grain in them.

There was one other area of policy dear to Stolypin, about which he did not have to argue a great deal, or face desperate resistance, because the results were swift and plain to see. This was the resettlement of peasants beyond the Urals—in Siberia, the Kirghiz lands, and Semirechye.

What could be more natural than pointing Russian peasants toward the unoccupied lands beyond the Urals? Why should they lie waste for century after century? The idea had in fact occurred to the ordinary peasant long ago. He had plucked out of thin air the reasons for it and the conditions which would find scientific confirmation half a century later. This eastward urge engendered dreams, legends, tales about the "Tsaritsa's lands," the "Gardens of Siberia," the "Mamur River." Peasants rushed there, sometimes even singly, often to be intercepted by the authorities, sometimes fleeing their native villages by night in carts with muffled wheels, with thousands of versts ahead of them, through strange places where they could not draw attention to themselves and so could not always find a night's lodging or beg for alms on their way to a completely unknown new home in the wilds. Ever since the Great Reform of 1861 the Russian government had obstructed the resettlement of its peasants on the rich, unoccupied lands at the selfish insistence of greedy landowners who feared that the cost of labor on their estates would rise tomorrow but never concerned themselves with what might happen to Russia the day after. Peasants were forbidden to leave European Russia, where there were thirty-one inhabitants per square verst, for Siberia, which had fewer than one, until the famine of 1891, when controls were relaxed and construction of the Trans-Siberian Railway began. All the same, a resettlement program had to wait for the heat wave of 1905 and the sacking of gentry estates.

Resettlement, like improved cultivation, was another way of relieving peasant poverty, and so made its claim on Stolypin's attention and his efforts. As soon as he became responsible for the whole nation's business the stream of settlers obtained many incentives: the government transported land spotters free, provided information, marked out holdings, subsidized the removal of families with their household goods and livestock, and even constructed special simplified passenger carriages for the purpose (Stolypin's name stuck to wagons of this type at a later date, when they were crammed full of lost souls). Loans were granted for building houses and buying machinery. A whole stratum of the peasantry, the most enterprising who were nonetheless insufficiently endowed in their old places, was drawn into the eastern areas. The "Cabinet" lands (strictly speaking, the Tsar's) in the Altai were made over for resettlement—an area about five times the size of Belgium. Soldiers crossing Siberia on their way back from the war with Japan swelled the number of interested peasants. One hundred thirty thousand migrated in 1906, and half a million or more annually after that. (When war broke out in 1914 more than four million had moved—as many as in the three hundred years since Yermak.) The settlers received their land gratis and as absolute property. Millions of desyatins were distributed at the rate of fifty to a family, yielding as much as sixty puds a desyatin. Pyotr Arkadievich's dream was coming true. Irrigation works were in progress on the Hungry Steppe. Only four years had gone by—an insignificant time in the scale of Russian history (it would fit seventy-five times over into the life span of the Romanov dynasty alone)—when Stolypin with his favorite minister, Krivoshein, his partner in all his work for the peasantry, spent August and September 1910 touring several of the resettlement areas in Siberia, traveling most of the way in a cart and rejoicing no less than the settlers themselves in their unfettered, healthy, prosperous lives in their new homes, flourishing farms and villages, even towns, where three years ago there had not been a single human being, their cheerful, eager work with the first fruits already visible, the inexhaustible forest, the fertile tilth, the abundant grazing land, the free hunting and fishing. After three years these people could scarcely believe that they had once lived in penury, and wondered why they had not set out for Siberia long ago.

If all this had been done in the first four years, and the annual grain harvest already raised to four billion puds, what might be achieved in twenty years of unhampered development?

The sight of so much prosperity all around him, the constant movement, and the air of the Siberian plains made this the most enjoyable experience in Stolypin's life—incomparably sweeter than the rewards which some day the throne might bestow on him, or the honor in which the Russian people might hold him. In those happy months, with no bodyguard around him, he was privileged to see how his hard labor at his desk was reflected in the new life of a great people on the rich expanses of Siberia. These people who had ventured boldly into remote and untamed places, stalwart and irrepressibly energetic people, a sound and sturdy offshoot of the Russian nation, were making themselves prosperous by the toil of their hands, free men, remote as could be from the miasma of revolution, freely declaring themselves for the Tsar and for Orthodoxy, asking for churches as well as schools. Russia was being built anew in this new place, and it was a cleaner Russia: beyond the Volga, Stolypin met a former Socialist Revolutionary member of the First Duma who was now an enthusiastic homesteader and a devotee of law and order. Throughout the journey Stolypin and Krivoshein were eagerly discussing further measures to ensure that this great tidal wave of resettlement rolled on unimpeded.

A month later Stolypin was sitting beside Kaiser Wilhelm at Potsdam, with the comfortable feeling of a thriving Siberia at his back, surprised over and over again to find how easily manageable international affairs were, how little there was to this much overrated "foreign policy." Relations with Germany could be put on as good a basis as anyone could wish.

Russia was on the way to recovery—and there was no stopping her. Awareness of this irreversible change had seeped into the minds and hearts of revolutionaries too. For thirty years on end those minds and hearts had been hungrily expecting imminent revolution in Russia. That one hope governed their lives and all their actions. Now they were high and dry, a prey to doubt, weariness, and apostasy. They were no longer listened to. The revolution was not a non-event—it had happened, and suffered defeat. It was no longer a rosy glow on the horizon of the future, but a fading blood-red blotch on that of the past. (This period has gone down in history as "the years of the Stolypin reaction." It was indeed a reaction—the reaction of souls not yet utterly lost against the obscenities around them, the reaction of the healthy part of the people against the diseased. Stand aside—let us work and live!)

The terrorists fell back from Stolypin himself. From 1910 on they no longer stalked him, no longer sought opportunities to kill him. Their many previous failures had not made them despair and abandon their intention, but a time had arrived in which terrorists no longer found an enthusiastic and grateful welcome even in intellectual households where they had been used to it. Among the population at large they felt not so much persecuted as unwanted, rejected. This robbed them of the strength to act.

Stolypin could turn his attention to preventing the pollution of the Neva by effluents and to the provision of free tea for down-and-outs in night shelters. Blessed with exuberant good health, he could never find enough work to do. No one ever saw him jaded.

In the winter of 1909–10 he was living on the Fontanka, no longer in hiding. His excursions to the Tauride Palace took place on fixed and generally known days and that summer he was able to visit the estate near Kovno of which he was so fond.

Once, while inspecting flying machines, he was introduced to the pilot Matsievich, with the warning that he was a well-known Socialist Revolutionary. (Membership in the SR Party did not preclude military service or work in any capacity.) With a sudden gleam in his eye the pilot challenged Stolypin to go up with him. He could not decline, although he was taking not just his own life but the fate of all Russia in his hands. A duelist's sense of honor weighed more heavily with him than prudence or duty, as he had shown more than once under threat of assassination. He agreed at once.

And up they went. They circled twice at considerable height. The pilot could have crashed and killed both of them at any minute. (It was quite usual for terrorists to sacrifice themselves with their victims.) Or he could have tried to kill just his passenger. But he did not. The antagonists merely eyed one another and carried on an unimportant conversation. (Shortly afterward Matsievich was killed flying solo. "It's sad to lose a brave flier," Stolypin remarked.)

In those days it was not the practice to trumpet the praises of statesmen throughout the land or to paste their portraits about the streets. Buried among the teeming hundred million, remote from politics, few of Russia's citizens were likely even to remember who was Chairman of the Council of Ministers. They knew only the Tsar (and Stolypin gladly remained in his shadow), but they could see for themselves that the country was calmer, that there was no more rioting and looting, that it was possible to live a quiet life in Russia.

The Kadets no longer dared revile Stolypin, and stopped attacking him altogether. They tacitly accepted the new situation—just as long as they did not have to give the victor credit. He had carved himself an inexplicably strange niche: too much of a nationalist for the Octobrists, too much of an Octobrist for the nationalists; a reactionary to all on the left yet practically a Kadet to the true right. His measures were too reactionary for the wreckers and too destructive for the reactionaries. But, alien as he was, "the public" had got into the habit of tolerating him.

There was, however, one stratum which remembered from day to day only too well who was Chairman of the Council of Ministers and marveled that he had lasted so long. They followed this extraordinary careerist's every new and promising move with indignation and envy—this lucky fellow, fortune's favorite, this self-confident go-getter, this outsider, this non-Petersburger whose services to the country they could not match, this incorrigible optimist with his parrot cries about the bright future while privileges and rights were being more and more menacingly undermined. This was the uppermost stratum of the courtiers and high bureaucrats—a thin top layer of the Russian population, but broad and thick enough to hamper the moves of the Prime Minister. They kept their own score, chalking it up like billiards or card players. The chalk marks looked as if they would be rubbed out or fade, but they burned with a white heat, outshining everything in the country and the whole universe outside the game room. On their scoreboard Stolypin was not a winner but an out-and-out loser: he had risen to the top too young; he insolently refused to recognize any obligation to anyone; in ad hominem situations—is so-and-so to be encouraged? promoted? transferred? mentioned in the honors list? protected from punishment?—he never made decisions ad hominem, like a good fellow among his peers and with their interests at heart—no, he took refuge behind some figment called "the interest of the state." He never joined in any intrigue, any comradely cabal, he posed as a completely independent individual, something that does not and cannot exist. . . . The figures of the unpayable account swelled in flaky chalk. This intriguer had bewitched and hoodwinked the Emperor, and somehow hung on to his post when, according to the reckoning, it was time for him to be gone. Translating into their chalky and waxy language, they counted every one of his successful reforms against him: he was blamed for releasing the peasants to set up smallholdings; he was blamed for his hobnobbing with the zemstvos—to whom he had begun to transfer part of the state's sacrosanct and indivisible administrative authority (the gentry hindered his efforts to reform local administration at county level, although half of the marshals of the gentry did not even live in their counties); he was blamed for increasing local taxation at the expense of landowners to pay for the consolidation of the peasantry; he was blamed for devising a system of worker's insurance at the expense of the industrialists and state revenues; he was blamed for protecting Old Believers and sectarians; he was blamed for his lack of respect for courtiers. Lastly—or firstly!—he had not earned the rank of chamberlain or state secretary.

He was an insufferable parvenu to all the gray-headed heavyweights of the State

Council, unapproachable to the whole court clique, and more and more unacceptable to Her Imperial Majesty. (Everybody who could obtain an audience whispered into her ear that Stolypin was building up his own popularity at the expense of the Tsar's.)

The distinguishing characteristic of this milieu is not steely, tensile strength but marsh-like viscosity. It gives beneath the foot, it becomes a tacky mess—but compress it enough and it is invincible. Not just the Emperor's mind and ears but the very air, the whole atmosphere, was filled and vibrated with suspicions, condemnations, indignant protests that it was unseemly to let one man hold on to such a lofty post so long and so powerfully. It was gradually brought home to the Emperor that the man who had been his Prime Minister for five years was not his well-wisher and the savior of the throne but one who reaped new laurels with every success and was eclipsing his sovereign.

In any quagmire there are untraceable sticky threads stretching from edge to edge. They come into action in unexpected places to give the marsh its unconquerable marshy resilience. Officialdom dared not openly oppose the lawful government's authority—so resistance to Stolypin suddenly made itself felt through the Church, in Saratov province, where not so long ago he had been governor. Bishop Germogen and the monk-priest Iliodor, a fanatic with insane eyes, preached against the holders of power as heretics and traitors to the Emperor—and who if not Stolypin was the first among them? They got rid of their provincial governor. It suddenly turned out that they were both in league with Rasputin, who was becoming influential at court. (They quarreled with him, and with each other later.) The Emperor chose to dismiss the Chief Procurator of the Synod, a member of Stolypin's cabinet, and gave orders that the secular authorities should abandon their persecution of Iliodor and let him resume his religious duties at Tsaritsyn. As Stolypin was heard to say at about this time:

> It is a mistake to think that the Russian cabinet holds power. It is only a reflection of power. One must know the combination of pressures and influences under which it has to operate.

The government was impotent against the anonymous "spheres," the obscure nests of opposition behind the scenes. There were those, like Guchkov, who urged Stolypin to break out of his cramped position and openly challenge the dark forces. But Stolypin could not do that without turning himself into another Iliodor.

The number of his enemies multiplied, though Stolypin did nothing to multiply them. He never gave free rein to his resentments and his reflexes. He would not be distracted from the real battle. For that reason, he avoided a head-on collision with Rasputin for as long as he could. (And did not protest too vehemently when police observation of Rasputin, his drinking bouts, his crooked business contacts, was ended on orders from on high, and the plan to rusticate him failed in 1908. The Emperor explained one day that he would "sooner have ten Rasputins than one of the Empress's fits of hysterics.") For a long time Stolypin simply tried to keep out of his way: Rasputin's path, and that of the government, must not cross. But it proved impossible: the sticky threads were everywhere, determining the appointments of archbishops, senators, governors, generals, members of the State Council. Even in his own Ministry of the Interior, Stolypin was hampered and kept under surveillance by the senior Vice-Minister, Kurlov. This unsuitable and unfriendly outsider appeared from nowhere, at the Emperor's wish, not

Stolypin's, to take over the Police Department and the Corps of Gendarmes, and so was nominally in charge of the security of Russia, which was much less dear to his heart than his murky private business deals. Suddenly—these things always emerged unexpectedly—Stolypin's senior deputy was found to be a close acquaintance of the same Iliodor, then of Rasputin, just when Rasputin had firmly entrenched himself at Tsarskoye Selo and was becoming an intolerable growth in the body politic. It was impossible to allow matters of state to be decided at the level of that clodhopper and Stolypin decided to send him home at the beginning of 1910. He was soon back, alas, and soaring to greater heights. (Krivoshein tried to warn Stolypin: "You can do many things, but don't fight Rasputin and his friends or you'll come a cropper." By doing so Stolypin finally forfeited the Empress's goodwill.)

The marsh was bound to get its own back. Intense conflicts usually become acute without warning and often for relatively unimportant reasons. You never know where you will trip up. The complicated and contentious affair of the western zemstvos arose—and the opposition came together on this ground in a single howling mob.

Aleksandr II had not felt able to extend the Zemstvo Act to the whole of the western region from Kovno to Kiev, and local governmental bodies there were still appointed, not elected. The advantage of that sort of zemstvo was supposedly its nonrevolutionary character: appointed officials worked conscientiously and never opposed the government. But there was more to it than that: appointed zemstvo men could not make such bold use of local forces as their elected counterparts, and did not consider themselves entitled to broaden the activity of their zemstvo, to strengthen their position by increasing local taxes, or to take over governmental functions. These, however, were things that Stolypin wanted to see the zemstvos doing throughout Russia. The broadening of zemstvos' rights was a stage on the highroad which he was following.

He could not authorize a simple geographical extension of the existing rules. Only four percent of the population in the western provinces was Polish, yet all nine representatives of the region in the State Council were Poles. Though the peasants there were Lithuanian, Russian, White Russian, or Ukrainian, the landowners were Poles to a man; it was they who owned the wealth, shaped the economy, employed labor, influenced the religion, education, and material existence of the inhabitants; it was they who had political experience and secure control of their regions, all of which welded them into a solid national group. For these reasons elected zemstvos in the nine provinces seemed likely to come under overwhelming Polish influence, and the provinces would drift away from Russia along a Polish road. What was necessary was to insure against an unfair preponderance and prevent the extended zemstvos from becoming an instrument of Polish policy.

Under Aleksandr II's Zemstvo Act the landowners' vote outweighed that of the peasants. Damage to the national interest now seemed to be the likely punishment for this exploitative anti-peasant law. If the Russian character of the western provinces was to be preserved, the old zemstvo law had to be turned inside out: the effects of the differential franchise must be neutralized so that the Polish landowners would not have preponderance over the peasants. This could be achieved by dividing the electorate into colleges by nationality, giving the vote to the clergy (none of them Poles), and also (unheard of, this) lowering the property qualification so that the poor non-Poles would choose more electors than the well-off Poles (who would, however, still have sixteen percent of the votes—four times as many as their numbers warranted). Steps must be taken to ensure that representatives of peasant communities, not rich Poles, had a majority on the zemstvo. It was particularly important for the chairman of the zemstvo board and the chairman of the schools council to be Russians (or Ukrainians or White Russians—nobody made any real distinction between the three groups in those days):

> We must assert openly and without hypocrisy that the western lands are and must remain Russian. We must protect the Russian population against the Polish landowning minority.

(What a good thing it would have been if they had thought of doing the same in Russia itself much earlier. Why had the question—how to protect peasants against landlords—not arisen in Russia half a century before?)

We can assume a certain political disingenuousness in Stolypin's thinking on this matter. Though his aim was as honest as can be (his three favorite lines of policy—advancement of the peasant, reinforcement of the zemstvos, encouraging Russian national awareness—converged in it), he did not forget for a moment that the democratization of the zemstvos by lowering the property qualification for the vote would mean an influx of Russian semi-intellectuals with revolutionary tendencies in place of the conservative Polish gentry, and so was bound to appeal to the State Duma. And indeed, although the Duma frowned on the nationalistic spirit of the draft law (and the left voted against it), it accepted a reduction of the property qualification by twice the amount proposed by Stolypin. The Duma was probably right, but farsighted conservatives were inevitably alarmed by the thought that this lowering of the property qualification might become an epidemic and infect Russia proper at a later date. The law was passed in the first chamber, but inevitably aroused opposition in the second, not to Stolypin's national policy, but precisely to his policy regarding the zemstvos.

The second chamber, the State Council, nominally existed to apply the brakes and bring wise second thoughts to bear on overhasty enactments by the Duma. Of its 150 members, half were elected and half nominated by the Emperor himself. (This arrangement generally creates a delaying mechanism through which a monarch can exert his own influence. In the case of Nikolai II it gave scope for his tendency to appoint congenial people to important posts in which they would act as a counterweight to bold men of action, and spare him the need to intervene personally.)

"An ice cap of tired souls," Stolypin called the State Council. Some of its members were ancients too decrepit and too deaf to pick up the subject under discussion in the chamber—they had to acquaint themselves with the agenda at rehearsals before the sessions. It was also the filter tank for ex-officeholders—dismissed, relegated, or honorably retired—among them, of course, many vainglorious failures. The most poisonous snake in the State Council at that time was Witte, who had a personal hatred of Stolypin. He was consumed by an arid, nagging, sterile envy of Stolypin's success in pacifying Russia and drawing her out of the hysteria and abasement into which she had sunk in his time. (It was not just that Stolypin had taken over his post and repaired the broken-down system. Witte was comically upset by the Odessa city government's decision to rename Witte Street. He begged Stolypin on his knees not to let them do it, but Stolypin would not intervene.) Witte it was who became, not the main spokesman of open opposition, but the main instigator of resistance behind the scenes.

Nonetheless, Stolypin had managed to avoid trouble with the State Council until his ill-fated bill on the western zemstvos provoked stubborn opposition. Selfish class interest prevailed over all else. Though the bill might not seem important enough to warrant it, they were ready to fight to the death and endanger the policies which Stolypin had followed for five years and planned to continue in years to come.

Most of the clauses were accepted by a majority even in the commission set up by the Council, but before the meeting of the full Council, Stolypin realized that a wall of hostility was rising in his path and got the Emperor to sign a letter to the chairman urging acceptance of the bill. One of his determined adversaries, V. Trepov, obtained an audience with the Tsar and asked whether the letter was to be understood as a command or whether the members of the Council could vote according to conscience. The Emperor, who loved balancing opposing forces against each other, bade Trepov (as he naturally would) to obey his conscience, but, since he loved secrecy no less, concealed the episode from Stolypin. In any case, he had by this time accumulated a number of grievances against the Prime Minister: his whole entourage and all those whom he received did their best to turn him against Stolypin. These months in 1911 also saw the most serious crises over Iliodor and Rasputin, in which Stolypin's actions upset the Tsar and he suffered defeat.

On 17 March, the State Council voted the bill down in plenary session, and on 18 March, Stolypin submitted his resignation.

There was nothing unusual here: states as well as individuals often come to grief over some avoidable side issue although more difficult obstacles have already been surmounted. After a long series of victories one's ability to assess resistance is impaired and hot impatience takes over.

The existing constitutional order did not require the government to resign in the case of a vote of no confidence in one of the chambers: the government was responsible only to the monarch. But that was just it: the voting in the State Council, and more particularly the atmosphere around him, made it clear to Stolypin that behind the scenes, and without revealing himself, the sovereign had already rejected his Prime Minister.

Four days went by without an answer to Stolypin's request. (Petersburg was already speaking of Kokovtsov as Prime Minister and photographs of him had appeared in the windows of shops selling engravings.) Then he was summoned by the Dowager Empress, who had always been his loyal and unwavering supporter. The Emperor, who was leaving, wiping tears from his eyes, as Stolypin arrived, passed him by without a word of greeting. Maria Fyodorovna warmly urged Stolypin to remain at his post: "I have conveyed to my son my profound conviction that you alone have the strength to save Russia." At two in the morning a courier brought Stolypin a sixteen-page letter from the Tsar in which he confessed his error, apologized, promised never again to conceal anything affecting the business of state from the Prime Minister, expressed his hope that they could work in partnership, and asked him to withdraw his resignation.

Stolypin now showed an uncharacteristic severity (the measure of his resentment or of his determination to clear the way for reforms far ahead?). He insisted that the Emperor should release the leaders of the opposition, Trepov and Durnovo, from the State Council on indefinite leave. And that the Council itself (together with the Duma—the law did not allow it to be done differently) should be suspended for three days only while the Western Zemstvo Act was promulgated under Article 87. This was done on 24 March. Hoary-headed, star-spangled elder statesmen were compelled to listen to the decree of the All-Highest dismissing them and to cheer the Emperor repeatedly.

Stolypin's step was constitutionally unjustifiable. Article 87 permitted the promulgation of laws by the Emperor *in the absence* of the legislative organs and in an emergency, but not the deliberate dismissal of the two chambers for this purpose.

We are bound to admit that Stolypin was too hotheaded and too stubborn, that he showed the impatience and high-handedness of a man of action prevented from acting, that he was utterly sick of the "spheres." With so much to be done, with the state's urgent needs before his eyes, obstruction from these old men vexed him beyond endurance. He probably felt an itch to teach the State Council a lesson, relying on the loyal support of the Duma. The occasion did not warrant his resignation, or the wrecking of the Council, or the application of Article 87. (V. Maklakov, writing at a cool distance of decades from the controversy, would try to show that Stolypin did not use the legal possibilities open to him correctly: all he had to do was wait patiently for the summer recess, *then* promulgate the law under Article 87. He would have avoided giving offense, the Duma would have had no reason to abrogate a law it had previously approved, and it would never have returned to the State Council.) But if you look at it, it was only by using Article 87 that Stolypin ever succeeded in getting any of his main enactments off to a quick start—and even then they got stuck either in the Duma or in the State Council, or were sunk never to resurface.

We can also see these impatient efforts to legislate without parliament as proof that Witte's constitution had miscarried. It was premature and those who had to operate it were not ripe for it, but for those with eyes to see there was a forewarning of the great trials which the twentieth century would visit upon all the parliamentary systems in the world, testing them for strength and malleability as red-hot iron must be tested under the hammer. Russia was overtaken by these trials earlier than any other country and at a time when she was less well prepared. It would be more discreet of us to postpone our pronouncement on the correct relation between parliamentary procedure and the individual will of the responsible statesman until the beginning of the twenty-first century.

Stolypin's high-handed suspension of the legislative chambers for three days antagonized the entire St. Petersburg "public": the left and the center by flouting the constitution, the right by humiliating them and punishing their leaders.

Guchkov, Stolypin's unpredictable ally, also behaved hotheadedly. Although the whole law as enacted corresponded with the political program of his Octobrist majority in the Duma, he gave up the presidency of that body in a rage (or a politically advantageous fit of feigned indignation) and went off all the way to Mongolia. He aggravated the incident even further by slamming the door in this way, and made the Third Duma rather more like the disloyal Second. (Stolypin was very surprised by Guchkov's resignation, and hoped for his speedy return. Guchkov would surely never betray him!)

In the Petersburg "spheres" Stolypin's success in getting his own way was variously seen as the *ne plus ultra* of self-infatuated dictatorial arrogance, or as a remarkable piece of luck in turning defeat to his own advantage.

A fortnight later Stolypin had to defend his decision in the State Council, which knew its strength, for after another six weeks it automatically annulled the law by not ratifying it. Stolypin was forced to listen to charges of vindictive spite, hysterical and reckless high-handedness, of behaving like an autocrat rather than a Prime Minister, ruthlessly maneuvering to retain his position, playing upon the revolutionary instincts of the Duma, persecuting independent, enlightened conservatism, fostering the growth of bureaucratic servility. He had to hear, too, detailed legalistic protests and emotional accusations that he had torn holes in the Manifesto of 30 October and reissued the Vyborg appeal turned inside out. But none of these accusations could shake Stolypin, and he answered as courageously and eloquently as ever, ranging much wider and deeper than the interpellation formally required him to, never evading any of the detailed issues or the great principles involved in the contest. He never failed to answer juridical arguments in kind, copiously quoting Western experts on constitutional law and pointing to precedents for his action—even the British parliament had been dissolved by Gladstone. Taking cover behind the throne (though its occupant had already betrayed his trust), he maintained that the will of the sovereign was above criticism, that it alone determined whether a law was urgently necessary or could wait its turn, that to deny the monarch's right to dissolve the two chambers was to expose the very life of the country to danger at critical moments in the future. Because Russia as yet lacked a political culture and the national assembly was in its infancy, wrangling devoured all the time which should be given to work, and the legislative chambers were apt to tie Gordian knots which only the monarch could undo—although that was as far from parliamentarism as one could get. (He slid around the principles of the Manifesto which he had tried in vain to preserve.)

Stolypin stood his ground in the State Council and seemed to have preserved intact his power at the head of the government. But toward the middle of May, as the last weeks for his bill approached and it was clearly doomed to annulment, it was in the Duma, on which he now mainly counted, that the most destructive voices were raised, though Stolypin had presented the bill in the Duma's formulation, hoping to find a common language.

Stolypin began by answering the interpellation objecting to his procedures. He put forward new arguments one after another, until the case for the bill's defense became a much more elaborate structure than the bill itself. He took particular care to defend the legality of his action, which he expected to be the main target of attack, but he also appealed to his listeners' feelings, reminding them that the legislature, because of its inexperience and the friction between it and the government, caused suffering to millions of Russians and prevented their prayers' being answered by holding up legislative proposals. In the present case, that of the law on the western zemstvos:

> Will the feeling of national solidarity, which is the great strength of our neighbors to east and west, prevail?

He hinted that in suspending the legislature he had been defending the Duma's own decision. Confronting this intensely hostile audience, he as always took the initiative and attacked first:

> Does the government too have the right to pursue clear-cut policies and fight for its political ideals? Would it become the government merely to keep turning the administrative wheel mechanically and efficiently? As in all things, there were two possibilities: to avoid responsibility or to accept responsibility and all the blows it would bring, if that was the cost of saving the object of our belief.

The heartfelt declaration once made to the Tsar by way of private rebuke now rang out publicly from the tribune:

> People in authority can commit no greater sin than that of pusillanimous avoidance of responsibility. Discharging my responsibilities is the greatest happiness in my life.

These were to be the last words he ever spoke in public.

He sat down in the government box to listen to the debate. Had he once again succeeded in overcoming the resistance of his listeners, winning them over or at least leaving them less sure of themselves? The very first speech from the Octobrist faction, left leaderless by Guchkov's departure, promised nothing good. The speaker referred to "the Prime Minister's *personal* crisis," and described him as playing games with legality:

> Even desirable measures, if carried out in a dubiously legal way, represent a return to the past. Our historical sin is lack of respect for the idea of law, for the sanctity of the law. If they meet with no opposition such measures have a tendency to repeat themselves.

The hardest work is not always that of the speechmaker. It may be more difficult to hear oneself spoken against and be unable to reply. How easy it is for legislators to *give their country laws* when they are exempt from the task of implementing them—or else to interrupt the operation of the law in order to look without hindrance for a way out of the country's agonizing situation. How easy it is, from the lacquered tribunal of the twentieth century, to put the unhurriedly chewed and mooed-over cud of legality above the most crying and immediate need. How easy it is in jacket, tie, and cuff links to present the bill for our millennium of sin without ever mentioning the impassable forests, the frosts, the Khazars, the Tatars, the Livonian Knights, the Poles. All those who have ever harried us had, no doubt, a respect for law!

Next in order of his party's importance but first in eloquence, the brilliant Vasily Maklakov spoke. Subtlest of lawyers, this was the very man to batter down the legalistic barriers raised by the Prime Minister. But he sprang one of those surprises of which only great orators are capable—he magnanimously ceded the ground on which he was thought to be strongest:

> I do not in fact believe that formally Article 87 has been infringed.

So there! The lawyer to end all lawyers acknowledged himself that the law had not been broken. What then?

> But as well as avoiding outright breaches of the law, one must apply it conscientiously and loyally.

The thrust of Maklakov's argument was that Stolypin, while formally observing the law, had perverted its meaning. He spoke passionately, and before he was halfway through was unhesitatingly proclaiming the Prime Minister's perversion of the law a political crime, saying that he was a victim of megalomania and had the morality of a Hottentot, not of a European Christian (like the Kadets there present). In the tense atmosphere of the packed chamber, Maklakov, given at last the chance denied him for the past five years to avenge the Kadets, aimed insults at the ministerial box like resounding slaps. (While the new President of the Duma, Rodzyanko, intoxicated with his office, looked important and dared not interrupt.) Maklakov did not refrain from a fine forensic flourish to touch his listeners' hearts:

> What a salutary demonstration it would be if the Chairman of the Council of Ministers, whose great energy and determination we know so well, would for once humbly bend his head.

After which he delivered another slap in the face—referring to Russia as "Stolypin's manorial demesne."

He landed blow after blow. But how the Prime Minister's position had changed: somehow he could not even show that he was offended and leave the box, let alone answer back. Not because this was a repetition of old insults, but because in the new circumstances it would be ridiculous and would seem to show that his adversary was right.

> The psychology of our ruling class does not change. All our provincial governors are miniature Stolypins. To him that way of thinking has become second nature, and he could not understand that the Duma might adopt a different position. But to the State Duma, whether there are to be zemstvos in the western provinces or not is a trivial matter in comparison with the question of whether the rule of law is to exist in Russia.

Yes, Stolypin had made a grave miscalculation. He had underestimated the Duma, had not realized that for it the western zemstvos, the canton zemstvos, and every other kind of zemstvo, indeed the nation's interests generally, were of no significance just as long as the parliamentarians could get their own back for a whole string of defeats inflicted on them by the Prime Minister. He had wrongly supposed that the Duma would want the Zemstvo Act, taken over by him as amended by the Duma itself, that it would be allured by the prospect of a lower property qualification and of democratization, not to mention the chance to strengthen its position against the State Council—but no, it had rejected all these opportunities. And although the lawyer-Kadet had just acknowledged that the law had not been broken, he read the Prime Minister a lesson:

> Every statesman must know how to give way in obedience to the law.

Such was the intolerable balance of forces, such the price for the Zemstvo Act, that he had to accept the reproof with bowed head.

> Only recently the Prime Minister was the most popular man in Russia.

(Except that the Duma had never recognized it.)

> Only recently his opponents respected his policies even while condemning them.

(Though that was not what they had said at the time.)

> And now just a few years later . . .

A few years later, Stolypin was for the first time at a disadvantage in a Duma debate. For the first time there had been a breakdown, though the ground had not seemed so very treacherous. With their howling in his ears he had dragged all Russia out of devilish chaos, and his strength had not failed him. And now a minor reform affecting half a dozen provinces had swept him off his feet.

> It shows great arrogance and great temerity to put one's own ideals above the law. History sometimes forgives those titans who overturn the laws of their country and carry it along with them; but he who has no great services to boast of should be more modest.

Had he, then, not carried the country along with him? Had he, then, done nothing for it? How could anyone measure his labor from the sidelines—anyone who had forgotten or never appreciated how close the country had been to the abyss, never shared the muscular strain?

> For four years past we have never wearied of exposing the disgraceful behavior of the administration which he heads. . . . He is the victim of exaggerated confidence in the correctness of his views, a perfect example of the over-ambitious ruler. . . . Instead of genuinely pacifying the country he has fanned the flames to make himself indispensable. . . .

That his path had been strewn with bombs was forgotten—he was a careerist who had obtained his post by guile. It was no good answering, "Yes, but they crippled my children and yours were never touched."

It was an extraordinary feeling. All that he had built up in five years of steady and successful work seemed to be lying in ruins. His whole achievement was in doubt. If five years ago he had left them talking shop they would all have perished. He had saved them with his firm hand and was now condemned to experience insecurity for the first time. Yes, he had made a mistake. He had lost his temper when he need not have done so. He had wanted to teach the arrogant State Council a lesson. . . .

Then, suddenly, one of those startling sophisms that distinguish the great orator from the small—Maklakov, the Kadet, cries out as though this was the sorest of his wounds:

> To think what has been done with the monarchic idea! I am just as much a monarchist as the Prime Minister.

(The Duma is taken aback.)

> I consider it madness to oppose monarchy where its roots are strong. But this champion of the monarchy has involved the sovereign's name in his conflict with the State Council. . . . That is an improper procedure. . . . A dubious action. . . . He tendered his resignation to obtain an unfair advantage. . . .

The ingenious sophisms, the throb in the courtroom voice were not meant for the Duma. His words soared over Rodzyanko's samovarlike person . . . higher . . . higher . . . they could not but reach *those* ears, din into them that the Prime Minister's dismissal was inevitable. He had risen to speak ostensibly in defense of the Duma, and brilliantly contrived to drive a wedge between the unworthy minister and the great Tsar. Only thus could the Duma overthrow Stolypin—in alliance with the invisible monarch and with the invisible "spheres." Having attained his chief aim, which would have been beyond the reach of the Duma alone even if it had voted with one voice, Maklakov now permitted himself a crowning insult:

> For statesmen *of this type* the Russian language has an expressive word—*vremenshchik* [timeserver]. He had his time—and his time is past. He may remain in office a little longer, but, gentlemen, we are witnessing his death throes.

He had judged his stroke well. He knew well that, having struck his victim and spat in his face, he would not be challenged to a duel, which would be the final proof of Stolypin's bankruptcy.

What an enormous effect a single speech by an apparently unarmed man can have: he contributed nothing in the way of argument, he added no makeweight to the scale. A nimble tongue, skillfully playing on the well-known weaknesses of his listeners, was enough to topple the giant who had wrestled with all Russia, enough to sweep onto the rubbish heap a government which was still far from exhausted.

Next on the rostrum was another monarchist, the hysterically erratic Purishkevich, with a crafty attempt to wring applause from his eternal enemies on the left, and to strike the fatal blow from where Stolypin least expected it.

There were insults enough here too: Stolypin had behaved like a coward, shielding himself with the sacred name of the Emperor, he had undermined the authority of Russia's autocratic ruler, he had not shown firmness in dealing with the disorders in Saratov province but flirted with revolutionaries(!), he was authoritarian, he did not understand Russia's political ideals, he was suffering from a failure of intelligence and will . . .

> But presumably he will depart someday!

(Pause for applause.) Purishkevich did not recognize Stolypin's right to call himself a Russian nationalist. Stolypin's nationalism was the most pernicious trend that had ever existed in Russia—he encouraged the smaller nationalities to hope for self-determination and a separate existence, he wanted to give self-government to the border regions, and this was insane, because the non-Russian peoples of the Empire could not have self-government on an equal footing with the Russian population of the heartland. The western territories had not asked for elected zemstvos—that was the Duma's idea, and to please the Duma the Prime Minister had introduced, with the Duma's amendments, a law which was disastrous for the Russian population and a triumph for the Poles and the leftists—Social Democrats, Socialist Revolutionaries, and separatists would flood the western zemstvos.

Not everyone has to endure even once in his lifetime a day of slow and public torture, with no chance to defend himself. But the staggering, the dizzying, the shattering thing is to be attacked with equal ferocity from opposite sides. The rebukes of each successive orator repeat and add weight to those of his predecessor. From all sides come an uninterrupted sequence of unbridled insults—and suddenly your confidence, which has never before wavered, is shaken. Blow after blow rains on you and softens your resistance. The familiar and unquestionable objective suddenly dips, twists, splits, and a fearful doubt comes over you: was it so fine and so uniquely important after all? You ask yourself not just whether it was worth risking your neck for that law but perhaps whether earlier, too, you had not seen things as they were.

Eager orators followed in quick succession—and not just ten, not just fifteen of them. The Third Duma had seized its chance to recoup all that all three Dumas had lost.

Stolypin heard from a socialist that he had drowned the Russian people in their own blood, that even its worst enemy could not have done so much harm to the Russian autocracy, that the law on the western zemstvos was the apex of a "pyramid of reprisals."

Another Kadet, a quite prominent one, asked:

> Where are the enormous services to his country which would entitle the Prime Minister to say that he is the vehicle of the national idea? We don't remember his Sadowa or his Sedan.

(Now they were even blaming him for not arranging a war.)

> His pretension that his ideas are uniquely correct for the Russian people is an affront to national sentiment.

From another rightist:

> Prime Minister, repent, approach the throne to beg forgiveness, for you have misled the supreme power.

It was as though all the hatred festering beneath the surface had suddenly burst through, as though they had all been just waiting for the chance to get their own back from the man who for so many years had been too much for them.

Some spoke for him, but many fewer, and they could not quiet the self-doubt in his heart. His feeling was one of utter defeat—not just over the zemstvo law but in all that he had tried to do in the five years of his administration, in the hopes and plans of a lifetime.

He had lived with the feeling that he had achieved a great deal. Now he saw that he had done nothing, that it was all dust and ashes.

Speakers came and went, the sitting dragged on into the evening, till midnight, beyond midnight, and only then did they give the floor—and then only to speak on voting procedure—to two western peasants whom Rodzyanko had refused to call all day, although the discussion would best have begun with them.

> You have gagged us. But we are very glad that we too are to have zemstvos. We don't care whether it's under Article 87 or any other—if we'd waited for you and your reforms, we should be waiting forever.

But it was too late; the deputies had no ears for that sort of thing, and it was high time to vote. Two hundred voted against Stolypin, eighty for. Only the Russian nationalists remained loyal.

(The bill sank from view, and it was only after Stolypin's death that it was passed without difficulty. The western zemstvos shortly proved very useful in the war years.)

Keen noses at court had sensed as early as April that the Emperor had cooled toward Stolypin once and for all, and was indeed full of hostility toward him. The "spheres" infused the atmosphere around him with doom. Seemingly all that was needed was a respectable excuse for retiring him to a post without influence. One possibility was the newly invented Vice-Regency of Eastern Siberia—why not send him to the part of the world he loved best?

Stolypin could simply have yielded, meekly departed, and (as we now know) saved his life and lived on to be recalled when Russia had need of him again. (And how sorely she would need him! In July 1914 to avert the war. At Petrograd and Mogilev in 1917 to prevent the debacle.)

But just as after the explosion on Aptekarsky Island he had refused to be bullied by revolutionaries, so now he would not take the weakling's way out under pressure from parliamentarians. He had to do his duty to the end.

After the Aptekarsky Island incident he said:

> I have been very remiss in not writing a memorandum for the Emperor to help prevent any doubt and confusion in the event of my death. I must do so without fail in case a second attempt is made.

Whether anything of the sort was written in anticipation of the second, the fourth, or the sixth attempt we do not know—it is doubtful whether from the time of the explosion and the journey under the Neva bridges to the Winter Palace he ever had a whole day free for it. The day's tasks were always urgent, the daily round was so demanding, and thought for the future could only patiently wait.

But after the defeats in the State Council and the Duma, Stolypin did feel ready to draw up and dictate a broad program—one which he had had in his head for a long time: the second stage, and a direct continuation, of his first, 1906, program, which he had expounded to the inattentive ears of the Second Duma, and which few had understood or appreciated. During the past sixty months the program had steadily become reality, growing in practice and in the author's mind, imperceptibly and inaudibly, as trees grow ring by ring. Only one who could take in the whole scene at a glance could discern what must be done next: the healing of the legs, the lower limbs, the peasantry, was proceeding splendidly; the time had now come to heal the bureaucracy.

Stolypin's second great program, dictated in May 1911 (punctuated with such phrases as "And this, all of it, can be done if only God so wills"), was arranged, accordingly, by branches of the state administration.

For the last year he had had in operation an advisory Council for Local Government, in which legislative proposals were drafted by central government officials, governors, marshals of the gentry, mayors, and zemstvo people sitting together. The object of this council, popularly known as the Pre-Duma, was to ensure that laws would be critically examined by practical people and not just be the creation of bureaucrats. Under the new program local administrative matters were assigned to a separate ministry, which would take over all agencies responsible for supervising them from the Ministry of the Interior (leaving it only with security, and relieving the police of functions which did not properly belong to them). Drawing on the experience of state governments in the United States, the new legislation would broaden the rights of the zemstvos. The zemstvos would take complete control of emergency food supplies (a new procedure to deal with famine was to be introduced: the better-off would be fed on credit, the physically strong in return for socially useful work, and the sick and disabled by charity). A special State Bank would be established to provide the zemstvos with credits for road building and other public works. Higher educational establishments would become the responsibility of the provincial zemstvos, middle schools would pass to the county zemstvos, and primary schools to the canton zemstvos (which the Duma would not for the present allow to be established). The property qualification for candidates in local elections was to be reduced by ninety percent, so that smallholders and workers with a little real estate could stand for election.

A new Ministry of Labor, with oversight of all enterprises, was to be created. Its tasks were to study the position of the working class in the West and draft laws to improve that of Russian workers, and to make the rootless proletarian a partner in the constructive work of the state and the zemstvos. There would be a Ministry of Social Insurance, a Ministry of Nationalities (on the basis of equal rights for all of them), a Ministry of Cults—all of them; and as for the Orthodox, the Synod would be converted into a council attached to the ministry, and plans for the restoration of the patriarchate would be worked out. Stolypin's belief was that the Russian people's religious needs were not being fully served, and that it was necessary to expand considerably the network of religious education, making the seminary an intermediate stage and ensuring that all priests graduated from an academy. The zemstvos and the municipal authorities would receive financial help from the Ministry of Health for the provision of free medical treatment to the rural population and the workers, the control of epidemics, and measures to improve the qualifications of medical personnel. Finally, there would be yet another new and independent ministry to survey and exploit mineral deposits.

To carry out their work all these ministries would need substantial budget allocations. Russia was unimaginably rich, but its budgetary policies were so misconceived that it relied partly on loans from poorer Western countries. And although the raw materials for them were abundant, the metal and mechanical engineering industries lagged far behind those of Western countries. Property in Russia was assessed for taxation at much less than its real value and its real yield, and foreign industrialists had no difficulty in exporting capital from the country. Correcting that state of affairs, increasing the duty on vodka and wines, and introducing a progressive income tax (the less-well-off would be practically exempt, and such indirect taxes as remained would not be high) would treble the state's revenues and provide the means of financing the program. The intention was to seek foreign loans only at the initial stage, and only in order to prospect for minerals and to build roads and railways, so that in fifteen or twenty years' time (by 1927–32) the transport network in European Russia would no longer be inferior to that of the Central Powers. The Ministry of Roads and Railways would finalize the appropriate plans—including canals and other waterways in its calculations—in 1912. Then the intention was to invite private concessionaires, Jewish banks, and joint-stock companies to participate. (The lifting of restrictions on the Jews was an essential part of Stolypin's program.) It was, however, expected that the operations of the State Bank would gradually supersede those of private banks.

The salaries of all state servants, the police, teachers, priests, and railway and postal officials were to be increased to keep up with the cost of living. (This would make it possible to attract educated people into these occupations.) Free primary education had already been widely introduced in 1908 and was expected to become universal by 1922. The number of intermediate educational institutions would be raised to 5,000, that of higher schools to 1,500. Minimal fees for higher education would give greater opportunities to the poorer classes. The number of scholarships was to be increased twenty times over in all universities. At the summit an academy would be established to train people for the higher government posts. This academy would offer two- or three-year courses in faculties corresponding to the various branches of the economy, and there would be precise regulations governing admission: each faculty would admit only the ablest graduates, with a knowledge of at least two foreign languages, from specified higher schools—the Faculty of Mineral Utilization, for instance, would take applicants from mining institutes, the Military Faculty graduates of military academies, the Faculty of Religious Studies graduates from theological academies. A dazzling array of specialists and experts would take their place in the Russian government machine. Pulling strings would no longer carry untrained incompetents to the top. No longer would the Tsar need to rack his brains and seek advice from his courtiers to find the right ministers. He would take them from a list submitted by the Council of Ministers. The Ministry of Nationalities would be headed by a public figure with influence in non-Russian circles. Stolypin even envisaged legalization of the Social Democrats. Only terrorists would still be outlawed.

The program also embraced foreign policy. Its basic assumption was that Russia had no need of territorial expansion, and should concentrate on assimilating what it already possessed, putting the state machine in order, and improving the condition of the population. Russia therefore needed a long period of peace. Developing the Tsar's initiative in establishing the Hague Peace Tribunal, Stolypin drew up in May 1911 a plan for the creation of an International Parliament, representing all countries, with its permanent seat in one of the smaller European states. Its commissions would function all the year round. It would have attached to it an International Statistical Bureau, which would collect and publish annually information for all states on the size and movement of populations, the development of industry and trade, natural resources, vacant land, export and import potential, living standards, the number of workers in industry and agriculture, the number of unemployed, average wages, incomes of particular sections of the population, taxes, internal indebtedness, savings. On the basis of this data the Parliament would be able to come to the aid of countries in difficulties, look out for sudden spurts of overproduction, shortages, signs of overpopulation—and Russia intended to cooperate in appropriate aid programs. An International Bank funded by the member states would offer credits in difficult cases.

The International Parliament would also set a limit on the armaments of each country and outlaw completely weapons which would cause suffering to the civilian population at large. When wars are waged with weapons of mass destruction there is the additional danger that established forms of government will be easily replaced by worse ones. The great powers might not, of course, agree to this system, but if they did not they would only damage their own standing, and the International Parliament would be able to achieve something even without their help.

Stolypin attached particular importance to relations with the United States, on which he placed his main hopes of support for the International Parliament. The United States had no cause to fear or envy Russia. Nowhere were the interests of the two countries in conflict. An aversion to Russia and the Russian people, and a belief that everyone in Russia was oppressed and that there was no freedom there, had been created by relentless Jewish propaganda. Stolypin intended to invite to Russia a large group of senators, congressmen, and journalists.

Forced retirement might get in the way of his plans, but he hoped to have the support of Maria Fyodorovna and, even if he were dismissed, to be recalled shortly afterward. The State Council and the Duma might oppose, *would* oppose his program with all their might, lacking as they were in political vision.

This program for the reconstruction of Russia by 1927–32, perhaps even more ambitious than the reforms of Aleksandr II, would have rendered Russia unrecognizable, enabling it to make full use of its natural and human resources for the first time.

(In the summer of 1911 it lay in a desk drawer at his country house near Kovno. After his death a government commission arrived there and, in the presence of witnesses, took it away, never to be seen again. His project vanished, was never published, discussed, exhibited, or indeed recovered—all that survived was the testimony of the man who helped Stolypin to draft it. The communists may possibly have found it and used a distorted version of some of Stolypin's ideas for their own purposes. Ironically, their first Five-Year Plan coincided exactly with what would have been the last five-year period of Stolypin's project.)

That summer, Pyotr Arkadievich was wearier than he had ever been, more subdued—and more affectionate to his children. In moments of depression he felt apprehensive, full of foreboding of his own death and of some catastrophe that awaited Russia. The first he had never feared, the second he dreaded. He complained wearily to Minister Timashev of his helplessness in the struggle with irresponsible influences at court. As he put it, "They'll go on living a few years longer on the capital I've accumulated, as camels live on their reserves of fat, then there will be a general collapse." He told Kryzhanovsky, his deputy at the Ministry of the Interior, "When I get back from Kiev we'll reorganize the police" (as envisaged in his program). In August he traveled to St. Petersburg for the last time, presided over the Council of Ministers in the Yelagin Palace, had his last meeting with Guchkov, to discuss ways of speeding up the passage through the Duma of a law on pensions for disabled rankers in the armed forces. In St. Petersburg he was warned that the Finnish revolutionaries had apparently sentenced him to death.

As if there were not enough of them already . . .

When the Tsar went to Kiev to enjoy several days of lavish celebrations, it did not occur to him to leave his Prime Minister behind to concentrate on serious matters, instead of wearing him like an extra shiny button among all his equerries and chamberlains.

This in spite of the fact that they were unveiling a monument to Aleksandr II to mark the fiftieth anniversary of the first great reform.

Stolypin was very sad as he took leave of his family, his Kovno neighbors, and his friends. He said that he had never been more reluctant to go away. (Though this trip made some sense inasmuch as Kiev was the most important town in the western region and it was necessary to recruit support for the new zemstvos there. Moreover, it was in Kiev in particular that the light of Russian nationalism shone most brightly in those years.)

For some reason the train stopped as soon as it left the station and could not get going again for half an hour.

Perhaps because he had not begun his journey from St. Petersburg he took with him not a gendarme officer but only a special aide, Staff Officer Yesaulov, not as a bodyguard but to assist his secretary in arranging interviews and official visits and with correspondence.

The security arrangements for the Kiev festivities (to which the Tsar had looked forward for so long, and which had therefore been the subject of much discussion at court) were altogether unusual: they were made not by the local authorities, which would have been normal, but by General Kurlov, who had usurped and monopolized this responsibility. The Tsar was greatly impressed by his zeal. Beginning early in the spring of 1911, Kurlov had toured the places on the Emperor's route and had been given authority over local departments in those regions. This had outraged the governor-general of Kiev, Fyodor Trepov, who had protested to Stolypin and offered his resignation. If the Emperor had been told about this threat it might have brought about a regularization of the arrangements (and things would have gone differently) but it would undoubtedly have cast a shadow on his pleasurable anticipations. Stolypin spared his childlike sovereign and persuaded Trepov to withdraw his resignation. So then security was taken out of the hands of a local official who knew everyone and everything in the place, and given to an outsider. Moreover, Kurlov was subordinate only to Dedyulin, the palace commandant, who attached to him Colonel Spiridovich as liaison officer for matters concerning the protection of the Emperor's person.

Kurlov was nominally Stolypin's subordinate, his deputy, but was now master of the police and the gendarmerie throughout the empire, independently of Stolypin—who preferred it that way. His mind was busy elsewhere and he had no time for police matters. Kurlov himself, his methods and his views, were diametrically opposed to those of the Prime Minister, and it was obvious that the man never took a professional decision without asking what was in it for himself. He was rather like a sharp-snouted boar challengingly standing his ground on his little trotters, and charging to rip his opponent. But he was firmly rooted, he had connections everywhere—with all of Stolypin's enemies, among others. This was no typical hushed and waxen bureaucrat: he had an enormous appetite for the life of a carefree gentleman. Carousals in restaurants were for him the measure of his success in life, and so in addition to his profession he was engaged in commerce and all sorts of shady deals and was up to his ears in debt. He was not clever. It was he who had swallowed Voskresensky's bait, released him from prison to act as a double agent, narrowly escaped being blown up with him on Astrakhan Street, and then fabricated accusations against other police generals.

But it would have required too much additional effort for Stolypin to rid himself of this tick. He had great tasks ahead of him and could not waste his strength on such things. It would all come out right in the end without any help from him.

The palace commandant, Dedyulin, magus and impresario of the celebrations, belonged to the "spheres"—that chain of muddy puddles—and was one of those who hated Stolypin. Knowing better than anybody how the Emperor had cooled toward his Prime Minister, Dedyulin could not wait to make this coolness obvious to the world at large—something he would find very enjoyable! The court was packed with experienced people who could detect the faintest sign of the Emperor's displeasure, add up the most elusive hints—but there was no need for any of that. It was made clear in the crudest way that Stolypin was no longer worthy of respect, or even of attention. From the moment he arrived in Kiev on 9 September he was ostentatiously and humiliatingly squeezed out of the court program and was not given even routine personal protection, let alone a bodyguard befitting his position.

He was assigned rooms on the easily accessible ground floor of the governor-general's house, with windows less than a meter from the ground and looking out on an almost unprotected garden, but Kurlov would not allow Yesaulov to post a gendarme outside—a superfluous measure, he said. Official personages and ordinary citizens, even peasants, turned up to sign the visitors' book in the entrance hall, a few steps from the Prime Minister's rooms and open to anyone who wished to enter, without a single officer or even an ordinary policeman on duty there. He was unguarded during his visits to the Cathedral of St. Sophia (to pray for the royal family) and to the Metropolitan, and also when he received deputations from the gentry, the zemstvos, and the municipality. Stolypin went on working whenever he had time free from ceremonies, governing the country from Kiev.

Bogrov had begun his little game—warning the police that an attempt on Stolypin's life was being planned—on 8 September, but no one informed the Prime Minister of this, and no one in the Kurlov-Verigin-Spiridovich-Kulyabko gang made any attempt to check whether the despised Stolypin was guarded or not.

When it became widely known that he had no guard, patriots volunteered to protect him. They were asked for lists of would-be bodyguards and submitted two thousand names. The lists were held back for confirmation and returned with some names crossed out. By that time it was too late. Yesaulov had difficulty in obtaining a policeman to stand guard in the lobby.

On the 11th, still unaware of the danger he was in, Stolypin rode to the station to join in welcoming the royal couple. He was not given one of the palace carriages, the police department could not afford a car (though it could afford Kurlov's drinking parties), so he and Yesaulov were compelled to share a cab, an open barouche, and travel without any bodyguard at all. The cab was stopped more than once by police officers who did not recognize Stolypin and would not let him through to join the guarded palace procession. Similarly, when the cortege began to leave no one had been told to look after a mere Prime Minister, and Yesaulov succeeded only with great difficulty in getting the Prime Minister's carriage placed behind the duty aide-de-camp's troika.

When the mayor of Kiev, Dyakov, heard of Stolypin's plight he sent him his own two-horse carriage for the rest of his stay.

It was around this time that Professor Rein implored Stolypin to wear a bulletproof vest under his uniform. Stolypin refused: it would be no good against a bomb. For some reason he always thought of himself being killed by a bomb, not by a revolver.

Neither on 12 September nor on the 13th, nor in the Merchants' Garden, did Stolypin have any idea that Bogrov had reported to the police or know anything about the information he had given . . .

Bogrov's ingenuity was uncalled for. He could never have imagined how defenseless the whole of imperial Russia was against a single individual—himself! In the first day or two, without waiting for the gala performance at the theater, he could have taken forty shots at Stolypin.

It was only on 14 September that a warning note came from Trepov, followed by a visit from Kurlov. Kurlov had really come to discuss official business generally and to get signatures to a long honors list. Somewhere in the middle of all the rest was the warning from secret agent Bogrov, in view of which the Prime Minister would do better to wait for a car from the security department.

Stolypin did not take it very seriously. Had they found a bomb? No.

One question it would never have occurred to him to ask was whether the police were inviting this secret informer to assist in surveillance. That was categorically forbidden, as Kurlov knew, and had never been done.

In any case, Stolypin was being hurried off to the day's festivities—maneuvers and horse racing. Because he had no place in the palace procession they wanted him to hurry along there an hour and a half in advance, before the road was closed to traffic. Stolypin refused to waste an hour and a half in that way.

In deference to court etiquette, he spent the last day of his tireless life on uninterrupted ceremonies.

Those accompanying Stolypin to the theater had no tickets of admission until the last moment (receiving them, probably, no sooner than Bogrov). Yesaulov was not placed next to Stolypin in the front row, left aisle, but wedged in the middle of the third row, and when he tried to claim it he found even this seat occupied by a colonel in the Bulgarian party. After a great deal of argument Yesaulov cleared up the misunderstanding and was given a seat on the right aisle. So Stolypin had none of his aides near him, let alone any sort of bodyguard.

He could have joined Trepov in his box, but refused, regarding excessive precautions as pusillanimous.

As he entered the theater Yesaulov asked Kulyabko whether the plotters had been arrested, and was told, "They are holding their conference tomorrow."

Stolypin also asked Kurlov whether there was any news of the plotters. Kurlov replied that he did not know, but would find out in the intermission. By then the curtain was about to rise.

In the first intermission Kurlov discovered nothing, and perhaps did not try to. Stolypin stopped thinking about it. He walked about the pit alone.

He had plenty to think about during those absurdly wasted September days when he should have been working at the beginning of the autumn in which the fate of his reforms would be decided.

In the second act Kokovtsov came along to say goodbye. He, lucky fellow, was leaving for St. Petersburg and his ministry.

"Take me with you," Stolypin said jokingly. "I feel out of place. We aren't wanted here—they could have managed very well without us."

Kokovtsov had always been an awkward and self-willed minister. As he saw it, the Finance Minister's role was not to expand the budget, to power the advance of Russia, but to curb expenditure, to save money. Stolypin was always having to overcome his resistance. But just at that moment seeing a man who had work to do and knew how to do it was like a breath of fresh air.

In the second as in the first intermission Stolypin did not leave the stuffy hall. There was nowhere to go if he had wanted to. He stood with his back to the orchestra, propped up on his elbows against the barrier, and facing the aisle. He was wearing a white, summer-weight frock coat (but felt as cramped and hot as though he were in armor).

Very few people remained in the auditorium; the whole length of the aisle was empty. Along it came, snakelike, a long thin person in tails, a black presence, standing out from the summery gathering, quite unlike the rest of the audience.

Stolypin stood chatting to a featherheaded courtier, who didn't yet know that talking to and being seen with this particular Prime Minister was a waste of time. No one more important had come near him.

They both simultaneously realized that the man almost upon them had murder in mind. He had a long face, and looked both suspicious and witty (such people often are witty). A young Jew.

As they realized it, the courtier plunged to one side to save himself.

While Stolypin removed his elbows from the barrier and rushed forward, hands outstretched, to grapple with the terrorist as he had grappled with others before him.

Bogrov had already produced his black Browning. His face twitched wryly, not in triumph, not in surprise, but as though some unspoken witticism had occurred to him.

A burning sensation. A jolt. His back was against the barrier again.

Another burn. Another jolt.

Stolypin stood steadily as though the shots had pinned him to the barrier.

The terrorist's black back was wriggling away up the aisle.

No one tried to pursue him.

Somebody shouted, "Stop him!" That cracked voice sounds like Count Frederiks's, yes it is. I saw him somewhere around here.

Stolypin stood there. He could not move, but standing still was easy enough.

They had stalked him so long—and finally caught him.

He still felt nothing, he stood as though untouched, but he knew that this was death.

The expression on the murderer's sensitive face had wounded him as much as the bullet.

Stolypin stood there, still alone. Professor Rein hurried up to him. Now a great bloodstain was spreading and getting stickier over his white frock coat.

There was a warm patch under the stain.

Stolypin raised his eyes to the right. He was aware of someone up above there—or was looking for someone he remembered seeing there.

Ah, there He was: standing at the parapet of his box and staring down in surprise.

What would happen to . . . ?

Stolypin tried to make the sign of the cross in his direction, but his right hand hung limply and refused to rise. His ill-fated right hand, crippled long ago, and now pierced again.

What would become of Russia . . . ?

Then he raised his left hand and fervently, slowly, deliberately, blessed his sovereign with it.

That was all. He could stand no longer.

A fatal pistol shot was no new event in Russian history.

But there was never one so fraught with consequences—for the whole of the twentieth century.

Neither at that moment nor later did the Tsar go down to the wounded man.

Didn't come to him. Didn't come near him.

But what those bullets had slain was the dynasty.

They were the opening shots of the fusillade at Yekaterinburg.

[6 6]

What can one say about state service? It is the most secure form of service, and the most rewarding of occupations, if you have the correct attitude. To serve the state is to bathe in the favors showered on you by your betters, and to rise gradually to their level. It is a stream of gratifying awards, and of even more welcome money, sometimes over and above your salary. If you know what is what.

Sitting down to a lavish spread among friends and colleagues, you could chuckle about it. Let's give the office sparrow his crumbs! A suckling pig to myself or don't ask me to dine!

Peter the Great, inaugurating the Russian state machine, bequeathed to us the great Table of Ranks: this is the way to the top, and its military and civil lanes ascend in parallel terraced steps so that there can be no dispute about anyone's status. The graduations on each of the stairways elevated above the amorphous Russian people are strictly comparable, and everyone in the state service has an exact understanding of his relative importance, the degree of authority he can exercise, the measure of deference he owes to his superiors, and his prospects of further advancement. The man who has interiorized these laws most successfully will ascend most easily toward the highest offices in the state.

But these laws should not be understood to mean anything so simple as that patient merit must have its reward. The patient submit too patiently to straining in the shafts, grow old and stale ambling too gently along, and never achieve anything notable in life. Truckling to superiors is a necessary condition of advancement, but you will never rise high enough by toadying alone: you must be capable of decisive action too. (Napoleon's rise illustrates this very well.) Again, perfect knowledge and unerring application of the laws are a necessary but not a sufficient condition of success. You must also be able to pull out and display the right clause at the right time. Knowledge of the laws arms you with a powerful set of teeth. You bare them when you should at enemies, competitors, inspectors, and if need be (heaven forbid!), against your judges—and every now and then, just to make sure they know your strength, you give those above you a little nip (but not, of course, anyone on whom the sun of the Tsar's favor never sets). Bold actions of this sort, in discreet measure, can greatly facilitate your movement upward.

On the lower rungs of the career ladder you may, because of circumstances or your own youthful inexperience, take false steps. Inspired by hopes of glory too naïvely conceived, you may make the mistake of beginning your career as a Guards officer, careless of difficulties in your way (even, perhaps, the disadvantage of low stature). You correct your mistake later by going through the Military Law Academy and becoming an army lawyer. But correcting errors always means delay, and you are already running late. You molder for thirteen years in a provincial procurator's office, you are forty-three and not nearly halfway up the ladder, in an overpopulated sector thronged with unsuccessful petty officials, all your knowledge of ways and means is of no avail, your thrusting energies will never be applied, those lofty seats will never be placed beneath you, the blessings you deserve never be poured out before you.

Till one day, despondently pacing your procurator's office at Vologda, with a good view of provincial misery outside, and counting for the ten thousandth time the links in the chain of your misfortunes, you are suddenly visited by a wonderful thought, one that must precipitately transform your whole career: was not Pleve himself, the mighty Minister of the Interior, once a procurator in Vologda? How then can the Vologda district court function a minute longer unless someone hangs portraits of all former Vologda procurators on its walls? And how else can you obtain the estimable portrait of the generally beloved minister for your gallery except by sending a special envoy to St. Petersburg to see him? And who more suitable for this task than the originator of this idea, me, Kurlov?

It all happens as planned! Kurlov is sent on his mission, Pleve feels flattered, the portrait itself is carefully wrapped to travel by train, but it will not be nailed to the wall by the loving hands of the initiator of the project (if indeed the gallery is ever established), for the all-powerful minister looks closely at the overripe Vologda procurator—a short figure with a small head, close-cropped hair, only moderately fierce mustaches, and a decidedly modest clean-shaven chin, very unsure of himself, but very honest, very loyal—and *unexpectedly* asks the question: "Look, we're short of people. Wouldn't you like to move from local justice to administration?" Kurlov's bags were already packed, and from 1903 he began his quiet ascent, becoming first vice-governor of Kursk, then governor of Minsk.

Everything was fine. One elegant somersault and he could have begun his surefooted, energetic climb up the higher rungs of the ladder, if only all who served the ladder and its cult had not been overtaken by a dark and dangerous time in which not just the careers but the very lives of high-placed public servants were under threat—as when, for instance, they had to take command of large parties of soldiers sent to defend big private estates. (This brings us back to Napoleon. What was Napoleon? A man who in spite of his small stature had an iron will and the ability to manipulate great masses of men. Finding shelter and comfort in an endangered nest of gentlefolk, and calming the fears of its fair inhabitants with a display of sangfroid, resolution, and profound understanding of the situation, also, of course, has its romantic side.) The creator of the

Table could never have foreseen such a perilous and troublous time; the rungs of the great ladder became treacherous, some people fell even from the topmost rung and broke their necks, like the never to be forgotten Pleve himself, others slipped down a rung or two, and the rest could not plant their feet on the next rung as freely and confidently as before; they had once known that nothing stood above them except the will of a superior, but now they had to be forever squinting at the general public and adjusting their stance to please it, or at least so as not to disgust it too much.

Kurlov, however, was so circumspect, so conscious of his adaptability in dealing with others that he felt capable of rising even with two contradictory laws in operation: you had to be a loyal servant of the throne and also *persona grata* with the liberals. Thus, when he took over the governorship of Minsk and ordered the dispersal of the wild young people, most of them members of the Bund, he was quick to let the world see that he was a staunch supporter of complete equality for the Jews. (The Jewish question was the master key to liberal hearts.) If he kept a couple of Cossack squadrons around the governor's residence, he did not fail to explain to a deputation of local residents that this was only because it was easier to stable horses there, and that in any case this came within the purview of the military, not his own. If troops guarding the station opened fire on an ugly crowd, you had to forestall public abuse of the governor by court-martialing the shooters. (The terrorists were not at all grateful for Kurlov's tact and hurled a bomb at him anyway, but it did not explode: as it was later discovered, von Kotten had removed the detonator with his own hands in good time.) As a result of this episode, he had momentarily lost his footing and the governorship of Minsk, but now he could make all on the right think of him as a victim of the influences of 30 October. However, when he was appointed to another governorship, this time of loyalist Kiev, he refused to be harnessed to the rickety wagon of the right, and indeed outraged it by supporting the enchanting General Sukhomlinov, who was accused of Judophilia.

There are no ladders too slippery for a truly gifted public servant to climb, no tangles so thorny that he cannot emerge unscratched, just as long as he keeps an eye out for himself and maintains his sangfroid. In the Russian bureaucratic hierarchy Kurlov knew many such operators; it was they who held the state together. It would, Kurlov thought, have been held together more firmly if all in high office always acted in concert, realized the need for complete cohesion at the top, stood up for one another in difficult situations, and never jeopardized each other by improper rebukes, as when Dmitri Trepov blurted out his accusation that Lopukhin and the Police Department had not allocated the necessary funds for the protection of Grand Duke Sergei Aleksandrovich. (And how heartlessly he had trampled on Lopukhin afterward, with no regard at all for his rank or the prestige of his department, just for giving away Azef. Lopukhin's destruction was contrary to all the laws because there was no penalty for divulging state secrets and no law punishing improper dealings with secret agents.) We all grieve for the Grand Duke and respect his memory, honor his saintly widow, who visited the murderer in prison—but that does not give us the right ever to besmirch one another's reputations.

Not every bureaucrat, however, possesses the special gift which Kurlov knew himself to have: he did not passively wait for advantageous transfers or vacancies to arise. Whether it was vacant or not he marked out the post which it would be good for him to occupy next, and pressed his claim to it. The tenderhearted Durnovo, when Minister of the Interior, had promised to move him from rebellious and Jewish Minsk to the prosperous and more important province of Nizhni Novgorod. Alas, Durnovo himself had fallen from office in the stormy early months of 1906, and the ruffianly parvenu Stolypin, who succeeded him (quite irregularly soaring to ministerial office directly from the same sort of gubernatorial post as Kurlov's own—and he was two years younger than Kurlov!), did not know, or pretended not to know, and did not want to carry out Durnovo's promises. Kurlov's information proved correct, and a vacancy duly occurred at Nizhni Novgorod, but someone else was appointed to it.

This was a fateful moment. He would, after all, be serving under this upstart from now on. He could not let himself be humiliated. He must forcibly extract what had been promised him. He must put himself in a strong position from the start. Besides, just staying on in revolutionary Minsk in those terrible months would mean ruining his career one way or another, losing his reputation and perhaps his life. There was nothing for it but to apply for leave.

At any other time it would have been suicidal. If you deliberately interrupted your service it could be forever. But at such an uncertain time the most sensible thing to do was probably to stand aside and see what happened. If there was to be general collapse it was better to get out from under the endangered edifice in good time. If the country recovered, fresh vacancies could be expected. (Kurlov, of course, did not retire completely, because he held the court rank of chamberlain.)

Being particularly farsighted, Kurlov used his prolonged leave of absence for a lengthy holiday abroad, in *la douce France*, needless to say. That was the vantage point from which he followed developments in Russia.

Here we must remember that although the bureaucratic hierarchy is an organic part of the Creation, the skeletal frame of mankind, the stone foundations on which the world firmly stands, it is not the vibrant vital tissue, not the living water that surges between the piers. Money is. Money gives the same incomparable power as high position in the state, but with it you enjoy also complete personal independence, you live in a rosy mist of anticipated delights. It is wrong in principle to let your life be bounded by service: service is merely the condition on which you enjoy life's gifts.

Realizing the two-sidedness of existence while still very young, Kurlov had given careful thought to his selection of a wife and married a factory owner's daughter with a large dowry. Not only could he now afford things beyond the means of many who had risen higher in the service, but he had obtained the moral right to watch and grieve over the probable demise of Imperial Russia at a comfortable distance, from Paris or Nice, while enjoying in the flesh the good things of this world. Even if there was a total collapse, he could, if he lived modestly, stay on in Europe for many years.

The country seemed to have gone mad. Fortresses and regiments mutinied. Whole provinces were up in arms. By way of climax the scene was lit by the glare of the unprecedented bomb outrage on Aptekarsky Island (which Stolypin, ever fortune's favorite, survived). But by the autumn of 1906 anarchy had undoubtedly lost ground. It was time for Kurlov to return to Russia and to duty, to continue his ascent in the Ministry of the Interior. It did, however, mean paying homage to the very same Stolypin.

When their relations got off to a bad start, Kurlov chose the course not of sycophancy but of unremitting pressure masked by businesslike politeness. He was inspired to behave like this by the realization (after a single audience) that the Tsar was well disposed toward him: he had not forgotten Kurlov's misfortune at Minsk, and had said more than once in the past months how distressed he was to have lost such a valuable administrator. Without waiting to see what second-class posts Stolypin would toss at him Kurlov came right out with his long-cherished desire to be chief of police in St. Petersburg or Moscow—in spite of the fact that those posts were occupied at the time. Stolypin must have known of the Emperor's predilection for him, but would not oblige, urging him instead to accept the post of governor of Kiev for a little while (the governor-general, Sukhomlinov, had requested the then governor's removal). Kurlov agreed most reluctantly: instead of the steep promotion which he deserved, this was if anything a step down—from his previous, independent gubernatorial post to one where he had a governor-general over him. This sort of thing always damages a man's standing in the eyes of fellow bureaucrats. He consented, but only for a short period, to help out at a difficult time, letting Stolypin know that he fully expected to become chief of police in St. Petersburg in the not too distant future.

The moment he reached Kiev he found himself facing a complicated situation, from which he emerged with flying colors, jailing the rampant rightists and showing favor to the Jews. (This was absolutely essential after the unfortunate events at Minsk: "look both ways" was now the rule for all on the hierarchical ladder.) His appointment to Kiev turned out in fact to have been most fortunate. He formed a lasting and cordial friendship with Governor-General Sukhomlinov, a prominent general launched on a great career. He made friends too with another outstanding general, Nikolai Iudovich Ivanov, whom the Emperor dearly loved. He had found in them two constant and effective advocates, who had the ear of the Tsar and would remind His Imperial Majesty from time to time of his honest and hard-done-by servant Kurlov.

Another not inconsiderable bit of luck was getting to know two agreeable and useful people through the Kiev Department of the Okhrana, Colonel of Gendarmes Spiridovich, who had won fame by arresting the terrorist Gershuni, and after being wounded had been promoted to take charge of security at court—another important post in which it was of great advantage to Kurlov to have a well-wisher!—and his sister's husband, the comic (some might say a little undereducated), heavy-handed (but perhaps a little light-fingered), possibly not very clever but ever so hospitable Kulyabko.

This Kulyabko had had no success in the army or the police, had misspent funds and made injudicious use of spurious documents, so Spiridovich had taken him on as a civilian clerk, then put him in charge of secret agents, and most recently, following the well-known and laudable custom of placing your own man at every turn along your path, had left him behind in Kiev as deputy head of the Okhrana. Kulyabko was the sort of lovable, loyal simpleton who bares his own soul to you, and, with his unquestioning loyalty, makes himself at home in yours—and in your financial affairs while he is at it.

On the subject of money there is a very fine line to be drawn. Some men you can trust with everything else, with your life and the lives of your family, but cannot trust in money matters—so that there is no real intimacy. The delicate tissue of your finances is a much more intimate matter than your love affairs: amorous secrets you can share with almost any pretty woman, money secrets only with a carefully chosen and devoted man. If you find such a man, he becomes truly close to you. (That was how it was with Kulyabko. When Kurlov found an opportunity he would make that loyal man a captain of gendarmes, raise him to a position of command, ease the burden of subordination, protect him when he was attacked, gently chide him when necessary, but steadily increase his privileges and his importance. If Kulyabko neglected his correspondence with the Police Department, if he was insolent to governors, if he put an ex-convict in charge of the Criminal Investigation Department, never mind: he would fully atone for his mistakes with his zeal and reliability.)

When it had begun to look as though the St. Petersburg police chief was never going to retire he was suddenly killed by terrorists. (They narrowly missed killing Stolypin with him.) Kurlov naturally expected to be appointed to the post as promised, but the days went by and no letter of appointment arrived. He then sent a telegram from Kiev to remind Stolypin (who was breaking his word for the second time). Stolypin's excuse (sincere or insincere?) was that the goodwill of the Highest toward Kurlov stood in the way of the appointment: the Emperor had seen fit to say how reluctant he would be to see such a loyal servant move to a new post only to be killed by villains in a matter of days. Meanwhile the Emperor was conferring on him the honorary rank of equerry.

Kurlov was deeply moved by His Imperial Majesty's concern, which exceeded anything he could have expected when seeking the post on which he had set his heart. He had not got the post this time around, but the Emperor's favor held the promise of a dazzling series of successes in years to come and even the all-powerful Stolypin could do nothing about it.

Kurlov became deputy director of the Police Department, but then was sidetracked to a dangerous dead-end post (yet again after the murder of his predecessor), that of head of the Prisons Administration. He had to contend with the hostility of the self-important director of police, Trusevich, and of the malevolent Minister of Finance, Kokovtsov, with the covert ill will of the Minister of Justice, Shcheglovitov, the continual aloofness and falsity of Stolypin, the envy of Stolypin's deputy Makarov; but Kurlov always kept his eye on the target and burst like a bullet through the tangle around him. And of course he now had loyal friends behind the scenes, zealous advocates at the foot of the throne, and they helped him to obtain, all at once, more than he had dared seek: when Makarov retired early, in 1909, Kurlov, to Stolypin's surprise, was promoted to Vice-Minister of the Interior, over the head of Trusevich, whose amour propre was so hard hit by this blow that he ricocheted into the Senate. (The Empress herself had wanted Kurlov. She said that only his appointment could still her anxieties for the life of the Tsar. The royal couple both felt that in Kurlov they would have a counterweight to Stolypin's excessive liberalism.) Under the terms of his appointment Kurlov had sole oversight of the Police Department and complete discretion in its management, which gave him the opportunity for large-scale transfers, demoting uncongenial people and promoting his favorites. (This was how that nice, comical Kulyabko came to head the security service of all of southwestern Russia, with a number of generals under him, although he was only a lieutenant colonel and had only recently been elevated even to that height. Just as abruptly the same imperious hand gave authority over the police of the whole Empire, in the post of deputy director of the Police Department, with a precipitate rise in rank and salary, to a certain Verigin, whom no one had ever before thought of the slightest importance, but who happened to be one of those ultra-loyal people to whom the most intimate monetary secrets could be entrusted.) Kurlov's keen eye picked out people he could trust for unusually rapid advancement, but his general practice was quite different: he avoided anything out of the ordinary and tried to subject the police to the normal working of the Table of Ranks; promotion by seniority would in due course raise every official to the next rank, without unfairness to the rest.

His first few weeks in the empyrean were a period of dizzy delight for Kurlov, but as he cooled down he began to see a gap in the powers which he had won: he could not exercise unchallenged authority over all police activity as long as the Corps of Gendarmes remained independent. There was a precedent for the subordination of the Police Department and the Corps to a single person by imperial decree—Dmitri Trepov in 1905. Kurlov would have liked to see that decree reissued: it gave the person appointed the right to report directly to the Emperor and to sit in the cabinet! Stolypin, of course, would not agree, fearing a rival, and the idea had to be dropped. But Kurlov was able to assume control of the Corps de facto with deft assistance from Sukhomlinov, by then Minister of War, who had the idea of appointing Baron von Taube (Trusevich's protégé) to the more suitable post of ataman of the Don Cossacks, and so clearing the way for Kurlov to take over the administration of the Corps. Kurlov's title was simultaneously changed from "counselor" to "general" (also, one must admit, rather reminiscent of Napoleon's rise), though his court rank remained that of equerry. And so an unprecedentedly wide area of official activity opened up before him—the whole field of police investigation and security throughout the empire. Moreover, Stolypin, increasingly preoccupied with the land, with the zemstvos, with resettlement, with industry, paid less and less attention to the Ministry of the Interior itself.

Possessed of such extraordinary power, and now that the country had become so much quieter, Kurlov could develop a policy of his own for further pacification; different from the blinkered policy of uncompromising struggle with revolutionaries by which Stolypin had exposed himself as well as others to their fury. Kurlov's was a carefully judged policy of disarmingly gliding around the problem until all the sharpened knives fell harmlessly into the sand, while the police authorities earned their moral reward in the absence of reprisals, *causes célèbres*, and recriminations from the "public." Kurlov behaved in this reasonable way toward Sletov's group of Socialist Revolutionaries, who arrived in St. Petersburg to kill the Tsar and disguised themselves as cabmen to observe his movements. Their number included one police agent. Kurlov could easily have arrested the whole group before they carried out their conspiratorial plan, and brought the terrorists to trial, which would certainly have ended with the death sentence. But bloody reprisals like that would not have hindered subsequent attempts on the precious person of the Emperor, and would have troubled the public eye with the red glare they shed on Kurlov's own person. He found an ingenious way out. Through the same collaborator he warned the terrorists that the police had them under observation, and gave all of them a chance to make good their escape abroad.

Following the example of the Emperor, who had personally forbidden any form of surveillance in the armed forces he adored, Kurlov further forbade the use of agents in higher educational institutions, again with the object of appeasing the public and forestalling recriminations.

There is always a great temptation, and a need, to use secret agents, but it must be done with care, since it is likely to go badly wrong. As, alas, it did in the case of the ungrateful Petrov, whose release and dispatch abroad to assist an investigation Kurlov had personally authorized, endeavoring as always to appease the enemy while also forestalling attempts on the Tsar. God in His mercy had seen to it that Kurlov was not among those who kept a rendezvous with Petrov and were blown up. But the cruel press had shown him no mercy.

With the public ever ready to find fault, the safest thing would have been not to use informers at all. Or if you did, not to have them at the center of a revolutionary party but to rely on inconspicuous local agents working for local branches of the security police. Kulyabko had operated in this way with splendid results, and it could never cause a scandal.

Kurlov's appetite for power and status was, then, for the time being fully gratified. But he began to feel a shortage of money for the free and gentlemanly pursuits which alone give you the assurance that you are living life to the full, in the only way befitting a scion of the landed gentry. Where, indeed, is life's tremulous flame more excitingly reflected than in sparkling wineglasses on a snowy tablecloth at an ex-Guards officer's exquisite dinner table, with attractive women around it? Not, of course, in boring domestic surroundings, but at the club or in a restaurant, or in masculine company with the young ladies of the ballet for dessert. Alas, that is a way of life that requires a lot of ready cash, and Kurlov's salary and gratuities were not so very big. Once his wife's dowry had been frittered away he was living on borrowed money.

This compelled him, even when he was Vice-Minister of the Interior, to carry on a business of his own, as he had informed Stolypin on taking up his duties. Uninterrupted attention to this private business, and the sometimes very laborious financial manipulations connected with it, of course tended to distract the general from his official duties (though he was an expert bookkeeper). It was not, however, this that mainly distracted him from the task of organizing the work of the secret police in the Empire efficiently: it was the Emperor's frequent journeys throughout Kurlov's years in office.

The disorders in the country had by then been largely quelled, and the Emperor felt the desire, after so many years of voluntary imprisonment, to travel abroad and also to show himself to his people. Strictly speaking, Kurlov's office did not oblige him to concern himself with the Tsar's security on his travels about the country, but he quickly realized that this was an entirely desirable duty: for one thing, the Tsar knew the chief protector constantly at his side and was full of goodwill toward him, and for another, such journeys called for complicated planning and could be so arranged that the general responsible personally took charge of the hundreds of thousands of rubles allocated for security purposes, to be disbursed as need arose, wherever and to whomever necessary, without disclosure and without receipts. This new financial procedure introduced by Kurlov (not without opposition and not without caustic comment from his enemies) had proved convenient in all respects. Since he had decided to do without a central network of agents (after the unfortunate business with Petrov), nothing was known about the intentions of the revolutionaries, and he had to make up for this by increasing visible security with large bodies of soldiers and policemen, many of them commandeered from other districts. This effective method at times required disbursals from operational funds, which could be carried out by such trustworthy people as Verigin and Kulyabko, particularly as they showed a talent for keeping costs down. (It was for this reason that Kurlov sometimes invited Kulyabko to places outside his own district—to Riga, for instance.) The Emperor was also pleased to pay state visits to the King of Italy and the Kaiser, to spend two months in the Empress's native Hesse, to attend the lavish celebration of the bicentenary of the Battle of Poltava, visit Riga, and in the autumn stay for months at a time in Livadia.

The keen pleasure which the Most August Family took in these holidays and excursions reinforced their gratitude and goodwill toward General Kurlov, which afforded him in turn the highest moral gratification. This came at a particularly crucial time because the exceptional favor which Stolypin had enjoyed was becoming more and more precarious and would soon be a thing of the past. With his relentless passion for reform he was doomed to fall, and Kurlov, whose rule it was to choose his next post in advance, knew that he must not miss the critical moment. When in the spring of 1911 Stolypin clashed with the State Council (in which Kurlov had many sympathizers) people began to say with certainty that the Prime Minister's departure was a matter of weeks, if not of days, that he would be transferred to some honorific sinecure, and that however you shuffled the cards no one but Kurlov could possibly take over the Ministry of the Interior. It seemed a matter of urgency to bring his claims to the attention of the All-Highest. But Kurlov took the precaution of sounding out the Grand Duke Nikolai Nikolaevich first—and, to his great disappointment, was informed that Stolypin was still firmly in place.

Because the man of the moment had no liking for him it became impossible for Kurlov or his protégés to move upward. The service was simply no place for honest men who refused to truckle to the Prime Minister.

To cap it all, Stolypin called for an audit of the Police Department's secret funds. That was intolerable.

This was the situation when the All-Highest decided to pay his ceremonial visit to Kiev for the consecration of the memorials to St. Olga and to Aleksandr II. Kurlov was all the more eager to take full personal responsibility for the security arrangements, cold-shouldering both the Police Department and the governor-general of the Southwestern Region, Fyodor Trepov, who let it be seen how deeply offended he was when his claim to look after security was ignored. By now Kurlov's aides had a great deal of experience, and Kulyabko was completely at home in Kiev. A lengthy provincial assignment would allow Kurlov to provide his cousin and other useful persons with living expenses and important-sounding functions, and to relieve the pressure on his own budget by living at the public charge for some weeks. Whole squadrons of gendarmes and a large number of uniformed and secret police officers were commandeered from the capitals and other parts of the Empire to reinforce the Okhrana in Kiev—forty-eight officers and two thousand other ranks in all. In the general supervision of security arrangements Kurlov received invaluable help from Colonel Spiridovich, who was attached to the court, and his own Verigin, now a gentleman of the bedchamber (it was time to get him promoted to chamberlain). On Kurlov's orders they were both included in the city's commission for allotting tickets to the gala performance at the opera—to ensure that the city let in no undesirables. Kurlov's cousin was in charge of all the other tickets: for the Cathedral, the Merchants' Garden, the racecourse, and the unveiling of the monuments.

Without a doubt all the revolutionary parties would mobilize their forces to make an attempt on the Tsar's life during these festivities, and it seemed likely that Savinkov himself would be in charge of their planning. But they were up against Kurlov's carefully organized and numerous security force.

In the event, the utmost exertions of the Okhrana's forces failed to unearth any deeply hidden terrorists, until on 8 September Kulyabko was suddenly phoned by Bogrov, an informer whose remarkable cleverness had earned him good marks in the past. The news caught up with the police chiefs at a private feast (every dinner was a feast at that time) which Kulyabko was giving in honor of Spiridovich and Verigin, with Senko-Popovsky among the other guests. The conversation with Bogrov was as cordial as that around the dinner table—understandably enough, since security officials are constantly in touch with secret informers and not only get used to them but begin to treat them as intimates. When such an informer comes along you cannot show distrust of him: if you do you will undermine his confidence and his usefulness. Bogrov was doubly precious because he had been lost and had now returned to the fold, clever fellow, with information about a crime in preparation. This was an unexpected cause for rejoicing, and no one need be blamed if his master was only too ready to trust him.

Kurlov could not be at the dinner because of a slight attack of rheumatism. (In spite of which he continued tirelessly directing the whole enormous security operation from his couch in the Yevropeiskaya Hotel, giving little dinners in his room for a small number of guests.) The trio therefore reported Bogrov's visit and his information only on the following day, when Kurlov fully resumed his duties. He immediately appreciated the extreme importance of the matter, and the rewards which might accrue from it. How should they deal with it? The "Sletov variant" could be used: Nikolai Yakovlevich could be warned through Bogrov that the police had discovered their plans, whereupon the terrorists would quietly take themselves off with their bombs and the festivities would go forward as smoothly as anyone could wish. But then again with no great risk, and with enormous credit to himself, he could lay hands on the whole group. Kulyabko's arrangements were approved, and supplemented by the dispatch of a team of ten policemen under a captain to Kremenchug to search for an amiable, dark-haired man who looked like an intellectual. Kurlov also cooled Kulyabko's eagerness to make a police apartment available to the terrorists: this could damage Bogrov, whose own apartment was obviously the most suitable, although external surveillance of Bogrov senior's enormous house was a complicated business. (It was so big that whole clinics rented accommodations in it.) The one thing they must not do, whatever happened, was to insult Bogrov by keeping watch on him personally. They could, in addition, check some of the facts—they could telegraph St. Petersburg and ask von Kotten whether there had been any such letter in the last year from the SR Central Committee to Kalmanovich.

By now the last-minute preparations for the festivities were in full swing, the royal guests were expected in two days' time, and our quartet were rushed off their feet getting ready for their arrival. General Kurlov, after several days of illness, had to make up for lost time, issuing instructions, briefing subordinates, making payments, surveying the locale, inspecting his forces, paying visits; nor could he let the festive flame burn low—nothing was more important than the jolly luncheons, the dinners, the champagne, the music, the gypsy ensembles with which the courtiers leavened to the best of their ability this most solemn festival. In this ambience General Kurlov could obviously not be expected to remember Stolypin's rather irksome request that he confer and cooperate with the governor-general of Kiev. He was still less likely to have any such ridiculous idea as reporting Bogrov's information to Stolypin himself: the standing of the Prime Minister had so conspicuously declined and the Tsar's coolness toward him was so obvious that Kurlov would almost have been demeaning himself by flying in the face of fashion and showing any consideration for his nominal chief. So many signs conspired to assure him that he himself would be sitting in Stolypin's chair as Minister of the Interior any day now! Besides, if he reported anything like this to the Prime Minister he would take the matter into his own hands and usurp the credit for catching the terrorists. And should Stolypin escape dismissal yet again, he was not the man to let it be known that Kurlov was his unsung savior! Anyway, there was no time left to report in person: only the presence, hour by hour, of that martyr-to-duty Kurlov in the streets through which the ceremonial cortege would pass, only Kurlov's valiant generalship ensured the safety of the Most August Family. Without him gendarmes and soldiers in whatever numbers would be too few.

Day after day was spent in drilling, patrolling, cordoning off, and inspecting; the whole Kiev Okhrana lived its life out in the streets, with only one man left behind a desk in the department.

A senior detective was assigned to deal with Bogrov, who had in any case added nothing worth mentioning to his original report. Meanwhile, the detectives sent to Kremenchug had failed to pick up the seasoned conspirator Nikolai Yakovlevich. He had evaded all those looking for him in Kremenchug and at the railway stations, and slipped into Bogrov's house unobserved. Anyone new to police work might have panicked at this point, brutally burst into Bogrov's apartment, and arrested Nikolai Yakovlevich. That, however, would have been not even a half-success, but a total failure: as on the eve of Aleksandr II's assassination, or that of Pleve, the arrest of one member of the group would only force the rest to act more quickly. The correct security procedure was to wait for the terrorists to make their next move, keeping a close watch on them through Bogrov, since resources were lacking to keep watch on Nikolai Yakovlevich himself.

The danger spot was the Merchants' Garden, the boundary of which ran at one point along the hilly riverbank and was difficult to guard. But all went well.

Further reports from Bogrov were not long in coming. On 14 September he turned up in the middle of the night to report the arrival of a woman bomb thrower. The young man was extraordinarily agitated—understandably, caught up as he was in a whirlwind conspiracy. Kulyabko's night was left in tatters. First thing in the morning he was with Spiridovich, and together they caught Governor-General Trepov before he left home to watch the troops rehearse. It was a mistake, of course, to bring Trepov into the affair after he had been excluded from the planning of security, but they were reluctant to disturb General Kurlov, especially as they had several hours in hand before the terrorists were due to meet on the boulevard. This was the first Trepov had heard of Bogrov and the assassination plan. He sent a message warning Stolypin to stay indoors and told Kulyabko to take him Bogrov's letter of the night before. Kulyabko, however, in company now with Verigin, naturally went off to see their own superior first. General Kurlov scolded Kulyabko for his misconceived initiative: by inviting Trepov to interfere he had created a risk of duplication and confusion in the security arrangements. They would, of course, have to tell Stolypin something now, but Kulyabko could obviously not approach the Prime Minister himself, only his adjutant. Even so, he should only summarize the news in general terms, leaving out such details as Bogrov's warning letter.

Kurlov himself had an appointment with Stolypin that morning to discuss routine matters (including Verigin's promotion to the court rank of chamberlain), and to obtain the Prime Minister's signature to a list of gratuities. He could not avoid some brief mention of Bogrov's story in the course of his report, but he made it as casual as he could, and suggested only that the Prime Minister should go about in a motorcar, not a carriage, that day.

Kurlov watched the Prime Minister while he was talking and was struck by the obvious signs of his irreversible decline. Stolypin even asked Kurlov to make room for him in his own compartment on the train journey to Chernigov.

"Surely Your Excellency has a place on the steamer with the royal party?"

"I haven't been invited."

Conclusive evidence that Stolypin was in disfavor and being deliberately humiliated! Obviously he was only days away from dismissal.

What did require extraordinary police measures was ensuring the safe return of the Emperor from the maneuvers, even changing his itinerary if necessary. (Spiridovich had already rushed around to warn the palace commandant and take the necessary precautions.) Next, he must be protected at the racecourse. Then en route to the theater. And during the performance. (With ninety-two Okhrana agents and fifteen officers on duty, he should be safer there than anywhere.)

Another piece of news awaited Kurlov when he got back to the Yevropeiskaya for lunch. The self-denying Bogrov, for whom no effort was too much, had come along again, directly to the hotel this time, to report another change in the terrorists' plan. Well, the thing to do was not to interfere, but to let matters take their course and wait for further information from Bogrov. And so that he would not lose the terrorists' confidence he must be supplied with the theater ticket for which he had asked. (Bogrov's remark about the terrorists' having *protectors in high places* was chilling. Kurlov and his friends had to plan very, very cleverly and act very, very cautiously. If they swam against the current they might ruin a record of long and impeccable service.)

However, with enormously complex arrangements to worry about there was no time to examine Bogrov's story in detail. Kurlov had hardly an hour free to relax in a restaurant of an evening. He had to make his presence and his efforts felt by personally supervising police operations whenever the Emperor rode out. He was doomed to spend a whole exhausting day on the streets: at one moment steering the gathering crowd in the wrong direction by loudly giving misleading instructions to the police, at another switching the Emperor to a less dangerous route on his own responsibility, or begging his friend Dedyulin, the palace commandant, to consult the Emperor about other possible changes of program. In all these operations Kurlov had the tireless, shrewd, and gallant help of Colonel Spiridovich.

Then came the lavish banquet at the palace. It would soon be time for the theater, and Kurlov had first to go and check whether the police had inspected the building thoroughly (making sure that nothing was hidden in the artists' dressing rooms or in their makeup kits), after which he had to ride to the palace, take command of the imperial cortege, and conduct it to the theater. Only then, a few minutes before the performance began, would he be able to take his prestigious and responsible place in the front row of the stalls, three seats away from the royal box. (The first seat would be occupied by Admiral Nilov, a favorite of the Tsar's, who was never quite sober, and the second by Dedyulin. These two were Kurlov's most useful well-wishers, and it was through them that he always received court news promptly.) Stolypin, who had the fifth seat in the row, repeated to Kurlov the somewhat incoherent message delivered to his adjutant, Yesaulov, by Kulyabko, that the terrorists would not after all be meeting on the boulevard that evening. Had they then perhaps met in the afternoon? Stolypin knew nothing about that.

Kurlov, however, did know. Kulyabko had brought him news from Bogrov at the racecourse that afternoon and on several occasions during the day, and Kulyabko's actions had earned the general's complete approval. Kurlov did know, but did not *have* to know, at least not in such detail, for the purpose of reporting to Stolypin. He spent the whole of the first act whispering to the palace commandant, not concealing from him the startling detail about protectors in high places, and when the act ended he did not dash off to make further inquiries for the Prime Minister but questioned Stolypin again to find out how much he knew. Only when the aisles were clear did he saunter off to look for Kulyabko.

Kulyabko, meanwhile, had been given plenty to worry about: Bogrov had announced on his arrival at the theater that the terrorists' evening rendezvous on Bibikov Boulevard, around which a net of agents had been thrown, was also canceled. Things were beginning to look gloomy. What should have been a brilliant success threatened to turn into defeat. The terrorists were slipping through the net. Kulyabko realized with a sinking heart that he needed Bogrov not in the theater but at home, to stay close to Nikolai Yakovlevich lest he get away altogether. But Bogrov was so happy in his fine clothes and so proud to be at the gala performance when so many of Kiev's worthiest citizens had failed to get tickets, squeezed out by the notables from St. Petersburg (the only other Jews present were two millionaires), that Kulyabko hadn't the heart to turn him away. The most he could bring himself to do was to send Bogrov home to make sure quickly before the performance began that Nikolai Yakovlevich was still there. Bogrov went off (it would have been awkward to send a policeman with him) and returned to announce that Nikolai Yakovlevich was having supper. Ah, good, there was nothing to worry about for the duration of that supper.

But during the first act Kulyabko felt the pinch of anxiety again. On the stage a queen was falsely accused and cast into the sea to drown with the prince, her son, but Kulyabko had no eyes for any of that. He could see nothing except the wily and elusive Nikolai Yakovlevich filtering like an invisible man through the net of detectives and vanishing into the distance with a suitcase containing pistols, and also Lieutenant Colonel Kulyabko's (and not only his) hopes of promotion, a medal, and a gratuity.

In the first intermission, although he felt rather embarrassed about it, Kulyabko was about to ask Bogrov to run home once more, but just then he saw his benefactor General Kurlov striding importantly about the foyer. Kurlov saw at once what must be done. He did not approve of sending Bogrov home: once, to get his gloves, was all right, but it must not happen again, as he would be found out. Then a shrewd thought occurred to him. For two days running the terrorists had been repeatedly changing their plans. No one had thought of asking Bogrov how they did it. It could of course be done by means of notes carried by inconspicuous people. The Bogrov house had several floors, and was always full of people. But it might just possibly be done by telephone. Surely in Kiev it must be technically feasible to listen in on calls to the Bogrov residence? Verigin popped up at that very moment and Kurlov ordered him to send for the Director of Posts and Telegraphs, to discuss the possibilities.

The intermission was not nearly over yet, and Verigin and Kulyabko crossed the street to the Café François, where the Director of Posts and Telegraphs (who had no ticket for the theater) joined them. Yes, of course, what they suggested could be done. He promised that by 11 p.m., which meant by the beginning of the third act, Bogrov's line would be monitored.

A police chief has the right, and it is in his interest, to keep all such details to himself: they may have hidden implications, and they might reveal some lapse which should certainly be concealed from outsiders.

So when he returned to the seats for distinguished guests Kurlov gave Stolypin a vague answer. Yes, the terrorists would be meeting later, somewhere else, he didn't know where, but would find out from Bogrov. (He said nothing about Bogrov being right there behind them.)

But then Kulyabko's anxiety began to grow again. It was nearing eleven o'clock, Nikolai Yakovlevich must have finished his supper by now, and after supper he could easily have gone off to another apartment. If so, the whole remarkable operation organized by the Okhrana would be a failure. As soon as the curtain began swaying at the end of the second act and he could decently rise, the restless lieutenant colonel crept away and nodded to Bogrov, inviting him to follow.

Stolypin, beginning at last to feel uneasy about the uncertainty surrounding the terrorists, broke into Kurlov's interesting conversation with the palace commandant and asked him to go and find out how matters stood. Kurlov had no choice but to obey, and went out into the corridor, where he sent a gendarme officer to look for Kulyabko. He noticed the telephone room and thought of ringing the Director of Posts and Telegraphs, but just then Kulyabko hurried up to him to report that Bogrov had been sent home to check for the second time. This greatly displeased Kurlov, who lengthily reprimanded Kulyabko for disobeying orders.

At that very moment an unidentifiable sound like the snapping of dry wood came from the theater, followed by loud cries, and people rushed out of the hall in agitation, shouting that Stolypin had been shot dead. Kulyabko lost control of himself, and Kurlov lost control of Kulyabko, who rushed into the hall to ask or see for himself what had happened. Kurlov restrained an impulse to fling himself into the flood of people—the danger was not yet past, there might be more shots to come. The audience were high-placed persons, many of whom naturally expected the next bullets to be aimed at themselves. General Sukhomlinov, for one, fled from the front row, and Verigin ordered the fire doors to be opened to assist his own retreat.

That it was Bogrov (crafty little Yid!) who had fired the shots Kurlov learned from Spiridovich as he sped past with saber bared. He had intended to use it on the assassin, who was being beaten up by officers in the aisle, but, recognizing Bogrov, stayed his hand and charged ahead to stand guard, saber in hand, beneath the Tsar's box.

When he heard that Stolypin had not been killed Kurlov abandoned all idea of going into the hall. Nothing could have been more unpleasant just then than having to exchange words or even a look with the wounded Prime Minister.

Kulyabko, meanwhile, dangerously out of control, stumbled around like someone lost, clutching his head, plucking at his revolver holster, and promising to shoot himself.

Only General Kurlov preserved perfect sangfroid and went off to give the necessary instructions. Outside he ordered his men to clear the square, cordon off the theater, and check everyone who left. He must make sure that the Emperor got away safely.

That may have been a mistake. He should have hurried to take charge of the assassin while he was still in the hands of the gendarmes.

During the extended intermission Stolypin was taken to the hospital, and the national anthem was played, with those onstage kneeling to the Emperor. Bogrov was led into the buffet and searched, and the gendarme officer who had saved him from being badly beaten began questioning him. Kulyabko hung around pointlessly, making excuses, desperately incapable of taking in the situation, imagining that he would palliate his own fault if he shifted the blame onto his superiors and tried to sink them. He readily took the blame for not having Bogrov under observation inside the theater. He had no answer to one very simple question—why did he not have Bogrov searched at the entrance?—and the nimbler Verigin answered for him, "It would be unethical to search *our own agents*, it could undermine the trust between the two sides, and it is contrary to accepted practice."

Kurlov felt afraid to go there himself. Something inside would not let him. But after hearing Verigin's report he began to see more and more clearly that if he did not take urgent steps everything, and every one of them, might be lost. The next few minutes could decide what would become of many years of service, could decide his whole future and that of his friends. The very best thing to do would be to take Bogrov along to the department for interrogation and keep the investigation entirely in their own hands. But if Kurlov himself appeared with this intent he would disclose a personal interest—which was undesirable. They somehow brought Kulyabko to his senses and sent him to the buffet to insist that Bogrov should be taken to Okhrana headquarters. Spiridovich, who had now returned his saber to its sheath, joined in explaining that Bogrov was primarily the concern of Kulyabko. But by then the procurator of the High Court had arrived, and he refused to hand Bogrov over. Kulyabko insisted passionately, desperately, that he must at least be allowed to speak to Bogrov alone and obtain certain important information from him. But he was not allowed to do even that. Kulyabko's plea for a tête-à-tête to get at the truth was then supported by Kurlov through a third person, and the procurator wavered for a moment but still refused.

Meanwhile Kurlov had to absent himself (with his heart in his boots!) to see that the Emperor returned safely from the theater to the palace. Things would have to take their course while he was away.

Only after all the carriages had left did the four of them assemble in the Yevropeiskaya Hotel to discuss the situation. In their haste they made another mistake; they should have concentrated on reassuring Kulyabko (what a boneless wonder he had turned out to be!), enlightening him, and showing him the right way to behave, but instead they decided to make another attempt to kidnap Bogrov and sent a police officer over to the theater to take him into custody on the authority of General Kurlov, head of the Police Department and commander of the Corps of Gendarmes, and deliver him to the Okhrana for interrogation. The result was disastrous: the procurator not only had the audacity to refuse (he had already been in touch with Shcheglovitov, the Minister of Justice) but, on learning from the same stupid policeman that Kulyabko was presently at the Yevropeiskaya, telephoned and summoned him to the theater for questioning.

Kulyabko had not had time in the few hours since the shooting to collect his wits. Unprepared and bemused as he was, he failed to see where his advantage lay when he went along to be questioned, and revealed that Spiridovich, Verigin, and Kurlov himself all knew that Bogrov was to be admitted to the theater, and that he, Kulyabko, had not taken a single step without their knowledge. This was an irreparable error, which complicated the investigation, and the position of his associates, without in any way improving his own.

Bogrov, with no one to influence or instruct him, also began by concealing from his interrogators where he had obtained his ticket, but then named both Verigin and Spiridovich.

In the meantime, a convincing apologia began to take shape in the cool and experienced heads of Kurlov and Spiridovich. Spiridovich, needless to say, knew nothing about Bogrov, and in theory was not called upon to know about him, because that was the business of the local security organs and *he* was in charge of *palace* security. Nor, indeed, did he have time for such things. Verigin was even less involved, since he had no special duties in the sphere of security and no connection with the investigation of political crime, but was simply a special assistant on Kurlov's staff. Where Bogrov was concerned, neither of them had ever given, and neither was formally entitled to give, any instructions. As for General Kurlov himself, he was indeed fully responsible for the general state of security during the festivities, but precisely because of the immensity of the task he could not look into every detail (he had been kept informed about Bogrov only in broad outline), and had to delegate authority to various executive officers without whom any attempt to run a department would be impossible. Investigatory procedures were not his direct responsibility. As for Kulyabko, he was an official of many years' standing and much experience, and Kurlov had every reason to rely on him.

If they had been thinking clearly and planning their defense from the first minute, the three senior men would have evaded any sort of accusation and been on firm ground. General Kurlov could then much more authoritatively and effectively have extended a hand to help and defend a subordinate (Kulyabko) who had landed in trouble because of his imprudence and certain minor oversights in the performance of his duties. There were powerful exculpatory arguments in Kulyabko's favor too: he could not possibly have anticipated Bogrov's treachery—the man had always been such a good and loyal servant; no one looking at that puny, wall-eyed intellectual could possibly take *him* for a terrorist; and subjecting him to flat-footed surveillance or a house search would have spoiled the whole game. A combination of unforeseeable circumstances explained the whole thing.

But Kulyabko was like a cow stung by gadflies. He lost all capacity for clear thought, rushed wildly from place to place, bellowed, foamed at the mouth, and was called for questioning before he could be primed.

The course of the investigation still depended to a great extent on what happened up above. How much (or how little) importance would be attached to the wounding (the death?) of State Secretary Stolypin? The indications in court circles, and close consideration of the Emperor's behavior, gave Kurlov grounds for supposing that the investigation would be a low-key affair, making it easier to escape unpleasant consequences if his testimony was discreet from the start (especially as the palace commandant, Dedyulin, had that very evening reaffirmed the promise spelled out in earlier conversations that if Stolypin fell—which now probably meant when Stolypin died—he, Dedyulin, would promote Kurlov's claim to the Ministry of the Interior—with every likelihood of success).

However you looked at it, one thing was beyond doubt: some of the gaps in security over the last few days must be stopped as quickly as possible, in fact that very night, to make sure that the investigation followed the right lines. An avalanche of house searches and arrests must be set rolling: anyone who could possibly be connected with Bogrov must be pulled in. For a start, his own apartment, so far spared, must be raided, and Nikolai Yakovlevich and the weapons found. Assign as many police officers as possible to the job! Pull in everybody found in the apartment, the aunt included! Arrest everybody in Kiev who had previously been hauled in as an anarchist. Detain everybody mentioned in Bogrov's notebooks, all his relatives, and all his acquaintances, even those who were barristers, though this would upset a lot of people. Never mind—he had a ready-made excuse: preoccupied as he was with important general measures for the preservation of order, General Kurlov, once again, could not inquire into every detail of his subordinates' actions. At the same time, all this activity in the course of the night would count against accusations of inaction earlier on.

Seventy-eight people in the categories listed were arrested that night. Not all of them were subsequently questioned.

There was another useful move he could make now: although he was heartily sorry for Kulyabko, Kurlov must personally suspend him from his duties.

Nor was that the end of the turbulent night. Kurlov was suddenly summoned to the apartment of Kokovtsov, hitherto Minister of Finance, but now, it turned out, already in the small hours appointed acting Prime Minister. It would, of course, be just as easy to appoint an acting Minister of the Interior! That, however, was not the purpose of Kokovtsov's summons: he did not even offer his hand but asked Kurlov in a frankly hostile tone, "Have you got what you wanted, then? Are you satisfied?" The whole conversation made it clear that the new Prime Minister would spare no effort to indict Kurlov for a nonexistent crime.

He greeted the dawn of 15 September with a heavy heart. Now that the unmanageable Kulyabko had dragged them all into the mud, Kurlov began to discern one last, straightforward and sure way of defending himself. If the State Secretary should die, die quickly (and the doctors' first impression was encouraging), he could confess that he, General Kurlov, had known everything, known even that Bogrov had been admitted to the theater, but had acted throughout with the knowledge and permission of Stolypin himself, keeping him systematically informed of the course of events.

It could do the dead Prime Minister no real harm, and it would make Kurlov's defense very much easier.

To make sure that this item of news did not sink without trace in the court record, it would be enough to whisper it discreetly to a couple of liberal reporters and the whole press would eagerly pick up and develop a theme so congenial to it—that Stolypin had perished because of the police system which he himself had created to deal with revolution!

[67]

Next morning Kiev was stunned by a hail of rumors, spoken and printed, a muddle of truth and fantasy. Questions raced about the city. Is he alive? Who killed him? How?

Rumor said that the bullets were poisoned! Rumor had it that the assassin had been seated in the fourth row, that he was one of the highest in the land! *The Stock Exchange Gazette* hastened to report that the murderer had been in the front rows, that he was a fanatical monarchist and had conferred with members of the Emperor's retinue.

The most reliable reports concerned Stolypin himself. He had not lost his presence of mind, but removed his coat unaided; the red patch on his waistcoat had quickly widened, he had clutched at this place and all at once his hand was covered with blood. He had sunk onto a seat as his strength began to fail. Rein, a professor of medicine, happened to be near, other doctors present in the theater had hurried to him, and between them they had stopped the hemorrhage and escorted him out of the theater themselves, bloodying their own suits. The ambulance had arrived at the theater in the meantime, and it had delivered the wounded man to the Makovsky Clinic, not far away on Malo-Vladimir Street.

There were two bullets. One had entered below the right nipple—it had struck the Order of St. Vladimir on his breast and dented it, which had reduced the force of entry. There was no exit wound, the bullet had lodged in the muscles along the backbone. There was reason to fear that it had grazed the diaphragm and the liver. The second bullet had pierced Stolypin's hand and the barrier between the stalls and the orchestra pit, and had wounded a violinist in the leg. Removal of the bullet from his back was not considered urgent, and they did not intend to operate just yet. During the night there was cause for alarm—the patient's heart, which was not strong, kept flagging. After his wounds were dressed, the injured man received the last rites, recited the Communion prayer out loud, and crossed himself with his left hand. He was in great pain, but bore it stoically.

An improvement set in toward morning, explicable perhaps by the patient's courage, and the doctors began to hope for a favorable outcome, indeed to think it was a ninety percent certainty. The patient asked for a mirror, inspected his tongue in it, and said, "It looks as if I shall pull through this time." Of his abdominal pains he said, "The governor-general's dinner is still lying heavy in my stomach." His nerves were badly shaken: every knock or rustle disturbed him. The roadway in front of the hospital was covered with straw. The doctors were not doing anything of importance, just waiting. The celebrated Zeidler had been summoned from St. Petersburg. The patient's appetite was poor, and he could not be given a laxative. He was given wine, black coffee, and a bromide, and morphine injections when he was in pain.

And the would-be assassin? A young assistant in a law firm, with a long record as a revolutionary. His home had been searched and he had been arrested on several occasions. Member of the Central Committee of the Socialist Revolutionary Party and its Fighting Organization.

But the public was not satisfied. One man, even the most desperately militant of SRs, could not carry out such an important and complicated "action" alone! People's minds naturally looked for a huge conspiracy, a large terrorist group. According to one rumor, the Socialist Revolutionaries had united with the Bund and the Finns and this was only the first of a series of major actions. Miscellaneous scraps of information were seized on and collated: some revolutionary had committed suicide a few days earlier on the Okhrana premises (he turned out to be a common criminal who had not fled abroad in time); some car or other (evidently it had nothing to do with the case) had been rushing up and down Fundukleev Street near the theater that night and the passengers had beaten up a watchman who would not let them into a yard; an electric wire had been cut in the theater, but the culprits had not managed to get at the main circuit and plunge the building in darkness so that the assassin (for whom a soldier's greatcoat and forage cap had been provided) could escape; the assassin himself had admitted the existence of such a plan under interrogation.

None of this was subsequently confirmed.

Then the news got around that the assassin was not a stranger from out of town but the son of a rich and respected citizen, and that he had entered the theater with a ticket. The Kiev establishment was badly frightened: the victim was, after all, the head of the government. They threatened to deprive Bogrov *père* of membership in the Nobles Club and the Concordia. (They soon found that there was no need to.) There were even muttered hints that the father ought to be excluded from the legal profession (the son was disbarred, but not immediately). The lawyer with whom Bogrov had been registered for eighteen months, ever since he had left the university, although he had never handled a single case but was only on the books to satisfy the authorities, announced that he was disowning Bogrov (he was in too much of a hurry—he needn't have done it at all).

A spate of reports in the national and local press contained a good deal that was true but in the general confusion remained unconfirmed, and a good deal that was untrue but in the general confusion went uncontradicted. There were reports that the assassination had nearly taken place on 11 September: twenty minutes before the arrival of the imperial family an unknown horseman had appeared on the square before the government buildings and removed himself only after an argument—and this horseman was said to be Bogrov. According to another report, Bogrov was noticed on 14 September at the cadets' parade on the racecourse, in the enclosure for spectators without full tickets. The secretary of the Trotting Horses Society, who had occasionally seen Bogrov at the races, was said to have been told by him that he was waiting for the "court photographer," and to have escorted him out of the enclosure, which was separated from the ministers' seats by only a few paces and a waist-high wire fence.

How much truth there was in any of this the general public would never discover.

The city felt that it was partly responsible, in that the Executive Board of the Duma had issued the theater tickets. An extraordinary meeting of the Duma was called on 15 September, and the mayor, Dyakov, rebutted accusations of negligence: the criminal had not been admitted to the theater by the city, but by another body, which had demanded a block of tickets for its own use. "*Which body?*" the deputies roared, although they knew very well. And the mayor happily unburdened himself: the Okhrana.

The Duma set up a howl. The Duma demanded a copy of the record of tickets issued and, without waiting to see which way the wind of public opinion would blow, made Stolypin an honorary citizen of Kiev.

What public opinion had to say was that there could be no happier denouement, no more salutary flea in the ear of authority. For the press too this was a game it could not lose. Were the assassins revolutionaries? That would teach reaction a lesson! Or were they secret policemen? Still more educational: they had killed their own Minister of the Interior and the head of the government! (Late on 16 September the medical communiqués took a sharp turn for the worse: inflammation of the peritoneum gave great cause for concern, and the action of the heart was becoming alarmingly weak. It became more and more natural to use the word "killed.") People had, after all, been saying ever since anyone could remember, among themselves and in print, that the Okhrana was rotten through and through, that it was a state within the state. The police in Russia depended entirely on provocation—and here was the result! A symbiosis of police and revolutionaries, the security organs and the terrorists! The *system itself* encouraged the police to organize such conspiracies, or not to put a stop to them.

What had happened was more and more clearly becoming a cause for liberal rejoicing: the suppressor of revolution had been removed by the Okhrana's own pistol!

(A new wave of rumors swept the city. An entry in Okhrana records was said to show that Kulyabko had issued the revolver to Bogrov. Kulyabko had left the theater immediately before the assassination and hurried off somewhere by car. Kulyabko had disappeared from Kiev, and could not be found. No, he hadn't vanished; he was still around giving orders in the streets—and a crowd was said to have shouted "Down with the provocateur!" at him.)

The center, the right, and the not quite so far right were all horrified—it was so glaringly obvious that others besides Stolypin were badly guarded, that all Russia was unguarded, defenseless, completely unprepared. Neither the secret agents nor the expensive outward show of the vainglorious Okhrana adequately guaranteed the safety of the state. (Milyukov was quick to declare that security during the celebrations had cost 900,000 rubles. This was later reduced to 300,000 and the actual cost proved to be still less.) The Russian public had to all appearances been gradually forgetting and recovering from terrorism. Terror, so people thought, was being deprived of its arms, and the power of the state had been reinforced. Then, suddenly, at a royal command performance, with the Okhrana present in extraordinary force, an audacious villain had fired on the very man who had brought the country a measure of peace!

The State Duma was in a quandary. The Octobrists would have liked to question the government on the general activity of the security police, while the left was for confining the question to police use of provocation to disrupt the revolutionary forces. The normal rules governing security operations had been so flagrantly ignored that even *The Land*, an extreme right-wing journal hostile to Stolypin and all he stood for, accepted at first that the attack had been instigated by the Okhrana.

How else could anyone make sense of it? It was established from scraps of information pieced together in the first few days that Bogrov had been allowed into the theater with a revolver to unmask, in some incomprehensible way, an unnamed criminal, who had gained entry to the theater by unknown (indeed unimaginable) means. Even if there had been no police plot against Stolypin there was no denying that there had been gross negligence. Either they had wanted to be deceived or they were monumental fools. The details that got into the press were more surprising all the time. When Bogrov was leaving home for the theater the ordinary detectives on duty had thought there was something suspicious about him but Kulyabko's deputy had reassured them, "He's our man." Tickets for the theater had been given to other dubious characters, such as Franz Pyavloka, at one time leader of a gang of robbers (with fourteen robberies on record) and now working for Kulyabko. It even appeared that the Police Department itself had been denied any part in security arrangements for the celebrations, as had the governor-general of the Southwestern Region: they and everybody else had been supplanted by the mysterious and all-powerful Kurlov, Verigin, and Spiridovich—little known hitherto, this cluster of names scurried across the pages like fat spiders. The upheaval, as always, brought hidden things to light: that right-wing enemies of Stolypin had lent Kurlov large sums of money which had not yet been repaid; that the minor official Verigin had been promoted far beyond his deserts on the very day Kurlov took office, that the whole Department truckled to this favorite, that he had been given tens of thousands of rubles to use at his own discretion, that he had now left Kiev as though he had nothing to do with what had happened and no responsibility for it; and that Rasputin had recently offered the post of Minister of the Interior to the governor of Nizhni Novgorod, saying that it would be "easy to remove" Stolypin.

At that moment an inky cloud seeped into the pages of the press. A "well-informed" source alleged that it was *Stolypin* who had kept the governor-general out of the security arrangements, and that Bogrov had been given his theater ticket with the approval of *Stolypin himself*.

Stolypin was by now beyond hearing and denying any of this, but the press seized on it triumphantly. This was twice as good! The government, not the police, were the provocateurs. Perhaps Azef himself had had some part in Stolypin's murder. (A rumor to that effect was put about.) Perhaps they had hoped to seize a hundred revolutionaries and hold a great show trial? Were the Kurlovs then merely by-products of Stolypin's policies? Was it Stolypin himself who had planted agents provocateurs all over Russia? Had he fallen victim to his own devious schemes? What more fitting end to the politics of nationalism and Orthodoxy!

A spasm of joyous excitement ran through the Kadet press. If the right-wing papers openly defended Kurlov, *Russia* and *Russian Banner* uninhibitedly vilified the Prime Minister, who was still not quite dead. The Kadet papers, with their refined skill in tricking the censor, were as you would imagine not at a loss for words:

> Stolypin was struck down at the very moment when he was in effect happily and merrily celebrating his own triumph. What does fate's angry gesture mean? Should we perhaps hear through the noise of these shots a warning voice? Russian society now has ways of protesting without shedding blood—but perhaps fate wished to remind us that the old methods still exist?

For decency's sake they reluctantly refrained from open rejoicing, but *The Russian Gazette* had not the slightest compunction about saying that terror was a natural expression of the public mood, a consequence of the profound disorder in the state, as a result of which every stratum of society was permeated by the profoundest discontent. This was a good opportunity to repeat that the government was "hostile to the people" (not just mistaken, not just blind, but hostile). While *Speech* could now finally conclude that "the nationalist policy lacks all positive content." In general, Stolypin had been wrong about everything for so long that the shot fired in Kiev had if anything rung out too late.

The Kadets seemed to have given up applauding terror in recent years (it had become fashionable to say that terrorists clear the way for reaction), but Bogrov's bullet set their pulses racing. (Secretly they were consumed by regret: if only *they*—the royal family—had been blown up!) All society indulged in atavistic gloating. The habit of extolling the "heroic deeds" and "selfless sacrifices" of the revolutionaries was so deeply rooted. Almost lost amid all the other revelations was the rumor that a certain member of the State Duma had once received a secret communication from the Central Committee of the Socialist Revolutionaries in exile, and no one thought this improper, let alone criminal.

Then the indefatigable telegraph began relaying reactions to the attempt from abroad, where people could say out loud just what they thought. The irrepressible Burtsev for one, with his much-vaunted insight into conspiratorial behavior, made his thoughts public. While the SR Central Committee thundered (and the legal press had no qualms about reproducing its statement) that although Bogrov had received no instructions from them to fire his shots, the Socialist Revolutionary Party welcomed the assassination of Stolypin, which had an important "agitational significance" and had sown confusion in ruling circles.

After that the lonely figure of Bogrov towered even more heroically in the public eye! If only he had not been linked with the Okhrana he would have been a national hero!

There were those who tried to give yet another twist to the story: now that the guilt of the Okhrana and the government was proven (through Bogrov), perhaps Bogrov himself was not guilty? For society at large, and still more for his family and friends, the main thing now was if possible to cleanse Bogrov of the Okhrana taint, to show that this was not another Azef case! They desperately wanted Bogrov to be clean—with blood on his hands, but otherwise clean. (They detested Kulyabko simply for his slanderous insistence that Bogrov was an agent of long standing. According to the press, this same Kulyabko had destroyed letters in Lev Tolstoy's own hand.)

Bogrov's brother publicly expressed his indignation that the newspapers had the audacity to use the word "murder" (for what, you were to infer, was a just execution in the name of the people). Bogrov's father, overtaken by the news in Berlin and obviously filled with pride in the son he had reared, gave an interview: my son loves horses, rowing, card playing, he is a clubman, a bon vivant, his way of life is not at all what has been said, he had no need of petty sums of money. There could be no doubt (Bogrov senior in Berlin had no doubt) that criminal activity on the part of Okhrana officers was at the bottom of it. He's killed a man? I can't bring myself to accept the thought. (Meaning: It can't have been a man he killed. He couldn't!)

Neither the estimable Bogrov senior, nor the worthy corporation of lawyers whose sole vocation was to see justice done, nor yet a single one of the respectable newspapers, the "professorial" press included, could spare time from the extremely important question of whether Bogrov was an honest revolutionary to consider another one: did a bumptious twenty-four-year-old have the right to decide all by himself what was best for the people and shoot at the heart of the state, to kill not only the Prime Minister but his whole program, to change the course of history for a country of 170 million people?

One thing only perturbed society: was he an honorable man or a police spy? How distressing if he was a police spy. But come to think of it, that was even better: that would make it all the more obvious that not he but the "milieu," the accursed "regime" was to blame, and Bogrov was only its tragic victim.

There were, however, limits set by the censorship: open glorification of the murderer was not permitted. But the press enthusiastically seized on every little laudable trait it could find. Rumor had it that Bogrov had shown perfect self-control under interrogation, that his demeanor was very calm, very ironical, the demeanor of a true revolutionary who had performed his civic duty. He had given his testimony, cigarette in mouth, arms Napoleonically folded. It was almost as though he hadn't a care in the world! He was sorry for his parents. He was taking an interest in what the papers were saying about him!

Since the right wing also had nothing to say in Stolypin's defense it was left to *New Times*, which had not been on the best of terms with him either, to strike a different note:

> The forces of darkness are on the march again. . . . We have lost our sense of security. . . . Stolypin did not hide, and that made it easier to strike him down. This is a challenge to the Russian people, a slap in the face of Russian parliamentarism. . . . This is not an isolated crime, but an assault on Russia. . . . It was not the sufferings of the proletariat that raised the hand of this murderer, the son of a millionaire, but a man's feeling for his own tribe, which has begun to encounter obstacles to its conquests. Stolypin was planning the nationalization of credit. Stolypin stood for Russian nationalism, and for that he became a martyr.

But a louder sound than any of these rolled farther over Russia—the sound of prayer. Some people had gone straight from the theater to the Monastery of St. Michael for a service of intercession that very night. There were countless services in the churches of Kiev on 15 September. Prayers were offered continuously in the crowded cathedrals of St. Sophia and St. Vladimir, and many of the congregation wept undisguisedly. The Academic Council at the University of St. Vladimir sent a telegram to say that it was offering up prayers. In St. Petersburg on the same day Guchkov organized a service in the Tauride Palace, and there were services in the hall of the City Duma, the chapel of the General Staff, and the Admiralty. A series of services was requested at the Cathedral of Our Lady of Kazan by the Octobrists, the nationalists, the State Council, the War Ministry, the Ministry of the Interior, the Ministry of Agriculture . . .

Who knows how many others there were, in other churches?

In Moscow too.

And in each and every city in the Russian Empire.

* * *

PRAY AS THEY WOULD, IT DID HIM NO GOOD

* * *

[68]

What were the newspapers saying about him? And what were they saying about Stolypin?

Surely Stolypin could not still be alive? Surely he would not survive? It was agony to think that it might all have been in vain.

Bogrov had been standing so close that he seemed to see the cloth of

Stolypin's coat near the unfastened top button twitch under the whirlwind impact of the bullet. He had a physical sensation not just of shooting but of driving the bullet into his enemy's torso. He did not fire all eight rounds, lost count of how many he had fired—he had had enough of it, he was certain of his success, and he took flight.

Why had he been in such a hurry? It now turned out that he had fired only two bullets, the second of them only at Stolypin's hand. (He had not felt the revolver wobbling. Was he, then, already running away when he fired?)

Even as he was shooting he suddenly saw clearly that he could still escape! The noble public in the half-empty hall was so terrified—people screamed hysterically, scattered and ran, hid behind seats as though they, not Bogrov, had to escape. The aisle before him was clear, and he started running, still carrying the revolver (if he had thrown it away perhaps he would not have been recognized?), and he was not far from the exit when an officer seized his wrist in an iron grip, and the Browning fell or was wrenched from his hand. By now he could no longer keep up with what was going on. Someone struck him on the head, apparently with a pair of opera glasses, and then he was thrown to the ground and beaten, by whom and with what he could not see.

Only afterward in the buffet, where he was first interrogated, did he realize that two of his teeth had been knocked out.

He had trained intensively to undergo harsh interrogation and was ready even to lose his life, but he had forgotten that he might be beaten up, he had not expected for a moment that his body would have to endure pain and torment before he was executed. Revolutionaries were not as a rule beaten. But even when they simply put handcuffs on him to take him to the jail it was so unexpectedly painful that Bogrov cried out and asked for them to be loosened. And that was on the first night, when he was too inflamed with pride to feel pain very much.

On the second and third days, when elation had given way to depression, he ached all over, and as he lay in his cell these pains depressed him more than the thought of what awaited him. Depressed and in pain as he was, the absence of comforts—a flushing toilet, running water, electric light, a soft bed, home cooking—seemed unbearable. His body felt neglected, martyred, abandoned.

Bogrov sent for a doctor.

He had been rescued from the military men who were beating him by an officer of gendarmes, Lieutenant Colonel Ivanov, who had slung him over the barrier into one of the boxes. Ivanov again had helped the chief investigating officer and taken a good-natured part in the interrogation. Nor had he refused to answer when Bogrov asked what they were saying about him in the papers, what his parents had been told, and what they had said. And . . . how Stolypin was.

Stolypin was not yet dead, but hope ran high: his liver had been damaged.

Most important of all, Bogrov had divined the sentiments of the public correctly and knew that "this victim will get no sympathy."

When hatred is indulged to the full it ceases to oppress us. A sense of duty done restores our equilibrium.

The end of the struggle. A feeling of pleasurable weakness. For the first time all sense of responsibility had drained away.

Yes, he had been right—once he had committed himself to the act all his doubts and internal debates were over. What gives a man's life value is knowing how to achieve his aim. One man's aim demands that he spare himself, another's that he sacrifice himself.

How simple it had proved in the end to change the course of history: all you had to do was get a theater ticket, walk past seventeen rows of seats, and press a trigger.

And he had done it entirely alone, carrying out his very own original idea! He had involved no one else, no one else would suffer for it. He would not let any of his acquaintances and patrons in the legal profession be pulled in.

Now that the main business—the main business of his whole life, evidently!—had been performed and the future was decided, the investigators' questions did not annoy him, indeed they came as a relief: a release from that unmanageably proliferating tangle of secrets and plans which had so unnerved him in the past week that every verbal contact was an irritant. Now at last he could talk about it all, if only to *them*! Now that his task was fulfilled, now that he could feel proud of himself and had no need to cringe or wriggle, he answered questions as easily as a bird flies. Before they left the buffet he had been quick to declare himself an anarchist. (Although he had not been one for a long time.)

It would, of course, have been much jollier to talk with people from his own circle (with reporters he would have been more brilliant still), now that he had succeeded in doing *something special*. But the investigators too were all intelligent, polite, and attentive listeners who showed nothing but respect for Bogrov's personality and his opinions. Moreover, everything of importance was recorded, bureaucratic procedure would take its inevitable course, and Bogrov's depositions would be most carefully preserved, to appear someday in the press explaining and justifying for the benefit of history his great and lonely feat.

He told the whole story, proudly and straightforwardly, without nervousness, without omission or invention or prevarication. Yes, I am Mordko Gershevich Bogrov, assistant to a barrister. I planned my attempt on Stolypin long ago, long before the Kiev ceremonies. Why Stolypin? Because he was an enemy of the people. I consider Stolypin more to blame than anyone for reaction in Russia, for the harassment of the press and of the non-Russian peoples. Stolypin ignored the views of the State Duma. I bought the revolver three years ago. I haven't been able to do much shooting, I've only fired into the air. I didn't work out any elaborate plan for the attack. I was sure that once in the theater I would find the right moment to approach him. I carried out the attack without consulting anyone else, and not as a member of any organization. (A note to that effect was found in his wallet when he was arrested: "I confirm that I carried out my attempt to kill State Secretary Stolypin single-handed, without accomplices, and not on the instructions of any political party.") The ticket was issued to me in my own name. The bullets were not poisoned.

Was it true that he was an Okhrana agent of long standing?

There was no getting away from that. Concealment was impossible.

Yes, I have cooperated with the Department. Yes, for four years now. Yes, I supplied information. Why? Well, er . . . I wanted a little extra money. Why did I need it? I prefer not to explain. (Because there was no explanation!)

He did not produce a single new name, did not mention a single secret meeting place or a single conspiratorial action. Nor indeed did anyone ask him about such things.

Over and over again he told them: Kulyabko did not know of my intentions. (He slipped up once, and told them that Kulyabko had offered him tickets to the Merchants' Garden and to the theater.) No, of course he didn't know. (What, after all, had Kulyabko ever done to him except encourage him and give him money? Now he too was in terrible trouble. Bogrov was aware of something more than gratitude or the need for discretion—he had begun to feel an unnatural affinity with Kulyabko. No true anarchist would ever lift a finger out of compassion for the head of an Okhrana department. Yet here he was . . .)

And that was it. The whole story of the sensational murder proved to be neither mysterious nor complicated. There was barely material enough for two or three crystal-clear statements.

On 15 September another deposition was taken down, to the effect that Bogrov had thought of making an attempt on the Emperor, but had put it out of his mind for fear of provoking a pogrom. As a Jew, he said, he did not think that he had the right to perform any action which might result in the slightest curtailment of the rights of the Jews.

There was no calculation, no invention in what Bogrov said on this matter. He was loyal to his people to the last; and this was obviously the main source of his inner strength.

So very loyal was he that he refused to sign this answer of his. (If the government learns of my statement it will have a weapon—it could use the threat of pogroms to deter Jews from terrorist acts. And terrorist acts must continue in Russia without hindrance.)

For this reason the statement had to be recorded in a separate protocol, bearing the signatures only of the investigating officer and the procurator.

"Do you wish to add anything of importance to your depositions, or to change anything?"

"No."

(His liver is damaged! He is dying! The deed is done!)

"One more question: how, I wonder, after serving the Department honorably for four years, could you bring yourself to commit such a murder?"

Bogrov answered as though he pitied their obtuseness. "I refuse to give my reasons." (Have you still not understood that I never served you? Do you still not understand the first thing about this whole business? I didn't serve you—you served me. That is how history will read and understand it.)

"That seems to conclude the investigation. The case can now be sent for trial."

Trial? Who needed a trial? He knew what an awkward figure he would cut. The real trial had already taken place. The Prime Minister had been the accused. But neither he nor any witnesses had been examined. The whole trial had taken place in Bogrov's seething brain. The sentence had been—death! And it had been carried out.

Meanwhile, his head and his reckless courage were cooling. And he felt such pain in his battered body. (The beating had shaken him badly.) And how he missed his two lost teeth.

Reality was returning. Trial, you say? How could he, who lived and worked among lawyers, he who had planned his attack so minutely, have failed to prepare for the trial? He had been completely absorbed in plans for the assassination. (Otherwise he would never have been able to do it.) But the trial was a splendid escape route (remember how Zasulich got off!). It left him so much room to maneuver. He would hire a defense counsel—the very best in Kiev—and through him make contact at once with his own world! Let them know the truth, get them to pass it on, learn what he needed to know.

No, that door had slammed in his face. He was a "police spy." That was the one stain that could never be wiped away, the one thing that "society" could never forgive, and any argument about it in open court would make him a pariah in the eyes of all decent people. Even talking about it with a well-wisher would be more than he could bear right now. What if he called Goldenweiser in tomorrow, wept on his shoulder, and told him that it was all an ingenious ploy, a move to subvert the Okhrana so that he could carry out the great murder? No, it would be no good! Neither Goldenweiser nor society at large was capable of overlooking it. The lawyers' minds would be his, but not their hearts. It would be impossible for them to make fiery speeches in his defense.

It was all over. He was a pariah. He had to take the consequences. He had to defend himself.

The case, however, was passed to the District Military Court.

Oh dear. This is a bit different from the High Court. This isn't going to be another Zasulich affair. The lightest sentence it will hand down is hard labor for life.

After interrogation he was consigned to a cell. The cells in the fortress were of the old-fashioned kind—no peepholes, no ventilation panes, locked with heavy padlocks, but light and spacious. This was the round Kosoy Kaponir [Crooked Tower] in a corner of the Pecherskaya Fortress on the cliffs overlooking the Dniepr. From the window he could see the ancient earthworks, and that lighter stripe over the coarse, sun-scorched grass was a little-used path. Beyond the ravine he could see the Bald Mountain. That was where those condemned to death by the Military Court were executed.

A bleak, wild mountain scarred with ravines. *The* Bald Mountain, legendary haunt of witches and scene of their sabbaths.

And then that evil-smelling wooden tub, left too long unemptied. No bath, no shower, no regular change of linen—all out of the question.

To make things worse, the appetite he had lost in the feverish days after his arrest came back with a vengeance. He hadn't felt so hungry in ages, he was simply starving. The "endless succession of rissoles" of which he used to speak ironically looked so tempting now. To think that he had found it so boring to eat them!

In fact, he had never appreciated his life of ease. Oh, to return to it now, to have everything there for the asking! How comfortable he would make himself.

The body (and that impalpable presence within it) recovers from overstrain, self-hypnosis, from an unnatural pose, from inertia, from shock. Feeling returns in jabs, in jolts, in spurts. But how to return to life? He must return.

He was oppressed by the stony emptiness of the bare expanse from the tub to the window looking out on the mountain of despair (the place where *you* will be executed!). The solitude he had previously longed for became a torment, and he was sad that all conversation with living people was over, sad that the investigation had ended.

Ah, but it had not! They took him off for further interrogation.

And as they took him across the circular vestibule and along the echoing corridor, the undamaged wheels of his inventiveness engaged and began to whirl. Exert yourself! Find a way!

The interrogator was the same Ivanov, the lieutenant colonel of gendarmes (Kulyabko's friend), who had saved him from a worse beating in the theater. He was by himself, without the chief interrogator. And as full of goodwill as before.

First question: a revolver has been found in your father's possession too; do you know whether he has ever used it, and why he had it? Second question: did so-and-so and such-and-such ever visit your house, and if so what was their business? None of the rest was of any importance. And with that, alas, the interrogation ended. Sign the protocol.

The investigation was over, but Ivanov had not finished. He gazed at Bogrov with great sympathy and understanding. He spoke to him almost affectionately. "Let me share some of my thoughts with you. You are a man of rare strength of character, of exceptional bravery. You have done something which no one else could have achieved. But your present attitude can do you no good. What is the point of your proud obstinacy, why do you persist in saying that it was all your own idea, and that you thought of it long ago? You are only aggravating your plight; that way lies certain death. Why put your neck in the noose? Out of loyalty to the revolutionaries? But they have all disowned you—not one of them has acknowledged you as a comrade. What you wanted to do, you have done. Nobody can take that from you. Why, then, are you so obstinate? It's time to think of yourself, to make things easier for yourself. Don't represent yourself as such a high-principled political offender, don't insist that you were so wholly committed to the idea of killing the Prime Minister. You could have done it on the spur of the moment, on a sudden impulse, almost accidentally. On the other hand, you have worked loyally for the Security Department against the revolutionaries—what have you to lose now in those circles? But you can do something to make your lot easier. Think it over. I strongly advise you to change your testimony when you get into court."

Surely it was too late to change his testimony?

"Certainly not. It is perfectly possible. It's often done. The court would reopen the investigation. You would risk nothing by contradicting yourself. Since you had no confederates, no accomplices, no witnesses, nobody can trip you up."

Bogrov was too cautious, too skeptical to answer precipitately. But this new idea sank into him like a broad-bladed knife, severing old trammels.

Then he was back within the thick stone walls of his cell. Unobserved, unseen. Pacing once again from door to window. With that blood-freezing view of the accursed mountain.

Had he really weakened so quickly, had the thought of death softened him, had he knuckled under? Well, whatever happened he must try to save himself. The death sentence on terrorists was often commuted to hard labor. It had happened even to Sazonov, Pleve's killer. If a beating was so painful, what would hanging be like?

No, he had not come out of the interrogation on top. He could see that now. He had handled it wrong. And since that whole crowd of revolutionaries had denied him their support, refused to inscribe his feat among their battle honors, he was surely free? When had he ever belonged to that gang anyway? He was a free individual, a supporter of evolution along liberal lines. And that was all.

Should he change his story? Change his whole explanation of his act? Belittle his feat and save himself? He had never been ambitious anyway. He had already sacrificed his life. That was not enough. He must sacrifice his public reputation. Well, it was already besmirched. It would not easily be cleansed.

How the world had shrunk! To a single barred window, a path up a deserted hillside. He couldn't even see the Dniepr. The wind blew and blew over the deserted witches' mountain—a scene as dismal, as wild, as hopeless as everything else in this accursed Russia. How far away they seemed, those enchanting bays on the Côte d'Azur—at Villefranche-sur-Mer, for example—seen from your balcony in the morning, after you had taken your shower, put on your narrow breeches and your spotless white shirt, feeling young and eager to live (eager for a life which was all promise, but which somehow never gave you what most mattered . . .). The palms of Nice, the colorful rows of stalls along the streets, the women who sold vegetables and winked at passersby . . . The Promenade des Anglais . . . The beaches of cozy little Menton . . . The enormous plane trees behind the casino at Monte Carlo . . . The overblown rococo opulence of the gaming rooms, the gilded walls, the golden dome . . .

In the first room, where the play was for low stakes, nerves were taut, a girl smoking a cigarette stood at the table, together with fluffy-headed old women, raddled men, fanatical system-builders with pencils, and whenever the ball stopped racing around the red and black circle in the dishlike depression rakes clutched by the croupier's assistants shot out like the bony hands of witches to scoop up in a twinkling all that had been lost by the patrons and, almost contemptuously, to shove their gains to the rare winners. The faces of the croupiers: dead-eyed men with crude features, bandits with black mustaches and caricatures of noses, or noble scholars in glasses. A youngish woman in a mauve dress, with blackened eyebrows and lashes, expels smoke toward the ceiling with powerful puffs and watches the game with wild-eyed absorption. Whenever she wins—the same small sums as she loses—a rapturous smile flits across her face, but any man who thought it was meant for him and tried to take her away from the table would soon discover his mistake.

Bogrov had gambled in this room as well as in others, watching the crazy little ball with mounting excitement. But when he had money to spare he went on to the inner rooms. The entrance fee was high. These were the private gaming rooms—for real gambling, where stakes were unlimited and there were no crowds, either of players or of watchers, but fewer than ten to a table, where any show of emotion was considered indecent, and the unlucky young player wore a devil-may-care look on his mad face as he strolled from table to table. Under a ceiling as inordinately high as the others, there was a brittle silence in the almost empty room. Here you did not use chips instead of money, and an apoplectically flushed old man at the baccarat table extracted wad after wad of new hundred-franc notes in sealed packets of a hundred from a bag at his feet, apparently without counting, while a lean Italian with an eloquent face dealt the cards with insidious skill, and just as stealthily and unerringly swept the packets of bank notes into a deep inner drawer.

There was no thrill like it! In half an hour you could live through a whole lifetime.

People there were more excited than Bogrov had been in the Kiev Opera House. The music of life itself rang in their ears!

Never again would he see any of this.

Glancing from face to face, moving from room to room, traveling from one little town to the next, whether you won or lost, whether you merely eyed the girls at a distance or bought yourself an Italian tart for the night—you would come to realize, if only later on, far away in sprawling, prodigal Kiev, or damp and gloomy Petersburg, or in this locked cell, that those were the only golden pages in your life.

And you had never appreciated them.

Let's go over it—all that happened, all you saw and felt and dreamed about, the perfumed pleasures you enjoyed on all your European journeys, all your stays in watering places.

1906? Munich . . . Paris . . . Wiesbaden

1907? Nice . . . Menton

1908? Merano . . . Montreux . . . Leipzig

1909? Paris . . . Nice . . . Monte Carlo

1910, and last spring, in February, the Côte d'Azur again.

Twenty-four years. Was that a short life? Or was it perhaps a long one?

If only there was some way to . . .

He must play on! The stakes were even higher than in the private gaming rooms.

Was Ivanov trying to trick him? Had he been picked for that purpose? It would suit *them* that way. But it would not be a bad thing for Bogrov either.

The pacing from stone wall to stone wall grew faster, as there was no one to see.

No, he wouldn't beat his head against the wall like a maddened ram. He could neither buy his way out nor burrow his way out. He would do it by the devious workings of his powerful mind.

His testimony would look implausible? Let them pin it on the Okhrana then! Since his name was linked with the Okhrana anyway, why not exact one last payment from them? Help me and my life is saved! Refuse to help me and I'll see you never live it down!

Yes! That was the best move left to him—to be a millstone around the neck of the Okhrana.

He would paint a picture of systematic collaboration—which had never existed. He would mix the Okhrana and the terrorists together so thoroughly that nobody would disentangle them in a hundred years. And the social significance of his act would grow immeasurably! He would have struck a double blow at the regime, and by blackening the Okhrana system he would be striking another blow at Stolypin! He would reach the man even from the next world. For this new great aim he would sacrifice the last shred of his personal reputation. What could be harder than putting together an assassination from nothing? He had done it—with his bare hands. Surely the rest would be simpler?

[69]

His eyes were fixed on one point on the ceiling—his body would permit no more. He could not turn onto his right side at all, and turning onto his left was painful. He had to lie supine, his weight crushing his backbone just as when he had been pinned to the barrier, aware the whole time of the bullet still there under his shoulder blade.

The first night had been a dangerous one. Death had stared him in the face. His heart had kept slowing down.

In the morning there was a remission. The wound stopped throbbing.

He was fully conscious, his mind was clear and moving freely, as our higher faculties always should be. He no longer believed that he was going to die.

When he looked in the mirror his color was good, his face was not that of a dying man. He had no temperature. The racking pains of the first few hours had subsided (or was that just the effect of the morphine?) and the feeling of nausea had diminished. He so wanted to forget his body's troubles and withdraw into his mind—how easily he could live there!

Where had the most damaging bullet struck? The doctors explained that it had struck his Order of St. Vladimir, which had reduced its impact and deflected it.

For the better, or for the worse?

They said that there was no blood in his sputum, no peritonitis—that was good.

A sick man or a wounded man immediately ceases to count as a grown-up independent person. He loses not only control over his situation but his right to know what is happening to him. If Stolypin had not remembered some Latin from student days he would not have understood from the doctors' cryptic utterances that the bullet had pierced the diaphragm and made a lesion in the liver.

At least it wasn't his heart or his throat, or he would have died immediately. It could have been worse.

But we have only one liver.

Enemies know the thing to peck out is the liver.

Was he really going to die?

They had got through to him after all.

His helpless right hand was maimed forever. He must have tried to shield himself with it.

He asked about the wounded musician. The man wasn't seriously hurt.

Though it no longer mattered, it would be "interesting" to know how the assassin had managed to get into the theater. The things of this world meant less and less to him, but this riddle still teased him.

Why the theater anyway, when it would have been so easy to kill him any day during the Kiev celebrations?

All those policemen were the same! Too busy chasing promotion. Remember Gerasimov in St. Petersburg, in the worst revolutionary years—how many times he had self-effacingly saved the Tsar and Stolypin and others. The terrorists had avenged themselves by slandering him, and Kurlov had gobbled him up.

Kurlov! That ignorant, muddled, conceited mediocrity, foisted on him as chief of all police forces! He had not dismissed the man when he should have done so, had not interfered with his crackpot security exercises because he didn't want to hurt the Emperor's feelings. But how he would like to look the man in the eye now!

He sent for Kurlov, but Kurlov was too crafty to come. He had gone off junketing with the Emperor.

What made Stolypin think that he still had the authority to summon people?

Did Stolypin really think that he had ever had complete authority even when he was head of the government?

How simple it all was: someone had killed the head of the Russian government—and no one even came along to tell him how and why.

Still, on the first day he felt reasonably well, so well that he expected to pull through and to look into the whole thing when he was up and about again. The doctors did not keep from their patient what they had read in the newspapers—that the shots had been fired by an Okhrana agent, Bogrov.

Bogrov? The man they had been talking about yesterday? The secret agent who had informed on the terrorists? It defied belief.

These questions would have intrigued him, would have set him fidgeting, if any of it had mattered any longer. What difference did it make who had done it and why? They had got through to him.

In fact, his spirit floated freely, unresentfully. His mind was clearer than ever.

Pyotr Arkadievich was waiting for the most important conversation in his life.

Waiting.

For the Emperor.

As soon as they had brought him to the hospital the night before and bandaged his wounds, and even before taking Communion, Stolypin had asked those around to let the Emperor know that he was ready to die for him.

Throughout that first dreadful night, with death hanging over him, he had expected the Emperor from hour to hour.

He had expected him all the more confidently that morning when he began to feel better.

There was so much to tell him, so much to warn him against. After what had happened Stolypin could talk to him as never before, frankly and without reservations.

But the day was running out and the Emperor did not come.

Stolypin knew his Emperor—how he knew him! He may have remembered that even on the day of the Khodynka catastrophe the French ambassador's ball had not been canceled. He may have remembered that the Emperor loved and enjoyed nothing more than military parades, that according to plan the main parade was to take place on 15 September, at some distance from the city, and that tens of thousands of men had been brought in for it. How could the schedule possibly be changed?

He knew all this. And he waited.

He waited even more confidently toward the evening of 15 September, when the Emperor was due to return to Kiev.

But still the Emperor did not come.

Stolypin's most lucid day went by and was lost.

Could the Emperor not have altered the program of the celebrations just a little bit?

Was it really of no importance to him to be told about matters of state? About what remained to be done? About future dangers? To hear a dying man's thoughts? Pyotr Arkadievich's wish was to explain his whole reform plan to the Emperor that very day—to bequeath it to him and commit him to carrying it out. Not in memory of Stolypin's past services, not as a reward to Stolypin for defeating revolution and restoring his country to him in good health, but for the sake of his own future! For his own sake! He obviously did not see what a tight corner Russia was in, even now, and what she must do to break out of it.

There was one visitor—an investigating officer, not a very high-ranking one. He questioned Stolypin and drew up a statement: what exactly had happened in the theater, where exactly and next to whom the Prime

Minister had been standing, how the assassin had approached him and in which hand he was holding . . .

Another visitor allowed in by the doctors was Kokovtsov, already acting Prime Minister.

It might have happened twice before, if Stolypin had been dismissed. Now it had. Kokovtsov was taking over his post.

He was not an enemy. But he was narrow, intellectually and emotionally. Was there any way of deepening his understanding, of enlarging his sympathies? He needed to be braver at heart if he was to pull this load.

Why not Krivoshein? . . .

The Emperor had so willed.

Stolypin shared some of his thoughts with Kokovtsov. Among the most important: Kokovtsov must get the Emperor to replace Sukhomlinov—it was becoming obvious that the War Ministry was in a state of chaos.

Into the vacuum created by the Emperor's absence a secretary brought bundles of telegrams—good wishes for his recovery from all corners of Russia.

In the hour of anguish we hear these encouraging cries from friends—always too late. How much more valuable it would have been to have one sixteenth of their number beside us while we were still capable of action.

Besides the telegrams there were newspaper reports of church services—in the capitals especially they went on uninterruptedly. Local people brought along icons, and more icons. The Bishop of Chernigov brought oil from the relics of St. Barbara the Martyr.

How Russia loved such excesses! But they were no substitute for the work of every day. It was easier to pray for someone than to give him support. Easier than doing what needed to be done.

Stolypin had always been conscious of a God above him, urging him on, inspiring him, guiding him.

His first endeavor had been to fill the peasant's barn.

Must he now take his leave? Before the most important of his reforms?

He longed to hear a clear, firm voice promising to continue his work with the same strength of purpose. But nowhere in Russia was such a voice raised. Perhaps there was no such voice?

To depart—at forty-nine, and still at the height of his powers. Leaving behind a Russia still rent by the rabid hostility of civil society toward the imperial power. By malicious lies. By ignorant prejudice.

It is as Thou hast ordered it, O Lord, Thou whose designs are beyond our understanding. However much it is Thy will for each of us to do, however many times we exceed the limit of all we had thought possible, at each new horizon, even at the final horizon of death, there is still more left undone to trouble us. . . . There is so much for which I feel myself needed, but Thou hast bidden me be still and struggle no more.

And what of Olga? What of the six children, some grown up, some still infants?

Whether it was a punishment from God or a mercy, there was no relief, except just occasionally in a short sleep, from his uninterrupted awareness that he was wounded and might die.

I shall surely die.

There was nothing new in the telegrams and rumors. It was no good trying to make sense of the pains and the murmurings inside him, to try to guess what was going on, whether *this* was breaking down or *that* was healing, whether the blood was clotting or whether the tired heart was pumping it away.

The doctors didn't seem to be giving him any treatment. Morphia and caffeine, that was all. They said he would be up in three weeks. They wouldn't disturb him to change his dressings. They thought of extracting the bullet, but left it there. They were waiting for an eminent colleague from St. Petersburg.

He who had been perpetually active found himself peremptorily cut off from everything. He had no one to talk to. Nor any way of sending messages. The mind destined never to have any part in the future reviewed his past.

1906. Mutinies and rebellions everywhere.

1907. "You can't frighten me."

How apt such unstudied phrases can be. The joy of standing fast! And the misery of stumbling about among quarreling factions instead of maneuvering flexibly with the serried ranks of state power behind you.

But how could he complain? He might have died on Aptekarsky Island without achieving anything. Instead, he had been granted five years to do his work.

Though the whole burden of Russia rested on his shoulders he had not hesitated for a moment to challenge that loudmouth to a duel.

This too had been a duel of sorts. Except that the enemy had crept up on him stealthily, and an active man's breast is always exposed.

He had been struck by the expression on the assassin's face, his triumphant certainty that he was right. Yet even as he exulted in victory there was a wry smile on his intellectual face: would the world realize how clever he had been?

They had all been perverted in this way. The corruptors had been at it for half a century.

What did Russia matter to them? What did they care about the tasks facing it?

No, no, this was no Okhrana agent.

In the course of our lives we receive prophetic warnings, adumbrations of what is to come. They seem irrelevant at the time yet affect us more than we think. We usually fail to recognize them. When he had made his speech on Azef he had refused to entertain the obscene notion that an Okhrana agent had directed terrorists. But his enemies in the Duma had prophesied that the government itself would perish at the hands of such informers! Perhaps there was a freakish resemblance between the Azef affair and what had happened to him.

They had been disappointed that time. Their triumph now would be complete. . . . For so many people Bogrov could not have timed his shot better. It put the finishing touch to the April sessions of the Duma.

He ought to have made time to deal with the police. He shouldn't have shrunk from it.

1909. Russia's development steadily gaining speed.

1910. A year of great achievements. Individual homesteads already spreading over the face of Russia, changing the face of nature. His own happy trip to Siberia, truly the supreme moment of his life, since he could tell himself, "All this is your creation."

Perhaps, then, he had done all that he was meant to do. It is not given to any single individual to do so very much. One man cannot change the whole course of history.

Yet even in that finest hour, indeed especially then, he was beset on all sides, tied hand and foot . . .

No, that was wrong. No, Lord, I thank Thee, giver of all good things, that it was granted to me to accomplish so much.

The high point of the journey had been in mid-September: the very days so boringly taken up this year by the Kiev ceremonies had last year been so spacious, so rich in incident, out on the Siberian steppe with the grain elevators rising around him, amid hills of grain.

If only he could go there again, just once!

The night of 15–16 September went by, with less cause for alarm than the night before. His temperature remained at thirty-seven, his pulse was not over ninety, and he tried hard to believe that his chances were as good as the doctors said. He was neither feverish nor delirious. It was just that his immobilized body seemed swollen and heavy, and he was so weak. His right side, around the wound, was as heavy as iron. What mysterious process was going on in the depths there? The bleeding had stopped, and they weren't changing the dressing. They weren't giving him any treatment at all. Perhaps there was nothing they could do?

Olga arrived from their Kovno estate.

"Well, you can see how it is, my dear . . . Well . . . There we are . . ."

But the Emperor did not appear late that evening after the parade, nor yet early next morning.

Would he come that afternoon?

What was on his program? Oh, yes, he would be going out of Kiev again—to Korosten and Ovruch.

So he wouldn't come?

He didn't come.

Yes, Pyotr Arkadievich knew his Emperor. But all the same he awaited his arrival. He made ready to speak, not like a subject but like a man on his deathbed, to say things he could say to no one else.

Your Majesty, do not delude yourself that all is now well. One violent storm will bring it all tumbling down again! The same two forces seek to disrupt us—the irresponsible and the insane. And one of the two is entirely at your mercy—clear away this rank growth, Your Majesty!

Pinned down as he was, right and left, with an excruciating, tearing pain in his shoulders, whom should he suggest to the Emperor as his own replacement? There was no one.

Did he regret not having raised his voice to shake the Emperor before this? Or did he, on the contrary, regret that he had not done more to retain the Emperor's goodwill?

He had always behaved as his feelings told him to. He could not dissemble, he could not falsify the facts.

Well, he had perhaps become too heated that spring over the western zemstvos.

Let the man who has governed a state condemn him.

Nobody could judge every little detail perfectly.

Why is it that if you get on successfully with the main task, all around become your enemies?

He had said once in a speech that the enemy furiously hacks away at the scaffolding as we try to build, and someday it will surely collapse—yes, he had said "surely"—and crush us beneath the wreckage (you too, vengeful Rodichev, will never get your scaffolding built, you will tumble first!), but let it be when the framework of the renewed Russia is already in being.

But was it yet in being? Had the main work been done? Oh God—only now did Pyotr Arkadievich see what was most important, only now, when he no longer had the strength to raise himself on one elbow.

There was nothing terrible about dying. He had not known the fear of death for a long time past, he was surprised himself how little he feared it, although he was still under fifty. His fears had always been for Russia.

Alas, he could no longer help her!

It was frightening to think that he would have no heirs and that his work would never be completed. Why are *we* never allowed to take a hand in the real work? Why instead of us are Germans planted everywhere, or decrepit Russian freaks, and if someone with a firm guiding hand sets out to build a road they fly at him from every side to knock compass, yardstick, pick, or shovel from his hold.

. . . Your Majesty, if the two sides are not made to see sense we may yet come to grief. It is unthinkable that the country should go on living so dangerously divided. I have dark forebodings, Sire—and not only because this bullet was my lot. The year 1905 may repeat itself, Your Majesty—God forbid there should be another war. You must tenderly nurture the new healthy growth. And put no trust in self-seeking people, of whom there are so many around you!

The day dragged on endlessly, and his mind was less clear than on the day before. At times everything went dark, or he felt sick, or broke into a sweat which left him weaker, and he was more conscious all the time of the heavy lump of iron where his liver should be, and even when Zeidler arrived from St. Petersburg the surgeons were still reluctant to do anything.

Meanwhile the Emperor was opening a church at Ovruch.

Stolypin longed for Guchkov to appear: he remembered the years when they had got on so well—perhaps now they could renew their understanding.

He was somewhere on the way or was just setting out, but he too was in no hurry. He sent an Old Believers' icon on ahead.

Stolypin was feeling worse all the time.

"Bury me in Kiev, Olga. I shall sleep peacefully in this city."

He had long ago expressed a solemn wish to be buried "where he was killed"—his intimates all knew of it. As it turned out, he had been killed in the cradle of Russia, the city in which Russia had its earliest roots. This, and not bureaucratic Petersburg, not Kadet-dominated Moscow, was where Russian national feeling had flourished most vigorously in recent years. It was for Kiev's sake that he had fought his battle over the western zemstvos last spring.

It had almost broken his heart at the time, but now it might even have helped stem the hemorrhage.

By evening his mind had begun to wander—just when it occurred to him that he could write down all that he wanted to say to the Emperor. Why hadn't he thought of it before! Sentences formed themselves more eloquently than when he was fully conscious. At last he knew how to convince the Emperor, who could not fail to do his bidding. What happiness!

He asked for paper, something to use as a pad, a pen—and suddenly he remembered that his right hand had always written with the support of his left, and now it was wounded. How could he write? His courage failed him.

Delirious dreams crowded in. His wife and Dr. Afanasiev, who had sat through both nights, were at his bedside.

In the morning consciousness returned. The doctors were alarmed, they found that his peritoneum was inflamed and that he had a pulse of 120. Three days late, they made up their minds to change his dressings, and operated to remove the murderous bullet from his back.

Pyotr Arkadievich asked to see it.

He was too weak by now to speak at any length and with any force, even if the Emperor did come.

The Emperor, it seemed, had been in the clinic late the previous evening, while the patient was unconscious. He had left Kiev yet again that morning, loyal to his timetable.

17 September was a day of interruptions, intermittent dozing, injections.

Broken thoughts passed through his mind.

He had thrown wide the gates to the Russian future. He could not be sure that they would not be shut again.

Oh God, how should I picture the future? Will it be sunlit and sublime or wreathed once more in dark mists? If only I could see the continuation of the changes I have set in motion, see which way it will go.

He yearned to fling himself into it, to become part of it. I belong there! I belong there, all of me!

But another feeling—of resigned detachment—was growing within him. It has nothing to do with me. It's over—and I am glad.

On the morning of the 18th Pyotr Arkadievich regained consciousness completely and asked the professors a question: "How can you lie to me on the last day of my life?"

The professors avoided answering. His right hand was bandaged, and with his left he could not feel his own pulse—if there was any pulse to feel. They gave him oxygen, and caffeine.

Stolypin lay there, conscious, thinking hard.

He knew very well that he was dying.

And that day the Emperor had simply not come.

He was a weak man, unhappy in the knowledge of his weakness, unable to face unpleasant realities—and he had just not come.

It was God's will to send us such an Emperor at such a time.

It is not for us, O Lord, to weigh Thy purposes.

O God, our Creator! Illuminate his mind and his heart! Grant him the strength to face great hardships!

All day on 18 September the sick man suffered dreadfully as his mind grew darker, groaning and tossing and turning. They were surprised that his heart was still holding out—at times it seemed to have stopped altogether and only caffeine started it beating again.

They should probably have operated the day before, when they discovered the hemorrhage under the diaphragm, to drain the blood and plug the liver. They had hesitated too long.

No more outsiders were allowed into the room.

In the evening as he was lapsing into oblivion, he asked for the electric light to be switched on. "Give me paper. . . . Give me a pen! . . . What's the good of a penholder without a nib?"

Then there was something about the way to rule Russia.

Several times he repeated the word "Finland" quite distinctly, and his left hand traced pictures on the bedsheet.

They brought him pencil and paper but he could not use them.

By 8 p.m. his extremities were getting cold. He was having great difficulty with his breathing.

At nine he spoke his last: "Turn me on my side." Dr. Afanasiev did so.

Then he lost consciousness altogether.

They began letting people in to make their farewells.

The archpriest read the prayer for the dying.

His face retained its fresh color to the very last.

His wife stood like a woman turned to stone.

At 10 p.m., at about the hour when the assassin had struck, after four days of struggle, Stolypin died.

Dr. Afanasiev, who had kept watch over him four nights on end, confided that he had seen many people of outstanding intelligence and talent when they were doomed to die, and most of them had clung desperately to life, betrayed their sense of helplessness, their lack of spirit, pleading with the doctors to save them, searching their faces for any sign of hope. But from this patient he had heard no entreaties. Knowing that he was doomed, he had shown a rare equanimity and self-possession.

Stolypin went to meet death as an equal. He passed like a sovereign from one kind of life to another.

* * *

HE WHO SHOWS THIS WORLD A PATH
ONLY EARNS THE WORLD'S WRATH

* * *

[7 0]

They wanted to delay the announcement of his death until the morning, but that proved impossible because of the panic that seized the Jews of Kiev (the news could not be prevented from leaking) and, shortly afterward, of Odessa. Those who could began to leave the city. Their representatives hastened to the authorities, imploring them to protect the Jews.

Protection was promised, and given. The authorities concentrated on measures to prevent a pogrom. (Bogrov had calculated correctly.) Patriotic demonstrations in the streets were broken up by the police, and, just in case, people suspected of planning a pogrom were arrested. More than

30,000 troops, who had not yet returned to base after the big parades, were brought into Kiev and stationed near the Jewish sections of the city. The acting Prime Minister, Kokovtsov, published a circular ordering the most determined measures to protect the Jews. The governor-general promulgated an order given by the Emperor as he was leaving Kiev: "The crowd, societies, and individual persons are forbidden to take any irresponsible action likely to result in disorders." The Union of St. Michael the Archangel issued an appeal to its members to preserve strict order in the streets. In the City Duma the leader of the right declared that any assault on any person contradicted the spirit and intention of Stolypin's policy—he had always fought for order and legality. "In this place we feel the heartbeat of the population of Kiev, we must do all we can to calm its passions." The right decided not even to allow public meetings, for fear of setting off disturbances. (The Kiev right had suddenly realized just before Stolypin died that the Makovsky Clinic, in which he lay, had been given no police protection: if he had begun to recover, Bogrov's accomplice—if he had one—would have found no difficulty in entering the clinic and planting a few extra bullets in him.)

What perhaps made this self-restraint easier for the right was that they had never regarded Stolypin as one of them, but on the contrary as a traitor: instead of rejecting the Manifesto of 30 October and trampling it in the mud he had tried to further the development of Russia within the framework of that forcibly extorted concession. Although he had hauled Russia out of the swamp of revolution he had always disappointed the intolerant extreme right, which did not want to know about reform and progress, about new ideas, and above all about concessions, which believed in nothing but prayerful prostration before the Tsar, in petrified immobility, century after century. Of course, being killed by a Jew made Stolypin more acceptable to the right. The local Kiev "Unionists"—members of the Union of the Russian People—planned a demonstration to prove the point at a performance of *A Life for the Tsar* in the opera house where Stolypin had been shot. (The authorities got wind of it and canceled both the matinee and the evening performance.) But the leaders of the right in St. Petersburg remained irreconcilable: the whole of the right faction in the Duma was demonstratively absent from his funeral—neither Markov the Second, nor Purishkevich, nor Zamyslovsky turned up. The right-wing papers said quite frankly, "Russia did not adopt Stolypin as her own . . . May his aberrations be a warning to anyone who takes his place—a warning not to succumb to the hypnosis of contemporary liberal influences."

At the requiem Mass in Zhitomir, Archbishop Antoni Khrapovitsky condemned Stolypin's reforms as leftist and called upon all Orthodox Christians to pray for the forgiveness of his sins; while the far-famed Iliodor of Tsaritsyn (who had a score of his own to settle with Stolypin) refused even to celebrate a requiem: "Stolypin is no kin of ours, no friend, and has done nothing for our good."

They were all taking their cue from the Emperor. No one had failed to notice that he had visited the clinic only once, and had not got as far as the sick man himself. The celebrations to which he had so looked forward went ahead undisturbed by the shots in the theater, never deviating by a hairsbreadth from the program elaborated long before. The military parade, the inspection of Kiev's institutions, the trip to Ovruch and Chernigov took place as planned. The Emperor got back only on 19 September—too late to say goodbye to the dying man, but too soon to wait around for the removal of the body to the Lavra on the following day. The Tsar carried out his program like a man tiptoeing between skittles. He missed seeing the wounded man during those first minutes in the theater, then again when he was so eagerly awaited in the clinic; he missed him on the day of his death, missed his removal to the Lavra, missed the day of his funeral. Everybody could see that the Autocrat of All the Russias had shown no pity for the wounded man.

The word went around, and filtered into the press: "They say the Emperor doesn't consider him much of a loss."

Not surprisingly, the country was not engulfed in waves of sympathy. Prayers for Stolypin's recovery throughout Russia were succeeded by requiems. The chanting ceased—and silence reigned.

And not surprisingly, the liberal press felt no need for the faintest murmur of commiseration, and every newspaper reported that Lieutenant Colonel of Gendarmes Ivanov was most favorably impressed by Bogrov's personality. Journalists took the opportunity to pontificate in this fashion:

> What went through the mind of the wounded minister as he lay dying? A clear vision, perhaps, of the true nature of the police system in which he lived and operated?

Or, in the name of history, to offer a stockbroker's quotation:

> Was the deceased a great statesman? Did he have a broad and profound governmental program with well-defined principles and systematically planned? No, the powerful sweep of a unifying idea was not one of his characteristics.

A government commission almost immediately visited Stolypin's Kovno estate and impounded his program for the development of Russia over the next twenty years. Newspapers passed judgment on him with the brash vulgarity in which, in the twentieth century, journalists have outshone the rest of the world. The Kadet press, for instance, admonished its readers:

> No one is entitled to forget that the *law* [meaning the Codex elaborated by graduates of law faculties and approved by their learned brothers sitting in a legislative body] stands above religion and above national sentiment.

Only Menshikov in *New Times* felt able to write:

> This shot has echoed throughout the world. He was killed in the prime of life and in the execution of his duties, when his career in politics was just beginning. He fought against revolution as a statesman, not as the head of the police. He was a new type of public servant. And our only response to this event is "rest in peace" and the blue smoke from the thurible. That is our only reaction to the decapitation of Russia. All these requiems are shadow play. Revolution must be resisted by more than theatricals.

Was there, then, nothing that could be called public opinion in the country besides the utterances of journalists and politicians? Had no one else anything to say? In Russia, Russia's loss went almost unexplained.

Some citizens of Kiev discussed the erection of a memorial to Stolypin. The state did not offer to contribute. While Russia buried its best head of government in a century, in two hundred years, the left, the semi-left, and the right jeered and sneered and turned their backs. All of them—from the émigré terrorists to the devout Tsar.

You had to look to the West to read that (as a statement from the French government put it) Bogrov's attack was not on an individual but on the foundations of ordered government. That Stolypin was a great statesman, a mainstay of order, who in an amazingly short time had put Russia back on the road to prosperity. That (in the words of *The Times*) he had adapted the political life of Russia to representative institutions more quickly and in a more orderly fashion than it had ever been done in any country. That he had died the death of a martyr for his beliefs, that his death was a national disaster for Russia, and that it could only be hoped that the Stolypin era would not end with his death. That (according to the Viennese newspapers) yet another great son of Russia had fallen victim to bestial passions, and that the Russian terrorist socialists—who had great influence in bourgeois and academic circles—called themselves freedom fighters in an attempt to conceal their revolting barbarism but succeeded only in hindering the work of peaceful development.

The dead Stolypin lay in an oak coffin, dressed in a white tunic. Out of all the wreaths sent, his widow chose a wreath of thorns to place on his breast. His dented Order of St. Vladimir lay on a cushion at his feet. It was difficult to get in or out of the crowded clinic, but people took turns paying their last respects.

He was to have been buried by Askold's grave, but the Emperor visited the clinic and gave orders that he should be laid to rest in the Lavra.

On 20 September, Stolypin's remains were taken from the clinic in an open coffin to the Lavra, the Monastery of the Caves a few versts away, through crowded streets lined with soldiers. The dead man was given the protection which he had been denied in life. Then there had been not a single gendarme—now there were hundreds of them, as many as could be assembled from St. Petersburg, Moscow, and Kiev, riding or marching before and behind the procession in ceremonial dress, because the deceased Prime Minister had also, after all, been Minister of the Interior. But they made an incongruous frame for one whose service to Russia was so very much greater. People whose support Stolypin had so sorely lacked in his lifetime were there in great numbers—deputations from government departments, senior officers of the armed services, senior civil servants. (Kurlov, however, had taken himself off to St. Petersburg, and Spiridovich to Yalta.)

Many brass bands played. Torchbearers went before the procession. Then came representatives of the gentry and zemstvo leaders dressed in white. The chorus from the ill-starred opera house. Cathedral choristers in dark blue cassocks. Ten banners. A tall cross. Sextons and deacons two by two, swinging censers. Three bishops and eight archimandrites, their miters flashing in the sun. In places people knelt as the hearse went by. It was drawn by six horses in white trappings and with white plumes. The procession stopped outside churches while bishops read from the Gospels. Behind the hearse walked members of the family, followed by generals and other officers, members of the monarchic organizations with flags, and people carrying hundreds of wreaths of silver or of fresh flowers. The procession took three hours to pass.

One little thing was missing. The Emperor had seen fit to leave Kiev for a holiday in the Crimea the day before. (Their Majesties did, however, send a wreath. As did the Dowager Empress.)

Deputations from St. Petersburg had arrived on 22 September, in time for the funeral. The ranks of the Duma delegation were rather thin—fifty members: a cross section of the Russian nationalists, the only group who were loyal to Stolypin from start to finish (but their leader in Kiev, Shulgin, was also traveling in the Crimea), and a handful of Octobrists led by a penitent Guchkov. There was no one from the left or from the extreme right of the Duma. Rodzyanko laid a wreath, but only on his own behalf. "Not on behalf of the Duma?" he was asked. "The deputies did not authorize it."

Not one of the grand dukes was there.

The coffin had stood for the past few nights in the Trapeznaya Church, with marshals of the nobility, zemstvo men, members of the City Duma, and (inevitably) officials of the Ministry of the Interior standing guard. True, loyal friends who had helped with the agrarian reform were also there—Krivoshein, the Minister of Agriculture, and Lykoshin, Stolypin's aide.

The Metropolitan conducted the service for the dead. Bishop Yevlogi of Kholmskaya Rus delivered an ardent valedictory in which he called Stolypin a crusader.

Before the coffin was carried out of the church, representatives of the press, photographers, and motion-picture cameramen had made themselves comfortable at the place of burial. The Unionists insisted that this was insulting and asked that they be removed. When they refused to go voluntarily they were escorted from the graveyard.

Bells tolled as the coffin was carried out of the church. The guard of honor (gendarmes again) presented arms. Stolypin's decorations were carried behind him on cushions. There were fifty-four priests, six deacons, four bishops, and the Metropolitan, all in white vestments. The coffin was carried by high—but not unduly high—dignitaries (the Emperor had instructed the most senior of them to leave Kiev). Two ministers, Shcheglovitov and Timashev, were pallbearers. Krivoshein escorted Stolypin's widow. Rodzyanko, Guchkov, Balashov, and Vladimir Bobrinsky were also there. Quite a gathering!

An Old Believer, apparently a peasant, tried to say something when the coffin was set down, but the gendarmes hustled him away.

After prayers had been read at the tomb—including "How Glorious Is He" and "Rest in Peace"—to three volleys of rifle fire Russia's great man was lowered into a vault between the Refectory and the Great Church. It was sealed at once.

They had never succeeded in frightening him.

Only in killing him.

[7 1]

The trial of Bogrov in camera began a few hours later in one of the bigger cells of the Kosoy Kaponir. The rumor that he would be given a public trial in St. Petersburg, so that all suspicions against the Okhrana could be examined in the full glare of publicity, proved false. The cowards, of course, tried him behind closed doors, and the indictment was not published. What better way of confirming the suspicions of the left? Only very guilty people could be so anxious to conceal the truth about the Bogrov case. Bogrov was obviously their man. The establishment itself had contrived the assassination!

Forget about the troops lined up at the funeral to present arms as the dead man's decorations were carried by on cushions. A public trial would have shown real respect.

It appeared that the defendant had asked for paper the night before, 21 September, to make "an extremely important statement." Since he had already been committed to the jurisdiction of the District Military

Court, the prison authorities refused his request. The prosecutor's office had been informed next morning, but had not modified the proceedings.

The trial was due to begin at 5 p.m. They had overlooked the fact that there was no electricity in Kosoy Kaponir, and the day turned dull. The judges began in twilight and shortly sent for oil lamps.

On the bench were four officers from the garrison, colonels and lieutenant colonels, with a major general presiding. The prosecutor was a lieutenant general. The president and the prosecutor had obviously not failed to note and digest the Emperor's repeatedly demonstrated lack of concern for the Prime Minister, when he was wounded and after his death. They may have drawn their own conclusions, but in all likelihood also sought advice—from someone who will remain forever unknown. However that may be, five of the twelve witnesses summoned did not appear. Kurlov was not even on the list: the court (like the investigators before it) dared not aim so high. Verigin, who of course had "absolutely nothing to do with the matter," had hurried off to St. Petersburg almost as soon as the shooting took place. Spiridovich was tied down by his responsibility for the security of the court during the celebrations, and so could not get away from Kiev immediately, but he had ignored two summonses to assist the investigation. When the Minister of Justice warned the Minister of the Court that he would go to the Emperor directly and demand that Spiridovich comply, he had appeared at once but (as the foursome had agreed) had given no concrete answers, having, you will remember, "no connection with the matter whatsoever." After that it was hardly to be expected that he would appear in court.

Not one of the contumacious witnesses received a second summons.

There was no defense counsel, since the defendant had waived his right to one. But, stranger yet, no record of the proceedings was kept, no full transcript of the evidence made. The trial might have been taking place in a theater of war, with the enemy's shells already shaking the tower to its foundations. Or else they could have been trying a pickpocket.

Some important local people were present: the governor-general, Fyodor Trepov; Nikolai Iudovich Ivanov, commander of the Military District (the Ivanov whose life Bogrov had once saved by betraying the would-be assassins); the governor of Kiev; the provincial Marshal of the Gentry; several procurators. The Minister of Justice, Shcheglovitov, also looked in for part of the time. Not one of these people pointed out that the court was being careless in not keeping records—if they thought of it as carelessness.

The facts were too unpalatable to the authorities to be written down in detail. And in accordance with the laws of the bureaucratic condition, an opinion on what had happened had already been imprinted on each of those minds. Bogrov (he was still wearing his frock coat, badly crumpled during the skirmish in the theater and his sojourn in prison, and was now minus collar, cuffs, and bow tie) suddenly asked for the witness Kulyabko to be kept behind in court while he made his own statement (this was forbidden by law, but the court agreed!), and coolly proceeded to blow sky-high everything that had been said to the investigating officer. They wouldn't give him any paper to put it all in writing the night before, so he was turning the case inside out orally.

His evidence now directly contradicted what he had said before.

Gone was the great plan to remove the enemy of the people, the enemy of the non-Russian peoples, the enemy of progress and the constitution. It had all been a matter of pure chance. He, Bogrov, had, it was true, been walking around for some days with a revolver in his pocket, but had not definitely made up his mind—far from it—to kill anyone, or, if he had, who it should be. He had assassinated Stolypin without premeditation, and it was as much a surprise to him as to anybody. He had always served the Okhrana honestly and conscientiously, because he sympathized with its aims, and he had received practically no remuneration.

(I'm one of you. More so than you ever thought. If I drown you will go down with me!)

Delegates from the anarchists in Paris had visited him twice that summer, asked him to account for his expenditure from party funds in 1908, accused him of having dealings with the Okhrana, and demanded that he commit some terrorist act, or else they would make his activity as agent provocateur public and kill him.

(Save me, I am yours! See how I have suffered for you.)

The anarchists had advised Bogrov to kill—Kulyabko!

(Kulyabko jumped as if he had received a charge of birdshot. Had he, then, been in such danger? He who had tearfully confessed his own unconscionable stupidity in the course of the investigation—anything to avoid being classified as a traitor to the state—had *he*, then, been the main intended victim?)

The oil lamps were brought in. They cast menacingly enlarged shadows. Movements and gestures, monstrously magnified in black, chased each other across the vaulted ceiling.

Bogrov had himself marked out Kulyabko—they were in constant contact, and this was a killing he could have carried out with complete impunity.

(Dear, clever Bogrov! Kulyabko saw it all now: if he himself was to have been the main victim he could not really be blamed for anything much!)

Kulyabko's trustfulness and his sympathy had stayed Bogrov's hand. He had gone to Kulyabko's home on the night of 13–14 September (how neatly it was all fitting in) to kill him—what other reason could he have had?—but was disarmed by his kindness, and his state of undress.

(I had pity on Kulyabko, on one of you! Accept me as one of you!)

He warmly defended Kulyabko for having believed in him. Kulyabko had made an honest mistake.

In the strange shadows on the ceiling you could not distinguish this world from the next.

All this was happening at nightfall, close to the Bald Mountain.

The court was taken aback by this sudden twist.

"Why, then, *did* you kill State Secretary Stolypin?"

"I chose him completely by chance. He was the most important person in the audience."

Why, then, his Napoleonic hauteur in the hours immediately afterward? Why had he wrapped himself in a hero's cloak for so many days and marched so resolutely toward the scaffold? Why had he heaped up the most damaging evidence against himself, invited the most scorching charges?

The court was taken aback, though not to the extent of asking any of these questions. But was the court really so surprised? Did anyone seek an explanation for this drastic change of testimony? Did anyone question Bogrov's motives?

Did they examine his statement searchingly? Start keeping a detailed protocol? Call for further investigation? Postpone their decision?

They did not.

If shells had been landing around the tower, the court could not have been in more of a hurry to get its work over as quickly and as quietly as possible. Its object might have been to confirm the gravest accusations of the left-wing press: "He's one of you."

Kulyabko, bleating with happiness, was given an easy run on the witness stand. (Now that he had heard the new version in full, it was all the easier for him to adjust his own story.) He was full of praise for his loyal collaborator Bogrov. He had, of course, said all along that Bogrov's activities were exceptionally useful to the Department. It would have been unthinkable not to believe Bogrov, and unethical to keep a check on him. Why, though, had Kulyabko not tried to arrest the revolutionaries allegedly in Bogrov's flat? Well, because he was not sure that they would be demonstrably preparing to commit a crime, and at the same time he would be giving Bogrov's secret away to them. As for admitting Bogrov to the theater (if Kurlov had not put it into his head Kulyabko would never have thought of it himself, or if he had would never have dared whisper it), *Bogrov was allowed into the theater with Stolypin's knowledge!*

The earth had been shoveled into Stolypin's grave and tamped down. Anyone could jump on it as much as he pleased.

It was all very simple and conclusively clear. (And remember, they had to be quick.) When Kulyabko's evidence agreed so closely with that of Bogrov, why should the court question any of the six witnesses present? As for those who had not appeared, the evidence of Spiridovich and

Verigin could be read out, and the court could retire to discuss its verdict.

This court was Kalyaev's brainchild, a heroic completion of the Act.

Had the defendant anything more to tell the court? Only that he suffered from hunger in the prison (more and more acutely as the hope of saving his life revived). He asked to be given better food.

The prison administrator was called and reported that Bogrov received officer's rations. The court ordered that Bogrov should be given as much to eat as he wanted.

After only twenty minutes they were back with their verdict: Mordko Gershevich Bogrov, lawyer's assistant, is found guilty of participation in an association formed for the purpose of attempting to change by force the form of government established by the Fundamental Laws of Russia (they had to have an "association" as required by Article 102: the Code nowhere made provision for revolutionary acts by individual assassins, although they had been occurring on and off for half a century; the Code, in fact, was ill adapted to the years of revolution) and of murder with malice aforethought, and is sentenced to deprivation of all the rights of his status, and to death by hanging.

Bogrov swayed.

Just like that? Was that all?

He had been confident that his ruse would work. It had not.

The worst had happened. The little ball had jumped out of the wheel.

(The court might have been glad to show clemency, but there was one law which Bogrov did not know about: martial law is always in force within a radius of two versts from the Emperor. It did not matter so much that the accused had killed the Prime Minister: he had used a firearm in the Emperor's presence!)

The court added a rider about Kulyabko: he had not taken the necessary steps . . . had not given instructions . . . had not instituted surveillance . . . These matters should be brought to the attention of the appropriate authorities.

That was all. No question of putting him on trial.

Bogrov was now given his final sheet of paper—once in his cell he would get no more—to write a last letter to his parents.

The court broke up. People were leaving one by one. Grotesque shadows from that other world flitted over the vaulted ceiling. Soldiers were waiting to take him away.

By the light of an oil lamp and with a table before him Bogrov managed to write.

For other people his story might vary, but he had one father and one mother—and for them there could be only one story. He had rung the changes, but this was the end. The opportunity to write such a letter would not recur.

It was not just to his parents that he was writing. The letter would be printed and reprinted dozens of times. It was a letter to the whole world.

But how could he put it all into words? And be sure that it would get through?

"Dear Mama and Papa, this is the one moment at which I have felt wretched. You must have been baffled by such a rush of real and unreal secrets . . ."

Real ones and unreal ones. That should be clear enough. Don't believe what they say about me, don't believe that I was an Okhrana agent. He could make it even clearer.

"Go on thinking of me as an honorable man."

"Honorable"—he couldn't possibly put it more clearly! For Bogrov senior, for the whole circle of Russian lawyers, for Russian "society" at large, to be honorable was to be an enemy of the organs of authority. "Honorable" meant that he had killed for idealistic reasons.

And it would get past the censor.

They had been in a great hurry with the trial and were eager now to have the execution behind them. It was to take place the following night, 23–24 September. (Stolypin's relatives asked in vain for a postponement until the results of the inquiry into the Kiev Okhrana Department were known. It was about to begin; Senator Trusevich had been appointed to conduct it on 23 September, and would arrive in Kiev on the 24th.) They would have done it at once but for the law forbidding executions just before Sunday. It would have to be on Monday morning.

No major terrorist had ever been tried and executed in Russia with such nervous haste. Quick, get him out of the way—we want no more interrogations, no more investigations, no more replays. The final version, the one produced at the trial, wasn't bad at all: hardly anybody was blamed for anything, hardly anybody had blotted his curriculum vitae.

But now the Okhrana was the subject of an inquiry, and the court had not taken the trouble to produce a record signed by the defendant. How, then, was the Okhrana's blamelessness to be proved?

So on Saturday, 23 September, in the silent fortress of Kosoy Kaponir, into the condemned man's cell, legally barred to everyone from *this* world, crept—no, boldly stepped—an investigating officer!

To interrogate the prisoner further! Nowhere else does this ever happen to a man already condemned to death! (We see here the character and the power of those lofty "spheres." Prison walls, however many bricks thick, have this peculiarity: though insurmountable to the prisoner they are easily permeable by those with authority.)

How Bogrov's heart fluttered! His last variant was working! There were winding ways he could still take!

The someone who crept in to him was yet again Lieutenant Colonel of Gendarmes Ivanov. He had almost come to love Bogrov in the past few days, and had informed the press, "He is one of the most remarkable people I have ever met in my life." (Many years later, thrown onto the scrap heap of emigration, after the revolution's long series of victories, he would write a letter of protest to a White newspaper which had the temerity to describe Bogrov's appearance as unprepossessing.)

Why had he penetrated the impenetrable doors? To show his gratitude for Bogrov's lifesaving prevarication in court?

No, he had come because Bogrov's courtroom version had proved insufficient.

Well, the court's decision was not as promised either.

Ah, but the court was not controlled by the Okhrana.

What was there left for him now that sentence had been passed?

He could run away! That would be even better than what he had first expected—emigration instead of hard labor in Siberia. And it was within the power of the Okhrana.

He found it hard to believe.

But if the lieutenant colonel had been allowed in to see a condemned man, regardless of regulations, and if "many influential persons" had an interest in the matter . . . And anyway, this would certainly not be the first time it had happened. How many escapes had the Okhrana organized in the past? There was Petrov, Solomon Ryss . . . and many others.

That was certain.

A man from outside, and a gendarme officer at that, has an incalculable advantage over a man locked up for the last time.

But this condemned man's heart palpitated hopefully, his mind vibrated with ingenious schemes.

Anyway, they weren't asking much more of him than he had already given—just to dot a few *i*'s. The way you put it in court did not carry complete conviction. You must make it clear that we had every reason to trust you until the very last moment. You must emphasize that you were suddenly coerced into committing your terrorist act by the revolutionaries, under threat of death. Give details.

And, of course, sign it.

This pregnant conversation is hidden from us and we shall never know anything about it since both participants went long ago to their graves. But a formal record has survived. According to this, the condemned man, so proud and obstinate a little while ago, willingly answered questions during this unscheduled interrogation, helped with the wording, and signed the record.

The interrogation began with a ploy which might have been transported by time machine from 1946 to 1911: Bogrov was simply shown a photograph and asked whether he knew the man.

Instead of fretting about eternity, communing with God, or repenting of his past, a man awaiting execution may just as well give a lieutenant colonel of gendarmes a little help with his snapshot collection. As though he had only been waiting to be shown this photograph, his story began to pour out without further prompting.

Yes, of course, that's the anarchist who came to see me last March after I got out of Lukyanovka prison and told me that people there were very annoyed with me: a letter renewing the accusations against me had reached them in prison a year back, and he had been given the job of questioning me all over again.

The subject was exhausted, but once the narrative flow had started there was no stopping it. And it wasn't like in court—there was time to get things on paper.

In May he had had another visit. Two anarchists turned up from Paris, a "revolutionary commission" making the rounds of places all over Russia where revolutionary work had come to a standstill, to determine the reasons for this collapse and concentrate the party's forces and its weapons. They had Bogrov down for a deficit of 520 rubles. Although he did not consider that he had overspent, he borrowed money from his parents and paid up. Nonetheless, at the end of July, when he was at the dacha near Kremenchug (where the whole extraordinary story originated—Nikolai Yakovlevich and the motorboat included), they had sent him a registered letter (in Kiev its delivery would have been recorded, but in a village there was no fear of that) demanding assurances in a hostile tone.

Would he not regret throwing away his victory, descending from his pedestal, rejecting all that he had achieved? Going down in history not even as just a bon vivant from Monte Carlo but as a petty police stooge? Totting up all over again the party funds he had squandered and repaid, remembering all his petty tale-telling, explaining the one great feat of his life by fear, pretending that he had killed to expiate an offense, to avoid being killed himself as a traitor? It was obvious enough that the record was not being made to be kept secret through the ages. Slightly modified in transition, this was what would very shortly be given to the newspapers. Should he choose the shameful version, which previously he himself had thought worse than death?

Death, staring him in the face, had turned out to be more dreadful than he had imagined.

And if I live—just watch me turn all this upside down again!

Oh, yes, another anarchist, a man he knew from the "Stormy Petrel" group, had turned up at Bogrov's apartment en route from Paris on 29 August. (A long and thorough and leisurely record was being made. His head, as on that earlier occasion, supplied him with plenty of realistic details.) This was what the anarchist had to say: Bogrov's betrayal had been conclusively established, and they had now decided to make the facts known in all the places he frequented—to tell both the lawyers and the public at large. This meant outlawry, followed by physical death at the hands of avengers. But "Stormy Petrel" would give him till 18 September to rehabilitate himself, preferably by killing Kulyabko.

Kulyabko . . . Kulya . . . He had grossly overdone the Kulyabko theme. Another little question followed. "Why were you so anxious to shield Kulyabko at the trial?" Bogrov: "Kulyabko was so flummoxed by the prosecutor's questions that he didn't know what to say. I felt sorry for him."

Had he really been so fond of Kulyabko, then? Loved him almost like a bedfellow? No answer. Think what you like.

"Then, as it happened, came the Kiev celebrations, and Stolypin turned up. I happened to know him by sight" (from the encounter at the St. Petersburg waterworks). "He was the center of public interest—so I decided. All the same, if I had seen anyone else in the aisle before him I might have killed him instead." (A terrorist always has wide freedom of choice!) "I committed my terrorist act almost unthinkingly." (The crime was virtually unplanned, it was a gesture of despair—that was how Kurlov wanted it.)

The virtuoso of mystification, the skilled creator of varying versions, had constructed yet another—and yet again dates, motives, actions fitted. (Not all, but enough of them—not all of them fitted the "definitive" version either.)

But if it was really like that, why didn't the anarchists boast that they had committed the murder? (A weak spot in his story, this.)

Yet another variant was possible: his own free decision was already ripening and the threat from the anarchists only hurried it along. That would be the best way to put it.

But that was not what the customer wanted.

With his sinuous ingenuity he had wriggled to the very summit of the pole and stung his enemy to the rapturous applause of the public. Was he now to flop down like a limp rag?

Oh, how he wanted not to die!

To have fired his shot, to have steered Russia's obtuse bulk onto a different course, then to walk lightly perfumed into the gilded hall at Monte Carlo . . . that was what he had wanted.

Dostoevsky explored many a spiritual abyss, unraveled many a fantasy—but not all of them.

Next day, Sunday, a rabbi was allowed in to see the condemned man. "Tell the Jews," Bogrov said, "that I didn't want to harm them. On the contrary, I was fighting for the benefit of the Jewish people."

That was the one and only part of his testimony to remain unchanged.

The rabbi said reproachfully that Bogrov might have caused a pogrom. Bogrov replied, "A great people must not bow down to its oppressors!"

This statement also was widely reported in the press.

* * *

The condemned man's final hours were running out, and no one else came to see him. No one came and opened the door for him to run away . . .

Had Ivanov tricked him?

Late on Sunday afternoon the wasteland below the fort on the Bald Mountain was searched, then cordoned off by infantry, Cossacks, and policemen. In addition to members of the execution party, permission to be present at the execution had been given to some twenty men from the Union of the Russian People, which had vocally doubted whether Bogrov would actually be hanged and some other criminal substituted for him. As he was put into the prison carriage, still wearing his frock coat, which by now looked rather comic, an electric torch was shone on him, and the Unionists chorused, "That's him all right," "I gave him a good one in the theater!"

It looked genuine enough.

They had four versts to ride. Bogrov complained that he felt feverish.

At the place of execution the assistant court secretary loudly read out the sentence (the same words with the passage about a criminal confederacy) by the light of blazing torches.

Bogrov was asked if he had anything more to say to the rabbi. Yes, he wanted to continue his conversation with the rabbi, but in private. "That's impossible." "In that case, get on with it."

Ivanov had tricked him.

He asked those present to say goodbye to his parents for him.

What he said after that was too quiet and too confused for anyone to make sense of it.

The executioner, a convict from Lukyanovka prison, tied Bogrov's hands behind his back. Led him to the gallows. Draped the winding sheet about him.

"Do you want me to hold my head up higher?" Bogrov asked from under the sheet.

The executioner sprang the trap.

The body danced for a while, and hung there for fifteen minutes as required by law. Torches flared and crackled in the deep silence.

"I don't think he'll shoot anybody else," said one of the Unionists.

He no longer needed to.

Some of the Unionists carried off lengths of rope as souvenirs.

Many Jewish students in Kiev went into mourning for Bogrov.

How well it had all ended, with Bogrov correctly testifying that there was nothing to the whole affair but the unhappy aberrations of a warped little man. Not the slightest blemish was left on the reputations of the police generals. Or on any high-ranking person.

There was no proud challenge to the country.

No undermining of the imperial power.

The imperial power loved bromide banalities. Anodyne conclusions. Trivial endings.

[7 2]

Alix had stayed at home in the palace on 14 September because both she and Aleksei were unwell. The Emperor himself had spent the afternoon at the racecourse watching one of his favorite shows—a display by cadets from classical high schools, modern secondary schools, the municipal school and the trade school, the orphanages and charity schools marching in four regimental columns. He had thanked them all. After a little rest it was time to move on to a lengthy banquet given by the governor-general. Another little rest, and he was away with his two older daughters to the gala performance at the opera.

In the second intermission they went out of the box into an antechamber. The Emperor smoked, while Olya and Tanya drank a cool drink, and functionaries came along to ask how they were enjoying the opera and whether they wanted anything.

At that moment they heard two shots fired in the hall. They all hurried into the box and, looking down over the velvet-upholstered rampart, saw Stolypin, quite near to them, still standing propped up against the orchestra barrier.

Slowly, slowed down by his wounds, Stolypin turned his head, saw the Emperor, and raised his hand, his left hand for some reason, to bless the wearer of the Russian crown.

The Emperor could see from the box that Stolypin was very pale, and that there was a big bloodstain on his white coat. Immediately afterward Stolypin took a step toward his seat, trying to unbutton his coat. Professor Rein and gray-headed Count Frederiks bent over him to help.

A noise reached the royal party from the far end of the hall: they had caught the murderer and were beating and reviling him. The hall rang with panicky shouting from all who were in it. Gallant Spiridovich rushed over at once, saber bared, pushing his way into the space before the first row, and took his stand, quivering with loyal zeal, directly beneath the royal box.

Just think of it! How splendid the security arrangements must have been! But there was no way of protecting yourself against that hell-brood.

Poor Stolypin. And how depressing that it should happen during these splendid celebrations.

The sad event prolonged the intermission. All the doctors in the audience gathered around Stolypin. They raised him and slowly led him toward the exit. The hall was filling up; the noise grew but was still somewhat restrained by the presence of the Emperor. Now every seat was occupied again, except Stolypin's, in the front row by the aisle. Even the martial Spiridovich sheathed his saber and took his seat in the third row.

The audience demanded that the national anthem be played as a retort to the dastardly outrage. The whole cast, in the costumes of Tsar Saltan's realm, with the stage Tsar among them, knelt and sang "God Save the Tsar." The whole audience rose to its feet. The Tsar stood at the very front of his box with the grand duchesses, so that everyone could see.

The anthem was repeated twice.

Then they went on with the third act, after which the Tsar and his daughters left. By then security precautions had been reinforced, if that was possible. The devoted General Kurlov was extremely active.

The Emperor went back to the palace very sadly. He realized that a tragic event had taken place.

Poor Stolypin.

But he was surprised, and annoyed with himself, to find that he was not overwhelmed by grief. He asked himself why.

It was all because Stolypin had clung to office too long. Why hadn't he resigned earlier? He knew very well that the time had come. Why had he waited to be dismissed?

If he had resigned he would have been safe and sound now.

Better make Kokovtsov acting Prime Minister for the time being. He had sometimes deputized for Stolypin during his absences.

Back in the palace Alix had not yet heard about the attempt. She was in bed with a bad headache and back pains, and the Tsarevich was in his cot in his own room. Neither of them, thank heaven, was worse than before he had left for the theater.

Nikolai told Alix what had happened, forcing his voice to express sorrow. While he was doing so Tanya and Olya burst in and began tearfully telling their mother the whole story.

But Alix took it calmly, and Nikolai stopped reproaching himself so harshly for his lack of feeling. Some sort of equilibrium was restored.

The girls went away, and he sat down beside Alix. Still obviously in pain, she wrinkled her forehead and said thoughtfully, "You know . . . this may not be the worst solution. I pray to God for his recovery—but he would have had to be retired anyway. True, all the newspaper talk and drawing-room gossip would have been distasteful. And of course your mama would have been against it."

What she said was factually correct, but there was something morally false in it.

"It's my fault," Nikolai said despondently. "I couldn't make up my mind to it. If I had dismissed him in time Stolypin would be unhurt."

Alix flashed him her look of profound understanding. But there was also a tinge of regret in her words.

"My husband is always just a little less firm than he should be. And firmness in a monarch is truly a blessing for his subjects. Firmness always settles problems in the least unkind way."

Nikolai sat there glumly, elbows on knees, head cupped in his hands.

"He would never have gone voluntarily. I would have been waiting forever."

Since last spring he had been waiting for Stolypin to set him free by resigning. How he regretted giving in to Mama in March! Never since the Duma had been in existence had any debate there so vexed him as that on the western zemstvos last spring, and especially Maklakov's words: "The Emperor sees himself made ridiculous, treated like a pawn in Stolypin's dubious game."

"He made such harsh conditions. He treated the State Council so rudely."

"He was never really our man, Nicky. He was always out to strengthen the unruly Duma. He stuck to that wretched Manifesto. Everybody kept telling you that."

"Well, he was a help at a very difficult time."

"Even then he wasn't as firm as Dumbadze."

But that very difficult time would never repeat itself. The troops were so devoted to the Emperor that they would never let themselves be swayed again. The people would not let their minds be poisoned by agitation a second time. The three-hundred-year-old dynasty had weathered the crisis and would now, perhaps, stand for three thousand.

"He refused to retract the Manifesto, he would only water it down. All the rightists condemn him for it."

"And he's never had any respect for Our Friend! He was quite heartless to him."

Nikolai had to agree. "Yes, he's never made life easy. He's always been very wearing."

So very tiresome! Why, oh why, should an autocratic ruler submit to such oppression?

There was a hushed silence in the royal couple's apartment. Not a sound could be heard from the palace or the city.

Alix spoke: "He would have liked to take your place."

"How could he do that?" Not just the absurdity of the idea but the tone of the whole conversation stung him to protest. "That's ridiculous."

"You know what I mean. He had too much of an appetite for glory and didn't hesitate to put you in the shade."

Alas, they had talked about this before.

"Let's say a prayer," he said emphatically, as though rejecting what she had said. "Let us pray for his recovery. And then, of course, we'll let him take his rest."

Tanya, however, cried a lot during the night, and both of the older girls slept badly.

The report on the wounded man next morning was that he had been in great pain during the night and had been given several morphia injections. The Emperor simply couldn't find the few minutes necessary to visit him: that day, 15 September, a large-scale parade had been arranged to mark the conclusion of the maneuvers, fifty-five versts from Kiev. The drive there and back by car would take a great deal of time, not to mention the parade itself. (The young grand duchesses all attended services of intercession in the Cathedral of St. Vladimir and in St. Andrei's Church.)

The parade was a huge success. Ivanov and Alekseev, fine generals both of them, presented for his inspection an immense rectangular formation of troops. Six airplanes soared overhead. Four army corps marched past the Tsar. There seemed to be no end to them: infantry, artillery, dragoons, uhlans, hussars, Cossacks (from the Don, the Kuban, the Terek, Orenburg), trotting or at walking pace. Then the horse artillery, the heavy transport, cars, motorcycles; not one an inch out of line. Finally a team of balloonists goose-stepped past, holding down a balloon carrying two officers which they released as they came abreast of the Emperor. As many as ninety thousand men took part, and every unit was thanked by the Tsar.

This parade was a fitting climax to the marvelous Kiev celebrations, which had been among the happiest days of Nikolai's life. In the heart of the Russian land, in the place of Russia's baptism, he had received everywhere an ecstatic welcome! He had witnessed with his own eyes the people's indestructible love for him! It was late when he got back from the parade, and then there was a big reception for officers, and a dinner for unit commanders later that evening. The following morning he had to leave very early for Ovruch, where the thirteenth-century Cathedral of St. Vasili, newly restored, awaited reconsecration.

This outing was just as marvelous in a different way. They went to Korosten by train, then just before eight went by car to Ovruch. The sky was overcast but it was not raining and there was a promise of brighter weather later. As they left Korosten the villagers offered them bread and salt. Farther along the road peasants had erected arches decorated with flowers and icons, bread and salt were brought out several times, enthusiastic crowds cheered, and they met religious processions.

Ovruch itself had apparently not slept all night. Processions from thirty-six churches, some thirty thousand peasants, had come in from the countryside round about, and the crowd on the approaches to the town was three versts long. A guard of honor from the local regiment was drawn up on the town square, together with cadets from the municipal school. The national anthem was played, and the Emperor inspected them. At the cathedral he was met by deputations from the gentry, the zemstvos, and the town, all bearing bread and salt. The clergy were headed by the archbishop. They had brought their most sacred treasure—the icon of St. Vasili, and relics of the saint. The service of consecration began. Afterward the Emperor visited the archbishop in his apartment.

It was evening when they got back to Kiev. On the way from the station to the palace the Emperor called at the clinic and saw Stolypin's wife, newly arrived, but the wounded man himself was in a poor state and the doctors advised against visiting him.

The Emperor felt a certain relief. He had no wish to talk to Stolypin just at that moment.

Back home in the palace a mound of telegrams awaited him—from the Kings of England and Serbia, the President of France, the Sultan, the Reichskanzler, the Austrian and other governments. They all expressed their sympathy with the Emperor of Russia in his profound grief, and the horror which the crime had inspired in them.

This spate of telegrams, however well-meaning, contributed to the exaggeration of the Prime Minister's importance. Nikolai remembered how Wilhelm and Edward had always asked enthusiastically about Stolypin. They had never experienced the discomfort of working with such a willful minister, always so sure of himself and so unyielding that his sovereign had the sensation of losing his independence.

The newspapers too in recent years had contracted an unhealthy habit of reporting in exaggerated detail what Stolypin was currently doing and what he was about to do, as though the life of the state revolved around him alone.

On Sunday, 17 September, after morning Mass in the governor-general's chapel, the Emperor visited Kiev's High School No. 1, which was celebrating its centenary, having been opened just before Napoleon's invasion of Russia. It was a very grand occasion, with the whole school and many invited guests present. Prayers of thanksgiving were offered in the school chapel. The school hall was adorned with a portrait of the Tsar and his coat of arms. A choir on the platform sang "Glory to Him." The Emperor bowed to them all, and examined the mementos on display. Kasso read out a decree of the Emperor graciously permitting the school to assume the honorific "Imperial." There were cheers and the whole audience sang "God Save the Tsar." Pleasant speeches followed. The Tsar signed his name in the school's "golden book" for very distinguished visitors, spoke a few words to the pupils nearest to him, and went around to a few classrooms. (It turned out, incidentally, that the murderer was an alumnus of this very school.)

He further attended the unveiling of the memorial to St. Olga—a gift to Kiev from the Emperor. On the same day he found time to go through the Museum of the History of War and the Museum of Peasant Crafts, in both of which very interesting information was supplied. At the palace he was at home to professors from the university.

That evening he had to embark on a steamer and sail away from the illuminated hills of Kiev to Chernigov. This river trip had been planned long ago, and a superannuated steam launch had been converted into a nice little miniature yacht, unlike anything in the local flotilla, so that the Tsar could sail up the Desna. They moved slowly against the current, and although the middle channel had been dredged specially, on one occasion they went aground in the shallows. The Desna is a winding, sandy-bottomed river, and navigation is difficult. (The whole of the Most August Family went out on deck to watch the sailors refloating the boat.) And the scenery along the banks was quite unspoiled, and at times very cozy.

The journey took longer than expected. It was after noon on 18 September when they got to Chernigov, greeted by the ringing of bells. A guard of honor awaited them at a landing place prepared specially for the Tsar, and the anthem was played. The Emperor inspected the guard of honor. Then he was greeted by children with flowers, and by members of his retinue who had arrived by train—Frederiks, the palace commandant, the head of his traveling chancery, Admiral Nilov, and a number of generals, among them those most amiable fellows Sukhomlinov and Ivanov, the obliging Kurlov in a state of high excitement, the chief procurator of the Holy Synod, the local governor, Nikolai Maklakov (a brother of that sneering Kadet but a very nice, very loyal fellow himself—it was hard to believe they belonged to the same family).

This governor had arranged a magnificent program, an unforgettable program, although it lasted only a few hours. Bread and salt from the mayor, the burgesses, the Jews. Then to the cathedral in an open carriage, through streets lined by row upon row of townsfolk. The whole center of the town was a sea of flags, foliage, flowers; balconies and shop windows were adorned with carpets and Ukrainian fabrics; busts and portraits of Their Majesties and the imperial arms were displayed in many places. The weather too was amazing! Autumn here was sunnier than the northern summer. And what a marvelous place the cathedral itself was! He kissed the icons and the coffin of St. Feodosi. Then he inspected the local infantry regiment and two thousand cadets on the town square. Then there was a visit to the Gentry Assembly, where lunch was served. He went through the museum. He walked among delegations from the peasants of Chernigov province—village headmen and elected representatives, more than three thousand in all. It was a repetition of Poltava two years earlier. How powerfully it moved him, what joy it gave him to see in the flesh and right before his eyes his own bearded, trusting, grateful people! Nothing else could have such a beneficial effect, so effectively restore his strength. Toward evening he returned to the river and sailed for Kiev. Crowds ran along the banks after the steamer, singing the anthem and shouting "Hurrah!"

However, the news that Stolypin's condition was deteriorating reached him even here. And when he disembarked at Kiev next morning, to an artillery salute, Kokovtsov was waiting on the quay to tell him that Stolypin had passed away the night before. So they hadn't saved him after all! Poor fellow, poor fellow, so young, and he had left his children fatherless. How sorry the Emperor felt for them! He would have to grant the widow a pension commensurate with the salary of the deceased.

But there was no time to spare, the Sevastopol train would be leaving in a few hours. The Emperor went to the clinic to hear the prayers for the dead, but Alix had no time at all, she had to hurry off to the palace with the rest of the family to get ready.

Stolypin was lying on a table under a sheet. His poor widow was standing like a stone statue, unable even to weep. "As you see, Your Majesty," she said, "Russia still has her Susanins." The Emperor, who was truly sorry for the unfortunate woman, did not, of course, demur. Stolypin's widow could be excused for such a remark, but mentioning him and Susanin in the same breath was overdoing it. Susanin had sacrificed himself for his Tsar; Stolypin had simply served the state, not always showing good judgment.

At the palace there were more telegrams from heads of state, deploring the Prime Minister's death.

Something, though, prevented Nikolai from grieving wholeheartedly. Ever since he had done violence to his own wishes last spring he had felt a constriction in his chest. Even now he could not remember without pain how the other man had seen him leaving his mother's room in tears.

The behavior of the crowds in Kiev's streets was amazing, right to the end. He could scarcely remember anything like it. In the center schoolboys once again lined the whole length of Aleksandrovskaya Street and Bibikov Boulevard. The Kievans were southerners, quite unlike the buttoned-up Petersburgers; the unrestrained enthusiasm of their greeting brought tears to Alix's eyes and Nikolai too was deeply moved.

The civil and military authorities and a large number of ladies had assembled at the station to see them off. They made the rounds of the gathering in the royal waiting room. There he informed Kokovtsov that his appointment as Prime Minister was now permanent. There was no one more suitable in the cabinet. Krivoshein was too much Stolypin's man, and Kokovtsov would be a contrast to the late Prime Minister. With him the Emperor would breathe more easily. Kokovtsov would rule his cabinet, but not the Empire. Who should take the dead man's place as Minister of the Interior? The Tsar suggested, somewhat hesitantly, Khvostov (the nephew of the governor of Nizhni Novgorod; Alix wanted him because Grigori Rasputin had asked her), but Kokovtsov unexpectedly said no. "Very well, let's leave the post vacant for the time being, Kurlov can be in charge temporarily, we can discuss it when you come down to the Crimea."

And now, much as he had enjoyed the dazzling events in Kiev, something still more joyful lay before him, the journey to the Crimea. (Remember, Alix, it was the Crimea that united us forever!) And, what was more, to a newly built palace which they had never even seen before.

The train moved out. At last Nikolai had a chance to rest completely, to recover from the celebrations as well as from everything else. However enjoyable all those receptions, deputations, salutations, flowers, and cheering crowds had been, rest and privacy were still better. There was nothing so soothing as a long, steady train ride, as Nikolai knew from the many journeys he had made by train during the war with Japan. After the forced confinement and humiliating inactivity of the revolutionary years, when he was truly an imprisoned Tsar—he could neither ride a horse nor drive out through his gates, and this in his own country! He had felt ashamed of his motherland, and indignant—after all that, he appreciated his country more than ever as it sped past his window. The long journey from St. Petersburg to the Crimea, and back, was always a delight.

As for the Crimea itself . . . !

They arrived at Sevastopol at teatime on 20 September, and went straight to South Bay. It was a lovely warm day. What a joy it was to be rowed out again to his favorite yacht on such a day, to go into his cabin and find everything just where it had been, to lie on his bunk for a while thinking, get up and take a stroll on deck, with a feeling of homecoming, of becoming himself again, with everything within him put back where it belonged. In the years of the troubles the *Standard* had been their only freedom, and they had loved it dearly and missed it since.

But right now it was impossible for the Emperor not to visit his Black Sea squadron. He turned his glasses on the battleships and other vessels. The brilliant polished look of the ships and the cheerful daredevil faces of the crews left Nikolai ecstatic. So different from the revolutionary filth of a few years ago. Things had righted themselves, thank God!

At dusk both city and ships were lit up. There were illuminated streamers with Their Majesties' monograms, and fireworks soared into the sky. Harbor approaches and city vied with each other in light effects, searchlights from the ships stabbed the darkness.

Much as they longed to go on they had to stay in Sevastopol, on the *Standard*, almost a week. The reason for the delay was that the architect who had built the new palace at Livadia begged to be given a few more days so that everything would be just as it should be. It seemed worth obeying his wish so that their first impressions would be perfect and without blemish. Anyway, Alix was so much at home on the yacht and would have more rest there than in a new palace where the rooms still had to be put in order.

So while they waited in Sevastopol the Emperor arranged to inspect the garrison troops on the north side, on Saturday the 23rd, again on Monday, and yet again on Tuesday after the rain stopped. While on Sunday, after Mass with prayers for departed emperors and for Stolypin, he received veterans of the siege of Sevastopol. There was a review of young gymnasts. And some cadets came aboard to show off their skill at arms drill and formation gymnastics. They ended with a rowing race.

Nikolai spent much of his time resting, and slept a great deal—a deep and healthy sleep with his porthole open, breathing the sea air, listening to the lapping of the waves. He wrote a long letter to Mama, describing the whole journey from Belgorod to Sevastopol, which had been the family's dream since spring, sharing all his impressions, most of them happy, some of them sad, giving her a minute and methodical account of all the events along the way—maneuvers, parades, receptions, Stolypin's murder, all in the order of their occurrence—not forgetting to mention the weather on each occasion (he had recorded it in a special notebook for inclusion later in his letters). He also told Mama about court ceremonies and weddings of which she had not yet been notified.

He had no real business for the time being, but ought to decide soon who should take Stolypin's place as Minister of the Interior. Dedyulin, the palace commandant, buttonholed him daily to recommend Kurlov. Kurlov really did thoroughly deserve the post, and was extraordinarily expert in police work: whom if not Kurlov did the Emperor have to thank for being able to travel in such marvelous security in recent years? And with what alacrity and sincerity he always declared his readiness to perish himself rather than let the Emperor come to any harm—though he always knew what dangers to guard against. In terms of seniority and qualifications Kurlov should be appointed. But unfortunately that business at Kiev seemed somehow to have shed a compromising light on him. He had, after all, been caught napping. So in spite of the palace commandant's urgings the Emperor could not quite make up his mind to it. Alix wanted to appoint Khvostov, a jolly and talented fellow with right-wing convictions, and friendly to Grigori; while Kokovtsov in his letters pressingly suggested Makarov, another of Stolypin's deputies, whom Alix disliked.

Though the days at Sevastopol passed so pleasantly, best of all was the anticipated move to the new palace at Livadia. Courtiers who had already been there brought back the most enticing news: it was dazzling outside and unbelievably comfortable inside.

One of the greatest joys a man can aspire to is moving with his beloved family to a new house after his own heart.

The Emperor had turned down, not for the first time, plans to build a railway line along the southern coast of the Crimea. He would not have the peace and quiet of Livadia disturbed. Iron and smoke must not be allowed to intrude on those magical places, which seemed to have remained untouched since the Creation.

He always strained to catch a glimpse of those cliffs, those peaks, those wild hills reaching for the sky, as soon as the ship began to approach the shore. He loved the way in which capes, some blue-green and wooded, some bare and craggy, alternated with deep-set light blue bays.

Intensive preparations had been made in Yalta for the arrival of the royal personages. (They had not come at all the year before while the palace was under construction.) A special pier had been built for the *Standard* to tie up and the Emperor's summerhouse on the mole had been redecorated. They were met by the local dignitaries and a delighted public. The bridge onto the Livadia road was adorned with a triumphal arch.

The road began to rise—and their hearts beat faster with anticipation. They had great faith in Krasnov, the architect. He was very able and he had already built Uncle Nikolai an excellent palace. But when their new home suddenly rose up before the Tsar and his family, dazzling white, joyous, elegant in its Italianate symmetry, they all gasped. They got out of the car, and inspected the palace thoroughly from the outside before entering, moving slowly to prolong their enjoyment. Alix could not contain herself and before they had half finished viewing it she said, "I've been dreaming of a palace like this since I was a child."

Walls you would love at first sight. Steps that simply invited you to go up and down them. Oh, and Alix's study—an enchanting corner room on the second story, full of light, with a balcony looking out over Yalta. And oh, the Emperor's larger study! All the bedrooms were so pretty, so light, so cheerful, and joined by a single balcony. Aleksei had a corner playroom. There was a little Moorish courtyard! With a dining room opening onto it!

"We shall come here every spring now!"

"Can we come in autumn sometimes?"

Ministers could come there if they had something really important to report. They would enjoy it too.

Winter in Tsarskoye Selo, summer at Peterhof, spring and autumn in Livadia. It would be wonderful there in March. There would be sleet and fog and blizzards in St. Petersburg—and in Livadia, glycineas, acacias, laburnum's golden rain, Italian anemones, tulips, irises!

Now they would take days over the delightful task of adapting the rooms to their liking, settling into them.

"It will soon be Olga's sixteenth birthday, we shall be giving a ball—why not here?"

Resting here would be wonderful, life would be all that could be desired. Here, among his beloved family, with his dearest love and best friend beside him, on their walks, at lunch, at tea, reading aloud to one another, occasionally holding intimate little parties with amiable, well-mannered friends—he could live his whole life that way if his duties were not so burdensome.

Alix's wonderful, proud eyes shone.

"We must show all this to Our Friend! I want Our Friend to see and bless this new palace. We shall be here for a long time yet, shan't we? December here is amazing. Shall we invite him here for your name day? And he'll tell us more about Palestine."

Grigori had traveled last spring to Palestine.

The imperial couple's position and duties did not permit them to go just where they pleased and just when. But Alix too very much wanted to go there.

The place itself had apparently not changed and his father's damp and dark wooden palace was close by, but this other one, this white one, closer to the sea, almost on the edge of the cliff, changed everything. And that marvelous bench made out of a single block of white marble, at a table also made out of a single block of white marble! Just to sit there facing the sea and forget yourself! The dear Black Sea—was there anything more blessed on earth? To sit in the shade of the oleanders, staring at it for hours on end! The muffled roar of the mighty rollers. Steamers and sailing ships in the distance. At this height you were alone in the world, and at one with the sea.

Nature as it passes through us day by day must inevitably leave some imprint on sensitive souls, and it affects us most profoundly when we are remote from humanity at large. Could anything compare with the splendid bluffs of Oreanda and Livadia soaring up from the sea? From them you could look down, holding your breath, at the immense, bewitching, ever-changing, restlessly rippling water like some fine fabric, dark blue one moment, then green, then mauve . . . Or you could stroll quietly conversing along the mountain path to Oreanda, which had been cunningly laid so as neither to rise nor to descend, never to get either wider or narrower, but always to leave room just for two. All the unpleasantnesses, the urgencies, the importunities, the frictions of St. Petersburg, all those mind-numbing political conundrums to which you simply couldn't devote yourself passionately and with all your heart, because any normal heart would burst and no normal brain could endure it—this was the only salvation from them, to distance yourself for a few months, to forget that any of it existed, to rest in this little corner, this likeness of God's heaven, breathing in the scent of the magnolias, peering at the sea through their branches.

Here, more than anywhere, you felt that you had left the world behind and were in Paradise.

But however hard you tried to forget, you were never completely free of care: beyond the sheltering mountains of the Crimea, spreading far to the north, the west, and the east, lay Russia, like the folds of a voluminous coronation robe weighing so cruelly on his shoulders that he could never entirely forget it.

After a few days Kokovtsov arrived. Since he was only taking his first tentative steps he raised a lot of questions.

Among other things he said that the inquiry into the murder was taking a quite unpleasant turn, that the shadow of suspicion had fallen on Kurlov and Spiridovich—it was suggested that they had not just been inefficient but had indirectly participated in the crime.

This was terrible.

Kurlov, then, could not take over from the murdered Stolypin as Minister of the Interior? Well, that in itself was punishment enough.

Who was it to be, then? He would have to accept Kokovtsov's candidate, Makarov.

For the time being at least.

Kokovtsov, however, thought that Kurlov and the others ought to be punished or even put on trial.

But they had broken no specific law.

The Emperor was dismayed and perplexed.

A thought occurred to him. Under the influence of the heady Crimean air the Tsarevich's health had mended rapidly during those few days in September. The Emperor felt a warm upsurge of gratitude, which demanded an outlet. He must do others a kindness. So he told Kokovtsov that he wanted to celebrate the Tsarevich's recovery with a good deed—and terminate the investigation of Kurlov, Spiridovich, Verigin, and Kulyabko.

Kokovtsov tried to persuade him that the investigation could not be suppressed but must take its natural course. The whole of "society" was watching closely.

Well, that was another good reason for not raising the sword too high. After all, the Tsar was forgiving them on his own behalf too. He might easily have been killed himself, either at the theater or in the Merchants' Garden.

And he forgave them all.

Perhaps because he was someone new after five years Kokovtsov was both more stimulating and easier to get on with. A change of ministers is always refreshing. The Emperor told him straight out: "I'm glad you don't behave like the late Stolypin."

"Your Majesty," Kokovtsov protested, "Stolypin died for you."

(Come, come, that is not strictly true, not true by a long shot.)

The Empress, who didn't like standing for long at a time, made Kokovtsov sit beside her, and graciously conversed with him.

"It seems to me that you attach too much importance to Stolypin's activities and to his character. There is no need to regret those who are no more. I am convinced that each of us has a part to play, and when one of us suddenly drops out, it is because he has played his part to the full and exhausted his usefulness. I am convinced that Stolypin died to make way for you, and that this is a blessing for Russia."

[73]

(THE TSAR SHOWS CLEMENCY)

Kokovtsov had not waited for Stolypin to die before ordering an inquiry into the activities of the Okhrana in Kiev. Shcheglovitov, the Minister of Justice, arrived and sealed the Okhrana offices before Kulyabko knew what was happening. And the commission of inquiry—Trusevich, with a team of lawyers and police officials—rolled up before Bogrov had been executed. It looked as though the investigators meant to spare no one; especially—and this was something unknown to the public at large but all-important in the official world—since Trusevich had been overtaken in the promotion race and elbowed out by Kurlov, and ought therefore to be his personal enemy. Kulyabko, however, had been appointed in Trusevich's time, which complicated matters. The diaries of agents and informers were called in. The commission began painstakingly questioning hundreds of policemen (many of whom had returned to St. Petersburg) about their assignments during the Emperor's travels. The murder and the hasty secret trial had mystified the general public and everybody expected sensational disclosures from Trusevich. In the State Duma (which reassembled exactly forty days after Stolypin's death, but began by paying its respects to a deputy who had died in the interim—only later did Rodzyanko mention Stolypin) Makarov, the new Minister of the Interior, promised that the government would conceal nothing, but would shed the brightest light possible on the affair.

These sweeping revelations, however, remained an unrealized possibility. Months went by, and not only was no bright light shed, not only was nothing official published, but when the newspapers occasionally printed what were allegedly authentic excerpts from the proceedings of the inquiry into the Kurlov clique (all four names were by then known, and connected in the public mind) their editors were threatened with prosecution if . . . yes, if their information proved in fact to be genuine! There was a rumor—wishful thinking on the part of the public—that Kulyabko had been put under house arrest, but even that never happened.

The inquiry took its course in deep secrecy. Kulyabko slowed it down as much as he could, lied whenever he had the chance, and even went back on his previous testimony. When first interrogated he went so far as to deny that Bogrov had been allowed into the

Merchants' Garden. But he admitted that all four had known (as Bogrov had testified that first night) about Bogrov's presence in the theater. Verigin, who lacked experience in these matters, was guilty of hesitation: he *thought* that Kulyabko had reported this to General Kurlov. Kurlov said that he knew absolutely nothing about it, and was just as emphatic that Spiridovich and Verigin knew nothing either. Kulyabko, with the room spinning about him, reminded Kurlov that both of them knew Bogrov by sight, had seen him in the theater and could not have failed to recognize him, and that this was why Spiridovich had spared Bogrov the saber poised over his head. This made Spiridovich still more insistent that certain things had been deliberately kept from him. As for Kurlov, he said that he had not known Bogrov by sight or by name, and that he knew nothing whatsoever about any aspect of the affair.

Though Trusevich was itching to get at the truth his commission was paralyzed by the Emperor's wishes. It recorded simply that "Colonel Spiridovich gave his explanation to the senator." Nothing more. (Spiridovich had not even been relieved of his duties as head of palace security while the inquiry was in progress.)

Trusevich let himself go only in his financial inquiries. He concluded that Kulyabko had expended huge sums on incompetently managed agents and surveillance operations, that Kurlov had handled sums of as much as 150,000 rubles at his own discretion and had used them to pay private debts, and that Verigin also was unable to account for 50,000 rubles.

Kurlov, however, produced receipts for all the sums concerned signed by people accountable to him, and offered proof that he was still deeply in debt, which confirmed that he was an honorable man. In any case, Senator Trusevich was not empowered to look into *private* economic operations.

Kurlov found it difficult and unpleasant having to explain so much to the commission, but it was not so bad as if he had had to see Stolypin in his last few days. He had been summoned by telephone three times to see the dying man, but had managed to stay away on each occasion. If he had gone there he would have had rather different questions to answer, and with witnesses inevitably standing by, and that would have made it so much more difficult for him to tie up loose ends now.

His clear mind, his legal training, and his long professional experience supplied Kurlov with irrefutable arguments in his own defense, and he remained vice-minister for three months while he fenced with the commission. He would have hung on longer if Makarov had not treacherously tripped him up. On his return from the Crimea he passed on to Kurlov something the Emperor was supposed to have said: "I'm surprised that such an honest and loyal servant as Kurlov hasn't resigned before now." How could he check this story? You couldn't ask the Emperor if he really had made such a remark. Kurlov felt compelled to resign. It was a costly decision: even if he was exonerated he would not receive compensation for loss of income while under investigation, or a full pension, nor would he be eligible for appointment to the Senate. (All these things would have been very useful now that he was about to marry for the second time. But a little later Rasputin, that simple Christian and great judge of men, readily promised to help Kurlov extricate himself from all unjust accusations.)

In view of Kurlov's high position the commission's findings were passed not to the

Senate, as the highest judicial instance, but to the State Council, where they languished for some months vainly awaiting a decision. By now there were nine thick volumes of documentation, but further explanations were still required from the foursome. None of them was brief, but Kurlov was extraordinarily prolix. Above all, he argued that all the charges against Verigin and Spiridovich were irrelevant on the grounds that although they had hovered over all the security arrangements they had had no specific duties in this connection. He further denied that Kulyabko was unsuitable for his post, saying that he was not a man of great ability—but what gendarme officer in Russia was? Kurlov asked a question of his own: where could he find a precise formulation of the actions with which he was charged? The only concrete fact mentioned was the breach of an instruction forbidding the use of informers in protecting state servants. To begin with, he had not known that Bogrov was being used in this way, and, secondly, this instruction was meant for his subordinates in the Police Department, and he as vice-minister was not bound by it. Equally misconceived was the charge that the Okhrana had failed to exploit the liaison between Bogrov's cook and the plainclothesman Sabaev in order to find out whether the alleged terrorists existed: the police could not be expected to use such methods, which contravened accepted moral norms. The main point was that the blame could not be put both on the superior officer and on his subordinates. If Kurlov knew nothing, only Kulyabko could be blamed. If Kurlov had known, then he was to blame and Kulyabko was clean. Well, Kurlov hadn't known about the planned assassination at all, right up to 14 September, and did not learn the details even then. He had had to spend the whole of that day outside, ensuring the Tsar's safety as he rode about the streets. General Kurlov, who was in charge of the whole security service, could not personally attend to such matters as shadowing Bogrov. It was impossible to run such an immense operation without delegating. Kurlov had in fact arrived at the theater after Stolypin, and learned only from him that the terrorists were to have met for some reason or other on some boulevard or other but had not in the event turned up. He asked the commission to note in this connection that no one had ever taken ultimate control of the police away from Stolypin. On the other hand, it was still not certain that the information given by Bogrov was a mere fabrication. There was nothing at all in the accusation that security inside the theater was inadequate: there were ninety-two Okhrana personnel with fifteen officers. It simply had to be admitted that even with ideal security arrangements it was not always possible to anticipate terrorist acts, especially those carried out by individual terrorists.

(Ten years later, and in emigration, he would put together a still more immaculate tale, and his remodeled version was even harder to fault. "Bogrov's statements," he said, "troubled me greatly and in spite of Stolypin's skepticism I insisted on summoning an officer belonging to the minister's personal bodyguard"—i.e., an extra body from St. Petersburg, in addition to the hundred already in Kiev. "But Stolypin considered that the measures taken to protect him were already exaggerated"—measures which left his anteroom and the garden under his ground-floor windows unprotected. After this Kurlov "had no intention of moving a single step from Stolypin's side" in the theater, but Stolypin himself, once more, sent him to find out what he could from Kulyabko—the one thing Kurlov had not managed to do in several days.)

As for Kulyabko, in his replies to the Senate he withdrew his original testimony that Kurlov "did know," and asked it to regard his new testimony, that Kurlov "did not know," as definitive.

All the same, the State Council did not find in favor of the foursome. Kurlov had not carried out Stolypin's instructions that he should take no action of importance affecting the Kiev Okhrana without consulting the governor-general. On the contrary he had delegated inordinately wide powers in security matters to Kulyabko, who was not up to his job at the best of times. He had negligently entrusted dealings with Bogrov to Kulyabko, without first checking information which appeared to be of the greatest importance—if he had done so the hoax would have fallen through immediately. Kurlov had not carried out a routine check on local Okhrana agents when he arrived in Kiev. He had ignored a warning message about Bogrov's character from the Police Department. He had attached no importance to the suspicious variability of Bogrov's reports. The tickets had been assigned by a commission of which both Spiridovich and Verigin were members. Bogrov, though known to be politically unreliable, had been admitted without being searched and without surveillance both into the Merchants' Garden and into the theater, where he strolled around freely, selecting his victim. Suspicious-mindedness was essential in Okhrana officers. It was lacking in this case. Instead, there was a systematic failure to take necessary action. Bogrov's movements and disappearances were accepted without question. The foursome had all joined in discussion of the terrorist act in preparation, and not one of them could be excluded from the inquiry. There was prima facie evidence of crimes which called for judicial scrutiny. Criminal charges should be brought, and an investigation set in motion.

Such judgments might sound like a merciless onslaught on defenseless people, but these people had such powerful hidden defenders that Kurlov did not fear even the hostility of the Prime Minister. The Minister of Justice was compelled to make two decisive concessions. Inasmuch as the foursome had made no deal with Bogrov in advance their alleged offense counted as dereliction of duty rather than a political crime. And since the actions complained of had been performed in the course not of military but of police duties they should be brought before a civilian not a military court.

All they had done was kill the Prime Minister of their country—obviously a mere bureaucratic misdemeanor. The blackest cloud was dispersed before lightning could strike.

Meanwhile, another sensible step was taken by order of the Emperor to the War Ministry dated 12 February 1912. Lieutenant Colonel Kulyabko was discharged from the Corps of Gendarmes "for domestic reasons," and transferred to the infantry reserve.

At long last (in spring 1912) a commission of inquiry was set up under Senator Shulgin. He began work in June and arrived in Kiev in August. All these delays greatly helped to allay public excitement. For many months people confidently assumed that justice was taking its course and would prevail. Meanwhile passions cooled. And whereas it had been advantageous to get the Bogrov case over in nine days the investigation of the foursome dragged on for fifteen months.

The wheels, however, began to turn more quickly. Kurlov, whose time was now his own, sat down to write a voluminous new work. With the practiced eye of the bureaucratic climber he spotted every handhold and foothold. His main defensive ploy was still the one he had devised that first September night, further amplified and sophisticated each time he used it.

He could not be accused of failure to act in a position of authority, because he had no direct control over local police operations. He only gave general guidance on matters referred to him. Further, all important security measures had been concerted with Adjutant General Trepov. Again, Bogrov had never been called in for questioning as a political suspect, so that there was no reason at all to regard him as politically unreliable. Nor were there any grounds for doubting the information supplied by Bogrov. Bogrov should have been watched? He should have been, of course, but Kurlov had thought that such an elementary police procedure would not be neglected by an experienced department chief in the Okhrana. There was nothing complicated about the crime itself. Every bit of information received, every order given, had been reported in detail to State Secretary Stolypin. Kurlov now recalled that Bogrov had been, or might have been, told to keep an eye on ministers in the Merchants' Garden; but he had certainly known nothing about the decision to admit Bogrov to the Garden. It would have been quite wrong to send police agents directly to Bogrov's apartment; they might have scared away a newly arrived group of terrorists. Before the performance, and again during the first intermission, Kurlov had made it his business to find out from Stolypin what he had learned from Kulyabko. His own attempt to obtain information from Kulyabko had produced nothing of importance, but he had subsequently passed on to Stolypin the incomplete information at his disposal. Kurlov had spent the first and second acts discussing with the palace commandant how they should proceed. The shooting came as a complete surprise and could not have been foreseen. It never could have entered his, Kurlov's, head that Bogrov might be in the theater. He had warned Kulyabko that Bogrov must not be allowed to lose sight of Nikolai Yakovlevich for a moment. It was perfectly possible that Bogrov had not known an hour earlier that he would have to kill someone. The demand had caught him unawares and made him the helpless instrument of someone else's will. The thing to do was to look for the underlying political reasons and the unknown secret forces instead of viciously attacking official persons. Bogrov could have no possible personal grudge against Stolypin and could not therefore have murdered him on his own initiative and at the risk of his life. Kurlov believed that Kulyabko had talked to Bogrov somewhere outside the theater entrance, perhaps during the performance. About gloves? Yes, Kulyabko had said something about gloves, but it was not clear that they were talking about white theater gloves rather than ordinary outdoor gloves. It was decided that Kulyabko would go and keep watch outside Bogrov's house after the performance. What about Spiridovich? Kurlov wasn't sure that anybody had talked to him, at any rate nothing had survived in his memory. After the attack Kurlov had ordered Kulyabko to draw up a detailed report on the whole affair, but Kulyabko had for some reason been slow about it, so that Kurlov was unable to piece together an exact account of what had happened. Why had Bogrov not been taken to the Okhrana section for questioning? Well, yes, Kurlov had been in favor of that, but the new Prime Minister, State Secretary Kokovtsov, had not shared his view. (When you are poised over the abyss you must hitch yourself to any helpful projection.) Governor-General Trepov (sling your rope around him!) had never said anything about Kulyabko's incompetence, and it was with his consent that Kulyabko was put in charge of security.

Senator Shulgin now attempted to assemble records of Bogrov's various interrogations, and it was suddenly found that for some reason there was no record of what he had said in court. For some reason none had been kept. Shulgin had to question the procurators and other functionaries who had been present at the trial, and do his best to reconstitute the proceedings.

In spite of Kurlov's amazingly ingenious explanations, his reputation as a policeman, and the correctness of all his methods and his theories of detection, the senator did not balk at renewing all the old charges against him: dereliction of duty; failure to take steps to prevent a crime; failure to order surveillance of Bogrov, search his apartment, and verify his information; failure to forbid the issue of tickets to Bogrov although he *did* know about it on both occasions; failure to have Bogrov searched for arms and kept under observation in the theater; failure to arrange protection for the two ministers after he had been warned that they were in danger.

Nor could the senator find any mitigating circumstances for the other three officers.

The hostile conclusions of the commission were drafted in August 1912. (As late as 1914 the censorship would not allow much of this to be published and carefully screened Spiridovich from the public gaze because he was close to the court.) Justice, when the trail is cold and the quarry too grand, is the slowest of chariots. Not until December 1912 did the relevant department of the State Council meet to deal with the case of the Kurlov four.

All those who had studied the case, both the senator, who acted as *rapporteur*, and the procurator, found against the accused. Bogrov had been given the opportunity to throw a device into the royal box, and only fear of a pogrom, not the police, had stopped him. If Kurlov "did not know" that Bogrov was in the theater it aggravated his offense. He should have known. His mission in Kiev was to deal with all security arrangements, and he could not shift the blame to his subordinates. Spiridovich and Verigin, whatever their immediate duties were at that moment, held extremely important posts in the state service; they knew who Bogrov was and they had seen him in the theater, yet they said nothing.

The wording of the judgment confined itself to charges of negligence with particularly grave consequences, but it stood out inescapably from the documentation that all four were *accomplices* in the murder, Kulyabko a very active one.

So although the Emperor had let it be known that he took a lenient view, the investigation had crept stealthily forward until it was almost at the throats of the four.

The indictment was, however, presented not to a court but to the elder statesmen of the State Council. Their well-earned repose depended on the Emperor's goodwill and they were still angry with Stolypin. Nor could their superannuated, bureaucratic hearts admit such a harsh indictment. Some of their number had themselves run into difficulties in the service of the state. Anybody might do so, none of us is a saint. And Kurlov had on more than one occasion stood up for people accused of negligence, abuse of authority, or diversion of funds. People who serve the same state machine for decades should always be ready to help each other out. One faint, quavering voice after another repeated the same argument: if Kurlov was to blame, these ancients bleated, then Kulyabko was not, and if Kulyabko was to blame—as he plainly was—then the other three were innocent. Kurlov had not been negligent, just unfortunate. No person in authority could be expected to do everything himself and never to rely on subordinates.

They unanimously found Kulyabko guilty on all charges, including theft of state funds, and sent him to prison for the terrible term of sixteen months (subsequently reduced to four months by imperial decree).

As for the other three, opinions were divided. Six members (including Shturmer, later so famous for his lachrymose piety) voted for acquittal; five, in spite of everything, for conviction. The five, however, included the president; and that stickler for honesty Makarov, Minister of the Interior, gave them his support. This tipped the scale very slightly, but sufficiently to produce a verdict of guilty. The six who had favored acquittal nonetheless demanded that their dissenting opinion be presented for the Emperor's consideration.

Although the proceedings had dragged on for fifteen months the public had not forgotten and, while it awaited the outcome, reports on what was happening, and denials of those reports, had found their way into the press: readers were told that there was a deadlock, with opinions evenly divided; that an indictment was already being drawn up; that there was to be a full-dress trial in the Catherine Hall of the Tauride Palace; that, on the contrary, the State Council's decisions had not been confirmed by the Emperor and that Kurlov would be promoted.

As always, the worst rumors were the most reliable. It became known early in 1913 that the Emperor had minuted the State Council's report in his own hand: "The case of General Kurlov, Colonel Spiridovich, and State Counselor Verigin is to be considered closed, with no further consequences for them."

An amnesty to mark the tercentenary of the dynasty was expected in two months' time. The accused men could have been convicted for the sake of decency and immediately amnestied. Instead, the Emperor was at pains to demonstrate his confidence, his goodwill, his particular predilection for these people by pardoning them in advance—pardoning that sharp-toothed weasel, that champion bureaucrat; that sycophant courtier, that giddy theorist of criminal investigation who had swallowed such trashy bait; and that phantom functionary, that faceless person who had sprung from nowhere and was on his way back there.

This moving act of clemency was the Emperor's way of symbolically marking the third centenary of the dynasty.

He could, of course, have pardoned them sooner. That in fact had been his wish: as far as he was concerned the interests of the state were not affected, only the fate of individuals, erring but loyal individuals to whom he should show mercy. He had decided to pardon them long before—during that happy September in the Crimea when one of the Tsarevich's remissions compensated for the loss of a Prime Minister who had grown tiresome. When Makarov, Stolypin's successor at the Ministry of the Interior, brought the Emperor the results of the investigation, from which it was clear that all the threads led to Kurlov, the Emperor conceived an instant dislike for him, retained all the documents to acquaint himself with the case in detail, took charge of the whole matter personally, and never raised it with Makarov again. (The new minister was dismissed immediately after voting against Kurlov in the State Council.) If the Tsar had not pardoned them earlier it was because he had hoped that the tried and true ancients would understand and do it for him.

They had, of course, done their best. Like all creatures of the dark, they recognized their kind by smell and by the red glint in the corners of the eyes. They rallied to protect and pull to safety a "fellow man"—a man like themselves, who had fallen as they might fall. They would have recoiled in amazement if they had been told that what they were deciding was not the fate of Kurlov but how soon their own houses were to be ransacked, they themselves shot, and their domestics hacked to pieces.

What hope had they of holding their own against revolutionaries? Against people who would sacrifice their lives at eighteen or twenty-five, who would face certain death to achieve their ends? Whereas not one among them, at forty or fifty or even seventy, thought of anything but his career, and of self-preservation at all costs in order to pursue it. Any concern for Russia was exceptional: the rule was to think only about the comforts of office. They did not overtax their minds, their actions were leisurely, they pampered themselves and lived in blissful ease, shone modestly on social occasions, intrigued and gossiped. What did they look up to? They made a show of Orthodox piety (standing through church services regularly so as to be like everybody else) and they were loyal to the Tsar, on whom their careers depended.

How could they fail to lose Russia? When servants of the state are so anxiously absorbed in monitoring the system of transfers, promotions, and awards that there is no room for any other thought in their heads—what can you call it except paralysis of power? Of the senior generals at the beginning of the war in 1914 hardly one is to be found in the White movement later on, and it is equally true that not one of the die-hard policemen, not one of the palace pets, not one of the Council elders will be glimpsed among the defenders of the tottering throne; those who had not scattered would be lying low. From 1907 to 1917 they had been more or less unaware of the danger threatening them and when revolution came they lacked the presence of mind for self-defense.

Fifteen months of investigation had merely confirmed what was known in the first red-hot moments, and the whole affair was consigned to oblivion. A timorous *finis* was written to the story of murderer and traitors alike, the page was squeamishly crumpled and lost. How characteristic of Russia's last Emperor was this evasion, this dismissal of unpleasant reality.

It suited Russian liberal "society" to regard Bogrov as an employee of the Okhrana, and—simply to avoid punishing sycophants—the Russian Tsar allowed this obscene version to lodge in Russia's memory and stain Russia's honor. To save three bureaucratic hides the Supreme Power accepted the whole filthy smear itself. The summit of the tree nonchalantly sacrificed the healthy shoots and flaunted the withered ones.

This long-drawn-out story of forgiveness for murderers is instructive for those who do not avert their eyes. Every act of clemency to that pack helped to drain the life from the state. The Emperor had shown often enough in the past that he was incapable of understanding Stolypin's aims. By departing from Stolypin's course after his death and, not least, by pardoning his murderers, the Emperor showed that he had no feel for the country and its 170 million for whose souls and minds and memories and honor God's anointed was answerable to the Judges of Earth and Heaven.

Coincidentally, on the very day it refused to condemn Kurlov the State Council made yet another sage decision: it denied the province of Archangel the right to establish a zemstvo organization. The most Russian, the most literate land of old peasant Russia, the most independent and least tainted by serfdom, a land which had flourished in ancient times under Novgorod and under Muscovy, was not granted the privilege of local self-government in the twentieth century because it was short of landowning gentry! The Russian crown could not bring itself to rely on the backward peasant class—why, they were practically children, incapable of living without the tutelage of the educated.

Those who had flouted Stolypin were now flouting his most cherished idea.

The "act of clemency" in January 1913 was the throne's final betrayal of Stolypin, his whole work and life, and people of all political persuasions were well aware of it. In the same year a memorial to the murdered man was unveiled in Kiev (erected by public subscription: the Emperor had not wanted it, and the treasury had not given a single kopeck), and this was the occasion for renewed discussion of his life and death. The liberal newspapers (the great majority) were more scurrilous now than they had dared to be at the time of the murder: he was called a power lover, a typical timeserver with no policies of his own who always chose to do whatever was profitable to him personally, so that every step he took was determined by careerist considerations and ruthless hostility to all who got in his way. The unveiling of the monument itself was called by liberal newspapers the "Kiev operation," at which Russian nationalists and one faction of the Octobrists (the other fought shy of the occasion) "fraternized over the dear corpse," because "people wished to hear the sound of their own voices around the monument." Rodzyanko brought a wreath—as before, on his own behalf, not for the Duma. Those ministers who turned up laid wreaths for themselves, not for the government. As for the court and the royal house, they were not represented.

Only two years had passed since Stolypin's death, but almost everything that appeared in print in Russia openly mocked his memory and ridiculed his absurd scheme for building a great Russian nation.

Bogrov's bullets had proved armor-piercing and unstoppable.

[74]

They had ended so soon, the carefree years, those incomparable Petersburg winters, ended when he was only twenty-six. He had languidly studied law and administration in the mornings, but had been relieved even of that when he was twenty-two. There were whole days of freedom, lunches, tea parties, dinners with titled persons and retainers, not a single evening at home; ballets, French farces, folksingers and gypsies (Hungarians, or Caucasians dancing the lezginka), wine, a flutter at the roulette wheel . . . Nikolai rarely went to bed before 1 a.m., and often enough it was at three; he rose reluctantly in the morning or even slept away half of his study period and never lamented the cancellation or abbreviation of a State Council session. (His father made him sit through them. He would make bets with himself on how many minutes the day's session would last and calculate whether he would have time to dash off somewhere afterward.) He fasted before Communion twice a year, and there were official receptions on certain holidays, but otherwise every day was free for boisterous fun on the rink at Anichkovo or hide-and-seek with the Sheremetev girls, looking out through the fence at the Nevsky, strolling with other young people on the embankment. He had early on made a habit of recording all these things in his diary—it would be amusing to look back at them sometime. He had also begun to enjoy reading Russian history—it seemed to him that there could be no more interesting books than those in which he felt the living presence of his forebears and saw events as though they were happening or about to happen before his eyes. Languages—English, German, French—seemed to cost him no effort, came to him very easily. He always preferred the practical to the theoretical side of his military training, and had served in turn in the infantry as a battalion commander (Preobrazhensky Regiment), in the cavalry as a squadron commander (Life Guards Hussars), and for two years in the Horse Artillery Brigade of the Guards Corps.

He had taken part in summer maneuvers with each of his units in turn. There were days in the saddle, mock attacks (he had photographs to remember it all by), occasional night alerts (and time to catch up with your sleep after dawn), shooting clay pigeons with other officers, music from trumpeters and songsters—an easy and a merry life for a healthy young man, a life of freedom in the open countryside, untrammeled by court ritual, where he could indulge in his own pleasures: jumping over the bonfire, playing skittles, rolling in the hay, scrambling up on the roof, canoeing, rowing pairs, fishing, duck shooting, and, when the weather was bad, playing billiards and telling stories. The evenings were free anyway, and Krasnoye Selo was nearby; he could go there every evening, have a few drinks and a hearty snack, or go for a ride in a hunting brake with musicians in attendance, or enjoy dancing with the young ladies from the finishing school, or watch Spanish or Ukrainian or gypsy dancers over supper and perhaps until six in the morning. Or in the season he could put in an appearance at the operetta or the ballet in the charming little Tsarskoye Selo theater and go behind the scenes. He was positively taken with little Kshesinskaya, she was more bewitching all the time.

Then those Septembers! September was the month when the Emperor and the grand dukes held their hunts. Hunting is one of the greatest pleasures a man can enjoy—the ride through the woods, the chase, taking up numbered positions, a volley, another volley, a stag falls in mid-gallop, falls like a hare. In a single outing they might kill dozens of stags, not to mention goats and wild boars. (Sometimes you might aim wildly and hit a dog.) The ladies would join them when they followed the hounds. There would be any number of pheasants, partridges, and of course woodcocks. Enthusiastic hunters never spare themselves—they will rise in the dark, they will ride thirty versts on a cold, wet morning. There were suppers with music, where toasts were drunk to the slain stags. The hunt musicians sounded their horns. You could chivy the Bialawieza bison. There was lawn tennis, Mass in the field chapel, exhibitions of conjuring. To help the time pass you could play cards or billiards for money. Local peasants came to pay their compliments with music; five hundred or more kerchiefs would be distributed and the women would scramble for them.

Then, at his father's wish and of his own choice, that unbelievably long journey, not to Europe, where everyone went, but to the East. With the two Georges, his own brother Georgi and Prince George of Greece (Georgie), and a young and merry retinue. In Greece they saw Olympus, in Egypt they climbed the pyramid of Cheops, visited Aswan and Memphis, secretly watched the dancing dervishes. They hunted panthers and tigers in India, elephants in Ceylon, and crocodiles in Java. (His brother had caught a severe chill in India, had been sent home, and had been ill on and off ever since.)

Enjoyable as these diversions were, other things left a more lasting impression. In India he could not endure the feeling of being surrounded by cocksure Englishmen, and seeing their red uniforms everywhere. In Siam it was impossible not to marvel at the country's extraordinarily subtle ancient culture. At Otsu in Japan he was suddenly attacked by a fanatic and only Georgie had kept his head and saved Nikolai (even a blow with the flat of the blade could have been fatal), a terrifying reminder that we are all defenseless against fate, all entirely in the hands of God.

The journey packed his mind with impressions of the many different civilizations that lived side by side with his own, each unique, each full of secrets; of the greatness and complexity of God's world, and of how much in it we do not understand.

Then the two-month journey back across Siberia, an expanse great enough to impress even a Russian imagination, a country belonging entirely to Russia, and known to hardly anyone. He inspected with delighted interest towns in which he never expected to find himself again: Irkutsk, Tobolsk, Yekaterinburg.

Meanwhile, he was maturing emotionally and longing for true love. When Uncle Sergei had married Aunt Ella, her twelve-year-old sister, the angelic Alix, a princess of the house of Hesse, had come with her to the wedding. The sixteen-year-old Nikolai had danced with her and tried to give her a brooch, which she was too shy to accept. They had carved their names in a gazebo. Nikolai had carried her ethereal image ever since in his heart, he rushed to see her whenever she visited St. Petersburg, and when he was twenty he had firmly resolved to seek her hand. As always happens with monarchs and their heirs, dozens of incidental political considerations stood in the Tsarevich's way and efforts were made to deflect his choice. Mama was very much against it, Papa was not happy, they had had something quite different in mind, but young Nikolai would not budge, sure that here was his only chance for happiness. After years of resistance he finally obtained permission, and in the happiest spring of his life, at the age of twenty-six, he went to Coburg to propose and plight his troth. Although a train of princes attended the Tsarevich, and the young Alix's grandmother Queen Victoria came from England to give her moral support, nothing was as yet really decided. The main doubt was whether Alix would agree to adopt the Orthodox faith. On Tuesday came the first difficult conversation with the now remarkably pretty but despondent Alix. She was unwilling to change her religion, and Nikolai became tired and disheartened. That she agreed to see him and talk to him at all on Wednesday was somewhat reassuring. He just managed to get through Thursday, helped by the wedding of a German prince, followed by a performance of *I Pagliacci*, and beer drinking, in the evening. Ah, but on Friday, the most unforgettable day of his life, what a weight fell from his shoulders, and how happy Mama and Papa would be: Alix had consented. He walked around in a daze all day, not fully realizing what had happened to him. Wilhelm congratulated the young couple on their engagement, and the whole many-branched royal family exchanged joyful kisses. The Tsarevich could not believe that at last he had a fiancée. What sublime, what heavenly happiness the betrothed state was! And how Alix's behavior toward him had changed. That alone made him deliriously happy. She could even write a couple of sentences in Russian almost without a mistake. They went riding together in an open carriage, sat by the pool, picked flowers or cut lilac blossoms, took photographs of each other. People flocked into the garden to watch, and bands (infantry or dragoons) played under their windows. It seemed so strange, riding, walking, sitting together, just the two of them, without the slightest feeling of awkwardness! Alix gave Nikolai a ring. How sweet she was with him! Now and again they sat up together, just the two of them, as late as midnight. He couldn't possibly imagine being separated from her now, for however short a time. But it had to be—and it was horrible. Alix went to stay with her grandmother in London, and Nikolai walked by himself in the places which would now always be dear to him, picking her favorite flowers and enclosing them in the letters he wrote in the evenings. At every step there was something to remind him of her. He carried a photograph of her, with a border of pink flowers, wherever he went and propped it up before him while he ate.

He found it impossible to live longer than two months without her in St. Petersburg, and he set off again, this time sailing to London, thoroughly enjoying his father's marvelous yacht *Polar Star*, but crazy with impatience. Then came a succession of delightful days when he and his darling Alix were inseparable, riding about Windsor Park in the Queen's carriage, visiting the Flower Show, blissfully rowing on the Thames, playing piano duets—and after all this the joy of falling asleep in a cozy room under the same roof as Alix. He seized every half hour in the daytime, every evening, sometimes even a little time before daybreak to sit alone with his beloved fiancée. His diary was no longer a secret from her and although she did not understand Russian she would occasionally take his pen from him and make an entry of her own (in English: . . . "with unending true devotion, better fare than I can say"), or she would go steadily through the blank pages ahead, writing a line here and there in her precious handwriting, so that her entries would intertwine later with his, just as their souls intertwined.

Es muss was Wunderbares sein
Ums Lieben zweier Seelen,
Sich schliessen ganz einander ein
Und nie ein Wort verhehlen.

Und Freud und Leid und Glück und Not
So mit einander tragen,
Vom ersten Kuss bis in den Tod
Sich nur von Liebe sagen. *

They went to lunches, to dinners, to parades, to theaters, he wearing a dolman, a Circassian coat, a pelisse, his full Hussar uniform, or his Guards dress coat, showing off Russia's military splendors and his own manly bearing. Dressing up in the uniforms of different regiments was a fascinating pastime—it was as though you had managed to serve in all of them, to live through their military experience. Then those marvelous peaceful evenings with sweet Alix. That month in England was like living in Paradise, and it had flown by before he knew it.

> [Drawing of a heart. In English] Never may you forget her, whose most earnest . . . prayer is to make you happy.

He visited an antique furniture shop and bought a beautiful bed, a washstand, and an Empire mirror, which she liked very much. He was

* There is something miraculous in the love of two souls which merge into one another, which share their joy and their suffering, and which from their first kiss to their last expiring breath sing to each other of their love.

simply dying with love for his priceless girl. He bought her pretty things from jewelers. One day he told her about Kshesinskaya—there would never be anything like that again.

> [In English] My own boysy boysy dear, never changing, always true. Have confidence and faith in Your girly dear . . . I love you even more since you told me that little story.

Then there were still those last days by the sea, sitting on the beach watching the tide come in, wading barefoot. He could not bear to be away from his beloved fiancée for a minute. He had to prolong his blissful stay by just one day. No sooner had he parted with his precious love, no sooner had he been rowed out to the yacht than—surprise!—he found a wonderful long letter from her waiting.

> [In English] Love is caught, I have bound his wings love! . . .
> Within our 2 hearts for ever love sings.

What heart could withstand these lines? He sent his reply immediately with a shore-bound Englishman. He was altogether worn out with grief and yearning. How could he survive two months of parting?

> [In English] Let the gentle waves rock you to sleep—your Guardian Angel is keeping watch over you.

On the voyage home he sent her letters by pilot boats.

That autumn, alas, Papa suddenly became seriously ill. Although he yearned passionately to fly to his dear Alix, Nikolai dutifully accompanied his parents to the Crimea. There he pined, fretted terribly on days when he received no letter from her, but felt doubly compensated when two letters arrived at once the following day. She tearfully lamented the postponement of her fiancé's arrival. Why, oh why, had they not got married that summer? September limped by. There were days when Papa was very much better, got to his feet, busied himself with his ministers and his documents. In his usual gruff way he refused all treatment, and kept the "sawbones" at arm's length. Nikolai went to see the carrier pigeons released, and rode a lot, to the vineyards, to the farm, to the waterfall, or farther on to the lighthouse, to Uchan-su and Alupka. Papa began feeling very poorly and became more and more confused. It grieved Nikolai to see his poor father so ill. Full of dismal thoughts and of longing, he sat on the pebble beach watching the huge waves roll in. There could be no question of going to Alix.

Shortly afterward there were five doctors on the spot. One day early in October, Papa felt so weak that he took to his bed without being told to. Dear Alix wrote to Mama, and with Papa's and Mama's consent he wrote to Darmstadt asking her to come. He was enormously touched by their kindness. What bliss it would be to meet again so much sooner than he had expected, in spite of the sad circumstances. Papa had started going back to bed after lunch, and for the first time ever Nikolai read for him the state papers brought by couriers. The papers were often boring, and often perplexing, and there were always lots of new names and incomprehensible references. How vexatious it all was. However did Papa remember it all? They went to Yalta to meet guests—seeing new faces is always refreshing. They lunched, incongruously, with music, and only afterward learned that Papa had received the last rites while they were doing so.

For the first time he was seized with dread. What if his father died? What would happen then? Oh God, how frightened and vulnerable he would be! Where would he, unprepared as he was, find the courage to rule an empire? How could he hope to acquire his father's heroic strength? But who else was there? The oldest son, the heir, could not evade his duty. And Georgi was consumptive.

A day later he met his adored Alix and went with her in a barouche to Livadia. What joy it gave him! Half of his cares and his grief seemed to fall away. Tatars welcomed them with bread and salt at every stop and the carriage was loaded with flowers and grapes. But Papa was weaker, and Alix's arrival fatigued him.

Again they were together afternoon and evening, up to the moment when he escorted her to her own suite. He was overjoyed with her presence. He even sat down to deal with official papers in her room. They took trips to Oreanda, enjoyed the sea views, played cards. Alix's presence calmed and fortified him. He loved her more and more deeply every day: what happiness to have such a treasure for a wife! He helped her embroider covers for the pyx and chalice in preparation for her first Communion.

> [In English] Your Sunny is praying for you and the beloved patient . . . Be firm and make the Drs. . . . come alone to you every day and tell you how they find him, and exactly, what they wish him to do, so that you are the first always to know . . . Don't let others be put first and you left out. You are Father dear's son . . . Show your own mind and don't let others forget who you are.

She was right. He had to learn to assert himself and make his wishes felt.

They strolled by the sea. There was no carriage and he was afraid that the climb back would be too much for Alix's legs.

Another day went by, and Papa received Communion again. Oh God! Was it really that serious? Might it be the end? His heart ached for his noble, strong, and generous father! O Lord, let this cup pass from me, lay not this unwanted burden on my frail shoulders!

He spent part of the evening with Papa, who was tormented by a heavy bronchial cough. Papa wanted to accustom him to the idea that his turn would soon come to rule. For the present they would work together every day, so that Papa could explain things to him. His whole body turned cold with fear at the thought of it all. He was so afraid and so sick at heart that he could take nothing in. Later on he sat with dear Alix again.

> [In English] When you feel low and sad, come to Sunny and she will try to comfort you & . . . warm you with her rays.

Papa did not sleep at all that night, and was so ill in the morning that they were all called in to see him, not to say goodbye, but it was as though they were doing just that. Those were terrible days! How would it end? That was the moment Nikolai had always dreaded.

They no longer dared leave the house. It was such a consolation to have dear Alix sitting by him all day while he read documents from various ministers. Then there was the conference of doctors in Uncle Vladimir's room. They took care to make no noise at lunch. Papa felt a little brighter, and spent the following day sitting up in his armchair while Nikolai worked with him again. There were so many names, so many things to think of, how could anybody grasp it all, give the necessary directions? How could anyone learn to make decisions? Papa went back to bed feeling terribly weak.

Next morning he had difficulty in breathing and was given oxygen.

He took Communion for the third time, and the Lord summoned him.

Oh God, this blow would shake Russia to its foundations! He could not imagine the country without his father. His head was spinning. He did not want to believe it. He felt as though the life had been drained out of him.

The Emperor's standard over the palace roof was slowly lowered for all Yalta to see and a cruiser in the harbor roads fired a salute.

Prayers for the dead were said that evening in the late Emperor's bedroom.

Such a dreadful change in the space of a day! Never again would his life be one of ease. All the cares of state would be his lot, as long as he lived.

To be Tsar of Russia was difficult beyond endurance.

But in this, as in all things, God's will must be done.

On a black autumn evening the dead man was carried from the palace to the church between two rows of torchbearers. A macabre sight.

But even in time of deep sorrow the Lord gives us quiet joy: dear Alix was received into the Orthodox Church. Then they spent the whole day together answering telegrams. It was cold, and the sea was roaring. For the second day running he had time only to struggle through the billowing clouds of telegrams. On the third day he was still drafting telegrams, there seemed to be no end to them. But in the afternoon he went for a drive with Alix. And in the evening he sat with her as usual and her companionship gave him the strength to bear his lot.

Gott geht mit dir, Seinem Kinde, fürchte dich nicht!*
[In English] Ask yourself often: how should I act, if I perceived the angels.

The family, conscious that it was also a dynasty, argued about arrangements for the wedding. Should it be solemnized with the usual pomp and circumstance, in St. Petersburg after the funeral? Or should it be a private ceremony, here and now? All the uncles, who together carried a great deal of weight, insisted that it should be in St. Petersburg, and Nikolai did not even think of disagreeing with them.

They left a week after the old Emperor's death. Cossacks and fusiliers took turns carrying the coffin from the church at Livadia to the quay in Yalta. The deceased Emperor was borne along the Crimean coast, covered by the flag of St. Andrei. The whole Black Sea fleet was drawn up in line at Sevastopol. The funeral train set out on its journey north. Services were held at the main stations along the line. The presence of Nikolai's dearest love, his beautiful bride-to-be, consoled him and gave him strength. He sat with her for whole days.

[In English] What love unites, no fate can separate . . . [I shall] be soon yr. own little Wife.

The coffin was borne through Moscow to the Kremlin on a gun carriage, with stops for prayers at ten churches. The first thing he had to do in his father's stead was to say a few words to representatives of the different estates assembled in the Hall of St. George. He had been in a state of agitation from early morning. He felt horribly nervous. But it went off well enough, thank God.

In St. Petersburg the solemn funeral procession from the station to the Peter and Paul Fortress took four hours. Then came the burial service in the fortress. Another requiem in the evening. Services day after day, in the presence of foreign royalty and delegations. The family were all drained of emotion, their aching eyes could weep no more.

With every service he attended Nikolai was more painfully aware of the burden laid upon him, never to be shed. He had to receive the whole State Council and make another speech. (Pobedonostsev wrote it for him and drilled him beforehand.) Receive his court officials, and speak yet again. Read ministers' reports, and for the first time listen to some of them delivered orally. Think up remarks to make to every member of the foreign delegations. The Kings of Serbia and Rumania between them took up the few free minutes in which he might have been seeing Alix. He was tired of never catching more than brief glimpses of her. He longed to be married so that there would be no more partings. Then came a requiem conducted by the Metropolitan, and on the twentieth day yet another requiem in the fortress, with prayers over the grave. Two of the

* The Lord is your guide, you are His child. Have no fear.

princes left, and he could not wait to be rid of the others. He received various foreigners, some bearing letters. He had to find answers to so much nonsense that he became quite confused and scarcely knew what he was saying; he felt heavy at heart and could almost have wept with vexation when he had to give a dinner for all the visiting princes in the concert hall of the Winter Palace. The flow of ministerial reports increased. He received the whole Senate in the palace ballroom. Received a steady procession of governors-general. Then governors. Army commanders. Cossack atamans. A flood of deputations from all over Russia, as many as five hundred people at a time in the Nicholas Hall. On his rest day, when there were no receptions and few if any reports were presented for him to read, he could take wonderful walks with Alix or sit quietly with her. In such painful circumstances it seemed strange to be thinking about his wedding. It was rather as though it were someone else's. The two of them would have felt rather cramped in the four rooms previously occupied by Nikolai—and he and Alix went to choose carpets and curtains together for two more rooms.

At last—the great day when he emerged from the big chapel in the Winter Palace a married man, and he and Alix rode in a state carriage along the Nevsky Prospect, lined with troops, to the Cathedral of Our Lady of Kazan. (He had given orders for police protection of bride and groom to be withdrawn on the day of the wedding.) Then wedding presents from the whole family had to be inspected, and another batch of telegrams, this time congratulatory, answered. He was unimaginably happy with Alix, they could not bear to be separated from each other, he would have spent his whole time with her if he could, but his duties called him away. To escape from the ministers and their reports they went to Tsarskoye for a week and had an indescribably delightful time, with no need to see anyone, day or night, and no need to read state papers. Their bliss knew no bounds. Man has no right to wish for any greater happiness on this earth.

> [In English] Never can I thank God enough for the treasure He has given me for my very Own . . . I cover yr. sweet face with kisses . . . If little wify ever did it anything that displeased you or unwillingly grieved . . . you . . . —forgive her *dushki*!

They strolled about the park, went for drives in a droshky, went tobogganing, went to see the Ceylon elephant. They played duets on the piano, drew, looked at albums, read out comic verses from old fashion magazines. There are no words to describe the bliss of living alone with a tenderly loved wife in such a splendid place as Tsarskoye. (It was also his birthplace.)

Back to St. Petersburg. They hung pictures and photographs on the walls of their new rooms. On the fortieth day there was a requiem Mass in the fortress. They looked over plans for rearranging rooms in the Winter

Palace, chose new furniture and materials. There seemed to be no end to governors' reports. He was mercilessly nagged for whole mornings at a time. If Pobedonostsev failed to appear with stern injunctions and dire warnings, ministers would be stupefying him with contradictory recommendations, or else it would be the turn of the military to present themselves, or he would have to receive the whole Board of Admiralty, or sign separately each item on an honors list drawn up by the Senate to mark his own name day. Then there were Christmas presents to be got ready for England and Darmstadt, his darling wife's belongings newly arrived from Darmstadt to be sorted out, his own presents under the Christmas tree to be examined. They also went for sleigh rides, just the two of them. Though they had been married more than a month, he was only just beginning to get used to the idea, and his love for Alix grew from day to day. But those piles and piles of paper were carried in with relentless regularity, and there was never time for Nikolai and Alix to read a nice little French book to each other, or for him to read one of his historical journals. (He so much enjoyed immersing himself in the remote history of his country! Most of all, Nikolai loved the reign of Aleksei Mikhailovich. He loved those ancient times before Peter, when the Moscow Tsar and his people spoke the same language and thought the same thoughts.) There were half-holidays when there was only one minister to be seen, or when by good luck a ceremonial meeting of the Academy of Sciences ended within the hour, leaving time for skating, or later in the day a moonlight sleigh ride to the islands.

In this way Nikolai was gradually drawn during the months of mourning—not suddenly inducted on one particular day—into his fated role as an omnipotent autocratic monarch. What ought he to do? What must he say? Whom should he appoint? And whom should he dismiss? With whom should he agree, and whose advice should he reject? Somewhere lay the one and only correct line, visible to Divine Providence but hidden from the eyes of men—and from the eyes of the youthful monarch and his advisers, for they too, of course, were often wrong. Nikolai had never received a word of political instruction from his late father, who when he was in good health had always thought it too soon (let the boy enjoy himself, wait till he's more grown-up) and when he was ill had never expected the outcome to be fatal. The one thing Nikolai remembered from his father's last days was "Listen to Witte." Nikolai had at one time dutifully sat through boring sessions of the State Council, but had made little effort to follow the debates of those gouty, diabetic, gray-haired or bald-headed ancients.

Uncle Vladimir told Nikolai not to worry: both Aleksandr II and Aleksandr III had come to the throne in troubled times, but now after thirteen years of peace all was quiet, there was no war, there were no revolutionaries on the scene, there was no need for hasty innovations, no need to change anything, nor even to move anyone from his present post—that would make it look as if the son was showing disapproval of his father's actions. Nikolai found this advice immensely congenial. What he had to do was the easiest thing imaginable: not rack his brains thinking up changes but let things follow their present course. (Except that the Minister of Roads and Railways had to be dismissed immediately for peculation—but the late Tsar had intended to do that.)

He could not, however, make a habit of relying on Uncle Vladimir; he was under Auntie Miechen's thumb, and she didn't get on with Mama. There were similar difficulties with Uncle Aleksei, Uncle Pavel, and Uncle Sergei: each of them had his own life, and each might think with some reason that he was better equipped to inherit the throne. Still less could he look for useful advice to the eight grand dukes who were his cousins, while his great-uncle Mikhail Nikolaevich, who was a field marshal and also President of the State Council, took nothing to heart unless it affected the artillery. There was always Pobedonostsev of course, who had so recently been in charge of his education as heir to the throne, and long before that his father's chief tutor. Nikolai told Pobedonostsev that what had most distressed him in those first few weeks was the avalanche of paper launched upon him by his subordinates, which he simply had no time to read. Pobedonostsev explained that much of it was trivial, that they just wanted his signature to avoid taking responsibility themselves, and that he must break them of the habit. But clever though Pobedonostsev was, there could be no question of submitting completely to his dictates, and anyway his views could not invariably be superior to those of other clever people close to hand—such as Witte, for instance. But Witte, as Nikolai soon discovered, had very definite opinions on everything, and enjoyed nothing more than expressing them, especially on matters which were not his business as Minister of Finance, perhaps to bring the concerns of other ministers under his control. But even on financial matters Witte was not the only one with ideas—whether, for instance, Russia should adopt the gold standard. Some said one thing, some another, and you had to call a conference to sort it all out, which you did not succeed in doing in the end. Witte might suggest setting up a commission to look into the condition of the peasants, and the young Emperor would readily agree, but then Pobedonostsev would turn up, point out the futility of this scheme, and the Emperor would quash it, whereupon Witte sent a carefully argued note on the urgent need for such a commission, and the Emperor, convinced by his arguments, minuted his complete agreement in the margin, after which Durnovo came along to insist that there should be no commission, and the Emperor minuted "no action for the present." Then Sandro (who was his cousin, his brother-in-law, and a friend of his own age) discovered a previously unknown outstanding patriot and connoisseur of Russian life who won the Emperor's enthusiastic support for his idea that every effort must be made to block the invasion of Russia by foreign capital. The Emperor had put several measures to this end on paper, and foreign firms had immediately got to know of his view, when an agitated Witte appeared with a memorandum from Professor Mendeleev on the immense benefits to be derived only from an influx of foreign capital, and insisted that the Emperor should express an opinion which would be binding on all ministers. A meeting of ministers was called, and they decided to permit further foreign investment.

Nothing in the monarch's role was more excruciatingly difficult than this—making the correct choice between the views of his advisers. Each man's opinion was set out so as to look convincing. Who could determine which of them was right? How easy and pleasant ruling Russia would be if the opinions of all his counselors coincided! Surely they could get together, clever people like these, and reach agreement among themselves? But no, they were somehow fated always to speak in different voices and leave their Emperor in an impossible position. All they could do was suffocate him with memoranda, reports, and more reports.

If Nikolai was particularly unsure of himself, it was because he had been so secure and so comfortable looking over his father's shoulder.

As if the disagreements among ministers were not enough, many who were remote from the throne, fired with hope now that the firm hand of the late Emperor was lifted from them, were just as eager to offer their views and participate in the conduct of Russia's affairs. Impertinent orators began uttering audacious ideas in provincial zemstvos and gentry assemblies, on occasion almost going so far as to demand a constitution and the limitation of the imperial power (too intoxicated with their rhetoric to realize that they would be the first victims of a constitutional order). What most offended him was that they obviously did not regard their young monarch as a force to be reckoned with. They wanted to take advantage of his initial weakness and denude him of his autocratic power feather by feather. But Nikolai was not too young to realize that the great power he had inherited existed only as long as it was intact and unshared. He must not let it be fragmented. He must be able to exercise it in its fullness if it was to be of use to his enormous country. He summoned up all his strength and decided to administer a rebuff, to receive deputations from gentry assemblies, zemstvos, and cities and flatly refuse any such suggestions. All the same, he felt more agitated than he had ever felt in his life. (Alix was also worried: she was unsure whether it was proper for her to bow to the deputies and decided not to.) He began to be afraid that he would not be able to memorize the short speech prepared for him. But he did not want to read it—it must sound as though these were words of his own, just thought of. Friends gave him the idea of keeping the text of his speech inside his cap, which protocol would require him to remove at a certain point. And so it was done, and he spoke, or read, his lines without stumbling, telling them that he would safeguard the principles of autocracy as firmly and unswervingly as his unforgettable father—only, at the most important point, he made one mistake, saying that some zemstvo men were under the spell of "senseless" (instead of "groundless") dreams. All went well. He had put them in their place. (And it wasn't much of a mistake, surely? Either way, he was saying no.) But they resented it, and kept reminding him of it for years.

The bad omens attending these ceremonies proved justified. When the Tver delegation (the most troublesome of all) were paying their respects the dish slipped from their leader's hand and rolled away noisily. The loaf and the salt were spilled on the floor. Nikolai made a movement as though to help by picking up the dish, but sensed that this was not fitting for an Emperor and would only embarrass everyone further. (It often occurred to him afterward that it was from this ceremony and the dropping of the dish that everything began to go wrong.)

It is hard being Tsar of Russia, especially at the beginning, when you are still a stranger to it. Domestic affairs by themselves would not have been too tiresome but there were also many foreign policy headaches—and there the personalities, opinions, permutations were even more bewilderingly varied, and however depressed you were, you had to keep to yourself your chagrin that it was beyond human wit to choose the correct course. Giers, the old and experienced Minister of Foreign Affairs, who would soon follow his master into the grave, told the young monarch at his first audience that Russia had been fettered to France for two years past by a military alliance so secret that in both countries most members of the government knew nothing about it, although the details had already been filled in; it was already decided, for instance, that in the event of war with Germany, France would field nearly one million and Russia eight million men. Burdened with this secret, Nikolai was now doomed to receive urgent, almost ardent letters from his warmly affectionate friend and devoted cousin Wilhelm, reminding him that Russia and Germany, and their ruling houses, had been linked by traditional ties of friendship for a century, and for good reason: they were at one in their resistance to anarchism and republicanism, in their loyalty to the monarchic principle, which alone kept their two countries on firm foundations, in a Europe which included France—where presidents ensconced themselves on the throne of beheaded kings, and evildoers were amnestied almost as soon as they were jailed—and England, where anarchists from all over the world found asylum, and governments tottered and crashed amid general derision.

There was something very attractive, very winning about Wilhelm. He was always so candid, so sure that every word of his was right—and that was no more than the truth! What he said helped Nikolai to understand many things. Although he had never been schooled in government, Nikolai knew instinctively that only monarchy kept Russia strong, and that if the country became a republic with regular changes of government, it would be destroyed by the comings and goings of irresponsible windbag merchants (concerned only to gratify their own ambitions in their brief interval of power) and by furtive capitalists with the money to buy newspapers and manipulate public opinion.

All very true, but Aleksandr III's heir was also governed by his father's will. His father must have had some reason for entering into an alliance with a president perched on the throne of guillotined kings, and listening to the "Marseillaise," cap in hand, at Kronstadt.

Wilhelm was so friendly, so affectionate, so lovey-dovey to Nicky and Alix, and Nikolai longed with all his heart to be just as frank himself, but the secret treaty was like a hidden magnet deflecting his answers from the truth. He dreaded to think what would happen when Willy got to know about this treaty.

Nikolai did manage to find out before the aged Foreign Minister died what had induced his father to make the strange alliance. There had previously existed a secret Mutual Insurance Treaty between Germany and Russia: if either country should be involved in a war, the other would observe benevolent neutrality. But as soon as the youthful Wilhelm succeeded his grandfather and sent Bismarck into retirement he took his new chancellor's advice not to renew the treaty in 1890.

Must he assume that Willy's fervent flattery and his presents were meant to hide a secret of his own? No one, however clever, could live like that. If you approached the whole thing with warm goodwill it might turn out to be a mere misunderstanding. You had to find room in your heart for both Germany and France, reconcile them to each other—that was it!

An opportunity quickly presented itself—the ceremonial opening of the Kiel Canal. All the other navies would be there—surely the French navy would want to be beside the Russian? He succeeded in persuading them. What a triumph! The first step toward European reconciliation! (Angry voices were raised afterward in the French parliament: the occasion coincided with the twenty-fifth anniversary of the Franco-Prussian War.)

Then came another opportunity. In the months when his father was dying, impetuous Japan, a previously unheard-of country not listed among the powers, suddenly made war on helpless China and quickly defeated her. The young Nikolai was the only one among the rulers of Europe to have seen that country with his own eyes, and for that reason he felt a special responsibility for it and a special predisposition toward it. There was no time to be lost, it could not be put off until he was more at home with the business of ruling—he must pull the predator up short. The same pacific impulse made him appeal to the two age-old enemies, France and Germany, to help him in this task. No one thought that they could possibly join in a common action, but they did, together with Russia, and it was a great success: Japan broke off the war which it was winning, renounced Korea and the Liaotung Peninsula, including Port Arthur, taking only Formosa, no mainland territory, and promising to show the greatest consideration for the interests of other powers.

See what wisdom there sometimes is in gentle hearts! The young monarch had achieved something of which old, experienced politicians would never have dreamed.

Cousin Wilhelm was even more incensed by Japan's impertinence than Nikolai himself. He acknowledged that Russia's great mission was undoubtedly the civilizing of the Asian continent and the defense of Europe and the Cross against the encroachment of the yellow race and Buddhism. Europe should be grateful to Nikolai for understanding Russia's vocation so readily, and Germany would see to it that there was peace on Russia's European frontiers while she carried out her task.

Until then Nikolai had not realized himself that this was Russia's vocation, but he began to think hard about it and see it more and more clearly. Why, of course, it was not for nothing that fate had taken him as a very young man to the mysterious Far East and bound him to it with so many threads. Even the assassination attempt at Otsu was a bond. The East was no longer an abstraction for him. It meant broad, warm, fertile expanses by warm seas, bordering on Russia's icy Siberia, which defied cultivation and had no way out to the sea. The two formed a single continuous land mass, and the link between them had a prophetic significance. (Witte contributed a golden idea: build the railway not around the Amur but along the shorter route across Manchuria. China would not be able to refuse.) It turned out, moreover, that his father had made a grant of two million rubles to an enterprising Buryat* for the peaceful conquest of Mongolia, China, and Tibet. The money had been spent, and another two million was now wanted for the continuation of the undertaking. It was a worthwhile investment. The Eastern idea became the young monarch's foible. And, of course, it was not weak little Japan that stood in Russia's way, but England's always obtrusive iron shoulder. (Witte suspected that the Japanese were so bullheaded only because of secret English promises.) It was a fact that England had been Russia's enemy through the ages, at all times and in all places. One of the few remarks Nikolai remembered his father making on political matters was that England, and only England, had always hindered Russia's every step, in Asia, in Persia, in Constantinople, in the Balkans—everywhere. (It had been very nice, though, staying with Queen Victoria.)

Secrets, of course, could never be kept in a republic. The secret of the Franco-Russian alliance was soon blurted out in the French parliament.

* P. A. Badmayev (1851–1919), Buryat Mongolian adventurer, quack doctor, financier, and political intriguer. [*Trans.*]

Nicky felt that he would be ashamed to face Willy, although the alliance had not been his idea. But their friendship stood the test. Willy magnanimously forgave him (and anyway there was nothing in the treaty to say that it was directed against Germany). Nicky did have to endure being told that one fine day he might find himself involved in the most terrible war Europe had ever seen, and wondering how it had ever happened.

A year had now passed since his father's death. He came out of mourning, feeling sorry and guilty, because mourning was his only tie with the dear past. In mourning, Nikolai had felt that his father was still trying to transfuse advice into him, to pass on some secret which he had not had time to impart on earth. Now the young monarch would have to discover these things for himself. With God's help, of course.

Preparations began for the coronation—twenty days of celebration in Moscow in May. Nikolai went there with a sinking heart, secretly dreading it, as he dreaded any social ordeal which required him to appear in public frequently and perhaps make speeches. (Alix, his sunshine, the only one who knew about it, did her best to put heart into him.) But he himself confidently expected that the moment the crown was placed on his head in the Cathedral of the Assumption he would change completely and become a true ruler with divinely instilled wisdom. Believing and thirsting for this, crowned and wearing the purple, holding the scepter and the orb, he recited the creed with a dry throat and listened to the coronation prayer: "Grant him understanding and wisdom that he may judge Thy people truly, kindle his heart to succor those who are afflicted, and do not disappoint us in our hopes." From the day of the coronation he felt that he had come of age. From the day of the coronation he began to ponder over divine election and the divine right of kings, whom only God could guide.

A misfortune which he had done nothing to deserve occurred on the fourth day after the coronation. A crowd which had gathered overnight to receive presents began pushing and jostling for no obvious reason early next morning, and within ten minutes had trampled thirteen hundred of its own number to death. This disaster cast a dark shadow on the celebrations. Nikolai was horrified and grief-stricken. Why had God sent this misfortune to mar the coronation—could it be an ill omen? Not only was there no time for such reflections but the rigid timetable of the festivities demanded his attendance that very evening at a ball given by the French ambassador. Alix considered, and all his uncles spoke up in support of her, that not to go would be impolite to the French.

A monarch's actions are governed by different rules from those of other people. Relations between states and peoples impinge upon his day-to-day routine. And he has to get used to this.

But it looked bad.

Nikolai showed leniency and not one of those who organized the gathering on Khodynka Field was punished. There was no point in increasing the number of sufferers even further.

But some sort of divine displeasure seemed to hang over the royal couple themselves. They went to Nizhni Novgorod that summer for the All-Russian Exhibition of Trades and Crafts, and at the very hour of their visit black clouds gathered and great hailstones battered the pavilions, breaking many windows and threatening to wreck the exhibition altogether.

That same summer they made a long and enjoyable journey abroad. Visits to the Emperors of Austria-Hungary and Germany and to the King of Denmark (Nikolai's grandfather), and a holiday in Scotland with Queen Victoria, were followed by a triumphant finale in Paris, where the French crowd received the Russian Tsar almost as enthusiastically as the Moscow crowd had. Pictures of him were distributed in the streets and printed on chocolate boxes. Crockery, soap, and toys bearing the Russian arms were on sale. Nikolai was so moved that he could not resist speaking at a military parade of Russia's "brotherhood in arms" with the French (although he could not remember being taught that any such thing had ever existed). They relaxed after all these excitements in Alix's native Darmstadt, and gloomy memories of Khodynka Field and the Nizhni Novgorod exhibition ceased to trouble the royal couple.

His reception in Paris was such a moving experience for Nikolai that his antipathy to the republic faded and he enthusiastically agreed to a friendly understanding on Turkey proposed by the French government, only to learn back in St. Petersburg that the French had tricked him and tied him hand and foot so that he could do nothing about the Straits.

You thought you were making a promise to honest people, and they cheated you. Nikolai was so indignant that he let his ministers persuade him to turn the tables and order an immediate landing on the Bosphorus. Turkey was dying, and he should make sure of his inheritance. The Russian envoy in Constantinople was particularly insistent, assuring him that resistance would be negligible. The Minister of War and the Minister of the Navy confirmed that strategically it was perfectly feasible. It was a very tempting idea—to begin the new reign by gloriously seizing Tsargrad, the city of Constantine, the unattainable dream of all his predecessors. Someone, someday must carry out Russia's historic task—to return to the ancestral home and make all the Slavs safe forever. Some sort of inner voice told Nikolai that the time had come and that the onus was on him. The Russian ambassador had already drawn up instructions for himself in the Emperor's name, giving him the right to summon the Russian fleet and a landing force of thirty thousand to Constantinople at a moment of his own choosing—and Nikolai signed them. What if the fleets of other countries appeared in the Dardanelles? Let them—Russia was ready to go to war with all Europe! (England, however, would not fight—it would prefer to partition Turkey and seize Egypt for itself.) At this point Uncle Aleksei, the admiral, came back from abroad in a state of high excitement: rumors were already going around Paris, it would be an enormous debacle. Nikolai withdrew the ambassador's plenipotentiary powers at once.

He was still unconvinced that his reactions were truly those of an Emperor. He longed to find the compelling and ungainsayable course, but somehow it always eluded him. He longed to know how to govern, but there was no one from whom he could obtain such knowledge. From the first day of his reign he had been helplessly borne along by the current. He would have dearly loved to understand the laws governing the events of his time, but did not know where to look for them. He knew and liked to meditate on many episodes in Russian history, but they never seemed to give him any clear indication. He was too shy to ask, even if his pride had allowed him to show that he did not know. Nor had his father bequeathed counselors of the kind he needed. The gaunt and gangling Pobedonostsev, with his hollow cheeks, his big glasses, his ears sticking out as though aghast at the growing wickedness of this hopeless world, was too heavy-handed and too rough—Nikolai had wearied of his sermonizing long ago, in his teens. The zealous, the indefatigable Witte, who was so overwhelmingly clever that it took your breath away to hear him talk, Witte who had invented the state liquor monopoly and was so adept at extracting money from the Rothschilds, had, alas, an alarming and demoralizing tendency to annex the whole state and life in general to the Ministry of Finance. He supported only those ministerial candidates who would not compete with him.

Nikolai was worse than fatherless. There was no one he could confide in, except his beloved Alix and his wise mama. The young royal couple had no friends in high society—perhaps because they chose whenever possible to spend their time quietly together rather than at the center of a noisy court. Even their habit of never missing Mass, or the service on the vigil of a saint's day, struck the aristocracy as a ridiculous affectation.

Perhaps he ought to show more affection and trust to his ardent friend Wilhelm, but there was something a little frightening in his ardor. Wilhelm was an Emperor and his peer, and his earnest and enthusiastic admonitions often echoed Nikolai's deepest feelings. The two found it convenient for purposes of rapid and candid communication to use their personal adjutants as envoys rather than relying on their awkward Foreign Ministries. Willy would speak of "our position in Asia," implying that Nicky's interests in that part of the world were his own. In 1897 Willy paid a lengthy visit to St. Petersburg. They opened their hearts to each other, concluded that their views on all matters were identical, and that for both of them their high ambition was the defense of the white race in Asia. One August evening as they were returning from Krasnoye Selo to Peterhof, just the two of them in an open carriage, Wilhelm, with his mustaches almost brushing his cousin's face, pleaded and pleaded and in the end persuaded Nikolai not to hinder his occupation of Kiaochow. It was impossible to hold out against such persistence!

But Russia had assured China after the Sino-Japanese War that there were no subjects of dispute between the two countries, that she wished to live in friendship with her neighbor and was prepared to defend her against the Europeans. It was in return for this that the Chinese had granted Russia permission to build the railway through northern Manchuria. China now appealed to Russia to defend her against Germany. This was a ticklish situation, but someone thought up an ingenious answer: Russia was ready to help China, but to do so would need a base of operations inside Chinese territory. The Chinese offered Port Arthur. Nikolai and his advisers conferred—should they take it or should they not? Nikolai knew that Russia had no claim—in ordinary human terms it was wrong—but can a great Emperor measure things by the common man's yardstick? There have never, anywhere, been any firm rules for the conduct of Emperors. Port Arthur was the ice-free port so urgently needed, far to the south of the present Russian seaboard. How could he fail to take it for the sake of Russia's greatness? Did he as Emperor have the right not to take it? Besides, Russia must be the sure bulwark against the yellow race. (Alix too was very much against the yellow men.) He decided to take it on lease for twenty-five years, with the right to join it up with the great Trans-Siberian Railway, which would soon reach that vicinity.

Wilhelm applauded. A masterly agreement! In effect you will be master of Pekin! Thanks to your great journey you have become the expert on the East. With your intelligence you will always manage to find a way out. All eyes are turned hopefully on the great Emperor of the East. He presented Nicky with an engraving made by himself and showing the two of them protecting Europe from the yellow peril.

There was much truth in what he said. Nikolai did have a special feeling for and a special understanding of the East. Anointment had opened his eyes to this before most things. Russia's mission was to expand further and further to the east. (Especially as she would never be allowed to take the Bosphorus.)

However, Germany's and Russia's territorial gains whetted Britain's appetite. Wilhelm, honorable as always, warned Nikolai that Britain was discussing an alliance with Germany—surely she would not succeed in separating the friends? Britain, Nikolai answered, had already tried to tie Russia's hands and curb her development in the Far East by offering her an alliance, and had been rebuffed. The diplomatic permutations made his head spin. Relations between individuals are never as mercurial and as subject to abrupt changes as relations between states. Yet the monarchs were all cousins or in-laws, all one big family.

Where was this endless arms race between the great powers leading?

Could it possibly ensure peace for anyone? No, it squandered the resources of all peoples and would end in a still worse war. The War Minister, Kuropatkin, reported to the Emperor that to keep up with the rest of Europe and with each other both Russia and Austria would soon have to introduce rapid-firing cannon, which would cost Russia at least a hundred million rubles. Why not, he asked with simple peasant common sense, reach an understanding with Austria that neither side would introduce those weapons? Both sides would benefit and the balance of forces would remain unchanged. Kuropatkin expected the Emperor to scold him for this unsolicited advice, but Nikolai responded eagerly: "You obviously don't know me very well yet. I have great sympathy with your marvelous idea. I stood for a long time against the introduction of the latest rifles."

He felt certain that he had finally found the feat of true statesmanship that God willed him to accomplish.

It wasn't just rapid-firing cannon; other innovations were imminent: field mortars, fougasse shells, concrete pillboxes, new types of machine guns. So much senseless expenditure! It would unbalance the budget, undermine the people's welfare—and to what end? Long intervals of peace simply meant the accumulation of unprecedented arsenals. And in a few years' time these armaments in their turn would lose all value and meaning, and new ones would be required. Why not appeal to all the powers simultaneously to sign a treaty barring the further development of arms? After all, Aleksandr II had proposed that the whole world ban dumdum bullets—and they had been banned. The appeal was now a matter of urgency, since the non-European nations too were quickly adopting the inventions of modern science. (Moreover, after her acquisitions on the Liaotung Peninsula, it was important for Russia to show the world that she was a peace-loving country.) As it was worked out in detail, the idea looked more and more attractive: Russia must be the country to take the initiative for peace. Russia was the one country that could afford even to fall behind in the arms race: she was too big for anyone to attack her. And Kuropatkin's dream—that the money saved on arms would go to improve peasant farming and strengthen Russia's roots—would become reality. He, Nikolai, would sow this great seed. Release billions for the welfare of ordinary people. Give posterity cause to remember him with gratitude. Stamp his own imperial name on the century about to begin.

So in August 1898, with no advance warning to Russia's ally France or to Nikolai's friend and cousin Wilhelm (no one must have an unfair start in thinking it over, and above all no one must have a chance to dissuade him), a note from the Russian government was sent to all the powers. (Nikolai, enamored of every word in it, read it to the Empress three times over, and loved it more each time.) The note called upon them, not to disarm—that would have aroused alarm and suspicion—but to set limits on the development of armaments, to replace armed tension with trust and stability, and to prevent the unproductive squandering of the spiritual and physical resources of their peoples, of labor and capital. To this end a conference should be called and an international court of arbitration established.

The whole world was taken by surprise. The press (and presumably the peoples?) reacted positively and in places enthusiastically, while governments were ironical or hostile: from the Tsar's throne it was easy enough to say what you liked, the Tsar's government did not depend on public opinion or on parliamentary approval of war credits. France was hurt, because Russia had concealed the planning of the note from her ally, and perturbed by the thought that twenty-seven years of preparations for the recovery of Alsace-Lorraine might go for nothing. England and America took it more calmly, since there was no suggestion that naval forces should be limited, and they relied on naval strength to attain their ends. At this point a dangerous conflict flared up between England and France in Africa, threatening to end in war. So confused were the accounts between nations that it was impossible to choose a moment equally advantageous to all for the abandonment of the arms race. Someone would always be left behind. Russia herself had problems—the Bosphorus, as always, and the Far East—and she ought to consider whether she should hasten to rearm with rapid-firing cannon in spite of everything; if she did not catch up, others might think that she was making her proposal to limit armaments because she had exhausted her means. Perhaps she should rearm first, and *then* set herself limits? Wilhelm sent a telegram welcoming the Russian Emperor's lofty ambitions, and promptly increased the size of his land forces.

The noble scheme either had to be abandoned or had to be pursued more purposefully. Nikolai received messages of gratitude from many societies and individuals, and these were encouragement enough for him to continue. In December 1898 he agreed to a second circular to the powers, proposing a general conference to deal with the limitation of each country's armed forces to a level determined by the size of the population; the prohibition of new firearms, new explosive devices, and the use of submarines in naval warfare; and the establishment of a court of arbitration between the powers.

It was all so incontestably desirable that the powers could not refuse to attend. But they had no intention of agreeing to anything. The world press praised the Russian Tsar's initiative as before. The conference took place at The Hague in 1899, but it did not set its mark on the new century. The German representative declared that *his* people were not languishing under the burden of military expenditure, nor was universal conscription a burden for Germans but an honor. A commission of the great powers turned down all of Russia's main proposals, and the idea of compulsory arbitration was also rejected. The only result was the creation of the Hague Tribunal.

The whole initiative was so right and so good, yet it was swallowed up so stupidly by quicksand. Nikolai took it as a personal failure. He was of two minds, inclined to regret that he had ever started the thing only to make a fool of himself and give people an opportunity to call his intentions comically sentimental or suspect that they concealed some crafty Russian scheme.

Even an anointed monarch cannot easily see the road marked out for him to follow. The most tempting step ends in empty space or in the slush. Truth is split in two in the struggle between powers, and in the arguments between your own advisers—and your heart is rent with it. Nikolai had dreamed only of doing what was right and good, but there was no one to tell him what and how. The only sure things were family life and the simplest occupations. Alix, his sunshine. Bathing his first little daughter. Morning and evening walks, enjoying God's world. Occasionally, canoeing, or cycling on the grounds of Tsarskoye Selo, or training a dog to the gun. Relaxing in the evening at a performance of some lovely opera, or a funny play, sometimes seeing the same show twice. What gave him great enjoyment and always raised his spirits was taking the salute at a ceremonial review. Then there was a round of regimental celebrations in the autumn, and another in the spring. (Nikolai's private calendar was divided up by regimental anniversaries.) How much better than sitting signing endless orders and authorizations until you ceased to see or understand them, or listening to two stupefying ministerial reports a day, stealing glances at your watch as they dragged on into the lunch hour, robbing a man of the time he needs just to be a man. Nobody knew for sure what ought to be done, but all those ministers and a host of their subordinates went on from day to day doing whatever it was with great assurance.

How unbearable it was to be an Emperor, and Emperor of all the Russias at that; how good and how natural to be a simple family man—to take an evening off now and then and sit reading the history of other times, which was so enjoyable because all the choices had been made already and you knew what had ensued.

Sometimes, though, you felt proud. Not only when even the German fleet was lit up and fired a salute on your name day, but when, for instance, war broke out between England and the Transvaal, and the eternal troublemaker and predator was caught in a trap. Nikolai was completely absorbed in the war, read the detailed reports in the British papers from the first line to the last, rejoiced in the English losses—they should have looked for the ford before they jumped in the water. He was fired with pride that he was the only man on earth who could change the course of the war in Africa to Britain's ruin. He had a very simple means at hand: he need only telegraph an order to his armies in Turkestan to mobilize and march toward the frontier. No more than that! And the strongest navy ever seen could not prevent him from punishing England in her most vulnerable spot!

But his advisers objected—that was what made him dislike them, they were always objecting, saying that Russia was unprepared for military operations, her army was technically behind, and anyway there was no continuous rail link between Turkestan and the Russian heartland.

In fact, it was no more than a pleasant dream. He lacked the resolution to initiate great actions on his own responsibility. But he was proud of his idea. What he must do was strengthen Russia's lines of communication, her military presence, her influence in Asia, to which the Siberian land mass gave her a natural entry. In Europe, the Bosphorus was his only inducement to make war—and the Bosphorus and the Dardanelles together would give him no more than entry to another enclosed sea, the Mediterranean. Whereas in Asia very small garrisons could bring great benefits. It was impossible not to expand in Asia when it could be done so easily, without great military effort. (And how much more valuable Russia's acquisitions would become once the great Trans-Siberian Railway was ready!) China was a great crumbling mass, from which any strong state could break off whichever pieces it needed. While his own government feebly drifted and floundered, and all his ministers wanted nothing better than to carry on that way, voices in China whipped up growing resentment at national humiliation, and in the summer of 1900, ignoring their government, the Chinese rose, cut Pekin off from the sea, laid siege to the diplomatic quarter, and were said to have killed several hundred white people through the length and breadth of China. The whole world howled in indignation at these Chinese atrocities. There was no wireless telegraph as yet, so it was impossible to find out what was happening in the unfortunate diplomatic compound, but obviously a massacre was in progress, and troops must be sent to the rescue. The European powers had never been so fully agreed on anything. An international expeditionary force was mustered. Russia contributed one-third of the troops and Russia took Pekin. To everyone's surprise, the diplomatic compound had not been touched; the Chinese government had thrown a weak cordon around it, and that was sufficient defense against the rebels. Nikolai felt guilty and disgusted with himself for having taken part in the combined attack. Witte insisted that hostilities against China were completely irrational when Russia could obtain all it needed by negotiations. (All the same, they did in the course of this little war annex the whole area between Manchuria and Port Arthur.) Nikolai then informed the powers that he was leaving Pekin, and proposed a general withdrawal. He warned the Western powers that their forces could expect no further help from Russia.

It was shameful. Russia had promised China protection, and then joined the rest in attacking her.

Stories were told that made things worse. When the rumors about Chinese atrocities got around, some of the inhabitants of Blagoveshchensk, which was under fire from the Chinese side, indignantly drove Chinese residents from their houses and forced them to swim the Amur. Many were drowned.

The Emperor's power was unbounded. He could not remain inactive; but if he acted, a careless hand could crush hundreds and thousands of people. Where he could refrain from action it was better to do so. The golden mean was preferable to drastic measures. A Christian could not do to China what he would not want done to Russia. But practical politics compelled him to act, to build the line across Manchuria, to fortify it with a defensive zone, to establish an overland link with Port Arthur.

In the same year Nikolai abolished Siberian exile. He wanted to clean up that great and healthy land, not use it as a dumping ground for unwholesome and turbulent elements. He had a mental vision of Siberia as the scene of Russia's growth in the near future.

Deciphering the machinations and intrigues and plots of the European powers naturally made the greatest demand on the Emperor's attention and his vigilance. Inside Russia there should be no enemies, only subjects awaiting their turn to enjoy his favor. Russia ought to be united. But no: in all those years, while Nikolai was taxing his mind to make sense of international crosscurrents, there had been no peace at home. They had not taken in his refusal to grant a constitution. Malcontent zemstvo employees, and gentlemen idlers who knew nothing of the country's real needs and could fill their leisure hours devising ways of satisfying imaginary needs, went on agitating. Worse still, the professors had corrupted their students, kidnapped them.

For the first four years of his reign Nikolai had believed that he could settle all problems, external and internal, by peaceful means—either by waiting patiently himself or by asking others to be patient. In the fifth year of his reign, 1899, he was cruelly disillusioned. The Hague Peace Conference did not bring world peace, and at home vicious hostility bared its teeth.

The trouble flared up without warning. At a degree ceremony at St. Petersburg University the students took offense at the rector's perhaps unnecessarily rude and clumsy warning that there must be no drunken horseplay afterward. They howled him down and disrupted the ceremony. At the exit the police for no good reason herded the students toward one of three bridges and rode into the crowd to break it up, using whips. Regrettable, but no excuse for what followed. The students declared the university closed for a long period, prevented their fellows from entering and their teachers from lecturing. Students in St. Petersburg, Moscow, and the provincial universities all came out in sympathy. Nikolai wanted to settle it paternally and appointed a commission of inquiry under an adjutant general known to be sympathetic to students. This might have been expected to restore peace, especially as the police were forbidden to interfere in the future, but the strike went on for a month, two months, there was a free-for-all in the lecture halls at Kiev, another month went by, and still no one listened to the conciliation commission, while the whole of educated society egged the students on.

How ridiculous you feel if you can stand up to the world powers but cannot take in hand the excitable young in your own country. And when you remember that most of those receiving higher education have no means of their own, that half of them are excused tuition fees and a quarter are helped by scholarships, you wonder angrily why the state should have to woo students, why, when everybody else is constrained by duty, they alone are spared. Nikolai gave his consent—they must be punished. Witte approved the proposals: those responsible for the disorders were to be excluded from their institutions for one, two, or three years, and sent into the army for the period of their suspension, even if they were exempt from the call-up and even if they were physically unfit. Military training would be the best corrective.

For four years he had thought that he might be able to rule in the spirit of his grandfather rather than that of his father. In four years no major problems had clamored for a decision. Then, suddenly, they began knocking at the door one after another.

Finland. If it was part of Russia, why could it not live according to Russian laws? Why should it accept and apply them only when they met with its approval? Finland called up only ten thousand soldiers, but Russia had no right to transfer a single one of them from one province to the next. Aleksandr I had been lavish with his gifts to Finland, but those were easier times, and what had been freely granted in the first year of the century had to be curtailed in its last. Perhaps Russia and Finland should lead separate lives. But who could take it upon himself to dismantle an inherited empire?

The zemstvos. His grandfather had not established zemstvos in all the provinces, and there was now apparently an urgent need to extend them to those without. But the inexhaustible Witte, always so brilliant and so sure of himself however often he changed his mind, whispered in the Emperor's ear that zemstvos were not really compatible with autocratic government. Instead of looking after local needs they had a tendency to outgrow their purpose and undermine the monarchy.

When problems crowd in, decisions are easier if they are all of a kind. Send unruly students into the army. Refuse to extend the zemstvo system. Change the Finnish call-up regulations. Most important of all, preserve the Russian peasant commune as if it were the apple of your eye.

The countryside's response was a series of bad harvests even in the richest and most fertile provinces. Finnish unrest grew to the point of demanding complete separation. "Society" was aroused to such a pitch of anger that it seemed not to care whether Russia itself survived if only it could get rid of the Tsar. What was written in the papers was so remote from traditional Russian ideas that it might have been in an unrelated language, with no possibility of translation or explanation. In the universities things were quiet for one and a half academic years; then in February 1901 a student ushered in the twentieth century by shooting the Minister of Education, Bogolepov!

What should the monarch do? Bow down to the students? Demand other shootings?

The assassin was tried in a civil court which was not empowered to sentence him to death. (In fact, he shortly afterward made good his escape.) Indeed, there had not been a single political execution in the six years of Nikolai's reign and he had never thought of resorting to them. Thousands of students gathered before the Cathedral of Our Lady of Kazan. They were surrounded, blows were exchanged here and there, and they were arrested in droves, eight hundred of them altogether, more than the prisons and the regimental drill halls combined could hold. Some were cautioned, others expelled, and still others sent back to their native places. It was hoped that with the most disorderly of them out of the way the others would quiet down. The Emperor also appointed an easygoing minister so that he would not appear to be avenging the murdered man. The new minister began by authorizing student meetings and looking for ways of improving university life.

Shortly afterward terrorists fired on Pobedonostsev (and missed). In response to the government's moderation, "society's" hostility to the regime grew fiercer from month to month and expressed itself in ruthless forms.

Early in the following year, 1902, another youth shot to death the Minister of the Interior, Sipyagin. "Society" was overjoyed, and made no attempt to conceal it.

This was when Nikolai began to feel really angry. These bullets were in effect aimed at him. They were refusing to let him lead the country, demanding his surrender. He never felt the slightest temptation to do so. He was the wearer of a historic crown, he had the whole people on his side, and only a handful of intellectuals against him. The Emperor made Pleve, who favored strong measures, his new Minister of the Interior.

These lethal splinters had lodged in the very heart of the country, where all were Russians, his own people, and things should have gone more smoothly than elsewhere. Why couldn't people who loved the country and wished it well live peacefully and comfortably together?

He liked to go hunting capercailzies on an April night. It didn't matter if he got no sleep, he was always wide awake the day after a hunt, and he could take a nap after his ministerial audiences. He liked going around the barracks and thanking the men for their service. He liked attending maneuvers and listening to the leisurely analysis afterward. Watching a rifle battalion fanning out in extended order. Galloping out to a place where he could expect to see the uhlans or the Jägers pass by on their way to camp. (Alix would follow in a charabanc.) Going for a row in a dinghy, just the two of them, in splendid weather, on a sea like glass. Watching a race between barges or whaleboats or skiffs. Seeing an amusing play in the evening—in the theater at Krasnoye Selo if it was summer. (He was always sad to leave Krasnoye Selo. It was the center of all the army camps.) But nothing was more delightfully relaxing than going to lunch in an officers' mess, staying on till supper or later, chatting informally, listening to an inexhaustible fund of army stories, or to gypsy musicians or a Russian choir, getting home at 2 a.m., and still enjoying the evening in retrospect when you rose the next day.

How easy life must be for the man with no responsibilities beyond his own immediate family! But the young monarch is responsible also for some dozens of grand dukes and grand duchesses, for his cousins and even for uncles and aunts much older than himself, for the income from their appanage lands, the posts they occupied, and even for their amours—Uncle Mikhail and later on Uncle Pavel had made light of their duty to keep up dynastic appearances, refused to curb their passions, and chosen the degrading course of morganatic marriage, so that they had to be removed from their posts, stripped of their rank, and banished abroad. How it had grieved the whole royal clan!

The heir to the throne, his gentle, contemplative brother Georgi, was consumptive and quietly wasted away in seclusion in the Caucasus, surviving their father only by a matter of months.

The difficulty of ruling was that of applying your mind not merely to the governance of your own obedient body, your own family, or the imperial household but to dominating an area far too great for any individual. Sometimes, while he was clearing the ice in the Winter Palace garden or taking a ride near Tsarskoye Selo, Nikolai strained his wits so much comparing the conflicting views picked up from subordinates or in actual conversation that if he could have transmitted all this tension into his crowbar it would have danced furiously on the ice, and if he could have communicated it to his horse it would have snorted and bolted.

What made ruling hard was the intolerable difficulty of addressing those you ruled. It was easy enough when he was with two or three others talking in a closed room, or when he had a guest or two to lunch. It was pleasant among military men, preferably Guardsmen; he had no difficulty in speaking up then, his words flowed freely. (The jubilee of the Corps of Pages fell around about this time and was celebrated lengthily and uproariously. Nikolai talked a great deal, and with enjoyment, on that occasion.) But he was awkward and constrained when he had to speak out in a gathering of civilians, especially if they were highly educated men of ideas. In those circumstances Nikolai felt as though his hands were tied behind his back. He could not make a natural gesture. His tongue would cleave to his palate, incapable of pronouncing a single gracious or affable word, and the Emperor even feared that he might be blushing, that his bashfulness was obvious, and would gladly have sunk into the earth just to get away. (The centenary of the State Council, and of the establishment of ministries, more or less coincided with the jubilee of the Corps of Pages, and Nikolai died a thousand deaths attending those other celebrations, but did not speak a single word on any of those occasions.) God had granted nearly half of mankind the gift of behaving unconstrainedly in a gathering, but Nikolai froze, was paralyzed, and could only hope that his silence would be sufficiently imposing.

The hard thing for a ruler was the cruel difficulty of making correct decisions and of choosing loyal people on whom he could rely. How often had he thought that he had finally found the correct solution, only to see it collapse under the pressure of events, or to find that the strength to carry it out was lacking. How often had he supposed that he had found the right man at last, only to hear others informing him in chorus that he had chosen badly. And then his advisers were never of one mind, they were forever contradicting one another, and the obvious inference was that they themselves did not know what it would be right to do. Nikolai had less and less faith in his advisers as the years went by. He no longer disclosed his thoughts in full, but simply sounded their opinions, assuming in advance that any one of them could be wrong. The Tsar's instinct was likely to be a more reliable guide.

Ministers, some more modestly, some more boldly, all made a show of decisiveness in their opinions and actions. They were always insisting that so-and-so should be given an award, and somebody else appointed to a council of trustees or some other profitable post, or sent into honorable retirement in the State Council. (The Emperor had dealt personally with Kshesinskaya's plea to be excused from a fine for wearing the wrong costume, and had been compelled to sacrifice the Director of Theaters.) Those who like Witte considered themselves brilliant urged the Tsar to rely solely on talent. Others tried to convince him that loyalty and devotion were all that was needed, and that the Tsar should have around him hardworking and scrupulously honest people of average ability. His was a difficult path to tread—listening patiently while three of them in succession contradicted each other, reading the reams of documents laid before him, when so often many ministers had already acted on their own initiative that the monarch's decision was no longer necessary. Because of the continual angry buzz of contradiction and disagreement between them Nikolai began to have less confidence in ministers than in anybody. The longer a minister had held his post, the less he was trusted, though once he had resigned the Tsar might begin to trust him again. Nikolai trained himself to make a show of listening attentively (more often than not he was bored, though he would liven up occasionally if there was anything amusing in the report), and was particularly affable if he intended to get rid of the minister shortly or to overrule him. He trained himself to conceal his feelings and his opinions from ministers, to seek reliable advice from some outsider, some good and perceptive man with no official position, and to promulgate important decisions without reference to the relevant minister or department.

If only he had some direct means of discovering what his people thought—that would be the way to make a decision. But the ministers stood like a fence between Emperor and people.

Then there were sometimes delays and changes of mind because Alix and Mama held different views. Worse still was the multitude of grand dukes, many of whom claimed a right to influence decisions. People with all sorts of axes to grind had to be given an audience. Shyly at first, but more assertively as time went on, Nikolai learned to say, "That is my wish, and I don't want to hear anything further about it."

He became more sure of himself from year to year. He was no more of a sinner, and no more prone to error, than any of them, and he was fortified by divine unction. He was an autocrat, and it was high time he realized it, as Alix was always telling him. He was God's elect from the day of his birth, and so could rule better than any of them. If only he believed in himself and followed the dictates of his conscience it would never let him down. There was truth in the saying that "the Tsar's heart is in the hands of God." Nikolai was also answerable to history—and history would understand the course he had taken. There was no cause for surprise if his ordinances did not please his contemporaries: they lived in an infidel milieu, with a totally different view of the world. It was fortunate that he and Alix found such ready understanding and support in each other.

Sometimes he was sinfully impatient and sought to know God's will more clearly through the occult channels open only to the enlightened. For that purpose it was permissible to use those mysterious people who communicated with the world beyond the grave and often learned infallible truths from it. One fascinating man of this sort was Monsieur Philippe, an occultist and doctor of medicine from Lyons, who had by good luck (and through the good offices of Uncle Nikolasha and the Montenegrin princesses) turned up at the court in St. Petersburg. He had no difficulty in summoning up spirits, among them the shade of Aleksandr III, who now made up for his omission in his lifetime by dictating instructions to his son on how to rule their fatherland. (One of the first was that he should assign the Montenegrin prince a pension of three million rubles.) Monsieur Philippe also promised to help them in their family misfortune: Alix had borne four girls and still there was no heir to the throne. The medium persuaded her that she was pregnant and carrying a boy, and the royal couple were happy for a few brief months. Then came the grievous discovery that she was not pregnant at all—and the sudden change gave rise to a slanderous tale in high society that she had given birth to a freak which had to be suffocated. This odious behavior on the part of the "best people" left a deep scar on the feelings of Alix and Nikolai. No section of the Russian population was more alien to them than the social elite, with their hypocritical bowing and scraping and their readiness to betray at any moment. Because high society and exaggerated protocol were so unpalatable to them, and because they liked to live modestly, the royal couple stopped giving palace balls. A happy evening for them was one spent in the family circle, or on Saturday at the late-night service.

Everybody in the world has enemies. Those of Monsieur Philippe supplied the information that he was not a doctor of medicine and that he had been prosecuted in France for fraud. This calumny against a man who had become dear to Alix and him angered the Emperor. He lost control of himself (a very rare thing with him), threw the papers on the floor and trampled them underfoot, then gave orders for the President of France to be asked to provide Philippe with the missing diploma. Negotiations began, but the French government was nervous about parliamentary questions, and it was decided to give Philippe a Russian degree, the rank of full state counselor, and the status of gentleman. At that point Russia's senior police agent in France, one Rachkovsky, whose duty it was to keep watch on Russian revolutionaries in that country, instead of minding his own business reported that Monsieur Philippe was apparently a simple butcher without education and that he had turned to hypnosis when the French police had forbidden him to treat the sick. This left a nasty taste, and Rachkovsky was removed from Paris and retired.

So a variety of unfortunate circumstances made it difficult for him to go on using Monsieur Philippe's brilliant talents, and the period of complete emancipation from ministerial opinions, when Nikolai could give categorical orders in the knowledge that his decision came from a higher power, lasted no more than a year. Unfortunately, Philippe had not managed to obtain definitive instructions on the best way for Nikolai to conduct himself in the Far East.

But he had seen those lands! That, obviously, was an indication of God's design. The same divine plan could be seen in the fact that Russia's eastern territories marched with those of China. The dormant and decadent East needed a strong hand from outside—and whose, if not Russia's, could it be? The grand design of Nikolai's reign was evidently meant to be the expansion of Russian influence far to the east: he must make rich Manchuria Russia, proceed to annex Korea, perhaps even extend his sway over Tibet. Alix gave him much encouragement. The best way of ensuring that war would not result was for Russia to make a show of strength. No one would dare to make a move against her anyway.

Strangely enough, it was not Nikolai's natural helpers, the Russian ministers, but the German Emperor who agreed with him about the grandeur and the urgency of these tasks. At this time the cousins met every year, and kept up a friendly correspondence which on Wilhelm's side could be better described as tender, almost amorous. It even seemed that Wilhelm's sole intention in building up his navy was to help Nikolai maintain peace in the world. He was only building the Berlin–Baghdad railway, it seemed, to put it at Russia's disposal so that she could move up troops against the British. Nikolai revealed the great Asian objective of his rule to his devoted, his humbly admiring cousin and friend at Reval in 1902, and as he sailed away Willy's flags signaled a courtly farewell: "The Admiral of the Atlantic Ocean salutes the Admiral of the Pacific!" He ended his letters with the words "Ever on watch—Willy," and he did pass on many secrets discovered by his agents in Asia about Britain's hidden hostility and Japan's preparations for war. He warned Nikolai again and again about the dangers of a "Crimean combination" of Russia's enemies. The democratic countries, ruled by parliamentary majorities, would always be against the stable imperial monarchies; as he moved further into Asia, Nikolai would find Britain and the United States hostile, and her useless ally, France, unsympathetic. It was, he said, obvious to everyone on the European continent that Russia must obey the laws of expansion and endeavor to obtain an ice-free harbor for her trade. For this she would need a "hinterland"—namely, Manchuria—and should also have Korea so that it could not threaten or hinder her trade. It was clear to every unprejudiced person on the continent that Korea should and would become Russian; how and when was no concern of anyone except Russia and her Emperor.

Alas, the Russian ministers were by no means so fully in agreement with their sovereign. The only consolation was that sooner or later they all, like the mercurial Witte, contradicted their former views and continually contradicted each other. Witte, who had been the first to suggest the line across Manchuria and originally asked for as large a Russian force as possible to be sent there, had subsequently backed down and insisted on the withdrawal of the troops, alleging that it would be financially ruinous to Russia to maintain them outside the country for a long period. No one, you might think, had a more obvious duty to support his sovereign's military plans than the War Minister, Kuropatkin, but he complained like an old woman that Russia was too weak to keep armies simultaneously on her western frontiers and all over Asia. His advice was not to touch Korea (which, however, held the promise of great gains for Russia in the future); to give up southern Manchuria and Mukden, a Chinese holy city, because Russia would not be able to defend them in any case, and would have the whole world against her if she tried to keep them; and to remain only in northern Manchuria, thereby ensuring the defense of the Amur and the railway, halving the length of the frontier, and avoiding a clash with Japan. Kuropatkin was particularly worried about the possibility of such a clash because Russia still needed several years to complete the Trans-Siberian line, and until it did only three trains every twenty-four hours could cross Lake Baikal by ferry in each direction. (He seemed not to understand that there would be no clash because Japan would never risk it!) Then Witte, contradicting himself again, agreed to the annexation of Manchuria, and even to the opening of a timber concession in Korea. Pleve's hope was that a clash in Asia would be a useful distraction and allay the ferment inside Russia. Kuropatkin, on the contrary, tried to alarm Nikolai by saying that war with Japan would be extremely unpopular and would aggravate the internal disorders. Whereas if Russia held on to northern Manchuria alone she would very probably avoid war altogether.

It would be easier to do without advisers than to have two or four of them. It would have been simply impossible for Nikolai to decide which of them was right, but for the fact that he knew the East far better than any of them, and that Russia's good and Russia's glory were closer to his heart.

Meanwhile, the unrest among educated people did not indeed subside but grew into a general discontent with the whole scheme of things: whatever you did, even if it was a reversal of what you had done before, was wrong. There was no way of disciplining the papers, though they were chock-full of foul libels, insulting lampoons, and incitement to disorder. What ought he to do in such cases? How would his father have acted? Nikolai had often been told that when someone called Tsebrikova had attacked the late Emperor in a pamphlet which was widely circulated in the two capitals, Aleksandr III's orders to those who wanted to arrest her were "Let the silly old creature go free!" But when the government tried ignoring the propaganda this time around it simply grew more voluble and more vicious. Then the government tried punitive measures—dismissing a zemstvo board here, arresting and banishing a few students there—and it grew still worse. The root of all these troubles was that as soon as a Russian citizen obtained even a rudimentary education he inevitably became an enemy of the government and neither fair words nor hard knocks would deter him. If you gave such people a job to do—for instance, to make a statistical study of rural conditions, with a view to improving them—they converted their statistics into propaganda for the burning of manor houses. Politically unreliable people were put in the army for corrective training, and as a result soldiers were corrupted and did not want to perform their duties. At a time when the whole of Japanese society was unreservedly and enthusiastically supporting its government against Russia, when it was unshakable in its patriotism, Russian society seemed to have gone mad: it cared nothing about Russia's glory, about her commercial advantage, about the expansion of her influence, and was ready to jeer at her every success and victory. On the subject of the Far East the air was thick with abuse.

And so there was no one to share the burden of the great plan to absorb the Asian Far East—the Emperor bore it alone. Still, he had to treat the unrest in society with contempt as an illegal, irrelevant, and temporary hindrance.

The great scheme was something you couldn't even explain to yourself in a few words. It soared in the high clouds above the expanses of Asia, and no living soul could say whether its bounds were set in Tibet or India or Persia. The Manchurian railway was the first step. Once you had the railway you had to have an ice-free port at the end of it. It had to be guarded, and the unstable Chinese regime, which was itself on the point of collapse, could hardly guarantee its security. The disturbances in China in 1900 had induced Russia to occupy Manchuria temporarily, against her own wishes, and only because of those alarming events. Delay in withdrawing Russian troops after the end of the troubles had, however, caused great indignation everywhere, and early in 1901 Russia had to announce that she would respect the territorial integrity of China and seek a means of evacuating Manchuria as soon as possible, once a central government was reestablished in Pekin and the situation in Manchuria returned to normal. At the same time, the statement went on, this was a matter between Russia and China, and no third party should presume to pass judgment on it. As it happened, China was so frightened of Japan that she would not sign the evacuation agreement, which meant that Russia's hands were free for the future. Thereafter, the imperial Russian government claimed complete freedom of action. There could no longer be any question of returning Manchuria to China unconditionally until order was completely restored throughout the country. Japan took this as a serious affront and assumed the role of China's ally, defending her integrity against Russia's ambitions. Japan could not reconcile herself to the fact that Russia had now taken what she herself had been compelled to cede six years earlier. The Russian ambassador in Tokyo did his best to persuade the Japanese that there was no need for alarm: only the Western European powers had colonialist designs on China, while Russia was an Eastern power like Japan, her interests in Asia were purely domestic, and the last thing she would wish was to annex Manchuria. (In spite of which Russia took soundings to see what the consequences of a declaration of intent to annex Manchuria might be. It was excruciatingly difficult for the Emperor to make up his mind whether to return Manchuria or not. Obviously none of the Western powers would intervene directly, but was Manchuria a big enough prize to make it worth accepting the Japanese challenge? On the other hand, Japan would certainly not bring herself to fight alone against almighty Russia. Then again, if Russia left Manchuria how could she prevent it from being given over to other powers to develop?) Besides Manchuria there was Port Arthur, which must unquestionably remain Russian. (Kuropatkin assured him that it could withstand a ten-year siege if necessary.) And then there was the most complicated problem: Korea. Under the 1896 agreement Russia and Japan were to enjoy equal rights in Korea, while according to the protocol of 1898 Korea was to remain independent. But Japan had become so brazen in the last few years that she was now demanding exclusive military and political rights. Russia's representatives made no impression on the Japanese with their warnings that Russia could not remain indifferent to the condition of a small neighboring country and allow a foreign government to establish its authority there. The recently appointed Japanese Foreign Minister, the very influential Marquis Ito, arrived in St. Petersburg. Nikolai received him and confirmed Russia's earlier statements, while Ito voiced Japan's suspicions of Russia's secret plans in Korea, where Japan needed political and military rights. The Marquis offered a new agreement, recognizing Japan's rights in Korea, which was too weak to exist independently, while omitting all mention of Manchuria so that Russia would have a free hand there. There would then be nothing to prevent Russia and Japan from being close friends, since Korea was the only subject of discord. Nikolai did not need his advisers to tell him that the Marquis's proposal was of no advantage to Russia: it gave her nothing she did not already have, since Manchuria was in her hands already and would remain so, whereas Japan, which as yet had no foothold on the mainland, would under the agreement obtain rights in Korea and be able to bar Russia's way there. Russia would certainly have to move into Korea in the course of her natural expansion, sending in troops in support of her commercial interests. No agreement with Japan was reached in December 1901.

It was immediately after this that Japan made her military alliance with Britain. That country would give Japan friendly support if she was at war with one power and military support if she was at war with two. Britain had only just extricated herself from the Transvaal, but undertook to support Japan if either France or Germany joined in a war against her. France hastened to make it clear that the Franco-Russian alliance had no reference to matters beyond Europe. And Germany, outside Wilhelm's tender letters, did not wish to help Russia too openly. Even old friends like the United States were turning against Russia, obviously under the influence of Jewish public opinion.

The world was a big place, and Russia was alone in it.

Russia was a big place, and the Emperor was alone in it.

In spite of it all he could not give up his great and secret Asian plan. Nikolai had to steer Russia along that unfamiliar channel by a great effort of will. If all the ministers he appointed turned out to be feeble and incompetent he would have to bypass them, and seek and use true and loyal helpers.

First among these was Sandro, his sister Ksenia's husband. Sandro eagerly set to work reinforcing the Russian Pacific fleet and organizing the timber concession in northern Korea in spite of the Korean government's unreasonable opposition. Another such was Admiral Alekseev, who was worried that excessive pliancy would only provoke fresh Japanese demands. (Nikolai was fully in agreement with this gallant man: they must not yield an inch!) If there was to be a war with Japan, Korea would be a better place to have it than Manchuria. Korea must become Russian. Nor must Russia's troops be withdrawn from the province of Mukden—that would leave Port Arthur exposed. A third splendid adviser was the non-seagoing Admiral Abaza. But the aide who most fully satisfied his needs was one presented to him by Sandro—Bezobrazov, a retired cavalryman, and therefore of course also well versed in military matters. He was a man of firm purpose and quick decision, and he promised to obtain all Manchuria and all Korea for Russia by "mere playacting." The Emperor made him his personal scout and plenipotentiary in the Far East, raised him to the rank of State Secretary, and authorized him to write in a code known only to the two of them, bypassing vacillating ministers. He was the sovereign's eye, watching keenly for things which should have been and had not been done to the greater power and glory of Russia, and for slackness in executing the Emperor's commands. Bezobrazov familiarized himself with the General Staff's secret files and decided that whatever that awkward War Minister said Russia had no need to strengthen her defenses on the western frontier, and could switch all her resources to the development of the East. He went on to explain that Russia's commercial ventures in Korea, especially the timber concession, would shortly begin to yield fantastic profits, and that the East would pay its own way. (In the meantime he accepted a credit of two million rubles.) Bezobrazov's energy inspired Nikolai. Surrounded by a large retinue of his own, Bezobrazov was here, there, and everywhere in the Far East, giving orders without reference to Russian ministers, or to agreements entered into by Russian diplomats, or to the impotent Chinese government. He acted as he thought fit, because a dictatorship of this sort was the only way of furthering the Emperor's Far Eastern ambitions. Nikolai could not have been more delighted with the man of his choice, and his own cleverness in escaping from ministerial tutelage. He was able now to bypass the overcautious Minister of Foreign Affairs and deal directly with Admiral Alekseev and with Bezobrazov, the only worry being that disagreements sometimes flared up between the two of them. He had never been lucky enough to have two aides who saw eye to eye in everything.

He was, however, becoming firmer and more self-assured, and for the first time began to feel truly an autocrat.

Anyway, things were going well in the Far East. Resistance to Russia's moves had existed only in the imagination of fainthearted ministers. Russia's influence was spreading, though far too slowly.

In the summer of 1903 Nikolai realized one of his most cherished ambitions: he personally participated in the canonization of a Russian saint, the Venerable Serafim of Sarov, who had died during his great-grandfather's reign. He went to the forest region of Tambov province in July to be present at the ceremonies, taking neither state officials nor state business nor courtiers with him. He was escaping from St. Petersburg, stagnant city of mockers and unbelievers, to immerse himself in holy things and in the simple faith of his people. His expectations were gratified to the full. The people gathered in the thousands, traveling from great distances on peasant carts for the glorification of the saint, an event which Russian "society" found hilarious. There was no need for masters of ceremonies or police or a bodyguard. The pilgrims unharnessed their horses and led them out of the way, then flooded the open space before the monastery and trickled along the sides of the forest path—men with beards and women wearing white kerchiefs—to see their Tsar helping to carry the saint's coffin. Services went on for four days in one church or another. The monastery precinct was always crowded, and many people knelt outside praying. A throng of worshippers escorted the saint's coffin from the monastery to the hermitage, their candles burning bravely in the windless darkness, and their harmonious singing ascending to the night sky. Nikolai couldn't remember being so happy and so much at peace. He saw before him the true Russian people, with their fervent faith, and knew beyond doubt that the people and he himself were at one in their prayers. From this distance, surrounded by people worshipping under the open sky, it seemed ridiculous to imagine that somewhere in the same country there existed a high society which had departed from God, a seditious academic establishment, loudmouthed students, a scurrilous press, and murderous revolutionaries. Seen from Tsarskoye Selo or the Winter Palace all these things were alarming, but from this place, from the depths of the real Russia, they looked insubstantial and unreal. What would these peasants say if they were asked to sit in judgment over students who were given the chance to study and broke up lectures instead? He was glad that he had defied those who had tried to deter him from doing something for these worthy peasants that spring, and had abolished the collective guarantee in the commune which made the innocent responsible for the guilty, the obedient for the contumacious. Away from state papers, government departments, and high society he was in contact with his people, he was the true people's Tsar for whom Russia longed. Truth resided in the people, and in the Tsar. If only he could always feel as close to his people as here at Sarov! Then what the Tsar willed would be what the people knew to be right.

"Do not disappoint us in our hopes . . ."

Nikolai returned from Sarov surer of himself and of his ideas than ever before. It was now clear to him beyond doubt that he must assert his sovereign will and not allow himself to be deflected, that he must simply sweep obstacles from his path. As soon as he got back he sent Witte into honorific semiretirement. (Witte had been pouring out new projects at the rate of one a week—and dissociating himself from his own measures whenever "society" made a fuss.) The Emperor now acted on an old idea of his—making the Far East a vice-regency, and so separating its affairs completely from those of Russia proper. The region was no longer within the purview of the central ministries: the viceroy, Admiral Alekseev, took over command of the army, the civilian administration, and also diplomatic relations with China and Japan, with full authority to act as he thought best. This new arrangement made the Emperor's life easier. Instead of racking his brains over policy he could sit back and await news of successes achieved. This was all the more fortunate in that he had to absent himself from state business, and indeed from Russia, for some months that autumn: the Princess of Hesse died before her time and he had to take Alix home (she was ill with grief, she had never experienced such a loss before) to mourn the dead woman.

You would have thought that the Japanese would resign themselves to the situation once they saw Russia's resolve. Strangely enough, they did not. Nikolai could only regard as sheer impertinence the proposals they made in August. Russia's agents reported from Japan that the country was preparing for war. Preparing to commit suicide? He could not see how war could possibly break out, but obviously steps must be taken to prevent it. Alekseev's tone with the Japanese was firm and dignified. (A pity that he had fallen out with Bezobrazov, though.) Russia would have to occupy Mukden again and introduce troops into Korea. In November things seemed to be quieting down completely. Then in December military intelligence reported that the Japanese government had decided to go to war. Wilhelm also picked up the story from somewhere and warned Nikolai that Japan would attack in late January. The Japanese papers were in a state of high excitement. Well, Russia had said "Back!" to them eight years earlier, and they had withdrawn: she must speak just as firmly now, and refuse to yield an inch! Time was Russia's best ally—she was getting stronger from year to year. In January the Japanese insolently proposed that the Russians should cede Korea to them, in return for which they would abandon all claims on Manchuria. His own Minister of Foreign Affairs was so unhelpful, indeed so much of a hindrance to any sort of active policy, that Nikolai had to devise a scheme of his own and act secretly: he sent two enterprising Kalmyks to incite the Tibetans against the British. (How bitterly he regretted not intervening in the Boer War—he had still not been sufficiently sure of himself.) The upshot was a situation full of excruciating uncertainty. If, God forbid, there had to be war, Russia must put it off for another eighteen months, until the gap in the Trans-Siberian Railway around Lake Baikal was closed. It would be better still, of course, to preserve the peace. These were the views he expressed in conference with his ministers on 8 February, after which he felt elated for the rest of the day. We must, he told them, outdo the Japanese in our zeal for peace, in our loyalty to the spirit of the Hague Conference, and then they too will come to their senses. He attended a performance of *Rusalka* that evening. The singing was very good. When he got home he was given a telegram from the viceroy informing him that the Japanese had treacherously attacked Port Arthur the night before, damaging two battleships and a cruiser, and so leaving the Russian fleet much weaker in comparison with their own.

We can never take in the magnitude of great disasters at first hearing. Nikolai's immediate reaction was one of indignation at the insolence of the aggressor and determination to punish his treachery as it deserved. The Minister of War, Kuropatkin, who was appointed to command the army in the field, was confident of a quick victory—he expected no serious resistance. Once the Japanese army on the mainland was routed Russian forces must land on the Japanese islands, occupy Tokyo, and smash Japan, and Britain and America into the bargain if necessary. Russia, land of heroes! They would feel her wrath! The only hurtful thing was that some people in Russia would form a poor opinion of their own navy.

Other habitual feelings and worries and preoccupations contended for a place in his mind in those first few weeks. Alix, now certainly pregnant, was very poorly. She lay in bed most of the time, tormented by a migraine, only occasionally moving to a sofa, and very rarely appearing at dinner. They no longer took the air together, on foot or in their carriage. He had to enjoy *Götterdämmerung*, and concerts by massed choirs or by Andreev's balalaika ensemble, without her, and was all the more eager to spend his other evenings alone with her, reading to her. His days were filled as always with ministerial reports, a constant succession of courtesy callers, documents to be read, tea parties and lunches, family dinners with Mama or others of his numerous royal relatives (sometimes they dined to music), regular church attendance, frequent memorial services, dedications. If he needed a walk it had to be in the Winter Palace gardens, or he could enjoy the kaleidoscopic succession of uniforms at the changing of the guard. Just once he went out on the roof. Winter in St. Petersburg that year was one thaw after another. There was no need to put carriages on runners. Murderous dust was blowing about the streets as early as March. Only on Sundays could he tear himself away to enjoy the nice little park at Tsarskoye, where there was plenty of snow, and spend delightful hours walking with some companion or alone with his dogs. He was out with the gun only twice that winter, in the pheasant shoot at Ropsha. True, both occasions were a great success—he himself brought down a hundred birds in a day. He visited the shipbuilders at Galerny Island, the New Admiralty, and the Baltic Works. The yards were hard at work, and the men had cheerful, honest faces. This did something to soothe the hurt inflicted by those forty wretches at Moscow University who had sent a telegram to the Mikado congratulating him on his victory over Russia, and by the schoolboys, seminarists, and even girls from church schools who had paraded the streets of Tiflis, Tver, and other towns shouting, "Long live Japan! Down with autocracy!" (What could be done with such people?)

He could only wait and try to be patient. Concentrating and equipping troops to fight in such a distant theater was a lengthy business. Movement along the Trans-Siberian line was still held up by the Baikal gap. The Baltic fleet would not be ready to sail around Africa and Asia to the Far East for some time yet. France had chosen this time to announce her *entente cordiale* with Britain, and was doing nothing to help Russia. (Wilhelm was right: those two countries would always come together in a "Crimean combination.") Yet it was Russia's obligations to France that made it impossible for her to withdraw troops from her western frontiers. Wilhelm, though, was warmer than ever, proud of his honorary rank of admiral in the Russian navy, and of Nikolai's readiness to confide in him. He invited the Tsar to look, as he himself did, to heaven for aid, and offered tactful solace when Russia suffered defeats which were greeted with malicious glee by the entire press in liberal Europe and America and by Russia's homegrown liberals.

The war took its course: a disastrous war for Russia. The Japanese seemed to be in no hurry, but every step they took brought victory, and every step Russia took ended in defeat. It was a blissful day when no telegrams at all came from the Far East, since there was nothing but bad news. Nikolai still had high hopes of Alekseev, wrote him long letters, and received encouraging telegrams in reply, which, alas, subsequently proved to be ill-founded. The Japanese were wearing the Russians down at Port Arthur and preventing movement into and out of Vladivostok. A first-class battleship, with the incomparable Admiral Makarov aboard, was blown up by a Japanese mine at Easter. As soon as they had built up their forces on the mainland the Japanese took the offensive. The Russian armies had still not closed up, and were short not only of equipment but even of food provisions, which had to be brought from Russia.

They shrank from the Japanese onslaught and backed away over the vast expanses of Manchuria, leaving cannon behind (Russia had lost none since Borodino!), retreating in disorder to the north or southward as far as Port Arthur, incapable of finding a defensible line and making a stand. Only yesterday Russia had seemed to the whole world, to herself, and to her Emperor a uniquely powerful country. Now, within a few weeks, her forces had been shown to be vulnerable, too small, and—disastrously—anywhere except where they were needed. The whole land army was in the wrong place. The fleet was in the wrong ocean and indeed shut up in the wrong port. The sailors made so many unforgivable blunders that they seemed poor substitutes for their old selves.

At this humiliating time Nikolai thought that it best became him to conceal his grief and his shame behind a mask of imperturbability. Nothing must be seen to disturb the performance of his daily duties. He went out into the garden to flatten what little was left of the snow, and as always fresh air and exercise put him in a better humor. He missed none of the ceremonies which he was expected to attend: a review at one of the military schools (he always enjoyed this because he knew that he had a fine bearing and sat his horse well), the parade and charge on Palace Square, the mounted parade of the cuirassiers on their anniversary, the regimental exercises of the Life Hussars or the Uhlans, and many other parades and regimental celebrations. He drank the traditional bumper on the parade ground, or in the other ranks' mess, took refreshments or lunched with the officers, received graduates from all the military schools, went to see an air balloon being inflated, inspected an ambulance train named after Her Majesty the Empress, inspected the new naval armaments, which were so cleverly designed and fitted that he went away with a high heart, feeling much more cheerful about the whole future of the armed forces. He was further encouraged by all the conversations he had with men who had returned from the Far East wounded or shell-shocked and were now on their way back again: such contacts made Nikolai feel that he had been there and played some part himself. He was cheered above all by the welcome St. Petersburg gave to the heroes of the *Varyag* and the *Koreets*. He himself entertained them at the Winter Palace.

There was the usual round of Saturday and Sunday services, of course. (There were seven hundred courtiers and rank-and-file members of his bodyguard at the main service on Easter Sunday.) Nikolai never missed a service. He put into earnest prayer all the effort which it was physically impossible for him to project across Siberia to help the army in the field. As in years past, he did not forget the service of thanksgiving in April on the anniversary of his miraculous deliverance from the Japanese assassin at Otsu. The remembrance of that incident had acquired a symbolic significance this time around: God had been merciful to him that day, and surely for some purpose.

Needless to say, the Emperor continued to receive verbal reports from ministers, some felicitously brief, some labored and tedious; he continued to read documents and minute them, sometimes to the point of stupefaction; he neglected none of the petty matters on which he was required to make decisions. When time went by with no encouraging telegram from Alekseev he relieved his feelings by conversing with the Admiral General, his Uncle Aleksei, or with Admiral Abaza, whom he had kept in St. Petersburg for that purpose.

There was no reason to interrupt the regular routine of family life and the annual migration—to Tsarskoye as soon as the spring thaw ended, to the seaside at Peterhof in high summer (traditionally an entire uhlan regiment would be drawn up in the Aleksandr Park to greet the royal family on arrival). This regular change of one well-loved place for another was one of life's greatest pleasures. Petersburg was more convenient for theatergoing, for visiting exhibitions of antiques or objets d'art, or archaeological museums, but there were few good walks, and there was nowhere to take a drive except along the embankments. In dear little Tsarskoye there were marvelous walks in any weather, even in pouring rain or high winds, but it was particularly delightful on mild sunny days; or you could ride your horse around Pavlovsk, or make up a party and go as far as the Venus Pavilion at Gatchina for tea or food cooked in the open air. That summer they had thought up a new amusement—trips in a motor train. He had hunted capercailzies in their mating places twice that spring. He joined in crow shooting on the grounds at Tsarskoye Selo—killing only one a day to begin with, then two. At Peterhof there were trips in launches, or by cutter out to the buoys, or you could play with the dogs on the beach, or wade and splash about in the stream. The whole routine was immensely soothing. He was only thirty-six, after all, and his young body made many demands. Sunday was a strictly private day of rest in the family circle, with no ministerial audiences, and his soul was utterly at peace, as though nothing bad or menacing was happening in the world. (Not that you escape such things altogether even at family dinners. Uncle Aleksei had perhaps acquired the power to interfere more than he should in Far Eastern matters generally and now in the war with Japan, but Mama was against removing him from the Admiralty; while Uncle Vladimir, undeterred by the distressing course of events, was asking him to let Kirill, who had miraculously survived when the battleship blew up and all aboard including Makarov perished, go abroad to rest and receive medical attention.)

That year they celebrated privately the tenth anniversary of their betrothal and the eighth of their coronation. (The memory of that moment also gave him new strength: he could not have been anointed to no purpose.) But the most special thing about the year was Alix's pregnancy, and the sixth blossoming of hope that the child would be a son! How tenderly Nikolai looked after her that year, pushing her wheelchair almost daily down the avenues of Tsarskoye Selo and Peterhof, through those charming grounds (sometimes with the girls on bicycles beside them), or when she felt strong enough he took her for a sail on the lake, or else she and the children went for a drive in a carriage accompanied by Nikolai on horseback. He could not have endured a single day without seeing her, and would never have left her side had he not been visited by a great and happy thought: that the monarch has in his hands a means of influencing the course of war more powerful than any available to the General Staff, and one which does not depend on equipment or military stores or provisioning.

He could do this by passing on the divine grace which God's anointed possesses. He must show himself to the troops and bestow his blessing on whole regiments, or batteries, or companies at a time, and indeed on each soldier individually, by seeing that he received a sacred likeness, that of Serafim of Sarov, for instance, from the Tsar. Seeing the Tsar with their own eyes and receiving his blessing would make up for many deficiencies in training and in leadership. Alix commended him on this idea, and they began choosing saints for the troops together. Those already fighting in the Far East were out of reach, but regiments awaiting posting were not, and Nikolai resolved not to let a single one leave without his blessing. He gave orders that they should be stationed for their farewell parades at different points along a railway line, so that he could visit and bless several regiments in a single journey, without leaving Alix for more than a week at a time. On his first journey he visited Belgorod, Kharkov, Kremenchug, Poltava, Orel, Tula, Kaluga, and Ryazan. The regiments and batteries gave an excellent account of themselves, and everything was in perfect order, even after the heavy rains. The review was always splendid (there were frequent cloudbursts and some heavy storms that summer, but the air was blissfully warm). Needless to say, the fact that the Tsar himself was seeing them off to the war and had left no one without his blessing was an inspiration to the troops. Still, life was empty and tedious away from his best beloved. What a joy it was to hurry home again, full of the marvelous memories of his journey, and see dear Alix. (But also, alas, to sit down again to read reports which had not been sent on to him while he was traveling.) The second time he went to Kolomna, Morshansk, Tambov, Penza, Syzran, Ufa, Zlatoust, and Samara. He was thrilled by the regiments on parade, admired their precision and their silence during the ceremonial marches (the Tambov and Morshansk regiments particularly distinguished themselves), and occasionally recognized reservists whom he had known or seen when he was a junior officer himself—the Emperor had an extraordinary memory for faces. Large deputations turned up to greet him at stations, local inhabitants sometimes lined the track, and he made a point of attending a cathedral service in every town. He returned from this trip profoundly moved, grateful to the Lord for all His mercies and sure that He would not abandon Russia. It was a greater joy than ever to be back in the bosom of his family and to wheel his little wife along the avenues again. His third trip took him to Staraya Russa and Novgorod, and, as before, he was delighted with the parades and especially the appearance of the men. His fourth journey was to the Don, to the Cossack camp at Novocherkassk. It was uncomfortably hot in the train. Representatives of the Don Army Command, the gentry, and the merchant class were on the platform to meet him. He had the Don division march past twice, and blessed them with icons. He found the Cossacks a splendid body of men, with excellent horses. They couldn't have made a better impression. Afterward many Cossacks galloped alongside the train, showing off their horsemanship. There were great crowds of enthusiastic and high-spirited people at stations along the route. Yes, Russia was invincible! God would never desert her!

By then the great, the unforgettable day had arrived, the day on which God's mercy to Russia was made manifest: at 1:15 p.m. on 12 August, Alix gave birth to a son! He had no words to thank God for the solace vouchsafed in that year of tribulation. They attended a service of thanksgiving. There was an avalanche of telegrams from all over the world, and it took three days to acknowledge them all. Wilhelm, invited to stand as godfather by proxy, was very flattered. (Wilhelm was his only loyal friend throughout that distressing year, grieving with Russia over her defeats and her casualties, promising to give the Russian Baltic squadron coaling facilities as it sailed around Africa, suggesting ways in which the Black Sea fleet might force the Dardanelles, relaying intelligence reports on British aid to Japan. He did, however, use the occasion to press hard for a trade agreement, which could be burdensome. Nikolai sent Witte to see him.) The heir to the throne was christened on the twelfth day. A cortege of gilded carriages formed up on the seafront, escorted by Cossacks (Hussars and a detachment of the ataman's cavalry). That day he finally abolished corporal punishment in Russia. On his fortieth day the baby had a dangerous hemorrhage. But Nikolai managed to look remarkably calm and cheerful, though he was sick at heart for some time afterward.

The Japanese had reached Port Arthur on the landward side and surrounded it completely before the Tsarevich's birth. The fleet was trapped. (Keeping it there had been Alekseev's unfortunate idea.) Nikolai ordered it to withdraw to Vladivostok, but it could not break out, and had to return damaged to doomed Port Arthur. The cruiser squadron at Vladivostok also suffered defeats. (Should he still send in the Baltic fleet? It would not stand the test.) The rainy spell further delayed the land battle. It took place at last in August at Liaoyang. The two sides were evenly matched, but Kuropatkin lost his nerve, let victory slip through his fingers, and took the humiliating decision to retreat because he was afraid that his flank might be turned. This was an unforeseen disaster.

It was a war of senseless defeats, unrelieved by a single victory. The sun of Russia seemed to have split and burned out. Russian arms seemed to have shivered to bits as soon as her Emperor's hand took them up—or that hand itself had disintegrated.

After Liaoyang something in men's eyes and on their faces said, "We may not win."

The losses were not so formidable in themselves. Russia had lost more in older battles, but lost them gloriously. These losses were unexpected, and disproportionate for a great country fighting a little one. They were shameful. They inspired caricatures in Western newspapers showing little monkeys taking down a full-grown giant's trousers, caning him, and chasing him away.

That summer there were two foul murders: terrorists killed first the governor-general of Finland, then the Minister of the Interior while he was on his way to Peterhof for an audience. In Pleve, Nikolai lost an irreplaceable minister. The Lord's hand is heavy when He visits His wrath upon us.

But how can we turn away His wrath? We do not know ourselves what false step we have taken. The troops had cheered their Tsar with unfeigned joy, village after village, district after district, had waved hands, hats, headkerchiefs, as his train went by—but perhaps he should not have let these millions make him lose sight of the educated class, which was so inexplicably hostile and growing angrier all the time. Perhaps he should have made some concessions to it? Pleve's line had been to suppress all signs of internal discontent, and he had stuck to it successfully. But perhaps the Minister of the Interior should be less heavy-handed while the war was going badly? Nikolai appointed Prince Svyatopolk-Mirsky, knowing that he was popular with the zemstvos and had liberal leanings himself, though not to the extent of wanting a constitution. Perhaps the right course would be to avoid conflict with anyone inside the country and to unite the government and educated society in a common effort? The most difficult question had always been how to deal with discontent among the educated. Endless repression was impossible, and so were endless concessions. If they could be fired with fervent love for Russia the problem would be solved. But they would not be moved.

If only he could shut his eyes tightly, and open them again to find that social discontent and, better still, the Japanese war were no more. There were some peaceful days. Why couldn't they all be like that? The daily round improved his spirits. He went mushrooming with Mama. He took Alix out in her wheelchair as he had before her confinement. He often sat reading to her in the evenings, while their little treasure lay by them in his cot. There were great complications with the English nurse, and lengthy debates as to whether they should dismiss her. If there was a beautiful sunset he sometimes went canoeing on the sea. To Nikolai nature was one great living creature. His first waking thought was always about the weather. Good or bad, he remained conscious of it all day long. It affected his mood, his reaction to others and to their ideas, it could sway his decisions. When he sat down to his diary in the evening the first thing he recorded was the past day's weather. After such a strange summer he felt cheated by the sudden and early onset of autumn, with piercing winds and a chill in the air even on sunny September days. Nikolai was so put out by this early change of season that he sometimes did not go out for his walk. It was October when they left the coast for Tsarskoye. There were shoots around Gatchina and at Peterhof. The beaters raised lots of game. He shot pheasants, woodcocks, partridges, and as many as fifty hares in a drive. He continued to visit regiments and review parades, watched the Horse Guards ride by at walking pace or at the gallop, sat for photographs with his officers, toasted regiments, went to the consecration of the dragoons' church, the inauguration of the Suvurov museum, the Hussars' gala in the manège. Georgie, the Greek prince who had saved his life at Otsu, came to stay and asked him to take Crete away from Turkey and give it to Greece. Nikolai was eternally grateful to him and would have acted as intermediary, but in that difficult year he could only support the prince's efforts to persuade European governments that there was no good reason why Crete should not be made over to Greece.

Nikolai could not stay idly aloof from the war. Time and time again he traveled great distances to bless with icons whole divisions or infantry brigades as they left for the East, receiving the greetings of gentry and peasant deputations as he alighted from the train, then making his way to the encampment on horseback. The troops were always in splendid condition, and their horses were good. As previously untouched military districts were called on to send troops to the front these journeys took him as far as Warsaw and Odessa. Driving through the streets of Odessa after a service in the cathedral, he was delighted with his reception, and by the orderliness of the crowds. He read a great deal on these long journeys, and always contrived to write to Alix however much the train shook.

If it were not for Alix and the little one, and, he supposed, his duty to control his ministers and supervise policy, he would have set out for the East himself. It made his heart ache that he was not sharing the hard lot of his troops in that distant place. Nothing would have pleased him more than to be with his army. He missed no opportunity to talk to people returning from Manchuria, always listening with interest, and showing his delight on the rare occasions when one of them had anything good to report (Stessel on the attacks he had repelled, Kuropatkin on the hills he had captured). He received the newly appointed army commanders, Grippenberg and Kaulbars, to wish them Godspeed. Alekseev insisted that they should take the offensive and save Port Arthur. He was right—but Kuropatkin kept putting it off, complaining that he hadn't enough troops, and that his forces were not yet all in position. Surely it was high time to make the Japanese bend to Russia's will! At the end of September, Kuropatkin launched a major offensive, but had advanced no more than twenty or thirty versts southward when he ran into the Japanese. That was the beginning of a nine-day battle on a front some dozens of versts long. By the Feast of the Patronage of the Blessed Virgin it had become clear that the Russian army was retreating with heavy losses. After a long internal struggle, which he allowed no one else to see, Nikolai brought himself to remove the magnificent admiral from the supreme command, and his vice-regency came to an end. This was the disastrous end of a year of high hopes, and of a man whom he himself had chosen and cherished. Port Arthur was still holding out (in spite of typhus, scurvy, and a shortage of ammunition), but its bitter fate was unmistakably clear. Defeatism was in the air, and Nikolai could not remain unaffected. Had the war ended almost as soon as it had begun? In fact, it had still not really begun, the fleet had not been deployed, much of the army had not yet reached the battlefield—but perhaps the war had passed its zenith, perhaps it was time to give up and make peace?

During the days of cruel doubt that autumn no one gave Nikolai more support than Cousin Wilhelm. A true friend, he simply refused to hear talk of ending the war, and sent word through his Russian aide-de-camp that even if Port Arthur fell an immediate peace would be a mistake on Russia's part and a triumph for her enemies. Surely Russia would not give in without scoring a single substantial success.

Nikolai replied gratefully that Wilhelm could be sure of Russia's determination to continue the war until the last Japanese was driven out of Manchuria.

The question on which he found it hardest of all to make up his mind was whether or not to send the 2nd Squadron around the world from the Baltic to the Pacific. It would have a voyage of many months before it, it would be vulnerable to the British and to the Japanese, and when it arrived it would be only a third as strong as the Japanese navy. All practical arguments were against sending it. But could he, when he had a large fleet, fail to send it where it was needed? Could he, when he had a fleet, abandon the sea to the enemy? He would be admitting then and there that the war was already lost.

That autumn one crisis of self-doubt succeeded another. He thought hard, he talked to people, he summoned conferences, and, several times over, reached a decision—not to send it! It was as though the weight of the world had fallen from his shoulders. He also decided, several times over, to send it! And the crushing weight was on his shoulders, no, in his breast again, inescapable, inexorable.

All the problems of his reign were like that: too heavy to carry, too big to avoid. Such was the cross God had called him to bear.

Nikolai had always loved his navy, but for the 2nd Squadron he had a special tenderness, almost as though he had a guilty foreboding. He used to visit it at Kronstadt in the last stages of fitting out. He visited it again before it set sail, inspected all the ships, and in wonderful weather—a good omen that—accompanied it out of Kronstadt on his yacht. (They raised Mama's standard, and the whole squadron, sailing in two lines, fired a salute. A solemn and beautiful picture.) A month later he took a train and caught up with the squadron at Reval, and again visited all the ships to make his final farewells, taking Alix with him to some of them. (The assembled ladies of Estland were afterward presented to her at the station.) He thought about the squadron hour by hour as it left Libau on its hazardous voyage. (Bless its voyage, O Lord, and bring it safely to port!) He made a special trip to see off two delayed cruisers, and received submarine crews separately. He followed the squadron's progress anxiously.

A mere ten days later a dreadful disaster occurred; the squadron sighted some four-funneled minelayers of unknown origin off the British coast at night, and opened fire on them, whereupon they vanished and British fishing boats took their place, like the windmills substituted for Don Quixote's giants. Russia was disgraced in the eyes of the world. Britain hurled threats at her. British cruisers sailed in pursuit of the Russian fleet, and war between the two countries seemed imminent. Britain had a plausible *casus belli*. Misfortunes never come singly.

How could he curb the insolence of arrogant foes? He learned now how true it was that if you always did good deeds they would someday be rewarded. When Nikolai had proposed and organized the Hague Court he had not foreseen anything of this kind—but now it came in useful, and the conflict was settled by arbitration.

This was ten years after his father's death. Lord, how much more difficult everything has become in Russia in these ten years! But if God is merciful to us there will yet be peaceful times!

As the 2nd Squadron sailed on, the danger of obstruction from the British, or of war, gradually subsided. But its progress depended on coaling facilities, which only Germany could provide, and Cousin Wilhelm suddenly announced that to do so would be a breach of neutrality, that it was getting more dangerous all the time, and that Britain and Japan might ask him not to, or use force to try to prevent him from doing it. Germany and Russia acting together could face that risk, but what of Nikolai's charming French ally and its *entente cordiale* with Britain?

Perhaps it was time to put France to the test by inviting her to adhere to an alliance of the continental powers: "Then we need fear no threat. Japan will be done for, and Russia will triumph."

Another idea that Wilhelm might have elicited from Nikolai's own head! Whose long-cherished thought was this, if not his own? One of his first steps had been to bring a reluctant French fleet to the Kiel celebrations in an attempt to reconcile the irreconcilable foes, round out the dual alliance into a solid triple alliance, and so deliver Europe from British high-handedness! And, of course, put the overweening Japanese in their place. Why, indeed, after twelve years as Russia's ally had France not hurried to her aid at this grave moment? A triple coalition would bring peace and quiet to the whole world. Nikolai asked Wilhelm to draft proposals for such an alliance.

Wilhelm did not keep him waiting. But the draft which he sent so promptly was not one of his best efforts: there was little of relevance to the war with Japan and much more about the way to handle France if she refused to join their two countries. The project as amended in St. Petersburg did not, alas, win Wilhelm's approval. He sent a fresh draft, and for some reason was insistent that France should be told nothing until Russia and Germany had signed. Once their agreement was made public France would be glad to adhere, but if it was divulged too soon war with Britain might break out before they were ready. As always in diplomatic negotiations, all sorts of incrustations formed around a simple proposal—incidental implications, the likely reactions of the European press, the responses and counterproposals of absent powers, the Foreign Minister's fears that Germany's object was to provoke a quarrel between Russia and France—and in the end this bold and valuable idea came to nothing.

Meanwhile there were warning tremors in the Russian capitals themselves. The noble and honorable Prince Svyatopolk-Mirsky's appointment to the Ministry of the Interior was well received at first by the press and by "society": messages of goodwill were sent to him, he made professions of goodwill and expressed confidence in the public, and it looked as though "society" was ready to trust him in return, so that Nikolai was quietly glad that he had ignored the advice of his stern Uncle Sergei and risked a measure of relaxation for the sake of national unity. Clemency, it seemed, was the answer to the eternally difficult internal problem.

Alas, the newspapers quickly departed from the policy of "mutual trust" and were soon awash in articles on Russia's artificially prolonged sleep and allegations that the government machine was responsible for her defeats. Suddenly, all restraint was abandoned and the whole press and all those who could make their voices heard began demanding immediate reform, war or no war, and a stiff dose of freedom which might completely emasculate the state. (One old proposal Nikolai remembered was the creation of a "Tsar's own newspaper," to explain the official point of view and the decisions of the Supreme Power. They had never got around to it.) People at once began talking more or less openly about the need to limit the monarch, while the revolutionary parties hailed Russia's defeats in the field and the outbreak of terrorism. For their part the liberals were not too squeamish to get together with the terrorists in Paris and demand the abolition of the monarchy.

Then Svyatopolk-Mirsky slipped up: he should have been firm enough to ban at once the unauthorized and unrepresentative congress of self-appointed zemstvo men in St. Petersburg. Nikolai would even have agreed to a national congress of true representatives of the zemstvos with a genuine mandate: it would be worth listening to them as in some sense representatives of the people, and the Tsar could not have closed his ears to them, but it would have taken four months to elect such a body and in the meantime the impostors had already assembled in Petersburg. Svyatopolk-Mirsky could not bring himself to put obstacles in their way, and so they met in open session without authorization to elaborate their "points," which would have left the government powerless—and which were without delay disseminated throughout Russia. Immediately afterward Svyatopolk-Mirsky made Nikolai very angry by asking to be relieved (pretending that he had successfully completed his task), and Uncle Sergei submitted his resignation on the grounds that he could not think of continuing as governor-general of Moscow under such a saccharine minister. One of them certainly had to go, they were obviously quite incompatible, but it was painful having to decide between them. To his surprise Nikolai found himself accepting Svyatopolk-Mirsky's proposal to summon a conference to discuss immediate reform.

Meanwhile an epidemic of so-called banquets had spread all over Russia: anybody and everybody subscribed to a dinner and made speeches calling for the limitation of the Tsar's prerogatives and the introduction of a constitution! It became clear that society was taking advantage of "mutual trust," not to unite with the government, but to change the state structure.

Suddenly crowds of young people were parading unhindered along the Nevsky Prospect carrying red flags and shouting, "Down with the autocracy!" While the Moscow City Duma insolently demanded that the whole state administration should be subject to the scrutiny of elected persons, and invited all Moscow to regard those of its members who refused to agree as having behaved disgracefully. Young people even shouted, "Down with the Tsar!" at concerts, and interrupted the performance with revolutionary songs. Proclamations were printed somewhere or other, and distributed everywhere. On one occasion thousands of people flooded Strastnaya Square, and red flags were seen again. Uncle Sergei ordered the police not to open fire, but to disperse them with sheathed sabers or the flat of the blade. The demonstrators retaliated with sticks, bludgeons, and iron bars.

This internecine struggle hurt Nikolai deeply, and he felt less sure than ever what he ought to do. (The weather too had once again taken an unpleasant turn. The thaw brought gray skies, a keen wind, and a horribly dull atmosphere.)

Two conferences were called in mid-December to discuss reforms which might put an end to the unrest. Those taking part were a few senior uncles, a few senior ministers and elder statesmen. To begin with, they were rather in favor of convening an Assembly of the Land, with representatives from all classes, but Uncle Sergei firmly discouraged this as uncalled-for by the situation and inappropriate in time of war. They then decided to involve elected representatives of local institutions in preliminary discussion of state matters. But Nikolai found it extremely difficult to make up his mind on this too. Uncle Sergei urged him to strike out the clause while Witte urged him to leave it in, because otherwise the decree would be a flimsy tissue of resounding phrases which would appease nobody. Witte insisted that every country in the world was moving in the same direction, toward representative government, and that Russia must do likewise. O God, why hast Thou burdened me with decisions which will determine Russia's future for ages to come? Russia had risen from the depths with quite different beliefs: that it was useful to listen to the people's voice but that decisions were for the Tsar and the Tsar alone. No, the parliamentary form of government would not be for Russia's good, but would lead only to a chaos of angry passions. These were all determined attempts to steer Russia along a path which was alien to the mind of her people. The clause was crossed out.

There was another reason for Nikolai's low spirits throughout November and December—that because of the seriousness of the situation he had stayed behind in the inspissated gloom of Petersburg instead of spending those months in the pleasant atmosphere of the Crimea. His courage failed him and it was more difficult than ever for him to make up his mind about anything. He could not give way to their demands. He would never have dared oppose them if the truth was on their side—but who could be sure of it? And in the midst of all this, dignity forbade him to let his dismay be seen. He had to preserve his composure, and even feign indifference, for all to see. He must not let his innermost feelings and anxieties become the subject of idle gossip. During those weeks he often visited Mama at Gatchina, had tea with her, and stayed on till dinnertime, talking and seeking her guidance. "What would my father have done in my place?"

They did not go to Bialowieza either, for the usual hunt. They only spent odd days shooting pheasants at Peterhof or at Ropsha, or hunting elk in the Tsarskoslavyansky Forest (on one occasion the beasts slipped through the ring, on another they killed an elk with big antlers but only four tines). Even on hunting days he could not put state business out of his mind—he sat through ministerial reports early in the morning, making sure not to be late for his outing, and listened patiently to others when he returned tired out yet refreshed.

In winter too he still had to carry out the duty which he had adopted voluntarily, but considered sacred: he never failed to visit troops leaving for the East and give them his blessing. That gloomy December, after bringing the conference on reform to some sort of conclusion and promulgating a decree, he went with his brother Mikhail and his usual traveling companions to Kiev province. With winter storms howling around them, the troops must see something miraculous in these sudden appearances of the ubiquitous Tsar on the frozen fields! Infantry divisions, rifle brigades, battalions of cavalry, sappers and bridge builders would parade at some distance from the local town. They all put on a brave show and were obviously in excellent condition. One day, near Zhmerinka, the cold was so dreadful and the wind so strong that the fingers of Nikolai's left hand were nearly frostbitten as he rode around the ranks. He made haste to bless each of the units on parade, but it still took an hour and a half! (The cold made Mikhail feel quite ill.) How pleasant it had been to board the warm train afterward! There was such a hard frost at Baranovichi next day that he decided not to go out into the country and ordered the troops to be brought to the station.

That night, near Bobruisk, he received the shattering news that Port Arthur had surrendered. There had been enormous losses, sickness was rife among the garrison, shells were running out—he knew all that, but had never for one moment stopped wanting to believe that the defenders would hold out. Evidently God had not so willed. He wept, and prayed.

After a week of travel how glad he was to find dear Alix and the children well! (Needless to say, there was no escaping ministerial reports the moment he arrived.) The only relief he got was being at home, lunching with the family, dining tête-à-tête with Alix, looking through photograph albums, choosing between vases sent from the porcelain works, watching the cinematograph, receiving an icon from the Ural Cossacks for the little treasure, reading aloud, occasionally playing duets with someone on the piano. Only in the family circle could a man find peace of mind and imagine that the worst would pass him by.

Christmas came. There was the children's Christmas tree, the Christmas tree for everybody else, the household guards' Christmas tree in the manège, and another visit to the same place to distribute presents to the second company on duty. The Metropolitan came to the palace at Tsarskoye Selo to celebrate Christ's birthday, and stayed to lunch. The Emperor visited soldiers back from the war in the hospital and gave them their Christmas presents. Poor Alix hurt herself tobogganing with the children.

On New Year's Eve he received Svyatopolk-Mirsky. It was all very upsetting. The banquets were still going on throughout the country—and there was no obvious way of banning them. He received Abaza to discuss what to do next in the Far East. He worked hard reading and signing decrees of every imaginable kind. He organized a memorial service in the Tsarskoye Selo cathedral for those who had fallen at Port Arthur.

He looked for God's blessing on the coming year, 1905, with a victorious end to the war, a lasting peace, and an untroubled life in the future. They went to the Communion service, and after lunch he answered greetings telegrams. They spent the evening alone together. They were so glad to be staying at Tsarskoye that winter, and not to have to move to the Winter Palace. There was a Christmas party for the officers, with all the children present, including the little treasure, who behaved very well. At New Year's he had to accept Uncle Sergei's resignation—he had consented to accept an army appointment as commander of the Moscow Military District. They took a long walk together, and Uncle Sergei prophesied that no good would come of the new liberal course. A trade school pupil had already taken a shot at Trepov. Next day Nikolai had a serious talk with Svyatopolk-Mirsky, whose only response was to offer his own resignation. Nikolai unburdened himself in a conversation with Abaza.

At Epiphany they went to Petersburg for a service in the chapel at the Winter Palace followed by the blessing of the water down by the Neva. A Horse Guards battery fired a salute from near the Stock Exchange, and one of the guns was loaded with live case shot, which fell close to the worshippers, wounded a policeman, and put holes in a flag. Some of the shot broke windows on the lower floor of the Winter Palace, and spent bullets even landed on the Metropolitan's dais.

The salute continued until it reached a hundred and one volleys. The Tsar didn't turn a hair, and no one took flight, although there might easily have been another hail of case shot.

Had a single live round found its way among the blanks, or was this an assassination attempt? Or just another ill omen? If they had aimed a little more accurately several hundred people would have been killed. It was a depressing event. Nikolai and Alix dined alone and went early to bed.

Next morning he was discussing whether to buy warships in Chile and Argentina. The fleet was running down and had to be reinforced quickly. There was no peace that day—he had to receive nine people in succession. (And the frost on the trees was so beautiful!) They had to deal with a serious strike which had broken out in Petersburg during the past week. It had started with some local problem at the Putilov works and something like a hundred thousand men, so he was told, were now involved. They were asking the impossible and some priest was for some reason making extravagant demands on behalf of all the factories—demands which if met would bring about the total collapse of Russian industry. They had no doubt been led into temptation when they saw how easily the Baku strikers had got their own way. Great crowds of strikers marched to every mill, every factory, every workshop, threatening the workers with violence if they too did not put down their tools. To prevent unnecessary bloodshed, the police themselves sometimes ordered workers to stop work. Printing presses also closed down, and in this vacuum (or during this respite) everybody obviously began to feel that the danger of disorders had been greatly exaggerated. Some people suggested arresting the ringleaders, but the police were too busy simply preserving order and could spare no men for the purpose, nor was such a measure justified in the present situation, which bore equally heavily on everyone. He and Alix went to kiss the icon of the Virgin Mary.

On the following day all Petersburg seemed to be on strike. It was incomprehensible—and not a bit sensible of them. If everybody stopped work, that would not put an extra crumb in anyone's mouth. (Unless perhaps they were being paid to do it?) It became known that the whole crowd of workers intended to march the next day, Sunday, to the Winter Palace, to talk to their Little Father, the Tsar, about their needs. None of his subordinates, of course, said anything out loud, but he could see the question in their eyes: would the Emperor go to Petersburg, to the Winter Palace, where they expected to find him? Would he speak to them? Nikolai had never even spoken to a single worker about his needs. He would not know how to. How could he talk to a hundred thousand or more at once? He could certainly face a gathering of that size if it was made up of several divisions, drawn up in good order under their officers, expecting simple commands and simple greetings. But to stand alone before an amorphous crowd, with no one in charge of it—his heart sank at the thought. How would he behave? What would he say? What would happen? His tongue would cleave to his palate, he would not be able to raise his eyes and look at them. It would, of course, give him great happiness—the Tsar talking to his people, face-to-face; he had often pictured such a scene—but not right now, not without preparation. And what would he talk to them about? Preoccupied as he was with a grueling war and the continuing friction with educated society, Nikolai had given too little thought to the factories, and they had rudely reminded him of their existence. In spite of everything, his inclination was to appear on the Winter Palace balcony and hear what they had to say—but the grand dukes were emphatically against it. His feeling then was that he should not go back to Petersburg at all. Alix agreed with him completely, and her instinct was never wrong. This crude challenge from dubious "leaders" such as this socialist priest—the revolutionaries were certainly behind it all. This conclusion was confirmed beyond doubt when the petition they had drawn up became public that evening. New demands had been added. Ordinary unsophisticated workers had needs of their own and would never dream of putting forward as their main demands universal, direct, equal, and free elections to a constituent assembly, freedom of the press, and a government responsible not to the Tsar but to the people. Moreover, the tone of it was insolent: swear that you will do these things or we shall all die here on the square before your palace! This petition, appearing at the last minute, took them by surprise. Had it been read to the workers? Were they even aware of it? Its whole content was taken from the Social Democratic program. Svyatopolk-Mirsky arrived at Tsarskoye to report on the measures he had taken, looking helpless and hopeless. He was at the end of his tether, and Nikolai was nearing the limit of his patience with this minister but could not find a suitable day to accept his resignation. Because the police had neither the numbers nor the training to deal with mass marches on this scale, and because the garrison also was small, troops from outside the city were ordered to enter Petersburg the next day to maintain order and keep the crowd away from the palace. Should martial law be proclaimed in the capital? There was no good reason for that. The city police chief put out a printed notice prohibiting large assemblies anywhere in the city and threatening to deal as the law prescribed with any crowd that gathered. There would no doubt be a general in charge at every key point who would know what to do—the Tsar could not concern himself with every step. (The only problem was that because of the printers' strike the notice was printed in too few copies, it was too small, and was not displayed everywhere.)

That evening Nikolai spent a long time in prayer. He was for some reason frightened by this sudden development—not by the socialist demands, but by the thought of two hundred thousand people taking to the streets of Petersburg unshepherded. He prayed again at Mass the next morning, torn between hope and fear. Everyone was looking to the monarch for decisions. How he longed not to have to make them! He hoped that everything would pass without trouble, and stayed at home that sunny day in the soothing surroundings of the park at Tsarskoye Selo. From there his ears did not hear the fatal salvos. O God, what a dreadful day! Horrible though it was, the troops had to open fire in some places, because neither persuasion nor warnings nor threats nor even blank cartridges could stop the singing crowds as they pressed on toward the center of the city and charged, cheering, at the soldiers lined up in their path. A sprinkling of students among the crowd of workers jeered at the soldiers, hurled insults and stones at them, and even fired pistols. The troops had to use their weapons at the Narva gate, on Troitskaya Square, on Vasilievsky Island (where barricades were erected) and even by the Admiralty, on the Pevchesky and Politseisky bridges, because large numbers infiltrated even that far. In the end there were perhaps a hundred dead, and others fatally wounded.

O God, how distressing, how sickening! Why had this disaster befallen him so suddenly and so undeservedly. But how could he have prevented it? The imperial government did not have hundreds of young aides to go into the midst of the crowd and explain that the petition had been foisted on them by evil men who had nothing in common with them, that the Tsar, their father, knew of their needs, but that he could not attend to them during this terrible war.

Then he thought that at least they had marched without red flags, and that those from the Putilov works had even carried religious banners and icons as though this were a saint's day procession, so that even the police were embarrassed and walked before the crowd with bare heads. Perhaps the workers had not understood the bugle call—why should they? Nor could they know that the Tsar was not in Petersburg. They were, after all, marching not to see the police chief or the ministers, but their Tsar, hence their assurance. Once they started their march they would be determined to finish it—they would not return empty-handed. And anyway, merely walking through the streets was surely not forbidden? Were there any rules about how many could or could not walk together? How unprepared everyone had been for this emergency! There had been far too little discussion with his ministers about what should be done. There had certainly been no understanding that the troops would necessarily open fire.

If two hundred thousand took to the streets, was that revolution? Could it begin as easily as that, from one day to the next?

He prayed, and wept: O God, why dost Thou not help me? Why is all around me dark? Enlighten me, O Lord! What should I do? What should I have done?

And could the same thing happen again, tomorrow or the day after? That was what was expected. Taking advantage of the discomfiture and absence of the police, people broke streetlamps and windows, looted shops, private houses, and one arsenal. They cut off the electricity supply in the evenings. Soldiers out by themselves were insulted and assaulted in the streets. If this was not the beginning of a revolution, what was it? Troops had to be posted in the streets for another two days. Svyatopolk-Mirsky was in a state of collapse. A strong man was needed at the helm. As it happened, Dmitri Trepov, who had resigned from his post in Moscow at the same time as Uncle Sergei, was in Petersburg, intending to join the army in Manchuria. Nikolai decided to remove the city and province of Petersburg from the jurisdiction of the Ministry of the Interior and put them under Trepov as governor-general.

He was given no cause to regret this decision. It proved a fortunate one. Trepov was firm and decisive, and knew what was needed. Things quieted down, and there were no more clashes. In places, workers began trying to return to work, though efforts were made to obstruct them.

Things were quieter, but there was no return to the old situation. The scene of the disturbances had now shifted partly to Moscow. Ministers reported that neither the police nor the military could restore order. Now that the streets of the capital had been dyed with blood ministers were no longer listened to. The voice of the autocrat was needed.

The voice of the autocrat? Yes, they were right. Tsar and people must be one. But how was he to make himself heard across the gulf between them? To whom was he to speak, and where and when if he did not use the normal machinery—government departments, the Senate, decrees, rescripts, the officials appointed for this purpose? Nikolai did not know how it was to be done.

His ministers insisted that the Emperor must say something. They drafted a manifesto expressing grief and horror at what had occurred, saying that the Tsar had not known in time what was happening, and (this was Witte's suggestion) that the troops had not been acting on his orders.

No! He could not say that about his troops. To betray his troops was something he could not do. And although it was true that he had not been fully informed about what was happening and had not fully understood it, others could say the same, everyone had been caught off balance.

Trepov saved the day by suggesting that he should summon a delegation of loyal workers from various enterprises. Not too many, of course—say thirty, that would be a manageable number. He brought them out to Tsarskoye ten days after the disaster, and the Tsar recited a carefully rehearsed piece. His language was firm, but his manner was mild and compassionate.

"You have been incited to rebel against me," he said. "Strikes and unlawful assemblies will always compel the authorities to resort to armed force, and that inevitably means innocent victims. I know that the worker's life is not an easy one. But have patience. If you wish to make your needs known to me you must not do it in a disorderly crowd—that is a crime."

But he showed no anger. Far from it: "I believe in the honest feelings of working people and their unshakable loyalty to me, and for that reason I forgive their offense."

Yet even after he had forgiven them the situation did not revert to normal. It was just at this time that Kuropatkin began his offensive, only to suffer another setback a few days later and withdraw with losses. The Emperor had to take some initiative. But he could not read the will of heaven. What, oh what, *should* he do?

Willy did not fail to show his concern in those weeks. Indeed, his eager interference would have been unforgivable in anyone else, but he was a loyal friend, he was Nicky's peer, and entitled to put himself in his place. Through his Russian aide-de-camp, then in a long, ardent, and strongly worded letter to the Tsar himself, and a little later, still in a state of high excitement, through Mama, Wilhelm outlined a plan of action and with his usual ungovernable impatience urged—no, practically ordered—Nikolai to carry it out. "Russia," he wrote, "is turning over a new page in its history. Svyatopolk-Mirsky slackened the reins too soon, hence the flood of outrageous articles bringing the government into disrepute. The revolutionary party captured the credulous workers, and they began making categorical demands which they did not understand themselves. But you," he said, "should have gone out onto the balcony of the Winter Palace to receive a few of these ignorant people and talk to them like a father. Your words would have inspired reverence in the masses and would have routed the agitators. Remember that the masses know nothing of the Tsar's thoughts. Under an autocratic regime the ruler must provide the program of government himself. If he does not, any reform proposals look like a smoke screen set up by ministers, and everyone is uneasy and feels the lack of a firm hand. When the monarch remains hidden, even the well-intentioned wildly misinterpret the situation and make him the target of their discontent. An autocratic ruler must be strong-minded and have a clear understanding of the results of his actions. As it is, everyone in Europe shares the view that the Tsar alone is entirely responsible for the war—for its sudden outbreak and for Russia's obvious unpreparedness. Reservists are reluctant to go and fight in a country whose name they had not even heard of before. It is a terrible thing to have to wage an unpopular war for which the flame of patriotism cannot be kindled. Everyone is looking to the Tsar for some great heroic self-sacrificial act—perhaps to assume the supreme command and restore the confidence of his soldiers. In times gone by your ancestors went to pray in your ancient churches and assembled the people in the Kremlin courtyard before setting off to a war. Moscow awaited some such summons from you after the Japanese attack—and waited in vain. The fact that war was not declared from the walls of the Kremlin has had a profound effect. But even now it is not too late for the Tsar to win back Moscow and with it all Russia. There must, of course, be no accommodation with rebels. God forbid that any concessions should be made to the riotous mob—even the slightest would have disastrous consequences. You must manifest your royal will, command the attention of the people and inspire the army. It is quite impossible to deal simultaneously with two such complicated matters as a major war and reform of the government system. And you cannot end the war with Japan without some substantial success. So, then, all measures of reform must be postponed. But your immutable decision to do so must be announced firmly and for all to hear. The most appropriate place for such an announcement is the Moscow Kremlin. You should make your appearance surrounded by a brilliant entourage of high clergy and gentry, and assemble right-thinking representatives of all classes. Then you should go out onto the balcony with religious banners and icons, and read out your manifesto to your loyal subjects. They would listen with bated breath. It is the Tsar's will that discussion of internal policies should end and all his people's endeavors be directed toward victory. Once the war is over there will be reforms—the reforms the Tsar himself wants, a habeas corpus act, a broadening of the powers of the State Council, but no constituent assemblies, no freedom without discipline. (Do not entrust the work of reorganization to wily characters like Witte: he has hidden ambitions of his own, he remembers every occasion on which his pride has been injured, and he is not inspired by the old gentry tradition.) If need be, tell them that you are going off to share the hardships of war with their brothers (the Tsar cannot stay in Peterhof or in Tsarskoye forever!), and the whole people will fall on their knees and pray for you! And the people's contributions to the war effort will come flooding in."

For every man, it is said, there is someone to whom by fate's decree he is inexplicably drawn, and with whom his destiny is inextricably entwined. For Nikolai this someone was more and more obviously Wilhelm.

He was offended, ashamed, and grateful all at once. If he and this man stood together and let nothing destroy their friendship, they could save Russia and Germany and the whole world from collapse.

But Nikolai did not feel in himself the strength of mind for bold steps, for challenging action. He had waited too long to address the people in the Kremlin (especially when he pictured those grinning liberals, with whom Moscow swarmed, among the crowd). And how could he bring himself to go for several months to the inhospitable end of the world, leaving his darling Alix and the little treasure behind?

No. Let things go as God willed.

It was in Moscow, in the Kremlin, in its empty courtyard that Uncle Sergei was blown to pieces by a bomb just a few days later. He was dead in less than a minute; there was almost nothing left of his body (and the coachman, who received something like eighty splinters, was still in agony). A deafening explosion. Ever since the criminals (nurtured somewhere in Russia, though Wilhelm was sure that it was in Geneva) had tasted blood, they had gone from murder to murder. First it was ministers, now it was grand dukes. They were killing off one by one all who stood in their way and kept sedition in check. It was perfectly possible that they intended to exterminate the whole royal house. For that reason, Nikolai himself could not go to his uncle's funeral, and it was agreed that none of the grand dukes and grand duchesses should even go to memorial services in Petersburg cathedrals, or to any place where someone might be lying in wait for them. They held services in their household chapels. The whole court wore mourning. (He and Alix recalled that they had first met at Uncle Sergei's wedding.) The whole royal family suddenly found themselves prisoners in their palaces—Uncle Vladimir in particular was harassed by threatening letters. Around this time a dozen revolutionaries were caught with a stock of explosives. It was not altogether safe even in Tsarskoye with its spreading grounds and they took good care to go nowhere else. Nikolai canceled all parades and all other outside engagements, and they did not leave Tsarskoye after the unfortunate events during the blessing of the waters at Epiphany. He had not the slightest fear of attempts on his life, but an autocrat has no right to expose himself.

But after 22 January there was still worse to come, though this did not become clear in a single day. The Petersburg workers seemed to have calmed down (although alarming rumors spread like wildfire, and troops were brought into the city on two occasions), but the strikes had shifted to Moscow, to the railways, to the Baltic lands. In Poland the railways were at a standstill. Looting, murder, arson, and minor disturbances spread to one Russian city after another, even to Yalta, so that in some of them it was dangerous to leave the house in the evening, and people might well wonder whether the country had a Tsar or not. There were no troops to keep order: they were flowing out at an ever-increasing rate, fourteen trainloads of them a day by now, to reinforce the army in Manchuria. It was as though evil people everywhere had by some mysterious means received word that now was the time when they could misbehave with impunity, that their Tsar would never again use force, and that he did not, as he strolled about his park, know what to do. The educated class were much more angry than the common people over 22 January, angry, it almost seemed, with themselves for falling behind and trying now to catch up. Lawyers, professors, even academicians issued protests and went on strike. Letters of protest were signed by as many as three hundred people at a time, teachers refused to teach (but not to draw their state salaries). Students in nearly all higher educational institutions called a strike to last until autumn (they too did not renounce their state grants), and there was no way of protecting those who wanted to study from the violence of the strikers. As if this were not enough, pupils both in classical high schools and in modern secondary schools went on strike. The parents of pupils at the modern school at Tsarskoye itself decided that their children should strike. The whole of Russian society seemed to be having hysterics. The newspapers all spoke as though the convocation of an Assembly of the Land was a foregone conclusion. Student rallies took place with official permission at St. Petersburg University. At one of them the students resolved that they did not want an Assembly of the Land but a Constituent Assembly—in other words, that they wanted to determine the form of government in Russia as though nothing of the sort had existed there before. Another meeting broke up after a portrait of the Emperor was torn down, ripped to shreds, and trampled underfoot.

What could be done with them? It was no good arresting them. It was decided to ignore them, to pretend that nothing had happened.

On those mild, overcast February days Nikolai strolled about the snow-covered avenues hunched and despondent, unable to make up his mind what to do. It was as though someone had opened a black sack and all these horrors had come pouring out of it. He was more and more horrified by the unbridled fury of the educated public, the venom with which it ridiculed and execrated him. He felt completely helpless. What could he do? How could he call on them to obey authority?

No one seemed able to help him. His advisers spoke with different voices. His joy in discovering a uniquely strong-minded and straightforward Governor-General, who had no fear for his life, was short-lived: the ministers to a man took a violent dislike to him, Witte most of all, and told him that Trepov would ruin everything with his intransigence. As always, there were only two ways: firmness or compromise. But he could not feel more than lukewarm about either, and so could not commit himself once and for all.

Nikolai now began summoning all his ministers to Tsarskoye Selo simultaneously, and chairing meetings at which he hoped that the right decision would emerge from the clash of opinions. They all advised him to make concessions and to summon representatives of society, saying that otherwise financial collapse was unavoidable, that foreign powers would lose faith in Russia, and that revolution would break out. All, however, might yet be well if an Assembly of the Land was convened within four months.

But Wilhelm's advice—that he should appeal to the people directly—still warmed his heart. If he could not do it by word of mouth he must publish a manifesto. He knew in his heart that Wilhelm was right: how could there be any reforms while the war lasted? Right, too, that Svyatopolk-Mirsky had been a mistake. It was his concessions that had opened the floodgates. Nikolai, therefore, drafted a manifesto without consulting his ministers but with the help of steadier people, and promulgated it. He called on all loyal subjects to help in eradicating sedition and vanquish the foreign foe. He said that it was Russia's mission to defend the interests of all Christian powers in the Pacific. He said that the foundations of the Russian state, sanctified by the Church, must not be shaken.

He had shown firmness, he had signed his manifesto, he had for a moment a comfortable feeling of security—and almost at once he regretted it. He felt sorry for all those good men who wanted to give him good and sensible advice: surely the Emperor did not mean to shut his ears to the voice of his people? It was just that he dared not break with the country's historical past, that he could not consent to put the country's fate in the hands of elected persons, expose it to party strife—but he would be very glad to listen to sensible advice, he was eager to receive it! The Tsar's will must express the mind of the people; he therefore bestirred himself to promulgate, together with his unyielding manifesto, a magnanimous decree granting all subjects the right to speak out openly and freely on ways of improving the government of the country, and instructing the Council of Ministers to receive and study all reform projects, whatever their authorship.

Pleased with this elegant balancing act, Nikolai, without calling a Council of Ministers, arranged for the manifesto and the decree to be published simultaneously on the morning of 3 March.

That same morning, however, the ministers gathered for a scheduled meeting. They behaved as though they had not noticed the decree, but were undisguisedly shocked that he had put out a manifesto which they had not helped to draft. Nikolai, so buoyant for a while, felt his heart sink again. They had brought along a proposed rescript (he had instructed them to produce it, but had forgotten) on preparations for the convocation of local representatives to take part in drafting legislation, in which there was not a word about the suppression of sedition and the exigencies of the war, and which suggested that, in spite of the war, reforms were about to begin. This rescript flatly contradicted the newly published manifesto, and was at cross-purposes with the decree, suggesting not that the Tsar was voluntarily seeking good advice but that he was being forced along the parliamentary road. Once again they were making a concerted effort to push their Emperor into intolerable concessions, and there was no way of evading or defending himself against their earnest harangues. Nikolai was always afraid that he would weakly give way instead of standing up for himself. It happened yet again: trapped by his ministers, he suffered agonies and ended by signing the rescript on the same day as the manifesto and the decree. God bless the manifesto and the decree! Godspeed to the rescript also!

He left the meeting disgusted with himself. When he got back to Alix he burst into tears.

Memorial services for Uncle Sergei were still going on. He acknowledged a mass of telegrams—condolences from abroad, of course: in Russia people were rejoicing in the Grand Duke's death. The little treasure had cut his first tooth. They packed parcels for Alix's hospital train. Stessel, the hero of Port Arthur, released by the Japanese, came to lunch at Tsarskoye, and they had a long talk about the siege.

The one thing that could save Russia now and transform the mood of the public was a brilliant victory in Manchuria. The public, enjoyably preoccupied with its rebellion, had almost forgotten the war, but Nikolai feverishly remembered and prayed—and waited. He knew that unprecedentedly large forces (some six hundred thousand men) now confronted each other. While he was putting his name to the patriotic manifesto, the warmhearted decree, and the ill-starred rescript Kuropatkin gave battle near Mukden.

O Lord, is there no end to the trials Thou visitest upon us! Why is Thy anger with us unbounded? Another defeat, and a dreadful one! Under pressure on three sides Kuropatkin retreated to avoid being surrounded completely, abandoning a hundred guns and even regimental flags, losing as many as sixty thousand men and leaving thirty thousand others in Japanese hands. It was practically a rout.

Since first the black sack had been untied, disaster after disaster had swarmed upon Russia.

He was forced to linger at Tsarskoye that spring so as not to expose himself to terrorists. His favorite place had turned into a prison. He felt as though real power was no longer in his hands, that what would or would not happen no longer depended on him. But the liberals were powerless too. Everything was in the balance. Neither side could feel firm ground underfoot.

They were forming what they called "unions." Then came the "Union of Unions." Preparations were being made to summon a congress of zemstvos, and no attempt was made to stop it this time. Their mouths were watering for the sweetest of sweets—universal, direct, equal, and secret voting, as though this would save the whole situation. Nikolai had hoped that the congress would be barred, but it was allowed. As for the decree calling on all who had the interests of the state at heart to submit their wise counsel, it was defiantly interpreted in many places as an invitation to assemble and loudly, rudely, propose the abolition of everything you could think of, not excluding the monarchy and Russia itself; while educated society and the newspapers debated whether Russia should now make peace, as though this was a matter for them and not for the Emperor to decide. They even discussed how much should be ceded to Japan.

Spring had set in, though—a marvelous, a magnificent spring. But early in May it was as if a chill ground wind blew through the country, bringing contradictory rumors at first, then more and more distressing news about a naval battle in the Tsushima Strait, in which the losses all seemed to be on the Russian side. Three days later the whole appalling picture was unveiled—the 2nd Squadron had been almost totally destroyed! The joyous spring weather only served to make this dark event still more painful.

Terrible is the Lord in His wrath! The war had brought no other blow to equal this. Evidently it was written in the heavens and could not be otherwise. The news arrived on the ninth anniversary of his coronation.

He rode a great deal, to blow the cobwebs away. Sometimes he went canoeing or took a bicycle ride. He received artillery officers who had just graduated from the Artillery Academy. He and Alix together gave an audience to the amiable Guchkov from Moscow. (He had been with the army and had many interesting things to say.) Uncle Aleksei decided to leave the Admiralty after the Battle of Tsushima. Nikolai grieved for the poor fellow (although it was he who had so far prevented the reform of the navy).

What should he now do about the war? One hundred and fifty thousand young soldiers had been called to the colors by the eighth partial mobilization order (there was no general mobilization), and they could be transported to Manchuria in three months' time, bringing the strength of the army up to half a million. They could call up a ninth contingent, but that would affect the dangerously restive western region. Japan was in command of the sea, there was no way of defending Kamchatka, Sakhalin, or the Amur estuary, and Vladivostok lacked troops, ammunition, and provisions to defend itself. The morale of the army, low enough before, had been sapped by Tsushima. Nikolai received advice from many quarters to make peace (his favorite admiral, Alekseev, the initiator of the whole Eastern enterprise, was more despondent than anyone). Others urged him at least to find out what Japan's terms would be. Nikolai was by now fully persuaded that he must endure humiliation if necessary for the sake of internal stability, which mattered more than anything else. Restoring peace with the world outside would bring peace at home and make it possible to deal effectively with problems at present insoluble. It had to be done quickly, before the Japanese occupied any part of Russian territory. Even the initiation of peace talks would have a positive effect on the mood of the people. If only he knew how to get this unhappy war off his hands! He had never realized how fortunate he was, and how easy it was to rule the country, before the war broke out.

Others, however, told him that, on the contrary, the internal disorders would not subside if the war ended without a victory: it would hardly improve the mood of the public if the army returned demoralized. Moreover, fresh humiliations could be expected once Japan learned that Russia was seeking peace.

It was a vicious circle: peace was necessary because the internal situation was so bad, but peace would only make the internal situation worse. How difficult everything was: complications beyond the wit of man to solve proliferated endlessly. And all of them were heaped upon Nikolai's head. "Your war is unpopular with your people," Wilhelm now wrote. "You cannot simply because of your own conception of national honor send more men to their deaths. You will have to answer to the King of Kings! Let me act for you, and begin negotiating for a peace treaty. The Japanese respect America, and President Roosevelt and I are great friends. I can make approaches informally."

That was obviously how it was meant to be. He had a good head on his shoulders, Wilhelm. He always knew what was best.

A few days later the American President offered to mediate, and talks began. Nikolai kept up appearances as much as possible, insisting in his replies to telegrams from patriots that he would never conclude a peace unworthy of Russia, and meanwhile sent the omnicompetent Witte to conduct the negotiations. He knew very well that Witte would not mind paying heavily at Russia's expense, but he had to send someone with a mind of his own and a good mind. Looking around him, he saw no one of that description close to the throne.

Having dispatched Witte, he lived in hopes that the negotiations would succeed, and also that they would fail. Either result would bring relief: one way he would be free of the war, the other he would escape humiliation. Either his people's faith in their fatherland would be shattered or the bloodshed would continue. He did not know which he preferred. It was one of those crippling choices life demanded of him. Only his trust in the All-Highest brought him consolation.

At home the situation continued to deteriorate. Barricades went up in Lodz. There were disturbances in Odessa. A mutiny on battleships of the Black Sea fleet, in which officers were murdered, left him stunned and bewildered; he could scarcely believe that anything so disgraceful had actually happened! On the other hand, the two latest call-ups had passed peacefully, there was a steady flow of reinforcements to Manchuria, the army was very much stronger than it had been, the country's finances were on a sound footing, the economy was unaffected, the higher age groups had not yet been called up, and Russia could go on fighting for another ten years if need be—but for the behavior of Russian "society." It was cruelly frustrating to have to sue for a humiliating peace in such circumstances. At first the Japanese asked for the whole of Sakhalin and heavy reparations, but Nikolai resolved at once not to give them a kopeck, and began to hope that this would wreck the negotiations and that "society" would blame the Japanese, not the Tsar, and abandon its rebellion. Japan, however, unexpectedly gave up its demand for reparations, and asked only for southern Sakhalin, Port Arthur, and Liaotung. Witte duly signed. Japan's agreement was a bolt from the blue, and the peace was concluded so abruptly that Nikolai took it as a further defeat and a fresh cause for grief. He walked around in a trance all day long, till a strong, chilly wind sprang up to cool the stuffy air and his burning brow. Perhaps it was just as well that they had signed. Perhaps that was how it had to be. A service of thanksgiving was held in the palace, but he felt no joy.

The war was ending as it had begun—like a dream.

They spent the summer, as always, at Peterhof. For one thing, it was safer there, in that confined space. There was glorious hot weather for some weeks. They bathed a lot, and Alix went wading with the children. They took trips in an electric launch. They played tennis.

In the course of those grueling weeks, Willy had suggested a meeting, and Nikolai, desperately anxious to share his feelings with someone close to him and also his peer, eagerly agreed. Because the situation in Russia was so tense each of them would go by yacht to a rendezvous close by, at Björkö in the Gulf of Finland. Nikolai expected support and friendly advice on the negotiations with Japan, and also on the disorders at home, since his cousin seemed enviably able to see some way out. Wilhelm turned up cheerful but preoccupied. As Russia extricated herself from the war with Japan, he said, there was a particular danger that Britain might attack her, so that the defensive alliance which Russia and Germany had still not finalized (and into which they would subsequently draw France) was more urgently necessary than ever. Amid all the anxieties of recent months Nikolai had somehow lost sight of this idea, and could not at first understand why Wilhelm thought such a treaty essential at this precise moment, from the very day when peace with Japan was concluded (and Germany could no longer be required to act against her). Willy, full of friendly solicitude, would not take no for an answer. He had, it seemed, even brought a full and final draft treaty with him! Yes, but hadn't they stipulated that France should be consulted first? Most certainly not, said Wilhelm, that was the last thing they should do; Britain would get wind of it immediately and would have time to declare war. They must sign it at once (he was signing as he said it) and then it would be easier for France to join them, if she had any conscience. At this he offered the pen to his friend—sign here! Nikolai, try as he might, could not keep up with Willy's reasoning. He had other things on his mind. It was true, though, that France had remained aloof during the years of war and disaster, behaving less like Russia's ally than like a cordial friend of her enemies. Whereas Willy was the sort of friend who never deserted you in trouble, and the war with Japan had made them firmer friends than ever—Willy always called Nicky his dear brother, and his one hope was to see Nicky successful. He said that Russia stood to gain from this treaty in the first place, and that this was why he was suggesting it. Later on the Dual and the Triple Alliances would fuse, forming an Alliance of Five—who could possibly stand up to that? After which all the minor states would naturally fall into line, confidently following the lead given by Russia and Germany. It was entirely possible that even Japan would join in due course. That day, said Willy, would be the beginning of a fresh page in history.

So Nikolai signed. The friends were beside themselves with joy. They embraced. "And now," said Wilhelm, "we must keep our treaty a deep secret. Please don't even tell your Minister of Foreign Affairs, or else it will get around." "Not even the Minister of Foreign Affairs?" "Not even him!" "But surely someone must witness our signatures?" "Well, you have your Navy Minister with you, he can sign without reading the text, and my adjutant can be my witness." They parted firm friends and Nikolai got home with the pleasantest memories of those few hours (glad to see his children again, but not his ministers). As a party to a Triple Alliance with France and Germany, Russia would be invincible.

But what was happening inside Russia? Anybody and everybody was holding a congress, and every congress tried to outdo the others in the outrageousness of its resolutions. The Congress of Zemstvos and Towns wanted to send a delegation to the Emperor, and it was no longer in the Emperor's power to refuse them: he had to meet his enemies, the constitutionalists, face-to-face, feeling like a schoolboy summoned by the headmaster. He stood before them and scanned their faces (they were no different from any other group of substantial citizens, nearly all from the gentry class, some of them indeed princes) and waited to see what they would shoot at him. Their words were respectful (or condescending?), but meant as a warning that the government of the country would be paralyzed until elected representatives of the people were convened, as the Emperor had promised.

Nikolai was touched in spite of himself by their unexpected restraint and answered cordially (they are Russians like myself—surely we can see eye-to-eye?). True, he had made such a promise, but it was a slow business; they were working on this Assembly of the Land, or perhaps they should use the modern term State Duma, but try as they would, they couldn't get it right, and anyway the two sides meant different things by it: the Emperor saw it as a consultative assembly of moderate and cooperative people, whose counsels would help him not to overlook any useful measure, while the rebellious gentry had in mind a turbulent Assemblée, which would usurp the Tsar's authority under cover of the general uproar.

A month later the same zemstvo men held another congress and issued a statement at odds with their message at Peterhof: that it was useless waiting for reform, that revolution was a fact, and that they must address their appeals not to the throne but to the people. Without waiting to be asked they adopted an arbitrary constitutional project of their own and rejected the Emperor's consultative Duma. This many-headed gathering gave Nikolai no clue as to whether he should believe yesterday's zemstvo representatives or today's. It was becoming clear that all these requests for popular representation were part of a cunning scheme for the seizure of power. The intellectuals at meetings of the Union of Unions openly called the existing government a gang of criminals. Liberal intellectuals sometimes used worse language than the revolutionaries themselves.

People expected from the Emperor a Duma in which all national groups and all classes were represented, while Nikolai was more and more inclined to create a body consisting almost entirely of peasants—levelheaded, unexcitable, steady fellows, preferably illiterate, who would not repeat hysterical newspaper talk or be taken in by provocateurs—and to deny fly-by-nights, hotheads, and the loudmouthed and insolent urban public generally any part in it. How, oh how, could he reestablish unity and understanding between the Tsar and Russia, between the Tsar and the people of the land? It used to exist of old! After the prayers which opened his summer conference with senior officials and experts, Nikolai tried to master every clause of the draft himself and determine its final form. He realized that he was about to take an unprecedented step, one for which in all probability neither his father, nor his grandfather, nor his great-grandfather would ever have forgiven him.

It was a hot summer, with many spectacular thunderstorms. What with ministerial reports and drafting sessions some days were unusually busy—he might be working for five or six hours at a stretch. On top of that he had to receive many wounded men. His relaxations were tennis with Misha and his officers or outings in a launch or an outboard motorboat. They had tea under a sunshade or on the balcony, or in the Chinese pavilion. But nothing raised his spirits more than visiting an army unit to enjoy a leisurely dinner with brother officers or calling out the Horse Guards and riding out to the training ground himself to watch them fall in.

It was about then that the sad news of Monsieur Philippe's death arrived.

On the Feast of the Transfiguration (also the day of the Preobrazhensky Guards Regiment's anniversary parade), after six months of preparatory work, they published the Law on the State Duma, and the outraged urban rabble, including princes descended from the house of Rurik, howled "Fraud!" Wilhelm, who had been urging him for so long to hurry up and publish it, congratulated him, but now began pressing him to hurry on with the elections and let the people's representatives reject or approve the conditions of the expected peace, so that responsibility for the decision would be theirs, the opposition would be left speechless, and the Emperor would be safe from attack whatever happened: no mortal ruler could take responsibility for such a decision without his people's help.

Wilhelm offered this advice with his usual self-assurance. But Nikolai knew that the real people always have faith in their Emperor, and he was in no hurry to shed the burden of lonely decisions. After eleven years he was used to them.

But another part of the nation, and a more mobile part, was doing unimaginable things in Russia. They had gone unpunished when they first began, and unchecked on two other occasions, and now there was no means of controlling them and stopping them. Many parts of the

Empire, and especially Poland, Finland, and the Baltic region, were convulsed by strikes, bomb outrages, murders, and robberies. Strikers organized street marches. Two-thirds of the oil wells at Baku had been fired, and there had been bloody clashes between Tatars and Armenians. A similar bloodletting had occurred in Tiflis. Arms were obviously being smuggled into Russia in large quantities. This became generally known when a ship carrying two thousand Swiss rifles went aground. As a concession to the students, to make it easier for them to begin the next academic year, the universities were granted autonomy: henceforth they would elect their rectors and their territory would be out of bounds to the police. The students were not at all grateful—they took advantage of these concessions to hold legal public meetings at which incendiary anarchist speeches were made.

All this was more than flesh and blood could bear. Nikolai had been wondering for some time how to get away for a few days and rest, to enjoy life privately for a little. The conclusion of peace with Japan made this dream realizable. They sailed on the comfortable yacht *Northern Star* to the Finnish skerries, taking all the children, and rode at anchor with the squadron. The children enjoyed it all greatly, played with the officers and sailors, and Nikolai himself was as happy as a child with all this freedom and leisure. His hope was that his little heir would come to love the sea as he did. There were trips around the islands, races between launches or sailing boats; he visited ships with Alix, raised the alarm from time to time ("shipping water," "enemy sighted," "fire!") and was pleased with the turnout. But the main recreation was hunting. They organized shoots on the islands with sailors as beaters. He killed blackcocks, hares, and a large fox. In the evening there were fireworks for the children, or else they played games or made music. One day they dined with the officers and midshipmen, and there was a great deal of laughter. And how well they slept! It was a very happy fortnight, as though they sensed that they would not be so carefree again for a long time. Then Witte was back from the peace talks and in a hurry to present himself. Nikolai invited him out to the skerries and bestowed the title of Count on him. Witte was overwhelmed, and made three attempts to kiss the Tsar's hand. They would probably have stayed longer but the glass was falling, the winds were freshening, and they had to return to Petersburg—to the same old round of audiences and receptions. They missed their dear little yacht dreadfully.

Nikolai had hoped that the country would calm down once peace was concluded. Far from it: the disturbances grew more and more serious. Students could now assemble, free from police interference, in authorized places, and five or seven thousand people at a time, including outsiders, would vociferate for weeks on end, going home each night and resuming the next morning. They might adopt resolutions calling for an end to the strike, but only because it was a passive and ineffectual form of struggle and the time had come to go over to active incitement, with the universities converted into political schools and revolutionary centers. "Why study, when all Russia is bleeding? Long live communism!" It was galling to hear these things and have no means of protesting: the Tsar could not make his voice heard, and the students were unknown to him and invisible. Besides, there were feelings that he could not disclose even to those nearest to him: Nikolai had been badly scalded by the bloodshed on 22 January and now eyed the government's every move carefully, to prevent a repetition. But the wild disorders went from bad to worse. Journalism had thrown off all restraints, and no one would seek redress through the courts. One printing press called a strike and the young compositors went off with a bunch of suspicious hangers-on to break windows in other printshops until they all stopped work. Policemen and gendarmes were occasionally killed. (No one was arrested, not even the ringleaders, for fear of exacerbating the general discontent!) Until the postal services went on strike letters full of obscene abuse were delivered to the grand dukes. Then the post office struck, followed by the telegraph, and soon lawyers, high school pupils, bakers were all for some reason or other out; the strike was spreading like wildfire from one institution to another. Even the Ecclesiastical Academy was on strike, and when the Metropolitan went along to appeal to their conscience the students jeered and sang revolutionary songs and denied him entrance. Some priests refused to read from the pulpit the Metropolitan's pastoral message calling for civil peace. Moscow had no respite from strikes and street fighting throughout September and on into October. The strikers wanted to have works deputies who were not subject to dismissal or arrest but would themselves have the power to dismiss the management. Unauthorized congresses were held by self-elected deputies. (The local authorities were strangely inactive.) Proclamations packed with extravagant promises were disseminated. Improvised street meetings heard demands not for an Assembly of the Land, nor yet for a Duma, but simply for the overthrow of the autocracy and for a Constituent Assembly. The police had orders to disperse the crowds without firing. Telegraph messages from agents reported nothing but murders (of policemen, Cossacks, soldiers), disturbances, and riots. But public prosecutors were not bringing political criminals to trial, nor indeed were the investigators identifying them—the law officers evidently sympathized with the culprits.

Perhaps the thing to do was to let the disturbances run their course. Russia would see for herself that they were ruinous and turn away from them.

A revolutionary Railwaymen's Union sprang up and began urging the whole mass of railway employees to strike. The call was an instant success, and between 20 and 23 October almost all the lines out of Moscow struck. The plan was to cause a general food shortage and to hinder the movement of troops should the government resort to force. Students ordered shops to put up their shutters. In Moscow subversives took advantage of the breakdown of communications to spread the rumor that the Emperor had "abdicated and left the country." Moscow was suddenly without water and electricity, and the pharmacists were on strike. In Petersburg itself Nikolai put Trepov in command of all garrison troops: one warning from him that disorder would be forcibly suppressed ensured that the city remained quiet. Meanwhile, the enemy had called for a general strike throughout the country. It was horrifying! The workers might well be justified in many of their demands, but nobody was willing to wait patiently for solutions to be found.

As though all this were not enough, the Emperor's cousin, the Grand Duke Kirill, chose that dangerous moment to shame the dynasty: he took it into his head to marry his divorced cousin Victoria, stubbornly defied the Emperor's veto, and had to be dispatched abroad. Indeed, Nikolai was so angry that he wanted to strip Kirill of his title.

What was he to do? The situation seemed if anything more intractable than in January. All communication with Moscow, by telegraph or telephone, was cut. His ministers were hesitant and confused. Their one subject of discussion during those days of turmoil was whether or not to create the post of Prime Minister (Witte wanted the job) and subordinate other ministers to him. Nerves were strained to breaking point. Everyone felt that a fearful storm was brewing.

On one such dreadful day Witte asked for an unscheduled audience and Nikolai summoned him with high hopes. When every link in the chain of power had become so weak, when officials throughout the country were either inert or busy doing irrelevant or damaging things, on whom could he pin his hopes if not on that bold and inexhaustibly knowledgeable man, his deliverer from a luckless war? Witte started coming to Peterhof early in the morning and staying almost until nightfall. On one of his visits he set out his ideas in full for Nikolai alone, on another occasion he repeated them with Alix in the room, and presented a memorandum. Only an outstandingly intelligent man could be of any help in this complicated situation, and Witte was certainly that. He had the ability to rise above the common round, the daily task, and see things from the vantage point of the historian or the political philosopher. He enlarged on his ideas fluently and fervently—it was a pleasure to listen to him. He said that what was happening in Russia showed that the country had reached a definite stage in the development of the human spirit, that the aspiration to freedom was inherent in every social organism, and that it was manifesting itself quite normally in the progress of Russian society toward civic freedom. This aspiration had come close to producing an explosion, and if it was not to end in anarchy the government must itself now boldly and openly take the lead. Whether it did so or not, freedom would shortly prevail. If it owed its victory to revolution the consequences would be fearful—socialist experimentation, the destruction of the family and religion, the country pulled to pieces by foreign powers. There was an easy way to avoid all this: the government only had to adopt society's demand for complete freedom as its own political slogan, and it would win enough support to bring the process under control. (Witte personally undertook to carry out this policy with a firm hand.) The offer of a consultative Duma had come too late and could no longer satisfy society, which had now moved on to embrace much more ambitious ideals. The Tsar must not rely on the loyalty of the peasantry and single them out for special treatment. No, he should fall in with the ideas of progressive society and move toward universal, equal, and secret voting as the ideal of the future. Nor was there any reason to fear the word "constitution." It only meant that the Tsar would share legislative power with elected persons, and he should be ready for this eventuality. The main thing was to choose ministers respected by the public. (Who, it went without saying, respected Witte more than anyone else.) Witte did not, of course, wish to disguise the fact that this would mean an abrupt departure from Russia's time-honored policies. But they could not go on clinging to tradition at this unprecedentedly dangerous moment. The Tsar really had no choice: if he did not place himself at the head of the liberation movement he would be condemning his country to anarchy.

Nikolai could not argue with Witte's merciless logic, and the situation did indeed suddenly seem desperate. (How and when had it come to this?) But his heart forbade him to give up his own power, age-old traditions, and the peasantry all at once. Somehow what Witte asked did not seem quite right, but there was no other equally clever person to consult.

Not one of his ministers, not even the serviceable and solicitous Minister of the Court, Frederiks, was of any use at all as an adviser. It had somehow come about that there were no really clever advisers close to the throne or indeed in the capital of the Russian Empire. Mama was away in Denmark. But she had always advised him strongly to cling to Witte at awkward moments. (And he had inherited the same advice from his father!)

Dmitri Trepov was, of course, honest and devoted, but he lacked Witte's breadth, his insight, his powers of persuasion, and could only obstinately insist that reform of any sort was unthinkable in the midst of the present uproar. Unless the disturbances were first put down by armed force, reforms would look like surrender. Since that terrible day, though, Nikolai could not bring himself to use troops against a civilian crowd.

After Witte's hypnotic suasions, and after failing to obtain a yes or no from Alix, Nikolai spent a day, and yet another day, seeking advice here and there, tormented by his inability to get a decisive answer from anyone. Days of uninterrupted discussion had left him very tired, indeed completely enervated. But there was a continued influx of inopportune visitors—Cossacks from the Urals with a gift of caviar, a heartwarming delegation bent on seeing the little one, various foreigners. In the evening they played snap or billiards as usual, but next morning even if he got up late there was no escape from the problem.

In the meantime, the railway strike had not only reached Petersburg but affected the line from there to Peterhof so that the people he wanted to see had to come either in horse-drawn carriages or by steamer. What a delightful time to live in! (The weather too was foul—cold winds and rain.) He fancied at times that Witte might be exaggerating, that he could avoid making any decision, or make a little, easy one. He sent Witte a telegram accordingly, telling him to coordinate the activities of all ministers (previously each of them had reported to the Emperor separately) and to restore order on the railways, and everywhere else while he was at it. It would seem more natural to summon elected deputies when things were quieter.

This, however, looked too much like Trepov's program to his enemy Witte. He arrived at Peterhof by sea next morning to repeat yet again that repression was a theoretical possibility (although it was unlikely to succeed), but that he, Witte, was not the man to carry it out. In any case, there were not enough troops in Russia to stand guard over every railway line—they were all beyond Baikal, kept there by the breakdown of the railways! This time Witte had wrapped up his ideas in a formal ministerial memorandum: if the Emperor approved it he would be opting for a new course—trying to cure Russia's ills by granting wide freedoms, beginning immediately with freedom of the press, of assembly, and of association, after which the political ideas of the right-minded majority would gradually become clear and the governmental system could be organized accordingly, though this would take many years, because the people at large would need time to get used to the responsibilities of citizenship.

They discussed it in the morning and again in the early evening. Much of what Witte proposed was alarming, but no one had any other suggestions, and there was nowhere to look for alternatives, so he had to appear acquiescent. But the idea of committing himself completely to a single pair of hands was frightening. Perhaps Witte would take someone with a different political outlook, Goremykin, say, as Minister of the Interior. Witte, however, was adamant that he must choose colleagues to suit himself, without restriction, some of them perhaps—there was nothing to be frightened of in that—from the ranks of the politicians.

No! Nikolai could not put his name to this memorandum. And anyway, there ought to be some statement by the Emperor that could be read out in churches, a manifesto addressed directly to the ears and hearts of the people, graciously bestowing the freedoms which they desired. For Nikolai what mattered most was the form in which his concessions were promulgated: let them come straight from the Tsar to meet the wishes of the people. Yes, that's it—let Witte produce a draft and bring it along tomorrow!

They played no games that evening. Early the following morning Uncle Nikolasha irrupted—he had traveled by post chaise all the way from his Tula estate, avoiding the strikes. He couldn't have timed it better! If a strong hand was needed, a dictator, who would be more suitable? Uncle Nikolasha had been colonel of the Life Hussar regiment in which Nikolai had commanded a squadron, and had remained for him a great authority on military matters ever since. In the heat of the first few moments Nikolasha seemed ready to accept the dictatorship. But Witte disembarked again to pour out more soothing syrup, and again Nikolai softened, became unsure of himself. As for Uncle Nikolasha, he was completely converted and declared himself wholeheartedly in favor of Witte and the civic freedoms, indeed went so far as to say that he would shoot himself if Nikolai did not sign. The fact was, Witte said—and they believed him—that if an energetic military man did manage to suppress the present rebellion it would be at the cost of much bloodshed, and even so would give them only a brief breathing space. Whereas Witte's plan would bring a peace that would last. He insisted on one thing only—that his own memorandum should be published, so that the Emperor would not be assuming personal responsibility (or was it so that Witte could exhibit himself to society in the most flattering light?). It was, he said, difficult to make all the points in a manifesto anyway. He had, nonetheless, been working on a manifesto. It had been thought out on the steamer, and his assistants were now putting the finishing touches to it down on the quay. They sent for the manifesto.

It contained some marvelous phrases: "The well-being of Russia's Emperor is inseparable from the well-being of his people, the people's sorrows are his sorrows." This was exactly what Nikolai himself sincerely thought, this was the message he had always wanted to bring home to his people, if only he could have found someone skillful enough to do it for him. He was genuinely at a loss to understand why men of ill will did not cease to trouble, why tolerance and the love of peace could not prevail on both sides, so that life would be good for peaceful people in town and country, and also for the multitude of loyal state servants, the multitude of amiable dignitaries, civil and military, the imperial court and the imperial family, all the grand dukes and grand duchesses—and no one need give up anything or change his way of life. (Mama was always particularly insistent that no one should raise the question of the appanage lands—which, according to their party programs, the swine wanted to take away from the family.)

The contents of the manifesto further included all the freedoms on which Witte had insisted, the enlargement of the electorate to the previously announced Duma, and the provision that no law could come into force without the approval of that body.

The Emperor knew, of course, that the Russian people were not ready for representative government! They were too ignorant and unthinking, and the intelligentsia were too thoroughly imbued with revolutionary ideas. But he was making his concessions, not to the mob in the street, not to the revolutionaries, but to the moderate elements with some feeling for the state.

This was in any case not quite the same as a constitution, because it came from the heart of the Tsar and had been granted by him of his own free will.

Though all present were in favor, Nikolai, cautious as ever, did not sign but kept the document by him while he prayed and thought, and talked it over with Alix, and with a few others, Goremykin for one. Two further drafts were prepared, although Witte had warned Nikolai as he left that no changes should be made without consultation, otherwise he could not undertake to implement the manifesto. On Sunday night old Frederiks was sent to see Witte in Petersburg. Witte would not accept a single one of the amendments. He chose to see them as proof of a lack of confidence in him and declined the post of Prime Minister.

Nobody, however, had any radically different solution to suggest at the time: except for the loyal Trepov, everyone—and Uncle Nikolasha more than anyone—was convinced of the need to grant civic freedoms and limit the Tsar's power. Nikolai was very conscious that it was a terrible decision to have to make. He was tormented by uncertainty, just as he had been over the peace with Japan. Would he be doing right? Or wrong? He had received the autocratic power intact from his ancestors, and now he was circumscribing it. It was like mounting a coup d'état against himself. He felt as though he was losing his crown. But his consolation was that God so willed it, that Russia would at least be delivered from the intolerable state of chaos in which she had now been for a year, that with this manifesto the Tsar was bringing peace to his country and strengthening the moderates against extremists of all varieties.

He therefore graciously bestowed the civic freedoms.

That was on Monday, 30 October, the seventeenth anniversary of the rail crash in which the dynasty had come close to extinction. (They commemorated the event every year.) He attended the anniversary of the Combined Guards Battalion. They held a service of thanksgiving at home, then sat waiting for Witte. Uncle Nikolasha was rather too cheerful. He kept repeating, as though someone still needed convincing, that with all the troops in Manchuria they lacked the means of establishing a dictatorship in any case. Nikolai's head ached and his thoughts were muzzy, as though he was intoxicated.

After praying again, and crossing himself, he signed, and his mood improved at once, as it always did when the ordeal of decision making was over. Once the manifesto was published the country would surely quiet down at last.

The following morning was sunny and cheerful—a good omen. Nikolai expected the first waves of popular joy and gratitude that very day. To his astonishment everything went wrong. Some did rejoice, but instead of thanking the Emperor tore up pictures of him in public, vilified him for retaining some of his power and making only insignificant concessions, and demanded a Constituent Assembly instead of the State Duma. There was no bloodshed in Petersburg thanks only to Trepov, who banned all processions (the press insisted on his dismissal), but in Moscow and in all other towns triumphal processions took place, with red banners, celebrating victory over the Tsar, treating him with derision, not gratitude. When on the following day the faithful responded spontaneously and took to the streets in every town with icons, portraits of the Emperor, Russian flags, and singing the national anthem, they too showed neither gratitude nor joy, but only consternation. The Synod tried in vain to halt this second upsurge, telling the people that the Tsar was mighty and could be trusted to deal with the situation: the two currents, the red and the tricolored, were bound to clash everywhere, there was bound to be fighting in the streets, and the local authorities took fright and seemed to disappear. In every town in Russia and Siberia the people reacted with extraordinary unanimity. They were exasperated by the hysterical cavortings of the revolutionaries, and since many of these were Jews their anger sometimes sought an outlet in pogroms. (The British press inevitably reported that the riots had been organized by the police.) Such was the fury of the crowd in some places that they set fire to official buildings in which revolutionaries had shut themselves up, and killed all those who tried to escape. Within a few days Nikolai was receiving telegrams from all over the country offering warm support—a clear indication that people wanted the autocracy preserved. The people's support had rescued him from isolation, but why had they waited till now, why had these good people remained silent in the past few days when both the practical Nikolasha and the devoted Goremykin had agreed that he must give in? What was he to think? That the autocracy was no more? Or that in some higher sense it continued to exist?

In that higher sense it was immovable. Without the autocracy there *was* no Russia.

Things had moved so quickly that there was still nothing on paper except the manifesto and Witte's memorandum. It was suddenly as if all the old laws had been summarily repealed and not a single new law, not a single new rule formulated. God in His mercy would surely help. Nikolai felt in his heart that God was sustaining him, and did not despair.

Witte appealed to the newspapers for help, and through them to "society": if they would just give him a few weeks' respite while he formed a government . . . "Society," however, demanded that normalization should begin with the termination of martial law and of special security measures, the dismissal of Trepov, the abolition of the death penalty for looting, arson, and murder, the withdrawal of troops and Cossacks from the capital ("society" regarded the troops as the main cause of the rioting), and the annulment of what was left of legal restraints on the press, so that the papers would in the future bear no responsibility for any statement they chose to make. Witte found no support anywhere, and within a few days didn't know where he stood. However warmly he invited them, not one of the liberals and zemstvo men would join his government and lead the way to freedom. And although he replaced half of the ministers and thirty-four governors, although he dismissed Trepov and several police officials, he did not succeed in pacifying the country, but only exacerbated the troubles. Strange that such a clever and experienced man should have miscalculated so badly. The new government was just like its predecessors—afraid to act, waiting to be told what to do. By now even Nikolasha was disillusioned with Witte.

Rather late in the day, it became clear that the Moscow strike had passed its peak and was subsiding on the eve of publication of the manifesto—the water had been turned on again, the horse trams were running, the slaughterhouses were working, the students had given in, the City Duma had ceased calling for a republic, the railwaymen on the Kazan, Yaroslavl, and Nizhni Novgorod lines had already voted to report for work . . . If only he had known all this in time! The country had been quieting down, there had been no need for any manifesto, but now the Emperor had poured gas on the flames, and Moscow flared up again. Even Governor-General Durnovo took off his hat for the "Marseillaise" and saluted the red flags. Very nearly a hundred thousand people turned out for the funeral of some medical orderly, and orators exhorted their hearers not to believe the manifesto but to overthrow the Tsar. Brand-new revolvers were being issued at the university (not all the gun runners had gone aground, and it was impossible to guard the whole of Russia's long maritime frontier). Back in Petersburg students threw a bomb at the Semyonov Guards from the premises of the Technological Institute.

Why couldn't someone have galloped in a few days ago and told him that the troubles were dying down? Why, indeed, had he not listened to Wilhelm that summer and hurried on with the election and convening of that consultative Duma? It might have been still better to call a halt! Now the conflagration had flared up more fiercely than ever. Crowds carrying red flags stormed prisons to free those inside. The national flag was torn down wherever it was seen. Those who had been on strike earlier demanded payment for the days they had lost, and meanwhile new strikes were called. The press had scaled new heights of impudence in its twisted accounts of government action, its downright lies, its vile slanders. Censorship in any form whatsoever had broken down completely, and revolutionary papers had now come out into the open. Rallies in higher educational institutions went on for weeks at a time. Traffic on the railways came to a halt again. Siberia was cut off altogether, and east of Omsk there was total anarchy. A republic was declared in Irkutsk. Reservists whose return home was delayed mutinied in Vladivostok, and indiscipline spread elsewhere. There was unrest even in one of the grenadier regiments in Moscow, and troops in Voronezh and Kiev were out of hand. Kronstadt was in the hands of a mob of drunken sailors (it was impossible to obtain detailed information because the telephone was out of action—all Nikolai knew was that the windows of the palace at Peterhof were rattled by gunfire), and naval personnel were running wild in Petersburg. In southern and eastern Russia armed gangs ran riot and took the lead in the destruction of gentry property. Agitators from the towns incited peasants to rob their landlords, and there was no one to hold them back. Jacqueries broke out in one locality after another. The revolutionary parties openly discussed plans to carry their propaganda to the troops and start an armed uprising. A self-styled Council of Workers' Deputies seized printing presses in the capital and demanded money. All Poland was in a state of rebellion, and in Finland and the Baltic states insurgents were already blowing up bridges and taking over whole districts. The governor-general of Finland had to take refuge on a battleship (Nikolai signed another manifesto, granting everything the Finns were asking). Then there was a mutiny in the fleet at Sevastopol. Another naval mutiny! (It was amazing how little concern the wretches showed for Russia's honor and how easily they forgot their oath of loyalty!) Then a nationwide strike of postal and telegraph services was called, and movement and communications became more difficult than ever. At Tsarskoye Selo they could only talk to Petersburg occasionally by wireless telegraph. It was impossible to understand how Russia had sunk so far in a single month—financially, economically, and in every other respect, not least in her international standing. If only the authorities would do their duty honestly and fearlessly! But as far as he could see, none of those in office were capable of self-sacrifice.

Meanwhile Witte, having failed to put himself at the head of the "natural march of progress," was now recommending hanging and shooting, which it was not in his power to carry out. A bloodletting was certainly imminent, the worst yet. It hurt and frightened the Tsar to think that the killed and wounded were all his own people. He felt ashamed for

Russia, forced to endure this crisis with the eyes of all the world on her. How low she had been brought in such a short time.

Nikolai was in an agony of despair, isolated and shut off from the world: he had never been in the habit of leaving Tsarskoye and Peterhof if he could help it, and would have been afraid to do so now. All these palaces, including Mama's dear old home at Gatchina, might shortly vanish. (Even the palace servants had now started making demands.) He must bear his heavy cross meekly. Once the peasants got into the Duma they might very well demand the restoration of the autocracy. He prayed for the strength and peace of mind to perform his labors, and it was at this time that he made the acquaintance of the man of God Grigori, an authentic son of the people from Tobolsk. He pardoned Stessel (someone had had the bright idea of investigating the poor fellow's surrender of Port Arthur and putting him on trial).

What in his heart he most missed in those bitter days was contact with the Guards, and a chance to imbibe their martial spirit. The humiliating need to take precautions against terrorists made it impossible for him to drive out to the Guards' depots. Nikolai, however, had a marvelous idea—he would invite whole regiments to be his guests at Tsarskoye Selo. No sooner said than done. Twice a week either the 1st Semyonovsky Regiment or the Preobrazhensky Regiment or the Moscow Regiment or the Horse Guards came along. On the first day the regiment made itself at home in the barracks, and all the officers dined with the royal couple. Conversation flowed freely, and seeing them put fresh heart into him. Next day, on the parade ground in front of the palace, or in the manège, depending on the weather, the regiment would perform its ceremonial drill, always brilliantly, magnificently. He had the Horse Guards ride past three times—at walking pace, at a trot, and at the gallop. They were marvelous! He rode along the ranks of the Finnish Guards carrying Aleksei, and all eyes were on their little colonel-in-chief. After every parade there was lunch with the officers, and sometimes he sat on till dinner or much later. The morale of these regiments was so high that the burdens of state sat more lightly on Nikolai's shoulders and leading Russia seemed less onerous. Wilhelm understood him very well: yes, he said, if you need relief from your cares and disappointments, you can do nothing better than parade your splendid Guards regiments.

Nikolai had, however, been having a very hard time with Wilhelm too that autumn. He had succumbed to temptation and revealed the Björkö agreement to the Minister of Foreign Affairs, who was horrified. Show France a treaty like that, all signed and sealed, and she would want to know against *whom* it had been concluded! It was all a cunning trick on Wilhelm's part to upset Russia's friendship with France, deliver Germany from isolation, and tie Russia to her! There was a glaring contradiction between this and the Franco-Russian treaty. France's sole aim was to recover her lost territories from Germany, and nothing and no one would induce her to agree to a pact of this sort.

Nikolai had not seen it like that, but now he began to wonder. On the one hand, France had not been a loyal ally, had deserted Russia in time of war, and because of complaints from Russian Jews was now reluctant to make her a new loan. On the other hand, Germany had taken advantage of Russia while she was tied down by the war to make a trade agreement under which the Russian grain crop was practically given away. In fact, Russia had no loyal friends. But surely his own best friend Wilhelm could not be guilty of such low trickery? Nikolai would never have expected it of him. Perhaps if he handled it cleverly, he could still free himself from the Björkö agreement?

Nikolai wrote to Wilhelm saying that valuable as the agreement was, it could not possibly come into force until France joined them, and here he had run into great difficulties. They must not push France into the arms of the enemy. Wilhelm did not rise to the bait. He answered in a very stern telegram that Russia's obligations with regard to France had no significance except insofar as France earned her friendship. But she had abandoned Russia during the war with Japan, whereas Germany had supported her in every possible way. That imposed certain moral responsibilities on Russia. The two parties had shaken hands and signed in the sight of God, who hears all promises. What was signed was signed, and the agreement must be carried out as it stood. Besides, it was hardly likely that France would refuse to join them.

He was in a tight spot and at first saw no way of releasing himself. But, with the help of the Minister of Foreign Affairs, he thought up a plan. Nikolai would say that he had not had with him at Björkö the text of his father's agreement with France, and that this precluded anything which might lead to a clash with that country. Thus the Björkö agreement must be regarded as conditional and could not come into force for the time being.

Wilhelm brusquely insisted that the treaty had been signed and must be implemented, adding that although Aleksandr III might have made some sort of agreement with France he had personally told Wilhelm more than once how he detested French republicanism.

That was, of course, true. Nikolai detested it himself. And the republican French had just as strong an aversion to monarchic Russia. But, for whatever reason, the father had nonetheless signed the treaty, and it was not for the son to undo it. Why had Germany not got in first and extended her treaty of friendship with Russia? There were complications here which it was impossible to unravel. Why, he asked himself, had Wilhelm behaved so disingenuously at Björkö, and why was he so insistent now? It was this high-handedness that most offended Nikolai and made him want to tear himself from Wilhelm's embraces. He would not be treated like a child!

* * *

Alas, they would never again be on such friendly terms as before and during 1905. Professions of friendship were renewed but they no longer meant much.

Russia's weakness after the war with Japan compelled Nikolai to seek an accommodation with Britain so that he would not have to worry about his Central Asian frontiers. Uncle Edward came to see him at Reval. (He had wanted to come to Petersburg, but Nikolai didn't like the idea of explaining that they couldn't set foot outside the palace together because there were terrorists everywhere.) This one meeting could hardly outweigh dozens of similar meetings with Wilhelm, yet to his surprise it seemed to be tipping the scale. Nikolai had never thought of Britain as a possible friend and ally, but in the eyes of Willy and the world at large it began to look as though Russia was slipping into a pointless alliance with Britain.

All this had its effect a year later, in 1908, when Austria annexed Bosnia and Herzegovina (craftily choosing a time when Nikolai was cruising on his beloved yacht, so that he was out of touch for quite a long while). Everybody in Europe was behaving as though Russia was no longer a power to be reckoned with. (And the War Minister, reporting on the state of the army, seemed to leave no alternative but to endure it all patiently.) Nikolai now wrote to Wilhelm, echoing Wilhelm's words to him: firmly united, Russia and Germany were the bulwark of monarchic institutions, and he would strive as long as he lived to strengthen the bonds between them. Wilhelm's reply, however, came not in a personal letter, nor through his adjutant, but in the form of crude pressure from the German government to make Russia humiliate herself by acknowledging the Austrian annexation instead of merely keeping silent about it. Russian "society," always neurotically at one on the Slav question, was unanimous in its indignation all the way from the far right to the Kadets, and now had yet another reason to despise the government. Even the Emperor, however, could see no way of avoiding this humiliation. He promised himself that he would not forget it (but held it against Austria, not Germany).

In spite of everything they continued to meet. He went to Potsdam to celebrate the centenary of Germany's liberation from the French with Russian assistance. They renewed their pledges to work together honestly and to maintain the brotherhood-in-arms which had begun so long ago—not, of course, that it had ever been Nikolai's intention to arm himself against Germany or go to war with her.

For Russia these were among her best years—years of rest and recovery, of rapid development, of prosperity. She was gaining strength from day to day. But suddenly the wheel of fortune came full circle, and history began to do what it is ordinarily supposed not to do—repeat itself, mockingly asking all the actors to begin the performance all over again, and try to get it right this time. Six years after the annexation of Bosnia,

Austria was now hovering threateningly, and with even less justification, over Serbia—and Nikolai had in his hand yet another telegram from Wilhelm . . .

July 1914

. . . invoking the warm and tender friendship which had kept them together for so long.

The telegram mentioned too their estrangement in more recent years, but still the professions of warm and tender friendship were there in black and white! News of the latest events had overtaken Wilhelm in the Norwegian fjords, and he was telegraphing Nikolai while still on his way home by sea, behaving like a friend, not merely like one head of state to another. How fortunate it was, thought Nikolai, that they had established such a close relationship and they could communicate directly and frankly at a moment's notice. Communication would be so much slower, more confusing, and in times of crisis more hazardous if it was conducted through two Ministers of Foreign Affairs or two ambassadors: such people never reacted sensitively enough, and long-nosed Sazonov's bald head contained a lively mind with a tendency to contradict, to look for objections and possible complications, which meant that time was wasted, and that clear-cut policies and straight talk became impossible. There could be no substitute for a direct link between the two Emperors themselves.

That the crisis found Wilhelm in the fjords was evidence in itself that he was not secretly plotting with Austria. Nikolai was more convinced than ever that Wilhelm really had not known in advance about Austria's intention to seize Bosnia. Austria always behaved in this shifty way—now, for instance, she had timed her ultimatum to Serbia so that it would not become public while Poincaré was giving his farewell dinner for Nikolai on board a French battleship. Who had ever heard of anything as rude and peremptory as the wording of that ultimatum? And why had Austria refused to extend the time limit beyond forty-eight hours?

You would think that Franz Josef, after sixty-six years on the throne, might have preferred to die quietly.

The previous Friday, Nikolai had authorized some preliminary measures: bringing troops back from summer camp to barracks, recalling officers from leave, alerting the fortresses and also the fleet (to avoid a repetition of Port Arthur), but he saw as yet no need to order even partial mobilization on the Austrian frontier. But now, on Monday, 27 July, Wilhelm's telegram had put his mind at rest, and he wrote to Sazonov instructing him as a matter of urgency to get Serbia to appeal to the Hague Court. This was a case eminently suitable for arbitration. Let Austria argue her case! Austria had made the Archduke's murder inevitable—she was simply reaping her reward for the annexation of Bosnia. Why bring poor Serbia into it? Serbia had made a conciliatory answer and accepted almost all of the humiliating conditions imposed on her.

The weather meanwhile was wonderful. He played a little tennis with Anya Vyrubova, then spent the whole evening reading.

Tuesday was another beautiful day. Sukhomlinov, the War Minister, and Yanushkevich, Chief of the General Staff, arrived with their regular, routine reports.

Nikolai had always greatly respected old Sukhomlinov, a brilliant soldier who had given him lessons when he was heir to the throne. Yanushkevich too was a clever fellow, a strong-minded and self-possessed general who knew his business, of the same age as the Tsar himself. They had nothing fresh to report, and things were left as they had been on Saturday; preparations for partial mobilization, should it prove necessary, would continue, but nothing more drastic must be done. In the hands of such cool and experienced generals there was no need to worry at all. Sukhomlinov said repeatedly that Russia need not fear war with anyone—she would win whoever the enemy might be.

That day, when he had finished with official business, he got in a game of tennis, and then went over to Strelna for tea with Aunt Olga. While he was there Sazonov telephoned to say that Austria had declared war on Serbia that afternoon.

It was like a thunderbolt. A dastardly war against a weak little country! The mischievous cat was up to its old tricks—rapped on its paws once, and then again, it was still trying to steal the milk.

He received Sazonov at Peterhof at an unheard-of hour in the evening. The Foreign Minister arrived in a bellicose mood, his sunken eyes darting stabbing glances, and insisted on immediate partial mobilization. He had insisted even earlier, as soon as the Austrians delivered their ultimatum, that Russia would get nowhere by behaving peacefully—she would be humiliated yet again by her surrender of Serbia, and if Germany was set on war anyway, she would damage Russia's interests at another sensitive point. Sazonov was sure that Austria's ultimatum had Germany's full approval. Nikolai refused to believe it; but he yearned with his whole being to teach Austria a lesson. A repetition of the Bosnian humiliation would be past endurance. He could not faintheartedly fail brother Slavs a second time. Russia was a great power and would behave like one.

Still, he must not lose his head—the consequences would be too serious, and it was still not too late to appeal to The Hague. But Sazonov was more emphatic than he would normally dare to be; he shook his little bald head, he came as near to pacing the floor as politeness allowed, and waved his arms, saying that the disgrace would be more than politically conscious Russia could bear. "Society's" spirits had risen amazingly and half measures could only dissipate its enthusiasm. It was this novel unity of feeling between Emperor and society that steeled Nikolai's resolve. It would in any case have been difficult to hold out against his people's urging. Reluctant though he was, he gave his consent to partial mobilization in districts adjoining Austria. His mind was on something else—the need to send a telegram to Willy as quickly as he could—but that was something he had to do with no minister present.

His hand trembled as he wrote his message (in English), corrected it, reread it, and handed it over to be coded. The telegram went off to Berlin in the night. Nikolai said that he was turning to Willy for help, fearing that he might soon have to yield to pressure from an extremely indignant Russia, and implored him for the sake of their old friendship not to let the Austrians go too far, to prevent the disaster of a European war while there was time.

He thought of their dozens of meetings, the lunches and dinners tête-à-tête, the friendly embraces, the jokes, the presents, the many occasions on which they had bared their souls to each other—and he thanked God for all this, which would surely save the situation now!

The following day, Wednesday, the 29th, was an extraordinarily disturbed one. Yanushkevich arrived early in the morning, plunging him into a torment of irresolution from the very start. The partial mobilization to which Nikolai had so reluctantly consented the day before was a practical impossibility—apparently the General Staff had never worked out plans for such an eventuality! And where would the line be drawn in the Warsaw Military District, which bordered on both Austria and Germany? Had they really been too busy to think of such things in peacetime? His anger, however extreme, would have been justified, but it was absolutely impossible to get angry with the velvet-smooth Yanushkevich, whose voice and appearance and manners were all equally enchanting (and who was very conscious of his charm). Besides, he had been Chief of the General Staff for only four months, so he couldn't be held responsible. But could it be true? Better check with Danilov, the Quartermaster General, he knew everything! They checked—Danilov returned from leave and told them that no such plan had ever existed. How strange that such a natural idea—partial mobilization against Austria—had never occurred to anybody. But what about Sukhomlinov? He had been War Minister for five years, hadn't he? Yanushkevich was embarrassed, covered with confusion; if there was one thing he didn't want it was to let his benefactor down. Obviously Sazonov had known as little or less when he was begging for partial mobilization the day before. So it could never have been discussed in the Council of Ministers either. How strange!

Perhaps, though, it was for the best? Nikolai even felt as though a load had slipped from his shoulders: he need not order mobilization at all for the time being. He could bide his time. (And it would probably all end well: his friend Wilhelm would not desert him, they would settle it all by negotiation. Finally, he had a trump up his sleeve. Britain had so far taken care not to show her hand, and Germany was assuming that she would remain neutral. He would appeal to Britain, and a prompt and firm declaration from her would mean that the danger was over.) Very well then, no mobilization at all.

Oh dear, dear! The sensitive Yanushkevich was suffering no less than the Tsar himself. In the first place, he had been given his instructions three whole days ago and was already drawing up plans for partial mobilization as required. Hm . . . Nikolai understood military matters well enough to know that mobilization procedures could not be worked out and relayed to military districts even in three months. But, then, in the second place, a switch from partial to general mobilization could cause chaos, the schedule for troop trains and the itineraries of committed units would be thrown into confusion . . . There was an extra thickness of velvet in the soft voice and the soft eyes . . . "In case of an alarm we should do better at once to order general mobilization . . . it would be better to make plans for general mobilization right away . . ."

A decree to that effect, ordering general mobilization, was what he had drafted and brought with him, all ready for the Tsar to sign.

Nikolai recoiled from him. He would not consent to general mobilization for anything! (It would be seen in Europe as a bullying gesture, an unnecessary threat.) What need was there for it, anyway? He had agreed to partial mobilization yesterday only with great reluctance.

Yes, but . . . it was impossible not to plan for mobilization at all. Some sort of scheme for partial mobilization would no doubt emerge. And obviously they should have a plan for general mobilization ready just in case . . . Here Yanushkevich's delicate eyelids drooped in horror to think how they might be caught out. The Emperor's signature did not mean immediate mobilization. It was only the beginning of the road. The signatures of three ministers still had to be obtained, and the decree passed to the Senate for promulgation. He only wanted to be prepared for any eventuality.

Well, in that case . . . If ministers also had to sign (they wouldn't sign without asking him) . . . And Yanushkevich was so persistent and so persuasive! Obviously, since there was no partial mobilization, and since they couldn't simply do nothing about mobilization at all . . .

"You won't let me down, my dear fellow, will you? You'll consult Sazonov . . . and keep me informed?"

He need be in no doubt about that!

He signed.

(And while he was about it he also signed, without reading them, because their conversation had gone on so long, standing orders for commanders of troops in the field.)

This morning's conversation was only the beginning of his troubles on that unquiet day. Everyone could now be reached by telephone. In the extraordinary circumstances the Emperor's subordinates made so bold as to ring him up, something which had never happened before, first one, then another, then a third; it went on all day long, and he felt as though he was pinned to the spot by their ringing, afraid to move in case there was another call . . . and he had to take all these calls in the valet's room. To speed things up he began using the same means of contacting his ministers. He had always hated the telephone and refused to use it. What could be more unpleasant and unnatural than a discussion, and an important one at that, over the telephone? You hadn't been expecting the call, you couldn't see the other person, and you were not at liberty to look about you, to walk around the room, to pause for thought, or just keep quiet.

Nikolai remained pinned down indoors in Peterhof, except for attending a graduation parade for naval cadets and playing a little tennis (he was morose, preoccupied, and off his game). The weather, though, was marvelous again. Meanwhile, things were happening in Petersburg, Vienna, Belgrade, Berlin, and other capitals, and everybody was sending letters and telegrams to everybody else (except poor Poincaré, who was still sailing home after his stay with Nikolai).

Next morning the German ambassador waited on Sazonov with the reassuring message that Germany would make every effort to persuade Vienna to back down (just as Nikolai had expected), but asked Russia not to create difficulties by mobilizing prematurely (Nikolai had no intention of doing that!). Sazonov replied that partial mobilization was imminent, but was not yet under way (which was true), adding that Russia's military measures were not aimed at Germany nor should they be taken to mean that she would necessarily move against Austria. After this, the Council of Ministers, when it met at midday, resolved not to proceed with the partial mobilization.

Another item of news arrived: Austria had refused to enter into any exchange of views with Russia, either directly or through intermediaries.

This was what came of giving way in 1908. Austria calculated that once again Russia would be afraid to stand up for Serbia. But if she failed again Austria would take Serbia and go straight on to the next outrage.

The German ambassador asked permission to call on Sazonov again, and read out a telegram from the Chancellor: if Russia went on with her military preparations, *even if she did not mobilize*, Germany would feel compelled to mobilize herself—and an immediate attack would follow!

It was a bright day, but there was darkness in his heart. Peterhof was spacious and peaceful, he could see the placid Gulf of Finland from his study window, but he was trapped. People talked to Russia not as they would to a great power but as they did to Serbia. She was forbidden even to take simple precautionary measures.

The shame of it left him gasping. He had one remaining hope—Sazonov had asked Britain to speak out at last and make her position clear.

But then came salvation in the shape of a telegram from Wilhelm. Of course Willy had not changed, and of course he had not changed sides! He promised to help smooth things over, asking only that Nikolai not let it come to war.

Nikolai was elated. Their friendship would save the day! He rushed to the telephone, to make sure that Sazonov and Sukhomlinov and Yanushkevich did nothing irreversible . . .

Then he began drafting his reply to Wilhelm. Their correspondence was so brisk that a telegram sometimes crossed the answer to its predecessor.

How, Nikolai wanted to know, can we reconcile your conciliatory telegram with the completely different tone of your ambassador's statement? Please inquire into this discrepancy. Let us refer the whole Austro-Serbian dispute to the Hague Conference. Let us avoid bloodshed. I put my trust in your wisdom and your friendship!

At this point the news arrived that the Austrians were shelling Belgrade. That was why they had been so unwilling to talk! That was why they had been so anxious to win time!

Meanwhile, Sazonov and Sukhomlinov had been with Yanushkevich at Staff Headquarters discussing partial mobilization, as authorized. They telephoned the Emperor to report that it could only be carried out at the risk of disrupting an eventual general mobilization. It would only confuse things. They asked him to sanction general mobilization.

And he had to make the decision chained like an idiot to the receiver, his mind too cramped to think. The Austrians were already shelling the peaceful inhabitants of Belgrade. Something must be done. And Russia found herself shamefully unprepared for partial mobilization. (He was too tactful to tell them over the telephone that they were to blame for the whole thing.) Well . . . I don't know . . . let's see . . . well, maybe . . . just preliminary steps for the present, remember, this isn't final approval . . . All right, then.

What made the decision hard was that he had to take it not with bombs falling around him, not on a good horse with the men lined up before him, but speaking into empty space through an ebonite tube. Yet once it was released with his bated breath the word he found it so hard to say would set millions in sudden motion.

The evening was lonely and miserable. No one arrived to report. He had no outside duties. He had spent the hours between lunch and teatime with his family. And somewhere out there something irremediable was being done. How could he go to bed and to sleep with that thought?

Then suddenly—relief, in a telegram from dear Willy again, the answer to his last but one. Naturally Willy shared Nikolai's desire to preserve peace! Russia could, of course, remain a spectator instead of involving all Europe in the most terrible war it had ever seen. A direct agreement between Vienna and Petersburg was possible and desirable, and Wilhelm was making every effort to bring it about. But preparations for war by Russia would make it difficult for him to mediate and would bring catastrophe much nearer.

Thank you, thank you for this happy release! The situation could yet be saved—unless his subordinates had already set things rolling. No, they would have had to wait for the ministers to sign and the Senate to publish.

At 10 p.m. Nikolai went down to the valet's room for the umpteenth time and asked to be put through to the War Ministry and the General Staff. Through the tube came a hoarse voice quite unlike Yanushkevich's amazingly velvety and deferential tones, stubbornly objecting that mobilizing was not like turning a wheel which you could stop or start as you pleased, and that the Chief of Staff could not assume the responsibility for such a measure . . . ("Then I shall assume it myself," Nikolai exclaimed) . . . and that it might now be too late to call a halt, because military districts had received telegraph orders to mobilize . . .

"How can that be? When did it happen? What about the ministers' signatures?"

Surely he couldn't have collected them in the past hour and a half? The telephone grudgingly crackled that all the necessary signatures had been collected earlier in the day as a precautionary measure. Paris and London had already been notified by Sazonov that general mobilization had begun, that orders were being telegraphed to military districts at that very moment. There was no going back now!

It must be stopped, at once! He was not, thank God, an elected president, tied hand and foot, but a monarch in his own fatherland. It must be stopped! There would be partial mobilization, no more—and the Emperor did not want to hear any further argument.

Once again, he felt an immediate sense of relief.

A still, warm, starry night. The sea was so calm that he could not hear the waves on the beach.

But before he went to bed it was his pleasant duty to reply to Wilhelm, to thank him warmly for his prompt replies. Russia's military precautions need cause no complications. They had been taken five days ago for purely defensive purposes. He hoped with all his heart that Wilhelm would mediate. But no, a telegram was not enough, an adjutant general would take a detailed letter to Wilhelm the next day. Send for him now, have him ready to leave tomorrow.

The telegram was sent in cipher at 1 a.m., and the Emperor's heavy day was over. (Only the next morning did he learn that at 1 a.m. Sazonov had been woken up by a telephone call from the German ambassador, asking to be received immediately.)

Thursday morning, thank God, began more quietly. There were no alarming telephone messages. Only a request from the Navy Minister for permission to lay mines in the Baltic—which Nikolai did not grant. He could give special orders to that effect if the time came.

He had put his trust in Willy—he must show that he did trust him, and take a risk.

There was also a comically inopportune call from the Minister of Agriculture, Krivoshein, asking for an urgent audience. (He discovered later that Sazonov had put Krivoshein up to it, and that he had meant to plead for general mobilization.) Nikolai refused him, he was far too busy.

He really was busy, but not with the schedule of previously arranged and unimportant audiences. What he must be sure to do was write his reply to Willy before the middle of the day so that it could go off with the adjutant general and help to clear every cloud from the horizon.

Before he could sit down to write it he was called to the telephone again. Sukhomlinov and Yanushkevich were ringing from the General Staff: they were unhappy with yesterday's order countermanding general mobilization and again asked permission to proceed with it. Nikolai lost his temper—he had never encountered such importunacy in subordinates before. Were they really so worried by the German threat, or just trying to palliate their unpreparedness for partial mobilization? He firmly rejected their pleas and simply declared the conversation at an end, but for some reason did not hang up immediately, so that Yanushkevich had time to tell him that Sazonov was in the room at his side and asking permission to take the receiver.

When an end must be made, happy the man who can do it abruptly and finally. Nikolai was incapable of making a sharp break even when he was angry. He said nothing, let Sazonov speak if he must.

Sazonov swiftly asked to be received that day, saying that he had an urgent report to make on the political situation.

He obviously could not refuse to see the Foreign Minister at such a time. If he did that, there would be no point in having a Foreign Minister. But to tie his hands in advance, and make sure that the outcome would be just the same, Nikolai told Sazonov to come at the very time when the adjutant general was to pick up the letter.

Then he sat down to his dialogue with Willy. In the turmoil of hopes and fears only the cord between their hearts held firm. Unhampered by telegraph language and code, Nikolai wrote. The murder of the Archduke was, of course, a horrible crime. (There was nothing to distinguish these terrorists from those who had killed Uncle Sergei and Stolypin and dozens of generals and high officials in Russia.) But what proof was there that the Serbian government had anything to do with it? Inquests often made mistakes. Why did Austria not reveal the results of the investigation to Europe at large instead of presenting Serbia with a curt ultimatum and declaring war? As it was, Serbia had made concessions which could not be expected of any independent government, but Austria was set on a punitive expedition, as though dealing with a colony. It would be a very difficult task to cool down the war fever in Russia. Nikolai appealed to Wilhelm . . .

When he had received Willy's telegram the night before, and when he awoke that morning, he had thought of this letter as an irresistibly persuasive outpouring of his soul. But after all those time-wasting audiences, all those telephone calls, and lunch, his thoughts had lost their freshness and the right words would not come. It no longer seemed likely that a letter reaching Wilhelm in two days' time would decisively change the whole course of events in Europe for the better.

By now the adjutant general was there to collect it. He and Sazonov had arrived together, and he received them together, as he had intended. Sazonov looked his age. He was bald except for a woolly crescent at the back of his head. His face, always sour and secretive, was distorted by neuralgia. In his nervous state Sazonov, regardless of etiquette and the impression he was making, began speaking excitedly, and went on and on without pausing for breath. Some of what he said was truly frightening. The tragic hour had come which would determine the fate of Russia and of the dynasty. Russia could not simply abandon her Slav policy all at once. War had been in the offing for a long time, and was now unavoidable. Vienna was already fully decided on it and had begun operations, while Berlin refused to say the words which might bring the Austrians to their senses, and wanted instead to see Russia capitulate yet again, to cover Russia's name with shame—something for which the country would never forgive its Emperor. Diplomacy had said its last word. It was perfectly obvious that Germany was on a collision course, and if the Russian state was to survive she must meet Germany fully armed. If Russia did not begin general mobilization at once it would be of no avail later, Russia would suffer catastrophe and lose the war before she could draw her sword. It was incomparably better to wait fully armed—after all, Russia was not starting the war—than to be caught off balance for fear of causing war. Besides, Russia could contrive to mobilize secretly, so that Europe would not even know about it.

Nikolai paced restlessly like a wounded man, not caring whether they saw him wringing his hands. He was on the rack, torn by conflicting forces, near to bursting. He had to make the greatest decision of his life, right now, that very moment! No one, present or absent, could advise and help him, and the voice of the Lord was indistinct. With all those ministers, generals, grand dukes, state secretaries around him he was doomed to make all the decisions himself, in his own tormented, vacillating mind. He felt the need of a single man of superior character and intelligence who would take responsibility for the decision, who would say at once, "This way and no other," and act accordingly.

There had been one such man—Stolypin! How sorely he needed Stolypin at that very minute.

The crux of the matter was that if Germany was deceiving him Russia was in deep trouble. (But with her immense frontiers where exactly would the trouble come from?) Whereas if Germany was sincere Russia might take a wrong step and cause a war on a scale which the mind could hardly grasp . . .

The adjutant general, who had remained silent till then, murmured sympathetically, "It is terribly difficult . . ."

Nikolai started, as though from a blow on a taut nerve, and cut him short. "It is I who have to decide!"

"And what about your Britain?" he asked Sazonov, suddenly remembering. What would it have cost her to make just one unambiguous declaration in the last few days? If she had, there would have been no problem.

Sazonov suddenly remembered something himself. He had been handed a fresh piece of news as he was setting out for Peterhof: the German fleet had left Kiel some hours earlier and was proceeding full steam into the Baltic to make a surprise attack!

Could it be? And Nikolai had refused permission to lay mines!

His overstretched nerves finally snapped. He could not forget the lesson of Port Arthur.

"Very well, you've convinced me. But this will be the hardest day of my life."

He felt immediate relief.

As always, when he finally gave way.

When he shed the burden of decision.

Sazonov asked permission to telephone Yanushkevich at once, from Peterhof, to tell him that general mobilization would begin at midnight.

Very well.

It was such a warm day. The sunlight danced on the waves so prettily. It was hard to imagine that not very far away a German squadron was furrowing the Baltic, stealing toward a second Port Arthur.

Was it true, though? The report could just as easily be false.

He went to bathe, and enjoyed it. But the relief which letting go had brought, the feeling of relaxation after his bath, quickly deserted him. His heart and his head were as heavy as ever.

Was it foreboding? At 6 p.m. a telegram from Wilhelm was brought in. There was no trace of affection this time, no discrepancy between its tone and that of the ambassador's demarche. "Your mobilization," it said, "will have serious and dangerous consequences. Austria has still not ordered general mobilization. The onus of decision now rests on you and you alone. The choice between war and peace is your responsibility."

Oh God, how hemmed in he felt, how cramped! Oh God, how frightening it was! Dear God, help me to bear this inhuman burden . . . !

His first impulse was to telephone Yanushkevich and cancel the mobilization order.

But he was afraid of what his subordinates would think.

Nikolai had a vivid picture of Wilhelm in his mind, his burning eyes, his rapid and passionate way of speaking, and try as he might he could not see him as the ultimate enemy. In twenty years Wilhelm had never behaved like an enemy. There had been a cruel misunderstanding, a fatal failure to talk things over fully, just as on 21 January 1905, when Wilhelm had urged him to check the mob but had not said how it was to be done.

And suddenly his mind was flooded with light and he saw . . . Willy, think what we are doing! We must come to our senses! We shall lose our thrones!

But to telephone countermanding mobilization was too embarrassing. (He did not know that Yanushkevich's telephone would be out of order for twenty-four hours.)

And there was the other side of it to consider. They had given in to Austria so often and so humiliatingly. They must behave differently sometime, must show firmness. It was possible to speak more firmly, now that the devil of revolution had been cast out from Russia.

What had Sazonov meant by promising to mobilize secretly? Notices had been put up in all the streets of Petersburg on the morning of the 31st, printed on red paper for some reason, as though suffused with the blood still to be shed. Or had the red flag sneaked into the Emperor's camp? All the foreigners noticed it, and the color red for some reason had a special effect. Both the German and the Austrian ambassadors rushed to see Sazonov, and their demarches were subsequently relayed to the Emperor by telephone. Sazonov assured the German that nothing irremediable would be done on the Russian side. He, however, had arrived with a note saying that Germany was taking certain steps, that Austria would not violate Serbia's territorial integrity, but that Russia must accept the localization of the conflict.

Localization? Meaning that Russia must let Serbia suffer her fate in isolation? Perhaps, though, all might yet be well with God's aid? If only it could be!

Oh God! How he regretted that they had not ordered partial mobilization! His unfaithful servants had made no plans for it! If only this crisis would pass him by!

The Austrian ambassador reported his government's readiness to discuss the ultimatum with Russia directly.

It was high time they did just that! But Sazonov for some reason—you couldn't put your own head on a subordinate's shoulders, you could never stay his hand in time—had recommended that the Austrians talk to London. And to suspend military operations.

It was a gray, heavy day, and his thoughts were funereal. He fully regretted agreeing to general mobilization. But demobilization was still a possibility: history told him that mobilization need not end in war.

At 11 a.m. all the ministers arrived at Peterhof to confer. They discussed who should be Supreme Commander. Who if not the Emperor himself? All his life he had felt like a prisoner among civilians. Inspections, parades, maneuvers, conversations with officers were his only happiness, the breath of life to him. He had decided long ago to put himself at the head of his troops. All that remained to be considered was the organization of the civil administration in his absence. Again they said no. Again his wishes were resisted! The ministers, even Goremykin, were against it to a man: the shadow of possible defeats must not fall on the Emperor. Goremykin quoted precedents—Aleksandr I had withdrawn from the army in 1812, Aleksandr II had never assumed Supreme Command.

It was entirely for him to decide, but, reluctant as he was to abandon his dream, he somehow could not go against the unanimous view of his ministers.

At that point Sazonov was called to the telephone to speak to the German ambassador. There was still hope!

Nikolai, there and then, while they were still in session, began drafting his next telegram to Wilhelm—he had seen in a flash of inspiration how he could explain things and put them right. "Thank you for your mediation. It seems to offer some hope of a peaceful outcome. It is impossible for technical reasons to halt our military preparations. But we do not want war, far from it! My troops will make no provocative moves, I give you my word on that. I put my faith in God's mercy. Your devoted . . ."

He sent it to be coded, then received the German ambassador, Count Pourtalès, affably. If at that moment it had depended on the two of them peace would have been assured. Pourtalès seemed crushed by the menacing course of events. He implored the Emperor to halt the mobilization and give the Kaiser room to mediate.

"Now you, Count, are a military man—how can anyone halt the machinery of mobilization once it has picked up speed?"

The interview only made him feel more depressed and helpless.

How anxiously he awaited Wilhelm's reply!

He went for a stroll with his daughters. He forced himself to deal with his papers.

There were two letters in the post. They could not have been worse timed. They pierced him to the heart. One was from Siberia, from the wounded Grigori, who implored him not to go to war, threatening all sorts of disasters. The second consisted of four words: "Fear God! A mother."

He was shattered. But what was he to do? What *could* he do?

Suddenly a telegram from Wilhelm was brought in. But yet again it was one which had crossed his own en route. They were no longer reacting in time. They were no longer listening to each other as they had for the last twenty years . . .

Wilhelm said that Russia's mobilization made his mediation futile. His friendship with Nikolai and Russia, bequeathed to him by his grandfather on his deathbed, had always been sacred to him, and it was not on him that the blame for all the disasters threatening the civilized world would fall. However, it was still possible for Nikolai to avert them by halting preparations for war.

Nikolai could not see *how*.

Inexorably, uncontrollably, an abyss was widening between them, carrying them farther and farther apart, each on the brink of his own precipice.

He sat there, alone in the world, his head bowed over the telegram, shedding tears for the end of their friendship.

He could no longer decide which of them had done more to end it.

That evening he received a dispatch from the Russian ambassador in Berlin reporting that within an hour of sending his last telegram Wilhelm had made a triumphal entry into the capital and delivered a speech from his balcony, saying that he was being forced to go to war. Leaflets with the text of Germany's ultimatum to Russia were already being distributed in the streets of Berlin, though Nikolai had still not seen it when he went to bed that night.

Pourtalès delivered it to Sazonov at midnight. Germany gave Russia a mere twelve hours, until midday on Saturday, to halt war preparations.

News of Austria's general mobilization order, issued at about the same time as Russia's, arrived on Friday evening.

Nikolai woke up in the morning of Saturday, the 1st, anxiously wondering whether war had broken out yet. It had not. Was there, then, still hope?

It was the anniversary of the discovery of the relics of St. Serafim. He could not think of that day without a lump in his throat.

Audiences with ministers, arranged long in advance, took their usual course, as though nothing important had happened. He did not have the strength to cancel them and give himself time to think.

He offered Sukhomlinov the post of Supreme Commander. To his surprise, Sukhomlinov said no, but strongly recommended Yanushkevich as Chief of Staff to the Supreme Command.

He then spoke to Nikolasha, who proudly accepted the appointment.

Nikolai surrendered the Supreme Command with tears in his eyes. But he meant it, of course, as a temporary appointment; he would join the army in the field himself later on.

The ultimatum had expired, but the hours went slowly by and nothing happened.

He must make one more try, just one more!

He sent yet another telegram to Willy. "I understand that you must mobilize. But promise me that this does not mean war, that we shall go on talking. Our friendship has stood the test of time, and must with God's help prevent bloodshed. I await your reply impatiently and hopefully."

He must pray. God was merciful. It would pass.

He and Alix went to the Diveevo monastery.

He took a walk with the children.

Later on, there was Vespers. They went to pray again.

He returned at peace with himself.

Returned in time for Sazonov's call: Pourtalès had waited on him, and Germany had declared war.

This was how it had happened. The elderly ambassador had arrived in a state of great agitation and asked whether His Imperial Majesty's government was in a position to give a favorable answer to the ultimatum. Sazonov had replied that the order for general mobilization could not be countermanded. Count Pourtalès, more and more agitated, had taken a folded piece of paper from his pocket and reiterated his question as though he had not heard the answer the first time. Sazonov, surprised, repeated it. Pourtalès, distraught, with the piece of paper trembling in his hand, asked the same question in the same words yet a third time, and when Sazonov answered it for the third time handed him a note declaring war, retreated to the window, and wept with his head in his hands: "I would never have believed that I should leave Petersburg under such circumstances." He embraced the minister, said that he did not feel capable of arranging the withdrawal of the embassy himself, and asked Sazonov to attend to it for him.

There were tears in Nikolai's eyes. It was as though his family was falling apart.

But life had to go on. They dined. At 11 p.m. he received the British ambassador and together they drafted a telegram to the King of England.

That was like moving into a different family.

He felt quite ill. He was about to take a bath at 2 a.m. when his valet knocked at the bathroom door: "A very, very urgent telegram from His Majesty the Emperor Wilhelm."

What could it mean? What was there left to talk about? His hands shook. No date, Potsdam, 10 p.m. Wilhelm hoped that Russian troops would not cross the frontier.

What could it possibly mean? Did it mean that there was still hope after all?

What hope could there be when Wilhelm himself had declared war on Russia that very evening?

Had he changed his mind? Might all yet be well? Miracles did happen! His prayers had been heard by St. Serafim of Sarov!

He telephoned Sazonov. Sazonov must call Pourtalès.

Time went by, and Nikolai was in a frenzy of excitement alone there—he did not wake his wife—wringing his hands and praying. Surely Wilhelm's conscience had smitten him? He had seen how close he was to plunging Europe into a nightmare!

Sazonov rang. Nikolai went down to the valet's room. Count Pourtalès had replied that he had no fresh instructions and could say nothing further. He assumed that the telegram had been sent a day earlier and had been held up in transit.

Nikolai's poor heart beat painfully.

Was such a thing possible—could it take twenty-four hours to get a message from Emperor to Emperor at a time like this? Of course not. His heart told him that the message really had been sent that evening. Could it be Wilhelm's intention to mislead him? To win time for his troops? Did he think that Nikolai might falter at the last minute, and make himself ridiculous by weakly backing down?

At this last minute Nikolai was cured of his friendship for Wilhelm. He suddenly felt cold. He slumped onto the bed and slept.

He woke on Sunday feeling as if he had recovered from an illness. His path in life had been chosen, and he must follow it and not give way to despondency. Despondency was a grievous sin.

Somehow he suddenly felt a great relief. The war would last no more than a year, perhaps only three months. War would strengthen patriotic sentiment and afterward Russia would be mightier than ever.

It was another sunny day. His spirits rose. He was purged of doubt and fear.

He went to Mass with two of his daughters. The service left him still calmer and surer of himself.

They lunched alone.

The whole world around Peterhof was infinitely still.

It was St. Ilya's day, but there was no hint of a storm in the air.

The same thought had occurred to all of them yesterday—they must show themselves to the people. The people would make for the Winter Palace like lost children looking for their parents. They must not find it deserted.

That afternoon they sailed on the royal yacht over a sparkling sea to

Petersburg, and went by launch straight to the Winter Palace landing stage. There was a large gathering in the Nikolai Hall—Guards officers, courtiers and their ladies. The manifesto was read out, and prayers were said before an icon of Our Lady of Kazan (to whom Kutuzov had prayed as he set out for Smolensk). The whole congregation sang "Lord Save Thy People" and "Long Live the Tsar." There were shouts of hurrah, and many people wept.

Then Nikolai and Alix went out onto the balcony overlooking Palace Square.

What a tremendous surge of enthusiasm! Such deafening shouts! The whole expanse from the palace to where the crescent of the General Staff building blocked the view was one great sea of heads, portraits of the Tsar, Russian flags, and religious banners.

Nikolai bowed to all sides. The crowd sang, and some people knelt before the palace.

He stood at last before them, the monarch face-to-face with his people, looking down upon his people, bestowing his blessing on them, as he had always dreamed. Why had he never shown himself to them since the coronation?

(Wilhelm came to mind again—not as his enemy, but as a prophet whose vision had proved true. You only have to step out onto the balcony, he had said, and your people will fall on their knees before their Tsar.)

Why had he not done this often? They sang as though they were in church, prayed, bowed down to him, and the bad years—was it five or ten or fifteen?—with all their griefs and terrors, were, he could see now, no more than a fleeting frown on the smooth, sparkling waters of memory.

It was as though the twenty years of his reign had never been, as though he had still made no mistakes, never quarreled with his people. Today he was a newly crowned Tsar, just beginning his glorious reign.

Document No. 8

July 1914

LETTER TO THE EMPEROR FROM RASPUTIN IN A SIBERIAN HOSPITAL

Dear Friend again I say to thee there is a storm cloud over Russia disaster much grief darkness and no break in the cloud. A sea of tears and is there no end to bloodshed? What shall I say? There are no words the horror is indescribable. I know that all want war from thee they know not that it is for ruin. God's punishment is heavy when He takes away reason. That is the beginning of war. Thou Tsar and father of thy people

do not let the madmen triumph and destroy thee and thy people. Germany will be beaten but what of Russia? If you think there has truly been no worse martyr through the ages always drowning in blood. Great destruction grief without end.

Grigori

[7 5]

After all that had happened in past years who would ever have expected such a display of national unity? Students kneeling and singing "God Save the Tsar"! Thousands of people waving Russian flags and enthusiastically cheering the Tsar! "Society" reconciled with the government! Wrangling between parties, classes, nationalities had stopped, and what was left was one great Russia! Could anyone have expected this even a little while ago? There had been no patriotic upsurge like it since 1812. How little we know ourselves—and we know Russia still less.

A student in a dress with a bold checkered pattern, a large girl with a determined manner and one of those large peasant faces with no refinement of feature yet full of character so often seen among Great Russians, was holding forth to her own group with broad gestures, and loudly enough for other groups and passersby to hear. If anybody had uttered such thoughts as little as a month ago they would have rung false, but no one ridiculed her and other voices were raised in support.

"The reconciliation of state and society is a miracle!"

"And what about the appeal to Poland? We are holding out the hand of friendship to the Poles!"

"This time we are not the 'gendarme of Europe.' We are defending Serbia from profanation!"

"The first cannon shots seem to have ushered in a new world!"

"Yes!" The big girl in the checkered dress tossed her head, which was tightly bound with thick braids of fair hair. "We needed this war! For the sake of the Serbs but even more for our own salvation! We were becoming characterless, we had lost faith in ourselves, grown flabby, sunk as low as we could get—to the level of the *Blue Magazine* and the tango! We need a heroic deed to renew ourselves! We need a victory to freshen the atmosphere in which we have been stifling!"

Yet no one hissed her or cried "shame!" because they had all passed through those amazingly different streets in bloom with the white headdresses and red crosses of nurses, the bandages of the first wounded men, and warmed by the sudden friendliness of everybody to everybody else, something never known in Petersburg. And they had come from houses where women were already meeting to make dressings and knit mittens and socks and jerseys for soldiers.

Seeing the first wounded had turned Veronika's thoughts elsewhere. How many more would there be before it ended?

One haughty voice was raised in protest: "How can you let yourself be swept along by all this patriotic milling around, like wood chips on a stream? After all the years we've spent learning to think and to look at things with open eyes."

A bold, thin-faced girl said in a vinegary voice: "Stifling, you say? You're right. But it was the muddle and neglect here at home that were stifling us. We need a long peace, not war! Why did we have to get mixed up in this war?"

Another student, older than the rest of them, almost shouted her down: "We have to think in terms of national survival. This is a duel to the death between Slav and German. Besides, if we had left France to fight alone the Germans would have smashed her by now and turned on us—and we would have had to face them single-handed! We are members of the *entente*, and the only way out is victory for the Allies."

Another girl, dark-complexioned and with a pigtail, protested: "You talk about national unanimity. That's a dangerous thing. It implies that one side or the other—either society or the state—must have been wrong. Which of them? We need to know."

The big girl turned to face her squarely and said triumphantly: "National unity is not dangerous, it's the normal condition of any people. It's a great pity we couldn't achieve it earlier, that we've had to pay such a price for it. The whole of Russian educated society has been anti-nationalist in outlook for decades. Perhaps now that we're united we shall discover the true way at last."

Others contradicted her—but one objector was not really in disagreement: "Patriotism isn't the point! What matters is the opportunity to merge with the people, to stand side by side with the people on equal terms, something we have dreamed of for decades . . ."

Merge with the people—many of those present wanted to, but had no clear idea how to do it. There was no obvious task for them to undertake and the administration of the Bestuzhev Women's Courses had put out no statement, suggested no contribution its students might make to the war effort. So, quite spontaneously, a number of them had gathered excitedly in the vestibule, although there were ten days to go before the school year began, hoping to clarify things for themselves in discussion or from some chance remark. There was some talk about tomorrow's "flag day"—a collection was to be taken up on the streets of the capital, and many women students had volunteered to help, but others said that carrying around the begging bowl for a single day was ludicrously little to be doing when so many young women were giving up everything to volunteer as nurses. It might seem an absurd thing for someone with a higher education to do, but then the war itself was a disruption of normal existence with no precedents. The first days of the war were like a great thunderclap, a warning of dreadful things to come, and the natural selfish reaction was to remain aloof, but that was quickly overtaken by a stronger impulse—to join in, body and soul. Some were simply eager to take part in the first war of their generation. It might only last three or four months! Russia is fighting for justice in the world—how can we stand aside? Russia is fighting for her existence—how can we refuse to help her?

There were others who said, "Yes, but we can best contribute to the war effort as critics of the government, warning it against the mistakes it could make—against restricting the rights of the Jews, for instance."

The institute's new premises, on Central Prospect, were, they were told, to be handed over for use as a hospital. So the offices were still in the old building, on the tenth line.

Normally there would have been no one in the vestibule as early as this, before the end of August, but they had flocked in, drawn by the need to learn more before making up their minds. A large number of students were standing in groups or strolling around. It was a warm sunny day, and they had nothing on over their summer dresses.

There was some argument too about the renaming of the capital—since the previous day it had been Petrograd, not Sankt-Peterburg. Here again, no one called this ridiculous jingoism. They only complained that the "Sankt" had been dropped, that whoever was responsible had substituted the Emperor Peter for the apostle, not realizing that "St. Peter's City" should be "Svyato-Petrograd." Others recalled that the city's name had originally been pronounced "Piterburkh," as though it was Dutch. The form "Peterburg," wished on them by the Germans, was a symbol of Russia's eternal subjection, and it was a good thing that it had been rejected!

No first-year students had arrived yet, so those about to begin their second year still felt like new girls, and their conversation was subdued. Somebody said that the schedule was already on the notice board. So far in advance? Evidently the administration was feeling the challenge of the times. The second-year students went to look, among them Veronika and Likonya, Varya from Pyatigorsk, the one with the bobbed hair and stubborn little chin, the other Varya, the yellow-haired one from Velikie Luki, and Liza from Tambov, who always looked melancholy and was as slender as a poplar sapling. They discussed the schedule.

The great event in the life of the school was the appointment of a new teacher of medieval history—a woman. Professor (!) Andozerskaya! She had obtained her doctorate, needless to say, in France, not in Russia, but things were beginning to move—she had recently been given a master's degree in Russia. On the schedule she was still described as "instructor," but the students knew that she was generally accorded the title of professor in university circles. In addition to her second-year course on medieval history she would be conducting a seminar titled "Use of Sources" for senior students.

All this was very exciting. The girls were eager to get a look at the professor and form some impression of her that very day. They were in luck. They were told in the registry that Andozerskaya was with the dean. They waited.

They drifted over to the window and began telling each other all that they had heard about her. Her appointment undoubtedly meant that some progress was being made toward emancipation, it was a victory for all the oppressed. Andozerskaya had helped obtain funds for the refectory, for a hostel, for scholarships. But in her seminar, which she had started last spring, she expected students to pore over eleventh-century papal bulls in Latin. Her published work was on the same sort of thing—the ecclesiastical community in the Middle Ages, pilgrimages to the Holy Land . . .

Both Varyas saw in this cause for wonder and perhaps amusement. How could anyone retreat so far from the life of today? How could anyone risk blunting the students' social awareness in such a way?

Since a woman could not obtain professorial rank in Russia and had to go to Europe for it, she might find herself studying medieval European history among other things—but why bring that stale stuff home, why lecture us on it?

"She wanted to emancipate herself, of course, but don't you think she's paid too high a price for it—retreating into those grim and useless Middle Ages?"

"Who says they're useless? What about Kareev and Greves?"

But although both Varyas were progressive they looked like reactionaries among the Bestuzhev students in 1913–14. The dialectic never stops! They had somehow not kept up with the philosophical debates among their fellow students, and their voices were too shrill. An imperceptible but irreversible change had taken place under the vaulted ceilings of those lecture rooms, and Liza from Tambov (a priest's daughter, as it happened), the tallest in their little group, shook her head, pityingly rather than reproachfully, and drawled: "My dear girls, aren't you sick of those hollow platitudes? In our circle we can enjoy intellectual freedom and do without narrow party ideology. We have been given the opportunity to open our ears to Truth itself, to become wiser than all those politicians—so why . . ."

The artless face looked even longer. The tip of her straight nose twitched in perplexity.

Before the argument could become heated Andozerskaya emerged from the dean's office. She was quite a short woman—only her piled-up hair made her taller than Likonya. She had taken some care over her appearance, but her dress was unadorned except for the sheen on gray shot silk, and was not meant to emphasize her figure.

She walked modestly by, holding a little book like a missal in an antique binding but with a pretty pink bookmark. She looked young for a professor, let alone a woman professor; perhaps a little over thirty.

That made it easier for them to cluster around her and address her all at once. "Excuse me, please . . ." "Is it you who are going to . . ." "What would you like us to call you?"

"Olda Orestovna." "Olga?" "No, Olda." "Scandinavian, perhaps?" "Perhaps—it was a whim of my father's." Andozerskaya seemed quite happy to be approached and her manner was casual.

Even the most eminent professors, in fact, were glad to stop and talk to students. It was a generally accepted law in Russian higher schools that a professor's standing was determined not by the favor or the ill will of the authorities but by student opinion. A professor who incurred the disfavor of his superiors might go on teaching for some considerable time and be treated as a hero, and when he was eventually dismissed he wore a martyr's crown. But woe betide the professor whose students identified him as a reactionary: general contempt, the boycotting of his lectures and books, and inglorious forced retirement were his destiny.

Varya from Pyatigorsk came straight out with what was troubling her: "Don't you think that such a minute interest in the dead and gone Middle Ages is too big a price to pay?"

Olda Orestovna's light purposeful step would have carried her past them, but she stood there, firmly and unreluctantly poised on her high heels on the same patch of parquet floor. The pseudo-prayerbook did not prevent her right hand from reinforcing the gestures of the left, and her face said that she was ready for a seminar or a debate there and then.

"It isn't a price we pay. If we leave out the Middle Ages, the history of the West is fragmented and you won't be able to understand the modern part either."

She looked into dark-eyed Veronika's calm face and glanced up at Liza's wide, thoughtful gaze.

Varya from Pyatigorsk: "But for practical purposes the history of the West, or all that we need of it, begins with the great French Revolution . . ."

Varya from Velikie Luki: "No, with the Enlightenment . . ."

"All right, with the Enlightenment. Why do we need to know about pilgrimages to Jerusalem? Or paleography?"

Olda Orestovna listened with a faint smile as though she had heard all this before.

"You mustn't jump to conclusions—don't mistake the branch for the tree. The Western Enlightenment is only one branch of Western culture, and by no means the most fruitful. It starts from the trunk, not from the root."

"What would you say is more important?"

"If you like, the spiritual life of the Middle Ages. Mankind has never experienced such an intense spiritual life, with the spiritual so far outweighing the material, either before or since."

The age of obscurantism? Of the Inquisition?

Both Varyas: "But . . . but . . . surely we shouldn't waste the present generation's powers on the Middle Ages in Western Europe? How can that contribute to the liberation of the people? To progress in general? Ought we to be studying papal bulls in present-day Russia? And in Latin at that!"

Olda Orestovna performed a smooth glissando on the edges of the pseudo-prayerbook's pages. It was a rare Latin work. She smiled, unabashed. "History isn't politics, my dears, with one loudmouth echoing or contradicting what another loudmouth has said. Sources, not opinions, are the material of history. And we must accept the conclusions as they come, even if they go against us. Independent scholarship must rise above . . ."

This was not at all what they expected. This was too much!

"But what if the conclusions are incompatible with the current needs of society?" "Analysis of today's society and today's material conditions is all we need to decide what we should be doing now. What more can the Middle Ages offer?"

Andozerskaya, whose small figure could not be seen above the heads of her interrogators, inclined her own head to one side and smiled confidently, meaningfully.

"What you say would be true if the life of the individual really was determined by his material surroundings. It would be a lot simpler if the milieu was always to blame, and all we had to do was change it. When you talk about 'what we should be doing today' you no doubt have revolution in mind? But physical revolution never means liberation—on the contrary, it is a struggle against the spiritual. There is something else besides the social milieu—there is our spiritual tradition, all the hundreds of traditions! There is also the spiritual life of the individual human being, and hence his personal responsibility, even if it means opposition to the society around him, for what he does himself and for what others do with his knowledge."

Veronika emerged from her reverie as though she had stepped through a wall. "For what others do as well?"

Olda Orestovna looked at her attentively again. "Yes, for what others do, too. Because we may have helped, or hindered, or washed our hands of what they were doing . . ."

Liza, the tall poplar sapling, swaying slightly on her long slender legs, said: "Will you be organizing a discussion group for us, Olda Orestovna?"

"If we can agree on a subject," she answered unhesitatingly.

"What do you suggest?" Liza's questioning gaze dwelt on her.

Andozerskaya looked around the circle, counting heads and wondering whether this was the place to make a suggestion. She thought a moment, pursing her small lips.

"Well, what about the religious transmutation of beauty in the Middle Ages and the Renaissance?" She looked at each of them again, and saw that many of them were perplexed. "Or the mystical poetry of the Middle Ages?" She gave another brief smile. "Well, let's think it over."

She bowed slightly, giving them, or herself, leave to go, and walked away, a small, narrow, straight figure, looking from behind almost like a student herself, except for an unintellectual dash of elegance.

Liza watched her go thoughtfully.

The others began talking loudly. Both Varyas were indignant. Were they meant to believe that the spiritual life of the Middle Ages did not derive from the social and economic conditions of the time? Just let her dare say anything of the sort in her lectures!

Liza tossed her head. "I can't bear the way you insist on explaining everything by economics. Give it a rest."

Varya from Pyatigorsk (very sure of herself after that summer): "It's amazing how people change! I had a friend, I've told you about him. I met him a week ago at Mineralnye Vody station . . ."

Veronika calmly defended the professor, as though talking to herself: "Still, surely personal responsibility is a good thing? If social circumstances are everything, what are we as individuals? Mere ciphers?"

Varya from Velikie Luki pulled her up short. "We are the molecules of society, and that's enough."

Likonya's eyes had strayed to the window. She looked absent. But they insisted on knowing what she thought. She raised her eyebrows, stretched her neck, and shrugged first one shoulder, then the other. "I liked her a lot. Especially her voice. She could be singing an aria. A complicated one—you can't catch the melody at first."

Her friends burst out laughing. "What about the words, though?" "Did you like her discussion subject?"

Likonya wrinkled her small forehead, but her full lips parted in a smile. "The words? I wasn't listening to them."

* * *

DON'T SEARCH THE VILLAGE,
SEARCH YOUR HEART

* * *

[7 6]

Aglaida Fedoseevna Kharitonova was a hard woman, used to a position of power, and power sat easily upon her. Her indulgence of Tomchak was an almost unique occurrence in her life. Her late husband, worthy fellow that he was, had been terrified of her from the moment he began courting her until he drew his last breath. He had invariably consulted her in his work as inspector of high schools and had in all matters deferred to her without a murmur. The children knew that only Mama could authorize or prohibit anything important. The city authorities took Kharitonova's views very seriously, and in spite of the left-liberal leanings of the school she ran, no one ventured to curb her or reprimand her. (In any case, the whole of educated society in Rostov, coexisting as it did with the capital of Cossackdom, was duty-bound to adopt a left-liberal stance.) The history teacher in Kharitonova's school was the wife of a revolutionary (who had during her time there been tried and sentenced, escaped, and arrived in Rostov to work underground), and the whole content of the history course had a frankly revolutionary bias. Russian literature was taught with the same bias. The teaching of Scripture could not be avoided, of course, but the priest called in for this purpose was no bigot, no fanatic, and more than half of the pupils were excused from these lessons because they were Jewish by religion. Of course, the pupils had to sing "God Save the Tsar" on special occasions, but they did so with an undisguised lack of enthusiasm. Aglaida Fedoseevna did not, however, permit this ironic disrespect of the powers that be to turn inward and threaten her own authority within the school, which was exercised relentlessly and was proof against any attempt to shake it. Not only did all her charges tremble before her, but high school boys and pupils from the Navigation School invited to parties crept upstairs timidly, knowing that the stony headmistress was at the top eyeing each of them intently through her pince-nez and ready to send him down again for the most trivial fault in his dress. Manners at Kharitonova's school were beyond praise, and since it would otherwise be impossible to maintain such high standards, fees were necessarily high. There were charitable places for only two girls in each class, and pupils were generally daughters of wealthy parents.

Ruling autocratically, as she did, over her school, the last thing Aglaida Fedoseevna had ever expected was rebellion in her own small and easily managed family. Her husband never kicked against the traces, but after his death his oldest son had done just that—Vyacheslav, as he was christened, or Yaroslav, as his mother later decided to call him. He had been duly steeped in the spirit of enlightenment from his earliest years, but while still in the fifth class he had developed an urge to become an officer cadet. Such a dominating and self-assured mother could not easily give way to any eccentric choice of career on the part of a son, but this aberration of his was particularly hurtful: behind what looked like a foolish boyish infatuation lurked the gray shadow of betrayal. Her older son wanted to leave her for, of all things, the benighted and obtuse officer caste, which had never been touched by the spirit of free critical thought or the passion for learning. The wholesome love of the people inculcated in Yaroslav had taken a freakish turn: his ambition was not to help liberate the common people, but to draw upon what he called its sacred strength, to take root, as he put it, in Russian soil. Yaroslav was a gentle boy, but this kink of his proved a stubborn one. His mother wrestled with him and nagged him for three years, but after school, in her maternal role, she could not bring enough authority and logic and anger to bear, so Yaroslav left home for Moscow and entered the Aleksandrov Military School.

The battle for her son did not have to end there. Free thought sometimes broke through even to the officer corps. Kropotkin, after all, had been educated in the Corps of Pages, and Chernyshevsky had taught in the Cadet Corps. But then came a second blow, this time from her daughter, Zhenya, and in the same year.

However great her enthusiasm for freedom in social relationships and for equal (if not superior) rights for women, Aglaida Fedoseevna had a retrograde respect for the rule that a girl should be married more than nine months before she bore a child. Zhenya broke this rule, and rushed into marriage afterward without waiting for her mother's blessing. Then the birth of the child had disrupted her studies at the Teachers' Training College in Moscow. To cap it all, Zhenya's husband, Dmitri Filomatinsky, son of a deacon and himself a first-year student, seemed nothing like the strong, manly fellow Aglaida Fedoseevna would have wanted for her lively, energetic, thoroughbred daughter. So she refused once and for all to recognize the marriage, and tried to behave as though it had never happened and her granddaughter had never been born. All three were condemned to perpetual banishment, and forbidden to visit Rostov. Zhenya nursed little Lyalka in some attic in Kozikhin Lane, while her husband studied for his final examinations and worked on his diploma project.

Ksenia Tomchak, who sympathized greatly with the exiled Zhenya, had been a frequent visitor in the past year, and had passionately defended her in letters and on visits to Rostov. She finally succeeded in swaying Aglaida Fedoseevna, who had that spring granted the outcasts leave to show themselves just once.

The headmistress had been extremely angry, but she was just. She had to acknowledge that Zhenya had put right her mistakes, or that they were not mistakes after all. The son-in-law was indeed a puny, unimposing creature, but Lyalka was a very healthy child, and like her mother. After almost wrecking the family by being born, Lyalka became its shining, vibrant, joyous center, usurping the place of her uncle, eleven-year-old Yurik. Once she had set eyes on Lyalka her grandmother refused to be parted from her. And the son-in-law turned out to be intelligent and businesslike. He was not just an engineer, but an up-to-date heating engineer; there was any amount of work waiting for the young graduate in the neighborhood, in Rostov and in Aleksandrovo-Grushevsk, and he had even been offered the use of a laboratory in the Don Polytechnic Institute. He had none of silly Yaroslav's bantam bravado—so much the better, the crossed hammer and wrench were becoming the emblem of the new age instead of the crossed swords or flags of old. Her son-in-law was conscious of it, and although he behaved modestly he had a strength of character invisible from outside. At meals he was overshadowed by his mother-in-law's person, but not daunted by her barbs, which he parried—she had to admit—quite wittily, though good-naturedly. Success at his work and delight in his wife and his child kept him in a permanent state of blissful magnanimity. Zhenya drifted around in a still more blissful state. Happiness suffused the Kharitonov apartment like a pink cloud, and no one who breathed that atmosphere could fail to be infected by it. Even Aglaida Fedoseevna, who went along the corridor from the school to her apartment three times a day, could not hold out against the pink cloud's embrace, try as she might. Her granddaughter would be crowing, her daughter humming to herself, her son-in-law quietly laughing, Yurik sitting at the table arguing in a more adult way every day—and the old wound left by her husband's death, and the new wound inflicted by her willful son, gradually healed.

That was how Ksenia had found the Kharitonov family when she came south from Moscow in July, before the war began. She had always felt happy with these people, but never so happy as now. Letters from Zhenya which had reached her at the farm had been full of the same crazy happiness, a happiness so great that it could hardly believe in itself. The war was not yet visible as the dividing line in their lives. Ksenia plunged in anticipation into that warm mist of happiness as she alighted at Rostov station on her way back from the Kuban, got into a cab, and checked that she still had the six articles she had brought with her.

True, she had winged home to the farm like a carefree bird, and was returning burdened with cares—but where else should she take them, where else should she look for help and protection and advice if not to the Kharitonovs? Her father's grim command had slammed down upon her like a black grave slab: not only would she not be allowed to study dance (she wouldn't have dared hint at it) but he had ordered her to give up her present studies, told her it was time she was married. With Irina's help she had won a respite till Christmas—and in the meantime war had broken out. While she was at home she could see no way out—she couldn't argue with her father. But as soon as she woke up in the train the next morning and saw through the window from Bataisk the streets of Rostov climbing down from the ridge to hang over the river—Rostov, where Ksenia's freedom, her joys, and her interests had first blossomed—her father's threats ceased to weigh upon her like a tombstone and the old man with the big nose and the loud voice ceased to be the sole, the dread and unchallengeable arbiter of her life.

Her heart always beat faster whenever she returned to Rostov, especially in the early mornings when the steep rise of the Sadovaya up to Dolomanovsky was fresh and clean and its leaves showed dark green and the cabdriver whipped up his horses so as not to fall behind the tram! The trams, too, were quite different from those in Moscow. They had power wheels instead of arms, and there were airy summer trams with no sides. Little boys hung on the back, perched on the coupling hook, and stole a ride as far as the policeman at the crossroads.

Beyond Nikolsky Lane the Great Sadovaya straightened out completely and became a three-verst arrow aimed straight at the border of Nakhichevan. There were the Arkhangorodskys' windows on the second floor, there was the balcony outside their drawing room, with a canvas awning over it, and that might very well be Zoya Lvovna moving her flowerpots around, but the trees were too luxuriant for Ksenia to see properly, and anyway the Arkhangorodskys could wait; first thing in the morning was not the time to visit them. There was that fashionable shop on the sunny side of the Sadovaya, a two-story building with a pebble-dash trim and striped awnings with fringes over each plate-glass window. The cabby wanted to turn into the Taganrog Prospect, but she told him to go straight on to Cathedral Lane. (The other way would have taken her past the Old Market and that overpowering smell from the rows of fish stalls. There was always such an abundance of huge bream and carp that stalls were erected down to the edge of the road, and in the early morning whatever of the night's catch remained unsold would still be alive, silvery, wriggling, floundering about the counters.) There was another modern building on the corner of the Taganrog Prospect—you wouldn't find many like it even in Moscow: the upper stories were almost without walls, all glass . . . The Grand Hotel . . . the Merchants' Garden . . . the San Remo. No, Rostov wasn't so very small and it *was* very comfortable! . . . Posters. Wonder what's on? A benefit performance for someone at the Mashonkin Theater . . . the Truzzi Circus . . . a French miniature theater . . . a powerful drama at the Solea . . . and a very funny Max Linder film. She had a day or two to go and see some of these things. They passed the City Park and turned onto the bumpier cobblestones of Cathedral Lane. There was the modern school, the one Yurik went to. The post office. The Old Cathedral stood out against the sky at the end of its lane, squat and ugly, and on the open space before it the statue of Aleksandr II with its octagonal surround. Then alluring, colorful Moscow Street, in which there was nothing but shops, with awnings over the windows—Moscow Street, Rostov, could dress you as well as any street in Moscow itself. And there, farther on across the road, past the drive-in for market carts, she could see Kharitonova's school. No, that's the main entrance, perhaps I'd better go around the other side, to the headmistress's door.

How she loved that staircase, loved every door! As soon as she crossed the threshold she was in that atmosphere of intellectual freedom and easy relationships which had always existed in the Kharitonov family. And there was Zhenya running to embrace her, rushing like a whirlwind as though she were the younger. Her eager, determined, happy face! "I'm so glad—we weren't expecting you just yet. What brings you here so soon? Trouble at home? . . . You must break with your father. Do what I did! They'll come around later! Listen, though . . . Lyalka is marvelous! She has musical talent, I swear she has! She keeps up an improvised recitative the whole time! It's practically singing! . . . Come on, come and listen to her . . . No, she's just talking for the moment. She never stops . . . I admit I'm the only one who can understand it all . . . Sometimes she hides under the blanket and says, 'Can't find me!' And her skin is so delicate, touch it . . . did you ever feel anything like it?"

Lissome, merry Zhenya with her ringing, happy laugh couldn't contain her happiness, she wanted to share it with everyone. They had never lived here at the same time: Zhenya had already left for the university when Ksenia moved into her room. There were five years between the Moscow student and the little savage from the steppe. Zhenya had grumbled a bit: this rich kid would probably be stuck-up. She would never have stood for that—she would have made Ksenia's life not worth living. But Ksenia wasn't a bit stuck-up; she was a worker, and she was eager to learn. Later on she was Zhenya's ambassador from Kozikhin Lane. The difference in age was smoothed over, but now there was another difference—Zhenya was a wife and mother, Ksenia an unmarried girl. (Will this ever happen to me? It will! Of course it will! Otherwise what is the point? . . . It could be better still. It could be a son. Dmitri Ivanovich is a very fine man, but someday I shall meet a man who . . . !)

If she could only forget her father's threats or rather just defy them (the very thought was terrifying), life could be so happy! Everything would be splendid!

Another new diversion—photography! They had a Kodak, and Mitya often took snapshots. They developed them together and Zhenya mounted them herself. There were photographs square, round, oval, and rhomboid, some with detailed backgrounds, some against artificial white backgrounds—Lyalka in a little bonnet, Lyalka with nothing on at all, Lyalka in her bath, Lyalka with a doll, Mama with Lyalka, Papa with Lyalka, Grandma with Lyalka, Zhenya and Mitya by the sea of Azov—"the bathing was splendid, and it isn't very far away, and it's cheap, we shall go every summer!"

There was one cloud in the sky. It was time to go and say hello to Aglaida Fedoseevna—and there was that one cloud . . . You see, Yaroslav

. . . No-o-o!!! He can't be . . . Not . . . ! No, not that . . . but two corps have been smashed, just in the area where he is . . . Go on, go and see Mama . . .

Mama? She would always be the headmistress to Ksenia. As long as she lived, Ksenia would be in awe of her, would smooth down her hair before facing her, would always feel a little afraid of her, would never dare argue or contradict.

Aglaida Fedoseevna was sitting primly on a double-backed chair at a round table, both with loose covers, and laying out a game of patience, "Cross Beats Crescent." She turned her majestic head slightly as Ksenia entered and offered a rather wrinkled, indeed a decidedly slack cheek to be kissed. (Ksenia had been granted the daughterly privilege of kissing her only on leaving school.) As she bent over her Ksenia saw that gray hairs, previously unnoticeable, had invaded the headmistress's temples and the fringe on her forehead.

Playing patience? She did that only on comfortably relaxed evenings, never in the morning. Aglaida Fedoseevna was always on her feet and active early in the morning. But now she sat deep in her armchair, elbows propped on the table, obviously disinclined to move. As always, she concentrated on questioning her companion, indicating that no news could be expected from herself. As always, she spoke austerely, taking care not to let her voice sound gentle and casual. Ksenia, standing before the table, was asked the unavoidable questions. What sort of summer had she had? How were all at home? Why was she traveling back earlier than she had intended? On what date would she be in Moscow? But Aglaida Fedoseevna was looking all the time not at her but at the nine little heaps of cards arranged in a crescent and the four little heaps representing the Cross, now and then slowly moving a card after much thought.

This seemed a good moment to tell her troubles and ask for protection against her father's unreasonableness. Ksenia made a start. It was a nightmare, it was all so ridiculous! It had been so difficult for her to get into the agriculture course, the girls they took were nearly all gold medalists, surely she couldn't be expected to give it all up and leave now? . . .

The headmistress made an effort to look thoughtful. Of course she understood, of course Ksenia was right, she would have to write to Zakhar Fyodorovich.

But behind the pince-nez there were dark semicircles under her eyes. Her lips were pursed grimly as though a whole class was about to feel her displeasure. Ksenia noticed an envelope held down by a vase, and recognized Yaroslav's handwriting. She felt herself blushing with shame, and cried impulsively: "Aglaida Fedoseevna! What's the date of your letter from Yarik? I've had one too! And such a happy one, I'll tell you what he says . . ."

The headmistress looked up sharply and raised one eyebrow. "What was the date on yours?"

"18 August. Postmarked Ostrolenka, 13th Corps . . ."

That accursed thirteen again.

Aglaida Fedoseevna returned to her patience.

She had a letter dated 18 August herself. Today was the 2nd of September. And today had come the communiqué from "the Supreme Commander's Headquarters."

She moved another card.

She looked at Ksenia, suntanned, but fair-haired. So animated a little while ago, now she was close to tears.

Yarik and she were after all like brother and sister. She was even closer to Yarik than to Zhenya. Aglaida Fedoseevna pointed. "Bring it here!"

"It" was a photograph. A mounted photograph, with a cardboard flap glued on to prop it up, standing on another little table. A graduation photograph of Yarik in second lieutenant's uniform!

Ksenia picked it up and they looked at it together.

Heavens! He looked even more like a little boy in that huge cap and with that high collar than he did in shirt sleeves around the house. He had tightened his straps till they were vertical, and looked so pleased with himself! A heavy revolver hung from his broad belt . . .

Aglaida Fedoseevna relaxed her uncompromisingly straight back and her uncompromisingly rigid shoulders and spoke to Ksenia like a daughter.

"You can see for yourself, it's gone too far just to be called obstinacy. He could have been a third-year student now, and no one would have touched him. The reports in the newspapers are deliberately written so that nobody can understand them . . . Where is this corps? Where is this Narva Regiment? Still, there's the Ostrolenka postmark, which means it's the southern army, Samsonov's . . . He's right in the middle of it all . . ." And suddenly the most ordinary of teardrops fell onto the seven of hearts.

And suddenly, for the first time ever, those warm, young arms were thrown round the aging neck. She was, after all, like a mother! More than a mother!

"Aglaida Fedoseevna! Dear Aglaida Fedoseevna! He's alive, I know he is! I'm sure of it, my heart tells me he is! And from the tone of his letter he's very happy! People like Yarik don't die so soon! He is destined to be happy! You'll see! We shall get a letter soon!"

The headmistress brushed her tear from the seven of hearts.

Destined? All she wanted to know was whether he still had a destiny at all, whether he was alive, whether there would be another letter. But Aglaida Fedoseevna had no channel of communication with the hidden forces that ordered these matters.

Unless perhaps her game of patience was one . . .

She stiffened into her normal posture. She frowned. Her brows indicated that the barriers were up again. But an almost inaudible plea escaped her lips.

"Have you seen Yuka yet? Go and take a look at him. Some volunteers were marching along the Sadovaya and he was keeping up with them on the sidewalk. There was another demonstration of some sort, some Cossacks rode in from their villages carrying banners, and there he was again. Some schoolboys had been sent along with flags to sing 'God Save the Tsar' but nobody had told him to go . . ."

He was called Yuka at home because in early childhood he couldn't pronounce the *r* in Yurka.

What used to be the boys' room had been given to Dmitri Ivanovich as his study, and Yurik had a corner in the big room, walled in by cupboards. He was not there, however, but lying prone on the balcony looking out on Nikolaev Lane, penciling black curves on a glossy green page of the big Marx atlas, and thinking.

"Hey there!" Ksenia greeted him cheerfully and squatted down by him, raising a breeze with her skirt. "Yuka, hello!"

She touched his head and ruffled his hair. It was not close-cropped, and spiky ends stuck out at different angles. Yuka politely rolled onto his side so that he could see her, but did not put his pencils down, and there was a faraway look on his face.

"Whatever are you doing? Why are you making such a mess of that beautiful atlas?"

"It's mine. And I can rub it all out afterward." Yurik made no effort to shake off his dream.

"What do those lines mean?" Ksenia asked cheerfully, ingratiatingly, still squatting, her skirt occupying half the balcony.

Yurik's greenish eyes looked at her seriously. She had never let him or Yarik down and they both trusted her.

"Only don't say anything to the family." He wrinkled his nose, and his grave, sunburnt face assumed the look of one making a great concession. "This is the front line. When one side or the other wins a victory I rub it out and redraw it!"

He had been rubbing it out when she had found him: one flank was caving in, but the center was holding well.

"But this is southern Russia! What are you thinking of? According to you, the Germans have taken Kharkov—and Lugansk!" She didn't want to upset the boy, but she couldn't help laughing. "You need a different map, there'll never be a war down there, Yurik!"

He gave her a pitying, patronizing, sideways look. "You needn't worry. We'll never surrender Rostov!"

He rolled over onto his stomach again and began moving the front northward from Taganrog.

[77]

(A GLANCE AT THE NEWSPAPERS)

WE MUST WIN!

Confusion in the German army . . .

. . . Germany seriously shaken since Gumbinnen . . . Large cavalry force transferred from Belgium . . .

GERMANS DESECRATE ORTHODOX ICONS. Germans put wounded men to death in Brussels . . . Austrians massacre Serbian civilians regardless of age or sex . . .

. . . Kaiser Wilhelm's sleepless nights. In the grip of a murderous fantasy . . .

. . . Knut Hamsun's prophetic words: "The Slavs are the people of the future, they will conquer the world after the Germans."

I, your darling, I, your dear one,
I will lead you to Berlin.
(Igor Severyanin)

WAR NEED NOT STOP WORK! We are selling Victoria quick-knitting machines as before . . .

DOUBLE YOUR INCOME! Buy a Mandel camera . . .

R A C I N G today

. . . News of Kozma Kryuchkov's glorious feat has reached all Russia. We, a group of schoolchildren . . . make our modest contribution . . . please find enclosed five rubles.

. . . Be sober, be alert! . . . Mobilization is proceeding everywhere . . . amid enormous popular enthusiasm. Apart from deeper reasons hidden in the secret recesses of the great Russian soul . . . the closing down of establishments selling alcohol . . .

. . . German schools in Petersburg . . . Harsh and cruel treatment of pupils . . .

. . . Crime in Petersburg is down 70 percent.

. . . One of the wounded tells us that the Russian forces did not meet a single German in twenty-four hours. An accordionist often walks in front and plays while the soldiers sing . . . You forget that this is war . . .

. . . We who have not been called to the colors must work both for ourselves and for those who have gone . . . The whole village must help to plow and seed the fields of those who are away, and reap the crop of those whose horses have been requisitioned. In case of doubt consult your local land captains.

Burtsev, a well-known Russian socialist in Paris, has appealed to all political parties in Russia to forget their differences and join in defending Russian nationhood . . .

. . . from words to deeds. The Germans owe their strength to their remarkable unity, their organizational skills, and their capacity for hard work . . . The time has come for all of us to work . . .

WAR DIARY. The Russian army today occupied Soldau, Neidenburg, Willenberg, and Ortelsburg, and is advancing to cut off the retreat of routed German troops . . . Several German corps are likely to be taken prisoner.

R A C I N G today

EXCHANGE THE SLAVERY OF WAGE LABOR for a business of your own with an income of 2,000–6,000 rubles a year. Buy this translation of Prince Kropotkin's well-known book . . .

. . . Our special braces will give you a majestic martial bearing . . .

WILL GERMANY BE DEFEATED BY HUNGER OR ON THE BATTLEFIELD? Article by an economist.

GERMAN ATROCITIES. The cruelest tortures and horrors of the Inquisition pale in comparison with . . . One of the wounded officers (name not given) who took part in the battle of (name omitted) informed the correspondent of *Stock Exchange Gazette* of the following common German practice: Russian soldiers taken prisoner with light wounds are made to undergo an operation for the severing of the tendons of their arms . . . This operation reassures the Germans that the wounded man will be unable in the future to handle weapons . . .

GERMANS ATTEMPT OFFENSIVE IN EAST PRUSSIA . . . German troops transferred from the French frontier . . .

Turkey scarcely conceals her hostility toward Russia. She will not, we hope, go unpunished. The Greeks will not resist the temptation to square accounts . . . the Arabs, obedient to Britain's instructions, and the Armenians in the Caucasus will want more than they have been given . . . It is doubtful whether anything will remain of the Ottoman Empire if it ventures to . . .

Cholera among Turkish troops . . . Refugees from Adrianople report . . .

. . . Unprecedented atrocities committed by German soldiers . . . great indignation among German colonists . . . in order to dissociate themselves from barbarous German behavior many colonists, especially in Kherson province, have decided to apply for permission to adopt Russian surnames and even forenames . . .

Soldiers of Latvia! Together with the heroic Russian army you are approaching Marienburg, the ancient capital of the Teutonic Knights. It was from there that the predator band held our motherland in its iron embrace . . . Latvian girls seized as hostages . . . Latvian maidens will welcome only heroes home.

Wheelchairs for war cripples.

Music Lovers. A collection of difficult pieces in simple arrangements . . .

Weakness in whatever form can be successfully treated with Stimulol.

BULLETPROOF VESTS

W E M U S T W I N ! ! !

THE WAR AND VODKA . . . In these times of great individual grief and great national rejoicing there is no serious psychological need for vodka . . .

CABMEN'S PETITION . . . Now that there is no vodka the customary rudeness has abated . . . people have started working with greater dispatch and more conscientiously . . . prolong these happy days at least until the end of the war . . . Also, now that the police are relieved of the duty of picking up drunks off the streets they can keep a sharper lookout for thieves . . . .

Issue of rations to reservists' families. Each member of an enlisted man's family . . . to receive monthly: 68 pounds of flour, 10 pounds of meal, 1 pound of sunflower seed . . .

WAR DIARY . . . The need for strict military secrecy compels the Supreme Commander to give only very meager information on the course of military operations. Whereas the German military authorities sometimes describe in their communiqués victories which have not taken place, our General Staff sometimes withholds news of victories won . . . German troops in the way of our southern units have succeeded in holding up General Samsonov's flanking columns temporarily . . . The Army Commander has been killed, as have Generals Pestich and Martos, Army HQ has been very seriously damaged by artillery fire, and some Russian regiments have suffered heavy losses.

This regrettable occurrence has not, however, damaged our strategic position in the least . . . The uninterrupted flow of troops from Russia has changed the balance of forces in our favor . . . To hold up Samsonov the Germans had to throw in two corps from Belgium.

Thus, General Samsonov's vigorous move can be seen as a blood sacrifice on the altar of comradeship-in-arms . . .

IN MEMORY OF A. V. SAMSONOV

Intent on the battle scene before you,
You watched the charge with eagle eye,
Ignored the menace hovering o'er you,
That hostile pinpoint in the sky.

. . . According to one who knew him well, the deceased was loved as few generals are by their subordinates. He was always even-tempered and courteous, he was always quick to grasp and size up a situation . . .

. . . By order of the Emperor, Cavalry General **P. K. Rennenkampf** has been awarded the Order of St. Vladimir, Second Class with Swords, for distinguished service in the field.

. . . No one expected a triumphal progress all the way to Berlin or Vienna, because the vicious enemies of the peace-loving peoples have staked everything on this war, which is bound to be desperately hard-fought. Our troops recently smashed three German corps at Gumbinnen, and now we learn that the enemy has fallen upon two of our corps with enormous forces and inflicted great losses on us. General Samsonov was among those killed. No one's courage will fail him on hearing this news; faintheartedness must cast no shadow on the deaths of the brave. Their blood can only reinforce our courage . . .

. . . We have suffered a misfortune, and the news has undoubtedly distressed us all. But at the same time it is quite natural that, as well as grief, another feeling swells within us, a feeling of joy. We rejoice that we have been told the truth without concealment. Those who do not fear to speak the truth, however bitter it is, are strong. It is the weak who lie!

Once more as of old we shall answer her call,
Shoulder to shoulder unflinching we'll stand,
Fight to the finish though millions fall,
Drive the invader from Russia's fair land.

Till the Swabian goblin, all puffed up with pride,
Shall lay down his arms and slink home to his den,
Let each of us fight with what weapon he finds,
The soldier with bayonet, the poet with pen.

. . . The Chief Administration of the General Staff is receiving large numbers of telegrams, reply prepaid, requesting exemption, postponement, or other concessions for persons called up under the general mobilization. The Chief Administration wishes to make it known through the press that there is a procedure established by law for determining the rights of those called up for active service, and that representations from relatives on their behalf will receive no attention.

MANIFESTO FROM THE PRESIDENT AND GOVERNMENT OF THE FRENCH REPUBLIC. Citizens of France! By the brave exertions of our valiant soldiers . . . under pressure from superior enemy forces . . . So that they can concern themselves more effectively with the welfare of the people, governmental and public bodies will be temporarily transferred from the city of Paris . . .

SITUATION IN EAST PRUSSIA. We learn from completely authoritative sources that the situation in East Prussia gives no cause for alarm. The serious losses suffered by two

Russian corps are explained by the long range of the enemy's heavy artillery and the large area under fire. This event cannot materially affect the general course of military operations in East Prussia.

FRENCH SUCCESSES! The French army, having reached Paris, has gone over to the offensive . . . The French government has moved to Bordeaux . . .

GREAT RUSSIAN VICTORY OVER THE AUSTRIANS. Successes all along a 300-verst front!

3 September. First flag day. As soon as the gray autumn day dawned a whole army of collectors selling Allied flags "in aid of victims of the war" poured out onto the streets of Moscow . . . In restaurants . . . in clubs . . .

NOW IS THE TIME TO THINK about a museum of the Second Fatherland War!

Our offensive into the heart of East Prussia continues. The steady stream of new forces from Russia enables us to continue our penetration . . . This will further weaken Germany's armies on the western front . . .

WAR TO THE FINISH . . . We must not conclude a separate peace with Germany, which would be mutual insurance against peace-loving peoples . . . Frequently in history magnanimous impulses have ruined what has been achieved at the cost of . . . Universal moral significance . . . Diplomatic oath sworn on bloody swords . . . The knightly fidelity of the three governments . . .

[7 8]

Ilya Isakovich had been alerted some weeks earlier by engineer friends in Kharkov, in Petersburg, and even at the Kolomna Machine Building Works, whose representative in southeastern Russia he was, among other things, not to miss while he was in Rostov the brilliant engineer Obodovsky, hitherto known in Russian engineering circles only for his books in German: on economics, on harbor design, on ways to concentrate industry, on the development of trade between Russia and Europe, on price fluctuations, all in addition to specialist works of interest only to mining engineers. All sorts of stories were told about him. How, for instance, wandering around the streets of Milan without a penny in his pocket, he had thought up a scheme for improving the efficiency of the tram service and sold it for a good price to the city fathers. Only yesterday Obodovsky had been an émigré, and the day before that a state criminal, a revolutionary with a price on his head, but he had taken advantage of the amnesty on the tercentenary of the Romanov dynasty, the file on one matter outstanding had been closed, and for the past three months he had been making an informal triumphal progress around the main engineering centers in Russia, warmly welcomed everywhere both for his outstanding talent and for his revolutionary past. The war found Obodovsky in the Donets Basin, the most important stop on his itinerary, but he had completed his program there and had now arrived in Rostov-on-Don with letters of introduction, to Arkhangorodsky among others. They arranged by telephone to spend the morning of 2 September together, then lunch at Ilya Isakovich's house. They met in his office (which was also that of the Southeastern branch of Erlanger & Co., the millers), leafed through drawings and atlases together, then went to inspect Arkhangorodsky's two proudest creations in Rostov, the new city elevator and the Paramonov mill, which had an annual turnover of a million rubles.

They got on well from the first, in spite of all the differences between them. Ilya Isakovich was the elder by ten years, rather short and rather fat, taciturn and restrained in his gestures, very particular about his dress (all his clothes were made by the best tailor in Rostov) and his carefully combed dark mustache, hair, and eyebrows. The thirty-nine-year-old Obodovsky was tall and fair-haired, casual in his dress, or rather incapable of thinking about it; while he was walking he sometimes waved his arms so violently that he staggered, and he always looked flustered as though one important matter had interrupted him while he was busy with another. He seemed to be bursting with excessive energy. As he shortly said himself: "You know, on this trip, I feel like a samovar with several taps. Anyone who turns one or two of them on and lets a little steam out is my benefactor. If I had stayed abroad any longer I would have blown up. This trip will give me a chance to reduce the pressure. I can't wait, as Gorky puts it, to stir up the lees of life. I'm sick to death of sitting abroad writing edifying things that Russia can't read. I've had a bellyful of being abroad. I want to turn my hand to making a life for Russia! I don't mind if I only sleep four hours a night. That's all the sleep I'm getting on this trip."

He had the easy smile of a man with nothing to hide. His features were in motion, and the pattern of wrinkles on his forehead changed continually all the time he talked.

His hair was close-cropped for comfort.

He had a ready and interesting reply to every question, talking eagerly, enthusiastically, as his thoughts raced off to explore byways which were strange to him, and pausing at every bend to let his companion know what the West did and what Russia had yet to see.

Their day would have bored an outsider, but they were exhilarated by the ceaseless uprush of ideas, information, conjectures. They talked through every carriage ride, every walk across a yard or up a flight of stairs or through a workshop, and even while they were discussing the machinery and operations before their eyes they continued their previous conversation between sentences. It is always gratifying to show your work to someone who appreciates it, and to feel yourself warming to him. Obodovsky missed nothing of importance—the way in which the Swiss rollers had been modified, the method of washing the grain. All that he saw he praised precisely as it deserved, and no more. But apart from that he had an extraordinary eye for the possibilities; he saw every process, every problem, in relation to the Russian economy at large and the development of Russia's trade with the West tomorrow (or, but for the war, today).

In their background, their experience of life, and in their technical qualifications, they were unlike, indeed there was no point of contact between them, but they were both inspired engineers and their shared enthusiasm raised them aloft like a powerful, invisible wing, and made them brothers.

They also found time for simple stories. Encouraged by his questioning, Arkhangorodsky told his guest that he had been among the first millers to graduate from the Kharkov Technological Institute—there had been only five of them, and each of them could look forward to an important and well-paid post. Arkhangorodsky, however, had not soared, but, to the dismay of his father, a small dealer, had worked as a laborer in a mill, rising to the position of assistant miller after a year, and that of miller after another two. It was only because of this, he said, that he had come to understand what mills were about and what their needs were.

They went, at the visitor's wish, to see the steep slope down to the Don where the Rostov City Council was thinking of putting a moving footpath to bring people up from the embankment. Obodovsky said that the war had interrupted the building of the metro: the plant to supply power for the underground trains had been under construction, and the first line, from the Bolshoi Theater to Khodynka Field, was to have been opened in 1915. In fact, building in Moscow had gone mad in the last few years, and a great deal had been completed.

Ilya Isakovich, his gaze as composed as ever, studied his restless companion appraisingly. Ilya Isakovich's life had been straightforward, untroubled, predictable, and Obodovsky's the very opposite, all dizzy turns, meteoric ascents, and sudden collapses. He even breathed jerkily, as though he was trying to take in air for a dozen pair of lungs, and although he complained bitterly about the war, a peaceful life would surely be too uneventful for him, which was why he was so eager to make things happen.

He did not once mention his revolutionary past, which had brought him two trials, imprisonment, banishment, and foreign exile. He talked mostly about recent impressions of foreign countries: he had visited America, studied the mining industry in Germany, held a post in a workers' insurance institution in Austria, and written a book (to be published in

Russia, but the publishers in Kharkov were several months late with it—first they had said they were short of type, then they had lost the preface). But nothing meant more to him than this present trip: a career in ore extraction or coal mining had, of course, always been open to him as a graduate of the Mining Institute, but in those days what mattered to him was making revolution, and he had nearly landed in a Siberian mine in chains, then later on in emigration he had yearned for the Donets Basin and a chance to get to work. He talked ecstatically about what could be done there in ten years, in twenty years, working according to a comprehensive plan, with an eye to long-term developments at every stage. Take, for instance, the underground gasification of coal . . .

"The main thing is we're out of the doldrums! Russia is no longer becalmed! Once you have a wind you can even sail against it if you must!" Obodovsky cried enthusiastically.

Everywhere he went, mining experts, graduates from his own class of 1902, had greeted him with a warmth that brought a lump to his throat, offered him work as an engineer, as a consultant, as a lecturer, even as director of the Department of Mines!

"Why are we always so short of qualified people?" he asked in dismay. "As soon as someone more or less competent turns up everybody tries to grab him, everybody makes him tempting offers. A funny country, this—any number of grandees, any number of bureaucrats, any number of drones, and nobody to do the work!"

"Well, what have you decided to do?"

"As a matter of fact I've turned down even the most glamorous offers. For the time being I'll just give a few lectures at the Mining Institute and do odd jobs in Petersburg. It's hard to say what's most important; students, insurance, the labor exchange, the ports, trade, banking, the professional associations—Russia needs all these things, you long to be doing everything at once. Speaking generally, there are two equally important tasks, and we have to put our backs into both of them: the development of our productive forces and the development of independent public activity!"

"Yes, if it weren't for the war."

"If only they were any good at that! The mainspring's rotten! Everybody relies on somebody else. They don't know which century they're living in. They treat this great country as though it was their private estate, they think they can make war or make peace just as they see fit, as they did against Turkey in the last century, and they assume that they'll always get away with it. Not one of the grand dukes even knows the words "productive forces"! Whatever the palace needs will always be delivered, no need to worry! They attach much more importance to anniversaries: celebrations at Kostroma, minting a medal . . ."

"All the same," Arkhangorodsky said slyly, "but for the Romanov anniversary your samovar would have blown up somewhere in the Ruhr."

Obodovsky laughed. "True enough. But if you look at the Russian intelligentsia their idea of economics is the eight-hour day, surplus value, interest. Concrete economics—mineral deposits, irrigation, transport—they don't understand at all. All these people are standing in the way! But now that the day of national reconciliation has dawned perhaps all our forces can be turned to construction. Give us ten years of peaceful development and you won't recognize Russian industry or the Russian countryside. We could have such an amazingly profitable trade agreement with Germany. Let me give you some details . . ."

They had reached Ilya Isakovich's house. He rang the bell and the door was unlocked automatically from upstairs (no doorman for Arkhangorodsky). Their apartment occupied several rooms on the second floor, all opening onto a dark corridor. Ilya Isakovich had brought his guest home ten minutes early in some trepidation—his wife, Zoya Lvovna, might embarrass him by not being ready. They had a cook, who left to herself would have produced lunch on time, but it would not have been sufficiently *recherché*—the provenance and ingredients of every dish would have been too obvious. For such an illustrious guest it would be too bad if Zoya Lvovna—"Madame Volcano"—could not make an effort herself: her fitful culinary ardor (primed by Molokhovets's cookbook) was reserved for such occasions.

Zoya Lvovna looked out into the corridor, glowing from the heat of the stove, and announced in a breathless whisper that lunch would be half an hour late. Ilya Isakovich meekly fetched a decanter, smoked salmon, bread, and butter from the dining room and put them on a tray in the study.

"Oh yes—what about the Engineers' Union?" the indefatigable Obodovsky asked him as he returned. "What's the situation here?"

"It's a bit anemic, I think."

"There are strong and lively groups in several places. In my opinion the Engineers' Union could become one of the leading forces in Russia. More important and more productive than any political party."

"And take part in government?"

"Not directly. We have no interest in power as such—in that I'm still loyal to Pyotr Alekseevich."

"Who?"

"Kropotkin."

"You know him personally?"

"Quite well. We met abroad. Clever, practical people don't exercise power, they create, they transform. Power is a dead toad. But if it obstructs the development of the country we might have to take over."

He laughed.

The first tot cheered them, the second still more. They began to see everything from a loftier vantage point, and more broadly. From the depth of his leather couch Obodovsky flung out his arm in protest and said with his usual directness, "Why are all your branches called Southeastern? I wonder. What makes you think you're in the Southeast of Russia? This is the Southwest!"

"The Southwest is the Ukraine. The railway line is called the Southeastern too."

"Where do you think you are, then? Where are you looking from? You obviously can't see Russia. To see Russia you have to look from a long, long way off, almost from the moon. Then you'd see that the northern Caucasus is the southwestern extremity of this great mass. All Russia's amplitude, all her wealth, all our hopes for the future are in the Northeast! Never mind the Straits, the exit to the Mediterranean, that's all stupidity! The Northeast is what matters—from the Pechora to Kamchatka, the whole Siberian North! The things we can do there! Build railways and motor roads—diagonal and circular routes—warm up the tundra and dry it out. Think of all we can dig out of the ground there, all we can plant and grow, all the people we can settle!"

"Ah, I remember now," said Ilya Isakovich. "Didn't you more or less set up a Siberian republic in 1905? Didn't you want to secede?"

Obodovsky laughingly denied it. "Not secede! We wanted to use it as a base to liberate Russia."

Arkhangorodsky sighed. "All the same, it's pretty chilly up there, I don't feel much like going. I'd sooner be here."

"Somebody will have to feel like it, Ilya Isakovich. Not at your age maybe, but the young will have to. The way the world's going, it will soon be unthinkable to keep those great expanses empty. Mankind won't allow Russia to be a dog in the manger. We shall either have to use the North, or give it up. Yermak didn't conquer Siberia—the conquest is still ahead. Russia's center of gravity will shift to the Northeast. That's a prophecy. There's no avoiding it. Incidentally, Dostoevsky came to the same conclusion at the end of his life, and dropped Constantinople—look at the last article in *Diary of a Writer*. Do you know Mendeleev's forecast that the population of Russia will be more than three hundred million in the middle of the twentieth century? One Frenchman forecasts that we shall have three hundred and fifty million by 1950!"

Arkhangorodsky, small, composed, and cautious, sat on his leather-cushioned swivel armchair with his small hands folded on his prominent stomach. "Always supposing, Pyotr Akimovich, that we don't take it into our heads to disembowel each other first!"

[7 9]

Ilya Isakovich had always known that if you want a happy family life you don't marry a beauty, that life with a beauty and a temperamental one at that is very uncomfortable. Sensible people had warned him against it, but he had not been able to resist golden-haired Zoya with her capricious moods, her "all or nothing" philosophy (either a collar up to her ears or a daring décolleté—and if she didn't like her face in a photograph she scribbled over it), her frustrated theatrical ambitions (her family had held her back), her unfinished studies at the Warsaw Conservatoire, her play readings from Schiller and her musical evenings, her passion for vases, rings, and brooches, and her disdain for darning needles and dusters. Jewelry certainly looked good on her—in her hair, about her neck, on her breast, around her wrists—but Ilya Isakovich had warned her when they married, and repeated it many times after, that he was an engineer, not a merchant. (He could, of course, have changed his line of business slightly and combined mill building with buying houses and land, but that would have meant losing touch with the engineering side.) Still, Zoya Lvovna's behavior provided her husband with relief and relaxation from his daytime concerns, although an outsider might have thought that for all its hangings and drapes and its satin wall coverings, there was something missing in the apartment, whether it was that there was not enough light from the lamps and the windows, or not enough warmth from the radiators, or that the broom had missed some of the corners, or that not all of the crumbs had been brushed from the sideboard.

Lunch, though a little late, appeared in the end. The table in the dark but roomy dining room (it would seat forty) was covered with a whiter cloth and had a more lavish service than usual. A handsome and dignified maidservant was adding the last items from the enormous old-fashioned sideboard to the seven places as they entered. (Zoya Lvovna liked everything to look beautiful and employed only good-looking maidservants, although she was jealous of her husband.)

The hostess, now out of her apron, went from room to room to announce lunch. Apart from the guest of honor, nearly all the others were members or practically members of the family: their daughter Sonya, her schoolfriend Ksenia, a young man called Naum Halperin, son of a well-known Rostov Social Democrat whom the Arkhangorodskys had concealed in 1905 (they had been close friends ever since), and finally Mademoiselle, who had been Sonya's governess when she was a little girl, and was one of the family. The son of the house was elsewhere.

Naum and Sonya resembled each other closely in some, though not in most, respects: each had a mop of black hair (Naum's was rather unkempt), flashing dark eyes, and an appetite for aggressive argument. They had agreed beforehand to show Sonya's father the error of his ways in participating in the disgraceful so-called patriotic demonstration of Rostov Jewry. This "demonstration" had taken place at the end of July and had begun in the synagogue. Ilya Isakovich had a seat of honor there, on the eastern side, and put in an appearance on the high holidays, out of respect for tradition, but he was not a believer and need not have turned out for the demonstration. Nonetheless, he had. The synagogue, which had a choir, was decorated with tricolors and a portrait of the Tsar; there were soldiers present and the service began with prayers for the victory of Russian arms. The rabbi's speech was followed by one from the chief of police, "God Save the Tsar" was sung, then some twenty thousand Jews paraded through the streets with flags and placards bearing the words "Long live great Russia, one and undivided," accompanied by a body of newly enlisted volunteers. They held a mass meeting by the statue of Aleksandr II, they sent greetings to the city police chief and a loyal telegram to the Tsar; nor was that the end of these abominations. Sonya had left Rostov shortly afterward, Ilya Isakovich had gone away for a time, but now they were together again, and fuel had been added to the flames by a newsreel, shown in two cinemas the day before, so full of sickening humbug, so intolerably false, that the young people were in a fever of impatience to hear what Sonya's father had to say for himself.

They had learned rather late that there would be a guest at lunch—a well-known renegade revolutionary. At first they had been a little put out and thought of postponing their assault, but on second thought they decided that his presence was an advantage: if this anarchist had retained any vestige of revolutionary conscience he would support them, and if he was an out-and-out traitor that would make the fight even hotter and more interesting. They sat down at the table looking for the first opportunity to lock horns and with no intention of waiting till the soup plates were removed.

The hors d'oeuvres had not improved with waiting, and Zoya Lvovna called for the soup (by telephone—the length of the corridor from dining room to kitchen made this necessary). It was no ordinary soup, but a clear borsch, appetizingly accompanied by shortcake tarts filled with cream cheese. The hostess sat at the head of the table, with the guest at her side. He praised her inventiveness, then told the company where he had come from and where he was bound, that he was trying to decide what commitments to undertake, and that there were arguments in favor of so many different things.

The shaggy Naum fixed the renegade with a menacing gaze and asked with heavy emphasis: "What sort of production do you want to develop? Capitalist production?"

Ilya Isakovich looked black. He guessed that the young people intended to make a scene, and he was anxious to check their impertinence before it went any further.

Obodovsky also guessed what was coming. He had a dozen things to do after lunch and would have liked to eat in peace. Besides, the taps of his eloquence were meant to be turned on for those who thought like himself. Refuting the immature ideas of the young seemed to him a stale and boring occupation. But he remembered that he was a guest and made an effort—it was not much of an effort for one with his ready flow—and answered in a full and friendly way: "I've heard that question before! It's at least twenty years old! We used to ask each other the same thing at student get-togethers in the late nineties. You could see the split coming even then—between revolutionaries and engineers, wreckers and builders. I was one of those who thought that constructive work was impossible. I had to spend some time in the West to see what an orderly life anarchists lead there and how conscientiously they work. Anyone who has done any real work, anyone who has ever made anything with his own hands knows that there is only one kind of production—not capitalist production, not socialist production, but production to create wealth for the nation, the common material base without which no people can live."

Good-natured eloquence could not quench the flame in Naum's black eyes.

"Under capitalism the people never see and never will see any of this national wealth you talk about! It slips through the people's hands and all goes to the exploiters."

"Well—who are the exploiters?" Obodovsky asked with a faint smile.

Naum shrugged one shoulder. "It seems only too obvious to me. You ought to be ashamed to ask such a question."

"Those who are in the thick of it don't have to be ashamed, young man. It's those who sit with their arms folded and judge from a distance who should be. Why, only today we've been looking at a great elevator and a modern mill where not long ago there was nothing but weeds. I can't tell you how much intelligence and knowledge and careful planning and experience and organizational skill has gone into them. Taken together, do you know what all that is worth? Ninety percent of the future profit. The labor of the workers who hauled the bricks and laid them is worth ten percent—and if you wanted to you could do the job with cranes. They got their ten percent. But then young people come along, humanitarians . . . you're a humanitarian, I suppose?"

"Call me that if you like. What difference does it make?"

"These humanitarians come along and explain to the workers that they've been given too little, while some miserable engineer in glasses who never lifted a crowbar in his life—nobody knows what he gets paid for, it's obviously graft of some sort! Untrained minds and simple natures are easily convinced and easily excited: they attach value to their own labor but can't appreciate anyone else's. Our unenlightened people are very easily stirred up and seduced."

"Well, why should Paramonov get the profit?" Sonya cried.

"It isn't all unearned, believe me. I mentioned organization. It isn't all unearned. And the part of it that is we must gradually divert by rational social measures into other channels. Not try to confiscate it with the aid of bombs, as we used to do."

He could not have proclaimed his apostasy and his defeatism more frankly. Naum's lip curled contemptuously and he exchanged a look with Sonya.

"So you've turned your back on revolutionary methods forever?"

Naum and Sonya were so tense and so full of scorn that they had forgotten to eat. Meanwhile, the stately maidservant had brought in the second course, and the hostess made Obodovsky admit that he could not begin to guess what it was and what it was made of. She expected compliments, she was beaming in anticipation, and it should have been his duty to produce them, but four fiery black eyes were still scorching the renegade from across the table and he returned to what he had been saying.

"I wouldn't put it that way. What worried me most at one time was how to share out what was produced with no help from me. Now I mainly worry about creating something. The best heads and hands in the country must devote themselves to that, poorer heads can attend to distribution. When enough has been created nobody will be left without a share even if distribution is erratic."

Naum and Sonya were sitting next to each other on the long side of the table, facing the two engineers. They exchanged glances and snorted. "Create! . . . Tsarism won't let you create!" They were ready to drop this subject and move on to the main point they had in reserve. But now it was Obodovsky's turn to ask questions.

"What is your own political persuasion, may I ask?"

Naum had to answer, but less boldly—it wasn't the sort of thing you shouted about: "I'm a Socialist Revolutionary."

He hadn't followed in his father's footsteps, finding Menshevism too pacific, too namby-pamby for his liking.

Ilya Isakovich never said anything loudly, not even the most important things, and not even when he wanted to stress their importance. He even scolded his children by tapping the table lightly with a fingernail, and they always heard. From under eyebrows just as thick and black he looked almost lovingly at Naum.

"May I ask where your party gets its funds? All those meeting places, safe houses, disguises, bombs, all the moving around, the escapes, the literature—where does the money come from?"

Naum shied indignantly. "I don't think that's a proper question to ask. And I think the public knows the answer anyway."

"Well, there we have it," Ilya Isakovich said, polishing his nail on the tablecloth. "There are thousands of you. It's a long time since any of you had a job. And we aren't supposed to ask any questions. Yet you don't consider yourselves exploiters—although you consume far more than your share of the national product. You'll tell me that the revolution will square the account . . ."

"Papa!" Sonya's voice was strident with indignation. "You don't have to do anything for the revolution"—not that she did anything for it herself—"but to talk about it in that way is insulting and unworthy of you."

She was sitting diagonally opposite her father, and Naum diagonally opposite Obodovsky. The two indignant stares crossed as they lunged at their targets.

By now, the next course had been ordered in by telephone—baked fish served in big shells. The guest was required to marvel yet again, and Zoya Lvovna, playing with the platinum-and-diamond lozenge on her ring, gaily informed him that politics bored her to extinction, that if there was one thing she hated it was politics!

Mademoiselle, on the other short side of the table, facing the mistress of the house, was just as bored by all this politics, indeed still more desperately, since except for thanking the maid she had not been able to say a word to anyone. When the president of the Kharkov judicial circuit had made her acquaintance in a Paris café and brought her back to Russia fifteen years earlier, she had not known a word of the language, and assuming that her first Russian charges would have no French, had sung them to sleep with ditties about someone slyly slipping into someone else's bed. Since then she had got to know the local idiom and the local customs well enough to understand and hate this endless talk about politics. By now the record of her conquests was a closed book and she had set foot firmly on the path of righteousness. For the past year she had been visiting a lonely hawker to teach him French, and Zoya Lvovna had been told that they intended to marry, but now he had been called up.

Ksenia sat demurely next to the indignant Sonya and near Mademoiselle, darting bright glances at the speakers. At school she and Sonya had been the pride of their class: they always sat together in the front row, always raised their hands together, always got top marks. But at school the answers had always been clear: whatever you needed to know, then and forever afterward, you were told beforehand, or could look up in a book, and there was never any doubt about it. Now, however, Ksenia was afraid that even if she had felt like saying something it would turn out to be a ridiculous howler. All these clever people at the table said different things, and it was impossible to decide that one of them was right and another wrong. Ksenia, the child of the steppe, had been trained of old in the Kharitonov household not to show by staring wide-eyed or by yawning that the conversation at table was incomprehensible or boring to her, but to indicate interest and understanding by such economical means as a quick turn of the head toward the speaker, an occasional nod of approval, an appreciative smile, or a startled lift of the eyebrows. Ksenia went carefully through her repertoire while taking care to employ the battery of knives, forks, and spoons correctly. And all the time she was busy with her own thoughts.

Her life was imbued with a feeling she could not put into words. Every day, every step she took brought her imperceptibly, inevitably closer to that higher happiness which is the only reason for being born into this world. And the happiness she looked forward to did not depend on war or revolution, on revolutionaries or engineers—it was simply something that would without fail come to pass.

Ilya Isakovich, not so much arguing as thinking aloud over his plate, said: "How impatient you are to have your revolution. Of course, shouting is easier and making a revolution is more fun than building Russia up, that's too much like hard work. It's a pity you aren't a bit older, you'd have seen what it was like in 1905 . . ."

Sonya was not going to let her father get off so lightly this time. He was in for a drubbing.

"You ought to be ashamed, Papa! The whole intelligentsia is for revolution!"

Her father spoke in the same quiet, reasonable way as before. "Don't we belong to the intelligentsia, then? We engineers who make and build everything of importance—don't we count as intellectuals? No one with any sense can be in favor of revolution, because it is just a prolonged process of insane destruction. The main thing about any revolution is that it does not renew a country but ruins it, for a long time to come. And the bloodier, the more protracted the revolution is, the more dearly the people have to pay for it—the better its claim to be called a 'Great Revolution.' "

An anguished wail from Sonya: "We can't go on living as we are! Life under this putrid monarchy is also impossible, and it will never go away of its own free will! Try explaining to the regime that revolutions ruin a country and see if it will go away voluntarily!"

Ilya Isakovich was still smoothing the same bit of tablecloth with a firm, circular movement of his fingernail. "Don't imagine that once the monarchy goes the good times will arrive immediately. There's no knowing what may happen! Your socialism will be no good to a country like Russia for a long time yet. A liberal constitution would be quite enough for us for the time being. Don't imagine that a republic would be all pie, a feast for the gods. A hundred lawyers would get together and try to outtalk each other. The people will never govern themselves whatever happens."

The maidservant, whom the whole family treated with careful politeness, was carrying around dessert in little baskets. Zoya Lvovna was telling Obodovsky about her travels in southern Europe with the children and Mademoiselle a year ago. Two emphatic fists banged the table, two loud and confident young voices cried, "They will! They will govern themselves!" There was still a lingering hope in the fiery dark eyes fixed on the ex-anarchist: could he really have fallen so low, was he beyond redemption?

He evidently wasn't in complete agreement with his host, and might have been about to argue with him if the hostess hadn't claimed his attention.

Ilya Isakovich began talking more emphatically, and a slight twitch of his eyebrows and mustache betrayed his growing agitation.

"The more violent the storm, the better, eh? That's simply irresponsible. I've built two hundred mills, steam or electric, in southern Russia, and if a violent storm breaks, how many of them will still be grinding? What will people, including those around this table, do for food?"

He had laid himself open! Scarcely holding back tears of shame and resentment, Sonya burst out: "Was that any reason to join the rabbi in demonstrating your loyalty to the city police chief and the monarchy? How could you? How could you bring yourself to do it? Do you want to reinforce the autocracy?"

Ilya Isakovich smoothed down the table napkin on his chest. His voice was quiet and controlled: "The paths of history are more complicated than you would like them to be. The country you live in has fallen on evil times. So what is the right thing to do? Let it perish, and to hell with it? Or say: 'I too want to help you. I belong to you'? Living in this country as you do, you must make up your mind and stick to your decision: do you, heart and soul, belong to it, or do you not? If not, you can work to destroy it, or you can leave—it makes no difference. But if you do, you must gear yourself to the laborious process of history: work, persuade others, and gradually change things."

Zoya Lvovna had also been listening. She had her own solution to the problem: if you ate matzohs at Passover you should also bake rice cakes and color eggs at the Christian Easter. A generous soul should be able to accept and understand all things.

The respect and gratitude he felt toward this family prevented Naum from rudely interrupting, but nothing could stop Sonya from blurting out her pent-up indignation.

"Living in this country! You live in Rostov because you are an honorary citizen, while those who haven't managed to fight their way into high school are left to rot in the Pale of Settlement! Do you think you're accepted as a Russian just because you've called your daughter Sonya and your son Vladimir? You're in a ridiculous, degrading, servile situation, but you might at least refrain from underlining your slavish loyalism! Town councillor! What sort of Russia is it you're supporting in its hour of trouble? What sort of Russia is it you're going to build? Patriotism, you say? Patriotism in *this* country? Patriotism and pogroms are never very far apart here. You can't even train as a nurse unless you're a Christian by religion. Read it for yourself! They're afraid Jewish girls might poison the wounded. And in the Rostov hospital there's a bed named in honor of Stolypin and another in honor of police chief Zvorykin! How idiotic can they get? Are there no limits to their absurdity? Take this colossal city of Rostov, with all its education, with *your* mills and *your* town council—one stroke of the pen and it's subordinated to the ataman of the Don Cossacks, the very same Cossacks who use their whips on us. Yet you can still stand around Aleksandr's statue singing 'God Save the Tsar'!"

Ilya Isakovich bit his lips, and his napkin slipped from under his tightened collar.

"In spite of all that . . . we have to rise above it. We must have the sense to see that there's more to Russia than the Union of the Russian People, that there's also . . ."

He seemed to be short of air or to have a sudden pain in his side. Obodovsky unhesitatingly supplied the end of the sentence: ". . . the Russian Engineers' Union, for instance," and flashed a glance at the young people.

Arkhangorodsky, bracing himself against the table, had recovered his speech. "That's right," he said. "What makes you think the Russian Engineers' Union is less important?"

"The Black Hundreds," Sonya cried, her sleeve brushing the untouched sweet. "They're what's important! You were paying homage to the Black Hundreds, not just to your country! And I'm ashamed of you!"

She had ended by making him lose his temper after all. His hands held edgeways on the table illustrated his point as he said in a trembling voice: "On this side you have the Black Hundreds, and on this side the Red Hundreds, and in between"—he cupped his hands to represent the hull of a ship—"a handful of practical people are trying to make their way through. They aren't allowed to!" He parted his hands and brought them together with a loud clap. "They will be crushed! They will be squashed flat!"

[8 0]

The Grand Duke Nikolai Nikolaevich had been out of favor under Aleksandr III. He had not even been included in the Tsar's suite. Under Nikolai II he stood head and shoulders above the swarm of grand dukes—just as he towered over them physically, his six feet five inches making him the tallest man in the royal family. His position, however, was somewhat precarious. At times he had a great influence on the Emperor, indeed dominated him: it was often said that Nikolai Nikolaevich had forced the Tsar to issue the Manifesto of 30 October and establish the Duma by threatening to shoot himself in the Tsar's study. He did not turn a deaf ear to public opinion, he was not afraid of political movements, he listened to what they had to say (though "society" regarded him to the last as a Black Hundreder). There were, however, times when his implacable opposition to the Empress (to which he was committed by his second wife, the strong-willed Montenegrin princess, and her sister) had cost him his post, his influence, and his footing and he had sunk into the shadows. In 1908, for instance, the State Defense Council, over which Nikolai Nikolaevich had (somewhat absentmindedly) presided, was abolished—and he had no further part in strategic planning or in matters affecting the army as a whole. He had subsequently lost his command of the Guards and become a general among other generals, commanding the St. Petersburg Military District.

But then came the war, and the Tsar's ministers talked the Tsar out of his decision to assume the Supreme Command. It was suddenly obvious to him and to everyone else that there was no one in Russia big enough for the post except Nikolai Nikolaevich. Once again the Grand Duke was elevated to the heights.

This last-minute decision had come too late for changes in the personnel of the Supreme Commander's staff. The Tsar's choice of Yanushkevich as a congenial Chief of Staff was bound to seem eccentric in a soldier's eyes. General Yanushkevich was a notable desk warrior. True, he had been a professor at the Military Academy, but his subject was military administration. He knew all there was to know about organization, filling out forms, and accountability, but did not understand the first thing about military leadership. An effective Quartermaster General would have compensated to some extent for this appointment, but the Emperor had selected a QMG to suit himself, the slow-witted, unimaginative, laborious Danilov ("Black" Danilov). And now, true to his habit of letting sleeping dogs lie, the Emperor had asked one trivial favor of the Grand Duke: to leave the Supreme Commander's staff as it was, which was just how he himself liked it.

How could Nikolai Nikolaevich refuse? It was essential for him to have the Supreme Command. No lesser post could satisfy him in this war, which he had so long desired because of his hatred of Germany. He had no wish to make unnecessary difficulties, and in any case he quite sincerely regarded the will of the Lord's Anointed as sacred. He had been brought up to think like that. Nikolai might be his nephew and a much younger man, but he was also his ruler, and to forget it would be to renounce the monarchic principle. When he had been Supreme Commander only in anticipation and imagination, Nikolai Nikolaevich had looked forward to astounding Russia with his appointments. His friend General Palitsyn would be Chief of Staff, and the unassuming and unglamorous General Alekseev, on whose military insight the Grand Duke greatly relied, would be Quartermaster General. As it was, he had to take over someone else's staff, as well as a strategy worked out without his participation.

But he was thrilled, he was heartened, he was enchanted by a heaven-sent omen. As soon as he and his staff arrived in Baranovichi the Grand Duke was granted a sign that he would be a successful Supreme Commander and so, of course, that Russia would win the war. This augury was vouchsafed in the form of an extraordinary, an almost impossible and therefore divinely inspired coincidence. It turned out that the little church in the railway settlement outside Baranovichi, which Petersburg had chosen as the staff's location, was dedicated to St. Nicholas—but not to St. Nikolai of Mirlikia, patron saint of churches in every corner of Russia, but Nikolai Kochan, the Novgorod wonder-worker and holy fool, whose feast on 9 August (close to the day of their arrival in Baranovichi!) was also the Supreme Commander's name day, which made this saint his heavenly protector. It was doubtful whether there was another church in all Russia named after St. Nikolai Kochan. This could not be a meaningless coincidence; it must be a supernatural sign.

To be sure that he read the message from heaven fully and correctly, the Supreme Commander obviously must not absent himself from this propitious place for any length of time. He must not dash about the front line from division to division and regiment to regiment but remain on this spot, where all the lines of command crossed and from which he would determine Russia's victory.

Having a permanent location made possible an unvarying and comfortable routine, a regular round of duties and relaxations. The staff's two trains stood on the edge of the forest, the Supreme Commander's own train almost in the forest. The small building chosen for the Quartermaster General's department, where all operational reports and plans were examined and discussed, was directly opposite the Supreme Commander's carriage, so that he had no more than twenty meters to go. The Grand Duke slept in the carriage. If telegrams or reports arrived in the night the Supreme Commander was not to be disturbed. When he rose, which was always at nine, he would first wash and say his prayers, and then messages would be brought in for his perusal while he drank his morning tea. This done, the Chief of Staff would arrive to present his report. There followed two hours of meditation and discussion on operational matters, and then it was noon and time for lunch. After that the Grand Duke lay down for a rest, then went for a ride in a motorcar (at no more than twenty-five versts per hour, for fear of accidents), returning in time for tea, after which there was no serious business to attend to. He dealt with miscellaneous minor matters affecting his suite, and devoted the rest of his time to private conversation. Before dining the Supreme Commander sat down in his carriage to write his daily letter to his wife, who was in Kiev, giving her a detailed account of the day's happenings. He would have found life unlivable if deprived of heart-to-heart exchanges with someone dear to him, and he would of course have to forfeit them if he went riding around army units. Having a permanent location meant also that the Supreme Commander received his wife's letters regularly. Dinner was at seven-thirty, as in St. Petersburg. The staff officers assembled in the dining car, there was always vodka and wine, and later on tea (optional) would be served for the third time in the day. The Supreme Commander attended his church for all-night services, and on feast days. (The choir had been recruited from the finest singers in the employ of the court and the Cathedral of Our Lady of Kazan.) Privately, he was always in communion with God: he never sat down to table without praying, and he spent a great deal of time on his knees, bowing to the ground in prayer, before retiring for the night. His prayers were heartfelt, and he had no doubt that they really helped.

The Grand Duke longed desperately for rapid and decisive victories, because of his martial and chevaleresque character, because of his hatred for German militarism, and because of the special obligations to friendly France which rested on Russia as a whole and on the Grand Duke personally. Since his brilliantly successful visit two years ago the French had loved him, they believed in him, they had always taken it for granted that he would be appointed Supreme Commander. France must not be abandoned in her hour of need! That was why the Grand Duke had ordered an immediate all-out attack by two Russian armies on East Prussia, and was making determined efforts to speed it up.

The expected victories, however, did not come. Even on the Austrian front an unfavorable situation had developed, while in Prussia no second, crowning success followed that at Gumbinnen—they could not, try as they might, push the enemy either into the sea or across the Vistula. Samsonov had taken a number of towns to begin with, but then stalled. Then came the news of Artamonov's removal (a rash step: if you remove corps commanders just like that you will never have an effective army).

Then there was total silence. On the 29th Zhilinsky had arrived in Baranovichi complaining that Samsonov had suspended communications without authorization and that now there was no news of him. Colonel Vorotyntsev, who had been dispatched to that sector, had for some reason not returned. These prolonged silences boded no good. On the 30th they were still no wiser: the whole long day went by without news from anywhere. That night the Supreme Commander was roused from his sleep: a strange, alarming telegram of uncertain reliability (it was properly encoded but had been sent by ordinary post office telegraph) had arrived without passing through Army Group HQ. It read as follows:

> After five days of fighting in the Neidenburg-Hohenstein-Bischofsburg region a large part of the 2nd Army has been destroyed. The Army Commander has shot himself. The remnants of the army are fleeing across the Russian frontier.

It bore a lowly signature—that of the CO communications of the 2nd Army. Why was it not signed by someone senior? The Army Chief of Staff, for instance? Was this an exercise in deception? A mistake on the part of a panicky officer? Why was there no word from Zhilinsky and Oranovsky, who should know more about it?

In their report on the 31st Zhilinsky and Oranovsky merely put all the blame on Samsonov and told the adventure story of the Army staff's escape from encirclement. "We have no information on the situation in either corps of the 2nd Army. It is to be presumed that the 1st Corps is giving battle at Neidenburg . . . Soldiers separated from the 15th Corps are arriving in Ostrolenka in droves . . ."

This was not enough to make the situation clear, but too much for the Grand Duke's peace of mind. Still, Danilov and Yanushkevich (who really were very agreeable fellows) joined in assuring him that no irreparable disaster had occurred and that the situation might still take a favorable turn. But the Supreme Commander's heart sank: if all they could say about the nearest and easily accessible units was "it is to be presumed . . ." what of those farther away? He sensed that a catastrophe had occurred and that nothing within the power of mere men could help—only heaven could save the situation. He went to Vespers, and afterward knelt for some time (a tall figure even on his bony knees) praying before the lighted icon lamps.

There was no formal report in writing on the destruction of the 2nd Army from Zhilinsky—so there was no basis for a formal written report to the Emperor. But the Grand Duke carried out his normal daily program only mechanically that day. Tall and straight as a poplar (especially when mounted on the hunters imported for him from England), he ranged the territory of Supreme HQ, and strolled in the little garden laid out beside his train. The alert soldierly expression which had always made him look so young had vanished, and it was suddenly obvious that he was nearing sixty. He conversed with members of his suite and of the staff with courteous reserve, but in accordance with HQ's security regulations no mention was made, outside the QMG department's building, of actual military operations. It was particularly important to keep them secret from the representatives of the allies—a Frenchman, an Englishman, a Belgian, a Serb, and a Montenegrin, who lived in one of the trains and took their meals with the staff. They must hear nothing to Russia's disadvantage. They need have no inkling of her discomfiture until it was judged necessary to tell them. Though ominous rumors were passed around sotto voce, though faces were gloomy, everybody took his cue from the Grand Duke and on the surface life at HQ seemed to follow its normal course. Count Mengden of the Horse Guards, one of the Grand Duke's adjutants, continued to fly his pigeons and recall them with a piercing whistle, and to teach his badger tricks in the space between the Grand Duke's carriage and the QMG's building.

On 1 September he had to report the catastrophe to the Emperor, and also to make some admissions to the press, which had already carried hints.

Uncertain how the Tsar, whose goodwill was so precarious, would react to what had happened, the Grand Duke sank into a state of gloomy paralysis. The Tsar never answered in a hurry, and there would be two or three days to wait. The young Empress, the whole Rasputin clique, and Sukhomlinov would certainly try to use the setback in Prussia against the Grand Duke and perhaps to dislodge him before he had a chance to make up for it with future successes. Seen from Petersburg, Neidenburg, Bialystok, and Baranovichi were a stone's throw from each other, and it would not be difficult to persuade the Tsar that the Supreme Commander had ruined everything.

If the wait for the Tsar's answer was hard to bear, the Grand Duke was even more devastated by his own helpless ignorance about the event for which he would be punished. He was as much in the dark as ever: what exactly had happened, and why, and how bad was it? Zhilinsky himself carried a great deal of weight in court circles, and the Grand Duke could not demand a quick and full account from him as he would from any other subordinate. Perhaps he knew the answers, and was deliberately concealing them, leaving the Grand Duke to take full responsibility.

On the night of 1–2 September, Supreme HQ again demanded the details from Northwestern Army Group HQ, but Oranovsky replied that he himself could not get a clear picture.

Every day so far had been oppressively hot, though the nights were cold. But on the morning of the 2nd the sun rose halfheartedly and gave only a dim light. The sky gradually became more and more overcast from hour to hour. It was difficult to see where the cloud was coming from and there was only a very light, if chilly breeze. The western horizon was ashen, and by midday all was gloom.

In spite of his heavy heart the Grand Duke tried to keep to his routine. He dressed and left his carriage at the appointed time to take the air, on horseback on this occasion. Catching sight of the officer in charge of military communications, an amiable sluggard who collected cigar bands, the Grand Duke remembered that he had saved some for him and went back to fetch them.

As he reemerged from the carriage he saw striding quickly toward him . . . —Was he dreaming? Could it be? Could the man really be alive and well? It was. The man he most wanted to see at that moment! Colonel Vorotyntsev!

Vorotyntsev advanced briskly, looking around as though to make sure that no one would intercept him. There was no one in sight, except the general gloating over his cigar bands, an adjutant near the Grand Duke, and a staff general a little farther away. Vorotyntsev, wearing nothing over his tunic, might never have left HQ. He walked with the characteristic gait which line officers never lose, but a little unsteadily, almost limping. One of his shoulders was noticeably higher than the other, there was a dry scab on his jaw, and his cheeks were unshaven.

Before he could come to a halt and salute, the Grand Duke hailed him with unconcealed delight.

"Vorotyntsev! You're back! Why didn't somebody let me know?"

Vorotyntsev, for the moment no longer the elegant staff officer, saluted just as unsteadily, as though his hand was heavier than usual.

"Your Imperial Highness! I've only just . . . I only got here ten minutes ago . . ."

(It wasn't "only just." He had been sitting in the forest for hours. He had left Blagodarev there with his greatcoat and pack. He knew the schedule at HQ, and had deliberately timed his appearance so as to avoid both Yanushkevich and Danilov and make sure of seeing the Grand Duke first.)

The Grand Duke glanced quickly at the bandage around Vorotyntsev's shoulder and raised his expressive eyebrows.

"Wounded?"

"Nothing serious."

His burning eyes devoured the Grand Duke.

Nikolai Nikolaevich's long face looked young again—though it was only apprehension that made it so.

"Well, how are things there? Come on now!" he said loudly, imperiously.

Vorotyntsev stood with his chest thrown out, in the regulation position for addressing a senior officer, but his eyes moved to the adjutant and to the general who was approaching from the other direction. In a moment they would all be flocking around. He must beat them to it.

"Your Imperial Highness! I ask you to hear what I have to say in confidence."

The Grand Duke nodded unhesitatingly and turned briskly on his heel. Agile as a boy, he was already mounting the steps to the carriage on long, slender, high-booted legs, looking around to tell the adjutant not to let anyone in.

The interior of the carriage had been completely reconstructed. They went into a study with windows at each end, an oriental carpet covering the whole floor, a desk, a bearskin on the wall, crossed presentation swords, several icons, and a portrait of the Emperor. The Supreme Commander of all Great Russia's armies and Vorotyntsev sat facing each other across the desk tête-à-tête, and the Grand Duke, free from interference by his advisers, waited eagerly for the news and the guidance which no one else could give him. Vorotyntsev had never been in such a situation in all his military career and never would be again. This was a moment too extraordinary ever to be repeated, a moment when an intelligent line officer might influence the performance of the whole military machine! His whole previous service career had obviously been leading up to this climax. His thoughts were marshaled, oriented, poised. He had slept the sleep of the dead for two nights and the day between them, his body ached and burned, but his head was clear. The auspicious way in which their conversation had begun set his mind working three times as quickly.

He began to pour out his thoughts freely, feeling not in the least nervous before his august companion (he was never nervous before anyone). He described concisely and concretely the failure to plan the 2nd Army's operation carefully; the excessive haste and the bewildering switches; how Samsonov had thought things were going, and what was happening in reality; what the other generals had been doing; the important opportunities missed, and those used to good effect. All the time he was with the encircled army, and afterward, among those who had escaped, Vorotyntsev had asked questions and collected every bit of information he could. It had all crystallized in the clear plan which he had so cheerfully presented to Samsonov nine days ago.

This thoughtful account was not all that Vorotyntsev had brought into the Grand Duke's study on wheels; more important, he had brought the scorching breath of battle, with which he had filled his lungs during the engagement at Usdau and the desperate defense of Neidenburg with those companies of the Estland Regiment. He had brought the passion which cannot be fueled merely by conviction, by the knowledge that you are right, but only by personal suffering. He spoke with the insight which no one could have unless he had seen Yaroslav's joy when he met brother Russians ("You aren't surrounded, then? Who's behind you—more of ours?"), seen Arseni panting like a blacksmith's bellows ("We'll be back in Russia soon! And we thought we'd never get out of this!"), seen Arseni again slump like an empty sack and dig the butcher's knife he no longer needed into the ground.

All that the Supreme Commander had called into being by a distant wave of his wand, without ever seeing or feeling it, Vorotyntsev had rolled home to him like a great cast-iron ball.

He now began describing the fate of almost every regiment, battalion by battalion—naming those known to him which had perished in rear-guard actions and those which had got away. The artillery was almost entirely lost, and at least several thousand men remained within the ring, but the surprising thing was that between ten and fifteen thousand had escaped with no general to lead them.

Did the Supreme Commander know nothing of all this? Hadn't HQ Northwestern Army Group reported any of it?

The Supreme Commander's lean, fine-drawn, aristocratic face began to look fierce, like that of a hunter sighting his quarry. He scarcely interrupted, he asked no questions (Vorotyntsev spoke smoothly and left no openings), he reached for his fountain pen several times, but made no notes. He smoked, chewing at his cigar impatiently, as though the length of it was between him and the truth. It was not just that his compassion was aroused, he was wholly absorbed, transformed into one of the unfortunate participants in that unhappy battle.

Vorotyntsev's hopes rose. Perhaps riding into that hell and wandering there like a lost soul had not been a futile and ludicrous caprice of his, perhaps he could make it worthwhile by raising the Grand Duke's heavy hand and letting it fall on all those wooden heads. Vorotyntsev had never suffered from exaggerated respect of persons, and never less than now. He spoke of corps commanders as though they were inefficient platoon leaders whom he himself could remove.

But suddenly, while he was speaking of Artamonov, whose behavior had angered him most, he saw in the Supreme Commander's eyes a hint of resistance, a frosty glint. Unlike as their features otherwise were, he remembered the impenetrable blankness of Artamonov's eyes.

Yes, Artamonov's failure to carry out orders was incomprehensible. But a junior officer might have been responsible for the confusion.

One of the Grand Duke's weaknesses was that he grew to like those he served with. In contrast to the Emperor, who was always capable of propelling yesterday's favorite into limbo with an embarrassed smile, the Grand Duke was proud of his chivalrous loyalty: once he had taken a liking to a man he would always defend him.

Even if the man was a ninny.

To bring it home to him more vividly, to help him feel it, Vorotyntsev named all the splendid regiments crushed at Usdau because someone had misled them, among them the Yenisei Regiment, with which the Grand Duke had so recently paraded at Peterhof! The reply he received was: "Of course there will be a strict investigation. But he is a brave general, and a believer."

Suddenly he was no longer keenly interested, no longer open-minded. He had retreated behind a smoke screen of grand-ducal majesty.

Vorotyntsev said no more. If even the order to withdraw from Usdau was a bagatelle, if ordering back soldiers who had spontaneously taken the offensive after hours under fire, causing an undamaged corps to fall back forty versts and bringing about the destruction of an army, did not amount to a betrayal of trust, if a general could not be stripped of his rank for it, if no heads were to roll, why had this army been put into uniform in the first place? Why had the country gone to war at all?

The Supreme Commander's carriage should have reared up in horror at Vorotyntsev's story. The whole stationary train should have jolted into motion and derailed itself. But it stood unrocked and what was left of the Grand Duke's tea did not wobble in the glass.

The Supreme Commander had not raised his hand to punish and to command. Vorotyntsev's daring plunge had only carried him into empty space. He had taken a long run, gathering the momentum to shift the heavy mass, and every fiber in his body had assured him that he could budge it, but the mass had turned out to be as smooth as it was heavy, and his outstretched hands could get no grip on its rounded surface.

He had had the temerity to attempt to move something which was proof against any such effort.

He had said a great deal in a hurry without losing his breath. But now he felt winded.

The Supreme Commander also sat there overwhelmed, his shoulders hunched, his arms dangling. He had entirely lost his soldierly bearing.

"Thank you, Colonel. Your report will not be forgotten. General Zhilinsky will be here tomorrow, and we shall examine the situation in the Operations Department. I should like you to be present and make a report."

Vorotyntsev's hopes revived. He looked at the thin form and bright blue eyes of the elderly general, the long horsy face so close to him across the desk. Perhaps it would all be seen in the right light tomorrow. Perhaps the discussion would result in some sort of action. Artamonov didn't really matter. What mattered were the lessons to be drawn from it all.

The Grand Duke indicated with a vague gesture, twice repeated, that the audience was at an end. Vorotyntsev rose and asked permission to withdraw. He was surprised to find that he had been sitting there for more than an hour and a half. He could not think that his report had had no effect at all.

The wry line of distress at the corner of the Grand Duke's large mouth was like a scar.

There was a knock at the door. Derfelden, the Grand Duke's adjutant, hurried in with a sealed telegram. He held it out with a reverent inclination of his tall Horse Guardsman's body.

"From the Emperor!" He took a step or two backward.

The Supreme Commander rose and read it standing up.

Vorotyntsev had ceased to think clearly. He forgot that he had no right to be present while the Grand Duke read a telegram from the monarch. He had a confused feeling that something had been left unsaid.

In the waning daylight (it was getting darker all the time outside) he saw the Grand Duke's quixotic face brighten, grow calmer, younger. The crooked scar etched by Vorotyntsev's story had disappeared.

The Grand Duke's long, long arm reached out to detain Derfelden.

"Captain! Call the archpriest in—he's just this minute walked by."

The tough old warrior's sinewy body had lost none of its elasticity. He stood solemnly before the portrait of the Emperor, God's plenipotentiary on Russian soil.

Vorotyntsev looked up at the Grand Duke, who was the taller by half a head. He saluted again, asking permission to withdraw. But the other man, radiantly happy now, answered solemnly, emphasizing certain words: "No, Colonel, since you are here, your distressing story has earned you the right to receive the healing unction before anyone. Listen to these words of succor—this is the Emperor's gracious reply to my report on the catastrophe!"

He read it out in a ringing voice, relishing every word of the text as if he had composed it himself: "Dear Nikolasha! I grieve deeply with you for the tragic loss of valiant Russian warriors. But we must submit to the will of God. He that endures to the end shall be saved. Yours, Nika."

"He that endures to the end shall be saved." The Grand Duke, a fine soldierly figure, standing at attention as though reporting to a senior officer, repeated the words like an incantation, pronouncing them in the Church Slavonic fashion, but looking and listening for something new in them.

An archpriest with an intelligent and gentle face came in.

"Listen, Father Georgi! Listen how kind the Emperor is, and what joy he bestows on us! 'Dear Nikolasha! I grieve deeply with you for the tragic loss of valiant Russian warriors. But we must submit to the will of God. He that endures to the end shall be saved. Yours, Nika.' "

The archpriest listened with the appropriate expression and crossed himself before the icon.

"There's a separate message informing us that the Tsar has ordered the immediate transfer of the icon showing the appearance of the Mother of God to the Blessed Sergius from the Monastery of the Trinity and St. Sergius to Supreme Command HQ. What joyful news!"

"That's wonderful news, Your Imperial Highness," the archpriest agreed with a dignified bow. "It is no ordinary icon—it is painted on a board from the coffin of the Blessed Sergius. It has accompanied our armies into battle for nearly three centuries. It went with Tsar Aleksei Mikhailovich on his Lithuanian campaign. It was with Peter the Great at Poltava, and with Aleksandr the Blessed on his European campaign. And . . . and . . . it was at the Commander-in-Chief's headquarters during the Japanese war."

"What joy! This is a token of God's mercy!" The Supreme Commander strode excitedly from one side of his study to the other. "With this icon we shall have the aid of the Mother of God!"

* * *

PRAYING KNEADS NO DOUGH

* * *

Document No. 9

(German leaflet dropped from an airplane)

RUSSIAN SOLDIERS!

THEY ARE CONCEALING THE FACTS FROM YOU.

THE 2ND RUSSIAN ARMY HAS BEEN SMASHED!

. . . 300 cannon, all the supply wagons, and 93,000 men have been captured.

The prisoners of war are very satisfied with their treatment and have no wish to return to Russia. They find life good in our country.

Belgium is defeated. Our armies are at the gates of Paris . . .

[81]

It is difficult to believe, so sudden was the transition to autumn, that only two days earlier summer was ablaze and a greatcoat was an encumbrance. Now it was the very thing. The autumn wind whistled through the stripped pines and there were sudden showers of fine rain from the changeable sky. It was good not to be crawling through marshes in such weather.

The two colonels, Vorotyntsev and Svechin, turned up the collars of their greatcoats, thrust one hand in a pocket and one under their coattails, and walked between the bare trunks of towering pines, which were stirred by the wind only at the summit where there were still branches.

Four days had gone by since the breakthrough, but Vorotyntsev was still anything but calm. He shrugged his good shoulder impatiently. "No!" he said. "To speak your mind, to say just what you think even if it's only once, is a delightful thing: It's also a duty! You must speak your mind just once, even if it kills you!"

Every part of Svechin's head—ears, nose, mouth—was on the large side. His brilliant black eyes were made to express passion, but he himself was phlegmatic, not easily persuaded.

"You can never say all you think, anyhow. Surely you realize that, left to himself, Zhilinsky would never have acted so absurdly? The whole operation was carried out on orders from the top . . . and it's no good pretending you don't know it."

"I don't have to pretend!"

"If the troops were rushed up in such an insane hurry, before they were ready, and never given a day's rest or time to look around themselves, it's because the orders came from the Grand Duke—if not from still higher. Do you really think that all the rush and all the miscalculations are simply the result of Zhilinsky's and Danilov's crassness? What they did must have been approved at the very top: get on with it, throw this corps in, throw that corps in, ready or not! That's our generous Russian nature—helping our noble allies at whatever cost to ourselves. Paris is worth a Mass. If we don't do it Europe will think badly of us. So what are you complaining about?"

"Oh no! As far as I'm concerned, Paris isn't worth that sort of Mass!" Vorotyntsev's lively eyes looked upward and his lips quivered as though he could taste something bitter. "They'll march tens of thousands of Russian prisoners through German towns, and German crowds will rejoice. I'm not in the army to provide that sort of Mass! Never in history has such a sacrifice been rewarded. How can we lay down our own people's lives so rashly?"

Svechin pursed his thick lips deprecatingly. "Well, everybody else will know exactly what and *whom* it's all about, and you'll go on blasting Zhilinsky. He's a not inconsiderable personage, of course. But you won't get very far with it. The Grand Duke will see the implications. He's the one who was so eager to please the allies, he's the one who kept proclaiming that he wouldn't leave France in the lurch."

"The Grand Duke was pushing them, I know that. But it was Zhilinsky who made the concrete mistakes. He showed neither intelligence nor consideration for the troops. He's one of those who will lay down anybody's life but his own. I want to destroy that way of thinking, and for that purpose Zhilinsky will do. Or Artamonov. Why should forty thousand Russian lives be thrown away just because that sheep's head married Bobrikov's daughter and went up in the world?"

"Yes, but it was the Grand Duke, if you remember, who gave the order to cross the frontier on 14 August," Svechin said coolly. "Zhilinsky actually asked for a postponement. He thought himself that the offensive was doomed."

Vorotyntsev's light gray eyes flashed fire. "So he shouldn't have carried out the order! He should have had the courage to speak his mind! And refuse!"

"Now you're asking rather a lot," said Svechin, almost laughing.

The evening before, after seeing the Grand Duke, Vorotyntsev had made a report to Yanushkevich and Danilov, but only a superficial one. Nor indeed did they try to elicit details—they would have been happier with no report at all. Dead men, and prisoners of war, do not report. Afterward, he had poured out his thoughts to Svechin, who had contributed an account of the way things looked from headquarters. They had returned to the subject early in the morning, in the few minutes before the conference.

"And who had the idiotic idea of blockading Königsberg, with not a soul in the place? Zhilinsky, of course! The 1st Army was wasted on that! Even within the limits set, so many things could have been done better! I understand what you mean about the Grand Duke. It's no good bringing up Artamonov with him. All the same, he's a soldier at heart. He's bound to be exasperated when he hears in detail what they've done."

In the Operations Section, in the Quartermaster General's department as a whole, and indeed among the whole headquarters staff, Svechin was the only man Vorotyntsev could confide in, and Svechin confided only in him. But confidences cannot be compartmentalized—if you admit someone into your confidence there can be no barriers.

"What makes everybody so sure that His Most August Lankiness can understand it all?" Svechin asked with a grin. "That he can take it into his own hands and save the situation? Just because he's gone all around Russia bringing the cavalry up to scratch . . . There's his stature, his looks, his voice, but he hasn't a thought of his own in his head, he just watches which way the wind blows . . ."

"Look at Yanushkevich! Mincing milksop! Never smelled powder in his life! Never commanded so much as a platoon! Or that genius of stupidity Danilov! Why doesn't somebody sweep them out? Why have they packed Supreme HQ with these characters?" Vorotyntsev asked in an agonized voice. "How can we go to war with generals like these?"

Svechin was neither carried away nor put out by Vorotyntsev's feverish, anguished intolerance.

"Unmasking them wouldn't suit the Grand Duke at all—it would rebound on him. Have you ever seen any higher-up in this country change his mind because somebody lower down makes a heated speech to him? A businesslike argument, a sensible memorandum may influence particular issues, but do they ever change the whole picture? You can never get through to everybody, never produce an upheaval. It just can't be done. It's like a dirty pool, a pool of tar—you can't even make the circles spread. Look, Yegori, an hour from now you have to make the choice of a lifetime. You have to speak up, of course, but there's a right way and a wrong way of doing it."

"I daresay you're right, Andreich," Vorotyntsev answered. But the feverish, haggard face, with the purple mark showing through his beard, was set in a grimace of agonized intransigence. "Only if you'd gone through it all yourself . . . All your reasonableness, and mine too . . . No, I daresay this is something a man experiences maybe once or twice in a lifetime. I want nothing in the world except to rub their noses in the truth! When I was escaping I swore that if I only came through alive . . ."

"Well, you'll destroy yourself, that's all."

"And if I do?" Vorotyntsev said with a twisted smile. He still had a vision of the Grand Duke so easily comforted. " 'He that endures to the end shall be saved!' . . . They can only banish me as far as a regiment. And I wasn't a bad regimental commander."

Svechin was two years the younger, but so staid and prudent that no one would ever have thought it.

"That's all very well. If only there were no nuisances-in-chief tripping you up at every turn. They'd be sending you idiotic orders, and you would have to carry them out, and make your soldiers pay the price. You'd be sending a telegram begging your old friend Colonel Svechin to step in and get you out of it. No, it's the *doers* who get things done, not the rebels, quietly, inconspicuously, but they get there. Suppose I amend just two stupid orders a day—clear the name of a brave regimental commander, say, and save a battalion of sappers from getting killed unnecessarily—that's a day I haven't lived in vain. And if you're sitting by me amending another two—that makes four! It's pointless fighting the powers that be, the thing to do is to keep them on course. There's nowhere you can be more useful than here. You've been amazingly lucky. The Grand Duke heard you give one commentary on a field exercise, remembered it ever after, and here you are at Supreme HQ, but if they turn you out you'll never get this high again."

Yes, that was how the bond of personal sympathy had been established. The Grand Duke had taken a liking to Vorotyntsev at first sight and remembered him ever since. And Vorotyntsev hadn't forgotten for a moment his gratitude to the Grand Duke. In this whole affair he wanted, if he could, to keep the Grand Duke and the tarry pool separate.

To Svechin's sober, ironical mind it all seemed so clear and straightforward.

"Well, you asked to be allowed to go, and you went. Why? Did you do any good there? Was it really necessary?"

"I had to find out. I couldn't let it go without a try," Vorotyntsev said lamely.

He had, it was true, been desperately anxious to go, and as things were now, it was hard to see any excuse for his expedition.

"If it was a purely military matter, a question of tactical errors, I would take your advice and hold my peace. We could have made up for them elsewhere. But, don't you see, it has ceased to be just that. The way they *feel* about things—that's what I can't put up with. I plunged in because I supposed that the outcome of a battle and the fate of an army are decided down below, in action. But when those at the top have that sort of feeling you're no longer in the realm of tactics and strategy. 'He that endures to the end'! *They* are willing to endure all *our* sufferings to the very end, without ever venturing into the front line. *They* are ready to endure three or four or five debacles on this scale, confident that in the end the Lord God will come to the rescue!"

He had not said all he could. There were things that he did not want even to think, let alone tell Svechin. But among those he could not forgive was—yes!—the Tsar himself. The Tsar was far too easily comforted—and that was unforgivable.

"There's still nothing you can do about it." Svechin, unmoved, hissed the words through clenched teeth. "You'll come a cropper and things will stay just as they are. In the heat of the moment, rebellion may seem the obvious and honest course, but in time you'll see that patience would have been better. Take my word for it, keep quiet and get on with the job."

Vorotyntsev could not be calmed down. "That's just what I can't do! I can't sit still! If you have an arrow through your chest can you help trying to pull it out?"

He stopped, turned toward Svechin, and gripped him by his sword belt.

"D'you know what . . . you may think it strange, but I'll tell you anyway. I was on guard one night, out in a clearing under the stars, and my men were all asleep. Suddenly I somehow couldn't understand what we were doing there. Not just in that clearing, not just in the German trap. I couldn't understand what business we had in the war at all."

"What do you mean?"

"I just had the wretched feeling that we were all somewhere we shouldn't be. That we were hopelessly lost. Doing the wrong thing."

His wounded shoulder rose still higher under his tunic in painful protest.

"I couldn't understand myself what was bothering me. Then I began thinking: We imagine that we are spending our lives just learning to fight but there is more to it than that, we are learning how best to serve Russia. If war comes we accept it as our lot—we can't wait to apply our knowledge. But what a Russian officer's honor demands and what is good for Russia are not necessarily the same thing. When you come to think of it, our last unavoidable and generally understood war was the Crimean. Since then . . . Don't you ever think like that?"

"Yes, but how can *we* serve Russia except by fighting?"

"I've asked myself that question. Simply by making sure that we have a strong standing army. I thought of Stolypin . . ."

He was becoming incoherent. Svechin wrinkled his bulging forehead and brought his friend down to earth again.

"They'd have dragged us in anyway. They'd have attacked just the same. It was because we mobilized that they did attack. We could be giving way all along the line, and we still wouldn't satisfy Germany's appetite."

"I wouldn't yield an inch!"

"Oh well . . . You were just delirious. Samsonov's battle shook you up badly. But, believe me, that will be just an episode in the history of this war. And as for *those* people, their minds are already elsewhere, not, like yours, dwelling on East Prussia and Samsonov. They're expecting a telegram any minute now, to say that Lvov has been taken. They know of course," he went on in his straightforward, pragmatic way, but with a fierce glint in his black eyes, "they know, but don't care, that butter-fingers Ruzsky has gone south of the city for safety's sake, let six hundred thousand Austrians slip from between the pincers, and politely sped Auffenberg and Dankel on their way instead of annihilating them, because that's what the textbooks told him to do . . . They'll pretend that Lvov makes up completely for the Samsonov debacle and expect medals for it. Church bells will ring all over Russia to celebrate our stupidity in capturing an empty city."

Vorotyntsev did not want to hear about the Austrian front or anything else except the encirclement at Neidenburg. He spoke more heatedly than ever: "What you say only makes things worse. I shall let them have it as soon as we get there!"

Svechin wagged his big head. "You really worry me. When we get into the conference room keep one eye on me and remain seated. Remember, your whole career may depend on what happens today. If you ruin your chances now you'll be sorry later."

They had reached the fringe of the forest and were walking back toward the trains and the settlement. (HQ was on wheels, and hidden by the trees, as the seriousness of the military situation demanded. The staff lived in the carriages but worked in buildings that resembled sheds.) It was five minutes to ten, and other officers were also converging on the building which housed the QMG's department.

A clerk was bustling like a flustered duck along the outermost path, skirting the area where he might bump into senior officers, and behind him, with the steady stride which was natural to him and had nothing to do with army training, taking one step to the clerk's two, came Arseni Blagodarev.

Now that his shoulders were relieved of all their burdens he swung his arms freely as he walked. He looked around inquisitively, quite unawed by Supreme HQ and the proximity of grand dukes.

Vorotyntsev's tension and exasperation vanished immediately. He held out his hand to detain the clerk. In a hurry to be about his business, the man anticipated Vorotyntsev's question. (His salute did not carry his hand to his temple or turn his elbow outward—HQ staff knew who was who.)

"We're getting it all written down, Your Honor—line of march, supply situation . . ."

"Uh-huh." Vorotyntsev let him go and looked affectionately at Arseni, who saluted the two colonels, his own and the stranger, head held high, elbow well back, but without the regulation do-or-die stare. He seemed to be treating it as a game rather than trying to impress.

"Well, then, Arseni, you're being posted to the artillery now, are you?"

"That's right," Arseni said with an indulgent smile.

"Every inch a grenadier, wouldn't you say?" Vorotyntsev asked Svechin, giving Arseni's chest an appreciative slap. "You'll be going to the Grenadier Artillery Brigade, I've arranged it."

"That's all right, then," Blagodarev said, moving his tongue around the inside of his cheek. Then, realizing that this was not the way to behave now that they were no longer back *there*: "Thank you very much indeed!" He saluted again, and his big lower lip jutted out in a barely perceptible smile.

It wasn't his experience of encirclement that made him behave like this. He had been just the same when Vorotyntsev had first met him at Usdau. He treated not just "his own" colonel but all officers in the same way: he used regulation language unerringly, and you felt certain that he would never overstep the mark, but his tone at times verged on the playful. Unschooled as he was, Arseni behaved as though he knew more than all the military academies had to teach.

"I may have a regiment of my own soon—wouldn't you like to be in it?"

Arseni's lip turned down. "Infantry?"

"Infantry."

Arseni made a show of thinking.

"No-o-o," he drawled. "Thanks all the same." Then, pretending to remember his manners: "It's whatever you say, sir!"

Vorotyntsev laughed, as he would at a child. He rested his good hand on Arseni's shoulder—he had to reach up to it—on the epaulet which had already been ironed smooth and stiffened with a strip of cardboard. "I won't be giving you any more orders, Arseni. Are you angry with me for taking you away from the Vyborg Regiment and dragging you into the trap?"

"Of course not," Arseni replied, as quiet and casual as if he was talking to someone from back home. His nose twitched.

There had never been time to talk when they were fighting their way out. Afterward they had been busy catching up on their sleep. Now each of them had to hurry off to do his duty, and in any case the difference in rank made it difficult to speak freely. But they both had the feeling that an opportunity had been missed. Vorotyntsev had a lump in his throat and swallowed hard. Potato-nosed Arseni rolled his tongue around as though it was too big for his mouth.

"Well . . . mountains don't meet but men do . . . We may see each other sometime . . . Be a good soldier . . . You may be a colonel yourself someday."

They both laughed.

"And get home in one piece."

"The same to you."

Vorotyntsev took off his cap. Arseni whipped off his own. A cold wind blew about them, with a few drops of rain in it.

They embraced. Their lips met.

Vorotyntsev hurried off to overtake Svechin. And Blagodarev turned to follow the disapproving duck-like clerk.

[8 2]

There were no large rooms in the building. The biggest of them would hold twenty in a pinch. There were in fact just twenty officers in the Quartermaster General's department, but more than half as many again had gathered that morning.

Two short tables had been placed at right angles to each other. At the head of one sat the Supreme Commander, even when seated the tallest man present. Next to him—they were inseparable—was his brother, Grand Duke Pyotr Nikolaevich, dutifully taking it all in (although everybody knew that for years past he had been preoccupied with church architecture and uninterested in military matters). Next to him was their cousin, the choleric Prince Pyotr of Oldenburg ("Poppycock Pasha"). Then came the Adjutant General, Illustrious Prince Dmitri Golitsyn (master of the royal hunt in recent years). Then General Petrovo-Solovovo, the debonair marshal of the Ryazan nobility, now a "general-in-waiting." Then Lieutenant General Yanushkevich, the Supreme Commander's Chief of Staff, deftly sorting his papers with an ingratiating little smile on his sly face. Then the Quartermaster General, Lieutenant General Danilov ("Black" Danilov), with his rectangular forehead, his spreading jowls, and his fixed glare. Then the "duty general" who dealt with awards and appointments. Immediately facing the Grand Duke, by the opposite wall, where the two tables met, sat the Commander-in-Chief Northwestern Army Group, General of Cavalry Zhilinsky, a man of sixty or so with a hard, sallow face and a coldly contemptuous manner. Also present were the head of the Diplomatic Section, the head of the Naval Section, and the Chief of Army Communications.

Those for whom there was no room at the tables—members of the Operations Section, the Supreme Commander's adjutant, the Kalmyk prince who was Yanushkevich's adjutant, and Zhilinsky's adjutant—had chairs by the window or the stove and held their notebooks on their knees.

The stove had been lit earlier that morning, and the room was not overheated. Bursts of cold rain pattered against the windowpane more and more frequently. It was so dull and cheerless outside that they wondered whether to switch the lights on.

They were wedged in so tightly that they agreed to speak sitting down. It looked more businesslike anyway. They were there to compare views, not to make speeches.

At the Grand Duke's invitation Zhilinsky spoke first. He did not once raise his gray eyelids fully. He could afford not to look at most of those present. For the most part he kept his eyes on his papers or on the Grand Duke. The head with the gray topknot moved only occasionally as he widened his field of vision. He spoke as he always did, without emotional emphasis. He evidently did not expect any of those present to treat him as though he was on trial. He lectured them in his harsh, crackling voice as though he was the Grand Duke's equal called in to discuss on equal terms an unpleasant but not very significant occurrence.

The deplorable failure of the 2nd Army, he said, was entirely the fault of the late General Samsonov. To begin with, he had failed to carry out Army Group HQ's basic directive about the line of advance. (Details followed.) By deviating without authorization from the specified direction General Samsonov had inadmissibly overextended his frontage, made his corps march unnecessarily long distances, and so lengthened his lines of communication. Worse still, he had opened up a gap between the 1st and 2nd armies, disrupting cooperation between them. Unlike the punctilious General Rennenkampf, Samsonov had interpreted several other orders to suit himself. (Details followed.) His order to the central corps on the night of 27–28 August to continue their advance, although he knew that the flanking forces had withdrawn, was incomprehensible to any normal, sensible person. This gross error was aggravated by his ill-considered order to cut off telegraph communication from Neidenburg, which made it impossible for Army Group HQ to prevent the shattering defeat of his army. When Army Group HQ had, after some delay, realized what the position was, he, Zhilinsky, had immediately telegraphed orders to all corps to withdraw to their starting lines, and it was entirely the fault of General Samsonov that the central corps were unable to receive this message.

The Commander-in-Chief Northwestern Army Group did not raise his croaking voice to denounce Samsonov, and this made what had happened seem still more simple and obvious: the deceased Army Commander was directly and grossly at fault. There was no real reason, then, for anyone there present to feel guilty or ill at ease.

Not a murmur of protest, not a skeptical cough was heard. The only sound was that of flies, brought to life by the heat of the stove, buzzing about the room and settling in black clusters on the whitewashed stovepipe and the ceiling.

Vorotyntsev writhed and fumed. No one in Russia, no one in the whole of warring Europe was more hateful to him at that moment than this Living Corpse. He hated the clipped voice, the clayey face adorned with an elaborate mustache that hid much of his cheeks and curled upward at the tips to make him look imposing, and his so far unchallenged haughtiness. But it was not only for today's work that Vorotyntsev hated this gravedigger. All the stupidities, the blunders, and the oversights of which he had been guilty during his tenure as Chief of Staff were so many links in a chain around the neck of the Russian army, dragging it down to destruction. And there he was, giving his meticulously weighed account with not the slightest fear of rebuttal or even demur, let alone of punishment. Even if he was dismissed another very agreeable post would be found for him. He had, after all, carried out his most important duty—his duty to his French allies and to General Joffre. If worst came to worst he could go to France to collect bouquets from French ladies and lunch with the President.

Still, General Zhilinsky would not leave his listeners altogether without hope. He would make up for the timorous Samsonov with his own boldness: he planned nothing less than a repetition of the combined operation of the 1st and 2nd armies around the Masurian Lakes! Rennenkampf, now deep inside Prussia, was excellently placed for it. It remained only to reinforce the 2nd Army, re-form certain corps, and dispatch Sheideman by the route chosen before hostilities began.

The Grand Duke sat, upright and majestic, as though he expected the national anthem to be played at any moment.

Zhilinsky seemed to have covered everything, but naturally General Danilov now felt called upon to speak, since everyone there regarded him as the best strategic thinker in the Russian army. In his position it was no good saying just anything. He had to exhibit the results of profound thought, let them see that a constant stream of ideas flowed through that head (the head was thick, the stream sluggish, the ideas stillborn!), and so the Quartermaster General, with the supreme self-assurance common in dimwits, began speaking in a voice that brooked no contradiction.

He agreed completely with the general picture drawn by the Army Group Commander. (And went over it again.) But some important additions were necessary. If Samsonov had crossed the Russian frontier earlier, as he had been ordered to, and if he had struck at the enemy's flank in the area of the Masurian Lakes, as instructed, instead of waiting until the Germans turned to face him, we would undoubtedly have thrown them into confusion and would now be celebrating a major victory. The fatigue of the 2nd Army had also played no small part, and General Samsonov must bear the blame for disregard of the normal rest days provided for in infantry regulations. Many errors of lesser importance could be laid at his door.

More eloquent than what he said was the stupefying silence into which he now lapsed, his features rectangular and lifeless, expressing nothing, his eyes staring fixedly, his shapeless ears flat against his head. Even the handlebar mustache did nothing to improve his appearance. The pomposity of the man! He behaved as though he had narrowly avoided disclosing a secret too deep to be mentioned in such a large gathering. Military secrets and the complexities of strategy were burdens which this martyr to duty shouldered alone. He was the expert, and he would unravel these matters when the time came. No one else had the key to this lock: officers lower in rank inevitably lacked both his knowledge and his talents, while above him there was only the sensible but ineffectual Yanushkevich and the impetuous and impractical Grand Duke.

In the natural order of things it was now the turn of the Supreme Commander's Chief of Staff to speak. How gladly dark-eyed Yanushkevich, with his puffy face and his fluffy mustache, his ingratiating manner, his affectionate handling of files and papers (and probably of women), would have forgone his turn! A kindhearted monarch had offered him this post in a generous moment. Suave Yanushkevich felt as much at home with strategy and operational planning as Little Red Riding Hood in the dark forest. His heart had missed a beat, but then at the thought of how delightful it would be to occupy such a high post his heart had jumped for joy. And anyway he could not possibly upset his blue-eyed Emperor, who was just as easily embarrassed as himself, by confessing that he understood nothing of such matters.

Whether he was riding in a carriage or walking over spacious parquet floors in the palaces of St. Petersburg, Yanushkevich was always conscious of the impression he was making, and would tell himself over and over again, and with dread and delight, that he was Lieutenant General Yanushkevich, Chief of the General Staff! He had held that position only four months, and the main effort so far required of him had been to prevent the war from failing to break out. That done, he had intended to remain aloof from subsequent menacing developments, but War Minister Sukhomlinov, that incorrigible optimist, had promoted him to be Chief of Staff to the Supreme Commander.

How could he bring himself to refuse what was undoubtedly a great advance in his career? From his first day at Supreme HQ, however, Yanushkevich had been in thrall to Danilov, the only one there who knew anything or could do anything. Danilov's tone was a constant reproach—why was Yanushkevich Chief of Staff, and not he himself? One thing Yanushkevich quickly grasped was that though there were better strategists than Danilov in the Russian army, he too was Sukhomlinov's choice, and it might be more advantageous to leave him where he was, deferring to him in private and promising to obtain for him awards and promotions equal to his own. They were like two boats tied together, and only together could they navigate this war, Yanushkevich dealing with organizational matters and Danilov with strategy.

But what torments he suffered every morning, when he was forced to endure strategic discussions and look sagacious. What an effort it cost him right now to rise and look important, taking care that no one noticed how frightened he was of slipping up and how tiresome and incomprehensible he found it all. In any case, he could say nothing against Zhilinsky, who though formally his subordinate was a full general and had been his predecessor as Chief of the General Staff, while he himself was an upstart, promoted over the heads of his seniors.

Yanushkevich simply repeated, and went on repeating, in rounded phrases and courteous tones all that had been said before, adding nothing and omitting nothing, merely rearranging it a little, so that it became clearer all the time to the conference how gravely at fault he had been, that deceased commander who had destroyed his own army. It was a relief that he had removed himself! Other generals, it seemed, could never make such mistakes, and the conference began to lose all sense of urgency. Every point had been covered, and the subject was exhausted.

Vorotyntsev's agitated pencil had noted all their evasions on a piece of paper resting on his map case—together with ways of hitting back at them. At the top of the page, more evenly and precisely written in black ink, were the main points he had jotted down with his Japanese fountain pen the night before. He made no notes on Yanushkevich's contribution, and scarcely listened to it. Sitting with his eyelids lowered so as not to see them all, he saw instead Samsonov's honest, vulnerable face, not as he was now, lying in some untraceable thicket, not even as he was when he took leave of his troops at Orlau, but back at Ostrolenka, when he was still free to act as he chose, when it was still possible for him not to lose the battle. Even then his helpless vulnerability was written on his face. Vorotyntsev had a vision of Kachkin's savage grin as he crashed through the thickets like a wild boar, carrying Ofrosimov over his shoulder. And of Blagodarev flopping down, plunging his knife into the ground as though it was the plowshare with which he had just turned up a hundred desyatins.

He was about to leap up from his chair and speak without permission, but Svechin, sitting beside him, gave his elbow a cautionary squeeze. The Supreme Commander did not even look at him. He was sitting with one lean cavalry officer's leg over the other, remote and unbending as always, expressionless, except that his pursed lips raised the ends of his mustache. He had eyes only for Zhilinsky's sallow face and stupidly raised eyebrows. It was not so long ago that he himself had authorized Zhilinsky to replace Samsonov if necessary. But since yesterday it had gradually become clear to him that Zhilinsky might well be the main culprit in the catastrophe, and that removing *him* at once would be the most effective way of asserting his own authority and teaching all the generals a lesson. It might, however, be a rash move. Zhilinsky considered his present post beneath him and would gladly relinquish it. He would dash off to St. Petersburg to whisper his complaint in the highest circles and tell tales to Sukhomlinov. In the viper's nest at court whatever happened next would be used against Nikolai Nikolaevich. If the war went badly he would be incompetent, ill equipped to hold the Supreme Command. If the war went well he would be called ambitious, and a threat to the Tsar and his family. God saw how he grieved for the flower of the officer corps and for the stout soldiers who had suffered so dreadfully in encirclement. But ninety thousand men surrounded and twenty thousand dead was not the whole of Russia. Russia had a hundred and seventy million people. To save all Russia he needed not just a victory or two in the field, but, more important still, to win the biggest battle of all, that at court for the heart of the Emperor: he had to get rid of the unscrupulous Sukhomlinov, exclude the vile Rasputin, and undermine the influence of the Empress. With all this in front of him he could not afford just now to reinforce the other side with a resentful Zhilinsky. Loyalty to the greater Russia made it the Grand Duke's immediate duty to suppress his compassion for the lesser Russia, for Samsonov's army, which was in any case beyond salvation.

But he would see to it that Zhilinsky had a rough time, he would scare him by setting Vorotyntsev on him. That much he must do! The Grand Duke had been aware of Vorotyntsev the whole time, and had noticed from the corner of his eye how restive he was.

Outside the gloom was thickening. Raindrops spattered the windows. It was getting dark in the room, and they turned the electric lights on. The whitewashed walls made the room very bright, and every man there could see the minutest detail in the appearance of his neighbors. The head of the Diplomatic Section, Supreme HQ, was the next to speak. He requested the generals not to lose sight of foreign policy implications and the country's international commitments. The French public was convinced that Russia could be making a greater contribution. The French government took the view that Russia had not fielded all available forces, that the East Prussian offensive was not an adequate effort, that the Germans had transferred two corps from the eastern to the western front, and not the other way around (on this point French and Russian intelligence reports conflicted), and that France had the right to remind her ally of the promise to launch an all-out attack on Berlin.

That last word the Grand Duke and the generals ignored as though it was one of those embarrassing noises which good manners require us not to notice in company, keeping their eyes on the window or the wall or the papers before them.

But if that one word had no resonance for them, the force of the Diplomatic Section's statement and the will of the Emperor were unmistakable: they must at all costs and with all speed save their French ally! Their hearts, of course, ached for Russia's losses, but it was important not to let her allies down.

The Chief of Army Communications then reported that the reinforcement of the East Prussian front was being treated as a matter of the greatest urgency. Troops were being continually transferred from the Asian borderlands for this purpose. Two corps from the Caucasus, one from Turkestan, and one from Siberia would arrive shortly. So that the immediate second offensive, which was morally imperative, was already materially provided for.

Zhilinsky said that this had been his reason for asking the gentlemen there present to sanction a repetition of the operation around the Masurian Lakes.

If it meant losing all he had, his career, the army, his epaulets—no, if they scalped him for it, tore the skin from his burning head, Vorotyntsev had to jump up. Lies! Lies! All lies! The man could not be allowed to go on lying indefinitely! He wrenched his elbow from Svechin's grip and, forgetting that on this occasion speakers were expected to keep their seats, rose to his feet in a rage with no idea what his first furious words would be—and heard the Grand Duke's commanding voice: "Now I shall ask Colonel Vorotyntsev to give us his personal impressions. He has been with the 2nd Army."

There was no explosion. The hissing steam of his fury escaped invisibly. He cautiously restrained his leaping heart, remembering the proverb that "the man who masters his wrath can master everything."

"Our review of the situation is all the more essential, Your Imperial Highness, in that Rennenkampf's army is under threat at this very minute, and may come to an even worse end than Samsonov's."

(Too loud. Must be quieter. Lower the steam pressure.)

It was as though someone had broken the window and a cold, wet wind had burst in on them. They shrank and shifted uneasily in their seats, the Grand Duke as well as the others.

But Vorotyntsev became more fluent with every sentence, and delivered what sounded like a carefully prepared and judiciously weighed speech: "Gentlemen! No one from the 2nd Army has been invited to our conference—there is hardly anyone left to invite. But I was with them at the time, and perhaps I may be permitted to say what I think those now dead or in captivity might have said. Dead men may be forgiven for speaking plainly, as we were all trained to do . . ."

(Just as long as his voice did not fail him! Just as long as he didn't choke on his words!)

". . . I am not going to talk about the valor of our soldiers and officers—no one here has called it into question. Among those whose names should be inscribed in the rolls of honor are regimental commanders Alekseev, Kabanov, Pervushin, and Kakhovskoy. If more than fifteen thousand men escaped from encirclement they owe it to a handful of colonels and staff captains, not to Army Group HQ! Except where the German artillery had a two-to-one advantage (and sometimes even where they did) our units came out on top in tactical engagements. They held their defensive positions under the heaviest fire—the Vyborg Regiment at Usdau, for instance. The 15th Corps, led by the brilliant General Martos, attacked, and attacked successfully, from first to last. Yet in spite of all this the battle ended not, as people here have put it, in failure but in a crushing defeat."

He hurled the word into the room like a bomb. The blast lashed their faces.

It was a challenge to the Grand Duke too. He could not acknowledge to the Emperor that "defeat" was the right word, although he was ready to "put his head on the block" if the Emperor thought he should. But though he could not admit the truth of what Vorotyntsev had said he did not interrupt. He sat there as tall and imposing and aristocratically haughty as ever (so close to the throne—and yet so far away).

"I am bound to say that we should have been on guard. The Russian General Staff knew from intelligence the assumptions on which the German High Command was acting: in German war games the Russians always took the offensive, just as the 2nd Army now did, and it was always against the left flank on the Narew that the Germans launched their successful counterattack. They even had General Samsonov moving as in fact he did. I have been told that the blame rests entirely on him. The dead cannot answer back—and if it were true it would be very convenient for us, there would be no need for us to mend our ways. But if we act on that assumption you must forgive me for predicting that the same thing will happen over and over again, and we are very likely to lose the war altogether!"

There was a rustle of protest. Zhilinsky's lusterless eyes rested on the Supreme Commander: it was time he interrupted this brash colonel and put him in his place.

But the Supreme Commander, who could be so peremptory, sat motionless with his head thrown back. His expression said only that he was in control of the situation.

"I must, though, object on behalf of the late Aleksandr Vasilievich to some of the things said here. He arrived in Bialystok straight from Turkestan and was presented with a ready-made plan, according to which the army would march deep into the Masurian wilderness, where there was nothing but fortresses and corridors between lakes. He saw that this was ludicrous and sent alternative suggestions of his own, intended for the Supreme Commander and submitted to Lieutenant General Oranovsky, Chief of Staff, Northwestern Army Group, on 11 August."

(Vorotyntsev's voice was rising steadily. He did his best to control it.)

"When several days went by with no response to his memorandum he did not know what to think. He asked me to be sure to inquire about it at Supreme HQ, and I learned yesterday that Samsonov's message had never reached the Grand Duke!"

The Living Corpse turned a death's-head grin on Vorotyntsev. Since the Supreme Commander was silent the time had come for him to intervene himself.

"I know nothing of this memorandum."

"That makes it even worse, Your Excellency!" Vorotyntsev seemed glad of the interruption and addressed Zhilinsky directly. "Obviously, we shall never know the truth of the matter without an inquiry. If there is one, I shall ask for that piece of paper to be produced!"

Generals' faces quivered indignantly. Everything had been sufficiently explained; what did the insolent fellow mean by his talk of an inquiry? They all looked at the Supreme Commander, mutely begging him to stop this crazy colonel.

But the Supreme Commander sat inscrutably, with his beautifully molded head in the air, looking somewhere above Zhilinsky.

Zhilinsky, usually so terse and phlegmatic, retorted with uncharacteristic heat: "General Samsonov probably retracted the memorandum."

"No, he didn't. I'm quite sure of that," Vorotyntsev insisted, looking only at Zhilinsky—a supraterrestrial being when seen, or rather not seen, from Ostrolenka or Neidenburg or Orlau, but now, within touching distance, just a bony old man with a bad back. "The plan which General Samsonov put forward, and as far as possible followed, was sound. It enabled him to outflank a large proportion of the enemy's forces, though still not enough of them. The inexplicable obstinacy of Army Group HQ in hanging on to that corner of the Masurian Lakes is at least equally to blame for the overextension of Samsonov's front."

Zhilinsky, more irritated still, interrupted. "Our main concern was to coordinate the operations of the two armies."

Vorotyntsev had sensed by now the Supreme Commander's tacit agreement not to interrupt him. No one else there would be able to talk him down. He had reached his goal! His journey hadn't been in vain! He became colder and more rational. His lips twisted in a mocking smile. He cast sentence after sentence at Zhilinsky, like so many nooses around his neck.

"How can you speak of coordination when one army was made to attack prematurely and the other practically stood down? When General Rennenkampf's five cavalry divisions were not thrown in to pursue the enemy after Gumbinnen, or sent to save the 2nd Army from disaster? Army Group HQ seems to have deliberately prevented the two armies from coordinating their movements, by making the 1st Army attack a week too early. Why? Do you call it coordination when Sheideman's corps is taken away from Samsonov and given to Rennenkampf on 23 August, then assigned to the Warsaw area on the 27th—as though apparently its presence had become unnecessary just when the 2nd Army was facing its decisive battle?"

How did Vorotyntsev know all this? These sins lay at the door of Supreme HQ. Danilov turned a suspicious eye on Svechin and said nervously: "There were good strategic grounds for that. We were getting the 9th Army ready to move on Berlin . . ."

"So the 2nd Army could be thrown to the wolves?" Vorotyntsev retorted. "Anyway, Sheideman's corps *was* sent to help the 2nd Army on the 28th—only Army Group HQ misdirected it! On the 29th the corps was assigned to Warsaw yet again, but on the 30th General Rennenkampf carried it off northward. Do you call that coordination between armies? Northwestern Army Group HQ was created solely for the purpose of coordinating them. General Samsonov has been accused of irresolution but the Army Group command was guilty of the worst kind of indecision when it kept back half of the army to protect the rear and maintain communications!"

"What do you mean, half of it? Where do you get that from?" Danilov clamored indignantly, with an obtuse colonel known as "Treacherous Vanka," a favorite of his, seconding him.

"Just think, gentlemen: two army corps, the right and the left, and three cavalry divisions—exactly half of the army. And Samsonov is ordered to attack and win with the other half. Since Army Group HQ had held back the flanks, it should have sent them to help the center out. General Samsonov made mistakes, certainly, but they were tactical mistakes. The strategic mistakes have to be laid at the door of Army Group HQ. Samsonov did not have forces larger than those of the enemy at his disposal, but Army Group HQ did—and still the battle was lost. We have to draw the inescapable conclusions, gentlemen; otherwise, what is the point of this conference? What are staff officers for? The conclusion I draw is that we are incapable of leading any unit bigger than a regiment!"

"Your Imperial Highness, I must ask you to put a stop to this colonel's nonsensical statement!" Zhilinsky proved that he was not quite a corpse by thumping the table.

The Grand Duke's big, eloquent, oval eyes surveyed him coldly. He spoke quietly but firmly.

"What Colonel Vorotyntsev says is very much to the point. I am learning a lot from him. As I see it, Supreme HQ" (he looked at Danilov, who lowered his bovine brow, while a shiver seemed to run down Yanushkevich's sensitive spine) "took practically no part in supervising the operation, but left it entirely to the Northwestern Army Group." He knew his Danilov. The Grand Duke often grasped the essentials long before Danilov had finished chewing the cud of reports he had written himself. "And if the colonel gets something wrong you can correct him immediately."

Zhilinsky grunted, rose, and went out to relieve himself.

The Supreme Commander was greatly tempted. He had the evidence before him. Why not set up a commission of inquiry to examine it further? Zhilinsky could be banished in disgrace, and Supreme HQ would be safe from all accusations.

But only the day before the Emperor's gracious telegram had shown the Grand Duke a different way: the way of forgiveness, with all recriminations laid aside. Besides, he had received an imperial decree (not yet made public) promoting Oranovsky to the rank of full general. Promotion procedures take their own course, independently of military operations, and there is no way of arresting them.

Once its charge has carried it beyond the enemy's defenses a cavalry unit's losses are behind it, and it has time in hand and an unimpeded gallop. So it was with Vorotyntsev. The real discussion was about to begin!

"However, I should like to deal with broader issues. What was the 2nd Army's strength squandered on? On subduing a deserted and pathless tract of our own territory! Before they could even reach the frontier or make contact with the enemy our corps had to flounder in the sands for five or six days. Ammunition, food, supplies would have to be lugged across the same expanse. How? Why didn't someone think of planting supply dumps along the frontier before the war?"

Yanushkevich frowned. Listening to this impertinent Young Turk from Golovin's class at the Academy caused him pain. The snake's tongue flickered under the fluffy mustache.

"If we had done that the enemy might have seized the supplies."

Vorotyntsev reared up, his jaw purple with anger. "So you would sooner lose twenty thousand dead and seventy thousand prisoners than a dozen quartermasters' stores?"

He could not look at the man without feeling sick. Every effeminate movement gave him away: "General" Yanushkevich was an impostor. How could such a man be Chief of Staff to the Supreme Commander?! And what was to prevent him from sending all of Russia's fighting forces to their destruction?

"The reason no stores were put near the frontier," Danilov said heavily, "was because we expected to be on the defensive in this region, not attacking."

That was true. But the supposition was part of a plan for the whole war which had been hastily changed, then further modified by Zhilinsky, when he was Chief of Staff, *and* by the War Minister, *and* by the Emperor! For that matter, the Grand Duke himself had favored the change. Vorotyntsev could not afford to let himself be sidetracked. He had more pointed and more provocative things to say now that Zhilinsky had reentered the room and was stumping back to his seat.

"But the main reason for the destruction of Samsonov's force is that neither it nor the Russian army as a whole was ready to take the offensive so soon. Everybody here knows that according to our original estimate the army was to have been ready to go into action two months from the day of mobilization. One month was the minimum."

Zhilinsky had reached his chair, but did not sit down. The contest had become too hot for that. He confronted Vorotyntsev, resting his clenched fists on the table. The colonel, crimson with tension, chest thrown out as though he too was ready for fisticuffs, flung his next words in Zhilinsky's face.

"We made a fatal decision just to please the French, thoughtlessly promising to begin operations a fortnight after mobilization, when we were only one-third ready. Only an ignoramus could have promised to lead our units into battle piecemeal and in a state of unreadiness!"

"Your Imperial Highness, this is an insult to the Russian state and to the Emperor, who approved of the decision! According to our convention with our French allies . . ."

Vorotyntsev, hurriedly taking advantage of the last second before the Grand Duke lost patience, retorted in a voice full of hatred: "Under the convention Russia promised to give 'resolute aid,' not to commit suicide! It was you who signed Russia's suicide note, Your Excellency!"

(Yanushkevich, forgotten by everyone, sat with his head lowered. It was he, though, who had demanded that the Northwestern Army Group should act four days earlier still.)

"It is also an insult to the Minister of War!" Zhilinsky yelled, but his voice was cracked and unfrightening. "And the decision had His Majesty's approval! There is no room for officers like you at GHQ! Nor indeed in the Russian army!"

The Grand Duke sat like a handsome statue, his legs crossed and turned away from the table. He spoke stonily, through stern lips: "Yes, Colonel. You have exceeded the limits of the permissible. It was not for this that I allowed you to speak."

He would not be allowed to say his last word, the last, perhaps, of his army career. He could not bear to forgo a single syllable, could not bear to know and not tell what he knew. He had nothing more to lose or to fear, he was free of all constraints. He saw only the men of the Dorogobuzh Regiment carrying a dead colonel and a wounded lieutenant on their shoulders; Staff Captain Semechkin, that merry, mettlesome bantam of a man, breaking through the enemy lines with two companies of the

Zvenigorod Regiment . . . and he answered the Supreme Commander in ringing tones: "Your Imperial Highness! I too am an officer of the Russian army, like you and like General Zhilinsky. And we, all of us, every officer in that army, share responsibility for our country's history. We cannot and must not lose one campaign after another. Those same Frenchmen will look on us with contempt tomorrow!"

The Grand Duke rarely lost his temper but now he flared up: "*Colonel!* Leave the conference room at once!"

Vorotyntsev felt only relief. The white-hot arrow tip had been plucked from his breast. Bringing flesh with it, but no matter. Not another sound. Thumbs along the seams of his trousers. About-face, with a stamp of the heel. March to the door.

As he reached it a beaming adjutant entered.

"Your Imperial Highness! A telegram from the Southwestern Army Group!"

This was it, what they had all been waiting for! The Grand Duke unfolded his limbs and rose. The others also got to their feet.

"Gentlemen! The Mother of God has not deserted our Russia! The city of Lvov has been taken. A colossal victory! We must issue a communiqué to the press."

Document No. 10

Telegram, 2 September

I am happy to give Your Majesty the glad news of the victory won by General Ruzsky's army at Lvov after seven days of uninterrupted fighting. The Austrians are returning in total disorder, in some places abandoning light and heavy weapons, artillery and supply wagons as they flee. The enemy has sustained enormous losses, and many prisoners have been taken . . .

Supreme Commander
Adjutant General NIKOLAI

* * *

UNTRUTH DID NOT START WITH US
AND WILL NOT END WITH US

* * *

1937 Rostov-on-Don
1969–70 Rozhdestvo on the Istya; Ilinskoye
1976; 1980 Vermont

INDEX OF NAMES

Adler, Viktor (1852–1918) Leader of the Austrian Social Democratic Party.

Alakayevka Village in the Samara (now Kuibyshev) province in which the Ulyanov family had a country house in the years 1889–93.

Aleksandr Mikhailovich ("Sandro") (1866–1933) Second cousin and brother-in-law of Nikolai II.

Aleksandrovo-Grushevsk (now Shakhty) Town in the Territory of the Don Cossacks.

Alekseev, Y. I. (1843–1918) Illegitimate son of Aleksandr II. Admiral. Viceroy in the Far East, 1903–5.

Aleksei Aleksandrovich (1850–1908) Grand Duke. Uncle of Nikolai II. Admiral. Commanded the Russian navy during the war with Japan.

Aleksinsky, G. A. (1879–1966) Bolshevik (until 1917). One of the leaders of the Ultimatists.

Aptekarsky Island Island in the Neva Delta on which Stolypin had a house.

Artamonov, Leonid (1859–1932) General. Commanded 1st Army corps in August 1914. Court-martialed for abandoning Soldau, forced into retirement.

Askold Ninth-century ruler of Kiev. A church on the banks of the Dniepr marks the spot known as "Askold's grave."

Azef, Y. F. (1869–1918) Double agent. Leading member of the Socialist Revolutionary Party who worked simultaneously for the Okhrana.

Bazarov, V. A. (real name Rudnev) (1874–1939) Bolshevik publicist. Supported Bogdanov against Lenin. Worked in planning organs after 1917.

Below, Fritz von (1853–1918) German general. Corps commander, 1914–18.

Bogdanov, A. A. (real name Malinovsky) (1873–1928) Doctor and philosopher. Bolshevik. Leading exponent of various political and ideological trends condemned by Lenin.

Bogrov, Grigori (1825–85) Grandfather of Stolypin's murderer, Mordko Bogrov. Author of a notable work on Jewish customs, *Memoirs of a Jew* (1871–74).

Bulygin, A. G. (1851–1919) Minister of the Interior from February to November 1905. Author of an abandoned project for a consultative Duma.

Burtsev, V. L. (1862–1942) Populist, member of People's Will, then of the Socialist Revolutionary Party. Denounced double agents in his periodical *Byloe* (*Times Past*).

Danilov, Y. N. (1866–1937) Quartermaster General, and in fact though not in name Chief of Staff to Grand Duke Nikolai Nikolaevich, Supreme Commander of the Russian armies.

Degaev, S. P. (1857–1920) Member of People's Will who informed on his comrades in 1882–83.

Dubasov, F. V. (1845–1912) Admiral. Governor-General of Moscow and suppressor of the rising in December 1905. Survived two attempts on his life.

Dubrovin, A. (1855–1918) Doctor. One of the founders of the Union of the Russian People.

Durnovo, P. N. (1844–1915) Vice-Minister, then Minister of the Interior in the years 1900–5.

Durnovo, P. P. (1835–?) Governor-General of Moscow.

Figner, V. N. (1852-1942) Populist. Member of the Executive Committee of People's Will. Imprisoned for twenty years in the Schlüsselburg fortress. Her memoirs are a major historical document.

François, Hermann von (1856–1923) German general.

Frederiks, V. B., Count (1838–1927) Minister of the Imperial Court, 1897–1917.

Georgi Aleksandrovich, Grand Duke (1871–1899) Younger brother of Nikolai II.

Gershuni, G. A. (1870–1908) Member of Socialist Revolutionary Party. Organized assassination of several high officials.

Golitsyn, D. B. (1851–1920) General. Master of the Imperial Hunt.

Golovin, N. M. (1875–1944) General. Military theorist. Professor at General Staff Academy, 1908–13. Author of works on First World War and Russian Civil War.

Goremykin, I. L. (1839–1917) Chairman of the Council of Ministers, April–July 1906 and January 1914–January 1916.

Grinevitsky, I. I. (= Griniewicki, Ignacy) (1856–81) Member of People's Will. Threw the bomb that killed Aleksandr II and was himself fatally wounded.

Guchkov, A. I. (1862–1936) Leader of the Octobrist Party (center-right party in the Duma). Member of the Provisional Government, March–May 1917. Emigrated in 1918.

Gurko, V. I. (1864–1937) General Corps Commander in 1914. Commander-in-Chief, March–May 1917.

Hanecki, Jakub (1879–1937) Member of both Polish and Russian Social Democratic parties. Close to Lenin in 1912–15; executed in Stalin's Great Purge.

Ivanov, N. I. (1851–1919) General. Commander of Kiev Military District, 1908–14, Commander-in-Chief Southwestern Front, 1914–March 1916.

Kadets The Constitutional Democratic (liberal) Party.

Kalyaev, I. P. (1877–1905) Member of Socialist Revolutionary Party's "Fighting Organization" (terror squad). Assassinated Grand Duke Sergei in 1905. Executed.

Kamenev, L. B. (real name Rosenfeld) (1883–1936) Bolshevik. Member of Politburo, 1918–26. One of the leaders of the Left opposition to Stalin. Executed 1936.

Kamo (nom de guerre of Simon Ter-Petrosian) (1882–1922) Georgian Bolshevik, organizer of "expropriations" (armed robberies to swell Party funds) in which Stalin participated.

Karakozov, D. V. (1840–66) Revolutionary. In 1866 made the first attempt on the life of Aleksandr II. Executed.

Kareev, N. I. (1850–1931) Historian and sociologist. Professor at St. Petersburg University.

Karpinsky, V. A. (1880–1965) Member of the RSDRP (Russian Social Democratic Workers' Party) from its foundation in 1898. Met Lenin in Geneva in 1904.

Kasso, L. A. (1865–1914) Minister of Education, 1910–14.

Kerensky, A. F. (1881–1970) Lawyer. Deputy in Fourth Duma. Minister in Provisional Government. Prime Minister, July–November 1917.

Khvostov, A. N. (1827–1918) Leader of the Right in the Fourth Duma. Minister of the Interior, 1915–16. Executed after the October Revolution.

Kibalchich, N. I. (1853–81) One of the four members of People's Will executed for the assassination of Aleksandr II.

Koba The young Stalin's nom de guerre.

Kokovtsov, V. N. (1853–1943) Minister of Finance, 1904–5 and 1906–14. Chairman of the Council of Ministers, 1911–14.

Konovalov, A. I. (1875–1948) Industrialist. Leader of the "Progressivist" group in the Fourth Duma. Minister in the Provisional Government, 1917.

Krasin, L. B. (1870–1926) Bolshevik. Expert in procurement and manufacture of weapons. Member of Central Committee, supported Bogdanov against Lenin. Held important diplomatic posts in early 1920s.

Krivoshein, A. V. (1857–1921) Minister of Agriculture, 1906–15. Close collaborator of Stolypin, with whom he toured Siberia to inspect results of their resettlement scheme.

Krupskaya, N. K. (1869–1939) Schoolteacher. Social Democrat. Married Lenin at Shushenskoye (eastern Siberia) in 1898. Played an important part in Soviet educational program after the October Revolution.

Kuropatkin, A. N. (1848–1925) Minister of War, 1898–1904. Commander-in-Chief in the Russo-Japanese War of 1904–5. Army commander and subsequently Army Group commander, 1914–16.

Kvyatkovsky, A. A. (1853–80) Member of People's Will. Executed 1886.

Lozovsky, A. (real name S. A. Dridzo) (1878–1952) Bolshevik. One of the group who favored reunification of Bolsheviks and Mensheviks in 1909–17. Vice-Minister of Foreign Affairs, 1934–46. Liquidated 1952.

Lunacharsky, A. V. (1875–1933) Bolshevik. From 1909 with Bogdanov and Maxim Gorky led left-wing faction opposed to Lenin. Commissar for Education, 1917–29.

Lvov, G. E., Prince (1861–1925) Kadet. Prime Minister, March–July 1917.

Lyadov, M. N. (real name Mandelstam) (1872–1947) Bolshevik. Member of leftist opposition to Lenin, 1909–11.

Lyubatovich, O. S. (1853–1917) and **Lyubatovich, V. S.** (1855–1907) Members of People's Will.

Mackensen, August von (1849–1945) Commander of German 17th Army Corps, 1914; later Army commander, Army Group commander, and Field Marshal.

Makarov, S. O. (1848–1904) Admiral. Commanded Pacific Squadron at outbreak of war with Japan. Perished in April 1904, when his flagship struck a mine.

Maklakov, N. A. (1871–1918) Acting Minister of the Interior, 1911–13. Minister, 1913–15.

Maklakov, V. A. (1870–1957) Leading member of Kadet Party. In emigration wrote an important study of late Tsarist Russia in which he deplored his party's disruptive radicalism.

Malinovsky, R. V. (1876–1918) Bolshevik from 1910, protégé of Lenin. Central Committee member, deputy in Fourth Duma. Had been an Okhrana agent from 1900 or earlier. Lenin defended him against accusations of double-dealing in 1914 and

1917. When the police archives were opened after the October Revolution, he was summarily executed.

Mamontov, S. I. (1841–1918) One of the Russian industrialists who provided revolutionaries with funds.

Manuilsky, D. Z. (1883–1959) Bolshevik.

Maria Fyodorovna (1847–1928) Daughter of Christian IX of Denmark, sister-in-law of Edward VII, wife of Aleksandr III, mother of Nikolai II.

Martov, Y. O. (real name Tsederbaum) (1873–1923) Social Democrat. Close associate of Lenin in 1894–1903. Leader of the Menshevik group when they parted company with the Bolsheviks in 1903.

Mien, G. General. Commanded the Semyonovsky Guards Regiment. Suppressed the rising in the Presnya district of Moscow in December 1905. Assassinated August 1906.

Mikhail Aleksandrovich, Grand Duke (1878–1918) Younger brother of Nikolai II. Refused the crown when Nikolai abdicated. Murdered by the Bolsheviks.

Mikhail Nikolaevich, Grand Duke (1832–1909) Great-uncle of Nikolai II. President of State Council, 1881–1905.

Mikhailov, T. M. (1859–81) Member of People's Will. Executed.

Mikhailovsky, N. K. (1842–1904) Liberal populist publicist and literary critic.

Moltke, Helmuth von (1800–1891) "Moltke the Elder." Field Marshal. Commanded the Prussian and subsequently the Imperial German forces in the wars of 1864–71.

Moltke, Helmuth von (1848–1916) "Moltke the Younger." Nephew of above. Chief of German General Staff in 1914, dismissed after the defeat on the Marne in September of that year.

"Montenegrins, The" Two daughters of Prince Nicholas of Montenegro. Militsa (1866–1931) and Anastasia (1867–1929), who married, respectively, Grand Duke Pyotr Nikolaevich and his brother Grand Duke Nikolai Nikolaevich.

Morozov, S. (1862–1905) Textile magnate, patron and benefactor of revolutionaries.

Nakhichevan, Khan of Aged Caucasian princeling in command of Guards cavalry corps in East Prussia in 1914.

Natanson, M. A. (1850–1919) Populist. One of the founders of the Land and Freedom Party in 1876 and of the Socialist Revolutionary Party in 1900.

Nechaev, S. G. (1847–82) Revolutionary. Author of the notorious *Catechism of the Revolutionary*. The murder of a fellow revolutionary organized by Nechaev in 1869 inspired Dostoevsky's novel *The Possessed*. Nechaev took refuge in Switzerland but was deported to Russia, was sentenced to twenty years' imprisonment, and died in the Peter and Paul Fortress.

Nikolai Nikolaevich, Grand Duke (1856–1929) "Nikolasha." Great-uncle of Nikolai II. Supreme Commander of Russian forces August 1914–August 1915.

Okhrana "Defense," colloquial name for the security police before 1917. Made much use of agents provocateurs in its campaigns against revolutionaries. Abolished after the February (March) Revolution of 1917.

Oldenburg, Pyotr, Duke of (1868–1924) Husband of Nikolai II's sister Olga.

Olga Konstantinova, Grand Duchess Second cousin of Nikolai II. Wife of George I of Greece, who was assassinated in 1913.

Sipyagin, D. S. (1853–1902) Minister of the Interior. Assassinated in 1902.

Spiridonova, M. A. (1884–1941) Socialist Revolutionary. Took part in terrorist campaigns, sentenced to forced labor for life, freed by February Revolution. From November 1917 to March 1918 she was the leader of the left Socialist Revolutionary faction allied to the Bolsheviks. Perished in Gulag.

Sukhomlinov, V. A. (1848–1926) General. Minister of War, 1909–15. Arrested 1916, accused of treason, acquitted, rearrested by Provisional Government 1917, sentenced to ten years' imprisonment, amnestied 1918, died abroad.

Svyatopolk-Mirsky, P. D. (1857–1914) Minister of the Interior, August 1904–June 1905.

Trepov, D. F. (1855–1906) Brother of F. F. Trepov. Governor-General of St. Petersburg in 1905.

Trepov, F. F. (1812–89) Chief of Police in St. Petersburg whom Vera Zasulich attempted to assassinate.

Trepov, F. F. (1854–1938) Son of the above. Governor-General of Kiev, 1908–14.

Ultimatists Ultimatism was one of the names given to the extreme left-wing faction in the Bolshevik Party critical of Lenin. It originated in 1908 and was led by Bogdanov and Lunacharsky. An "ultimatum" was to be delivered to the party's Duma faction, demanding more militant tactics.

Union of the Russian People Extreme right-wing nationalist and anti-Semitic organization established in 1905 by A. Dubrovin and others to defend absolutism. Provoked pogroms.

Zasulich, V. I. (1849–1919) Populist, then with Plekhanov founder of the League for the Liberation of Labor. Menshevik after 1903.

Zetkin, Klara (1857–1933) German Social Democrat and later Communist.

Zinoviev, G. Y. (1883–1936) Bolshevik. Collaborator of Lenin from 1907. Executed in Stalin's Great Purge.

MAP

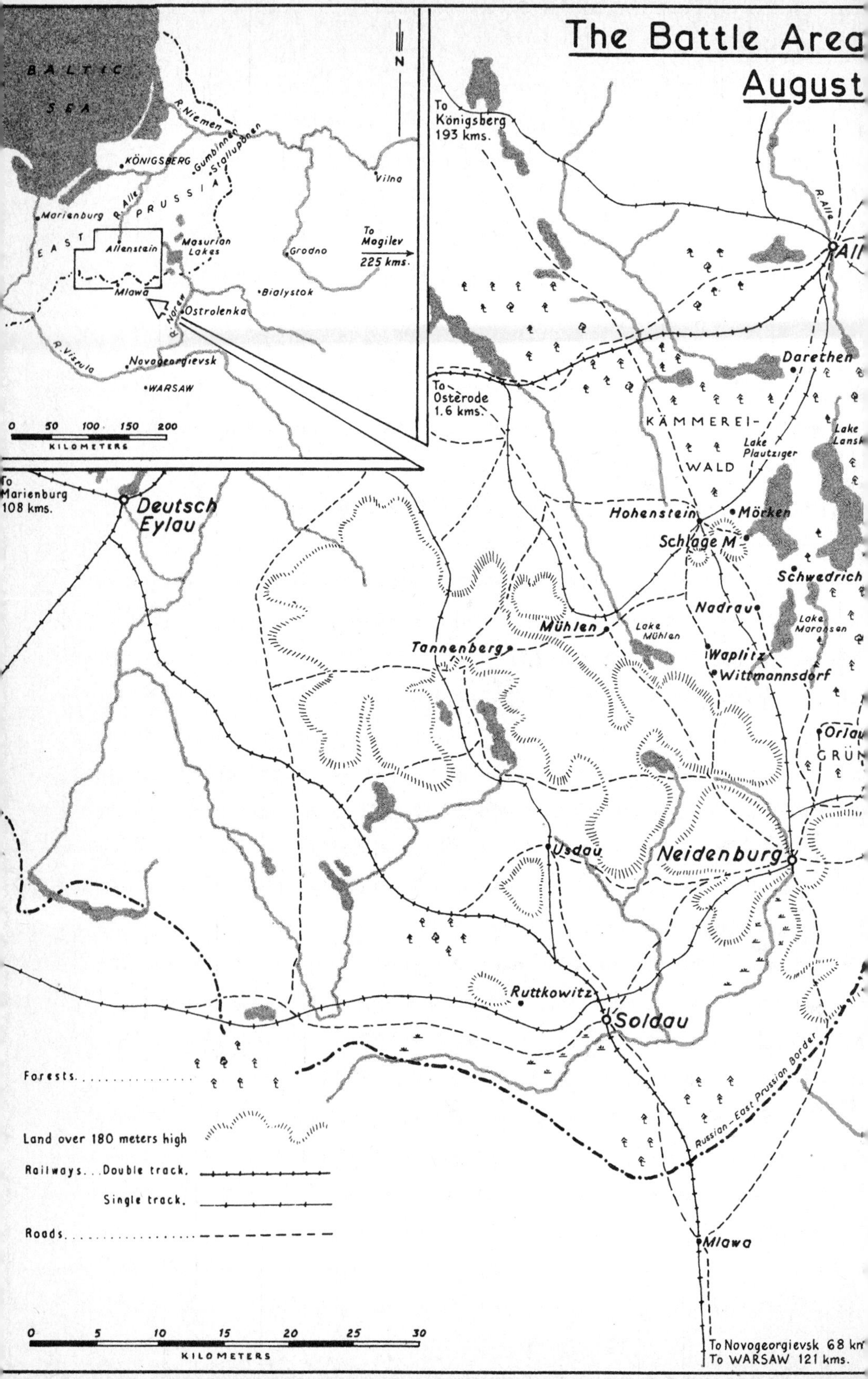

The Battle Area
August
BALTIC SEA
R. Niemen
KÖNIGSBERG
Gumbinnen
Stallupönen
EAST PRUSSIA
R. Alle
Marienburg
Allenstein
Masurian Lakes
Vilna
Grodno
To Mogilev 225 kms.
Mlawa
R. Narew
Ostrolenka
Bialystok
R. Vistula
Novogeorgievsk
WARSAW
0 50 100 150 200
KILOMETERS
N
To Königsberg 193 kms.
To Osterode 1.6 kms.
To Marienburg 108 kms.
Deutsch Eylau
Darethen
KÄMMEREI-WALD
Lake Plautziger
Lake Lansk
Hohenstein
Mörken
Schlage M
Schwedrich
Nadrau
Mühlen
Lake Mühlen
Lake Maransen
Tannenberg
Waplitz
Wittmannsdorf
Orlau
GRÜN
Usdau
Neidenburg
Ruttkowitz
Soldau
Russian-East Prussian Border
Mlawa
To Novogeorgievsk 68 km
To WARSAW 121 kms.
Forests
Land over 180 meters high
Railways... Double track.
Single track.
Roads
0 5 10 15 20 25 30
KILOMETERS

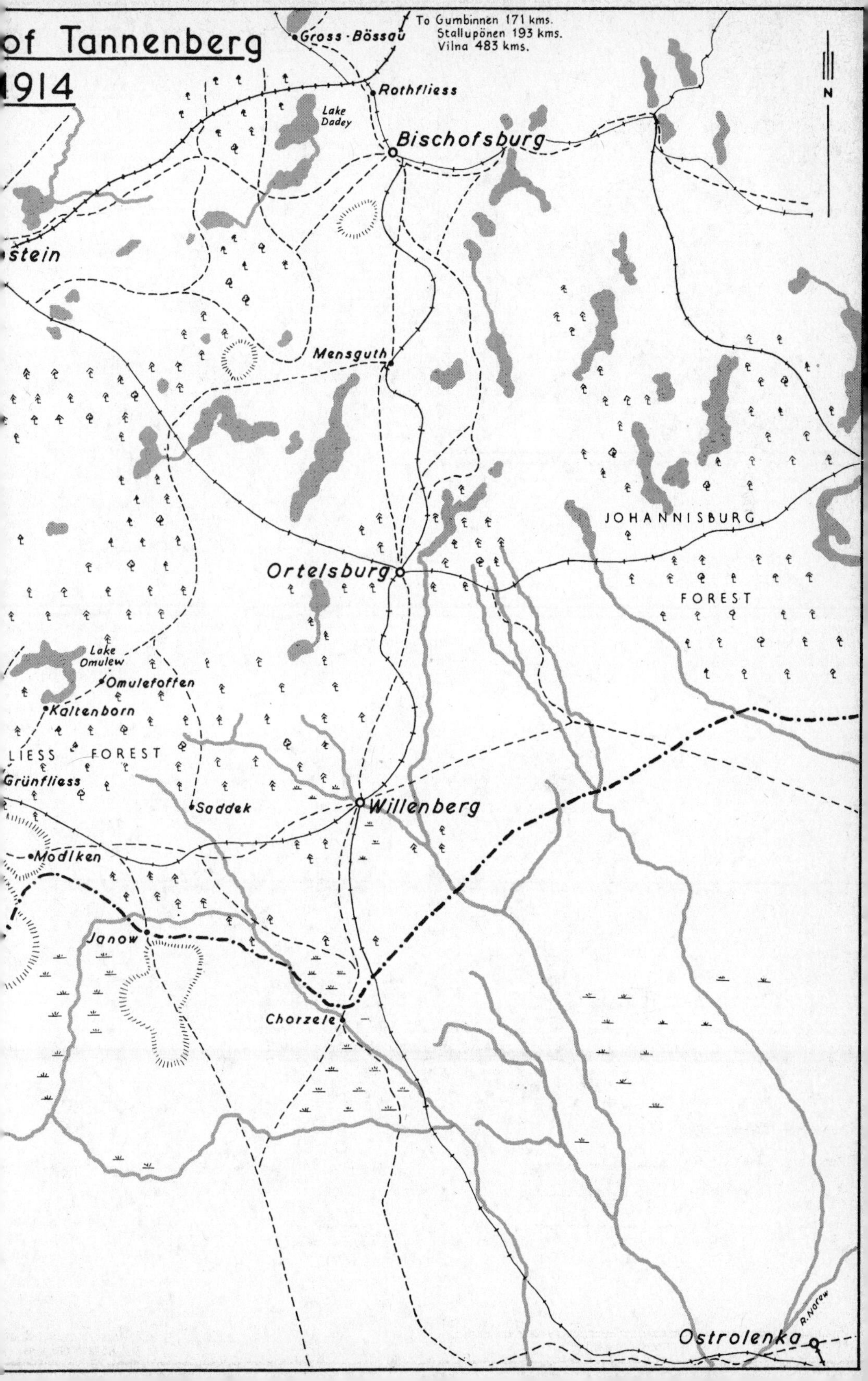

of Tannenberg
1914
To Gumbinnen 171 kms.
Stallupönen 193 kms.
Vilna 483 kms.
N
Gross-Bössau
Rothfliess
Lake Dadey
Bischofsburg
stein
Mensguth
JOHANNISBURG
Ortelsburg
FOREST
Lake Omulew
Omulefoffen
Kaltenborn
LIESS FOREST
Grünfliess
Saddek
Willenberg
Modlken
Janow
Chorzele
R. Narew
Ostrolenka